LOUIS-FERDINAND CÉLINE

Journey to the end of the night

&

Death on the Installment Plan

Classipublica

Louis-Ferdinand Céline
(1894-1961)

THE TWO MASTERPIECES

Journey to the end of the night *(1932)*
&
Death on the Installment Plan *(1936)*

Published by
Omnia Publica International LLC
OMNIAPUBLICA
www.omniapublica.com

TABLE OF CONTENT

JOURNEY TO THE END OF THE NIGHT

To Elisabeth Craig

Our life is a journey
Through winter and night,
We look for our way
In a sky without light.

(Song of the Swiss Guards 1793)

    Travel is useful, it exercises the imagination. All the rest is disappointment and fatigue. Our journey is entirely imaginary. That is its strength.
    It goes from life to death. People, animals, cities, things, all are imagined. It's a novel, just a fictitious narrative. Littré[1] says so, and he's never wrong.
    And besides, in the first place, anyone can do as much. You just have to close your eyes. It's on the other side of life.

---

[1] Littré. Emile Littré (1801-81), French lexicographer. His Dictionnaire de la langue français enjoys the prestige of Webster in the United States and of the Oxford English Dictionary in England.

Preface to 1952 Gallimard Edition

Hey, they're putting Journey on the rails again. What a feeling it gives me.

A lot of things have happened in fourteen years...

If I weren't under so much pressure, forced to earn my living, I can tell you right now, I'd suppress the whole thing, I wouldn't let a single line through.

Everything gets taken the wrong way. I've been the cause of too much evil.

Just think of all the deaths, the hatreds around me... the treachery... the sewer it adds up to... the monsters...

Oh, you've got to be blind and deaf!

You'll say: but it's not Journey! It's your crimes that are killing you, Journey has nothing to do with it. You yourself have been your ruin! your Bagatelles! your abominable lingo! your imaging, clowning villainy! The law's clutching you, strangling you? Hell, what are you complaining about? You jerk!

Oh, many thanks! Many thanks! I'm raging! Fuming! Panting! With hatred! Hypocrites! Jugheads! You can't fool me! It's for Journey that they're after me! Under the ax I'll bellow it! between "them" and me it's to the finish! to the guts! too foul to talk about... pissed with Mystique! What a business!

If I weren't under pressure, forced to earn my living, I'm telling you right now, I'd suppress the whole lot. A homage I paid to jackals!... That's right!... A free gift... A tip... I threw my luck away... in '36... gave it to the executioners' wives! the prosecutors! the undertakers! One two three admirable books to cut my throat with! And listen to my groans! I made them a present! I was charitable, that's all!

The world of intentions amuses me... used to amuse me... not anymore.

If I weren't under such pressure, such duress, I'd suppress the whole lot... especially Journey... Of all my books it's the only really vicious one... That's right... The heart of my sensibility...

It'll all start over again. The Sarabbath![2] You'll hear a whistling from up above, from far away, from places without names: words, orders...

You'll get an eyeful of their machinations!... You'll come and tell me about it...

Oh, don't imagine that I'm playing! I've stopped playing... I've even stopped being amiable.

If I weren't under duress, as though standing with my back to something... I'd suppress the whole lot.

---

[2] Sarabbath. A combination of witches' sabbath and saraband.

Here's how it started. I'd never said a word. Not one word. It was Arthur Ganate[3] that made me speak up. Arthur was a friend from med school. So we meet on the Place Clichy. It was after breakfast. He wants to talk to me. I listen. "Not out here," he says. "Let's go in." We go in. And there we were. "This terrace," he says, "is for jerks. Come on over there." Then we see that there's not a soul in the street, because of the heat; no cars, nothing. Same when it's very cold, not a soul in the street; I remember now, it was him who had said one time: "The people in Paris always look busy, when all they actually do is roam around from morning to night; it's obvious, because when the weather isn't right for walking around, when it's too cold or too hot, you don't see them anymore; they're all indoors, drinking their cafés crèmes or their beers. And that's the truth. The century of speed! they call it. Where? Great changes! they say. For instance? Nothing has changed. They go on admiring themselves, that's all. And that's not new either. Words. Even the words haven't changed much. Two or three little ones, here and there…" Pleased at having proclaimed these useful truths, we sat looking at the ladies in the café.

After a while the conversation turned to President Poincaré,[4] who was due to inaugurate a puppy show that same morning, and that led to *Le Temps*[5] where I'd read about it. Arthur Banate starts kidding me about Le Temps. "What a paper!" he says. "When it comes to defending the French race, it hasn't its equal." And quick to show I'm well informed, I fire back: "The French race can do with some defending, seeing it doesn't exist."

"Oh yes, it does!" he says. "And a fine race it is! the finest in the world, and anybody who says different is a yellow dog!" And he starts slanging me. Naturally I stuck to my guns.

"It's not true! What you call a race is nothing but a collection of riffraff like me, bleary-eyed, flea-bitten, chilled to the bone.

They came from the four corners of the earth, driven by hunger, plague, tumors, and the cold, and stopped here. They couldn't go any further because of the ocean. That's France, that's the French people."

"Bardamu," he says very gravely and a bit sadly. "Our forefathers were as good as we are, don't speak ill of them!…"

"You're right, Arthur, there you're right! Hateful and spineless, raped and robbed, mangled and witless, they were as good as we are, you can say that again! We never change. Neither our socks nor our masters nor our opinions, or we're so slow about it that it's no use. We were born loyal, and that's what killed us! Soldiers free of charge, heroes for everyone else, talking monkeys, tortured words, we are the minions of King Misery. He's our lord and master! When we misbehave, he tightens his grip… his fingers are around our neck, that makes it hard to talk, got to be careful if we want to eat… For nothing at all he'll choke you… It's not a life… "

"There's love, Bardamu!"

"Arthur," I tell him, "love is the infinite placed within the reach of poodles. I have my dignity!"
"You do, do you? You're an anarchist, that's what you are!"

A wise guy, as you see, with only the most advanced opinions.

"That's right, you windbag, I'm an anarchist. And to prove it, I've written a kind of prayer of social vengeance, it'll bowl you over. The Golden Wings! That's the title!" And I recite:

"A God who counts minutes and pennies, a desperate sensual God, who grunts like a pig. A pig with golden wings, who falls and falls, always belly side up, ready for caresses, that's him, our master. Come, kiss me."

"Your little piece doesn't hold water," he says. "I'm for the established order, and I'm not interested in politics. What's more, the day my country asks me to shed my blood, it'll find me ready, and no slacker."

That's what he said.

---

[3] Ganate. Probably derived from ganache, meaning "blockhead."

[4] Poincaré. Raymond Poincaré (1860-1934). Then President of France, a largely ceremonial office at the time.

[5] *Le Temps*. A daily newspaper. Regarded as the semiofficial organ of the Third Republic. Liberal in tendency. Became rightist after the First World War.

It so happened that the war was creeping up on us without our knowing it, and something was wrong with my wits. That short but animated discussion had tired me out. Besides, I was upset because the waiter had sort of called me a piker on account of the tip. Well, in the end Arthur and I made up. Completely. We agreed about almost everything.

"It's true," I said, trying to be conciliatory. "All in all, you're right. But the fact is we're all sitting in a big galley, pulling at the oars with all our might. You can't tell me different!... Sitting on nails and pulling like mad. And what do we get for it? Nothing! Thrashings and misery, hard words and hard knocks. We're workers, they say. Work, they call it! That's the crummiest part of the whole business. We're down in the hold, heaving and panting, stinking and sweating our balls off, and meanwhile! Up on deck in the fresh air, what do you see?! Our masters having a fine time with beautiful pink and perfumed women on their laps. They send for us, we're brought up on deck. They put on their top hats and give us a big spiel like as follows: "You no-good swine! We're at war! Those stinkers in Country No. 2! We're going to board them and cut their livers out! Let's go! Let's go! We've got everything we need on board! All together now! Let's hear you shout so the deck trembles: 'Long live Country No. 1!' So you'll be heard for miles around. The man that shouts the loudest will get a medal and a lollipop! Let's go! And if there's anybody that doesn't want to be killed on the sea, he can go and get killed on land, it's even quicker!"

"That's the way it is exactly," said Arthur, suddenly willing to listen to reason.

But just then, who should come marching past the cafe where we're sitting but a regiment with the colonel up front on his horse, looking nice and friendly, a fine figure of a man! Enthusiasm lifted me to my feet.

"I'll just go see if that's the way it is!" I sing out to Arthur, and off I go to enlist, on the double.

"Ferdinand!" he yells back. "Don't be an ass!" I suppose he was nettled by the effect my heroism was having on the people all around us.

It kind of hurt my feelings the way he was taking it, but that didn't stop me. I fell right in. "Here I am," I says to myself, "and here I stay."

I just had time to call out to Arthur: "All right, you jerk, we'll see"—before we turned the corner. And there I was with the regiment, marching behind the colonel and his band. That's exactly how it happened.

We marched a long time. There were streets and more streets, and they were all crowded with civilians and their wives, cheering us on, bombarding us with flowers from café terraces, railroad stations, crowded churches. You never saw so many patriots in all your life! And then there were fewer patriots... It started to rain, and then there were still fewer and fewer, and not a single cheer, not one.

Pretty soon there was nobody but us, we were all alone. Row after row. The music had stopped. "Come to think of it," I said to myself, when I saw what was what, "this is no fun anymore! I'd better try something else!" I was about to clear out. Too late! They'd quietly shut the gate behind us civilians. We were caught like rats.

* * *

When you're in, you're in. They put us on horseback, and after we'd been on horseback for two months, they put us back on our feet. Maybe because of the expense. Anyway, one morning the colonel was looking for his horse, his orderly had made off with it, nobody knew where to, probably some quiet spot that bullets couldn't get to as easily as the middle of the road. Because that was exactly where the colonel and I had finally stationed ourselves, with me holding his orderly book while he wrote out his orders.

Down the road, way in the distance, as far as we could see, there were two black dots, plunk in the middle like us, but they were two Germans and they'd been busy shooting for the last fifteen or twenty minutes.

Maybe our colonel knew why they were shooting, maybe the Germans knew, but I, so help me, hadn't the vaguest idea. As far back as I could search my memory, I hadn't done a thing to the Germans, I'd always treated them friendly and polite. I knew the Germans pretty well, I'd even gone to school in their country when I was little, near Hanover. I'd spoken their language. A bunch of loud-mouthed little halfwits, that's what they were, with pale, furtive eyes like wolves; we'd go out to the woods together after school to feel the girls up, or we'd fire popguns or pistols you could buy for four marks. And we drank sugary beer together. But from that to shooting at us right in the middle of the road, without so much as a word of introduction, was a long way, a very long way. If you asked me, they were going too far.

This war, in fact, made no sense at all. It couldn't go on.

Had something weird got into these people? Something I didn't feel at all? I suppose I hadn't noticed it...

Anyway, my feelings toward them hadn't changed. In spite of everything. I'd have liked to understand their brutality, but what I wanted still more, enormously, with all my heart, was to get out of there, because suddenly the whole business looked to me like a great big mistake.

"In a mess like this," I said to myself, "there's nothing to be done, all you can do is clear out... "

Over our heads, two millimeters, maybe one millimeter from our temples, those long tempting lines of steel, that bullets make when they're out to kill you, were whistling through the hot summer air.

I'd never felt so useless as I did amid all those bullets in the sunlight. A vast and universal mockery.

I was only twenty at the time. Deserted farms in the distance, empty wide-open churches, as if the peasants had gone out for the day to attend a fair at the other end of the county, leaving everything they owned with us for safekeeping, their countryside, their carts with the shafts pointing in the air, their fields, their barnyards, the road, the trees, even the cows, a chained dog, the works. Leaving us free to do as we pleased while they were gone. Nice of them, in a way. "Still," I said to myself, "if they hadn't gone somewhere else, if there were still somebody here, I'm sure we wouldn't be behaving so badly! So disgustingly! We wouldn't dare in front of them!" But there wasn't a soul to watch us! Nobody but us, like newlyweds that start messing around when all the people have gone home.

And another thought I had (behind a tree) was that I wished Déroulède[6]—the one I'd heard so much about—had been there to describe his reactions when a ball tore open his guts.

Those Germans squatting on the road, shooting so obstinately, were rotten shots, but they seemed to have ammunition to burn, whole warehouses full, it looked to me. Nobody could say this war was over! I have to hand it to the colonel, his bravery was remarkable. He roamed around in the middle of the road, up and down and back and forth in the midst of the bullets as calmly as if he'd been waiting for a friend on a station platform, except just a tiny bit impatient.

One thing I'd better tell you right away, I'd never been able to stomach the country, I'd always found it dreary, those endless fields of mud, those houses where nobody's ever home, those roads that don't go anywhere. And if to all that you add a war, it's completely unbearable. A sudden wind had come up on both sides of the road, the clattering leaves of the poplars mingled with the sharp crackling sounds aimed at us from down the road. Those unknown soldiers missed us every time, but they spun a thousand deaths around us, so close they seemed to clothe us. I was afraid to move.

That colonel, I could see, was a monster. Now I knew it for sure, he was worse than a dog, he couldn't conceive of his own death. At the same time I realized that there must be plenty of brave men like him in our army, and just as many no doubt in the army facing us. How many, I wondered. One or two million, say several millions in all? The thought turned my fear to panic. With such people this infernal lunacy could go on for ever... Why would they stop? Never had the world seemed so implacably doomed.

Could I, I thought, be the last coward on earth? How terrifying!... All alone with two million stark raving heroic madmen, armed to the eyeballs? With and without helmets, without horses, on motorcycles, bellowing, in cars, screeching, shooting, plotting, flying, kneeling, digging, taking cover, bounding over trails, root-toot-tooting, shut up on earth as if it were a loony bin, ready to demolish

---

[6] Déroulède. Paul Déroulède (1847-1914). Writer and politician. Extreme nationalist, supporter of General Boulanger and founder of the League of Patriots.

everything on it, Germany, France, whole continents, everything that breathes, destroy destroy, madder than mad dogs, worshiping their madness (which dogs don't), a hundred, a thousand times madder than a thousand dogs, and a lot more vicious! A pretty mess we were in! No doubt about it, this crusade I'd let myself in for was the apocalypse!

You can be a virgin in horror the same as in sex. How, when I left the Place Clichy, could I have imagined such horror? Who could have suspected, before getting really into the war, all the ingredients that go to make up the rotten, heroic, good-for-nothing soul of man? And there I was, caught up in a mass flight into collective murder, into the fiery furnace... Something had come up from the depths, and this is what happened.

The colonel was still as cool as a cucumber, I watched him as he stood on the embankment, taking little messages sent by the general, reading them without haste as the bullets flew all around him, and tearing them into little pieces. Did none of those messages include an order to put an immediate stop to this abomination? Did no top brass tell him there had been a misunderstanding? A horrible mistake? A misdeal? That some-body'd got it all wrong, that the plan had been for maneuvers, a sham battle, not a massacre! Not at all! "Keep it up, colonel! You're doing fine!" That's what General des Entrayes,[7] the head of our division and commander over us all, must have written in those notes that were being brought every five minutes by a courier, who looked greener and more shitless each time. I could have palled up with that boy, we'd have been scared together. But we had no time to fraternize.

So there was no mistake? So there was no law against people shooting at people they couldn't even see! It was one of the things you could do without anybody reading you the riot act. In fact, it was recognized and probably encouraged by upstanding citizens, like the draft, or marriage, or hunting!... No two ways about it. I was suddenly on the most intimate terms with war. I'd lost my virginity. You've got to be pretty much alone with her as I was then to get a good look at her, the slut, full face and profile. A war had been switched on between us and the other side, and now it was burning! Like the current between the two carbons of an arc lamp! And this lamp was in no hurry to go out! It would get us all, the colonel and everyone else, he looked pretty spiffy now. but he wouldn't roast up any bigger than me when the current from the other side got him between the shoulders.

There are different ways of being condemned to death. Oh! What wouldn't I have given to be in jail instead of here! What a fool I'd been! If only I had had a little foresight and stolen something or other when it would have been so easy and there was still time. I never think of anything. You come out of jail alive, out of a war you don't! The rest is blarney.

If only I'd had time, but I didn't. There was nothing left to steal. How pleasant it would be in a cozy little jailhouse, I said to myself, where the bullets couldn't get in. Where they never got in! I knew of one that was ready and waiting, all sunny and warm! I saw it in my dreams, the jailhouse of Saint-Germain to be exact, right near the forest. I knew it well, I'd often passed that way. How a man changes! I was a child in those days, and that jail frightened me. Because I didn't know what men are like. Never again will I believe what they say or what they think. Men are the thing to be afraid of, always, men and nothing else.

How much longer would this madness have to go on before these monsters dropped with exhaustion? How long could a convulsion like this last? Months? Years? How many? Maybe till everyone's dead? All these lunatics? Every last one of them? And seeing events were taking such a desperate turn, I decided to stake everything on one throw, to make one last try, to see if I couldn't stop the war, just me, all by myself! At least in this one spot where I happened to be.

The colonel was only two steps away from me, pacing. I'd talk to him. Something I'd never done. This was a time for daring. The way things stood, there was practically nothing to lose. "What is it?" he'd ask me, startled, I imagined, at my bold interruption. Then I'd explain the situation as I saw it, and we'd see what he thought. The essential is to talk things over. Two heads are better than one.

---

[7] General des Entrayes. Entrayes derives from entrailles, "entrails." (Old Blood and Guts.) As will be seen later on, his first name was Céladon, which suggests a languishing lover.

I was about to take that decisive step when, at that very moment, who should arrive on the double but a dismounted cavalryman (as we said in those days), exhausted, shaky in the joints, holding his helmet upside-down in one hand like Belisarius,[8] trembling, all covered with mud, his face even greener than the courier I mentioned before. He stammered and gulped. You'd have thought he was struggling to climb out of a tomb, and it made him sick to his stomach. Could it be that this spook didn't like bullets any more than I did? That he saw them coming like me?

"What is it?" Disturbed, the colonel stopped him short; the glance he flung at that ghost was of steel.

It made our colonel very angry to see that wretched cavalryman so incorrectly clad and shitting in his pants with fright. The colonel had no use for fear, that was a sure thing. And especially that helmet held in hand like a bowler was really too much in a combat regiment like ours that was just getting into the war. It was as if this dismounted cavalryman had seen the war and taken his hat off in greeting.

Under the colonel's withering look the wobbly messenger snapped to attention, pressing his little finger to the seam of his trousers as the occasion demanded. And so he stood on the embankment, stiff as a board, swaying, the sweat running down his chin strap; his jaws were trembling so hard that little abortive cries kept coming out of him, like a puppy dreaming. You couldn't make out whether he wanted to speak to us or whether he was crying.

Our Germans squatting at the end of the road had just changed instruments. Now they were having their fun with a machine gun, sputtering like handfuls of matches, and all around us flew swarms of angry bullets, as hostile as wasps.

The man finally managed to articulate a few words: "Colonel, sir, Sergeant Barousse has been killed."

"So what?"

"He was on his way to meet the bread wagon on the Etrapes road, sir." "So what?"

"He was blown up by a shell!" "So what, dammit!"

"That's what, colonel, sir." "Is that all?"

"Yes, sir, that's all, colonel, sir."

"What about the bread?" the colonel asked.

That was the end of the dialogue, because, I remember distinctly, he barely had time to say "What about the bread?" That was all. After that there was nothing but flame and noise. The kind of noise you wouldn't have thought possible. Our eyes, ears, nose, and mouth were so full of that noise I thought it was all over and I'd turned into noise and flame myself.

After a while the flame went away, the noise stayed in my head, and my arms and legs trembled as if somebody were shaking me from behind. My limbs seemed to be leaving me, but then in the end they stayed on. The smoke stung my eyes for a long time, and the prickly smell of powder and sulfur hung on, strong enough to kill all the fleas and bedbugs in the whole world.

I thought of Sergeant Barousse, who had just gone up in smoke like the man told us. That was good news. Great, I thought to myself. That makes one less stinker in the regiment! He wanted to have me court-martialed for a can of meat. "It's an ill wind," I said to myself. In that respect, you can't deny it, the war seemed to serve a purpose now and then! I knew of three or four more in the regiment, real scum, that I'd have gladly helped to make the acquaintance of a shell, like Barousse.

As for the colonel, I didn't wish him any hard luck. But he was dead too. At first I didn't see him. The blast had carried him up the embankment and laid him down on his side, right in the arms of the dismounted cavalryman, the courier, who was finished too. They were embracing each other for the moment and for all eternity, but the cavalryman's head was gone, all he had was an opening at the top of the neck, with blood in it bubbling and glugging like jam in a kettle. The colonel's belly was wide open, and he was making a nasty face about it. It must have hurt when it happened. Tough shit for him! If he'd beat it when the shooting started, it wouldn't have happened.

---

[8] Belisarius. Byzantine general (500-65). According to the legend, he was blinded by order of Emperor Justinian. Numerous paintings show him as a beggar, holding out his reversed helmet for alms.

All that tangled meat was bleeding profusely.

Shells were still bursting to the right and left of the scene.

I'd had enough, I was glad to have such a good pretext for making myself scarce. I even hummed a tune, and reeled like when you've been rowing a long way and your legs are wobbly. "Just one shell!" I said to myself. "Amazing how quick just one shell can clean things up. Could you believe it?" I kept saying to myself. "Could you believe it!"

There was nobody left at the end of the road. The Germans were gone. But that little episode had taught me a quick lesson, to keep to the cover of the trees. I was in a hurry to get back to our command post, to see if anyone else in our regiment had been killed on reconnaissance. There must be some good dodges, I said to myself, for getting taken prisoner... Here and there in the fields a few puffs of smoke still clung to the ground. "Maybe they're all dead," I thought. "Seeing they refuse to understand anything whatsoever, the best solution would be for them all to get killed instantly... The war would be over, and we'd go home... Maybe we'd march across the Place Clichy in triumph... Just one or two survivors... In my dream... Strapping good fellows marching behind the general, all the rest would be dead like the colonel... Like Barousse... like Vanaille (another bastard)... etc. They'd shower us with decorations and flowers, we'd march through the Arc de Triomphe, We'd go to a restaurant, they'd serve us free of charge, we'd never pay for anything anymore, never as long as we lived! We're heroes! we'd say when they brought the bill... Defenders of the Patrie! That would do it!... We'd pay with little French flags!... The lady at the cash desk would refuse to take money from heroes, she'd even give us some, with kisses thrown in, as we filed out. Life would be worth living."

As I was running, I noticed my arm was bleeding, just a little though, a far from satisfactory wound, a scratch. I'd have to start all over.

It was raining again, the fields of Flanders oozed with dirty water. For a long time I didn't meet a soul, only the wind and a little later the sun. From time to time, I couldn't tell from where, a bullet would come flying merrily through the air and sunshine, looking for me, intent on killing me, there in the wilderness. Why? Never again, not if I lived another hundred years, would I go walking in the country. A solemn oath.

Walking along, I remembered the ceremony of the day before. It had taken place in a meadow, at the foot of a hill; the colonel had harangued the regiment in his booming voice: "Go to it, boys," he had cried. "Go to it, boys," and "Vive la France!" When you have no imagination, dying is small beer; when you do have an imagination, dying is too much. That's my opinion. My understanding has never taken in so many things at once.

The colonel had never had any imagination. That was the source of all his trouble, and of ours even more so. Was I the only man in that regiment with any imagination about death? I preferred my own kind of death, the kind that comes late... in twenty years . , . thirty... maybe more... to this death they were trying to deal me right away... eating Flanders mud, my whole mouth full of it, fuller than full, split to the ears by a shell fragment. A man's entitled to an opinion about his own death. But which way, if that was the case, should I go? Straight ahead? My back to the enemy. If the M.P.s were to catch me roaming around I knew my goose was cooked. They'd give me a slapdash trial that same afternoon in some deserted classroom... There were lots of empty classrooms wherever we went. They'd play court-martial with me the way kids play when the teacher isn't there. The noncoms seated on the platform, me standing in handcuffs in front of the little desks. In the morning they'd shoot me: twelve bullets plus one. So what was the answer?

And I thought of the colonel again, such a brave man with his breastplate and his helmet and his mustache, if they had exhibited him in a music hall, walking as I saw him under the bullets and shell-fire, he'd have filled the Alhambra, he'd have outshone Fragson,[9] and he was a big star at the time I'm telling you about. That's what I was thinking. My heart was down in the dumps.

After hours and hours of cautious, furtive walking, I finally caught sight of our men near a clump of farmhouses. That was one of our advance posts. It belonged to a squadron that was billeted nearby. Nobody killed, they told me. Every last one of them alive! I was the one with the big news: "The

---

[9] Fragson. Popular cabaret singer early in the century.

colonel's dead," I shouted, as soon as I was near enough. "Plenty more colonels where he came from." That was the snappy comeback of Corporal Pistil, who was on duty just then, what's more, he was organizing details.

"All right, you jerk, until they find a replacement for the colonel, you can be picking up meat with Empouille and Kerdoncuff[10] here, take two sacks each. The distribution point is behind the church... the one you see over there... Don't let them give you a lot of bones like yesterday, and try and get back before nightfall, you lugs!"

So I hit the road again with the other two.

That pissed me off. "I'll never tell them anything after this," I said to myself. I could see it was no use talking to those slobs, a tragedy like what I'd just seen was wasted on such stinkers! It had happened too long ago to capture their interest. And to think that a week earlier they'd have given me four columns and my picture in the papers for the death of a colonel the way I'd seen it. A bunch of halfwits.

The meat for the whole regiment was being distributed in a summery field, shaded by cherry trees and parched by the August sun. On sacks and tent cloths spread out on the grass there were pounds and pounds of guts, chunks of white and yellow fat, disemboweled sheep with their organs every which way, oozing intricate little rivulets into the grass round about, a whole ox, split down the middle, hanging on a tree, and four regimental butchers all hacking away at it, cursing and swearing and pulling off choice morsels. The squadrons were fighting tooth and nail over the innards, especially the kidneys, and all around them swarms of flies such as one sees only on such occasions, as self-important and musical as little birds.

Blood and more blood, everywhere, all over the grass, in sluggish confluent puddles, looking for a congenial slope. A few steps further on, the last pig was being killed. Already four men and a butcher were fighting over certain of the prospective cuts.

"You crook, you! You're the one that made off with the tenderloin yesterday!"

Leaning against a tree, I had barely time enough to honor that alimentary dispute with two or three glances, before being overcome by an enormous urge to vomit, which I did so hard that I passed out.

They carried me back to the outfit on a stretcher. Naturally they swiped my two oilcloth sacks, the change was too good to miss.

I woke up to one of the corporal's harangues. The war wasn't over.

* * *

Anything can happen, and I in my turn became a corporal at the end of that same month of August. Many a time I was sent to headquarters with five men for liaison duty under General des Entrayes. He was a little man, he didn't say much, and at first sight he seemed neither cruel nor heroic. But it was safer to suspend judgment... What he seemed to value most of all was his comfort. In fact he thought of his comfort all the time, and even when we'd been busy retreating for more than a month, he'd chew everybody out in every new stopping place if his orderly hadn't found him a nice clean bed and a kitchen with all the modern appliances.

This love of comfort gave our chief of staff a lot of trouble. The general's domestic requirements got on his nerves. Especially since he himself, yellow, gastritic in the extreme, and constipated, wasn't the least bit interested in food. But he had to eat his soft-boiled eggs at the general's table all the same, and listen on that occasion to his complaints. Those are the things a soldier has to put up with. But I couldn't feel sorry for him, because as an officer he was a first-rate swine. Judge for yourself. After a whole day spent dragging ourselves uphill and down glade, through carrots and clover, we'd finally stop so the general could get to sleep somewhere, We'd find him a quiet, sheltered village, where no

---

[10] Kerdoncuff. Ker = "house" in the Breton language. The name suggests a Breton yokel. "Doncuff" seems to be a transliteration of the German Dummkopf —jughead.

troops had been billeted yet, or if they had been, they'd have to move on in a hurry, we'd throw them out even if they'd already stacked their rifles, and they'd just have to spend the night in the open.

The village was reserved for the general staff, its horses, its mess, its luggage, and not least for that stinking major. The bastard's name was Pinçon, Major Pinçon.[11] I hope they've killed him off by now (and not pleasantly). But at the time I'm talking about Pinçon was disgustingly alive. Every evening he'd send for us liaison men and give us a good chewing out, to keep us on our toes and fire us with enthusiasm. Then he'd send us all over the place, after we'd run errands for the general all day. Dismount! Mount! Dismount again! And more of the same, carrying his orders in all directions. They might just as well have drowned us. It would have been more convenient for everybody.

"Dismissed!" he'd yell. "Get back to your regiments! And on the double!" "Where is the regiment, sir?" we'd ask...

"At Barbigny."[12] "Where's Barbigny?" "Over there!"

Over there, where he pointed, there'd be nothing but darkness, same as everywhere else, an enormous darkness that swallowed up the road two steps ahead of us, only a little sliver of road about the size of your tongue was spared by the darkness.

This Barbigny of his was at the end of the world. Try and find it! To find his Barbigny you'd have had to sacrifice at least a whole squadron! A squadron of brave men, what's more! And I wasn't brave at all, I couldn't see any reason to be brave, so obviously I had less desire than anyone else to find his Barbigny, the situation of which, incidentally, was pure guesswork as far as he was concerned. Maybe they thought they could make me go and commit suicide if they yelled loud enough. But either you have it in you or you don't.

I knew only one thing about that blackness, which was so dense you had the impression that if you stretched out your arm a little way from your shoulder you'd never see it again, but of that one thing I was absolutely certain, namely, that it was full of homicidal impulses.

As soon as night fell, that big-mouth major couldn't wait to send us to our deaths; it was something that came over him at sundown. We'd try a bit of passive resistance, we'd pretend not to understand, we'd try to take root in that cozy little billet, but when we finally couldn't see the trees, we had to resign ourselves to going away and dying a little; the general's dinner was ready.

From then on, it was all a matter of luck. Sometimes we'd find Barbigny and the regiment and sometimes we wouldn't. When we found it, it was mostly by mistake, because the squadron sentries would start shooting at us. So naturally we'd advance and be recognized, and usually spend the night doing all sorts of details, carrying numberless bales of oats and buckets of water, and getting chewed out till our heads reeled, in addition to dropping with sleep.

In the morning, our liaison team, all five of us, would report back to General des Entrayes and get on with the war.

But most of the time we didn't find the regiment and we'd circle around villages on unknown trails, keeping away from evacuated hamlets and treacherous thickets—as much as possible we avoided those kinds of things because of German patrols. We had to be somewhere though while waiting, somewhere in the darkness. Some things couldn't be avoided. Ever since then I've known how wild rabbits must feel.

Pity comes in funny ways. If we'd told Major Pinçon that he was nothing but a cowardly stinking murderer, we'd only have given him pleasure, the pleasure of having us shot without delay by the M.P. captain, who was always following him around and who lived for nothing else. It wasn't the Germans thai M.P. had it in for.

So for night after idiotic night we crept from ambush to ambush, sustained only by the decreasingly plausible hope of coming out alive, that and no other, and if we did come out alive one thing was sure, that we'd never, absolutely never, forget that we had discovered on earth a man shaped like you and me, but a thousand times more ferocious than the crocodiles and sharks with wide-open jaws

---

[11] Major Pinçon. Pinçon = louse in argot, but Céline probably had in mind the expression "gai comme un pinçon"—merry as a louse.

[12] Barbigny. Connected no doubt with "barbant," "barbe," meaning "boring," "annoying."

that circle just below the surface around the shiploads of garbage and rotten meat that get chucked overboard in the Havana roadstead.

The biggest defeat in every department of life is to forget, especially the things that have done you in, and to die without realizing how far people can go in the way of crumminess. When the grave lies open before us, let's not try to be witty, but on the other hand, let's not forget, but make it our business to record the worst of the human viciousness we've seen without changing one word. When that's done, we can curl up our toes and sink into the pit. That's work enough for a lifetime.

I'd gladly have fed Major Pinçon to the sharks and his M.P. with him, to teach them how to live; my horse too while I was at it, so he wouldn't have to suffer anymore; the poor fellow didn't have any back left it was so sore, only two plaques of raw flesh under the saddle, as big as my two hands, oozing rivers of pus that ran from the edges of his blanket down to his hocks. I had to ride him all the same, trot trot... That trot trot made him wriggle and writhe. But horses are even more patient than people. His trot was an undulation. I had to leave him out in the open. In a barn the smell of his open wounds would have been asphyxiating. When I mounted him, his back hurt him so badly that he arched it, oh, very politely, and his belly hung down to his knees. It felt like mounting a donkey. It was easier that way, I have to admit. We were plenty tired ourselves with all the steel we had to carry on our heads and shoulders.

General des Entrayes was waiting for his dinner in his specially requisitioned house. The table had been set, the lamp was in its place.

"Beat it, Christ Almighty, the whole lot of you!" Pinçon yelled at us one more time, shaking his lantern under our noses. "We're sitting down to table! I'm telling you for the last time! Are those swine ever going to go!" he screamed. The passion of sending us to our death put a little color into his diaphanous cheeks.

Sometimes the general's cook would slip us a bite before we left. The general had too much to eat, seeing the regulations allowed him forty rations all for himself! He wasn't a young man anymore. In fact he must have been close to retirement age. His knees buckled when he walked and I'm pretty sure he dyed his mustache.

The veins in his temples, we could see in the lamplight as we were leaving, described meanders like the Seine on its way out of Paris. He had grown-up daughters, so it was said, unmarried and like himself not rich. Maybe those were the thoughts that made him so crotchety cranky, like an old dog disturbed in his habits, who goes looking for his quilted basket whenever anyone opens the door for him.

He loved beautiful gardens and rosebushes. Wherever we went, he never passed up a rose garden. When it comes to loving roses, generals haven't their equal. It's a known fact.

Anyway we finally set out. It was hard to get the plugs started. They were afraid to move because of their wounds, but in addition they were afraid of us and the darkness, afraid of everything, to tell the truth. So were we! A dozen times we went back to ask the major for directions! A dozen times he cursed us for goldbricks and goof-offs. Finally, with the help of our spurs, we'd pass the last outpost, give the sentries the password, and plunge into our murky adventure, into the darkness of this no man's land.

After wandering a while from side to side of the darkness, we finally got part of our bearings, or so at least we thought... Whenever one cloud seemed lighter than another, we were convinced that we'd seen something... But up ahead of us there was nothing we could be sure of but the echo that came and went, the echo of our horses' hoof beats, a horrendous sound you wanted so bad not to hear that it stopped your breath. Those horses seemed to be trotting to high heaven, to be calling everybody on earth to come and massacre us. And they could have done it with one hand, just steady a rifle against a tree and wait for us. I kept thinking that the first light we'd see would be the flash of the shot that would end it all.

In the four weeks the war had been going on, we'd grown so tired, so miserable, that tiredness had taken away some of my fear. In the end the torture of being harassed night and day by those monsters, the noncoms, especially the low-ranking ones, who were even stupider, pettier, and more hateful than usual, made even the most obstinate among us doubt the advisability of going on living.

Oh, how you long to get away! To sleep! That's the main thing! When it becomes really impossible to get away and sleep, then the will to live evaporates of its own accord. Seeing we were still alive, we'd just have to look as if we were looking for our regiment.

Before a thought can start up in the brain of a jughead, a lot of cruel things must happen to him. The man who had made me think for the first time in my life, really think, practical thoughts that were really my own, was undoubtedly Major Pinçon, that torture master. I therefore thought of him as hard as I could as I clanked along, crushed by the weight of my armor, an extra in this incredible international extravaganza, into which, I have to admit, I had leapt with enthusiasm.

Every yard of darkness ahead of us was a promise of death and destruction. But how would it come? The only element of uncertainty was the uniform of the killer. Would he be one of us? Or of them?

I hadn't done anything to Pinçon! No more than I had to the Germans... With his face like a rotten peach, his four bands that glittered all over him from his head to his belly button, his scraggly mustache and his bony knees, with the field glasses dangling from his neck like a cowbell and his 1/1000 map. I kept wondering why he was so intent on sending other people to their death. Other people who had no maps, We four horsemen on the road were making as much noise as a battalion. They must have heard us coming ten miles away, or else they didn't want to hear us. That was always a possibility. Maybe the Germans were afraid of us? Why not?

A month of sleepiness on every eyelid, that's what we were carrying, and as much again in the backs of our heads, plus all those pounds of tin.

The men in my party didn't express themselves very well. Actually they hardly spoke at all. They'd come from the ends of Brittany, and what they knew they hadn't learned at school but in the army. That night I tried to make a little conversation about the village of Barbigny with the one next to me... his name was Kersuzon.

"Kersuzon," I say. "We're in the Ardennes now... Do you see anything in the distance? I don't see a damn thing... "

"It's as black as an asshole," Kersuzon says. That was enough...

"But," I suggest, "haven't you heard anyone mention Barbigny in the course of the day? Give you an idea where it is?"

"No."

That was that.

We never did find Barbigny. We went around in circles until morning and ended up in another village, where the man with the field glasses was waiting for us. The general was taking his black coffee in the arbor outside the mayor's house when we got there.

"Ah, Pinçon!" he says in a loud voice to his chief of staff as he sees us pass, "Youth is so wonderful!" After that he went out for a leak and then, stooped over, his hands behind his back, he took a little stroll. The general was very tired that morning, the orderly confided to me, he'd slept badly, some trouble with his bladder, so it seemed.

Kersuzon always gave me the same answer when I questioned him at night, as if I'd pressed a button, it kind of tickled me. Two or three times more he said the same thing about the asshole darkness and a while after that he was killed, on his way out of some village we'd mistaken for some other village by some French soldiers who'd mistaken us for somebody else.

It was a few days, I remember now, after Kersuzon was killed that we dreamed up a little trick that suited us fine to keep from getting lost in the darkness.

So they were throwing us out of the billet. All right all right. We don't say a word. No griping, no come-back. "Clear out!" old wax face yelled as usual.

"Yes sir, very good sir."

And off we'd go in the direction of the gunfire, we didn't wait to be asked twice, all five of us. You'd have thought we were going to pick cherries. It was rolling country around there, the Meuse with its vine- covered hills, grapes that weren't ripe yet, and autumn, wooden villages well dried by three months of summer, highly inflammable.

We'd noticed that one night when we couldn't figure out where to go. There was always a village burning in the direction of the gunfire. We didn't go too close, we gave that village a wide berth and just watched, like an audience, so to speak, from maybe seven or eight miles away. And every night from then on all kinds of villages would burst into a blaze on the horizon, one after another, we'd be surrounded by them, dozens of burning villages in a circle, up ahead and on both sides, like a crazy carnival, sending up flames that licked the clouds.

We'd watch the flames as they swallowed up everything, churches and barns, one after another. The haystacks burned higher and livelier than anything else, the beams reared up in the darkness, throwing off sparks, before crashing into a sea of light.

Even from ten or fifteen miles away you get a good view of a burning village, It was a merry sight. A tiny hamlet that you wouldn't even notice in the daytime, with ugly, uninteresting country around it, you can't imagine how impressive it can be when it's on fire at night! You'd think it was Notre-Dame! A village, even a small one, takes at least all night to burn, in the end it looks like an enormous flower, then there's only a bud, and after that nothing.

Smoke rises, and then it's morning.

We'd leave the horses saddled in a field close by, and they wouldn't move. We'd go and saw wood in the grass, all but one, naturally, who'd take his turn on guard. But when you've got fires to watch, the night passes a lot more pleasantly, it's not a hardship anymore, you're not alone.

Unfortunately, the villages didn't last... After a month's time there wasn't a village left in that neck of the woods. The forests were shelled too. They didn't last a week. Forests make nice enough fires, but they don't last.

After that the roads were all clogged with artillery columns going in one direction and civilians running away in the other.

So naturally we couldn't go either way, we could only stay where we were.

We'd line up for the privilege of getting killed. Even the general couldn't find any billets with no soldiers in them. In the end we were sleeping in the fields, general or no general. Those who still had a bit of spirit lost it. That was when they started shooting men to bolster their morale, whole squadrons, and when our M.P. got a citation for the way in which he was carrying on his little private war, the real honest-to-goodness war.

* * *

They gave us a short rest, and a few weeks later we climbed back up on our horses and started north. The cold came with us. The gunfire was never far away. But we never came across any Germans except by accident, a hussar or a squad of riflemen here and there, in yellow and green, pretty colors. We seemed to be looking for them, but we beat it the moment we laid eyes on them. At every encounter two or three horsemen bit the dust, sometimes theirs, sometimes ours. And from far in the distance their riderless horses, with loose clanking stirrups, would come galloping toward us, we'd see their saddles with the peculiar cantles and all their leather as fresh and shiny as pocketbooks on New Year's Day. They were coming to see our horses, they made friends in no time. They were lucky. We couldn't have done that.

One morning when they rode in from a reconnaissance patrol, Lieutenant de Sainte-Engence[13] swore to the other officers that he hadn't made it up. "I carved 'em I tell you. Two of them!" he insisted, showing everybody his saber, and true enough, the little groove was full of caked blood, that's what it's made for.

Captain Ortolan backed him up. "He was splendid! Bravo, Sainte-Engence!... Ah, messieurs, if you'd only seen him! What a charge!"

Ortolan was in command of the squadron.

"I saw every bit of it! I wasn't far away! A thrust to the right... Zing! The first one drops!... A thrust full in the chest!... Left! Cross! Championship style!... Bravo again, Sainte-Engence! Two lancers! Less than a mile from here! Still lying there! In a plowed field! The war's over for them, eh, Sainte-Engence?... A double thrust! Beautiful! I bet they spilled their guts like rabbits!"

---

[13] Lieutenant de Sainte-Engeance. "La sainte engeance" means roughly "the no-good crew."

Lieutenant de Sainte-Engence, whose horse had galloped a long way, received his comrades' compliments with modesty. Now that Ortolan had authenticated his exploit, his mind was at rest, so he rode off some distance and cooled off his mare by circling slowly around the assembled squadron as if he were just coming in from a steeplechase.

"We must send another patrol over there!" cried Captain Ortolan. "Immediately!" He was terribly excited.

"Those two poor devils must have been lost to come this way, but there must be more behind them... Ah, Corporal Bardamu. Go take a look, you and your four men!"

The captain was talking to me.

"And when they fire at you, try to make a note of their position and come right back and tell me where they are! They must be Brandenburgers!... "

The regular army men told me that in peacetime this Captain Ortolan hardly ever showed up for duty. Now that a war was on, he made up for it. He was indefatigable. His vigor and verve, even among all those other lunatics, were getting more unbelievable from day to day. It was rumored that he sniffed cocaine. Pale, rings under his eyes, always dashing around on his fragile legs... Whenever he set foot on the ground, he'd stagger at first but then he'd get hold of himself and stride angrily over the furrowed fields in search of some new feat of daring. I wouldn't have been surprised if he'd sent us to get a light from the muzzles of the enemy's guns. He was in cahoots with death. I'd have sworn they had a contract, death and Captain Ortolan.

He'd spent the first part of his life (I had made it my business to find out) breaking his ribs in horse shows several times a year. And his legs, because of also being broken and not being used for walking, had lost their calves. When he walked, it was with nervous, pigeon-toed steps, as though walking on eggs. Seeing him in his enormous greatcoat, stooped over in the rain, you'd have taken him for the phantom hindquarters of a race horse.

It needs to be said, though, that at the start of that monstrous enterprise, during the month of August and through September, certain hours, whole days now and then, certain stretches of road and parts of forest were still propitious to the doomed... In those places you could toy with the illusion that you were more or less safe, you could finish eating your bread and bully beef without being too much plagued by the foreboding that this was the last time. But from October on there were no more of these little lulls, the hail fell thicker and sharper and faster, spiced with shot and shell. Soon we'd be at the heart of the storm, and the very thing we were trying not to see, our death, would be so close to our noses that we couldn't see anything else.

The night, which had terrified us at first, seemed almost pleasant by comparison. In the end we longed for the night and waited for it. It was harder for them to shoot at us then than in the daytime. That was the only difference that counted.

It's hard to face the facts, even in connection with war the imagination holds its own for a long time. Cats who've been threatened by fire for too long end up by jumping in the water.

During the night we'd cadge a few minutes here and there that came pretty close to the blessed days of peace, those days that now seem too good to be true, when everything was benign, when nothing really mattered, when we did so many things that had come to seem so marvelously, superlatively delightful. Days of peace, days of living velvet...

But soon the nights as well were a merciless torment. Almost every night we'd have to keep our weary bones at work, put up with a little extra torture, just so as to eat or catch a little nap in the darkness. The food convoys moved up to the front lines at a disgraceful crawl, long limping lines of shaky wagons, bursting with meat, prisoners, wounded, oats, rice, and M.P.'s, and don't forget the wine in big jiggling pot-bellied jugs that reminded us of high old times.

Behind the rolling forge and the bread wagon men came dragging themselves on foot, prisoners in handcuffs, some of theirs and some of ours, condemned to this or that, lashed by the wrists to the M.P.s' stirrups, some due to be shot the next day and no downer in the mouth than the others. It didn't spoil their appetites either, they ate their ration of that tuna fish that's so indigestible (they wouldn't have time to digest it) while waiting by the side of the road for the convoy to shove off—and they ate their last chunk of bread, too, with a civilian chained to them, who was said to be a spy but he didn't know it. Neither did we.

The military torture continued in its nocturnal aspect... Groping our way through the hump-backed streets of a village without light or face, bent under sacks that weighed more than a man, from one unknown barn to another, threatened and yelled at, haggard, with no better prospect than to end in a sea of liquid manure, sickened at the thought that we'd been tortured, duped to the entrails by a gang of vicious lunatics, who had suddenly become incapable of doing anything else than killing and spilling their guts without knowing why.

We'd flop down between two manure piles, but the noncoms would soon kick and bellow us to our feet, and send us to a different part of the convoy, to load or unload something else.

The village darkness was gorged with food and soldiers, bloated with fat, apples, oats, sugar, that we had to haul around and distribute to this squad and that squad. That convoy had brought everything except a ticket home.

Our detail was dead tired, we'd drop right next to our cart, and the sergeant-major would come around and shine his lantern on the corpses. He was an ape with a double chin. Regardless of the chaos, he had to find a watering place for the horses! Oh yes, the horses had to drink! But I've seen four men, ass and all, drop with fatigue, and fall fast asleep with the water up to their necks.

After the watering we had to find the alley we'd come by and get back to the farm, where we thought we'd left the rest of our squad. If we didn't find it, we could always pass out at the foot of some wall and sleep for an hour, if there was an hour left. In this business of getting killed, it's no use being picky and choosy... You've got to act as if life were going on, and that lie is the hardest part of it.

The wagons started back to the rear. In flight from the dawn, they hit the road again. Squeaking in every crooked wheel, off they drove, and with them went my prayer that they'd be ambushed, cut to pieces, burned that same day, the way you see in war pictures, supply column wiped out for ever and ever, with its escort of M.P. gorillas, horse soldiers, and lantern-swinging noncoms, with its work details, its sacks of lentils and flour that would never be cooked and never be seen, again. Because there are many different ways of kicking in, of exhaustion or something else, but the worst is to do it while hauling enough sacks to fill the night with.

The day when those motherfucking wagons would be shattered to the axles, they'd leave us alone, I thought, and even if only for one night, we'd be able to sleep with body and soul.

This food supply business was just one more nightmare, a nasty little monster on top of the big one, the war. Brutes to the right of us, brutes to the left of us, they were all over the place. Condemned to a deferred death, the only thing that really mattered was an enormous longing for sleep, all the rest was torture, even the time and effort it took to eat. A bend in the brook, a familiar-looking wall... But mostly it was the smells helped us find our farm, we'd reverted to dogs in the wartime night of the deserted villages. The smell of shit was the best guide of all.

The quartermaster top kick was the guardian of the regiment's hatreds, he, until further notice, was master of the world. Anybody who talks about the future is a bastard, it's the present that counts. Invoking posterity is like making speeches to worms. There in the wartime village night the top kick was corraling human cattle for the big slaughterhouses that had just opened. The top sergeant was king. King of Death! Sergeant Cretelle! Absolutely! Nobody more powerful! And nobody as power-ful, except one of their top sergeants on the opposite side.

Nothing was left of the village, no living thing except terrified cats. First the furniture went, smashed up for firewood, chairs, tables, sideboards, from the lightest to the heaviest. And anything that the boys could carry, they made off with. Combs, lamps, cups, silly little things, even bridal wreaths, everything went. As if we'd had years of life ahead of us. They looted to take their minds off their troubles, to make it look as if they had years before them. Everybody likes that feeling.

As far as they were concerned, gunfire was nothing but noise. That's why wars can keep going. Even the people who make them, who fight in them, don't really get the picture. Even with a bullet in their gut, they'd go on picking up old shoes that "might come in handy." The way a sheep, lying on its side in a meadow, will keep on grazing with its dying breath. Most people don't die until the last moment; others start twenty years in advance, sometimes more. Those are the unfortunates.

I wasn't very bright myself, but at least I had sense enough to opt for cowardice once and for all. I imagine that's why people thought I was so uncommonly calm. Be that as it may, I inspired a paradoxical confidence in our Captain Ortolan, who decided that night to entrust me with a delicate mission. It consisted, he told me in confidence, of trotting before daylight to Noirceur-sur-la-Lys,[14] a city of weavers, situated some ten miles from the village where we'd camped. My job was to find out at firsthand whether the enemy was there or not. All that day patrols had been contradicting one another, and General des Entrayes was good and sick of it. For that reconnaissance mission I was allowed to pick one of the less purulent horses in the platoon. I hadn't gone out alone in a long time. It made me feel as if I were starting on a trip. But my feeling of deliverance was illusory.

I was so tired when I set out that hard as I tried I couldn't properly visualize my own murder, I couldn't fill in the details. I moved from tree to tree, accompanied by the clanking of my hardware. All by itself my pretty saber made as much noise as a piano. I don't know if I was deserving of sympathy, but for sure I was certainly grotesque.

What could General des Entrayes have been thinking, sending me out alone into that silence, all clothed in cymbals?

The Aztecs, so the story goes, routinely disemboweled eight thousand faithful a week in their temples of the sun, a sacrifice to the god of the clouds to make him send them rain. Such things are hard to believe until you get mixed up in a war. Once you're in a war, you see how it is: the Aztecs' contempt for other people's bodies was the same as my humble viscera must have inspired in our above-mentioned General Celadon des Entrayes, who, thanks to a series of promotions, had become a kind of chickenshit god, an abominably exigent little sun.

The one tiny bit of hope I had left was of being taken prisoner. It didn't amount to much, a shred. A shred in the night, because the circumstances weren't conducive to polite preliminaries, far from it. The foe would shoot first and introduce himself afterward. Besides, what would I say to this soldier, hostile by definition, who'd come from the other end of Europe for the express purpose of murdering me?... Suppose he hesitated for one second (that was all I'd need), what would I say to him?... And come to think of it, what would he be? A sales-clerk?... A professional soldier?... A gravedigger?... In civilian life... A cook?... Horses are lucky, they're stuck with the war same as us, but nobody expects them to be in favor of it, to pretend to believe in it. Unfortunate, yes, but free! Enthusiasm, the stinker, was reserved for us!

I could see the road clearly just then and, plunked down on the mud beside it, big squares and cubes of houses, their walls whitened by the moonlight, like big unequal blocks of ice, pale and silent. Would this be the end of it all? How much time would I spend in this desolation after they'd done for me? Before it was all over? In what ditch? Beside which one of these walls? Would they come and finish me off? With a knife? Sometimes they gouged out your eyes, cut off your hands, and so on... There were all sorts of rumors on the subject, and they were no joke! A hoofbeat... Another... would be enough!... This beast makes a noise like two men with iron boots fastened together, running with a jerky, uneven step...

My heart, a rabbit, warm in its little rib cage, fearful, cowering, bewildered... You must feel pretty much the same way when you jump off the top of the Eiffel Tower. You'd like to stop yourself in mid-air.

That village kept its menace secret, but not entirely. In the center of a square a tiny fountain gurgled just for me.

That night I had everything to myself. I was the owner of the moon, the village, and of an enormous fear. I was about to break into a trot with a good hour's ride ahead of me to Noirceur-sur-la-Lys, when I caught sight of a well-veiled light over a door. I headed straight for that light, surprised to detect inside myself a kind of daring, a deserter's daring to be sure, but more than I'd ever suspected. The light disappeared the next second, but I'd seen it all right, I knocked, I kept at it, I knocked again, I called out in a loud voice, half in German, half in French to be on the safe side, to those strangers locked in the darkness.

The door finally opened by just a crack.

---

[14] Noirceur-sur-la-Lys. The Lys River is partly in Belgium and partly in northern France. The word lys = "lily." In French as in English lilies are proverbially white. Noirceur — blackness.

A voice asked: "Who are you?" I was saved. "A dragoon..."

"French?" A woman speaking. I could see her now... "Yes, French... "

"Some German dragoons were here this afternoon... They spoke French too... " "Yes, but I'm really French... "

"I see!"

She seemed to have her doubts. "Where are they now?" I asked.

"They left at about eight o'clock, heading for Noirceur... " She pointed north. A young girl, shawl and white apron, emerged from the shadow.

"What did the Germans do to you?" I asked.

"They burned a house next to the town hall, and they killed my little brother, ran a lance through his belly... He was playing on the Red Bridge, watching them go by... Look!" She showed me. "There he is."

She didn't cry. She relit the candle, that was the light I had seen. At the back of the room I saw— it was true—the little corpse lying on a mattress; it was dressed in a sailor suit with a big square collar, the face and throat were as livid as the candlelight. The child's arms and legs and back were bent, he was all doubled up. The lance had passed, like an axis for death, through the middle of his belly. His mother was on her knees beside him, crying her heart out. So was the father. Then they all started moaning at once. But my trouble was thirst.

"You wouldn't have a bottle of wine to sell me?" I asked.

"You'll have to ask my mother... She may know if there's any left... The Germans took a lot just now... " The two women talked it over in an undertone.

The daughter came back and announced: "There's none left... the Germans took it all... We'd given them plenty without being asked, but even so... "

"Oh yes, they drank and they drank," said the mother, who'd suddenly stopped crying. "They're crazy about it... "

"Must have been more than a hundred bottles," said the father, still on his knees.

"And there's not a single one left?" I kept at it, still hoping, because of my terrible thirst, especially for white wine with a good bitter tang that wakes you up a little. "I don't mind paying... "

"There's nothing left but the best!" the mother conceded. "It costs five francs a bottle." "That's fine!" I said, taking a big five-franc piece out of my pocket.

"Go and get one!" she said to the sister in a whisper.

The sister took the candle and a moment later brought up a bottle from the hiding place. I had what I wanted, there was nothing more to stay for.

"Will they come back?" I asked, anxious again.

"Maybe!" they all said together. "If they do, they'll burn everything in sight... They promised they would when they left... "

"I'll just go and see what they're up to!"

"You're very brave... It's that way," said the father, pointing in the direction of Noirceur-sur-la-Lys... He even stepped out on the road to see me on my way. The girl and her mother stayed behind, fearful, watching over the little corpse.

"Come back in!" they called out to him. "Joseph, come in. You've no business out there on the road... " "You're very brave!" the father said to me again, shaking me by the hand.

I started off again, northward, at a trot.

"At least don't tell them we're still here!" The girl was shouting. She'd come out just for that.

"They'll see for themselves tomorrow whether you're here or not," I called back. I wasn't happy about giving them my five francs. There was five francs between us. Five francs is reason enough to hate people and make you want them dead... There won't be any love to spare in this world as long as there's five francs.

"Tomorrow!" they repeated, fearing the worst...

Tomorrow, for them too, was far away, there wasn't much sense in that kind of tomorrow. The one thing any of us really cared about was living for one more hour, one more hour is a big deal in a world where everything has reduced itself to murder.

I didn't have far to go after that. I trotted from tree to tree, expecting to be challenged or shot from one minute to the next. Nothing happened.

It must have been about two in the morning, not much more, when I got to the top of a little hill, at a walk. Suddenly, looking down from there, I saw rows and rows of burning gas jets, and then in the foreground a station all lit up with its cars and its buffet, but not a sound came up to me... Nothing. Streets, avenues, street lamps, and more lights in parallel lines, whole neighborhoods, and everything else a black voracious void, with this city plunked down as if it had been lost, lying there all lit up in the heart and center of the darkness. I got down off my horse, made myself comfortable on a little hummock, and sat there looking at that city for quite some time.

That didn't tell me if the Germans had moved into Noirceur, but since I knew that in a case like that they usually set fire, I figured if they'd moved in and hadn't set fire to the place right away, they must have something very unusual up their sleeve.

No gunfire either. All very suspicious.

My horse wanted to lie down too. He tugged at his bridle and that made me turn around. When I turned back to the city, something about the look of the hummock in front of me had changed, not much, but enough to make me sing out: "Hey! Who goes there?" That change in the layout of the darkness had taken place a few steps away... Must be somebody there...

"Don't shout too loud!" came a deep, hoarse voice, very French. "You lost too?" he asked me. Now I could see him, a foot slogger, the peak of his cap was cracked in "goodbye to the army" style. After all these years I remember that moment, his silhouette emerging from the grass the way targets used to in shooting galleries, soldier targets.

We came closer. I was holding my revolver, for two beans I'd have fired, don't ask why. "Hey," he asks. "You seen them?"

"No, but I've come here to see them." "You from the 145th Dragoons?"

"That's right. You?" "I'm a reservist... "

"Oh!" I said. That amazed me. He was the first reservist I'd met in the war. We'd always been in with the Regular Army men. I couldn't see his face, but his voice was different from ours, sadder, which made him sound nicer. Because of that, I couldn't help trusting him a little. Which was something.

"I'm fed up," he said. "I'm going to get myself captured by the Boches... " He wasn't keeping any secrets.

"How are you going about it?"

All of a sudden his plan interested me more than anything else. How was he fixing to get taken prisoner? "I don't know yet."

"How'd you manage to get away?... It's not easy to get taken prisoner." "To hell with that! I'll just surrender."

"What's wrong? You scared?"

"I'm scared, and besides, the war is stupid. I don't give a damn about the Germans, they never did anything to me... "

My feeling was that I should be polite to the Germans. I'd have liked this reservist to explain, while he was about it, why I had no stomach either to make war like everybody else... But he didn't explain a thing, he just kept saying he was fed up.

Then he told me how his regiment had been dispersed at dawn the day before because some of our sharpshooters had fired on his company by mistake. They hadn't been expected just then, they'd arrived three hours ahead of schedule. So these sharpshooters, tired and taken by surprise, had fired across the fields and riddled them with bullets. I knew the story. I'd been through it myself.

"Never fear," he went on. "I saw my chance, and I took it. Robinson, I says to myself—Robinson's my name, Leon Robinson—it's now or never, I say to myself. This is the time to get going... Right? So I started through a little clump of woods and pretty soon, what do you think, I run into our captain... he's leaning against a tree, in very bad shape!... Dying!... He was holding his pants in both hands and vomiting...

Bleeding all over and rolling his eyes... There was nobody with him. He was through... 'Mama! Mama!' he was sniveling, all the while dying and pissing blood...

"'Shut up! I tell him. Mama! Mama! Fuck your mama!'... Just like that, on my way past, out of the corner of my mouth!... I bet that made him feel good, the bastard!... What do you think of that!... It's not every day you can tell the captain what you think... Too good to miss... A rare opportunity!... To get out of there faster I chucked my pack and gun... dropped 'em in a duck pond... You see, I don't take to killing people, I never learned to... even in peacetime, I never cared for fights... I'd walk away... See what I mean?... In civilian life I tried to go to the factory regularly... I was kind of an engraver, but I didn't like it because of the arguments, I was happier selling the evening papers in a quiet neighborhood where I was known, around the Bank of France... Place des Victoires, if you want to know... Rue des Petits-Champs ... that was my territory... I never went beyond the Rue du Louvre and the Palais-Royal on one side, get the idea?... In the morning I'd run errands for shopkeepers... sometimes a delivery in the afternoon, odd jobs, see?... kind of unskilled... But one thing I don't want is weapons... If the Germans see you with a weapon, you're cooked , . . But if you're dressed free and easy like I am now... Nothing in your hands... nothing in your pockets... they get the idea that it won't be hard to take you prisoner, see? They know who they're dealing with... If you go up to the Germans mother naked, that would be even better... Like a horse! They wouldn't know what army you belong to... "

"That's a fact!"

I caught on that being older is good for the mind. It puts sense into you.

"So you say they're down there?" We figured, we estimated our chances and looked for our future in the great luminous expanse of the silent city as though consulting the cards...

"Let's get started!"

First we'd have to cross the railroad tracks. If there were sentries, they'd see us. Or maybe they wouldn't. We'd soon find out. Maybe there'd be an overpass, or maybe we'd take the tunnel.

"We'll have to hurry," said Robinson... "Gotta do these things at night, people aren't friendly in the daytime, everybody plays to the gallery in the daytime, even in the war, the daytime is a circus... You taking your horse?"

I took the horse. A precaution... to get away quicker if the reception was bad. We got to the grade crossing, the big red and white arms were up. I'd never seen that kind of gate before. They weren't like that around Paris.

"Think they've moved in already?"

"Positive!" he says. "Anyway, keep going."

Now we were forced to be as brave as the brave, because of the horse who was plodding slowly behind us and seemed to be pushing us with his noise, we couldn't hear anything else. Clop! clop! went his hooves. He'd put his foot down in the middle of the echo, as if he hadn't a care in the world.

So this Robinson was counting on the night to save us... The two of us were walking down the middle of the street, with no attempt at concealment, in step what's more, we could have been drilling...

Robinson was right, the daytime was pitiless, from the earth to the sky. The way we were walking in the street, we must have looked perfectly harmless, as innocent as if we'd been coming back from a leave. "Did you hear about the 1st Hussars, taken prisoner in Lille, every last one of them... Marched right in... the way I heard it... they didn't know... the colonel in the lead... Down the main street, boy oh boy!... And then the trap closed!... In front of them... behind them... Germans everywhere!... At the windows!... Everywhere!... There they were!... Caught like rats!... Like rats! Talk about luck!" "The bastards!"

"Yeah, wasn't that something!... " We couldn't get over that marvelous capture, so neat, so conclusive... It really floored us... The shops had all their shutters closed, so did the houses, with their little gardens in front, all so neat and prim. But after the post office we saw a house, a little whiter than the rest, with all the lights on at all the windows, upstairs and down. We went and rang the doorbell, we still had our horse behind us. A thickset man with a beard opened. "I am the mayor of Noirceur," he told us right away without our asking, "and I am expecting the Germans!" This mayor steps out into the moonlight to look at us. When he saw we weren't Germans but still French, he wasn't so solemn any more. Friendly yes, but embarrassed. Obviously he hadn't been expecting us, we didn't quite fit in with the arrangements he must have made, the decisions he'd taken. The

Germans were supposed to enter Noirceur that night, he'd been notified and he'd settled everything with the Prefecture, their colonel here, their field hospital there, etc. And what if they turned up now? With us there? There'd certainly be trouble! Dreadful complications!... He didn't come out and say all that, but we could see what he was thinking.

So there in the darkness he starts talking to us about the interests of the public at large... in that enveloping silence... the public at large, that's all he would talk about... the material interests of the community... the artistic patrimony of Noirceur, entrusted to his care, a sacred trust if ever there was one... especially the fifteenth century church... suppose they burned it down!... like the one in Condé-sur-Yser!... Had we thought of that?... In a fit of temper... annoyed at finding us there... He impressed us with the full extent of our responsibility... harebrained youngsters that we were!... the Germans had no use for unsavory towns with enemy soldiers still prowling around in them. That was common knowledge...

While he was lecturing us like that in an undertone, his wife and two daughters, luscious hefty blondes, put in a word here and there to back him up... The long and the short, they didn't want us there... In the air between us there hovered sentimental and archaeological considerations, suddenly sprung to life since there was no one in Noirceur that night to contest them... patriotic, ethical, word-propelled considerations, ghosts that the mayor tried to hold fast, but they faded away, undone by our fear and selfishness, and by the plain truth for that matter.

The mayor of Noirceur himself was knocking himself out with his touching effort to convince us that our Duty was to clear out instantly... he wasn't as brutal about it as our Major Pinçon, but in his way he was every bit as determined.

The only argument we could have pitted against all those wielders of power was our contempt-ible little wish not to die and not to be burned alive. Which didn't amount to much, especially when you consider that you can't come out with sentiments like that in the middle of a war. So we wandered off into other deserted streets. Everyone I'd met that night had bared his soul to me.

"Just my luck!" said Robinson as we were pushing off. "If only you'd been a German, you're an obliging sort, you'd have taken me prisoner and we'd be all set... It's hard for a man to get rid of himself in a war!"

"What about you?" said I. "Wouldn't you have taken me prisoner if you had been a German? Maybe they'd have given you the Médaille Militaire! Some funny word the Germans must have for their Médaille Militaire..."

Seeing there was absolutely no demand for us as prisoners, we finally sat down on a bench in a little park and opened up the can of tuna fish Robinson had been warming in his pocket since morning. Now we could hear gunfire far in the distance, very far. If only both sides could have stayed in the distance where they were and left us alone!

Then we walked by the river, and alongside of some half-unloaded barges we urinated long streams into the water... We were still leading the horse by the bridle, he tagged behind us like a great big dog... Near the bridge, in the ferryman's one-room house, there was a dead man stretched out on a mattress all alone, a Frenchman, a major of light cavalry, actually he looked something like Robin-son.

"Ugly son of a bitch!" says Robinson. "I don't know about you, but I don't like dead people."

"The funny part of it," I said, "is that he looks something like you. The same long nose, and you're not much older... "

"Well, you see, it's being so tired that makes us all look alike, but oh if you'd seen me before!... In the days when I went bicycle riding every Sunday!... I was really handsome! You should have seen the calves on me! You can't beat bicycling! It develops the thighs too... "

We left the house, the match we'd lit to look at the stiff had gone out. "You see?... it's too late... you see?"

Already, in the darkness at the end of the town, a long gray and green line marked the crest of the hill: Day! One more! One less! We'd have to try and get through this one the same as the rest, the days had got to be like hoops, tighter and tighter to get through, and filled with bursts of shrapnel.

"Coming back this way tomorrow night?" he asked before we separated.

"Tomorrow night? There's no such thing... What do you think you are, a general?"

"I don't think about anything," he says. "No thoughts at all! I think about not getting killed... that keeps me busy... One more day is one more day—that's what I think!"

"You're right... So long, pal, and good luck!"

"Good luck to you too! Maybe we'll meet again!"

We each went back to his own war. And then things happened, and a lot more things that it's not easy to tell about now, because people nowadays wouldn't understand them anymore.

* * *

If you wanted to be respected and looked up to, you had to hurry up quick and pal up with the civilians, because they were becoming more and more vicious as the war went on. I saw that as soon as I got back to Paris. It also became clear to me that the women had ants in their pants and that the old men were talking big, and their fingers were all over the place, in assholes, in pockets...

The civilians back home were infected with the idea of glory, they picked it up from the soldier boys and soon learned how to bear up under it, bravely and painlessly.

Nurses and martyrs by turns, mothers were never without their long dark veils and those little diplomas the Ministry never failed to send by special messenger. In short, the home front was getting organized.

At a well-conducted funeral, you're sad too, but you think of other things, the will, your next vacation, the widow, who's a good-looker and said to be passionate, and your plans for continuing to live a great deal longer by contrast, and maybe never dying... You never can tell.

And as you follow the hearse, everybody lifts his hat to you. It's heart-warming. Then's the time to behave properly, to look dignified, not to laugh out loud, to gloat only internally. That's permissible. Everything's permissible internally.

During the war, instead of dancing on the mezzanine, you danced in the cellar. The boys had no objection, in fact they were all for it. They demanded it as soon as they got to town, and nobody thought it indecent. The one thing that's really indecent is bravery. You expect physical bravery? Then ask a worm to be brave, he's pink and pale and soft, just like us.

For my part, I had nothing to complain of. Actually, thanks to the Médaille Militaire I'd won and my wound and all, I was about to lose my innocence. They'd brought me the medal while I was in the hospital convalescing. And that same night I went to the theater, to let the civilians see it during intermissions. A triumph! Those were the first medals seen in Paris. It floored them!

That was when I met little Lola from America in the lobby of the Opéra-Comique, and it was thanks to her that I really found out what was what.

There are certain dates that stand out after months and months when you might just as well have been dead. That evening at the Opera-Comique with my medal was a turning point in my life.

Lola made me curious about the United States, because of the questions I started asking right away and that she hardly answered at all. When you start traveling that way, you never know when or how you'll get back...

At the time I'm speaking of, everybody in Paris wanted a uniform. Practically nobody was without one, except neutrals and spies, which to all intents and purposes were identical. Lola had a genuine official uniform, and it was really natty, decorated with little crosses all over, on the sleeves and on the tiny cap that she perched at a rakish angle on her wavy hair. She'd come to help us save France, as she told the hotel manager, to the best of her humble ability but with all her heart! We understood each other right away, but not completely, because the transports of the heart were beginning to give me a pain, I was more interested in the transports of the body. You can't trust the heart, not at all. I'd learned that in the war, and I wasn't going to forget it in a hurry.

Lola's heart was tender, weak, and enthusiastic. Her body was sweet, it was adorable, so what could I do but take her all together as she was? Lola was a good kid all right, but between us stood the war, the monstrous frenzy that was driving half of humanity, lovers or not, to send the other half to the slaughterhouse. Naturally this interfered with our relationship. For me, who was dragging out my convalescence as long as possible and wasn't the least bit eager to go back on duty in the flaming graveyards of no man's land, the absurdity of our massacre was glaringly obvious at every step I took in town. Whichever way I looked, I saw cynical grasping cunning.

Still, I hadn't much chance of keeping out of it, I lacked the indispensable connections. The people I knew were all poor, people whose death is of no interest to anybody. And I could hardly count on Lola to keep me safe at home. Even if she was a nurse, I couldn't have conceived of anyone more bellicose than that sweet young thing—except maybe Ortolan. If I hadn't been through the muddy fricassee of heroism myself, her little Joan of Arc number might have stirred and converted me, but since my enlistment on the Place Clichy I had grown phobically allergic to heroism, verbal or real. I was cured. Radically cured.

For the convenience of the ladies of the American Expeditionary Force, the group of nurses Lola belonged to were quartered in the Hôtel Paritz[15] and, to make things even more delightful for her personally, she had been put in charge (she had connections) of a special service, whose mission it was to supply the Paris hospitals with apple fritters. Every morning thousands of dozens of them were handed out. Lola performed this benign duty with a touching zeal, which, as it turned out, was later to have disastrous consequences.

Lola, it has to be admitted, had never made a fritter in all her life. She therefore hired a number of mercenary cooks, and after a few trials the fritters were ready for delivery, as juicy and sweet and golden as anyone could wish for. All Lola actually had to do was taste them before they were delivered to the various hospital wards. Every morning Lola got up at the stroke of ten, took her bath, and went down to the kitchens, which were situated deep in the basement. This, I repeat, she did every morning, clad only in a black-and-yellow Japanese kimono that a boyfriend in San Francisco had given her the day before she left.

In short, everything was running smoothly, and we were happily winning the war, when one fine day at lunch I found her shattered, refusing to touch so much as a single dish. I was seized with foreboding: what misfortune or sudden illness had befallen her? I begged her to entrust herself to my watchful affection.

After conscientiously tasting fritters every day for a month Lola had put on two pounds! Her little belt bore witness to the disaster, she found herself obliged to move on to the next notch. She burst into tears. I did my best to comfort her. In a turmoil of emotion we repaired by taxi to several pharmacies, situated at a considerable distance from one another. The scales proved implacable. As ill luck would have it, they all confirmed that two pounds had indeed and undeniably been gained. I suggested that she turn her job over to a friend who, on the contrary, was eager to enlarge her allurements. Lola wouldn't hear of such a compromise, which she regarded as shameful, as a kind of desertion. That, I recall, is when she told me that her great-great uncle had been a member of the crew of the eternally glorious Mayflower which landed in Boston in 1677,[16] and that in view of such a past she couldn't dream of shirking her fritter duty, which may have been humble but was nevertheless a sacred trust.

The fact remains that from that day on she barely touched her teeth—which, incidentally, were evenly set and very very enticing—to the fritters. Her dread of putting on weight completely destroyed her enjoyment of life. She began to waste away. Soon she was as afraid of fritters as I was of bullets. Because of the fritters we spent most of our time taking long healthful walks on the riverbanks and boulevards, and we stopped going to the Napolitain, because ice cream is another thing that makes ladies put on weight.

I had never dreamed of a place so comfortable to live in as her room, all pale blue with a bathroom adjoining. Photographs of her friends were all over, with dedications, not many women, lots of men, handsome, dark with curly hair, that was her type, she'd talk to me about the color of their eyes and read me the dedications, which were tender, solemn, and every last one of them absolutely irrevocable. At first those effigies embarrassed me, I felt I was being rude, but then I got used to it, The

---

[15] Hôtel Paritz. A combination of Paris and Ritz.
[16] Boston 1677. This is typical of Celine's cavalier treatment of history. He was well aware that the Mayflower landed neither in Boston nor in 1677.

moment I stopped kissing her, I was in for it, she'd start on the war and her fritters. France figured prominently in our conversation. To Lola's way of thinking, France was some sort of chivalric being, not very clearly defined in space or time, but at the moment dangerously wounded and for that very reason too too exciting. When anybody mentioned France to me, I instantly thought of my guts, so I wasn't nearly so open to patriotic ardor. Each man to his fears. Nevertheless, since she was sexually accommodating, I listened and never contradicted her. But when it came to my soul, she wasn't at all satisfied with me. She'd have liked to see me bubbling and bursting with enthusiasm, whereas I couldn't see a single reason for adopting that sublime state of mind, in fact I could see a thousand, all equally irrefutable, for persevering in the exact opposite disposition.

Obviously Lola was nuts with happiness and optimism, like all people on the good side of life, the ones with privilege, health, security, who still have à long time to live.

She kept bothering me with the soul, she was always going on about it. The soul is the body's vanity and pleasure as long as the body's in good health, but it's also the urge to escape from the body as soon as the body is sick or things are going badly. Of the two poses, you take the one that suits you best at the moment, and that's all there is to it! As long as you can choose between the two, you're all right. But I couldn't choose anymore, my die was cast! I was up to my neck in the truth; death dogged my every step, so to speak. It was very hard for me to think of anything but my suspended sentence to be murdered, a fate which everyone else regarded as just the right thing for me.

In this kind of deferred death agony that hits you when you're lucid and in good health, the mind is open to nothing but absolute truths. Once you've been through it, you'll know what you're talking about till the end of your days.

My conclusion was that if the Germans were to come and pillage, massacre, and burn everything in sight, the hotel, the fritters, Lola, the Tuileries, the cabinet ministers, their little boyfriends, the Coupole, the Louvre, the department stores, if they were to swoop down on the city and unleash the wrath of God and the fires of hell on this putrid carnival, to which nothing in the way of sordidness could possibly be added, I would have nothing to lose and everything to gain.

You don't lose much when the landlord's house burns down. Another landlord will always turn up, unless it's the same one, German or French, English or Chinese, to collect the rent... In marks or francs? What difference does it make, seeing you've got to pay...

In short, my morale was low. If I'd told Lola what I thought of the war, she'd have taken me for a monster and banished me from the ultimate joys of her boudoir. So I was careful to keep my sentiments to myself. Besides, I had outside difficulties and rivalries to worry about. Quite a few officers were trying to filch her away from me. Their competition was redoubtable, armed as they were with the seduction of their Legions of Honor. And just then the American papers were beginning to be full of this damned Legion of Honor. She cuckolded me two or three times, and I'd go so far to say that our relationship would have been in serious danger on those occasions, if it hadn't dawned on her that I could be put to a higher use, namely, made to taste the fritters every morning in her stead.

This last-minute specialization saved me. She could accept me as a substitute, for I was a valiant comrade- in-arms, hence worthy of so sacred a mission. From that moment on we were more than lovers, we were partners as well. The modern age had dawned.

To me her body was a joy without end. I never wearied of exploring that American body. I have to admit that I was a terrible lecher. I still am.

And I formed the pleasant and fortifying conviction that a country capable of producing bodies so daringly graceful, so tempting in their spiritual flights, must have countless other vital revelations to offer, of a biological nature, it goes without saying.

I made up my mind, while feeling and fondling Lola, that sooner or later I'd take a trip, or call it a pilgrimage, to the United States, the sooner the better. And the fact is that I knew neither peace nor rest (in an implacably adverse and harassed life) until I managed to go through with that profound and mystically anatomical adventure.

So it was in the immediate vicinity of Lola's rear end that I received the message of a new world. Of course Lola wasn't all body, she also had a wee little face that was adorable and just a bit cruel because of her gray-blue eyes that slanted slightly upward at the corners like a wildcat's.

Just looking at her made my mouth water, like a sip of dry wine, that flinty taste. There was a hardness in her eyes, unrelieved by the amiably commercial orientalo-Fragonard vivacity you find in nearly all the eyes in these parts.

We usually met in a cafe nearby. There were more and more wounded men hobbling through the streets, many of them very bedraggled. Collections were taken for their benefit, "days" for this group and "days" for that group, especially for the organizers of the "days." Lying, fucking, dying. A law had just been passed prohibiting all other activity. The lies that were being told surpassed the imagination, far exceeded the limits of the absurd and preposterous—in the newspapers, on posters, on foot, on horseback, on pleasure boats. Everybody was doing it. In competition, to see who could lie the most outrageously. Soon there wasn't a bit of truth in the city.

The little that had been left in 1914, people were ashamed of now. Everything you touched was phony, the sugar, the aeroplanes, the shoes, the jam, the photographs... Everything you read, swallowed, sucked, admired, proclaimed, refuted, defended was made up of hate-ridden myths and grinning masquerades, phony to the hilt. The mania for telling lies and believing them is as contagious as the itch. Little Lola's French consisted of only a few phrases, but they were all patriotic: "On les aura!... ," "Madelon, viens!... "[17] It was enough to make you cry.

Stubbornly, shamelessly she harped on the deaths of those doomed to die, actually all the women did, as soon as it became fashionable to be brave for other people.

Just as I was looking within and discovering such an extraordinary taste for everything that took me away from the war! I often asked Lola questions about America, but her answers were vague, pretentious, and manifestly unreliable, calculated to make a brilliant impression on me. But by that time I distrusted impressions. I'd been taken in once by an impression, and nobody was going to hoodwink me again. Nobody.

I believed in her body, I didn't believe in her soul. I thought of Lola as a charming goldbrick, miles away from the war, miles away from life.

She flitted across my nightmare with the mentality of the patriotic press: the poilus in the trenches, our own Lorraine, the cadets in their white gloves... In the meantime I made love to her more and more, I'd convinced her it was a good way to lose weight. But she set more store by our long walks. I hated long walks. But she insisted.

So we spent several hours every afternoon being athletic in the Bois de Boulogne, walking around the lakes and back.

Nature is a frightening thing... Even when it's solidly domesticated as in the Bois, it gives real city dwellers an eerie, anxious feeling. And that puts them in a confiding mood. The Bois de Boulogne may be damp, fenced in, greasy, and trampled, but there's nothing like it for sending memories rushing irresistibly to the minds of city dwellers strolling under the trees. Lola was not immune to that melancholy, confidential anxiety. As we walked along she told me, more or less truthfully, a thousand things about her life in New York and her little girlfriends over there.

I couldn't quite make out how much of the potpourri of dollars, engagements, divorces, dresses, and jewelry that seemed to have made up her existence was worth trying to believe.

That day we headed for the race track. In those days and that neck of the woods you still saw lots of horse- drawn carriages, children on donkeys, other children kicking up dust, and cars full of soldiers on furlough, always in desperate haste, between two trains, to track down the women strolling on the side paths, raising more dust in their hurry to go to dinner and make love, jumpy, oily, peering this way and that, tormented by the implacable clock and the lust for life. They sweated with passion, but also with the heat.

The Bois wasn't as well cared for as usual, it was neglected, in a state of administrative suspense.

"It must have been pretty here before the war," Lola observed... "So chic!... Oh, tell me about it, Ferdinand!... Your races here... Were they like ours in New York?"

---

[17] Madelon, viens, "Madelon, come." An allusion to the words "Quand Madelon vient nous servir à boire... " ("When Madelon comes and serves us drinks... "), from the popular First World War song.

To tell the truth, I'd never been to the races before the war, but to amuse her I instantly made up dozens of colorful details, drawing on stories various people had told me. The toilettes... the ladies of fashion... The gleaming carriages... The start!... The joyous, imperious horns... The water jump... The President of the Republic... The undulant betting fever, etc.

My idealized account was so much to her liking that it brought us together. At that moment Lola seemed to discover that we had at least one taste in comon, well concealed in my case, namely, a taste for social functions. She went so far as to kiss me in a burst of spontaneous emotion, something, I have to admit, that she seldom did. And then she was touched by the sadness of bygone fashions. Everyone has his own way of mourning the passage of time. It was through dead fashions that Lola perceived the flight of the years.

"Ferdinand," she asked, "do you think there will be races here again?" "When the war is over, Lola, I should think... "

"We can't be sure, can we?" "No, we can't be sure."

The possibility that there would never again be races at Long-champ overwhelmed her. The sadness of the world has different ways of getting to people, but it seems to succeed almost every time.

"Suppose, Ferdinand, suppose the war goes on a long time, maybe for years... Then it'll be too late for me... to come back here... Do you understand, Ferdinand?... You know how I love beautiful places like this... so grand, so chic... It'll be too late... Forever too late... Maybe... Maybe I'll be old, Ferdinand... When the races start up again... I'll be old... You'll see, Ferdinand, it will be too late... I can feel it will be too late..."

She was as desolate as if she'd put on two more pounds. I said everything I could think of to comfort her and give her hope... She was only twenty-three after all... The war would be over soon, oh very soon... Good times would come again... as good as before, even better... For her at least... being so adorable ... the lost years... she'd catch up with no harm done... She wouldn't run short of admirers... so soon... To please me she pretended she wasn't sad anymore.

"Do we have to keep walking?" she asked. "Your weight!... "

"Oh, that's right, I'd forgotten... "

We left Longchamp, the children had gone. Nothing left but dust. The furlough boys were still chasing Happiness, but no longer in the copses, the pursuit of Happiness had moved to the cafe ter-races around the Porte Maillot.

We headed for Saint-Cloud along the riverbank, shrouded in a dancing halo of autumn mists. As we approached the bridge, some barges loaded to the gunwales with coal and lying low in the water were thrusting their noses under the arches...

Above the fences the park deployed a great fan of greenery. Those trees are as vast and gentle and strong as dreams. But trees were something else I distrusted, ever since I'd been ambushed. Be-hind every tree a dead man. Between two lines of roses the avenue, rising gently, led to the fountains. Outside the kiosk the soda-water lady seemed to be slowly gathering the evening shadows around her skirt. Further on, along the side paths, great cubes and rectangles of dark-colored canvas were flap-ping, carnival booths, which the war had taken by surprise and suddenly filled with silence.

"It's been a whole year since they went away!" the soda-water lady told us. "You won't see two people here in a whole day now... I come out of habit... There used to be so many people!... "

That was all the old lady knew, the rest of what had happened was a blank to her. Lola wanted to go and look at the empty tents, one of those funny sad impulses.

We counted about twenty of them, a long one full of mirrors and a lot of small ones, candy stands, lotteries, even a small theater traversed with drafts. There was a tent in every space between the trees; one of them, near the Grand Avenue, had lost its flaps, it was as well ventilated as a punc-tured mystery.

These tents were leaning close to the mud and fallen leaves. We stopped near the last, the one that was bent lowest, it was pitching on its poles like a ship in the wind, with wildly flapping sails ready to snap the last of its cables. It swayed in the rising wind, a sheet of canvas flew up above the roof and flapped and flapped. The old name of the stand was written on the front in green and red letters; it had been a shooting gallery, the Gallery of the Nations. There was no one to take care of it now. Maybe the owner had gone shooting with the rest of them, with his customers.

What a lot of bullets the little targets in the stand had taken! All of them riddled with little white dots! A wedding, that always got a laugh out of them: tin figures in the first row, the bride with her flowers, the cousin, the soldier, the groom with a big red face, and in the second row the guests, who must have been killed a good many times when the carnival was still operating.

"I bet you're a good shot, aren't you, Ferdinand? If the carnival were still running, I'd challenge you... You are a good shot, aren't you, Ferdinand?"

"No, I'm not a very good shot... "

In the last row behind the wedding, another row was daubed in, the town hall with its flag. People must have shot at the town hall, too, when the gallery was working, at the windows, they'd open and a bell would clang, and they even shot at the little tin flag. And they'd shot at the regiment marching on an incline nearby, like mine on the Place Clichy, this one was between the pipes and the little balloons. People had shot at those things for all they were worth, and now they were shooting at me, yesterday and tomorrow.

"They're shooting at me, too, Lola!" I cried. It slipped out of me.

"Let's be going," she said... "You're talking nonsense, Ferdinand, and we'll catch cold."

We descended the main avenue, the Avenue Royale, toward Saint-Cloud, avoiding the mud. She held me by the hand, hers was tiny, but I couldn't think of anything but the tin wedding at the shooting gallery up there, which we had left behind us in the shadow of the trees. I even forgot to kiss Lola, something had come over me, I felt very funny. I think it was then that my head became so agitated, with all the ideas going around in it.

It was dark when we got to the Pont de Saint-Cloud.

"Ferdinand, would you like to have dinner at Duval's? You like Duval's, don't you... It would cheer you up... There's always such a big crowd... Unless you's rather eat in my room..." She was being very considerate that evening.

We finally decided on Duval's. But we'd hardly sat down when the place struck me as monstrous. I got the idea that these people sitting in rows around us were waiting for bullets to be fired at them from all sides while they were eating.

"Get out!" I warned them. "Beat it! They're going to shoot! They're going to kill you! The whole lot of you!" I was hurried back to Lola's hotel! Everywhere I saw the same thing... The people in the hallways of the Paritz all seemed to be on their way to be shot and so did the clerks behind the big desk, all of them just ripe for it, and the character down at the door with his uniform as blue as the sky and as golden as the sun, the doorman, and the officers and generals walking this way and that not nearly so gorgeous of course, but in uniform all the same, all ripe to be shot, there'd be shooting from every side, no one would escape, not this one, not that or the other. The time for joking was past...

"They're going to shoot!" I yelled at the top of my lungs in the middle of the lobby. "They're going to shoot! Beat it, all of you!... " I went to the window and shouted some more. What a disturbance! "Poor soldier boy!" the people said. The concierge led me gently to the bar, by suasion. He gave me something to drink and I drank quite a lot, and then the M.P.'s came and took me away, not so gently. There'd been M.P.'s at the Gallery of the Nations, too. I'd seen them. Lola kissed me and helped them to take me away with their handcuffs.

Then I fell sick, I was delirious, driven mad by fear, they said at the hospital. Maybe so. The best thing to do when you're in this world, don't you agree, is to get out of it. Crazy or not, scared or not.

* * *

There was quite a commotion. Some people said: "That young fellow's an anarchist, they'll shoot him, the sooner the better... Can't let the grass grow under our feet with a war on!... But there were others, more patient, who thought I was just syphilitic and sincerely insane, they consequently wanted me to be locked up until the war was over or at least for several months, because they, who claimed to be sane and in their right minds, wanted to take care of me while they carried on the war all by themselves. Which proves that if you want people to think you're normal there's nothing like having an all-fired nerve. If you've got plenty of nerve, you're all set, because then you're entitled to do practically anything at all, you've got the majority on your side, and it's the majority who decide what's crazy and what isn't.

Even so my diagnosis was very doubtful. So the authorities decided to put me under observation for a while. My little friend Lola had permission to visit me now and then, and so did my mother. That was all.

We, the befogged wounded, were lodged in a secondary school at Issy-les-Moulineaux, especially rigged to take in soldiers like me, whose patriotism was either impaired or dangerously sick, and get us by cajolery or force to confess. The treatment wasn't really bad, but we felt we were being watched every minute of the day by the staff of silent male nurses endowed with enormous ears.

After a varying period of observation, we'd be quietly sent away and assigned to an insane asylum, the front, or, not infrequently, the firing squad.

Among the comrades assembled in that suspect institution, I always wondered while listening to them talking in whispers in the mess hall, which ones might be on the point of becoming ghosts.

In her little cottage near the gate dwelt the concierge, who sold us barley sugar and oranges as well as the wherewithal for sewing on buttons. She also sold us pleasure. For noncoms the price of pleasure was ten francs. Everybody could have it. But watch your step, because men tend to get too confiding on such occasions. An expansive moment could cost you dearly. Whatever was confided to her she repeated in detail to the Chief Medical Officer, and it went into your court-martial record. It seemed reliably established that she'd had a corporal of Spahis, a youngster still in his teens, shot for his confidences, as well as a reservist in the corps of engineers, who had swallowed nails to put his stomach out of commission, and a hysteric, who had described his method of staging a paralytic seizure at the front. One evening, to sound me out, she offered me the identification papers of a father of six, who was dead, so she told me, saying they might help me to a rear echelon assignment... In short, she was a snake. In bed, though, she was superb, we came back again and again, and the pleasure she purveyed was real. She may have been a slut, but at least she was a real one. To give royal pleasure they've got to be. In the kitchens of love, after all, vice is like the pepper in a good sauce; it brings out the flavor, it's indispensable.

The school buildings opened out on a big terrace, golden in summer, surrounded by trees, with a magnificent panoramic view of Paris. It was there that our visitors waited for us on Thursdays, including Lola, as regular as clockwork, bringing cakes, advice, and cigarettes.

We saw our doctors every morning. They questioned us amiably enough, but we never knew exactly what they were thinking. Under their affable smiles as they walked among us, they carried our death sentences.

The mealy-mouthed atmosphere reduced some of the patients under observation, more emotional than the rest, to such a state of exasperation that at night, instead of sleeping, they paced the ward from end to end, loudly protesting against their own anguish, convulsed between hope and despair, as on a dangerous mountain spur. For days and days they suffered, and then suddenly one night they'd go to pieces, run to the Chief Medical Officer, and confess everything. They'd never be seen again. I wasn't easy in my mind myself.

But when you're weak, the best way to fortify yourself is to strip the people you fear of the last bit of prestige you're still inclined to give them. Learn to consider them as they are, worse than they are in fact and from every point of view. That will release you, set you free, protect you more than you can possibly imagine. It will give you another self. There will be two of you.

That will strip their words and deeds of the obscene mystical fascination that weakens you and makes you waste your time. From then on you'll find their act no more amusing, no more relevant to your inner progress than that of the lowliest pig.

Beside me, in the next bed, there was a corporal, a volunteer like me. Up until August he had been a teacher at a secondary school in Touraine, teaching history and geography, so he told me. After a few months in the front lines this teacher had turned out to be a champion thief. Nothing could stop him from stealing canned goods from the regimental supply train, the quartermaster trucks, the company stores, and anywhere else he could find them.

So he'd landed there with the rest of us, while presumably awaiting court martial. But since his family persisted in trying to prove that he had been stupefied and demoralized by shell shock, the prosecution deferred his trial from month to month. He didn't talk to me very much. He spent hours combing his beard, but when he spoke to me it was almost always about the same thing, about the method he had discovered for not getting his wife with any more children. Was he really insane? At a time when the world is upside down and it's thought insane to ask why you're being murdered, it obviously requires no great effort to pass for a lunatic. Of course your act has got to be convincing, but when it comes to keeping out of the big slaughterhouse, some people's imaginations become magnificently fertile.

Everything that's important goes on in the darkness, no doubt about it. We never know anyone's real inside story.

This teacher's name was Princhard. What can the man have dreamed up to save his carotids, lungs, and optic nerves? That was the crucial question, the question we men should have asked one another if we'd wanted to be strictly human and rational. Far from it, we staggered along in a world of idealistic absurdities, hemmed in by insane, bellicose platitudes. Like smoke-maddened rats we tried to escape from the burning ship, but we had no general plan, no faith in one another. Dazed by the war, we had developed a different kind of madness: fear. The heads and tails of the war.

In the midst of the general delirium, this Princhard took a certain liking to me, though he distrusted me of course.

In the place and situation we were in, friendship and trust were out of the question. No one revealed any more than he thought useful for his survival, since everything or practically everything was sure to be repeated by some attentive stool pigeon.

From time to time one of us disappeared. That meant the case against him was ready and the court-martial would sentence him to a disciplinary battalion, to the front, or, if he was very lucky, to the Insane Asylum in Clamart.

More dubious warriors kept arriving, from every branch of service, some very young, some almost old, some terrified, some ranting and swaggering. Their wives and parents came to see them, and their children too, staring wide-eyed, on Thursdays.

They all wept buckets in the visiting room, especially in the evening. All the helplessness of a world at war wept when the visits were over and the women and children left, dragging their feet in the bleak gas-lit corridor. A herd of sniveling riffraff, that's what they were; disgusting.

To Lola it was still an adventure, coming to see me in that prison, as you might have called it. We two didn't cry. Where would we have got our tears from?

"Is it true that you've gone mad, Ferdinand?" she asked me one Thursday. "It's true," I admitted. "But they'll treat you here?"

"There's no treatment for fear, Lola." "Is it as bad as all that?"

"It's worse, Lola. My fear is so bad that if I die a natural death later on, I especially don't want to be cremated. I want them to leave me in the ground, quietly rotting in the graveyard, ready to come back to life... Maybe... how do we know? But if they burned me to ashes, Lola, don't you see, it would be over, really over... A skeleton, after all, is still something like a man... It's more likely to come back to life than ashes... Reduced to ashes, you're finished!... What do you think?... Naturally the war... "

"Oh, Ferdinand! Then you're an absolute coward! You're as loathsome as a rat... "

"Yes, an absolute coward, Lola, I reject the war and everything in it... I don't deplore it... I don't resign myself to it... I don't weep about it... I just plain reject it and all its fighting men. I don't want anything to do with them or it. Even if there were nine hundred and ninety-five million of them and I were all alone, they'd still be wrong and I'd be right. Because I'm the one who knows what I want: I don't want to die."

"But it's not possible to reject the war, Ferdinand! Only crazy people and cowards reject the war when their country is in danger... "

"If that's the case, hurrah for the crazy people! Look, Lola, do you remember a single name, for instance, of any of the soldiers killed in the Hundred Years War?... Did you ever try to find out who any of them were?... No!... You see? You never tried... As far as you're concerned they're as anonymous, as indifferent, as the last atom of that paperweight, as your morning bowel movement... Get it into your head, Lola, that they died for nothing! For absolutely nothing, the idiots! I say it and I'll say it again! I've proved it! The one thing that counts is life! In ten thousand years, I'll bet you, this war, remarkable as it may seem to us at present, will be utterly forgotten... Maybe here and there in the world a handful of scholars will argue about its causes or the dates of the principal hecatombs that made it famous... Up until now those are the only things about men that other men have thought worth remembering after a few centuries, a few years, or even a few hours... I don't believe in the future, Lola... "

When she heard me flaunting my shameful state like that, she lost all sympathy for me... Once and for all she put me down as contemptible, and decided to leave me without further ado. It was too much. When I left her that evening at the hospital gate, she didn't kiss me.

Evidently the thought that a condemned man might have no vocation for death was too much for her. When I asked her how our pancakes were doing, she did not reply.

On my return to the dormitory, I found Princhard at the window with a crowd of soldiers around him. He was trying out a pair of dark glasses on the gas light. The idea, he explained, had come to him last summer at the seashore, and since it was summer now, he was planning to wear them next day in the park. That park was enormous and exceedingly well policed by squads of vigilant orderlies. The next day Princhard insisted on my going for a walk on the terrace with him to try out his beautiful glasses. A blazing afternoon beat down on him, defended by his opaque lenses. I noticed that his nose was almost transparent at the nostrils and that he was breathing hard.

"My friend," he confided, "time is passing and it's not on my side. My conscience is immune to remorse, I have been relieved, thank God, of those fears... It's not crimes that count in this world... people stopped counting them long ago... What counts is blunders... And I believe I've made one... that's absolutely irremediable... "

"Stealing canned goods?"

"Yes, just imagine... I thought I was being so clever... My idea was to abstract myself from the battle and return, disgraced but still alive, to peace, as one returns, exhausted, to the surface of the sea after a long dive... I almost succeeded . , . but this war, undoubtedly, has been going on too long... So long that cannon fodder disgusting enough to disgust the Patrie is no longer conceivable... She has begun to accept every offering, regardless of where it comes from, every variety of meat! Today there's no such thing as a soldier unworthy to bear arms and, above all, to die under arms and by arms... They're going, latest news, to make a hero out of me!... How imperious the homicidal madness must have become if they're willing to pardon—no, to forget!—the theft of a can of meat! True, we have got into the habit of admiring colossal bandits, whose opulence is revered by the entire world, yet whose existence, once we stop to examine it, proves to be one long crime repeated ad infinitum, but those same bandits are heaped with glory, honors, and power, their crimes are hallowed by the law of the land, whereas, as far back in history as the eye can see—and history, as you know, is my business— everything conspires to show that a venial theft, especially of inglorious foodstuffs, such as bread crusts, ham, or cheese, unfailingly subjects its perpetrator to irreparable opprobrium, the categoric condemnation of the community, major punishment, automatic dishonor, and inexpiable shame, and this for two reasons, first because the perpetrator of such an offense is usually poor, which in itself connotes basic unworthiness, and secondly because his act implies, as it were, a tacit reproach to the community. A poor man's theft is seen as a malicious attempt at individual redress... Where would we be? Note accordingly that in all countries the penalties for petty theft are extremely severe, not only as a means of defending society, but also as a stern admonition to the unfortunate to know their place, stick to their caste, and behave themselves, joyfully resigned to go on dying of hunger and misery down through the centuries for ever and ever... Until today, however, petty thieves enjoyed one advantage in the Republic, they were denied the honor of bearing patriotic arms. But that's all over now, tomorrow I, a thief, will resume my place in the army... Such are the orders... It has been decided in high places to forgive and forget what they call my momentary madness, and this, listen carefully, in consideration of what they call the honor of my family. What solicitude! I ask you, comrade, is it my family that's going to serve as a strainer and sorting house for mixed French and German bullets?... It'll just be me, won't it? And when I'm dead, is the honor of my family going to bring me back to life?... I can see how it will be with my family when these warlike scenes have passed... as everything passes... I can see my family on fine Sundays... joyfully gamboling on the lawns of a new summer... while three feet under papa, that's me, dripping with worms and infinitely more disgusting than ten pounds of turds on the Fourteenth of July, will be rotting stupendously with all my deluded flesh... Fertilize the fields of the anonymous plowman—that is the true future of the true soldier! Ah, comrade! This world, I assure you, is only a vast device for kidding the world! You are young! Let these minutes of wisdom be as years to you! Listen well, comrade, and don't fail to recognize and understand the tell-tale sign, which glares from all the murderous hypocrisies of our Society: 'Compassion with the fate, the condition of the poor... ' I tell you, little man, life's fall guys, beaten, fleeced to the bone, sweated from time immemorial, I warn you, that when the princes of this world start loving you, it means they're going to grind you up into battle sausage ... That's the sign... It's infallible. It starts with affection. Louis XIV, at least, and don't forget it, didn't give a hoot in hell about his beloved people. Louis XV ditto. He smeared his asshole with them. True, we didn't live well in those days, the poor have never lived well, but the kings didn't flay them with the obstinacy, the persistence you meet with in today's tyrants. There's no rest, I tell you, for the little man, except in the contempt of the great, whose only motive for thinking of the common people is self-interest, when it isn't sadism... It's the philosophers... another point to look out for while we're at it... who first started giving the people ideas... when all they'd known up until then was the catechism! They began, so they proclaimed, to educate the people... Ah! What truths they had to reveal! Beautiful! brilliant! unprecedented truths! And the people were dazzled! That's it! they said. That's the stuff! Let's go and die for it! The people are always dying to die! That's the way they are! 'Long live Diderot!' they yelled. And 'Long live Voltaire!' They, at least, were first-class philosophers. And long live Carnot,[18] too, who was so good at organizing victories! And long live everybody! Those guys at least don't let the beloved people molder in ignorance and fetishism! They show the people the roads of Freedom! Emancipation! Things went fast after that! First teach everybody to read the papers! That's the way to salvation! Hurry hurry! No more illiterates! We don't need them anymore! Nothing but citizen-soldiers! Who vote! Who read! And who fight! And who march! And send kisses from the front! In no time the people were good and ripe! The enthusiasm of the liberated has to be good for something, doesn't it? Danton wasn't eloquent for the hell of it. With a few phrases, so rousing that we can still hear them today, he had the people mobilized before you could say fiddlesticks! That was when the first battalions of emancipated maniacs marched off!... the first voting, flagmatic suckers that Dumouriez[19] led away to get themselves drilled full of holes in Flanders! As for Dumouriez himself, who had come too late to these new-fangled idealistic pastimes, he discovered that he was more interested in money and deserted. He was our last mercenary. The free-gratis soldier... was something really new... So new that when Goethe[20] arrived in Valmy, Goethe or not, he was flabbergasted. At the sight of those ragged, impassioned cohorts, who had come of their own free will to get themselves disemboweled by the King of Prussia in defense of a patriotic fiction no one had ever heard of, Goethe realized that he still had much to learn. This day,' he declaimed grandiloquently as befitted the habits of his genius, 'marks the beginning of a new era!' He could say that again! The system proved successful... pretty soon they were mass-producing heroes, and in the end, the system was so well perfected that they cost practically nothing. Everyone was delighted. Bismarck, the two Napoleons,

---

[18] Carnot. Lazare Carnot (1753-1823). Statesman and general. Member of the Convention and of the Committee of Public Safety under the French Revolution. Surnamed "Organizer of Victory" for his work in organizing and directing the Revolutionary armies.
[19] Dumouriez.. Charles-François Dumouriez (1739-1823). Went over to the Revolution and in collaboration with Kellermann won the battle of Valmy against the Prussians in 1792. In the following year he was defeated at Neerwinden and denounced to the National Assembly as a traitor. Whereupon he deserted to the Austrians.
[20] Goethe. Goethe was indeed present at the battle of Valmy, and Céline's quotation is reasonably accurate.

Barrès,[21] Elsa the Horsewoman.[22] The religion of the flag promptly replaced the cult of heaven, an old cloud which had already been deflated by the Reformation and reduced to a network of episcopal money boxes. In olden times the fanatical fashion was: 'Long live Jesus! Burn the heretics!'... But heretics, after all, were few and voluntary... Whereas today vast hordes of men are fired with aim and purpose by cries of: 'Hang the limp turnips! The juiceless lemons! The innocent readers! By the millions, eyes right!' If anybody doesn't want to fight or murder, grab 'em, tear 'em to pieces! Kill them in thirteen juicy ways. For a starter, to teach them how to live, rip their guts out of their bodies, their eyes out of their sockets, and the years out of their filthy slobbering lives! Let whole legions of them perish, turn into smidgens, bleed, smolder in acid—and all that to make the Patrie more beloved, more fair, and more joyful! And if in their midst there are any foul creatures who refuse to understand these sublime truths, they can just go and bury themselves right with the others, no, not quite, their place will be at the far end of the cemetery, under the shameful epitaphs of cowards without an ideal, for those contemptible slugs will have forfeited the glorious right to a small patch of the shadow of the municipal monument erected by the lowest bidder in the central avenue to commemorate the reputable dead, and also the right to hear so much as a distant echo of the Minister's speech next Sunday, when he comes around to urinate at the Prefecture and sound off over the graves after lunch... "

But from the end of the garden someone was calling Princhard. The head physician had sent his orderly to get him on the double.

"Coming," Princhard cried. He had barely time enough to hand me the draft of the speech he had been trying out on me. A ham if there ever was one.

I never saw Princhard again. He had the same trouble as all intellectuals—he was ineffectual. He knew too many things, and they confused him. He needed all sorts of gimmicks to steam him up, help him make up his mind.

It's been a long time... since that night when he went away. But I remember it well. Suddenly the houses

at the end of our park stood out sharply, as things do before the night takes hold of them. The trees grew larger in the twilight and shot up to the sky to meet the night.

I never made any attempt to get in touch with Princhard, to find out if he had really "disappeared," as they kept saying. But it's best if he disappeared.

* * *

While the war was still on, the seeds of our hateful peace were being sown.

A hysterical bitch, you could see what she'd be like just by watching her cavorting in the dance hall of the Olympia. In that long cellar room, you could see her squinting out of a hundred mirrors, stamping her feet in the dust and despair to the music of a Negro-Judeo-Saxon band. Britishers and Blacks, Levantines and Russians were everywhere, smoking and bellowing, military melancholies lined up on the red plush sofas. Those uniforms that people are beginning to find it hard to remember were the seeds of the present day, of something that is still growing and that won't become total shit for a while yet, but will in the long run.

Every week, after spending a few hours at the Olympia, warming up our desires, a few of us would go calling on our friend Madame Herote,[23] who kept a lingerie, glove, and bookshop in the Impasse des Bérésinas[24] behind the Folies Bergère, a covered passage that isn't there anymore, where little girls brought little dogs on leashes to do their business.

---

[21] Barrès. Maurice Barrès (1862-1923). Writer and politician. Extreme French nationalist, obsessed by the German menace.

[22] Elsa the Horsewoman. *Elsa la Cavalière*, the title of a novel by Pierre MacOrlan (1882-1970). A slight anachronism because the novel did not appear until 1921.

[23] Madame Herote. From érotique—"erotic."

[24] Impasse des Bérésinas. This street figures prominently in Death on the Installment Plan and is no doubt the Passage Choiseul, where Céline grew up.

We went there to grope for our happiness, which all the world was threatening with the utmost ferocity. We were ashamed of wanting what we wanted, but something had to be done about it all the same. Love is harder to give up than life. In this world we spend our time killing or adoring, or both together. "I hate you! I adore you!" We keep going, we fuel and refuel, we pass on our life to a biped of the next century, with frenzy, at any cost, as if it were the greatest of pleasures to perpetuate ourselves, as if, when all's said and done, it would make us immortal. One way or another, kissing is as indispensable as scratching.

My mental state had improved, but my military situation was still uncertain. I had leave to go out now and then. Anyway, the name of our lingerie lady was Madame Herote. Her forehead was low and so narrow that at first you felt uneasy in her presence, but her lips were so smiling and voluptuous that after a while you didn't see how you could get away from her. Under a surface of staggering volubility and unforgettable ardor, she concealed a set of simple, rapacious, and piously mercantile aims.

In a few months she piled up a fortune, thanks to the Allies and thanks above all to her uterus. Her ovaries had been removed; to put it plainly, she had been operated for salpingitis the year before. That liberating castration had made her fortune. Gonorrhea in a woman can be providential. A woman who spends her time worrying about pregnancy is a virtual cripple, she'll never go very far.

Old men and young men thought, and so did I, that love was easily and cheaply available in the backrooms of certain lingerie-bookshops. That was still true some twenty years ago, but today a lot of things aren't done anymore, especially some of the most agreeable. Every month Anglo-Saxon puritanism is drying us up a little more, it has already reduced those impromptu backroom carousals to practically nothing. Now marriage and respectability are the thing.

In those days, for the last time, there was still freedom to fuck standing up and cheap, and Madame Herote put it to good use. One Sunday an auction room appraiser with time on his hands sighted her shop and went in; he's still there. He was slightly gaga, and gaga he remained, but nothing more. Their happiness aroused no interest in the neighborhood. In the shadow of the newspapers with their delirious appeals for ultimate patriotic sacrifices, life went on, strictly rationed, larded with precautions, and more trickily resourceful than ever before, Those are the heads and tails, the light and shade, of the same coin.

Madame Herote's appraiser invested money in Holland for his better-informed friends, and for Madame Herote as well once they became intimate. Her stock of neckties and brassieres and almost-chemises attracted customers of both sexes and brought them back time and time again.

Any number of national and international encounters took place in the pink shadow of those curtains, amid the incessant loquacity of Madame Herote, whose substantial, talkative, and overwhelmingly perfumed person would have put the most bilious of males in a lecherous mood. Far from losing her head in these miscellaneous gatherings, Madame Herote turned them to her advantage, first in terms of money, since she levied a tithe on all sentimental transactions, but also through her enjoyment of all the lovemaking that went on around her. She took pleasure in bringing couples together and as much or more in breaking them up by means of tale-telling, insinuations, and out and out treachery.

She never wearied of fomenting happiness and tragedy. She stoked the life of the passions, and her business prospered.

Proust, who was half ghost, immersed himself with extraordinary tenacity in the infinitely watery futility of the rites and procedures that entwine the members of high society, those denizens of the void, those phantoms of desire, those irresolute daisy-chainers still waiting for their Watteau, those listless seekers after implausible Cytheras. Whereas Madame Herote, with her sturdy popular origins, was firmly fastened to the earth by her crude, stupid, and very specific appetites.

Maybe, if people are so wicked, it's only because they suffer, but years can elapse between the time when they stop suffering and the time when their characters take a turn for the better. Madame Herote's impressive material and amatory success hadn't had time yet to soften her rapacious instincts.

She was no more hateful than most of the shopkeeping ladies about, but she took so much trouble convincing people of the contrary that one doesn't tend to forget her. Her shop was more than a meeting place, it was a kind of secret gateway to a world of wealth and luxury, in which, much as I had wanted to, I had never set foot until then, and from which I was promptly and embarrassingly ejected after one furtive incursion, my first and last.

In Paris the rich live together. Their neighborhoods adjoin and coalesce, so as to form a wedge of urban cake, the tip of which touches the Louvre and the rounded outer edge is bounded by the trees between the Pont d'Auteuil[25] and the Porte des Ternes. That's the good part of the city. All the rest is shit and misery.

At first glance the rich neighborhoods don't look so very different from the rest of the city, except that the streets are a little cleaner. But if you want to go deeper in your excursion, to get inside the people who live there, you'll have to rely on chance or on intimate connections.

Madame Herote's shop could give you some little access to this preserve, through the Argentines who came in from the privileged neighborhoods to buy shirts and underwear and flirt with the unusual selection of ambitious, theatrical, musical, and well-built young friends whom Madame Herote deliberately gathered around her.

I, who, as they say, had nothing to offer but my youth, became too much interested in one of them. Little Musyne they called her in her crowd.

In the Passage des Bérésinas, the shopkeepers all knew one another, it was like a provincial village wedged for years between two Paris streets, in other words, everybody slandered and spied on everybody else as much as was humanly and deliriously possible.

What the shopkeepers mostly talked and complained about before the war was the petty, desperately thrifty life they all led. Among other sordid hardships, the chronic complaint of those shopkeepers was being obliged by the prevailing gloom to light their gas at four in the afternoon because of their showcases. But inside the shops, the selfsame twilight made for an atmosphere conducive to off-color suggestions.

Nevertheless, a good many of the shops were being ruined by the war, while Madame Herote's, thanks to the young Argentines, to officers with per diem allowances, and to the advice of her friend the appraiser, enjoyed a prosperity on which, as you can easily imagine, the whole neighborhood commented in the most vitriolic terms.

It was just about then, for instance, that the famous pastry shop at 112 lost its best customers. The latest mobilization was to blame. So many horses had been requisitioned that the ladies with the long gloves, who had dropped in regularly at teatime, would have been obliged to walk. They stopped coming, and they never came back. Sambanet, the music binder, was suddenly unable to resist the urge, which had long tormented him, to sodomize a soldier. A bungled attempt one night did him irreparable harm with certain patriotic gentlemen, who accused him forthwith of being a spy. He was obliged to close up shop.

Then Mademoiselle Hermance, at No. 26, who had hitherto specialized in the sale of a certain mentionable or unmentionable item made of rubber, would have been doing all right under the prevailing circumstances, if she hadn't found it so unconscionably difficult to procure her "merry widows," which were made in Germany.

In short, it was only Madame Herote who, on the threshold of a new era of lighter-than-air democratic lingerie, found an easy way to prosperity.

Plenty of anonymous letters were written from shop to shop, and they didn't mince words. Madame Herote preferred for her entertainment to write to highly placed persons, so demonstrating that a virulent ambition was the cornerstone of her character. She wrote several to the Premier, for instance, just to convince him that he was a cuckold, and some to Marshal Pétain[26] in English, with the help of

[25] Pont d'Auteuil. Céline's geography is as free and easy as his history, though he knew Paris like the back of his hand. Both extremities of the wide end of the wedge are slightly displaced, the one linguistically, the other geographically. Pont d'Auteuil should be Porte d'Auteuil, which is far away, and Porte des Ternes should be Porte Maillot, which isn't far at all. Then you get the eastern edge of the Bois de Boulogne, hence the trees.

[26] Pétain. Philippe Pétain (1856-1961), general. Took part in the battle of the Marne. Commanded victorious French troops at Verdun. Made commander-in-chief of the French armies in 1916 and created a marshal of France

a dictionary, to drive him crazy. But what's an anonymous letter? Water off a duck's back. Every day Madame Herote received a whole packet of these unsigned letters, which didn't smell good, I assure you. She'd be pensive, upset, for about ten minutes, but then she'd recover her composure, she didn't care how or by what means, but she got it back good and solid, for there was no place for doubt in her inner life, and still less for truth.

Among her customers and protégées, there were several young ladies from the entertainment world— actresses and musicians—who came with more debts than clothes. Madame Herote gave them advice, and it helped them no end. One of them was Musyne, the most attractive of the lot for my money. Musyne was a musician, she played the violin, a very shrewd little angel, as I was soon to learn. Implacable in her determination to succeed here on earth and not in heaven, she was doing all right at the time of our first meeting in an adorable, exceedingly Parisian, and now completely forgotten little act at the Variétés.[27] She'd appear with her violin in a kind of impromptu prologue in melody and verse. A charming, complicated genre.

Smitten as I was, my days became a frenzy, dashing from the hospital to the back door of her theater. I was seldom alone in waiting for her. The ground forces would snatch her away in a twinkling, the flyers had an even easier time of it, but undoubtedly the seduction prize went to the Argentines. As more and more soldiers swarmed to the colors, their cold-storage meat business assumed the proportions of a tidal wave. Little Musyne made a good thing of those profiteering days; she knew what she was doing, since then the Argentines have gone out of existence.

I didn't understand. I was being hornswoggled by everything and everybody, women, money, and ideas. I was a sucker, and I didn't like it. I still run into Musyne now and then, every two years or so she crosses my path, as people one has known well tend to. Two years is the time it takes to perceive at one glance, a glance as sure as instinct, the ugliness that can come over a face, even one that was delicious in its day.

For a moment you hesitate, then you accept the face as it has become, with its repugnant cumulative disharmony. What can you do but acquiesce in this slow, painstaking caricature which two years have etched, but accept the passage of time, that portrait of ourselves. Then we can say that we've really recognized each other (like some foreign banknote that one hesitates to accept at first sight), that we hadn't taken a wrong turn, that each on his own we'd traveled the right road, the inevitable road to decay, for another two years. That's all there is to it.

When she ran into me like that, I frightened her so with my big head it looked as if she wanted to run away, to avoid me, to turn aside, anything... Obviously, as far as she was concerned, I stank of a whole past. But I've known her age for too long, and try as she will she absolutely can't escape me. She stands there, evidently put off by my existence, as if I were a monster. She, so sensitive, feels obliged to ask me crude, stupid questions, the kind that a housemaid caught stealing sugar might ask. All women are domestics at heart. But possibly she imagines this revulsion more than she feels it; that's the only consolation I can find. Maybe I'm not really repulsive, but only give her the illusion that I am. Maybe I'm an artist in that line. After all, why wouldn't there be an art of ugliness as well as beauty? Maybe it's a gift that needs to be cultivated.

For a long time I thought little Musyne was stupid, but that was only because I was vain and she had run out on me. Before the war, you know, we were all a lot more ignorant and conceited than today. A little nobody like me was much more likely to take rubbish for rainbows than he would be today. I thought being in love with somebody as adorable as Musyne would give me every kind of strength and virtue, especially the courage I lacked, just because she was so pretty and such a gifted musician. Love is like liquor, the drunker and more impotent you are, the stronger and smarter you think yourself and the surer you are of your rights.

Dozens of Madame Herote's cousins had made the supreme sacrifice, so she never left her passage except in deep mourning. To tell the truth, she seldom went out, because the appraiser was pretty

in 1918. After French defeat in World War II became premier of unoccupied France. Tried and sentenced to death in 1945. Sentence commuted to life imprisonment by de Gaulle.
[27] Variétés. Theatre des Variétés, a theater in Montmartre devoted chiefly to operettas and light comedies. Several of Offenbach's operas were performed there.

jealous. We gathered in the dining room behind the shop, which with the coming of prosperity had taken on the appearance of a little salon. There we would chat and pass the time in a pleasant, well-behaved kind of way under the gas jet. Little Musyne at the piano would charm us with classical pieces, only classical music was thought fitting in those sorrowful times. We'd sit there for whole afternoons, side by side, the appraiser in the middle, musing over our secrets, our fears and hopes.

Madame Herote's maid, whom she had hired only a short time before, was always bursting with impatience to find out when this one would finally make up his mind to marry that one. In her village free love was unheard of. All those Argentines and officers and slippery-fingered customers filled her with an almost animal terror.

More and more often Musyne was monopolized by the South American customers. What with waiting for my angel, I soon got to know the caballeros' kitchens and servants very well. Naturally the valets took me for a pimp. In the end everybody took me for a pimp, including Musyne and, I'm pretty sure, the regulars at Madame Herote's shop. There was nothing I could do about it. Sooner or later people are bound to classify you as something.

I wangled another two months' convalescent leave, and there was even some talk of a medical discharge. Musyne and I decided to go and live together in Billancourt. This was actually a subterfuge to ditch me, because she took advantage of its being so far away to come home less and less frequently. She was always finding some pretext for spending the night in Paris.

The nights in Billancourt were soft and sweet, enlivened now and then by those childish airplane or zeppelin alarms which provided the civilian population with thrills and self-justification. While waiting for Musyne, I'd walk as far as the Pont de Grenelle,[28] where the darkness rises from the river to the overhead Métro tracks, with their strings of lights traversing the darkness and their enormous metallic hulks, hurling themselves like thunder at the flanks of the big buildings on the Quai de Passy.

There are neighborhoods like that in big cities, so stupidly ugly that you're almost always alone there.

In the end Musyne was showing up at our so-called home only once a week. More and more often she'd spend the evening accompanying some lady singer at the house of some Argentine. She could have made a living playing at the movies, and it would have been a lot easier for me to call for her, but the Argentines were lively and paid well, while the movie houses were dismal and the pay was wretched. Life is made up of those little preferences.

To complete my misery, the Theater of the Armies came along. In no time Musyne got to know dozens of people at the Ministry. More and more often she went off to entertain our soldier boys at the front and stayed away for weeks on end, serving up sonatas and adagios to the troops. The front seats in the orchestra would be occupied by top brass, well placed to admire her legs, while the soldiers, seated on wooden stands behind their commanders, had to make do with melodious echoes. After the performance, of course, she would spend exceedingly complicated nights in the hotels of the army area. One day she came home as happy as a lark, brandishing a certificate of heroism, signed if you please by one of our glorious generals. With that diploma she became a real success.

It made her ever so popular with the Argentine colony. They feted her, they were mad about my Musyne, oh, what an adorable little front-line violinist! So rosy-cheeked and curly-headed, and a heroine to boot. Those Argentines knew which side their bread was buttered on, their admiration for our glorious generals knew no bounds, and when my Musyne came back to them with her authentic document, her pretty phiz, and her nimble, heroic little fingers, each tried to love her more than the next, they tried to outbid each other, so to speak. The poetry of heroism holds an irresistible appeal for people who aren't involved in a war, especially when they're making piles of money out of one. It's only natural.

Ah, jaunty heroism! Strong men have swooned away! The shipbuilders of Rio offered their names and their shares to the adorable young thing who feminized the warlike valor of the French so charmingly for their benefit. Musyne, I have to admit, had managed to outfit herself with a delightful

---

[28] Pont de Grenelle. The bridge with the Métro on it is not the Pont de Grenelle but the next one in a northwesterly direction, the Pont de Bir-Hakeim, then called the Pont de Passy.

little repertory of war adventures, they were wonderfully becoming, like a jaunty little cap. Sometimes she amazed me with her skillful touch, and listening to her I had to own that when it came to tall stories I was a clumsy faker compared to her. She had a gift for locating her fantasies in a dramatic faraway setting that gave everything a lasting glow. It often struck me that when we combatants spun yarns they tended to be crudely chronometric and precise. Her medium was eternity. Claude Lorrain[29] was right in saying that the foreground of a picture is always repugnant and that the interest of an artwork must be seen in the distance, in that unfathomable realm which is the refuge of lies, of those dreams caught in the act, which are the only thing men love. The woman who can turn our despicable nature to account has no difficulty in becoming our darling, our indispensable and supreme hope. We expect her to preserve our illusory raison d'être, but on the other hand she can make a very good living while performing this magic function. Instinctively, Musyne did just that.

The Argentines lived in the Ternes area and on the fringes of the Bois, in small private houses, resplendent and well fenced-in, which were kept so delightfully warm in that wintry weather that when you came in from the street your thoughts suddenly took an optimistic turn, you couldn't help it.

In my jittery despair, I had taken to waiting for Musyne in the butler's pantry as often as possible, a stupid thing to do. Sometimes I waited until morning, I was sleepy, but jealousy kept me awake, and so did the quantities of white wine the servants poured out for me. I seldom saw the Argentine masters of the house, I heard their songs and their blustering Spanish and the piano which never stopped but was usually being played by other hands than those of my Musyne. What, meanwhile, was she doing with her hands, the slut?

When she saw me at the door in the morning, she made a face. I was still as natural as an animal in those days. I was like a dog with a bone, I wouldn't let go.

People waste a large part of their youth in stupid mistakes. It was obvious that my darling was going to leave me, flat and soon. I hadn't found out yet that mankind consists of two very different races, the rich and the poor. It took me... and plenty of other people... twenty years and the war to learn to stick to my class and ask the price of things before touching them, let alone setting my heart on them.

So as I warmed myself in the pantry with the servants, I was unaware that the people dancing over my head were Argentine gods, they could have been German, French, or Chinese, that didn't mean a thing, the point was that they were gods, rich people, that's what I should have realized. Them upstairs with Musyne, me downstairs with nothing. Musyne was thinking seriously of her future, and naturally she preferred to do that kind of thinking with a god. I, too, was thinking of my future, but in a kind of delirium, because my constant companion was a muted fear of being killed in tbe war or of starving when peace came. I had a death sentencé hanging over me, and I was in love. A nightmare, to put it mildly. Not far away, less than seventy miles, millions of brave, well-armed, well-trained men were waiting to settle my hash, and plenty of Frenchmen were waiting, too, to pump me full of lead if I declined to be cut into bleeding ribbons by the opposite side.

A poor man in this world can be done to death in two main ways, by the absolute indifference of his fellows in peacetime or by their homicidal mania when there's a war. When other people start thinking about you, it's to figure out how to torture you, that and nothing else. The bastards want to see you bleeding, otherwise they're not interested! Princhard was dead right. In the shadow of the slaughterhouse, you don't speculate very much about your future, you think about loving in the days you have left, because there's no other way of forgetting your body that's about to be skinned alive.

Since Musyne was slipping away from me, I took myself for an idealist, which is the name we give to our little instincts clothed in high-sounding words. My leave was drawing to an end. The newspapers were summoning every conceivable combatant to the colors, first of all, it goes without saying, the ones without connections. An official order had gone out that no one should think of anything but winning the war.

---

[29] Claude Lorrain. Claude Gellée, known as le Lorrain (1600-82). French landscape painter who spent most of his life in Rome.

Musyne, like Lola, was extremely eager to have me get back to the front on the double and stay there, and since I seemed to be dragging my feet, she decided to expedite matters, which was unusual for her.

One night when for a change we went home to Billancourt together, the fire brigade came by blowing bugles, and everybody in our house went scrambling down to the cellar in honor of some zeppelin.

Those petty panics, when a whole neighborhood in pajamas would pick up candles and vanish, cackling and clucking, into the bowels of the earth to escape a peril that was almost entirely imaginary, showed up the terrifying futility of those people, who behaved by turns like frightened hens and sheepish sheep. These preposterous inconsistencies ought to disgust the most patient, the most tenacious of sociophiles for good and all.

At the first blast of the bugle, Musyne forgot every bit of the heroism for which she had been cited at the Theater of the Armies. She insisted on rushing into some hole and dragging me with her, into the Métro, the sewers, anywhere, as long as it was sheltered and deep enough under ground! After a while the sight of all those people, our fellow tenants, fat and thin, jovial and majestic, descending four by four, into the salutary pit, armed even me with indifference. Brave or cowardly— there's not much difference. A poltroon in one situation, a hero in another—it's the same man, and he doesn't think any more in one aspect than in the other. Everything unrelated to making money is infinitely beyond him. The question of life and death escapes him completely. Even on the subject of his own death his cogitations are feeble and ass-backward. He understands money and theatricals, nothing else.

Musyne whined when I resisted. Other tenants urged us to come along, and in the end I gave in. There were several cellar compartments to choose from, and various suggestions were made. The majority finally favored the butcher's storage cellar, it was deeper down, so they said, than any of the others. On the stairs I caught a whiff of an acrid odor that I knew only too well and which I absolutely couldn't bear.

"Musyne," I said, "are you really going down there? With all that meat hanging on hooks?" The question surprised her. "Why not?"

"Well," I said, "I have certain memories. I'd rather go back upstairs... " "You mean you're leaving me?"

"You'll join me as soon as it's over." "But it may go on a long time... "

"I'd rather wait for you upstairs," I said. "I don't like meat, and it'll be over soon."

During the alert, sheltered in their dens, the tenants exchanged sprightly comments. Some ladies in kimonos, the last to arrive, swept with elegance and grace into that odoriferous chasm, where the butcher and his wife bade them welcome, at the same time apologizing for the artificial cold, indispensable for the conservation of their merchandise.

Musyne vanished with the rest. I waited in our apartment, a night, a whole day, a year... She never came back to me.

From that time on I became harder and harder to please. I had only two thoughts in my head: to save my skin and go to America. But getting away from the war was a first step which kept me busy and breathless for months and months.

The patriots kept clamoring: "Guns! Men! Ammunition!" They never seemed to get tired. It looked as if they wouldn't be able to sleep until poor Belgium and innocent little Alsace were wrested from the German yoke. It was an obsession which, so we were told, prevented the best of our fellow citizens from breathing, eating, or copulating. But it didn't seem to prevent the survivors from swinging business deals. Morale was doing all right on the home front.

There was every reason to ship us back to our regiments in a hurry. But when the medics looked me over, they still found me subnormal, barely good enough to be sent to another hospital, this one for the bones and nervous system. One morning six of us, three artillerymen and three dragoons, all of us sick and wounded, left the depot in quest of this institution where shattered courage, demolished reflexes, and broken arms were repaired. First, like all wounded soldiers at the time, we stopped for a checkup at the Val- de-Grâce,[30] that noble pot-bellied citadel, with its beard of trees. The corridors smelled like a third-class railway carriage—a smell that's gone today, forever no doubt, compounded of feet, straw, and oil lamps. We didn't hang fire at the Val, they'd barely caught sight of us when two administrative, bedandruffed, and overworked officers chewed us out good and proper, threatened us with a court-martial, and projected us via other administrators into the street. They had no room for us, so they said, and directed us, very vaguely, to a bastion situated somewhere in the outskirts.

From bistrot to bastion, from absinthe to café crème, the six of us wandered about, at the mercy of every misdirector, in search of this new refuge which seemed to specialize in the treatment of incompetent heroes like us.

Only one of us had even the most rudimentary personal property, and that fitted nicely into a little tin box marked "Pernot Biscuits," a well-known brand at the time, though I never hear it mentioned anymore. In that box our comrade kept a few cigarettes and a toothbrush. Come to think of it, we used to kid him about the care he took of his teeth, which was most unusual at the time. "Homosexual" we used to call him'.

Finally, in the middle of the night, we approached the outworks, swollen with darkness of the Bicêtre bastion. No. 43 it was called. That was the place.

It had just been renovated to serve as a home for elderly cripples. They hadn't even finished laying out the garden.

When we got there, there wasn't a living soul in the military section, only the concierge. The rain was coming down in buckets. The concierge was terrified when she heard us, but we made her laugh by touching her in the right place. "I thought it was the Germans," she said. "They're miles away," we told her. "Where are you wounded?" she asked with concern.—"All over, but not in the cock!" said one of the artillerymen. That, I don't mind telling you, was real wit, just the kind the concierge liked.

Later on some old men on welfare were lodged in that bastion with us. New buildings with miles and miles of window glass had been thrown up for them in a hurry, and there they were kept like insects until the end of the war. On the surrounding hills a rash of skimpy housing lots vied for possession of the seas of mud inadequately contained by rows of precarious shacks, in the shadow of which one would occasionally see a head of lettuce and three radishes, of which, it is hard to say why, the nauseated slugs were making the houseowner a present.

Our hospital was clean. You have to hurry to see that kind of thing, move in at the beginning, the first few weeks, because maintenance isn't a French virtue, we have no taste for it, in fact, we're downright disgusting in that respect. We flopped on six metal beds, at random and by moonlight, the building was so new the electricity hadn't been put in yet.

Early next morning the doctor came and introduced himself, he seemed delighted to see us and exuded cordiality. He had reasons for being pleased, he'd just been promoted to major, and in addition he had the most beautiful eyes you ever saw, supernatural velvet, he made use of them to flutter the hearts of several volunteer nurses, who surrounded him with attentions and sympathetic mimicry and feasted on every word and move of their dear doctor. At the very first meeting he took our morale in hand and told us as much. Taking one of us by the shoulders and shaking him with paternal familiarity, he explained the regulations in a comforting tone and indicated the quickest and surest way of getting ourselves sent back to the front to be lambasted some more.

Wherever they came from, no two ways about it, that was their only thought. It seemed to give them a kick. It was the new vice. "France, my friends," he proclaimed, "has put her trust in you. France is a woman. She is counting on your heroism! She has been a victim of the most cowardly, the most abominable aggression. She has a right to expect her sons to avenge her to the hilt! To restore, even at the cost of the extreme sacrifice, every square inch of her territory! All of us here in the hospital, my friends, will do our duty, and we expect you to do yours! Our science is at your disposal! It is yours! All its resources will be devoted to curing you! Help us with your good will! I know we can count on your good will! We hope, we trust, that each one of you will soon resume his place side by

[30] Val-de-Grâce. A former abbey, converted into a military hospital in 1795.

side with his dear comrades in the trenches! Your sacred place! Defending your beloved soil! Vive la France! Forward to battle!" He knew how to talk to soldiers.

We were all standing at attention at the foot of our beds. Behind him a brunette, one of his group of pretty nurses, was having a hard time controlling her feelings, which were made visible by three or four tears. The other nurses, her friends, tried to comfort her: "Don't worry, sweetie, he'll be back... I'm sure he will!"

Her cousin, a plumpish blonde, was consoling her the most. As she passed us, holding her up with both arms, the plump one told me this weakness had overcome her pretty cousin because her fiancé had just gone off to the navy. Our impassioned medical authority tried to soothe the tragic and beautiful emotion aroused by his short, vibrant speech. He was embarrassed and grieved. The apprehension he had awakened in this profound and noble heart, all sensibility and tenderness, was too painful. "If we had only known, Doctor," the blonde cousin whispered, "we'd have warned you... They love each other so dearly, you can't imagine!" The group of nurses and the Master went their way. Chattering and swishing they receded down the corridor. They had finished with us.

I tried to recollect, and to fathom the meaning of, the speech the man with the beautiful eyes had just made, but far from depressing me, when I thought it over, his words struck me as just what was needed to disgust me with the whole idea of dying. My comrades were of the same opinion, but they did not, like me, see a kind of challenge or insult in them. They made no attempt to understand what was going on around us; all they saw, and that unclearly, was that the usual delirium of the world had so increased in the last few months that there was nothing stable left for a man to build his existence on.

Here in the hospital, just as in the Flanders night, death stalked us. Here, to be sure, it threatened from a distance, but just as implacably, once the Administration set it in pursuit of your trembling carcass.

Here, it was true, they didn't bawl us out, in fact they spoke gently, and they never talked about death, but our death sentence showed up distinctly in the corner of every paper they asked us to sign and in all the precautions they surrounded us with... those tags around our necks and wrists... whenever they let us out for a few hours. And all the advice they gave us!... We felt counted, watched, serial-numbered, enrolled in the vast multitude that would soon be leaving for the front. So naturally all the civilian and medical personnel around us seemed more cheerful than we were. The nurses, the bitches, weren't in the same boat, their only thought was to go on living, to live longer and longer, to live and love, to stroll in the park and to copulate thousands and thousands of times. Every one of those angelic creatures had a plan all worked out in her perineum, like a convict, a little plan for love later on, when all of us soldier boys should have perished in God knows what mud and God knows how!

Then they would sigh with a very special commemorative tenderness that would make them more attractive than ever; interspersed with heartbreaking silences, they would evoke the tragic days of the war, the ghosts... "Do you remember little Bardamu?" they would say in the gathering dusk, thinking of me, the lad who had coughed so much and given them such a time to make him stop... "Poor boy, his morale was way down... I wonder what became of him?"

A few poetic regrets, if adroitly placed, are as becoming to a woman as gossamer hair in the moonlight.

What I couldn't help hearing under their spoken words and expressions of sympathy was this: "Nice little soldier boy, you're going to die... You're going to die... This is war... Everyone has his own life... his role... his death... We seem to share your distress... But no one can share anyone else's death... A person sound in body and soul should take everything that happens as entertainment, neither more nor less, and we are wholesome young women, beautiful, respected, healthy, and well bred... For us the automatism of biology transforms the whole world into a joyous spectacle, into pure joy! Our health demands it!... We can't afford the ugly dissipations of sorrow... We need stimulants and more stimulants... You'll soon be forgotten, dear little soldier boys... Be nice, die quickly... and let's hope the war will be over soon, so we can marry one of your charming officers... preferably one with dark hair... And long live the Patrie that Papa's always talking about! . . , How wonderful love must be when Johnny comes marching home!... Our little husband will be decorated!... cited for bravery...

You can shine his lovely boots on our happy wedding day if you like... if you're still in existence, soldier boy... Won't you be happy about our happiness, soldier boy?... "

Every morning we saw our doctor, time and again we saw him surrounded by his nurses. He was a scientific light, we were told, The old men from the charity hospital next door would come jerking past our rooms, making useless, disjointed leaps. They'd go from room to room, spitting out gossip between their decayed teeth, purveying scraps of malignant, worn-out slander. Cloistered in their official misery as in an oozing dungeon, those aged workers ruminated the layer of shit that long years of servitude deposit on men's souls. Impotent hatreds grown rancid in the pissy idleness of dormitories. They employed their last quavering energies in hurting each other a little more, in destroying what little pleasure and life they had left.

Their last remaining pleasure! Their shriveled carcasses contained not one solitary atom that was not absolutely vicious!

As soon as it was settled that we soldiers were going to share the relative comfort of the bastion with those old men, they began to detest us in unison, but that didn't stop them from begging for the crumbs of tobacco on our window sills and the bits of stale bread that had fallen under our benches. At mealtimes they pressed their parchment-skinned faces against the windows of our mess hall. Over their crinkled rheumy noses, they peered in at us like covetous rats. One of those invalids seemed smarter and wickeder than the rest, he'd come and entertain us with the songs of his day, Pere Birouette[31] he was called. He'd do anything we asked provided we gave him tobacco, anything except walk past the hospital morgue, which incidentally was never idle. One of our jokes was to make him go that way, while supposedly taking him for a little stroll. "Won't you come in?" we'd say when we got to the door. He'd run away, griping for all he was worth, so fast and so far we wouldn't see him again for at least two days. Pere Birouette had caught a glimpse of death.

Professor Bestombes, our medical major with the beautiful eyes, had installed a complicated assortment of gleaming electrical contraptions which periodically pumped us full of shocks. He claimed they had a tonic effect, and we had to put up with them on pain of banishment. It seems that Bestombes was very rich; he must have been to be able to buy all those expensive electrocution machines. He could afford to throw money around because his father-in-law, a political bigwig, had done some heavy finagling while purchasing land for the government.

Naturally the doctor exploited his advantages. Crime and punishment, it all adds up. We took him as he was, and we didn't hate him. He examined our nervous systems with meticulous care and questioned us in a tone of polite familiarity. This sedulously cultivated good nature enchanted the nurses in his section, who all came of excellent families. Every morning these cuties looked forward to his displays of affability, which were just so yummy. In short, we were all actors in a play—he, Bestombes, had chosen the role of a benevolent, profoundly human and humane scientist. We pulled together, that was the essential.

In this new hospital I shared a room with Sergeant Branledore,[32] a re-enlisted man. He was an old hospital hand. He'd been dragging his perforated intestines around for months and had been in four different hospitals.

He had learned in the process how to attract and to hold the active sympathy of the nurses. He vomited, pissed, and shat blood with astonishing frequency; he also had a lot of trouble breathing, but none of that would have sufficed to win him the special good graces of the nurses, who had seen worse. So between two choking fits, if a doctor or nurse was passing, Branledore would sing out: "Victory! Victory! Victory will be ours!" Or he'd murmur those same words with one corner or the whole of his lungs, as the circumstances required. Thus attuned to the ardently aggressive literature of the day by a well-calculated bit of histrionics, he enjoyed the highest moral standing. That man knew his stuff.

Since all the world was a stage, acting was the thing. Branledore knew what he was doing. And indeed nothing looks more idiotic, nothing is more irritating than a sluggish spectator who turns up

---

[31] Père Birouette. From hiroute, a familiar term for the male sex organ.
[32] Sergeant Branledore. From branler, to masturbate.

on stage by mistake. When you're up there, you've got to join in, come to life, act a part, take the plunge or clear out. Especially the women demanded a show, the bitches had no use at all for clumsy amateurs. Unquestionably war went straight to their ovaries, they demanded heroes, and if you weren't a hero you had to pretend to be one or be prepared for the most ignominious fate.

After a week in this new hospital we realized that we would absolutely have to change our image, and thanks to Branledore (a lace salesman in civilian life) the selfsame men, who on our arrival had been terror- stricken, shunning the light, haunted by disgraceful memories of slaughterhouses, meta-morphosed ourselves into an incredible gang of swashbucklers, determined to conquer or die, and, take my word for it, armed with derringdo and the most outrageous language. Our speech had indeed become vigorous and so obscene that the ladies sometimes blushed, but they never complained be-cause it is generally agreed that a soldier is as brave as he is wild and cruder than there is any need to be, so much so that his bravery can be measured by the crudeness of his language.

At first, though we copied Branledore to the best of our ability, our patriotic act wasn't quite right, it wasn't really convincing. It took a good week, two in fact, of intensive rehearsing before we had fully caught on.

As soon as that scientific luminary, our Professor Major Doctor Bestombes, noticed the striking improvement in our moral attitudes, he decided to encourage us by admitting a few visitors, our par-ents to begin with.

To judge by stories I had heard, certain soldiers, really gifted types, experienced a kind of intox-ication, you might even speak of an exotic thrill, in combat. Whenever I tried to imagine this particular brand of pleasure, just trying laid me low for at least a week, I felt so incapable of killing anyone that I thought I might just as well give it up right away and abandon the whole idea. Not that I lacked experience, they'd done everything possible to inculcate a taste for killing, but I simply had no talent in that direction. Maybe my initiation should have been more gradual.

One day I decided to tell Professor Bestombes how hard I was finding it, body and soul, to become as brave as I should have liked to be and as the undoubtedly sublime circumstances required. I was uneasy, afraid he would think I was being insolent and talking out of turn. Not at all! The great man said he was delighted that I'd come to him and bared my troubled soul so fully and frankly, "You're better, friend Bardamu!" he concluded. "You're better, that's all there is to it! Yes, Bardamu, I regard your coming to me like this, absolutely of your own free will, as a most encouraging sign of a marked improvement in your mental state... Vandesquin,[33] that modest but infinitely wise observer of moral breakdown in the soldiers of the Empire, summed up his findings, back in 1802, in a memoir that is quite unjustly neglected by students of the present day, but must nevertheless be regarded as a classic. In it he describes, with remarkable insight and precision, the so-called 'confessional crises' met with in moral convalescents, and terms them the most encouraging of all symptoms... Almost a century later our great Dupré[34] established his now celebrated nomenclature of the same symptom and characterized the identical crisis as a 're-collection of memories'; according to the same author, this crisis, if the cure is properly administered, should soon be followed by a massive break-up of anxiety percepts and the definitive liberation of the area of consciousness, this being the second stage in the process of psychic recovery. Elsewhere, employing the bold terminology that was his special gift, Dupré devises the formula 'disencumbering cogitative diarrhea' for this crisis, which is accom-panied by intense euphoria, a marked resumption of relational activity, a sudden and striking restora-tion, among other things, of sleep, which in some cases has been known to go on for days at a time, and lastly, at a more advanced stage, by conspicuous hyperactivity of the genital functions, amount-ing, sometimes in patients who were previously frigid, to a positive sexual frenzy: 'The patient recov-ers not by easy stages, but at a gallop.' Such was the magnificently descriptive metaphor by which another of our great French psychiatrists of the last century, Philibert Margeton,[35] characterized this recuperative triumph, this sudden resurgence of normal functions in a patient recovering from the fear

---

[33] Vaudesquin. Probably fictitious.
[34] Dupré. Ernest Dupré (1862-1921). An eminent specialist in neurology and psychiatry.
[35] Margeton. Probably fictitious.

syndrome... As for you, Bardamu, I already, at the present moment, regard you as a true convalescent... Would it interest you, Bardamu, since we have arrived at this gratifying conclusion, to know that I shall be reading a paper on the fundamental characteristics of the human mind at the Society for Military Psychology tomorrow?... It is not without its merits, I venture to believe."

"Oh yes, Professor, I take a passionate interest in these questions... "

"Well then, Bardamu, to make a long story short, the thesis I put forward is that before the war man was an unknown quantity for the psychiatrist and the resources of his psyche an enigma..."

"That is also my humble opinion, Professor..."

"You see, Bardamu, the war, by providing us with such unprecedented means of trying men's nervous systems, has been a miraculous revealer of the human mind... Recent pathological disclosures have given us matter for centuries of meditation and study... Let's face it , . . Up until now we hardly suspected the richness of man's emotional and spiritual resources! Today, thanks to the war, all that has changed! By a process of breaking and entering, painful to be sure, but decisive, nay providential for science, we have penetrated his innermost depths'. Ever since the first revelations came to my attention, the duty of the modern psychologist and moralist has been clear to me, Bestombes, beyond any possible doubt! Our psychological conceptions are in need of total revision!"

I, Bardamu, was of exactly the same opinion.

"Yes indeed, Professor, I am convinced that... "

"Ah, you think so too, Bardamu... You say so yourself! In man, you see, there is a balance between good and evil, between egoism on the one hand and altruism on the other... In elite subjects more altruism than egoism. Am I right? Don't you agree?" "Exactly, Professor, you've hit the nail on the head... "

"And what, Bardamu, I ask you, what is the highest known concept, the concept best suited to arousing the altruism of the elite subject and compelling it to manifest itself unequivocally?"

"Patriotism, Professor!"

"Ah, you see? The word is yours, not mine. You understand, Bardamu!... Patriotism and glory, which is its corollary and proof!"

"How true!"

"Ah! our soldier boys... at their first baptism of fire they spontaneously cast off all sophisms and subsidiary concepts, in particular the sophism of self-preservation. Instinctively and immediately they merge with our true raison d'etre, the Patrie. For the attainment of truth, Bardamu, intelligence is not only superfluous, it is in the way. Like all essential truths, the Patrie is a truth of the heart! The common people understand that... and that is where the inept scientist goes wrong... "

"It's beautiful, Professor! Too beautiful! I am reminded of the Ancients!"

Bestombes pressed both my hands almost affectionately. And in a fatherly tone he added for my special benefit: "That, Bardamu, is how I mean to treat my patients, electricity for the body, and for the mind massive doses of patriotic ethics, injections as it were of invigorating morality!"

"I understand, Professor!"

I was indeed beginning to understand more and more.

On leaving him I joined my invigorated companions at Mass in the brand-new chapel, I caught sight of Branledore in a corner, demonstrating his moral vigor by giving the concierge's little girl lessons in enthusiasm. He beckoned me to join him, and I did. That afternoon some of our parents came from Paris for the first time since we'd been there, and from then on they came every week.

I had finally written to my mother. She was glad to see me again and whimpered like a bitch whose puppy has been given back to her. She thought she was doing me a lot of good by kissing me, but she was miles behind the bitch, because she believed what they said when they took me away from her. A dog only believes what it can smell. One afternoon my mother and I took a long walk through the streets around the hospital, dawdling down half-finished byways, with lampposts that hadn't been painted yet, between long, oozing house fronts with their windows full of gaudy dangling rags, the shirts of the poor... We listened to the crackling song of the frying pans, a tempest of rancid fat. In the great shapeless desert surrounding the city, the rot in which its false luxury ends, the city shows everyone who wants to look the garbage piles of its enormous posterior. There are factories one avoids when out for a stroll, which emit smells of all sorts, some of them hardly believable. The air roundabout couldn't possibly stink any worse. Nearby a little street carnival molders between two chimneys of unequal height, the wooden horses cost too much for the rickety dribbling children with nosefuls of fingers, who long for them and stand spellbound, sometimes for weeks on end, attracted and repelled by their forlorn rundown look and the music.

What efforts are made to keep the truth away from these places, but it comes back again and again, to grieve for everybody. Drinking is no help, red wine as thick as ink, nothing helps, the sky in those places never changes, it's a vast lake of suburban smoke, shutting them in.

Under foot the mud drags you down with fatigue, and the sides of existence are also closed, shut off by hotels and more factories. Even the walls in that section are coffins. With Lola gone for good and Musyne too, I had nobody left. That's why I finally wrote to my mother, just to see somebody. I was only twenty, and all I had was a past. The two of us together, my mother and I, walked through dozens of Sunday streets. She told me little things about her business, what the people around her were saying about the war, that it was sad, "horrible" in fact, but that with plenty of courage we'd all come through in the end, the ones that got killed were an accident, like in the races, if you kept your seat properly you wouldn't fall. To her the war was just one more affliction, she tried not to think about it too much, because it frightened her in a way, it was full of terrifying things she didn't understand. She had no doubt that poor people like her were born to suffer in every way, that that was their role on earth, and that if things had been going so badly of late, the cumulative faults of the poor must have a good deal to do with it... They must have been very naughty, of course they hadn't meant to be, but they were guilty all the same, and giving them a chance to expiate their transgressions by suffering was a great kindness... My mother was an "untouchable."

That resigned, tragic optimism was her only faith and the foundation of her character.

The two of us, in the rain, went down streets of vacant lots. The sidewalks in that part of the world sink and evade your step, in winter the branches of the little ash trees at the edge hold the raindrops a long time, a tenuous fairyland trembling in the breeze. Our way back to the hospital led past a number of newly built hotels, some had names, others hadn't even gone to that much trouble. "Rooms by the week" was all they had to say for themselves. The war had suddenly emptied them of all the workers and wage slaves who had lived there. They wouldn't even come back to die. Dying is work, too, but they'd do it somewhere else.

My mother was tearful as she took me back to the hospital. She accepted the accident of my death, and not content to acquiesce, she wondered if I was as resigned to it as she was. She believed in fate as implicitly as she did in the beautiful standard meter at the Conservatoire des Arts et Métiers, which she had always spoken of with respect, because she had learned in her youth that the one she used in her notions shop was a scrupulous copy of that superb official original.

Between the housing lots in that degraded countryside there were still a few fields and gardens here and there and, attached to those scraps of land, a few aged peasants wedged in between the new buildings. When there was time left before I had to be back, my mother and I went to watch them, those comical peasants obstinately poking iron into the earth, that soft grainy substance, where the dead are laid to rot but which gives us our bread all the same. "The ground must be terribly hard," my mother said every time she saw them. She was puzzled. You see, she only understood miseries that resembled her own, city miseries, and she tried to figure out what the country kind could be like. That was the only curiosity I ever saw in my mother. It was all the diversion she needed for a Sunday, and she took it back to the city with her.

I never heard from Lola, or from Musyne either. Those sluts were on the good side of the situation, from which we, the flesh earmarked for sacrifice, were barred by smiling but implacable orders. Twice I'd been sent back to the places where the hostages were coralled. My future was all settled.

* * *

As I've told you, Branledore, my neighbor at the hospital, enjoyed permanent popularity with the nurses. He was swathed in bandages and dripping with optimism. All the other patients envied him and copied his manner. Once we'd become presentable and ceased to be moral lepers, we all began to get visits from socialites and political bigwigs. People started telling each other in the drawing rooms that Professor Bestombes' Neuro-Medical Center had become a temple and home, as it were, of the most intense patriotic fervor. Our visiting days came to be patronized not only by bishops, but also by an Italian duchess, a big munitions magnate, and before long by the personnel of the Opera and the Comedie Franchise. A beautiful young actress from the Comedie, who recited poetry like nobody's business, came to my personal bedside and declaimed some superlatively heroic lines for my special benefit. As she spoke, her perverse red hair (she had the complexion that went with it) was tossed by extraordinary waves that sent vibrations straight to my perineum. When this divine creature questioned me about my feats of arms, I gave her so many poignant details that she began to devour me with her eyes. Deeply moved, she asked leave to have the most intense passages in my narrative framed in verse by a poet who happened to be one of her admirers. I consented without hesitation. Informed of this project, Professor Bestombes expressed his special approval. He even granted an interview on the subject to an "illustrated national weekly," whose photographer took our picture all together on the hospital steps with the beautiful actress beside us. "In these tragic days," cried Professor Bestombes, who never missed a trick, "it is the poet's highest duty to revive our taste for the epic! This is no time for trivial artifice! Down with emasculated literature! A new soul has been born to us in the great and noble tumult of battle! The great patriotic renewal... The lofty summits to which our glory is destined!... We demand the sustaining grandeur of the epic!... For my part, I find it admirable that this sublime, creative, and never to be forgotten collaboration between a poet and one of our heroes should have taken place under our very eyes in this hospital which I direct!"

Branledore, my roommate, whose imagination had been rather outdistanced by mine and who didn't figure in the photograph, was seized with a keen, tenacious jealousy. He became my embittered rival for the palms of heroism. He made up new stories, he surpassed himself, no one could stop him, his exploits verged on delirium.

It was difficult for me to get the jump on him, to improve on his extravagances, yet none of us at the hospital resigned himself to defeat; in a fever of emulation we all vied with one another in composing brilliant pages of military "history" in which to figure sublimely. In those heroic romances we wore the skins of phantasmagoric characters, but deep within them our ludicrous selves trembled body and soul! I'd like to have seen people's faces if they had found out what we were really like. The war had been going on too long.

Our great friend Bestombes received the visits of innumerable foreign celebrities, neutrals, skeptics, and scientists of all persuasions. Spruce, besabered inspectors from the War Ministry passed through our wards, their military careers had been extended, they had been rejuvenated and revitalized with pay increases. So naturally they were generous with praise and citations. Everything was perfect. Bestombes and his wounded heroes were the pride of the medical profession.

My fair admirer from the Comédie came back and paid me a private visit, while her pet poet was completing the rhymed narrative of my exploits. One day I finally ran into this pale, anxious young man in one of the corridors. The doctors, he told me, had assured him that the fragility of his heart strings was well-nigh miraculous. Consequently these same doctors, always concerned with the protection of the frail, had kept him out of the army. To make up for which our young bard had undertaken, at the risk of his health and last spiritual energies, to forge "The Moral Cannon of Our Victory." A magnificent— and it goes without saying—unforgettable weapon. Practically everything was unforgettable in those days.

I wasn't going to complain, since he had picked me from among so many undeniably brave men as his hero! And, I have to admit, they honored me royally. It was magnificent. The recitation was given at the Comédie Française itself, as part of a so-called poetic afternoon. The whole hospital was invited. When my vibrant redhead appeared on the stage, striding grandly, her figure draped in the for once voluptuous folds of the tricolor, the whole audience, flushed with desire, rose to its feet and gave her one of those ovations that never seem to end. Naturally I had known what to expect, but my amazement was real all the same. I could not conceal my stupefaction from my neighbors at hearing her, my magnificent friend, thrill and throb and sigh in such a way as to make the dramatic effect of the episode I had dreamed up for her more vivid and more moving. Her poet was miles beyond me for fantasy, he had monstrously magnified mine, enhanced it with flamboyant rhymes and high-sounding adjectives, which fell with a solemn reverberation on the breathless, admiring silence. Coming to the climax of a period, the most impassioned of the lot, the actress turned toward the box where Branledore and I and a few other wounded men were sitting, and held out her two magnificent arms as though offering herself to the most heroic among us. At that particular moment the poet was faithfully rendering a deed of awe-inspiring bravery that I had attributed to myself. I don't remember exactly what it was, but I'm sure it was something pretty good. Luckily, when it comes to heroism, people are willing to believe anything. The audience caught the meaning of her symbolic offering, turned in our direction, ecstatic, stamping, bellowing with joy, and clamored for the hero.

Branledore took up the whole front row of the box and blotted out the rest of us. He hid us almost completely with his bandages. He did it on purpose, the bastard.

But two of our comrades climbed up on chairs behind him so the crowd could admire them over his head and shoulders. They brought the house down.

I came close to crying out: "But it's all about me! Me and nobody else!" I knew my Branledore, we'd have exchanged insults in front of all those people, we might even have used our fists. So in the end he was the winner, he triumphed. Just as he'd planned, he had the whole storm of applause to himself. Defeated, we took refuge backstage, where fortunately we were feted again. That was some comfort. But our actress and inspiration wasn't alone in her dressing room. The poet, her poet, our poet was with her. He had the same weakness for young soldier boys as she did. They made it clear to me very artistically. A handsome offer. They repeated it, but I ignored their kind suggestions. I was the loser, because they had influence and things might have worked out very well. I left them abruptly, I was nettled. Silly of me, I was young.

To recapitulate: the aviators had snatched Lola away from me, the Argentines had taken Musyne, and now this harmonious invert had filched my magnificent actress. Sadly I left the Comédie as the last torches were being extinguished in the corridors and returned alone, without recourse to the streetcar, to our hospital, that mantrap plunked down in the tenacious mud of the rebellious suburbs.

* * *

The plain truth, I may as well admit it, is that I've never been really right in the head. But just then such fits of dizziness would come over me for no reason at all that I could easily have been run over. The war had given me the staggers. When it came to pocket money, all I could count on during my stay at the hospital was the few francs my mother managed to scrape up for me each week. So as soon as I could I went looking for little extras here and there, wherever I could find them. One of my old bosses looked like a likely prospect, and I went right over to see him.

I remembered opportunely that in a certain obscure period of my life shortly before the war I had worked as a helper for this Roger Puta[36] who owned a jewelry shop near the Madeleine. My work for that loathsome jeweler consisted of menial jobs, such as polishing the silverware in the shop. There was lots of it, every shape and size, and it was hard to take care of in the gift-giving holiday season because it was always being handled.

As soon as my classes were out at medical school where I was engaged in exacting and (because I kept flunking the exams) interminable studies, I hightailed it to the backroom of Monsieur Puta's shop, where I labored for two or three hours, until dinnertime, applying whiting to his chocolatières.

In return for my work, I was fed, copiously I have to admit, in the kitchen. Then in the morning before school, I had to take the watchdogs out for a piss. All that for forty francs a month. Puta's jewelry shop on the corner of the Rue Vignon sparkled with thousands of diamonds, each one of which cost several decades of my salary. They're still sparkling in the exact same place, by the way. When everybody was mobilized, this Puta got himself assigned to the auxiliaries and put under the special orders of a certain cabinet minister, whose car he drove from time to time. But he also made himself useful, unofficially of course, by supplying the ministry with jewels. The higher officials speculated, with gratifying results, on present and future transactions, and the longer the war went on,

---

[36] Puta. From pute, putain, meaning "whore."

the more jewels were needed. Monsieur Puta got so many orders that he sometimes had trouble filling them.

When he was overworked, Monsieur Puta managed to look slightly intelligent because of the fatigue that tormented him, but only then. When rested, his face, in spite of his undeniably fine features, became so harmonious in its idiotic placidity that it would be hard not to carry a despairing memory of it with one to the grave.

His wife, Madame Puta, seldom left the cashier's desk, in a manner of speaking she and the desk were one. She had been brought up to be a jeweler's wife. That had been her parents' ambition. She knew her duty inside and out. The prosperity of the cash drawer brought happiness to husband and wife. Not that Madame Puta was bad looking, not at all, she could even, like so many others, have been rather pretty, but she was so careful, so distrustful that she stopped short of beauty just as she stopped short of life—her hair was a little too well dressed, her smile a little too facile and sudden, and her gestures a bit too abrupt or too furtive. You racked your brains trying to figure out what was too calculated about her and why, you always felt uneasy when she came near you. This instinctive revulsion that shopkeepers inspire in anyone who goes near them and who knows what's what is one of the few consolations for being as down at heel as people who don't sell anything to anybody tend to be.

The petty cares of business were everything to Madame Puta; in this she resembled Madame Herote, but with a difference; in her case, they possessed her body and soul, just as God possesses his nuns.

And yet from time to time, she would give a thought to the world around her. For instance, she might indulge in some little expression of sympathy for parents with sons at the front. "How dreadful this war must be for people with grown-up children!"

"Think before you shoot your mouth off!" her husband responded without delay. Such mawkishness found him ready and resolute. "I suppose there's no need of defending France?"

Good as gold, but first and foremost good patriots, stoics in short, they went to sleep every night of the war directly above their shop with its millions, a French fortune.

In the brothels that he visited now and then, Monsieur Puta, though demanding, refused to be taken for a spendthrift. He'd set them straight at the outset. "I'm no Englishman, dearie, and I know the score. I'm just a little French soldier, and I'm not in a hurry." That was his opening statement. The girls respected him for his well-regulated way of taking his pleasure. He liked to enjoy himself, but couldn't be taken in, a real man. He knew human nature and took advantage of his knowledge to sell a few jewels to the assistant madame, who had no faith in stocks and bonds. As for his military career, Monsieur Puta was making impressive progress, from temporary discharges to permanent deferments. After God knows how many providential medical examinations, he was finally exempted for good. One of the highest joys of his existence was to contemplate and if possible to handle a shapely thigh. In this one pleasure at least he got the better of his wife, who took no interest in anything but the business. Take a man and woman with otherwise equal qualities, you always seem to find a little more uneasiness in a man, however stagnant and narrow-minded. This Puta had just a dash of the artist in him. Lots of men are like that, their artistic leanings never go beyond a weakness for shapely thighs. Madame Puta was glad she had no children. She voiced her pleasure in being sterile so often that one day Monsieur Puta spoke of their satisfaction to the assistant madame. "Yes," said the assistant madame. "But after all somebody's children have to go. It's a duty." That was true, the war involved duties.

The cabinet minister whose car Puta drove had no children either. Cabinet ministers never have children.

Around 1913, at the same time as me, there was another helper doing menial jobs in the shop; his name was Jean Voireuse.[37] At night he was some kind of super in the little theaters, and in the afternoon he delivered parcels for Puta. The pay was small, but he didn't mind. He managed to make ends meet thanks to the Metro. He delivered his parcels on foot almost as quickly as if he'd taken the

---

[37] Voireuse. From foireux, argot for "coward."

Metro, and kept the price of the ticket. All velvet. True, his feet smelled a little, quite a lot in fact, but he knew it and asked me to let him know when there were no customers in the shop so he could safely go in and settle his accounts with Madame Puta. As soon as she had the money, she'd send him out to the backroom with me. During the war again his feet stood him in good stead. He was reputed to be the fastest courier in his regiment. While on convalescent leave, he came to see me at the Bicêtre fort, in fact it was then we decided to get in touch with our old boss. We didn't let the grass grow under our feet. When we got to the Boulevard de la Madeleine they had just finished dressing the shop window...

"Well, well! Who'd have expected... !" Monsieur Puta was rather surprised to see us. "But I'm glad to see you all the same. Come right in! You're looking well, Voireuse! Fine and dandy. But you, Bardamu, you look sick, my boy! Oh well, you're young! You'll recover! You youngsters are in luck when all's said and done! Great days, great experience for you! Up there! And out in the open too! This is history, my boys. Make no mistake! And what history!"

We didn't answer, we thought we'd let Monsieur Puta go on a while before touching him... And on he went:

"It's rough in the trenches, I won't deny that... But it's no bed of roses here either, you know!... You boys have been wounded? All right, but I'm absolutely bushed. For two years now I've been on night duty! Do you know what that means? Exhausted! Worn to a frazzle! Oh my God! The streets of Paris at night! No lights... Driving a car, as often as not with the Minister in it! In a hurry! You simply can't imagine!... I could get killed a dozen times every night!... "

"Oh yes," Madame Puta put in, "and sometimes he drives the Minister's wife too... " "Oh yes, and it's not over yet... "

"Dreadful!" we said in unison.

"What about the dogs?" Voireuse asked to be polite. "What's become of them? Does somebody still take them out in the Tuileries?"

"I've had them put away! They were bad for business... German shepherds... the customers, you see... "

"A pity!" said his wife. "But the new dogs we have now are very nice, they're Scotch... they smell a little... not like our German shepherds, do you remember, Voireuse?... They hardly smelled at all. We could shut them up in the shop even after the rain... "

"That's right!" said Monsieur Puta. "Not like old Voireuse here with his feet! Do your feet still smell, Jean? You young scamp!"

"They still smell a little, I think," said Voireuse. At that moment some customers came in.

"I won't keep you any longer, my boys," said Monsieur Puta, intent on getting Jean out of the shop as quickly as possible. "Keep well, that's the main thing! I won't ask you where you've come from! Certainly not! Security first is my motto!"

At the word "security" Puta made a very serious face, like when giving back change... So that was the end of our visit. As we were leaving, Madame Puta gave us each twenty francs. The shop was polished as spick- and-span as a yacht, we were afraid to walk through because of our boots, which looked monstrous on the fine carpet.

"Oh, Roger! Look at them!" Madame Puta cried out. "Aren't they comical!... They're not in the habit anymore! They walk as if they'd stepped in something!"

"The habit will come back!" said Monsier Puta amiably, glad to be rid of us so quickly and cheaply.

Out in the street we realized we wouldn't go far with our twenty francs each, but Voireuse had another idea.

"Come on," he says, "we'll go and see a lady I know, her son was a buddy of mine, killed on the Marne. I go and see his parents every week and tell them how their son was killed... They're rich... The mother gives me a hundred francs or so every time... They say it makes them happy... So... "

"But what'll I do? What'll I say to this lady?"

"Well, you'll tell her that you were there too... She'll give you another hundred francs... They're the right kind of rich... Take it from me... Not like that stinking Puta... They don't count their pennies... "

"All right," I said. "But are you sure she won't ask me for details?... Because I didn't know her son, see?... I'll be flummoxed if she asks for... "

"No, no... don't worry... Say the same as me... Just nod your head and say yes... Nothing to worry about! The woman is brokenhearted, so if someone comes and talks about her son it makes her happy... That's all she wants... Anything at all... It's easy... "

I wasn't very enthusiastic, but I badly wanted the hundred francs, which struck me as providential and unusually easy to come by.

"All right," I said finally. "But don't expect me to make anything up, I'm warning you! Promise? I'll say the same as you, not a word more... How did he get killed anyway?"

"A shell hit him smack in the face, a pretty big one, at Garance the place was called, on the Meuse front, on the bank of some river... Boy, they didn't find 'this much' of him! Absolutely nothing left... a memory. And you know, he was a big man, strong and husky and athletic, but what would you expect? Nobody can stand up against a shell!"

"That's a fact!"

"Wiped off the face of the earth!... His mother still finds it hard to believe! I've told her over and over again... She insists that he's just missing... Crazy idea!... Missing!... It's not her fault, she never saw a shell, she doesn't see how a man can vanish into thin air... like a fart, and that it's all over, especially when the man is her son... "

"It's only natural."

"By the way, I haven't been to see her for two weeks... But you'll see how it is when I go in... The mother receives me right away in the drawing room... It's a beautiful house... You'll see... so many curtains and carpets and mirrors you'd think you were in a theater... A hundred francs is nothing to them, they'll hardly miss it... About like five francs to me... Today she'll be good for two hundred... because she hasn't seen me for two weeks... You'll see, the servants with gilded buttons... "

At the Avenue Henri-Martin we turned left and went on a little way, then we came to a gate surrounded by trees in a little private road.

"See?" said Voireuse, when we were standing in front of it, "it's practically a chateau... What did I tell you? The father's supposed to be high up in the railroads... a big shot... "

"You sure he's not a stationmaster?" I said, making a joke.

"Don't be stupid!... There he is now... he's coming to meet us... "

But the old man didn't come out right away. He was walking around the lawn, stooped over, talking to a soldier. We went nearer. I recognized the soldier, it was the reservist I had met that night at Noirceur-sur-la-Lys, when I was on reconnaissance. I even remembered the name he'd given me: Robinson.

"Do you know that footslogger?" Voireuse asked me. "Yes, I know him."

"Maybe he's a friend of theirs... They must be talking about the mother. I hope they don't prevent us from going to see her... Because she's the one mostly that forks over the money..."

The old gentleman came over to us.

"My dear friend," he said to Voireuse in a quavering voice. "It grieves me to tell you that since your last visit my poor wife has succumbed to our great sorrow... Last Thursday we left her alone for a moment, she had asked us to... She was in tears... "

He couldn't finish his sentence. Suddenly he turned away and left us.

"I know you," I said to Robinson, as soon as the old gentleman was far enough away. "And I know you... "

"What happened to the old lady?" I asked him.

"Well," he informed us, "she hanged herself the day before yesterday, that's all." He added: "Of all the lousy luck!... She was my army godmother!... Such things only happen to me; A calamity! My first leave!... For six months I'd been looking forward to this day... "

Voireuse and I couldn't help laughing at Robinson's discomfiture. A nasty surprise if there ever was one, but her being dead didn't give us our two hundred smackers, and we'd made up a new story special for the occasion. So none of us was very happy.

"You and your big mealy mouth!" We were ragging Robinson, trying to get a rise out of him, "You thought you had a good thing, didn't you? A sweet little feed with the old folks? Or maybe you thought you'd screw your fairy godmother?... serves you goddam right!"

We couldn't stay there all day looking at the grass and laughing, so we all three together started off in the direction of Grenelle. We all counted our money, it didn't come to much. Seeing we had to get back to our respective hospitals and barracks that same evening, there was just enough for dinner at a bistro, and maybe there'd be a little something left over, but not enough to go upstairs at the cathouse. We went in anyway, but we only had a drink at the bar.

"Say," said Robinson, "it's good to see you again. But what do you think of that kid's mother? The bitch, hanging herself just when I'm due to arrive!... I won't forget her in a hurry!... Do you see me hanging myself?... Unhappy, you say?... I'd hang myself every day!... What about you?"

"Rich people are more sensitive," said Voireuse.

Voireuse had a good heart. "If I had six francs," he went on, "I'd go upstairs with the brunette over there by the slot machine... "

"Go ahead," we told him, "you'll tell us if she knows how to suck... "

We rummaged in our pockets, but counting the tip there wasn't enough to give him his piece. Just enough for another coffee each and a cassis. When we'd finished, we went out and roamed around some more.

We broke up on the Place Vendôme and went our separate ways. Saying good-bye, we couldn't see one another, and we spoke softly because of the echoes. No light, it wasn't allowed.

I never saw Voireuse again. I've often run into Robinson. As for Jean Voireuse, it was the gas that got him on the Somme. He died two years later by the sea, in Brittany, in a navy sanatorium. He wrote to me twice when he first got there, but no more after that. He'd never seen the ocean. "You can't imagine how beautiful it is," he wrote me. "I bathe a little, it's good for my feet, but I think my voice is gone for good." That made him unhappy, because his big ambition was to get into a theater chorus some day.

The chorus is better paid and more artistic than being an ordinary super.

* * *

The army finally dropped me, I'd saved my guts, but my brains were scrambled for good. Undeniably. "Beat it!" they said. "You're no good for anything anymore."

"To Africa!" I said to myself. "The further the better." The ship that took me on board was a ship like any other, Consolidated Corsairs, that was the line. It was bound for the tropics with a cargo of cotton goods, officers, and civil servants.

That boat was so old that the copper plate with its birth date had been removed from the upper deck; the date was such ancient history it had inspired the passengers with fear and witticisms.

So they shoved me on board in the hope that I'd recuperate in the colonies. My well-wishers were dead set on my making my fortune. Personally I just wanted to get away, but a man should always try to look useful if he's not rich, it didn't look as if my studies would ever end, and I couldn't go on forever. I didn't have enough money to go to America. So "Africa it is," I said, and let myself be steered to the tropics where, I was told, you were sure to get ahead fast, provided you behaved and were reasonably temperate.

Those prognostics gave me food for thought. There wasn't much to be said for me, but my manners were all right, and I was self-effacing; deference came easy to me, I lived in constant fear of not being on time, but took good care never to get ahead of anybody. In short, I had delicacy.

After all, if you manage to escape alive from an international slaughterhouse run rampant, it's a sign of tact and discretion. But let's get back to our trip. It looked fairly promising as long as we were in European waters. In small, adenoidal, mutually suspicious groups, the passengers lolled and lounged in the shade between decks, in the toilets and in the smoking room. From morning to night they steeped themselves in Picon and gossip. They belched, they dozed, they shouted, and never expressed the least regret for anything they had left behind in Europe.

Our ship's name was the Admiral Bragueton.[38] If it kept afloat on those tepid seas, it was only thanks to its paint. Any number of coats laid on, layer after layer, had given the Admiral Bragueton a kind of second hull, something like an onion. We were heading for Africa, the real, grandiose Africa of impenetrable forests, fetid swamps, inviolate wildernesses, where black tyrants wallowed in sloth and cruelty on the banks of never-ending rivers. I would barter a pack of "Pilett"[39] razor blades for big long elephant's tusks, gaudy-colored birds, and juvenile slaves. Guaranteed. That would be life! Nothing in common with the emasculated Africa of travel agencies and monuments, of railways and candy bars. Certainly not! We'd be seeing Africa in the raw, the real Africa! We the boozing passengers of the Admiral Bragueton.

But as soon as we'd passed the coast of Portugal, things started going bad. One morning we woke up in the midst of a steam bath, pervasive and alarming. The water in our glasses, the sea, the air, our sheets, our sweat, everything was hot, sultry. From then on, by night and day, it was impossible to have anything cool in your hands, under your ass, or in your throat, except the ice from the bar in your whisky. A dull despair descended on the passengers of the Admiral Bragueton, condemned to sitting permanently in the bar, held fast by little pieces of ice, exchanging threats and incoherent apologies after their card games.

It didn't take long. In that despondent changeless heat the entire human content of the ship congealed into massive drunkenness. People moved flabbily about like squid in a tank of tepid smelly water. From that moment on we saw, rising to the surface, the terrifying nature of white men, exasperated, freed from constraint, absolutely unbuttoned, their true nature, same as in the war. That tropical steam bath called forth instincts as August breeds toads and snakes on the fissured walls of prisons. In the European cold, under gray, puritanical northern skies, we seldom get to see our brothers' festering cruelty except in times of carnage, but when roused by the foul fevers of the tropics, their rottenness rises to the surface. That's when the frantic unbuttoning sets in, when filth triumphs and covers us entirely. It's a biological confession. Once work and cold weather cease to constrain us, once they relax their grip, the white man shows you the same spectacle as a beautiful beach when the tide goes out: the truth, fetid pools, crabs, carrion, and turds.

Once we had passed Portugal, everybody on board started unleashing his instincts, ferociously; alcohol helped and so did the blissful feeling conferred, especially on soldiers and civil servants, by the knowledge that the trip was absolutely free of charge. The knowledge that for four consecutive weeks their bed, board, and liquor won't cost a thing is in itself enough to make most people delirious with thrift. Consequently, when it became known that, alone of all the ship's passengers, I had paid my own fare, I was looked upon as a shameless and intolerable swine.

If on leaving Marseille I had had some experience of colonial society, I would have gone down on my knees and begged the pardon and indulgence of the colonial infantry officer I kept running into, the highest in rank of those on board, for my un-worthiness, and perhaps, for safety's sake, I'd also have humbled myself before the senior civil servant. Then those phan-tasmagorical passengers might have tolerated my presence in their midst and nothing would have happened. But I was ignorant, and my foolhardiness in supposing that I was entitled to breathe the same air as they almost cost me my life.

One can never be too anxious. Thanks to a certain ingenuity, I lost nothing but what self-respect I had left. This is what happened. Some time after the Canary Islands, I learned from one of the stewards that my fellow passengers, by common accord, thought me affected, not to say insolent... that they suspected me of being a pimp and a pederast... something of a cocaine addict on the side... but only on the side... Then the suspicion made its way around that I must have left France to escape the consequences of certain heinous crimes. But I was only at the beginning of my troubles. At that point I learned that on this line it was customary to view paying passengers with extreme caution, accompanied by persecution; I'm speaking of those who were not traveling free, either on military

---

[38] Bragueton. From braguette, meaning "fly" (of trousers).
[39] Pilett. Transmogrification of Gillette.

transportation orders or on the basis of some bureaucratic arrangement, for as everyone knows, the colonies belong to the upper reaches of the administration.

After all there are few plausible reasons for an unknown civilian to venture into those parts... A spy, a suspicious character... they found a thousand reasons for giving me sinister looks, the officers straight in the eye, the ladies with a knowing smile. After a while, even the deck hands and stewards, encouraged by the passengers, took to exchanging heavily caustic remarks behind my back. In the end no one doubted that I was the biggest and most intolerable, in fact the only out and out blackguard on board. A promising outlook.

My neighbors at table were four toothless and bilious postal officials from Gabon. They had been friendly to me, chummy in fact at the start of the voyage; now they never said a word to me. They had tacitly agreed that I was a man to be watched. I seldom left my cabin, and then only with infinite precautions. The air was so hot it weighed on our skins like a solid. Behind my bolted door I lay naked, trying to imagine what plan those diabolical passengers had cooked up to destroy me. I didn't know anyone on board, yet they all seemed to know me. An exact description of me must have taken instant form in their minds, like that of a famous criminal published in the newspapers.

Through no fault of mine, I had been cast in the indispensable role of the "foul and loathsome villain," shame of the human race, whose presence has been recorded down through the centuries, who is as well known to everyone as God and the Devil, but who during his passage on this earth is so polymorphous and evasive as to elude everyone's grasp. For this "villain" to be at last isolated, identified, and cornered, exceptional circumstances had been needed, such as were to be met with only in the narrow confines of this ship.

A great moral carnival was in the offing aboard the Admiral Bragueton. The "unclean beast" would not escape his fate. That was me.

This in itself made the trip worthwhile. Isolated among these spontaneous enemies, I labored to identify them without their noticing. Especially in the morning, I was able to watch them with impunity through the porthole of my cabin. Before breakfast, covered with hair from pubis to eyebrows and from their rectums to the soles of their feet, they would emerge to take the air in pajamas that were transparent in the sunlight; or glass in hand, sprawled against the rail, they would belch and retch, especially the captain with the bulging bloodshot eyes, whose liver started plaguing him at daybreak. Regularly at dawn he would ask his cronies about me, curious to know if I hadn't been "tossed overboard" yet, "like a gob of spit"! And he'd illustrate his remark by projecting a turgid oyster into the frothing sea. Boy oh boy!

The Admiral wasn't getting ahead very fast, just groaning along from roll to roll. It was more like a sickness than a voyage. As I examined the members of the morning council from my porthole, they all seemed rather seriously ill, malarial, alcoholic, syphilitic in all likelihood; at a distance of thirty feet, their visible decay was some consolation for my own troubles. These bigmouths, after all, were just as defeated as I was... still bragging, nothing more! That was the only difference!... The mosquitoes had worked them over, sucking their blood and pumping their veins full of poisons that would never go away... Treponemas were filing away their arteries... Alcohol was corroding their livers... The sun was cracking their kidneys... Crab lice were clinging to their pubic hair and eczema to the skin of their bellies... The searing light would scorch their retinas!... In not so long a time what would be left of them? A bit of brain... To do what with, I ask you!... where they were going?... To commit suicide? Where they were going a brain wouldn't do them a bit of good... No two ways... it's no joke growing old in a place where there's nothing to do... but look at yourself in a mirror with verdigris for silvering, and see yourself getting seedier and seedier, more and more decrepit... Rot sets in quickly in the green mansions, especially when it's atrociously hot.

The North at least preserves your flesh; Northerners are pale once and for all. Between a dead Swede and a young man who has had a bad night there's not much to choose. But the day after a colonial lands, he's already full of maggots. Those infinitely laborious little worms have been waiting for him personally, and they'll stay with him a lot longer than life will. He's a bag of worms, that's all.

We had another week at sea before putting in to Bragamance, the first of the promised lands, I felt as if I were living in a case of dynamite. I had just about given up eating for fear of sitting down at their table or crossing the deck in the daytime. I'd stopped talking altogether. I was never seen taking the air. It would have been hard to be as little in evidence on that ship as I was and yet stay on board.

My cabin steward, a family man, was kind enough to inform me that those dashing colonial officers had lifted their glasses and sworn a solemn oath to slap my face at the first opportunity and then chuck me overboard. When I asked him why, he didn't know and asked me in turn what I had done to warrant so much hard feeling. We were left with our perplexity. It was unlikely to be cleared up. They didn't like my face, that's all.

You won't catch me taking another trip with people so hard to please. In addition, they had so much time on their hands, sequestered with themselves for thirty whole days, that it didn't take much to stir them up. And besides, when you stop to think about it, at least a hundred people must want you dead in the course of an average day, the ones in line behind you at the ticket window in the Métro, the ones who look up at your apartment when they haven't got one themselves, the ones who wish you'd finish pissing and give them a chance, your children and a lot more. It happens all the time, and you get used to it. On a boat this same impatience is more noticeable, which makes it more upsetting.

In that bubbling cauldron, the suint of those scalded beings is concentrated, the presentiment of the vast colonial solitude that will soon bury them and their destinies and make them groan like the dying. They cling, they bite, they rend, they froth at the mouth. My importance on the ship increased prodigiously from day to day. My rare appearances at table, silent and stealthy as I tried to make them, took on the magnitude of significant events. The moment I entered the dining room, the hundred and twenty passengers gave a start and began to whisper...

Advancing from malignant suppositions to slanderous conclusions, the colonial officers at the captain's table, fortified with apéritif after apéritif, the tax collectors, and especially the lady school-teachers on their way back to the Congo (of these there was quite an assortment on board the Admiral Bragueton) puffed me up to infernal proportions.

On boarding the ship in Marseille, I had been nothing, just a dreamy sort of nobody, but now, thanks to the concentrated attention of all those alcoholics and frustrated vaginas, I found myself changed beyond recognition, endowed with alarming prestige.

The captain of the ship, a shady, breezy, racketeering type, had gone out of his way to shake hands with me at the start. When he crossed my path now, he didn't even seem to know me, it was as if I'd been wanted for some sordid crime, guilty from the start... Guilty of what? When men can hate without risk, their stupidity is easily convinced, the motives supply themselves.

From what I seemed to discern of the compact malevolence that held me in its vise, the female section of the conspiracy was masterminded by one of the schoolteachers. She was going back to the Congo to die, or so at least I hoped, the bitch. Almost always she was trailing around after the officers, so handsome in their resplendent tight-fitting tunics and further embellished by the oath they had sworn to crush me like a noisome slug well before the next port of call. They wondered out loud whether I would be as repulsive flattened out as I was erect. In short, they were having a fine time. The schoolteacher whetted their fury, called down thunders on the deck of the Admiral Bragueton, resolved to know no rest until I had been picked up gasping, punished forever for my imaginary impertinence, chastised for daring to exist, brutally beaten, bruised and bleeding, imploring pity under the boot and fist of one of those heroes, whose muscular prowess and spectacular rage she was burning to admire. A scene of high carnage, from which her weary ovaries promised themselves an awakening. As good as being raped by a gorilla. Time was passing, and it's dangerous to keep the afficionados waiting too long. I was the bull. The whole ship was clamoring, quivering from port to starboard.

The sea enclosed us in that boiler-plated circus. Even the engine-room crew knew what was going on. And since we only had three days ahead of us before putting into port, three decisive days, several matadors volunteered. The more I avoided the showdown, the more aggressive, the more im-pending they became. The executioners began to rehearse. They cornered me between two cabins, at a bend in the corridor. I escaped by the skin of my teeth, but going to the toilet was getting downright dangerous. With only three days to go, I decided to forgo the needs of nature. The portholes were all I needed. Crushing hatred and boredom were all around me. It can't be denied, the boredom on ships is something unbelievable; to tell the truth, it's cosmic. It fills the sea, the ship, the heavens. It's enough to unhinge the soundest of minds, so what would you expect of those chimerical deadheads?

A sacrifice! And I was the victim. Things came to a head one evening after dinner, at which, ravaged by hunger, I had put in an appearance. I bent over my plate and didn't budge, I didn't even dare to take out my handkerchief to wipe the sweat off my brow. Nobody had ever eaten his dinner more discreetly. From the engines a faint, continuous vibration rose up under my behind. My table companions must have known what sentence had been passed on me, for to my surprise they started talking to me freely and amiably about duels and stabbings, and asking me questions... Just then the schoolteacher from the Congo, the one whose breath was so strong, appeared in the lounge. I had barely time to notice that she was wearing a sumptuous lace evening dress. With nervous haste she sat down at the piano and played, if you can call it playing, a number of pieces, always skipping the finale. The atmosphere became intensely furtive and strained. I jumped up and ran, hoping to take refuge in my cabin. I had almost reached it when one of the colonial officers, the chestiest and most muscular of the lot, barred my way, without violence but firmly. "Suppose we go up on deck!" he enjoined me. We had only a few steps to go. For the occasion he was wearing his gold-braidiest cap, and he had buttoned his buttons from collar to fly, something he hadn't done since our departure. So this was to be a full-dress dramatic ceremony! A tight spot for me, my heart was pounding on a level with my belly button.

This preamble, this abnormal full dress made me foresee a slow and painful execution. That officer looked to me like a chunk of the war, obstinate, inexorable, murderous, which someone had suddenly plunked down in front of me.

Behind him, blocking the doorway, appeared four junior officers, vigilant in the extreme, the escort of Doom.

Flight was impossible. The speech that followed must have been carefully rehearsed. "Sir, you have before you Captain Frémizon[40] of the colonial army! In the name of my comrades in arms and of the passengers on this ship, who are justly indignant at your unspeakable behavior, I have the honor to demand an explanation!... Certain remarks you have made about us since we left Marseille are intolerable!... If you have any grievances, sir, the time has come to state them out loud! , . . to proclaim audibly what you have been saying in a shameful undertone for the last twenty-one days! To tell us at last what you think!... "

On hearing these words I was very much relieved. I had feared some sudden deathblow impossible to parry, but in talking, the major was offering me a way out. Any possibility of cowardice becomes a glowing hope if you're not a fool. That's my opinion. Never be picky and choosy about means of escaping disembowelment, or waste your time trying to find reasons for the persecution you're a victim of. Escape is good enough for the wise.

"Captain!" I replied, putting into my voice all the conviction of which I was capable under the circumstances. "What an extraordinary mistake you are in danger of making! You! Me! How can you think me capable of such ignominious sentiments? How monstrously unjust! Indeed it is more than I can bear! When only yesterday I was fighting for our beloved country! When over the years my blood has mingled with yours in innumerable battles! Oh, Captain, sir, how could you think of crushing me beneath such an injustice?"

Then, addressing the whole group:

"What abominable slander has abused you, gentlemen? Leading you to imagine that I, to all intents and purposes your brother, would dream of spreading foul calumnies about heroic officers! This is too much! Really too much!" And I went on: "Oh, for such a thing to happen at the very moment when these heroes, these incomparable heroes, are preparing to resume, with what courage I need not say, their sacred duty of safeguarding our immortal colonial empire! Where the most glorious

---

[40] Frémizon. From frémir, to quiver, quake, shake (with passion).

soldiers of our race have covered themselves with eternal glory. The Mangins![41] the Faidherbes![42] the Gallienis![43]... Oh, Captain! To suspect me! Of this!"

At that point I pulled up short. I hoped my silence would impress them. Luckily it did for a moment. Thereupon, without delay, taking advantage of the oratorical armistice, I went straight up to the captain and, in an access of emotion, gripped both his hands.

With his hands enclosed in mine I felt fairly safe. Still clasping them, I continued, as volubly as ever, and while assuring him that he was right, a thousand times right, suggested that we make a fresh start, but get our signals straight this time. This unbelievable misunderstanding, I assured him, had been brought about by my stupid though natural timidity! I admitted that my behavior could reason-ably have been interpreted as unconscionable disdain by the ladies and gentlemen present, these "he-roes and charmers... this providential conclave of astounding characters and talents... Not forgetting the incomparably musical ladies, the ornaments of our good ship!... " After making this profuse and elaborate apology, I implored them to admit me without delay or restriction to their joyous patriotic brotherhood... in which I hoped, now and forever, to cut an admirable figure. And of course without releasing the major's hands, I redoubled my eloquence.

As long as a soldier isn't killing, he's a child and easily amused. Since he is not in the habit of thinking, it costs him a crushing effort to understand when spoken to. Captain Frémizon wasn't killing me, he wasn't drinking, and he wasn't doing anything with his hands or feet. He was only trying to think. For him that was much too much. In short, I'd caught him by the head.

Gradually, during this ordeal by humiliation, I felt my self-respect weakening, weakening a little more, seeping away, and finally abandoning me completely, officially as it were. Say what you please, that's a beautiful moment. After that incident I became infinitely light and free, morally speaking of course. Fear is probably, more often than not, the best means of getting you out of a tight spot. Since that day I've never felt the need of any other weapons, or virtues for that matter.

The captain couldn't make up his mind, and his friends, who had come there expressly to wipe up my blood and play knucklebones with my dispersed teeth, had to content themselves with catching words in mid-air. The civilians who had come rushing, tingling with eagerness at the news of an impending corrida were looking very dangerous. Since I didn't know exactly what I was talking about, but only that I'd better keep it lyrical at all costs, I held on to the captain's hands and stared at an imaginary point in the cottony fog through which the Admiral Bragueton was making its way, puffing and spitting from one turn of the propeller to the next. Finally, to wind up my harangue, I ventured to raise one arm above my head, releasing one of the captain's hands, but only one, and flung myself into my peroration: "Gentlemen: Aren't we all agreed that brave men will always come to an under-standing in the end? So damn it all, Vive la France! Vive la France!" That was Sergeant Branledore's gimmick. And once again it worked. That was the only time France ever saved my life, otherwise the opposite has been closer to the truth. I observed a moment's hesitation in my audience—after all, it's hard for an officer, however ill-disposed, to strike a civilian who has just shouted "Vive la France!" as loud as I had. That hesitation saved me.

I reached into the group of officers, grabbed two arms at random, and invited everybody to come to the bar and drink to my health and our reconciliation. The heroes resisted for barely a minute, and then we drank for two hours. But the females, silent and increasingly disappointed, kept their eyes on us. Through the portholes of the bar I saw the obstinate schoolteacher-pianist prowling like a hyena, surrounded by other females. The bitches had a strong suspicion that I'd conned myself out of the trap, and were determined to nab me at the next turn. Meanwhile, men among men, we went on drink-ing under the useless but stupefying electric fan, which since the Canaries had been wearing itself out churning the tepid, cottony atmosphere. Still, I had to keep up my verve and spout the kind of talk , .

---

[41] Mangin. Charles Mangin (1866-1925). General Mangin owes his fame largely to his prowess in the First World War, but he began his career in Africa and Indochina.
[42] Faidherbe. Louis Léon César Faidherbe (1828-89). General and colonizer. Began his career in Algeria and Guadeloupe.
[43] Galliéni. Joseph Galliéni (1849-1916). General and administrator. Distinguished career in the colonies. It was he who requisitioned the Paris taxicabs to carry reinforcements to the battle of the Marne.

. nothing too difficult... that would appeal to my new friends. For fear of putting my foot in it, I overflowed with patriotic admiration, and kept asking those heroes, one after another, for stories and more stories of colonial feats of arms. War stories, like dirty stories, appeal to the military of all countries. The best way to make a sort of peace, a fragile armistice to be sure, but precious all the same, with men, officers or not, is to let them bask and wallow in childish self-glorification. There's no such thing as intelligent vanity. It's an instinct. And you'll never find a man who is not first and foremost vain. The role of admiring doormat is about the only one that one man is glad to tolerate in another. With these soldiers I had no need to tax my imagination. It was enough to appear impressed. It's easy to ask for more and more war stories. Those boys were crammed full of them, It was like the good old hospital days. After each story I made sure to express my approbation, as Branledore had taught me, with a glowing phrase: "Splendid! Why, that deserves to go down in History!" There's a formula that can't be beat! Little by little, the group I had wormed my way into decided that I was all right. They started telling the same kind of cock-and-bull war stories as I had heard in the old days and later dished out myself in imagination contests with my pals in the hospital. Except their setting was different, their fairy tales happened in the jungles of the Congo instead of the Vosges or Flanders.

Once Captain Frémizon, the one who a moment before had volunteered to purge the ship of my putrid presence, perceived that I listened more attentively than anyone else, he began to give me credit for no end of delightful qualties. His arterial flux seemed attenuated by the effect of my original praises, his vision cleared, his bloodshot, alcoholic eyes even began to sparkle despite his besotted state, and the sprinkling of doubts about his own worth, which he had somehow conceived deep within him and which assailed him in times of extreme depression, were for a time adorably dissipated by the miraculous effect of my intelligent and pertinent comments.

No doubt about it, I was a creator of euphoria! I had them slapping their thighs for all they were worth! I alone knew how to make life worth living in spite of the agonizing humidity! Wasn't I the most inspired of listeners?

As we were thus shooting the shit, the Admiral Bragueton began to slow down, she seemed to be making hardly any headway; not an atom of breeze around us, we must have been skirting the coast, moving as sluggishly as if the sea had been molasses.

The sky above us was molasses too, a black, viscous mass that I eyed hungrily. I'd have liked best to get back into the night, even sweating and groaning, no matter how! Frémizon went on and on with his stories, I had the impression that land was near, but my plan for escape filled me with alarm... Gradually our conversation ceased to be military and became first ribald, then frankly filthy, and in the end so incoherent that it was hard to keep it going. One after another of the company gave up and fell asleep, crushed under the weight of their snores, a nasty kind of sleep that scraped the caverns of their noses. That was the time to get away. One must never miss up on those remissions of cruelty that nature manages to impose on the most vicious and aggressive of this world's organisms.

By then we were anchored a short distance from the coast. All we could see of the shore was some lanterns moving back and forth.

Very quickly a hundred bobbing canoes full of screeching black men came crowding around the ship. There were black men all over the decks, offering their services. In a few seconds I carried the few bundles I had done up in secret to the gangway and slipped down it behind one of the boatmen, whose features and movements were almost entirely hidden from me by the darkness. At the bottom of the steps, on a level with the plashing water, I wondered anxiously where we were going.

"Where are we?" I asked.

"At Bambola-Fort-Gono,"[44] the shadow answered.

We pushed off and paddled hard. To make us go faster I helped him.

I had time to get one last look at my menacing fellow passengers. In the light of the cabin lamps, laid low by apathy and gastritis, they grunted and fermented in their sleep. Bloated and sprawling, they all looked alike now, officers, civil servants, engineers, and traders, pimply, potbellied and swarthy, intermingled and more or less identical. Dogs look like wolves when they're asleep.

---

[44] Bambola-Fon-Gono. From bamboula, meaning roughly "whoopie," and "gonococcus."

A few moments later I was back on land. Under the trees the night was thicker than ever, and behind the night lay all the complicities of silence.

* * *

In this colony of Bambola-Bragamance the Governor reigned triumphant over everybody. His soldiers and civil servants hardly dared breathe when he deigned to let his eyes fall on them.

Far below these notables, the resident traders seemed to thieve and thrive more easily than in Europe. Not one coconut, not one peanut in the entire colony evaded their brigandage. As fatigue and ill health overcame the civil servants, it began to dawn on them that they'd been had, that all they had gained by being sent out here was braid and forms to fill out and very little pay. So naturally they looked at the traders with a bilious eye. The military faction, even more dull witted than the other two, subsisted on a diet of colonial glory, washed down by quantities of quinine and miles of red tape.

Understandably, a life spent waiting for the thermometer to go down made everybody more and more cantankerous. The consequence was private and collective quarrels, preposterous and interminable, between the military and the administration, between the administration and the traders, between these two in temporary alliance and the military, between the whole lot of them and the black population, and finally between blacks and blacks. The little energy that hadn't been sapped by malaria, thirst, and the heat was consumed by hatred so fierce and deep seated that it wasn't uncommon for these colonials to drop dead on the spot, poisoned by themselves like scorpions.

Nevertheless, this virulent anarchy was held in check, like crabs in a basket, by a hermetic police structure. The civil servants griped in vain, for the Governor, to keep his colony in subjection, was able to recruit all the moth-eaten mercenaries he needed, impoverished blacks driven to the coast by debts, defeated by the law of supply and demand, and needful of something to eat. These recruits were taught the law and how to admire the Governor. The Governor seemed to wear all the gold in his treasury on his uniform... in the blazing sunshine, it surpassed belief, even without the plumes.

He went to Vichy for the cure every year, and he never read anything but the Official Gazette. A number of the civil servants cherished the hope that he'd sleep with their wives some day, but the Governor didn't care for women. He didn't care for anything. He survived each new epidemic of yellow fever like a charm, while so many of the men who'd have liked to bury him died like flies at the first whiff of fever.

There was a story that one Fourteenth of July, as he was reviewing the troops of the Residency, caracoling up ahead of his Spahi guards who were carrying a flag as big as a house, some sergeant, delirious with fever no doubt, rushed out in front of him, shouting: "Get back, you jerk!" It seems the Governor was very much upset by this outrage which, as it happened, was never satisfactorily explained.

It is hard to get a faithful look at people and things in the tropics because of the colors that emanate from them. In the tropics colors and things are in a turmoil. To the eye, a small sardine can lying upon the road at midday can take on the dimensions of an accident. You've got to watch out. It's not just the people who are hysterical down there, objects are the same way. Life only becomes tolerable at nightfall, but then almost immediately the darkness is taken over by swarms of mosquitoes. Not one or two or a hundred, but billions of them. Survival under those conditions is quite an achievement. A carnival by day, a colander by night, a quiet war.

When the hut you sleep in has filled at last with silence and the air is almost fit to breathe, the termites, those loathsome beasts eternally engaged in eating away the uprights of your cabin, get to work. The day a tornado hits this treacherous filigree, whole streets will go up in dust.

The town of Fort-Gono where I'd landed, the capital of Bragamance, was perched precariously between sea and jungle, but supplied, adorned, so to speak, with enough banks, brothels, cafés, café terraces, and even a recruiting office, to make it a small metropolis. There was even a Place Faidherbe and a Boulevard Bugeaud,[45] in case you wanted to take a walk. The whole was a clump of gleaming edifices surrounded by jagged rocks, riddled with larvae, trampled by generations of soldiers and officials.

At about five o'clock the military element would grouse and gripe over their apéritifs, the price of which, as it happened, had just gone up when I arrived. A delegation of consumers was about to petition the Governor to issue a decree enjoining the cafe owners from playing fast and loose with the prices of absinthe and cassis. If some of the regulars were to be believed, the very foundations of colonization were threatened by ice. Indeed it cannot be denied that the introduction of ice into the colonies has sparked off a process of devirilization. Riveted by force of habit to his iced apéritif, the colonial could no longer hope to dominate the climate by stoicism alone. The Faidherbes, the Stanleys, the Marchands,[46] be it noted in passing, had nothing but good to say of the tepid, muddy beer, wine, and water they drank for years without complaining. There you have it. That's how colonies are lost.

I learned plenty more in the shade of the palm trees which, all along those avenues of precarious dwellings, throve in provocative contrast. It was only that garish raw greenery which prevented the place from looking exactly like La Garenne-Bezons.

At nightfall the native hookers came out in strength, wending their way between clouds of hungry mosquitoes armed with yellow fever. There were Sudanese girls as well, offering the passerby the treasures under their loincloths. For extremely moderate prices you could treat yourself to a whole family for an hour or two. I'd have liked to flit from twat to vagina, but necessity obliged me to look for work.

The director of the Compagnie Pordurière[47] du Petit Congo, so I heard, was looking for an inexperienced man to take charge of one of the trading posts in the bush. I went without delay to offer my incompetent but enthusiastic services. The director's reception of me was not exactly friendly. That lunatic —I may as well call a spade a spade—lived not far from the Government House in a spacious straw bungalow built on piles. Before even looking at me, he fired several questions about my past, then, somewhat appeased by my naive answers, his contempt took a more indulgent turn. Still, he did not yet see fit to offer me a seat.

"To judge by your papers, you know something about medicine?" he observed. I replied that I had indeed studied for a time in that field.

"It'll come in handy," he said. "How about some whisky?"

I told him I didn't drink. "Smoke?" Again I declined. Such abstinence surprised him. In fact he scowled.

"I'm suspicious of employees who don't smoke and drink... Are you a pederast by any chance?... No? Too bad!... They don't steal as much... That's been my experience... They get attached... Well," he was kind enough to hedge. "By and large I seem to have noticed that quality, that advantage, in pederasts... Maybe you'll prove me wrong..." And changing the subject: "You're hot, aren't you? You'll get used to it. You'll have to. How was your trip?"

"Uncomfortable!" I said.

"Well, my friend, you haven't seen a thing. Come and tell me what you think of this country when you've spent a year in Bikomimbo, the place where I'm sending you to replace that joker... "

His Negress, squatting beside the table, was fiddling with her feet and scraping them with a little piece of wood.

"Beat it, you slut!" her master flung at her. "Go and call the house boy! And get me some ice while you're at it!"

The boy took his time coming. Infuriated, the Director sprang to his feet and received him with two brutal slaps in the face and the same number of resounding kicks in the gut.

---

[45] Bugeaud. Thomas Robert Bugeaud, Marquis de la Piconnerie (1784-1849). Figured prominently in the conquest of Algeria.

[46] Marchand. Jean-Baptiste Marchand (1836-1934). General and explorer. Took part in various expeditions in West Africa. In the course of an expedition begun in 1897 reached Fashoda on the Upper Nile, but the French government ordered him to evacuate when British troops arrived under Kitchener.

[47] Pordurière. A combination of port, meaning "seaport," and ordures, meaning "garbage."

"These people will be the death of me," the Director predicted with a sigh and slumped back into his armchair that was covered with dirty, rumpled, yellow canvas.

"Look, old man," he said, suddenly grown friendly, as though liberated for a while by his access of brutality. "Would you mind handing me my whip and my quinine... there on the table... I oughtn't to get so excited... It's stupid to fly off the handle like that... "

From his house we overlooked the river port, which shimmered through dust so dense, so compact, that we heard the clanking and thumping more clearly than we could see what was going on. On the shore files of black men were busy, encouraged by whips and curses, unloading hold after hold of ships that were never empty, climbing up flimsy, teetering gangplanks with big baskets balanced on their heads—like vertical ants.

Through a scarlet haze I saw them coming and going in jerky lines. Some of these working shapes carried an extra black spot on their backs, those were mothers toting their babies along with their sacks of palm cabbage. I wonder if ants can do that.

"Doesn't it always seem like Sunday here?" the Director joked. "So jolly! So colorful! And the females always naked. You've noticed? Good-lookers too, don't you agree? Of course it seems strange when you've just arrived from Paris, I won't deny it. And look at us! Always in white ducks. Like at the seashore! Aren't we a sight for sore eyes? All dressed up for First Communion! It's always a holiday here, take it from me! Day in and day out, just one glorious Fourteenth of July! And it's like this all the way to the Sahara! Think of it!"

He stopped talking, sighed, grunted, said "Shit!" two or three times, mopped his forehead, and started in again.

"Out where the Company's sending you, it's deep in the bush. Very damp! . . , Ten days' trip from here... First by sea... Then up the river... The river's all red, you'll see!... And on the other side it's the Spaniards... The man you're replacing at the post up there is a rotter... just between you and me... He simply won't send us his accounts... Nothing we can do... we've sent him letter after letter!... A man doesn't stay honest long when he's alone!... You'll see!... He's written, says he's sick... Big deal! Sick! I'm sick too! What does he mean sick? We're all sick. You'll be sick yourself before you know it! That's no excuse! What do we care if he's sick!... The Company comes first! When you get there, take inventory, that's the essential!... There's food enough for three months and merchandise for at least a year... You won't run short!... Don't start at night, whatever you do!... Be on your guard!... He's got his own niggers, he'll send them down the river to pick you up, maybe they'll chuck you overboard. I bet he's trained them! They're as rascally as he is! Fact! He's probably dropped a hint to those niggers about you!... That's the kind of thing they do around here! And be sure to take your quinine with you, your own, get it before you leave!... He might doctor his, I wouldn't put it past him!"

The Director thought he'd given me enough advice and stood up to say good-bye. The tin roof over our heads seemed to weigh at least two thousand tons, it absorbed all the heat of the day and sent it down on us. We were both making faces with the heat. We could just as well have dropped dead.

"Perhaps," he said, "there's no point in our meeting again before you leave, Bardamu! Everything wears one out so down here! Well, no, maybe I'll run down to the warehouses before you go and see how you're making out... You'll hear from us when you get there... There's a mail every month... The mail goes out from here... Well, good luck!"

And he vanished into the shadow between his tropical helmet and his jacket. I could clearly see the tendons in the back of his neck, curved like two fingers pressing against his head. He turned around again:

"Don't forget to tell that loafer to come back here in a hurry... I've got a few things to say to him!... And not to waste time on the way! Oh, the rat! I only hope he doesn't croak before he gets here!... That would be a shame! A bleeding shame! Oh, the blackguard!"

One of his blacks went ahead of me with a big lantern and took me to the place where I was to live before leaving for the Bikomimbo of my dreams.

We passed through avenues full of people who seemed to have come out for a stroll after dark. The night, hammered by gongs, was all around us, interspersed by brief snatches of song as incoherent as sobs, the big black night of the hot countries, with its brutal tom-tom heart that always beats too fast.

My young guide glided along easily on bare feet. There must have been Europeans in the bushes, you could hear them wandering about, their easily recognizable white men's voices, aggressive and hypocritical. The bats came whirling and weaving through the swarms of insects attracted by our light. Under every leaf of the trees there must have been at least one cricket, to judge by the deafening din.

Halfway up a hill we were stopped at a crossroads by a group of native riflemen arguing around a coffin draped in a big French flag.

It was somebody who had died in the hospital, and they didn't know exactly where to bury him. Their orders were vague. Some wanted to put him in one of the fields down below, some insisted on a garden at the top of the hill. The question had to be decided one way or the other, so the boy and I joined in the discussion.

In the end the pallbearers decided for the lower rather than the upper burial ground, because it was easier to walk downhill. Then we met three young white boys, the kind that in Europe go to rugby matches on Sunday, enthusiastic, noisy, pale-faced spectators. Like myself they were employed by the Societé Pordurière and were kind enough to show me the way to the unfinished shanty where my portable folding bed was temporarily situated.

The edifice when we got there was absolutely empty except for a few utensils and my so-called bed. As soon as I lay down on that wobbly filiform object, two dozen bats emerged from the corners and took to whishing back and forth like a volley of fans over my apprehensive repose.

The young black, my guide, came back to offer me his intimate services. Then, disappointed when I told him I wasn't in the mood that evening, he offered to introduce me to his sister. I'd have been curious to know how he expected to find his sister in such darkness.

Not far away the village tom-tom chopped my patience into little bits. Thousands of hard-working mosquitoes took possession of my legs, but I didn't dare set foot on the ground because of the scorpions and snakes which, I assumed, had started on their abominable hunting expeditions. The snakes had plenty of rats to choose from, rats were gnawing away at everything that can be gnawed, I heard them on the wall, on the floor, and quivering, ready to drop, on the ceiling.

Finally the moon rose, and things were a little quieter in the shanty. All things considered, life in the colonies was no great shakes.

Nevertheless, the next day came, a steaming cauldron. An enormous desire to go back to Europe took hold of me body and soul. Only one thing prevented me from clearing out—lack of money. That was enough. Anyway, I only had another week to spend in Fort-Gono before going to my job in Bikomimbo, which I'd heard described so delightfully.

The biggest building in Fort-Gono after the Governor's Palace was the hospital. I ran into it wherever I went; I couldn't walk a hundred yards in the town without coming across one of its pavilions, smelling faintly of carbolic acid. From time to time I ventured down to the docks to watch my anemic young colleagues, whom the Compagnie Pordurière recruited in France by emptying whole settlement houses, at work. They seemed possessed by a bellicose haste to unload freighter after freighter without stopping. "Harbor fees are so dreadfully costly!" they kept saying, sincerely distressed, as if it had been their own money.

They belabored the black porters with a will. They were conscientious, you couldn't deny it, and they were also flabby, heartless sons-of-bitches. In other words, they were well chosen, as mindlessly enthusiastic as any employer could dream of. Sons that would have delighted my mother, worshiping their bosses, if only she could have had one all to herself, a son she could have been proud of in the eyes of the world, a real legitimate son.

Those half-baked little specimens had come to tropical Africa to offer their flesh, their blood, their lives, their youth to their bosses, martyrs for twenty-two francs a day (minus deductions), and they were happy, yes, happy down to their last red corpuscle, for which ten million mosquitoes were lying in wait.

The colonies make these little clerks fat or make them thin; either way they hold them fast; there are only two ways to die under the sun, the fat way and the thin way. There's no other. You may have a preference, but it's your constitution that decides whether you get fat or whether the bones jab at your skin.

The Director up there on the red cliff, cavorting diabolically with his Negress under the tin roof with the ten thousand kilos of sunshine on it would be no better off when his time was up. He was the skinny kind. Sure, he was putting up a fight. It looked as if he could beat the climate. Looked! In reality he was crumbling even faster than the others.

The story was that he'd thought up a beautiful scheme that would make him a fortune in two years... But he'd never have time to carry it out, even if he applied himself to defrauding the company day and night. Twenty-two directors before him had tried to make a fortune, each with his own system, like at roulette. All this was well known to the stockholders, who were keeping an eye on him from up above, still higher up, from the Rue Moncey in Paris. The Director made them laugh. How childish! The stockholders were the biggest bandits of all, they knew their Director was syphilitic and much too horny for the tropics, they knew he downed enough quinine and bismuth to burst his eardrums and enough arsenic to make his gums drop out.

In the Company's bookkeeping the Director's months were numbered, numbered like the months of a pig's life.

My little colleagues never exchanged ideas. Only set formulas, baked and rebaked like dry crusts of thought. "Worry won't get us anywhere!" they said. "Never say die!... " "The Director's a jerk!... " "Nigger skin is good for tanning!" etc.

In the evening after work we'd meet for apéritifs with an "assistant manager," a Monsieur Tandernot from La Rochelle. If Tandernot hobnobbed with the traders, it was only because they'd pay for his drinks. He was a pitiful case, stone broke. His position in the colonial hierarchy was the lowest possible, overseeing road construction in the middle of the jungle. His militiamen had clubs, and naturally the natives worked. But since no white man ever used the new roads that Tandernot built, and since the blacks preferred their own tracks through the jungle where it was harder to lay hands on them for tax purposes, and since Tandernot's government roads didn't actually go anywhere, they soon vanished under a dense growth of vegetation, from month to month if the truth be known.

"Believe it or not," that astonishing pioneer would say, "last year I lost a hundred and twenty-two kilometers of them."

During my stay, I only heard Tandernot boast about one thing, the one achievement he was humbly vain about: he was the only European capable of catching cold in Bragamance with the thermometer at a hundred and ten in the shade... That one distinction consoled him for many sorrows. "I've caught another rotten cold!" he'd announce proudly over his apéritif. "You don't see that happening to anyone else!" And other members of our sickly group would cry out: "Good old Tandernot! What a man!" This little satisfaction was better than nothing. Where vanity is at stake, anything is better than nothing.

Another way the Company's petty clerks amused themselves was putting on fever contests. It wasn't difficult. These matches could go on for days, and they whiled away the time. When evening came and, almost always, the fever with it, they'd take their temperatures. "Hey, I've got a hundred and one!"... "Hell, that's nothing. I can work up a hundred and three any time I feel like it!"

These readings were absolutely accurate and above board. By the light of hurricane lamps they'd compare thermometers. The winner would tremble and gloat. "I'm sweating so much I can't piss," said the most emaciated of the lot, a skinny young fellow from the Pyrenees, a champion of febrility who had come to Bragamance, so he told me, to get away from a seminary where he hadn't enough freedom. But time was passing, and none of my companions could tell me exactly what species of freak the man I was replacing in Bikomimbo belonged to.

"He's funny!" they told me, and that was all.

"When you start out in a job like that," said the little Pyrenean with the high fever, "you've got to show what you're good for! It's all one way or the other. As far as the Director's concerned, you'll either be solid gold or solid shit! And another thing. He'll judge you right away."

I was very much afraid of being put down as "solid shit" or worse.

These young slave drivers, my friends, took me to see another employee of the Pordurière, who deserves special mention. He operated a store in the European quarter. Moldering with fatigue, oily and decrepit, he dreaded the slightest ray of light because of his eyes, which two years of uninterrupted baking under a tin roof, had dried out atrociously. It took him a good half hour every morning to open them, so he told me, and another half hour before he could see more or less clearly. Every ray of light was torture. A big mangy mole.

Suffocation and suffering had become second nature with him, and so had thieving. If he'd suddenly woken up healthy and honest, it would really have thrown him off balance. Even today, at this distance, I'd call his hatred for the Director General one of the most violent passions it has ever been given me to observe. At the thought of the Director, a violent rage would make him forget the pain he was in, and on the slightest pretext he'd rant and rave, all the while scratching himself from top to toe.

He never stopped scratching, in ellipses so to speak, from the lower end of his spinal column to the top of his neck. He dug furrows into his epidermis and dermis with his bloody fingernails, while continuing to wait on his numerous customers, most of them virtually naked blacks.

With his free hand he would plunge busily into various repositories to the right and left of him in the dark shop. Without ever making a mistake, deft and admirably quick, he would take out exactly what the customer wanted, stinking leaf tobacco, damp matches, cans of sardines, a ladleful of molasses, super- alcoholic beer in phony bottles, which he'd suddenly drop if overcome by the desire to scratch in the cavernous depths of his trousers. Then he would thrust in his whole arm, and it would emerge through the fly, which he always left partly open as a precaution.

He referred to the ailment that was eating away his skin by its local name, "corocoro." "This miserable corocoro! When I think that the stinking Director hasn't caught it yet, it makes me itch a hundred times worse! The corocoro can't get a hold on him!... He's too rotten already. That pimp isn't a man. He's a smell!... Pure unadulterated shit!"

When he said that, we'd all burst out laughing, the black customers too, in emulation. He frightened us a little. But he had one friend, a wheezing, graying little fellow who drove a truck for the Pordurière. He used to bring us ice that he'd stolen here and there from ships tied up at the wharf.

We'd drink his health at the bar, surrounded by the black customers, who looked on enviously. These customers were the more sophisticated blacks, who'd lost their fear of doing business with white men, a kind of elite so to speak. The other blacks, not so smart, preferred to keep their distance. Matter of instinct. But the most enterprising, the most contaminated of the blacks got taken on as clerks in the store. You could recognize the black clerks by the way they cursed and yelled at other blacks. My colleague with the corocoro traded in crude rubber, it came in sticky balls that the natives would bring in from the bush in big sacks.

While we were in the store, listening to him by the hour, a family of rubber gatherers came to the door and froze with timidity, the father in the lead, wrinkled, girt in a skimpy orange loincloth and holding his long machete.

The savage was afraid to come in despite the encouragements of one of the native clerks: "C'mon in, nigger! Come look see! We no eat savages!" Won over by these kind words, they stepped into the sweltering shack, at the back of which our corocoro man was ranting.

Apparently that native had never seen a store or possibly even a white man before. One of the women, with a big basket of crude rubber balanced on her head, followed him with downcast eyes.

Quickly the recruiting clerks grabbed her basket and put the contents on the scales. The savage didn't know what the scales were about or anything else. His wife was still afraid to raise her head. The rest of the family waited outside. The clerk told them to come in, too bad if they missed the show.

That was the first time they had all trekked in from the bush to the white man's town. It must have taken them a good long time to collect all that rubber. So naturally they were interested in the outcome. You hang little cups on the trunks of the trees, and the rubber oozes into them very very slowly. Sometimes you don't get so much as a small glassful in two months.

After the weighing, our scratcher dragged the bewildered native behind the counter, did a little reckoning with a pencil stub, and shoved a few coins into the man's hand. Then he said: "Beat it! That's it!"

All his little white friends were convulsed to see how cleverly he had handled the transaction. The black man stood there by the counter, looking lost in his skimpy orange underdrawers.

One of the black clerks yelled at him to wake him up: "You no savvy money? You savage?" This clerk knew his onions, he was used to these peremptory transactions, he had probably been trained. "You no speakie French?" he went on. "You missing link, eh?... What you speakum anyway? Couscous? Mabillia? Jackass! Bushman! You heap big jackass!"

The savage just stood there with his hand closed on his coins. He would have run away if he had dared, but he didn't dare.

"What you buy with dough?" the scratcher put in. "I haven't seen such a jughead in a long time! He must have come a long way,—What you wait for? Gimme that dough!"

He grabbed the money, and in place of the coins gave the black man a bright green handkerchief that he had deftly spirited from some secret hiding place under the counter.

When the black man hesitated to leave with the handkerchief, the scratcher went a step further. He certainly knew all the tricks of the conqueror's trade. Shaking the big square of muslin before the eyes of a wee black child, he said: "Ain't it pretty, you little turd? Did you ever see one like it, little sweetie, little stinkpot, little fart?" And one-two-three he tied it around the child's neck. Now the child was dressed.

The whole family stared at the child, decked out in the green cotton object... There was nothing more they could do, because the handkerchief had come into the family. They could only accept it, take it, and go.

They all backed slowly out. They crossed the threshold. When the father, who was last, turned around to say something, the sharpest of the clerks, who was wearing shoes, helped him leave with a swift kick in the ass.

The entire little tribe stood silently on the other side of the Avenue Faidherbe, under the magnolia tree, watching us finish our apéritifs. It looked as if they were trying to understand what had happened to them.

The corocoro man was treating us. He even played his phonograph for us. You could find anything in his store. It made me think of the supply depots in the war.

* * *

As I've told you, there were lots of blacks and small whites like myself working in the warehouses and plantations of the Compagnie Porduriere du Petit Togo at the same time as me. The natives, by and large, had to be driven to work with clubs, they preserved that much dignity, whereas the whites, perfected by public education, worked of their own free will.

Wielding a club is fatiguing in the long run. The white men's hearts and minds, on the other hand, have been crammed full of the hope of becoming rich and powerful, and that costs nothing, absolutely nothing. We've heard enough about Egypt and the Tatar tyrants! In the art of squeezing the last ounce of labor out of a two-legged animal, those primitive ancients were pretentious incompetents! Did they ever think of calling their slave "Monsieur" or letting him vote now and then, or giving him his newspaper? And especially had they thought of sending him to war to work off his passions? After twenty centuries of Christianity (as I personally can bear witness) your modern man simply can't control himself when a regiment passes before his eyes. It puts too many ideas into his head.

Accordingly, I decided to keep a close watch on myself from then on and learn to keep my mouth scrupulously shut, to conceal my longing to get away, in short, to prosper if possible and come what may, in the service of the Compagnie Porduriere. Not a moment to lose.

Alongside our warehouses, on the muddy river banks, whole nests of crocodiles, insidious and unmoving, lurked in wait. Built of metal, they enjoyed the delirious heat, and so apparently did the blacks.

At midday you couldn't help wondering if all this bustle of toiling masses, this hubbub of screeching, overexcited blacks on the docks was possible.

To learn the secret of numbering sacks before taking to the bush, I had to submit to gradual asphyxiation in the Company's main warehouse along with the other clerks, between two scales wedged into the alkaline crowd of ragged, pustulous, singing black men. Each one of them drew a little cloud behind him and shook it in cadence. The dull thuds of the overseers' clubs descended on their magnificent backs without provoking the least complaint or protest. Dazed and passive, they suffered pain as unquestioningly as the torrid air of that dusty furnace.

The Director came by from time to time, always aggressive, to make sure I was mastering the techniques of numbering sacks and falsifying weights.

With sweeping blows of his club he cleared his path to the scales through the press of natives. "Bardamu," he said to me one morning when he was in high spirits. "You see these niggers all around us?... Well, when I came to Little Togo almost thirty years ago, those loafers still lived by hunting, fishing, and intertribal massacres!... I was a small trader then . , . Well, as true as I'm standing here, I'd seen them coming home to their village after a victory, loaded with more than a hundred baskets of bleeding human flesh to stuff their bellies with!... Hear that, Bardamu?... Bleeding!... Their enemies! A feast!... Today, no more victories! We've accomplished that much!... No more tribes!... No more flimflam and foolishness! Today we've got a labor force and peanuts! Good hard work! No more hunting! No more guns! Peanuts and rubber!... To pay taxes with! Taxes to get us more rubber and peanuts! This is life, Bardamu! Peanuts! Peanuts and rubber!... And say... Well, I'll be damned. There's General Tombat!"[48] True enough, he was coming our way, an old man crumpling under the enormous weight of the sun.

The general wasn't exactly a soldier anymore, but he wasn't exactly a civilian either. Confidential agent of the Porduriere, he took care of liaison between the Administration and the business community, an indispensable function although the two lived in a state of permanent competition and hostility. But the general was a shrewd maneuverer. For instance, he had disentangled a shady deal in enemy holdings, which had been judged inextricable in high places.

At the beginning of the war General Tombat's ear had been split, not very badly, just enough to get him honorably retired after Charleroi.[49] He had immediately offered his services to "Greater France." But long after Verdun,[50] that epic battle was still on his mind. He was always shuffling a handful of telegrams. "Our little poilus will hold on! They are holding on!" It was so hot in the warehouse and France was so far away that we could have done without General Tombat's predictions. But just to be polite we all, and the Director with us, declared in chorus: "They're marvelous!" On these words Tombat left us.

A few moments later the Director opened up another violent path through the tightly packed torsos and vanished in his turn into the peppery dust.

The Director had eyes like glowing coals, he was consumed with a passion to hornswoggle the Company. He frightened me a little, and I had difficulty in getting used to his presence. I found it hard to believe that in all the world there could be a human carcass capable of such maximum-tension greed. He seldom said anything to us straight out, he spoke only in muffled hints, and he seemed to live and breathe for the sole purpose of conspiring, spying, and betraying. I was told that he stole, swindled, and peculated incomparably more than all the other officials put together, and they were no slouches, I assure you. But I can easily believe it.

During my stay in Fort-Gono, I had a little leisure in which to roam around. The only really desirable spot I came across in the whole town was the hospital.

Whenever you get to a new place, certain ambitions turn up inside you. My ambition was to be sick, just plain sick. Every man to his taste. I walked around those promising hospital pavilions, so doleful, withdrawn, and unmolested, and I never relinquished their antiseptic charm without regret. The lawns around them were brightened by furtive little birds and anxious multicolored lizards. An earthly Paradise in its way.

As for the blacks, one soon gets used to them, their sluggish good nature, their slow gestures, and the protuberant bellies of their women. Those blacks stink of their misery, their interminable

---

[48] Tombat. A combination of tomber, meaning "to fall," and combat, meaning "combat."
[49] Charleroi. City in Belgium. Scene of a battle in 1914, ending in a French withdrawal.
[50] Verdun. City in eastern France. Scene of a long drawn-out, and extremely bloody battle in which the French withstood a powerful German offensive and were finally (1917) victorious.

vanities, and their repugnant resignation; actually, they're just like our poor people, except they have more children, less dirty washing, and less red wine.

When I'd finished inhaling and sniffing at the hospital, I followed the native crowd and stopped for a while outside the pagodalike edifice near the fort that a restaurant owner had built for the entertainment of the sexy young jokers of the colony.

The prosperous whites of Fort-Gono went there at night and gambled doggedly, meanwhile drinking and yawning and belching with a will. For two hundred francs you could lay the luscious patronne. The young jokers had a lot of trouble with their trousers when they wanted to scratch, because their suspenders kept sliding off.

At night big crowds poured out of the native huts and collected around the pagoda, never weary of seeing and hearing the whites jigging around the mechanical piano as off-key waltzes wheezed from its moth- eaten strings. When she heard the music, a blissful look came over the patronne, meaning that she felt like dancing.

After trying in vain for several days, I managed to have a few talks with her in private. Her periods, she confided, lasted no less than three weeks. Fault of the tropics. In addition, her customers wore her out. Not that they made love very often, but since drinks at the pagoda were on the expensive side, they tried to get their money's worth by pinching her ass something terrible before leaving. That was what wore her out mostly.

As a competent businesswoman, the patronne knew all the gossip of the colony, all the desperate love affairs that transpired between the fever-harried officers and the handful of civil servants' wives, they too menstruating interminably and languishing for days on end in the deep reclining chairs of their verandas.

The streets, offices, and shops of Fort-Gono were awash with mutilated desires. To do everything people did in Europe despite the abominable temperature and their own progressive, insurmountable decay seemed to be the prime obsession, satisfaction, and grimace of those maniacs.

The fences could hardly contain the swollen, wildly aggressive vegetation of the gardens; the rampant foliage molded delirious lettuces around the houses, those chunks of dried-out egg white, in which some jaundiced European was rotting away. All along the Avenue Fachoda,[51] the liveliest and most fashionable street in Fort-Gono, there were as many overflowing salad bowls as Government officials.

Every night I went to my no doubt unfinished shack, where my skeleton of a bed had been put up by my depraved boy. He set traps for me, he was as sensual as a cat, he wanted to become part of my family. I, however, was haunted by other, far more pressing preoccupations, especially by my plan to take refuge for a while in the hospital, the only armistice within my reach in that torrid carnival.

In peace as in war, I took no interest at all in futile pastimes.

Even the sincerely and eminently obscene offers that came to me through the boss's cook struck me as colorless.

For the last time I made the rounds of my young friends at the Porduriere, trying to cull some information about that disloyal employee, the one I had orders to replace at all costs in the bush. Empty chit-chat.

Nor did I learn anything substantial in the Café Faidherbe at the end of the Avenue Fachoda, abuzz at the twilight hour with hundreds of slanders, rumors, and calumnies. Nothing but impressions. Whole dustbins full of impressions were overturned in that half-light encrusted with multicolored lamps. Shaking the lace of the giant palm trees, the wind blew clouds of mosquitoes into the customers' saucers. The Governor, thanks to his exalted rank, figured prominently in the discourse round about. His inexpiable crumminess was the mainstay of the apéritif conversation in which the nauseated colonial liver seeks relief before dinner.

At that hour all the cars in Fort-Gono, ten in all, drove back and forth past the cafe. They never seemed to go very far. The Place Faidherbe had the characteristic atmosphere, the overdone décor,

---

[51] Avenue Fachoda. See note on Marchand above, p. 109 [note 46]. A bit of a joke. Since Fashoda represented a French humiliation, an Avenue Fachoda in France or the French colonies was unthinkable.

the floral and verbal excess, of a subprefecture in southern France gone mad. The ten cars left the Place Faidherbe only to come back five minutes later, having once more completed the same circuit with their cargo of anemic Europeans, dressed in unbleached linen, fragile creatures as wobbly as melting sherbet.

For weeks and years these colonials passed the same forms and faces until they were so sick of hating them that they didn't even look at one another. The officers now and then would take their families for a walk, paying close attention to military salutes and civilian greetings, the wives swaddled in their special sanitary napkins, the children, unbearably plump European maggots, wilted by the heat and constant diarrhea.

To command you need more than a kepi; you also need troops. In the climate of Fort-Gono the European cadres melted faster than butter. A battalion was like a lump of sugar in your coffee; the longer you looked the less you saw. Most of the white conscripts were permanently in the hospital, sleeping off their malaria, riddled with parasites made to order for every nook and cranny in the body, whole squads stretched out flat between cigarettes and flies, masturbating under moldy sheets, spinning endless yarns between fits of painstakingly provoked and coddled fever. Poor bastards, they were having a rough time, a pitiful crew in the soft half-light of the green shutters, re-enlisted men soon fallen from celebrity, side by side—the hospital was mixed—with civilians, all hunted men in flight from the bosses and the bush.

In the apathy of those long malarial siestas, the heat is such that the flies also rest. From bloodless, hairy arms on both sides of the beds dangle grimy books, all in tatters. Half the pages are missing because of the dysentery cases, who never have enough paper, and also because of the sourpuss nuns, who have their own way of censoring wicked books. The military crabs victimize the nuns as much as everybody else. When they want a good scratch, they lift up their habits behind the screen where this morning's stiff is still so hot that he hasn't yet managed to grow cold.

Depressing as the hospital was, it was the only place in the whole colony where you could feel forgotten, safe from the people outside, the bosses. A vacation from slavery, that was the main thing, anyway the only happiness within my reach.

I made inquiries about the requirements for admission, the habits and idiosyncracies of the doctors. By that time the prospect of leaving for the bush filled me with despair and thoughts of revolt; already I was planning to contract every available fever as soon as possible, to return to Fort-Gono desperately ill and so emaciated, so repulsive that they'd not only have to take me, but also to ship me back to France. I already knew some wonderful tricks for getting sick, and I was learning special new ones for the colonies, I prepared to overcome a thousand difficulties, for neither the directors of the Compagnie Pordurière nor the military authorities were easily discouraged from tracking their chill-racked, cadaverous prey and pouncing on them as they played cards between the pissy beds.

They would find me resolved to rot with whatever disease proved necessary. Unfortunately you didn't usually stay in the hospital for long, unless you wrote finis there to your colonial career once and for all. Sometimes the toughest and smartest of the fever patients, those with the greatest strength of character, managed to slip aboard a transport bound for France. That was a happy miracle. Most of the hospital patients gave up, recognized that the regulations had defeated them, and went back to the bush to lose what weight they had left. If the quinine relinquished them to their maggots while they were still in the hospital, the chaplain would simply close their eyes at about six in the evening, and four Senegalese would carry the bloodless husks to the plot of red clay beside the church in Fort-Gono. That church, incidentally, was so hot under its tin roof that you never went there twice, more tropical than the tropics. To stand up in that church you'd have to pant like a dog.

That's the way it goes. You can't deny it, men have a hard time doing all that's demanded of them: butterflies in their youth, maggots at the end.

I tried here and there to get a little more information, a few facts to go by. Because what the Director had told me about Bikomimbo seemed incredible. Apparently the place was an experimental trading post, an attempt to penetrate the bush, at least ten days' journey from the coast, isolated in the midst of the natives and their jungle, which had been described to me as an enormous reservation, crawling with animals and diseases.

I wondered if my young friends at the Pordurière, who oscillated between aggressiveness and extreme depression, weren't simply jealous of me. Their idiocy (which is all they could call their own) varied with the amount of liquor they had ingested, the letters they had received, and the amount of hope they had lost during the day. As a general rule, the more moribund they felt, the more they swaggered and strutted. If they'd been ghosts (like Ortolan at the front) their gall would have known no bounds.

Our apéritifs went on for three whole hours. We always talked about the Governor, the pivot of all our conversations; then we talked about possible and impossible swindles, and lastly about sex: the three colors of the colonial flag. The civil servants present made no bones about accusing the military of wallowing in peculation and abuse of authority, but the military paid them back in kind. The traders, for their part, regarded all these prebendaries as hypocritical imposters and bandits. A rumor that the Governor was being recalled had been in circulation every morning for the past ten years, yet the delightful telegram announcing his disgrace never arrived, and this in spite of the at least two anonymous letters mailed to the Minister for the Colonies each week, imputing a thousand meticulously described atrocities to that local tyrant.

The blacks are lucky with their onion skins; the white man, encased between his acid sweat and his tropical shirt, poisons himself. It's not safe to go near him, I'd learned my lesson on board the Admiral Bragueton.

In only a few days I heard some sweet stories about my Director! His past was as full of low dodges as a prison in a seaport town. His past had just about everything in it, including, I imagine, some magnificent miscarriages of justice. True, his looks were against him, his face had the terrifying look of an undeniable murderer, or rather, to be fair, the look of a reckless man in a terrible hurry to get ahead—which amounts to the same thing.

If you passed by at siesta time, you might see, sprawled in the shade of their houses on the Boulevard Faidherbe, a few white women, the wives of officers or settlers, who were even more devastated by the climate than the men, frail creatures with pleasingly hesitant voices, infinitely in-dulgent smiles, their pallor coated with rouge, as though happy on their deathbeds. These transplanted middle-class women showed less courage and pride of bearing than the patronne of the Pagoda, who had no one but herself to lean on. The Compagnie Pordurière consumed quantities of small clerks like me, every year it lost dozens of these subhumans in the jungle trading posts not far from the swamps. Pioneers!

Every morning the Army and Business came to the office of the hospital, whimpering and beg-ging for their men. Not a day went by but some captain came threatening and calling down God's thunders on the Head Physician to make him send those three malarial card-playing sergeants, and two syphilitic corporals back to their units on the double, because how could he put a company to-gether without noncoms? If told that his gold-bricks were dead, he'd stop bothering the hospital man-agement and go back to the Pagoda for a few more drinks.

Men, days, things—they passed before you knew it in this hotbed of vegetation, heat, humidity, and mosquitoes. Everything passed, disgustingly, in little pieces, in phrases, particles of flesh and bone, in regrets and corpuscles; demolished by the sun, they melted away in a torrent of light and colors, and taste and time went with them, everything went. Nothing remained but shimmering dread.

At last the freighter, which was to take me along the coast to the vicinity of my trading post, anchored within sight of Fort-Gono. The Papaoutah was her name. A small ship, wood-burning and flat-bottomed, built for estuaries. I was the only white on board, and they assigned me a small space between the kitchen and the toilet. We moved so slowly that at first I thought we were being cautious in getting out of the roadstead. But we never went any faster. This Papaoutah was incredibly short on power. We edged along within sight of the coast, an endless gray line tufted with small trees in the dancing heat mists. What a trip! The Papaoutah plowed through the water as slowly and painfully as if she herself had sweated it all. She would undo one little wave after another as cautiously as if they'd been bandages. The pilot, it seemed to me from a distance, must have been a mulatto; I say "seemed" because I never summoned up the energy to go up on the bridge and see for myself. Until about five o'clock I stayed in the shaded gangway, wedged in among the blacks who were the only passengers. If you don't want the sun to burn your brains through your eyes, you have to blink like a rat. After five you can indulge in a look around—the good life. That gray fringe, that tufted country at the water's edge, looked like flattened dress shields and didn't appeal to me at all. The air was unbreathable, even at night it was hot, sultry, and salty. Everything was so cloying it raised my bile, what with the smell of the engine and in the daytime the water that was too brown on one side and too blue on the other. This was even worse than the Admiral Bragueton, minus of course the murderous officers.

At last we approached the port of my destination. Its name, I was told, was Topo. After coughing, spitting, and quaking on the surface of that oily dishwater for three times as long as it takes to eat four canned meals, the Papaoutah finally pulled up at the landing.

Three enormous thatched huts stood out from the shaggy banks. From a distance and at first glance the place was rather attractive. This, I was told, was the mouth of a big sandy river, which I was to mount by canoe on my way to the heart of the jungle. I was scheduled to spend only a few days here at Topo by the sea, just time enough to frame my last colonial resolutions.

We headed for a flimsy dock, and before reaching it the Papaoutah scraped a sand bar with its fat belly. Well I remember that dock, it was made of bamboo, a story in itself. They told me it had to be rebuilt every month, because of the tricky, nimble little mollusks that came by the thousands and ate it up. This endless rebuilding, in fact, was one of the heartbreaking occupations that weighed on Lieutenant Grappa,[52] Commander of the Topo station and the surrounding territory. The Papaoutah called only once a month, but a month was all the mollusks needed to eat up her dock.

As soon as I landed, Lieutenant Grappa took possession of my papers, checked them for authenticity, copied them into a virgin register, and invited me in for an apéritif. I was the first traveler, he informed me, to come to Topo in two years. Nobody came to Topo. There was no reason to come to Topo. Sergeant Alcide was Lieutenant Grappa's second in command. In their isolation there was no love lost between them. "I always have to watch that subordinate of mine," said Lieutenant Grappa at our first meeting, "or he tends to get too familiar."

Since any happenings they might have imagined in that wilderness would have been too implausible (for what could happen in such a place?), Sergeant Alcide prepared in advance a whole sheaf of "Nothing to report" reports, which Grappa signed without delay, and the Papaoutah carried them away to the Governor General.

Among the lagoons round about and in the depths of the jungle several moth-eaten tribes lived in misery and stagnation, decimated and befuddled by trypanosoma and chronic poverty; even so, these tribes paid a small tax, collected of course with clubs. From among their younger set a few militiamen were recruited to wield these same clubs. The militia consisted of twelve men.

Lucky bastards! I know whereof I speak. I knew them well. Lieutenant Grappa equipped them in his own way and fed them regulation rice. One rifle for all twelve, but each had his own little flag. No shoes. But, since all things are relative and comparative in this world, the native recruits thought Grappa was treating them splendidly. Every day, in fact, he turned away volunteers and enthusiasts, young men who had had their fill of the bush.

The hunt in these parts didn't yield much, and at least one grandmother a week was eaten for want of gazelles. At seven o'clock every morning Alcide's militiamen reported for drill. Since I lived in one corner of his hut, where he had made room for me, I had a ringside seat for the fantasia. Never has any army in the world had more willing soldiers. In response to Alcide's commands, those primitives would wear themselves out pacing the sand in columns of four, eight, and finally twelve, imagining they had packs, shoes, and even bayonets, and better still, going through the motions of using them. Barely emerged from a nature so vigorous and so close at hand, they wore nothing but an apology for khaki shorts. They had to imagine all the rest, and did. At Alcide's peremptory command, these ingenious warriors deposited their imaginary packs on the ground and lunged into empty space to disembowel illusory enemies with illusory bayonets. Then, after simulating the unbuttoning of jackets, they would stack invisible rifles and in response to another sign, fling themselves with unfeigned passion into an abstraction of rifle drill. To see them disperse, gesticulating with studied precision, and lose themselves in intricate, epileptic, and insanely useless movements was deeply

---

[52] Lieutenant Grappa. From the well-known Italian alcoholic spirit.

depressing. Especially when you remember that in Topo the raw, stiffling heat, so perfectly concentrated in that sand pit between the conjugated polished mirrors of the sea and the river, would have made you swear by your bleeding buttocks that you were being forced to sit on a chunk of sun that had just fallen off.

But these implacable conditions didn't stop Alcide from sounding off. Not at all. Passing over the heads of his incredible drill squad, his roars mounted to the tops of the venerable cedars at the edge of the jungle. And the thunder of his "Ten-shun!" reverberated still further, further still.

Meanwhile Lieutenant Grappa was administering justice. We'll have more to say about that. Or from a distance, from the shade of his hut, he'd be supervising the ephemeral construction of his ill-fated dock. He had ordered complete uniforms and equipment for his recruits, and every time the Papaoutah showed up, he went down to the dock with sceptical optimism to take delivery. For two years he'd been clamoring for those uniforms. It may have been especially humiliating for Grappa as a Corsican to see that his militiamen were still stark naked.

In our hut, Alcide's I mean, a small, semiclandestine trade was carried on in small objects and miscellaneous odds and ends. As a matter of fact, all the commerce of Topo passed through Alcide's hands, for he and he alone possessed a small stock of tobacco, both packaged and in the leaf, several liters of brandy, and a few bolts of cotton goods.

It was plain that the twelve militiamen felt a real liking for Alcide though he chewed them out interminably and kicked their rear ends rather unjustly. But those nudist soldiers had discerned in Alcide the unquestionable signs of kinship, of fellow membership in the great family of the innately, incurably poor. Black or not, tobacco created a tie, it always does. I had brought a few newspapers with me from Europe. Alcide looked through them, trying to take an interest in the news, but though he tried three times to fix his attention on those ill-assorted columns, he couldn't get through them. "You know," he confessed to me after his vain effort, "I don't really give a shit about the news anymore! I've been here for three years now!" It shouldn't be thought that Alcide was trying to impress me by playing the hermit. Actually, the ruthlessness, the manifest indifference of the whole world where he was concerned, had driven him, in his capacity as a re-enlisted sergeant, to regard the whole world outside of Topo as a distant planet.

Alcide was a good sort, obliging, generous and all. I realized that later, a little too late. He was crushed by his enormous resignation, that basic quality that makes it as easy to kill poor bastards in and out of the army as to let them live. Poor people never, or hardly ever, ask for an explanation of all they have to put up with. They hate one another, and content themselves with that.

Around our hut, scattered over the lagoon of torrid pitiless sand, there were strange little flowers, fresh and short-lived, green, pink, or purple, the kind that in Europe you only see painted on certain pieces of porcelain, a kind of primitive no-nonsense morning glory. Closed on their stems, they endured the long abominable days, then opened in the evening and trembled in the first balmy breezes.

One day when Alcide saw me picking a little bunch of them, he warned me: "Pick them if you want to, but don't water the little bitches, it kills them... They're delicate, not at all like the sunflowers we used to grow for the army kids in Rambouillet!... You could piss on them!... They'd drink anything!... If you ask me, flowers are like men... The bigger the dumber!" That was an obvious dig at Lieutenant Grappa, whose body was bulky and ramshackle, his hands short, purple, and terrifying. The kind of hands that would never understand anything. And indeed, Grappa made no attempt to understand.

I stayed in Topo for two weeks, during which I shared not only Alcide's existence and food, his bed fleas and sand fleas (two species), but also his quinine and the inexorably tepid and diarrheic water of the nearby well.

One day when Lieutenant Grappa was feeling convivial he invited me to his house for coffee. Grappa was jealous, he never let anyone see his native concubine. Consequently, he picked a day when his Negress was visiting her parents in their village. It was also the day when his court of justice convened, and he wanted to impress me.

The motley mass of complainants and screeching witnesses had arrived early in the morning. In bright- colored loincloths they crowded around the hut. Defendants and mere public stood mixed helter-skelter, all smelling strongly of garlic, sandalwood, rancid butter, and saffron-scented sweat.

Like Alcide's militiamen, all these people seemed intent first and foremost on frenzied illusory motion; in transports of imaginary argument, they spewed castanet language and shook their clenched fists.

Deep in his creaking, groaning cane chair, Lieutenant Grappa smiled at all this assembled incoherence. He trusted for guidance in the post interpreter, who in a loud and barely intelligible mumbo-jumbo communicated unbelievable complaints.

Take, for instance, the one-eyed sheep that a certain girl's parents refused to return despite the fact that their daughter, though married in due form, had never been delivered to her husband, because in the meantime the bride's brother had somehow seen fit to murder the bridegroom's sister, who had been guarding the sheep at the time. And many similar but even more complicated grievances.

Around us a hundred faces, impassioned by these questions of custom and interest, bared their teeth with little clicking or big gurgling sounds, black-African words.

The heat was nearing its height. I looked up past the edge of the roof to see if some disaster was approaching in the sky. Not even a storm.

"I'm going to straighten this whole thing out immediately!"' Grappa finally declared; the heat and interminable palavers had driven him to a decision. "Where's the bride's father? Bring him here!"

"Here he is!" cried a dozen natives, pushing an elderly, decrepit-looking black man swathed with great dignity in a yellow pagne—Roman style—to the front. With one clenched fist the old man beat time to everything that was being said around him. He didn't look as if he'd come to make a complaint, more likely he hoped for a bit of entertainment long after he'd given up expecting any tangible results from his lawsuit.

"All right," said Grappa. "Twenty strokes! Let's get this over with! Give this old pimp twenty strokes! That'll teach him to pester me every Thursday for the last two months with his batty sheep story!"

The old man saw four husky militiamen coming toward him. At first he didn't understand what they wanted with him, but then he began to roll his eyes, which were bloodshot like the eyes of a terrified old animal that has never been beaten before. He made no real attempt to resist, but neither did he know what position to take so the scourge of justice would inflict the least pain.

The militiamen pulled him by the toga. Two of them wanted him to kneel, but the other two told him to lie prone. In the end, they just laid him out on the ground any which way, lifted up his toga, and subjected his back and buttocks to a score of blows with a flexible rod that would have made a healthy mule bellow for a week. He wriggled and writhed, the fine sand spurted all around him mixed with blood, he spat sand as he howled, he made me think of an enormous pregnant basset bitch being tortured.

The public was silent while this was going on. All you could hear was the sound of the beating. When it was over, the old man, though half unconscious, tried to get up and cover himself with his Roman pagne. His mouth and nose and most of all his back were bleeding profusely. Droning their comments and chit-chat in funereal tones, the crowd led him away.

Lieutenant Grappa relit his cigar. In my presence, he affected an air of aloofness from these things. I don't believe he was more Neronian than anyone else, but he disliked being obliged to think. That infuriated him. What exasperated him when performing his judicial functions was the questions he was asked.

The same day we witnessed another two memorable thrashings pursuant to further disconcerting reports of dowries taken back, poisonings threatened... promises unfulfilled... children of uncertain origin, etc.

"Oh!" Grappa cried. "If they only knew how completely cold their bickerings leave me, they'd stay in their jungle where they belong instead of chewing my ear off with their cock and bull stories! Do I bother them with my troubles?" But then he started on a different idea: "You know, I'm almost beginning to think those apes are developing a taste for my justice... For two years I've been trying to get them disgusted with it, but every Thursday they come back for more... Believe it or not, young man, it's almost always the same ones who keep coming!... A bunch of perverts if you ask me!"

Then the conversation turned to Toulouse, where he spent all his leaves and where he was planning to settle in six years when he retired. It was all right with me. We had pleasantly arrived at the

Calvados stage when we were disturbed again by a native who'd been sentenced the week before but was late in having his sentence carried out. Now, two hours after everyone else, he'd come of his own free will to get his thrashing. He'd been on the trail for two days and two nights, and he had no intention of going back to his village with his business undone. But he was late, and in matters of penal punctuality Grappa was uncompromising: "He asked for it! Why didn't he wait his turn last time?... I sentenced the motherfucker to those fifty strokes last Thursday, not today!"

Still, the client protested, for he had a good excuse; he'd had to hurry back to his village to bury his mother. He had three or four mothers all to himself. Excellent arguments!...

"It will have to wait till the next session!"

But our client would barely have time for the trip to his village and back before the following Thursday. He went on protesting, he wouldn't budge. It took several violent kicks in the ass to get that masochist out of the camp. They gave him some pleasure, but not enough... In the end he went to Alcide, who took advantage of the situation to sell him a whole assortment of tobacco, in the leaf, in packages, and in the form of snuff.

Well entertained by these various incidents, I took my leave of Grappa. It was time for his siesta, and he withdrew to the interior of his hut, where his native housekeeper, who had just come back from her village, was already reclining. That black woman had a magnificent pair of tits, and she had been well schooled by the Sisters in Gabon. Not only did the young lady speak French (with a lisp), she also knew how to administer quinine in jam and to dig chiggers out of the soles of one's feet. She knew a hundred ways of making herself agreeable to a white man without tiring him or by tiring him, whichever he preferred.

Alcide was waiting for me. He was rather miffed. It was probably the invitation with which Grappa had honored me that decided him to confide in me. What he told me was pretty strong stuff. Unasked, he modeled Grappa's portrait in steaming cow flop. I replied that he had taken the words out of my mouth. Alcide's vulnerable point was that in defiance of army regulations, which strictly forbade it, he was trading with the natives in the jungle round about and with his twelve militiamen as well. He mercilessly sold those people tobacco on credit. When payday came around, there was no pay for the militiamen to collect, they had smoked it all up. They smoked up advances. This petty irregularity, what with the rarity of cash in the region, hampered the collection of taxes.

Lieutenant Grappa was too cautious a man to provoke a scandal in Topo while he was in command, but he was definitely pissed off, maybe he was jealous. Understandably enough, he felt that whatever negligible sums of money the natives called their own should remain available to the tax collector. Each man to his taste and humble ambitions.

At first this system of credit against their pay had seemed rather strange and even outrageous to the riflemen, whose sole purpose in working was to smoke Alcide's tobacco, but he had got them used to it by kicking them in the ass. By that time, they'd given up trying to collect their pay, they calmly smoked it up in advance, among the bright-colored flowers outside Alcide's hut, between two stints of imaginary drill.

In short, there was room in Topo, small as it was, for two systems of civilization, Grappa's, which you might call Roman and which consisted of flogging your subjects for the sole purpose of extracting tribute, of which, if Alcide was to be believed, Grappa retained a disgraceful percentage for his own strictly personal use, and the more elaborate Alcide system bearing witness to a higher stage of civilization, in which every soldier becomes a customer. This military-commercial complex is much more modern and hypocritical; it is, indeed, the basis of our own system.

Lieutenant Grappa was no great shakes at geography. For his knowledge of the vast territories committed to his charge, he relied on a few rudimentary maps that he had at the post. He was none too eager to know more about those territories. After all, we know what trees and the jungle are, we can see them very nicely from a distance.

Tucked away in the fronds and hollows of that immense steam bath, a few thinly disseminated tribes stagnated amid their fleas and flies, stultified by their totems and unflaggingly gorging themselves with putrid manioc... Utterly naïve, frankly cannibalistic, maddened by poverty, and ravaged by a thousand plagues. No earthly reason to go near them. Nothing to justify troublesome administrative incursions, which could yield no results whatsoever. When Grappa had finished meting out justice, he preferred to turn toward the sea and contemplate the horizon from which he had come one day and across which he would sail one day if all went well.

Familiar and all in all agreeable as the place had become to me, the time came when I had to think of leaving Topo for the post that was to be my dwelling place and occupation after several days of fluvial navigation and sylvan peregrinations.

Alcide and I were getting on fine together. We tried to fish for swordfish, a variety of shark that infested the waters in front of our hut. He was just as clumsy as I was. We never caught anything.

The only furnishings in his hut were his folding bed, mine, and a few crates, some empty, some full. I had the impression that what with his little business he must be putting quite a lot of money aside.

"Where do you keep it?" I asked him several times. "Where do you hide your filthy lucre?" Just to get his goat. "Planning a big spree when you get back?" I was only teasing him. Twenty times at least, as we dug into the inevitable canned tomatoes, I'd entertain him with amazing episodes of the heroic joyride from cathouse to cathouse that would celebrate his return to Bordeaux. He never said anything. He'd only laugh, as though my little stories amused him.

Apart from the drill and the court sessions, nothing happened in Topo, nothing whatever, so naturally, for want of other subjects, I'd take up the same old joke as often as possible.

Once toward the end of my stay, I thought of writing to Monsieur Puta to touch him for some money. Alcide promised to mail my letter the next time the Papaoutah called. Alcide kept his writing materials in a small biscuit tin, just like the one Branledore had had, exactly the same. All re-enlisted sergeants seemed to have them. When he saw me start opening the box, Alcide made a movement to stop me. I was surprised and embarrassed. I had no idea why he wouldn't let me open it, but I put it down on the table. "Oh, all right, open it!" he said finally. "Hell, it doesn't matter." The photograph of a little girl was pasted to the inside of the lid. Just the head, a sweet little face with long curls, the way they wore them in those days. I took out pen and paper and quickly closed the lid. I was embarrassed at my indiscretion, but I also wondered why it had upset him so.

First I figured that the child must be his and he hadn't wanted to talk about her. I asked no questions, but then I heard him behind my back, trying to tell me something in a strange bumbling voice I'd never heard. I felt very uncomfortable. I knew I ought to help him tell me his story, but I didn't know how to go about it. I knew it would be a painful story to listen to, and I wasn't looking forward to it.

"It's nothing!" I finally heard him say. "It's my brother's daughter... They're both dead... " "Her parents?" "Yes, her parents... "

"Then who's bringing her up? Your mother?" I asked him that to show I was taking an interest. "My mother's dead too." "Who then?" "Well, me!"

He grinned and blushed crimson, as if he'd done something absolutely indecent. Then he hastened to rectify:

"All right, I'll explain... I'm having her brought up in Bordeaux by the Sisters... But don't get me wrong, they're no Sisters of Charity... High-class Sisters... She's my responsibility and you needn't worry. She'll want for nothing! Her name is Ginette... Sweet little girl... Like her mother... She writes to me, she's making good progress, but you know, those schools are expensive... Especially now that she's ten... I want her to have piano lessons at the same time... What do you think of the piano?... Well, in my opinion the piano is the right thing for girls... Don't you agree?... And what about English? English can come in handy... Do you know English?"

As Alcide confessed his failing—not being generous enough— I began to look at him more closely, with his little cosmetic mustache, his eccentric eyebrows, and his burnt-black skin. The delicacy of the man! And how he must have scrimped and saved on his meager wages... his pitiful allowances and tiny clandestine business... for months and years in this infernal Topo!... I didn't know what to say, I had no experience, but his heart was so much superior to mine that I went red in the face... Next to Alcide I was an impotent slob, boorish and vain... No two ways... Plain as day...

I didn't dare speak to him anymore. Suddenly I felt unworthy to say a word to him. I, who only yesterday had kept him at a distance and even looked down on him a little.

"I haven't been lucky," he went on, unaware that he was embarrassing me with his confidences. "Imagine, two years ago she had infantile paralysis... You know what infantile paralysis is?"

He went on to explain that the child's left leg was atrophied and that a specialist in Bordeaux was treating her with electricity.

"You think she'll get it back?" he asked me.

I assured him that she would recover completely with time and electricity. He spoke very circumspectly of his dead mother and of the child's infirmity. He was afraid, even at a distance, of harming her.

"Have you been to see her since her illness?" "No, I've been here the whole time."

"Will you go and see her soon?"

"I don't think I'll be able to go for another three years... You see, I do a little business here... That's a big help to her... If I went on leave now, my place here would be taken before I got back... Especially with that bastard... "

So Alcide had asked to do a double hitch, to stay in Topo for six consecutive years instead of three, for the sake of his little niece, of whom he had nothing but a few letters and that little photograph.

"What bothers me," he said after we'd gone to bed, "is that she hasn't anybody for the holidays... That's hard on a little girl... "

Obviously Alcide was perfectly at ease, at home so to speak, in the higher regions, on terms of familiarity with the angels. You wouldn't have known it to look at him. With hardly a thought of what he was doing, he had consented to years of torture, to the crushing of his life in this torrid monotony for the sake of a little girl to whom he was vaguely related. Motivated by nothing but his good heart, he had set no conditions and asked nothing in return. To that little girl far away he was giving enough tenderness to make the whole world over, and he never showed it.

Suddenly he fell asleep in the candlelight. After a while I got up to look at his face. He slept like everybody else. He looked quite ordinary. There ought to be some mark by which to distinguish good people from bad.

* * *

There are two ways of getting into the jungle. One is to cut a tunnel through it, the way rats do in a bale of hay. That's the stifling way. I jibbed at that. Or you can endure the misery of sitting huddled in a hollow tree trunk, while they paddle you up the winding river from copse to snag, waiting for the endless days to pass and laying yourself open without defense to the deadly glare. And finally, dazed by the yapping of the black men, you reach your destination in some sort of condition.

At first your paddlers always need time to catch the cadence. Arguments. A paddle strikes the water, two or three rhythmic howls, the jungle sends back an answer, eddies, she's gliding, two paddles, three, still groping for the rhythm, waves, inarticulate burblings, a backward glance at the sea, flattening out as it recedes, and up ahead the long smooth expanse into which you're toiling. And for a while yet, far away on his dock, almost swallowed up by the sea mists, Alcide under his enormous bell-shaped pith helmet, a chunk of head, the face a small cheese, and below it the rest of him, floating in his tunic, lost in a strange white-trousered memory.

That's all I have left of the place, of Topo.

Have they managed to defend that scorching hamlet against the insidious scythe of the yellowish-brown river? Are its flea-bitten huts still standing? Are new Grappas and unknown Alcides still training new recruits in imaginary combat? Is the same plain-dealing brand of justice still being meted out? Is the drinking water still so rancid? So tepid? So bad that whenever you try to drink it, it leaves you disgusted for days on end... Is there still no refrigeration? And what of those acoustic battles between the flies and the everlasting hum of the quinine... Sulphate? Chloride?... in your ears?... But most of all: Are there still black people sweltering and pustulating in that caldron? Who knows? Maybe not.

Maybe none of all that is there anymore, maybe a tornado broke loose one night, maybe the Little Congo, just in passing, gave Topo one good lick with its muddy tongue and it was all over.

Maybe the whole place is dead and gone, the very name wiped off the maps, and nobody left to remember Alcide... Maybe his little niece has forgotten him too. Maybe Lieutenant Grappa never saw his Toulouse again... Maybe the jungle, which has always, year after year when the rainy season sets in, had designs on the dune, has recaptured the whole settlement, crushed it beneath the shade of its giant mahogany trees, even those unexpected little sand flowers that Alcide didn't want me to water... Maybe it's all gone... I'll long remember those ten days going up the river... Huddled in the bottom of the canoe, watching out for muddy whirlpools, picking furtive passages between enormous drifting branches, nimbly avoided. A labor for convicts on the lam.

After every sundown we'd camp on a rocky promontory. Finally one morning we left that filthy native canoe and slipped into the forest by a hidden path that twined through the moist green gloom, lit only here and there by a ray of sunlight falling from the roof of that vast cathedral of leaves. Monstrous felled trees forced us to make frequent detours. Whole Metro trains could have maneuvered with ease in the hollows left by their roots.

Suddenly the full light was on us again, we had come to a clearing and had to climb, an additional effort. The rise we had come to overlooked the endless forest, rolling over red, yellow, and green peaks, modeling and smoothing hill and dale, as monstrously spacious as the sea and the sky. I was given to understand by signs that the man whose habitation we were looking for lived just a little further on... in another valley. And there he was waiting for us.

He had built a sort of hut between two big boulders, sheltered, as he informed me, from the eastern tornadoes, which were the worst, the most furious. That, I was willing to admit, was an advantage, but the hut itself definitely belonged to the lowest, most ramshackle category, an almost theoretical edifice, coming apart at every seam. I had foreseen something of the sort, but this surpassed all my expectations.

The man must have thought I looked downcast, because he addressed me rather brusquely, to shake me out of my thoughts. "Come off it, you'll be better off here than in the trenches! Here at least you can worry along. The food is rotten, I can't deny it, and there's nothing to drink but pure mud, but you can sleep as much as you like... There's no big guns here and no bullets! All in all, it's a bargain!" He talked something like the Director General, but he had pale eyes like Alcide's.

He must have been close to thirty, with a beard... I hadn't taken a good look at him on arriving, because on arriving I'd been thrown off by the dilapidation of the setup he was supposed to bequeath me and which might possibly be my home for years... But observing him later on, I found a distinctly adventurous face with sharply accentuated angles, one of those rebellious faces that plunge into life head-on instead of rolling with the waves, with a big round nose, and cheeks like coal barges, plashing against destiny with a soft babbling sound. That was an unhappy man.

"It's true," I said. "There's nothing worse than war."

I thought we'd said enough for the moment. I had no desire to say any more. It was he who went on:

"Especially now that they make them so long. Well anyway, friend, you'll see that it's no joke here! There's nothing to do... It's a sort of vacation... Except who'd want to spend a vacation in a place like this? Well, maybe it's a matter of temperament. I wouldn't know... "

"How about the water?" I asked. The water I saw in the cup I had poured myself had me worried, it was yellowish. I drank some, it was sickening and as warm as in Topo. A three-day sediment of mud.

"Is this the water?" The water torture was starting all over again.

"Yes, that's all there is, except rain water... But when it starts raining, the shack won't last long. You see the condition it's in?"-I saw.

"The food," he went on, "is all canned. That's what I've been eating for a whole year... It hasn't killed me. Convenient in a way, but it doesn't stick to the ribs... The natives eat putrid manioc, that's their business, they like it... For the last three months it's been running through me... Diarrhea... Maybe it's fever too, I've got both... Around five o'clock I'm more lucid... That's how I know I've got fever, because it's hard to feel hotter than you do already in this climate!... Actually, it's probably the chills that tell you you've got a fever... And not being quite so bored, maybe that's another sign...

but that's a matter of temperament too... maybe a few drinks would cheer us up... but I don't go for drink... it doesn't agree with me... "

He seemed to think very highly of what he called "temperament."

Then while he was at it, he gave me a little more of his delightful information: "By day it's the heat, at night it's the noise that's hard to bear... It's unbelievable . , , The animals go chasing round and round, to fuck or to kill each other, how do I know?... Either way, you never heard such a hulla-baloo!... The loudest are the hyenas... They come up close to the shack... You'll hear them!... You won't have any doubts... It's nothing like the quinine music , . , Sometimes you can mistake birds or big flies for quinine... It's conceivable... But hyenas, the enormous way they laugh... They're smelling your flesh... That's what makes them laugh... They're in a hurry to see you pass on!... You can even see their eyes shining, so I'm told... They feed on dead bodies... I've never looked into their eyes... I'm sorry in a way... "

"Sounds delightful!" I said.

But he hadn't finished with the night life.

"Then there's the village," he went on... "There aren't a hundred niggers in it, but they make enough rumpus for ten thousand. You'll tell me what you think of it! And man! If it's tom-toms you're after, you've come to the right place!... If they're not beating them because the moon is out, they're beating them because the moon has gone by... There's always some reason!... The sons-of-bitches seem to be in cahoots with the animals to drive us crazy! So help me, I'd shoot the whole lot of them if I weren't so tired... As it is, I put cotton in my ears... That's even better... As long as I had vaseline in my medicine chest, I greased the cotton with it, now I use banana oil... Banana oil does the trick... That way they can gargle with thunderstorms if it makes them happy! It's no skin off my ass with my ears full of greased cotton! I don't hear a damned thing! These niggers are sick, they're perverts! You'll see!... All day long they squat on the ground, you wouldn't think them capable of moving as far as the nearest tree to piss against, but the minute it's dark, surprise! Vice! Nerves! Hysteria! Chunks of the night gone hysterical! That's niggers for you, take it from me! Degenerate scum!... "

"Do they often come and buy from you?"

"Buy? You're out of your mind! The trick is to rob them before they rob you! That's business! At night of course they do as they please... with greased cotton in both ears!... they'd be fools to stand on ceremony!... Besides, as you see, my shack has no door... so naturally they help themselves... for them it's the good life... "

"But what about your inventory?" I asked, utterly dismayed at what he had told me. "The Direc-tor General told me... he made himself very clear... to draw up a meticulous inventory the moment I got here... "

"I have the honor," he replied with perfect calm, "of telling you that the Director can kiss my ass... " "But won't you have to see him on your way through Fort-Gono?"

"I will never see either Fort-Gono or the Director again... It's a big forest, my young friend... " "But where will you go?"

"If anyone asks you, tell them you don't know. But since you seem eager to learn, let me give you some very good advice before it's too late! Don't worry about the company any more than the Company worries about you! If you can run as fast as the Company screws its employees, I can tell you right now that you're due to win the Grand Prix!... So be thankful that I'm leaving you a little cash and ask no more!... As for the stock, if it's true that the Director told you to take charge of it... tell him there isn't any left, and that's that!... If he won't believe you, who cares?... They take us all for thieves anyway! So it won't make any difference to public opinion if for once we get a little something out of it... And besides, don't worry, the Director knows more about financial monkey-shines than anybody, so why contradict him? That's my opinion! What's yours? Everybody knows that for a man to come here he has to be prepared to kill his father and mother! Am I right?"

I wasn't so sure all he'd been telling me was true, but either way this predecessor of mine struck me as an out-and-out bandit.

I wasn't at all easy in my mind. "Another mess I've fallen into!" I said to myself with increasing conviction. I stopped talking with that thug. In one corner, stowed every which way, I found the merchandise he was leaving me, a few scraps of cotton goods... But loincloths and shoes by the dozen, some boxes of pepper, several lamps, a douche can, a staggering quantity of canned "Cassoulet à la Bordelaise," and lastly a picture post card of the Place Clichy.

"Next to the ridgepole you'll find the rubber and ivory I've bought from the niggers... I worked hard at first... And oh yes, here are three hundred francs... That's what's coming to you... " Coming to me for what? I had no idea, but I didn't bother to ask him.

"You may still be able to manage a bit of barter," he said. "Because, you know, you'll have no use for money out here, only when you want to clear out... "

He started laughing. Not wanting to cross him at the moment, I did likewise, I chimed in as if everything were hunky-dory.

In spite of the extreme destitution in which he'd been living for many months, he had surrounded himself with an elaborate domestic staff, consisting mostly of young boys, who fell all over themselves in their eagerness to bring him the household's one and only spoon or the matchless cup, or to extract with consummate skill the classical and inevitable burrowing chiggers from the soles of his feet. In return, he would often oblige them with a kindly hand between their thighs. The only work I ever saw him do was scratching himself, but that, like the shopkeeper at Fort-Gono, he did with the marvelous agility that can be observed only in the colonies.

The chairs and tables he bequeathed me showed me what ingenuity can do with crushed soapboxes. That sinister individual also taught me how it is possible, for want of anything better to do, to propel those ungainly, caparisoned caterpillars which, quivering and foaming at the mouth, kept assailing our forest cabin, far into the distance with a short swift kick. God help you if you are clumsy enough to crush one.

You'll be punished with an entire week of intense stench, which rises slowly from that unforgettable mash. He had read somewhere that those horrible monsters were the oldest animals in the world, dating, so he claimed, back to the second geological period! "When we've come as far as they have, my boy, won't we stink too?" His exact words.

The sunsets in that African hell proved to be fabulous. They never missed. As tragic every time as a monumental murder of the sun! But the marvel was too great for one man alone. For a whole hour the sky paraded in great delirious spurts of scarlet from end to end; after that the green of the trees exploded and rose up in quivering trails to meet the first stars. Then the whole horizon turned gray again and then red, but this time a tired red that didn't last long. That was the end. All the colors fell back down on the forest in tatters, like streamers after the hundredth performance. It happened every day at exactly six o'clock.

Then the night set in with all its monsters and its thousands and thousands of croaking toads.

The forest is only waiting for their signal to start trembling, hissing, and roaring from its depths. An enormous, love-maddened, unlighted railway station, full to bursting. Whole trees bristling with living noisemakers, mutilated erections, horror. After a while we couldn't hear each other talk in the hut. I had to hoot across the table like a hoot owl for my companion to understand me. I was getting my money's worth. And remember, I didn't like the country.

"What's your name?" I asked him. "Did you say Robinson?"

He had just been telling me that the natives in those parts suffered horribly from every conceivable disease and that the poor bastards were in no condition to engage in any kind of trade. While we were talking about the natives, so many flies and insects, so large and in such great numbers, dashed against the lamp in such dense squalls that we finally had to put it out.

Before dousing the lamp, I caught a glimpse of Robinson's face, veiled by a curtain of insects. That may be why his features impressed themselves more sharply on my memory, whereas before that they hadn't reminded me of anything in particular. He went on talking to me in the darkness, while I retraced the steps of my past with the sound of his voice as a charm with which to open the doors of the years and months and finally of my days, wondering where I could have run into this man. But I found nothing. No answer. You can lose your way groping among the shadows of the past. It's frightening how many people and things there are in a man's past that have stopped moving. The living people we've lost in the crypts of time sleep so soundly side by side with the dead that the same darkness envelops them all.

As we grow older, we no longer know whom to awaken, the living or the dead.

I was trying to identify this Robinson when gales of hideously exaggerated laughter, not far away in the night, made me jump.

Then they fell silent. It must have been the hyenas he'd told me about.

And then there was nothing but the villagers and their tomtoms, those crazy drums made of hollow wood, termites of the wind.

The name Robinson gnawed at me more and more insistently. In the darkness we talked about Europe and the meals you can order if you've got the money, not to mention the drinks! so deliciously cool! Not a word about the next day, when I was to be left alone, for years perhaps, with all those cans of cassoulet... Would war have been better? No, worse! Definitely worse!... He thought so too... He'd been in the war himself... And nevertheless he was getting out of here... He was fed up with the forest, and that was that... I tried to bring him back to the war... But he wouldn't oblige...

Finally, as we were getting ready for bed, each in his corner of that shambles of leaves and partitions, he came right out with it: he preferred the risk of being haled into court for theft to living on cassoulet as he'd been doing for almost a year. Then I saw the lie of the land.

"Haven't you any cotton for your ears?" he asked me... "If not, you'd better make some with the nap of a blanket and a drop of banana oil. You can make very nice little plugs that way... I for my part refuse to put up with the bellowing of those baboons... !"

Actually that concert had everything in it but baboons, but he clung to his inept generic term.

It suddenly occurred to me that this business with the cotton must be a cloak for some fiendish trick. I was seized with fear that he'd murder me there on my folding bed and make off with what was left in the money box... The idea paralyzed me. But what could I do? Call for help? Call who? The village cannibals?

... I thought of myself as missing. Even in Paris a man without money, without debts, without hope of an inheritance, hardly exists, he's missing to all intents and purposes... So what could I expect here? Who'd bother to come to Bikomimbo and even honor my memory by spitting in the water? Nobody of course.

Hours of intermittent terror. He didn't snore. All those sounds, those calls from the forest made it hard for me to hear him breathe. No need of cotton. I kept puzzling, and finally the name Robinson revealed a body, a posture, a voice I had known... And just as I was giving in to sleep, the whole man stood before my bed, I held him fast, not him of course, but the memory of this Robinson, the man at Noirceur-sur-la-Lys in Flanders, who'd been with me on the fringes of that night when we went looking for a hole through which to escape from the war, and then the same man later in Paris... It all came back to me. Years passed in a few moments. I'd been unhappy, sick in the head... Now that I knew, now that I'd placed him, I couldn't help it, I was thoroughly scared. Had he recognized me? In any case he could count on my silence and complicity.

"Robinson! Robinson!" I cried out cheerfully, as if I had good news for him. "Hey, old man! Hey, Robinson!"... No answer.

With pounding heart I got up, expecting a mean jab in the gut... Nothing. Then, rather bravely, I groped my way to the other end of the shack, where I'd seen him go to bed. He was gone.

Striking a match now and then, I waited for daybreak. The day came in a burst of light and so did the black servants, laughing and offering me their enormous uselessness. At least they were cheerful, I'll admit that. From the first, they tried to teach me the art of not giving a damn. I did my best to explain with a series of carefully studied gestures how terribly Robinson's disappearance had me worried. No use. It was all the same to them. True, it's senseless to worry about anything that isn't right in front of your nose. What bothered me most about all this was the money box. But when someone walks off with a money box, you seldom see him again... I therefore decided that Robinson was most unlikely to come back and murder me. Which was that much gained.

So the whole landscape was mine! I'd have all the time I needed., I thought, to study the surface and the depths of this leafy immensity, this ocean of red, of mottled yellow, of flamboyant hams and head cheeses, magnificent no doubt for people who love nature. I definitely didn't. The poetry of the tropics turned my stomach. The thought of all those vistas repeated on me like tuna fish. Say what you like, it will never be anything but a country for mosquitoes and panthers. And not for me.

I preferred to go back to my shack and fix it up in anticipation of the tornado that could not be long in coming. But I was soon obliged to abandon my attempts at reinforcement. The standard parts of the structure were amenable to further disintegration but defied repair, the vermin-infested thatch was coming apart, you couldn't have made a decent urinal out of my home.

After I had described a few listless circles in the bush, the sun forced me to go back in and silently collapse. The same old sun! At the noon hour everything falls silent, everything is afraid of burning up. And it wouldn't take much, grass, animals, and people are heated through. Meridian apoplexy.

My one and only chicken, bequeathed to me by Robinson, dreaded the noon hour the same as I did, he'd go back in with me. For three weeks the chicken lived with me like that, following me like a dog, clucking constantly, seeing snakes wherever he went. One day of extreme boredom, I ate him. He had no taste at all, his flesh had been bleached by the sun like an awning. Maybe he was what made me so sick. Be that as it may, the morning after that meal I couldn't get up. Around noon, completely groggy, I dragged myself to the medicine chest. There was nothing in it but some iodine and a map of the Nord-Sud Métro.[53] I hadn't seen a single customer in the store, only a few villagers who came to look-see, interminably gesticulating and chewing cola, ridden with sex and malaria. They gathered in a circle around me and seemed to be discussing my ugly mug. I was a hundred-percent sick, I felt as if I had no further use for my legs, they just hung over the edge of my bed like unimportant and rather ridiculous objects.

All the runners brought me from the Director in Fort-Gono was letters stinking with insults and idiocy, and threatening what's more. Businessmen all think of themselves as big or little professional wizards, but in practice they usually turn out to be hopeless incompetents. My mother, writing from France, admonished me to take care of my health, as she had during the war. My head could be all set for the guillotine, and still my mother would scold me for forgetting my muffler. She never missed an opportunity to try and convince me that the world is a kindly place and that she'd done a good job in conceiving me. This alleged Providence was the great subterfuge of maternal thoughtlessness. It was easy for me, I have to admit, to leave all my boss's and mother's hogwash unanswered, and the fact is I never did answer their letters. Clever of me, but it didn't improve my situation.

Robinson had made off with almost everything that fragile edifice had contained, but who'd believe me if I said so? Write letters? What for? To whom? At about five every afternoon I shook with a violent fever, my bed jiggled and rattled as if I'd been vigorously jerking off. A bunch of blacks from the village had come to wait on me and taken possession of the hut; I hadn't sent for them, but to send them away would have been too much of an effort. They squabbled over the remains of the stock, rummaged through the kegs of tobacco, tried on the last of the loincloths, felt the material, and took them off, adding, if that was possible, to the general disorder of my establishment. The rubber was all over the ground, mingling its juice with the bush melons and those sickly-sweet papayas that taste like pissy pears... I ate so many of them in place of beans that now, fifteen years later, the memory of them still turns my stomach.

I tried to gauge the degree of hopelessness to which I had fallen. I couldn't. "Everybody steals!" Robinson had said to me three times before disappearing. The Director was of the same opinion. In my fever those words ran through me like shooting pains. "You've got to figure the angles!" He'd said that too. I tried to get up, I couldn't make it. He'd been right about the water we had to drink, it was concentrated muck. Little black boys brought me bananas, big ones, little ones, red ones, and more and more papayas, but I was so sick of all that and everything else! I'd have vomited up the whole globe.

As soon as I felt a tiny bit better and not quite so dazed, I was seized again with a horrible fear, the fear that the Company would call me to account. What would I say to those devils? How would I get them to believe me? They'd have me arrested for sure! And who would try me? A bunch of special judges, something like a court-martial, armed with terrible laws they had gotten from God knows

---

[53] Nord-Sud Métro. One of the earliest Métro lines, crossing Paris from north to south. Since unification of the Métro lines, known as Line 12.

where, who never tell their real intentions and who for the sheer fun of it make you drag your bleeding steps up the steep path overlooking hell, the path that leads poor bastards to their death. The Law is a big Luna Park of suffering. When a poor man lets himself get caught in it, you'll hear him screaming for centuries on end.

I preferred to lie there in a stupor, trembling and foaming at the mouth with a 104° fever, than to be lucid and forced to think of what would happen to me in Fort-Gono. I even stopped taking my quinine because I figured the fever would keep life away from me. You get drunk on what you've got. While I lay there sweltering, I ran out of matches. They'd been in short supply. Robinson hadn't left me a thing, only "Cassoulet à la Bordelaise." But plenty of that, I assure you. I threw up whole tins of it. And even to arrive at that result, you had to heat them.

The shortage of matches provided me with one little amusement, watching my cook light his fire with two pieces of flint and some dry grass. It was while I was watching him that the idea came to me. With plenty of fever added, my idea became wonderfully vivid. Though clumsy by nature, I was able after applying myself for a month to light a fire with two sharp stones like a savage. In short, I was learning how to make do under primitive conditions. Fire is the first thing; then there's hunting, but I wasn't interested in that. My flame was all I needed, and I practiced conscientiously. Day after day I had nothing else to do. I never got nearly as good at the sport of propelling those "secondary" caterpillars. I didn't quite get the knack. I squashed a lot of them, and then I lost interest. I gave them the run of the house—like old friends. There were two big storms, the second went on for three days and, worse, for three nights. At last I had drinking water in the bucket, tepid to be sure, but even so... In the deluge the scraps of goods in my little stock began to run and intermingle, a disgusting mess.

Some of the natives obligingly brought me lianas from the forest to anchor my shack to the ground, but in vain; at the slightest wind, the leafy walls would flap wildly against the roof like wounded wings. There was nothing I could do about it. Never a dull moment.

Blacks big and small decided to join me in my downfall, they got more and more familiar. And they were so very happy. What fun! They came and went as they pleased in my so-called home. Freedom! As a sign of perfect understanding we exchanged signs. If I hadn't had fever, I might have started learning their language. There wasn't time enough. I made very good progress in fire-making, but I hadn't yet mastered their best manner. I wasn't very quick about it. Showers of sparks still flew into my eyes, which gave my black friends a good laugh.

When I wasn't moldering with fever on my folding bed or working my primitive tinderbox, I thought of the Company's accounts. It's funny how hard it is to throw off one's dread of irregular accounts. I'd undoubtedly inherited that from my mother, she'd contaminated me with her "He who steals a pin will steal a pound... and end up murdering his mother." We all find it hard to throw off those ideas. We pick them up in childhood, and they come back to terrify us later on, in every crisis. Our only hope of getting rid of them is the force of circumstances! Luckily the force of circumstances is enormous. Meanwhile the store and I were sinking. One of these days we'd be swallowed up by the mud, which got thicker and more viscous with every downpour. The rainy season. What looked like a boulder yesterday was oozy molasses today. Tepid water fell in cascades from dangling branches and followed one everywhere, it invaded the hut and spread round about as in an old abandoned riverbed. The rain made a porridge of my merchandise, my hopes, and my accounts, and so did my fever, which was also very moist. The rain was so compact that when it hit you it stopped your mouth like a lukewarm gag. But the flood didn't stop the animals from getting together, the nightingales started making as much noise as jackals. Anarchy all over the ark, and I a doddering Noah. This, I thought, had been going on long enough.

Ah my mother's adages weren't about honesty. As I remembered opportunely, she used to say when burning old bandages: "Nothing purifies like fire!" A mother leaves you something for every turn of Fate. You just have to take your pick.

The time had come. My pieces of flint were not very well chosen, not sharp enough, most of the sparks struck my hands. In the end, however, some of my merchandise took fire in spite of the dampness: a parcel of sopping wet socks. It happened after sundown. The flames rose impetuously. Wildly jabbering, the villagers gathered around the blaze. The crude rubber that Robinson had bought was sizzling in the middle, and the smell reminded me invincibly of the famous Telephone Company fire on the Quai de Grenelle that I'd gone to see with my Uncle Charles, who sang sentimental ballads so well. That was the year before the big Exposition, when I was very young. Nothing brings memories to the surface like smells and flames. My shack smelled exactly that way. Though drenched, it burned very thoroughly to the ground, merchandise and all... No more accounts. The owls and leopards, toads and parrots must have been flabbergasted. It takes something to impress that crowd. Like war with us. Now the forest could come back and cover the wreckage with its thundering leaves. I hadn't saved anything but my personal belongings, my folding bed, the three hundred francs, and naturally, sad to say, a few cans of cassoulet for the road.

When the fire had been burning for an hour, hardly anything was left of the shack. A few tongues of flame in the rain and a few jabbering black men poking about in the ashes with the tips of their spears amid gusts of the smell that clings to all catastrophes, emanates from all the defeats of this world, the smell of smoking gunpowder.

Now was the time to make quick tracks. Back to Fort-Gono, retrace my steps? Try to explain my conduct and the circumstances of the present disaster? I hesitated... Not for long. Nothing can be explained. The world only knows how to do one thing, to roll over and kill you, as a sleeper kills his fleas. That would be a stupid way to die, I said to myself, to let myself be crushed like everybody else. To put your trust in men is to get yourself killed a little.

In spite of the condition I was in, I decided to head straight into the bush in the direction taken by that infernal Robinson.

* * *

Often on my way I heard the beasts of the jungle with their plaints and calls and tremolos, but I hardly ever saw them. I don't count the little wild pig I almost stepped on one day not far from my shelter. Hearing those torrents of calls and screams and roars, you had the impression that they were close by, hundreds and thousands of them. And yet, when you got to the place where the hubbub came from, there was nobody there, except for those big blue guinea fowl, all trussed up in their plumage as if they were going to a wedding and so clumsy when they jumped coughing from branch to branch that you thought they must have had an accident.

Lower down, in the musty undergrowth, big heavy butterflies, bordered like death notices, quivered with the effort of opening their wings, and lower still it was us, sloshing through the yellow mud. We had trouble getting ahead, especially because the blacks were carrying me in a litter made of sacks sewn end to end. They could easily have tossed me in the drink while we were crossing a stream. Why didn't they? I found out later. Or they could have eaten me, since that was one of their customs.

Now and then I'd question them with my thick tongue, and every time they answered: Yes, yes. Always glad to oblige. Good fellows. Whenever my diarrhea let me go for a while, the fever took hold. You wouldn't believe how sick I was. I couldn't see things clearly anymore, or rather, everything was beginning to look green. After nightfall all the animals of creation surrounded our camp. We'd make a fire. But here and there, even so, a cry would pierce the great black awning that stifled us. Despite its horror of men and fire, a wounded, dying animal would manage to complain to us, seeing we were right there.

After the fourth day I stopped even trying to distinguish reality from the absurd fever images that went chasing one another through my head along with fragments of people and endless tatters of resolutions and disappointments.

Even so, I tell myself today when I think about it that the bearded white man we met one morning on a stony promontory near the meeting of two rivers must have been real. A cataract nearby was making a hellish din. He was a sergeant, something like Alcide, except this one was Spanish. Worrying along from trail to trail, we'd ended up in the colony of Rio del Rio, an ancient possession of the Crown of Castile. That poor Spanish soldier also had a shack. I seem to remember that he laughed when I told him about my misadventures and what I'd done with my shack! His, I have to admit, looked a little better, but not much. His special cross was the red ants. On their annual migration those little bitches had elected to pass straight through his shack, and they'd been at it for going on two months.

They took up practically all the space; you could hardly turn around, and if you got in their way, they pinched you hard.

He was overjoyed when I gave him some of my cassoulet, because he'd been living on tomatoes for the last three years. I couldn't better that. All by himself, he told me, he had downed more than three thousand cans. Tired of preparing the tomatoes in different ways, he had taken to sucking the cans like eggs, through two little holes in the lid.

When the red ants discovered that a new variety of canned goods had arrived, they mounted guard around the cassoulet. It wouldn't have been advisable to leave a freshly opened can standing; they'd have summoned the whole nation of red ants to the shack. There are no bigger communists anywhere. And they'd have eaten up the Spaniard too.

My host informed me that the capital of Rio del Rio was called San Tapeta,[54] a seaport famous all along the coast for its transoceanic galleys.

It so happened that the track we were on ended there, we would just have to go straight ahead for three days and three nights. I was good and sick of my delirium, so I asked the Spaniard if he knew of some good native medicine that would straighten me out. My head was acting up something terrible. But he wouldn't hear of any such mumbo jumbo. For a Spanish colonial he was strangely Africanophobic, so much so that when he went to the toilet he refused to use banana leaves and kept a whole sheaf of the Boletín de Asturias, cut up in little pieces for that express purpose. And he didn't read the paper... same as Alcide.

For three years he'd been living there alone with the ants, a few little kinks, and his old newspapers. What with his awful Spanish accent, which was so strong it was like having somebody else in the room, it was hard to get him stirred up about anything. When he chewed out his natives, it was like a tempest. For loudness of mouth, Alcide couldn't hold a candle to him. I took such a liking to that Spaniard that in the end I gave him all my cassoulet. Out of gratitude he made me a lovely passport on grainy paper stamped with the arms of Castile, with a signature so elaborate, so finicky, that it took him at least ten minutes to get it right.

He'd told the truth, you couldn't miss the road to San Tapeta, you only had to follow your nose. I don't remember the trip, but of one thing I'm sure, that as soon as we got there they handed me over to a priest who was so gaga that having him beside me gave me a kind of comparative self-confidence. But not for long.

The town of San Tapeta was plunked down on the side of a rock, directly facing the sea. It was hard to believe how green the place was. A magnificent spectacle no doubt, seen from the roadstead, splendid from a distance... On the spot, though, there was nothing to admire but the same overworked carcasses as in Fort-Gono, everlastingly sweating and pustulating. In a lucid moment I dismissed the blacks of my little caravan. They'd crossed a long stretch of jungle and feared for their lives going back, so they said. In leaving me, they wept in advance at the thought of the journey, but 1 hadn't the strength to feel sorry for them. I had suffered and sweated too much. And I was still at it.

By day and by night, to the best of my recollection, a lot of jabberers—they were decidedly in plentiful supply—crowded around my bed, which had been set up for that very purpose in the presbytery, since entertainment was rare in San Tapeta. The priest filled me with tisanes, a long gilded crucifix dangled over his belly, and when he came near me a loud clinking of coins rose from the depths of his soutane. Conversation with those people was out of the question. It exhausted me completely just to mumble a word or two.

I really thought it was all up with me, and I tried to take a last look at what could be seen of the world through the priest's window. I doubt if I could describe those gardens today without gross and outlandish mistakes. The sun was there, I can vouch for that, always the same, as if somebody had opened a big furnace in your face, and then behind it there was more sun and insane trees, whole avenues of them, those lettuces as big as oaks and those African dandelions, three or four of which would add up to a perfectly good chestnut tree in France. Throw in a toad or two, as hefty as spaniels, waddling furtively from one flowerbed to the next.

---

[54] San Tapeta. From tapette, argot for "homosexual."

People, countries, and objects all end up as smells. I kept my eyes closed because I really couldn't open them anymore, Then from night to night the sharp smell of Africa was blunted. It became harder for me to recapture that heavy mixture of decaying soil, human crotches, and ground saffron.

Time, patches of the past, then more time, and then at a certain moment I felt a series of jolts and twists, and then the jolting became more regular, a swaying, a rocking...

I was still lying down, that was sure, but whatever I was lying on was moving. I let myself go, I vomited, then I woke up again and fell asleep again. I was on the sea. I felt so faint that I barely had the strength to catch the new smell of ropes and tar. It was cool in the heaving niche where I was lying directly under a wide- open porthole. They'd left me alone. Evidently my journey was continuing... But what journey? I heard steps on the deck, a wooden deck right over my nose, and voices, and the waves lashing and melting against the ship's side.

Life seldom comes back to your deathbed, wherever you may be, except in the form of a low-down trick. The one those people in San Tapeta had played on me filled the bill. Taking advantage of my befuddled state, they'd sold me to the captain of a galley. A fine galley, to be sure, high of hull, well fitted with oars, crowned with beautiful purple sails, gilded figurehead, superbly upholstered officers' quarters, and on the prow a magnificent cod-liver-oil painting of the Infanta Combitta[55] dressed for polo. The Infanta, I was told later on, was the ship's sponsor, offering it the protection of her name, her tits, and her royal dignity. It was flattering.

After all, I reflected when I realized what had happened, in San Tapeta I was as sick as a dog, the whole world was spinning, and I'd certainly have died in that presbytery where the natives had left me... Return to Fort-Gono?... Those accounts would certainly have got me fifteen years... Here at least I was moving, and that was ground for hope . . • Come to think of it, the captain of the Infanta Combitta had taken a big chance in buying me, even dirt cheap, from that priest before weighing anchor. It was a risky investment, for that captain could have lost all his money... He was counting on the brisk sea air to revive me. He deserved a reward and obviously he was winning his bet, for I was already recovering. I could see he was as pleased as Punch. I still raved quite a lot, but with a certain logic... After I opened my eyes, he often came to see me in my cubbyhole. He was always wearing his plumed hat. That's how I saw him.

It amused him to see me try to raise myself on my pallet in spite of my fever. "All right, shitass!" he'd say. "You'll soon be able to row with the rest of them!" A kindly thought. He roared with laughter, giving me little strokes of his whip, but in a friendly kind of way, on the back of my neck, not on my rear end. He wanted me to laugh too, to share his pleasure at the business acumen he'd shown in acquiring me.

The food on board struck me as quite acceptable. My speech was still muddled. Soon, as the captain had foreseen, I recovered enough strength to join the boys at the oars. But where there were ten oarsmen, I saw a hundred: multiple vision.

The crossing wasn't fatiguing, because most of the time we were under sail. Our conditions between decks were no more nauseating than those of the usual third-class passengers on a Sunday excursion train, and not nearly as perilous as what I'd endured on the Admiral Bragueton coming out. There was always plenty of breeze on this voyage from the east to the west of the Atlantic. The temperature dropped. Nobody complained about that between decks. The only trouble was that the trip seemed to be taking a long time. For my part, I had seen enough seascapes and jungle vistas to last me an eternity.

I'd have liked to ask the captain a few questions about the aim and purpose of this trip, but once I was definitely on the mend, he lost interest in me. Anyway, I was still driveling too much for conversation. From then on I saw him only from a distance, like a real boss.

I started looking for Robinson among the galley slaves, and several times in the silence of the night I called him in a loud voice. There was no answer except for a few insults and threats from the other galley slaves.

---

[55] Combitta. From con = the female sex organ and bite = the male sex organ.

Still, the more I thought about the details and circumstances of my adventure, the more likely it seemed to me that the same thing must have happened to him in San Tapeta. Except that Robinson must be rowing on some other galley. Those jungle niggers, I thought, must all have a hand in the racket. Why shouldn't they take their turn? They've got to live, haven't they?... so naturally they sell the things and people they can't eat right away. The natives' relative kindness to me could be attributed to the most sordid of motives.

For weeks and weeks the Infanta Combitta sailed over the rolling Atlantic from fit of fever to fit of seasickness, and then one evening all was calm around us. My delirium was gone. We were bobbing at anchor. Waking next day, we realized on opening the portholes that we had reached our destination. And what a sight it was!

* * *

Talk of surprises! What we suddenly discovered through the fog was so amazing that at first we refused to believe it, but then, when we were face to face with it, galley slaves or not, we couldn't help laughing, seeing it right there in front of us...

Just imagine, that city was standing absolutely erect. New York was a standing city. Of course we'd seen cities, fine ones too, and magnificent seaports. But in our part of the world cities lie along the seacoast or on rivers, they recline on the landscape, awaiting the traveler, while this American city had nothing languid about her, she stood there as stiff as a board, not seductive at all, terrifyingly stiff.

We laughed like fools. You can't help laughing at a city built straight up and down like that. But we could only laugh from the neck up, because of the cold blowing in from the sea through a gray and pink mist, a brisk sharp wind that attacked our pants and the chinks in that wall, I mean the city streets, which engulfed the wind-borne clouds. Our galley spun its narrow wake just outside the docks, at the end of the shit- colored bay, asplash with schools of rowboats and avid, tooting tugs.

When you're down at heel, it's never much fun landing anywhere, but for a galley slave it's a lot worse, especially in America, because those people don't like the galley slaves that come over from Europe at all. "They're anarchists!" That's what they say. The only people they really welcome are tourists, who bring them dough, because all the currencies of Europe are relatives of the Dollar.

I might have tried what others had succeeded in doing, swimming across the harbor and once on land start shouting: "Long live Dollar! Long live Dollar!" It's a gimmick. A lot of people have landed that way and made a fortune. It's not certain, but so they say. Even worse things happen in dreams. I had a different plan in my head, along with my fever.

On board the galley I'd become an expert at counting fleas (not just catching them but adding and subtracting them, in short, compiling statistics), a subtle skill, which looks like nothing at all, but still it's a technique and I thought I'd make use of it. You can say what you like about the Americans, but when it comes to techniques, they're connoisseurs. They'd be crazy about my way of counting fleas, I was sure of that in advance. I was convinced that I couldn't fail.

I was about to offer them my services when suddenly our galley was ordered to its quarantine station, a sheltered cove nearby, within hailing distance of a small village at the end of a quiet bay, two miles east of New York.

There we remained under observation for weeks and weeks, long enough to acquire a daily routine. Every evening after supper, for instance, our water squad would go ashore and make its way to the village. To attain my ends I'd have to go along.

My shipmates knew what I had in mind, but the adventure didn't tempt them. "He's mad but harmless," they said. The food wasn't bad on board the Infanta Combitta, they got clubbed now and then, but not too badly, and all in all it was bearable. An average sort of job. And it had one sublime advantage, you couldn't be fired from a galley, and the king had even promised them a small pension at the age of sixty-two. That prospect made them happy, it gave them something to dream about, and another thing: they played at voting on Sundays, it gave them a feeling of freedom.

We were kept in quarantine for weeks, the men bellowed between decks, they fought and buggered one another by turns. But their main reason for not wanting to escape with me was that they were absolutely down on this America that I was so smitten with. We all have our bugaboos, and theirs was America. They even tried to sour me on it. I told them I knew people there, my little Lola among others, who must have been loaded by then, and Robinson no doubt, who had surely carved himself a niche in the business world, but they clung to their aversion for the United States, their disgust, their hatred: "You'll always have a screw loose," they said. One day I made as if to join their expedition to the village water tap, and then I told them I wasn't going back to the galley. Good-bye!

They were a good bunch all in all, hard workers. They told me again that they didn't approve one bit of what I was doing, but they wished me good luck and plenty of fun all the same, in their own way. "Go!" they said. "Go right ahead! But we're warning you: You haven't got the right ideas for a beggar! It's your fever that scrambles your brains! You'll come back from that America of yours in worse condition than we are! Your fancy ideas will be the end of you! You want to learn things? You know too much already for the likes of you!"

I tried to tell them I had friends who were expecting me. I spluttered and stammered.

"Friends?" they said. "Your friends couldn't care less! Your friends forgot you long ago!... "

"But I want to see Americans," I insisted. "And besides, they've got women like nowhere else in the world!"

"Wise guy!" they said. "Come on back with us. Believe us, it's not worth it. You'll make yourself sicker than you are. We'll tell you what Americans are like! They're either millionaires or skunks! There's nothing in between! The shape you're in you certainly won't be seeing any millionaires! But don't worry, you'll get your fill of skunks, you can be sure of that! And it won't be long, oh no!"

That's the way they spoke to me. A bunch of jerks, cock-suckers, subhumans, they made me sick! "Beat it, the whole lot of you!" I told them. "You're green with envy, that's all! We'll see if the Americans skin me alive! But one thing is sure, you've all got ladyfingers between your legs, and limp ones at that!"

I told them off, and after that I felt fine.

Night was coming on, and the galley was blowing the whistle for them. They all started rowing in cadence, all but one, me. I waited till I couldn't hear them anymore, then I counted up to a hundred and ran to the village as fast as I could. That village was a pretty little place, well lit, wooden houses just waiting to be used, lined up to the right and left of a chapel, all perfectly silent. Unfortunately I was shivering with malaria and fear. Here and there I came across a sailor from the garrison—those people seemed to be taking it pretty easy—and even a few children and then a young girl with delightful muscles. That was America! I had arrived! It's a pleasure to see that sort of thing after so many parched adventures. It's as life-giving as fruit. I'd stumbled on the one useless village in the whole country. A small garrison of sailors and their families kept its installations hi readiness for the conceivable day when a raging plague, imported by a boat like ours, would threaten the metropolis.

Those installations would be used for killing off as many foreigners as possible, so as to keep the city population from catching anything. They even had a cemetery ready, with flowers all over. They were waiting. For sixty years they'd been waiting. Waiting was all they did.

Finding an empty shack, I slipped in and fell asleep instantly. In the morning the streets were full of sailors in short pants, sturdy, well-built fellows, wielding brooms and sloshing water around my refuge and on all the streets and squares of that theoretical village. I tried to look unconcerned, but I was so hungry that in spite of my fears I headed for a place where there was a smell of cooking.

That's where I was spotted and cornered between two squads of sailors, determined to identify me. Their first idea was to chuck me in the water. Taken straight to the Head Quarantine Officer, I was in a bad way. Though constant adversity had led me to develop a certain crust, I still felt too steeped in fever to risk any of my brilliant improvisations. My mind was wandering, and my heart wasn't in it.

The best policy was to lose consciousness. Which I did. In the office where I later came to, some ladies in light-colored dresses had replaced the men around me. They put me through a vague and benevolent interrogation, which would have been plenty for me. But benevolence never lasts in this world, and the next day the men started talking prison to me again. I took the opportunity to bring up fleas, just in passing, so to speak... How I could catch them... and count them... my specialty... as well as classify these parasites and compile flawless statistics. I saw that my approach interested my guards, I had captured their attention. They were listening. But as for believing me, that was a different kettle of fish.

Finally, the commanding officer of the station turned up. He was called the "Surgeon General," which would be a good name for a fish. He spoke roughly, but with more authority than the others. "What's this you're telling us, boy?" he said. "You say you can count fleas? Really now!" He thought that would shut me up, but not at all. One two three I reeled off the little spiel I had prepared. "I believe in the enumeration of fleas! It's a civilizing factor, because enumeration is the basis of the most invaluable statistical data!... A progressive country must know the number of its fleas, broken down according to sex, age group, year and season... "

"Come, come, young man! Enough of your hogwash!" the Surgeon General broke in, "You're not the first! Other young scamps from Europe have been here before you, telling us the same kind of fairy tales, but in the end they turned out to be anarchists like the rest of them, only worse... They didn't even believe in Anarchy any more! Enough of your boasting!... Tomorrow we'll try you out on the immigrants over there on Ellis Island, in the shower room! Major Mischief, my assistant, will tell me if you've been lying. For two months now Major Mischief has been clamoring for an expert flea counter. We'll assign you to him for a try! Dismissed! And if you've lied to us, we'll chuck you in the drink! Dismissed! And watch your step!"

I withdrew from the presence of that American authority as I had withdrawn from so many authorities, by presenting first my pecker and then, by a deft about-face, my rear end, accompanying the whole with a military salute.

This statistics racket, it seemed to me, was as good a way as any other of getting me to New York. The very next day, Mischief, the major in question, told me in a few words what my work would be. He was a fat, jaundiced-looking man, as nearsighted as it's possible to be, with enormous smoked glasses. He must have recognized me the way wild animals recognize their victims, by the general outline, because with those glasses he was wearing he couldn't possibly have distinguished any features.

On the job we got along fine. I even think that by the end of my stay Mischief had taken quite a liking to me. In the first place, not seeing a person is an excellent reason for taking a liking to him, and besides he was delighted at my brilliant flea-catching technique. Nobody else in the whole station could hold a candle to me when it came to catching and boxing the most restive, keratosed, and impatient of fleas. I was able to classify them by sex before they had even been removed from the immigrant. I don't mind telling you, my work was amazing... In the end Mischief trusted my skill implicitly.

By late afternoon the nails of my thumb and forefinger were bruised from crushing fleas, but my day's work wasn't over, I still had to line up the columns of my daily statistical table: So-and-so many Polish... Yugoslavian... Spanish fleas... Crimean crabs... Peruvian chiggers... every furtive, biting thing that travels on human derelicts ended under my fingernails. As you see, my work was both monumental and meticulous. Our calculations were completed in New York in a special office equipped with electrical flea- counting machines. Every day the little quarantine tug crossed the whole harbor, carrying our figures to be processed or checked.

Days and days passed, my health picked up, but, as my fever and delirium abated in those comfortable surroundings, my craving for adventure and daring exploits revived and became imperious. At ninety-eight point six everything is boring.

Yet I could have stayed there, with not a thing to worry about, well fed at the station mess. Best of all, it seems worth adding, Major Mischief's daughter, a stunning young lady of fifteen, used to turn up in extremely short skirts after five o'clock and play tennis directly under the window of our office. I've seldom seen finer legs, still slightly on the mannish side perhaps, yet on their way to becoming more delicate, a splendid specimen of burgeoning flesh. A challenge to happiness, a promise to make a man shout for joy. Some of the young ensigns of the detachment followed her everywhere.

Those young scamps had no need to justify themselves by doing useful work like me! I didn't miss the slightest detail of their caperings around my little idol. Just watching them, I found myself blanching several times a day. After a while, I began to think that maybe at night I could pass for a sailor myself. I was still fondling that hope when, one Saturday in the twenty-third week of my stay, the situation ripened. The man in charge of shuttling the statistics back and forth, an Armenian, was suddenly promoted to the post of executive flea counter in Alaska, where he'd be dealing with the prospectors' dogs.

A fine promotion if ever there was one, and true enough, the man was delighted. The Alaskan dog teams are invaluable. Since they are always needed, they are well cared for. Whereas nobody gives a damn about immigrants, of whom there are always too many.

That left no one to take our figures to New York, and in a twinkling I was assigned to the task. Before I shoved off, Mischief, my boss, shook hands with me and urged me to be good and behave myself in town. That was the last bit of advice that estimable man ever gave me, and just as he had never seen me up to that time, he never saw me again. As soon as we went ashore, the rain came down in buckets, penetrated my thin jacket, and soaked the statistics, which gradually melted away in my hand. Nevertheless, I made a big wad with some of them and let it stick out of my pocket to make me look more or less like a businessman when I hit town. Thereupon, trembling with fear and emotion, I hurried off in quest of new adventures.

Raising my eyes to the ramparts, I felt a kind of reverse vertigo, because there were really too many windows and so much alike whichever way you looked that it turned my stomach.

Flimsily clad, chilled to the bone, I made for the darkest crevice I could find in that giant façade, hoping that the people would hardly notice me in their midst. My embarrassment was quite superfluous. I had nothing to fear. In the street I had chosen, really the narrowest of all, no wider than a good-sized brook in our part of the world and extraordinarily dirty, damp and dark at the bottom, there were so many other people, big and little, thin and fat, that they carried me along with them like a shadow. They were going to town like me, on their way to work no doubt. Poor people like everywhere else.

* * *

As if I knew where I was going, I put on an air of choosing and changed my direction, taking a different street on my right, one that was better lit. "Broadway" it was called. I read the name on a sign. High up, far above the uppermost stories, there was still a bit of daylight, with sea gulls and patches of sky. We moved in the lower light, a sick sort of jungle light, so gray that the street seemed to be full of grimy cotton waste.

That street was like a dismal gash, endless, with us at the bottom of it, filling it from side to side, advancing from sorrow to sorrow, toward an end that is never in sight, the end of all the streets in the world.

There were no cars or carriages, only people and more people.

This was the priceless district, I was told later, the gold district: Manhattan. You can enter it only on foot, like a church. It's the banking heart and center of the present-day world. Yet some of those people spit on the sidewalk as they pass. You've got to have your nerve with you.

It's a district filled with gold, a miracle, and through the doors you can actually hear the miracle, the sound of dollars being crumpled, for the Dollar is always too light, a genuine Holy Ghost, more precious than blood.

I found time to go and see them, I even went in and spoke to the employees who guard the cash. They're sad and underpaid.

When the faithful enter their bank, don't go thinking they can help themselves as they please. Far from it. In speaking to Dollar, they mumble words through a little grill; that's their confessional. Not much sound, dim light, a tiny wicket between high arches, that's all. They don't swallow the Host, they put it on their hearts. I couldn't stay there long admiring them. I had to follow the crowd in the street, between those walls of smooth shadow.

Suddenly our street widened, like a crevasse opening out into a bright clearing. Up ahead of us we saw a great pool of sea-green light, wedged between hordes of monstrous buildings. And in the middle of the clearing stood a rather countrified-looking house, surrounded by woebegone lawns.

I asked several people in the crowd what this edifice was, but most of them pretended not to hear me. They couldn't spare the time. But one young fellow right next to me was kind enough to tell me it was City Hall, adding that it was an ancient monument dating back to colonial times, ever so historical... so they'd left it there... The fringes of this oasis formed a kind of park with benches, where you could sit comfortably enough and look at the building. When I got there, there was hardly anything else to see.

I waited more than an hour in the same place, and then toward noon, from the half-light, from the shuffling, discontinuous, dismal crowd, there erupted a sudden avalanche of absolutely and undeniably beautiful women.

What a discovery! What an America! What ecstasy! I thought of Lola... Her promises had not deceived me! It was true.

I had come to the heart of my pilgrimage. And if my appetite hadn't kept calling itself to my attention, that would have struck me as one of those moments of supernatural aesthetic revelation. If I'd been a little more comfortable and confident, the incessant beauties I was discovering might have ravished me from my base human condition. In short, all I needed was a sandwich to make me believe in miracles. But how I needed that sandwich!

And yet, what supple grace! What incredible delicacy of form and feature! What inspired harmonies! What perilous nuances! Triumphant where the danger is greatest! Every conceivable promise of face and figure fulfilled! Those blondes! Those brunettes! Those Titian redheads! And more and more kept coming! Maybe, I thought, this is Greece starting all over again. Looks like I got here just in time.

What made those apparitions all the more divine in my eyes was that they seemed totally unaware of my existence as I sat on a bench close by, slap-happy, drooling with erotico-mystical admiration and quinine, but also, I have to admit, with hunger. If it were possible for a man to jump out of his skin, I'd have done it then, once and for all. There was nothing to hold me back.

Those unlikely midinettes could have wafted me away, sublimated me; a gesture, a word would have sufficed, and in that moment I'd have been transported, all of me, into the world of dreams. But I suppose they had other fish to fry.

I sat there for an hour, two hours, in that state of stupefaction. I had nothing more in the world to hope for.

You know about innards? The trick they play on tramps in the country? They stuff an old wallet with putrid chicken innards. Well, take it from me, a man is just like that, except that he's fatter and hungrier and can move around, and inside there's a dream.

I had to look at the practical side of things and not dip into my small supply of money right away. I didn't have much. I was even afraid to count it. I couldn't have anyway, because I was seeing double. I could only feel those thin, bashful banknotes through the material of my pocket, side by side with my phony statistics.

Men were passing, too, mostly young ones with faces that seemed to be made of pink wood, with a dry, monotonous expression, and jowls so wide and coarse they were hard to get used to... Well, maybe that was the kind of jowls their womenfolk wanted. The sexes seemed to stay on different sides of the street. The women looked only at the shopwindows, their whole attention was taken by the handbags, scarves, and little silk doodads, displayed very little at a time, but with precision and authority. You didn't see many old people in that crowd. Not many couples either. Nobody seemed to find it strange that I should sit on that bench for hours all by myself, watching the people pass. But all at once the policeman standing like an inkwell in the middle of the street seemed to suspect me of sinister intentions. I could tell.

Wherever you may be, the moment you draw the attention of the authorities, the best thing you can do is disappear in a hurry. Don't try to explain. Sink into the earth! I said to myself.

It so happened that just to one side of my bench there was a big hole in the sidewalk, something like the Metro at home. That hole seemed propitious, so vast, with a stairway all of pink marble inside it. I'd seen quite a few people from the street disappear into it and come out again. It was in that underground vault that they answered the call of nature. I caught on right away. The hall where the business was done was likewise of marble. A kind of swimming pool, but drained of all its water, a fetid swimming pool, filled only with filtered, moribund light, which fell on the forms of unbuttoned men surrounded by their smells, red in the face from the effect of expelling their stinking feces with barbarous noises in front of everybody.

Men among men, all free and easy, they laughed and joked and cheered one another on, it made me think of a football game. The first thing you did when you got there was to take off your jacket, as if in preparation for strenuous exercise. This was a rite and shirtsleeves were the uniform.

In that state of undress, belching and worse, gesticulating like lunatics, they settled down in the fecal grotto. The new arrivals were assailed with a thousand revolting jokes while descending the stairs from the street, but they all seemed delighted.

The morose aloofness of the men on the street above was equaled only by the air of liberation and rejoicing that came over them at the prospect of emptying their bowels in tumultuous company.

The splotched and spotted doors to the cabins hung loose, wrenched from their hinges. Some customers went from one cell to another for a little chat, those waiting for an empty seat smoked heavy cigars and slapped the backs of the obstinately toiling occupants, who sat there straining with their heads between their hands. Some groaned like wounded men or women in labor. The constipated were threatened with ingenious tortures.

When a gush of water announced a vacancy, the clamor around the free compartment redoubled, and as often as not a coin would be tossed for its possession. No sooner read, newspapers, though as thick as pillows, were dismembered by the horde of rectal toilers. The smoke made it hard to distinguish faces, and the smells deterred me from going too close.

To a foreigner the contrast was disconcerting. Such free-and-easy intimacy, such extraordinary intestinal familiarity, and up on the street such perfect restraint. It left me stunned.

I returned to the light of day by the same stairway and went back to the same bench to rest. Sudden outburst of digestive vulgarity. Discovery of a joyous shitting communism. I ignored both these disconcerting aspects of the same adventure. I hadn't the strength for analysis or synthesis. My pressing desire was to sleep. O rare, delicious frenzy!

So I joined the line of pedestrians entering one of the neighboring streets. We progressed by fits and starts because of the shopwindows, which fragmented the crowd. At one point, the door of a hotel created a great eddy. People poured out on to the sidewalk through a big revolving door. I was caught up and poured the other way, into the big lobby inside.

Instant amazement... You had to divine, to imagine the majesty of the edifice, the generous proportions, because the lights were so veiled that it took you some time to know what you were looking at.

Lots of young women in the half-light, plunged in deep armchairs as in jewel cases. Around them attentive men, moving silently, with timid curiosity, to and fro, just offshore from the row of crossed legs and magnificent silk-encased thighs. Those miraculous beings seemed to be waiting for grave and costly events. Obviously they weren't giving me a thought. So, ever so furtively, I in my turn passed that long and palpable temptation.

Since at least a hundred of those divine leg owners were sitting in a single row of chairs, I reached the reception desk in so dreamy a condition, having absorbed a ration of beauty so much too strong for my constitution that I was reeling.

At the desk, a pomaded clerk violently offered me a room. I asked for the smallest in the hotel. I can't have had more than fifty dollars at the time. Also, I was pretty well out of ideas and self-assurance.

I hoped the room the clerk was giving me was really the smallest, because his hotel, the *Laugh Calvin*,[56] was advertised as the most luxurious and sumptuously furnished on the whole North American continent!

Over my head, what an infinity of furnished rooms! And all around me, in those chairs, what inducements to multiple rape! What abysses! What perils! Is the poor man's aesthetic torment to have

---

[56] *Laugh Calvin*. The reason for this odd name is that Calvin Coolidge, president of the United States from 1923 to 1929, was never known to smile, much less laugh.

no end? Is it to be even more long-lasting than his hunger? But there was no time to succumb; before I knew it, the clerk had thrust a heavy key into my hand. I was afraid to move.

A sharp youngster, dressed like a juvenile brigadier general, stepped, imperious and commanding, out of the gloom. The smooth reception clerk rang his metallic bell three times, and the little boy started whistling. That was my send-off. Time to go. And away we went.

As black and resolute as a subway train, we raced down a corridor. The youngster in the lead. A twist, a turn, another. We didn't dawdle. We veered a bit to the left. Here we go. The elevator. Stitch in my side. Is this it? No. Another corridor.

Even darker. Ebony paneling, it looks like, all along the walls. No time to examine it. The kid's whistling. He's carrying my frail valise. I don't dare ask him questions. My job was to keep walking, that was clear to me. In the darkness here and there, as we passed, a red-and-green light flashed a command. Long lines of gold marked the doors. We had passed the 1800s long ago and then the 3000s, and still we were on our way, drawn by our invincible destiny. As though driven by instinct, the little bellhop in his braid and stripes pursued the Nameless in the darkness. Nothing in this cavern seemed to take him unawares. His whistling modulated plaintively when we passed a black man and a black chambermaid. And that was all.

Struggling to walk faster in those corridors, I lost what little self-assurance I had left when I escaped from quarantine. I was falling apart, just as I had seen my shack fall apart in the African wind and the floods of warm water. Here I was attacked by a torrent of unfamiliar sensations. There's a moment between two brands of humanity when you find yourself thrashing around in a vacuum.

Suddenly, without warning, the youngster pivoted. We had arrived. I bumped into a chair, it was my room, a big box with ebony walls. The only light was a faint ring surrounding the bashful greenish lamp on the table. The manager of the *Laugh Calvin* Hotel begged the visitor to look upon him as a friend and assured him that he, the manager, would make a special point of keeping him, the visitor, cheerful throughout his stay in New York. Reading this notice, which was displayed where no one could possibly miss it, added if possible to my depression.

Once I was left alone, it deepened. All America had followed me to my room, and was asking me enormous questions, reviving awful forebodings.

Reclining anxiously on the bed, I tried to adjust to the darkness of my cubbyhole. At regular intervals the walls on the window side trembled. An Elevated Railway train was passing. It bounded between two streets like a cannonball filled with quivering flesh, jolting from section to section of this lunatic city. You could see it far away, its carcass trembling as it passed over a torrent of steel girders, which went on echoing from rampart to rampart long after the train had roared by at seventy miles an hour. Dinnertime passed as I lay thus prostrate, and bedtime as well.

What had horrified me most of all was that Elevated Railway.

On the other side of the court, which was more like a well shaft, the wall began to light up, first one, then two rooms, then dozens. I could see what was going on in some of them. Couples going to bed. These Americans seemed as worn out as our own people after their vertical hours. The women had very full, very pale thighs, at least the ones I was able to get a good look at. Before going to bed, most of the men shaved without taking the cigars out of their mouths.

In bed they first took off their glasses, then put their false teeth in a glass of water, which they left in evidence. Same as in the street, the sexes didn't seem to talk to each other. They impressed me as fat, docile animals, used to being bored. In all, I only saw two couples engaging, with the light on, in the kind of thing I'd expected, and not at all violently. The other women ate chocolates in bed, while waiting for their husbands to finish shaving. And then they all put their lights out.

There's something sad about people going to bed. You can see they don't give a damn whether they're getting what they want out of life or not, you can see they don't even try to understand what we're here for. They just don't care. Americans or not, they sleep no matter what, they're bloated mollusks, no sensibility, no trouble with their conscience.

I'd seen too many puzzling things to be easy in my mind. I knew too much and not enough. I'd better go out, I said to myself, I'd better go out again. Maybe I'll meet Robinson. Naturally that was an idiotic idea, but I dreamed it up as an excuse for going out again, because no matter how much I tossed and turned on my narrow bed, I couldn't snatch the tiniest scrap of sleep. Even masturbation, at times like that, provides neither comfort nor entertainment. Then you're really in despair.

The worst part is wondering how you'll find the strength tomorrow to go on doing what you did today and have been doing for much too long, where you'll find the strength for all that stupid running around, those projects that come to nothing, those attempts to escape from crushing necessity, which always founder and serve only to convince you one more time that destiny is implacable, that every night will find you down and out, crushed by the dread of more and more sordid and insecure tomorrows.

And maybe it's treacherous old age coming on, threatening the worst. Not much music left inside us for life to dance to. Our youth has gone to the ends of the earth to die in the silence of the truth. And where, I ask you, can a man escape to, when he hasn't enough madness left inside him? The truth is an endless death agony. The truth is death. You have to choose: death or lies. I've never been able to kill myself.

I'd better go out into the street, a partial suicide. Everyone has his little knacks, his ways of getting sleep and food. I'd need to sleep if I wanted to recover the strength I'd need to go to work next day. Get back the zip it would take to find a job in the morning, and in the meantime force my way into the unknown realm of sleep. Don't go thinking it's easy to fall asleep when you've started doubting everything, mostly because of the awful fears people have given you.

I dressed and somehow found my way to the elevator, but feeling kind of foggy. I still had to cross the lobby, to pass more rows of ravishing enigmas with legs so tempting, faces so delicate and severe. Goddesses, in short, hustling goddesses. We might have tried to make an arrangement. But I was afraid of being arrested. Complications. Nearly all a poor bastard's desires are punishable by jail. So there I was on the street again. It wasn't the same crowd as before. This one billowed over the sidewalks and showed a little more life, as if it had landed in a country less arid, the land of entertainment, of night life.

The people surged in the direction of lights suspended far off in the darkness, writhing multicolored snakes. They flowed in from all the neighboring streets. A crowd like that, I said to myself, adds up to a lot of dollars in handkerchiefs alone or silk stockings! Or just in cigarettes for that matter! And to think that you can go out among all that money, and nobody'll give you a single penny, not even to go and eat with! It's heartbreaking to think how people shut themselves off from one another, like houses.

I, too, dragged myself toward the lights, a movie house, and then another right next to it, and another, all along the street. We lost big chunks of crowd to each of them. I picked a movie house with posters of women in slips, and what legs! Boyohboy! Heavy! Ample! Shapely! And pretty faces on top, as though drawn for the contrast, no need of retouching, not a blemish, not a flaw, perfect I tell you, delicate but firm and concise. Life can engender no greater peril than these incautious beauties, these indiscreet variations on perfect divine harmony.

It was warm and cozy in the movie house. An enormous organ, as mellow as in a cathedral, a heated cathedral I mean, organ pipes like thighs. They don't waste a moment. Before you know it, you're bathing in an all-forgiving warmth. Just let yourself go and you'll begin to think the world has been converted to loving-kindness. I almost was myself.

Dreams rise in the darkness and catch fire from the mirage of moving light. What happens on the screen isn't quite real; it leaves open a vague cloudy space for the poor, for dreams and the dead. Hurry hurry, cram yourself full of dreams to carry you through the life that's waiting for you outside, when you leave here, to help you last a few days more in that nightmare of things and people. Among the dreams, choose the ones most likely to warm your soul. I have to confess that I picked the sexy ones. No point in being proud; when it comes to miracles, take the ones that will stay with you. A blonde with unforgettable tits and shoulders saw fit to break the silence of the screen with a song about her loneliness. I'd have been glad to cry about it with her.

There's nothing like it! What a lift it gives you! After that, I knew I'd have courage enough in my guts to last me at least two days. I didn't even wait for the lights to go on. Once I'd absorbed a small dose of that admirable ecstasy, I knew Yd sleep, my mind was made up.

When I got back to the *Laugh Calvin*, the night clerk, despite my greeting, neglected to say good evening the way they do at home. But his contempt didn't mean a thing to me anymore. An intense inner life suffices to itself, it can melt an icepack that has been building up for twenty years. That's a fact.

In my room I'd barely closed my eyes when the blonde from the movie house came along and sang her whole song of sorrow just for me. I helped her put me to sleep, so to speak, and succeeded pretty well... I wasn't entirely alone... It's not possible to sleep alone...

* * *

To eat cheaply in America, you can buy yourself a hot roll with a sausage in it, it's handy, they sell them on street corners in the poor neighborhoods, and they're not at all expensive. I didn't mind eating in poor neighborhoods, but never meeting those splendid creatures designed for the rich, that bothered me. Under those conditions it wasn't worth eating.

True, at the *Laugh Calvin*, on those thick carpets, I could pretend to be looking for somebody among the too pretty women in the lobby. After a while I was able to face that sultry atmosphere without quailing. Thinking about it, I had to admit that the boys on the Infanta Combitta had been right; experience was teaching me that I didn't have sensible tastes for a poor slob. My shipmates on the galley had been right in giving me hell. Anyway, my morale was still low. More and more I dosed myself on movies, in this street or that street, but all they gave me was enough energy for a little stroll or two. No more. The loneliness in Africa had been pretty rough, but my isolation in this American anthill was even more crushing.

I'd always worried about being practically empty, about having no serious reason for living. And now, confronted with the facts, I was sure of my individual nullity. In that environment, too different from the one where my petty habits were at home, I seem to have disintegrated, I felt very close to nonexistence. I discovered that with no one to speak to me of familiar things, there was nothing to stop me from sinking into irresistible boredom, a terrifying, sickly sweet torpor. Nauseating.

On the point of dropping my last dollar in this adventure, I was still bored. So profoundly that I even refused to envisage the most urgent steps I should have been taking. We are so trivial by nature that only amusements can stop us from dying for real. I clung to the movies with desperate fervor.

Leaving the delirious gloom of my hotel, I attempted a few excursions in the main streets round about, an insipid carnival of dizzy buildings. My weariness increased at the sight of those endless house fronts, that turgid monotony of pavements, of windows upon windows, of business and more business, that chancre of the world, bursting with pustulent advertisements. False promises. Driveling lies.

Along the river I explored other streets, more and more of them. Here the dimensions were more normal; for instance, from the sidewalk where I was standing I might have smashed every window in the house across the street.

Those neighborhoods were full of the smell of constant frying, the shops dispensed with side-walk displays for fear of theft. Everything reminded me of the streets around my hospital in Villejuif, even the children with their crooked swollen knees all along the sidewalks, and the barrel organs. I'd have been glad to stay there with them, but poor people wouldn't have fed me any more than the rich; besides, I'd have had to look at them all, and their too much misery frightened me. So I finally went back to Richtown. "You no- good!" I said to myself. "Really, you have no virtue!" A man should be resigned to knowing himself a little better each day if he hasn't got the guts to put an end to his sniveling once and for all.

A streetcar was running beside the Hudson, heading for the midtown section, an ancient vehicle, trembling in every wheel and all its terrified carcass. It took a solid hour to get there. The passengers submitted without impatience to a complicated ritual, you paid by tossing coins into a kind of coffee mill stationed at the entrance. The conductor, dressed like ours, in the uniform of a Balkan prisoner of war, watched them doing it.

At last we arrived. Returning exhausted from those populist excursions, I once again passed that inexhaustible double row of beauties in my Tantalian lobby. Again and again I passed, pensive and prodded by desire.

My poverty was such that I didn't dare rummage through my pockets to make sure. If only, I thought, Lola hasn't picked this particular moment to leave town... But will she want to see me in the first place? Should I touch her for fifty or for a hundred dollars as a starter?... I hesitated. I felt that I wouldn't have the nerve till I'd eaten and slept properly for once. And then, if this first touch was successful, I'd go looking for Robinson right away, that is, as soon as I got my strength back. Robinson was nothing like me. He was determined! Courageous! Oh yes! I could bet he knew all about America by now, all the ins and outs! Maybe he knew some way of acquiring the certainty, the peace of mind, in which I was so sadly lacking...

If, as I supposed, he too had come on a galley and trodden these shores before me, he'd be well launched on his American career by now. These jumpy lunatics wouldn't faze him! I myself, come to think of it, might have looked for a job in one of those offices, whose dazzling signs I saw outside... But at the thought of having to enter that sort of building I crumpled with fear. My hotel, that gigantic, loathsomely animated tomb, was enough for me.

Maybe those vast accretions of matter, those commercial honeycombs, those endless figments of brick and steel didn't affect the habitues the way they did me. To them perhaps that suspended deluge meant security, while to me it was simply an abominable system of constraints, of corridors, locks and wickets, a vast, inexpiable architectural crime.

Philosophizing is simply one way of being afraid, a cowardly pretense that doesn't get you anywhere.

I went out and watched my last three dollars wriggling in the palm of my hand under the electric signs on Times Square, that amazing intersection where the crowds engaged in picking their movie show are bathed in floods of advertising. In search of a cheap restaurant, I went into one of those rationalized public refectories, where the service is reduced to a minimum and the alimentary rite is cut down to the exact measure of nature's requirements.

They hand you a tray at the entrance, and you take your place in a line. You wait. The girls around me, delightful candidates for dinner, didn't say a word to me... It must feel really funny, I thought, to be able to go right up to one of those young ladies with the tidy, prettily shaped noses, and say: "Miss, I'm rich, very rich... just tell me what it might please you to accept... "

Everything that was so complicated a moment before would suddenly become so simple, so divinely simple... Everything would be changed, the forbiddingly hostile world would turn into a playful, docile, velvety ball, rolling at your feet. Then and there, perhaps, you'd throw off the exhausting habit of dreaming about successful people and enormous fortunes, because then you'd be able to put your hands on all that. The life of people without resources is nothing but one long rebuff and one long frenzy of desire, and a man can truly know, truly deliver himself only from what he possesses. As for me, I'd picked up and dropped so many dreams, my mind was cracked and fissured, full of drafts and disgustingly out of order.

In the meantime I was afraid to attempt even the most inoffensive conversation with these young things in the restaurant. I went ahead with my tray in well-behaved silence. When it came my turn to pass the earthenware hollows filled with sausages and beans, I took what was given me. That restaurant was so clean and well lighted that, skimming its mosaic floor, I felt like a fly on milk.

Waitresses dressed like nurses stood behind the noodles, rice, and stewed fruit. Each had her specialty. I took what the most attractive ones were dishing out. To my regret, they didn't smile at the customers at all. As soon as you were served, you had to leave your place in line and find yourself a table. You balance your tray and take little mincing steps as if it were an operating room. It was a change from the *Laugh Calvin* and my gold-bordered ebony cubbyhole.

But if they showered the customers with so much light, if they lifted us for a moment from the habitual darkness of our condition, there was method in their madness. The owner was up to something. I had my suspicions. After days of darkness it feels very strange to be suddenly bathed in torrents of light. It made me a little giddier than usual. Which wasn't difficult, I admit.

I couldn't manage to hide my feet under the immaculate little enamel-topped table I had landed at; they stuck out in all directions. I'd have liked my feet to be somewhere else, because we were being watched through the window by the line of people we had just left in the street. They were waiting for us to finish eating so they could come and take our tables. Actually that was the reason, to keep up their appetite, why we were so well lighted and displayed so prominently; we were living advertisements, so to speak. The strawberries on my cake shimmered and sparkled so brightly that I couldn't bring myself to eat them.

You can't get away from American business enterprise.

Yet despite the dazzling glare and my cramped posture I perceived the comings and goings in my immediate vicinity of a very nice waitress and decided not to miss a single one of her delightful movements.

When my turn came to have her clear my table, I took careful note of the unusual shape of her eyes, the outer ends of which tilted upwards more sharply than is common among French women. The eyelids also inclined slightly toward the eyebrows on the temple side. A sign of cruelty, but just enough, the kind of cruelty you can kiss, an insidious tartness like the Rhine wines one can't help liking.

When she came close to me, I made little gestures of complicity, as if I knew her. She looked me over as if I'd been an animal, without indulgence but with a certain curiosity. "This," I said to myself, "is the first American woman who has been forced to look at me."

Once I'd finished my luminous cake, there was no help for it, I had to give up my place to someone else. Reeling slightly, instead of taking the obvious way to the exit, I braced myself and circled round the man at the cash desk who was waiting for all of us and our money. Sticking out like a sore thumb in the bright, disciplined light, I headed for the blonde.

The twenty-five waitresses at their posts behind the simmering dishes all signaled to me in unison that I was mistaken, headed the wrong way. In the plate-glass window I saw a great stir among the people waiting, and the people behind me, who were supposed to start eating, hesitated to sit down. I had broken the foreordained order of things. All the people around me cried out in consternation: "It must be a foreigner!"

But I had my idea for what it was worth, I wasn't going to lose the beauty who had waited on me. The sweet thing had asked for it, she had looked at me. I was sick of being alone. I was sick of dreams. I wanted sympathy! Human contact! "Miss," I said, "you hardly know me. But I already love you. Shall we get married?... " That's how I addressed her, most respectfully.

Her answer never reached me, for a giant guard, he too dressed all in white, stepped up at that exact moment and simply shoved me out into the night, without insults or brutality, like a dog that has misbehaved.

The whole thing went off like clockwork, there was nothing I could say. I went back to the *Laugh Calvin*.

In my room the same thunders were still shattering their echoes, first the roar of the "El," which seemed to hurl itself at us from far away, smashing the city every time it passed by carrying away the aqueducts; and, in between, incoherent, mechanical sounds from far below, coming up from the street, plus the soft murmur of the eddying crowd, hesitant, monotonous, always starting up again, then hesitating again and starting up again. The great stewpot of people in a city.

From up high where I was, you could shout anything you liked at them. I tried. They made me sick, the whole lot of them. I hadn't the nerve to tell them so in the daytime, to their face, but up there it was safe. "Help! Help!" I shouted, just to see if it would have any effect on them. None whatsoever. Those people were pushing life and night and day in front of them. Life hides everything from people. Their own noise prevents them from hearing anything else. They couldn't care less. The bigger and taller the city, the less they care. Take it from me. I've tried. It's a waste of time.

* * *

I have to admit it was only for need of money, but how very pressing, how imperious a need! that I started looking for Lola. If it hadn't been for that pitiful need, man! would I have let that little bitch of a girlfriend grow old and die without ever setting eyes on her again! All in all—and when I thought about it I had no doubt whatsoever—her behavior to me had been most crummily ruthless.

When, grown older, we look back on the selfishness of the people who've been mixed up with our lives, we see it undeniably for what it was, as hard as steel or platinum and a lot more durable than time itself.

As long as we're young, we manage to find excuses for the stoniest indifference, the most blatant caddishness, we put them down to emotional eccentricity or some sort of romantic inexperience. But later on, when life shows us how much cunning, cruelty, and malice are required just to keep the body at ninety- eight point six, we catch on, we know the score, we begin to understand how much swinishness it takes to make up a past. Just take a close look at yourself and the degree of rottenness you've come to. There's no mystery about it, no more room for fairy tales; if you've lived this long, it's because you've squashed any poetry you had in you. Life is keeping body and soul together.

I finally, with a good deal of trouble, found my little bitch on the twenty-third floor of a building on 77th Street. It's incredible how revolting people seem when you're about to ask a favor of them. Her place was posh, pretty much what I'd imagined.

Having steeped myself in large doses of cinema, I was mentally in pretty good shape, almost out of the depression that had weighed on me ever since I landed in New York, so our first contact wasn't as unpleasant as I'd expected. Lola didn't even seem terribly surprised at seeing me, it was only when she recognized me that she seemed rather put out.

By way of preamble, I tried to strike up an inoffensive sort of conversation, drawing on our common past. I kept it as discreet as possible and mentioned the war just in passing, without any particular emphasis. There I was putting my foot in it. She didn't want to hear about the war, not one word. It aged her, and she didn't like that. She lost no time in getting back at me; age, she said, had so wrinkled, bloated, and caricatured me that she wouldn't have known me in the street. In short, we exchanged compliments. If the little tart thought she could get me down with such foolishness! I didn't even deign to react to her sleazy impertinence.

Her furnishings didn't bowl me over with their elegance, but the place was cheerful enough, or at least I thought so after the *Laugh Calvin*.

There always seems to be a certain magic about getting rich quickly. Since the rise of Musyne and Madame Herote, I knew that a poor woman's ass is her gold mine. Those sudden female metamorphoses fascinated me, and I'd have given Lola's concierge my last dollar to make her talk.

But there was no concierge in the house. There were no concierges in the whole city. A city without concierges has no history, no savor, it's as insipid as a soup without pepper and salt, nondescript slop. O luscious scrapings! O garbage, O muck oozing from bedrooms, kitchens, and attics, cascading down to the concierge's den, the center of life—what luscious, tasty hell-fire! Some of our concierges are victims of their profession, laconic, throat-clearing, delectable, struck dumb with amazement, martyrs, stupefied and consumed by the Truth.

To counter the abomination of being poor, why deny it, we are in duty bound to try everything, to get drunk on anything we can, cheap wine, masturbation, movies. No sense in being difficult, "particular" as they say in America. Year in year out, we may as well admit, our concierges in France provide anyone who knows how to take it and coddle it close to his heart with a free-gratis supply of all-purpose hatred, enough to blow up the world. In New York, they're cruelly lacking in this vital spice, so sordid and irrefutably alive, without which the spirit is stifled, condemned to vague slanders and pallid bumbled calumnies. Without a concierge you get nothing that stings, wounds, lacerates, torments, obsesses, and adds without fail to the world's stock of hatred, illumining it with thousands of undeniable details.

What made this lack all the more deplorable was that Lola, surprised in her native environment, inspired me with a new sort of disgust. I longed to pour out my revulsion at the vulgarity of her success, at her trivial, loathsome pride, but how could I? In that same moment, by the workings of an instant contagion, the memory of Musyne became equally hostile and repugnant to me. An intense hatred for those two women arose in me, it's still with me, it has become part and parcel of my being. I'd have needed a whole panoply of evidence to rid myself on time and for good of all present and future indulgence for Lola. We can't live our lives over again.

Courage doesn't consist in forgiveness, we always forgive too much. And it does no good, that's a known fact. Why was "the Housemaid" put in the last row, after all other human beings? Not for nothing, we can be sure of that. One night while they're asleep, all happy people, believe me, ought to be put to sleep for real, that'll be the end of them and their happiness once and for all. The next day they'll all be forgotten, and we'll be free to be as unhappy as we please, along with the Housemaid. But what's all this I'm telling you? Lola was pacing the floor without many clothes on, and in spite of everything her body still struck me as very desirable. Where there's a luxurious body there's always a possibility of rape, of a direct, violent breaking and entering into the heart of wealth and luxury, with no fear of having to return the loot.

Maybe she was just waiting for me to make a move, and then she'd have shown me the door. Anyway, I was careful, mostly because I was so abominably hungry. Eat first! Besides, she was going on and on about the vulgar trivia of her daily life. The world would certainly have to be shut down for at least two or three generations if there were no more lies to tell. People would have practically nothing to say to one another. She finally got around to asking me what I thought of her America. I owned that I'd become so weakened, so terror-stricken, that almost everyone and almost everything frightened me, and that her country as such terrified me more than all the direct, occult, and unforeseeable menaces I found in it, chiefly because of the enormous indifference toward me which to my way of thinking was its very essence.

I had my living to make, I told her, so I'd soon have to cure myself of my excessive sensibility. In that respect, I admitted, I was very backward, and I assured her that I'd be exceedingly grateful if she could recommend me to some possible employer among her acquaintances... But please, as soon as possible... I'd be quite satisfied with a modest salary... And considerably more of this insipid hogwash... She took my modest but nevertheless indiscreet suggestion pretty badly. Her replies were discouraging from the start. She couldn't think of anyone at all who might give me a job or help me. Naturally that drove us back to talking about life in general and hers in particular.

We were still sizing each other up morally and physically when the bell rang. And then, with practically no pause or interval, four women swept into the room, painted, corpulent, middle-aged, muscular, bejeweled, and very free and easy. Lola introduced us very summarily, she was visibly embarrassed and tried to drag them away somewhere, but, thwarting all her efforts, they competed for my attention, telling me everything they knew about Europe. Europe was an old-fashioned garden, full of old-fashioned, erotic, grasping lunatics. They knew all there was to know about the Chabanais[57] and the Invalides.[58] Personally, I hadn't been to either of those places, the first being too expensive, the second too out of the way. In replying, I was overcome by a blast of automatic patriotism that made me even sillier than usual on such occasions. I told them their city gave me the creeps. An unsuccessful carnival, a nauseating flop, though the people in charge were knocking themselves out to put it over...

While perorating thus artificially and conventionally, I couldn't help realizing that there were other reasons than malaria for my physical prostration and moral depression. There was also the change in habits; once again I was having to get used to new faces in new surroundings and to learn new ways of talking and lying. Laziness is almost as compelling as life. The new farce you're having to play crushes you with its banality, and all in all it takes more cowardice than courage to start all over again. That's what exile, a foreign country is, inexorable perception of existence as it really is, during those long lucid hours, exceptional in the flux of human time, when the ways of the old country abandon you, but the new ways haven't sufficiently stupefied you as yet.

At such moments everything adds to your loathsome distress, forcing you in your weakened state to see things, people, and the future as they are, that is, as skeletons, as nothings, which you will nevertheless have to love, cherish, and defend as if they existed.

---

[57] Chabanais. Le Chabanais on the rue Chabanais was one of the most celebrated and luxurious of Paris brothels.
[58] Invalides. A group of buildings put up in 1670 by Louis XIV as a home for wounded soldiers. The tomb of Napoleon is situated in the church of Saint-Louis des Invalides, the most prominent building in the compound.

A different country, different people carrying on rather strangely, the loss of a few little vanities, of a certain pride that has lost its justification, the lie it's based on, its familiar echo-no more is needed, your head swims, doubt takes hold of you, the infinite opens up just for you, a ridiculously small infinite, and you fall into it...

Travel is the search for this nothing, this bit of intoxication for numbskulls...

Lola's four visitors had a good laugh listening to my wild confessions, my little Jean-Jacques act. They called me all sorts of names that I hardly understood because of their American mispronunciation and oily, indecent way of speaking. Loudmouthed cats.

When the Negro servant came in with tea, we all fell silent.

One of the visitors must have had more discernment than the others, for she announced in a loud voice that I was shaking with fever and must be frightfully thirsty. In spite of my shakes, I loved the food that was served. Those sandwiches, I can say without exaggeration, saved my life.

The conversation turned to the relative merits of the Paris brothels, but I didn't bother to join in. The ladies dabbled in various complicated drinks and then, flushed, warmed, and communicative, started talking about "marriages." Busy as I was with the food, I couldn't help realizing in one corner of my mind that these were marriages of a very special kind, matings, I was pretty sure, between juveniles, and that the ladies collected a commission on them.

Lola saw that this talk caught my attention and aroused my curiosity. She gave me a pretty mean look. She had stopped drinking. The American men Lola knew weren't like me, they never showed curiosity. Under her watchful eye I controlled myself with some difficulty. I'd have liked to ask those ladies a hundred questions.

Finally the guests left us, moving heavily, enlivened by drink, sexually stimulated. Bouncing and wriggling, they held forth with a curiously elegant and cynical eroticism. I sensed an Elizabethan something deep down, and I'd have liked to feel its undoubtedly choice and concentrated vibrations at the end of my organ. But much to my regret and increased sadness, I got no more than a presentiment of that biological communion, that vital message so essential for a traveler. Incurable melancholy!

As soon as they had left, Lola made no secret of her exasperation. That intermezzo had really annoyed her. I didn't say a word.

"Those hags!" she cried a few minutes later. "How did you get to know them?" I asked her. "I've always known them... "

No inclination to tell me more at the moment.

Judging by their rather arrogant manner toward her, I had the impression that in a certain society these women must have enjoyed greater prestige than Lola, a considerable authority, in fact. I never found out any more about it.

Lola said something about going downtown, but told me I could stay and wait for her and have some more to eat if I was still hungry. Seeing that I'd left the *Laugh Calvin* without paying my bill and had no intention of going back—for good reason—I was delighted with her suggestion—a few more moments of warmth before going out and facing the street, and oh my aching back! what a street!

As soon as I was alone, I made for the hallway leading to the place the Negro servant had emerged from. We met halfway to the pantry, and I shook hands with him. He trusted me right off and led me to the kitchen, a fine, well-arranged place, much more logical and attractive than the living room.

Right away he started spitting on the beautiful tile floor as only black men know how to spit, abundantly and consummately. As a matter of politeness, I too spat as best I could. That did it, he took me into his confidence. Lola, he informed me, had a yacht on the river, two cars in the garage, a cellar stocked with liquor from all over the world. The Paris department stores sent her their catalogues. That was the story. And he proceeded to repeat the same meager information over and over again. I stopped listening.

I dozed beside him, and the past came back to me, the days when Lola had left me in wartime Paris. The chase that sly, glib, lying minx had led me, Musyne, the Argentines, their ships full of meat. Topo, the bedraggled cohorts on the Place Clichy, Robinson, the waves, the sea, poverty, Lola's gleaming white kitchen, her Negro servant. And me sitting there as if I were somebody else. Everything would go on. The war had burned some and warmed others, same as fire tortures you or comforts you, depending on whether you're in it or in front of it. You've got to work the angles, that's all.

It was true what she'd said about my having changed, I couldn't deny it. Life twists you and squashes your face. It had squashed her face too, but less so. It's no joke being poor. Poverty is a giant, it uses your face like a mop to clear away the world's garbage. There's plenty left.

Still, it seemed to me that I'd noticed something new in Lola, moments of depression, of melancholy, gaps in her optimistic stupidity, the moments when a person has to stop and gather the strength to carry his life, his years, a little further, because they've become too heavy for the vitality he has left, his lousy little bit of poetry.

Suddenly the Negro began to jiggle and hop. Something had come over him. I was his new friend, and he was determined to stuff me full of cakes and load me with cigars. Finally, with infinite precautions, he removed a round, leaden object from a drawer.

"The bomb!" he cried furiously. I retreated. "Liberia! Liberia!" he shouted exultantly.

He put it back where it belonged and spat again, superbly. What emotion! What jubilation! His laughter, that gut sensation, infected me. Why not? A little thing like that, I said to myself, doesn't mean a thing. When Lola finally got back from her errands, she found us in the living room, plunged in smoke and laughter. She pretended not to notice.

The Negro quickly made himself scarce. She took me to her room. I found her sad, pale, and trembling. Where could she have been? It was getting late. The time of day when Americans are at a loss because the pulse of life around them has gone into slow motion. Every second car is back in the garage. It's the time for half-confidences. But to benefit by it you've got to hurry. To put me in the mood she questioned me, but the tone she took when asking certain questions about the life I'd been leading in Europe stuck in my craw.

She made it quite clear that she thought me capable of every kind of beastliness. That hypothesis didn't make me angry, it only embarrassed me. She had a good idea that I'd come to ask her for money, and that in itself created a natural animosity between us. Such feelings verge on murder. We stuck to commonplaces, and I did my level best to avoid an out and out quarrel. She asked among other things about my sexual escapades, wanting to know if, somewhere in the course of my bummings around, I hadn't abandoned a child she could adopt. A bug that had got into her. She was obsessed with the idea of adopting a child. She thought rather naively that a tramp like me must have sired clandestine families all over the world. She was rich, she confided, and not having a child to devote herself to was more than she could bear. She had read every available book on child care, especially the ones that go into a lyrical swoon about motherhood, those books that cure you, if you really assimilate them, of all desire to copulate for ever and ever. Every virtue has its contemptible literature.

Since she wanted to sacrifice herself exclusively for a "little creature," I was out of luck. All I had to offer her was a big creature and one who struck her as too disgusting for words. Poverty doesn't draw unless it's properly presented, swathed in imagination. Our conversation languished. "Look, Ferdinand," she finally suggested, "we've had enough talk. I'm going to take you across town to see my little protege. I enjoy looking after him, but his mother drives me crazy... " It was a strange time to be visiting. In the car on the way, we talked about her catastrophic Negro.

"Did he show you his bombs?" she asked. I owned that he had put me through that ordeal.

"He's a maniac, Ferdinand, but not dangerous. He fills his bombs with my old bills... Years ago in Chicago he had his day... He belonged to a dangerous secret society for black emancipation... Horrible people, to judge by what he's told me... The police broke up the gang, but he still has a weakness for bombs... He never puts explosives in them... The spirit of the thing is enough for him... He's really an artist... He'll be a revolutionary as long as he lives. But I keep him, he's an excellent servant. And all things considered, he's probably more honest than the ones who aren't revolutionaries... "

And she came back to her adoption mania.

"It's really too bad you haven't a little girl somewhere. A dreamy nature like yours is no good at all for a man, but it would be fine for a woman... "

The rain poured down, closing the night around our car as it glided over the long band of smooth concrete. Everything was hostile and cold to me, even her hand, which I was holding tight in mine all the same. Everything came between us. We pulled up in front of a house that looked very different from the one we had just left. In an apartment on the second floor a little boy of about ten was waiting for us with his mother. The furniture had pretensions to Louis XV, and the cooking smells of a recent meal were still in the air. The child jumped up on Lola's lap and kissed her affectionately. The mother also seemed very fond of Lola. While Lola was talking to the child, I managed to take the mother into the next room.

When we came back, the boy was performing for Lola's benefit a dance step he had just learned at the Conservatory. "He'll need a few more private lessons," Lola observed, "then I may introduce him to my friend Vera at the Globe Theater. I wouldn't be surprised if the child had quite a future ahead of him." After these kind, encouraging words the mother thanked her tearfully and profusely. At the same time she accepted a small wad of green dollars, which she tucked away in her bosom like a love letter.

"I'd be rather pleased with that little boy," said Lola, once we were outside, "but I have to put up with the mother at the same time, and I don't care for mothers who are too sharp for their own good... Besides, the kid is too depraved... That's not the sort of attachment I want... What I long for is a purely maternal feeling... Do you understand me, Ferdinand?" When it comes to making a living, I can put up with anything, it's not a matter of intelligence, I just know I have to adapt.

She couldn't stop talking about her desire for purity. A few streets further on she asked me where I was planning to sleep that night and took a few more steps beside me. I said that if I didn't get hold of a few dollars I wouldn't be sleeping anywhere.

"All right," she said. "Come home with me. I'll give you a little change, then you can go where you please."

She was determined to put me out into the night as soon as possible. The usual thing. Always getting shoved out into the night like this, I said to myself, I'm bound to end up somewhere. That's some consolation. "Chin up, Ferdinand," I kept saying to myself, to keep up my courage. "What with being chucked out of everywhere, you're sure to find whatever it is that scares all those bastards so. It must be at the end of the night, and that's why they're so dead set against going to the end of the night."

After that it was very cold between us in her car. The streets we passed threatened us with all the armored silence of their infinitely towering stone, with a kind of suspended deluge. A city lurking in ambush, an unpredictable monster, viscous with asphalt and rain. At last we slowed down. Lola went in ahead of me.

"Come up," she said. "Follow me."

Her living room again. I wondered how much she'd part with to get this business over with and be rid of me. She took some banknotes out of a small handbag she had left on the table. I heard an enormous rustling of crumpled bills. Great moments! In the whole city there was no other sound. But I was so embarrassed that I asked her—I don't know why and it was most out of place—for news of her mother whom I had forgotten.

"My mother is ill," she said, turning around and looking me full in the face. "Where is she now?"

"In Chicago."

"What's wrong with her?"

"Cancer of the liver... I've put her in the hands of the finest specialists in town... They're costing me a fortune, but they'll save her. They promised."

More and more details of her mother's condition in Chicago poured out of her. Her feeling for her mother made for familiarity, and in spite of herself she appealed to me for comfort. I had her where I wanted her.

"And you, Ferdinand, you believe they'll cure her, don't you?"

"No," I said briskly and firmly. "Cancer of the liver is absolutely incurable."

At that she went deathly pale. The bitch, that was the first time I'd ever seen anything disconcert her.

"But Ferdinand, the specialists assured me she'd recover! They guaranteed it! They gave it to me in writing! They're great doctors, Ferdinand... "

"For cash, Lola, there will always be great doctors... luckily... I'd do the same for you myself if I were in their place... And so would you, Lola... "

Suddenly what I was saying struck her as so incontrovertible, so obvious that she couldn't even put up a fight.

For once, maybe for the first time in her life, she lost her nerve.

"But Ferdinand, don't you realize how terribly you're hurting me?... I love my mother, didn't you know that I love her?"

Glad to hear it! Good grief! Who the hell cares whether she loves her mother or not! Lola was sobbing in her emptiness.

"Ferdinand, you're a worthless monster!" she shouted in a rage. "You're wicked! Wicked! Saying awful things like that is just your cowardly way of avenging yourself for the rotten situation you're in... And I just know you're doing my mother a lot of harm by talking that way!"

In her despair I sniffed vestiges of the Coue method.[59] Her fury didn't frighten me as much as that of the officers on the Admiral Bragueton, who'd wanted to annihilate me to give the bored ladies a kick.

I watched Lola closely as she was calling me every name in the book, and it gave me a certain feeling of pride to observe that by contrast the more she insulted me the more my indifference, no, my joy, increased. We're nice people deep down.

"Now," I figured, "she'll have to give me at least twenty dollars to get rid of me... Maybe even more... "

I took the offensive: "Lola, lend me the money you promised or I'll sleep here, and you'll hear me repeat all I know about cancer, its complications, its hereditary character, because you know, Lola, cancer is hereditary, and don't forget it!"

As I developed and refined on the details of her mother's case, I saw Lola blanch, weaken, crumple before my eyes. "Oh, the bitch!" I said to myself. "Keep a good hold on her! For once you've got the good end!... Don't let her off the line! You won't find such a good one in a hurry!... "

She was beside herself. "Here!" she screamed. "Take it! Take your hundred dollars and get out and never come back, hear, never!... Out! Out! Out! You beast!"

"Won't you kiss me all the same, Lola... Come on! We're still friends, aren't we?" I suggested, to see how far I could go in disgusting her. At that point she took a revolver out of a drawer, and she wasn't joking. The stairs were good enough for me, I didn't even ring for the elevator.

That good solid fight restored my taste for work and picked up my morale. The next day I took the train to Detroit., where, I'd been assured, it was easy to get hired and there were lots of little jobs that were well paid and didn't take too much out of you.

* * *

The passers-by spoke to me the way the sergeant had spoken to me in the forest. "You can't go wrong," they said. "Just follow your nose."

And true enough I saw some big squat buildings all of glass, enormous dollhouses, inside which you could see men moving, but hardly moving, as if they were struggling against something impossible. Was that Ford's? And then all around me and above me as far as the sky, the heavy, composite, muffled roar of torrents of machines, hard, wheels obstinately turning, grinding, groaning, always on the point of breaking down but never breaking down.

"So this is the place!" I said to myself... "It's not very promising..." Actually, it was worse than everywhere else. I went closer, up to a door where it was written on a slate that men were wanted.

---

[59] Coué method. A method of self-healing devised by Emile Coué (1857-1926), pharmacist and psychotherapist. Very popular in the United States for a time. You repeated to yourself several times a day: "Every day in every way I'm getting better and better."

I wasn't the only one waiting. One of the men cooling their heels told me he had been there, on the same spot, for two days. The poor sucker had come all the way from Yugoslavia for this job. Another dead beat spoke to me, he said he'd decided to work just for the fun of it—a nut, a phony.

Hardly anybody in that crowd spoke English. They eyed each other distrustfully like animals who had often been beaten. They gave off a smell of urinous crotches, like in the hospital. When they spoke to you, you kept away from their mouths, because in there poor people smell of death.

Rain was falling on our little crowd. The files of men stood compressed under the eaves. People looking for work are very compressible. What he liked at Ford's, an old Russian in a confiding frame of mind told me, was that they didn't care who or what they hired. "But watch your step," he added for my instruction, "don't get uppity, because if you get uppity they'll throw you out in two seconds and in two seconds you'll be replaced by one of those mechanical machines that he always keeps on hand, and it's no soap if you try to get back!" That Russian spoke good Parisian, because he'd been a taxi driver for years, but then he'd been fired because of some cocaine business in Bezons, and in the end he'd staked his cab in a game of zanzi with a fare and lost it.

It was true what he told me, that they took on anybody at all at Ford's. He hadn't lied. I had my suspicions, though, because down-and-outers like that tend to be off their rockers. There's a degree of destitution when the mind doesn't always stay with the body. It's too uncomfortable. What's talking to you is practically a disembodied soul. And a soul isn't responsible for what it says.

Naturally they stripped us stark naked for a starter. The examination was given in a kind of laboratory. We filed slowly past. "You're in terrible shape," said the medical assistant the moment he laid eyes on me, "but it doesn't matter."

And me with my worry about being turned down because of my African fevers in case they chanced to palpate my liver! Not at all, they seemed delighted at the cripples and weaklings in our batch.

"For the kind of work you'll be doing here," the doctor assured me, "your health is of no importance."

"Glad to hear it," I said. "But you know, doctor, I'm an educated man, I even studied medicine at one time... "

At that he gave me a dirty look, I saw that I'd put my foot in it again, to my detriment.

"Your studies won't do you a bit of good around here, son. You're not here to think, you're here to make the movements you're told to. We don't need imaginative types in our factory. What we need is chimpanzees... Let me give you a piece of advice. Never mention your intelligence again! We'll think for you, my boy! A word to the wise."

Lucky for me that he warned me. It was just as well that I should know the manners and customs of the house. I'd already made enough stupid blunders to last me at least ten years. From then on I was determined to pass for a quiet little drudge. When we had our clothes back on, we were sent off in slow- moving files, hesitant groups, in the direction where the stupendous roar of machinery came from. Everything trembled in the enormous building, and we ourselves, from our ears to the soles of our feet, were gathered into this trembling, which came from the windows, the floor, and all the clanking metal, tremors that shook the whole building from top to bottom. We ourselves became machines, our flesh trembled in the furious din, it gripped us around our heads and in our bowels and rose up to the eyes in quick continuous jolts. The further we went, the more of our companions we lost. In leaving them we gave them bright little smiles, as if all this were just lovely. It was no longer possible to speak to them or hear them. Each time three or four of them stopped at a machine.

Still, you resist; it's hard to despise your own substance, you'd like to stop all this, give yourself time to think about it and listen without difficulty to your heartbeat, but it's too late for that. This thing can never stop. This enormous steel box is on a collision course; we, inside it, are whirling madly with the machines and the earth. All together. Along with the thousands of little wheels and the hammers that never strike at the same time, that make noises which shatter one another, some so violent that they release a kind of silence around them, which makes you feel a little better.

The slow-moving little car full of hardware has trouble passing between the machine tools. Gangway! The workers jump aside to let the hysterical thing through. And the clanking fool goes on between the belts and flywheels, bringing the men their ration of servitude.

It's sickening to watch the workers bent over their machines, intent on giving them all possible pleasure, calibrating bolts and more bolts, instead of putting an end once for all to this stench of oil, this vapor that burns your throat and attacks your eardrums from inside. It's not shame that makes them bow their heads. You give in to noise as you give in to war. At the machines you let yourself go with the two three ideas that are wobbling about at the top of your head. And that's the end. From then on everything you look at, everything you touch, is hard. And everything you still manage to remember more or less becomes as rigid as iron and loses its savor in your thoughts.

All of a sudden you've become disgustingly old.

All outside life must be done away with, made into steel, into something useful. We didn't love it enough the way it was, that's why. So it has to be made into an object, into something solid. The Regulations say so.

I tried to shout something into the foreman's ear, he grunted like a pig in answer and made motions to show me, very patiently, the simple operation I was to perform forever and ever.

My minutes, my hours, like those of the others, all my time, would go into passing linchpins to the blind man next to me, who had been calibrating these same linchpins for years. I did the work very badly from the start. Nobody reprimanded me, but after three days of that first job, I was trans-ferred, already a failure, to pushing the little trolley full of washers that went jolting along from ma-chine to machine. At one machine I left three, at another a dozen, at still another only five. Nobody spoke to me. Existence was reduced to a kind of hesitation between stupor and frenzy. Nothing mat-tered but the ear-splitting continuity of the machines that commanded all men.

At six o'clock, when everything stops, you carry the noise away in your head. I had enough noise to last me all night, not to mention the smell of oil, as if I'd been given a new nose and a new brain for all time.

By dint of renunciation I became, little by little, a different man... a new Ferdinand. It took several weeks. But then the desire to see people came back to me. Naturally not the factory hands, they were mere echoes and smells of machines like myself, lumps of flesh convulsed with vibrations. I wanted to touch a real body, a pink body made of soft, quiet life.

I didn't know a soul in that city, least of all any women. Finally, after a good deal of trouble, I obtained the vague address of a "house," a clandestine brothel, at the north end of town. On several evenings in a row, after work, I strolled around the neighborhood on reconnaissance. The street was like any other, though maybe a little cleaner than the one where I lived.

I located the house in question, it had a garden around it. To get in, you had to move quickly so the cop on duty nearby wouldn't notice. That was the first place in America where I was received without brutality, amiably in fact, for my five dollars. And what beautiful young women, well rounded, bursting with health and graceful strength, almost as beautiful, come to think of it, as the ones at the *Laugh Calvin*.

And these, at least, you could come right out and touch, I couldn't help myself. I got to be a regular customer. It used up all my pay. When night came, I needed the erotic promiscuity of those splendid, welcoming creatures to restore my soul. The movies were no longer enough, that mild anti-dote was powerless to fight the physical horror of the factory. To survive, I needed lecherous tonics, drastic elixirs. In that house I didn't have to pay much, they gave me friendly terms, because I brought the girls a few little refinements from France. Except on Saturday night, then there was no time for refinements, business boomed, and I had to make way for baseball teams on a spree, magnificently vigorous young bruisers, to whom happiness came as easily as breath. While the baseball teams were at it, I, likewise in high spirits, would sit alone in the kitchen, writing my short stories. I'm sure those athletes' enthusiasm for the ladies of the establishment didn't measure up to my own slightly impotent fervor. Confident in their own strength, those baseball players were blase about physical perfection. Beauty is like drink or comfort, once you get used to it, you stop paying attention.

They visited the brothel mostly to make whoopee. Often they'd end up having terrible fights. The police would burst in and take them all away in little trucks.

Toward Molly, one of the lovely girls there, I soon developed an uncommon feeling of trust, which in frightened people takes the place of love. I remember her kindness as if it were yesterday, and her long, blond, magnificently strong, lithe legs, noble legs. Say what you like, the mark of true aristocracy in humankind is the legs.

We became intimate in body and mind, and took walks around town for a few hours every week. She was comfortably off, since she took in about a hundred dollars a day in the cat-house, while I made barely ten at Ford's. The lovemaking she did for a living didn't tire her in the least. Americans do it like birds.

In the evening, when I'd finished pushing my little delivery wagon around, I'd meet her after dinner and force myself to put on a cheerful face. You've got to be cheerful with women, in the beginning at least. A vague desire came over me to suggest things we could do, but I hadn't the strength. She understood the industrial blues, she was used to factory workers.

One evening, just like that, a propos of nothing, she presented me with fifty dollars. First I looked at her. I didn't dare. I thought about my mother and what she'd have said. And then it came to me that my mother, poor thing, had never given me that much. To please Molly, I went right out with her dollars and bought a lovely tan "four-piece" suit, which was what they were wearing that spring. They had never seen me arrive at the cathouse looking so natty. The madame played her big phonograph just to teach me how to dance.

Later Molly and I went to the movies to break in my new suit. She asked me on the way if I was jealous, because the suit made me look sad and so did not wanting to go back to the factory. A new suit always throws you off. She gave my suit passionate little kisses when nobody was looking. I tried to think of something else.

What a woman my Molly was! What generosity! What a body! What fullness of youth! A feast of desires! And then I was worried again. Was this pimping?

To make matters worse, Molly pleaded: "Don't go back to Ford's. Get yourself a little job in an office... as a translator, for instance... That's the thing for you... You like books... "

Her advice was kindly given, she wanted me to be happy. For the first time somebody was taking an interest in me, looking at me from the inside so to speak, taking my egoism into account, putting herself in my place, not just judging me from her point of view like everyone else.

If only I had met Molly sooner, when it was still possible to choose one road rather than another. Before that bitch Musyne and that little turd Lola crimped my enthusiasm. But it was too late to start being young again. I didn't believe in it anymore. We grow old so quickly and, what's more, irreme- diably. You can tell by the way you start loving your misery in spite of yourself. Nature is stronger than we are, no two ways about it. She tries us in one particular mold, and we're never able to throw it off. I had started out as the restless type. Little by little, without realizing it, you begin to take your role and fate seriously, and before you know it, it's too late to change. You're a hundred-percent restless, and it's set that way for good.

Very lovingly Molly tried to keep me with her, to dissuade me... "Life can be just as pleasant here as in Europe, Ferdinand. We won't be unhappy together." And in a sense she was right. "We'll invest our savings... We'll buy a little business... We'll be like other people... " She said that to quiet my scruples. Plans for the future. I agreed with her. I was even rather ashamed of all the trouble she was taking to hold me. I was very fond of her, but I was even fonder of my vice, my mania for running away from everywhere in search of God knows what, driven, I suppose, by stupid pride, by a sense of some sort of superiority.

I was afraid of hurting her. She understood and anticipated my concern. She was so nice that I finally told her about the mania that drove me to clear out of wherever I happened to be. She listened to me for days and days while I held forth, laying myself disgustingly bare, fighting with phantasms and points of pride, and she never lost patience, far from it. She only tried to help me get over my foolish and futile anxiety. She didn't quite get the point of my ravings, but she always took my part against my phantoms or with them, whichever I preferred. She was so gentle and persuasive that I grew accustomed to her kindness and took it almost personally. But I felt that I was beginning to cheat on my so-called destiny, my raison d'être as I called it, and stopped telling her everything that passed through my mind. I crawled back into myself all alone, just delighted to observe that I was even more miserable than before, because I had brought a new kind of distress and something that resembled true feeling into my solitude.

All that is commonplace. But Molly was gifted with angelic patience and had an unshakable belief in "vocations." For instance, her younger sister at the University of Arizona had been smitten with a craze for photographing birds in their nests and wild animals in their dens. So to enable her to study that astonishing specialty, Molly regularly sent this photographer sister of hers fifty dollars a month.

A really unbounded heart, containing something sublime, convertible into cash and not phony like mine and so many others. Molly would have liked nothing better than to take a financial interest in my dotty career. Though at times I struck her as pretty well off the beam, she thought my convictions real and not to be discouraged. She offered me an allowance and only asked me to draw up a little budget. I couldn't make up my mind to accept. A last vestige of delicacy prevented me from banking any further, from speculating, on her really too noble and kindly nature. And that's how I deliberately got myself in bad with Providence.

I was so ashamed of myself that I even made a feeble attempt to go back to Ford's. Nothing came of my heroic little gesture. I got as far as the factory gate but at that liminil point I froze. The thought of all those machines whirring as they lay in wait for me demolished my feeble work impulse once and for all.

I stationed myself outside the glass front of the main power plant, that multiform giant which roars as it pumps something or other God knows where and brings it back again through a thousand gleaming pipes as intricate and menacing as lianas. One morning as I stood there in drooling contemplation, my Russian taxi driver came by. "Hey, you old rascal," he says to me. "You've been fired!... It's been three weeks since you showed up... They've already put a machine in your place... I warned you... "

"At least," I said to myself, "that finishes it... No need to come back... " And I beat it back to town. On the way home I dropped in at the Consulate to ask if by any chance they'd had news of a Frenchman by the name of Robinson.

"Oh yes!" said the consuls. "Yes indeed! He's been in here to see us twice, with false papers what's more... Actually he's wanted by the police! Do you know him?... " I let it go at that.

After that I expected to meet Robinson any minute. I felt it in my bones. Molly was as kind and affectionate as ever. Once she felt sure I was planning to go away for good, she was even nicer than before. There was no point in being nice to me. Often on Molly's free afternoons we took trips to the outskirts.

Bare little hills, clumps of birches around tiny little lakes, people here and there reading dingy magazines under a sky heavy with leaden clouds. Molly and I avoided elaborate confessions. She knew the score. She was too sincere to say much about her grief. She knew what went on inside, in her heart, and that was enough for her. We kissed. But I didn't kiss her properly as I should have, on my knees if the truth be known. I was always partly thinking about something else at the same time, about not wasting time and tenderness, as if I wanted to keep them for something magnificent, something sublime, for later, but not for Molly and not for this particular kiss. As if life would carry away everything I longed to know about it, about life in the thick of the night, and hide it from me, while I was expending my passion in kissing Molly, and then I wouldn't have enough left, I'd have lost everything for want of strength, and life—Life, the true mistress of all real men—would have tricked me as it tricks everyone else.

We went back to the crowds, and then I'd leave her outside her house, because the customers would keep her busy all night until early morning. While she was taking care of them, I can't deny I was sad, and my sadness spoke to me so plainly of her that I felt she was with me even more than when she really was. I went to the movies to kill time. After the show, I'd board a streetcar going this way or that way and tour around in the night. After two o'clock flocks of timid passengers would get on, a type you seldom see before or after that hour, always pale and sleepy, in docile groups, bound for the suburbs.

With them you could go a long way. Much further than the factories, to vague housing developments, little streets of shapeless bungalows. On pavements sticky with the small rain of dawn the daylight glistened blue. My streetcar companions vanished along with their shadows. They closed their eyes on the day. It was hard to make those specters talk. Too tired. They didn't complain, not at all, they were the men who cleaned stores and more stores during the night, and all the offices in the city, after closing time. They didn't seem as anxious as we day people. Maybe because they'd sunk to the very bottom of things.

One of those nights when I'd taken still another streetcar and we'd got to the last stop and everybody was quietly getting off, I thought I heard someone calling me by name: "Ferdinand! Hey, Ferdinand!" Naturally it sounded outrageous in that dim light, I didn't like it. Above the rooftops the sky was coming back in cold little patches, cut out by the eaves. Sure enough, someone was calling me. I turned around and instantly recognized Leon. He came over to me, speaking in a whisper, and we filled each other in.

He'd been cleaning an office like the rest of them. That was as much of a gimmick as he'd managed to find. He walked heavily, with a certain true majesty, as if he had been doing dangerous and in a way sacred things in the city. Actually I'd noticed that all those night cleaners had that look. In fatigue and solitude men emanate the divine. His eyes were also full of it when, in the bluish half-light where we were standing, he opened them wider than eyes usually open. He, too, had cleaned endless rows of toilets and made whole mountains of silent offices sparkle.

"Ferdinand," he said. "I recognized you right away. By the way you got into the car... By the sad look on your face when you saw there were no women on board. Am I right? Isn't that your style?" He was right, it was my style. Unquestionably, my soul was as obscene as an open fly. So his observation was apt and nothing to be surprised at. What I hadn't expected was that he too was a failure in America. That came as a surprise.

I told him about the galley at San Tapeta. But he didn't know what I was talking about. "You're delirious!" he said simply. He'd come over on a freighter. He'd have tried for a job at Ford's, but his papers were just too phony, he wouldn't have dared show them. "They're barely good enough to keep in my pocket," he said. For cleaning offices they didn't much care who you were. They didn't pay much either, but they looked the other way... This night work was a kind of Foreign Legion, "What about you?" he asked me then. "What are you doing? You still cracked? Still chasing rainbows? Still got the travel bug?"

"I want to go back to France," I said. "I've seen enough, you're right... "

"Best thing you can do," he said. "For us the jig is up... We've aged without noticing it, I know... I'd like to go home too, but there's still this trouble with my papers... I'll wait a while and try and get hold of some good ones... I can't complain about the work I'm doing... There's worse. But I'm not learning English... Some of the guys have been at it for thirty years and all they've learned is 'Exit,' because it's written on the doors they polish, and 'Lavatory.' You get the drift?"

I got the drift. If Molly should ever fail me, I'd have to go into night work myself. No reason why that should ever stop.

The fact is that when you're at war you say peace will be better, you bite into that hope as if it were a chocolate bar, but it's only shit after all. You don't dare say so at first for fear of making people mad. You try to be nice. When you're good and sick of wallowing in muck you speak up. Then everybody thinks you were raised in a barn. And there you have it.

I met Robinson two or three times after that. He wasn't looking at all well. A French deserter, who made bootleg liquor for the gangsters of Detroit, let him occupy a corner of his shop. The business tempted Robinson. "I'd make a little rotgut for those bastards to pour down their throats," he confided, "but you know, I've lost my nerve... The first going-over a cop gave me, I know I'd fold up... I've been through too much... Besides, I'm sleepy all the time... Not to mention the dust in those offices, my lungs are full of it... See what I mean? It wears you down... "

We arranged to meet another night. I went back to Molly and told her the whole story. She tried not to show how bad I was making her feel, but it wasn't hard to see she was miserable. I kissed her more often now, but her unhappiness was deep, more real than in other people, because most of us tend to talk as if things were worse than they are. American women are different. We're afraid to understand, to admit it. It's rather humiliating, but this is real unhappiness, not pride, not jealousy, there are no scenes, it's genuine heartbreak. We may as well admit that we haven't got it in us and that when it comes to the pleasure of being really unhappy we're bone dry. We're ashamed of not being richer in heart and everything else, and also of having judged humanity worse than it really is.

Now and then Molly would let go and say something mildly reproachful, but it was always said gently and kindly.

"You're sweet, Ferdinand," she'd say. "I know you try hard not to be as beastly as other people, but sometimes I wonder if you really know what you want. Think it over. You'll have to find a way of earning your living when you get back there, Ferdinand... You won't be able to roam around all night dreaming the way you do here... the way you enjoy so much... while I'm working... Have you thought of that, Ferdinand?"

In a way she was dead right, but I couldn't help being the way I was. I was afraid of hurting her. She was so easy to hurt.

"Believe me, Molly, I love you, I always will... as best I can... in my own way."

My own way didn't amount to much. And yet Molly had a perfect body, she was very tempting. But I had that lousy weakness for phantoms. Maybe I wasn't entirely to blame. Life forces you to spend too much of your time with phantoms.

"You're very affectionate, Ferdinand," she reassured me. "Don't worry about me... You've got this sickness... always wanting to know more and more... That's all... Anyway, you have to live your own life... Out there, all alone... You'll go further traveling alone... Will you be leaving soon?"

"Yes, I'll finish medical school in France, and then I'll come back," I had the gall to assure her. "No, Ferdinand, you won't be back... And I won't be here either... "

She was nobody's fool.

It came time for me to go. One evening shortly before she'd have to start working, we went to the station. I'd said good-bye to Robinson during the day. He wasn't happy either to see me go. I was always leaving people. On the station platform, while we were waiting for the train, some men passed, they pretended not to know her, but they exchanged whispers.

"You're already far away, Ferdinand. You're doing exactly what you want, aren't you? That's the main thing. It's the only thing that counts... "

The train pulled in. I wasn't so sure of my plans once I saw the engine. I kissed Molly with all the spirit I had left... I was sad for once, really sad, for everybody, for myself, for her, for everybody.

Maybe that's what we look for all our lives, the worst possible grief, to make us truly ourselves before we die.

Years have passed since I left her, years and more years... I wrote many times to Detroit and all the other addresses I remembered, where I thought she might be known. I never received an answer.

The house is closed now. That's all I've been able to find out. Good, admirable Molly, if ever she reads these lines in some place I never heard of, I want her to know that my feelings for her haven't changed, that I still love her and always will in my own way, that she can come here any time she pleases and share my bread and furtive destiny. If she's no longer beautiful, hell, that's all right too! We'll manage. I've kept so much of her beauty in me, so living and so warm, that I've plenty for both of us, to last at least twenty years, the rest of our lives.

To leave her I certainly had to be mad, and in a cold, disgusting way. Still, I've kept my soul in one place up to now, and if death were to come and take me tomorrow, I'm sure I wouldn't be quite as cold, as ugly, as heavy as other men, and it's thanks to the kindness and the dream that Molly gave me during my few months in America.

* * *

Getting back from the Other World isn't the half of it. You pick up the sticky, precarious thread of your days just as you left it dangling. It's waiting for you.

For weeks and months I hung around the Place Clichy, where I'd started from, and environs, the Batignolles for instance, doing odd jobs. Ghastly! Under the rain, or in the heat of the cars when June came, that burns your throat and nose, almost like at Ford's. For entertainment I'd watch them pass, people and more people, on their way to the theater or the Bois in the evening.

Always more or less alone in my free time, I'd mull over books and newspapers and all the things I'd seen. I resumed my studies, all the while working for a living, and finally managed to pass my examinations. Science, take it from me, is closely guarded, the Faculty of Medicine is a well-locked cupboard. Plenty of jars and very little jam. But after braving five or six years of academic tribulations I got my degree, a very high- sounding piece of paper. Then I put up my shingle in the suburbs, my sort of place, at La Garenne- Rancy,[60] right after the Porte Brancion[61] on your way out of Paris.

I had no great opinion of myself and no ambition, all I wanted was a chance to breathe and to eat a little better. I put my name-plate over the door and waited.

The neighborhood people came and eyed my name-plate suspiciously. They even went to the police station to ask if I was a real doctor. Yes, they were told. He's filed his diploma, he's a doctor all right. The news spread all over Rancy that a real doctor had set up shop in addition to all the others. "He'll never make a living," my concierge predicted. "There are too many doctors around here already!" She was perfectly right.

In the suburbs it's mostly by streetcar that life turns up in the morning. Starting at dawn, whole strings of them would come clanking down the Boulevard Minotaure, carrying loads of dazed citizens to work.

The young ones actually seemed happy about it. They'd cheer the traffic on and cling to the running boards, laughing for all they were worth, the darlings! It's hard to believe. But when you've known the telephone booth of the corner cafe for twenty years, so filthy you always mistake it for the crapper, you lose all desire to joke about serious things and about Rancy in particular. Then you realize where they've put you. These houses are your prison, pissy within, flat facades, their heart belongs to the landlord. You never see him. He wouldn't dare show his face. The bastard sends his agent. Yet the neighborhood people say he's affable enough when you meet him. It doesn't cost him a thing.

The sky in Rancy is the same as in Detroit, a smoky soup that bathes the plain all the way to Levallois. Cast- off buildings bogged down in black muck. From a distance the chimneys, big ones and little ones, look like the fat stakes that rise out of the muck by the seaside. And inside it's us.

You need the courage of a crab at Rancy, especially when you're not as young as you used to be and you know you'll never get away. There at the end of the streetcar line a grimy bridge spans the Seine, that enormous sewer which displays everything that's in it. Along the banks, on Sunday and at night, men climb up on the piles of garbage to take a leak. Flowing water makes men meditative. They urinate with a sense of eternity like sailors. Women never meditate. Seine or no Seine. In the morning the streetcar carries away its crowds to get themselves compressed in the Metro. Seeing them all fleeing in that direction you'd think there must have been some catastrophe at Argenteuil, that the town was on fire. Every day in the gray of dawn it comes over them, whole clusters cling to the doors and handrails. One enormous rout! Yet all they're going to Paris for is a boss, the man who saves you from starvation. The cowards, they're scared to death of losing him, though he makes them sweat for their pittance. For ten years you stink of it, for twenty years and more. It's no bargain.

Plenty of bitching and beefing in the streetcar, just to get into practice. The women gripe even worse than the kids. If they caught somebody without a ticket, they'd stop the whole line. It's true that some of those women are already stinko, especially the ones headed for the market at Saint-Ouen, the semibour-geoises. "How much are the carrots?" they ask long before they get there, to show they've got money to spend.

Compressed like garbage in this tin box, they cross Rancy, stinking good and proper especially in the summer. Passing the fortifications,[62] they threaten one another, they let out one last shout, and then they scatter, the Métro swallows them up, limp suits, discouraged dresses, silk stockings, sour

---

[60] La Garenne-Rancy. There actually is a La Garenne (La Garenne-Columbes) in the Paris suburbs, not far from where this imaginary town seems to be. The word garenne means "rabbit warren." Rancy suggests rance, meaning "rancid."

[61] Porte Brancion. All other indications are that La Garenne-Rancy was situated north-northwest of Paris. The Porte Brancion is on the southern rim of the city.

[62] Fortifications. These fortifications were built between 1841 and 1844, in the reign of Louis-Philippe, to protect Paris from foreign invasion. They consisted of a circular wall thirty-nine kilometers long with ninety-four bastions. Used during the siege of Paris by the Prussians in the war of 1870, they were destroyed after the First World War.

stomachs, dirty feet, dirty socks. Wear-ever collars as stiff as boundary posts, pending abortions, war heroes, all scramble down the coal-tar and carbolic-acid stairs into the black pit, holding their return ticket which all by itself costs as much as two breakfast rolls.

The nagging dread of being fired without ceremony, something (accompanied by a tight-lipped reference) that can happen to a tardy worker any time the boss decides to cut down on expenses. Never-dormant recollections of the "Slump," of the last time they were unemployed, of all the newspapers they had to buy for the want ads, five sous a piece... the waiting in line at employment offices... Such memories can strangle a man, however well protected he may seem in his "all-weather" coat.

The city does a good job of hiding its crowds of dirty feet in those long electric sewers. They won't rise to the surface again until Sunday. You'd better stay indoors when they emerge. Just one Sunday watching their attempts to amuse themselves will permanently spoil your taste for pleasure. Around the Métro entrance, near the bastions, you catch the endemic, stagnant smell of long drawn-out wars, of spoiled, half- burned villages, aborted revolutions, and bankrupt businesses. For years the ragpickers of the "Fortified Zone"[63] have been burning the same damp little piles of rubbish in ditches sheltered from the wind. Half- assed barbarians, undone by red wine and fatigue. They take their ruined lungs to the local dispensary instead of pushing the streetcars off the embankment and emptying their bladders in the tollhouse.[64] No blood left in their veins. When the next war comes, they'll get rich again selling rat skins, cocaine, and corrugated-iron masks.

For my practice I had found a small apartment at the edge of the "Zone," from which I had a good view of the embankment and the workman who's always standing up top, looking at nothing, with his arm in a big white bandage, the victim of a work accident, who doesn't know what to do or what to think and hasn't enough money to buy himself a drink and fill his mind.

Molly had been right, I was beginning to understand her. Study changes a man, puts pride into him. You need it to get to the bottom of life. Without it you just skim the surface. You think you're in the know, but trifles throw you off. You dream too much. You content yourself with words instead of going deeper. That's not what you wanted. Intentions, appearances, no more. A man of character can't content himself with that. Medicine, even if I wasn't very gifted, had brought me a good deal closer to people, to animals, everything. Now all I had to do was plunge straight into the heart of things. Death is chasing you, you've got to hurry, and while you're looking you've got to eat, and keep away from wars. That's a lot of things to do. It's no picnic.

In the meantime I wasn't getting many patients. It takes time to get started, people said to comfort me. At the moment the patient was mostly me.

Nothing, it seemed to me, can be gloomier than La Garenne-Rancy when you've got no patients. No doubt about it. You shouldn't think in a place like that, and I'd come, from the other end of the earth what's more, precisely to think at my ease. Wasn't I in luck! Stuck-up simpleton! Black and heavy it came over me... No joke, and it stayed with me. There's no tyrant like a brain.

Below me lived Bézin, the little junk dealer. Whenever I stopped outside his door he said to me: "You got to choose, doctor! Play the races or drink, it's one or the other!... You can't have everything!... I prefer my apéritif! I don't care for gambling... "

His favorite apéritif was gentiane-cassis. Not a bad-natured man ordinarily, but unpleasant after a few drinks... When he went to the Flea Market to stock up, he'd stay away for three days, his "expedition" he called it. They'd bring him back. And then he'd prophesy:

"I can see what the future will be like... An endless sex orgy... With movies in between... You can see how it is already... "

On those occasions he could see even further: "I also see that people will stop drinking... I'll be the last drinker in the future... I've got to hurry... I know my weakness... "

---

[63] Fortified Zone. Propertly "le Zone Militaire de Paris," commonly referred to simply as la Zone, "the Zone." The strip of land between the fortifications and the suburbs, where for military reasons construction was prohibited. In late popular usage the more depressing suburbs on the outskirts of Paris.
[64] Tollhouse. Up to the late twenties a tax was levied on certain foodstuffs entering Paris. There were toll stations (octroi) at all the city gates.

Everybody coughed in my street. It keeps you busy. To see the sun you have to climb up to Sacré-Coeur at least, because of the smoke.

From up there you get a beautiful view; then you realize that way down at the bottom of the plain it's us and the houses we live in. But if you try to pick out any particular place, everything you see is so ugly, so uniformly ugly, that you can't find it.

Still further down it's always the Seine, winding from bridge to bridge like an elongated blob of phlegm.

When you live in Rancy you don't even realize how sad you've become. You simply stop feeling like doing anything much. What with scrimping and going without this and that, you stop wanting anything.

For months I borrowed money right and left. The people were so poor and so suspicious in my neighborhood that they couldn't make up their minds to send for me before dark, though I was the cheapest doctor imaginable. I spent nights and nights crossing little moonless courtyards in quest of ten or fifteen francs.

In the morning there was such a beating of carpets the whole street sounded like one big drum.

One morning I met Bébert on the sidewalk; his aunt, the concierge, was out shopping, and he was holding down the lodge for her. He was raising a cloud from the sidewalk with a broom.

Anybody who didn't raise dust at seven o'clock in the morning in those parts would get himself known all up and down the street, as an out-and-out pig. Carpet beating was a sign of cleanliness, good housekeeping. Nothing more was needed. Your breath could stink all it liked, no matter. Bebert swallowed all the dust he raised in addition to what was sent down from the upper floors. Still, a few spots of sunlight reached the street, but like inside a church, pale, muffled, mystic.

Bebert had seen me coming, I was the neighborhood doctor who lived near the bus stop. Bébert had the greenish look of an apple that would never get ripe. He was scratching himself, and watching him made me want to scratch too. The fact is I had fleas myself, I'd caught them from patients during the night. They like to jump up on your overcoat, because it's the warmest and dampest place available. You learn that in medical school.

Bébert abandoned his carpet to come and say good morning. From every window they watched us talking.

If you've got to love something, you'll be taking less of a chance with children than with grownups, you'll at least have the excuse of hoping they won't turn out as crummy as the rest of us. How are you to know?

I've never been able to forget the infinite little smile of pure affection that danced across his livid face. Enough gaiety to fill the universe.

Few people past twenty preserve any of that affection, the affection of animals. The world isn't what we expected. So our looks change! They change plenty! We made a mistake! And turned Into a thorough stinker in next to no time! Past twenty it shows in our face! A mistake! Our face is just a mistake.

"Hey, doctor," Bébert sings out. "Is it true that they picked up a guy on the Place des Fêtes last night. Throat cut open with a razor. You were on duty, weren't you? Is it true?"

"No, Bébert. I wasn't on duty, it wasn't me, it was Dr. Frolichon[65]... "

"That's too bad, 'cause my aunt said she wished you'd have been on duty and you'd have told her all about it... "

"Maybe next time, Bébert."

"Do they often kill people around here?" Bebert asked.

I passed through the dust, but just then the municipal street sweeper whished past and, whirling up from the gutters, a howling typhoon filled the whole street with new clouds, more dense and stinging than the others. We couldn't see each other anymore. Bébert jumped up and down, sneezing and shouting for joy. His haggard face, his greasy hair, his emaciated monkey legs, the whole of him danced convulsively at the end of his broom.

---

[65] Dr. Frolichon. From folichon = "frolicsome."

Bébert's aunt came home from shopping, she had already downed a glass or two. I have to add that she sniffed ether now and then, a habit contracted when she was working for a doctor and having such trouble with her wisdom teeth. The only teeth she had left were two in front, but she never failed to brush them. "When you've worked for a doctor like I have, you don't forget your hygiene." She gave medical consultations in the neighborhood, and as far away as Bezons.

I'd have been interested to know if Bébert's aunt ever thought of anything. No, she thought of nothing. She talked enormously without ever thinking. When we were alone with no one listening, she'd touch me for a free consultation. It was flattering in away.

"Bébert, doctor, I have to tell you because you're a doctor, he's a little pig!... He 'touches' himself! I noticed it two months ago, and I wonder who could have taught him such a filthy habit... I've always brought him up right!... I tell him to stop... but he keeps right on... "

I gave her the classic advice: "Tell him he'll go crazy." Bébert, who'd been listening, wasn't pleased. "I don't touch myself, it's not true. It's the Gagat[66] kid who suggested... "

"See?" said the aunt. "I suspected as much. The Gagats, you know, the people on the fifth floor... They're all perverts. It seems the grandfather runs after female lion tamers... Really, I ask you, lion tamers... Look, doctor, while you're here, couldn't you prescribe a syrup to make him stop touching himself... "

I followed her to her lodge to write out an antivice prescription for Bébert. I was too easy with everybody, I knew that. Nobody paid me. I treated them all free of charge, mostly out of curiosity. That's a mistake. People avenge themselves for the favors done them. Bébert's aunt took advantage of my lofty disinterestedness. In fact she imposed on me outrageously. I let things ride. I let them lie to me. I gave them what they wanted. My patients had me in their clutches. Every day they sniveled more, they had me at their mercy. And while they were at it they showed me all the ugliness they kept hidden behind the doors of their souls and exhibited to no one but me. The fee for witnessing such horrors can never be high enough. They slither through your fingers like slimy snakes.

I'll tell you the whole story some day if I live long enough.

"Listen, you scum! Let me do you favors for a few years more. Don't kill me yet. Looking so servile and defenseless; I'll tell the whole story. You'll fade away like the oozing caterpillars in Africa that came into my shack to shit... I'll make you into subtler cowards and skunks than you are, and maybe it'll kill you in the end."

"Is it sweet?" Bébert asked about the medicine.

"Don't make it sweet whatever you do," said the aunt. "For that little creep... He don't deserve to have it sweet, he steals enough sugar from me already. He has every vice, he'll stop at nothing. He'll end up murdering his mother!"

"I haven't got a mother," said Bébert peremptorily. He had his wits about him.

"Damn you!" cried the aunt. "None of your back talk, or I'll give you the cat o'nine tails!" Then and there she takes it down off the hook, but he'd already beat it out into the street. "Cock-sucker!" he shouted back at her from the corridor. The aunt went red in the face and came back to me. Silence. We changed the subject.

"Maybe, doctor, you ought to go and see the lady on the mezzanine at 4 Rue des Mineures... He used to be a notary's clerk... She's heard about you... I told her what a wonderful doctor you are, so nice to the patients."

I know she's lying. Her favorite doctor is Frolichon. She always recommends him when she can and runs me down at every opportunity. As far as she's concerned, my humanitarianism has earned me an animal hatred. Because, don't forget, she's an animal. Except that this Frolichon she admires makes her pay cash, so she consults me on the run. If she recommends me, this must be a strictly nonpaying patient, or there's something very shady somewhere. As I'm leaving, I remember Bébert, "You ought to take him out," I said. "The child doesn't get out enough."

"Where do you want us to go? I can't go very far on account of my lodge... " "Take him to the park at least on Sunday... "

---

[66] Gagat. From gaga, feeble-minded.

"But there are even more people and more dust in the park than here... It's so crowded." There's some sense in what she says. I try to think of another place to suggest.

Diffidently I propose the cemetery.

The cemetery of La Garenne-Rancy is the only open space of any size in the neighborhood with a few trees in it.

"Say, that's a fact, I hadn't thought of that. Maybe we'll go." Bébert had just come in.

"How about it, Bébert? Would you like to go for a walk in the cemetery? I have to ask him, doctor, because I don't mind telling you, he's as stubborn as a mule about taking a walk... "

Actually, Bébert has no opinion. But the idea appeals to his aunt, and that's enough. She has a weakness for cemeteries, like all Parisians. It looks as if she were about to start thinking. She examines the pros and cons. The fortifications are too low class... The park is definitely too dusty... While the cemetery, sure enough, isn't bad... The people who go there on Sunday are mostly respectable folk who know how to behave... And another thing that makes it really convenient is that on the way back you can shop on the Boulevard de la Liberté, where some of the stores keep open on Sunday.

And she concluded. "Bébert, take the doctor to see Madame Henrouille on the Rue des Mineures... You know where Madame Henrouille lives, don't you, Bébert?"

Bébert knew where everything was, if only it gave him a chance to roam around.

* * *

Between the Rue Ventru and the Place Lénine it's all apartment houses. The contractors have taken over practically all the fields that were left around there, at Les Garennes, as the area was called. There was just a tiny bit of country at the end, a few empty lots after the last gas lamp.

Wedged in between apartment buildings, a few private houses are still holding out, four rooms with a big coal stove in the downstairs hallway; true, for reasons of thrift, the stove is seldom lit. The dampness makes it smoke. These remaining private houses belong to people who have retired on small incomes... The moment you go in, the smoke makes you cough. The people who've stayed in the neighborhood haven't got big incomes, especially these Henrouilles I was being sent to. They had a little something though.

In addition to the smoke, as you stepped in, the Henrouilles' house smelled of the toilet and stew. They'd just finished paying for the place, it represented the savings of at least fifty years. The first time you saw them, you noticed something was wrong and wondered what it was. Well, the unnatural side of the Henrouilles was that for fifty years they had never spent one sou without regretting it. They'd put their flesh and spirit into that house of theirs, like a snail. But the snail doesn't know what he's doing.

The Henrouilles had spent a lifetime acquiring a house, and once it was theirs they couldn't get over it. Like people who've just been dug out of an earthquake, they were flabbergasted. Folks who've just been let out of a dungeon must get a funny look on their faces.

The Henrouilles had thought about buying a house even before they were married. First separately, then together. For half a century they had refused to think about anything else, and when life had forced them to think about something else, the war for instance and especially their son, it made them very unhappy.

When as newlyweds they had moved into their house, each with the savings of ten years, it wasn't quite finished and it was still in the middle of the fields. To reach it in winter, they had to put on sabots; they'd leave them at the grocery store on the corner of the Rue de la Révolte in the morning when they set out for work in Paris, three kilometers distant, by horse car, two sous a ticket.

You need a sturdy constitution to get through a whole lifetime on such a schedule. There was a picture of them over the bed on the upper floor, taken on their wedding day. Their bedroom furniture had all been paid for, ages ago in fact. All the receipted bills that had accumulated in the last ten, twenty, forty years, He pinned together in the top bureau drawer, and the account book, fully up to date, is downstairs in the dining room where they never eat. Henrouille will show you all that if you ask him. On Saturdays he balances the accounts in the dining room. They've always eaten in the kitchen.

I learned these things little by little from them and other people and some from Bébert's aunt. When I knew them a little better, they themselves told me about the terror that had haunted them all their lives, the fear that their only son, who was in business, might find himself in difficulties. For thirty years that ugly thought had more or less kept them awake nearly every night. The boy had set himself up in the feather business! The ups and downs of feathers in the last thirty years are almost unimaginable. Perhaps there's no worse, no more unstable business in all the world than feathers.

Some businesses are so shaky that no one would think of borrowing money to put them back on their feet, but there are others where the question of a loan keeps coming up almost constantly. When it occurred to them, even now that the house was paid for, that their son might approach them for a loan, the Henrouilles stood up from their chairs, looked at each other, and went red in the face. What would they do if that happened? They would refuse.

Their minds had been made up from the first to turn down all requests for a loan , . . Because of their principles and so as to have a nest egg waiting for him, a legacy, a house, an inheritance. That was their way of thinking. There was no nonsense about their son, but in business it's so easy to go wrong...

When they asked me for my opinion, it was the same as theirs.

My own mother was in business; her business had never brought us anything but misery, a little bread and a lot of trouble. So naturally I was down on business. I had no difficulty in understanding the perils facing the boy, the risk involved in a loan he might be forced to envisage if hard pressed. I needed no explanations. For fifty years old man Henrouille had been a petty clerk in a notary's office on the Boulevard Sébastopol. He knew how fortunes can go to rack and ruin, and told me some hair-raising stories about it. Beginning with his own father, whose bankruptcy had prevented Henrouille from studying to be a teacher on leaving school and obliged him to go right into clerking. You remember things like that.

Well, now that their house was bought and paid for and they didn't owe a single sou, they had nothing to worry about on the security side. They were both sixty-five.

Just then Henrouille became aware of a strange ailment, or rather, he'd felt it for a long time but hadn't thought about it because there was still the house to be paid for. Once that was all settled and signed, he began to dwell on his strange trouble—dizzy spells and a whistling as of steam in both ears.

About that time he began buying the newspaper, because then they could afford it. And in the paper he saw an advertisement describing exactly what he felt in his ears. He bought the medicine it recommended, but it didn't do his ailment a bit of good; on the contrary, the whistling seemed to get worse. Maybe just from thinking about it. They finally decided on a visit to the dispensary. "It's high blood pressure," the doctor told them.

Those words came as a shock. But his new obsession came at just the right time. He had worried about the house and his son's bills for so many years that they had left a kind of hole in the tissue of fears that had gripped him body and soul for forty years and raised him to the same pitch of anguished trepidation every time a bill came due. Now that the doctor had spoken of blood pressure, he listened to the pressure beating against his ears from deep inside. He'd get up out of bed to feel his pulse and stand motionless beside his bed, feeling a faint quaver run through his body at every heart beat. All this, he said to himself, was his death. He had always been afraid of life, and now he attached his fear to something different, to death, to his blood pressure, just as for forty years he had attached it to the peril of not being able to finish paying for the house.

He had always been just as unhappy, but now he had quickly to find a good new reason for being unhappy. That's not as easy as it sounds. Just saying: "I'm unhappy" won't do. You've got to prove it, to make absolutely sure. That's all he wanted: to be able to state a good substantial motive for his fear. According to the doctor, his blood pressure was twenty-two. Twenty-two is something. The doctor had taught him to find the way to his own death.

Their son in the feather business hardly ever came to see them. Once or twice around New Year's, no more. There wasn't much point in his coming anymore. His father and mother had nothing left to lend. So he hardly ever turned up.

It took me longer to get to know Madame Henrouille; she had no fears, not even the fear of her own death, which she couldn't conceive of. She only complained of old age, but without really thinking about it, just to be like other people, and about the high cost of living. Their life's labor was behind them. The house was paid for. To speed up the final payments she'd even taken to sewing buttons on waistcoats for one of the department stores. "The amount of buttons you've got to sew on for five francs, you wouldn't believe it!" she'd say. And delivering her work on the bus, she rode second class and things were always happening. One afternoon a woman had bumped into her. Madame Henrouille had given her a piece of her mind. The woman was a foreigner, the first and only foreigner Madame Henrouille had ever spoken to.

The walls of the house had kept good and dry in the old days when there was still air circulating around them, but now that there were tall apartment buildings next door, everything oozed and trickled with humidity, even the curtains had a musty smell.

Once the house was really theirs, Madame Henrouille had been all smiles for a whole month, as blissful as a nun after communion. In fact she was the one who had suggested: "Look, Jules, suppose we buy a newspaper every day, now we can afford it!" Just like that. She had thought of her husband, she had looked at him. But then she looked around her and after a while she thought of his mother, her mother-in-law Henrouille. At that the daughter-in-law went suddenly serious again, the way she had been before they finished paying for the house. That thought brought them back to square one, it meant they would have to go on saving for the old woman, her husband's mother, whom the two of them never mentioned to each other or to anyone outside.

She lived at the far end of the garden with an accumulation of old brooms, old chicken crates, and the shadows of buildings. Her home was a low shed, from which she seldom emerged. Just getting meals in to her was a long complicated business. She wouldn't admit anyone to her antrum, not even her son. She was afraid of being murdered, so she said.

When the daughter-in-law thought of embarking on a new course of savings, she first said a few words to her husband to sound him out: Why, for instance, wouldn't they send the old woman to St. Vincent's Convent where the Sisters took care of feeble-minded old women like her. The son said neither yes nor no. He was busy with something else at the moment, those sounds in his ears that never stopped. What with thinking about that abominable whistling and listening to it, he'd convinced himself that it would prevent him from sleeping. And true enough, instead of falling asleep, he'd listen to his whistling, drummings, and hummings—a new torture that kept him busy day and night. He had all those noises inside him.

Little by little, though, his anxiety wore itself out, and there wasn't enough left to keep him busy all by itself. So then he and his wife started going back to the market at Saint-Ouen. Everyone said it was the cheapest for miles around. They'd leave home in the morning, and it took them all day, because of all the figures they added up and the discussions they'd have about the prices of things and the money they might have saved by buying one thing rather than another... Back home at about eleven that night, they'd be seized again by the fear of being murdered. That fear hit them regularly, especially the wife. He was more concerned with the sounds in his ears, he'd cling to them desperately at that hour when the street was perfectly still.

"I'll never be able to sleep!" he'd repeat to himself out loud to increase his terror. "You can't imagine!"

But she never tried to understand what he meant, or to imagine why this buzzing in his ears should trouble him so. "You hear me when I speak, don't you?" she'd ask him.

"Yes," he'd say.

"Well, then you're all right!... And it would make more sense to start thinking about your mother who's been costing us a fortune what with prices going up every day... And the stink in that shack of hers!"

The cleaning woman came in for three hours a week to do the washing, she was the only visitor they had had for years. She also helped Madame Henrouille to make her bed. Every time they had turned the mattress in the last ten years, Madame Henrouille, wanting it to be repeated all over the neighborhood, had told the cleaning woman in the loudest voice she could manage: "We never keep money in the house!" Just as a precaution, to discourage thieves and prospective murderers.

Before going up to their room together, they would close all the doors and windows with great care, each checking up on the other. Then they'd go out in the garden to make sure the mother-in-law's lamp was still burning. A sign she was still alive. She consumed quantities of oil. She never put her lamp out. She, too, was afraid of murderers and afraid of her son and daughter-in-law. In all the twenty years she'd been living there she had never opened her windows summer or winter and never let her lamp go out.

Her son kept his mother's money, a small pension. He took care of it. They left her meals outside the door. They kept her money. Not a bad arrangement. But she complained about the arrangement, and that wasn't all; she complained about everything. She'd shout through the door at anybody who approached her shack. The daughter-in-law would try to pacify her: "It's not our fault if you're getting old. All old people get the same pains... "

"Old yourself! You slattern! You scum! It's you that's killing me with your filthy lies!"

She denied her age ferociously. And through her door she battled irreconcilably against the evils of the whole world. She rejected the fatalities and compromises of the life outside as a base imposture. She refused all contact with such things, she wouldn't hear of them. "It's all a pack of lies!" she'd scream. "You made it up!"

She defended herself bitterly against everything that happened outside her hovel and rejected all temptation to compromise or be reconciled. She was sure that if she opened the door hostile forces would burst in, grab her, and finish her off once and for all.

"They're sly nowadays!" she would scream. "They have eyes all around their heads and mouths all the way down to their assholes and then some, all to tell lies with... It's them all over... "

She had the gift of gab, she had picked it up as a girl, peddling bric-a-brac at the Temple Market with her mother... She harked back to the days when the common people hadn't yet learned to listen to themselves growing old.

"If you won't give me my money I'm going out to work!" she'd shout at her daughter-in-law. "Hear, you slut? I'm going out to work, I want to work!"

"But grandmother, you're not strong enough!"

"Oh! I'm not strong enough! Try and get in here and you'll see if I'm not strong enough!"

So one more time they left her barricaded in her shack. But they were dead set on my seeing the old woman, that's what I'd come for. It took some doing before she let us in. To tell the truth, I couldn't quite see what they wanted of me. It was the concierge, Bébert's aunt, who had told them what a nice doctor I was, so kind and considerate... They asked me if I couldn't give her some medicine to keep her quiet...

But what they (especially the daughter-in-law) wanted even more was for me to get the old woman committed once and for all. After we'd knocked for a good half hour, she suddenly flung the door open, and there she was in front of me with her watery red-rimmed eyes... But there was a look in those eyes that danced merrily over her gray, shrunken cheeks, it caught your attention and made you forget the rest; it gave you a feeling in spite of yourself of lightness and pleasure, a feeling of youth that you tried instinctively to hold on to.

That bright look lit up everything in the darkness around her with a youthful joy, a frail but pure delight that we no longer have at our command. Her voice, which cracked when she screamed, gave her words a cheery ring when she consented to talk like other people, it made her phrases and sentences hop skip and jump as brightly as you please, the way people were able to do with their voices and the things around them in the days when not being able to sing or tell a story properly was looked upon as stupid, shameful, and sick.

Age had covered her, like a sturdy old tree, with smiling branches.

Grandma Henrouille was merry; discontented and filthy, but merry. The destitution in which she had lived for more than twenty years had not marked her soul. Her dread, on the contrary, was the outside world, as though cold, horror, and death could come to her only from that direction and not from within. She evidently feared nothing from within, she seemed absolutely sure of her mind, as of something undeniable, acknowledged, and certified, once and for all.

And to think that I had been chasing mine halfway around the world.

They called the old woman "mad"; that's easy to say. She hadn't set foot outside her den more than three times in the last twelve years, and that's all there was to it. She may have had her reasons... She was afraid of losing something... She wasn't going to tell them to people like us, people who were no longer inspired by life.

Her daughter-in-law brought up her commitment project again. "What do you say, doctor? Don't you think she's mad?... We can't get her to go out anymore!... It would do her good to get out now and then!... Oh yes, grandmother, it would do you good!... Don't say it wouldn't!... It would do you good... I assure you!" The old woman shook her head. She shut herself in, stubborn and savage, when that kind of pressure was put on her...

"She won't let us take care of her... She'd rather relieve herself in the corners... It's cold in her shack, and there's no fire... We really can't let her go on like this... Don't you agree, doctor, that we can't... ?"

I pretended not to understand. Henrouille had stayed home beside the stove, he preferred not to know exactly what his wife and mother and I were cooking up...

The old woman flew off the handle again.

"Give me back everything that's mine and I'll go away... I have money to live on... And that's the last you'll ever hear of me!... "

"Money to live on! But grandmother! You can't expect to live on your three thousand a year!... The cost of living has gone up since the last time you went out!... You tell her, doctor, wouldn't it be better for her to go and live with the Sisters like we told her , . . The Sisters are good and kind... "

But the thought of the Sisters gave her the creeps.

"The Sisters! The Sisters!" she rebelled. "I've never stayed with any Sisters... Why not send me to live with the priest while you're at it!... If I haven't got enough money, as you say, I'll go to work!"

"Work, grandmother? Where? Oh, doctor, would you listen to her! Work at her age! She'll soon be eighty! It's madness, doctor. Who'd want her? Why, you're insane, grandmother!... "

"Insane! Nobody! Nowhere!... Aren't you somewhere?... You lump of shit, you!"

"Listen to her, doctor! She's raving and insulting me! How can you expect us to keep her here?" The old woman turned to confront me, the new peril.

"How does he know if I'm crazy or not? Is he inside my head? Is he inside yours? He'd have to be to know!... Beat it, both of you!... Get out of my home!... The way you keep at me you're meaner than six months of winter!... Go and examine my son instead of standing there jabbering in the henbane! He needs a doctor a sight more than I do! Not a tooth left in his head, and they were perfect when I was taking care of him! Go on, beat it, get out, the both of you!" And she slammed the door in our faces.

From behind her lamp she watched us retreating across the yard. When we'd reached the other side, when we were far enough away, she started snickering again. She'd given a good account of herself.

When we got back from that disagreeable incursion, Henrouille was still standing by the stove, with his back to us. His wife went on pestering me with questions, all aimed in the same direction... She had a dark, sly little face. Her elbows hugged her body when she spoke. She never gestured. She was determined that this medical consultation shouldn't be wasted, she wanted it to serve some purpose... The cost of living was going up all the time... Her mother-in-law's pension wasn't enough anymore... They were getting old themselves after all... They couldn't go on forever living in fear that the old woman would die without proper care... that she'd set the house on fire... in her fleas and filth... instead of going to a perfectly good institution, where she'd be taken care of...

Since I put on an air of agreeing with them, they were both as affable as could be... they promised to sing my praises in the neighborhood... if only I'd help them... take pity on them... rid them of the old woman... who was miserable herself, living in the conditions she brought on herself with her obstinacy...

"We could even rent her little house," suggested the husband, who had suddenly woken up... He'd put his foot in it, saying that in front of me. His wife stepped on his foot under the table. He didn't understand why.

While they were wrangling, I thought about the thousand francs I could pocket just by making out a certificate of commitment. They seemed to want it badly... Bébert's aunt had probably told them all about me and assured them that I was the down-at-heelest doctor in all Rancy... and would do anything they asked... They'd never have expected Frolichon to do a thing like that! He was virtuous!

I was deep in these reflections when the old woman burst into the room where we were plotting. She must have suspected something. What a spectacle! She had bunched her ragged skirts over her belly, and there she was, all tucked up, screaming at us and at me in particular. She'd come in from the far end of the garden for that express purpose!

"Blackguard!" she yelled at me point blank. "You can go home! Didn't I tell you to beat it! You won't gain anything by hanging around!... I'm not going to the nuthouse!... Nor to the Sisters either!... Do your damnedest, lie your head off!... You won't get me, you bought and paid-for pimp!... They'll go before I do, the thieves, robbing an old woman!... And you, too, you rotter, you'll end up in jail, I'm telling you, and it won't be long!"

I was certainly out of luck. For once I'd had a chance of making a thousand francs at one stroke! I took to my heels.

When I was out in the street, she leaned over the little peristyle to shout after me in the darkness. "Scoundrel!... Scoundrel!" she shrieked. And the echo came back. The rain was coming down. I ran from lamppost to lamppost as far as the urinal on the Place des Fêtes. The first available shelter.

* * *

In that aedicula at hip height, I found Bébert.

He too had gone there for shelter. He had seen me running out of the Henrouille house. "So that's where you've been... " he said. "Now you'll have to go up and see the people on the fifth floor of our house, it's their daughter... " The girl he was referring to, I knew her well... wide hips, beautiful thighs, long and silky... There was something tender yet willful about her, and in her movements the precise grace that you often find in women who are sexually fit. She had consulted me several times about her pains in the abdomen. At twenty-five, after her third abortion, she was having complications. Her family called it anemia.

You should have seen her, so solidly built and with a taste for coitus unusual in females. Discreet in her ways, modest in dress and speech. Not the least bit hysterical. But well endowed, well fed, well balanced, a champion in her line. An athlete of pleasure. No harm in that. She only went with married men. And only with connoisseurs, men capable of recognizing and appreciating nature's triumphs, who won't settle for some vicious little slut. No, her soft skin, her sweet smile, her way of walking, and the nobly mobile fullness of her hips earned her the heartfelt, well-merited enthusiasm of certain office managers who knew their stuff.

Unfortunately these office managers couldn't divorce their wives on her account. On the contrary, she helped them to stay happily married. So every time she found herself three months gone, it never failed, she went to the midwife. When you're a hot number and you haven't got a sucker handy, life is no bed of roses.

Her mother opened the door by a crack, as cautiously as if she'd been expecting a murderer. She spoke in whispers, but they were so loud, so intense, she might just as well have been cursing.

"Oh, doctor, what have I done to deserve such a daughter! Oh, doctor, you won't breathe a word to anyone in the neighborhood, will you?... I trust you... " She went on and on, airing her fears and spluttering about what the neighbors might think... She was having an attack of knuckleheaded anxiety. Those attacks last a long time.

She gave me time to get used to the dim light in the hallway, the smell of leeks in the soup, the wallpaper with its idiotic leaves and flowers, and her strangled voice. Finally, amid bumblings and exclamations, we reached her daughter's bedside. She lay prostrate, her mind wandering. I'd have like to examine her, but she was losing so much blood, there was such a gooey mess I couldn't see anything in her vagina. Blood clots. A glug-glug between her legs like in the decapitated colonel's neck in the war. All I could do was put back the big wad of cotton and pull up the blanket.

The mother was looking at nothing and listening to nothing but herself. "It'll kill me, doctor! I'll die of shame!" I made no attempt to dissuade her. I didn't know what to do. We could see the father pacing back and forth in the little dining room next door. Apparently he hadn't finished composing his attitude for the occasion. Maybe he was waiting for things to come to a head before selecting a posture. He was in a kind of limbo. People live from one play to the next. In between, before the curtain goes up, they don't quite know what the plot will be or what part will be right for them, they stand there at a loss, waiting to see what will happen, their instincts folded up like an umbrella, squirming, incoherent, reduced to themselves, that is, to nothing. Cows without a train.

But the mother had the leading part as intermediary between her daughter and me. The stage could cave in, she didn't give a damn, she was happy and convinced of her goodness and beauty.

I couldn't count on anyone but myself to break this sickening spell.

I risked suggesting that the girl should be sent straight to the hospital for an emergency operation. A big mistake! I'd given her the cue for her finest speech, the one she'd been waiting for.

"Oh God, the disgrace! The hospital! Oh, doctor! The disgrace of it! All we needed! The last straw!"

There was nothing I could say. I sat down and listened to the mother thrashing about more tumultuously than ever, entangled in her tragic absurdities. Too much humiliation, too much misery culminate in total inertia. The world is too much for you to bear. You give up. While she invoked and provoked Heaven and Hell, thundering disaster, I looked down in defeat and, looking, saw a small puddle of blood forming under the girl's bed, from which a thin trickle oozed slowly along the wall toward the door. A drop fell regularly from the bed springs. Drip drip. The towels between her legs were soaked red. I managed to ask, very timidly, whether the whole placenta had been ejected. The girl's hands, pale and bluish at the tips, hung down on either side of the bed. It was the mother again who answered my question with a flood of disgusting jeremiads. I should have reacted, but I hadn't the strength.

I myself had been so obsessed by my bad luck for so long, I was sleeping so badly that I was just drifting, I didn't care whether one thing happened rather than another. My only thought was that if I had to listen to this screeching mother I was better off sitting than standing. It doesn't take much to please you once you're thoroughly resigned. And anyway, where would I have found the fortitude to interrupt this wild woman who "didn't know how she was going to save the family's honor." What a part! And how she ranted! After every abortion, I knew from experience, she let loose in the same way, trying, it goes without saying, to outdo herself each time! How long it went on she alone could decide! Today she seemed determined to decuple the effect!

She, it occurred to me, must have been beautiful herself, as luscious as you please in her day; but more verbose, I'm pretty sure, more wasteful of energy, more demonstrative than her daughter, whose concentrated intimacy had been one of nature's truly admirable achievements. Those things haven't been studied as closely as they deserve. The mother sensed her daughter's animal superiority and instinctively condemned it out of hand, the unforgettable depth of her fucking, her way of coming like a continent! In any case she was delighted with the theatrical aspect of the disaster. Her mournful tremolos monopolized the attention of our little group, as thanks to her we floundered in chorus. And there was no hope of getting her out of there. I ought to have tried, though. To do something. It was my duty, as they say. But I was too comfortable sitting and too uncomfortable standing.

Their place was a bit more cheerful than the Henrouilles', just as ugly but more comfortable. Cosy. Not sinister like the Henrouilles'. Just plain ugly.

Dazed with fatigue, I glanced around the room. Little things without value that had always been in the family, especially the mantelpiece cover with its little pink velvet bells that you can't buy anymore, and the porcelain Neapolitan, and the sewing table with the beveled mirror, a present no doubt from an aunt in the provinces who had had two of them. I said nothing to the mother about the puddle of blood I saw forming under the bed or the drops that kept falling punctually, she'd have screeched even louder and wouldn't have listened to me anymore. She was never going to stop complaining and venting her indignation. She was dedicated.

Just as well to keep still and look out of the window as the gray velvet of evening took hold of the avenue, house by house, first the smallest, then the others; in the end the big ones are taken, too, and the people moving about in between, more and more faint, vague and blurred, hesitating as they pass from sidewalk to sidewalk before vanishing into the darkness.

Further away, far beyond the fortifications, strings and rows of lights scattered through the night like tacks to hang forgetfulness over the city, and other little lights, red and green, boats and more boats, a whole flotilla come from all directions, tremulously waiting for the great gates of night to open behind the Tower.[67] If that mother had taken a moment to breathe, or better still, if there had been a long moment of silence, I might have dropped everything and tried to forget that it was necessary to live. But she kept at me.

"Couldn't I give her an enema, doctor? What do you think?" I didn't say yes or no, but once again, since she gave me a chance to speak, I advised immediate removal to the hospital. The only response was more yelping, sharper, more resolute, more strident than ever. There was nothing to be done.

I made slowly and quietly for the door.

The shadows now lay between us and the bed.

I could scarcely see the girl's hands resting on the sheet, because the two pallors were so much alike.

I went back and felt her pulse, which was weaker, more furtive than before. Her breath came in gasps. I could still hear her blood dripping on the floor like a watch ticking more and more slowly, more and more faintly. I couldn't do a thing. The mother went ahead of me to the door.

Especially, doctor," she said in a paroxysm of terror, "promise you won't say a word to anyone!" She implored me. "Give me your word!"

I promised anything she wanted. I held out my hand. She gave me twenty francs. She closed the door behind me, little by little.

Downstairs Bébert's aunt was waiting for me with her most solemn expression. "Is it bad?" she inquired. I realized that she'd been waiting for half an hour to collect her usual commission of two francs. To make sure I wouldn't get away. "And how about the Henrouilles? Everything all right?" she asked. She was hoping to collect a tip for them too. "They didn't pay me," I replied. Which was true. Her prepared smile turned to a pout. She suspected me.

"It's really too bad, doctor, if you can't get people to pay you. How can you expect people to respect you?... Nowadays people pay right away or not at all!" That, too, was true. I beat it. I had put my beans on to cook before leaving. Now was the time, at nightfall, to go and buy my milk. During the day people smiled to see me with my bottle. Naturally. No maid.

Winter dragged on, stretching out over months and months. We were always deep in rain and mist, they were at the bottom of everything.

There were plenty of patients, but not many who were willing and able to pay. Medicine is a thankless profession. When you get paid by the rich, you feel like a flunky, by the poor like a thief. How can you take a fee from people who can't afford to eat or go to the movies? Especially when they're at their last gasp. It's not easy. You let it ride. You get soft-hearted. And your ship goes down.

When the quarterly rent came due in January, I first sold my sideboard, I told the neighborhood people I needed the space, because I was planning to give physical culture classes in my dining room. I wonder if anyone believed me. In February, to pay my taxes, I sold my bicycle and the phonograph Molly had given me as a going-away present. It played "No More Worries." The tune is still running through my head. It's all I've got left. As for the records, Bézin had them in his shop for a long time, and then in the end he sold them.

To make myself sound even richer, I told people I was going to buy a car as soon as the warm weather set in and in preparation I wanted to take in a little cash. I suppose I just didn't have the gall to practice medicine seriously. When I was being escorted to the door after giving the family plenty of advice and handing them my prescription, I'd start talking about everything under the sun just to postpone the moment of payment a little longer. I was no good at playing the prostitute. Most of my patients were so wretchedly poor and foul smelling, so disagreeable too, that I always wondered where

[67] The Tower. The Eiffel Tower.

they would ever find the twenty francs owing to me and whether they mightn't murder me to get them back. And yet I needed those twenty francs badly.

Shameful! I still blush to think of it.

"Fees!... " as my colleagues persisted in saying. It didn't stick in their craw. As if the word made it perfectly natural and there were no need to explain... "Shameful!" I couldn't help thinking, you can't get around it. Everything can be explained, I know that. But that doesn't change the fact that the man who takes five francs from the poor and the wicked will be a louse to his dying day. Ever since then, in fact, I've been sure of being as slimy a customer as anyone else. It's not that I've committed orgies and follies with their ten francs. Certainly not. The landlord took most of it, but that's no excuse either. I wish it were, but it isn't. The landlord is shittier than shit, but that's another story.

What with eating my heart out and navigating in the icy showers of the season, I was beginning to look tubercular myself. Naturally. That's what happens when you have to forego practically every pleasure. Now and then I'd buy a few eggs, but my diet consisted mainly of beans and lentils. They take a long time to cook, I'd spend hours in the kitchen watching them boil after my visiting hours, and since I lived on the second floor I had a fine view of the back court. Back courts are the dungeons of row houses. I had plenty of time to look at my court, and especially to hear it.

That's where the shouts and yells of the twenty houses round about crash and rebound, even the cries of the concierges' little birds, rotting away as they pipe for the spring they will never see in their cages beside the privies, which are all clustered together out at the dark end with their ill-fitting, banging doors. A hundred male and female drunks inhabit those bricks and feed the echoes with their boasting quarrels and muddled, eruptive oaths, especially after lunch on Saturday. That's the intense moment in family life. Shouts of defiance as the drink pours down. Papa is brandishing a chair, a sight worth seeing, like an ax, and Mama a log like a saber! Heaven help the weak! It's the kid who suffers. Anyone unable to defend himself or fight back, children, dogs, and cats, is flattened against the wall. After the third glass of wine, the black kind, the worst, it's the dog's turn, Papa stamps on his paw. That'll teach him to be hungry at the same time as people. It's good for a laugh when he crawls under the bed, whimpering for all he's worth. That's the signal. Nothing arouses a drunken woman so much as an animal in pain, and bulls aren't always handy. The argument starts up again, vindictive, compulsive, delirious, the wife takes the lead, hurling shrill calls to battle at the male. Then comes the melee, the smash-up. The uproar descends on the court, the echo swirls through the half-darkness. The children yap with horror. They've found out what Mama and Papa have in them! Their yells draw down parental thunders.

I spent whole days waiting for what sometimes happens after these family scenes to happen. It happened on the fourth floor, across from my window, in the house on the other side.

I couldn't see a thing, but I heard it clearly.

There's an end to everything. It's not always death, it's often something else and possibly worse, especially when there are children.

That's where those tenants lived, at the level where the shadow begins to pale. If the father and mother were alone on the days when this kind of thing happened, they'd first have a long argument and then there'd be a long silence. The situation was building up. They had a bone to pick with the little girl. They called her. She knew. She started whimpering right away. She knew what she was in for. To judge by her voice, she must have been about ten. It took me quite a few times before I understood what the two of them did to her.

First they tied her up; it took a long time, like getting ready for an operation. That gave them a kick. "You little skunk!" cried the father. "The filthy slut!" went the mother. "We'll teach you!" they'd shout together, and bawl her out for all sorts of things that they probably made up. I think they tied her to the bed posts. Meanwhile the child was squeaking like a mouse in a trap. "That won't help you, you little scum. You've got it coming! Oh yes! You've got it coming!" Then came a volley of oaths, you'd have thought she was cursing at a horse. All steamed up. "Stop talking, Mama," said the little girl gently. "Stop talking, Mama! Hit me, but stop talking!" They gave her a terrible thrashing. I listened to the end to make sure I wasn't mistaken, that this was really happening. I couldn't have eaten my beans with that going on. I couldn't close the window either. I was no good for anything. I was helpless. I just stayed there listening, same as everywhere and always. Still, I believed I gained strength listening to such things, the strength to go further, a strange sort of strength, next time I'd be able to go down even deeper and lower, and listen to other plaints that I hadn't heard before or had had difficulty in understanding, because beyond the plaints we hear, there always seem to be others that we haven't yet heard or understood.

When they had beaten her so much she couldn't howl anymore, a little sob continued to come out every time she breathed.

And then I heard the man saying:

"All right, old girl! Step lively! In there!" As happy as a lark.

He said that to the mother, and then the door into the next room would slam behind them. Once she said to him, I heard her: "Oh, Julien, I love you so much, I could eat your shit, even if you made turds this big... "

That was their way of making love, their concierge told me, they'd do it in the kitchen, leaning against the sink. They couldn't do it any other way.

I learned those things about them little by little in the street. When I met them, the three of them together, there was nothing to attract notice. They'd be out for a walk like a normal family. And now and then I'd see the father outside his shop on the corner of the Boulevard Poincaré, where they sold "shoes for sensitive feet." He was the head salesman.

Most of the time our court had only unrelieved horrors to offer. Especially in the summer, it thundered with threats and echoes and blows, with falling objects and people, and unintelligible insults. The sun never reached the bottom. The walls seemed to be painted with dense blue shadows, especially in the corners. The concierges had their own little privies, clustered like so many beehives. At night when they went out to pee they'd bump into the garbage cans, which would boom like thunder.

Washing, strung from window to window, would be trying to dry.

After dinner, when there were no brutalities under way, what you heard was mostly arguments about the races. But those sporting polemics also ended badly as often as not, with assorted swats and wallops, and behind one of the windows, for one reason or another, someone was always knocked cold in the end.

In the summer everything smelled strong. There was no air left in the court, only smells. The prevailing smell by far is cauliflower. A cauliflower can beat ten toilets, even if they're overflowing. It's a known fact. The ones on the third floor were always overflowing. Madame Cézanne, the concierge at No. 8, would come up with her rattan unplugger. I'd watch her working away, and in the end we got to talking. "If I were you," she advised me, "I'd take care of the pregnant women on the quiet... Some of the women in this neighborhood really live it up... You'd hardly believe it!... They'd like nothing better than to use your services... Take it from me... It's better than treating cheap clerks for varicose veins... Besides, they pay cash."

Madame Cézanne had an enormous aristocratic contempt, I don't know where she got it, for anybody who worked...

"The tenants here are never satisfied, you'd think they were in jail, they've got to make trouble for everybody!... One day their toilets are plugged up... Another day their gas leaks... Or their letters are being opened!... Always making nuisances of themselves... Pests! The other day one of them spat in his rent envelope... Did you ever hear the like?"

Sometimes she'd have to give up trying to unplug a toilet, it was too hard. "I don't know what they put in there, but at least they shouldn't let it dry!... I know them... They always send for me too late... If you ask me, they do it on purpose!... In the place where I used to work, it was so hard they had to melt the pipe!... I can't imagine what those people eat... It's double strength... "

* * *

You'd have a hard time talking me out of the idea that Robinson wasn't mostly to blame for my trouble starting up again. At first I didn't pay much attention to my spells. I somehow kept dragging myself from one patient to the next, but I'd become even uneasier than before, more and more so, like in New York, and I was beginning to sleep even worse than usual.

In short, meeting Robinson again had given me a shock, and I seemed to be falling sick again.

With the misery painted all over his face, I felt he was bringing back a bad dream that I'd been unable to get rid of all those years. It was driving me nuts.

All of a sudden he turned up. I'd never see the last of him. He must have been looking for me in the neighborhood, I certainly wasn't looking for him... He was bound to come back again and make me think about his rotten life. Actually everything conspired to make me think of his repulsive substance. Even those people I saw out the window, who didn't look like anything much, just walking in the street, chewing the fat in doorways, rubbing shoulders, made me think of him. I knew what they were after and what they were hiding behind their innocent look. To kill and get killed, that's what they wanted, not all at once of course, but little by little like Robinson, with all the old sorrows they could summon up, all the new miseries and still nameless hatreds, except when they do it with out-and-out war, and then it's quicker.

I didn't even dare go out, for fear of meeting him.

My patients would have to send for me two or three times in a row before I'd make up my mind to visit them. Usually they had called in someone else by the time I got there. My head was a shambles like life itself. I was called to 12 Rue Saint-Vincent, fourth floor, where I'd been only once before. Actually, they came to get me in a car. I recognized the grandfather right away, he wiped his feet elaborately on my doormat. A furtive type, gray and stooped, his grandson was sick and he wanted me to hurry.

I remembered his daughter too, another strapping wench, a little faded, but strong and silent, she always came home to her parents for her abortions. They never scolded her, but all the same they wished she'd finally get married, all the more so since she already had a little boy of two staying with the grandparents.

For no reason at all this child was always getting sick, and when he was sick, the grandfather, the grandmother, and the mother wept together. What made them weep all the more was that he had no legitimate father. It's at times like that that families are most afflicted by irregular situations. The grandparents were convinced, without quite admitting it to themselves, that illegitimate children are more delicate and prone to illness than others.

The father, at any rate the putative father, had cleared out for good. They had talked marriage to him so much that he couldn't take it anymore. He'd beat it so fast that if he was still running he must have been far away by then. Nobody could understand why he had run out on her like that, least of all the girl herself, because he had really enjoyed fucking her.

Now that the fickle lover had gone, all three of them contemplated the child and blubbered. She had given herself to that man "body and soul," as they say. In her opinion that explained everything, it was bound to happen. The baby had come out of her body and left her thighs all wrinkled. The mind is satisfied with phrases, but not the body, the body is more fastidious, it wants muscles. A body always tells the truth, that's why it's usually depressing and disgusting to look at. It's true that I've rarely known a single childbirth to demolish so much youth. All that mother had left, in a manner of speaking, was feelings and a soul. No one wanted her anymore.

Before that clandestine birth, the family had lived in the Filles du Calvaire quarter, they had lived there for years. If they exiled themselves to Rancy, it wasn't for the pleasure of it, it was to hide, to get themselves forgotten, to disappear.

As soon as it became impossible to conceal the pregnancy from the neighbors, they decided to leave their Paris neighborhood to avoid all comments. A removal for honor's sake.

In Rancy they didn't need the respect of their neighbors. In the first place no one knew them in Rancy, and in the second place the municipal government was known all over France for its abominable politics; not to mince words, they were anarchists, thugs. In that kind of community public opinion is of no account.

The family had punished themselves voluntarily, cutting themselves off from all their old relations and old friends. Their tragedy was complete. Nothing more to lose, so they said. Declassed. When you're determined to lose your name, you go among the common people.

They found no fault with anyone. They merely tried to discover by feeble little acts of rebellion what Destiny could have had in mind the day it had played them such a dirty trick.

Living in Rancy gave the daughter only one consolation, but that was a big one. Now she could talk freely to all and sundry about "her new responsibilities." In deserting her, her lover had awakened a passion for heroism and singularity that had lain dormant in her nature. As soon as she felt sure that she would never for the rest of her days lead the same sort of life as most women of her class and background, and that she would always be in a position to invoke the tragedy of a life ruined by her very first love, she adjusted with alacrity to the great disaster that had befallen her and, all things considered, the ravages of fate became tragically welcome. She glorified in her unmarried-mother act.

In the dining room, as her father and I went in, the economy lighting stopped at half-tints and faces appeared only as pale spots, blobs of flesh mumbling words that hung suspended in a penumbra heavy with the smell of old pepper that all heirloom furniture exudes.

The child, lying swaddled on his back in the middle of the table, let me palpate him. To begin with, I pressed the wall of his abdomen, ever so carefully and slowly, from the navel to the testicles, and then still very gravely I auscultated him.

His heartbeat was like a kitten's, sharp and nervous. Then the child had enough of my exploring fingers and began to yell as children can do at that age, incredibly. That was too much. Since Robinson's return I'd been feeling very funny in body and mind, and the little innocent's screams made an abominable impression on me. What screams! Heavens above, what screams! I was at the end of my rope.

Another idea must have helped to provoke my idiotic behavior. In my exasperation, I couldn't stop myself from blurting out all the rancor and disgust I had been holding in for too long.

"Hey," I said to that little bellower, "don't be in such a hurry, you little fool, you'll have plenty of time for bellowing! Never fear, you little idiot, there'll be time to spare. Save your strength. There'll be enough misery to melt your eyes and your head and everything else if you don't watch out!"

The grandmother gave a start:

"What are you saying, doctor?" I repeated simply: "There will be plenty!"

"What?" she asked in horror. "Plenty of what?"

"You have to understand!" I said. "You have to understand. You're always having things explained to you! That's the whole trouble! Try to understand! Make an effort!"

"What will be left... What's he saying?" they all three asked one another. The daughter "with the responsibilities" made a strange face and started emitting prodigiously long screams. Here was a marvelous occasion for a fit, and she wasn't going to miss it. She meant business. She kicked! She choked! She squinted horribly! I'd done it all right! You should have seen her! "Mama, he's mad!" She bellowed so hard she almost choked. "The doctor's gone mad! Mama, take my baby away from him!" She was saving her child.

I shall never know why, she began in her agitation to take on a Basque accent. "He's saying such awful things! Mameng!... He's insane!... "

They snatched the baby out of my hands as if they were rescuing him from the flames. The grandfather, who had been so deferential only a short while ago, unhooked an enormous mahogany thermometer from the wall, it was as big as a club... And he pursued me at a distance to the door, which he slammed violently behind me with a big kick.

Naturally they took advantage of the incident not to pay for my call...

When I found myself back on the street, I wasn't exactly pleased with what had happened. Not so much because of my reputation, which couldn't have been worse in the neighborhood than people had already made it with no help from me, as because of Robinson, from whom I had hoped to deliver myself with my outburst of frankness, to find the strength never to see him again by deliberately creating a scandal, by stirring up this hideous scene with myself.

Here's what I figured: by my little experiment I'd see how much of a stink it's possible to kick up at one throw. The trouble with scenes and tantrums is that you're never finished, you never know how far you'll be forced to go in your frankness . , . What people are still hiding from you... And what they'll show you some day... if you live long enough... if you go far enough into the heart of their cock-and-bull stories... The whole business would have to be started all over again.

I, too, just then, was in a hurry to hide. I started for home by way of the Impasse Gibet, then I took the Rue Valentines. It was quite a distance. Time to change my mind. I headed for the lights. On the Place Transitoire I met Péridon the lamp lighter. We exchanged a few innocent remarks. "On your way to the movies, doctor?" he asked me. That gave me the idea. A good one, I thought.

The bus gets you there quicker than the Métro. After that shameful incident I'd have been glad to leave Rancy for good if I'd been able to.

When you stay too long in the same place, things and people go to pot on you, they rot and start stinking for your special benefit.

* * *

In spite of everything it was just as well that I went back to Rancy next day, because of Bébert, who fell sick just then. My colleague Frolichon had just gone off on his vacation. Bébert's aunt hesitated, then she asked me to take care of her nephew after all, probably because I charged less than any other doctor she knew.

It was after Easter. The weather was looking up. The first south winds were passing over Rancy, the ones that blew all the soot from the factories down on our windowpanes.

Bébert was sick for weeks and weeks. I went to see him twice a day. The neighborhood people would wait for me outside the lodge, pretending to be just passing by, and on the doorsteps of their houses. It gave them something to do. People would come a long way to find out if he was better or worse. The sunshine has too many things to pass through; it never gives the street anything better than an autumn light full of regrets and clouds.

People gave me lots of advice in connection with Bébert. The fact is, the whole neighborhood took an interest in his case. Some thought well, others poorly, of my intelligence. When I went into the lodge, a critical, rather hostile, and most of all crushingly stupid silence set in. The lodge was always full of the aunt's cronies, it smelled strongly of petticoats and rabbit piss. Each had her own favorite doctor, who was cleverer and more learned than any other. I presented only one advantage, but one that's hard to forgive, I charged hardly anything. A free-gratis doctor is bad for the reputation of a patient and his family, however poor they may be.

Bébert wasn't delirious yet, he had just lost all desire to move. He was losing weight by the day. A bit of yellow, flabby flesh still clung to his bones and quivered from top to bottom every time his heart beat. He'd got so thin in over a month of illness that his heart seemed to be all over his body. He'd look at me with a lucid smile when I came to see him. Sweetly he ran a temperature of 102, then of 103, and there he lay with a pensive look on his face for days and weeks.

After a while Bébert's aunt had shut up and stopped bothering us. She had said everything she knew. That took the wind out of her sails, so she'd go and blubber in one corner of her lodge after another. Grief had come to her when she ran out of words, and she didn't seem to know what to do with it. She'd try to wipe it off with her handkerchief, but it came back in her throat all mixed with tears, and she'd start all over again. She'd get it all over her and manage to be a little dirtier than usual. That would upset her and she'd cry out: "Oh dear! Oh dear!" That was all. She had cried so much she was exhausted, her arms would fall to her sides, and she'd stand there in front of me, absolutely bewildered.

But then after all she'd go back into her grief and give herself a jolt and start sobbing again. These comings and goings in her misery went on for weeks. I couldn't dispel the feeling that this illness would end badly. It was a kind of malignant typhoid that baffled all my efforts, baths, serum, dry diet, vaccines... Nothing helped. I did everything I could think of... all in vain. Bébert was going, being carried away irresistibly, smiling all the while. He was high up, balanced on top of his fever, and I was down below making a fool of myself. Naturally a lot of people were advising the aunt, pressing her to fire me in no uncertain terms and call in another, more imposing and more experienced doctor in a hurry.

The incident of the girl "with the responsibilities" had gone the rounds and been liberally commented on. The whole neighborhood was gargling with it.

But since the other doctors, once informed of the nature of Bébert's illness, showed no eagerness to take the case, I was kept on in the end. As long as Bébert had fallen to my lot, my colleagues figured, I might as well see him through.

All I could do was go to the bistrot now and then and phone various doctors in the Paris hospitals, with whom I was more or less acquainted, and ask those sage, widely respected luminaries what they would do if faced with a case of typhoid like the one that was driving me mad. They all gave me excellent, ineffectual advice, but all the same it pleased me to hear them making an effort free of charge for the benefit of the unknown child I had taken under my wing. After a while you start taking pleasure in the merest trifles, the small consolations life deigns to give us.

While I was busying myself with such subtleties, Bébert's aunt was collapsing on every chair and staircase in the house; she'd emerge from her daze only to eat. But she never missed a meal. Her neighbors wouldn't have let her forget. They watched over her. They stuffed her between sobs. "It'll keep your strength up!" they declared. She even began to put on weight.

Speaking of Brussels sprouts, the smell rose to orgiastic heights at the peak of Bébert's illness. It was the season. Everyone was making her presents of Brussels sprouts, ready cooked and steaming hot. "It's true,"
she was glad to admit, "they give me strength. And besides, they make me urinate."

Before bedtime, because of the doorbell, so as to sleep lightly and hear the very first ring, she'd fill herself full of coffee. That way the tenants wouldn't wake Bébert by ringing two or three times. Passing by the house in the evening, I'd go in to see if maybe it was all over. She'd speculate out loud: "Don't you think it may have been the rum and camomile tea he drank at the fruit store the day of the bicycle race that made him sick?" That idea had been plaguing her from the start. The stupid fool.

"Camomile!" Bébert murmured faintly, an echo submerged in his fever. Why try to tell her different? I'd go through the two or three professional motions she expected of me, and then I'd go and face the night, not at all pleased with myself, because, like my mother, I could never feel entirely innocent of any horrible thing that happened.

About the seventeenth day I decided that it might not be a bad idea to drop in at the Joseph Bioduret Institute[68] and ask them what they thought about a typhoid case of this kind. Maybe they'd give me a bit of advice or recommend some vaccine. That way, if Bébert were to die, I'd have done everything possible, tried everything, however out of the way, and then perhaps I wouldn't feel eternally guilty. At about eleven o'clock one morning I arrived at the Institute near La Villette at the other end of Paris. First they sent me wandering through laboratories and more laboratories, looking for a man of science. There wasn't a soul in those laboratories at that hour, neither laymen nor men of science, only various objects in wild disorder, the gutted bodies of small animals, cigarette butts, chipped gas jets, cases and jars with mice suffocating inside them, retorts, bladders, broken stools, books, dust, and more cigarette butts, which, mingled with the effluvia of the urinals, made up the prevailing smell. Since I was early, I thought while I was at it, I'd go and visit the tomb of that great scientist, Joseph Bioduret, which was right there in the basement of the Institute, in with the gold and marble. A bourgeoiso-Byzantine fantasy in the best of taste! The collection was taken on your way out of the crypt, and the guard was grumbling because someone had slipped him a Belgian coin. In the last half-century the shining example of this Bioduret had led any number of young people to choose the scientific career. And the scientific career had produced as many failures as the Conservatory. After a certain number of years of failure, scientists turn out to be pretty much alike. In the mass graves of the great débâcle a Doctor of Medicine is as good as a "Prix de Rome." The only difference is that they don't take the bus at exactly the same time of day. That's all.

I had to wait quite a long while in the garden of the Institute, a combination of prison yard and city square, with flowers carefully lined up along malignantly decorated walls.

At last some underlings began to turn up. Several, dragging their feet listlessly, were carrying provisions from the nearby market in large shopping bags. Then, in small, unshaven, whispering groups, the men of science came sauntering through the gate, more slowly and diffidently than their humble assistants, and dispersed down different corridors, scraping the paint off the walls as they

---

[68] Joseph Bioduret Institute. Bioduret seems to suggest the prolongation of life. The institute is clearly the Pasteur Institute. True, the Pasteur Institute is at the opposite end of Paris from La Villette. But this is just Célinian mystification. The institute is accurately located off the Rue de Vaugirard a few pages further on.

passed. Gray-haired, umbrella- carrying schoolboys, stupefied by the pedantic routine and intensely revolting experiments, riveted by starvation wages for their whole adult lives to these little microbe kitchens, there to spend interminable days warming up mixtures of vegetable scrapings, asphyxiated guinea pigs, and other nondescript garbage.

They themselves, when all's said and done, were nothing but monstrous old rodents in overcoats. Glory, in our time, smiles only on the rich, men of science or not. All those plebeians of Research had to keep them going was their fear of losing their niches in this heated, illustrious, and compartmented garbage pail. What meant most to them was the title of official scientist, thanks to which the pharmacists of the city still trusted them more or less to analyse, for the most niggardly pay incidentally, their customers' urine and sputum. The slimy wages of science.

Arriving in his compartment, the methodic researcher would spend a few moments gazing ritually at the bilious, decaying viscera of last week's rabbit, which was on classic and permanent display in one corner of the room, a putrid font. When the smell became really intolerable, another rabbit would be sacrificed, but not before, because of the fanatic thrift of Professor Jaunisset,[69] who was then Secretary General of the Institute.

Thanks to this thrift, some of the rotting animals gave rise to unbelievable by-products and derivatives. It's all a matter of habit. Some of the more practiced laboratory technicians had become so accustomed to the smell of putrefaction that they would have had no objection to cooking in an operational coffin. These modest auxiliaries of exalted scientific research sometimes outdid the thrift of Professor Jaunisset himself, taking advantage of the Bunsen burners to cook themselves countless ragouts and other, still riskier concoctions.

After absently examining the viscera of the ritual guinea pig and rabbit, the men of science slowly proceeded to the second act of their scientific daily life, the smoking of cigarettes. Thus they strove to neutralize the ambient stench and their boredom with tobacco smoke, and managed, from butt to butt, to get through the day. At five o'clock they put the various putrefactions back in the ramshackle incubator cabinet to keep them warm. Octave, the technician, hid the string beans he had cooked behind a newspaper to get them safely past the concierge. Subterfuges. Taking them home to Gargan all ready for supper. The man of science, his master, was still writing a little something, diffidently, doubtingly in one corner of his laboratory book, with a view to a forthcoming and utterly pointless paper that he would feel obliged to present before long to some infinitely impartial and disinterested Academy and that would serve to justify his presence at the Institute and the meager advantages it conferred.

A true man of science takes at least twenty years on an average to make the great discovery, that is, to convince himself that one man's lunacy is not necessarily another man's delight, and that all of us here below are bored with the bees in our neighbors' bonnets.

The coldest, most rational scientific madness is also the most intolerable. But when a man has acquired a certain ability to subsist, even rather scantily, in a certain niche with the help of a few grimaces, he must either keep at it or resign himself to dying the death of a guinea pig. Habits are acquired more quickly than courage, especially the habit of filling one's stomach.

I ransacked the Institute for Parapjne, I'd come all the way from Rancy to see him, so naturally I kept on looking. It was no small order. I made several false starts, hesitating a long while before choosing among so many corridors and doors.

Parapine was an old bachelor, he never ate lunch and I doubt if he ate dinner more than two or three times a week, but then enormously, with the frenzy of the Russian student, all of whose outlandish ways he had retained.

Parapine was an undisputed eminence in his special field. He knew all there was to know about typhoid in animals as well as human beings. His reputation went back twenty years to the day when certain German authors claimed to have isolated the Eberthella in the vaginal excreta of an eighteen-month-old girl, so creating an enormous stir in the Halls of Truth. Only too delighted to take up the challenge in the name of the National Institute, Parapine had outdone those Teutonic braggarts by

---

[69] Jaunisset. From jaunisse, "jaundice."

breeding the same microbes, now in its pure form, in the sperm of a seventy-two-year-old invalid. Instantly famous, he managed to hold the limelight for the rest of his life by publishing a few unreadable columns in various medical journals. This he had done without difficulty ever since his day of audacity and good fortune.

The serious scientific public trusted him implicitly and consequently had no need to read him. If those people were to start getting critical, no further progress would be possible. They would spend a whole year over every page.

When I came to the door of his cell, Serge Parapine was spitting steady streams into all four corners of his laboratory, with a grimace of such disgust that it made you wonder. Parapine shaved now and then, but he always had enough hair on his cheeks to make him look like an escaped convict. He was always shivering or at least he seemed to be, though he never removed his overcoat, which presented a large assortment of spots and still more of dandruff, which he would scatter far and wide with little flicks of his fingernails, at the same time bringing his always oscillating forelock back into position over his red-and-green nose.

In the course of my laboratory work in medical school, Parapine had given me some instruction in the use of the microscope and had shown me unquestionable kindness on several occasions. I hoped he had not forgotten me completely since those remote days and that he might consent to give me valuable advice in connection with Bébert, with whose case I was really obsessed.

Undoubtedly, I was much more interested in preventing Bébert from dying than if he had been an adult. You never mind very much when an adult passes on. If nothing else, you say to yourself, it's one less stinker on earth, but with a child you can never be so sure. There's always the future.

Once acquainted with my difficulties, Parapine asked nothing better than to help me and to orient my perilous therapy, but unfortunately, in twenty years, he had learned so many, so diverse, and so often contradictory things about typhoid that by that time he was just about unable to formulate any clear and definite opinion concerning that most commonplace ailment and its treatment.

"First of all, my dear colleague," he said. "Do you believe in serums? Huh? Give me your honest opinion... And vaccines?... What do you really think?... Some of the best minds today have no use for vaccines at all... That of course is a bold way of thinking... Yes, indeed... but even so... in the last analysis... Don't you think there's a certain truth in that sort of negativism?... "

The sentences issued from his mouth in terrifying bursts, amid avalanches of tremendous R's.

While he was struggling like a lion against other enraged and desperate hypotheses, Jaunisset, the illustrious Secretary General of the Institute, who was still alive at the time, passed our windows frowning superciliously.

At the sight of him, Parapine turned if possible paler than ever and abruptly changed the subject in his haste to show me all the disgust aroused in him by the mere daily sight of this Jaunisset, who was glorified by just about everyone else. In half a second he disposed of Jaunisset as a crook and maniac of the first water, accusing him of enough monstrous, unprecedented, and secret crimes to fill a penal colony for a century.

I was powerless to stop Parapine from giving me hundreds of hate-ridden pointers about the clownish trade of medical research, which he was obliged to practice if he wanted to eat. This hatred of his was more precise, more scientific you might say, than the hatreds emanating from other men occupying similar positions in offices or shops.

He spoke in a very loud voice, and I was amazed at his outspokenness. His technician was listening to us. He, too, had finished his bit of cookery and was still moving about, for form's sake, between incubator and test tubes, but he had grown so accustomed to listening to Parapine pouring out his more or less daily maledictions that he had come to regard these tirades, however extravagant, as absolutely academic and meaningless. Certain little private experiments that this technician pursued with great seriousness in one of the laboratory's incubators struck him, on the other hand, as prodigiously and deliciously instructive compared to Parapine's outpourings. Parapine's rages in no way tempered his enthusiasm. Before leaving, he tenderly, scrupulously shut the door of the incubator on his private microbes, as if it were a tabernacle.

"Did you notice that technician of mine, my dear colleague?" said Parapine as soon as he had gone. "Did you notice that old fool? He's been cleaning up my rubbish for almost thirty years, and all he ever hears people talk about is science, but that most abundantly and sincerely... well, far from being disgusted, he, unlike everyone else in the whole place, has come to believe in it! After handling my cultures for years, he thinks they're marvelous! He dotes on them... The most meaningless of my buffooneries enchants him! Isn't it the same with all religions? Hasn't the priest stopped believing in God years ago, while his sacristan goes on believing... Heart and soul!... It's sickening!... That old fool carries absurdity to the point of aping the dress and goatee of the illustrious Joseph Bioduret! Did you notice?... Between you and me, the great Bioduret wasn't so very different from my technician except for his worldwide reputation and the intensity of his manias... That giant of experimental science with his mania for rinsing his bottles with care and observing the hatching out of moths in incredible detail, has always struck me as monstrously vulgar... Take away his prodigious pettiness, his housekeeping and, I ask you, what's left to admire about the great Bioduret? All right, I'll tell you: The hateful look of a malignant, cantankerous concierge. That's all. In his twenty years of membership in the Academy he had ample time to exhibit his vile, contemptible character.

. . nearly everyone hated him, he quarreled... and what quarrels!... with just about everyone in sight. The man was an ingenious megalomaniac, nothing more... "

Parapine was slowly getting ready to leave. I helped him put a scarf around his neck and a sort of mantilla over his eternal dandruff. Then he remembered that I'd come to see him about something precise and urgent. "My word!" he said. "Here I've been boring you with my own little problems and forgetting your patient. Forgive me, colleague, and let's get back to our subject. But after all, what can I tell you that you don't already know? Among so many shaky theories and questionable experiments, reason, in the last analysis, forbids us to choose. Just do your best, colleague! Since you have to do something, do your best! Personally, I must tell you in confidence that typhoidal infections have come to disgust me beyond all measure! Beyond all imagination! When I came to typhoid as a young man, there were only a few of us prospecting the field, we were able to help one another... to advance one another's reputations... While now, what can can I say? They pour in from Lapland, my friend! from Peru! More and more every day! Specialists are turning up from all over the world! In Japan they roll off the assembly line! In less than a few years I've seen the world become a hotbed of universal and preposterous publications on this same hackneyed subject. To maintain and more or less defend my position I've resigned myself to writing and rewriting my same little article from congress to congress, from journal to journal, throwing in a few subtle, innocuous, and quite tangential modifications toward the end of each season... Believe me, colleague, typhoid in our time is as botched and bungled as the mandolin or banjo. It's maddening. Everyone wants to play some little tune in his own way. I may as well admit it, I haven't the strength to drive myself anymore, what I'm looking for, to see me through to the end of my days, is some quiet little backwater of research that will bring me neither enemies nor disciples, but only the mediocre celebrity without jealousy, which I sorely need and with which I shall gladly content myself. Among other absurdities, I have considered studying the comparative influence of central heating on hemorrhoids in northern and southern countries. What do you think of it? The role of hygiene? Of diet? That kind of thing is fashionable nowadays. Such a study, properly handled and ingeniously dragged out, is sure to be favorably received by the Academy, since the majority of its members are old men to whom these problems of heating and hemorrhoids can hardly be indifferent. Look what they've done for cancer, which concerns them so closely... Don't you think the Academy might vote me one of its hygiene awards? Why not? Ten thousand francs? Not bad... Enough for a trip to Venice... Yes, my young friend, I was in Venice once as a young man... Oh yes! You can starve there just as well as anywhere else... But you breathe a sumptuous aroma of death that's not easy to forget... "

By then we were out on the street, but had to hurry back for his galoshes, which he'd forgotten. That delayed us. Then we rushed through the streets, but he didn't tell me where we were going.

Making our way down the long Rue de Vaugirard[70] strewn with vegetables and other encumbrances, we approached a square surrounded by chestnut trees and policemen, and we slipped into the back room of a small cafe, where Parapine sat down at a curtained window.

---

[70] Rue de Vaugirard. Here the institute is correctly situated.

"Too late!" he moaned. "They've gone." "Who?"

"The little girls from the Lycée... Some of them are charming... I know their legs by heart. I ask for nothing more at the end of my day... Let's get out of here! I'll see them another day... "

* * *

I'd have been glad if I'd never have had to go back to Rancy. Since the morning when I'd left it, I had almost forgotten my daily cares; they were so deeply incrusted in Rancy that they didn't follow me. Perhaps they'd have died of neglect like Bébert if I hadn't gone back. They were suburban cares. Even so, on the Rue Bonaparte, reflection came back to me, the gloomy kind, though it's a street that would normally be pleasing to a passer-by. Few streets are so smiling and so gracious. But on approaching the Seine, I began to worry. I strolled aimlessly about. I couldn't make up my mind to cross the river. Everybody can't be Caesar! Across the bridge, on the opposite bank, my troubles would begin. I reserved the right to wait on the left bank until nightfall. At least, I said to myself, I'd be saving a few hours of sunlight.

The water lapped against the bank where the fishermen were, and I sat down to watch them. I really was in no hurry at all, no more than they were. I'd pretty well come to the point, the age, you might say, when a man knows what he's losing with every hour that passes. But he hasn't yet built up the wisdom to pull up sharp on the road of time, and anyway, even if you did stop you wouldn't know what to do without the frenzy for going forward that has possessed you and won your admiration ever since you were young. Even now you're not as pleased with your youth as you used to be, but you don't yet dare admit in public that youth may be nothing more than a hurry to grow old.

In the whole of your absurd past you discover so much that's absurd, so much deceit and credulity, that it might be a good idea to stop being young this minute, to wait for youth to break away from you and pass you by, to watch it going away, receding in the distance, to see all its vanity, run your hand through the empty space it has left behind, take a last look at it, and then start moving, make sure your youth has really gone, and then calmly, all by yourself, cross to the other side of Time to see what people and things really look like.

The fishermen on the bank weren't catching anything. They didn't even seem to care very much whether they caught any fish or not. The fish must have known them. They were all just pretending. A fine last glow of sunshine maintained a little warmth around us and sent reflections sprinkled with blue and gold leaping over the water. A cool wind came over to us through the big trees on the far side, a smiling wind blowing through thousands of leaves in gentle gusts. A nice place to be. For two whole hours we stayed there, catching nothing, doing nothing. Then the Seine darkened and the corner of the bridge turned red with the sunset. The people on the qua! above had forgotten us as we sat there between the embankment and the water.

The night came out from under the arches and climbed along the château,[71] taking the façade and, one by one, the sunset-flaming windows.

Again there was nothing I could do but go away.

The booksellers on the quai were shutting up their boxes. "Are you coming?" a woman shouted over the parapet to her fisherman husband beside me, who was putting away his tackle, camp chair, and worms. He grumbled and the other fishermen grumbled after him, and up we went, all of us grumbling, to the quai. I spoke to his wife, just to be saying something pleasant before night took everything away. Then and there she wanted to sell me a book. She had forgotten, so she said, to put it away in her box. "I'll let you have it at half price, for next to nothing." A little old Montaigne, absolutely authentic, for one franc. For that little money I was glad to give her pleasure. I took her Montaigne.

Under the bridge the water looked dark and heavy. I had lost all desire to go anywhere. On the boulevards I drank a cafe crème and opened the book she had sold me. I just chanced to open it at a letter Montaigne once wrote to his wife after a son of theirs had died. That passage caught my interest

---

[71] The château. The Louvre, which is never referred to as a château.

at once, probably because it made me think of Bébert. Roughly, this is what Montaigne says to his wife: "Ah, my dear wife, don't eat your heart out! Cheer up!... Everything will turn out all right!... It always does... And by the way, rummaging through some old papers belonging to a friend of mine, I've just found a letter that Plutarch wrote to his wife under circumstances very similar to ours... That letter, dear wife, struck me as so apt, so much to the point, that I'm sending it on to you!... A splendid letter! Well, I won't keep you waiting any longer, just let me know if it doesn't do a good job of healing your sorrow!... Dear wife! I'm sending you Plutarch's fine letter! It's really something! I'm sure you'll like it!... Pay close attention, dear wife! Read it carefully! Show it to your friends! And read it over! Now my mind is at rest... I'm sure it will set you up! Your devoted husband, Michel." Now that, I said to myself, is a good job. How happy his wife must have been to have a husband like her Michel, who never let anything get him down. Well, it's their business. Maybe we go wrong when we try to judge other people's hearts. Maybe they felt real grief. Period grief?

But as far as Bébert was concerned, my day hadn't been so good. I had no luck with Bébert, dead or alive. It seemed to me that there was nothing for him on earth, not even in Montaigne. Maybe, come to think of it, it's the same for everybody, nothingness. No getting around it, I'd left Rancy that morning, and now I had to go back, empty-handed. I had absolutely nothing to offer him, or his aunt either.

A short stroll around the Place Blanche before going back.

I see people all up and down the Rue Lepic, even more than usual. So I go up too, to see what's going on. The crowd was outside a butcher shop. You had to squeeze into the circle to see what was going on. It was a pig, an enormous pig. He was groaning in the middle of the circle, like a man who's being pestered, but louder. The people were tormenting him, they never stopped. They'd twist his ears just to hear him squeal. He'd tug at his rope and try to escape and squirm and wriggle his feet in the air. Other people would poke him and prod him, and he'd bellow even louder with the pain. Everybody was laughing more and more.

The pig couldn't manage to hide in the little straw he had, it would fly away when he grunted and puffed into it. He couldn't escape from those people, and he knew it. He kept urinating the whole time, but that didn't help him either. Any more than his grunting and bellowing. No hope, Everybody was laughing. The butcher back in his shop was exchanging signs and jokes with his customers and gesticulating with a big knife.

He was happy too. He had bought the pig and tied it up as an advertisement. He couldn't have had a better time at his daughter's wedding.

More people kept arriving outside the shop to watch the pig crumpling in big pink folds after every attempt to escape. But that wasn't enough yet. They put a vicious little dog on the pig's back and incited it to jump and snap at the fat dilated flesh. They were having such a wonderful time that they blocked off the street completely. The police had to come and disperse the crowd.

When you get to the top of the Caulaincourt Bridge[72] at about that hour, you see the first lights of Rancy beyond the great lake of night that covers the cemetery. To get there you have to go all the way around. It's a long way. You need so much time and so many steps to get around the cemetery to the fortifications, you get the feeling you're going around the night itself.

When you get to the Porte and the toll station, you pass the stinking old office where the little green official is rotting away. The dogs of the Zone are at their barking posts. In spite of everything you see some flowers in the light of a gas lamp, they belong to the flower woman who is always there, waiting for the dead who pass from day to day, from hour to hour. The cemetery, another cemetery next to it, and then the Boulevard de la Revoke with all its street lamps, heading straight into the night. You just turn left and follow it. That was my street. There was really no fear of meeting anyone. Even so, I'd have liked to be somewhere else and far away. I'd also have liked to be wearing slippers so no one would hear me going in. Yet I was in no way to blame if Bébert wasn't getting better. I had done all I could. I had nothing to reproach myself with. It wasn't my fault if such cases are hopeless. I

[72] Caulaincourt Bridge. From this point one would look out over the Montmartre cemetery and the "great lake of night." But only in a dream is one anywhere near the fortifications or the suburbs.

passed his door—without being noticed, I thought. Upstairs I didn't open the blinds, I looked through the slits to see if there were still people talking outside Bébert's. Some visitors were still coming out of the house, but they didn't look the same as yesterday's visitors. A neighborhood cleaning woman I knew was crying as she left. "It looks bad." I said to myself. "He's certainly no better... Maybe he's dead... if one of them is in tears already." The day was over.

I racked my brains: was I really not at all to blame? It was cold and still in my place. Like a little night just for me, in a corner of the big one.

Now and then the sound of steps rose up to me and the echo came in louder and louder, droning, then dying away... Silence. I looked out again to see if anything was happening across the way. Nothing was happening except inside me, still asking myself the same questions.

I was so tired from walking and finding nothing that I finally fell asleep in my coffin, my private night.

* * *

Why kid ourselves, people have nothing to say to one another, they all talk about their own troubles and nothing else. Each man for himself, the earth for us all. They try to unload their unhappiness on someone else when making love, they do their damnedest, but it doesn't work, they keep it all, and then they start all over again, trying to find a place for it. "You're pretty, Mademoiselle," they say. And life takes hold of them again until the next time, and then they try the same little gimmick. "You're very pretty, Mademoiselle... "

And in between they boast that they've succeeded in getting rid of their unhappiness, but everyone knows it's not true and they've simply kept it all to themselves. Since at that little game you get uglier and more repulsive as you grow older, you can't hope to hide your unhappiness, your bankruptcy, any longer. In the end your features are marked with that hideous grimace that takes twenty, thirty years or more to climb from your belly to your face. That's all a man is good for, that and no more, a grimace that he takes a whole lifetime to compose. The grimace a man would need to express his true soul without losing any of it is so heavy and complicated that he doesn't always succeed in completing it.

Just then I was busy improving my soul with bills I couldn't pay, insignificant as they were, my impossible rent, my overcoat that was much too light for the season, and the grocer who laughed up his sleeve every time he saw me counting my pennies, hesitating to buy a piece of Brie and blushing when the price of grapes started going up. And then my patients, who were never satisfied. Bébert's death hadn't done me any good in the neighborhood. His aunt didn't hold it against me, though. No, I can't say she behaved badly under the circumstances. It was more from the Henrouilles in their private house that trouble and worry suddenly began raining down on me.

One day Grandma Henrouille walked out of her shack without so much as a by-your-leave, ignoring her son and daughter-in-law, and decided entirely on her own to come and see me. She had a head on her shoulders. After that she came many times and asked me if I really thought she was insane. Questioning me like that gave the old woman something to do. She'd wait in my so-called waiting room. Three chairs and a little three-legged table.

When I got back that evening, I found her in the waiting room, comforting Bébert's aunt by telling her all about the relatives she herself had lost along the way before arriving at her age, nieces by the dozen, an uncle here and there, a father way back in the middle of the last century, any number of aunts, and her daughters, who had passed on here and there, she couldn't quite remember where or how. Her own daughters had become so vague in her mind that she had to imagine them more or less, but still with deep sorrow when she spoke of them to someone else. By that time her own children were even less than memories. Around her aged loins she gathered a whole nation of humble ancient deaths, shades long silent, imperceptible sorrows, which, when I arrived, she was trying with considerable difficulty to rouse to a little life for the consolation of Bébert's aunt.

And then Robinson dropped in to see me. Introductions all around. Friends.

In fact it was then, as I later recollected, that Robinson got into the habit of meeting Grandma Henrouille in my waiting room. They'd sit and talk. Bébert was to be buried the next day. "Are you coming?" the aunt asked everyone she met. "I'd appreciate it if you came."

"Of course I'll come," said the old woman. "It's nice to have people around one at such times." There was no keeping her in her hovel. She'd turned into a gadabout.

"Oh, I'm so glad you're coming," the aunt thanked her. "And you, Monsieur, will you come too?" she asked Robinson.

"Oh, I'm afraid of funerals, Madame, you mustn't take it amiss," he said to get out of it.

And then each of them talked a lot, all about his own affairs, almost violently, even Grandma Henrouille joined in. They all talked much too loudly, like in a nuthouse.

So I went in and took the old woman to my consulting room next door.

I didn't have much to say to her. But she had questions for me. I promised not to go through with the commitment proceedings. We went back to the waiting room and sat down with Robinson and the aunt. We all talked for a good hour about the sad case of Bébert. Everyone in the neighborhood agreed that I had knocked myself out trying to save him, that you can't fight fate, and that all in all, to everybody's surprise, I had behaved pretty well. When Grandma Henrouille heard the child's age, seven, she seemed to feel better, that relieved her in a way. The death of so young a child was just an accident in her opinion, not the same as a normal death, which might have given her food for thought.

Robinson started in again telling us about the acids that burned his stomach and lungs, suffocated him, and made him spit black phlegm. But Grandma Henrouille didn't spit anything at all, and she didn't work with acids, so what Robinson had to say on the subject was of no interest to her. She had only come to size me up. She looked at me out of the corner of her lively bluish eyes as I spoke, and none of the latent tension between us escaped Robinson. It was dark in my waiting room, the big building on the other side of the street was paling before giving in to the night. After that there were only our voices between us, and all that voices seem on the point of saying but never say.

Once alone with Robinson, I tried to make it plain that I had no desire whatever to see him anymore, but that didn't stop him from coming back toward the end of the month, and almost every evening after that. It's true that his lungs were in bad shape.

"Monsieur Robinson has been asking for you again," said my concierge, who liked him. "He doesn't seem to be getting better, does he?" she added. "He was coughing again when he came." She knew it annoyed me to hear her talk about him.

It's true that he coughed. "It's hopeless," he himself said. "I'll never get over it... " "Wait till summer! A little patience! You'll see... It'll just stop... "

You know... the kind of thing you say in such cases. I couldn't cure him as long as he was working with acids... But I tried to cheer him up all the same.

"It'll just stop?" he'd say. "You give me a pain. Do you think it's funny breathing like I do... I'd like to see you with a thing like this in your chest... This kind of thing in the chest get a man down... Take it from me... "

"You're depressed, you're having a bad time, but when you feel better... Even a little better, you'll see... "

"A little better? I'll feel a little better when I'm eight feet under! I should have got killed in the war, then I'd feel really better! For you there was some sense in coming back! You can't complain!"

People cling to their rotten memories, to all their misfortunes, and you can't pry them loose. These things keep them busy. They avenge themselves for the injustice of the present by smearing the future inside them with shit. They're cowards deep down, and just. That's their nature.

I stopped answering him. That made him angry. "You see? You think the same as I do."

To get him to leave me in peace, I made him up some cough syrup. It seems his neighbors complained that he coughed all the time and it kept them awake. While I was filling the bottle, he went on wondering out loud where he could have caught this stubborn cough. He also wanted me to give him injections of gold salts!

"If the injections killed me, I wouldn't mind, you know... "

Naturally I wouldn't have anything to do with this heroic therapy. Mostly I wanted him to go away.

Just seeing him hanging around, I'd lost all my pleasure in life. It was already hard enough for me to keep from drifting with the current of my own failure, from giving in to my impulse to close up shop once and for all. Twenty times a day I'd say to myself: "What for?" So listening to his lamentations in addition was really too much.

"You haven't any spirit, Robinson," I finally told him... "You ought to get married, maybe that would give you some zest for life... " If he'd got himself a wife, it would have taken him off my hands. The suggestion made him angry, and he left me. He didn't care for my advice, especially that kind. On the marriage issue he didn't even answer me. And I must admit, that was a pretty silly piece of advice.

One Sunday when I wasn't on duty we went out together. We settled on the terrace of a cafe at the corner of the Boulevard Magnanime and ordered a small cassis and a diabolo.[73] We didn't talk much, we didn't have much to say to each other. What good are words anyway when you know the score? You'll only come to blows. There aren't many buses on Sunday. Sitting on the terrace, it's almost a pleasure to see the boulevard so neat and clean, all rested like the people. The phonograph was playing in the café behind us.

"Hear that?" says Robinson. "His phonograph is playing American tunes. I recognize them. It's the ones they played at Molly's place in Detroit... "

In the two years he'd spent there he hadn't gone very far into American life. Still, he'd been touched in a way by their brand of music, where they, too, try to get away from the weight of routine and the crushing misery of having to do the same thing every day... While it's playing, they can shuffle about for a while with a life that has no meaning. Bears on both sides of the ocean...

He was thinking so hard about all that that he had hardly touched his cassis. A little dust was rising on all sides. Some children with big bellies and smudged faces were wandering around under the plane trees; they too were attracted by the phonograph records. Nobody can really resist music. You don't know what to do with your heart, you're glad to give it away. At the bottom of all music you have to hear the tune without notes, made just for us, the tune of Death.

A few shops still have the obstinacy to open on Sunday... the slipper woman comes out of her shop and parades her pounds of varicose veins from display to display, stopping to chat here and there.

At the newsstand the morning papers hang yellow and limp, an enormous artichoke of news going bad. A dog takes a quick piss on them, the news woman is dozing.

An empty bus is heading back to its depot lickety split. Thoughts have their Sunday too, come to think of it. We're even more dazed than usual. Here we sit, empty, bewildered, contented. We have nothing to talk about, because nothing happens to us anymore, we're too poor, maybe life is sick of us. Why not?

"Can't you think of something I could do to get out of this job that's killing me?" He had surfaced from his reflections.

"I want to get out of that racket, see? I'm sick of working like a mule... I want to roam around too... Wouldn't you know somebody who needs a chauffeur by any chance?... You know so many people... "

Sunday ideas, gentleman's ideas had come over him. I was afraid to argue, to insinuate that no one would entrust his motorcar to a man with the mug of an impoverished murderer, that with or without a uniform he would always look too peculiar.

"You're not very encouraging, are you?" he said. "So you think I'll never get out of the ditch?... You think there's not even any point in my trying?... In America you said I was too slow... In Africa I couldn't stand the heat... Here I'm not intelligent enough... But that's all a lot of hooey, you can't tell me different! If only I had plenty of money!... Everybody would think I was adorable... here... there... and everywhere... Even in America... Ain't it the truth? What about you?... All we need is to own an apartment house with half a dozen tenants paying good stiff rents... "

"You've got something there," I said.

---

[73] Diabolo. A mixture of limonade (fizz water with synthetic lemon flavoring) and some sort of syrup, usually mint or grenadine.

He had come to that major conclusion all by himself, and he couldn't get over it. Then he gave me a funny look, as if he had suddenly discovered something too-too nauseating about me.

"Come to think of it," he said, "you've got the good end. You sell your hokum to sick people, and you haven't a thing to worry about... Nobody riding you... You come and go when you like, you're free... You're nice enough on the surface but what a bastard underneath!"

"You're unjust, Robinson... "

"All right, then find me something... "

He was determined to pass on his acid job to someone else...

We started off through the little side streets. In the late afternoon you'd think Rancy was a village. The big house door is ajar. The yard is empty, and so is the dog's kennel. One afternoon like this, years ago, the peasants left their homes, driven away by the city creeping out from Paris. There are only one or two taverns left from those days, unsalable, crumbling away, overgrown by limp wisteria vines, hanging down over walls reddened with posters. The grating hung between two gargoyles has rusted till it can't rust anymore. All this past—nobody touches it anymore. It's dying without any help from anyone. The present tenants are much too tired when they come home at night to do anything about the outside of their house. They just pile up, family by family, in what's left of the common rooms and drink. The ceiling is marked with rings of smoke left by the wobbly hanging lamps of those days. The whole neighborhood is shaken uncomplaining by the continuous rumble of the new factory. Moss-covered tiles crash down on high, humpbacked cobblestones, the kind you'll find today only in Versailles and in venerable prisons.

Robinson accompanied me to the little town park hemmed in by warehouses, where all the strays in the neighborhood come and misbehave on the mangy lawn, on the senile boules[74] ground, around the incomplete Venus, and on the sandpile for playing and peeing.

The conversation started up again, about this and that. "My trouble is that drink doesn't agree with me." A bee in his bonnet. "When I drink, I get cramps, it's unbearable. Worse!" And by throwing up several times he demonstrated that even our little cassis that afternoon hadn't agreed with him. "See what I mean?"

He left me outside his door. "The Palace of Drafts," he said and vanished. I thought I wouldn't be seeing him for a while.

That night it looked as if my business might be picking up.

I got two urgent calls from the same house, the one over the police station. On Sunday evening everybody lets go... their sighs, their feelings, their impatience. Human dignity goes on a holiday spree. After a whole day of alcoholic freedom the slaves are stirring, there's no holding them, they sniff, they snort, they clank their chains...

In the house over the police station two tragedies were in progress at once. On the second floor a man was dying of cancer, on the fourth there had been a miscarriage that was more than the midwife could handle. That worthy matron was giving everybody absurd advice, all the while washing out napkins and more napkins. Between two douches she'd slip away to give the cancer patient downstairs an injection, at ten francs an ampule, of camphorated oil if you please. A good day for her.

Every family in the house had spent the day in dressing gowns and shirt sleeves, lending a helping hand, well reinforced by highly seasoned food. Every stairway and corridor smelled of garlic and other more obscure odors. The dogs were having a fine time, running up as far as the seventh floor. The concierge was determined to keep abreast of events. You couldn't move without running into her. She only drank white wine, because red wine gives you discharges.

The elephantine midwife in her smock was directing both tragedies, on the second floor and on the fourth, bounding, sweating, delighted, vindictive. My arrival infuriated her. She had been holding her audience since morning, she was the star.

I tried my best to spare her feelings, to make myself as inconspicuous as possible, to approve of everything (when in reality everything she had done was preposterous), but my being there and every

---

[74] Boules. Boules is the same as boccie and something like the English bowls. Played mostly by men on provincial village squares and in Paris parks.

word I said went against her grain. It was to be expected. A supervised midwife is as friendly as a hangnail. You can't think of any place to put her where she'll do as little harm as possible. From the kitchen the family overflowed through the apartment and out on to the staircase, where they mingled with the relatives of other tenants. And what multitudes of relatives! Fat ones and thin ones gathered in somnolent clusters under the hanging lamps. It was getting late, and more were arriving from the provinces where people go to bed earlier than in Paris. They were fed up. Everything I said to the relatives of those tragedies... upstairs and down... was taken amiss.

The death agony on the second floor didn't last long. Which had its good side and bad side. Just as his last gasp was coming up, Dr. Omanon, his regular doctor, drops in to see if his patient was dead, and starts bawling me out or pretty near for being there at the bedside. I explained to Omanan that I was on municipal Sunday duty, so my presence was perfectly natural. Whereupon, with dignity, I climbed up to the fourth floor.

Upstairs the woman's ass was still bleeding. It wouldn't have surprised me if she too had taken it into her head to die without bothering to wait. A minute to give her an injection, and down again to Omanon's patient. It was definitely all over. Omanon had just left. But the bastard had pocketed my twenty francs. Another dud. After that I was determined to stick to my post beside the miscarriage. So I ran upstairs as fast as I could.

Her vulva was still bleeding, and I explained a few things to the family. Naturally the midwife disagreed. It almost looked as if she were being paid for contradicting me. But there I was, I had to do something, who cared if she was happy or not? So let's not fool around! This case was worth at least a hundred francs to me if I handled it right and stuck to my guns. A man of science keeps his temper, damn it! It's hard work standing up to the remarks and questions steeped in white wine that hurtle implacably through the air over your innocent head... it's no joke. Belching and sighing, the family impart their opinions. The midwife is waiting for me to make a fool of myself, clear out, and leave her the hundred francs. But the midwife has another think coming. What about my rent? Who's going to pay it? This labor had been twiddling its thumbs since this morning, I won't deny it. She's bleeding, I won't deny that either, but it's not coming out, I've got to hold my ground.

Now that the cancer patient has died downstairs, his deathbed audience has crept up here. As long as you're losing a night's sleep, as long as you're making the sacrifice, you may as well take in all the entertainment the neighborhood has to offer. The downstairs family comes up to see if maybe this tragedy is going to end as badly as theirs. Two deaths in the same house, on the same night, would be a sensation to last them a lifetime. Nothing less. Everybody's dogs can be heard tinkling their bells as they scamper up and down the stairs. They come in too. More people from far away pour in, whispering. Some teenage girls have suddenly discovered the "facts of life," as their mothers put it and now, in the face of tragedy, they're putting on a tenderly knowing air. The female consoling instinct. A cousin has been watching them since morning. He's fascinated, he hasn't stirred from their side. They come as a revelation in his fatigue. Everyone's clothes are askew. The cousin will marry one of them, he wishes he could see their legs while he's about it, to make it easier to choose.

The fetus refuses to come out, the passage must be dry, it won't slip through, nothing but blood. This would have been her sixth child. Where's the husband? I ask for him.

The husband had to be found if I was going to send his wife to the hospital. A relative had suggested the hospital. She had a family at home and wanted to get to bed on account of the children. But when the word hospital was brought up, they couldn't get together. Some were in favor, others were dead set against, because of what people would say. They wouldn't even hear of it. Some very hard words were exchanged between relatives, words that would never be forgotten and would go down in the family. The midwife despised everybody. What preoccupied me was finding the husband, I wanted to consult him, so we could make up our minds one way or the other. He finally emerges from one of the groups, even more undecided than everyone else. But the decision was up to the husband. Hospital? No hospital? What does he think? He doesn't know. He wants to look. So he looks. I show him his wife's hole, the blood clots, the glug-glug, his whole wife seeping away. She's groaning like a big dog that's been run over by a car. He doesn't know what he wants. Somebody gives him a glass of white wine to pick him up. He sits down.

He still can't make up his mind. He's a man who works hard all day. Everyone knows him in the market and especially at the freight station, where he totes sacks, and no small loads, big heavy things, been toting them for the last fifteen years. He's famous. His trousers are vast and shapeless, likewise his jacket. They don't fall off, but he doesn't seem to be very much attached to his trousers and jacket. He only seems attached to the earth and standing upright on it, with his two feet spread wide as if the earth were going to start quaking under him any minute. His name is Pierre.

We're all waiting. "Well, Pierre," they all ask him. "What do you think?" Pierre scratches himself and goes and sits down right next to his wife's face, as if he had trouble recognizing this woman who was always bringing so much pain into the world, and then he sheds a kind of tear and stands up. We all fire the same question. I make out a certificate of admission for the hospital. "Try and think, Pierre!" everyone pleads. He tries but makes a sign meaning it won't come. He gets up and staggers out to the kitchen, taking his glass with him. Why wait any longer? That husband's indecision, everybody realized, was likely to go on all night.

We might as well be going.

For me it was a hundred francs lost, that's all. But one way or another I'd have had trouble with the midwife... that was sure. On the other hand, I wasn't going to risk any surgical manipulations in front of all those people and in my state of fatigue. "Too bad," I said to myself. "No use hanging around. Maybe next time... May as well resign myself... Let nature take her course, the bitch!"

I'd hardly reached the stairs when they all called me back and he came running after me. "Hey, doctor!" he yelled, "don't go!"

"What do you want me to do?" I asked him.

"Wait, I'll go with you, doctor!... Please, doctor!"

"All right," I said, and let him go down with me. I was in the lead, so I stopped at the second floor to say good-bye to the dead cancer patient's family. The husband went into the room with me, and we came right out again. In the street he fell into step with me. There was a nip in the air. We came across a puppy who was practicing how to answer the other dogs of the Zone with long howls. He was very persistent and very plaintive. He had already mastered the art. He'd soon be a real dog.

"Hey, that's Egg Yolk," says the husband, delighted at recognizing him and at changing the subject... "The daughters of the laundryman on the Rue des Gonesses brought him up on a baby's bottle... Do you know the laundryman's daughters?"

"Yes," I said.

As we were walking he told me about ways they had of feeding puppies on milk without its costing too much. But behind those words he was looking all the while for an idea in connection with his wife.

A bar was open near the Porte.

"Coming in, doctor? I'll buy you a drink."

I wasn't going to hurt his feelings. "All right," I said. "Two coffees." I took the opportunity to talk about his wife. My talking about her turned him dead serious, but I still couldn't get him to make up his mind. There was a big bouquet on the bar counter. For Martrodin's birthday, Martrodin was the owner. "A present from the children," he himself told us. So we had a vermouth with him and drank his health. The Drunkenness Law and a framed school diploma were hanging on the wall. When he saw that, the husband absolutely insisted on the owner reciting the Subprefectures of the Loir-et-Cher Department, because he had learned them in school and still knew them. Then he claimed it wasn't the owner's name on the diploma but somebody else's, that made the owner sore, so the husband came back and sat with me. He was in the throes of doubt again, so tormented that he didn't even see me leave...

I never saw that husband again. Never. I was badly disappointed by the events of that Sunday and tired besides.

I had hardly gone a hundred yards in the street when I saw Robinson coming my way, loaded down with all kinds of boards, big ones and little ones. I recognized him in spite of the darkness. He was embarrassed at seeing me and tried to get away, but I stopped him.

"Why aren't you in bed?" I asked him.

"Not so loud!" he said. "I've come from the building site... "

"And what are you doing with all that wood? Building what? A coffin... You stole it, I bet?"
"No. A rabbit hutch... "

"You raising rabbits now?"

"No, it's for the Henrouilles... "

"The Henrouilles? They've got rabbits?"

"Yes, three. They're going to keep them in the little yard, you know, where the old woman lives... " "You're fixing to build them a rabbit hutch at this time of night? Funny time to... "

"It was his wife's idea... "

"Some idea!... What's she going to do with rabbits? Sell them? Make top hats?"

"You'll have to ask her when you see her. As long as she comes across with the hundred francs, I... " This business with the rabbit hutch struck me as very odd... at that time of night. I kept at him.

He changed the subject.

"But what were you doing at their house?" I asked. "You didn't know the Henrouilles."

"The old lady took me to see them... that day I met her in your office... The old woman is a big talker once she gets started... You can't imagine... No getting away from her... So now I'm sort of pals with her and with them too... Some people like me, you know... "

"You never said a word about all that... But since you see them, maybe you know if they're managing to get the old woman committed... "

"No, not from what they tell me... "

He wasn't enjoying this conversation at all, I could feel that, he didn't know how to get rid of me. But the slipperier he got the more I wanted to know... "

"Life is hard, you got to admit it... the things a man has to do... " he said vaguely. But I brought him back to the subject. I was determined to make him come clean...

"They say the Henrouilles have more money than meets the eye... What do you think, now that you've been seeing them?"

"Yes, maybe they have, but one thing is sure, they want to get rid of the old woman." Robinson had never been much good at deception.

"It's because of the cost of living, you know, that keeps going up... that's why they want to get rid of her. They told me one time that you refused to certify her... Is that true?"

Then quickly, without insisting on an answer, he asked me which way I was going. "Been visiting a patient?"

I told him something about my adventures with the husband I had just lost by the wayside. That gave him a good laugh, but it also made him cough.

His cough doubled him up so bad I could hardly see him though he was right next to me. All I could vaguely make out was his hands, folded in front of his mouth like a big livid flower, trembling in the night. He couldn't stop. "It's the drafts," he finally said when the cough had spent itself and we'd come to the door of his house.

"One thing my pad is full of is drafts! And fleas! Have you got fleas in your place too?" I had. "Naturally," I told him. "I bring them home from my patients."

"Sick people smell of piss, don't they?" he said. "Yes, and sweat... "

"All the same," he said slowly after thinking it over. "I'd have liked to be a hospital orderly."
"Why?"

"I'll tell you... because people with nothing wrong with them, you can't get around it, are frightening... Especially since the war... I know what they're thinking... They don't always know it themselves... but I know what they're thinking... As long as they're up, they think about killing you... but when they're sick, no two ways, they're not as frightening... You've got to be prepared for anything, I tell you, as long as they're up. Don't you see it that way?"

"Yes," I had to say.

"Is that why you decided to become a doctor?" he asked.

Thinking it over, I realized that maybe Robinson was right. But then he had another of his coughing fits.

"Your feet are wet," I said. "You'll come down with pleurisy wandering around like this at night. Go home," I advised him. "Go to bed."

His nerves were on edge from all that coughing.

"I wouldn't be surprised if Grandma Henrouille came down with the flu," he said, laughing and coughing into my ear.

"What makes you say that?" "You'll see," he said.

"What have they dreamed up now?"

"That's all I can tell you. You'll see... "

"Come on, Robinson, you stinker, tell me. You know I never repeat anything... "

Suddenly he wanted to make a clean breast of it, maybe in part to convince me that he wasn't as resigned and lily-livered as he looked.

"Go on!" I prodded him in a whisper. "You know I never talk... " That was all the encouragement he needed.

"That's a fact," he admitted. "You know how to keep your mouth shut." And right away he starts to come seriously clean. You wanted it, here it is...

There wasn't a soul around us at that time of night on the Boulevard Coutumance. "Do you remember," he starts in, "the story about those carrot peddlers?" Offhand I didn't remember any story about carrot peddlers.

"Come off it," he insists. "You know... You told me the story yourself!"

"That's right!"... All at once it came back to me. "The brakeman on the Rue des Brumaires?... The one who got his balls blown off while stealing rabbits?"

"Yes, that's it, from the grocer on the Quai d'Argenteuil... " "Yes," I say. "I remember now. So what?"

I still didn't see the connection between that ancient incident and Grandma Henrouille.

He came out with it soon enough. "Don't you see?"

"No," I said. But soon I was afraid to see. "You're being awfully slow . , ."

"It's just that it looks like a nasty business for you to be getting into. You can't be going to murder Grandma Henrouille just to please the daughter-in-law?"

"Of course not. I'm just building the rabbit hutch they asked for... The fireworks are up to them... They'll do the rest... if they want to... "

"How much have they given you for all this?"

"A hundred francs for the wood and two-fifty for my work and a thousand more for the idea... And, you understand... this is only a beginning... a story like that... if properly told... is as good as a pension!... Well, son... now do you see?"

I saw very well, and I wasn't surprised. It only made me sad, a little sadder than before. Anything you can say to dissuade people in a case like that is bound to be feeble. Has life been kind to them? So why would they take pity on anybody? What for? What are other people to them? Has anybody ever been known to go down to hell to take someone else's place? No. They send other people down, that's all.

The vocation for murder that had suddenly come over Robinson struck me in a way as an improvement over what I'd observed up until then in others, always half hateful, half benevolent, always boring with their vagueness, their indirection. I had definitely learned a thing or two by following Robinson in the night.

But there was a danger: the Law. "The Law is dangerous," I told him. "If you're caught, you with the state of your health, you'll be sunk... You'll never leave prison alive... It'll kill you... "

"That's just too bad," he said. "I'm fed up with honest work... I'm getting old... still waiting my turn to have some fun, and when it comes... if it does, with plenty of patience... I'll have been dead and buried long ago... Honest work is for suckers... You know that as well as I do... "

"Maybe... but crime, you know, everybody'd go in for it if there weren't risks... And the police are rough... There's the pro and con... " We examined the situation.

"I won't say different, but doing my kind of work, in my condition, coughing, not sleeping, doing jobs that no horse would touch... Nothing worse can happen to me now... That's how I feel about it... Nothing... "

I didn't dare tell him that all in all he was right, because he'd have held it up to me later on if his new racket misfired.

To cheer me up he listed a few good reasons why I shouldn't worry about the old woman, first of all because any way you looked at it she hadn't long to live, she was already too old as it was. He would just be arranging for her departure.

All the same it was a very nasty business. The whole thing had been worked out between him and the couple. Seeing the old woman had taken to leaving her shack, they'd send her to feed the rabbits one evening... The fireworks would be carefully placed... They'd go off full in her face the moment she touched the door... Exactly what happened at the grocer's... The neighborhood people already thought she was mad, the accident wouldn't come as a surprise to anybody... They'd say they had warned her never to go near the rabbits , . . And she had disobeyed them... At her age there was certainly no chance of her surviving an explosion like the one they were fixing for her... right square in the puss. No two ways, that was some story I had told Robinson.

* * *

And the music came back with the carnival, the music you've heard as far back as you remember, ever since you were little, that's always playing somewhere, in some corner of the city, in little country towns, wherever poor people go and sit at the end of the week to figure out what's become of them. "Paradise" they call it. And music is played for them, sometimes here, sometimes there, from season to season, it tinkles and grinds out the tunes that rich people danced to the year before. It's the mechanical music that floats down from the wooden horses, from the cars that aren't cars anymore, from the railways that aren't at all scenic, from the platform under the wrestler who hasn't any muscles and doesn't come from Marseille, from the beardless lady, the magician who's a butter-fingered jerk, the organ that's not made of gold, the shooting gallery with the empty eggs. It's the carnival made to delude the weekend crowd.

We go in and drink the beer with no head on it. But under the cardboard trees the stink of the waiter's breath is real. And the change he gives you has several peculiar coins in it, so peculiar that you go on examining them for weeks and weeks and finally, with considerable difficulty, palm them off on some beggar. What do you expect at a carnival? Gotta have what fun you can between hunger and jail, and take things as they come. No sense complaining, we're sitting down, aren't we? Which ain't to be sneezed at. I saw the same old Gallery of the Nations, the one Lola caught sight of years and years ago on that avenue in the park of Saint-Cloud. You always see things again at carnivals, they revive the joys of past carnivals. Over the years the crowds must have come back time and again to stroll on the main avenue of the park of Saint- Cloud... taking it easy. The war had been over long ago. And say, I wonder if that shooting gallery still belonged to the same owner? Had he come back alive from the war? I take an interest in everything. Those are the same targets, but in addition, they're shooting at airplanes now. Novelty. Progress. Fashion. The wedding was still there, the soldiers too, and the town hall with its flag. Everything. Plus a few more things to shoot at than before.

But the people were getting a lot more fun out of the Dodge'em cars, a recent invention, because of the collisions you kept having and the terrible shaking they gave your head and innards. More howling lunatics kept pouring in for the pleasure of smashing ferociously into one another and getting scattered in all directions and fracturing their spleens at the bottom of their tubs. Nothing would make them stop. They never begged for mercy, it looked as if they'd never been so happy. Some were delirious. They had to be dragged away from their smash-ups. If they'd been offered Death as an extra attraction for their franc, they'd have gone right in. At about four o'clock the town band was supposed to play in the middle of the carnival ground. It took some doing to collect the musicians, because of the neighborhood bars, all of which wanted a turn at them. A last one was always missing. The rest waited. Some went looking for him. While waiting for them to come back, the others would be stricken with thirst and two more would disappear. They had to start all over again.

Incrusted with dust, the gingerbread pigs turned into relics and gave the prize-winners a devastating thirst.

Family groups are waiting for the fireworks before going home to bed. Waiting is part of the carnival too. Thousands of empty bottles jiggle and clink in the shadow under the tables. Restless feet consent or say no. The tunes are so familiar you hardly hear the music or the wheezing motor-driven cylinders behind the booths, which put life into things it costs two francs to see. When you're tipsy with fatigue your heart pounds in your temples. Bim! Bim! It beats against the velvet around your head and inside your ears. One of these days you'll burst. So be it! One of these days, when the movement inside catches up with the movement outside, when your thoughts scatter far and wide and rise up at last to play with the stars.

A lot of crying went on all over the carnival, children getting accidentally squeezed between chairs and others being taught to resist their longings, to forego the enormous little pleasure of another ride on the merry-go-round. For character building the carnival hasn't its equal. It's never too soon to start. The little darlings don't know yet that everything costs money. They think it's pure generosity that makes the grownups behind the brightly lit counters incite the public to treat themselves to the marvels which they have amassed and which they guard with their raucous smiles. Children don't know the law. Their parents slap them to teach them the law and protect them from pleasure.

There's never a real carnival except for the shopkeepers, and then it's deep down and secret. The shopkeeper rejoices at night when all the unsuspecting yokels, the public, the profit fodder, have gone home, when silence returns to the avenue and the last dog has squirted his last drop of urine at the Japanese billiard table. That's when the accounts are totted up, when the shopkeepers register their receipts and take stock of their powers and their victims.

On the last Sunday evening of the carnival, Martrodin's barmaid cut her hand pretty badly cutting sausage.

Late that night, the things around us suddenly became quite distinct, as if they were sick of wobbling from one side of fate to the other and had all come out of the shadow at once and started talking to me. But you'd better not trust things and people at such times. You think objects are going to talk but they don't say a thing, and often enough the night swallows them up before you can understand what they were trying to tell you. Anyway that's been my experience.

Be that as it may, I ran into Robinson that same night at Martrodin's café just as I was getting ready to dress the barmaid's wound. I remember the circumstances exactly. There were some Arab customers nearby, a whole raft of them were dozing on the benches. They didn't seem interested in anything that was going on around them. Speaking to Robinson, I was careful not to bring up our conversation of the other night, when I'd caught him carrying boards. I had trouble sewing up the barmaid's cut, because I couldn't see very well at the back of the bar. I had to pay close attention and that kept me from talking. As soon as I'd finished, Robinson drew me into a corner and informed me without my asking that everything was all set for his scheme, it would be coming off soon. His telling me that didn't suit me at all, I could have easily done without it.

"Soon? What?"

"You know as well as I do."

"What? The same old business?"

"Guess how much they're giving me?" I had no desire to guess.

"Ten thousand!... Just to hold my tongue!" "That's a lot of money!"

"It'll save my life, that's all," he said. "Those are the ten thousand francs I've needed all along!... The first ten thousand!... See?... I've never really had a trade, but now with ten thousand francs!..."

He must have started blackmailing them already...

He listed his projects, all the things he'd be able to do with ten thousand francs... Leaning against the wall, in the shadow... He gave me time to think about them. A new world. Ten thousand francs!

Yes, but thinking it over, I wondered if I wasn't running some risk myself, if I wasn't slipping into some sort of complicity by not trying to talk him out of his scheme. Actually I should have reported him. Not that I gave a damn about morality, any more than anyone else. What business was it of mine? But all the nasty stories, all the complications the law stirs up when a crime has been committed, just to entertain the taxpayer, the prurient bastard!... When that happens, it's hard to clear yourself... I'd seen it happen...

Trouble for trouble, I preferred the quiet kind that's not splashed all over the newspapers.

To make a long story short, I was fascinated and horrified at the same time. I'd gone this far, and once again I hadn't the courage to get really to the bottom of things. Now that the time had come to open my eyes in the darkness, I almost preferred to keep them shut. But Robinson seemed to want me to open them, to know all about it.

To change the subject a bit, as we roamed around the room, I started talking about women. He didn't think much of women.

"You know," he said, "I can get along fine without women, their big asses, their fat thighs, their rosebud lips, their bellies that always have something growing in them, if it's not a brat it's a disease... Their smiles won't pay your rent for you! Take me in my pad; if I had a woman, it wouldn't do me a bit of good to show the landlord her ass on the fifteenth of the month, he wouldn't reduce the rent!..."

Robinson had a thing about independence. He said so himself. But Martrodin was getting sick of our private conversation, our little plots in the corner.

"Robinson, dammit, the glasses!" he sings out. "Do you expect me to wash them for you?" Robinson starts up.

"You see," he informs me, "I'm filling in here."

It was carnival time all right. Martrodin was having a hard time counting up the take, it was getting on his nerves. The Arabs left except for the two who were still dozing by the door.

"What are they waiting for?" "The barmaid," says Martrodin.

"How's business?" I asked to be saying something, "Pretty fair... But it's not easy! See, doctor, I bought this place for sixty thousand before the crash. I'd need to get at least two hundred out of it... See what I mean?... It's true, the place is full, but it's mostly Arabs... And those people don't drink... They haven't caught the habit yet... Poles is what I need... Take it from me, doctor, the Poles are drinkers... In the Ardennes where T was before, I had Poles, they worked in the enameling ovens, get the idea?... Those ovens really heated them up!... That's what we need here!... Thirst!... On Saturdays they spent everything they had!... Christ! That was something! Their whole pay! Bing!... These greasers here aren't interested in drinking, they're more interested in buggering each other... It seems drinking's prohibited by their religion and buggery isn't... "

Martrodin had it in for the Arabs. "A bunch of perverts! It seems they even do it to my barmaid!... They're fanatics!... Crazy way to behave! Doctor, I ask you... "

With his stubby fingers Martrodin squeezed the little serous pouches he had under his eyes. "How are your kidneys doing?" I asked him when I saw him doing that. I was treating him for his kidneys. "I hope you've cut out the salt at least."

"There's still some albumen, doctor. I had the pharmacist analyze it only the other day... Oh, I don't care if I conk out, from albumen or something else, what bugs me is working the way I do... for practically nothing... "

The barmaid had finished washing her dishes, but her bandage had got so greasy I had to change it... She held out a five-franc note. I didn't want to accept her five francs, but she insisted. Her name was Severine.

"Why, Séverine," I observed. "You've had your hair cut."

"Had to," she says. "It's the style. And besides, with the cooking in this place, long hair picks up all the

smells... "

"Your ass smells a damn sight worse!" Martrodin breaks in. Our chatter was interfering with his accounts. "And it doesn't keep your customers away... "

"Yes, but it's not the same thing," says Séverine, who was good and mad. "Every part has its own smell... And look here, boss, you want me to tell you what you smell like... Not just one part, all over?"

Séverine was really worked up. Matrodin didn't want to hear the rest. He just grumbled and went back to his wretched accounts.

Séverine's feet were so swollen from the day's work that she couldn't manage to get out of her felt slippers and into her shoes. She prepared to leave in her slippers.

"I'll sleep all right with them on," she finally said aloud.

"Go put the light out in back!" Martrodin ordered her. "Anybody could guess that you don't pay the light bills,"

"I'll sleep all right," Séverine repeated with a sigh, as she was getting up.

Martrodin was still at his accounts. To reckon better he'd taken off his apron, then his vest. He was sweating blood. From the invisible depths of the bar we could hear a clatter of saucers, that was Robinson and the other dishwasher at work. Martrodin was tracing his big childish numbers with a blue pencil squeezed between his thick murderer's fingers. In front of us the barmaid was dozing, sprawled all over her chair. Now and then she'd regain a spark of consciousness in her sleep.

"Oh, my feet! Oh, my feet!" she'd say and fall back into her dose. But then Martrodin woke her with a yell.

"Hey, Séverine! Get your greasers out of here! I'm sick of them!... Clear out, the whole lot of you, Christ almighty! It's time!"

The Arabs didn't seem to be in any hurry at all in spite of the hour. Séverine finally woke up. "It's true I gotta go," she finally agreed. "Thanks, boss." She took both greasers along with her. They had joined forces to pay her.

"I'll do them both tonight," she told me as she was leaving. " 'Cause next Sunday I won't be able to on account of I'm going to Acheres to see my kid. 'Cause next Saturday is visiting day."

The Arabs got up and followed her. They didn't seem the least bit insolent. Still, Séverine looked at them kind of dubiously because she was so tired. "I don't agree with the boss," she says. "I like greasers better. Arabs aren't brutal like Poles, but they're perverts... Boy, are they perverts!... Well, let 'em do what they please, I don't think that'll keep me from sleeping!"-"All right, boys!" she called them. "Let's go!"

Off they go, all three, she a step or two ahead of them. We saw them cross the square, littered with the wreckage of the carnival, the last gas lamp at the end whitened their group for an instant, and then the night took them in. We heard their voices for a while and then nothing at all. There was nothing left.

I left the bistrot without talking to Robinson again. Martrodin bade me a polite good night. A policeman was pacing the boulevard. In passing each other we stirred up the silence. Here and there the sound startled a shopkeeper bogmired in his aggressive figuring, like a dog gnawing a bone. A family on a bender filled the whole street, yelling on the corner of the Place Jean-Jaurès. They weren't getting ahead at all, they stood at the end of an alley, hesitating to go in, like a fishing fleet in a gale. The father went stumbling from one side of the street to the other and couldn't seem to stop urinating.

The night had come home.

* * *

I remember another night about that time because of what happened. First, shortly after dinnertime, I heard an enormous sound of garbage cans being moved. People often made a racket with the garbage cans in my stairway. Then a woman moaning, sighing. I opened my door a crack, but I didn't move.

If I came out after an accident without being called, they'd probably think of me as a helpful neighbor, and my medical assistance wouldn't have to be paid for. If they wanted me, they'd just have to send for me officially, and then it would cost them twenty francs. Poor people persecute altruism implacably, meticulously, and the kindest impulses are punished without mercy. So I waited for someone to ring my bell, but no one came. For reasons of economy no doubt.

I had almost stopped waiting when a little girl appeared at my door, trying to read the names on the bells. As it turned out, she was looking for me. Madame Henrouille had sent her.

"Who's sick?" I asked.

"A gentleman. He's hurt himself... "

"A gentleman?" I thought of Henrouille himself, "The husband?... Monsieur Henrouille?" "No... A friend, but he's in their house…"

"Somebody you know?"

No, she'd never seen this friend.

It was cold out, the child ran, I walked fast. "How did it happen?"

"I don't know."

We skirted a small park, the remains of an old forest, where at night the long, slow winter mists would catch between the trees. One little street after another. We soon came to the house. The child didn't say good-bye to me, she was afraid to go nearer. Madame Henrouille, the daughter-in-law, was standing on the front steps under the awning, waiting for me. Her oil lamp was flickering in the wind.

"This way, doctor... This way... " she called out. "Has your husband hurt himself?" I asked her.

"Go right in!" she said rather brusquely, without even giving me time to think. I ran smack into the old woman, who began to yap and light into me while I was still in the hallway. A broadside.

"Oh, the monsters! The bandits! Doctor! They tried to kill me!" So they'd come a cropper.

"Kill you?" I said with an air of surprise. "Why would they want to do that?"

"Because I was taking too long to die! Use your brains, dammit! Naturally I don't want to die!"

"Mother! Mother!" the daughter-in-law broke in. "You've taken leave of your wits! How can you say such awful things to the doctor!"

"Awful things, is it? Well, you slut, you've got an all-fired nerve! Taken leave of my wits, have I? I've got wits enough to see the whole lot of you hanged! Believe you me!"

"But who's hurt? Where is he?"

"You'll see who!" the old woman puts in. "The murderer! He's upstairs on their bed! A fine mess he's made of your bed, you hussy! Got his no-good blood all over your mattress! His blood, not mine! What filthy rotten blood that must be! You won't wash that out in a hurry! Take it from me, that murderer's blood will stink for a long time to come! Some people go to the theater for excitement! Not us, we've got a theater right here! It's upstairs, doctor! Real theater, no make-believe. Don't miss it! Hurry hurry! Maybe the dirty dog will be dead before you get there! And then you won't see a thing!"

The daughter-in-law tried to hush her up, for fear she'd be heard on the street. In spite of the situation, the daughter-in-law didn't seem terribly upset, only put out that their scheme had misfired, but her opinions were unchanged. In fact she was dead sure she'd been right.

"Oh doctor, listen to her! Isn't it shameful! When I've always tried so hard to make her life pleasant! You know that! Didn't I keep urging her to go and stay with the Sisters... "

Hearing about the Sisters again was too much for the old woman.

"To Paradise! Yes, you slut, that's where you all wanted to send me! Oh, you bandits! That devil upstairs! That's why you and your husband brought him here! To kill me, that's right, not to send me to any Sisters! He botched it, the man's all thumbs if you ask me! Go on, doctor, go and see what that bastard upstairs has done to himself, oh yes, him and nobody else!... I hope he croaks! Go on, doctor! Go see him before it's too late!"

If the daughter-in-law didn't seem dejected, the old woman was even less so. The plot had almost wiped her out, but she wasn't as indignant as she put on. It was all an act. Actually that bungled murder had revived her, raised her up from the creeping tomb she'd been shut up in all those years at the back of the moldering garden. Late in life an indestructible vitality had come back and was running through her veins. She was indecently relishing not only her victory but also the prospect of having something to torment her mean-hearted daughter-in-law with for the rest of her life. She had her where she wanted her now. She was bent on my knowing every detail of the miscarried plot and how it had all happened.

"And do you know where I met that murderer?" she went on in the same exalted register, especially for my benefit. "In your waiting room!... That's right, doctor, and I didn't trust him!... I didn't trust him this far!... Do you know what he first suggested to me? He wanted to bump you off, you bitch! That's right, you slut! And cheap too! I assure you! He has the same propositions for everybody! It's common knowledge!... So you see, you hussy, I know how he makes his living! I know all about him! His name is Robinson!... Deny it if you dare! , . . Tell me that's not his name!... As soon as I saw him whispering in corners with you two, I had my suspicions... And a good thing too!... If I hadn't been suspicious, where'd I be now?"

Over and over again the old woman told me how it had all happened. The rabbit had moved while he was fastening the fireworks to the door of the hutch. Meanwhile she had been watching him from her shack, she'd had a "ringside seat," as she put it. The contraption was loaded with buckshot...

it had gone off in his face while he was connecting it up, right in his eyes. "A man's not easy in his mind when he's plotting murder," she concluded. "What would you expect?"

Anyway, for butter-fingered incompetence, it took the cake.

"That's what they've done to men lately," the old woman went on. "That's right! Matter of habit! They have to kill to eat!

They're not satisfied anymore to steal their daily bread! . , . Or kill their grandmothers!... Nobody's ever seen anything like it!... Never!... It's the end of the world!... Wickedness is all they're good for! And you now! Up to your necks in it!... And him gone blind! You'll have him on your hands for the rest of your days!... What do you think of that?... Him and his slimy tricks!... "

The daughter-in-law didn't say a word, but she must have worked out her plan. She was a really concentrated villain. While we were busy with our reflections, the old woman went looking through the rooms for her son.

"And you know, doctor, I have a son! Where's he got to? What's he up to now?" She staggered down the corridor, shaken by nonstop laughter.

Old people don't usually laugh so hard except in the bughouse. When you hear a thing like that, you wonder what the world's coming to. She was bent on finding her son. He'd escaped into the street. "All right, let him hide! He can live forever for all I care! Now he'll have to live with that scum upstairs, serves him right, live with the two of them, including our friend who'll never see again! And support him! Hee hee! Square in the face! I saw it! I saw it from start to finish! Boom boom! I saw it all right! And it wasn't a rabbit, I assure you! Damn it all, doctor, where's my son? Haven't you seen him? There's another dirty dog, always been even deeper than her, but now finally the viciousness of his crummy character has come out, oh yes, it's come out all right. It takes a long time for a low character like his to come out! But when it does, it's rotten to the core! You can't deny it, doctor! Something worth seeing!" She was having a fine time. She wanted to impress me with her superiority to the situation and to confound us all, to humiliate us, so to speak.

She had hit on a good role and was working it for all it was worth. An emotional binge. Which is always a pleasure. There's no limit to our happiness as long as we're capable of playing a part. She was sick of old folks' jeremiads, the only part she'd been given in the last twenty years. She'd never let go of this new, virulent, unhoped-for role that had come her way. Old age means not having a passionate role to play anymore, seeing your theater fold up on you, so there's nothing but death to look forward to! All of a sudden the old woman's zest had come back to her with her new and ardent role: the avenger. She didn't want to die anymore, not in the least. She radiated the desire to live, the affirmation of life. In melodrama she had found new fires, real fire.

She was wanning herself, she had no desire to leave the new fire, to leave us. For a long while she had almost ceased to be-lieve there was any fire. She hadn't known what to do to stop herself from dying at the back of her dim-witted garden. And then suddenly this tempest of hard hot reality had hit her.

"My death!" Grandma Henrouille was shrieking now. "That's something I want to see! Do you hear! I've still got my two eyes! I want to get a good look at it!"

She never wanted to die! Never! That was definite! She had stopped believing in her death.

* * *

Everybody knows that such situations are hard to manage and that managing them is always very expensive. In the first place we didn't even know where to put Robinson. In the hospital? Obviously that would make for loose tongues, all sorts of gossip... Send him back to his pad?... Unthinkable, with his face in that condition. Like it or not, the Henrouilles had to keep him.

He lay in bed upstairs, in a pitiful state. He was terrified of being thrown out and prosecuted. Not hard to see why. It was one of those things that you really can't tell anyone about. We kept the blinds in his room carefully drawn, but people, the neighbors, started passing through that street more often than usual, just to look up at the shutters and ask for news of the injured man. We gave them news all right, we told them fairy stories. But how were we to stop them from smelling a rat? From gossiping? Besides, they embroidered on what we told them. How could we stop them from speculating? Luckily nobody had gone to the law. That was something. As far as his face was concerned, I was doing all right. The wound was very jagged and a lot of dirt had got into it, but no infection had set in. As for his eyes, I foresaw scars in the corneas, through which light would pass with difficulty, if at all.

We'd manage to patch up some sort of eyesight if there was anything left to patch. For the moment we'd concentrate on what was most urgent, above all we'd have to prevent the old woman from getting us all into trouble with her horrible yapping in front of the neighbors. True, most of them thought she was mad, but that doesn't always account for everything.

If the police really started prying, God knew where it would lead us. Preventing the old woman from making a spectacle of herself in her little yard had become a ticklish business. We all took turns trying to calm her down. It was no good if she thought we were browbeating her, but gentleness didn't always work very well either. In a frenzy of vindictiveness, she was blackmailing us, neither more nor less.

I went to see Robinson at least twice a day. He groaned under his bandages as soon as he heard me climbing the stairs. He was really in pain, but not as much as he wanted me to think. He'd have cause, I foresaw, for much worse distress when he realized exactly what had happened to his eyes... I was evasive about the future. He complained of stinging in his eyelids. He thought that was what prevented him from seeing anything.

The Henrouilles were taking good care of him, in accordance with my instructions. No trouble on that score.

Nobody mentioned the plot anymore. We didn't speak of the future either. As I was leaving them in the evening, we all took turns looking at one another, so intensely I always had a feeling that we were about to do away with one another once and for all. When I thought it over, that culmination struck me as logical and expedient. I could scarcely imagine the nights in that house. But there they would be in the morning, and together we'd face the world together just where we left it together the night before. Madame Henrouille would help me renew the dressing with permanganate, and we'd open the blinds a bit as a test. The result was always the same. Robinson didn't even notice that we had just opened the blinds...

So the earth makes its way through the vastly menacing, silent night.

Every morning the son would welcome me with a little peasant phrase: "Well, well, doctor... Looks like another late frost!" he would observe, glancing up at the sky from under the little peristyle. As if the weather mattered. His wife would go out and try again to parley with her mother-in-law, but only succeed in redoubling her fury.

While we kept Robinson's eyes bandaged, he told me about his beginnings in life. When he was eleven, his parents had apprenticed him to a high-class shoemaker. One day he delivered a pair of shoes to a lady customer, and she invited him to share a pleasure which up until then he had known only in his imagination. He was so horrified by what he had done that he never went back to his boss. In those days fucking a customer was still an unforgivable crime. Especially the lady's chemise, all of chiffon, had had a phenomenal effect on him. Thirty years later he remembered that chemise in every detail. The lady swishing through her apartment full of cushions and fringed portieres, her pink and perfumed flesh, had given young Robinson food for interminable and despairing comparisons to last him the rest of his life.

Yet a good many things had happened since. He'd seen continents and been through whole wars, but he'd never recovered from that revelation. It gave him pleasure to think about it, to tell me about the minute of youth he had enjoyed with the lady customer. "Having my eyes closed like this makes me think," he observed. "It's like a parade... Like having a movie show in my bean... " 1 didn't dare tell him that he'd have time to get awfully sick of his little movie show. Since all thought leads to death, a day would come when he'd see nothing else in his movie show.

Not far from the Henrouilles' house there was a little factory with a big engine in it. It shook their house from morning to night. And there were other factories a little further away that thumped and pounded the whole time, even at night. "We'll be gone when the roof caves in," Henrouille would joke, but he was kind of worried all the same. "It'll happen sooner or later!" It was true that bits of plaster were falling from the ceiling. An architect tried to reassure them, but whenever you stopped in that house to listen to what was going on, you felt as if you were on a ship, sailing from one fear to another. Passengers, shut up between decks, making plans even sadder than life, economizing and dreading the darkness as well as the light.

Henrouille would go up to the bedrooom after lunch to read a while to Robinson, as I'd asked him to. The days passed. He treated Henrouille, too, to the story about that marvelous lady customer he had laid in the days of his apprenticeship. After a while the story became a kind of collective joke for everyone in the house. That's what happens to our secrets when we spread them abroad. There's nothing terrible inside us or on earth or possibly in heaven itself except what hasn't been said yet. We won't be easy in our minds until everything has been said once and for all, then we'll fall silent and we'll no longer be afraid of keeping still. That will be the day.

In the weeks while his eyelids were suppurating, I was able to entertain him with fairy tales about his eyes and the future. Sometimes I'd pretend the window was closed when it was wide open and sometimes that it was very dark outside.

But one day when my back was turned he went to the window himself to see what was what, and before I could stop him he had slipped the bandage off his eyes. He hesitated for quite a while. He touched the window frame first on the right, then on the left. He couldn't believe it, but in the end he had to. There was no getting around it.

"Bardamu!" he shouted. "Bardamu! It's open! The window's open, I tell you!"—I didn't know what to say. I stood there like an idiot. He was holding both arms out of the window, in the fresh air. Naturally he couldn't see a thing, but he felt the air. He stretched his arms out in his darkness as far as he could, as if he were trying to touch the end of it. He didn't want to believe it. His own private darkness. I pushed him back into his bed and said things to comfort him, but he didn't believe me anymore. He was crying. He, too, had come to the end. There was nothing more we could say to him. A time comes when you're all alone, when you've come to the end of everything that can happen to you. It's the end of the world. Even grief, your own grief, doesn't answer you anymore, and you have to retrace your steps, to go back among people, it makes no difference who. You're not choosy at times like that, because even to weep you have to go back where everything starts all over, back among people.

"What will you do with him when he's better?" I asked the daughter-in-law at lunch after this scene. They had asked me to stay and eat with them in the kitchen. Neither of them had any serious idea of how to get out of the mess they were in. The cost of buying him a pension terrified them, especially her, because she knew more about the price of arrangements for invalids. She had even gone to the Public Welfare and "taken steps." Steps they avoided mentioning to me.

One evening after my second visit Robinson did everything he could think of to keep me with him, he wanted me to stay a bit later than usual. He went on rehashing all the memories he could muster about the things we had done and the places we had been together, even things we had never tried to remember before. He remembered things we had never had time to bring up. In his seclusion the world we had explored seemed to pour back on him with all the moans, the kindnesses, the old clothes, the friends we had left behind us; in his eyeless head he had opened a shop full of outworn emotions.

"I'll kill myself!" he notified me when his misery seemed too great to bear. And yet he managed to bear his misery a little longer, like a weight that was much too heavy and infinitely useless, misery on a road where he met no one to whom he could speak of it, it was just too big and complicated. He couldn't have explained this misery of his, it exceeded his education.

He was a natural-born coward, I knew it and so did he; he kept hoping we'd save him from the truth, but on the other hand I was beginning to wonder if there was anywhere such a thing as a real coward... It looks like any man has things he is willing to die for, quickly and gladly. Except that a chance to die pleasantly, the chance he's looking for, doesn't always materialize. So he goes off somewhere to die as best he can... He sticks around on earth and everybody takes him for a jerk and a coward, but the truth is that he simply lacks conviction. He only seems to be a coward.

Robinson was not prepared to die under the conditions offered. Under different conditions he might have been delighted.

All in all, death is something like marriage.

This particular death didn't appeal to him, that was the long and the short of it.

Then he'd have to resign himself and accept his helplessness and distress. But for the moment he was frantically busy splotching his soul with misery and distress. Later he'd put order into his misery and then a real new life would begin. He'd have to.

"You may not believe me," he said to me that evening after dinner, piecing bits of memories together. "I've never had much of a gift for languages, but do you know, toward the end in Detroit I managed to carry on a bit of a conversation in English... I've forgotten it now, all except one little phrase... Two words... They've been coming back to me ever since this thing happened to my eyes... 'Gentlemen first!' That's just about all I can say in English now, I don't know why... of course, it's an easy thing to remember... 'Gentlemen first!" To take his mind off his troubles, we tried talking English together. We kept repeating "Gentlemen first" over and over again like idiots a propos of everything and nothing. A private joke. In the end we even taught it to Henrouille, who'd come up for a while to keep tabs on us.

While stirring up memories, we started wondering what might be left of all that... of all the things we'd known together... We wondered what could have become of Molly, our sweet Molly... As for Lola, I'd just as soon have forgotten her, but come to think of it I'd have welcomed news of them all, even little Musyne while I was at it... who was probably living in Paris, nearby... practically next door, in fact... Still, I'd have had to bestir myself to find out about her... There were so many people whose names, mannerisms, and addresses I had lost, whose friendliness and even their smiles, after so many years and years of trouble and worrying about the next meal, must have turned into pathetic grimaces, like old cheeses... Even memories have their youth... When you let them grow old, they turn into revolting phantoms dripping with selfishness, vanity, and lies... They rot like apples... So we talked about our youth, mulling it over. We didn't trust it... Which reminded me, I hadn't been to see my mother in a long time... And those visits had never done my nervous system any good... When it came to sadness, my mother was worse than me... Still in her little shop, she seemed after all those years and years to make a point of piling up disappointments around her... When I went to see her, she'd say: "You know, Aunt Hortense died two months ago in Coutances... Maybe you should have gone... And Clémentin, you remember Clémentin?... The floor polisher who played with you when you were little... Well, they picked him up the day before yesterday on the Rue d'Aboukir... He hadn't eaten in three days... "

Robinson's childhood had been so dismal he didn't know what to say when he thought of it. Except for the episode with the lady customer, he couldn't find anything, even in the far corners, that didn't make him sick with despair; it was like a house full of repugnant, foul-smelling objects: brooms, slop jars, housewives, and smacks in the face... Monsieur Henrouille had nothing to say of his own youth including his military service, except that he'd had his picture taken with a pompom, and that picture was still hanging over the wardrobe.

When he'd gone back down, Robinson told me how worried he was that he'd never get the promised ten thousand francs now... "Don't count on them!" was my advice. I thought it best to prepare him for that new disappointment.

Some bits of shot left over from the explosion kept surfacing at the edges of his wound. I removed them in several installments, a few each day. The pain was bad when I probed just above the conjunctiva.

We had taken every possible precaution, but the neighborhood people gossiped right and left all the same. Luckily Robinson suspected nothing, it would have made him a lot sicker than he was. No doubt about it, there was suspicion all around us. Moving about the house in her slippers, Madam Henrouille was quieter and quieter. You weren't expecting her and then she'd be right on top of you.

What with the reefs all around us, the least doubt could wreck us all. Then the whole ship would crack, split, crash, come apart at the seams, and wash up on the shore. Robinson, the grandmother, the fireworks, the rabbit, his eyes, the unlikely son, the murdering daughter-in-law—we'd all end up with our garbage and our rotten secrets in the office of some furibund examining magistrate. I wasn't very pleased with myself. Not that I'd done anything positively criminal. I hadn't. But I felt guilty all the same. I was especially guilty of wishing deep down that this whole business would go on. In fact I couldn't see any objection to all of us together drifting deeper and deeper into the night.

To tell the truth, there was no need of wishing, things were moving all by themselves, and moving fast.

* * *

The rich don't have to kill to eat. They "employ" people, as they call it. The rich don't do evil themselves. They pay. People do all they can to please them, and everybody's happy. They have beautiful women, the poor have ugly ones. Clothing aside, they're the product of centuries. Easy to look at, well fed, well washed. After all these years, life can boast no greater accomplishment.

It's no use trying, we slide, we skid, we fall back into the alcohol that preserves the living and the dead, we get nowhere. It's been proved. After all these centuries of watching our domestic animals coming into the world, laboring and dying before our eyes without anything more unusual ever happening to them either than taking up the same insipid fiasco where so many other animals had left off, we should have caught on. Endless waves of useless beings keep rising from deep down in the ages to die in front of our noses, and yet here we stay, hoping for something... We're not even capable of thinking death through.

The women of the rich, well fed, well lied to, well rested, tend to be good looking. That's a fact. And maybe, after all, it's enough. How do I know? Maybe that's a reason for living.

"Don't you think the women in America were prettier than the ones here?"—Robinson had been asking me things like that ever since he'd started chewing on his travels. He was getting curious, he even started talking about women.

I wasn't going to see him quite so often now, because about that time I was put in charge of a small neighborhood dispensary for tuberculosis. I may as well call a spade a spade, it brought in eight hundred francs a month. My patients were mostly people from the zone, that village of sorts, which never succeeds in picking itself entirely out of the mud and garbage, bordered by paths where precocious snotnosed little girls play hookey under the fences to garner a franc, a handful of French fries, and a dose of gonorrhea from some sex fiend. A setting for avant-garde films where the trees are poisoned with laundry and lettuces drip with urine on Saturday night. In those few months of specialized practice I performed no miracles. Miracles were sorely needed. But my patients weren't at all eager for me to perform miracles, they were banking on their tuberculosis to move them from the state of absolute misery in which they'd been moldering ever since they could remember to the state of relative misery conferred by microscopic government pensions. Their more or less positive sputum had been getting them periodically rejected for military service ever since the war. They got thinner and thinner, thanks to fever maintained by eating little, vomiting a lot, drinking enormous quantities of wine, and working in spite of it all, one day out of three, to tell the truth.

The hope of a pension possessed them body and soul. One day a pension would come to them like grace if only they had the strength to wait a little while before snuffing out completely. You can't know what it is to come back and wait for something if you haven't seen all the coming back and waiting poor people expecting a pension can do.

While the rain came down outside, they'd spend whole afternoons and evenings hoping in the corridor and doorway of my rundown dispensary, stirring up their hopes of percentages, their longing for definitely positive sputum, genuine hundred-percent tubercular sputum. Their hope of getting cured came far behind their hope for a pension... Of course they also thought about getting cured, but very little, they were much too dazzled by their dreams of an income, however infinitesimal. This ultimate, uncompromising desire left room only for negligible wishes, and even their death became by comparison a side issue, a sporting risk. Death after all is only a matter of a few hours, a few minutes, but a pension is like poverty, it lasts a whole lifetime. Rich people are drunk in a different way, they can't understand this frenzy about security. Being rich is another kind of drunkenness, the forgetful kind. That, in fact, is the whole point of getting rich: to forget.

Little by little I'd broken my bad habit of promising my patients good health. The prospect of getting well didn't thrill them. Good health can't be anything but second best. Getting well means you can work. Isn't that lovely? While a government pension, however negligible, is purely and simply divine.

When you have no money to offer the poor, you'd better keep your trap shut. If you talk to them about anything but money, you'll almost always be deceiving them, lying. It's easy to amuse the rich, all you need, for instance, is mirrors for them to see themselves in, because in the whole world there's nothing better to look at than the rich. To keep the rich cheerful all you've got to do is move them up a notch in the Legion of Honor every ten years, like a sagging tit, that'll keep them busy for another ten years. And that's the truth. My patients were poor and selfish; they were materialists, shrunk to the measure of their sordid hope that positive sputum streaked with blood would get them a pension. Nothing else meant a thing to them. Not even the seasons meant a thing. They were aware of the seasons only insofar as the seasons affected their cough and the state of their health; in the winter, for instance, you're a good deal more likely to catch cold than in the summer, but on the other hand you're more likely to spit blood in the springtime, and during the summer heat it's not difficult to lose as much as five pounds a week , . . Sometimes I heard them talking among themselves when they were waiting for their turn, and they thought I wasn't there... They told endless horror stories about me and lies that would make you blow your imagination out. Running me down like that probably picked them up, gave them some sort of mysterious courage that they needed to be more and more ruthless, hard and vicious, to stick it out, to last. Having someone they could slander, despise, and threaten seems to have made them feel better. And yet I did all I could to please them, I went to bat for them, I tried to help them, I gave them plenty of iodine to make them spit up their filthy bacilli, but I never succeeded in neutralizing their cussed-ness...

When I questioned them, they stood there in front of me, smiling like servants, but they didn't like me, mostly because I was helping them, but also because I wasn't rich, and having me for a doctor meant they were being treated free of charge, which is never flattering for a sick person, even if he is hoping for a pension. No slander would have been too great for them to spread behind my back. Most of the doctors in the neighborhood had cars, I didn't, and to their way of thinking my walking was a kind of infirmity. If anyone gave them the slightest encouragement, something my colleagues were always glad to do, they'd avenge themselves, or so it seemed, for all my kindness, for my devotion and readiness to help. Which is perfectly normal. Nevertheless the time passed.

One evening when my waiting room was almost empty, a priest came in to see me. I didn't know that priest, I almost showed him the door. I didn't like priests, I had my reasons, especially since the time they'd shanghaied me at San Tapeta. But hard as I tried to place this one, searching my mind for something definite to reproach him with, the fact is that I'd never seen him before. Still, he must, like me, have gone about quite a lot in Rancy by night, he lived nearby. Maybe he avoided me on his rounds. I thought it over.

Maybe somebody had told him I didn't like priests. You could see that by the weaseling way he started his spiel. One thing is sure—we had never jostled each other around the same sickbeds. He had been officiating, he told me, at a church nearby for the last twenty years. Plenty of parishioners, but not many who paid. A kind of beggar, come to think of it. We had that much in common. The soutane he was wearing struck me as a most uncomfortable sort of drapery for plodding through the muck of the Zone. I said as much. I went so far as to stress the extravagant discomfort of such a garment.

"You get used to it," he said.

The impertinence of my remark didn't put him off, he became more affable than ever. Obviously he had something to ask of me. His voice seldom rose above a certain confidential monotone which, or so at least I imagined, came from his calling. While he was cautiously preambling, I tried to form a picture of all he did each day to earn his calories, all his grimaces and promises, pretty much like my own... And then, to amuse myself, I imagined him all naked at his altar... It's a good habit to get into: when somebody comes to see you, quick, reduce him to nakedness, and you'll see through him in a flash, regardless of who it is, you will instantly discern the underlying reality, namely, an enormous, hungry maggot. It's good sleight-of- the-imagination. His lousy prestige vanishes, evaporates. Once you've got him naked, you'll be dealing with nothing more than a bragging, pretentious beggar, talking drivel of one kind or another. It's a test that nothing can withstand. In a moment you'll know where you're at. There won't be anything left but ideas, and there's nothing frightening about ideas.

With ideas nothing is lost, everything can be straightened out. Whereas it's sometimes hard to stand up to the prestige of a man with his clothes on. Nasty smells and mysteries cling to his clothes.

This Abbé had very bad teeth, decayed, discolored, ringed with greenish tartar, in short, a fine case of alveolar pyorrhea. I was going to talk to him about his pyorrhea, but he was too busy telling me things. The things he was telling me kept squirting against the stumps of his teeth under the impulsion of a tongue, no movement of which escaped me. In a number of spots the edges of his tongue were bruised and bleeding.

This kind of meticulous observation was a habit, you might say a hobby, of mine. When you stop to examine the way in which words are formed and uttered, our sentences are hard put to it to survive the disaster of their slobbery origins. The mechanical effort of conversation is nastier and more complicated than defecation. That corolla of bloated flesh, the mouth, which screws itself up to whistle, which sucks in breath, contorts itself, discharges all manner of viscous sounds across a fetid barrier of decaying teeth— how revolting! Yet that is what we are adjured to sublimate into an ideal. It's not easy. Since we are nothing but packages of tepid, half-rotted viscera, we shall always have trouble with sentiment. Being in love is nothing, it's sticking together that's difficult. Feces on the other hand make no attempt to endure or to grow. On this score we are far more unfortunate than shit; our frenzy to persist in our present state—that's the unconscionable torture.

Unquestionably we worship nothing more divine than our smell. All our misery comes from wanting at all costs to go on being Tom, Dick or Harry, year in year out. This body of ours, this disguise put on by common jumping molecules, is in constant revolt against the abominable farce of having to endure. Our molecules, the dears, want to get lost in the universe as fast as they can! It makes them miserable to be nothing but "us," the jerks of infinity. We'd burst if we had the courage, day after day we come very close to it. The atomic torture we love so is locked up inside us with our pride.

Since I was silent, stunned by the thought of these biological ignominies, the Abbé, thinking he had me in his pocket, assumed a benevolent, almost familiar manner. With infinite precautions he broached the subject of my medical reputation in the neighborhood. My reputation, he gave me to understand, might have been better if I had taken a very different course at the start, during the first few months of my practice in Rancy.

"Don't forget, my dear doctor, that the sick are basically conservative... As you must doubtless know, they live in fear that heaven and earth will fail them…"

In other words, I should have made my peace with the Church from the start. That was his eminently practical as well as spiritual conclusion. Not a bad idea. I was careful not to interrupt him but waited patiently for him to come to the point of his visit.

The weather couldn't have been gloomier or more confidential. It was so vile, so coldly and emphatically vile, it gave you the feeling that if you went out you'd never see the rest of the world again, that the world would have melted away in disgust.

My nurse had finally brought her case histories up to date, every last one. She had no excuse whatever for staying there listening to us. So she left us, but miffed, slamming the door behind her, and plunged into a furious downpour.

* * *

In the course of our conversation this priest told me his name, Abbé Protiste he called himself. Between exercises in evasiveness, he informed me that he and Madame Henrouille had for some time been taking steps with a view to getting the old woman and Robinson, the two of them together, into an inexpensive religious institution. They were still at it.

Looking closely at this Abbé Protiste, I might have taken him for a salesman in a department store, maybe even a section manager, wet, greenish, and many times dried. There was something really plebeian in the humility of his insinuations. In his breath, too. When it comes to breath, I never go wrong. There was a man who ate too fast and drank white wine.

Madame Henrouille, he told me as a starter, had called on him at the presbytery soon after the incident so see if he could help them out of the mess they had got themselves into. In telling me that, he seemed to be looking for excuses, explanations, as if he were ashamed of his part in the affair. There was really no need of putting on airs on my account. I knew the lie of the land. He was simply joining us in the night, that's all. That was his lookout. Little by little, what with the money involved, this priest had developed an extraordinary crust. That too was his lookout! Since my dispensary was steeped in silence and night had settled on the Zone, he lowered his voice to a whisper, wanting to confide in me alone. But whisper or not, everything he said struck me as monstrous and intolerable, probably because of the quiet all around me, which seemed to be full of echoes. Or were they only in my head? "Hush!" I kept wanting to say in the intervals between his words. I was so frightened my lips trembled a little, and at the end of his sentences I made myself stop thinking.

Now that he had joined us in our terror, the priest didn't quite know how to go about following the four of us in the darkness. A small group. He wanted to know how many of us were already mixed up in the affair. And where we were headed. So that he too, hand in hand with his new friends, might direct his steps toward the goal we would have to reach all together or not at all. We were all in the same boat now. The priest would have to learn to walk in the dark like the rest of us. He was still unsteady on his pins. He asked me what he should do to keep from falling. He didn't have to come if he was afraid. We'd get to the end together, and then we'd know what we'd been looking for in our adventure. That's what life is, a bit of light that ends in darkness. But on the other hand, maybe we'd never know, maybe we wouldn't find anything. That's death.

The essential for the moment was to grope our way carefully. At the point we had got to we couldn't go back. We had no choice. Their lousy justice with its Laws was everywhere, at the bend of every corridor. Madame Henrouille was holding the old woman's hand, her son and I were holding theirs and Robinson's as well. We were all in it together. I explained all that to the priest without delay. And he understood.

Like it or not, I told the Abbé, in our present situation it wouldn't do us a bit of good to be noticed and exposed by the passers-by, I made that very clear. If we met anybody, we should pretend to be just taking a walk. Those were the instructions. Act natural. So now the Abbé knew the ins and outs, he understood. He gave me an ardent handshake. Naturally he too was scared to death. A beginner. He hesitated, he floundered like an innocent. At that point there was neither road nor light, and in their place only words of caution, which we passed back and forth but didn't greatly believe in ourselves. The words people say to reassure each other at times like that fall on empty air. The echo sends back nothing, you've walked out on Society. Fear says neither yes nor no. Fear swallows up everything we say, everything we think.

Nor does it help at times like that to stare wide-eyed into the darkness. It's horror wasted, that's all. The night has taken everything, even the light of our eyes. It has drained us. Even so, we have to join hands or we'll fall. Day people can't understand us. Between them and us stands our fear, which will weigh on us until this thing ends one way or another and we can get back together, in death or life, with the other motherfuckers of this world.

For the moment the Abbé had only to help us and find things out in a hurry, that was his job. Actually that's what he had come for, to knock himself out finding a home as quickly as possible, first for Grandma Henrouille and then for Robinson, with the nuns in the provinces. He thought such an arrangement possible, and so did I. Except we'd have to wait months for a vacancy, and we were sick of waiting. We were fed up.

The daughter-in-law was quite right, the sooner the better. They should beat it and good riddance! So Protiste came up with another scheme which, I agreed on the spot, seemed most ingenious. Best of all, it would mean a commission for both of us, the priest and me. The arrangement was to go into effect almost immediately, and I'd have my own little part to play. It consisted in persuading Robinson to go south, to give him a bit of friendly but firm advice.

Not knowing either the bottom or the underside of Protiste's scheme, I ought perhaps to have expressed certain reservations, tried to protect my friend a little... Because the scheme Abbé Protiste put forward was indeed pretty wild. But we were all so harried by circumstances that our chief concern was haste. I promised everything they asked, to help and to keep my mouth shut. Ticklish situations of this kind seemed to be nothing new to this Protiste, and something told me that he would make things a lot easier for me.

But where were we to begin? We'd have to arrange for Robinson to leave quietly for the South. How would Robinson feel about the South? Not to mention leaving with the old woman, whom he had come very close to murdering... I'd insist... That's all!... He'd simply have to, for all sorts of reasons, not all of them very good, but sound, yes, sound...

The job that had been found for Robinson and the old woman in the South was certainly weird. In Toulouse. A beautiful city Toulouse! We'd be seeing Toulouse! We'd go visit them down there. I promised I'd go to Toulouse as soon as they were settled in their lodgings and their work and all.

Then, thinking it over, it bothered me a little that Robinson should be leaving so soon, but at the same time I was glad, mostly because for once I was making a bit of real profit on the deal. A thousand francs they were giving me. It was all settled. All I had to do was work up Robinson's enthusiasm for the South, convince him that there was no better climate for damaged eyes, that he'd be blissfully well off down there, and that all things considered he was pretty damn lucky to get off so easily. That ought to do it.

After five minutes of rumination along these lines, I myself was steeped in conviction and prepared for a decisive interview. Strike while the iron is hot, that's my opinion. After all, he'd be no worse off down there than here. Protiste's idea, when I thought it over, seemed perfectly reasonable. You've got to admit it, those priests know how to bury the worst scandals.

All things considered, the deal being offered Robinson and the old woman wasn't so bad. If I wasn't mistaken, it was some sort of mummy show. The mummies were in the cellar of some church, and tourists could visit them for a fee. A fine business, Protiste assured me. I almost believed him, and that made me a little jealous. It's not every day that you can get the dead to work for you.

I locked up the dispensary and started resolutely through the sludge with the priest, heading for the Henrouilles. This was really something new. A thousand francs' worth of hope! I had changed my mind about the priest. When we got to the house, we found the Henrouilles, man and wife, with Robinson in his room on the second floor. But what a state Robinson was in!

"So there you are!" he screeches frantically as soon as he hears my steps on the stairs. "There's something going on! I can feel it!... Tell me the truth!" he gasps.

He starts sniveling before I can say a word. The Henrouilles are making signs while he appeals to me for help: "A pretty mess!" I say to myself. "They're in too much of a hurry... Always have been!... They've broken it to him cold! Without preparation! Without waiting for me!... "

Luckily I was able to retell the whole story, so to speak, in different words. Robinson was more than willing to see the same facts in a different light. All right by him. The priest in the hallway didn't dare come into the room. He was reeling with fright.

"Come in!" the daughter-in-law finally called out. "Come right in! You're very welcome, Monsieur l'Abbé! You've caught a poor, stricken family, that's all!... The doctor and the priest!.., Always together in life's most painful moments! Isn't that right?"

She was making phrases. Her new-found hope of extricating herself from the shit and the darkness was making the old bag lyrical in her repulsive way.

The bewildered priest lost all control and started sputtering with excitement at some distance from the sickbed. His excitement communicated itself to Robinson, who resumed his raving: "They're lying! They're all lying to me!" he yelled.

Talk! Talk! And about what? Appearances! Emotional outpourings. Always the same. Still, it sparked me up, revived my nerve. I drew the daughter-in-law into a corner and put it to her plainly, because I saw that the only person capable of getting them out of this mess was yours truly. "A down payment!" I said to her. "And I want it now!" When there's no trust, as the saying goes, there's no reason to use kid gloves. She got the drift and deposited a thousand-franc note right in the middle of my palm. And then another to be on the safe side. I had thrown my weight. So while I was at it, I set to work, bringing Robinson around. He'd just have to go south, and that was that.

It's easy to speak of betrayal. But to betray somebody you need an opportunity, and once you have it you've got to take it. It's like opening a window in jail. Everybody would like to, but you don't often get the chance.

* * *

Once Robinson had left Rancy, I thought things would pick up, for instance that I'd have a few more patients than usual, but nothing of the kind. In the first place, there was a slump in those parts, a wave of unemployment, which is the worst thing that can happen. And then, in spite of the winter, the weather turned dry and mild, when what the medical profession needs is damp cold. No epidemics either, in short a bad season, a flop.

I even saw some of my colleagues making their rounds on foot, which goes to show, smiling as if it amused them to walk, but actually very much put out, their only purpose being to save money by giving their cars a rest. All I had to wear outside was a raincoat. Was that what gave me my obstinate cold? Or could it have been the habit I'd got into of eating much too little. How do I know? Or had my fevers come back? Be that as it may, there was a cold snap just before spring, and after that I never stopped coughing, I was really sick.

A disaster. One morning I simply couldn't get up. Bébert's aunt was just passing the house. I got someone to call her. She came up. I sent her to collect a small bill that was still owing to me in the neighborhood. The last and only. I collected half, and it did me for ten days, in bed.

Flat on your back for ten days you have time to think. As soon as I felt better, I'd get out of Rancy, that's what I decided. I hadn't paid my rent for six months... So good-bye my four sticks of furniture! I'd slip quietly away, naturally without a word to anyone, and I'd never be seen again in La Garenne-Rancy. I'd leave without trace or address. When the hyenas of poverty are on your trail, why argue? If you're smart, you'll shut up and clear out.

With my M.D., it was true, I could practice anywhere... But anywhere else it would be neither better nor worse... Yes, a little better at first, because it takes a while for people to find out about you, to get into the swing, and pick up the knack of doing you harm. While they're still looking for your most vulnerable spot, you have a little peace, but once they've found your funny bone it's the same all over. All things considered, the best time is the few weeks while you're still unknown in a new place. After that, the crumminess starts all over. It's their nature. The main thing is not to wait till they've spotted your weaknesses. Squash a bedbug before it can slip into its crack. Am I right?

As for sick people, patients, I had no illusions... In another neighborhood they'd be no less grasping or jugheaded or weak-kneed than the ones here. The same wine, the same movies, the same sports talk, the same enthusiastic submission to the natural needs of the gullet and the ass would produce the same crude, filthy horde, staggering from lie to lie, bragging, scheming, vicious... brutal between two fits of panic.

But just as a sick man changes sides in bed and in life, so we too are entitled to move from side to side, it's the only thing we can do, the only defense that's ever been found against Fate. No good hoping to drop off your misery somewhere on the way. Misery is like some horrible woman you've married. Maybe it's better to end up loving her a little than to knock yourself out beating her all your life. Since obviously you won't be able to bump her off.

Anyway, I slipped away from my mezzanine pad in Rancy very quietly. At my concierge's they were all sitting around the table over wine and chestnuts when I passed the lodge for the last time. They didn't see a thing. She was scratching herself, and he, bent over the stove, befuddled by the heat, was so far gone in drink that he couldn't keep his eyes open.

As far as those people were concerned, I was slipping into the unknown, a kind of endless tunnel. It feels good to have three less people knowing you, that is, spying on you and doing you dirt, three people without the faintest idea what's become of you. It's great. Three, because I'm counting their daughter, their little girl Thérèse, who scratched her fleas and bedbug bites so hard that she was all broken out and festering with boils. It's true that you got so badly bitten at my concierge's that going into their lodge was like crawling into a scrubbing brush.

Falling on the people who passed in the street, the long, naked, whistling finger of gas in the entrance turned them instantly into ghosts, gaunt or stout, framed in the black doorway. The same passers-by would then go and find themselves a bit of color here and there, in the light of windows or street lamps, and finally lose themselves, as black and shapeless as myself, in the night.

I was no longer under any obligation to recognize these passers-by. Still, I'd have liked to stop them for just one second in their aimless roaming, just long enough to tell them once and for all that

I was clearing out, getting lost far far away, so far that I didn't give a shit for any of them and they had no way of hurting me now, it was no use trying...

When I got to the Boulevard de la Liberté, the vegetable wagons were bumping along the road to Paris. I went the same way. I was almost out of Rancy. It was kind of chilly, so to warm myself I made for Bébert's aunt's lodge, which was a little out of my way. Her lamp was a spot in the darkness at the end of the corridor. "I really have to say good-bye to his aunt," I said to myself. "Then it'll really be over."

She was sitting as usual in her chair, among the smells of her lodge. A small stove warmed the room, and there was her old old face that always seemed about to burst into tears now that Bébert was gone. On the wall, over her sewing box, hung a big school photo of Bébert in his school smock, with his beret and his cross. It was an enlargement, she'd paid for it with coffee coupons. I woke her.

She started up. "Good morning, doctor." I still remember her exact words. "You look sick," she said first thing. "Sit down... I'm not very well myself... "

"I was taking a little walk," I said, feeling silly to be turning up like that.

"It's late for a little walk, especially being you're headed for Place Clichy... There's a cold wind on the avenue at this time of night... "

She stood up and, stumbling this way and that way, started making us a hot grog, at the same time talking about everything under the sun, but mostly the Henrouilles and Bébert.

There was nothing I could do to make her stop talking about Bébert, though it made her miserable and was bad for her and she knew it. I listened without interrupting, I was in a torpor. She wanted to remind me of all Bébert's endearing qualities, she set them out in a kind of display, taking a great deal of trouble because she was determined not to forget a single one of Bébert's qualities. She kept starting over, and when she had them all in order and had told me everything that could possibly be told about bottle feeding him as a baby, she'd remember some little quality that would have to be lined up beside the others. She'd start once again from the beginning, and even so she'd forget something, and when that happened she had no recourse but to burst into tears of frustration. She was so tired her mind wandered. She sobbed herself to sleep. She hadn't strength enough to retrieve her little memories of little Bébert, whom she had loved so dearly, from the darkness for very long. Nothingness was always close to her now and to some extent upon her. A bit of grog and fatigue and there it was, she fell asleep and snored like a distant airplane being carried away by the clouds. She had no one left on earth.

While she sat crumpled among the smells, I thought I'd go away and probably never see Bébert's aunt again. After all, Bébert had slipped away, quietly and for good, and his old aunt would be following him before long. Her heart was sick and very old. It pumped blood into her arteries as best it could, but then the blood had a hard time climbing back into the veins. She'd be going to the big cemetery nearby, where the crowds of dead are waiting. That's where she took Bébert to play before his illness. And then it would really be over. They'd come and repaint her lodge, and then it would seem as if we had all retrieved ourselves like Japanese billiard balls on the brink of the hole, shilly-shallying before they end it all.

Billiard balls also start out with vigor and brio, but they never get anywhere in the end. Neither do we, and the whole earth is good for nothing else than to help us all get together. Bébert's aunt no longer had far to go; there was practically no vigor left in her. We can't get together while we're alive. There are too many colors to distract us and too many people moving around us. We can only get together in silence, when it's too late, like the dead. I knew all that, but it didn't help. I too had to move and go somewhere else I couldn't stay there with her.

My diploma in my pocket made a big bulge, much bigger than my money and my papers. Outside the police station the patrolman was on duty, waiting to be relieved at midnight. He kept spitting. We bade each other good evening.

After the on-and-off light over the gas pump on the corner of the boulevard came the toll station with its clerks, verdant in their glass cage. The streetcars had stopped running. This was a good time to drop in on the toll clerks and talk about life, which is getting harder and harder, more and more expensive. There were two of them, a young one and an old one, both with dandruff, bent over enormous ledgers. Through their window you could see the fortifications, enormous shadowy piers jutting far out into the night as they waited for ships from so far away, ships so noble that you'll never see such ships. That's for sure. But we can hope for them.

I chewed the fat for quite a while with those clerks, we even drank a bit of coffee that was warming on the cast-iron stove. They asked me as a joke if I was going on vacation, at night like that with my little bundle. "That's right," I said. No use talking to those clerks about anything too peculiar. They couldn't have helped me to understand. Still, I was miffed at their little joke and felt the need of saying something striking, of impressing them sort of, so I started talking off the cuff, about the campaign of 1816,[75] the one that had brought the Cossacks to the exact spot where we were then, to the Barrier, on the heels of the great Napoleon.

All this, of course, as nonchalantly as you please. Having convinced those lugs of my superior culture and sprightly erudition, I felt reassured and started down the avenue to the Place Clichy.

You've doubtless noticed the two prostitutes waiting at the corner of the Rue des Dames. They fill in the few weary hours separating deep night and early dawn. Thanks to them, life perseveres through the darkness. With their handbags chock-full of prescriptions, all-purpose handkerchiefs, and photos of children in the country, they are the connecting fink. Be careful when approaching them in the darkness, for those women are so specialized—barely alive enough to respond to the two or three sentences which sum up everything one can do with them —that they barely exist. They are insect ghosts in buttoned boots.

Don't speak to them, don't go too near them. They're dangerous. I had plenty of room. I started running between the car tracks. The avenue is long.

At the end of it you'll see the statue of Marshal Moncey. He has been defending the Place Clichy since 1816 against memories and oblivion, against everything and nothing, with a wreath of not very expensive beads. I came running down the deserted avenue and got there one hundred and twelve years too late. No more Russians, no more battles, no more Cossacks, no more soldiers, nothing except a ledge of the pedestal that you could sit down on, just under the wreath. And the little brazier with three shivering derelicts around it, squinting into the acrid smoke. Not a very good place to be.

A few cars now and then raced desperately for the exits.

In times of crisis you remember the Grands Boulevards as a place that's not as cold as other places. What with my fever, it cost me an effort of the will to make my brain function. Under the influence of Bébert's aunt's grog, I descended the slope in flight from the wind, which isn't quite so cold when it comes at you from behind. Near the Saint-Georges Métro station an old woman in a little round hat was wailing about her granddaughter in the hospital, stricken with meningitis, so she said. With that as an excuse, she was taking up a collection. With me she was out of luck.

All I could give her was words. I told her about little Bébert and also about a little girl I'd taken care of in Paris, who had died of meningitis while I was in medical school. It had taken her three weeks to die, and her mother in the bed next to hers was so unhappy she couldn't sleep, so she masturbated the whole three weeks, and even when it was all over there was no way of stopping her.

Which goes to show that we can't do without our pleasures for so much as a second, and that it's very hard to be really unhappy. Life is like that.

The grieving old woman and I parted outside the Galeries. She was on her way to Les Halles to unload carrots. She'd been plodding the vegetable trail and so had I, the same.

But I was drawn to the Tarapout.[76] It's plunked down on the boulevard like a big luminous cake. And people come to it from all directions, in a frantic hurry, like grubs. They emerge from the night with wide- open eyes, all ready to stock up on images. The ecstasy that never ends. It's the same people as in the Métro. But here outside the Tarapout they're happy, same as in New York they scratch their bellies at the box office, secrete a little change, and rush, happy and resolute, into the glaring apertures. There was so much light on the people, on their movements, globes, and garlands of light,

---

[75] Campaign of 1816. In 1814, and not in 1816 as Céline whimsically says, Marshal Moncey (Adrien Jeannot de Moncey, due de Conegliano) defended the Clichy Barrier against the invading troops of the anti- Napoleonic coalition. There is a monument commemorating the event in the middle of the Place Clichy. The invading troops included Cossacks, who were long remembered with horror.

[76] Tarapout. The Paramount Theater.

that it practically undressed them. You couldn't have talked about anything personal in that lobby, it was the exact opposite of night.

Rather dazed myself, I went to a cafe nearby. At the table next to mine, when I looked up, who should I see but Parapine, my onetime professor, having a beer with his dandruff and all. We get together. There have been big changes in his life. It takes him ten minutes to tell me about them. No laughing matter. Professor Jaunisset had been so mean to him, had so persecuted him that he, Parapine, had been obliged to leave, to resign, and give up his laboratory. And then the mothers of the little girls at the Lycée had waylaid him at the gates of the Institute and beaten him up. Scandal. Investigation. Trouble.

At the last moment, thanks to an ambiguous advertisement in a medical journal, he had managed in the nick of time to secure another paltry means of support. Nothing much, of course, but down his alley and not fatiguing. The job was based on an ingenious application of Professor Baryton's recent theories concerning the role of the cinema in the education of cretin children. A significant step forward in the exploration of the unconscious. The latest thing. The talk of the town.

Parapine took his special patients to the Tarapout, because it was so modern. He picked them up at Baryton's rest home in the suburbs, and after the show took them back again—dazed, glutted with visions, safe, happy, sound, and wonderfully modernized. That was all he had to do. Once they were seated in front of the screen they needed no supervision. A perfect audience. Everybody was happy. The same film ten times in a row would have delighted them. They were without memory. Continuous surprise—what a joy! Their families were delighted. So was Parapine. So was I. We chortled with well-being and drank beer after beer to celebrate the material reinstatement of Parapine in the modern world. We'd stay there, we decided, until two in the morning, until after the last show at the Tarapout, then we'd pick them up and hurry them back to Dr. Baryton's establishment at Vigny-sur-Seine by cab. A good deal.

Delighted to see each other, we started talking just for the pleasure of exchanging fantasies, first about our travels and then about Napoleon, who cropped up in connection with Moncey on the Place Clichy. Everything becomes a pleasure when two people want nothing more than to get on together, because then you finally feel free. You forget your life, that is, you forget all about money.

One thing leading to another, we even thought up some funny things to say about Napoleon. Parapine knew the history of Napoleon well. It had fascinated him in secondary school back in Poland, he told me. Parapine had been properly educated, not like me.

So Parapine told me that during the retreat from Russia Napoleon's generals had a hell of a time stopping him from going to Warsaw to get himself sucked off just once more by the Polonaise of his heart. That was Napoleon all over, even in the midst of the worst reverses and calamities. Absolutely irresponsible! Think of his Josephine! He was her eagle, but it made no difference! Ants in his pants, come hell and high water! If you've got a taste for wine and women, nothing can stop you. And we all have it, that's the sad part. That's all we think about! In the cradle, at the cafe, on the throne, in the toilet. Everywhere! Everywhere! Our peckers! Napoleon or not! Cuckold or not! Pleasure first! To hell, says the Great Defeated One, with those four hundred thousand fanatics, emberesina'd[77] to the gills... as long as old 'Polion gets one last squirt! What a swine! Never mind! Life is like that! That's how everything ends. In absurdity. Long before the audience, the tyrant is bored with the play he's acting. When he's good and sick of secreting delirium for the benefit of the public, he goes and gets laid. When that happens, he's washed up. Destiny drops him in two seconds flat! His fans have no objection to his massacring them with might and main! None whatever!

That's nothing! They forgive him a hundred percent! What they won't forgive is when he starts boring them all of a sudden. Good work is tolerated only when hammed up! Epidemics stop only when the microbes get disgusted with their toxins. Robespierre was guillotined because he kept saying the same thing, and what did for Napoleon was over two years of Legion-of-Honor inflation. That

---

[77] Emberesina'd. A reference to the crossing of the Berezina River by Napoleon in 1812, in the course of his retreat from Moscow. More than twenty thousand French troops were lost.

lunatic's headache was having to supply half of sedentary Europe with a longing for adventure. An impossible job. It killed him.

Whereas the cinema, that new little factotum of our dreams, can be bought, hired for an hour or two like a prostitute.

Nowadays people are so bored that artists have been posted everywhere as a precaution. People are bored even in the houses where artists have been installed, with their overflow of emotion, their sincerities tumbling from floor to floor till the doors rattle. Each one of them is out to throb more outrageously and passionately, to abandon himself more intensely than his neighbor. Nowadays they decorate the crappers and slaughterhouses and pawnshops, and all that to entertain you, to cheer you up, to distract you from your Fate.

Just plain living, what a drag! Life is a classroom, and boredom is the monitor, always keeping an eye on you, you have to look busy at all costs, busy with something fascinating, otherwise he comes and corrodes your brain. A day that's nothing more than a lapse of twenty-four hours is intolerable. Like it or not, a day should be one long, almost unbearable pleasure, one long coitus.

Disgusting thoughts of this kind come to you when you're crazed by necessity, when a desire for a thousand other things and places is squeezed into each one of your seconds.

Robinson, too, in his way, was harried by the infinite before his accident, but now he was through, or so I thought.

Seeing we were quietly settled at the cafe, I talked, I told Parapine everything that had happened since our last meeting. He understood things, even my kind, and I confessed to him that I had broken my medical career by leaving Rancy so cavalierly. That was the only way to put it. It was no joke. Under the circumstances I couldn't dream of going back to Rancy. Parapine agreed.

While we were talking thus pleasantly, confessing as it were, the Tarapout had an intermission, and all in a heap the movie house musicians came over to the bistrot. So we all had a drink together. Parapine was well known to the musicians.

In the course of the conversation, it came out that a pasha was needed for the stage show. A silent part. The guy who'd played it before had left without notice. Yet it was a good part, and well paid. Not at all strenuous. And in addition, let's not forget, charmingly surrounded by a sumptuous flock of English dancing girls, thousands of precise and agile muscles. Just my line and just what I needed.

I smirked and smiled and waited for the manager to make me an offer. In other words, I applied for the job. Since it was late and they hadn't time to go looking for another actor at the Porte Saint-Martin,[78] the manager was delighted to have me right on the spot. It saved him shoe leather. Me too. He barely looked at me. In fact he took me then and there. And put me to work. It might have bothered them if I'd limped, but even there I'm not so sure...

Penetrating the lovely warm padded basement of the Tarapout, I found a veritable hive of perfumed dressing rooms, where the English girls, while waiting for their number, passed the time romping suggestively and swearing. Overjoyed to have reconnected with my bread and butter, I hastened to make friends with my easy-going young colleagues. They welcomed me charmingly. Angels. Discreet angels. Besides, it's pleasant to be neither confessed nor despised. That's England for you.

The Tarapout was raking it in. Even backstage all was luxury, well-being, legs, lights, soaps, and sandwiches.

I believe the sketch we appeared in was set in Turkestan. It was a pretext for choreographic monkeyshines, musical contortions, and violent drumming.

My part was slight but essential. Puffed up with gold and silver, I had some difficulty at first in finding a place to stand in among so many unstable lamps and doodads, but I got used to it, and thus displayed to my best advantage, I had nothing to do but daydream under the opalescent spotlights.

For a good fifteen minutes twenty cockney bayaderes knocked themselves out with song and bacchanalian dance, supposedly to convince me of the reality of their charms. I'd have been satisfied

---

[78] Porte Saint-Martin. The Theatre de la Porte Saint-Martin. A theater situated on the Boulevard Saint-Martin. One of the holy places of the Romantic drama. Burned down under the Commune in 1871. Rebuilt in 1873.

with less. It seemed to me that going through that routine five times a day was a lot to expect of a poor girl. Those girls never weakened, they waggled their bottoms implacably, with the slightly boring energy typical of their race, the unflagging persistence of an ocean liner, plowing its way through endless seas...

* * *

Why struggle, waiting is good enough, since everything is bound to end up in the street. Basically, only the street counts. Why deny it? It's waiting for us. One of these days we'll have to make up our minds and go down into the street, not one or two or three of us, but all. We stand on the brink, we simper and fuss, but never mind, the time will come.

Interiors are no good. As soon as a door closes on a man, he begins to smell and everything he has on him smells too. Body and soul, he deteriorates. He rots. It serves us right if people stink. We should have looked after them. We should have taken them out, evicted them, exposed them to the air. All things that stink are indoors, they preen themselves, but they stink all the same.

Speaking of families, I know a pharmacist on the Avenue de Saint-Ouen who had a marvelous sign in his window, a lovely advertisement: One bottle (price three francs) will purge the whole family. Isn't that great! They all belch!... and shit together, familywise. They hate one another's guts, the essence of home life, but no one complains because after all it's cheaper than living in a hotel.

Which brings us to hotels. A hotel is more unsettled, less pretentious than an apartment, you don't feel so guilty. The human race is never free from worry, and since the last judgment will take place in the street, it's obvious that in a hotel you won't have so far to go. Let the trumpeting angels come, we hotel dwellers will be the first to get there.

In a hotel you try not to attract too much notice. It doesn't do a bit of good. As soon as you shout too loud or too often, they put their finger on you. Pretty soon, the way sound carries from room to room, you'll almost be afraid to piss in the washbasin. So naturally you improve your manners, the way officers do in the navy. Heaven and earth can start quaking from one minute to the next, we'll be prepared, it won't faze us, for already, just colliding in the hotel corridors, we beg and obtain pardon ten times a day.

I'd advise you to familiarize yourself with the toilet smell of everyone on your floor; it comes in handy. It's hard to harbor illusions at a rooms-by-the-month hotel. The guests don't cut much of a figure. They journey discreetly through life from day to day, the hotel is a ship that's rotting and full of holes, and they know it.

The one I moved to was patronized mostly by students from the provinces. As soon as you set foot on the stairs, it smelled of breakfast and old cigarette butts. At night you could recognize the place from a distance, because of the flame of gray light over the door and the gap-toothed gilt letters hanging from the balcony like an enormous dental plate. A monstrous lodging machine, distempered by sordid goings-on.

We'd pay one another visits from room to room. After years of crummy undertakings in the world of practical affairs, of so-called adventures, I was back again with students.

Their desires were still the same, intense and putrid, neither more nor less insipid than in the old days when I'd left them. The people had changed, but the ideas were the same. They still went at more or less regular hours to the other end of the neighborhood to nibble bits of medicine, odds and ends of chemistry, a pill or two of law, and heaps of zoology. The war, in passing over their age group, hadn't changed a thing, and if out of sympathy you took an interest in their dreams, they led you straight to their fortieth birthday. These young men gave themselves twenty years, two hundred and forty months of dogged thrift, in which to achieve happiness.

Their notions of happiness and success were conventional images, but carefully drawn. They saw themselves at the last square, surrounded by a small but incomparably precious family. Yet they would seldom have looked at this family. What for? One thing a family isn't meant for is to be looked at. And a father's distinction and happiness consist in kissing his family —his poetry—without ever looking at it.

By way of novelty, they'd have motored to Nice with their dowered bride and possibly have adopted the use of checks for making payments. As for the shameful reaches of the soul, they would no doubt have taken their wife to a whorehouse one evening. No more. The rest of their world would be shut up in their daily papers and guarded by the police.

Staying at that flea-bitten hotel made my friends a trifle shameful and irritable for the moment. The young bourgeois student feels that he's being punished, and since it's taken for granted that he can't start saving yet, he drowns his sorrow in Bohemia and more Bohemia, in coffee-house despair.

At the beginning of each month we went through a short but acute fit of eroticism, the whole hotel shook with it. We washed our feet. An erotic expedition was arranged. Money orders arrived from the provinces, and that is what made up our minds. I might have obtained just as good coituses from my English chorus girls at the Tarapout, and free of charge at that, but thinking it over, I rejected the easy way because of the complications and the rotten jealous little pimps who were always hanging around backstage, waiting for the girls.

Since we read several pornographic magazines at our hotel, we knew the ropes and addresses needed for getting fucked in Paris. You have to admit that addresses are fun. You let yourself be tempted... even I, who had known the Passage des Bérésinas and traveled and experienced no end of complications in the pornographic line, never seem to have exhausted the hope of intimate revelations. Where the ass is concerned, there's always a residue of curiosity. You say to yourself that the ass has nothing more to tell you, that you haven't one more minute to waste on it, and then you start in again just to make absolutely sure that the subject is exhausted, you learn something new about it after all, and that suffices to launch you on a wave of optimism.

You pull yourself together, you think more clearly than before, you start hoping again even if you'd given up hope altogether, and inevitably you revert once more to the ass, the same old story. Indeed, there are always, at all ages, discoveries to be made in the vagina. So one afternoon three of us from the hotel set out in search of an inexpensive piece. It was quick work, thanks to the connections of Pomone,[79] who operated an agency in the Batignolles quarter for every kind of erotic arrangement or combination that anyone could desire. His books were full of offers at all prices. This providential man officiated without ostentation of any kind at the back of a court; his exiguous premises were so poorly lit that you needed as much tactile sense and gift of dead reckoning to find your way as in an unfamiliar urinal. Your nerves would be unsettled by the layers of curtain you had to part before reaching the procurer, who was always to be found seated in an artificial confessional twilight.

Because of that dim light, to tell the truth, I never really managed to get a good look at Pomone, and though we had long conversations and even worked together for a time, though he made me all sorts of propositions and confided any number of sensitive secrets, I should be quite incapable of recognizing him today if I met him in hell.

I remember only that the furtive enthusiasts in the sitting room, waiting their turn for an interview, always behaved correctly, never any familiarity between them, in fact they were as reserved as if they'd been waiting for some eccentric dentist who disliked noise and didn't care much for light either.

I made the acquaintance of Pomone through a medical student. The student cultivated him as a means of making a bit of extra money out of his cock, because, you see, the lucky bastard was gifted with a monumental penis. He and his amazing equipment would be hired to bring animation into little intimate gatherings in the suburbs. The ladies made a great fuss over him. especially those who wouldn't have believed that anyone could have "such a big one." Overwhelmed young girls would dream and rave. In the police records our student figured under the alarming pseudonym of Belshazzar![80] The watting customers seldom strike up a conversation. Suffering exhibits itself; pleasure and the needs of the flesh hang their heads in shame.

Say what you please, it's a sin to be a lecher and poor. When Pomone heard about my situation and my medical past, nothing could stop him from telling me about his suffering. A vice was wearing

---

[79] Pomone. From Pomona, goddess of fruit trees.
[80] Belshazzar. The wicked king of Babylon, who saw the handwriting on the wall (Daniel 5:25).

him out. It consisted in "touching" himself continuously under his desk, while conversing with his customers, hunters afflicted with an itching perineum. "It's my work, you see! How do you expect me to control myself... with all the horrors they tell me, the swine!... " In short, his customers tempted him to vice, like those obese butchers who can't help gorging themselves on meat. In addition, I believe his bowels were constantly inflamed as a result of a malignant fever originating in his lungs. And the fact is that he was carried off fay tuberculosis a few years later. He was also exhausted in a different sense by the chatter of his pretentious lady customers, always cheating, always making up ridiculous stories about nothing or about their sexual apparatus, the like of which, to hear them talk, you wouldn't find if you ransacked all four corners of the earth.

What the men wanted most and what had to be found for them was mostly consenting and admiring partners for their erotic wrinkles. Incredible the quantities of love those men had to share, as much as Madame Herote's customers. A single morning's mail would bring the Pomone Agency enough unsatisfied love to extinguish all the wars in the world forever. But these deluges of sentiment never went beyond the ass. The more's the pity.

His desk disappeared beneath that mass of passionate banalities. In my desire to know more, I decided to help him for a while in classifying that vast epistolary ragout. Just as with neckties or diseases, he explained, you grouped them according to types, the lunatics on one side, the masochists and sadists on another, the flagellants over here, the ones looking for a "governess" on a different page, and so on. It's not long before your amusement becomes a chore. We've been expelled from Paradise all right! No doubt about that! Pomone was of the same opinion with his moist hands and his everlasting vice, which gave him pleasure and remorse at the same time. After a few months I knew enough about his business and himself. My visits became less frequent.

At the Tarapout they continued to regard me as quite acceptable, a quiet, punctual super, but after a few weeks of calm, my customary ill luck sought me out from an unusual quarter, and I was obliged to abandon my work as a super and resume my miserable journey.

Seen in perspective, those days at the Tarapout were only a sort of forbidden and insidious port of call. Admittedly, I was always well dressed during those four months, once as a prince, twice as a centurion, one day as an aviator, and well and regularly paid. At the Tarapout I ate enough to last me for years. I led the life of a coupon clipper without the coupons. Treachery! Disaster! One night, I don't know why, they changed our number. The scene of the new sketch was the London Embankment. My misgivings were immediate, our little English girls were expected to sing, off key and ostensibly on the banks of the Thames at night, while I played the part of a policeman. A totally silent role, walking up and down in front of the parapet. Suddenly, when I'd stopped thinking about it, their singing grew louder than life itself and steered fate in the direction of calamity. While they were singing, I couldn't think of anything but all the poor world's misery and my own, those tarts with their singing made my heart burn like tuna fish. I thought I'd digested it, forgotten the worst! But this was the worst of all, a song that couldn't make it... And as they sang, they wiggle-waggled, to try and bring it off. A fine mess, all of a sudden we were knee deep in misery... No mistake! Mooning about in the fog! Their lament was dripping with misery, it made me grow older from minute to minute. Panic oozed from the very stage set. And nothing could stop them. They didn't seem to understand all the harm their song was doing us all... They laughed and flung out their legs in perfect time, while lamenting their whole life... When it comes to you from so far, with such sureness of aim, you can't mistake it and you can't resist.

Misery was everywhere, in spite of the luxurious hall; it was on us, on the set, it overflowed, it drenched the whole earth. Those girls were real artists... Abject misery poured out of them, and they made no attempt to stop it or even understand it. Only their eyes were sad. The eyes aren't enough. They sang the calamity of existence, and they didn't understand. They mistook it for love, nothing but love, the poor little things had never been taught anything else. Supposedly, they were singing about some little setback in love. That's what they thought! When you're young and you don't know, you mistake everything for love trouble...

Where I go... where I look...
It's only for you... ou...

Only for you... ou...

That's what they sang.

It's a mania with the young to put all humanity into one ass, just one, the dream of dreams, mad love. Maybe later they would find out where all that ended, when their rosiness had fled, when the no-nonsense misery of their lousy country had engulfed them, all sixteen of them, with their hefty mare's thighs and their bobbing tits... The truth is that misery already had the darlings by the neck, by the waist, they couldn't escape. By the belly, by the breath, by every cord of their thin, off-key voices. Misery was inside them. No costume, no spangles, no lights, no smile could fool her, delude her about her own, misery finds her own wherever they may hide; it just amuses her to let them sing silly songs of hope while waiting their turn... Those things awaken misery, caress and arouse her...

That's what our unhappiness, our terrible unhappiness comes to, an amusement.

So to hell with people who sing love songs! Love itself is misery and nothing else, misery lying out of our mouths, the bitch, and nothing else. She's everywhere, don't wake her, not even in pretense. She never pretends. And yet those English girls went through their routine three times a day, with their backdrop and accordion tunes. It was bound to end badly.

I didn't interfere, but don't worry, I saw the catastrophe coming.

First one of the girls fell sick. Death to cuties who stir up calamity! Let 'em croak, we'll all be better off! And while we're at it, don't hang around street corners near accordion players, as often as not that's where you'll catch it, where the truth will strike. A Polish girl was hired to take the place of the sick one in their act. The Polish chick coughed too, when she wasn't doing anything else. She was tall and pale, powerfully built. We made friends right away. In two hours I knew all about her soul, as far as her body was concerned, I had to wait a while. This girl's mania was mutilating her nervous system with impossible crushes. Naturally, what with her own unhappiness, she slid into the English girls' lousy song like a knife into butter. Their song began very nicely, like all popular songs it didn't seem to mean a thing, and then your heart began to droop, it made you so sad that listening to it you lost all desire to live, because it's true that everything, youth and all that, comes to nothing, and then you started harking to the words, even after the song was over and the tune had gone home to sleep in its own bed, its honest-to-goodness bed, the tomb where everything ends. Two choruses, and you felt a kind of longing for the sweet land of death, the land of everlasting tenderness and immediate foggy forgetfulness. As a matter of fact their voices were foggy too.

All of us in chorus repeated their plaint, reproachful of everybody who was still around, still dragging their living carcasses from place to place, waiting along the riverbanks, on all the riverbanks of the world, for life to finish passing, and in the meantime doing one thing and another, selling things to other ghosts, oranges and racing tips and counterfeit coins... policemen, sex fiends, sorrows, telling each other things in this patient fog that will never end...

Tania was the name of my new pal from Poland. Her life at the moment, I gathered, was one compact frenzy, because of a little forty-year-old bank clerk, whom she had known since Berlin. She wanted to go back to Berlin and love him in spite of everything and at all costs. She'd have done anything to get back to him.

She pursued theatrical agents, those promisers of engagements, to the ends of their pissy stairways. While waiting for answers that never came, those rotters pinched her buttocks. But she was so totally enthralled by her faraway love that she hardly noticed their manipulations. This state of affairs hadn't prevailed for a week when disaster struck. For months she had been loading Destiny with temptations, like a cannon.

Flu carried off her marvelous lover. The news came to us one Saturday afternoon. Disheveled and haggard, she dragged me to the Gare du Nord. That in itself was nothing unusual, but in her frenzy she clamored at the ticket window, insisting that she had to be in Berlin in time for the funeral. It took two station-masters to dissuade her, to get her to understand that it was much too late.

In the state she was in, I couldn't think of leaving her. She was intent on her tragedy, and still more intent on exhibiting it to me in full flood. What an opportunity! Love thwarted by poverty and distance is like a sailor's love; no two ways, it's irrefutable and sure fire. In the first place, when you're unable to meet too often, you can't fight, which is that much gained. Since life consists of madness spiked with lies, the farther you are from each other the more lies you can put into it and the happier you'll be. That's only natural and normal. Truth is inedible.

Nowadays, for instance, it's easy to talk about Jesus Christ. Did Jesus Christ go to the toilet in front of everybody? It seems to me his racket wouldn't have lasted very long if he'd taken a shit in public. Very little presence, that's the whole trick, especially in love.

Once Tania had been thoroughly assured that there was no possible train to Berlin, we made up for it in telegrams. At the Bourse[81] post office, we composed an extremely long one, because we didn't know whom to address it to. We didn't know anybody in Berlin except the dead man. From that moment on, there was nothing we could do but exchange words about the dead man's death. Words helped us to walk around the Bourse two or three times. Then we had to do something to soothe Tania's sorrow, so we strolled slowly up toward Montmartre, garbling words of grief.

On the Rue Lepic you start meeting people on their way to the top of the city in search of merriment. They're in a hurry. When they get to Sacré-Coeur, they look down at the night, a big dense hollow with houses piled at the bottom, On the little square we went into the cafe that looked the least expensive. By way of consolation and gratitude Tania let me kiss her wherever I pleased. She also liked to drink. Tipsy merrymakers were already asleep on the benches around us. The clock at the top of the little church started striking the hours and more hours, and on and on. We had reached the end of the world, that was becoming obvious. We couldn't go any further, because further on there were only dead people.

The dead began on the Place du Tertre, two steps away. From where we were it was easy to see them. They were passing over the Galeries Duf ayel,[82] to the east of us.

Even so, you've got to know how to find them—namely, from inside with your eyes almost closed, because the electric signs with their great copses of light make it very hard to see the dead, even through the clouds. I realized at once that these dead had Bébert with them. Bébert and I even gave each other the high sign, and then not far from him I saw the pale girl from Rancy, she had finally finished aborting, this time her guts had been taken out of her, and we, too, signaled to each other.

There were old patients of mine here and there, male and female, that I'd long stopped thinking about, and still others, the black man in a white cloud, all alone, the one they had given one lash too many down there in Topo, and old man Grappa, the lieutenant of the virgin forest! I'd thought of them all from time to time, of the lieutenant, the tortured black, and also of my Spaniard, the priest, he had come down from heaven that night with the dead to say prayers, and his golden crucifix was getting in his way, making it hard for him to fly from sky to sky. It got tangled up in the clouds, the dirtiest and yellowest of them, and as time went on I recognized more dead people, more and more... So many you can't help feeling ashamed of not having had time to look at them while they were living here beside you, all those years...

There's never enough time, it's true, not even for thinking of yourself.

Well, anyway, all those sons of bitches had turned into angels without my noticing! Whole clouds full of angels, including some very far-out and disreputable ones, all over the place. Roaming around, high over the city! I looked for Molly among them, a golden opportunity, my sweet, my only friend, but she hadn't come with them... She'd always been so nice that she probably had a little heaven all to herself, right next to God... I was glad not to find her with all those thugs, oh yes, the ghosts assembled over the city that night were really just the dregs of the dead, just scoundrels, scum and riffraff. Especially from the cemetery nearby they came, more and more of them, though it's not a big cemetery, not at all high class. There were even Communards, all drenched with blood, with their mouths wide open as if they wanted to yell some more and couldn't... The Communards were waiting with the others, waiting for La Pérouse, La Pérouse of the Islands, who was in command of

---

[81] Bourse. The Stock Exchange.
[82] Galeries Dufayel. A large furniture store in Montmartre. The name was regarded as symbolic of cheap luxury.

the whole rally that night... La Pérouse[83] was taking a hell of a long time to get ready, because of his wooden leg, which he'd put on backward... he'd always had trouble with that wooden leg, and besides he couldn't find his big spyglass.

He refused to come out of the clouds without his spyglass around his neck, crazy idea, the famous spyglass of his adventures, a laugh, it made you see people and things far away, further and further away through the small end, and naturally becoming more and more desirable because and in spite of your getting closer to them. Some Cossacks, who were tucked away not far from the Moulin,[84] couldn't manage to get clear of their graves. They were trying so hard it was terrifying, but they had tried many times before... They kept toppling back into their graves, they'd been drunk since 1820.

Nevertheless, a shower made them shoot up, and there they were over the city, refreshed. Then they scattered far and wide and painted the night with their turbulence, from cloud to cloud... The Opera in particular seemed to attract them, with its enormous brazier of electric signs in the middle. Spurting from it, the ghosts bounded to the other end of the sky, so numerous and so active they made your head spin. Ready at last, La Pérouse wanted them to hoist him up at the last stroke of four. They held him in place and strapped him to the saddle. Finally astride and settled, he went right on waving his arms and gesticulating. The clock striking four almost made La Pérouse lose his balance as he was buttoning his coat. But then he led the mad rush across the sky. A hideous rout. Twisting and turning, the phantoms pour from all directions, the ghosts of a thousand heroic battles... They pursue, they challenge, they charge one another, centuries against centuries. For a long while, the north is cluttered with their abominable mêlée. The bluish horizon detaches itself, at last the day rises through the big rent they've made in the night while escaping.

After that it becomes very hard to find them. You have to get outside of Time.

If you do manage to find them, it will be over toward England, but on that side the fog is always so dense, so compact that it's like sails rising one after another from the earth to the highest heaven and for all time. With practice and close attention you can find them even so, but never for very long, because of the wind that keeps blowing rain squalls and mists from the open sea.

The tall woman who is there, guarding the island, is the last of all. Her head is even higher than the uppermost mists. By now she is the only halfway living thing on the island. Her red hair, high over everything else, still puts a little gold into the clouds; that's all there is left of the sun.

They say she's trying to make herself a cup of tea.

She may as well try, because she'll be there for all eternity. She'll never bring her tea to a boil because of the fog, which has become too dense and penetrating. For a teapot she uses the hull of a ship, the most beautiful, the largest of ships, the last she could find in Southampton, and she heats up her tea in it, waves and waves of it... She stirs... She stirs it about with an enormous oar... That keeps her busy.

Serious for all time, bent over her tea, she doesn't look at anything else.

The whole dance has passed over her, but she hasn't even moved, she's used to having these ghosts from the Continent losing themselves over there... That's the end of it.

With her fingers she stirs, that's good enough for her, the coals under the ashes between two dead forests. She tries to revive the fire, it's all hers now, but her tea will never boil again.

There's no life left for the flames.

No more life in the world for anyone, only a wee bit for her... everything is almost over...

* * *

---

[83] *La pérouse.* Jean-François de Galaup, Comte de la Pérouse (1741-88), French navigator. Died in the course of a voyage around the world, probably massacred by the inhabitants of the island of Vanikoro. He did not have a wooden leg. The wooden leg seems to have been borrowed from Nelson.

[84] The Moulin, Le Moulin de Galette. A famous dance hall built in the nineteenth century beside a windmill so-called. Immortalized by Renoir's painting of it.

Tania woke me up in the room where we had finally gone to bed. It was ten in the morning. To get rid of her I told her I wasn't feeling very well and wanted to stay in bed a while.

Life was starting in again. She pretended to believe me. So soon as she'd gone, I went out myself. There really was something I wanted to do. The saraband of the night before had left me with a strong taste of remorse. The memory of Robinson came back to plague me. It was true that I'd abandoned the man to his fate and worse, to the mercies of Abbé Protiste. No need to say more. True, I'd heard that everything was just fine down there in Toulouse and that Grandma Henrouille was being good and kind to him now. In certain situations, however, you only hear what you want to hear and what seems most convenient... Come right down to it, those vague rumors didn't prove a thing.

Anxious and curious, I headed for Rancy in quest of news, something definite, the real thing. To get there I had to take the Rue des Batignolles, where Pomone lived. It was on my way. As I approached his house, I was surprised to see Pomone in person on the corner, apparently shadowing a little man at some distance. Since Pomone never went out, I figured something big must be going on. I recognized the character he was following, a client, in his correspondence he referred to himself as "the Cid." But we had been tipped oft", "the Cid"[85] worked in the post office.

For years he'd been pestering Pomone to find him a well-bred chick, that was his dream. But the young ladies that were introduced to him were never well bred enough to suit him. They committed gaffes, so he claimed. On close consideration, there are two main classes of chick, the "broad-minded" ones and the ones who've had "a good Catholic upbringing." Two equally crummy ways of feeling superior, two ways of titillating anxious, frustrated men, the "shrinking violet" type and the girl about town.

This search had gone on month after month and engulfed all "the Cid's" savings. His transactions with Pomone had brought him to the end of his resources and the end of his hopes. Later on I heard that "the Cid" had committed suicide in a vacant lot that same afternoon. Actually, I knew something cockeyed was afoot the moment I saw Pomone leave his house. So I followed them quite a way through that neighborhood, which loses its shops as it goes along, and even its colors one after another, till there's nothing left but ramshackle bistrots as you approach the toll gate. When you're not in a hurry, it's easy to get lost in those streets, befogged by the sadness and utter indifference of the place. So great is your ennui that if you had a little money you'd jump into a cab and escape. The people you pass are burdened with a fate so heavy that you feel embarrassed on their account. It's practically certain that behind their curtained windows some of those small pensioners have left their gas on. Nothing you can do about it. "Christ!" you say. Which isn't much.

There's not even a bench to sit down on. Everywhere you look it's brown and green. When it rains, it rains from all directions, from the front and sides, and the street is as slippery as the back of a big fish with a parting of rain in the middle. You can't even speak of disorder in that neighborhood, it's more like an almost well-kept prison, a prison that has no need of doors.

Roaming around like that, I finally lost Pomone and his suicide, right after the Rue des Vinai-griers. That put me so near La Garenne-Rancy I couldn't resist the temptation to cast a glance across the fortifications.

From a distance, La Garenne-Rancy doesn't look bad, you can't deny it, because of the trees in the big cemetery. You could swear you were in the Bois de Boulogne.

When you really want information about someone, you have to go to the people who know. After all, I said to myself, what have I got to lose by paying the Henrouilles a little visit? They must know what's going on in Toulouse. So then I made a mistake. You can never be careful enough. Before you know it, you're deep in the noisome regions of the night. It doesn't take long for disaster to strike. The merest trifle can bring it on, and besides, in the first place, there are certain people you shouldn't dream of going back to see. Especially those people! Once it's done, you're sunk.

Roaming at random, I was finally drawn by habit to the vicinity of the Henrouilles' house. Still in the same place, I couldn't get over it. Suddenly the rain was coming down. There was no one in

---

[85] "The Cid." The leading character in Corneille's tragedy Le Cid (1636), inspired by the life of the Cid Campeador, an eleventh-century Spanish hero.

the street but me. I didn't dare go any closer. I was about to turn back when the door of the house opened just enough for the daughter-in-law to motion me to come in. That woman saw everything. She'd seen me on the opposite sidewalk, looking fuddled. I had lost all desire to go closer, but she insisted. She even called me by my name.

"Doctor!... Oh, hurry!"

That's how she called me, not a moment's hesitation... I was afraid of attracting attention, so I hurried up her front steps. Again I saw the little corridor with the stove in it, the whole layout. I have to admit, it gave me the same old uneasy feeling. Then she started telling me that her husband had been very sick for two months and was getting steadily worse.

Naturally I had my suspicions.

"What about Robinson?" I hastened to ask her.

At first she eluded my question. Then finally she decided to answer. "They're both fine... Their business in Toulouse is doing well," she finally said, but talking very fast. That was all, then she shifted back to her sick husband. She wanted me to see him that minute, there was no time to lose... seeing that I was so devoted... that I knew her husband well... that he had confidence in no one but me... that he'd refused to see any other doctor... that they didn't have my address... Bullshit, in short.

I had good reason to suspect that there was more to her husband's illness than met the eye. I knew the lady well and the ways of the household. Nevertheless, my idiotic curiosity made me climb the stairs to the bedroom.

He was lying in the same bed where I'd treated Robinson after his accident some months before.

A room changes in a few months, even if you don't move anything. Old and rundown as things may be, they still find the strength, the Lord knows where, to get older. Everything had changed around us. Not that anything had moved, no, of course not, the things themselves had actually changed, in depth. Things are different when you go back to them, they seem to have more power to enter into us more sadly, more deeply, more gently than before, to merge with the death which is slowly, pleasantly, sneakily growing inside us, and which we train ourselves to resist a little less each day. From moment to moment, we see life languishing, shriveling inside us, and with it the things and people who may have been commonplace or precious or imposing when we last left them. Fear of the end has marked all that with its wrinkles, while we were chasing around town in search of pleasure or bread.

Soon our past will be attended only by inoffensive, pathetic, disarmed things and people, mistakes with nothing to say for themselves.

The wife left me alone with her husband. He was in bad shape. Not much circulation left. The trouble was in his heart.

"I'm going to die," he said simply.

Cases like this were my special form of luck. I listened to his heartbeat just to be doing something, the few gestures people expect under those circumstances. His heart was racing, no doubt about it; shut up behind his ribs, it ran after life in fits and starts, but run or not, it would never catch up with life. His goose was cooked. Soon, the way it was stumbling, his heart would fall in the muck, all juicy and red, gushing like a crushed pomegranate. That's how his flabby old heart would look on the marble, cut open with a knife at the autopsy that would take place in a few days. All this would end in a lovely court-ordered autopsy. That's what I foresaw, considering that everyone in the neighborhood would be relaying some highly seasoned rumors after his death, which would look very fishy after the other business.

The neighbors were laying for his wife with all the accumulated and still undigested suspicions aroused by the previous affair. This would come up a little later. At the moment the husband didn't know how to live or die. He was already part way out of life, but he couldn't quite get rid of his lungs. He expelled air, and air came back. He'd have been glad to let himself die, but he had to live to the end. It was rough work, and it was driving him up the wall.

"I can't feel my feet anymore!" he groaned... "I'm cold up to my knees... " He tried to touch his feet, but he couldn't.

He couldn't drink either. It was almost over. Handing him the tisane his wife had made him, I wondered what she could have put in it. That tisane didn't smell very good, but smell proves nothing.

Valerian smells vile all by itself. And the way he was suffocating, it didn't make much difference whether the tisane was spiked or not. Still, he was going to a lot of trouble, working like mad with all the muscles he had left under his skin to keep suffering and breathing. He was struggling as much against life as against death. In a case like that the right thing would be to burst. When nature stops giving a damn, there wouldn't seem to be any limits. Behind the door his wife was listening to our consultation, but I knew his wife like a book. I tiptoed over and caught her. "Caughtcha!" I said. She wasn't the least bit put out, she even whispered something in my ear.

"You should get him to remove his plate," she murmured... "It must interfere with his breathing... " It was all right with me. Why indeed shouldn't he remove his plate?

"But you tell him," I advised her. It was ticklish saying a thing like that to someone in his condition.

"No! No! It would be better coming from you," she insisted. "Coming from me it would upset him to know I knew... "

"Really?" I asked in amazement. "Why?"

"He's been wearing it for thirty years and never said a word about it to me... "

"In that case," I suggested, "why not let him keep it? As long as he's used to breathing with it in... " "Oh no, I'd never forgive myself," she replied with a kind of quaver in her voice...

I went quietly back into the room. He heard me approaching. He was glad I'd come back. Between fits of suffocation he spoke to me. He made an effort to be friendly, asked how I was getting along, if I had built up a new clientele... "Oh, yes!" I said in reply to all his questions. It would have been much too long and complicated to go into detail. Not the right time. Hidden behind the door, his wife made signs at me, meaning I should ask him to remove his plate. I went close to his ear and whispered, advising him to remove it. Mistake! "I threw it down the toilet!" he said, his eyes more frightened than ever. Vanity, that's what it was. After that he let out a long rale.

An artist makes do with what happens to be at hand. All his life Henrouille had taken aesthetic pains with his dental plate.

That was a good time for confessions. I'd have liked him to take advantage and give me his opinion about his mother and what had been done to her. But he couldn't. His mind was wandering. He began to drool copiously. The end. Impossible to get another sentence out of him. I wiped his lips and went back downstairs. His wife in the corridor wasn't at all pleased, she almost lit into me about the plate, as if it were my fault.

"It was gold, doctor!... I know! I know how much he paid for it!... They don't make them like that anymore!"... She went on and on! She made me so nervous I offered to go up and try again. But only if she went with me.

That time the husband hardly recognized us. Just a little. The rales weren't as loud when we were both with him; it was as if he wanted to hear everything his wife and I said to each other.

I didn't go to the funeral. The autopsy that I had kind of feared never came off. It was all done on the quiet. But after that the widow Henrouille and I were on the outs for good because of the dental plate.

* * *

Young people are always in such a hurry to go and make love, in such a rush to grab hold of anything that's been advertised as a pleasure. When it comes to sensation they never think twice. It's a little like those travelers who go and eat anything that's given them at the station buffet while waiting for the whistle to blow. As long as you provide young people with the two or three phrases likely to steer a conversation in the direction of fucking, that's all they need, they'll be as happy as larks. Happiness comes easy to the young, why wouldn't it when they come as often as they please?

Youth is a glorious beach at the edge of the water, where women seem at last to be freely available, where they're so beautiful they don't need the falsehood of our dreams.

So naturally when winter comes it's hard for us to go home, to tell ourselves that it's all over, to admit it. We'd be glad to stay on, even in the cold of age... we go on hoping. That's not hard to understand. We're contemptible. No one's to blame. Pleasure and happiness come first. I think so too.

When you start hiding from people, it's a sign that you're afraid to play with them. That in itself is a disease. We should try to find out why we refuse to get cured of loneliness. A character I met in the hopsital during the war, a corporal, spoke to me about that kind of feelings. Too bad I never saw him again! "The earth is dead," he said to me.

"We people are just worms on top of it, worms on its fat, revolting carcass, eating its entrails and all its poisons... Nothing can help us, we were born rotten... There you have it!"

True, they hauled this thinker off to the fortress one night, proof that he was still good enough to be shot. I even remember that it took two M.P.'s to hold him, a tall one and a short one. At the court-martial they said he was an anarchist.

Sometimes, when you think about it years later, you wish you could retrieve the words certain people said and the people themselves, so as to ask them what they were trying to tell you... But they're as gone as gone can be!... We weren't educated enough to understand them... We'd like to know if maybe they've changed their minds... But it's much too late... It's over and done!... Nobody knows anything about them anymore. So we just have to go on alone in the night. We've lost our true companions, and we didn't even ask them the right question, the real one, when there was still time. When we were with them, we didn't know. Lost men. Anyway, we're always late. Vain regrets won't make the kettle boil.

Well, luckily at least Abbé Protiste came to see me one fine morning to split the commission we'd made on Grandma Henrouille's crypt. Actually I'd given up expecting that priest. He dropped like a gift from heaven... We each had fifteen hundred francs coming to us. At the same time he brought me good news of Robinson. It seems his eyes were a good deal better. The lids had even stopped suppurating. And they were all asking for me down there. True enough, I'd promised to go and see them. Even Protiste insisted.

From what he told me I also gathered that Robinson was going to be married soon to the daughter of the woman who sold candles in the church next to the burial vault, the one that had jurisdiction over Grandma Henrouille's mummies. The thing was as good as done.

Naturally all this started us talking about the death of Monsieur Henrouille, but we didn't go into it very deeply. More pleasantly, the conversation came back to Robinson's future, and then to the city of Toulouse, that I didn't know at all and that Grappa had talked about in the old days, and then to the weird business the two of them were engaged in down there, and finally to the young girl who was due to marry Robinson. In other words, we talked about everything under the sun, a little of this and a little of that... Fifteen hundred francs! That made me indulgent, and optimistic, so to speak. Everything he told me about Robinson's plans struck me as wise, sensible, judicious, and well suited to the circumstances... Everything would be all right. So at least I thought. And then the priest and I started talking about age. We had both spent more than thirty years on inhospitable and little regretted shores. There was no point in even turning around to look back on those shores. We hadn't lost much by growing older. "A man, after all, must be very degraded," I concluded, "to regret one year more than another!... You and I, Mr. Priest, can grow old with gusto! And enthusiasm! Was yesterday such a bargain? Or last year?... What did you think of it?... Regret what?... I ask you!... Youth?... You and I never had any youth!

"The poor, it's true, get younger inside as they go along, and toward the end, provided that on the way they've made some attempt to jettison all the lies and fear and contemptible eagerness to obey they were given at birth, they're less revolting than at the start. The rest of what exists on earth isn't for them! It doesn't concern them. Their job, their only job, is to get rid of their obedience, to vomit it up. If they manage that before kicking in, then they can boast that they haven't lived for nothing."

I was definitely in good form... Those fifteen hundred francs had sparked me off. I went on: "The only real youth, Mr. Priest, is loving everyone without distinction, that alone is true, that alone is young and new. Well, Mr. Priest, do you know many young people who are like that?... I don't!... All I see is crusty old stupidities fermenting in more or less recent bodies, and the more these sordid absurdities ferment the more they stimulate the young and the more they boast how fantastically young they are! But it's not true, it's bullshit... They're young the way a boil is young, no more, because of the pus inside that hurts and makes them swell up."

My talking to him like that upset Protiste, and not wanting to irritate him anymore, I changed the subject... For one thing, he'd been very kind to me, providentially so in fact... It's hard to stop yourself from going back to a subject that's as much on your mind as that was on mine. It scrambles your brains. To get free, you try to unload some part of it on everybody who comes to see you, and that exasperates them. Being alone is to train for death. "A man," I went on, "should die more abundantly than a dog and take a thousand minutes to do it. Each minute will be new all the same and laced with enough fear and trembling to make him forget all the pleasure he may have had in making love during the preceding thousand years... Happiness on earth would be to die with and while having pleasure... The rest is nothing at all, a fear that we don't dare avow, art."

Hearing me rave that way, Protiste thought I must have fallen sick again. Maybe he was right and maybe I was wrong about everything. In my isolation, searching for a way to punish man's universal egoism, it's true that I was jerking off my imagination, looking for punishment everywhere, even in death. You amuse yourself as best you can when you're short of friends and don't often get a chance to go out, much less to emerge from yourself and fuck.

I admit it wasn't exactly sensible to needle Protiste with philosophical ideas contrary to his religious convictions. But the fact is his whole person exuded a nasty little smell of superiority that must have got on quite a few people's nerves. As he saw it, all we humans on earth were in a kind of waiting-for-eternity room, each with a number. His number, I don't have to tell you, was first class, good for Paradise. He didn't give a shit about anything else.

Such convictions are unbearable. On the other hand, when he offered that same afternoon to advance me the price of the trip to Toulouse, I stopped needling and contradicting him. My dread of having to face Tania and her ghost again at the Tarapout made me accept his invitation without a word of argument. A week or two of the easy life, if nothing else, that's what I said to myself. When it comes to tempting you, the Devil has millions of tricks. We'll never know them all. If we lived long enough, we wouldn't know where to go to start a new happiness. We'd have strewn aborted happinesses all over, the whole earth would stink of them, unbreathably. The ones in the museums, the real abortions, turn some people's stomachs, the mere sight of the things makes them want to vomit. And our loathsome attempts to be happy are miscarried enough to sicken you long before you die for real.

If we didn't forget them, we'd simply waste away. Not to mention the trouble we've taken to get where we are, to make our hopes, our degenerate joys, our passions and lies interesting... Want some? Help yourself. And what of our money? And our little affectations that go with it... And the things we get other people to swear to and that we ourselves swear to, things we thought no one had ever said or sworn to before, before they filled our minds and mouths, and perfumes and caresses and mimicries, in short, everything it takes to hide all that as much as possible, so we'll never have to speak of it again, for fear it will come back at us like vomit. Our trouble isn't lack of perseverance, it's that we're not on the right road that leads to an easy death.

Going to Toulouse was another piece of damn foolishness. Thinking it over, I suspected as much. So I had no excuse. But following Robinson in his adventures, I had developed a taste for shady undertakings. Already in New York when I couldn't sleep, I racked my brains wondering if it mightn't be possible to go further and still further with Robinson. You sink, at first you're afraid in the darkness, but all the same you want to understand, and after that you never leave the depths. But there's too much. You can't understand so many things at once. Life is too short. You don't want to be unjust to anyone. You have scruples, you hesitate to make snap judgments, and worst of all, you're afraid to die while you're hesitating, because then you'd have been on earth for nothing whatsoever. And that's the worst of all.

Hurry, hurry, don't be late for your death. Sickness, the poverty that disperses your hours and years, the insomnia that paints whole days and weeks gray, the cancer that may even now, meticulous and blood-spotted, be climbing up from your rectum.

You'll never have time, you tell yourself. Not to speak of war, which is also, what with the criminal boredom of men, ready to rise up from the cellar that poor people shut themselves up in... you can never be sure... It's a moot point... Maybe all those who don't understand should have their throats cut... And perhaps other, new poor people should be born, and so forth and so on, until we get a crowd who understand the joke, the whole joke... Just as you mow a lawn until the grass is really right, really soft.

On leaving the train at Toulouse I was in doubt what to do. But a bottle of beer at the station buffet set me strolling through the streets. An unfamiliar city is a fine thing. That's the time and place when, you can suppose that all the people you meet are nice. It's dream time. And because you're in a dream you can afford to waste a little time in the park. Still, after a certain age, unless you have gilt-edged reasons, people will think you've gone to the park to chase little girls like Parapine. So better not. You'll be safer in the pastry shop just before the park gate, the beautiful shop on the corner, as fancy as a brothel stage set, beveled mirrors studded with little birds. Deep in thought, you catch yourself eating burnt almonds ad infinitum. A place for seraphim. The young ladies who work there babble furtively about their private affairs as follows:

"So I told him he could call for me on Sunday... My aunt heard him and made a terrible stick because of my father... "

"But hasn't your father remarried?" her friend breaks in.

"What has that got to do with it?... Even if he's remarried, he still has a right to know who his daughter's going out with... ' The other young lady in the shop was of the same opinion. The consequence was an impassioned controversy involving all three. Not wanting to disturb them, I sat quietly in my corner, stuffing myself uninterruptedly with tarts and cream puffs, which were excellent by the way, hoping that my discretion would help them solve their delicate problem of family priorities more quickly, but they made no progress. Nothing came of their discussion. Their speculative incompetence restricted them to an imprecise sort of hatred. Those shopgirls were bursting with illogicality, vanity, and ignorance. Drooling with rage, they whispered insults by the dozen.

I couldn't help it, I was fascinated by their nasty passion. I attacked the rum babas. I stopped counting the babas. So did they. I was hoping they'd come to some conclusion before I had to leave... But passion made them deaf and soon dumb.

Tense, their venon spent, they rested in the shelter of the pastry counter, each one invincible, shut up in her shell, pinched, ruminating plans for a still more embittered comeback. At the first opportunity, she would—promptly this time-spew out all the angry, cutting absurdities she happened to know about her little friend. And the occasion wouldn't be long in coming, she'd see to that... Scrapings of arguments aimed at nothing at all. In the end I sat down, the better for them to befuddle me with the unceasing sound of their words, intentions, thoughts, as on a shore where the ripples of unceasing passions never manage to get organized...

You listen, you wait, you hope, here, there, in the train, at the cafe, in the street, in drawing rooms, at the coincierge's, you listen and wait for evil to get organized as in wartime, but there's only waste motion, nothing is ever done, either by those unfortunate young ladies or by anyone else. No one comes to help us. An enormous babble, gray and monotonous, spread over life like an enormously discouraging mirage. Two ladies came in, and the muddle-headed charm of the ineffectual conversation spread out between the counter girls and myself was broken. The girls gave the new arrivals their eager and undivided attention, anticipating their requests and their least desires. They chose here and there and nibbled at the tarts and petits fours. When it came time to pay, they gushed polite phrases, and each insisted on offering the others little pastries to nibble that very minute.

One declined most graciously, explaining at length and in confidence to the other ladies present, who took a keen interest, that her doctor had forbidden her all sweets, that her doctor was a genius, that he had done wonders in combating constipation in Toulouse and elsewhere, that he was well on his way to curing her of a retention of "number two," from which she had been suffering for more than ten years, thanks to a very special diet and a miraculous medicine known to him alone. The other ladies were not going to let themselves be outdone so easily in matters of constipation. Their own constipation defied comparison. They were up in arms. They demanded proofs. In response to their doubts, the lady observed simply that when moving her bowels she now broke wind, that it sounded like fireworks... that because of her new- style bowel movements, all well molded, solid, and substantial, she was obliged to take extra precautions... Sometimes these marvelous new feces of hers were so hard they gave her excruciating pain in the rectum... a tearing sensation!... So now she had to use vaseline before moving her bowels. Irrefutable.

Thus convinced, the voluble ladies left the Petits Oiseaux pastry shop, accompanied to the threshold by the smiles of the entire staff.

The park across the way was a good place in which to rest, meditate briefly, and put my thoughts in order before going to look for my friend Robinson.

In provincial parks the benches, offering a view of flowerbeds overstuffed with cannas and daisies, are almost always empty on weekday mornings. Near the rock garden, on strictly captive waters, a small tin boat, encircled by floating ashes, was moored to the shore by a moldy rope. A sign announced that the skiff operated on Sunday and that a tour of the lake cost two francs.

How many years?... students?... phantoms?

In the corners of all parks there lie forgotten any number of little coffins engarlanded with dreams, thickets charged with promises, handkerchiefs full of everything. All a big joke.

But that's enough daydreaming. Let's go looking for Robinson and his church of Sainte-Eponime, and that crypt where he and the old woman are taking care of mummies. That's what I'd come for, so I'd better get going.

I took a carriage, and we meandered this way and that at a leisurely sort of trot, through the dark sunken streets of the old town, where the light catches between the roofs. Over cobbles and bridges we drove with a great clatter of wheels, behind a horse that was all shoes. They haven't burned any cities in the South for a long time. They've never been so old. Wars don't pass that way anymore.

We pulled up in front of Sainte-Eponime[86] on the stroke of noon. The crypt was a little further on, under a calvary. It was pointed out to me, in the middle of a small, parched garden. You entered the crypt through a sort of barricaded hole. From a distance I saw the caretaker, a young girl, and asked for news of my friend Robinson. She was just closing the door. She answered with a friendly smile, and the news she gave me was good.

From where we were standing in that noonday light everything around us turned pink, and the worm-eaten stones of the church rose skyward, as though ready to melt into the air.

Robinson's little friend must have been about twenty, with firm, wiry legs, a small, perfectly charming bust, and surmounting it a delicate, precisely etched face. Just the eyes may have been a little too black and attentive for my taste. Not at all the dreamy type. It was she who wrote Robinson's letters, the ones I had received. She went ahead of me to the vault with her precise gait, her shapely feet and ankles. She had the build of a good lay, and must have spread her legs very nicely when circumstances demanded. Short, hard hands with a strong grip, the hands of an ambitious working girl. A brisk little movement to turn the key. Shimmering heat all around us. Once she had the door open, she decided, in spite of the lunch hour, to show me through the vault. I was beginning to feel a little more relaxed. Behind her lantern we descended into increasing coolness. It was real nice. I pretended to stumble between two steps as an excuse for grabbing her by the arm. That made us laugh, and when we reached the clay floor at the bottom I kissed her a little on the neck. She protested at first, but not very much.

After a brief moment of affection, I wriggled round her belly like a love worm. Lecherously we moistened and remoistened our lips for our soul conversation. With one hand I crept slowly up her tensed thighs, it's fun with the lantern on the floor, because at the same time you can watch the muscles rippling over her legs. It's a position I can recommend. Ah! Such moments are not to be missed. They put your eyes out of joint, but it's worth it. What gusto! What sudden good humor! The conversation resumed in a new tone of confidence and simplicity. Now we were friends. Asses first. We had just saved ten years.

"Do you often show people around?" I asked, puffing and putting my foot in it. But I quickly covered up: "Doesn't your mother sell candles at the church next door?... Father Protiste has told me about her."

"I only take Madame Henrouille's place during lunch hour," she answered. "In the afternoon I work for a dressmaker... On the Rue du Theatre... Did you pass the theater on your way here?"

---

[86] Sainte-Eponime. From "eponym"—the mythical or historical person after whom a tribe, city, country, etc. is named. In this instance, "etc." means "church."

Again she reassured me about Robinson. He was much better, in fact the specialist thought he'd soon see well enough to go out by himself. All that was most encouraging. As for Grandma Henrouille, she seemed delighted with the vault. She was doing good business and saving money. Only one difficulty, in the house where they were living, the bedbugs kept everybody awake, especially on stormy nights. So they burned sulfur. It seemed that Robinson often spoke of me, pleasantly what's more. One thing leading to another, we came around to the projected marriage, the circumstances and all.

I have to admit that with all that talk I still hadn't asked her name. Her name was Madelon.[87] She'd been born during the war. Their marriage plans, after all, suited me fine. Madelon was an easy name to remember. I figured she must know what she was doing in marrying Robinson... Even if he was getting better, he'd always be an invalid... And besides, she thought only his eyes were affected... But his nerves were shot, and so was his morale and everything else! I was almost going to tell her so, to warn her... I've never known how to steer conversations about marriage, or extricate myself from them.

To change the subject, I expressed a keen and sudden interest in the cellar and its occupants. People came a long way to see it, so as long as I was there why not take a look?

With her little lantern Madelon and I made the shadows of the corpses emerge from the wall one by one. They must have given the tourists food for thought! Those ancient stiffs were lined up against the wall as if a firing squad had worked them over... They weren't exactly skin and bone anymore, or clothing either... Just a little of all that... In a very grimy state, and full of holes. Time had been gnawing at their skin for centuries and was still at it... Here and there it was still tearing away bits of their faces... enlarging all the holes and even finding long strips of epidermis that death had left clinging to their cartilage. Their bellies had emptied of everything, and now there were little cradles of shadow where their navels had been.

Madelon explained that to get into this condition the bodies had had to spend more than five hundred years in a quicklime cemetery. You wouldn't have taken them for corpses. Their corpse days were far behind them. By easy stages they had come closer and closer to dust.

In that cellar there were big ones and little ones, six and twenty in all, who asked for nothing better than to enter into Eternity. They weren't being admitted yet. Two women with bonnets perched on top of their skeletons, a hunchback, a giant, and even a complete baby, with a kind of bib, lace if you please, around his tiny dried-out neck, and some bits and pieces of swaddling clothes.

Grandma Henrouille was making a lot of money out of these scrapings of the centuries. To think that when I last saw her she herself had looked very much like these spooks... So then Madelon and I went slowly back, passing them by again. One by one their so-called heads stood silent in the harsh circle of lamp light. It's not exactly night they have in their eye sockets, it's almost a gaze, but gentler, like the gaze of those who know. More disturbing is their smell of dust, it catches in your nose.

Whenever a party of tourists showed up, Grandma Henrouille was on the spot. She made those stiffs work like circus performers. At the height of the summer season, they brought her in a hundred francs a day.

"Don't they look sad?" Madelon asked me. A ritual question.

Death didn't mean a thing to that cutie. She had been born during the war, when death came easy. But I knew well how people die. Something I had learned. It's very painful. It's all right to tell the tourists that these dead are happy. They can't speak for themselves. Grandma Henrouille even clouted them on the belly when there was enough parchment left on it, and it went "boom boom." But even that's no proof of good cheer.

Finally Madelon and I got back to our own affairs. So it was true that Robinson was better. That was good enough for me. Our little friend seemed bent on this marriage. She must have been bored to death in Toulouse. You didn't often meet a man who had traveled as much as Robinson. What stories he had to tell! True ones and not so true. He'd already spoken to them at length of America and the Tropics. Lovely!

---

[87] Madelon. See above, note 17.

I'd been in America and the Tropics too. I knew stories about them too and proposed to tell her some. Come to think of it, I had traveled with Robinson, and that's how we'd got to be friends. The lantern went out. We lit it ten times while arranging the past and the future. She wouldn't let me touch her breasts, said they were much too sensitive.

But seeing that Grandma Henrouille would be coming back from her lunch any minute, we had to climb back to the daylight over the steep, rickety staircase, which was as difficult to negotiate as a ladder. I made a note of those stairs.

* * *

Because of the treacherous narrow stairs Robinson didn't often go down to the mummy cellar. Most of the time he stood at the door, giving the tourists a bit of sales talk and getting used to taking in a few specks of light here and there.

Meanwhile in the depths, Grandma Henrouille managed very well. She knocked herself out with the mummies., enlivening the tourists' visit with a little speech about her parchment stiffs. "They're not at all repulsive, ladies and gentlemen, because, as you see, they were preserved in quicklime... for more than five centuries... Our collection is the only one of its kind in the whole world... The flesh is gone, of course... Only the skin is left, but it's tanned... They're naked, but not indecent... You will observe that a baby was buried at the same time as its mother... The baby is also extremely well preserved... And that tall man with the lace shirt that he still has on... He's got every one of his teeth... You will observe... " At the end of the tour she clouted them all on the chest—it sounded like a drum. "Observe, ladies and gentlemen, that this one has only one eye left... all dried out... and the tongue too... it's like leather!" She gave it a pull. "He's sticking his tongue out, but he's not nasty... You can give what you like as you leave, ladies and gentlemen, but the usual is two francs each and half price for children... You can touch them before you go... convince yourself... but please, ladies and gentlemen, don't pull too hard... they're extremely fragile... "

Grandma Henrouille had wanted to raise the prices as soon as she got there, she applied to the Diocese. But it wasn't so simple, because of the priest at Sainte-Eponime, who demanded a third of the take all for himself, and also because of Robinson, who kept griping, because in his opinion she wasn't giving him a big enough rake-off.

"I've been took!" he concluded. "Took for a sucker!...

Again!... I never have any luck!... The old bag's cellar, you know... it brings in a fortune! . . , Believe you me, she's raking it in!"

"But you didn't put any money into the business," I argued to calm him down and put some sense into him... "And you're well fed! Well taken care of!"

But Robinson was as stubborn as a mule, he felt persecuted and that was that. He refused to understand, to resign himself.

"All in all," I said, "you've come out of a nasty business pretty well! So don't complain! You'd have gone straight to Cayenne[88] if they'd nabbed you... Here nobody's bothering you!... And you've found little Madelon who's a sweet kid and willing to put up with you... despite the state of your health... So what have you got to complain about?... Especially now that your eyes are getting better..."

"You seem to be saying I don't know what I'm complaining about," he said then. "But I feel I've got to complain... that's the way it is... it's all I've got left... that's right... It's the only thing they let me do... Nobody's forced to listen."

True enough, he did nothing but complain whenever we were alone. I had come to dread those confidential moments. I looked at him with his blinking eyes which still oozed a little in the sunlight, and I said to myself that all things considered Robinson was not endearing. There are animals like that, they can be innocent, unhappy, anything you please, you know it, and still you don't like them. There's something wrong with them.

"You could have died in jail... " I tried again, determined to make him think.

---

[88] Cayenne. Capital of French Guiana, a penal colony up to 1942.

"I've been in jail... It's no worse than where I am now!... You're out of date... "

He hadn't told me he'd been in jail. That must have been before we met, before the war. He pressed his point and concluded: "Take it from me. There's only one kind of freedom, only one, to see properly and have your pockets full of money. The rest is bullshit!... "

"So what, exactly, do you want?" I asked him. When he was challenged like that to make up his mind, to speak up, he deflated. And that's just when it might have been interesting...

During the day, while Madelon was working for the dressmaker and Grandma Henrouille was exhibiting her mummies, we went to a cafe under the trees. Robinson was crazy about that cafe under the trees, probably because of the noise the birds made up above us. Millions of them! Especially about five o'clock when they came home to their nests, all keyed up by the summer. They swooped down on the square like a storm. There was a story about a barber who had his shop across from the park and had gone crazy just from hearing them cheep for years and years. It's true we couldn't hear each other talk. Robinson thought it was cheerful.

"If only she'd give me twenty centimes per visitor and be regular about it, I'd be satisfied."

About every fifteen minutes he'd get back to his preoccupation. In between, the colors of times past seemed to come back to him, incidents too, stories, among others, about the Compagnie Pordurière in Africa, which both of us had known well after all, and some hairy tales that he'd never told me before. Maybe he hadn't dared. He was kind of reticent in a way, I'd even say secretive.

Speaking of the past, what I remembered best when I was in good spirits was Molly, like the echo of a clock striking in the distance. When something pleasant popped into my mind, I always thought of her.

After all, when our egoism lets us go for a while, when it comes time to throw it off, the only women whose memory you cherish in your hearts are the ones who really loved men a little, not just one man, even if it was you, but the whole lot.

When we left the cafe that evening, we hadn't done a thing, we could have been retired noncoms.

During the season, there was a steady flow of tourists. They hung around the crypt and Grandma Henrouille always got them to laugh. Her jokes weren't exactly to the priest's taste, but, since he was collecting more than his share, he didn't say boo, and besides smutty jokes were over his head. Be that as it may, Grandma Henrouille was worth seeing and hearing in the midst of her corpses. She looked you straight in the eye, she wasn't in the least afraid of death; wrinkled and shriveled as she was, you'd have thought she was one of them, coming along with her lantern to shoot the shit right in what passed for their faces.

When we got back to the house and foregathered for dinner, we discussed the day's take, and Grandma Henrouille called me her "little old Dr. Jackal" because of the dealings we'd had in Rancy. All in a bantering tone, of course. Madelon bustled about in the kitchen. That joint where we were staying got only the measliest light, it was an annex of the sacristy, very cramped, all cluttered with joists and struts and dusty crannies. "Yes," said the old woman, "it's practically always night in here, so to speak, but you can still find your bed, your pockets, and your mouth. That's good enough for me."

She hadn't grieved for long after her son's death. "He was always very delicate," she said to me one evening. "Look, I'm seventy-six and I've never complained!... He complained all the time, it was his way, exactly like your Robinson... just to give you an example. Take the stairs to the crypt, for instance... They're tough, you'll agree... You've been down there... They knock me out, of course they do, but some days they're worth as much as two francs a step to me... I've figured it out... Well, for that price I'd climb up to heaven if anyone asked me to!"

Madelon put lots of spices in our food, and tomatoes as well. It was great. And we drank rosé. Even Robinson had taken to wine now that he was living in the South. He had already told me everything that had happened since his arrival in Toulouse, so I had stopped listening. To tell the truth, I was kind of disappointed in him, and disgusted. "You're a bourgeois!" I told him finally (at that time I could think of no worse insult). "All you ever think of is money... Once you recover your eyesight, you'll be the worst of the whole bunch."

Hard words couldn't get him down. They seemed on the contrary to give him a lift. Besides, he knew it was true. The man's all set, I said to myself, no need to trouble my head about him... You can't get around it, a little woman like that, slightly on the violent, depraved side, will change a man beyond recognition... For a long time, I said to myself, I thought this Robinson was made for adventures, but cuckold or not, blind or not, he's only a cheap punk... Neither more nor less.

In addition, Grandma Henrouille had contaminated him with her mania for saving, and so had Madelon with her desire to be married. That settled it. He was washed up. Especially as he'd got to like the girl more and more. I knew something about that. I'd be lying if I said I wasn't a little jealous, it wouldn't be true. Madelon and I got together for short moments now and then, before dinner in her room. But those interviews were hard to arrange. We never spoke of them. We were as discreet as could be.

Don't go thinking on that account that she didn't love her Robinson. There's no connection. It was just that he was playing at being engaged, so naturally she played at being faithful. That's how it was between them. As long as they saw eye to eye, that was the main thing. As he told me, he wasn't going to touch her until they were married. It was his idea. So he'd have eternity, and I'd have the here and now. He was also planning, so he told me, to set himself up in a small restaurant with Madelon, and run out on Grandma Henrouille. He really meant business. "She's nice, the customers will like her," he foresaw in his more cheerful moments. "And say, you've tasted her cooking... When it comes to the eats, she hasn't her equal."

He even thought he could touch Grandma Henrouille for a bit of capital to start with. All right with me, but I suspected that he'd have a hard time persuading her. "You see everything through rose-colored glasses," I said, just to calm him down and make him think a little. At that he began to cry and call me a heartless bastard. To tell the truth, you should never discourage anybody. I admitted that I was wrong, that my trouble was my black thoughts, and that all things considered, they were what had wrecked my life. Robinson's gimmick before the war had been copperplate engraving, but he wouldn't have anything more to do with it, not at any price. That was his business. "With my lungs I need fresh air, and anyway my eyes will never be the same." In a way he was right. What could I say? When we walked through busy streets together, people turned around to pity the blind man. People have plenty of pity in them for the infirm and the blind, they really have love in reserve. I'd often sensed that love they have in reserve. There's an enormous lot of it, and no one can say different. But it's a shame that people should go on being so crummy with so much love in reserve. It just doesn't come out, that's all. It's caught inside and there it stays, it doesn't do them a bit of good. They die of love—inside.

After dinner Madelon would devote herself to her "little Léon," as she called him. She read the newspaper out loud. He was wild about politics at the time, and the papers in the South pustulated with politics, of the juciest kind.

Around us in the evening the house would sink into the dilapitude of the centuries. That's the time, after dinner, when the bedbugs come out for the corrida and also the time to test the corrosive formula which I hoped to sell to some pharmacist at a small profit later on. A modest racket. My invention amused Grandma Henrouille, and she helped me with my experiments. Together we went from nest to nest, from crack to cranny, and sprayed their swarms with my vitriol. They scurried and vanished in the light of the candle that Grandma Henrouille conscientiously held for me.

While at our work, we talked about Rancy. Just thinking about the place gave me the collywobbles, I'd have stayed in Toulouse for the rest of my life. What more did I want, after all, than my daily bread and some time to myself? Happiness in short. Still, I had to think about going back to work. Time was passing, and so were the Abbé Protiste's bonus and my savings.

Before leaving, I thought I'd teach Madelon a thing or two, and give her a bit of advice. Of course it's better to give money when you can afford it and you want to help. But you can also do good by warning a person, telling them exactly what's what and especially about the risks of fucking right and left. That's what I said to myself, because I was really worried about Madelon catching something. She was a smart little number, but no one could have been more ignorant about microbes. So I started explaining in great detail that she should take a close look before responding to advances. If it was red... if there was a drop at the end... In short, the classical and exceedingly useful things that everyone should know. After listening attentively and hearing me out, she protested for the sake of form. She even made something of a scene, assuring me... that she was a "respectable" girl... that I should be ashamed of myself... that I had a foul opinion of her... because she'd done it with me... that I despised her... that all men were beastly...

Anyway, the kind of thing they say in a case like that... I might have expected it... Window dressing. What mattered to me was that she had listened carefully to my advice and grasped the essential. The rest didn't mean a thing. After hearing what I had to say, what really saddened her was that you could catch all those things I'd been telling her about just from affection and pleasure. Even if nature was to blame, she thought I was fully as disgusting as nature, and that offended her. I carried the matter no further, except for a few words about condoms, which are so convenient. After that we played psychologist and tried to analyze Robinson's character just a little. "He's not exactly jealous," she said to me. "But he has his difficult moments."

"That's neither here nor there," I said, and launched into a description of Robinson's character, as if I knew

his character, but I noticed right away that I didn't know Robinson at all, except for a few obvious and glaring features. Nothing more.

It's amazing how hard it is to imagine what can make one person pleasing to another... You want to do someone a favor, to be helpful, and all you do is make a fool of yourself... It's pitiful, the moment you open your mouth... you flounder.

Nowadays it's not easy to be La Bruyère.[89] The whole unconscious skedaddles the moment you go near it.

* * *

Just as I was about to buy my ticket, they got me to stay... for another week, we agreed. The idea was to show me the country around Toulouse, the cool banks of the river I'd heard so much about, and especially they wanted me to see the beautiful vineyards on the outskirts, that everyone in town seemed to take pleasure and pride in, as if they were all part owners. They wouldn't think of letting me leave like that, when I hadn't seen anything but Grandma Henrouille's corpses. It was unthinkable! Well anyway, soft soap...

I was paralyzed by so much kindness. I didn't dare seem too eager to stay, because of my intimacy with Madelon, which was getting kind of dangerous. The old woman was beginning to suspect something between us. A strain in the air.

But the old woman wasn't coming with us on this excursion. In the first place she didn't want to close her crypt, not for a single day. So I agreed to stay on, and one Sunday morning we set out for the country. Robinson walked between us, we held him by the arms. At the station we took second-class tickets. Even so, the compartment smelled strongly of sausage, just the same as third class. We got off at a place called Saint-Jean. Madelon seemed familiar with the region, and right away she began meeting acquaintances from this village and that village. It looked like a fine day coming on. As we walked along, we had to tell Robinson everything we saw. "Here there's a garden... That's a bridge over there, and on top of it there's a man fishing... He's not catching anything... Watch out for the bicycle... " But the smell of French fries gave him his direction all right. In fact it was he who dragged us to a bar where they served French fries for fifty centimes a portion. I'd always known that Robinson was fond of French fries. So am I. It's a Parisian taste. Madelon preferred vermouth, dry and straight.

Rivers aren't happy in the South. They seem to be sick, always drying up. Hills, sun, fishermen, fish, boats, ditches, wash troughs, vines, weeping willows—all want some, all clamor for water. Much too much water is demanded of them, so there isn't much left in the riverbed. In places it looks more like a badly flooded road than a genuine river. Seeing we'd come for pleasure, we had to hurry up and find some. When we'd finished our French fries, we thought we'd take a little boatride before lunch,

---

[89] La Bruyère. Jean de La Bruyère (1645-96). Moralist. Author of Les Caractères, a book of maxims and portraits of contemporary figures, which gained great popularity.

that would be fun, me rowing of course, the two of them, Robinson and Madelon, facing me, hand in hand.

So off we go, merrily down the stream as they say, scraping the bottom here and there, she letting out squeals and he not quite easy in his mind either. Flies and more flies. Dragonflies everywhere, watching the river out of their big eyes and giving frightened little flicks of their tails. Amazing heat that makes the surface steam. We glide over the water from those long flat eddies back there to this tangle of dead branches... We hug the burning bank, looking for whiffs of shade that we grab as best we can under a few trees not too riddled with sunshine. Talking makes you even hotter, if that's possible. On the other hand, you're afraid to admit you're not comfortable.

Robinson, naturally enough, was the first to be fed up with navigation. I suggested landing near a restaurant. We weren't the only ones to have that little idea. Every fisherman on that reach of the river was already settled at the bistrot before us, jealously nursing his apéritif, entrenched behind a siphon. Robinson didn't dare ask me if this cafe I had chosen was expensive, but I set his mind at rest by assuring him that the prices were posted and perfectly reasonable. It was true. He never let go of his Madelon's hand the whole while.

Now it can be told that we paid our bill at the restaurant as if we had eaten, but we had only tried to eat. The less said of the dishes they served us the better. They're still there.

After that, to spend the afternoon, it would have been too complicated to arrange a fishing party, and it would have made Robinson unhappy because he wouldn't even have seen his float. As for me, I was sick and tired of rowing, just from the morning's effort. That had been plenty. The training I'd had on the rivers of Africa was far behind me. I had aged in that as in everything else.

For a change of exercise, I suggested that a little walk along the bank would do us a lot of good, at least as far as the tall grass you could see up there less than a mile away, not far from that line of poplars.

So there we went, Robinson and I arm in arm, and Madelon a few steps ahead of us. It was easier that way through the grass. At a bend in the river we heard accordions. The sound came from a barge, a beautiful barge moored at that point in the river. The music attracted Robinson. Which was understandable in his situation, and besides he had always had a weakness for music. Glad to have found something that amused him, we parked right there on the grass, which wasn't as dusty as on the slanting bank nearby. We could see that it wasn't any ordinary barge. It was neat and well turned out, not meant for hauling anything, more of a houseboat than a barge, with flowers all over it and even a spanking little kennel for the dog. We described the houseboat to Robinson. He wanted to know all about it.

"I'd like to live on a clean little boat like that myself," he said then. "How about you?" he asked Madelon...

"I see what you mean," she replied. "But that's an expensive idea you've got, Léon! I'm sure it would cost you a lot more than an apartment house... "

We all started reckoning how much that kind of a houseboat might cost, and we couldn't get together... Each of us insisted on his own figure... Regardless of what we were counting, our class of people used to do it out loud... Meanwhile, the accordion music came over to us as caressingly as you please, we could even hear the words of a song they were singing... Finally we agreed that the houseboat, just as it was, must be worth at least a hundred thousand francs... A figure to set you dreaming...

Close your lovely eyes, for the hours are short...

In the wonderful land, the beautiful land of drea-eams...

That's what they were singing inside the boat, men's and women's voices mixed, a little out of tune, but very pleasant all the same because of the setting. It went with the heat and the country and the time of day and the river.

Robinson persisted in driving his estimates sky-high. The way we'd described the houseboat, he was sure it would cost a lot more... Because it had a big glass window to let in more light and brass fittings all over, luxury in short...

"Léon, you're knocking yourself out." Madelon tried to quiet him. "Why don't you stretch out on this nice thick grass and rest a while... A hundred thousand or five hundred thousand, who cares?... You haven't got it and neither have I... So really there's no sense in working yourself up... "

He lay down, but he kept working himself up about the price all the same, he wanted to know for sure, and he wanted to see this houseboat that cost so much...

"Has it got a motor?" he asked... We didn't know.

Just to please him, since he insisted, I took a look at the stern, to see if I'd see the exhaust pipe of a small motor.

Close your lovely eyes, for life is a dream... Love is a fan-ta-sy...

Close your lovely eyes!

The people in there went on singing. We were drooping with fatigue... They were putting us to sleep.

Suddenly the spaniel came bounding out of the kennel and stood on the gangplank barking in our direction. We woke with a start, and we gave the spaniel hell. He had frightened Robinson.

So then a character who seemed to be the owner came out on deck through the little cabin door. He said he wouldn't stand for anybody shouting at his dog, and we talked back. But when he noticed that Robinson was as good as blind, the man calmed down and felt foolish. He changed his mind about bawling us out and even let us call him a few names to get even. To make up for his rudeness, he invited us to come and have coffee on his boat, to celebrate, he added, his birthday. He wouldn't hear of our baking out there in the sun, and so forth and so on... And besides it was lucky we'd turned up, because they were thirteen at table... He was a young man, an eccentric... He liked boats, he explained... We could see that. But his wife was afraid of the sea, so they had moored their boat out here, on the beach, so to speak... We went aboard, and everybody seemed glad to have us... First of all his wife, a fine-looking woman, who played the accordion like an angel. Anyway, it was nice of them to have us over for coffee. We could have been almost anybody. It was trusting of them... We realized right off that it wouldn't do to shame our charming hosts... Especially in front of their guests... Robinson had his faults, but as a rule he had a certain fine feeling. Just by the sound of their voices he realized that we had to behave and abstain from bad language. True, we weren't very well dressed, but we were neat and clean. The owner of the houseboat, I looked him over, must have been about thirty, with poetic brown hair and a nice sailor-type suit, but custom-made. And his attractive wife had really "velvety" eyes.

They had just finished lunch. Plenty of leftovers. We didn't say no to a piece of cake, certainly not. Or a glass of port to go with it. I hadn't heard such high-class voices in a long time. High-class people have a certain way of talking that intimidates you and frightens me personally, especially their women. It's really just a lot of half-baked, pretentious phrases, but as highly polished as antique furniture. Meaningless as they are, their phrases are terrifying. When you try to answer, you're afraid of slipping up. And even when they take the tone of the gutter and amuse themselves singing the songs of the poor, they hang on to that high-class accent, which inspires suspicion and antipathy. That accent always has the kind of whiplash that's needed for talking to servants. It's sexy, but it makes you want to tumble their women, just to see their dignity, as they call it, melt away.

In a whisper I told Robinson about the furniture, all antiques. The place reminded me a little of my mother's shop, except naturally it was cleaner and more orderly. My mother's shop always smelled of old pepper.

The walls all around were hung with paintings by the owner. A painter, as his wife told me with lots of simper and gush. His wife loved her man all right. He was an artist, nice penis, nice hair, nice income, everything needed to make a woman happy; in addition, she had her accordion, her friends, her reveries on the meager, swirling water, she was quite content never to go anywhere... Here they had all that plus all the sweet coolness in the world, enclosed between the half-curtains and the breath of the ventilator. And God-given security besides.

Seeing we were there, we thought we might as well make ourselves at home. Iced drinks, then strawberries and cream, my favorite dessert. Wriggling and simpering, Madelon accepted a second helping. She too was improving her manners. The men were taken with Madelon, especially the rich father-in-law. He seemed delighted to have Madelon beside him and went to no end of trouble to give her pleasure. He ransacked the whole table for delicacies just for her, and she lit into them with such enthusiasm that the tip of her nose was soon covered with whipped cream. To judge by the conversation, the father-in-law was a widower. If so, he'd forgotten it. Soon, what with the liqueurs, Madelon was tipsy. The suit Robinson was wearing and mine, too, showed signs of fatigue, of seasons and more seasons, but maybe in that dim light no one would notice. Still, I felt rather humiliated among those people, so comfortable in all respects, as clean as Americans, so well washed and well groomed, fit for a fashion parade.

Once liquored up, Madelon didn't behave so well. Aiming her little profile at the pictures, she started talking rubbish. The hostess noticed and took to the accordion again to gloss it over. Everybody sang, the three of us joined in under our breaths, but listlessly and out of tune, the same song as we'd been listening to outside, and then another.

Robinson had managed to strike up a conversation with an elderly gentleman who seemed to know all there was to know about growing cacao trees. A splendid subject. A get-together between colonials. To my amazement I hear Robinson saying: "When I was out in Africa—I was working for the Compagnie Pordurière in those days as their agronomist in chief—I used to mobilize a whole village to harvest the crop... " And more of the same. He couldn't see me, so he gave himself free rein... The sky was the limit... Phony memories... He really gave the old gentleman an earful... A pack of lies... Anything he could think of to put himself in the class of the old gentleman, who was really an expert. It exasperated and dismayed me to hear Robinson, who had always been rather reserved in company, shooting off his mouth like that.

They'd given him a place of honor in the depths of a big scented sofa. In his right hand he held a glass of brandy, while his left hand, with sweeping gestures, evoked the majesty of the untamed forests and the fury of the equatorial tornado. He was launched, well launched... Alcide would have had a good laugh if he could have been there in the corner. Poor Alcide!

I can't deny it, we were very comfortable on their houseboat, especially as a light breeze had come up on the river and, framed in the windows, the fluted curtains began to flutter like merry and cool little flags.

More ices were served and then another round of champagne. It was the owner's birthday, he told us so a dozen times. For once he had decided to give everyone, even the wayfarer, pleasure. For once that was us. For an hour or two or possibly three, we would all be reconciled under his aegis, we'd all be pals, the known, the unknown, even strangers, even we three whom they had picked up on the riverbank faute de mieux, so as not to be thirteen at table. I was going to start singing my little song of good cheer, but then I changed my mind, suddenly too proud, too conscious. At that point, to justify their invitation that lay heavy on my mind, I saw fit to reveal that in my person they were entertaining one of the most distinguished physicians of Greater Paris! They could hardly have suspected it from my dress! Or from the low estate of my companions for that matter! But the moment they knew who I was, they declared themselves delighted and flattered, and every one of them started telling me about his very special little ailments. I took the opportunity to make friends with a tycoon's daughter, a sturdy young cousin of the skipper's, who suffered from hives and developed acid stomach on the slightest provocation.

When you're not used to the comfort and luxuries of the table, they go to your head in no time. Truth is always glad to leave you. With next to no encouragement it will set you free. And we manage very nicely without it. Amid this sudden plethora of comforts a fine megalomaniacal delirium finds no difficulty in overwhelming you. I started telling tall ones in my turn, intermittently discussing hives with the young cousin. You extricate yourself from your daily humiliations by trying, like Robinson, to put yourself on a level with the rich by means of lies, the currency of the poor. We're all ashamed of our ungainly flesh, our inadequate carcasses. I couldn't make up my mind to show them my truth; it was as unworthy of them as my rear end. I had to make a good impression at all costs.

I started answering their questions with fantasies, same as Robinson had done in his confab with the old gentleman. I, too, was invaded by pride!... My enormous clientele!... The dreadful overwork!... My friend Robinson... the agronomist who had offered me the hospitality of his chalet... on the outskirts of Toulouse...

And besides, when your table companion has eaten well and had plenty to drink, he's easily convinced. Luckily! Anything goes! Robinson had preceded me in the furtive delights of impromptu cock-and-bull; it cost me very little effort to follow in his footsteps.

Because of the smoked glasses he was wearing, the people couldn't see exactly what was wrong with Robinson's eyes. We generously attributed his misfortune to the war. From then on we were sitting pretty, raised first socially, then patriotically, to the level of the other guests, who had been rather taken aback at first by the whimsy of the painter husband, though to be sure his status as a fashionable artist obliged him now and then to do something weird and unexpected... The guests began to find all three of us ever so charming and inconceivably interesting.

Maybe Madelon didn't play her role of fiancee as modestly as she should have; she got everybody including the women so hot and bothered I was afraid the party would end in an orgy. It didn't. Gradually the sentences became undone, defeated by slobbering attempts to go beyond words. Nothing happened.

Tangled in phrases and cushions, fuddled by our collective effort to make one another happy, more deeply, more warmly happier by the spirit alone since our bodies were replete, we did everything possible to suffuse the present moment with all the pleasure in the world, with every marvel known to us in and outside of ourselves, so that our neighbor might at last get the full advantage of it and confess to us that this was the very miracle he was looking for, that this gift from us was just what had been lacking for so and so many years to his eternal happiness! That we at last had revealed to him the reason of his own being! And he was going to tell all and sundry that he had found the reason of his being. So we'd down another bumper together to celebrate our joy! May our joy endure forever! And may this charm never be broken! May we, above all, never never relapse into those abominable days when there were no miracles, the days before we met and miraculously found one another!... All of us together from this moment on! At last! And for ever!

The skipper couldn't restrain himself from breaking the charm.

He had this mania for talking about his painting, it was really too much on his mind, about his pictures, come what may and a propos of anything or nothing. Thanks to his obstinate idiocy, crushing banality returned, drunk as we were, to our midst. Defeated, I went over to the skipper and delivered myself of a few heartfelt and high-flown compliments, the sweet words in which artists delight. Just what he needed. My compliments hit him like an orgasm. He slumped down on one of the overblown sofas and fell asleep almost instantly, as sweetly as you please, palpably happy. The others meanwhile studied the contours of one another's faces with a leaden gaze of mutual fascination, torn between almost irresistible somnolence and the delights of heaven-sent digestion.

As for me, I suspended my desire to doze, saving it up for the night. Only too often the day's lingering fears banish sleep, so when you're lucky enough to build up a small stock of beatitude, you have to be a born fool to squander it in futile preliminary catnaps. Keep it for the night, that's my motto! Always be thinking of the night. Besides, we'd been invited to dinner, so it was time to be working up a fresh appetite...

We took advantage of the prevailing stupor to slip away. The three of us managed a discreet exit, dodging the slumbering guests dispersed around the hostess's accordion. Softened by music, the hostess's eyes blinked in search of darkness. "See you later," she said as we passed. Her smile ended in a dream.

We didn't go very far, only to the place where I'd noticed a bend in the river, between two rows of tall, pointed poplars. From there you can see the whole valley, and in the distance a village in its hollow, huddled round a church tower planted like a nail in the reddening sky.

Madelon was anxious. "What time is there a train back?" she asked.

"Don't worry," we assured her. "They'll take us by car. It's all arranged. The skipper said so... They've got one... "

That was enough for Madelon. She was dreamy with happiness. It had really been a splendid day. "Léon," she asked him. "How do your eyes feel now?"

"Much better. I didn't want to tell you before because I wasn't sure, but I think, especially with the left eye, it's getting so I can count the bottles on the table... I drank quite a lot, did you notice? Good stuff too!"

"The left is the heart side!" said Madelon joyfully. Naturally she was happy about his eyes being better.

"Come," she suggested, "you kiss me and I'll kiss you." Their effusions were making me feel in the way. But it was hard for me to leave because I didn't know where to go. I made as if to do my business behind a nearby tree and stayed there, waiting for their seizure to pass. They said things full of tenderness. I heard them. The dullest love dialogues are kind of amusing when you know the people. And I'd never heard them talk like that before.

"Do you really love me?" she asked.

"I love you as much as I love my eyes!" was his answer.

"Oh Léon, that's a beautiful thing to say!... But you haven't seen me yet, Léon... Maybe when you see me with your own eyes and not just through other people's, you won't love me so much... When that time comes, you'll see other women, and maybe you'll love them all... The way your friends do... "

That remark, made in an undertone, was a dig at me... I hadn't the slightest doubt. She thought I was far away and couldn't hear her... So she let loose... She lost no time... Robinson started protesting. "Hey there!" Slander, malicious gossip, he assured her.

"Me! Certainly not! Oh no, Madelon!" he defended himself, "That's not my way at all! What makes you think I'm like him?... When you've been so good to me!... I'm the faithful sort! I'm no skirt chaser! When I give my word it's for always! You're beautiful, I know that already, but you'll be even more beautiful when I see you... There! Are you happy now? Not crying any more? What more can I tell you?"

"Oh Léon! You're so sweet!" she said, cuddling up to him. Then they were swearing to love each other forever and ever and nothing could stop them, the heavens weren't big enough.

"I want you to always be happy with me!... " he said very gently. "With nothing to do and everything you need all the same... "

"Oh, how good you are, my sweet Léon! You're even better than I thought... So tender!... So faithful!... So everything!"

"It's because I adore you, my pussycat... "

And they worked each other up even further by necking. And then, as if to shut me out of their intense happiness, they gave me a kidney punch...

She started off: "Your friend the doctor! Isn't he a nice one!" And then she repeated, as if the thought of me stuck in her craw. "He's a nice one all right!... I wouldn't want to say anything against him, because he's a friend of yours... But I have a feeling that he's a brute with women... I don't like to say anything bad about him, because I think he's really fond of you... But, you know, he's not my type... I'll tell you something... You're sure it won't make you mad?" No, nothing would make Léon mad. "Well, I'd say the doctor is too hot on women... Kind of like a dog, see what I mean?... What do you think?... I get the feeling that he's ready to jump every last one of them! He does his nasty business, and then he makes himself scarce...

Don't you think so? Don't you think he's like that?"

The bastard thought everything she wanted him to think, in fact he agreed that in addition to being right everything she said was screamingly funny. So funny he could die laughing. He encouraged her to go on and almost split a gut.

"Yes, Madelon, what you say is perfectly true! Ferdinand isn't a bad sort, but delicacy isn't his strong point, I don't mind telling you, nor fidelity either!... Take my word for it!... "

"Has he had lots of mistresses? You must know, Léon." The bitch. She was fishing for information.

"Plenty," he replied with assurance, "but you know... he's not hard to please... "

Some conclusion had to be drawn from this exchange, and Madelon proceeded to draw one. "Doctors are mostly all pigs, everybody knows that... But if you ask me, he's a champion!"

"You've never said truer words," my good and faithful friend approved her. And he went on: "It's so bad, he's such a sex fiend, I've often thought he took drugs... And say, the man's equipment! If you could see it! Huge! Monstrous! It's not natural!... "

"Really?" said Madelon, perplexed, trying to remember my equipment. "You think he's got some disease?" She was worried, suddenly dismayed by those intimate revelations.

"I don't know about that," he was regretfully obliged tc admit. "I can't tell for sure... But it wouldn't surprise me with the life he leads."

"Yes, you're right... he must take drugs... That must be why he's so strange sometimes... " Madelon's little head was working hard, and she added: "We'd better be careful from now on... "

"What's the matter?" he asked. "You afraid of him? He isn't anything to you, I hope?... He hasn't ever made you any advances, has he?"

"No, of course not. I wouldn't have let him. But you never know what he might take it into his head... Suppose he threw a fit, for instance... Those dope fiends have fits, you know!... But one thing is sure, I'd never go to him if I were sick!"

"Neither would I, now you bring it up!" Robinson approved. After which there was more mushing and petting...

"Honey lamb!" she cooed.

"Kitten... Kitten!" he replied. And silences in between, punctuated by barrages of kisses.

"See how many times you can tell me you love me while I kiss you as far as your shoulder... " That little game began at the top of the neck.

"I'm as red as a beet!" she cried, panting. "I'm suffocating! Air! Air!" But he didn't let her breathe. He started all over again. Sitting in the grass nearby, I tried to see what would happen. He took her nipples between his lips and toyed with them. Innocent pastimes. I was all red in the face myself for a variety of reasons and in addition amazed at my own indiscretion.

"We'll be very happy, won't we, Léon? Tell me you're sure we'll be happy."

Then came an intermission. And then endless plans for the future, enough plans to make a whole new world, but a world only for the two of them. I, most especially, wasn't in it at all. It looked as if they'd never finish getting rid of me, sweeping my nasty image out of their life.

"Have you been friends with Ferdinand a long time?" The question was nagging at her...

"Oh yes, for years... in different places... " he answered. "First we just happened to meet, on our travels... He likes going to strange places... So do I in a way, and for a long time we traveled together... See?" He reduced our life together to the flattest banality.

"Well," she said with crisp determination. "You're not going to be such good friends anymore... From now on!... It's going to stop! It is going to stop, isn't it, pussycat?... From now on I'll be your only companion... Understand?... How about it, sweetie?"

"What's wrong? You jealous of him?" In spite of himself he was rather disconcerted, the dope.

"No, I'm not jealous of him, but you see, Léon, I love you too much, I want you all to myself... I don't want to share you with anybody... And he's not the kind of person you should associate with now that I love you, Léon... He's too immoral... Understand? Tell me you adore me, Léon! Tell me you understand!"

"I adore you... "

"That's good."

* * *

We got back to Toulouse that same night.

The accident happened two days later. It was time for me to be leaving after all, and I was just packing my suitcase before starting for the station when I heard someone shouting outside the house. I listened... They wanted me to come quick and hurry down to the crypt... I couldn't see the person who was shouting that way. But to judge by the tone of voice, it must have been terribly urgent... They wanted me to go there right away!

"Just a minute," I say. "Where's the fire!" I didn't feel like hurrying. It must have been about seven o'clock, just before dinnertime. We were supposed to say good-bye at the station, we'd arranged it that way... That was convenient for everybody, because the old woman would be coming home a little later than usual. She was expecting a whole crowd of pilgrims at the crypt that evening.

"Come quick, doctor!" The voice in the street shouted again. "Madame Henrouille has had an accident!" "Okay! Okay! Okay!... I'll be right down."

But in less than a moment I'd thought it over. "You go ahead," I said. "Tell them I'm coming right away... Soon as I put my pants on... "

"But it's terribly urgent!" the voice cried... "She's unconscious, I tell you! . . , She seems to have broken a bone in her head!... She fell down the stairs!... down to the bottom of her vault!"

"That'll do!" I said to myself when I heard that lovely story. No need to think any longer. I beat it straight to the station. I knew all I wanted to know, I caught my train at seven-fifteen, but only by the skin of my teeth.

We never did say good-bye.

* * *

The first thing Parapine said when he saw me was that I wasn't looking well.

"You must have worn yourself to a frazzle in Toulouse," he said, suspicious as usual.

It's true that I'd had a scare down there in Toulouse, but nothing to complain about, since I'd managed to keep clear of serious trouble, or so I thought, by slipping away at the critical moment.

I told Parapine the story in detail and aired my suspicions as well. He wasn't convinced that I'd been very bright, but we didn't have time to go into it very thoroughly, because by then the question of a job for me had become so urgent that I had to do something about it. There was no time to be lost in discussion... I had only a hundred and fifty francs left to my name and no idea where to turn... The Tarapout?... They weren't hiring anymore... the Depression. Back to La Garenne-Rancy? Try and retrieve my practice? I considered it for a while in spite of everything, but only as a last resource and very reluctantly. Nothing is quenched so easily as the sacred fire.

It was Parapine who finally came to the rescue. He found me a small job at the institution where he himself had been working for some months.

Their business was still pretty good. In addition to taking cretins to the movies, Parapine was in charge of the sparks. Twice a week, at scheduled hours, he unleashed magnetic storms over the heads of the melancholies assembled for that purpose in a hermetically sealed and pitch-black room. Mental gymnastics in sum, a brilliant idea emanating from Dr. Baryton, his boss. A skinflint, incidentally, this colleague of ours. He took me on at a very low salary but with a contract a mile long, full of clauses entirely to his advantage. In short, a boss.

We were hardly paid at all at that rest home, but the food wasn't at all bad and the lodging was excellent, with facilities for laying the nurses, which was tolerated and tacitly permitted. Baryton, the boss, had no objection whatever, in fact he had noticed that erotic tolerance attached the staff to the house. A wise man looks the other way.

And besides, in the first place, it was no time to ask questions or make demands when he was offering me a nice little chunk of wherewithal in the nick of time. Thinking it over, I couldn't quite see why Parapine was suddenly taking such an active interest in me. His attitude weighed on my mind. To give him credit for brotherly love... would really be gilding his character... It had to be something more complicated. But you never can tell...

We all ate lunch together, that was the custom, gathered around Baryton, our boss, the esteemed alienist, with his pointed beard and short beefy thighs, a nice man except for his thrift, but on that point he could be utterly revolting, all he needed was a pretext or opportunity...

He certainly gave us plenty of noodles and rasping Bordeaux. Somebody had left him a whole vineyard, so he told us. Which was our tough luck. A very inferior vintage, I assure you.

His asylum at Vigny-sur-Seine was always full. It was called a "Rest Home" in the prospectuses, because it was in the middle of a big garden, where the nuts went walking on nice days. They walked as if they had trouble keeping their heads balanced on their shoulders, they seemed in constant fear of stumbling and spilling the contents. All sorts of misshapen things, things they were dreadfully attached to, were bobbing and bumping about in there.

When the patients spoke of their mental treasures, it was always with anguished contortions or airs of protective condescension that made you think of powerful and ultrameticulous executives. Not for an empire would those lunatics have gone outside their minds. A madman's thoughts are just the usual ideas of a human being, except that they're hermetically sealed inside his head. The world never gets into his head, and that's the way he wants it. A sealed head is like a lake without an outlet, standing, stagnant.

Baryton bought his noodles and vegetables wholesale in Paris. So naturally we weren't very popular with the shopkeepers of Vigny-sur-Seine. I'd go so far as to say that they detested us. Their animosity didn't spoil our appetites. At the beginning of my stay, Baryton, at the table, would distill philosophical conclusions from our disjointed remarks. But seeing that he had spent his life among lunatics and made his living by his association with them, sharing their meals, neutralizing their lunacies as best he could, nothing bored him so much as having to talk about their manias at table. "They have no place in the conversation of normal people!" he declared in peremptory self-defense. He himself observed that rule of mental hygiene strictly.

He was fond of conversation, and there was a kind of terror in the way he insisted on its being amusing, reassuring, and above all thoroughly sane. He just didn't want to think about the loonies. His feeling toward them was one of instinctive antipathy, and with that he contented himself once and for all. On the other hand, he loved hearing us talk about our travels. We couldn't tell him enough. My arrival liberated Parapine from the need to talk. For him it was providential, for now I could entertain the boss during meals. All my peregrinations were served up, related at length, doctored of course, made suitably literary, amusing. Baryton made an enormous amount of noise with his tongue and mouth in eating. His daughter Aimee always sat at his right. Though only ten, Aimee already seemed faded. Something lifeless, an incurable grayness blunted our image of Aimee, as though unhealthy little clouds were always passing over her face.

There were moments of friction between Parapine and Baryton. But Baryton never bore anyone a grudge, as long as they laid no claim to the profits of his establishment. For many years his accounts had been the only element of the sacred in his existence.

Once, in the days when Parapine still spoke to him, he had told him bluntly at table that he was lacking in Ethics. At first that remark had nettled Baryton, but then the whole thing had been smoothed over. You don't quarrel about such trifles. Listening to the story of my travels, Baryton not only relished a surge of romantic emotion but rejoiced at the money he was saving. "You're such a fine storyteller, Ferdinand, that after listening to you T don't have to visit those countries anymore!" To him no prettier compliment was conceivable. Only easily managed lunatics were admitted to his institution, never vicious, out-and-out homicidal maniacs. The place wasn't absolutely sinister. Hardly any bars and only a few isolation cells. Maybe the most worrisome case was little Aimee, his own daughter.

The child wasn't regarded as a patient, but the environment haunted her.

A howl or two would sometimes reach us in the dining room, but the cause of those screams was always something quite insignificant. And they never lasted long. Then occasionally a group of inmates would suddenly, for no reason at all, be shaken by a prolonged wave of frenzy in the course of their interminable wanderings between the pump, the clumps of bushes, and the begonia beds. Those incidents would be handled without great alarums and excursions by means of tepid baths and buckets of opium extract.

Now and then the lunatics would stand at the few dining hall windows that opened out on the street and terrify the neighborhood with their bellowing, but mostly they kept their horror to themselves. They took good care of their horror, defending it against our therapeutic efforts. That resistance of theirs was the spice of their lives.

When I think now of all the lunatics I knew at Baryton's, I can't help suspecting that the only true manifestations of our innermost being are war and insanity, those two absolute nightmares.

Maybe what makes life so terribly fatiguing is nothing other than the enormous effort we make for twenty years, forty years, and more, to be reasonable, to avoid being simply, profoundly ourselves, that is, vile, ghastly, absurd. It's the nightmare of having to represent the halt subhuman we were fobbed off with as a small-size universal ideal, a superman from morning to night.

In our nuthouse we had patients at all prices, the most opulent living in heavily padded Louis XV rooms. Baryton paid these a daily, highly priced visit. They'd be expecting him. Now and then he'd be welcomed with a titanic, truly magnificent, and long-premeditated sock in the jaw. which he'd enter on the bill under "special treatment."

At table Parapine maintained an attitude of reserve. Not that he was the least bit put out by my oratorical triumphs; quite the contrary, he seemed less preoccupied than in times past, in his microbe days, and all in all, almost happy. Don't forget that he'd had a bad scare over his business with the minor maidens. It had left him rather disconcerted in his dealings with the sex. In his free time, he'd wander around the grounds of our institution just like a patient. He'd smile at me when I passed, but his smiles were so vague, so pale, you'd have thought he was bidding me good-bye.

By taking us on as technical aides, Baryton had made a good bargain, for in addition to our unflagging devotion, we brought him entertainment and the echoes of adventure, for which deprivation had left him with such a craving. And indeed, he often took pleasure in expressing his satisfaction with us. Yet on Parapine's score he had certain reservations.

He had never felt entirely comfortable with Parapine. "Parapine, you see, Ferdinand," he confided in me one day, "Parapine is a Russian." To Baryton the fact of his being Russian was as descriptive, morphological, and irreparable as "diabetic" or "nigger." Launched on a topic that had been tormenting him for months, he set his brain to working enormously in my presence and for my special benefit... You wouldn't have recognized the old Baryton. We were on our way to the local tobacco store for cigarettes.

"Parapine, you see, Ferdinand, of course he's intelligent... but really, you know, there's something dreadfully arbitrary about his intelligence! Don't you agree, Ferdinand? In the first place, he simply refuses to adapt... You can see that at a glance... And he's not at ease in his work... For that matter, he's not at ease in the world... Admit it!... And there he's making a mistake! A big mistake!... Because it makes him unhappy!... That proves it. Take me, Ferdinand, think how adaptable I am!... " (He thumped his sternum.) "Suppose, for instance, the earth starts turning the wrong way tomorrow. What will I do? Well, Ferdinand, I'll adapt! Instantly! And do you know how, Ferdinand? I'll just sleep twelve hours more, that'll turn the trick! One two three! It's as simple as that! I'll have adapted! Whereas your Parapine, you know what he'd do in such a situation? He'd ruminate projects and grudges for another hundred years!... I'm certain!... I assure you!... Don't you agree?... If the earth starts going backward, he won't be able to sleep!... He'll see some sort of special injustice in it!... Injustice, injustice! That's his bug!... He was always talking about injustice in the days when he still deigned to speak to me... And do you think he'll content himself with sniveling? Which wouldn't be so bad!... Oh no! Before you know it he'll start looking for a way to blow up the planet! To get even, Ferdinand! And the worst of it, I'll tell you the worst of it, Ferdinand!... But just between you and me... Well, the worst of it is that he will find a way! That's right! Look here, Ferdinand, I'm going to tell you something. Try to imprint it on your mind!... There are simple lunatics and there are others, tortured by an obsession with civilization... It grieves me to think that Parapine belongs to the latter class!... Do you know what he said to me the other day?... "

"No, sir... "

"Well, here's what he said: 'Between the penis and mathematics, Monsieur Baryton, there's nothing! A vacuum!' And another thing!... Do you know what he's waiting for before starting to speak to me again?"

"No, Monsieur Baryton, I have no idea... " "He hasn't told you?"

"No, not yet... "

"Well, he has told me... He's waiting for the dawn of the mathematical age! Neither more nor less! His mind is made up! What do you think of such impertinence? To me! His senior! His chief!"

Of course I had to laugh a little, to join him in laughing off this extravagant fancy. But Baryton was no longer dwelling on such trifles. He had bigger and better things to get indignant about.

"Ah, Ferdinand! I see this kind of thing strikes you as innocuous. Innocent words... just one more case of idle foolishness... That's what you seem to think... Just that! Am I right? Oh, thoughtless Ferdinand! Let me take pains to put you on your guard against such aberrations, which only appear to be trivial! You are absolutely mistaken! Absolutely!... A thousand times mistaken!... You will believe me, I trust, when I tell you that in the course of my career I have heard, here and elsewhere, just about everything that can be heard in the way of hot and cold delirium! Nothing has been lacking... You'll give me credit for that, won't you Ferdinand? And you have surely observed, Ferdinand, that I am not given to anxiety... to exaggeration... Not at all... A word or group of words carries very little weight with me! And the same goes for sentences and whole speeches!... Though a simple man by birth and nature, I am, and no one will deny it, one of those amply inhibited persons who are not frightened by words!... Well, Ferdinand, conscientious analysis has obliged me to conclude that I must be on my guard against Parapine! And formulate the most express reservations... His variety of extravagance resembles none of the common, inoffensive varieties... It is, I believe, one of the few dangerous forms of eccentricity, a highly contagious mania, to be precise, of the rampant social variety! In your friend's case, we may not yet be dealing with out-and-out insanity... No... Maybe his trouble is only exaggerated conviction... But the contagious manias are well known to me!... I've known a good many sufferers from conviction mania... Of many different types... And in the last analysis, those who talk about justice seem to be the maddest of the lot!... At first, I must confess, I took a certain interest in justice fanatics... Today those particular maniacs annoy and exasperate me more than I can tell , . , Don't you feel the same way?... Human beings show a strange aptitude for transmitting this mania. It terrifies me, and we find it, mind you, in all human beings! Bear that in mind, Ferdinand, in all of them! Same as with liquor and sex... The same predisposition... The same fatality... Infinitely widespread... Are you laughing, Ferdinand? If so, you frighten me! Fragile! Vulnerable! Thoughtless! Dangerous Ferdinand! When I think that I took you for a serious-minded man! Don't forget that I'm old, Ferdinand, I could afford the luxury of thumbing my nose at the future! I'd have every right to! But you?!"

As a matter of principle, in all things and for all time, I agreed with the boss. I haven't made much practical headway in the course of my harassed existence, but I had learned the essential principles of servile etiquette. Consequently, we had become good friends. I never opposed him, and I didn't eat much at the table. A pleasant sort of assistant, in sum, economical, not the least ambitious, no threat to anyone.

* * *

Vigny-sur-Seine is situated between two sluice gates, between two hillsides stripped of vegetation, a village turning suburb. Paris will swallow it up.

It loses a garden a month. On the approaches, billboards splash it with all the colors of the Russian ballet. The town clerk's daughter has learned to make cocktails. Only the streetcar seems intent on becoming historical; nothing short of a revolution will make it give up. The people are anxious, the children no longer have the same accent as their parents. It embarrasses the inhabitants to think that they're still attached to the Seine-et-Oise[90] Department. Miracles are under way. The last garden globe vanished when Laval became premier, the local cleaning women have just raised their prices by twenty centimes an hour. A bookmaker has been sighted. The postmistress buys pederastic novels and imagines others that are even more realistic. The priest says "shit" at the drop of a hat and gives stock market tips to his parishioners when they are very very good. The Seine has killed its fish and is becoming Americanized between files of pusher-puller-selfloading barges that look like ghastly sets of rotten tin false teeth along both banks. Three developers have just gone to jail. Progress sweeps on!

The real-estate situation has not escaped Baryton. He bitterly regrets not having had the foresight to buy up lots in the next valley twenty years ago, when the owners were begging you to take them away, like rotten fruit, at twenty centimes a square meter. The good old days. Luckily his Psychotherapeutic Institute was holding its own very nicely. Nevertheless there were problems. Those insatiable families were always demanding, always insisting on newer and newer methods of treatment, more electrical, more mysterious, more everything... The most recent, most impressive machines and contraptions. And he had to submit, on pain of being outdone by his competitors... those similar institutions tucked away in the neighboring groves of Asnières, Passy, Montretout, lying in wait for the deluxe class of nuts.

---

[90] Seine-et-Oise. At that time the immediate suburbs of Paris belonged to the Seine Department, which in turn was surrounded by a wider belt, also regarded as suburban—the Seine-et-Oise Department.

Under the guidance of Parapine, Baryton did his best to modernize his establishment, as cheaply as possible to be sure, buying electrical, pneumatic, hydraulic devices, second hand, at a discount, at clearance sales, but indefatigably, so as to seem at all times better equipped than before and so appeal to the manias of his captious, well-to-do inmates. Many a moan was wrung from him by the necessity of acquiring useless equipment... of currying favor with the very lunatics.

"I opened my institution," he confided in me one day in an outpouring of sorrow, "just before the Exposition,[91] the big one, Ferdinand... we alienists in those days were, or, if you will, constituted a very small group, much less curious, I can assure you, and less depraved than today!... None of us in those days tried to be as crazy as his patients... It was not yet the fashion for the healer to go off his rocker on the pretext that it furthered the cure, an obscene fashion, mind you, like almost everything that comes to us from foreign countries...

"You see, Ferdinand, in the days of my beginnings, French medical men still had self-respect. They didn't feel obliged to rave along with their patients... In the interest of harmony?... Don't ask me! To make them happy? Where will it lead us?... If we persist in being more ingenious, more morbid, more perverse than the most persecuted lunatic in our asylums, in wallowing with some sort of obscene pride in every form of dementia paraded before our eyes, what will become of us?... Do you feel able, Ferdinand, to reassure me about the future of human reason? Or even of plain common sense?... At this rate what will be left of plain common sense in a few years? Nothing. I foresee it. Absolutely nothing! I can predict it... It's obvious...

"For one thing, Ferdinand, from the standpoint of a truly modern intelligence, haven't all differences and distinctions been effaced? No more white! No more black! Everything dissolves. That's the new approach! The fashion! If that's the case, why not go mad ourselves?... Right this minute! As a starter! And brag about it! Proclaim total psychic chaos! And advertise it with our own madness! Who's going to stop us? I ask you, Ferdinand!... What last superfluous human scruples?... What flabby misgivings? Well? . . , Sometimes, Ferdinand, when I listen to certain of our colleagues, and, mind you, among the most esteemed, the most sought-after by the clientele and the academies alike, I wonder where they're leading us! It's infernal! Those madmen disconcert, terrify, diabolize, and above all disgust me! Just hearing them at one of their modern congresses report on the results of their habitual researches, I'm seized with livid panic, Ferdinand! I listen and my reason deserts me! Diabolical, prurient, captious, and dishonest, these minions of modern psychiatry are hurling us into the abyss with their superconscious analyses... I say it again, into the abyss. One fine morning, Ferdinand, unless you younger men do something about it, that's where we'll end up! What with stretching ourselves thin, with sublimating ourselves and torturing our minds, we'll end up on the far side of intelligence, the infernal side, that there's no coming back from!... And the fact is, what with masturbating their intelligence day and night, those ultrasuper wise men seem even now to have shut themselves up in the dungeons of the damned!

"I say day and night, because you know, Ferdinand, they fornicate themselves all night in their dreams... Need I say more!... They dig at their minds! They dilate them! They tyrannize them!... All around them there's nothing left but a foul slumgullion of organic debris, a marmalade of madness and symptoms that drip and ooze from every part of them... The remains of the mind are all over our hands, and there we are, sticky, grotesque, contemptuous, fetid. Everything's going to collapse, Ferdinand, everything is collapsing, I, old man Baryton, am telling you, and it won't be long now!... You'll see the end, Ferdinand, the great debacle! Because you're still young! You'll see it! Oh, you'll enjoy it, I can promise you!... You'll all end up in the nuthouse! Zoom! Just one more outburst of madness! One too many! And wham! off you go to the loony bin! At last! You'll be liberated, as you put it. It has tempted you too much and too long! That will be the act of daring you've been clamoring for! But once you're in the nuthouse, my little friends... take it from me, you'll stay there!

"Make a note of this, Ferdinand, the beginning and end of all things is the lack of moderation! Want me to tell you how the big débâcle started?... It started when men played fast and loose with their sense of proportion! With foreign exaggerations! When moderation's gone, power goes with it!

---

[91] The Exposition. The Exposition Universelle (World Exhibition) held in Paris in 1900.

It was inevitable! Is then everyone doomed? Why not? All of us? Definitely! Going to the dogs? No, running! A mad stampede!

I saw the human mind, Ferdinand, losing its balance little by little and dissolving in the vast maelstrom of apocalyptic ambitions! It began about 1900... mark that date! From then on, the world in general and psychiatry in particular have been one frantic race to see who could become more perverse, more salacious, more outlandish, more revolting, more creative as they call it, than his neighbor... A pretty mess!... Who would be first to throw himself into the arms of the monster, the beast without heart and without restraint!... The beast will devour us all, Ferdinand, it's a certainty and a good thing too!... What is this beast?... A big head that goes where it pleases!... Even now its wars and its flaming slobber are pouring in on us from all sides!... Here and now we are in the midst of a deluge! Neither more nor less! Apparently we were bored with consciousness! Well, we won't be bored any longer! We've started buggering each other for variety's sake... And we've been going in for 'impressions' and 'intuitions' ever since... like women...

"And come to think of it, is there any need for us to weigh ourselves down with the least bit of logic?... Of course not!... Logic can only be an encumbrance to the infinitely subtle, truly progressive psychologists that our times are turning out... Don't get me wrong, I'm not saying that I look down on women, Ferdinand! Certainly not! You know that! But I don't care for their 'impressions'! I'm a testiculate animal, Ferdinand, and when I have a fact, I hang on to it for dear life... In that connection I had an interesting experience the other day... I was asked to admit a writer... He was cracked... You know what he'd been shouting for over a month? They're liquidating!... They're liquidating!... ' That's what he was shouting all over the house! He was a case all right. He had crossed over to the far side of the intelligence!... His trouble was that he simply couldn't liquidate... An old stricture was poisoning him with urine, stopping up his bladder... I had to relieve him drop by drop with a catheter... it took hours... But the family insisted that the cause of it all was his genius... I tried my level best to convince them that their writer's trouble was in his bladder, they clung to their idea... that he'd blown his top in a moment of excessive genius... In the end I had to fall in with their opinion... you know what families are like... You'll never get a family to understand that a man, related to them or not, is nothing but suspended putrefaction... No family will pay bills for suspended putrefaction... "

For twenty years Baryton had been wrestling with the quarrelsome vanity of families. They gave him a hard time. Patient and well balanced as I knew him to be, he nevertheless nursed a vestige of well-fermented hatred toward families... At the time when I was living close to him, he was exasperated and trying obstinately, though in secret, to free himself, to escape once and for all, one way or another, from the tyranny of those families... Everyone has his reasons for trying to escape his private unhappiness, and each of us, to that end, coaxes some ingenious method from the circumstances. Blessed are those who can content themselves with whorehouses!

Parapine, for his part, seemed happy to have chosen the way of silence. Baryton, as I came to understand only later, doubted in his heart whether he would ever succeed in freeing himself from families, from their hold on him, from the thousand repulsive servitudes involved in alimentary psychiatry, in short, from his condition. He so longed for something new and absolutely different that he was thoroughly ripe for flight and escape. This accounted no doubt for his critical tirades... Routine was death to his ego. Sublimation was no longer possible, he just wanted to go away, to take his body somewhere else. There was nothing of the musician in Baryton, and in the end he had to upset everything like a bear.

He, who thought himself so reasonable, set himself free by means of a scandalous and thoroughly regrettable action. Later on, at leisure, I shall try to tell what happened.

For the moment the job of assistant to Baryton struck me as quite bearable. The therapeutic routine was far from strenuous, though now and then, as you'd expect, I'd feel pretty sick after talking too long with one of the patients, a kind of dizzy spell would come over me, as though the patients, from one commonplace little remark to another, had, without seeming to, led me away from my usual dwelling place to the heart and center of their dementia. For a short moment I wondered how I would ever get out of there and whether I hadn't, unsuspecting, been locked up with them in their madness once and for all.

Because I was always kind to the inmates, which was my nature, I lived on the dangerous rim of madness, on the brink, so to speak. I didn't go under, but I felt in constant danger, as if they had lured me by stealth into their unknown city. A city whose streets became softer and softer as you penetrated further between its slobbery houses, with their melting, ill-closed windows and their dubious sounds. The doors and the ground are unstable, shifting . . , And yet something makes you want to go further, to see if you'll have the strength to retrieve your reason from the wreckage. Reason can easily become an obsession, as good humor and sleep are for neurasthenics. All you can think of is your reason. Everything's out of kilter. It's no joke.

So I was worrying along from doubt to doubt when the fourth of May came up. A big day. I was feeling wonderfully well that day. Pulse 78. Like after a good lunch. Then suddenly the world began to spin. I held tight. Everything turns to bile. People start looking weird. As if they'd gone sour like lemons and more malignant than ever before. From climbing too high, no doubt, to the very peak of health, I had fallen in front of the mirror and with passionate fascination was watching myself grow old.

On rotten days like that, mountains of fatigue and disgust accumulate between your nose and your eyes, enough in that one spot to last several men for years. Much too much for one man.

Just then, all in all, I'd have been glad to go back to the Tarapout. Especially as Parapine had also stopped talking to me. But I was in their bad books at the Tarapout. It's hard to have no source of spiritual or material comfort but your boss, especially when he's an alienist and you're not so sure of your own head. All you can do is hold tight. And not say anything. We could still talk about women together. That was a benign subject, which gave me a chance to make him laugh now and then. In that field he gave me credit for a certain experience, for some slight and nasty competence.

It had its advantages that on the whole Baryton should consider me with a certain contempt. A boss always finds the crumminess of his staff rather reassuring. A slave must at all costs be slightly, if not superlatively, contemptible. An assortment of chronic moral and physical defects justifies the horrible treatment he is getting. Then the earth turns more smoothly, for each man occupies the place he deserves.

A person you make use of should be dull and abject, a born failure. It comes as a relief to the boss, especially since Baryton paid us very badly. An employer with his degree of acute avarice tends to be suspicious and uneasy. Failure, debauchee, black sheep, loyal!... Now there's a perfect combination that will justify anything. Baryton wouldn't have been displeased if I had been kind of wanted by the police. Those are the things that guarantee an employee's loyalty.

I had cast off all self-respect long ago. That sentiment had always struck me as far above my station, much too costly for my resources. I'd made that sacrifice once and for all and had no regrets whatever.

By then I was quite content if I could keep myself in a tolerable state of alimentary and physical balance. I had stopped worrying my head about anything else. Nevertheless, I found it hard to get through certain nights, especially when the memory of what had happened in Toulouse prevented me from sleeping.

At such times I couldn't help it, I imagined all sorts of dramatic sequels to Grandma Henrouille's fall into the mummy crypt. Fear rose up from my bowels, seized hold of my heart, and made it pound so hard that I'd jump out of bed and pace the floor, this way and that way into the depths of darkness and into the dawning light. During those attacks I despaired of ever recapturing enough peace of mind to fall asleep again. If someone tells you he's unhappy, don't take it on faith. Just ask him if he can sleep... If he can, then all's well. That's good enough.

I would never again succeed in sleeping fully. I had lost, so to speak, the habit of trust, the enormous trust you need to sleep soundly among human beings. I'd have needed at least an illness, a fever, a specific catastrophe to retrieve some small part of my old indifference, neutralize my anxiety, and recapture the divine stupidity of an easy mind. The only bearable days I remember over a period of many years were a few days of heavy feverish flu.

Baryton never asked me about my health. For that matter he chose to disregard his own. "Science and life form disastrous mixtures, Ferdinand! Always avoid taking care of your health, believe me!... Every question asked of your body becomes a breach... through which anxiety, obsession, will enter...

" Such were his simplist biological principles... He thought he was clever. "The known is good enough for me" was another of his frequent sayings. He was trying to impress me.

He never mentioned money to me, but in his secret heart he thought of it all the time.

Though I didn't exactly understand them at the time, Robinson's dealings with the Henrouille family were on my conscience, and from time to time I tried to tell Baryton bits and pieces of the story. But it didn't interest him in the least. He preferred my stories about Africa, especially the ones relating to colleagues of ours whom I'd run across here and there and to the strange and questionable medical practices of those very freakish colleagues.

At the rest home we had an alarm now and then in connection with his little girl Aimée. Suddenly at dinner time she was nowhere to be found, neither in the garden nor in her room. I fully expected to find her dismembered body in a clump of bushes one evening. She roamed all over the place with our lunatics, so there was reason to fear the worst. And indeed she had narrowly escaped being raped quite a number of times. When that happened, there'd be no end of screams and shower baths and warnings. Time and again she'd been told to avoid certain hidden paths, but the child was irresistibly attracted to nooks and crannies. On those occasions her father never failed to give her a memorable spanking. All in vain. I think she enjoyed the excitement.

We of the staff always had to be on our guard when passing the lunatics in the corridors. Madmen are more prone to murder than ordinary people. We got into the habit of turning our backs to the wall when they passed, prepared to give them a good kick in the groin at the slightest suspicious move. Watching you out of the corners of their eyes, they pass on. Madness apart, we understood each other perfectly.

Baryton deplored the fact that none of us played chess. Just to please him, I had to take it up.

During the day he distinguished himself by an active petty chicanery that made life in his entourage extremely fatiguing. Every morning some new and abysmally practical idea would spring from his brain. One day he decided to replace our rolls of toilet paper with folded folios, and we were obliged to ponder and waste a whole week with contradictory resolutions. Finally we decided to wait for the sales at the department stores. The next futile bother had to do with flannel vests: should they be worn over or under the shirt?... And what was the proper way to administer Epsom salts?... Parapine evaded these subintellectual controversies by stubborn silence.

In the end, inspired by boredom, I told Baryton about many more adventures than my travels had ever provided. My stock was exhausted. From then on it was up to him to fill in the conversational vacuum with his niggling pros and cons. Of which there was no end. He had defeated me by exhaustion. And I had no such defense as Parapine's total indifference. In spite of myself I had to answer him. I couldn't hold myself back from bickering with him for hours on end about the relative merits of cocoa and coffee... He was bewitching me with foolishness.

We'd start in again about something or other, about elastic stockings for varicose veins, about optimum faradic currents, or the treatment of cellulitis in the region of the elbow... It got so that I'd jabber about anything under the sun in line with his tastes or recommendations, like a human talking machine... He would keep abreast or just ahead of me in those infinitely idiotic meanderings. He saturated me with conversation for all eternity. When Parapine heard us embark on quibbles as long as the noodles we were eating, he'd guffaw to himself and sputter the boss's Bordeaux all over the tablecloth.

But peace to the memory of Monsieur Baryton., the bastard. In the end I got rid of him. But what genius it took!

The frothier of the female patients entrusted to my care gave me a hell of a time... When it wasn't cold showers, it was catheters... Their little vices and perversions, their big apertures that always had to be kept clean... One of our young inmates regularly earned me a reprimand from the boss... She'd wreck the garden by pulling up flowers, that was her mania, and I didn't care for the boss's observations...

"The betrothed," they called her, she was an Argentine, physically not bad at all, but as for her head, she had only one idea, she wanted to marry her father. One by one she picked all the flowers in the garden and stuck them in the big white veil that she wore day and night, wherever she went. Her family, who were religious fanatics, were dreadfully ashamed. They hid their daughter from the world and her idea with her. According to Baryton, she had succumbed to the absurdity of too strict and rigid an upbringing. The unbending morality of her parents had exploded in her head, so to speak.

At dusk we'd read the roll call at great length and send the boarders to their quarters. Then we'd make the rounds of the rooms, mostly to stop the more agitated ones from masturbating too frantically before falling asleep. You have to watch closely and keep them in check on Saturday night, because the families come visiting on Sunday and it's bad for the reputation of the establishment if they find the patients masturbated white.

All that reminded me of Bébert and the antimasturbation syrup. I administered quantities of that syrup in Vigny. I had kept the formula and ended by believing in it.

The concierge at the rest home kept a little candy shop with her husband, a big bruiser who was called in now and then when an inmate got violent.

And so life and the months went by, pleasantly enough all in all, and we'd have had nothing to complain about if Baryton hadn't suddenly conceived another of his big ideas.

He had no doubt been wondering for quite some time if it mightn't be possible to make more and better use of me for the same money. And he finally found the answer.

One day after lunch he came out with his idea. First he had them dish up a whole salad bowl full of my favorite dessert, strawberries and cream. Already my suspicions were aroused. And true enough, I had no sooner downed the last strawberry than he attacked.

"Ferdinand," he says. "I've been wondering if you mightn't consent to give my little girl Aimee a few English lessons... What do you say?... I know you have an excellent accent... And in English a good accent is what counts, don't you think?... You see, Ferdinand, without wishing to flatter you, I know how obliging you are... "

He had caught me off balance. "Why, certainly, Monsieur Baryton," I said.

It was agreed then and there that I'd give Aimee her first English lesson the very next morning. And others followed, one after another, for weeks...

Those English lessons marked the beginning of a thoroughly murky, dubious period, during which event followed event at a rhythm quite different from that of ordinary life.

Baryton insisted on attending the lessons I gave his daughter, every one of them. In spite of my conscientious efforts, poor little Aimee made no headway in English, none at all. She had no interest whatever in discovering what all these new words might mean. In fact she wondered what we nasty men wanted of her that made us insist so on her remembering their meanings. She didn't cry, but she was very close to it. She'd have been a lot happier if we had left her alone to manage what little French she already knew, the difficulties and facilities of which were quite sufficient to keep her busy all her life.

But her father didn't see it that way, not at all.

"You must grow up to be a modern young woman, my dear," he kept insisting. That was supposed to comfort her. "I, your father, have lost a good deal by not knowing enough English to handle my foreign patients . . , Come come, don't cry, my darling!... You'd do better to listen to Monsieur Bardamu, who's so patient, so kind, and when you're able to say 'the' with your tongue the way he has shown you, I'll buy you a beautiful nickel-plated bicycle... "

But Aimée had no desire to say "the" or "enough," none whatever... It was the boss who said "the" and "rough" in her place, and that wasn't all he learned in spite of his Bordeaux accent and his mania for logic, which is really no help in English. This went on for a month, two months. As the father's passion for learning English developed, Aimée had less and less need to struggle with the vowels. Baryton monopolized me. In fact he took up all my time, he never let me go, pumped all my English out of me. Since his room was next to mine, I could hear him first thing in the morning, converting his whole private life into English as he dressed. "The coffee is black . . , My shirt is white... The garden is green... How are you today, Bardamu?" he would shout through the partition. He soon acquired a taste for the most elliptical forms of the language.

With that perversion he took us a long way... Once he had made contact with great literature, there was no stopping him... After eight months of such abnormal progress, he had refashioned himself almost completely along Anglo-Saxon lines. In this way he managed to get me completely disgusted with him. Twice in a row.

Little by little we had come to leave little Aimée out of the conversation almost entirely, in other words, in peace. She was quite content to go back to her clouds. She'd never learn English, and that was that. Baryton would learn it all.

Winter returned, and with it Christmas. The travel agencies were advertising return trips to England at bargain prices... While walking on the boulevards, accompanying Parapine to the movies, I'd notice those advertisements... I even went in and asked about the prices.

Then at table, in the course of the conversation, I dropped a word or two to Baryton. At first my bit of information didn't seem to interest him. He let it pass. I thought he'd forgotten all about it, but then one evening he himself brought it up and asked me to bring him a folder when I had a chance.

Between two English literature sessions, we often played Japanese billiards or bouchon in one of the isolation rooms situated just above the concierge's lodge and equipped with good iron bars.

Baryton excelled in games of skill. Parapine regularly challenged him to play for drinks and as regularly lost. We spent whole evenings in that improvised little game room, especially in the winter when it was raining, so as not to mess up the chief's big drawing rooms. Sometimes an excitable patient would be put in the same little room for observation, but not very often.

While Parapine and the boss were matching their skills at bouchon on the carpet or on the floor, I would amuse myself, if you want to call it that, trying to experience the same sensations as a prisoner in his cell. That was one sensation I had never known. If you really want to, you can work up friendly feelings toward the few people who pass through those suburban streets. At the end of the day, your heart goes out to the bit of movement created by the streetcars, bringing back docile clusters of office workers from Paris. Their débâcle ends at the first bend in the street, right after the grocery store. Then they flow quietly into the darkness. You've barely had time to count them. But Baryton seldom let me daydream at my leisure. In the middle of his game of bouchon,[92] he'd come to life with some ridiculous question.

"How do you say 'impossible' in English, Ferdinand?"

When it came to improving his English, he was insatiable. With every ounce of his native imbecility he aspired to perfection. No approximations or concessions for him. But then luckily events took a turn which brought me deliverance.

In the course of our readings in the history of England, I saw that he was losing some of his assurance and even the greater part of his optimism. As we were feeling our way into the Elizabethan poets, his mind and personality underwent great though imponderable changes. At first I found it hard to believe, but in the end I, like everyone else, was obliged to see Baryton as he had become, in truth a pitiful spectacle. His mind, formerly razor-edged to the point of severity, had begun to wander, leading him into incredible, interminable digressions. Little by little, he developed the habit of daydreaming for hours on end, he'd be right there in his Institute, before our very eyes, and his thoughts would be off in the distance... Though he had long and decisively repelled me, I felt a certain remorse at seeing him go to pieces like that. I felt partly responsible for his decline... I felt that his spiritual confusion had something to do with me... So much so that one day I suggested interrupting our study of literature, on the pretext that a break would give us time and leisure to renew our documentary sources... He wasn't fooled by my feeble ruse. His response was a friendly but categorical refusal... He was determined to carry on with the discovery of spiritual England under my guidance... Just as he had begun... What could I say?... I acquiesced. He was afraid the hours of life remaining to him might not suffice for complete success... In short, though I feared the worst, I was obliged to pursue our dismal academic peregrination to the best of my ability.

The fact is that Baryton was no longer himself. The persons and things around us became fantasmagoric and slow, losing their importance and even the colors they had formerly worn for us, and taking on a dreamlike, ambivalent softness...

---

[92] Bouchon. A game once especially popular among Beton fishermen. Coins or other valuables are placed on top of a large cork. Standing at some distance from it, the contestants toss disks; the player who first overturns the cork takes the coins.

Baryton had come to concern himself only occasionally and more and more languidly with the administrative details of his own establishment, though it was his life work and for over thirty years the object of his literally passionate interest. He now relied entirely on Parapine to manage the administrative end. The increasing confusion of his mind, which he still tried to conceal in public, soon became obvious to us, a physical reality.

One day Gustave Mandamour, a policeman we knew in Vigny because we sometimes employed him for certain heavy work, and undoubtedly the least discerning person I have ever come across though I've known many of his kind, asked me if the boss hadn't received some terrible news... I did my best to reassure him, but without conviction.

Baryton had lost his interest in gossip and chitchat, All he wanted was not to be disturbed on any pretext whatever . . , At the very beginning of our studies we had perused, too quickly to his way of thinking, Macaulay's compendious History of England, a seminal work in sixteen volumes. At his command and under quite alarming conditions, we went back to it. Chapter by chapter.

It seemed to me that Baryton was more and more dangerously contaminated by meditation. When we came to that merciless passage where the Pretender Monmouth disembarks on the blurred shores of Kent... Where his venture starts revolving around itself... Where Monmouth the Pretender no longer knows exactly what he's pretending to... Or what he wants to do... Or what he has come here for... Where he starts telling himself that he'd be glad to beat it... but he doesn't know where to or how... when defeat rises up before him... in the pale dawn... When the sea carries his last ships away... When for the first time Monmouth starts thinking... then likewise the lowly Baryton couldn't get to the end of his own decisions... He read and reread that passage and mumbled it over again... Overwhelmed, he closed the book and came over and lay down beside us.

For a long time, with half-closed eyes, he ran through the whole text from memory, and then in his English accent, the best among the Bordeaux accents I had given him to choose from, he recited it again...

Face to face with Monmouth's adventure, where all the pitiful absurdity of our puerile and tragic nature discloses itself in the mirror of Eternity, Baryton was seized with vertigo. Only the merest thread had attached him to our common lot, and now that thread snapped... From that moment on, I can say without exaggerating, he ceased to be one of us... He'd had it...

Late that night he asked me to join him in his directorial office... At that point I expected him to communicate some monumental decision, my immediate dismissal, for instance... Not at all... On the contrary, the decision he had arrived at was entirely favorable to me. Believe it or not, I was so unaccustomed to being surprised by good news that a tear or two escaped me... Baryton chose to interpret my emotion as sadness. That reversed the roles, and he began to comfort me...

"Will you doubt my word, Ferdinand, if I assure you that it took far more than courage on my part to resolve to leave this Institute?... I, whose sedentary habits are known to you. I, a man on the brink of old age, whose whole career has consisted of long, tenacious, scrupulous verification of innumerable slow or sudden inspirations?... In the space of a very few months, I have come to abjure all that... It seems hardly believable... Yet here I am, body and soul, in such a state of detachment, of exultation . , . Ferdinand! Hurrah, as you say in English! My past has ceased to exist! I shall be reborn, Ferdinand! Neither more nor less! I am going away! Oh, kind friend, your tears are powerless to attenuate the definitive disgust I feel for everything that has kept me here for so many lackluster years... Enough! I can bear it no longer! I repeat, I am going away! Fleeing! Escaping! True, I am torn! I know it! I bleed! I can see it! And yet, Ferdinand, not for anything in the world, do you hear me, Ferdinand? Not for anything would I turn back!... Even if I had dropped an eye somewhere in this muck, I would not come back to pick it up! That's the long and the short of it! Do you doubt my sincerity now?"

I doubted nothing whatsoever. Baryton was unquestionably capable of anything. Besides, I am sure that in the state he had worked himself up into, any contradiction on my part would have been fatal to his reason. I left him alone for a little while. But then, on second thought, I tried to influence him just a little, risked a last attempt to bring him back to us... by means of a slightly transposed, amiably oblique... argument...

"I beg you, Ferdinand, abandon all hope of my going back on my decision! It is irrevocable, I tell you! You will give me no end of pleasure by never speaking of it again... For the last time, Ferdinand, do you wish to please me? At my age, I know, a sense of mission is most unusual... That's a fact... But when it comes, it's irremediable... "

Those were his very words, almost the last he uttered. I cite them verbatim.

"Perhaps, my dear Monsieur Baryton," I nevertheless ventured to break in. "Perhaps in the end this sort of impromptu holiday you are preparing to take will be nothing more than a rather romantic episode, a welcome diversion, a happy intermezzo in the course of your undoubtedly somewhat austere professional activity... perhaps after tasting a different life... more varied, less banally methodic than the life we lead here, then perhaps you will simply come back to us, pleased with your journey, surfeited with the unforeseen... And then, quite naturally, you will resume your place at our head... proud of your recent acquisitions... refreshed in a word, and henceforth, no doubt, prepared to accept, to look with indulgence upon the daily monotony of our laborious routine... An older and a wiser man! If you'll forgive me, Monsieur Baryton, for putting it that way... "

"Oh Ferdinand, you flatterer!... Somehow you still manage to touch my masculine pride, which, I discover, remains sensitive, exigent in fact, despite all my weariness and past trials... No, Ferdinand! With all your ingenuity you cannot in one moment make the abominably hostile and painful essence of our whole striving look benign to me. And moreover, Ferdinand, the time for hesitation is past, it is too late to turn back!... I have been drained, I admit it, I shout it from the rooftops, Ferdinand: drained! stultified! defeated! by forty years of prudent paltriness!... That is far too much! What I aim to do? You want to know?... No reason why I shouldn't tell you, you, my last friend, you who have been willing to take a disinterested part in the sufferings of a defeated old man... What I want, Ferdinand, is to try and lose my soul, as you might try to lose a mangy dog, your stinking dog, the companion who disgusts you, and to get far away from him before you die... To be alone at last... At peace... Myself... "

"But, my dear Monsieur Baryton, I have never, in any of your words, caught an inkling of the violent despair whose uncompromising demands you have suddenly revealed to me. I am amazed! On the contrary, your daily remarks still strike me as perfectly pertinent... All your spirited, fruitful suggestions... Your splendidly judicious and methodical medical treatments... I would search your daily actions in vain for any sign of depression, of defeat... Really and truly, I discern nothing of the kind... "

But for the first time since I'd known him, Baryton derived no pleasure from my compliments. He went so far as to dissuade me, quite amiably, from pursuing the conversation in a laudatory vein.

"No, my dear Ferdinand, I assure you... True, your last professions of friendship have given my last moments here an unhoped-for sweetness, and yet with all your kindness you cannot reconcile me to the memory of a past which overwhelms me and which this place stinks of... At any cost and, do you hear? under any conditions, I am determined to go away... "

"But Monsieur Baryton, this institution, what will we do with it? Have you thought of that?"

"Yes, of course I've thought of it, Ferdinand... You will take over the management for as long as I'm away, that's all!... Haven't you always had excellent relations with our clientele? They will gladly accept you as director... Everything will be splendid, you'll see, Ferdinand... Parapine, since he can't abide conversation, will take care of the mechanical end, the apparatus, the laboratory... He has a way with those things... So everything's in the best of order... And you know, I've stopped believing that anyone's presence is indispensable... Even on that score, you see, my friend, I've changed considerably... "

True enough, he was unrecognizable.

"But aren't you afraid, Monsieur Baryton, that your departure will provoke malicious comments on the part of your competitors in the region?... In Passy, for instance? In Montretout?... In Gargan-Livry? All those people around us... Always keeping an eye on us!... Those indefatigably treacherous colleagues!... What construction will they put on your noble voluntary exile?... What will they call it? An escapade? How do I know? Mischief? Flight? Bankruptcy?... ; That eventuality had no doubt given him occasion for long and painful reflections. It still troubled him, and he turned pale before my eyes at the thought of it...

His daughter, Aimée, our little halfwit, was in for a pretty rough time. He was entrusting her to the care of an aunt in the provinces, a total stranger if the truth be known. So, once his private affairs had been settled, Parapine and I would only have to look after his interests and property as best we could. Adrift in a ship without a captain!

After all he had told me, I thought it permissible to ask him which way he was heading in his quest for adventure...

"To England, Ferdinand!" he replied, without batting an eyelash.

So much had happened to us in so short a time, I thought we'd have trouble digesting it, but it was clear that we'd have to adapt quickly to our new mode of life.

The very next day Parapine and I helped him with his luggage. The passport with all its little pages and visas startled him somewhat. He had never seen a passport before. But while he was at it, he'd have liked to apply for a few spares. We managed to convince him that this was impossible.

One last time he stumbled over the question: should he take hard collars or soft collars away with him and how many of each? This problem, still undecided, brought us almost to train time. All three of us jumped into the last streetcar for Paris. Baryton took only a small suitcase, intending to travel light and preserve his mobility wherever he went.

On the platform he was impressed by the noble elevation of the car steps on the international trains. Hesitating to mount those majestic structures, he contemplated the car as though gazing at a monument. We helped him a little. Having taken a second-class ticket, he made a comparative, practical, and cheerful observation: "First is no better," he said.

We shook hands with him. The time was at hand. The whistle blew, and the train pulled out on the dot with an enormous jolt and crashing of steel, abominably mutilating our farewells. He had barely time to say: "Good-bye, boys!" and his hand broke loose, carried away from ours...

Then his hand was waving in the smoke, rushing through the noise, already in darkness, further and further down the rails, white...

* * *

In a way we weren't sorry to see him go, but all the same the house seemed very empty without him.

In the first place, the way he'd gone made us sad, in spite of ourselves so to speak. It wasn't natural. After such a blow we wondered what might happen to us.

But we didn't have time to wonder very long. Only a few days after we'd taken Baryton to the station, I'm informed that there's someone asking to see me personally in the office. Abbé Protiste.

So I tell him the news, and what news! Especially the way Baryton had run out on us to go gallivanting around in the septentrional regions... When Protiste heard that, he couldn't get over it, and when it finally sank in, the altered situation meant only one thing to him, namely, the advantage I could derive from it. "Such trust on the part of your director," he kept saying over and over, "strikes me as the most flattering sort of promotion, my dear doctor."

I tried to calm him down, but once launched he persisted in his view of the matter and predicted that the most glorious of futures lay in wait for me, a magnificent medical career, as he put it. I couldn't stop him.

Nevertheless, though with considerable difficulty, we finally got back to serious matters, that is, to the city of Toulouse, whence he had arrived only the day before. Of course I gave him his turn to speak and tell me all he knew. I even pretended to be astonished, nay, stupefied, when he told me about the old woman's accident.

"What?! What's that?!" I interrupted. "Dead? Heavens above! When did this happen?" Little by little, he had to come clean.

Without telling me in so many words who had pushed the old woman down her little staircase, he said nothing to deter me from guessing... It seems she hadn't had time to say boo.

We understood each other... It was a good job, handled with care. This time he had done for her... He hadn't botched his second try.

Luckily everyone in the neighborhood had thought Robinson was still stone-blind. So they hadn't suspected anything more than an accident, a very tragic one to be sure, but quite understandable when you thought it over, given the circumstances, the old woman's age and the time of day, the late afternoon when she must have been tired... Just then I had no desire to hear more. He had told me plenty.

But it wasn't so easy getting the Abbé to change the subject. The thing was on his mind. He kept coming back to it, apparently in the hope that I'd make some kind of slip and give myself away... Nothing doing! He could keep trying... So after a while he gave up and contented himself with talking about Robinson and his health... His eyes... In that department he was much better... But his morale was still low. In fact his morale was terrible! In spite of the kindness and affection the two women never stopped showing him... he never stopped complaining about his own hard lot and life in general.

It didn't surprise me to hear Protiste telling me all that. I knew Robinson. He had a lowdown, ungrateful nature. But I distrusted the Abbé even more... I didn't say a word while he was talking to me. All his confiding didn't get him anywhere.

"I must admit, doctor, that your friend, in spite of a material life that has become pleasant and easy and the prospect of a happy marriage, has disappointed all our hopes... Once again he is succumbing to the same fatal penchant for escapades, the perverse impulses you detected in the past?... What do you think of those tendencies of his, my dear doctor?"

In short, if I got the drift, Robinson's only thought was to drop everything. At first his fiancee and her mother were angry, then they were stricken with grief. That's what Abbé Protiste had come to tell me. All this was rather upsetting, and for my part I made up my mind to hold my tongue and steer clear of these people's little family affairs at all costs... After an abortive interview we parted at the streetcar stop, rather coolly to tell the truth. Not at all easy in my mind, I went back to the rest home.

Only a short time after this visit, we had our first news of Baryton. From England. A few postcards. He wished us all "good health and good luck." After that a few vapid lines from one place and another. A card with no message on it informed us that he had gone to Norway, and a few weeks later there was a somewhat reassuring telegram: "Good crossing!" From Copenhagen.

As we had foreseen, the chief's absence provoked the most vicious comment in Vigny and environs. It seemed best for the future of the Institute that we should provide the patients and our colleagues round about with only the barest minimum of information regarding the reasons for this absence.

Months passed, months of extreme caution, dull and silent. Among ourselves we stopped mentioning Baryton altogether. To tell the truth, thinking about him made us feel rather ashamed.

And then it was summer again. We couldn't spend all our time in the garden supervising the patients. To prove to ourselves that we had some freedom in spite of it all, we ventured as far as the banks of the Seine, just to get out.

After the embankment on the far shore, the great plain of Gennevilliers begins, a beautiful expanse of gray and white, with chimneys softly outlined in the dust and mist. Right beside the towpath you'll see the bargemen's bistrot. It guards the entrance to the canal. The yellow current comes pushing against the lock.

For hours on end we'd look down at all that, and off to the side at the long swamp, the insidious smell of which reaches as far as the motor road. You get used to it. That muck was so old, so worn out by the river floods that it had no color left. Sometimes on summer evenings when the sky went pink and sentimental the mud would take on a kind of gentle look. It was there on the bridge that we'd listen to the accordion music they'd play on the barges while waiting at the lock gates for the night to be over so they could pass through to the river. Especially the ones coming down from Belgium are musical, they have color all over, green and yellow, and clotheslines full of shirts and drawers and raspberry-colored slips, puffed up by the wind as it leaps and gusts into them.

I'd often go to the bargemen's bar at the slack houf after lunch, when the owner's cat is blissfully at peace within four walls, shut up in a little blue-enamel heaven that belongs to him alone.

There I too sat drowsing in the early afternoon, forgotten, I thought, by all the world, waiting for the time to pass.

I saw someone coming in the distance, coming up the road. I wasn't long in doubt. He had hardly set foot on the bridge when I recognized him. It was Robinson, his very own self. No possible doubt. "He's come looking for me," I said to myself... "The priest must have given him my address!... I'll have to get rid of him quick!"

At that particular moment I thought it was foul of him to come around bothering me just as I was starting to build up a cosy bit of self-indulgence. We're always suspicious of things approaching on a road, and we're right. By then he had almost reached the bistrot. I went outside. He seemed surprised to see me. "Where in hell have you come from?" I ask him, not at all friendly. "From La Garenne... " he says. "Okay. Have you eaten?" He didn't look as if he'd eaten, but he didn't want to seem to be starving the moment he got there. "So you're on the loose again?" I ask him. Because, believe me, I wasn't at all glad to be seeing him again. It didn't suit me one bit.

Just then Parapine came up from the canal, looking for me. That was a good thing. Parapine was tired from being on duty so often at the asylum. It was true that I'd been taking my responsibilities rather lightly. Be that as it may, we'd both have given a good deal to know exactly when Baryton would be coming back. We hoped he'd stop gadding about pretty soon so he could relieve us of the business and start looking after it himself. It was too much for us. Neither of us was ambitious, and we didn't give a good goddamn about the prospects for the future. Which was wrong of us, I admit.

I have to give Parapine credit, he never asked questions about the financial management of the institution or my dealings with the clientele, but I filled him in just the same, in spite of him so to speak, and when that happened it was like talking to myself. About Robinson now, it was important to put him in the picture.

"I told you about Robinson, remember?" I asked him by way of introduction. "You know. My war buddy."

He'd heard me tell my war stories and stories about Africa a hundred times and in a hundred different ways. That was my style.

"Well," I went on, "This is Robinson in the flesh, come all the way from Toulouse to see us... We're all having dinner together at the house." To tell the truth, I felt kind of uneasy about inviting him in the name of the Institute. It was a sort of indiscretion. The situation called for a winning, ingratiating air of authority, something I didn't have at all. Besides, Robinson wasn't making things any easier for me. On our way back to the village he seemed curious and anxious, especially in regard to Parapine, whose long, pale face intrigued him. At first he thought Parapine was one of the lunatics. As soon as he found out where we were staying in Vigny, he began to see lunatics everywhere. I reassured him.

"What about you?" I asked him. "Have you found some sort of work at least, now that you're back?" "I'm going to start looking" was all the answer I got.

"How about your eyes? Cured? You can see now?" "Yes, I can see. Almost as good as before."

"Then you must be happy," I said.

No, he wasn't happy. He had other things to do beside being happy. I was careful not to mention Madelon right away. That was still a ticklish subject between us. We spent quite some time over our apéritifs, and I took the opportunity to tell him a good deal about the rest home and various other things. I've never been able to stop shooting my mouth off right and left, pretty much like Baryton, come to think of it. Our dinner went off cordially. And when it was over I couldn't very well put Robinson out in the street. I decided that for the present we'd set up a folding bed for him in the dining room. Parapine as usual expressed no opinion. "All right, Léon," I said. "You can stay here until you find a job... " "Thanks," he said simply. And every morning from then on he took the streetcar in to Paris, to look for a job as a salesman.

He was "sick of factories," he said, he wanted to be a salesman. I've got to be fair, he may have knocked himself out looking for a salesman's job, but he certainly didn't find one.

One day he came back from Paris earlier than usual. I was still in the garden, supervising my charges near the big pond. He came out and joined me. There was something on his mind.

"Listen!" he began. "I'm listening."

"Couldn't you give me some little job right here?... I can't find one anywhere else... " "Have you really tried?"

"Yes, I've really tried... "

"You want a job here in the nuthouse? Doing what? Can't you find some little thing in Paris? Would you like Parapine and me to ask some people we know?"

My offer to help him find a job wasn't to his liking.

"It's not that there's absolutely no jobs to be had," he said. "Maybe I'd find one... some little job... Sure... But don't you see... I absolutely have to make it look like I'm off my rocker... It's urgent, it's indispensable! It's gotta look like I'm off my rocker... "

"All right, " I said. "Say no more!"

"Don't try to shut me up, Ferdinand. I've got to say more," he insisted, "because I want you to understand. And as I know you, it takes you a long time to understand anything and decide to do something about it."

"In that case, shoot," I said. "Tell me all about it." I was resigned.

"If I don't make it look like I'm nuts, I'll be out of luck, I assure you... Big trouble!... She's perfectly capable of having me arrested... Now do you get the drift?"

"Madelon, you mean?" "Madelon! Who else?" "That's great!"

"You can say that again... "

"So you're really on the outs?" "As you see... "

"Come this way if you want to tell me more," I interrupted and led him off to one side. "It's safer because of the nuts... Mad as they are, they understand certain things that'll sound even wilder when they repeat them... "

We went up to one of the isolation rooms, and once there it didn't take him long to reconstitute the whole machination, especially as I already knew that he'd stop at nothing, and Abbé Protiste had hinted at the rest...

He hadn't bungled his second try. No one could accuse him of goofing again. Not by a long shot!

"You see, the old bag was getting on my nerves more and more... Especially after my eyes got a little better and I could go out in the street by myself... After that I could see things... I could see the old bag too... I could see her all right, in fact I never saw anything else!... All day long I had her there in front of me!... She was poisoning my life!... I honestly think she hung around on purpose... to bug me... I can't explain it any other way... And that house we were all living in, you know the house, it's a hard place to keep from fighting in... You saw how small it is!... We were all on top of each other!... You can't say different!"

"And the cellar stairs weren't very solid, were they?"

I myself had noticed how dangerous those stairs were, when I visited the crypt for the first time with Madelon. They'd been shaky even then.

"Yes, it was practically a setup," he admitted very frankly.

"And what about the people down there?" I asked him. "The neighbors, the priests, the reporters... Didn't their tongues wag some when it happened?... "

"No, it seems they didn't... Besides, they didn't think I was up to it... They thought I was a washout... Blind... You understand... "

"Well, you can thank your stars for that, because otherwise... But what about Madelon?... Was she in it with you?"

"Not exactly... But just a little, yes, of course, because we were supposed to inherit the whole crypt once the old bag passed on... Things had been settled that way... The two of us were going to take over... "

"So what went wrong between you?" "Well, that's hard to explain... "

"Was she sick of you?"

"Not at all, she was crazy about me and still dead set on getting married... Her mother was all for it too, more than ever. She wanted us to do it quick because we had come into the old bag's mummies and there'd be enough for the three of us to live on and then some... "

"So what went wrong between you?"

"Well, I just wanted them to leave me in peace! It's as simple as that! The mother, the daughter, both of them... "

"Look here, Léon!" I stopped him when I heard that. "Listen to me!... Your story doesn't make sense!... Think of Madelon and her mother, put yourself in their place... How would you feel in their place?... I ask you... When you got there, you hardly had a pair of shoes to your name, no job, nothing, all day long you complained, about the old woman keeping all the money, and so forth and so on... She passes on, or rather, you pass her on... And right away you start making faces again and putting on airs... Put yourself in the place of those two women, stop and think... It's unbearable!

Boy, would I have told you what you could do!... They should have sent you to jail, that's what you really deserved, I don't mind telling you!"

That's what I said to Robinson.

"Maybe so," Robinson answered back. "But even if you're a doctor and educated and all that, you'll never understand my nature... "

"You shut up," I finally told him. "You poor jerk, don't talk to me about your nature. You talk like a nut. I'm sorry Baryton has gone away God knows where, or he'd have taken you in! Best thing that could happen to you! Lock you up! See what I mean? Baryton would have known how to handle your nature!"

"If you'd had what I had and been through what I've been through," he came back at me, "you'd have been nuts yourself, I assure you! Maybe worse than me!... A softie like you!" And he began to bawl me out as windily as if he'd had a right to.

I watched him closely while he was gassing. I'd often been abused that way by the patients. It didn't bother me any more.

He'd got a good deal thinner since Toulouse, and something had happened to his face, something I'd never seen before, a kind of portrait had settled on his features, with forgetfulness and silence all around it.

In all this Toulouse business there was something else that bothered him, it was only a minor part of the story, but it had gone against his grain, and when he thought about it now it came back at him like bile. It was having to grease the palms of a whole bunch of operators for nothing. When they'd taken over the crypt, he'd had to dish out commissions right and left, to the priest, the chair woman, the town hall, the vicars, and God knows who else, all to no end, and that had stuck in his craw... Just talking about it threw him into a fit. Thieving he called it.

"And now tell me, did you finally get married?" I asked him. "I've told you already, no! I didn't want to anymore."

"But your little Madelon wasn't bad? You can't tell me different... " "That's not the question..."

"Oh yes it is. You said you were free, didn't you? If you were dead set on leaving Toulouse, you could have left her mother in charge of the crypt for a while... you'd have come back later... "

"Physically yes, you're right," he went on. "I admit it, she was first class. You told me the truth. Especially because it so happened that when I got my sight back, the first thing I saw was her, in a mirror... Can you imagine?... In the light!... About two months after the old woman fell... I was trying to look at Madelon's face, and then suddenly my sight came back... Like a flash of light... You get the picture?"

"Wasn't it nice?"

"Sure, it was nice... But that's not everything." "And you cleared out all the same?... "

"Yes, but let me explain, seeing you want to understand... She started it... she started thinking I was acting funny... that I'd lost my zip... that I wasn't nice to her anymore... that kind of crap... "

"Maybe your conscience was troubling you... " "Conscience?"

"Sure, why not?"

"Call it anything you want, I was feeling rotten, that's all... But I don't think it was conscience... " "Were you sick?"

"Yeah, sick, that's what it probably was. For the last hour I've been trying to make you say I'm sick... Admit you're pretty slow... "

"Okay, okay," I tell him. "Let's say you're sick if you think it's the safest way... "

"It would make sense," he assured me. "Because I wouldn't put anything past her... She could start singing to the cops any day now."

He sounded like he was giving me advice, and I didn't want his advice. That kind of thing didn't appeal to me at all, because of the complications it would lead to.

"Do you really think she'd talk?" I asked him, just to make sure... "After all, she was your accomplice in a way... That ought to make her think twice before shooting her mouth off... "

"Think twice!" Those words made him jump sky-high. "I can see you don't know her... " I handed him a laugh. "Hell, she wouldn't hesitate for one second... Like I'm telling you! If you knew her as well as I do, you wouldn't doubt it! She's in love, I tell you! Haven't you ever known a woman in love? When she's in love, she's crazy. Crazy, I tell you! And it's me she's in love with and crazy about!... Do you know what that means? It means that anything crazy is just her meat! Craziness won't stop her! Hell no!"

I couldn't tell him it rather surprised me to hear that Madelon had reached such a pitch of frenzy in a few months, because after all I'd known her slightly myself... I had my own ideas on the subject, but I couldn't tell him that.

From the way she had handled herself in Toulouse and the things I'd heard her say when I was hidden behind the poplar tree on the day of the houseboat, it was hard for me to imagine that she could have changed so completely in so short a time... She had struck me as more shrewd than tragic, a smooth article, only too glad to get what attention she could with her fantasies and pretensions, wherever they seemed to wash... But in that particular situation there was nothing I could say, I had to let it ride. "All right! All right!" I said. "And how about her mother? She must have let out a squawk when she realized you were clearing out for good?... "

"I'll say! All day long she went on about my rotten character and, mind you, just when I'd have needed to be treated kindly!... You should have heard her!... Anyway, on account of the mother too, it couldn't go on, so that's when I suggested to Madelon that I'd leave them in the crypt while I went off by myself for a while to travel around and see the country... "

"'Then you'll take me with you,' she protested... I'm your fiancée, aren't I?... You'll take me with you or you won't go at all!... And besides, you're not well enough yet'..."

"I'm all well,' I said, 'and I'm going by myself.' It dragged on and on."

"'A wife always goes with her husband,' said the mother. 'Why don't you just get married?' She backed her up just to bug me.

"Listening to that flapdoodle made me miserable. You know me! As if I needed a woman when I want to go to war! Or to run out on the war! Did I have women in Africa? Did I have a wife in America?... Hearing them go on like that for hours gave me a pain in the gut! A bellyache! I know what women are good for! And so do you! For nothing! I've traveled and I know. So one evening when they'd been driving me up the wall, I couldn't stand it anymore and I told the mother what I thought of her! 'You're an old fool,' I told her... 'You're even more dimwitted than Grandma Henrouille!... If you'd traveled a little more and known a few more people like I have, you wouldn't be in such a hurry to give people advice, and it's not by picking up little pieces of tallow in the corner of your stinking church that you'll learn about life! You ought to get out of there yourself, it would do you good. Why don't you take a walk once in a while, you old bag? A little fresh air would do you good. You'd have less time for your prayers and you wouldn't smell so much like a cow... ' "That's what I said to her mother! I can assure you, I'd been aching a long time to tell her off, and what's more she needed it bad... But all in all, it's me that got the most out of it... It sort of helped me out of the situation... It looked as if the old battle-ax had just been waiting for me to fly off the handle so she could call me all the names for son-of-a-bitch she knew! So she let loose and said a lot more than she needed to. 'Thief! Lounge lizard!' she yelled... 'You haven't even got a trade!... It's going on a year that I've been supporting you and my daughter!... Pimp!... ' Get the idea? A regular family scene... She seemed to be thinking it over for a while, and then she blurted out, she really put her heart in it: 'Murderer! Murderer!' That kind of gave me the shivers.

"When her daughter heard that, she was afraid I'd kill her mother on the spot. She flung herself between us and closed her mother's mouth with her own hand. Which was just as well. So the two of them are in cahoots, I said to myself. It was obvious , . , Well, I let it go... The time for violence was past... And anyway, what did I care if they were in cahoots?... Maybe you think that after letting off all that steam they'd leave me alone... Not at all! If that's what you think, you don't know them... The daughter started up again. Her head was on fire and so was her cunt... She started up worse than ever...

"'I love you, Léon... Can't you see that I love you?' "That's all she knew, her 'I love you' jazz. As if that was the answer to everything.

"'What! You still love him?' her mother put in. 'Can't you see that he's nothing but a thug? The lowest of the low! Now that he's got his eyesight back, thanks to our care, he'll bring you nothing but misery. Just take it from me, your mother!... ' "To finish up the scene, we all cried, even me, because whatever happened I didn't want to get in too bad with those chippies, I didn't want us to be too much on the outs.

"So I went out for a walk. We'd said too much, and staying in the same room we couldn't have controlled ourselves for long. Even so we kept wrangling off and on for weeks, and keeping an eye on each other, especially at night.

"We couldn't make up our minds to break up, but our hearts weren't in it anymore. It was mostly fear that kept us together.

"'You must love somebody else!' Madelon would say now and then.

"I'd try to reassure her: 'Not at all! Of course not!' But it was obvious that she didn't believe me. The way she saw it, you had to love somebody, there was no getting around it.

"'Just tell me this,' I'd say. 'What would I do with another woman?' But she had love on the brain. There was nothing I could say to calm her. She dreamed up stuff I'd never heard before. I'd never have suspected she was hiding such rubbish in her head.

"'You took my heart, Léon!' she'd fire at me in all seriousness. 'You want to go?' she blustered. 'All right, go! But I warn you, Léon, I'll die of grief!... ' Die of grief on my account? Where's the sense in that, I ask you. 'No, no,' I'd say. 'You won't die. And in the first place I never took anything at all. I haven't even knocked you up! Think it over. I haven't given you any diseases either! Or have I? Well then! All I want is to go away, that's all! A kind of vacation... What's wrong with that?... Try to be reasonable... ' But the more I tried to make her understand my point of view, the less she thought of my point of view. In fact we didn't understand each other at all anymore... It drove her crazy to think that I might really feel the way I said I did, that everything I said was true, simple, and sincere.

"Besides, she thought it was you who was trying to get me to beat it... And seeing that she couldn't hold me by making me ashamed of my feelings, she tried a different way of holding me.

"'Don't go thinking I want you because of the crypt and the business,' she'd say. 'You know I don't really care about money... What I want, Léon, is to stay with you... And to be happy... That's all... It's perfectly natural... I don't want you to leave me... It's too cruel for people to separate when they've loved each other like we have... Swear to me at least that you won't be gone for long... ' "It went on like that for weeks. She was in love all right, a real pest... Every evening she came back to her love jazz... In the end she was willing to leave her mother in charge of the crypt, on condition that the two of us went to Paris together to look for work... Always together!... A screwball! She was willing to put up with anything you could think of except that we should go our separate ways... On that subject the answer was strictly no... So naturally the harder she dug in the sicker I got of the whole business!

"It was no use trying to put any sense into her. I knew I was wasting my time and only getting her more stirred up. So I had to start thinking up ways to get rid of her love as she called it... That was what made me think of telling her that I kind of went out of my mind now and then... That fits would come on... without warning... She gave me a funny look... She didn't rightly know if this was another fish story or not. But anyway, considering the adventures I'd told her about and what the war had done to me and my latest exploit with Grandma Henrouille and the funny way I was acting with her, it gave her food for thought...

"She thought for more than a week and didn't bother me all that time... She must have said a word or two to her mother about my fits... Anyway, they didn't seem so eager to hang on to me anymore… 'Good deal!' I said to myself. 'It's going to be all right! Free at last!...' I could already see myself slipping quietly away in the direction of Paris without any breakage... But not so fast!... I started overdoing it... Frills!... I thought I'd hit on a smart way of proving to her once and for all that I'd been telling the truth... That I really went nuts when the spirit moved me... 'Feel!' I said to Madelon one evening. 'Feel the bump on the back of my head! And the scar on top of it! Some bump, eh?' "When she'd had a good feel of the bump on the back of my head, it really started her off, I can tell you... But imagine, it didn't disgust her at all, far from it, it gave her hotter pants than ever... 'That's where I was wounded in Flanders,'I said. That's where I was trepanned... ' "'Oh, Léon!' she cried out, still feeling the bump. 'Can you ever forgive me, Léon?... I doubted you up to now, but now I beg your forgiveness with all my heart! I see it all now! I've been beastly to you! Oh yes, I have! I've been awful! .. , I'll never be mean to you again! I swear it! I want to make it up to you, Léon. Right away! You'll let me make it up to you, won't you?... I'll make you happy again... Oh, how I'll take care of you! Starting today! I'd be ever so patient with you! So gentle! You'll see, Léon! I'll be so good to you you won't be able to get along without me! I'll give you back all my heart, I belong to you!... Every bit of me! I'll give you my whole life, Léon! Only tell me you forgive me, tell me, Léon!' "I hadn't said any of that, she'd said it all herself, so naturally she had no trouble answering herself... How in God's name was I to stop her?

"It looked like feeling my scar and my bump had made her drunk with love all of a sudden! She wanted to take my head in both hands and never let it go and make me happy from then to Eternity, whether I liked it or not! After that scene her mother wasn't allowed to bawl me out anymore. Madelon didn't even let her mother talk. You wouldn't have known her, she wanted to protect me to the bitter end!

"It couldn't go on. Naturally I'd rather we parted friends... But it was no use... She was bursting with love, and she was stubborn. One morning when she and her mother were out shopping, I did the same as you, I made up a little bundle and beat it on the quiet... After all I've told you, you won't try to tell me I wasn't patient enough... Believe me, there was nothing I hadn't tried... Now you know the whole story... When I tell you that girl would stop at nothing and that she's likely to come here looking for me any minute, don't try and tell me I'm seeing things... I know what I'm talking about! I know her! And we'd be a lot safer in my opinion if she found me locked up with the nuts... That way I could pretend not to understand... With her that's the only way... Just let on that you don't know what she's talking about... "

Two or three months before, I'd have been interested in what Robinson was telling me, but I seem to have aged all of a sudden.

I guess I'd been getting more and more like Baryton, I didn't give a damn. What Robinson had been telling me about his adventure in Toulouse didn't strike me as a very real danger anymore. I tried in vain to get excited about his situation, but his situation had a musty smell about it. Maybe we like to think different, but the world leaves us long before we leave it... for good.

One fine day you decide to talk less and less about the things you care most about, and when you have to say something, it costs you an effort... You're good and sick of hearing yourself talk... you abridge... You give up... For thirty years you've been talking... You don't care about being right anymore. You even lose your desire to keep hold of the small place you'd reserved yourself among the pleasures of life... You're fed up... From that time on you're content to eat a little something, cadge a little warmth, and sleep as much as possible on the road to nowhere. To rekindle your interest, you'd have to think up some new grimaces to put on in the presence of others... But you no longer have the strength to renew your repertory. You stammer. Sure, you still look for excuses for hanging around with the boys, but death is there too, stinking, right beside you, it's there the whole time, less mysterious than a game of poker. The only thing you continue to value is petty regrets, like not finding time to run out to Bois-Colombes to see your uncle while he was still alive, the one whose little song died forever one afternoon in February. That horrible little regret is all we have left of life, we've vomited up the rest along the way, with a good deal of effort and misery. We're nothing now but an old lamppost with memories on a street where hardly anyone passes anymore.

If you've got to be unhappy, you may as well keep regular habits. I insisted on everybody in the house being in bed by ten o'clock. I was the one who turned out the lights. The business took care of itself.

We didn't overtax our imaginations. The Baryton system of taking cretins to the movies kept us busy enough. Under our management the institution wasn't run as economically as it had been. Wanton waste, we figured, might bring the chief back, since it gave him such nightmares.

We had bought an accordion, so Robinson could play music for the patients to dance to in the garden during the summer months. It was hard to keep the inmates busy day and night. We couldn't send them to church all the time, they got too bored.

We received no further reports from Toulouse. Abbé Protiste never came back to see us. The asylum settled down to a life of furtive monotony. We weren't easy in our minds. Too many ghosts around.

Months passed. Robinson was looking better. At Easter time our patients became rather agitated, women in light-colored dresses had taken to strolling back and forth outside the garden. Harbingers of spring. I gave them bromides.

At the Tarapout the cast had been changed several times since the days when I'd worked there. The little English girls were far away, I was told. In Australia. We'd never see them again...

I wasn't allowed backstage since the business with Tania. I didn't press the point.

We started writing letters all over the place, especially to the consulates of the northern countries, to try and get some news of Baryton's movements. There were no answers of any interest.

Meanwhile Parapine performed his technical duties in dignified silence. I doubt if in twenty-four months he had uttered more than twenty sentences in all. I was obliged to attend to the daily material and administrative details practically unaided. I made a few mistakes. Parapine never held them up to me. We got along fine together by dint of sheer indifference. An adequate turnover of patients kept the institution going nicely. After paying for supplies and rent, we still had more than enough to live on, and it goes without saying that Aimee's aunt was paid regularly for the child's board.

Robinson, I had the impression, was suffering much less from anxiety than when he got there. He was looking better and had gained three kilos. On the whole it seemed that as long as families had little lunatics in their midst, they would keep coming to us, conveniently situated as we were, at two steps from the capital. Our garden alone was worth the trip. On fine summer days people would come from Paris just to admire our flowerbeds and our clumps of roses.

It was on one of those Sundays in June that I thought I recognized Madelon for the first time, in the middle of a group of strollers. For a moment she stood there, just outside our gate.

At first I didn't want to mention this apparition to Robinson, for fear of frightening him, but then, thinking it over, I advised him, for a time at least, to give up the aimless strolls in the neighbor-hood that he'd got in the habit of taking. My advice had him worried. But he didn't ask to know more. Toward the end of July we received a few postcards from Baryton, this time from Finland. We were glad to hear from him, but he didn't say one word about coming back, he only wished us good luck and sent us friendly greetings, Two months passed and then more... Again the roads were covered with summer dust. Around All Saints' Day one of our lunatics caused something of a stir outside our Institute. This patient had always been quiet and well behaved, but the mortuary excitement of All Saints was too much for him. We weren't quick enough to stop him from standing at the window and shouting that he didn't ever want to die... The passers-by thought he was too funny for words... In the midst of this ruckus I again had the unpleasant impression, but much more definitely than the first time, of having recognized Madelon in the front row of a group at the exact same place outside the gate.

In the night that followed I was awakened by a feeling of distress. I tried in vain to forget what I had seen. There was no point in trying to get back to sleep.

I hadn't been back to Rancy in a long time. As long as I was being pursued by a nightmare, I wondered if it mightn't be a good idea to take a look out there, where all misfortunes came from sooner or later... I'd left plenty of nightmares behind me out there... In a pinch you might think of going to meet them halfway as a kind of precaution... Coming from Vigny, the shortest way to Rancy is along the Seine as far as the Gennevilliers Bridge, the low flat one. The slow river mists break up just over the water, rise, drift, race, stagger, and fall on the other side of the parapet, around the little dim lamps. The big tractor factory on the left is hiding in a great chunk of darkness. The windows have been opened by a dismal conflagration that is burning it away from inside and goes on and on. After the factory you're alone on the riverbank... But you can't lose your way... Your degree of fatigue gives you a pretty good idea that you've reached your destination.

At that point you just have to turn left into the Rue des Bournaires, and then it's not far. It's easy to get your bearings because of the green and red signal lights at the grade crossing, which are always lit.

Even in the middle of the night I could have found the Henrouilles' house with my eyes closed. I'd gone there often enough in the old days...

But that night, just outside their door, I started to think instead of going ahead...

Madame Henrouille, it came to me, was living there alone now. They were all dead, all of them... She must have known, or at least suspected, how the old woman had died in Toulouse... I wondered how she had felt about it...

The street lamp whitened the glass top of the little portico over the doorstep like a snowfall. I stood on the street corner for a long time, just looking. I could have gone and rung the bell. I'm sure she'd have let me in. We hadn't quarreled after all. It was freezing cold where I was standing...

The street still ended in a bog, same as in my time. They'd promised to send workmen, but they never had. No one passed that way anymore.

It wasn't that I was afraid of Madame Henrouille. No. But all of a sudden I had lost all desire to see her. Wanting to see her had been a mistake. There, outside her house, I suddenly realized that there was nothing more she could tell me... Listening to her would have bored me, it was as simple as that... We were nothing to each other anymore.

By then I'd gone further into the night than she had, further even than Grandma Henrouille, who was dead. We weren't all together anymore... We had left each other for good... Death had come between us and so had life... Inevitably... Each man for himself, I mumbled... and started back to Vigny.

Madame Henrouille hadn't had enough education to follow me any further... Character, yes, she had plenty of that... But no education! That was the rub. No education! Education is indispensable! That's why she couldn't understand me anymore, or understand what was going on around us, vicious and stubborn as she was... That's not enough... You need a heart and a certain amount of knowledge to go further than other people... To get back to the Seine I took the Rue des Sanzillons and then the Impasse Vasson. My worry was all straightened out. I was pleased, almost happy, because now I knew that there was no point in batting my brains out over the Henrouille woman, I'd finally dropped her by the wayside, the bitch!... What a number! We'd been pretty good friends in our own way... We had understood each other for quite some time... But now she wasn't low enough for me, and she couldn't go down any further... To catch up with me... She had neither the education nor the strength. You don't go up in life, you go down. And she couldn't get down to where I was... There was too much night around me.

Passing the house where Bébert's aunt had been the concierge, I'd have liked to go in and see who was living now in the lodge where I'd taken care of Bébert and where he had died. Maybe his schoolboy picture was still hanging over the bed... But it was too late to be waking people up. I went on without showing myself...

A little further on, on the Faubourg de la Liberté, I saw the light still burning in Bézin's junk shop... I hadn't expected that... But it was only a gas jet in the middle of the window. Bézin knew all the news and gossip of the neighborhood from hanging around the cafés... He was known all the way from the Flea Market to the Porte Maillot.

He could have told me some good ones if he'd been awake. I pushed his door. The bell rang, but no one answered. I knew that he slept in the back room, his dining room actually... And there he was in the dark with his head between his arms on the table, sitting twisted beside his cold dinner that was still waiting, lentils. He had begun to eat. Sleep had grabbed hold of him the moment he started. He was snoring loudly. True, he'd been drinking. I well remember what day it was, a Thursday, the day of the market at Les Lilas... He had a green cloth full of his acquisitions spread out at his feet.

I had always liked Bézin, he was no crummier than most. Obliging, easygoing... I wasn't going to wake him up just out of curiosity, just to get answers to my few little questions... So I turned off the gas and left.

I'm sure he had a hard time making ends meet in that business of his. But at least he found no difficulty in falling asleep.

I can't deny that I felt sad as I started back to Vigny at the thought that all those people, those houses, those dirty, dingy, dismal things no longer spoke to me at all, no longer spoke straight to my heart as they had in the old days, and that, chipper as I might seem, I quite possibly didn't have the strength to go on much further like that alone.

* * *

About meals at Vigny, we had stuck to the same arrangements as in Baryton's day, that is, we all got together at table, except that now we usually ate in the billiard room above the concierge's lodge. It was cosier than the regular dining room, where unpleasant memories of English conversations still hung in the air. And besides, the furniture in the dining room was too good for us—genuine "1900" pieces with opaline stained-glass windows.

From the billiard room you could see everything that was going on in the street. That could come in handy. We'd spend whole Sundays in that room. Now and then we'd invite a doctor from the neighborhood to dinner, but our usual guest was Gustave, the traffic cop. He was regular. I can vouch for that. We'd got acquainted out of the window one Sunday, watching him on duty at the crossroads coming into town. The cars were giving him trouble. First we just exchanged a few words, and then from Sunday to Sunday we really got acquainted. It so happened that I'd cared for his two sons in Paris, one with measles, the other with mumps. Gustave Mandamour, that was his name, from Cantal, was our faithful friend. Conversation with him could be kind of trying, because he had trouble with his words. He could find them all right, but he couldn't get them out, they'd stay in his mouth making noises.

One evening Robinson invited him into the billiard room, as a joke I think. But it was Gustave's nature to keep on with anything he had started, so after that he came every evening at the same time, eight o'clock. He felt at ease with us, better than at the café, as he himself told us, because of the political discussions at the cafe that often got out of hand. We, on the other hand, never talked politics. In Gustave's case politics was a ticklish subject. It had got him into trouble at the cafe. The fact is, he should always have steered clear of politics, especially when he had a few drinks under his belt, which sometimes happened. In fact he had a reputation for drinking, that was his weakness. While with us he felt safe in every respect. He admitted it. We didn't drink. At our place he could let himself go and no harm would come of it. He knew he could trust us.

When Parapine and I thought of the situation we had escaped from and the one that had fallen into our laps at Baryton's, we didn't complain, there was no call to, because all things considered we'd had a miraculous stroke of luck, and we had all the social standing and material comfort we needed.

Still, for my part, I had never imagined that the miracle would last. I had a crummy past behind me, and already it was coming back at me like the belchings of fate. At the very start in Vigny I had received three anonymous letters that had seemed as suspicious and as menacing as could be. And then scads of other equally vicious letters. It's true that we often received anonymous letters at Vigny and didn't pay much attention to them as a rule. Usually they came from former patients, whose persecution mania had followed them home.

But these letters and their turns of phrase had me worried, they weren't like the others, their accusations were precise, and they were all about me and Robinson. To come right out with it, they accused us of shacking up together. A crummy insinuation. At first I was reluctant to mention them to Robinson, but I finally decided to when I kept receiving more and more letters of the same kind. So then the two of us tried to figure out who could have sent them. We drew up a list of all the possible people we both knew. That didn't get us anywhere. Anyway, this accusation didn't make sense. Homosexuality wasn't my line, and Robinson didn't give a damn about sex one way or the other. If anything was bugging him, it certainly wasn't sex. Only a jealous woman could have dreamed up such rotten calumnies.

In short, of all the people we knew, only Madelon seemed capable of pursuing us all the way to Vigny with such foul fabrications. She could go on writing her poisoned letters for all I cared... What

I feared was that, exasperated at getting no answer, she'd come around in person one of these days and kick up a ruckus at the Institute. You had to expect the worst.

For several weeks we jumped every time the bell rang. I was expecting a visit from Madelon, or still worse, from the police.

Every time Gustave Mandamour came around for his game a little earlier than usual, I wondered if he didn't have a summons tucked in his belt, but in those days Mandamour was still as friendly and easygoing as could be. It wasn't until later that he too underwent a striking change. At that time he came almost every day and lost every game he played with perfect equanimity. If his disposition changed, it was definitely our fault.

One evening, just out of curiosity, I asked Mandamour why he never won at cards. I had no serious reason for asking him, only my mania for knowing the why and the wherefore . . , Especially seeing that we didn't play for money. While we were talking about his bad luck, I stepped up to him, studied him closely, and saw that he was extremely farsighted. The fact is that with the lighting we had there he could barely distinguish clubs from diamonds. Something was bound to happen.

I corrected his infirmity by giving him a nice pair of glasses. At first he was delighted with them, but not for long. Since he played better with his glasses, he didn't lose as often as before, and then he took it into his head to stop losing altogether. That was impossible, so he cheated. And when, as sometimes happened, he lost in spite of his cheating, he sulked for hours. In short, he became impossible.

I was aghast, he'd get sore for no reason at all, and to make matters worse he'd try to upset us, to give us things to worry about. When he lost, he'd get even, in his own way... And yet, I repeat, we weren't playing for money, only for fun and glory... But he was furious all the same.

One evening when his luck had been bad, he harangued us before leaving: "Gentlemen, I'm warning you to watch your step!... Considering the people you associate with, if I were you, I'd be careful!... Among others, there's a dark-haired woman who's been passing your house for days!... A lot too often, if you ask me!... She must have her reasons!... I wouldn't be surprised if she had a bone to pick with one of you gentlemen!... "

That's the pernicious way Mandamour threw this thing in our faces before leaving the room. That got a rise out of us all right!... Nevertheless, I pulled myself together in an instant. "Oh, thank you Gustave," I answered calmly. "I don't see who this dark-haired woman you refer to can be... None of our former female patients, as far as I know, has had reason to complain of our care... It must be some poor deranged creature... We'll find out... Anyway, you're right, it's always best to know... Thanks again for telling us, Gustave... And good evening."

Robinson's consternation was such that he couldn't get up from his chair. When the policeman had gone, we examined the information he'd given us from every angle. After all, it could be another woman, it didn't have to be Madelon... There were others who used to hang around under the windows of our nuthouse... Still, there was good reason to believe it was she, and the mere possibility scared us out of our wits. If it was Madelon, what was she up to now? And what could she have been living on all these months in Paris? And supposing she was going to turn up in person, we'd better talk it over right away and decide what to do.

"Look here, Robinson," I said. "Make up your mind, it's high time, and don't change it... What do you want to do? Do you want to go back to Toulouse with her?"

"No, I tell you. No no no!" That was his answer. Plain enough.

"Okay," I said. "But in that case, if you really don't want to go back with her, the best thing, in my opinion, would be for you to leave the country for a while and try and make a living somewhere else. That's the surest way to get rid of her... She wouldn't follow you out of the country, would she?... You're still young... You've recovered your health... You're rested... We'll give you a little money, take it and shove off... That's my advice... Besides, you must be aware that this is no job for you... You can't go on like this forever... "

If he had listened to me, if he had cleared out then and there, it would have suited me, I'd have been really glad. But he wouldn't buy it.

"Why are you so mean to me, Ferdinand?" he said. "It's not nice of you at my age... Just look at me!... " He didn't want to shove off. He was sick of moving around.

"This is as far as I'll go," he said. "Say what you please... do what you please... I won't go... "
That was how he requited my friendship. Still, I kept trying.

"But what if Madelon were to turn you in, just supposing, in connection with old Madame Henrouille?... You told me yourself that you wouldn't put it past her."

"That would be just too bad," he said. "She can do as she pleases... "

That kind of talk was something new, coming from Robinson. Up until then he had never been a fatalist...

"At least go find yourself some little job nearby, in a factory, then you won't have to be here with us all the time... If somebody comes looking for you, we'll have time to warn you."

Parapine was in complete agreement with me. The matter must have struck him as really grave and urgent because he even went so far as to say a few words to us. We'd have to figure out some place to put Robinson, where he wouldn't be noticed... One of our business connections was a carriage maker not far away who owed us a small debt of gratitude for certain little favors we'd done him in awkward situations. He agreed to give Robinson a trial at hand painting. It was delicate work, not hard and nicely paid.

"Léon," we told him the morning he started in. "Don't make a fool of yourself in your new job, don't attract attention with your screwed-up ideas... Arrive on time... Don't leave before the others... Say good morning to everybody... In other words, behave. It's a decent shop, and you've been well recommended... "

But right away he got himself spotted, though you can't say it was his fault. A stool pigeon, who worked in one of the other workshops, saw him going into the boss's private office. That did it. Reported. Undesirable element. Fired.

So a few days later Robinson came back to us, jobless. It was bound to happen.

Then, just about the same day, he started coughing again. We auscultated him and found a whole collection of rales all up and down his right lung. Calling for bed rest.

One Saturday evening just before dinner someone asked for me personally in the reception room. A woman, they tell me.

It was her all right, wearing a little three-cornered hat and gloves. I remember well. No need of preliminaries. She couldn't have picked a worse moment. I give it to her straight before she can say a word.

"Madelon," I said, "if you've come to see Léon, I can tell you right away to forget it... Just turn around and go home... His lungs are affected and so is his head... Quite seriously, I might add... You can't see him... Anyway, he has nothing to say to you... " "Not even to me?"

"No, not even to you... Especially not to you," I added.

I expected her to flare up. No, she only stood there in front of me, shaking her head from side to side and compressing her lips. With her eyes she tried to find me where she had left me in her memory. I wasn't there anymore. I, too, had moved in her memory. In that situation I'd have been afraid of a husky man, but from her I had nothing to fear. She was only a weak woman, so to speak. I had always wanted to slap a face consumed with anger, to see what a face consumed with anger would do under the circumstances. A slap or a fat check is what it takes if you want to see all the passions that go beating about behind a face take a sudden tack. It's as beautiful as watching a sailing ship maneuvering in a stormy sea. The whole person keels over in the changed wind. That's what I wanted to see.

For at least twenty years that desire had been goading me. On the street, in cafés, wherever aggressive, touchy, boastful people quarrel. I'd never have dared for fear of getting hit back and even more of the shame that comes of getting hit. But here for once I had a golden opportunity.

"Get out!" I said, just to raise her fury to white heat.

She couldn't get over my talking to her like that. She started to smile, hideously, repulsively, as if she thought me ridiculous and really contemptible... "Smack! Smack!" I slapped her face twice, hard enough to stun a mule.

She slumped down on the big divan on the other side of the room, against the wall, with her head between her hands. Her breath came in short gasps and she moaned like a puppy that's been beaten too much. Then, as if she'd thought it over, she jumped up, light and bouncy, and went out the door without even turning her head. I hadn't seen a thing. I'd have to try again.

* * *

But regardless of what we did, she was smarter than all of us together. She saw her Robinson again, she saw him as often as she pleased... It was Parapine who first spotted them together. They were on the terrace of a cafe across from the Gare de l'Est. I'd suspected they were seeing each other, but I didn't want to seem to be taking the slightest interest in their relations. After all, it was none of my business. He was doing his work at the rest home, and not at all badly, taking care of the paralytics, a nasty job if ever there was one, wiping them, sponging them, changing their underwear, helping them slobber. We couldn't expect any more of him.

If he chose to see his Madelon on the afternoons when I sent him to Paris on errands, that was his business. We definitely hadn't seen her at Vigny-sur-Seine since those slaps in the face. But I was pretty sure that since then she must have told him some rotten things about me.

I stopped talking to Robinson about Toulouse, as if none of all that had ever happened.

Six months passed for better or worse, and then there was a vacancy on our staff, and we suddenly needed a nurse, skilled in massage. The old one had gone off to get married without giving notice.

Quite a few fine-looking girls applied for the job. In fact, so many strapping young women of all nationalities flocked to Vigny as soon as our ad appeared that we were hard put to it to choose among them. In the end we picked a Slovak by the name of Sophie, whose complexion, energetic yet gentle bearing, and divine good health struck us, I have to admit, as irresistible.

This Sophie knew only a few words of French, but I undertook without delay, the least I could do, to give her lessons. And lo and behold, in contact with her youth and freshness I felt my interest in teaching revive, though Baryton had done everything in his power to disgust me with it. Impenitent! But what youth! What vigor! What muscles! What an excuse! Supple! Springy! Amazing! Her beauty was diminished by none of that false or true reticence that impedes ail-too occidental converse. Frankly, I couldn't admire her enough. From muscle to muscle, I proceeded by anatomical groups... By muscular slopes, by regions... I never wearied of pursuing that concentrated yet relaxed vigor, distributed in bundles which by turns evaded and consented to the touch... Beneath her satin, taut or relaxed, miraculous skin!...

The era of these living joys, of great undeniable physiological and comparative harmonies is yet to come... The body, a godhead mauled by my shameful hands... The hands of an honest man, that unknown priest... Death and Words must give their permission first... What foul affectations! A cultivated man needs to be rolled in a dense layer of symbols, caked to the asshole with artistic excrement, before he can tear off a piece... Then anything can happen! A bargain! Think of the saving, getting all your thrills from reminiscences... Reminiscences are something we've got plenty of, one can buy beauties, enough to last us a lifetime... Life is more complicated, especially the life of human forms... A hard adventure. None more desperate. Compared with the addiction to perfect forms, cocaine is a pastime for stationmasters.

But let's get back to our Sophie! Her mere presence seemed a feat of daring in our sulking, fearful, unsavory household.

After she had been with us for some time, we were still glad to number her among our nurses, yet we could not help fearing that she might one day disturb the fabric of our infinite precautions or suddenly, one fine morning, wake up to our sleazy reality. Sophie still failed to suspect the depth of our fetid resignation! A gang of failures! We admired her, so alive in our midst... just her way of getting up from a chair, coming to our table, leaving it again... She charmed us...

And every time she performed those simple gestures, we experienced surprise and joy. We made strides in poetry, so to speak, just marveling at her being so beautiful and so much more obviously free than we were. The rhythm of her life sprang from other wellsprings than ours... Our wellsprings were forever slow and slimy.

The joyful strength, precise yet gentle, which animated her from her hair to her ankles troubled us, alarmed us in a charming sort of way, but definitely alarmed us, yes, that's the word.

Though our instinct reveled in her innate joy, our peevish knowledge of the things of this world rather frowned on it, that essentially frightened, ever-present knowledge which cowers in the cellars of existence, accustomed to the worst by habit, by experience.

Sophie had the winged, elastic, precise gait that is so frequent, almost habitual, among the women of America, the gait of heroic creatures of the future, whom life and ambition carry lightly toward new kinds of adventure... Three-masters of joyful warmth, bound for the Infinite...

Parapine, who was hardly given to lyricism on the subject of attractive women, would smile to himself when she left the room. Just to look at her did your soul good. Especially mine, I must say, which had lost none of its aptitude for desire.

Wishing to take her by surprise, to ravish a little of her pride, of the prestige and power she had acquired over me, to diminish her, in short to humanize her a little and reduce her to our paltry proportions, I would go into her room when she was sleeping.

At such times, Sophie offered a very different sight—more commonplace, yet surprising and reassuring as well. Without ostentation, almost uncovered, lying crosswise on the bed, legs every which way, skin moist and relaxed, she was battling with fatigue.

In the depths of her body she dug into sleep, so hard that it made her snore. That was the only time when I found her within my reach. No more enchantment. No joking. This was serious. She toiled as though to pump more life out of existence... At such times she was greedy, drunk with wanting more and more. You should have seen her after those sleeping bouts, still swollen, her organs exultant, ecstatic under her rosy skin. At such times she was funny, as laughable as other people. For some minutes she'd reel with happiness, then the full light of day would come to her and delivered, as if too heavy a cloud had just passed, she'd resume her glorious flight...

All that can be fucked. It's extremely pleasant to grasp this moment when matter becomes life. You rise up to the endless plateau that spreads out before men. "Whew!" you go. And again "Whew!" You come the limit up there, and then it's like an enormous desert...

Among us, her friends rather than employers, I, I believe, was the most intimate. True, she was regularly unfaithful to me with the orderly in charge of the violent ward, an ex-fireman. For my own good, she told me, so as not to put too great a strain on me, considering all the brain work I had under way, which wasn't exactly compatible with the demands of her fiery temperament. Entirely for my own good. She cuckolded me in the interest of hygiene. What could I say?

All this, when I think of it, could have given me nothing but pleasure if the Madelon business hadn't been weighing on my mind. One fine day I told Sophie the whole story to see what she'd say. Telling her my troubles made me feel a little better. I was sick of the endless quarrels and resentments growing out of that wretched passion, and Sophie thought I was perfectly right.

Seeing that Robinson and I had been such good friends, she thought we should all have one big reconciliation, just patch the whole thing up as quickly as possible. Her advice came from a good heart. Central Europe is full of good hearts. The only trouble was that she didn't know much about the characters and reactions of the people around here. With the best intentions in the world she gave me the worst possible advice. I came to realize that she'd been wrong, but too late.

"You should see Madelon," she advised me. "From what you've told me, I'm sure she's a good girl deep down... It's just that you provoked her, and you were really brutal and mean to her... You owe her an apology and a nice present too, to make her forget... " That's the way things were done in her country. Everything she advised me to do was exquisitely polite but not at all practical.

I took her advice, mostly because behind all the frills and foolishness, behind the diplomatic maneuvers, I envisaged the possibility of a little foursome that would have been most entertaining, in fact it would have made a new man of me. Under the pressure of age and circumstances, I note to my sorrow, my friendly feelings were taking an insidiously erotic turn. Betrayal. And Sophie, without meaning to, was abetting me in this betrayal. There was so much curiosity in Sophie she couldn't help being attracted by danger. An excellent nature, nothing Protestant about her, she never tried to belittle the opportunities life offered and was never suspicious of them. Just my type. She went further. She understood the need for variety in the distractions of the rear end. An adventurous disposition of that sort, you'll have to agree, is most unusual in women. We had definitely picked the right one.

She wanted me, and I thought it perfectly natural, to give her some idea of Madelon's physique. She was afraid of seeming awkward in an intimate situation with a Frenchwoman, in view of the stupendous reputation in this line that has been pinned on Frenchwomen in foreign parts. As for enduring Robinson's attentions at the same time, it was only to give me pleasure that she consented. Robinson didn't send her at all, so she said, but on the whole we were in agreement. That was the main thing. Okay.

I waited a while for a good opportunity to approach Robinson with my plan for a general reconciliation. One morning when he was in the office copying medical reports into the big book, the moment struck me as propitious, and I interrupted him to ask him very simply whether he thought it would be a good idea for me to see Madelon and suggest that we let our violent bygones be bygones... Whether on the same occasion I might introduce her to Sophie, my new friend? And lastly, if he didn't think it was time we all got together and patched up our quarrels.

At first, I could see, he hesitated, then he replied, but without enthusiasm, that he saw no objection... I suspect Madelon had told him that I'd try to see her soon on one pretext or another. About the slap in the face I'd given her the day she came to Vigny, I didn't breathe a word.

I couldn't run the risk of his yelling at me there and calling me a brute in public, because after all, though we'd been friends a long time, there in the institution he was under my orders. Authority first.

January was a funny time for that sort of operation. Because it was most convenient, we decided to meet in Paris one Sunday and go to the movies together. We thought maybe we'd drop in at the Batignolles carnival for a while first if it wasn't too cold out. Robinson had promised to take her to the Batignolles carnival.

Madelon, he told me, was wild about carnivals. That was a lucky thing. Meeting again for the first time, a carnival was the best possible place.

* * *

We sure got an eyeful of that carnival! And a headful too! Bim bam! And bam again! We whirl around! And we're carried away! And we scream and we yell! There we were, in the crowd with lights and noise and all the rest of it! Step up, step up! Show your skill, show your daring, and laugh laugh laugh! Wheel Everyone tried in his overcoat to appear to his best advantage, sharp and just a little aloof, to show that he usually went elsewhere for his entertainment, to more "expensif" places, as they say in English.

You tried to make the impression of knowing, lighthearted young blades in spite of the icy wind, just one more humiliation, and the depressing fear that you were spending too much money on these amusements and might have occasion to regret it for a whole week.

The merry-go-round sends up a big belch of music. It can't quite deliver itself of the waltz from Faust, but it tries hard. The waltz plumps down and shoots up again and swirls around the circular ceiling, which spins with its thousands of pastry light bulbs. The steam calliope's having a bad time. The music is giving it a pain in its pipe, its stomach. Would you care for a piece of nougat? Or would you rather try another target? Take your choice.

In our group at the shooting gallery it was Madelon, with the brim of her hat turned up over her forehead, who showed the most skill. "Look," she says to Robinson. "My hand isn't shaking. And we had plenty to drink, didn't we?"... Just to show you the kind of things we were saying. We'd just come out of a restaurant. "One more try!" And Madelon won the bottle of champagne. Bing bang! Bull's-eye! Then I bet her she can't catch me on the Dodge'em cars. "I'll take you up on that," she says as chipper as you please. "We'll take separate cars!" And there we go! I was glad she'd accepted. It was a way of making up to her. Sophie wasn't jealous. She had her reasons.

So Robinson climbs into the back car with Madelon and I get into another up front with Sophie. Man, do we collide! And it's crash! And hold tight! But I see right away that Madelon doesn't enjoy being shaken up. Neither does Léon for that matter, he used to like it, but no more. It's plain that he doesn't feel comfortable with us. While we're clutching at the rail, some sailorboys come along and start feeling us up, men and women alike, and making propositions. We're freezing. We shake them off. We laugh. More and more feeler-uppers come from all directions with music and rhythm and excitement. You get such jolts on these barrels on wheels that your eyes pop out of your head every time you clash. Great fun! Violence and joy! The whole accordion of pleasures! I want to make up with Madelon before we leave the carnival. I want to very much, but she doesn't respond to my overtures anymore. It's no soap. She's snubbing me. Keeping me at a distance. I can't make her out. These moods that come over her. I'd had hopes of something better. Physically, come to think of it, she has changed completely.

She can't bear comparison with Sophie, no sparkle, no luster. Good humor was more becoming to her, but now she has an air of possessing superior knowledge. That irritates me. I'd gladly give her another slap in the face, maybe that would bring her around or maybe then she'd tell me what she knows that's so superior. Come on, smile! This is a place of merriment, we haven't come here to weep! Let's whoop it up!

She's found work with an aunt of hers, so she tells Sophie while we're strolling later on. On the Rue du Rocher. Her aunt is a corset maker. May as well believe her.

It wasn't hard to see that if reconciliation was the idea, this meeting was a failure. My little scheme was a washout too. In fact, a gigantic flop.

Seeing each other again had been a mistake. Sophie hadn't really grasped the situation. She hadn't realized that this get-together would just make everything more complicated... Robinson should have warned me,

told me how stubborn she was... Too bad! Oh well! Barn! Bam! The carnival goes on! Let's try the "Caterpillar," as they call it. My idea and my treat! One more attempt to make up with Madelon. But she keeps slipping away from me, avoiding me. Taking advantage of the crush, she climbs into another seat up front with Robinson, I'm flummoxed again. We're dazed by waves and whirls of darkness. I mutter under my breath that it's hopeless. Sophie finally agrees with me. She realizes that in this whole affair I had been led away by my lecherous fantasies. "You see how it is? She's sore. I think we'd better leave them alone now... You and I could drop in at the Chabanais before we go home... " That suggestion appealed to Sophie, because while still in Prague she had often heard people talking about the Chabanais, and she was delighted at the thought of trying the Chabanais and judging for herself. But then we figured that considering the amount of money we had brought with us, the Chabanais would be too expensive. We'd just have to try and revive our interest in the carnival.

While we were in the Caterpillar, Robinson must have had a scene with Madelon. They were both in a foul humor when they got out. You really couldn't have touched her with a ten-foot pole that evening. To smooth things over I suggested an absorbing amusement—fishing for bottlenecks. Madelon accepted sulkily. Even so she beat us all hollow. She got her ring just over the cork and slipped it on just before the bell rang. Click! And that was that. The stand owner couldn't get over it. He gave her a half bottle of Grand- Due de Malvoison.[93] Just to give you an idea of how skillful she was. But it didn't make her happy. Right away she announced that she wouldn't drink it. "It's no good," she said. So Robinson uncorked the bottle and drank it. Down the hatch! At one gulp. A funny thing for him to do, because he practically never drank.

Then we came to the tin wedding. Biff! Bang! We all had a try with hard balls. It's depressing how clumsy I am at these things... I congratulate Robinson. He beats me at any game. But not even his skill could make him smile. They both looked as if we were leading them off to slaughter. We tried hard, but nothing could put any life into them. "This is a carnival!" I yelled at them. For once I was completely out of ideas.

My shouting things in their ears and trying to cheer them up didn't mean a thing to them. They didn't even hear me. "What about youth?" I asked them. "What are we going to do about it?... Has youth stopped making merry? Look at me, ten years older than the rest of you! All right, sweetheart, what do you say?" He and Madelon looked at me as if I were drunk, gassed, nuts, and there was no point in even answering me... no point in trying to speak to me, because I'd certainly be incapable of

---

[93] Grand-Duc de Malvoison. This is a take-off on the fancy names often given to poor-quality wines.

understanding anything they could say... I wouldn't understand a thing... maybe they're right, I said to myself, looking anxiously at the people around us.

But all those people were doing the things you do to have fun, they weren't nursing their little troubles like us. Far from it. They were getting something out of the carnival. A franc's worth here!... Fifty centimes' worth there!... Lights! Music, spiel, and candy... They were buzzing around like flies, scads of them, with their little grubs in their arms, livid, pasty-faced babies, so pale in the glaring light that you could hardly see them. Just around their noses those babies had a bit of pink, in the area for colds and getting kissed.

Among all the stands I immediately recognized the Gallery of the Nations... A memory, I didn't mention it to the others.—That makes fifteen years that have gone by... A long time... And what a lot of friends I've lost along the way! I'd never have thought the Gallery of the Nations could drag itself out of the mud it was sunk in out there in Saint-Cloud... But now it was all refurbished, as good as new, with music and everything. You gotta hand it to them. And all these people shooting. A shooting gallery always does business. And the egg was back again like me, there in the middle, supported by practically nothing, bobbing up and down. It cost two francs. We passed it by, we were too cold to try, it was best to keep moving. But not because we were short of change, our pockets were still full of change, our little pocket music.

I'd have tried anything just then to put some life into us, but no one was doing a thing to help. If Parapine had been with us, it would probably have been worse, seeing how gloomy he was with people. Luckily he'd stayed home to look after the loonies. I was sorry I'd come. Then Madelon started laughing after all, but there was nothing funny about her laugh. Robinson, who was beside her, snickered so as not to be different. Then Sophie started making jokes. That was all we needed.

As we were passing the photographer's booth, he noticed our hesitation. We had no great desire to go in, except Sophie maybe. But a moment later, thanks to our hesitation, we were at the mercy of his camera. He drawled out his commands, and we submitted on the cardboard bridge—he must have built it himself— of a purported ship, La Belle France. The name was written on imitation life belts. We stood there for quite some time, staring straight ahead, challenging the future. Other customers were waiting impatiently for us to come down off the bridge, and already they were avenging themselves for having to wait by not only finding us too ugly for words, but telling us so out loud.

They thought they could take advantage of our not being able to move. But they couldn't faze Madelon, she slanged them back with the full force of her Southern accent. She could be heard for miles around. She told them where to get off!

A magnesium flash. We all flinch. We each get a picture. We're even uglier than before. The rain comes through the canvas roof. Our feet are footsore and frozen stiff. The wind had found holes all over us while we were posing, so much so that there's hardly anything left of my overcoat.

All we can do is keep walking among the booths. I didn't dare suggest going back to Vigny. It was too early. Our teeth were already chattering with the cold and the heart-throb organ of the merry-go-round jangled our nerves till we were shivering even more. The end of the whole world—that's what the damned organ is laughing about. It bellows its message of disaster through its silver-plated kazoos, and the tune goes out to die in the environing darkness, along the pissy streets that come down from Montmartre.

The little housemaids from Brittany are definitely coughing a lot more than they did last winter when they'd just arrived in Paris. Their green-and-blue mottled thighs do their best to decorate the flanks of the wooden horses. The boys from Auvergne, who treat them to their rides, are cautious post-office clerks and, as everyone knows, never lay them without a rubber. They have no desire to catch it a second time. In expectation of love, the housemaids squirm and wiggle in the disgustingly melodious din of the merry-go-round. They're kind of sick to their stomachs, but that doesn't stop them from posing in the freezing cold, because this is the great moment, the time to try their youthful charms on the definitive lover, who may be there, already smitten, tucked away among the yokels in this frozen crowd. Love is still hanging back... but it'll come, same as it does in the movies, and happiness with it. If the rich man's son loves you for just one evening, he'll never leave you... It's been known to happen, and it's good enough. Naturally he's sweet, and naturally he's handsome, and naturally he's rich.

The old woman who keeps the newsstand over by the Métro doesn't give a damn about the future, she scratches her old conjunctivitis and slowly festers her eyes with her fingernails. An obscure pleasure that costs nothing. It's been going on for six years now, and her itching gets worse and worse.

Strollers, driven into groups by the bitter cold, gather around the lottery booth. A brazier of rear ends. They can't get in. So quickly, to warm themselves, they run, they bound into the knot of people across the way, waiting to get in to see the two-headed calf.

Under cover of the urinal, a young candidate for unemployment quotes his price to a provincial couple flushed with excitement. The morals cop knows what's going on, but he doesn't care, his assignment at the moment is the entrance to the Café Miseux.[94] He's been watching the Café Miseux for a week. The instigator must operate in the tobacco shop or in the backroom of the feelthy bookshop next door. Anyway it was reported long ago. Either one or the other of them, it seems, procures underage girls, who appear to be selling flowers. Anonymous letters again. The chestnut vendor on the corner does a bit of informing too. He has to. Everything that's on the sidewalk belongs to the police.

That machine-gun kind of, that you hear over there, shooting in crazy short bursts, is only the guy who runs the "Wheel of Death" on his motorcycle. An escaped convict, so they say, but I'm not sure. Anyway, he has crashed through his tent twice in this same spot and once a couple of years ago in Toulouse. Why can't he and his contraption smash up for good! Why can't he break his neck and spinal column once and for all! That noise would put anybody in a temper! The same goes for the streetcar with its bell, in less than a month it's killed two old folks in Bicêtre, hugging the walls of the shanties. The bus on the other hand is quiet, it pulls up slowly on the Place Pigalle, taking every possible precaution, staggering a little, blowing its horn, all out of breath, with its four passengers, who get off as slowly and carefully as choir boys.

Strolling from booth to booth, from clump to clump of humanity, from merry-go-rounds to lotteries, we'd come to the end of the carnival, to the big dark vacant lot where the families go to pee... Nothing to do but turn back. Retracing our steps, we ate chestnuts to work up a thirst. We got sore mouths but no thirst. There was a worm in the chestnuts, a cute little fellow. Naturally it was Madelon who got it. That was exactly when things started going really badly between us. Up until then we had kept ourselves more or less under control, but that worm really made her furious.

As she was going over to the gutter to spit out the worm, Léon said something to stop her, I don't remember what he said or what had got into him, but all of a sudden her going over to spit went against Robinson's grain. Like a damn fool he asked her if she'd found a seed in it... Honestly, that was no question to ask her... And then Sophie sees fit to join in their argument... She couldn't see what they were fighting about... She wanted to know.

Being interrupted by Sophie, a foreigner, exasperated them even more, what would you expect? Just then a bunch of hoodlums come between us, and we're separated. Actually they were young fellows trying to pick up customers, but with mimicry, kazoos, and assorted cries of terror. When we managed to get back together, she and Robinson were still fighting.

"It looks like time to go home," I thought... "If we leave them here together for another few minutes, they'll disgrace us right here in the middle of the carnival... Better call it a day... " The whole thing had been a failure, you couldn't deny it. "Let's go home," I suggested to Robinson. He gave me a look of surprise, but it still struck me as the wisest, most sensible course. "Haven't you had enough?" I added. He made a sign meaning that I should ask Madelon how she felt about it. I had no objection to asking Madelon, but I didn't think it was a very bright thing to do.

"We'll take Madelon with us," I finally said.

"Take her?" he asked. "Where do you want to take her?" "To Vigny, of course," I said.

That was a blunder. I'd done it again. But once I'd said it, I couldn't take it back.

"We have an empty room for her in Vigny," I went on. "There's no shortage of rooms out there!... We could all have a bite to eat before going to bed... At least it'll be more cheerful than freezing around here, like we've been doing for the last two hours... No trouble at all... " Madelon made no

---

answer to my suggestions. She didn't even look at me while I was speaking, but I know she hadn't missed a word of what I'd said. Anyway, I'd said it and it couldn't be helped.

Then when I'd wandered a few steps away from the group, she came over to me quietly and asked if I wasn't trying to put something over on her, inviting her out to Vigny. I didn't answer her. No sense trying to reason with a jealous woman. Anything I could say would only be a pretext for another endless scene.

Besides I didn't even know whom or what she was jealous of. It's often hard to localize feelings of jealousy. Come to think of it, she was probably jealous of everything, same as everyone else.

By that time Sophie didn't know where she was at, but she went on trying to be agreeable. She even took Madelon's arm, but Madelon was much too furious and much too glad to be furious to let herself be diverted by friendly gestures. We fought our way through the crowd to the streetcar stop on the Place Clichy. Just as we were about to board a car, a cloud burst right over the square, and the rain came down in cascades. The heavens emptied.

In half a second every taxi in sight had been grabbed. I heard Madelon right near me asking Robinson in an undertone: "You're not going to insult me in front of all these people?... Are you, Léon?" She was in bad shape. "You're sick of me, aren't you? Why don't you say so?" she went on. "Say you've had enough of me... That you'd rather be alone with these two... You all go to bed to-gether, I bet, when I'm not there, don't you?... Say you like it better with them than with me... Go on, say it so I can hear you... " After that she stood silent, her face contracted into a grimace around her nose, which pointed upward and tugged at her mouth. We were waiting on the sidewalk. "You see how your friends treat me?" she started in again. "You see, Léon?"

Léon, I have to give him credit, didn't answer back, he didn't do anything to provoke her, he could be very violent at times, but he just looked the other way at the house fronts and the boulevard and the cars.

And yet Léon had his violent moments. When she saw she wasn't getting anywhere with threats, she came back at him in a different way, with love talk, while we were all waiting. "I love you, Léon, hear, I love you... Do you realize at least what I've done for you?... Maybe I shouldn't have come today... but you do love me just a little, don't you? You must love me just a little... You have a heart, haven't you, tell me, Léon, tell me you have a heart... Then why do you despise my love?... We had a beautiful dream, the two of us together... And now you're so cruel to me!... You've trampled my dream, Léon!... You've soiled it!... You've destroyed my ideal, you can't say different... I suppose you don't want me to believe in love anymore... Is that it? And now you want me to go away for good... Is that what you want?... " All these questions while the rain was dripping through the awning of the café.

It was coming down on us all. He had warned me all right, she was exactly the way he had said. He hadn't made anything up. I'd never have thought them capable of rising to such an emotional paroxysm in so little time.

Seeing the cars and all were making so much noise, I was able to whisper a few words in Robinson's ear. I suggested that we try to run out on her and get this shindig over with as quickly as possible, because it was a flop and we'd better break up quietly before the situation soured in earnest and people got really angry as there was good reason to fear. "You want me to find you a pretext?" I whispered. "Then we'll all beat it separately?"—"No!" he answered. "Don't do that! Don't! She's capable of throwing a fit right here and we'd never be able to stop her!" I let it go at that.

Come to think of it, maybe Robinson enjoyed being yelled at in public, and besides he knew her better than I did. As the shower was letting up, we found a taxi. We jumped in, and there we were all squeezed together inside. First we didn't say a word to each other. The air was too heavy between us and I felt I'd put my foot in it enough. I thought I'd better wait a while before doing it again.

Léon and I took the folding seats, the two women sat in back. On weekend nights the road to Argenteuil is badly congested, especially as far as the Porte. After that you have to count a good hour before you get to Vigny, on account of the traffic. It's no fun sitting face to face and eye to eye without saying a word, especially when it's dark and everyone's kind of suspicious of everyone else.

Even so, if we had stayed like that, nettled, but keeping each to himself, nothing would have happened.

That's still my opinion when I think of it today.

It was my doing, I have to admit, that we started talking again and the quarrel resumed, worse than ever. We're never suspicious enough of words, they look like nothing much, not at all dangerous, just little puffs of air, little sounds the mouth makes, neither hot nor cold and easily absorbed, once they reach the ear, by the vast gray boredom of the brain. We're not suspicious enough of words, and calamity strikes.

Certain words are hidden in with the rest, like stones. They're not very noticeable, but before long they make all the life that's in us tremble, every bit of it in its weakness and its strength... The outcome is panic... An avalanche... You're left dangling like a hanged man, over a sea of emotion... A tempest comes and goes, much too powerful for you, so violent you'd never have thought mere emotions could lead to anything like it... I therefore conclude that we're never suspicious enough of words. But now let me tell you what happened: The taxi was slowly following a streetcar, because the road was being repaired... "Hum... hum" went the motor. A pothole every hundred yards... But the streetcar up ahead of us wasn't enough for me. Always childish and talkative, I was impatient. The snail's pace and the indecision all around me were more than I could bear... So, quick, I shattered the silence like a piggy bank to see what might be inside. I watched, or rather, since by then you could hardly see, I tried to watch Madelon in the left-hand corner of the cab. She kept her face turned toward the outside, toward the landscape, toward the darkness would be more like it. I noted with annoyance that she was as stubborn as ever. I, on the other hand, acted like a regular pest. Just to make her turn her head my way, I spoke to her.

"Look, Madelon. Maybe you've got some idea how we could amuse ourselves, but you're afraid to tell us? Would you like us to stop somewhere before we go home? Come on, tell us!... "

"Amuse ourselves! Amuse ourselves!" she said, as if I'd insulted her. "All you people think of is amusing yourselves... " Then she let out a whole barrage of sighs, deep and so touching that I've seldom heard the like.

"I'm doing my best," I said. "It's Sunday."

"How about you, Léon?" she asked him. "Are you doing your best too?" Straight from the shoulder. "Are you kidding!" was his comeback.

I looked at them both when we passed a streetlamp. What I saw was anger. Madelon leaned foward as if to kiss him. It was written that no one would miss a chance to put his foot in it that night.

The taxi had slowed down again because of the trucks that were strung out all along the road. It exasperated him to be kissed, and he pushed her away, rather roughly, I must say. Of course that wasn't a nice thing to do, especially in front of us.

When we came to the end of the Avenue Clichy, to the Porte, night had fallen, the lights were going on in the shops. Under the railroad bridge, in spite of the echo that's always so loud, I could still hear her asking: "Don't you want to kiss me, Léon?" She kept at him. He still didn't answer. So then she turned to me and harangued me directly. The affront was too much for her.

"What have you done to Léon to make him so mean? Tell me this minute!... What kind of stories have you been telling him?" That's the way she lit into me.

"Nothing at all," I told her. "I haven't told him anything!... Your quarrels are no concern of mine!"

The worst of it was that it was true, I hadn't said anything to Léon about her. He was free, it was up to him whether he stayed with her or left her. It was none of my business, but it was no use trying to tell her that, she had stopped listening to reason. Again we fell silent, sitting face to face in the cab, but the air was so charged with fury that it couldn't go on for long. She had spoken to me in a thin sort of voice I'd never heard her use before, the monotonous voice of a person whose mind is fully made up. Scrunched up as she was in the corner of the cab, I couldn't see her movements anymore, and that troubled me.

All that time Sophie had been holding my hand. With these goings on the poor kid didn't know what to do with herself.

Right after Saint-Ouen Madelon resumed her catalog of grievances against Léon. In long-winded frenzy she asked him questions and more questions, now at the top of her lungs: Did he love her, had he been faithful, and so on. For the two of us, Sophie and me, it was hopelessly embarrassing. But she was so excited she didn't care at all whether we were listening or not. If anything she welcomed it. On the other hand, it hadn't been very bright of me to shut her up with us in that box... every word resounded and, with her character, that made her want to put on a big act for our benefit. The taxi had been another of my brainstorms.

Léon had stopped reacting. He was tired after the evening we'd spent together, and he was always a little short of sleep, he'd always had that trouble.

"For God's sake calm down," I managed to shout at Madelon. "The two of you can have it out when we get there... You'll have plenty of time!"

"Get there! Get there!" she said in a tone that would make your hair stand on end. "We'll never get there, I tell you!... And anyway," she went on, "I'm sick of your dirty nasty ways... I'm a decent girl... I'm better than the whole lot of you together!... Pigs!... You can't make a fool out of me!... You can't understand a girl like me, you're not good enough... You're too rotten the whole lot of you to understand someone like me!... You'll never understand anything that's clean and beautiful!"

In sum, she attacked us in our self-esteem. She went on and on. I kept strictly quiet on my folding seat, I didn't so much as let out a murmur. But it did no good, every time the driver shifted gears she'd start yapping again. At times like that the least little thing can provoke disaster. Just making us miserable seemed to be giving her a big kick, she followed out her nature to the bitter end, she couldn't help it.

"Don't imagine you're going to get off so easy!" she threatened us. "That you're going to get rid of me on the quiet! Oh no! I may as well tell you right away! No, you won't get away with it! You no-good scum!... You've ruined my life! I'll wake you up, you bastards!"

Suddenly she bent over toward Robinson, grabbed him by the lapels of his overcoat, and started shaking him. He made no attempt to break loose. You wouldn't catch me interfering. It almost looked as if Robinson enoyed seeing her getting more and more excited on account of him. He was grinning, it wasn't natural. She was yelling at him, and he was jerking back and forth on his seat like a marionette, nose down, all the starch gone out of his neck.

Just as I was going to attempt some little gesture of remonstrance to stop the rough stuff, she bristled and started giving me a piece of her mind... Unloading things she'd been storing up for a long time... I was in for it all right. And there in front of everybody. "You shut up, you lecher!" she screams at me. "This is between Léon and me, and it's none of your business! I'm not having any more of your brutality! If you ever again lift a finger against me, Madelon will teach you how to behave!... First you cuckold your friends, then you beat their women!... Of all the blasted nerve! Aren't you ashamed of yourself?" Hearing these truths, Léon kind of woke up a bit. He wasn't grinning any more. For a second I even wondered if he and I weren't going to bash each other to kingdom come, but for one thing, with four of us packed into that cab, there wasn't room enough for a fight. That reassured me. Too cramped.

Especially since we were making pretty good time over the cobblestones of the boulevards along the Seine. The taxi was jolting so bad you couldn't even move.

"Come, Léon," she commanded him. "I'm asking you for the last time, come! Drop these people! Do you hear what I'm saying?"—A riot!

"Make him stop, Léon! Stop the car, or I'll stop it myself!" But Léon didn't stir from his seat. He was screwed on tight. "So you won't come?" she said again. "You won't come?"

She'd warned me that I'd better lie low. I'd had enough. "Are you coming?" she repeated. The cab was still going fast, the road was clear in front of us, and the jolting was worse than ever. We were bouncing around like crates in a truck.

"All right!" she concluded when he didn't answer. "All right, that does it! You asked for it! Tomorrow! You hear, no later than tomorrow, I'm going to the police and telling them exactly how Madame Henrouille fell down the stairs! Do you hear me now, Léon?... You happy now?... Not playing deaf anymore? Either you come with me right away or I go to the police tomorrow morning!... So are you coming or aren't you? Speak up!" She couldn't have made her threat any plainer.

So then he decided to say something after all.

"You were involved in it yourself," he said. "You can't say a thing... "

That didn't quiet her in the least, far from it. "I don't care!" she said. "What if I was? You mean we'll both go to jail?... That I was your accomplice?... Is that what you mean?... Well, that suits me fine!... "

And she started laughing hysterically, as if nothing could have been funnier...

"That would suit me to a T, I tell you! I'm crazy about jail, I tell you!... Don't go expecting me to back down because of your jail talk!... I'll go to jail any time you say!... .. But you'll go too, you bastard!... At least you won't be able to give me the run-around any longer!... I belong to you, okay! But you belong to me too! You should just have stayed with me down there! I can only love once, Monsieur! I'm no tart!"

In saying that she was defying me and Sophie too. Making a point of fidelity and respectability. In spite of it all the taxi was driving on, and he still made no move to stop the driver.

"Then you're not coming? You'd rather go to the pen? Okay!... You don't care if I turn you in?... You don't care if I love you or not?... You don't care about my future? You don't care about anything, do you?... "

"No," he says. "In a way you're right... But it's not just you... I don't care about anyone else either... Christ, don't take it as an insult!... I know you're a sweet kid... But I don't want to be loved anymore... It disgusts me!... "

She didn't expect to have that kind of thing thrown in her face... She was so surprised that she didn't know how to pick up the tirade she'd already begun. She'd been thrown off balance, but she recovered quick enough. "Oh! It disgusts you, does it?... What do you mean by that?... Tell me a little more, you ungrateful weasel!"

"No!" he said. "It's not you that disgusts me, it's everything. I don't want anything... You can't hold that against me... "

"What's that you say? Say it again! Me... everything?" She was trying to understand. "Me, everything? Don't talk Chinese!... Tell me in French, in front of these people. Why do I disgust you now? Don't you get a hard-on like everybody else, you big pig, when you make love? Oh, so you don't get a hard-on, is that it?... Out with it!... In front of these people... Tell us you don't get a hard-on!"

In spite of her fury, her way of arguing her case made you want to laugh. But I didn't have time to laugh very long, because she started up again. "And him there! I suppose he doesn't squirt every time he catches me in a corner! The beast! The sex fiend! I dare him to say it's not true!... You're all looking for something new!... Admit it!... Variety, novelty! That's what you want! A daisy chain! Why not a virgin! You degenerate pigs! Why look for pretexts?... You're jaded, that's all. You haven't even got the courage of your vices! You're scared of your vices!"

At that point Robinson took it on himself to answer. By that time he, too, had lost his temper, and he shouted as loud as she had.

"Wrong!" he shouted. "I've got plenty of courage, as much as you!... Only, if you want the whole truth... everything, absolutely everything! disgusts me and turns my stomach! Not just you!... Everything!... And love most of all!... Yours as much as anyone else's!... The sentimental tripe you dish out... Want me to tell you what I think of it? I think it's like making love in the crapper! Do you get me now?... All the sentiment you trot out to make me stick with you hits me like an insult, if you want to know... And to make it worse, you don't even realize it, you're the one that's rotten because you don't understand!... You're satisfied repeating the rubbish other people say... You think it makes sense... People have told you there's nothing better than love, they've told you it'll go down with everybody, everywhere and always, and that's good enough for you... Well, I say fuck their love!... You hear?... Their putrid love doesn't go down with me... not anymore!... You've missed the train! You're too late! It won't go down anymore, and that's that!... What a stupid thing to get steamed up about!... Why do you have to make love, considering all the things that are happening?... All the things we see around us!... Or are you blind?... More likely you just don't give a damn! You wallow in sentiment when you're a worse brute than anybody... You want to eat rotten meat?... With love sauce?... Does that help it down?... Not with me!... If you don't smell anything, it's your hard luck! Maybe your nose is stuffed up! If it doesn't disgust you, it's because you're stupid, the whole lot of you... You want to know what it is that comes between you and me?... All right, I'll tell you! A whole life is what comes between you and me... Isn't that enough for you?"

"My house is clean!" she comes back at him. "A person can be poor but clean, can't they? When did you ever see that my house wasn't clean? Is that what you're insinuating with your nasty remarks?... My rear end is clean, Monsieur!... Maybe you can't say as much for yourself!... Nor your feet neither!"

"I never said that, Madelon! I never said anything like that!... About your house not being clean!... You see that you don't understand a thing!" That was all he could think of saying to calm her down.

"So now you say you haven't said anything? You haven't said anything, have you? Would you listen to him! He insults me worse than garbage and then he claims he hasn't said anything! You'd have to kill him to make him stop lying! Jail isn't bad enough for a skunk like him! A lousy rotten pimp!... It's not enough! What he needs is the guillotine!"

Nothing could stop her. I couldn't make anything of what they were saying in that taxi. All I could hear was curses and insults in with the roar of the motor and the sloshing of the wheels in the wind and rain that came beating against our door in ferocious gusts. The air between us was charged with threats. "It's vile!... " she said several times. She couldn't say anything else. "It's vile!" And then she raised the stakes, double or quits. "You coming?" she said. "You coming, Léon? One... You coming? Two... " She waited. "Three?... So you're not coming?... " "No," he said, without moving an inch. He even added: "Do what you like!" That was an answer of sorts.

She must have moved back a little on the seat, as far as she could go. I guess she was holding the revolver in both hands, because when the shot went off it seemed to go straight into his belly. Then, almost at the same time, there were two more shots, one after the other... and then the car was full of acrid smoke.

But we kept right on going. Robinson slumped down on me, sideways, jerking and gasping: "Hep! Hep!" And more of the same: "Hep! Hep!" The driver must have heard.

First he slowed down a little to see what had happened. Then finally he stopped right under a gas lamp.

The moment he opened the door, Madelon gave him a violent push and jumped out. She scrambled down the embankment and beat it across the fields in the darkness, right through the mud. I tried to call her back, but she was already far away.

I didn't quite know what to do with my wounded man... In a way it might have been wisest to take him back to Paris... But by then we weren't far from our place... The townspeople wouldn't know what was going on... So Sophie and I bundled him up in overcoats and settled him in the corner where Madelon had fired her shots. "Take it easy!" I said to the driver. But he kept driving much too fast. He was in a hurry. The bumps made Robinson groan still worse.

When we pulled up in front of the rest home, the driver didn't even want to give us his name, he was worried about trouble with the police, having to testify and all that... He also said there were sure to be bloodstains on the cushions. He wanted to beat it right away without waiting. But I'd taken his number.

Two bullets had gone into Robinson's gut, maybe three, I wasn't quite sure yet how many.

She had fired straight in front of her, I'd seen that. The wounds weren't bleeding. Though Sophie and I were holding him up between us, he got a bad shaking and his head was wobbling. He spoke, but it was hard to understand him. He was already delirious. "Hep! Hep!" he kept chanting. He'd have time enough to die before we got there.

The street had been freshly paved. As soon as we came to our gate, I sent the concierge to get Parapine from his room in a hurry. He came down right away, and he and a male nurse helped us carry Robinson to his bed. Once we'd undressed him we were able to examine him and palpate the wall of his abdomen. It was already distended, and soft in places. I found two holes practically on top of each other, but no third; one of the bullets must have gone astray.

If I had been in Leon's place, I'd have preferred an internal hemorrhage, it floods the abdomen and doesn't take long. The peritoneum fills up, and that's the end. With peritonitis on the other hand an infection sets in, and it takes forever.

It was still too soon to tell how he'd go about dying. His belly was swelling up, he was staring at us, his eyes were already set, he was groaning, but not very much. He was having a sort of calm spell. I'd already seen him very sick in a lot of different places, but this time everything was different, his moans and his eyes and everything. It looked as if we couldn't hold him much longer, he was slipping away from minute to minute. He was sweating big drops that made it look as if his whole face were crying. At times like that you're sorry you've become as poor and as hard as you have. We're short of practically everything we'd need to help someone die. All we have left inside is the things that are useful in our everyday life, a life of comfort, a life all for ourselves, a life of viciousness. We've lost our confidence along the way. We've harried and goaded what pity we had left, driven it to the bottom of our body like some nasty pill. We've pushed pity to the bottom of our bowels along with our shit. That's a good place for it, we say to ourselves.

I stayed with Léon to commiserate, I had never felt so embarrassed. I couldn't manage it... He couldn't find me... it was driving him wild... He must have been looking for another Ferdinand, some-body much bigger than me, to help him die more easily. He was straining to figure out if there'd been any progress in the world... Poor fellow... Drawing up an inventory in his mind... Wondering if people hadn't changed just a little for the better during his lifetime, if maybe he had been unfair to them without meaning to... But there was only me, just me, me all alone, beside him, the genuine Ferdinand, who was short of everything that would make a man bigger than his own bare life, short of love for other people's lives. Of that I had none, or so little there was no use showing it. I wasn't as big as death. I was a lot smaller. I had no great opinion of humanity. I think I'd have found it easier to grieve for a dying dog than for Robinson, because a dog isn't tricky, and Robinson, in spite of everything, was tricky in a way. I was tricky myself, we were all tricksters... Our other qualities had left us along the way, I'd even lost the grimaces that can come in handy over deathbeds, I'd lost everything along the way, I couldn't find any of what we need to help a man die, all I could find was cunning. My feelings were like a house where you only go on holidays. Scarcely inhabitable. Besides, a dying man is demanding. Dying isn't enough for him. He has to get a kick out of it... At the very bottom of life, with his arteries already full of urea, he has to get a kick out of his last gasps.

And the dying snivel, because they're not having as much fun as before... They make demands... they protest. The dramatics of misery wants to carry over from life into death.

He came partly to his senses when Parapine gave him his injection of morphine. He even talked a little about what had happened. "It's best to have it end like this," he said. And later: "It doesn't hurt as much as I'd have thought." When Parapine asked him exactly where the pain was, you could see he wasn't all there anymore, but even so there were still things he wanted to tell us... He hadn't the strength, his head wasn't clear enough... He wept, he gagged, and a moment later he laughed. He wasn't like the usual sick man, we didn't know how to act in front of him.

It looked as if he were trying to help us live. As if he'd been trying to find us pleasures to go on living for. He held us by the hands. One hand each. I kissed him. That's all you can do in a case like that without going wrong. We waited. He didn't say anything more after that. A little later, maybe an hour, the hemorrhage came, internal and profuse. It carried him off.

His heart started beating faster and faster, and then very very fast. His heart was running after his exhausted, diminished blood, chasing it to the ends of his blood vessels, throbbing in his fingertips. The pallor rose up from his neck and took hold of his whole face. He died in a choking fit. He went as if he had taken a running start, squeezing the two of us in his arms.

Then, almost immediately, he was back again in front of us, already taking on the weight of a dead man.

We stood up. We disengaged ourselves from his hands. They stopped in mid-air, stiff, yellow, and blue in the light of the lamp.

Then Robinson was like a stranger in the room, someone who had come from a horrible country and you wouldn't have dared speak to.

* * *

Parapine kept his wits about him. He managed to send someone to the police station for a cop. The cop just happened to be Gustave, our Gustave, who was on stand-by after his traffic duty.

"OhmyGod!" said Gustave when he entered the room and saw Robinson.

Then he sat down at the nurses' table that hadn't been cleared yet to get his breath and take a little drink. "Seeing it's a crime," he said, "we'd better take him to headquarters." Then he remarked: "Robinson was all right, he wouldn't have hurt a fly. I wonder why she killed him... " Then he drank some more. He shouldn't have. Drink didn't agree with him. But he liked the bottle. It was his weakness.

We went up to the storeroom to get a stretcher. By then it was too late to disturb the staff, so we decided to carry the body to the police station ourselves. It was far away, at the other end of town, after the grade crossing, the last house.

We started out. Parapine held the front of the stretcher, Gustave Mandamour the other end. But neither of them walked very straight. Going down the little stairway, Sophie had to steady them a bit. It was then I noticed that she didn't seem terribly upset. Yet it had happened right beside her, so close that one of that madwoman's bullets could have gone right into her. But Sophie, as I'd noticed on other occasions, needed time to get her emotions started. Not that she was cold. When it hit her, it was like a ton of bricks, but she needed time.

I wanted to follow the body a little way to make sure it was really over. But instead of actually following as I should have, I veered from side to side of the road and finally, after passing the big school building near the grade crossing, I slipped into a side street that leads down to the Seine, first sloping gently between hedges and then taking a steep plunge.

Over the fences I saw them moving off with their stretcher.

They looked as if they'd suffocate in the sheets of mist that slowly closed behind them. Along the riverbank the current was driving hard against the barges, which had been wedged tight as a precaution against the flood water. More cold came from the Gennevilliers plain, in puffs of mist that spread over the swirling river and made the water glisten under the arches.

Down there in the distance lay the sea. But there was no more room in me for imaginings about the sea. I had other things to do. I had tried to lose myself, I hadn't wanted to be face to face with my own life anymore, but everywhere I kept finding it. I was always coming back to myself. My wanderings were over. No more knocking about for me... The world had closed in... We had come to the end! Like at the carnival! It's not enough to be sad; there ought to be some way to start the music up again and go looking for more sadness... But not for me... We may not admit it, but what we really want is to have our youth back again... We ought to be ashamed... Anyway, I wasn't prepared to endure any more!... Yet I hadn't gone as far in life as Robinson!... All in all, I hadn't succeeded... I hadn't conceived even one good, sound idea, like his idea of getting himself bumped off... That idea was bigger than my big head, bigger than all the fear that was in it, a fine, a magnificent idea to die with... How many lives would I need to make myself an idea more powerful than anything in the world? No saying. A flop! My ideas went rattling around in my head with lots of space between them. They were like faint, flickering little candles, trembling throughout a lifetime in the middle of a ghostly, abominable universe.

Maybe things were a little better than twenty years ago, nobody could say that I hadn't made a wee beginning of progress, but there seemed no possibility of my ever managing, like Robinson, to fill my head with one single idea, but that one superb, a thought far stronger than death, and of my succeeding, just with my idea, of exuding joy, carefreeness, and courage wherever I went. A scrumptious hero!

I'd be brimful of courage then. I'd be dripping with courage, and life itself would be just one big idea of courage, that would be the driving force behind everything, behind all men and things from earth to heaven. And by the same token there would be so much love that Death would be shut up inside it with tenderness, and Death would be so cosy-comfortable in there, the bitch, that she'd finally start enjoying herself, she'd get pleasure out of love along with everyone else. How wonderful that would be! What a production! I was laughing to myself all alone on the riverbank, when I thought of all the things I'd have to do if I wanted to inflate myself like that with infinite resolutions... An idealistic toad! Fever, you know.

My friends had been looking for me for at least an hour. Especially because they'd noticed that I wasn't in very good shape when I left them... Gustave Mandamour was the first to sight me under my gas lamp. "Hey, doctor!" he shouted. Mandamour, I can assure you, had some voice! "This way!

They want you at the police station. They want your deposition. —You know, doctor," he added, but now he was whispering in my ear, "you're not looking well." He walked beside me, in fact he held me up. Gustave was fond of me. I never found fault with him for his drinking. I was full of understanding. Whereas Parapine was rather severe and sometimes made him feel ashamed of himself for drinking so much. Gustave would have done practically anything for me. He admired me in fact. He told me so. He didn't know why. Neither did I. But he admired me. He was the only one.

We went down two or three streets together until we saw the lantern outside the police station. After that you couldn't go wrong. Gustave was worrying about the report he'd have to write. He didn't dare tell me so. He'd already made everyone sign at the bottom, but a lot of things were still missing from his report.

Gustave had a big head. Like me. I could actually wear his kepi, which goes to show, but he tended to forget details. Ideas didn't come easy to him, it cost him a struggle to speak and even more to write. Parapine would have been glad to help him write his report, but he hadn't seen the crime, he didn't know the circumstances. He'd have had to invent, and the inspector didn't want any inventions in his reports, he wanted nothing but the truth, so he said.

Climbing the stairway at the police station, I was shivering. I couldn't tell the inspector much either. I really wasn't feeling so good.

They'd put Robinson's body down beside the rows of big filing cabinets.

All around the benches the floor was littered with printed matter and cigarette butts. On the wall the inscription "Fuck the Fuzz" was only partly erased.

"Did you get lost, doctor?" the secretary asked me, quite amiably I must say, when I finally got there. We were all so tired we couldn't really talk straight.

Finally we were agreed about the phrasing and the trajectory of the bullets, one of which was still embedded in the spinal column. It hadn't been found. He'd be buried with it. They looked for the other bullets. The other bullets were embedded in the wall of the taxi. It was a powerful revolver.

Sophie came and joined us. She'd gone back for my overcoat. She kissed me and pressed me close to her, as if I were going to die too or fly away. "I'm not going away," I kept saying. "Be reasonable, Sophie, I'm not going away." Nothing I said could set her mind at rest.

Standing around the stretcher, we chewed the fat with the inspector's secretary, who'd seen worse in his time, crimes and noncrimes and disasters, and he wanted to tell us about all his experiences in one breath. We didn't dare leave for fear of offending him. He was so affable. It gave him pleasure to be talking with educated people for a change instead of thugs. We didn't want to hurt his feelings, so we hung around.

Parapine had no raincoat. Listening to us lulled Gustave's mind. His mouth hung open, and his thick neck was thrust out as if he was pulling a hand cart. I hadn't heard Parapine pour out so many words for many years, not since my student days, to tell the truth. All the things that had happened that day went to his head. But we decided to go home all the same.

We took Mandamour with us and Sophie too. Now and then she gave me a hug, her body was filled with the strength of worry and tenderness, and so was her heart. Her strength was all over her, it was wonderful. I, too, was full of her strength. That bothered me... it wasn't mine, and it was my own I'd need if I were to go and die magnificently one day, like Léon. I had no time to waste on grimaces. To work! I said to myself. But nothing came of it.

She even wanted me to go back and look at the corpse again. So I left without turning around. A sign said: "Close the door." Parapine was thirsty. From talking, no doubt. From talking too much for him. Passing the bistrot by the canal, we knocked on the shutters for a while. It made me think of the road to Noirceur during the war. The same little light over the door, on the point of going out. Finally the owner in person came and opened. He hadn't heard anything. We told him all the news, ending up with the murder. "A crime of passion!" Gustave called it.

The bar opened just before dawn for the benefit of the bargemen. As the night draws to an end, the locks open slowly. And then the whole countryside comes to life and starts to work. Slowly the banks break away from the river and rise up on both sides. Work emerges from the darkness. You begin to see it again, all very simple and hard. Over here the winches, over there the fences around the work sites, and far away on the road men are coming from still farther away. In small chilled groups they move into the murky light. For a starter they splatter their faces with daylight as they walk past the dawn. All you can see of them is their pale, simple faces... the rest still belongs to the night. They, too, will all have to die some day. How will they go about it?

They move toward the bridge. Then little by little they vanish across the plain, and other men come along, paler and paler as the light rises all around them. What are they thinking about?

The owner of the bar wanted to know all about the tragedy. He wanted us to tell him everything. Vaudescal was the owner's name; he was from the North and very clean.

Gustave gave him an earful.

Gustave kept chewing over the details. But that wasn't the essential, again we were losing ourselves in words. Besides, he was drunk and kept starting all over from the beginning. But there really wasn't any more to say, nothing at all. Even so, I'd have listened to him for a while yet, quietly half asleep, but the others started contradicting him and that made him mad.

In his rage he clouted the little stove. The whole thing collapsed and turned over: the stovepipe, the grate, the glowing coals. Mandamour was as strong as an ox.

To make matters worse he wanted to show us the genuine Fire Dance. He wanted to take off his shoes and prance around on the coals.

There had been some bad blood between Gustave and the bar owner about a slot machine that hadn't been licensed... Vaudescal was a snake in the grass. You couldn't trust him. His shirts were too clean for him to be really honest. He was vindictive and he was a stool pigeon. The riverbanks are full of that kind.

Parapine suspected that he was laying for Mandamour, hoping to take advantage of his drunkenness and get him fired.

Parapine had stopped him from doing his Fire Dance and made him feel ashamed. We pushed Mandamour to the end of the table. There he finally collapsed, as quiet as a mouse, amid Gargantuan sighs and smells. And fell asleep.

Far in the distance the tugboat whistled; its call passed the bridge, one more arch, then another, the lock, another bridge, farther and farther... It was summoning all the barges on the river, every last one, and the whole city and the sky and the countryside, and ourselves, to carry us all away, the Seine too —and that would be the end of us.

* * *

DEATH ON THE INSTALLMENT PLAN

Here we are, alone again. It's all so slow, so heavy, so sad... I'll be old soon. Then at last it will be over. So many people have come into my room. They've talked. They haven't said much. They've gone away. They've grown old, wretched, sluggish, each in some corner of the world.

Yesterday, at eight o'clock, Madame Bérenge, the concierge, died. A great storm blew up during the night. Way up here where we are, the whole house is shaking. She was a good friend, gentle and faithful. Tomorrow they're going to bury her in the cemetery on the rue des Saules. She was really old, at the very end of old age. The first day she coughed I said to her: "Whatever you do, don't stretch out. Sit up in bed." I was worried. Well, now it's happened... anyway, it couldn't be helped...

I haven't always been a doctor... crummy trade. I'll write the people who've known her, who've known me, and tell them that Madame Bérenge is dead. Where are they?

I wish the storm would make even more of a clatter, I wish the roofs would cave in, that spring would never come again, that the house would blow down.

Madame Bérenge knew that grief always comes in the mail. I don't know whom to write to anymore... Those people are all so far away... They've changed their souls, that's a way to be disloyal, to forget, to keep talking about something else.

Poor old Madame Bérenge; they'll come and take her cross-eyed dog away.

For almost twenty years all the sadness that comes by mail passed through her hands. It lingers on in the smell of her death, in that awful sour taste. It has burst out... it's here... it's skulking through the passageway. It knows us and now we know it. It will never go away. Someone will have to put out the fire in the lodge. Whom will I write to? I've nobody left. No one to receive the friendly spirits of the dead... and let me speak more softly to the world... I'll have to bear it all alone.

Toward the end the old lady was unable to speak. She was suffocating. She clung to my hand... The postman came in. He saw her die. A little hiccup. That's all. In the old days lots of people used to knock on her door and ask for me. Now they're gone, far away into forgetfulness, trying to find souls for themselves. The postman took off his cap. I know I could talk about my hatred. I'll do that later on if they don't come back. I'd rather tell stories. I'll tell stories that will make them come back, to kill me, from the ends of the world. Then it will be over and that will be all right with me.

At the clinic where I work, the Linuty Foundation, I've had a lot of complaints about the stories I tell... My cousin Gustin Sabayot makes no bones about it, he says I should change my style. He's a doctor too, but he works across the Seine, at La Chapelle-Jonction. I didn't have time to go see him yesterday. The fact is I wanted to talk to him about Madame Bérenge. I got started too late. Seeing patients is a rough job. At the end of the day we're both pooped. Most of the patients ask such tedious questions. It's no use trying to hurry, you've got to explain everything in the prescription twenty times over. They get a kick out of making you talk, wearing you down... They're not going to make any use of the wonderful advice you give them. But they're afraid you won't take trouble enough, and they keep at you to make sure; they want suction cups, X rays, blood tests... they want you to feel them from top to toe... to measure everything, to take their blood pressure, the whole damn works. Gustin has been at it for thirty years. One of these days I'm going to send those pests of mine to the slaughterhouse at La Villette for a good drink of warm blood, first thing in the morning. That ought to knock them out for the day. I can't think of any other way to discourage them...

The day before yesterday I finally decided to go and see Gustin at home. The suburb where he lives is a twenty-minute walk from my place once you've crossed the Seine. The weather wasn't so good but I started out just the same. I thought I'd take the bus. I hurry through my consultation. I'm slipping out past the accident ward when an old bag spots me and latches on to me. She drags out her words, like me. That comes of fatigue. She has a voice like a grater. That's from liquor. She starts whining and whimpering, she wants me to go home with her. "Oh, Doctor, please come, I beg of you!... My little girl, my Alice!... it's on the rue Rancienne, just around the corner..." I didn't have to go. My office hours were over, supposedly. She insists... By that time we're outside... I'm fed up with sick people; I've been patching up those pests all day, thirty of them... I was all in. Let them cough. Let them spit. Let their bones fall apart... Let them bugger each other. Let them fly away with forty different gases in their guts... To hell with them... But this sniveling bitch holds me tight, falls on my neck, and blows her despair in my face. Her despair reeks of red wine... I haven't the strength to resist. Anyway, nothing would have made her let go. I thought maybe when we got to the rue des Casses, which is a long street without a single lamp, I'd give her a good kick in the ass... So for the hundredth time I weaken... And the record starts up again. "My little girl!... Please, Doctor, please! My little Alice... You know her?" The rue Rancienne wasn't around the corner... It was completely out of my way... I knew exactly where it was. It's after the cable factory... She's still talking, and I listen through my private haze... "Eighty-two francs a week... that's all we've got to live on... with two children. And my husband is such a brute. It's shameful, Doctor."

I knew it was all a lot of hokum. Her whole story stank of booze and sour stomach.

By that time we'd got to their hangout. I climb the stairs. At last I could sit down... The kid wore glasses. I sit down beside her bed. She's sick all right, but even so she was playing with her doll, kind of. I thought I'd cheer her up. I'm always good for a laugh when I put my mind to it... She's not dying, but she does have trouble breathing... She's certainly got an inflammation... I make her laugh. She gags. I tell her mother there's nothing to worry about. The bitch! Now she's got me cornered, she decides she can use a doctor too. It's her legs, all covered with black-and- blue marks where she's been beaten. She hikes up her skirts. Enormous bruises and deep burns. Her unemployed husband did that with the poker. That's the way he is. I tell her what she can put on them... I take a piece of string and make a kind of swing for the miserable doll. Up and down she goes, from the bed to the doorknob and back. It was very funny... that was better than talking.

I apply the stethoscope. She's wheezing pretty bad, but it's nothing dangerous. I tell the mother there's nothing to worry about... exactly the same words as before. That's what gets you down. The kid begins to laugh. She gags again. I have to stop. Her face is all blue... Mightn't she have a little diphtheria? I'll have to see... Take a specimen?... Tomorrow.

The father comes in. With his eighty-two francs they can't afford wine, all they've got to drink is cider. "I drink it out of a bowl," he says right off the bat. "It makes you piss." And he takes a swig from the bottle to show me... . We all say how lucky it is that the little angel isn't too sick. What interested me most was the doll... I was too tired to bother about grown-ups and diagnoses. Grown-ups are a pain in the ass. I was determined not to treat a single one until next day.

I guess they think I don't take my work seriously. To hell with what they think. I drink their health again. The consultation is absolutely free, gratis, for nothing. The mother brings up her legs again. I give her a last piece of advice. Then I go down the stairs. On the sidewalk there's a little dog with a limp. He follows me without a moment's hesitation. Everything attaches itself to me today. It's a little fox terrier, black and white. Seems to be lost. Those unemployed punks upstairs, what ingratitude! They don't even see me to the door. I bet they're fighting again. I can hear them yelling. He can stick the whole poker up her ass for all I care. That'll teach her to waylay me at closing time.

I turned off to the left, toward Colombes. The little dog was still following me... After Asnières comes La Jonction, and then it's not far to my cousin's. I couldn't stand seeing him drag along like that. Maybe I'd better go home after all. We turned back by way of the Pont Bineau. skirting the row of factories. The dispensary was shut up tight when we got there... "We'll feed the little mutt," I said to Madame Hortense. "Somebody'll have to get some meat... We'll call up first thing in the morning. The S.P.C.A. will send a car for him. We'd better lock him up for tonight." Then I went out again, easy in my mind. But that dog was too scared. He'd been beaten too much. Life is hard on the streets. When we opened the window next day, he wouldn't wait, he jumped out, he was even afraid of us. He thought we'd locked him up to punish him. He couldn't understand. He didn't trust anybody anymore. It's bad when that happens.

Gustin knows me well. When he's sober, he has good ideas. He has a sense of style. His judgments are reliable. There's no jealousy in him. He doesn't ask much of this world. He's got an old sorrow... disappointment in love. He doesn't want to forget it. He seldom talks about it. She was a floozie. Gustin is good as gold. He'll never change till his dying day.

Meanwhile he drinks, kind of.

My trouble is insomnia. If I had always slept properly, I'd never have written a line.

"You could talk about something pleasant now and then." That was Gustin's opinion. "Life isn't always disgusting." In a way he's right. With me it's kind of a mania, a bias. The fact is that in the days when I had that buzzing in both ears, even worse than now, and attacks of fever all day long, I wasn't half so gloomy... I had lovely dreams... Madame Vitruve, my secretary, was talking about it only the other day. She knew how I tormented myself. When a man's so generous, he squanders his treasures, loses sight of them. I said to myself: "That damn Vitruve, she's hidden them some place..." Real marvels they were... bits of Legend, pure delight... That's the kind of stuff I'm going to write from now on... To make sure they're as good as I think, I rummage through my papers. I can't find a thing... I call Delumelle, my agent; I want to make him hate me... to make him groan under my insults. But he's not so easily fazed. It's all one to him, he's loaded. All he says is that I need a vacation... Finally Vitruve comes in. I don't trust her. I have my reasons. I light into her, point blank: where did you put my masterpiece? I had several hundred reasons for suspecting her...

The Linuty Foundation was across the way from the bronze balloon at the Porte Péreire. Almost every day when I'd finished with my patients, she'd come up to deliver my typescripts. A little temporary structure that's been torn down since. I wasn't happy there. The hours were too regular. Linuty, who had founded it, was a big millionaire, he wanted everybody to have medical treatment and feel better without money. Philanthropists are a pain in the ass. I'd have preferred some municipal dispensary... a little vaccinating on the side... a modest racket in certificates of good or bad health... . or maybe I could have supervised a public bath... in other words, something soft. Well, so be it. I'm not a Yid[95] or a foreigner or a Freemason, or a graduate of the École Normale; I don't know how to make friends and influence people, I fuck around too much, my reputation's bad. For fifteen years now they've seen me struggling along out here in the Zone;[96] the dregs of the dregs take liberties with me, show me every sign of contempt. I'm lucky they haven't fired me. Writing picks me up. I'm not so badly off. Vitruve types my manuscripts. She's attached to me. "Listen," I say, "listen, old girl, this is the last time I'm going to give you hell... If you don't find my Legend, it's the parting of the ways, it's the end of our friendship.

No more intimate collaboration… No more grub and bub, no more dough."

She bursts into lamentations. She's a monster in every way, her looks are awful and her work is awful. She's an obligation. I've had her on my neck since I was in England. She's the fruit of a promise. Our acquaintance goes way back. It was her daughter Angèle in London who made me swear to look after her forever. I've looked after her all right. That was my vow to Angèle. It dates back to the war. Besides, come to think of it, she knows what she knows. Okay. Supposedly she's tight-lipped, but she remembers... Angèle, her daughter, was quite a number. It's amazing how ugly a mother can get. Angèle came to a bad end. I'll explain if I'm forced to. Angele had a sister, Sophie, a big tall screwball, she's settled in London. And Mireille, the little niece, is over here. She has the combined vices of the whole family, she's a real bitch... a synthesis.

When I moved from Rancy to Porte Péreire, they both tagged along. Rancy has changed, there's hardly anything left of the walls or the Bastion. Big black scarred stones; they rip them out of the soft ground like decayed teeth. It will all go... the city swallows its old gums. The bus—the P.O. *bis* they call it now—dashes through the ruins like a bat out of hell. Soon there won't be anything but sawed-off dung-colored skyscrapers. We'll see. Vitruve and I used to argue about our troubles. She always claimed she'd been through more than I had. That isn't possible. Wrinkles, yes, she's got more. There's no limit to the amount of wrinkles people can get: the loathsome traces that the good years dig in their flesh. "Mireille must have put your papers away."

I leave with her and escort her out to the rue des Minimes. They live together, near the Bitrounelle chocolate factory, in a joint that calls itself the Hôtel Méridien.

Their room is an inconceivable mess, a junk shop full of miscellaneous articles, mostly underwear, all very flimsy and cheap.

Madame Vitruve and her niece both do it. They have three douche bags fully equipped and a rubber bidet. They keep it all between the beds; there's also an enormous atomizer that they've never

---

[95] "Yid." French *"Zizi."* The translation here is uncertain. The "normal" meanings of the word are the male sex organ and "wise guy."' In search of a meaning that would make sense in both passages, I came to the conclusion that this may have been a private word with Céline.

[96] The Zone *(la Zone [militaire de Paris])*. Originally the strip of land between the Paris fortifications and the suburbs, where for military reasons construction was prohibited. In later popular usage, the more depressing suburbs on the periphery of Paris.

succeeded in getting to work. I wouldn't want to be too hard on Vitruve. Maybe she has had more trouble than I have. That's what makes me control myself. Otherwise, if I were sure, I'd lick the hell out of her. She used to keep the Remington in the fireplace; she hadn't finished paying for it. So she said. I don't pay her too much for my typing, I've got to admit that... sixty- five centimes a page, but it mounts up in the end... especially with big fat books.

When it comes to squinting, though, I never saw the like of Vitruve. It was painful to look at her.

That ferocious squint gave her an air when she laid out the cards... tarots. She sold the little ladies silk stockings... and the future too, on credit. When she puzzled and pondered behind her glasses, she had the wandering gaze of a lobster.

Her fortune-telling gave her a certain influence in the neighborhood. She knew all the cuckolds. She pointed them out to me from the window, and even the three murderers—"I have proof." I'd also given her an old blood-pressure contraption and taught her a little massage for varicose veins. That added to her income. Her ambition was to do abortions or to get involved in a bloody revolution, so everybody would talk about her and the newspapers would be full of it.

I'll never be able to say how she nauseated me as I watched her rummaging through that junk pile of hers. All over the world there are trucks that run over nice people at the rate of one a minute... Vitruve gave off a pungent smell. Redheads often do. It seems to me that there's an animal quality in redheads; it's their destiny: something brutal and tragic; they've got it in their skin. I could have laid her out cold when she went on about her memories in that loud voice of hers... She had hot pants, and it was hard for her to do much about it. Unless a man was drunk and it was very dark, she didn't have a chance. On that point I was sorry for her. I myself had done better in the way of amorous harmonies. That, too, struck her as unjust. When the time came, I'd have almost enough put by to settle my accounts with death... I had my esthetic savings. What marvelous ass I'd enjoyed, I've got to admit it, as luminous as light. I had tasted of the Infinite.

She had no savings, that goes without saying. To earn her keep and get a little enjoyment on the side, she had to take a customer by surprise or corner him when he was too tired to resist. It was hell.

By seven o'clock the good little workers have gone home. The women are doing the dishes, the males are tied up in radio waves. That's when Vitruve abandons my beautiful book and goes out in pursuit of her livelihood. She pads from landing to landing with her slightly damaged stockings and her crummy lingerie. Before the crash she managed to get along, what with credit and the way she terrified her customers, but today the identical crap is given away at street fairs to stop the gripes of losers at the shell game.

That's unfair competition. I tried to tell her it was all the fault of the Japanese. She didn't believe me. I accused her of doing away with my wonderful Legend on purpose, even of throwing it in the garbage...

"It's a masterpiece," I added. "We've got to find it."

That handed her a laugh. We rummaged through the pile of merchandise.

Finally her niece came in. She was very late. Christ Almighty, what a rear end. That ass of hers was a public scandal. Her pleated skirt helped to bring it out... A rounded accordion. The unemployed are desperate, sex-starved; no dough to take a girl out with... They were good and mad. "What about giving me some of that ass!" they'd shout at her. Square in her face as she comes through the hall. It's rough always getting a hard-on for nothing. The youngsters with finer features than the rest feel entitled to it, they expect life to coddle them. It wasn't until later that she began to go down and hustle... after no end of calamities... For the present she was just having fun.

She didn't find my beautiful Legend either. She didn't give a damn about "King Krogold"... the only one who cared was myself. Her school of life was the Petit Panier, a dance hall near the Porte Brandon, just before the railroad.

They didn't take their eyes off me when I got mad. In their opinion I was a champion creep. A stick-in-the-mud, jerk-off intellectual, and so on. But now, surprisingly enough, they were scared I'd clear out. If I had, I wonder what they'd have done. I have no doubt that the aunt thought about it plenty. Lord, the winning smiles they treated me to when I began to talk about a change of air...

In addition to her amazing ass, Mireille had romantic eyes and a bewitching look, but a hefty nose... a beezer. That was her cross. When I wanted to humiliate her a bit, I'd say: "No kidding, Mireille, you've got a nose like a man..." But she was good at telling yarns, like a sailor. She made up all sorts of things, at first to amuse me, later to make trouble for me. I like to hear a good story. That's my weakness. She went too far, that's all. I got violent in the end, but she certainly deserved the thrashings I gave her, and if I'd killed her, she'd have deserved that too. She finally admitted it. The fact is I was pretty generous... I socked her for good reason. Everybody said so... at least the ones who were in the know.

I'm not being unfair to Gustin Sabayot when I say that he didn't knock himself out with his diagnoses. He got his ideas from the clouds.

The first thing he did when he stepped out of his house in the morning was to look up at the sky. "Ferdinand," he'd say, "today it's going to be rheumatism, one case after another. You want to bet?" He read that in the heavens. He was never very far off, because he had a thorough knowledge of the climate and the human temperament.

"Aha! a bit of hot weather after a cold spell. That calls for calomel, take my word for it. There's jaundice in the air. The wind has changed... From north to west. From cold to rain... That means two weeks of bronchitis... There's no point in their even getting up. If I were in charge, I'd make out my prescriptions in bed... After all, Ferdinand, when they come to see us, all they do is gab... For doctors who get paid by the call there's some point in it... but for us?... on a monthly salary... what's the use?... I could treat them without stepping out of the house. Damn pests. I don't have to see them. They wouldn't wheeze any more or less. They wouldn't vomit any more, they wouldn't be any yellower or redder, or paler, or less idiotic... That's the way it is and nobody's going to change it!" That's how Gustin felt about it, and he was damn right.

"Do you think they're sick?... They moan... they belch... they stagger... they fester... You want to clear them out of your waiting room? On the double? Even the ones who damn near suffocate every time they cough?... Offer them a free pass to the movies... or a free drink across the street... you'll see how many you've got left... If they come around and bother you, it's mostly because they're bored. On the day before a holiday you never see a soul... Mark my words, the trouble with those poor bastards isn't their health, what they need is something to do with themselves... they want you to entertain them, cheer them up, fascinate them with their belches... their farts... their aches and pains... they want you to find explanations... fevers... rumblings... new and intriguing ailments... They want you to get interested, to expatiate... that's what you've got your diplomas for... Ah, getting a kick out of his death while he's busy manufacturing it: that's Man for you, Ferdinand! They cling to their clap, their syphilis, their T.B. They need them. And their oozing bladders, the fire in their rectums. They don't give a damn. But if you knock yourself out, if you know how to keep them interested, they won't die until you get there. That's your reward. They'll come around to the bitter end." When the rain slanted down between the chimneys of the power plant, he'd say: "Ferdinand, this is sciatica day... If I don't get ten cases today I'll send my parchment back to the dean!" But when the soot came back at us from the east, which is the driest quarter, over the Bitrounelle chocolate factory, he'd crush a smudge against his nose and say: "I'll be buggered if the lungers don't start bringing up clots before the night is out. Damn it all, they'll wake me up a dozen times..."

Sometimes in the late afternoon he'd make things easier for himself. He'd climb up the ladder to the enormous cabinet where the samples were kept. And he'd start distributing medicines directly, free of charge, and absolutely without formality. "Hey you, Stringbean, you got palpitations?" he'd say to some sloven. "No." "Haven't you got a sour stomach?... A discharge?... Sure you have. Just a little? Well then, take some of this, you know where, in two quarts of water... it'll do you a world of good!... How about your joints? Don't they ache?... No hemorrhoids? And how about your bowels?... Here are some Pepet suppositories. Worms too? You think so? Well, here are some wonder drops... Take them before you go to bed."

He suggested something from every shelf... There was something for every disorder, every symptom, every obsession... Patients are amazingly greedy. As long as they've got some slop to put in their mouths, they're satisfied, they're glad to get out. They're afraid you might call them back.

With his Santa Claus act I've seen Gustin reduce to ten minutes a consultation that would have taken hours if handled conscientiously. But I myself had nothing to learn in that line. I had my own system.

I wanted to talk to him about my Legend. We'd found the first part under Mireille's bed. I was badly disappointed when I reread it. The passage of time hadn't helped my romance any. After years of oblivion a child of fancy can look pretty tawdry... Well, with Gustin I could always count on a frank, sincere opinion. I tried to put him in the right frame of mind.

"Gustin," I said. "You haven't always been the mug you are today, bogged down by circumstances, work, and thirst, the most disastrous of servitudes... Do you think that, just for a moment, you can revive the poetry in you?... are your heart and cock still capable of leaping to the words of an epic, sad to be sure, but noble... resplendent? You feel up to it?"

Gustin stayed where he was, half dozing on his step-ladder, in front of his samples and the wide-open medicine cabinet. Not a word out of him, he didn't want to interrupt me.

"It's the story," I informed him, "of Gwendor the Magnificent, Prince of Christiania... Here we are... He is breathing his last... as I stand here talking to you... his blood is pouring from a dozen wounds... Gwendor's army has just suffered a terrible defeat... King Krogold himself caught sight of him in the thick of the fray... and clove him in twain... Krogold is no do-nothing king... He metes out his own justice... Gwendor had betrayed him... Death comes to Gwendor and is about to finish his job... Get a load of this:

"The tumult of battle dies down with the last glow of daylight... The last of King Krogold's guards vanish in the distance. The death rattles of a vast army rise up in the shadows. Victors and vanquished give up their souls as best they can... The silence stifles their cries and moans, which become gradually weaker and less frequent...

"Crushed beneath a heap of his followers, Gwendor the Magnificent is still losing blood. At dawn Death stands before him." 'Hast thou understood, Gwendor?'" 'I have understood, O Death. I have understood since the beginning of this day... I have felt in my heart, in my arm as well, in my friends" eyes, even in the step of my charger, a slow, sad spell akin to sleep... My star was failing in thine icy grip... Everything began to leave me! O Death! Great is my remorse! Endless my shame... Behold these poor corpses!... An eternity of silence will not soften my lot...'" 'There is no softness or gentleness in this world, Gwendor, but only myth! All kingdoms end in a dream...'" 'O Death, give me a little time... a day or two. I must find out who betrayed me...'" 'Everything betrays, Gwendor... The passions belong to no one, even love is only the flower of life in the garden of youth.'

"And very gently Death gathers up the prince... He has ceased to resist... His weight has left him... And then a beautiful dream takes possession of his soul... The dream that often came to him when he was little, in his fur cradle, in the Chamber of the Heirs, close to his Moravian nurse in the castle of King René..."

Gustin's arms dangled between his legs. "Well, how do you like it?" I asked him.

He was on his guard. He wasn't too eager to be rejuvenated. He resisted. He wanted me to explain the whole thing to him, the whys and wherefores. That's not so easy. Such things are as frail as butterflies. A touch and they fall to pieces in your hands and you feel soiled. What's the use? I didn't press the matter.

In going on with my Legend I might have consulted some sensitive soul... well versed in fine feelings... in all the innumerable shadings of love...

I prefer to manage on my own.

Sensitive souls are often impotent. They need to be whipped. There's no getting away from it. Anyway, let me describe King Krogold's castle:

"... A great monster cowering in the heart of the forest, vast crushing hulk, hewn out of the rock... kneaded from bilging foulness, credences edged with friezes and redans... dungeons upon dungeons... from the distant seashore the crests of the forest ride in to break like waves against the outer walls...

"The lookout, wide-eyed for fear of being hanged... Higher... still higher... On the summit of More-hande, on the tower of the Treasure House, the banner flaps in the gale... It bears the royal arms. A snake beheaded, bleeding at the neck. Traitors, beware! Gwendor has paid for his crime... ."

Gustin was done in. He was dozing. In fact, he was sound asleep. I locked up his medicine cabinet. "Let's get out of here," I said to him. "We'll take a walk by the Seine. It'll do you good." He didn't want to move. I kept at him and he finally agreed. I suggested a little café on the other side of the Île aux Chiens. When we got there, he fell asleep again in spite of the coffee. Not a bad idea, I admit. It feels pretty good in those bistros around four o'clock... Three artificial flowers in a tin vase. The riverfront is deserted. Even the old soak at the bar is beginning to accept the idea that the *patronne* won't listen to him any more. I leave Gustin alone. The next tugboat is sure to wake him. The cat jumps off the old woman's lap and comes over to sharpen his claws.

The way Gustin turns up his hands when he sleeps, it's easy to read his future. A man's whole life is in his palms. With Gustin it's the life line that's prominent. With me it's luck, the fate line. My chances of long life don't look too good. I wonder when it will be. I've got a furrow at the base of my thumb... Will it be an arteriole bursting in my encephalon? Or in the central gyrus?... Or in that little convolution of the third ventricle?... Metitpois often used to point out that spot in the morgue... A stroke is a tiny little thing... A little break in the gray mass, no bigger than a pinprick... But the soul has passed through, carbolic acid and all... Unfortunately it might turn out to be a neoplasm of the rectum... I'd give a lot for the arteriole... Your health!... Metitpois was a real master. We used to spend whole Sundays poking around in the grooves... investigating the different ways of dying... That fascinated the old man... He wanted to get an idea of how it would be. He personally hoped for a nice cozy flooding of both heart ventricles at once when his time came... He was laden with honors!...

"The most exquisite deaths, remember that, Ferdinand, are those that attack us in our most sensitive tissues..." He had a precious, elaborate, subtle way of talking, like the men of Charcot's day. His prospecting of the Rolandic, the third ventricle, and the gray nucleus didn't do him much good... in the end he died of a heart attack, under circumstances that were anything but cozy. An attack of angina pectoris that lasted twenty minutes. He held out for a hundred and twenty seconds with his classical memories, his resolutions, the example of Caesar... But for eighteen minutes he screamed like a stuck pig... his diaphragm was being ripped out, his living guts... a thousand open razors had been plunged into his aorta... He tried to vomit them out at us... I'm not exaggerating. He crawled out into the living room... He damn near hammered his chest in... He bellowed into the carpet... in spite of the morphine... You could hear him all over the house and out in the street... He ended up under the piano. When the cardiac arterioles burst one by one, it's quite a harp... it's too bad nobody ever comes back from angina pectoris. There'd be wisdom and genius to spare.

We'd done enough meditating, it would soon be time for the venereal patients. That was at La Pourneuve, out past La Garenne. We worked together there. Just as I had foreseen, a tugboat whistle blew. It was time for us to be going. The venereal clinic was quite a place. While waiting for their injections, the clappers and syphilitics got acquainted. There was embarrassment at first, then they got to enjoy it. As soon as it was dark in the winter, they'd rush out to meet near the slaughterhouse down the street. Those people are always in a terrible hurry. They're afraid that sweet little erection won't come back. Mother Vitruve had figured it all out on her way to see me... The youngsters with their first dose... it makes them melancholy, it really gets them down... She used to wait for them at the exit... Motherly tenderness was her act... touching sympathy..." It burns pretty bad, doesn't it, boy? I know how it is... I've nursed them... I've got an amazing kind of herb tea... Why don't you come home with me, I'll make you some..." Two or three cups of coffee and the kid would come across. One night there was a terrible shambles down by the wall, an Algerian with a hard-on like a horse was buggering a little baker's boy for the hell of it, right near the night watchman's cabin. The watchman, who was an old hand at watching, took it all in... first the kid sighed, then he whimpered, and then he began to howl. He writhed and struggled, there were four of them holding him... Even so he got away and ran into the old man's cabin for protection. And the watchman locked the door.

"He got himself finished off. Believe it or not," said Vitruve. "I could see the watchman through the blinds. The two of them were at it. Birds of a feather if you ask me."

She didn't believe in sentiments. She took the lowest view and she was right. To get to La Pourneuve you had to take the bus. "You can spare five minutes," Gustin said. He wasn't in any hurry. We sat down in the bus shelter, the one before the bridge.

It was right there on the riverfront, at Number 18, that my parents went broke in the winter of '92. That was a long time ago. Their business was "Notions, Flowers, Feathers." There was only one shop window and all they had in it was three hats. The Seine froze over that year. I was born in May. The springtime—that's me. I suppose it's our fate, but you get sick of growing old, of seeing everything around you change, the houses, the numbers, the streetcars, the hairdos. Short dresses, creased hats— who cares?—the horseless carriage, the future belongs to aviation—it's all the same! It's all a drain on your attention. I don't feel like changing anymore. There are plenty of things I could complain about, but I'm stuck with them. I'm a mess, but I adore myself as much as the Seine stinks. The day they remove the hook-shaped lamp post from the corner by Number 12, I'll be very sad. Man is temporary, I know that, but we've already temporized enough for my money.

There come the barges... Nowadays each one has a heart of its own. It thuds loud and sullen in the echoing darkness of the arches. Enough of that. I'm falling apart. I'll stop complaining. But don't let them pile on any more. Things seem pretty crummy, but if they could carry us away with them, we'd die of poetry. In a way that wouldn't be bad. Gustin agreed with me about all those endearing little things, except that he looked to the bottle for forget-fulness. Why not?... There was always a little beer and nostalgia in his Gallic moustache.

At the venereal clinic we used to mark vertical bars on a big sheet of paper as we went along... That was all there was to it. A red stroke: Salvarsun. Green: mercury. And so on. The rest was routine... All we had to do was pump the juice into their buttocks or the bend of their arms... It was like larding a roast. Green!... Arm! Yellow... get those pants down!... Red!... Both buttocks... Another one in the ass!... Ditto! Bismuth! Blue! Dripping vein! Swine! Get those pants on!... Swab that arm!... The rhythm was merciless. Batches and batches of them... Endless lines... Limp cocks... pricks... dripping peckers... oozing. Festering... Starched sheets, as stiff as cardboard! Clap!... Queen of the world! The ass is its throne! Heated summer and winter!...

Sometimes the poor bastards are good and worried... but after a while they start passing each other sucker's remedies and screwing harder than ever... as long as Julienne doesn't notice

... They'll never come back... lying to us... howling for joy... urethra full of razor blades! Prick split in two! Cock in mouth. Get that crack ready!

Here's case history Number 34, timid little white-collar worker with dark glasses, wise guy. Every six months he goes to the Cour d'Amsterdam and gets a dose on purpose, so as to expiate by the rod... he pisses his razor blades into the little halfwits he meets through the ads... It's his way of saying his prayers, as he puts it. Number 34 is nothing but one big microbe. Here's what he wrote in our toilet: "I'm the terror of all cunts... I've buggered my big sister... I've had it twelve times." He's a punctual customer, quiet, well behaved, and always glad to be back.

That's our bread and butter. It's not as bad as working on the railroad.

When we got to La Pourneuve, Gustin said: "Say, Ferdinand, just now... while I was dozing, don't try to tell me different, you read the lines of my hand... Well, what did you see?"

I knew what was worrying him: his liver. It had been sensitive around the edges for a long time, and lately he'd been having awful nightmares... He was building up to a cirrhosis. In the morning I heard him throwing up in the sink... I told him it was nothing, why upset him? The damage was done. The main thing was that he should keep his jobs.

At La Jonction he'd landed his job in the welfare bureau soon after taking his degree. Thanks to a little abortion, that's the long and the short of it... the girl friend of a city councillor who was very conservative at the time... Gustin had just set himself up next door, he was poor as a churchmouse. It had come off smoothly, his hand hadn't begun to shake. The next time it was the mayor's wife. Another triumph!... Out of gratitude they had appointed him charity doctor.

In the beginning everybody had liked him in his new job. And then all of a sudden they didn't like him... they were sick of his mug and everything about him... they couldn't stand him. So they did everything in their power to make life miserable for him. They ran him down, accusing him of everything imaginable, of having dirty hands, of getting his doses wrong, of not knowing which drugs were poisonous... of bad breath... of wearing buttoned shoes... When they'd tormented him so much he was ashamed to be seen in the street and after threatening a thousand times to fire him like a fart, they changed their minds and began to tolerate him for no good reason, except that they were sick of regarding him as a punk…

All the filth, the envy, the vexation of the district had put its mark on his map. He'd suffered all the gall and rancor of the pen-pushers in his clinic. The hangovers of the 14,000 alcoholics of the district, the gastric catarrhs, the excruciating stoppages of the 6,422 cases of clap that he wasn't able to cure, the ovarian pangs of the 4,376 menopause cases, the querulous anxiety of 2,266 sufferers from high blood pressure, the irreconcilable contempt of 722 bilious headaches, the persecution mania of 47 tapeworm owners, plus the 352 mothers of children with worms, and the nondescript mob, the vast horde of masochists with manias of every kind, the eczema patients, the albuminous, the diabetic, the fetid, the palsied, the vaginous, the useless, the "too muches," the "not enoughs," the constipated, the repentant queers, whole shipments of murderers had been flowing over his face, cascading under his glasses morning and afternoon for thirty years.

At La Jonction he lived right in the middle of the shit-house, directly over the X-ray room. He had his three-room apartment, and it was a good solid stone building, not a plywood box like nowadays. But to hold your own against life you need dikes ten times higher than in Panama and little invisible sluices. He'd been living there since the Exposition, the big one, since the happy days of Argenteuil.

Now there were big *"buildings"* all around the place.

Occasionally Gustin would still attempt a little distraction… He'd bring in a little cutie, but that didn't happen too often. His great sorrow came back to him as soon as any sentiment started up… after the third meeting. He preferred to drink… There was a bistro across the street with a green front and a banjo player on Sundays. It was handy for the French fries, the girl really knew how to make them. The rotgut burned his innards… For my part, I haven't even tried to drink since I've had that buzzing in my ears day and night. It knocks me out, it makes me look like I had cholera. Gustin auscultates me now and then. He doesn't tell me what he thinks either. That's the one thing we're discreet about. I've got my troubles too, I have to admit it. He knows my case, he tries to cheer me up: "Go on, Ferdinand, go ahead and read, I'll listen to the damn thing. Not too fast, though. And cut out the gestures. It wears you out and it makes me dizzy."

"After the battle King Krogold, his knights, his pages, his brother the archbishop, the clerics of his camp, the whole court, went to the great tent in the middle of the bivouac and dropped with weariness. The heavy gold crescent, a gift from the caliph, was nowhere to be found… Ordinarily it surmounted the royal dais. The captain entrusted with its safekeeping was beaten to a pulp. The king lies down, tries to sleep… He is still suffering from his wounds. He wakes. Sleep refuses to come… He reviles the snorers. He rises. He steps over sleepers, crushing a hand here and there, leaves the tent… Outside he is transfixed with the cold. He limps, but still he makes his way. A long file of wagons rings the camp. The sentries have fallen asleep. Krogold moves along the deep trenches that defend the camp… He talks to himself, he stumbles, recovers his balance just in time. Something is glistening at the bottom of the ditch, an enormous blade. It trembles… A man is there, holding the glittering object in his arms. Krogold leaps, overturns him, pins him down, it's a common soldier, and slits his throat like a pig with his short sword. 'Glug, glug!' the thief gurgles through the hole. He drops everything. It's all over. The king bends down, picks up the caliph's crescent. He climbs out of the ditch. He falls asleep in the mist… The thief has had his just deserts."

About that time the crash came and I almost got fired from the clinic. Gossip again.

I heard about it from Lucie Keriben, who had a dress shop on Maidenform Boulevard. Lots of people came to her shop and they gossiped a good deal. She let me in on some pretty rotten rumors. So vicious in fact that it couldn't have been anybody but Mireille… I wasn't mistaken. Pure calumny of course. She was spreading it around that I had been organizing orgies with some of my female patients in the neighborhood. Really lousy stuff… Secretly Lucie Keriben was kind of glad to see me having a little trouble… She was jealous.

So I wait for Mireille to come home, I hide in the Impasse Viviane, where I knew she'd have to come by. I wasn't making enough money yet to go off and write full time… I was still good for another hitch of bad luck. I was in a foul humor. I see her coming… she passes in front of me. I give her a kick in the seat that sends her sailing off the sidewalk. She gets my meaning, but she won't talk. She wanted to see her aunt first. The little bitch wouldn't come clean. I couldn't get a word out of her.

She'd spread all that gossip to get me worried... then I'd hurry up and give them what they were after. Violence was no use. Especially with Mireille, it only made her more spiteful than ever. She wanted to get married. To me or somebody else. She was fed up with factories. At sixteen she'd already worked in seven of them in the western suburbs.

"No more job," she'd announce. At the Goody Gum-drops English candy factory she'd caught the director getting sucked off by an apprentice. What a place! For six months she tossed dead rats into the big sugar vat. At Saint-Ouen she'd been snagged by a forelady, who'd taken to swotting her in the washroom. They had walked off the job together.

Mireille knew all about capitalism before she even began to menstruate. At the free camp in Marty-sur-Oise there had been fingerplay, fresh air, and rousing speeches. She had developed nicely. On Federates' Day,[97] she was an honor to the settlement house, it was she who brandished Lenin on a pole from La Courtine to Père-Lachaise. The way she came swaggering down the street... the cops were flabbergasted. And with those luscious legs she had the whole boulevard horning out the *International*.

The little pimps at the dance hall where she hung out didn't realize what a number they had on their hands. She was still a minor and scared of the vice squad. For a while she tagged along with Robert, Gégène, and Gaston. But they were building up to a mess of trouble... She would be their downfall.

I could expect just about anything from Vitruve and her niece, especially Vitruve; she knew too much about me not to make use of it some day.

I appeased them with money, but the kid wanted more, she wanted the whole works. When I tried to get around her with affection, it looked mighty suspicious to her. I'll take her out to the Bois, I said to myself. She's got a grudge against me. I've got to do something to catch her interest. I had my plans for the Bois, I'd tell her a nice story, I'd flatter her vanity.

"Ask your aunt," I say. "You'll be home before midnight... Wait for me at the Café Byzance."

So there we go.

After the Porte Dauphine she was already in a better humor. She liked the swanky neighborhoods. At the Hôtel Méridien it was the bedbugs that got her down. When she picked up a little boyfriend and had to take her slip off, the marks made her feel ashamed. They all knew it was bedbug bites... They were all familiar with the liquids and the stuff you burn... Mireille's dream was a room without bugs... If she had cleared out then, her aunt would have had her brought back. She relied on her for the dough she brought in, but there was also a little pimp, Bébert from Val-du-Grâce, who had the same ideas. He ended up on snow. He'd been reading the *Journey*...

As we were approaching the Cascade, I began to get confidential...

"I know you've got a boyfriend in the post office who gets a kick out of letting you whip him..."

She was too happy to put on airs or beat about the bush. She told me all about it. But when we got to the Pré Catalan, she was afraid to go on, the' darkness frightened her. She thought I was taking her into the woods to beat her up. She felt in my pockets to see if I had a rod. I didn't have a thing. She felt my pecker. On account of the passing cars, I suggested we go over to the island where we could talk more at our ease. She was a slut, she had a hard time coming and danger appealed to her. The youngsters rowing on the lake lost control, got tangled in the branches, cursed, tipped, and ruined their little lanterns.

"Listen to the ducks gagging in the diluted urine!"

"Mireille," I say, once we were settled. "I know you're a champion liar... one thing you don't trouble your head about is the truth..."

"Go on," she says. "If I were to repeat a tenth of what I heard..."

---

[97] Federates' Day *(le jour des Fédérés)*. Fédérés was the name given to the Paris members of the National Guard at the time of the Commune. Many thousands of them were executed by MacMahon's troops after the fall of the Commune. *Le jour des Fédérés* (May 27) is a day devoted to their memory by left-wing parties and organizations.

"Okay," I say, "you can turn that off... I'm full of indulgence for you... I'd even call it weakness. Not on account of your body... or your face or your nose... What attracts me is your imagination... I'm a voyeur. You tell me dirty stories... And I'll tell you a beautiful legend... Is it a bargain?... fifty-fifty... you'll be getting the best of it..."

That appealed to her. She liked talking business... I filled her in... I guaranteed there'd be plenty of princesses, yards and yards of genuine velvet, brocade to the very linings, furs and jewels... beyond imagining... we were in perfect agreement about the setting and even the costumes. And then at last our story started in:

"We are in Bredonnes in Vendée... The city is making ready for a tournament...

"Here come the courtiers in fine array... naked wrestlers... mountebanks... their coach rides by... plowing through the crowd... Pancakes frying... three knights in damascened armor… they have come from far away… . from the South... from the North... their bold challenges ring out...

"Here comes Thibaud the Wicked, a troubadour... at daybreak he reaches the city gate along the towpath. He is weary and footsore... He has come to Bredonnes in quest of haven and shelter... and to seek out Joad the Dissembler, the sheriff's son, to remind him of a sinister affair, the murder of an archer in Paris, near the Pont aux Changes, in their student days...

"Thibaud enters the city... At Sainte-Geneviève ferry he flatly refuses to pay the fee... he comes to blows with the ferryman... The archers appear... they overpower him and drag him away... Here he is, bound hand and foot, foaming at the mouth, in tatters, dragged before the sheriff. He struggles furiously, and flings the ugly story in his face..."

The tone appealed to Mireille, she wanted more. We hadn't got along so well in a long time.

Finally it was time to go home.

There were only a few couples left on the paths. Mireille was all cheered up. She wanted to catch them in the act. We abandoned my beautiful Legend for a furious discussion about whether what women really wanted was to shack up with each other... Mireille, for instance, wouldn't she like to lay her girl friends a little?... goose them maybe?... especially the dainty little ones, the gazelles... what with those athletic haunches of hers... that sumptuous ass...

"What about dildoes?" she remarked. "Sure, that's why we watch. Why we look so hard when girls are having fun. To see if they won't grow one... So they can tear each other to pieces, the bitches. So they can rip each other's guts out. And bleed all over the place. So all their rottenness can come pouring out of them!..."

My sweet little Mireille was well informed. She followed my little show perfectly... I thought I'd better warn her: "If you repeat one word of this in Rancy, I'll make you eat your shoes!" And I grabbed hold of her under the gas lamp. I could already see the triumphant look on her face. I could feel it in my bones that she was going to tell the whole world that I had behaved like a beast... in the Bois de Boulogne! I began to see red... To think that she'd taken me for a ride again. I give her a good smack. She grins. Defiantly.

From the thickets and copses, from all sides, people run out to watch us, by twos and fours, in droves. All brandishing their cocks. The ladies have their skirts hiked up front and back. The brazen, the loose, and the cautious...

"Attaboy, Ferdinand!" the whole lot of them shout. What a noise! It rose up out of the woods. "Give her the works. Clout her! Sock her!" Naturally all that encouragement made me rough.

Mireille begins to shriek and run. I run after her. I knock myself out. I give her some wicked kicks in the rear end. They land with a dull thud. Hundreds of Ranelagh sex-fiends come running up, they collect by the prickloads in front of us, they pull up from behind...

The grass is full of them, thousands are pouring down the drive. More and more of them come stepping out of the darkness... The women's dresses are in tatters, tits torn and dangling… little boys without pants... they knock each other down, trample each other, toss each other up in the air... some are left dangling from the trees... along with smashed-up chairs... An old bag, English, comes along in a little car and sticks her head out the window so far it almost falls off... she was beginning to get in my way. Never had I seen eyes so full of happiness. "Hurray! Hurray!" she shouts without even stopping her car. "Great stuff! You'll crack her ass open. You'll send her sky-high. You'll knock the eternity out of her. Hurray for Christian Science!"

I ran still faster. I ran faster than her car. I gave it everything I had, I was dripping with sweat. As I charged, I thought of my job... I'd be sure to lose it. That gave me the chills: "Mireille! Have pity! I adore you! Will you wait for me, you damn slut! Will you listen to me?"

When we got to the Arc de Triomphe, the whole crowd began to whirl like a merry-go-round. The whole mob was chasing Mireille. The square was littered with corpses. The living were tearing off each other's pricks. The Englishwoman was toting her car over her head at arm's length. Hurray, hurray! She knocks over a bus with it. The traffic is blocked by three files of Mobile Guards with shouldered rifles. All for our benefit. Mireille's dress flies away. The Englishwoman flings herself on the kid, claws at her breasts... trickling, pouring, red all over. We fall, we writhe all together, we strangle each other. Pure bedlam.

The flame under the Arc de Triomphe rises, rises higher, breaks, scatters through the sky... The whole place smells of smoked ham... Then Mireille whispering in my ear, speaking to me at last: "Ferdinand, my darling, I love you!... I admit it, you have wonderful ideas!" The flames rain down on us, everyone picks up a big chunk... We stuff them sizzling and whirling into our flies. The ladies put on bouquets of fire... We fall asleep inside each other.

Twenty-five thousand policemen clear the Place de la Concorde. It was too much for us inside each other. It was too hot. There was smoke coming out. It was hell.

My mother and Vitruve in the next room were worried, they kept coming and going, waiting for my fever to go down. An ambulance had brought me home. I had collapsed on top of a sewer grating on the Avenue Mac-Mahon. The bicycle cops had found me.

Fever or not, I always have such a buzzing in both ears that it can't get much worse. I've had it since the war. Madness has been hot on my trail... no exaggeration... for twenty-two years. That's quite a package. She's tried a million different noises, a tremendous hullabaloo, but I raved faster than she could, I screwed her, I beat her to the tape. That's how I do it. I shoot the shit, I charm her, I force her to forget me. My great rival is music, it sticks in the bottom of my ear and rots... it never stops scolding... it dazes me with blasts of the trombone, it keeps on day and night. I've got every noise in nature, from the flute to Niagara Falls... Wherever I go, I've got drums with me and an avalanche of trombones... for weeks on end I play the triangle... On the bugle I can't be beat. I still have my own private birdhouse complete with three thousand five hundred and twenty-seven birds that will never calm down... I am the organs of the Universe... I provide everything, the ham, the spirit, and the breath... Often I seem to be worn out. My thoughts stagger and sprawl... I'm not very good to them. I'm working up the opera of the deluge. As the curtain falls, the midnight train pulls into the station... The glass dome shatters and collapses... The steam escapes through two dozen valves... The couplings bounce sky-high… In wide-open carriages three hundred musicians soused to the gills rend the air, playing forty-five bars at once...

For twenty-two years she's been trying to carry me off... at exactly midnight... But I can fight back... with twelve pure symphonies of cymbals, two cataracts of nightingales... a whole troupe of seals being roasted over a slow fire... It's bachelor's work... that's for sure. It's my second life. Anyway it's *my* business.

If I mention it now, it's to explain that I had a little attack in the Bois de Boulogne. I often make a lot of noise when I talk. I talk too loud. People make signs at me to lower my voice. I drool a little, I can't help it... It's very hard for me to take an interest in my friends. I tend to forget their existence. I'm preoccupied. Sometimes I puke in the street. Then it stops. It's almost quiet. But the walls begin to shake and the cars go into reverse. The whole earth trembles and me with it. I don't speak... Life begins again. When I get to see God in his place, I'll blast his ear, the inner ear, I've studied those things. I wonder how he'll like that. I'm the Devil's Stationmaster. The day I go, wait and see how the train jumps the track. Monsieur Bizonde, the trussmaker, whom I do little jobs for, will find me paler than ever. He'll get used to it.

I was thinking about all that in my room while my mother and Vitruve were padding about next door.

The gate of hell in your ear is a little atom of nothing. Move it a quarter of a hair's breadth… a micron... and look through. You're done for! That's all. You're damned forever. You ready? No? Do you think you can make it? Kicking in isn't free of charge. A beautiful shroud embroidered with tales—that's what the Pale Lady wants. The last gasp is very demanding. It's the last movie and nothing more to come. A lot of people don't know. You've got to knock yourself out. I'll be up to it soon... I'll hear my ticker give its last slobbery *pfutt*... and then plop! It'll wobble in its aorta... like an old broom handle... It'll be all over. They'll open it up to check... on that sloping table... They won't see my beautiful legend, nor my music either. The Pale Lady will have taken it all... Here I am, madame, I'll say to her, you're the greatest connoisseur of all...

I was dead to the world, but even so I couldn't get Mireille off my mind. I had no doubt about her spilling the dirt all over the place.

"My oh my!" they'd be saying at the clinic... "Ferdinand's been overdoing it. He goes out to the Bois to get laid... (the way they always exaggerate). With Mireille of all people... debauching all our young women... They're putting in a complaint... He's a disgrace to his profession! A rapist and an anarchist..."

No less! It made my blood boil in my bed to think about those fairy tales, I was oozing all over like a toad... I was suffocating... I wriggled and thrashed... I threw off all the covers... Suddenly I felt strong as an ox. But it's perfectly true that those devils were following us! That charred smell all over. An enormous shadow shuts off my view... It's Léonce's hat... An agitator's hat... with a brim as wide as a race track... He must have put out the fire... It's Léonce Poitrat! I'm positive. He's always been shadowing me... He's out to get me. He hangs around the Préfecture a damn sight more than legitimate business warrants... After six o'clock… He's all over the place, always active, organizing the apprentices, doing abortions... He doesn't like me... I give him the creeps. He's out to get me. He admits it.

He's the bookkeeper at the clinic. He wears a flowing bow tie. That hat blocks off part of my sleep... My temperature must be rising... I'm going to explode... At meetings he's the life of the party, you should see him... He can shout for two hours on end at those trade-union blackmail sessions. No one can make Léonce shut up... if anybody tries to change a single word in one of his motions, he blows his top. He can shout louder than a colonel. He's built like a brick shithouse. He can't be beat for hot air and his cock has no equal either, comes up harder than thirty-six biceps. Cast iron. That's him. He's secretary of the Bricklayers and Roofers' Union of Vanves La Révolte. Elected no less. His buddies are proud of Léonce, the lazy pugnacious bastard. For pimping on the labor movement he hasn't his equal.

With all that he wasn't satisfied, he was jealous of me, my ideas, my spiritual treasures, my looks, the way people call me "Doctor." There he was with the ladies, waiting... for me to make up my mind, for me to kick in... Nothing doing. Just to burn him up... I'd stay right on the ground where I was... It would be a miracle... I'd even kiss him in the hope of killing him... by contagion!

What's that noise upstairs... various noises... It's the pianist giving lessons... No, practicing... He's nervous. He must be alone... C... C... C! Not so hot. B... B... Come, come. Try again... E...E...D... It'll come out all right in the end! an arpeggio with the left hand... and now the right hand's perking up... B-sharp! Christ almighty!

Through my window I can see Paris... spread out below me... And then it begins to climb… toward us... toward Montmartre... One roof pushes the next, sharp, cutting, bleeding in the light, streets blue, red, and yellow... Lower down, the Seine, pale mists, a tugboat buffeting the current... with a tired wail. Still farther off, the hills... Everything looks alike... The night will take us in. Is that my concierge banging on the wall?

I must be in pretty bad shape for her to come up... Mother Bérenge is too old for all those stairs... Where can she be coming from?... She crosses my room ever so softly... She doesn't touch the floor. She doesn't even look to right or left... She leaves by the window, out into the void... There she is, off in the darkness above the houses... there she is, over there...D... F... G-sharp... E... Shit! Isn't he ever going to stop? That must be his pupil starting in... When fever spreads through you, life gets as flabby as a barkeeper's belly... You sink into a muddle of entrails. I hear my mother rubbing it in... She's telling Madame Vitruve the story of her life... Over and over again, to make it clear what a time she's had with me. Extravagant... irresponsible... lazy... nothing like his father... he so conscientious... so hardworking... so deserving... so unlucky... who passed on last winter... Sure... she doesn't tell her about the dishes he broke on her bean... Oh no! D... C... E... D-flat! That's his pupil, in trouble again...

skipping sixteenths... he's tangled up in the teacher's fingers... He's skidding... he can't straighten out... his nails are full of sharps... "Watch that beat!" I roar.

My mother doesn't say a word about how he used to drag her through the back room by the hair. The place was really too small to argue in... Not one word about all that... nothing but poetry... Yes, we lived in cramped quarters, but we loved each other so. That's what she was saying. Papa was fond of me, he was so sensitive about every little thing that my behavior... so much to worry about... my alarming propensities, the terrible trouble I gave him... hastened his death... all that grief and anguish affected his heart. Plop! The fairy tales people tell each other... they make a certain amount of sense, but they're a pack of filthy stinking lies... The stinking bitches get so het up filling each other full of bullshit that they drown out the piano... I can puke in peace.

Vitruve is no slouch at telling whoppers either... she lists her sacrifices... Mireille is her whole life... I can't catch it all... I'd better go to the can to vomit... probably a touch of malaria too... brought it back from the Congo... I'm pretty far gone in all directions...

By the time I get back to bed, my mother is in the middle of her courtship... the days when Auguste rode a bike... not to be outdone, the other one goes on shamelessly... about her desperate efforts to save my reputation... at Linuty's... Oh no! I can't stand it! I sit up... I'm at the end of my rope... I can't move... I just lean over and vomit on the other side of the doss. If I've got to be delirious, I'd rather wallow in stories of my own... I see Thibaud the Troubadour... He's always in need of money... He's going to kill Joad's father... Well, at least that will be one father less in the world... I see splendid tournaments on the ceiling... I see lancers impaling each other... I see King Krogold himself... He has come from the north... He had been invited to Bredonnes with his whole court... I see his daughter Wanda, the Blonde, the Radiant... I wouldn't mind jerking off, but I'm too sticky... Joad is horny in love... Oh well, why not... I've got to get back... A sudden surge of bile... The effort makes me bellow... This time my old bitches can't help hearing... They come in and patch me up. I throw them out... in the hallway they start shooting the shit again. After the way they'd been running me down, the tide changes... they discover my good points... they're dependent on me for a good many things...

Better be realistic... they'd been overdoing it... After all, who brings home the bacon?... My mother wasn't making much, working for Monsieur Bizonde, the famous trussmaker... Not enough to get by on... It's hard at her age to make ends meet on a commission basis. And who keeps Madame Vitruve and her niece going with his clever ideas?... Suddenly a new wave of suspicion. They begin to hedge...

"He's a scatterbrained brute... but good-hearted..." You've got to admit that. Yes, of course. There's the rent and groceries to think about... Mustn't exaggerate. They hasten to put each other's minds at rest. My mother is no workingwoman... She says that over and over again, it's her litany... She's a small businesswoman... Our family ran itself ragged for the glory of small business... We're no drunken workers, up to our ears in debt... Oh no! Certainly not... There's a big difference and don't forget it... Three lives, mine, hers, and most of all my father's were ground down by sacrifice... Nobody even knows what became of them... they paid our debts...

And now my mother knocks herself out trying to recapture those lives of ours... she's reduced to her imagination... they've disappeared... our pasts as well. Whenever she has a free moment, she tries to put things back on their feet... but inevitably they collapse again...

She flies into terrible rages if I even begin to cough, because my father had a chest like a bull, good strong lungs... I can't stand the sight of her anymore, she gives me the creeps. She wants me to share in her fantasies... I'm not in the mood. One of these days I'm going to do something bad! I want to have my own fantasies... C! E! A! the pupil is gone. The pianist is relaxing... Doing a *berceuse*... I wish Emilie would come up... She comes every evening to straighten out... She hardly says anything... I forget she's there... Ah, here she is! She wants me to take some rum... The drunks next door are bawling again...

"He has a high fever... I'm terribly worried," my mother repeats for the hundredth time. "He's so kind to his patients," yacks Vitruve.

At that point I was so hot I dragged myself to the window.

On a long tack across the Étoile my gallant ship glides through the dusk... under full sail... she is heading straight for the Hôtel-Dieu... The whole town is on deck, still and calm. All those dead—I know them all... I even know the helmsman... He's my buddy... The pianist has caught on... He's playing the tune we need: "Black Joe"... for a cruise... to catch the wind and weather... and the lies... If I open the window, it will be cold... Tomorrow I'm going to kill Monsieur Bizonde, who keeps us going... the trussmaker, in his shop... I want him to travel... he never goes out... My vessel groans and pitches over the Parc Monceau... She's slower than last night... She's going to hit the statues... Two ghosts go ashore at the Comédie Française... Three enormous waves carry off the arcades of the rue de Rivoli. The siren screams against my windowpanes... I close my door... A roar of wind... My mother appears with her eyes popping out... She scolds me. Misbehaving as usual. Vitruve comes running... More good advice. I rebel... I give them hell... My fair ship is limping. Those females can wreck the infinite... She's off course, it's shameful... Nevertheless she heels over to port... there's no more graceful craft afloat... My heart follows her... Those bitches would do better to run after the rats that are fouling the rigging... She'll never make that tack with her ropes so taut... got to slacken them... let out three turns before the Samaritaine! I shout all that out over the rooftops... My room is going to sink. I've paid for it, haven't I? Every last cent. With my lousy rotten existence... I shit in my pajamas... What a mess! Things are bad. I'm going to founder at the Bastille. "Ah, if only your father were here"... I hear those words. I explode. It's her again. I turn around. My father, I say, was a skunk! I yell my lungs out... "There was no lousier bastard in the whole universe! from the Galeries-Lafayette to Capricorne..." At first she was stupefied. Transfixed... Then she gets hold of herself. She calls me the lowest of the low. I don't know which way to look. She bursts into tears. She rolls on the carpet in anguish. She rises to her knees. She stands up. She comes at me with the umbrella.

She hauls off and gives me a couple of cracks full in the face. The handle breaks in her hands. She bursts into tears. Vitruve throws herself between us. She never wants to see me again. That's what she thinks of me. She sobs so hard the whole place shakes... All my father left behind him was his memory and carloads of trouble. Memory is an obsession with her. The deader he is the more she loves him. Like a she-dog that can't get enough... But I won't put up with it... I'll protest if it kills me. I repeat that he was a sneak, brute, hypocrite, and yellow in every way. She starts up again. She's ready to die for her Auguste. I'll smash her face. Hell! I haven't got malaria for nothing. She upbraids me, she lets herself go, she has no consideration for the state I'm in. I'm in a blind rage. I bend over and lift up her skirt. I see her calf as skinny as a poker, without any flesh on it. her stocking all sagging, it's foul... I've seen it all my life... I puke on it, the works...

"Ferdinand, you're out of your mind!" She backs away, gives a start and runs for it. "You're out of your mind!" she cries again from the stairs.

I stagger and fall flat. I hear her limp all the way down. The window is still wide open... I think of Auguste, he liked boats too... He was an artist at heart... He had no luck... he drew storms now and then on my blackboard...

The maid is still there beside my bed. "Lie down here in your clothes," I say. "We're cruising... My ship has lost all her lights over the Gare de Lyon... I'll give the captain a receipt, so he'll come to the Quai d'Arago when they set up the guillotines... the quay of morning..."

Emilie laughs... she doesn't get it... "Tomorrow," she says. "Tomorrow..." And she goes back to her kid.

Then I was really alone!

Then I saw the thousands and thousands of little skiffs returning high above the Left Bank... Each one had a shriveled little corpse under its sail... and his story... his little lies to catch the wind with.

The last century—I can talk about it, I saw it end... It pulled out by the road past Orly... Choisy-le-Roy... Rungis, where my aunt Armide lived, the eldest of the family...

She talked about all sorts of things that nobody remembered. The day we picked for our visit was a Sunday in the fall, before the hardest months. We wouldn't be back until spring for the surprise of finding her still alive...

Old memories stay with you... but they're delicate, fragile... I'm sure we took the horsecar in front of the Châtelet... We and our cousins would climb up to the top deck. My father stayed home.

My cousins would joke; we'd never find Aunt Armide in Rungis, they said. All alone in the house without a maid, she was sure to have been murdered, and what with the floods we probably wouldn't be notified until it was too late.

So we'd jog along to Choisy along the river. It took hours. That gave me a little fresh air.

We'd be taking the train back.

When we got to the end of the line, we'd have to hurry. Over the big cobblestones... my mother would tug at my arm to make me keep up... We'd meet other relatives, also on their way to visit the old lady. My mother would have trouble with her bun, her veil, her straw hat, and her hairpins and hatpins... When her veil was wet, she'd chew at it in irritation. The avenues on the way to my aunt's were full of chestnuts.] couldn't pick any up, we hadn't a moment to lose... Beyond the road there were trees, fields, an embankment, clods of earth, and then the country...

farther still, countries unknown... China... and after that nothing at all.

We were in such a hurry to get there that I made in my pants... To tell the truth I was in such a hurry all through my childhood that I had shit on my ass until I was drafted... We were all wringing wet by the time we got to the first houses. It was a sweet little village, I realize that now; with quiet little nooks, winding lanes, moss, all picturesque as hell. The fun was over when we reached her gate. It squeaked. My aunt had sold "ready to wear" at the Carreau du Temple for close on fifty years... All her savings had gone into her cottage in Rungis.

She lived at the back of one room, beside the fireplace, always in her armchair, waiting for people to come to see her. She kept the blinds drawn on account of her eyes.

Her cottage was in the Swiss style; that was all the rage in those days. Out in front there were some fish pickling in a smelly pool. A little more walking and you'd be at the door. Then darkness swallowed you up. You touched something soft. "Come closer. Don't be afraid, little Ferdinand..." That meant smooching. I couldn't get out of it. It was cold and prickly and then kind of warm at the corner of her mouth; the taste was awful. Somebody lighted a candle. The relations huddled together and began to gossip. It gave them a kick to see the relic kiss me... I was sick to my stomach from just that one kiss... and from walking too fast. But when she began to talk, they all had to shut up. They didn't know how to answer her. My aunt conversed only in the imperfect subjunctive. Old-fashioned. It cramped everybody's style. It was time for her to be moving along.

There had never been a fire in that fireplace behind her. "The draft was never quite sufficient..." The real reason was economy.

Before we left, Armide offered little cakes. Dry-as-dust cookies taken from a tightly covered receptacle that was opened twice a year. Everyone declined of course... they weren't children anymore... The cookies were for me, Ferdinand!... To show my pleasure and appreciation I had to jump up and down for joy... My mother pinched me, that was my signal to perform... I ran out into the garden, always the little imp, and spat it all out to the fish.

Everything that's washed up was there in the darkness, behind my aunt, behind her armchair. There was my grandfather Leopold, who never came back from India, there was the Virgin Mary, Cyrano de Bergerac, Félix Faure, Lustucru,[98] and the imperfect subjunctive. That's how it was.

I let the relic kiss me once again before leaving... And then hurried departure; out through the garden at breakneck speed. In front of the church we ditched some cousins, the ones who were going to Juvisy. In kissing me they gave off every known smell, rancid breath between beard and shirt front. My mother's limp was worse from sitting still a whole hour, her leg had gone to sleep.

When we came to the cemetery at Thiais, we'd dash in for a minute. There were two more of our dead at the end of one of the lanes. We scarcely looked at their tombs and lit out like thieves. We'd catch up with Clotilde, Gustave, and Gaston after the crossroads at Belle-Épine. My mother was dragging her bad leg and bumping into things. She even sprained her ankle once trying to carry me just before the grade crossing.

---

[98] Lustucru. An old-time clown. The name was manufactured from *"L'eûsses-tu cru?"*—"Would you have believed it?"

In the darkness our only thought was to reach the big apothecary jar at the pharmacy. That was on the main street, it meant we were saved... Against a background of raw gaslight gusts of music flew from the clattering doors of the wineshops. We felt threatened and quickly crossed the street. My mother was afraid of drunks.

The inside of the station was like a box, the waiting room was full of smoke, with a rickety oil lamp dangling from the ceiling. Huddled together around the little stove, the travelers hawked and coughed and sizzled in their heat. There's the humming of the train, it crashes in like thunder, you'd think it was tearing the whole place apart. The travelers shake themselves, break into a run, and storm the carriages like a hurricane. We're the last two. I get a good clout to teach me not to play with the door handle.

At Ivry we have to get out; we take advantage of our day out to drop in on Madame Héronde, the seamstress. She mends all our lace, especially the old things that are so fragile and hard to dye.

She lived in a shack at the far end of Ivry, on the rue des Palisses, in the middle of the fields. This was a good chance to stir her up a little. Her work was never ready on time. The customers were ferocious; nowadays nobody would dare to gripe the way they did then. I used to see my mother in tears almost every night over the seamstress and the lace that never came back. If our customer got peeved about her torn Valenciennes, she wouldn't be back for a whole year.

The plain beyond Ivry was even more dangerous than the way to Aunt Armide's. No comparison. Sometimes there were toughs. They'd insult my mother. If I turned around, I'd get a smack. When the mud got so soft and mushy that your shoes came off in it, it meant we hadn't far to go. Madame Héronde's shack was in the middle of an empty lot. Her mutt heard us and began to bark like mad. We caught sight of the window.

Our visit always came as a great surprise to Madame Héronde; she couldn't get over it. My mother upbraided her, unloaded her grievances. Finally both of them burst into tears. There was nothing for me to do but wait and look out... as far as possible... across the plain, heavy with darkness, that stretched out as far as the banks of the Seine and ended in a long cluttered line of housing lots.

Our seamstress did her mending by the light of an oil lamp. The smoke choked her and the light was ruining her eyes. My mother kept after her to have gas put in. "It's really indispensable," she said again as we were leaving.

Mending tiny little insets, pieces as delicate as spider webs, she was certainly ruining her eyes. It wasn't only self-interest that made my mother say these things, but friendship as well. I never visited Madame Héronde's shack when it wasn't dark.

"They're installing it in September," she said every time. It was a lie to make my mother leave her alone... my mother thought well of her for all her faults.

My mother was in mortal terror of thieving seamstresses. Madame Héronde had no equal for honesty. She never did us out of a single penny. And yet she was poor as a church-mouse and we entrusted her with treasures! Whole chasubles of Venetian lace, such as you wouldn't even see in a museum nowadays. When my mother spoke of her later on in the family circle, it was with enthusiasm. It brought tears to her eyes. "She was a real fairy, I've got to admit. It's too bad she couldn't keep her word. She never delivered anything on time, never once..." The fairy died before the gas was installed, of fatigue, carried off by the flu, and also no doubt by the sorrow of having a skirt chaser for a husband... She died in childbirth... I remember her funeral well. It was at Le Petit Ivry. There were only the three of us, me and my parents, her husband hadn't bothered! He was a handsome man, he drank up every cent he ever owned. He spent whole years at the bar on the corner of the rue Gaillon. We saw him there for at least another ten years every time we passed. And then he disappeared.

When we left Madame Héronde's, it wasn't the end of our visits. At Austerlitz we had another gallop and then a bus ride to the Bastille. The Wurzems had their workshop near the Cirque d'Hiver. They were Alsatians, cabinetmakers, a whole family of them. It was Wurzem who antiqued all our small pieces of furniture, the kidney-shaped tables, consoles, and so on. For the last twenty years he'd done nothing else, first for Grandma, then for other people. Marquetry doesn't last, it's a perpetual headache. Wurzem was an artist, an excellent craftsman. They all of them lived in the shavings, his wife, his aunt, a brother-in-law, two female cousins, and four children. He was never on time either. His vice was fishing. He'd often spend a whole week by the Canal Saint-Martin instead of filling his orders. My mother would shout herself blue in the face. He always had some insolent comeback. Then he'd apologize. The whole family would burst into tears; there'd be nine of them crying and we were only two. They were a shiftless lot. They never paid their rent. In the end they were thrown out and had to take refuge in the "jungle" off the rue Caulaincourt.

Their shack was down at the bottom of a pit, you had to walk over planks to get to it. We'd start shouting from far off and head for their lantern. What tempted me at their place was to upset the glue pot that was always teetering on top of the stove. One day I made up my mind. When my father heard about it, he told my mother that I'd strangle her one day, it was my nature. He could see it all.

The nice thing about the Wurzems was that they never bore a grudge. After the worst bawlings out, as soon as you'd give them a little money, they'd be singing again. Nothing ever got them down. Shiftless, never a look ahead. That's the working class for you. No sense of responsibility like us. My mother always seized on these incidents as object lessons to show me how not to live. I thought they were very nice. I went to sleep in their shavings. My mother had to shake me when it was time to race down to the boulevard and jump into the Halle-aux-Vins bus. I loved the inside of it, because of the big crystal eye that lit up the faces all along the benches. Pure magic.

The horses gallop down the rue des Martyrs, the people move aside to let us pass. Even so we're very late in getting back to the shop.

Grandma is griping in her corner, Auguste, my father, pulls his cap way down over his eyes. He's pacing about like a lion on the bridge of a ship. My mother collapses on the stool. She's in the wrong, there's no use explaining. Nothing we had done that day appeals to them. Finally we close the shop... We say good-bye politely. The three of us set out for home and bed. It's still an awful hike. We lived on the other side of the Bon Marché.

My father wasn't an easy man to get along with. When he wasn't in his office he always wore a cap, the nautical kind. It had always been his dream to be the captain of an ocean liner. That dream made him mighty bitter.

Our apartment on the rue de Babylone looked out on the Mission. The priests sang a good deal, even at night they'd get up to sing a few more hymns. We couldn't see them on account of the wall that was right against our window. That made it kind of dark.

My father didn't make much at the Coccinelle Fire Insurance Company.

When we got to the Tuileries, he often had to carry me. The cops all had big bellies in those days. They hung around under the lamps.

The Seine is surprising to a kid, the way the wind ruffles the reflections, and the black emptiness below, shifting and grumbling. We turned down the rue Vaneau, and then we were home. There was always a to-do about lighting the hanging lamp. My mother didn't know how. My father Auguste fumbled, cursed, swore, and kept upsetting the holder and the mantle.

My father was a stout, blond man who'd fly into a rage over nothing, with a chubby round nose like a baby's over an enormous moustache. He rolled his eyes ferociously when he was angry. He never remembered anything but troubles. He'd had plenty. He made a hundred and ten francs a month at the insurance company.

With his yen to serve in the navy, he had pulled seven years in the artillery. He would have liked to be imposing, well-off, and respected. At the Coccinelle office they treated him like dirt. His pride tormented him and he couldn't stand the monotony. He had nothing in his favor but his school diploma, his moustache, and his lofty principles. To make things worse I got born. We were on the downgrade.

We still hadn't eaten. My mother was pottering about with pots and pans. She had stripped to her petticoat for fear of grease spots. She kept muttering that her Auguste didn't appreciate her good intentions and the difficulties of the business... He sat with his elbows on one corner of the oilcloth table cover, mulling over his troubles... From time to time he put on a scowl to show that he couldn't hold himself in much longer... Still she kept trying to mollify him. But when she tried to pull down the beautiful yellow globe of the hanging lamp, he really flew off the handle. "Clémence! Stop that! Christ almighty! You're going to start a fire. Haven't I told you to use both hands?" He began to bellow something awful, he was so mad I thought he was going to bite his tongue off. In his bad spells he used to turn purple and swell up all over, he rolled his eyes like a dragon. It was horrible to look at. My mother and I were scared stiff. Then he broke a dish and went to bed.

"Turn toward the wall, you little pig! Don't turn around." I had no desire to... I knew... I was ashamed... it was my mother's legs, the skinny one and the fat one... She continued to limp about from one room to the next... He was trying to pick a fight... she insisted on finishing the dishes... She tried to clear the air with a little tune...

And through the holes in the roof The sun shone down upon us...

Auguste, my father, read *La Patrie*. He sat down beside my crib. She came over and kissed him. His storm was subsiding... He stood up and went to the window. He pretended to be looking for something down in the court. He let a resounding fart. The tension was down.

She let a little fart in sympathy and fled kittenishly into the kitchen.

Later they closed their door... the door to their bedroom... I slept in the dining room. The missionaries' hymn came in over the walls... And in the whole rue Babylone there was only a walking horse... clop clop... that late cab...

To raise me my father was always taking on extra jobs. Lempreinte, his boss, humiliated him in every possible way. I knew Lempreinte, he was a redhead who had gone pale, with long golden hairs, just a few of them, instead of a beard. My father had style, elegance came natural to him. That vexed Lempreinte.- He avenged himself for thirty years. He made him do nearly all his letters over again.

When I was still smaller, at Puteaux where they'd put me out to nurse, my parents used to come and see me on Sunday. There was plenty of fresh air. They always paid in advance. Never a cent owing. Not even when things were at their worst. But in Courbevoie, what with worrying and doing without all sorts of things, my mother began to cough. After that she never stopped. It was slug syrup and later on the Raspail method[99] that saved her.

On account of my father's style Monsieur Lempreinte suspected him of fancy ambitions. From the garden of the nurse's place in Puteaux you could look down over the whole of Paris. When Papa came to see me, the wind ruffled his moustache. That's my earliest memory.

After the fashion shop in Courbevoie went bankrupt, my parents had to work twice as hard, they really ran themselves ragged, she as my grandmother's saleswoman, he doing all the overtime he could at La Coccinelle. But the more he exhibited his high-class style, the more Lempreinte detested him. To keep from getting bitter, he took up watercolors. He used to paint at night after supper. They brought me back to Paris. I'd see him in the evening drawing, mostly boats, ships at sea, three-masters in a heavy breeze, black and white or in color. He had it in his blood... later on, memories of his days in the artillery, batteries galloping into position... or he'd do bishops... at the request of his customers... because of the bright robes... And dancing girls with hefty legs... My mother would offer a selection of his watercolors to the peddlers at lunch hour... She did all she could to keep me alive, I just shouldn't have been born.

At Grandma's on the rue Montorgueil she sometimes spat blood in the morning while arranging the sidewalk display. She'd hide her handkerchiefs. Grandma came out... "Wipe your eyes, Clémence. Crying won't help matters..."To get there early enough, we'd get up at daybreak and cross the Tuileries as soon as the housework was done; Papa would turn the mattresses.

The days were no joke. It was exceptional if I didn't cry a good part of the afternoon. In that shop I came in for more slaps than smiles. I apologized for everything I did, I was always apologizing.

We had to be on the lookout for theft and breakage. Junk is fragile. I ruined tons of the stuff, never on purpose. The thought of antiques still makes me sick, but that was our bread and butter. The scrapings of time are sad... lousy, sickening. We sold the stuff over the customer's dead body. We'd wear him down. We'd drown his wits in floods of hokum... incredible bargains... we were merciless... He couldn't win... If he had any wits to begin with, we demolished them... He'd walk out stunned

---

[99] Raspail method. François-Vincent Raspail (1794- 1878) was a chemist and an ardent republican. He wrote books popularizing the principles of medicine and devised a simple, inexpensive method of therapy, intended chiefly for the working class and based principally on camphor and aloes. He was prosecuted (1846) for the illegal practice of medicine.

with the Louis XIII cup in his pocket, the openwork fan with cat and shepherdess wrapped in tissue paper. You can't imagine how they revolted me, grown-ups taking such crap home with them.

During working hours Grandma Caroline ensconced herself behind the Prodigal Son, an enormous tapestried screen. Caroline had an eye for light fingers. Customers are low characters, especially the women. The fancier they dress, the worse crooks they are. A little piece of Chantilly slips like a breeze into a practiced muff.

The shop was hardly a blaze of light... And in the winter it's especially treacherous on account of the ruffles... velvet, furs, canopies big enough to enfold three bosoms... not to mention the long-range boas of all kinds starting from the shoulders, the waves of diaphanous chiffon... Birds of overwhelming sorrow... The lady struts, plowing through piles of bric-a- brac, clucks, retraces her steps... scatters things all over the place... pecking, cackling... finding fault for the hell of it. We were goggle-eyed trying to find something that would appeal to her, there was plenty to choose from... Grandma was always out rustling... looking for white elephants at the auction rooms... she brought back everything, oil paintings, amethysts, whole forests of candelabras, cascades of embroidered tulle, cabochons, pyxes, stuffed animals, armor, parasols, gilded monstrosities from Japan, alabaster bowls and worse, gimcracks without a name, and objects nobody ever heard of.

The lady gushes and burbles in this treasure-house of shards. The heap settles back into place behind her. She overturns, she jingles, she twists and turns. She's just come in to look. It's raining, she's come in out of the rain. When she's had enough, she leaves, promising to come again. Then we have to gather up the rubbish in a hurry. We crawl around on our knees, scraping under the furniture. If nothing's missing, if every handkerchief, knick-knack, piece of cut glass, every gewgaw is accounted for, we heave a great sigh of relief.

Mother slumps down, massaging her leg cramped from standing, speechless with exhaustion. And then just before closing time, the furtive customer steps in out of the darkness. He slips in softly, explains his business in a whisper, he has a small object to sell, a family keepsake, he undoes the newspaper wrapping. We don't think much of it. We'll wash his treasure in the kitchen sink, we'll pay him in the morning. He leaves with a mumbled good-bye... The Panthéon-Courcelles bus races past, almost grazing the shop.

My father comes in from his office. He keeps looking at his watch. He's on edge. We've got to make it fast.

He puts down his hat. He takes his cap from the nail.

We still have to eat our noodles and make our deliveries.

We'd put the light out in the shop. My mother was no cook, but she managed to work up some sort of mess. When it wasn't egg soup it was sure to be macaroni. No mercy. After the noodles we sat still for a moment, a little meditation is good for the stomach. My mother tried to entertain us, to dilute our embarrassment. If I didn't answer her questions, she'd keep on trying. "There's butter in them, you know," she would say gently. The light came from a naked gas jet behind the screen. The plates were in darkness. Stoically my mother helped herself to some more noodles to encourage us... It took a good swig of red wine to keep them down.

The alcove where we ate was also used for the washing and for storing the junk... There were heaps of it, mounds... The stuff that couldn't be patched up, that couldn't be sold, that wasn't fit to be shown, the worst monstrosities. From the transom draperies hung down into the soup. There was also, for some reason or other, a big coal range with an enormous hood that took up half the room. In the end we'd turn over our plates for a smidgin of jam.

It was like living in a filthy museum.

After we moved away from Courbevoie, Grandma and my father stopped talking to each other. Mama kept talking the whole time to keep them from throwing things at each other. Once we had downed our noodles and enjoyed our sampling of jam, we hit the road. The sold article would be wrapped in a big canvas. Usually it was some piece of drawing-room furniture, a "kidney," or occasionally a *poudreuse*. Papa hoisted it up on his shoulders and we'd start for the Place de la Concorde. After the Splashing Fountains I'd be kind of scared. As we headed up the Champs-Élysées, the darkness was immense. He sped along like a thief. I had trouble keeping up. It seemed like he was trying to ditch me.

I'd have liked him to talk to me, all he did was grunt insults at strangers. By the time we reached the Étoile, he was in a sweat. We took a little rest. When we got to the customer's house, we had to look for the service entrance.

When we delivered in Auteuil, my father was in a better humor. He didn't take out his watch so often. I'd climb up on the parapet and he'd tell me all about tugboats... the green lights, the whistle signals between the strings of barges. "She'll be down at the Point-du-Jour in no time." We'd admire the wheezing old tub and wish her a happy journey...

It was when we were going to the Ternes section that he really got into a foul mood, especially if it was a dame... He couldn't stand them. He'd be in a temper before we even got started. I remember one time we were going to the rue Demours. Outside the church he gives me a clout and a vicious kick to make me shake a leg crossing the street. When we got to the customer's house, I couldn't keep from crying. "You little bastard," he shouts at me, "I'll give you something to cry about!..." He climbed up the stairs behind me with his little tea table on his neck. We rang at the wrong door. All the maids looked out. I was squealing like a stuck pig... On purpose... to get his goat! What a ruckus! At last we find the right bell. The maid lets us in. She sympathizes with me. The lady of the house swishes in. "My, what a naughty little boy! He's made his papa angry." He didn't know which way to look. He would have liked to crawl into a drawer. The lady tries to comfort me. She pours my father a glass of cognac. Then she says: "Polish it up, my good man. I fear the rain will leave spots... ." The maid gives him a rag. He gets to work. The lady gives me a piece of candy. I follow her into the bedroom. The maid comes in too. The lady lies down in a mess of lace. All of a sudden she hikes up her dressing gown and shows me her fat legs, her behind, and her clump of hair. Whew! She goes poking around inside with her fingers...

"Come, little darling!... Come, little love!... Come, suck me in there!..." Her voice was ever so soft and tender, no one had ever spoken to me like that before. She opens it out. Oozing.

The maid was doubled up with laughter. That's what held me back. I ran off to the kitchen. I wasn't crying anymore. They gave my father a tip. He didn't dare to put it in his pocket, he just looked at it. The maid was laughing again. " I guess you don't want it," she asked him. He ran out to the stairs. He forgot all about me, I had to race after him in the street. I called him all the way down the avenue. "Papa! Papa!" I caught up with him on the Place des Ternes. We sat down. It wasn't very often that he kissed me. He squeezed my hand.

"Yes, my boy!... Yes, my boy!" he kept repeating as if to himself, looking off into space... He had feelings deep down. I had feelings too. Life has nothing to do with feelings. We went straight back to the rue de Babylone.

My father distrusted his imagination. He talked to himself in corners. He was afraid of being carried away... He must have been steaming inside...

He was born in Le Havre. He knew all about boats. A name that kept coming back to him was that of Captain Dirouane, who had been in command of the *City of Troy* . He'd seen his boat putting out to sea, moving out of the basin. She never came back. She had been lost with all on board off the coast of Florida. "A fine three-mast bark!"

Another, the *Gondriolan*, a Norwegian, overloaded, had crashed into the locks... Bad handling. He told me all about it. Twenty years later the incident still filled him with horror and indignation... And then he'd go back into his corner. And mull things over some more.

His brother Antoine was something else again. With real heroism he had crushed every impulse to wander. He too had been born right near the Great Semaphore... When their father died... he taught French at the lycée... he'd gone straight into the Bureau of Weights and Measures, a steady job. To play it absolutely safe he'd married a young lady in the Statistics Division. But a yearning for far-off places kept plaguing him... He still had adventure in his bones, he never felt buried enough, he kept digging in deeper and deeper.

He and his wife would come to see us on New Year's Day. They were so thrifty, they ate so miserably and never spoke to a soul, that the day they conked out nobody in the neighborhood remembered them. Everybody was surprised. They died in secret, he of cancer, she of abstinence. They found Blanche, his wife, on the Buttes-Chaumont.

That was where they used to spend their vacations. Just the same, it took them forty years, always together, to commit suicide.

My father's sister, Hélène, was a different story. She had wind in her sails. She ended up in Russia. She got to be a whore in St. Petersburg. For a while she had everything, a carriage, three sleighs, a village all her own, with her name on them. She came to see us at the Passage twice in a row, done up like a princess, stunning and happy and all. She came to a tragic end, shot by an officer. She had no willpower. She was all flesh, desire, music. It made my father puke just to think of her. When she heard of her death, my mother said: "What a terrible end! But it's a fit end for an egotist."

Then there was Uncle Arthur. He was no model either. The flesh was too much for him too. My father had a certain liking for him, a kind of weakness. He lived like a regular bohemian, on the fringe of society, in a shanty, shacked up with a housemaid. She worked at the restaurant outside the École Militaire. Thanks to her, there's no denying it, he managed to eat very well. He was a dandy, with a goatee, corduroy pants, pointed shoes, and a long slender pipe. Nothing ever got him down. Making women was his main occupation. He was sick a good deal, seriously so when the rent came due. He'd stay in bed for a week or more at some girl friend's house. When we went to see him on Sundays, he didn't behave very well, especially with my mother. He'd take little liberties with her. That made my old man see red. When we left, he'd swear by eighty thousand devils that we'd never go back.

"Really, that brother of mine! His manners are disgusting!..." But we'd go back all the same.

He would draw boats on his big drawing board, under the skylight; yachts cutting through the foam, that was his style, with gulls all around... Now and then he'd do some work for a catalog, but he had so many debts he always felt discouraged. He was cheerful when doing nothing.

From the cavalry barracks next door you could hear all the bugle calls. Arthur knew all the words that went with them by heart. He'd start in again at every refrain. He made up some smutty ones. My mother and the housemaid went: "Oh! Oh!" Papa was furious because of my tender years.

But the screwiest member of the family was certainly Uncle Rodolphe, he was really off his rocker. He would titter quietly when you spoke to him. He only answered his own questions. That could go on for hours. He insisted on living in the open air. He never consented to have anything to do with a store or an office, not even as a watchman, not even at night. He preferred to take his meals out-of-doors, on a bench. He distrusted the insides of houses. When he was really too hungry, he'd come to see us. He'd turn up in the evening. That meant things were pretty rough.

He made his living carrying baggage in the railroad stations. It was a job that took stamina and he kept at it for more than twenty years. He had an in with the "Urban Express." He ran like a rabbit after cabs and baggage as long as he was able to. His high season was when people were coming back from vacation. His job made him hungry, and always thirsty. The coachmen liked him. He was screwy at the table. He'd stand up with glass in hand, clink it all around, and strike up a song... He'd stop in the middle and burst out laughing without rhyme or reason... and drool all over his napkin.

We'd take him home. He'd still be laughing. He lived on the rue Lepic at the Rendez-vous du Puy de Dôme, a shack on the court. He kept his belongings on the floor, there wasn't a single chair or a table. At the time of the Exposition he became a "troubadour." He'd stand outside the papier-mâché grottoes along the Seine, drumming up trade for "Old Paris." His coat was a patchwork of rags of every color. He'd keep warm by bellowing and stamping his feet. In the evening, when he came to dinner in his carnival rig, my mother made him a hot-water bottle. His feet were always cold. To make matters worse, he took up with the "wench." She was a spieler too. She stood in a painted cardboard grotto at the other entrance. Poor thing, she'd already begun to cough her lungs out. She didn't last three months. She died right there in his room at the Rendez-vous. He didn't want them to take her away. He bolted his door. He came home every night and lay down beside her. It was the smell that put them wise. Then he went raving mad. He didn't understand that things die. They buried her by force. He wanted to carry her all the way to Pantin himself, on a hod.

Finally he went back to work by the Esplanade. My mother was horrified. "Dressed like a scare-crow, in this cold. It's a crime." What upset her most was that he wouldn't wear his overcoat. He had one of Papa's. They sent me to have a look. I was underage, so I could get through the gate without paying.

He was there behind the fence, dressed like a troubadour. All smiles again. "Hello," he said. "Hello, son... D'you see her? D'you see my Rosine?..." He pointed a finger across the Seine... the plain, a point in the mist... "You see her?" I said yes. I never crossed him. I told my parents he was all right. Pure spirit, that was Rodolphe!

Late in 1913 he went away with a circus. We could never find out what had become of him.

We never saw him again.

We left the rue de Babylone to open another shop, to try our luck again. This time it was in the Passage des Bérésinas, between the Stock Exchange and the Boulevards. Our living quarters were over the shop, three rooms connected by a spiral staircase. My mother was always limping up and down those stairs. Tip-tap-plunk, tip-tap-plunk. She'd hold on to the banister. The sound gave my father the creeps. He was always in a temper anyway, because the time wouldn't pass. He kept looking at his watch. With Mama and her leg in addition, it didn't take much to start him off.

Our top room was above the glass roof of the Passage; the windows looked out on an open space, so they had bars to keep out burglars and cats. That was my room, and it was also the place where my father could draw and paint when he came home after his deliveries. He'd fuss over his watercolors, and when he was finished, he'd often make as if to come down and catch me playing with myself. He'd lurk in wait on the stairs. I was quicker than he was. He only caught me once. But he'd always find some excuse for giving me a licking. It was a battle between us. In the end I'd always apologize for my insolence... It was an act, I hadn't done anything.

He'd ask me questions and answer them for me. When he was through licking me, he'd stay there behind the bars, looking out at the stars, the atmosphere, the moon, the night high above us. That was his quarterdeck. I knew that. He'd be commanding the Atlantic.

If my mother interrupted him, if she called him to come down, he'd start griping again. They'd collide in the darkness, in the narrow cage between the second and third floors. She'd be in for a good smack and a volley of insults. Tip... tap... plunk! Tip... tap... plunk! Whimpering under the onslaught, she'd run down to the basement and count her wares. "Why can't you leave me alone! Godammit to hell! What have I done to deserve this?..." His bellowing shook the whole house. In the narrow kitchen he'd pour himself a glass of red wine. Nobody let out a peep. That was how he wanted it.

In the daytime I had Grandma, she taught me to read a little. She herself wasn't very good at it, she had learned late, after her children were born. I can't say she was tender or affectionate, but she didn't talk much, which is a good deal, and she never hit me... She hated my father's guts. She couldn't abide him with his education, his high principles, his idiotic rages, and his catalog of complaints. For her money her daughter was an ass to have married such a prick... making seventy francs a month in an insurance company. As for me, the kid, she hadn't quite made up her mind what to think of me, she was keeping me under observation. She was a woman of character.

At the Passage she helped us as long as she could with what junk she still had left from her stock. We only lighted one window, that was as much as we could fill... It was a discouraging lot of bric-a-brac, decrepit with age, gray elephants, crap; if that was all we had to sell, we were sunk. We only kept going by scrimping... always noodles and pawning Mama's earrings at the end of every month... It was a wonder we had anything to eat at all.

We took in a little money doing repair jobs. We did them a lot cheaper than anybody else, we'd take them at any price. And we delivered day and night. For a profit of two francs we'd hike out to the Pare Saint-Maur and back.

"It's never too late for the brave," said my mother cheerfully. Her specialty was optimism. But Madame Héronde was always holding things up, she went too far. Every time she kept us waiting there was a crisis, the whole lot of us damn near starved. By five in the afternoon my father would be back from the office, trembling with anxiety, looking at his watch the whole time.

"Clémence, I repeat for the hundredth time, if that woman gets robbed, what's going to become of us?... Her husband will sell it all!... He spends all his time in the whorehouse, I know it for a fact!... Everybody knows..."

He dashed up to the top floor, bellowing the whole time. Then back down to the shop. Our house was like an accordion. The amplification was terrific.

I'd go scouting for Madame Héronde as far as the rue des Pyramides. If I didn't see her coming with her bundle bigger than she was, I'd run back empty-handed. Then I'd go look again. Finally, when all hope was gone, when it was plain that she had been lost with all on board, I'd sight her off the rue Thérèse, gasping in an eddy of the crowd, listing under her bundle. I'd tow her to the Passage. In the shop she'd collapse. My mother gave thanks to heaven. My father couldn't bear to witness these scenes. He'd climb up to his attic, looking at his watch at every step, refurbishing his obsession. He was building up to the next outburst, the Deluge that wouldn't be long in coming... Getting into trim...

The Pinaises screwed us. My mother and I go traipsing over to show them our selection of lace. For a wedding present.

They lived in a palace across from the Pont Solférino. I remember what struck me first... the vases, some were so big and fat you could have hidden inside. They'd stuck them all over the place. Those people were very rich. We were shown into the salon. The beautiful Madame Pinaise and her husband were there... they were expecting us. They give us a friendly reception. My mother spreads her stuff out in front of them... on the carpet. She gets down on her knees, it's handier. She talks herself blue in the face, she really knocks herself out. They stall, they can't make up their minds, they simper, they put on the dog.

Madame Pinaise reclines on the sofa in a dressing gown with a lot of ribbons. He takes me around in back, gives me a few friendly little pats, cuddles me a little... My mother on the floor is doing her damnedest, plowing through the pile, brandishing the merchandise... Her bun comes undone, her face is dripping wet. She's awful to look at. She gasps for breath, she loses her head, she clutches at her stockings, her bun topples, falls in her eyes.

Madame Pinaise comes over to me. They both start tickling me. My mother is still at it. Her spiel isn't getting her anywhere. I'm about to come in my pants... A flash! I see her... Madame Pinaise... She's swiped a handkerchief. It's disappeared between her tits. "My compliments, madame. You have such a nice little boy!..." That was to throw the dust in her eyes. They'd seen all they wanted. We quickly did up our bundles. My mother was sweating big drops but smiling just the same. She didn't wish to offend anyone... "Another time perhaps," she excused herself ever so politely. "I'm so sorry I couldn't tempt you..."

In the street, outside the doorway, she asked me in a whisper if I hadn't seen her slip the handkerchief into her corset. I said no.

"Your father will be sick. We had that handkerchief on consignment. Valenciennes openwork. It belonged to the Grégues. It wasn't ours. But imagine! If I had taken it away from her, we'd have lost her as a customer... and all her friends too... there would have been a scandal!"

"Clémence, look at your hair. It's undone. It's all over your eyes. You're green around the gills, poor thing. You're falling apart. You're running yourself ragged..." Those were his first words when we came home.

So as not to lose sight of his watch, he hung it up in the kitchen above the noodles. He gave my mother another look. "You're positively green, Clémence." The watch was so's we'd get through with the eggs, the stew, the noodles... with our tiredness and the future. He was fed up.

"I'll go get dinner," she suggested. He didn't want her to touch anything... He couldn't stand the thought of her handling the food... "Your hands are dirty! Hell, you're played out!" She went to set the table. She dropped a plate. Infuriated, he rushed to help her. The place was so small we were always bumping into things. There was never room enough for a wild man like him. The table rocked, the chairs began to waltz. It was a terrible mess. They collided. They got up full of black-and-blue marks. We went back to our leek salad. It was confession time...

"So you didn't sell anything?... All your trouble was for beans?... You poor dear..."

He began to sigh something awful. He was feeling sorry for her. He envisaged a future full of shit, we'd never get out of it.

Then she gave it to him straight... a handkerchief had been stolen... and the circumstances...

"What's that?" He couldn't take it in. "You didn't say anything? You let them get away with it? The fruits of our toil!" He was in such a rage that he cracked at the seams. His jacket burst. "It's abominable!" he roared. In spite of the uproar my mother kept yelping some kind of excuses... He had stopped listening. He seized his knife and brought it down in the middle of his plate... it split, the noodle juice ran all over the place. "No, no! I can't stand it." He rushed around, waving his arms. He took hold of the little sideboard, the Henri III. He shook it like a plum tree. There was an avalanche of dishes.

Madame Méhon, the corsetmaker who had the shop across from us, came to the window to enjoy the fun. She was an indefatigable enemy, she had detested us from the start. The Pérouquières, who had a bookstore two shops further down, make no bones about opening their window. Why should they stand on ceremony? They prop their elbows on the windowsill... My mother's going to catch it, that's a safe bet. As far as I'm concerned, I have no preferences. For yelling and boneheadedness, there's nothing to choose between them... She doesn't hit so hard, but more often. Which of the two I'd rather somebody killed? Well, all in all, my father, I guess.

They don't want me to see. "Get up to your room, you little pig... Go to bed! Say your prayers..."

He bellows, he rushes, he explodes, he bombards the kitchen. There's nothing left on the nails... Pots, pans, dishes, crash, bang, everything goes... My mother on her knees implores heaven for mercy... He overturns the table with one big kick... It lands on top of her...

"Run, Ferdinand," she still has time to shout. I run, passing through an avalanche of glass and debris... He charges into the piano that a customer had left us as security... he's beside himself. He bashes his heel into it, the keyboard clangs... Then it's my mother's turn, now she's getting hers... From my room I can hear her howling...

"Auguste! Auguste! Stop!" And then short stifled gasps...

I come part of the way down to look... He's dragging her along the banister. She hangs on. She clutches his neck. That's what saves her. It's he who pulls loose... He pushes her over. She somersaults... She bounces down the stairs... I can hear the dull thuds... At the bottom she picks herself up... Then he takes a powder... He leaves through the shop... He goes out in the street. She struggles to her feet... She goes back up to the kitchen. She has blood in her hair. She washes at the sink... She's sobbing... She gags... She sweeps up the breakage... He comes home very late on these occasions... Everything is very quiet again.

Grandma realized that I needed a little fun, that it wasn't good for me to be in the shop all the time. It made me sick to my stomach to listen to my lunatic father shouting his inanities. She bought a little dog for me to play with while waiting for the customers. I wanted to treat him like my father treated me. When we were alone, I'd give him wicked kicks. He'd slink away to whimper under the furniture. He'd lie down to beg pardon. He acted exactly like me.

It didn't give me any pleasure to beat him, I'd much rather have kissed him. In the end I'd fondle him and he'd get a hard-on. He went everywhere with us, even to the movies, to the Thursday matinee at the Robert Houdin.[100] Grandma treated me to that too. We'd sit through all three shows. It was the same price, all the seats were one franc, one hundred percent silent, without words, without music, without titles, just the purring of the machine. People will come back to that, you get sick of everything except sleeping and daydreaming. *The Trip to the Moon*[101] will be back again... I still know it by heart.

Sometimes in the summer there were only the two of us, Caroline and myself, in the big hall up one flight of stairs. In the end the usher would motion us to leave. I'd have to wake up Grandma and the dog. Then we'd hurry through the crowd and the bustle of the Boulevards. We were always late in getting home. We'd come in panting.

"Did you like it?" Caroline would ask me. I didn't say anything. I didn't like personal questions. "The child is secretive..." That's what the neighbors said.

On the way home she'd stop at the corner of our Passage and buy me a copy of *Illustrated Adventure Stories* from the newspaper woman with the charcoal footwarmer. She'd hide it for me in her panties, under her three thick petticoats. My father didn't like me to read such hogwash. He claimed it corrupted you, that it didn't prepare you for life, that I'd do better to learn the alphabet out of something serious.

---

[100] Théâtre Robert Houdin. Theater founded by Robert Houdin, the famous magician, specializing in magic and prestidigitation. Georges Méliès, the film pioneer, was for many years its director.
[101] *The Trip to the Moon*, film by Georges Méliès (1902) after Jules Verne's novel *De la Terre à la Lune* (1865). It lasted fifteen minutes and was an enormous success both in France and the United States.

I was going on seven, I'd soon be going to school, I shouldn't be given any wrong ideas... the other shopkeepers' children would also be going to school soon. The time for tomfoolery was past. On our way home from deliveries he'd make me little sermons about the seriousness of existence.

Whacks alone won't do it.

Foreseeing that I'd be a thief, my father blared like a trombone. One afternoon Tom and I had emptied the sugar bowl. It was never forgotten. But that wasn't my only fault. In addition my behind was always dirty, I didn't wipe myself, I didn't have time, that was my justification, we were always in too much of a hurry... I never wiped myself properly, I always had a sock coming to me... and hurried to avoid it... I left the can door open so as to hear them coming... I shat like a bird between two storms...

I bounded upstairs and they couldn't find me... I'd go around for weeks with shit on my ass.

I was conscious of the smell, I'd be careful not to get too close to people.

"He's as filthy as thirty-six pigs! He has no self-respect! He'll never make a living. Every boss in the world will fire him!..." He saw a shitty future in store for me.

"He stinks!... We'll always have him on our hands..."

My father looked far ahead and all he saw was gloom. He put it in Latin for emphasis: "*Sana... corpore sano.*" My mother didn't know what to say.

A little further down the Passage there was a family of bookbinders. Their children never went out.

The mother was a baroness. De Caravals was her name. She didn't want her children to learn bad language at any cost.

They played together all year long behind the window-panes, putting their noses in each other's mouths and both hands at the same time. Their complexions were like celery.

Once a year Madame de Caravals took a vacation all by herself. She'd go visiting her cousins in Périgord. She told everybody how her cousins came to meet her at the station in their "break" drawn by four prize-winning horses. They would drive together through endless estates... The peasants would troop out to kneel on the castle drive as they passed... that was the kind of stuff she dished out.

One year she took the two kids with her. She came back alone in the wintertime, much later than usual. She had on deep mourning. You couldn't see her face behind all the veils. She offered no explanation. She went straight up to bed. She never spoke to anybody after that.

The change had been too much for those children who never went out. The fresh air had killed them... That disaster gave everyone pause. From the rue Thérèse to the Place Gaillon all you heard about was oxygen... for more than a month.

As for us, we often had the chance to go to the country. Uncle Édouard, my mother's brother, was only too delighted when he could do something for us. He'd suggest excursions. My father never accepted. He always found some pretext for getting out of them. He didn't want to be beholden to anybody, that was his motto.

Uncle Édouard was up-to-date, he had a way with machinery. He was mighty clever with his hands. He wasn't extravagant, he wasn't the kind to involve us in a spending spree, but even so the slightest outing is bound to be rather costly... "A hundred francs," my mother would say, "don't last long when you go out."

Nevertheless the sad story of the Caravals had got the whole Passage so upset that something had to be done. It was suddenly discovered that everybody looked "peaked." Advice was passed from shop to shop. No one could think of anything but microbes and the perils of infection. The kids came in for a wave of parental solicitude. They were made to take whole jugfuls, whole barrelfuls of cod-liver oil, reinforced, in double doses. Frankly, it didn't do much good... it made them belch. It made them greener than ever; they could hardly stand up to begin with, now the oil killed their appetite.

I have to admit that the Passage was an unbelievable pesthole. It was made to kill you off, slowly but surely, what with the little mongrels' urine, the shit, the sputum, the leaky gas pipes. The stink was worse than the inside of a prison. Down under the glass roof the sun is so dim you can eclipse it with a candle. Everybody began to gasp for breath. The Passage took cognizance of its asphyxiating stench... We talked of nothing but the country, hills and valleys, the wonders of nature...

Édouard offered once more to take us out one Sunday, all the way to Fontainebleau. Papa finally gave in. He got our clothes ready and the provisions.

Édouard's first three-wheeler was a one-cylinder job, as massive as a field howitzer, with half a coachman's seat in front.

We got up that Sunday much earlier than usual. My ass was given a thorough wiping. We waited a whole hour at the meeting place on the rue Gaillon before the contraption got there. Our departure was something. It had taken at least six men to push the thing from the Pont Bineau. The tanks were filled. The carburetor spewed in all directions, the steering wheel quaked... There was a series of terrible explosions. They tried it with the crank, they tried it with a strap... They harnessed themselves to it by three and sixes... Finally a tremendous explosion... the engine began to turn. Twice fire broke out... and was quickly extinguished. My uncle said: "Pile in, ladies and gentlemen, I think she's warm now. Now we can get started..." It took nerve to stay put. The crowd pressed in on us. Caroline, my mother, and I wedged ourselves in. We were tied so tightly to the seat, so squeezed in among the clothes and gear that only my tongue protruded. But I came in for a good little whack before we moved off, just to keep me from getting any ideas.

The three-wheeler bucked and settled back... It gave two, three big jolts... A terrible crashing and belching were heard... The crowd shrank back in terror... They thought we were goners... But the monster was climbing the rue Reaumur in frantic fits and starts... My father had rented a bike... Since he couldn't pedal up the hill, he pushed us from behind... The slightest stop would have been the end... he had to push with all his might... At the Square du Temple we stopped a while. We started off again with a crash. In full flight my uncle poured grease, straight out of the bottle, into the connecting rods, the chain, and the whole works. It always had to be swimming in grease, like the engine of an ocean liner. There's trouble in the front seat. My mother has a bellyache. Jf she takes time out, if we stop, the engine is perfectly capable of conking out... if it stalls, our goose is cooked... My mother bears up heroically. My uncle, perched on his infernal machine, looking like a shaggy deep-sea diver surrounded by a thousand tongues of flame, adjures us over the handlebars to hold tight... My father is tagging after us. He pedals to the rescue. He picks up the parts as they fall off, pieces of levers and pedals, nuts, cotter pins—and some bigger things. We hear him cursing and swearing louder than the clatter of the machine.

The cobblestones were the cause of our disaster... At Clignancourt they snapped all three chains... At the Vanves tollgate they demolished the front springs... We lost all our lamps and the big horn shaped like a dragon's maw in the rills where the road was being repaired at La Villette... Near Picpus and on the highway we lost so much stuff that my father missed some of it...

I could hear him cursing behind us: that it was the end of the world and night would catch us on the road.

Tom ambled along ahead of our expedition, we took our bearings by his asshole. He had time to piss wherever he pleased. Uncle Édouard was more than clever, he had real genius for repairs of all sorts. Toward the end of our outings he had everything in his hands, his fingers were doing all the work, between jolts he juggled with splinters and wrist pins, he played the leaks and pistons like a trumpet. His acrobatics were marvelous to watch. But at a certain moment everything came tumbling out on the road all the same... We'd go into a drift, the steering gear would founder, we'd run plunk into the ditch. Crashing, gushing, snorting, the thing would run us all into the mud.

My father came up bellowing... The tin can let out one last BWAAH... And that was all.

The bastard passed out on us.

We stank up the countryside with crankcase oil. We disentangled ourselves from the catafalque... and then we pushed the whole thing back to Asnières. That's where the garage was. My father was magnificent in action, his calves bulged in his ribbed woolen stockings... The ladies along the road couldn't take their eyes off him. My mama was proud of him... The engine had to be cooled off, we had a small collapsible canvas bucket for the purpose. We'd take water from fountains. Our three-wheeler looked like a factory mounted on a pushcart. There were so many hooks and pointed gadgets sticking out on all sides that we ripped our clothes to tatters pushing...

At the tollgate my uncle and Papa went into a bar for a beer. The ladies and myself collapsed wheezing and panting on a bench outside and waited for our pop. Everybody was in a foul temper. In the end I was the victim. Storm-clouds hung over the family. Auguste was aching for a tantrum. He was just looking for a pretext. He was pooped, he was sniffing like a bulldog. No one but me would do. the others would have told him where to get off... He took a stiff drink of pernod. He wasn't used to it, it was a dumb thing to do... On the grounds that I'd torn my pants

he gave me a royal thrashing. My uncle stuck up for me, kind of. That only added to his fury.

It was on the way back from the country that I got my worst lickings. There are always crowds of people at the city gates. I screeched as loud as I could just to get his goat. I stirred up mob sentiment, I rolled under the café tables. I heaped mountains of shame on him. He blushed from head to foot. He hated attracting attention. I hoped it would make him bust. We started off again with our tails between our legs, our backs bent over the infernal machine.

There were always such scenes on the way back from our trips that my uncle gave up the whole idea.

"Of course the air is good for the little fellow," they said, "but the automobile gets him upset..."

Mademoiselle Méhon had the shop straight across from us. You can't imagine what a dog she was. She was always trying to pick a fight with us, she never stopped plotting, she was jealous. And yet she was doing all right with her corsets. She was an old woman and she still had her faithful clientele, handed down from mother to daughter for the last forty years. Women that wouldn't have let just anybody see their bosoms.

Things came to a head over Tom, who'd got into the habit of pissing against the shopwindows. Still, he wasn't the only one. Every mutt in the neighborhood did worse. The Passage was their promenade.

The Méhon woman crossed the street for no other purpose than to provoke my mother, to make a scene. It was scandalous, she bellowed, the way our mangy cur befouled her window... Her words resounded on both sides of the shop and up to the glass roof. The passersby took sides. It was a bitter brawl. Grandma, ordinarily so careful about her language, gave her a good tongue-lashing.

When Papa came home from the office and heard about it, he flew into such a temper you couldn't bear to look at him. He rolled his eyes so wildly in the direction of the old bag's shop window we were afraid he was going to strangle her. We did our best to stop him, we clung to his overcoat... He had developed the strength of a legionnaire. He dragged us into the shop... He bellowed loud enough to be heard on the fourth floor that he was going to make hash out of that damn corsetmaker... "I shouldn't have told you about it," my mother wailed. The harm was done.

In the weeks that followed my life was a little more peaceful. My father was absorbed. Whenever he had a moment's free time, he'd glare at the corset shop. She did the same. They'd spy on each other from behind the curtains, floor by floor. The moment he got home from the office, he'd begin to wonder what she might be up to. It was directly across the street... When she was in her kitchen on the second floor, he'd be standing in the corner of ours, muttering ferocious threats...

"Will you look at the rotten old bag! Isn't she ever going to poison herself?... Couldn't she take some mushrooms? Couldn't she swallow her false teeth? Hell! She even examines her food for ground glass..." He couldn't stop staring at her. He had no time for my propensities... It was better in a way.

The neighbors were afraid to commit themselves. Dogs urinated all over the place, on their windows too, not just on hers. It was no use sprinkling sulphur, the fact is that the Passage des Bérésinas was a kind of sewer. Piss brings company. Anybody who felt like it pissed on us, even grown-ups, especially if it was raining out in the street. They came in just for that. People even crapped in the little side alley, the Allée Primorgueil. What call had we to complain? Often a pisser, with or without a dog. gets to be a customer.

After a while my father wasn't satisfied with bristling at the corsetmaker, he'd work himself up against Grandma. "The dirty old bag—huh!—with her stinking mutt, you want me to tell you what she's been doing?... You don't know?... She's sly... she's underhanded! She's an accomplice. Well, there you have it. They're in it together, cooking up some lousy trick... and it's nothing new! Ah, those two bitches!... What for? You really want to know? To drive me raving mad. That's all. That's the long and the short of it."

"Come, come, Auguste. I assure you... You're imagining things. You make a mountain out of the least word..."

"I'm imagining things? Why don't you come right out and say I'm nuts! Go ahead! Imagining things! Ah, Clémence, you're incorrigible. Life goes on and you don't learn a thing... We're being persecuted, that's what! Stepped on! Ridiculed! They're dishonoring me. And what have you to say? That I'm imagining things! No! Oh, it's too much!"

And damned if he didn't burst into tears. It was his turn.

We weren't the only ones in the Passage with stands, kidney-shaped tables, little chairs, and fluted Louis XVI pieces. Our competitors, the junk dealers, sided with Méhon. That was to be expected. My father couldn't sleep anymore. His nightmare was cleaning the sidewalk outside our shop. He'd wash down the flags every morning before going to work.

He'd come out with his pail, his broom, his rag, and the little trowel he'd slip under the turds, to pick them up and throw them in the sawdust. What a humiliation for a man with his education! The turds increased in number and there were many more in front of our shop, lengthwise and crosswise, than anywhere else. Obviously a plot.

Mademoiselle Méhon was at her second-floor window grinning from ear to car as she watched my father battling the shit. It gave her a kick that lasted all day. The neighbors collected to count the turds.

Bets were laid that he wouldn't be able to clean it all up.

He'd make it fast, then he'd rush in to put on his collar and tie. He had to be at La Coccinelle before anyone else to open the mail.

Baron Méfaise, the director, counted on him implicitly.

This was when tragedy hit the Cortilènes. A drama of passion at Number 147 in the Passage. It was in the papers; for a whole week there was a dense crowd parading, grunting, pondering, and spitting outside their shop.

I'd seen Madame Cortilène lots of times, my mother made her blouses of fine Irish linen with lace insets. I remember well her long eyelashes, her eyes full of gentleness, and the looks she gave even a kid like me. I'd often jerk off thinking of her.

During fittings you get to see shoulders, skin... The moment she left, it never failed, I'd run up to the can on the fourth floor and masturbate strenuously. I'd come down with big rings under my eyes.

Those people had scenes too, but they were over jealousy. Her husband didn't want her to go out. He did the going out. He was a former officer, small and dark-haired, with a terrible temper. They sold rubber goods at 147, drainage tubes, instruments, and "articles"...

Everyone in the Passage said she was too pretty to keep that kind of shop...

One day her jealous husband came home unexpectedly. He found her upstairs starting up with two men; it gave him such a shock that he pulled out his revolver and shot her first and then himself, straight in the mouth. They died in each other's arms.

He hadn't been out more than fifteen minutes.

My father's revolver was a military model, he hid it in the bedside table. The caliber was something enormous. He had brought it home from the army.

The Cortilène tragedy might have given my father grounds for the worst tantrums, something to yell about. Actually it made him clam up. He hardly spoke at all.

There was no lack of turds on the sidewalk outside our door. With all the people who passed, there was so much spit it made the pavement sticky. He cleaned it all up. And not a peep out of him. That was such a revolution in his habits that my mother began to watch him when he locked himself up in his room. He'd stay there for hours. He neglected his deliveries, he gave up drawing. She'd look in through the keyhole. He'd pick up his gat, he'd turn the cylinder. You'd hear "click, click"... He seemed to be practicing up.

One day he went out alone and came back with cartridges, a whole box of them. He opened them up in front of us, to make sure we'd got a good look. He didn't say a word, he just put the box down on the table beside the noodles. My mother was scared stiff; she flung herself on the floor, she clasped his knees and implored him to throw it all in the garbage. It was no use. He was as stubborn as a mule. He didn't even answer. He shook her off roughly and swilled a quart of the red stuff all by himself.

He refused to eat. When my mother kept after him, he pushed her against the cupboard. Then he beat it down to the cellar and closed the trap over his head.

We heard him shooting: Ping! Ping! Ping!... He took his time, the shot rang out, followed by a tremendous echo. He must have been shooting at the empty barrels. My mother called down to him, screaming through the cracks...

"Auguste! Auguste! I implore you! Think of the child! Think of me! Call your father, Ferdinand!"

"Papa! Papa!" I bellowed...

I wondered whom he was going to kill. Mademoiselle Méhon? Grandma Caroline? Both of them like at the Cortilènes? He'd have to find them together.

Ping! Ping! Ping!... He went right on shooting. The neighbors came running. A bloodbath, they thought...

He ran out of ammunition. In the end he came upstairs... When he raised the trap, he was as pale as a corpse. We clustered around him, we held him up, we settled him in the Louis XIV armchair in the middle of the store. We spoke to him ever so gently. His revolver, still smoking, dangled from his wrist.

When she heard the shooting, Madame Méhon shat in her skirts... She came over to see what was going on. Then right in front of all the people my mother told her good and loud what she thought of her. And my mother wasn't the bold kind.

"Come right in! Take a good look! Look at the state you've driven him to. A good man! A family man! Aren't you ashamed of yourself? Oh! You're a wicked woman!"

Madame Méhon hadn't much to say for herself. She went back home in a hurry. The neighbors gave her hard looks. They comforted my father. "My conscience is clear," he kept mumbling under his breath. M. Visios, the pipe dealer who had been in the navy for five years, tried to placate him.

My mother wrapped the weapon in several layers of newspaper and then in a cashmere shawl.

My father went up to bed. She cupped him. He went on trembling for a couple of hours at least.

"Come, child... come!" she said when we were alone.

It was late. We ran down to Pont Royal by way of the rue des Pyramides... We kept looking to left and right to see if anybody was coming. We threw the package in the drink.

We returned home even faster than we'd come. We told my father we'd been taking Caroline home.

The next day he had terrible aches and pains... it killed him to stand up. For the next week at least, it was Mama that had to scrub the sidewalk.

Grandma had her doubts about the forthcoming Exposition. The last one in '82 hadn't done anything but screw up small business by making a lot of damn fools spend their money in the wrong way. After all that ballyhoo, all that fuss and bother, there was nothing left but two or three empty lots and a pile of rubbish so disgusting looking that even twenty years later nobody was willing to take it away... not to mention the two epidemics that the Iroquois, the blue, the yellow, and the brown savages had brought over.

The new exposition was bound to be even worse. There was sure to be cholera. Grandma was positive.

The customers were already beginning to save up, they were putting pocket money aside, finding a thousand pretexts for not buying anything... they were waiting for the "opening." A rotten bunch of griping blackguards. My mama's earrings never left the pawnshop.

"If the idea was to get the peasants to come in from the country, why couldn't they arrange dances for them at the Trocadéro?... It's big enough for everybody. They didn't have to rip the whole city open and plug up the Seine... Should we throw money out the window because we've forgotten how to have fun by ourselves? No!"

That was how my Grandmother Caroline saw it. The moment she left, my father began racking his brains, trying to figure out what she had meant by her bitter words...

He discovered a hidden meaning... personal insinuations... threats... He was on his guard. "At least I forbid you to discuss my private affairs with her!... Exposition hell! You want me to tell you, Clémence? It's a pretext. What she's getting at? You want to know? Well, I had a hunch the moment she opened her mouth. Divorce!... That's what she wants!"

Then he pointed across the room at me in my corner. Ungrateful wretch! Sneaky little profiteer... getting fat on other people's sacrifices... Me... with my shitass... my boils... my insatiable consumption of shoes... There I was! All this was about me, the scapegoat for all their misfortunes...

"Oh! Godammit! Godammit to hell! If it weren't for him! Oh! What's that? I'd clear out so fast. Bah! I can promise you that. I'd have done it long ago... long ago. Not tomorrow, see! This minute! Godammit! If we didn't have this little hunk of shit on our hands! She wouldn't keep harping, believe you me. Divorce! Oh! DIVORCE!..."

He was all shriveled, shaken with spasms. He was like the villain in the movies, only worse because he swore out loud...

"Oh! By all the whorehouses in hell! Freedom! Bah! Self-abnegation? Yes. Sacrifice? Yes. Privation? Yes. The whole shooting match and then some. And all for this perverted little shitass! Oh! Oh! Freedom! Freedom!..." He disappeared into the wings. On his way upstairs he belabored his chest with great dull blows.

The mere mention of "divorce" threw my mother into convulsions...

"Why, Auguste, I do everything I can! You know that! I work my fingers to the bone. I do the work of ten, you can see that for yourself. Things will get better! I promise you! I implore you! One day we'll be happy, all three of us!

"What about me?" he shouted down from upstairs, "I suppose I don't do my best. And a lot of good it does..."

She surrendered to her sorrows. The floodgates burst.

"We'll bring him up properly, you'll see, I swear it, Auguste! Don't work yourself up!... He'll do his best too... He'll be like us! He'll be like you! You'll see! He'll be like us. Won't you, child?"

We started delivering again. We saw the big monumental gate going up at the corner of the Place de la Concorde. It was so delicate, so fancy, so full of frills and gingerbread from top to bottom, it made you think of a mountain in bridal dress. Every time we passed by, we saw something new being done to it.

Finally they took the scaffolding away. Everything was in readiness for the public... At first my father pooh-poohed the whole thing, and then he went after all, all alone one Saturday afternoon. To everybody's surprise he was delighted... Pleased, happy, like a kid who's been to fairyland...

All our neighbors, except Madame Méhon of course, came running over to hear him tell about it. At ten that night he still had them spellbound. In less than an hour on the grounds, he had seen everything, been everywhere, understood it all and a lot more, from the Pavilion of Black Snakes to the Gallery of Machines, and from the North Pole to the Cannibals...

Visios, the sailor who had been all over the world, said the whole thing was marvelous. He'd never have believed it... and he knew a thing or two. My uncle Rodolphe, who had been working in the sideshow done up as a troubadour ever since the Exposition opened, was nonexistent as a storyteller. He was there in the shop with the rest of them. Draped in his finery, he'd grin for no reason, he'd make paper birds and wait for supper to be served.

Madame Méhon was at her window, worried sick to see all the neighbors coming over our way. For her money, it was sure to end in some plot. Grandma stayed away a whole week. Papa's bumptiousness gave her a pain. And every night he started his lecture all over again, adding new touches. Rodolphe got hold of some free tickets. So one Sunday the three of us dove into the crowd.

At the Place de la Concorde the mob got hold of us and really pumped us in. We came to, breathless and half unconscious, in the Gallery of Machines. It was terrifying! Hanging in midair in a transparent cathedral with little panes of glass that went way up to the sky. The racket was so awful we couldn't hear my father, and he was shouting his lungs out. Steam gushed and spurted on all sides. There were giant kettles as big as three houses, gleaming pistons that came charging at us out of the bottom of hell... In the end we couldn't stand it, we were scared, we beat it... We passed the Ferris wheel... but what we liked best was the bank of the Seine.

It was weird the way they had rigged up the Esplanade... terrific... Two rows of enormous cakes, fantastic cream puffs, full of balconies crammed with gypsies swathed in flags, music, and millions of little light bulbs that were lit in broad daylight. That was wasteful. Grandma was right. We moved on, crushed worse and worse. I was right near all the feet, the dust was so thick I couldn't see where I was going. I swallowed whole mouthfuls and spat cement... Finally we got to the North Pole... An explorer, real friendly, was explaining the show, but so confidentially, so softly, all wrapped up in his furs, you could hardly hear a thing. My father told us what was what. Then the seals came out for their dinner. They bellowed so loud there was nothing else in the world. So we beat it.

In the big Refreshment Palace lovely orangeade was being dished out in a long line at a little moving counter absolutely free of charge... Between us and it a riot was going on... A seething mob struggling to get at the glasses. Thirst has no mercy. If we'd attempted it, there wouldn't have been anything left of us. We fled through another door... We went to see the natives...

We only saw one, behind a fence, he was boiling himself an egg. He wasn't looking at us. He had his back turned. It was quiet there, so my father started gabbing again with lots of animation, trying to enlighten us about the curious customs of tropical countries. He wasn't able to finish, the nigger was fed up too. He spat in our direction and disappeared into his cabin... I couldn't see straight or open my mouth. I had breathed in so much dust all my passages were blocked. From one eddy to the next we made it to the exit. Even after we'd passed the Invalides I was still being jostled and trampled. We were so shaken, so shattered by fatigue and excitement we hardly recognized each other. We took the shortest way home... by way of the Marché Saint-Honoré. Then we went straight upstairs and drank all the water in the kitchen.

Our neighbors, with Visios, our sailor, in the lead, the perfume dealer from Number 27, Madame Gratat from the glove shop, Dorival the pastrycook, and Monsieur Pérouquière, popped right over to hear about it. They wanted us to tell them all about it and then some... Had we been to see all the exhibits?... Hadn't they lost me?... How much had we spent?... What! At every turnstile?...

Papa told them the whole story with thousands of details... some of them true and others not so accurate... My mother was happy, it had been worth it... for once Auguste was being really appreciated... She was mighty proud for his sake... He puffed himself up... he laid it on thick... She knew he was telling fairy tales... but that's what it is to be an educated man... she hadn't suffered for nothing... the man she had given herself to was somebody... a thinker... there was no denying it. All those poor bastards sat there with their tongues hanging out... Pure admiration!

Papa made it all up as he went along, without the slightest effort... There was magic in our shop... with the gas turned off. All by himself he put on a show a hundred times more amazing than four dozen Expositions... But he didn't want the gas... Just candles. Our shopkeeper friends brought their own glims, dug out of their storerooms. They came back night after night to listen to Papa and kept asking for more...

His prestige was enormous... They could think of nothing better. In the end, I guess, Madame Méhon must have taken sick over there in her hovel, haunted by bitter thoughts... They'd told her everything, down to the last syllable...

About two weeks later she couldn't stand it anymore... One night she came down all alone and crossed the Passage... She looked like a ghost... She was in her nightgown. She banged on our window. We all turned around. She didn't breathe a word. She stuck a piece of paper on the glass. The inscription was brief, in big capital letters: LIAR...

Everybody burst out laughing. The charm was broken. They all went home... Papa had nothing more to say...

The pride of our shop was the coffee table in the middle, Louis XV, the only piece we were really sure about. People were always making us offers. We didn't try very hard to sell it. We couldn't have replaced it.

The Brétontés, our fancy customers from the Faubourg Saint-Germain, had noticed it a long time ago... They asked us to lend it to them for a play they were putting on, a comedy, with some other society people in their private house. The Pinaises were in it, and the Courmanches, the Doranges whose daughters were so crosseyed, and a lot of others who were customers more or less. The Girondets, the Camadours, the De Lambistes, who were related to the ambassadors... The cream of the cream!... It was going to be put on one Sunday afternoon. Madame Brétonté was sure their play would be a howling success.

She came back more than ten times, always to pester us about that table. We couldn't refuse, it was for charity.

To make sure nothing would happen to it, we took a cab and delivered it ourselves in the morning, wrapped in three blankets. Then in the afternoon we came back just in time to take our seats, three stools near the door.

The curtain hadn't gone up yet, but already it was marvelous. The ladies, dressed fit to kill, all burbling and sashaying. They smelled so good you almost fainted... Looking around, my mother recognized all the best pieces from her shop. Her boleros, her neckbands, her Chantilly lace. She even remembered the prices. And hadn't they had them made up nicely! Lace could be so lovely... And wasn't it becoming to them!... She was in seventh heaven.

Before we left the shop, I had been warned that if I gave off any smells, I'd be thrown out one-two-three. I had given myself such a wiping the toilet was all stuffed up. Even my feet were clean in my dress shoes...

Finally the people took their seats. Somebody called for silence. The curtain rolled up... Our coffee table appeared... plunk in the middle of the stage... same as in our shop... That set our minds at rest... A few bars on the piano and the actors were saying their lines... Oh, how beautifully they spoke... all the characters coming and going and posturing in the bright light... They were marvelous... They started bickering and arguing... they were getting madder and madder... but it made them more charming than ever... I was carried away... I wanted them to start all over again. I didn't quite get it all... But I was captivated, body and soul... Everything they touched... their slightest gestures... the most commonplace words were enchanted... The people around us applauded, my parents and I didn't dare...

On the stage I recognize Madame Pinaise, she's absolutely divine... There were her legs again and those throbbing tits... She's lying on a deep silk divan... sheathed in an airy négligé... She's desperate, she's sobbing... All on account of Dorange, another of our customers... He's bawling the hell out of her, she has no one to turn to... The heartless blackguard slips around behind her and takes advantage... she's bent over our coffee table, bawling... he steals a kiss... and starts to bill and coo... It was nothing like home... Finally her resistance breaks down... She sinks back gracefully on the couch... He gives her another buss, square on the lips... She swoons, she passes out... Whew!... and him waggling his ass... I really caught on... the polite passion... the deep luscious melody... All those visions to jerk off on...

Our coffee table, I've got to admit, looked mighty good there. The hands, the elbows, the bellies of the plot all rubbed against it... La Pinaise clutched it so hard you could hear it crack all the way across the room, but the worst was when handsome young Dorange, in a very tragic moment, made as if to sit down on it... Mama's heart jumped in her throat... Luckily he bounced up again... almost instantly... During the intermission she kept worrying... what if he did it again?... My father understood the whole play... But he was too far gone to talk about it just then.

It did something to me too. I didn't touch the soft drinks or even the cookies that the society people passed around... Those socialites are used to mixing grub with magical emotions... They're pigs. It's all one to them as long as they're chewing. They gulp it all down at one sitting, the rose and the crap it grows in...

We went back to our seats... The second act passed like a dream... Then the miracle was over... We were back again among plain ordinary things and people.

We waited, all three of us on our stools, we didn't dare let out a peep... We waited patiently for the crowd to drift out, so we could take our table... Then a lady came in and asked us to wait just a little while... We agreed... The curtain went up again. We saw all the actors, all the people in the play. They were all sitting around our table... all playing cards together. The Pinaises, the Coulomanches, the Brétontés, the Doranges, and Kroing, the old banker... They all sat there facing each other...

Kroing was a funny little old man, he often came to my grandmother's shop on the rue Montorgueil, always very friendly and polite and completely shriveled up. He used violet perfume, it stank up the whole shop. He collected only one thing, it was his only interest in life: Empire bell-pulls.

The game on our table started quite amicably. They gave each other cards as politely as can be. Then things went kind of sour, they began to speak sharply, not at all like in the play... They weren't talking for the fun of it anymore. They shouted numbers at each other. The trumps resounded like somebody getting a licking. Behind their father the Dorange girls were squinting something awful. The mothers and wives were left strictly to themselves, sitting with their chairs against the wall, all tensed up and scared to breathe. A command rang out. The players exchanged places. On the table the dough was piling up... Heaps and mounds of it... Old man Kroing was pounding the tabletop with both hands... In front of the Pinaises the pile kept growing and swelling... like an animal... They were red in the face with excitement... With the Brétontés it was the exact opposite... They were losing their pazazz... They were as pale as ghosts... They didn't have a cent left in front of them... My father went pale too. I wondered what he was going to do. We'd been waiting at least two hours for the game to end... They'd forgotten us...

Suddenly the Brétontés stood up... They offered to stake... their castle in Normandy! They announced it solemnly... on three cards!... And little Kroing won... He didn't seem happy about it... Brétonté stood up again... "I'm staking the house," he muttered. "The house we live in!"

My mother was thunderstruck... She jumped up like a spring. My father couldn't hold her back...

She climbed up on the stage with her limp... in a voice still shaken with emotion she addressed those big gamblers: "Ladies and gentlemen, we've got to take our little boy home... he ought to have been in bed long ago... We're going to take our table..." Nobody raised any objection. They all acted as if they'd been hit on the head... They were staring into the void... We picked up our table and whisked it out fast... We were afraid they'd call us back...

When we got to the Pont Solférino, we stopped a moment for breath...

Years later my father was still telling that story... with priceless gestures... My mother didn't care for it... It stirred up too much emotion in her... He always pointed out the exact place in the middle of the table where we plain people had seen millions and millions vanish in a few minutes, and all a family's honor and all its castles go up in smoke.

I didn't learn very quickly with Grandma Caroline. Even so, the day came when I could count up to a hundred and read better than she could. I was ready to take up addition. It was time for me to go to school.

They chose the grade school on the rue des Jeûneurs, right near the shop, the dark door on the other side of the Carrefour des Francs-Bourgeois.

You went down a long corridor and there was the classroom. It looked out on a little court, and on the other side there was a wall so high that the blue sky was blotted out. To keep us from looking up, there was also the big tin shed that covered part of the yard. We were expected to concentrate on our lessons and not to bother the teacher. I hardly got to know him, all I remember is his spectacles, his big stick, and his cuffs on the desk.

It was Grandma who took me to school for eight days, on the ninth I fell sick. In the middle of the afternoon the matron brought me home...

Once I got to the shop, I couldn't stop puking. Waves of fever ran through me... a heat so dense that I thought I had turned into somebody else. It was kind of fun if I only hadn't had to throw up so much. My mother was suspicious at first, she thought I had eaten too much nougat... It wasn't my way... She begged me to control myself, to make an effort not to vomit so much. The shop was full of people. When she took me to the can, she was afraid somebody'd swipe her lace. I was feeling worse than ever. I threw up a whole basinful. My head began to boil. I couldn't hide my joy... All sorts of funny things were going on in my head.

I'd always had a big head, a good deal bigger than other children. I could never wear their berets. Suddenly, as I was puking, my mother remembered this monstrous deformity of mine... She was worried sick.

"Auguste, do you suppose he's coming down with meningitis on us? That would be just our luck... it's all we needed... That would really be the end!..." I finally stopped vomiting... I was baked in heat... I was terribly interested... I'd never suspected so much stuff could fit inside my noodle... fantasies... weird sensations. At first everything looked red... Like a cloud all swollen with blood... right in the middle of the sky... Then it disintegrated... and took the form of a Lady Customer... enormous... gigantic... She began to order us about... up there in the sky... She was waiting for us... hanging in midair... She commanded us to get busy... she made signs... to get a move on, the whole lot of us!... to clear out of the Passage p.d.q... . Every last one of us... There wasn't a moment to lose!

And then she came down, she came toward us under the glass roof... She filled the whole Passage... an enormous strutting figure... She didn't want a single shopkeeper left in his shop... not one of our neighbors was allowed to stay put... Even Madame Méhon came along. She had grown three hands and four gloves... I could see we were going out for a good time. Words danced around us like around actors... Impassioned cadences, surprise effects... magnificent, irresistible inflections

The gigantic Lady Customer had stuffed her sleeves full of our lace... She cleared out the showcase... right out in the open... She wrapped herself in point lace, whole mantillas, enough chasubles to cover twenty priests... And amid the frills and finery she grew and grew...

All the little good-for-nothings in the Passage... the umbrella vendors... Visios of the tobacco pouches... the girls from the pastry shop... they were waiting... The tragic and glamorous Madame Cortilène was there beside us... her revolver slung on a strap... It was full of perfume and she was spraying the whole place... Madame Gounouyou with the veils, the one who'd been shut up indoors for years on account of her runny eyes, and the caretaker in his cocked hat... they were all in a huddle as though getting ready for some shindig, all in their Sunday best, and even little Gaston, one of the bookbinder's kids that had died, he had come back for the occasion... his mother was just nursing him. He was sitting on her lap good as gold, waiting to be taken for a walk. She was holding his hoop for him.

Old Aunt Armide drove in from the cemetery in Thiais; she drew up in a brougham at the end of the Passage. She had just come for the drive... She had grown so old since the previous winter that she had no face at all, only a lump of soft dough in its place... I recognized her anyway by the smel!... She gave my mama her arm. My father Auguste was all ready, slightly ahead of time as usual. His watch hung from his neck, as big as an alarm clock. His rig was something very special, morning coat, straw hat, hard rubber bicycle, cock in evidence, stockings molded by his calves. All spiffed up like that, with a flower in his buttonhole, he got on my nerves worse than ever. My poor mother, overcome with embarrassment, returned his compliments... Madame Méhon, the old battle-ax, was carrying Tom balanced on her hat in among the feathers... She made him bite everybody who came by.

As we trooped along behind the enormous Customer, there got to be more and more of us. We pushed and jostled in her wake... And the Lady kept growing... If she hadn't bent down, she'd have gone through the glass roof... As we were passing by, the printer... death notices and visiting cards... popped out of his cellar, pushing a baby carriage with his two brats in it... there wasn't much life in them either... All bundled up in paper money... Nothing but hundred-franc notes... all counterfeit... so that was his racket... The music dealer from 34, who owned a phonograph, six mandolins, three sets of bagpipes, and a piano, refused to leave anything behind... He wanted us to take the whole lot with us... We harnessed ourselves to his showcase, and the whole thing collapsed under the strain. There was a terrible crash.

An orchestra of brilliant soloists pours from the stage door of the Plush Barn, the café- concert across from 96... They get together a long way from the giantess... they blare out three terrific chords... violins, bagpipes, and harps... the trombones and double basses blow and scrape so loud and lovely that we all howl with delight...

Slender, trim usherettes with fragile little caps are bouncing all around us... They fly through the air and land in the tangerines... At 48 the three elderly sisters, who hadn't set foot outside their shop in fifty-two years, who are always so courteous, so patient with their customers, suddenly start driving out the clientele with big sticks... Two old bags conk out on their sidewalk, disembowelled... The three old ladies tie footwarmers on their asses to make them run faster... Objects rain in all directions from the gigantic Customer... stolen knickknacks. They drip from every fold in her clothing... Her accessories keep falling off and she keeps picking them up... Outside Cesar's jewelry shop she repairs her dress and wraps herself in chains and pearls, all phony... Everybody laughs... She takes a whole salad bowl full of amethysts and throws them by the fistful through the skylight... We all turn violet. She bombards the glass roof with topazes from the next tray... We all turn yellow... We were almost at the end of the Passage. There's an enormous crowd ahead of our procession and a howling mob behind us... The woman from the stationery store at 86—I had swiped some pencils from her—fastened on to my pants... And the widow with the antique cupboards went for my dick... It was no fun... It was the umbrella man that saved me, he hid me under his parasol.

If Aunt Armide had found me again, I'd have had to kiss her right in the headcheese...

This time Uncle Édouard and his three-wheeler were chasing my father... he had his nose so close to the road that it almost bent his bicycle. A big pebble lodged in one of his nostrils. The engine cooed as softly as a lovesick pigeon, but Uncle Édouard had his eyes attached to two strings and was dragging them smack over the road for fear of missing something... On the front seat Aunt Armide, wedged in among the cushions, was passing the time of day with a gentleman all in black. He was hugging a thermometer three times as big as me... That was the doctor from the Hespérides, who had come for a consultation... He was filled with consternation... Thousands of luminous particles darted from his face... At the sight the neighbors took off their hats and bowed down to the ground. And then they showed their backsides... He spat on them. He didn't have time to stop. We stormed the entrance all together... We invaded the Boulevards...

As we were crossing the Place Vendôme, a fierce gust of wind inflated the Customer. At the Opéra she swelled up twice as big... a hundred times!... All the neighbors scurried under her skirts like mice... No sooner were they settled than they dashed out again in a panic... then they rushed back again to hide in the caverns... The confusion was awful.

The little dogs from the Passage ran squirting in all directions, doing their business, going for people's asses, nipping ferociously. Madame Juvienne, Number 72, toiletries, expired before our eyes, under a mountain of mauve flowers, jasmine... from suffocation... Three passing elephants trampled her slowly to death, a thousand little rivulets of perfume came pouring out...

Four little baker's apprentices who worked for Largen-teuil, the pastrycook, came running up... carrying the enormous pipe from the Mohammed Tobacco advertisement that lit up at six o'clock... They smashed the bowl against the Marché Saint-Honoré, trying to move the buildings out of the way... First they bashed in the one on the right—POULTRY—and then the one on the left—FISH.

But we had to keep going—especially the giantess. Our giantess... with two planets for tits... I was being knocked around pretty bad... my father tried to hold me up but it was no use... He got caught in the spokes of his bike... He bit Tom's tail. He trotted along ahead of us barking, but no sound came out...

The caretaker put me back on my feet, all he had on was the top of his uniform... The lower end of him was thin air... We got a good laugh out of him with his long pole for lighting the gas with... He stuck it up his nose, every inch of it.

As we were crossing the rue de Rivoli, the Customer missed her step, she tripped over a bus stop shelter and smashed a building... the elevator squirted out and gored her eye... We passed over the ruins. On the rue des Jeûneurs, my little friend Émile Sarsaparilla, popped out of my school... a hunchback... that's how I'd always known him... and green around the gills, with a big wine-colored smudge running out of his ears... Now he didn't look bad at all. He was handsome, pink, and natty... I was glad for his sake.

Now all those people we had known were running in the caverns underneath the Lady, in her drawers, through whole streets and neighborhoods, compressed inside her petticoats... They went where she chose. We were squeezed tighter than ever. My mother held me by the hand... Faster and faster... At the Place de la Concorde I realized she was taking us to the Exposition... It was mighty kind of her... She wanted us to have fun...

The Lady, our Customer, had all the money, all the shopkeepers' cash, stashed away on her... She was going to treat us... It was getting hotter and hotter, and we were still wedged against the Lady... In among the drapery, next to the lining, I saw thousands of things hanging. All the stolen goods in the world... As we galloped, the little "Byzantine" looking-glass, the one we'd been looking for for months on the rue de Montorgueil, fell on my head... it left a bump... If I'd been able to, I'd have sung out that it was found, but we were already so penned in I'd never have been able to pick it up...

The time had come, we all realized, to squeeze a little tighter. We were shoved into the gate, the monumental gate, the arrogant gate, that rose into the sky like the bun on a lady's hair... Going in like that without paying, we were all scared shitless... Luckily we were swept in by the swish of petticoats... We were crushed, suffocating, crawling on our bellies... Up above, our Customer bent down when it came time to go through. Was it all over? Were we under the Seine? Would the sharks be coming to ask us for a penny? What do you think? When do you ever get admitted to anything for free?... it just doesn't happen... I let out a yell so sharp, so piercing that the giantess lost her head. All of a sudden she picked up her skirts, every single frill and ruffle... and her drawers... and lifted them sky-high, way over her head... A tempest rushed in, a wind so glacial we screamed for pain... There we were on the quai, frozen stiff, abandoned, shivering, helpless. Down below, between the embankment and the three barges, the Customer had flown away!... Our neighbors from the Passage turned so white I couldn't recognize a single one of them... The giantess had fooled us all with her magnificent thefts... There wasn't any more Exposition... it had been over long ago... Already we could hear the howling of the wolves on the Cours de la Reine...

It was time to get going... But we couldn't run right... A lot of feet were missing... Small as I was, I ran Madame Méhon over...

My mother lifted her skirts... But she ran more and more slowly... on account of her calves... suddenly they were as thin as wire... and so hairy they got tangled up in each other like spiders... The people up ahead wound her into a ball... and let her roll... But the buses were coming... at fiendish speed... They thundered down the rue Royale... blue ones, green ones, lemon-colored ones... The shafts broke, the harnesses gushed out across the Esplanade and fell against the trees in the Tuileries. I sized the situation up at a glance... I harangued... I exhorted... I rallied my troops... I laid down my plan of attack... We try to back up on the sidewalk outside the Orangerie... But it's hopeless. Almost instantly poor Uncle Édouard and his motorcar are run over at the foot of the statue of Bordeaux[102]... A few minutes later he comes out of the Solférino métro station with his three-wheeled tub welded on to his rear end like a snail... We lead him away... He has to hurry, to crawl faster and faster on account of the hundreds of motorcars... Reine-Serpollets from the automobile show. They bombard the Arc de Triomphe. Hell-bent for the cemetery, they descend on our routed army...

For a split second I caught sight of Rodolphe, leaning against the pedestal of the statue of Joan of Arc, smiling happily... He's auctioning off his troubadour costume... He wants to be a general... This is no time to disturb him... The asphalt is all ripped up... A chasm opens... Everything falls in... I skirt the precipice... I catch Armide's pocketbook just as it's about to disappear... There's an inscription on it in beads: "In fond remembrance"... Her glass eye is inside... We're so surprised we all laugh like hell... But the avalanche of punks is coming on from all sides... This time there are so many of them the rue Thérèse is full up to the fourth floor... a hill of packed meat... we start climbing... It buzzes like a manure pile all the way up to the stars...

But to get back home we have to bend back four thoroughly padlocked iron gates... We push by the hundreds and thousands... We try to get in through the transom... Nothing doing... the bars bend but jump right back into place, they snap in our faces like rubber bands... A ghost has hidden our key... He wants a prick and won't settle for anything else... We tell him to go to hell. "Fuck you," he says. We call him back. There are ten thousand of us trying to argue with him.

Echoing down the rue Gomboust, a hundred thousand cries of disaster come to us in bursts... That's the crowds that are being massacred off the Place Gaillon... the buses are still raging... the apocalypse goes on... the Clichy-Odéon plows through the desperate mob... the Panthéon-Courcelles storms in from the rear, sending the pieces sky-high... they rain down on our shopwindow. My father beside me moans: "If only I had a trumpet!"... In despair he sheds his clothes, in a second he's mother-naked, climbing up the Bank of France... he's perched on top of the clock... He rips off the minute hand and brings it down with him... he dandles it on his knees... It fascinates him... it gives him a kick... we're all feeling pretty gay... But a detachment of Guards bursts in through the rue Méhul... the Madeleine-Bastille goes into a spin, tips, and crashes into our gate... Luckily the whole thing collapses. The axle catches fire, the van bursts into crackling flames... The conductor is whipping the

---

[102] Statue of Bordeaux. The east side of the Place de la Concorde is bordered by eight statues symbolizing French cities. Bordeaux and Nantes are the work of Callouet.

driver... They're coming faster and faster... They take the rue des Moulins, they climb the grade, they take the fire with them... a hurricane... The cyclone strikes, weakens, rises up again, and breaks against the Comédie Française... The whole building bursts into flame... the roof comes loose, rises, flies away in flames... In her dressing room La Screwball, the beautiful actress, is frantically poring over her lines... Her soul has to be saturated with poetry before she can appear on the stage. She gargles her crack so hard that she stumbles... she falls plunk into the fire... She lets out a terrible scream... The volcano has swallowed up everything...

Nothing is left in the world but our fire... we're all cooking in it... A ghastly redness rumbles through my brain with a crowbar that dislodges everything... blinding me with terror... It gobbles up the inside of my bean like fiery soup... using the bar for a spoon... It will never go away...

It took me a long time to recover. My convalescence dragged on for another two months. I had been very sick... it ended with a rash... The doctor came often. In the end he insisted they send me to the country... That was easy to say, but we hadn't the cash... They took me out in the fresh air whenever possible.

When the January quarter came due, Grandma Caroline went out to Asnières to collect the rent. She took me with her. She owned two brick and stucco houses out there on the rue de Plaisance, a little one and a medium-size one, she rented them out to working-class people. They were her property, her income, her savings.

We started off. We had to go slow on my account. I was weak for a long time, I'd get nosebleeds for no reason at all, and I peeled all over. After the station it's straight ahead... Avenue Faidherbe... Place Car-not... At the Town Hall you turn left and then you cross the park.

At the bowling alley between the fence and the waterfall, there's always a crowd of funny old codgers... lively old grampas full of spunk, always good for a joke, and some that grouse the whole time, retired shopkeepers... Every time they knocked the ninepins over, the jokes flew thick and fast... I understood all their gags... better and better as time went on... The funniest thing was when they had to pee... they'd trot behind a tree, one at a time... They had an awful hard time of it... "Hey, Toto, watch out you don't lose it..." That's the kind of thing they said. The others took up the refrain. To me they were irresistible. I laughed so loud my grandmother was embarrassed... Standing around in that wintry blast listening to their cracks... it was a good way to catch your death...

Grandma didn't laugh much but she wanted me to enjoy myself... It was no joke at home... she realized that... and this was cheap entertainment... We stayed a little while longer... When the game was over and we finally left the little old-timers, it was almost dark...

Caroline's houses were beyond Les Bourguignons... after the Market Gardens, which in those days extended all the way to the dikes at Achères.

So as not to sink into the muck and manure, we had to walk single file on a line of planks... You had to be careful not to bump into the frames... whole rows of them full of seedlings... I went behind her, still laughing but careful to keep my balance, remembering all those cracks... "Did you enjoy it all that much?" she asked. "Tell me, Ferdinand. Did you really?"

I didn't care for questions. I shut up like a clam... To own up brings bad luck.

We got to the rue de la Plaisance. That's where the work began. Collecting the rent was a headache... the tenants were in full revolt. They fought every inch of the way and they never paid in full... never... they tried every slimy trick... The pump was always out of order. The discussions were interminable... They started griping about everything under the sun before Grandma even opened her mouth... The shithouse was stuffed up... They were very dissatisfied... they shouted their complaints from every window in the place... they wanted it fixed... and right away!... They were afraid we'd put one over on them... They hollered to prevent us from mentioning the rent... They wouldn't even look at the bills... Their shithouse was really stopped up, it was overflowing into the street... In winter it froze and the bowl cracked under the slightest pressure... Every time it cost eighty francs... The bastards wrecked everything in sight... That was the tenants' way of getting even... And making children... Every time we came back there were new ones... with less and less clothes on... Some of them were stark- naked... Lying in the bottom of a cupboard...

The worst drunks and slovens treated us like dirt... They watched every move we made as we unplugged the drain. They followed us to the cellar when we went down for the bamboo pole to clean out the siphon... Grandma pinned up her skirts with safety pins and stripped to her shift on top. Then we went to work... We needed lots of hot water. We had to get it from the shoemaker across the street and bring it over in a pitcher. The tenants wouldn't give us a drop. Then Caroline started poking down into the drain. She worked her pole back and forth and dislodged the muck. The pole alone wouldn't do it. She plunged in with both arms, the tenants all came out with their brats to watch us cleaning out their shit... and the papers... and the rags... They'd wad them up on purpose... Caroline was undaunted... what a woman! Nothing could get her down...

She fought her way through. The tenants saw the drain was working again. They couldn't help admiring her energy... not to be outdone, they began to help us... They brought out wine... Grandma clinked glasses with them... she wasn't one to bear grudges... We wished each other Happy New Year... it was all very cordial and friendly... That didn't bring in any money… They were unscrupulous... If she'd given them notice, they'd have had time for vengeance before moving out... They'd have wrecked the whole joint... Both houses were full of holes... Every time we went out there we tried to fill them in... it was a waste of time... they kept making more... We took putty with us... Pipes, attics, walls, and floors were all shreds and patches... But what they attacked most viciously was the toilet bowl... The whole thing was full of cracks... It made Grandma cry to look at it... Same with the garden gate... They'd bent it double... it looked like licorice... For a while we'd given them a concierge, a friendly, obliging old woman... she hadn't lasted a week... She was so horrified she cleared out. In less than a week two of the tenants had gone up to strangle her... in her bed... some nonsense about doormats.

Those houses are still there. Only the name of the street has changed... from "Plaisance" to "Marne"... That was the fashion for a while...

Lots of tenants have come and gone, bachelors and spinsters, whole families, generations... They've gone on making holes, and so have the rats, the little mice, the crickets and woodlice... No one has plugged them in ages... Uncle Édouard inherited the houses. They've taken so much punishment they've got to be regular sieves... no one paid his rent anymore... the tenants had grown old, they were tired of arguing... so was my uncle... they were even sick of fighting about the shit-house... there was nothing more to wreck, there was nothing left. They turned them into storerooms. They put in their wheelbarrows, their watering cans and coal... At the moment we don't even know exactly who's living there... they've been condemned to widen the street... they're going to be torn down... As far as we know, there are four families... Portuguese, so they say.

Nobody's bothered to try to keep them up... Grandma knocked herself out, it didn't do her any good... when you come right down to it, that's what killed her... messing around that day in January even later than usual, first in cold water, then in boiling water... always in the draft, putting oakum in the pump and thawing out the faucets.

The tenants came out with their candles to needle us and see if the work was getting ahead. The rent? Well, they wanted a little more time. We should come around next week... We started back to the station.

At the ticket window Grandma Caroline had a dizzy spell. She clutched the railing... it wasn't like her... She had chills all over... We went back across the square to a café... While we were waiting for the train, the two of us shared a grog... When we got to Gare Saint-Lazare, she went straight home to bed... she was all in... she came down with a high fever, same as I'd had in the Passage, but hers was grippe and it turned to pneumonia... The doctor came morning and evening... She was so sick that we in the Passage didn't know what to tell the neighbors when they asked.

Uncle Édouard shuttled back and forth between her place and the shop... She was worse than ever... She was sick of having her temperature taken, she didn't even want us to know what it was... She still had all her wits about her. Tom hid under the furniture. He didn't budge, he hardly ate... My uncle came to the shop. He had a great big balloon full of oxygen.

One night my mother didn't even come home for supper... Next morning it was still dark when Uncle Édouard shook me in my bed and told me to get dressed quick. To go and kiss Grandma, he explained... I didn't know exactly what he meant... I was still half asleep... We walked fast... It was on the rue du Rocher... second floor... The concierge hadn't been to bed... She came out with a lamp to light the hallway... We went upstairs. Mama was in the first room crying… . down on her knees, slumped against a chair. She was moaning softly, mumbling in her grief... Papa was standing... he didn't say a word... He went out to the landing... then he came back again... He looked at his watch... He tugged at his moustache... Then I caught a glimpse of Grandma in her bed in the next room... She was breathing hard, gasping, suffocating, making a disgusting racket... The doctor was just leaving... He shook hands with everybody... Then they led me in. I could see she was fighting for breath. She was all yellow and red, her face was covered with sweat, like a wax mask beginning to melt... Grandma stared at me, but her look was still friendly... They had told me to kiss her... I was already leaning against the bed. She motioned me not to... She smiled a little... She wanted to tell me something... There was a rasping sound in her throat... it wouldn't come out... in the end she made it... she spoke as softly as she could... "Work hard, my dear little Ferdinand," she whispered... I wasn't afraid of her. We understood each other deep down... The fact is that I have worked hard, all in all... That's nobody's business...

She wanted to say something to my mother too. "Clémence, my little girl... take care... don't let yourself go... please, for my sake..." That was all she could manage. She couldn't breathe at all... She motioned us to leave... to go into the other room... We obeyed... We could hear her... The whole apartment was full of it... We stayed there at least an hour, stunned and silent. My uncle went to the door. He wanted to see her, but he didn't dare disobey. He only pushed open one of the double doors, that way we could hear her more distinctly... There was a kind of hiccup... My mother jumped up... She went *eek*, as if her throat were being cut. She crumpled up in a heap on the carpet between her chair and my uncle... Her hand was clenched so tight over her mouth that we couldn't take it away...

When she came to, she screamed: "Mama's dead"... over and over... she didn't know where she was... My uncle stayed on to keep watch... We went back to the Passage in a cab...

We closed the shop. We rolled down all the blinds... We felt kind of ashamed... kind of guilty... We didn't dare to move... for fear of spoiling our grief... Mama and all of us cried with our heads on the table... We weren't hungry... We didn't want anything... We didn't take up much room, but we'd have liked to make ourselves even smaller... to apologize to somebody, to everybody... We forgave each other... We begged and promised to- love each other... We were afraid of losing each other... forever... like Caroline.

Then came the funeral... Uncle Édouard attended to everything all by himself... he had made all the arrangements... He had his grief too... He didn't show it... He wasn't demonstrative... He called for us at the Passage just as they were taking away the body...

Everybody... neighbors... and people with nothing else to do... came over and said: "Be brave." We stopped on the rue Deaudeville to pick up our flowers... We took the best... Nothing but roses... They were her favorite flower...

We couldn't get used to her absence. Even my father was shattered... There was nobody but me to have scenes with... I was getting better but I was still so weak it was no fun to pick on me. Seeing me so wobbly, he hesitated to bellow at me...

I dragged myself from one chair to another... I had lost six pounds in two months... I was wasting away. I puked up all the cod-liver oil...

My mother couldn't think of anything but her grief. The shop was sinking beyond rescue... Even at rock-bottom prices we couldn't sell our trinkets... The customers were all stone broke… they were making up for their wild extravagance at the Exposition... They had as little mending done as possible. They thought twice before spending five francs...

My mother would sit there for hours without moving, on her bad leg, in an impossible position, benumbed... When she got up, it hurt so bad that she'd limp the whole time... My father would pace about upstairs in the opposite direction. The sound of her limp drove him nuts…

I'd pretend I had to do something. I'd go to the can and play with myself... I'd give it a tug or two... I couldn't get it up...

Aside from the two houses that had gone to Uncle Édouard, there were three thousand francs left from Grandma's estate... But that money was sacred... Mama said so right away... We must never part with it... We unloaded the earrings, they went for loans, one in Clichy, the other in Asnières... And yet our stock was getting sleazier and skimpier... enough to break your heart... it was hardly fit to show...

Grandma at least had been enterprising, she'd bring us stuff to sell on consignment... white elephants that other dealers were willing to lend her... But with us it wasn't the same... They were suspicious... no get-up-and-go, that's what they thought of us... We were going to the dogs...

When my father came home from the office, he'd dream up solutions... some pretty grim ones... it was he who cooked our bread soup... Mama wasn't up to it... he'd be stringing the beans... why wouldn't we turn on the gas and all commit suicide?... My mother just sat there... He blamed it all on the Freemasons... and Dreyfus!... and all the other criminals who were out to get us.

My mother was off her rocker... even her movements were weird... She'd always been clumsy, now she dropped everything. She'd break three dishes a day... She never came out of her daze... She was like a sleepwalker... If she went into the shop she'd be afraid... She didn't want to move, she'd stay upstairs the whole time...

One night when we were going to bed and not expecting anybody anymore, Madame Héronde turned up. She began to hammer at the shop door and sing out... We'd forgotten all about her. I went to open. My mother didn't want to be bothered, she even refused to see her... She just went hobbling around the kitchen. So then my father spoke up:

"How about it, Clémence? Make up your mind. If you leave it to me, I'll just send her home, you know that." She thought it over a minute, then she went down. She tried to count the pieces Madame Héronde had brought back... She couldn't count right... She was all muddled with grief... ideas, figures, it was all a fog... Papa and I helped her...

Then she went up to bed... Later she got up and came down again... She spent the whole night straightening out the shop, furiously, obstinately putting the stuff away.

In the morning everything was in perfect order... She was a different woman... You wouldn't have recognized her... All of a sudden she felt ashamed...

What a terrible humiliation to have let Madame Héronde see her so frazzled!

"When I think of my poor Caroline!... of the energy she had up to the last minute. Ah, what if she'd seen me like that!"

Suddenly she bucked up. During the night she had even made all sorts of plans... "Well, Ferdinand, son, if the customers won't come to us anymore, we'll go find them!... spring is coming, we'll close the shop for a while... We'll do all the markets in the suburbs... Chatou!... Le Vésinet!... Bougival!... where they're putting up all those fine villas... where all the fancy people live... That will be better than stewing in our own juice... than hanging around here waiting for nothing!... Besides you'll get some fresh air!"

The idea of doing the markets didn't appeal to my father one bit!... A risky business... It panicked him to think about it... He foresaw the worst complications... We were sure to get our last remnant of merchandise stolen!... We'd be stoned by the local shopkeepers... Mama let him talk... She'd made up her mind.

Anyway, we had no choice. We were skipping every other meal... We'd taken to lighting the stove with tapers instead of matches.

One morning the time came and we raced off to the station. My father carried the big bundle, an enormous piece of canvas stuffed with merchandise... Everything we had left that wasn't too disgusting... Mama and I lugged the cartons... On the platform at Saint-Lazare he ran through the list of his fears again. Then he beat it to the office.

In those days Chatou was quite a trip. We were there at the crack of dawn... We bribed the local cop... he rolled out the red carpet and found us a place... We found a stand for our stuff... We had a pretty good spot... between a butcher and a man selling little birds. But they didn't want us there... that was plain from the start.

The butter-and-egg man behind us kept griping the whole time. For his money we were screwballs with piles of rubbish. He made some very crummy remarks!

The alley we were in wasn't the best place, but it was near the park... in the shade of magnificent linden trees... About noontime the ladies appeared... simpering and my-dearing... If a wind started up, we were lost. At the first breeze all our stuff blows away, all the bonnets and hankies and ribbons... Those things are just waiting to take off, they're as light as clouds... We fastened them with mountains of clasps and clothespins. Our stand looked like a hedgehog... The ladies strolled by... capricious creatures... butterflies followed by one or two cooks... then they'd turn and come back... my mother tried to catch them with her spiel... to draw their attention to her embroideries... to the boleros she was taking orders for... to her "Brussels type" lace... or Madame Héronde's gossamer marvels...

"Isn't it amusing to meet you here!... In this drafty market!... Oh, you have a shop?... Do give me your card!... Of course we'll come to see you!"

They went on to gush somewhere else, we didn't sell them much... Well, it was publicity... Now and then a tornado would pick up our doodads and drop them on the veal cutlets next

door... The butcher gave us a piece of his mind...

We'd have made out better if we'd brought along our handsome dressmaker's dummy with the firm bust... that would have brought out our exquisite treasures... the muslin and satin frills, the creations of Madame Héronde's fairy wand... To maintain a Louis XV flavor, an atmosphere of refinement, amid the tripe and vegetables, we'd haul out a real museum piece, a diminutive masterpiece, the rosewood doll's cupboard... We kept our sandwiches in it.

Our dread, maybe even worse than the wind, was showers... All our finery turned to pancakes... The ochre ran out in rivers... the sidewalk was all sticky with it... The stuff felt like a lot of sponges... The trip home was awful. We never complained in my father's hearing.

The following week it was Enghien and certain Thursdays Clignancourt... the Porte... We were right next to the Flea Market... I liked the markets all right... they made me miss school. The fresh air pepped me up... When we saw my father in the evening, he gave me a pain in the neck... He was never satisfied... He met us at the station... I felt like dropping the little cupboard on his dogs to make him jump.

At Clignancourt it was an entirely different clientele... We'd only lay out our junk, our worst crap, the stuff that had been in the cellar for years. We let it go for beans...

It was at the Flea Market that I met little Paulo. He worked for a woman two rows behind us. He sold buttons up and down the avenue, near the Porte, or he'd stroll around the market with his tray on his belly, held up by a string around his neck. "Thirteen for two sous, ladies..." He was younger than me but awfully smart... We made friends right away... What I admired about Popaul was that he didn't wear shoes, just boards tied on with tapes... They didn't hurt his feet... So I took off mine too when we went out on expeditions together on the fortifications.

He sold his buttons quick, in baker's dozens, bone and mother-of-pearl, you didn't have time to look... After that we were free.

In addition he had a little racket. "It's easy," he explained as soon as we had no secrets from each other. In Bastion 18 or in the streetcar shelters near La Villette, he'd make little dates with soldiers and butchers and soften them up. He asked me to come and meet them. I couldn't, because it was too late when he did those things... You could make five francs, sometimes more.

Behind the weighing house he showed me, I didn't ask him to, the way grown-ups sucked him off. Popaul was lucky, he had juice, I didn't have any yet. One time he made fifteen francs in a single evening.

I had to lie to get away, I said I was going for French fries. My mother knew Popaul well, she couldn't abide him even at a distance and she forbade me to go with him. We went just the same, we'd go wandering around as far as Gonesse. I found him irresistible... Every time he got a little scared, he had a tick, he'd suck in his tongue, and suck and suck, it made him look awful. In the end, from seeing so much of him, I began to do it too.

Popaul's boss, the one that sold the drygoods, had a funny little jacket she put on him; it was very special, like a blazer, all covered with buttons, big ones and little ones, thousands of them, in front, in back, a whole sample case, mother-of-pearl, steel, and bone...

Popaul's idea of heaven was absinthe; his boss poured him a little aperitif whenever he came back sold out. It made him spunky. He smoked army tobacco, we made our own cigarettes out of newspaper... he didn't mind sucking people, he had a dirty mind. Every man we passed, we'd bet how big it was. My mother couldn't leave her stand, especially in that kind of neighborhood. I'd slip away more and more... And then here's what happened:

I'd thought Popaul was a regular guy, loyal and faithful. I was mistaken. He behaved like a queer. Why not face it? He was always talking about an arquebus. I didn't know exactly what he meant. So one day he brings it over. It was a big rubber band on a forked stick, a kind of slingshot, for shooting sparrows. "Let's practice," he says. "Then we'll smash a window!... There's an easy one on the avenue... After that we'll try a cop!..." OK, it seemed like a good idea. We go off by the school... "We'll start here," he says. School was just out and it was handy for a getaway. He passes me his beanshooter... I put in a big stone. I pull it way back... as far as the rubber will go... "Take a gander up there!" I say to Popaul. And ping!... crash!... right square in the clock!... the whole thing flies into smithereens... I stand there frozen like an asshole The racket and the dial going to pieces like that... I'm flabbergasted. People come running... I'm screwed... cornered like a rat... They all start tugging at my ears. "Popaul!" I holler... He's melted into thin air... He's gone!... They drag me off to my mother. They raise hell with her. She'd better pay for the breakage... or they'll take me off to jail. She gives her name, her address... I try to explain: "Popaul!"... The slaps rain down so thick and fast I can't see straight...

At home it starts up all over again, a tempest... My father beats the hell out of me, kicks me in the ribs, steps on me, takes my pants down. In addition he keeps bellowing that I'm killing him!... that I ought to be in jail! that I should have been there from the start!... My mother pleads, clings to him, falls at his feet, and screams that in prison "they get even worse." I was the lowest of the low. I was a gallowsbird. That's what I'd come to!... Popaul had a good deal to do with it, but there was the fresh air too and the freedom... I won't try to justify myself.

We spent a whole week like that, absolutely frantic. Papa was so mad, he got so red in the face, we were afraid he'd have an attack. Uncle Édouard came in from Romainville just to reason with him. Uncle Arthur didn't have enough influence, he was too frivolous. Rodolphe was far away, touring the provinces with the Capitol Circus.

Our neighbors and relations, everybody in the Passage, thought the best thing would be to give me a good physic and my father too, it would be good for both of us. They racked their brains and finally decided it was worms that made me so wicked... They gave me some substance... I shat yellow, I shat brown. It sort of calmed me down. It affected my father too... he was struck dumb for at least three weeks. All he did was give me a long suspicious look now and then... from a distance. I was still his bane, his cross. We took another physic, each of us had his own. He took Rochelle Salts, me castor oil, she took rhubarb. Then they decided that we wouldn't do the markets anymore, that gadding about would be my downfall. I made everything impossible with my criminal instincts.

My mother took me back to school, giving me lots of advice on the way. She was in a terrible state when we got to the rue des Jeûneurs. Everybody had warned her they wouldn't keep me a week... But I played it safe, they didn't throw me out. But I have to admit that I didn't learn anything. School made me miserable, the teacher with his goatee, always bleating his problems. It gave me the creeps just to look at him. After all the fun I'd had with Popaul it made me sick to sit still for hours on end listening to a lot of tripe.

The kids tried to have a little fun in the yard, but it was pitiful, the wall in front was so high it crushed you, it killed their desire to play. They went back in to struggle for good conduct tokens... Hell!

In the yard there was only one tree with one branch and one bird. The kids got it with a slingshot. The cat spent a whole recreation period eating it. My marks were average. I was afraid of being put back. I was even commended for good behavior. We all had shitty asses. I taught them how to keep their pee in little bottles.

In the shop the jeremiads got worse and worse. My mother kept mulling over her sorrow. She thought of her mother on every possible occasion, she remembered the slightest details... If somebody came in at closing time to sell some knickknack, she'd burst into tears... "If only my mother were here," she'd blubber, "she knew just what to buy..." Those remarks were disastrous...

We had an old friend who knew exactly how to take advantage of Mama's melancholy... Her name was Madame Divonne, she was almost as ancient as Aunt Armide. After the war of 1870 she and her husband had made a fortune selling lambskin gloves in the Passage des Panoramas. The shop was famous and they had another one in the Passage du Saumon. At one time they had eighteen people working for them. "All day long there are customers pouring in and out," Grandma used to say. Handling so much dough had gone to her husband's head. One fine day he lost everything and then some in the Panama Canal. Men have no guts... instead of fighting it out, he ran off with a skirt. They'd sold everything at a loss. After that she was down and out. Madame Divonne lived on this one and that one. Her only solace was music. She had a little something left, but so little that she barely got enough to eat and not every day at that. She sponged on her friends. She had married her glove man for love. She wasn't a tradeswoman by birth, her father had been a prefect under the Empire. She played the piano beautifully. She never took off her fingerless gloves because her hands were so delicate, and in the winter she wore thick mittens, but of openwork and decorated with pink pompons. She was always careful about her appearance.

She turned up at the shop... she hadn't been to see us in a long time. Grandma's death had moved her deeply. She couldn't get over it. "So young!" she'd say at the end of every sentence. She spoke with delicacy of Caroline, of their past, their husbands, of the Passage du Saumon and the Boulevards... with fine shadings and exquisite tact... She really had nice manners, I could see that... As she reminisced, everything turned into a fragile dream. She didn't take off her veil or her hat... on account of her complexion, she said. The real reason was her wig. We never had much on hand for dinner... We'd invite her all the same... But when she'd finished her soup, she'd take off her veil and her hat and the whole works... she'd pick up her soup plate and drink it down... That seemed the handiest way... on account of her false teeth, I guess. You could hear her wiggling them... She distrusted spoons. She was crazy about leeks but we had to cut them up for her, that was a bore. When we were through eating, she still didn't want to go home. She'd get gay. She'd turn to the piano, a pledge one of our customers had forgotten to redeem. It was never tuned, but it worked pretty well.

Everything got on my father's nerves and so did the old lady with her playful ways. But he softened when she struck up certain arias from *Lucia di Lammermoor*, and especially the Moonlight Aria.

She took to coming all the time. She didn't wait to be invited... She was perfectly aware of the havoc. While we put the shop in order, she'd race upstairs, she'd settle herself on the piano stool and toss off two or three waltzes and then *Lucia* and then *Werther*. She had quite a repertory, the whole *Châlet* and Fortunio's song. We had to go up sometime. She'd never have stopped if we hadn't sat down to table. "Peekaboo," she'd call out when she saw us. During dinner she'd do a good job of crying in unison with Mama. It didn't spoil her appetite. She didn't mind noodles. I was always aghast at the way she kept asking for more. She pulled the same game all over town, sharing memories with bereaved shopkeepers... She had vaguely known the dear departed of any number of neighborhoods. That was her way of keeping body and soul together.

She knew the history of every family in the Passages. And when there was a piano, she couldn't be beat... At past seventy she could still sing *Faust*, but she took precautions. She stuffed herself full of gumdrops to keep from going hoarse... She sang the choruses all by herself, making a megaphone with her hands. "Glory and fame to the men of old!"... Without taking her hands off the keys, she managed to pound it out with her feet.

In the end it was so funny we couldn't control ourselves, we'd die laughing. But once she was started, a little thing like that couldn't faze Madame Divonne. She was a born artist. Mama felt ashamed, but she laughed too... It did her good.

For all her faults and kittenishness, my mother couldn't do without her. She took her along wherever she went. At night, we'd take her as far as the Porte de Bicêtre. She'd walk the rest of the way, to Kremlin, not far from the Old People's Home.

On Sunday morning she'd call for us and we'd all go to the cemetery together. Ours was Père Lachaise, 43rd Division. My father never went in. He couldn't stand graves. He'd never go any farther than the square outside La Roquette prison. He'd read his paper and wait for us to come back.

Grandma's vault was very well kept. Sometimes we'd empty out lilacs, sometimes it was jasmine. We always brought roses. That was the family's only luxury. We'd change the vases, we'd polish the windows. Inside it was like a Punch and Judy show with colored statues and real lace altar cloths. My mother kept bringing new ones, that was her consolation. She was always putting the house in order.

While we were cleaning up, she sobbed the whole time... Caroline was down there, not very far away... I always thought of Asnières... The way we'd knocked ourselves out for those tenants. I could see her, so to speak... The place was spic and span, we washed it out every Sunday, but there was a funny little smell from down below... pungent, subtle, kind of sour, insinuating... once you'd caught it, you smelled it all over... in spite of the flowers... mixed in with the scent... clinging to you... It makes your head spin... it comes from the tomb... you think you must have been mistaken. And there it is again!... It was I who went down to the end of the lane to fill the pitchers for the vases... When we'd finished, I didn't say a word... And then that little smell came back at me... We'd close the door... We'd say a prayer... And we'd start down the hill to Paris...

Madame Divonne never stopped chattering the whole way... Getting up so early, working on the flowers, and all that crying whetted her appetite... Besides there was her diabetes... In any case she was hungry... The moment we left the cemetery, she wanted to have a snack. She couldn't stop talking about it, it got to be an obsession with her. "'You know what I feel like, Clémence? Not meaning to be greedy... A little slice of galantine on a nice fresh roll... How does it strike you?"

My mother didn't answer. She was embarrassed. I felt like throwing up on the spot... I couldn't think of anything else but vomiting... I thought of the galantine... of what Caroline must be looking like now down there... of all the worms... the big ones... the fat ones with feet… gnawing, swarming about in there... All that decay... millions of them in all that swollen pus, the stinking wind...

Papa was there... He had barely time to take me behind a tree... I threw it all up... everything... on the grating... My father jumped fast... but he didn't dodge it all...

"You damn pig!" he yelled. He had it all over his pants... The people were looking at us. He was mortified. He went off by himself in the other direction, toward the Bastille. He didn't want to have anything to do with us after that. We went to a little café for a cup of verbena to settle my stomach. It was a tiny little café just across from the prison.

I've often gone by there since. I always look inside. And I never see a soul.

Uncle Arthur was up to his ears in debt. From the rue Cambronne to Grenelle he had borrowed so much without ever returning it that his life was impossible. He was shiftless. One night he moved on the q.t. A friend helped him. They tied his stuff on a donkey cart. They were going out to the suburbs. We were already in bed when they came to notify us.

Arthur took advantage of the occasion to ditch his housemaid... She'd been talking about vitriol... Anyway, it was time he took a powder.

He and his pal had found a shanty where nobody would come around, in the hills around Athis-Mons. The very next day his creditors descended on us. The bastards, they never budged out of the Passage... They even went after my father at the insurance company. It was disgraceful. My father was in a terrible state... We were in for it again...

"What scum! What a family! What a crummy lot they all are. Never a minute's peace! They even come and hound me on the job!... My brothers act like a bunch of jailbirds! My sister sells her ass in Russia! My son has every known vice! It's a fine how-do-you-do! Christ almighty!..." My mother couldn't think of anything to say... She'd given up trying to argue with him. He could go on to his heart's content.

The creditors realized that Papa set store by his honor... They wouldn't give an inch. They never left our shop... As if things weren't rough enough already... If we'd paid his debts, we'd have really starved...

"We'll go and see him next Sunday," my father decided. "I'll give him a piece of my mind… as man to man!"

We left at daybreak to make sure of finding him before he started on his rounds... First we got lost... Then we picked up the trail again... Finally we located him... I expected to find Uncle Arthur all shriveled up, repentant, scared out of his wits, hiding in some cave, hunted by three hundred cops... eating stewed rats... That was what happened to escaped convicts in *Illustrated Adventure Stories*... It was a little different with Uncle Arthur... Early as it was, we found him at a table outside a bistro— La Belle Adèle. He gave us a royal welcome in the arbor… He was drinking hard on credit, and no vinegar either... A nice little *muscadet rosé*... first class... he was in the best of health... He'd never felt better... He had the whole neighborhood in stitches... they were crazy about him... they ran over to listen to him... La Belle Adèle had never had so many customers... Every single seat was taken, the overflow was sitting on the steps... Small homeowners from as far as Juvisy... in phony Panama hats...

And all the fishermen from the canal, in wooden shoes, would come out to La Belle Adèle just to meet Uncle Arthur. They'd never had so much fun in all their lives.

He had something up his sleeve for everybody! Every imaginable game from quoits to pitching pennies... Speeches... riddles... under the trees... for the ladies. Uncle Arthur was the life of the party, the ladies' delight... He knocked himself out, he spared no effort... But he never took his hat off, his artist's sombrero, though it was midsummer... the sweat ran down his face in rivers... He was always dressed the same... pointed shoes, corduroy pants... and that tie, an enormous bow like a lettuce leaf.

With his taste for domestic help he had floored all three waitresses... Happy to wait on him and love him... He didn't want to hear one word about his troubles in Vaugirard... Let bygones be bygones... He was going to start a new life... My father was all set to chew his car off... he wouldn't even let him get started... He kissed us each in turn... He was mighty glad to see us... "Arthur! Will you listen to me for one moment!... Your creditors are blockading our doorway... from morning to night!... They're driving us crazy... Do you hear me?" Arthur disposed of all those sordid memories with a sweeping gesture. And the way he looked at my father! Like he was a poor obstinate crackpot... The truth is he felt sorry for him! "Come along

now, the whole lot of you!... Come on, Auguste. You'll talk later. I'm going to show you the most beautiful view in the whole region... Saint-Germain is nothing... Just another little hill... The path on the left and then down the covered lane... My studio's at the end."

That's what he called his shanty. He wasn't lying, the situation was all right... A view of the whole valley... The Seine as far as Villeneuve-Saint-Georges and on the other side the forest of Sénart. You couldn't conceive of anything better. He was lucky. He didn't pay rent, not a sou.

Supposedly he was the caretaker, looking after the landlord's pond...

The pond only had water in it in the winter, in the summer it was dry. He was popular with the fair sex. He helped the local servant girls to wise up. His place was full of food... *muscadet* like down below, sausage, artichokes, and mountains of the little cream cheeses my mother was so fond of. He wasn't badly off... He told us about the orders he was getting... signs for every bar, grocery store, and bakery for miles around... "They do the useful things, I supply the charm!" That was his philosophy... There were sketches all over the walls: "At the Sign of the Stuffed Pike" with an enormous fish in blue, red, and vermilion... "The Fair Sailor Lass" for a laundress friend, with luminous nipples, a mighty ingenious idea... His future was assured. We could all be pleased.

Before we started back for the village, he stashed everything away in three or four big crocks, the food, and the white wine, as though burying treasure in a furrow... He didn't want to leave a trace. He was suspicious of the people who came by. On his door he'd written in chalk: "Never coming back."

We went down to the locks, he knew the bargemen. It was a long hike on steep paths, my mother limped along behind us. When we got there, she felt dizzy and sat down on a stone. We watched the tugboats maneuvering barges through the locks, they looked so frail and delicate against the walls... they don't dare to touch the sides...

The pudgy lockkeeper spits tobacco juice three times, takes off his coat, clears his throat, and curses over his windlass... The gate trembles on its pivot, groans, and starts moving in little jerks... The whirlpools hold it back... a trickle of water and finally she opens... the *Artémise* lets out a long whistle... the string of barges pulls in.

Further on you see Villeneuve-Saint-Georges... Little hills and then the gray bridge over the Yvette... Down below, the country... the plain. The wind starts up, stumbles over the river, whips up water in the floating washhouse... an endless lapping... branches beating triplets in the water... From the valley... from all sides... The modulated song of the breezes... Forgotten the debts... we don't even mention them... The air has gone to our heads... We bat the breeze with Uncle Arthur... He wants to take us across. My mother won't let us go... He jumps into a scow all by himself. He wants to show us his talents. He starts rowing against the stream. My father jumps with excitement and fires advice at him, exhorts him to be careful. Even my poor mother's interest is aroused. She fears the worst. Limping, she follows us up the bank... The shore is lined with fishermen casting worms through the air... Uncle Arthur gets in their way... They give him hell... He gets caught in the water lilies, he flounders... He starts up again, sweating like a whole football team. He turns, slips into the narrows, he has to row like hell toward the gravel pits, "the big eggbeater" is coming, the *Pride of the Quarries*, you can hear her in the distance, grinding up the river with a terrible clanking of chains... She drags at the bottom, bringing everything to the surface... every known kind of mud and corpses and pike... She kicks up waves that hit both banks at once... Wherever she goes, she spreads terror and disaster... The boats by the shore toss furiously and crash into the stakes... All three basins are rocking at once... It's death on the boats. There she is, the *Pride of the Quarries*, coming out from under the bridge. All the hardware, all the catapults and steering gear in hell are rattling inside her carcass and on her balconies. She's dragging at least twenty barges loaded with clinkers... This is no time to show off... My uncle gets tangled in a rope... He hasn't time to reach the shore... His boat rises on the swell... his beautiful lid falls in the soup... He bends forward, this is going to be the great stroke... He loses his oar... he loses his head... He tries again... He tips... He falls flat on his ass in the drink, exactly like a water fencer. Luckily he knows how to swim!... We all come running, we comfort him, we congratulate him... the Apocalypse has passed... By now she's sowing havoc up by Ris-Orangis.

We all repair to the Lost Minnow, where the lockkeepers hang out, we congratulate each other... It's aperitif time... Hardly taking the time to dry, Uncle Arthur gathers all his friends around him... He has an idea!... Wants to start a club called the "Brethren of the Sail." The fishermen are less enthusiastic. He takes up a collection... His little girl friends come over and kiss him. We stay on for supper... Under the Japanese lanterns, between soup and mosquitoes, he breaks into song: "A poet once told me..." Nobody wants Uncle Arthur to go back to his pond... Everybody wants his company... He doesn't know whom to please first...

We started for the station... We slipped away quietly while he was still warbling... But my father wasn't happy... especially when he thought it over... He was burnt up inside. He was furious with himself for not having spoken up... He'd been lacking in firmness. We went out to see him one more time. Arthur had a new boat with a real sail... and even a little jib up front... He tacked about singing "O Sole Mio." The gravel pits echoed with his singing. He was as happy as a lark... My father couldn't stand it... This couldn't go on... Long before the aperitif we slunk away with our tails between'our legs... Nobody saw us leave... We never went back... It was impossible to associate with him anymore... He would have debauched us...

My father had been working for La Coccinelle exactly ten years. That entitled him to a vacation, two weeks with pay...

It wasn't very sensible for the three of us to go away like that... it cost a fortune... But that was a terrible summer, the heat was killing us in the Passage, especially me, I looked the greenest, I was growing too fast. I was so anemic I could hardly stand up. We went to see a doctor, he was alarmed. "What he needs isn't two weeks, but three months of fresh air!..." That's what he said.

"Your Passage," he went on, "is a pesthole... You couldn't even get a radish to grow there.

It's a urinal without doors or windows... You've got to get out of there."

He was so outspoken about it that my mother came home in tears... We needed more money... They didn't want to dig too deeply into the three thousand francs we had inherited... So they decided to try the markets again: Mers... Onival, and especially Dieppe... I had to promise to watch my behavior... to stop bombarding clocks... to stop going with hoodlums... not to stir from my mother's side. I promised the moon and the stars... I'd be good, I'd even be grateful... and I'd work hard for my school diploma when we got back...

That reassured them and they decided we could go. We closed the shop. First my mother and I would spend a month in Dieppe and look around... Madame Divonne would come in from time to time to see that nothing went wrong while we were gone... Papa would join us later, he'd make the trip on his bicycle... He'd spend two weeks with us...

Once we were there, the two of us got settled very quickly, we really didn't have too much trouble. We found lodgings in Dieppe over a café, the Tomtit, in an apartment that belonged to a clerk in the post office. We had two mattresses on the floor. The only trouble was the sink. It didn't smell good.

When it came time to unload our stuff on the main square, my mother got jittery. We had brought a complete collection of embroideries, frills, and baubles, all very light and airy. It seemed awfully risky to display all those things out in the open in a strange city... After thinking it over, we decided it would be better to go straight to the customers, it was a lot of trouble of course, but there was less chance of being taken... We did the whole length of the Esplanade, along the ocean front, from door to door... It was hard work. Our stuff was heavy. We'd wait outside the villas, on a bench across the way. The best time to go in was when they'd just filled their bellies... You had to hear the piano... Now they're moving into the drawing room...

My mother would jump up and race to the doorbell... The reception could be good or bad... Anyway she managed to sell a certain amount...

I got plenty of air. There was so much of it and so strong that it made me drunk. It even woke me up at night. I saw nothing but cocks and asses and boats and sails... The laundry floating on the clothes lines gave me a terrible hard-on... It swells out... it drives you crazy... all those women's panties...

At first we were afraid of the sea... We'd stick to the little sheltered streets as much as we could. The gale makes you delirious. I never stopped playing with myself...

A traveling salesman's kid lived in the room next to ours. We did all our homework together. He felt me up a little, he jerked off even more than I did. He came to Dieppe every year, so he knew all the different kinds of boats. He taught me all about their rigging and their sails... Three-master barks... square-riggers... schooners... I studied the ships with passion while my mother was doing the villas...

She got to be as well known on the beach as the coconut man... always hobbling around with her bundle... Inside there were embroideries, patterns, needlework sets to keep the ladies busy, and even irons... She'd have sold kidneys, rabbit skins, hot air, anything, to help us last out the two months.

In our comings and goings we also had our qualms about the port. We were afraid to go too close to the edge on account of the bollards and ropes that are so easy to trip over. It's a mighty treacherous place. If you fall into the muck, it sucks you down, you sink to the bottom, the crabs eat you, they never find you again...

The cliffs are dangerous too. Every year whole families get squashed under them. A moment's carelessness, a false step, a thoughtless remark... and the mountain falls down on top of you. We took as few chances as possible, we seldom left the streets. In the evening, right after supper, we'd start ringing bells again. We'd make a grand tour... starting first at one end, then at the other... We'd do the whole Avenue du Casino...

I'd wait on a bench outside the villas... I'd hear my mother shouting herself hoarse inside... She really knocked herself out... I knew all her arguments by heart... I knew all the stray dogs... They turn up, they sniff, they beat it... I knew all the peddlers, that's the time when they come home with their carts... They pull, they push, they run themselves ragged... Nobody takes any notice of them... They're free to curse and swear all they like... They grunt and groan and tug at the shafts... One more pull... just to the next corner... The lighthouse blinks its big eye in the night... The flash passes over the old man... On the beach the surf sucks up pebbles... crashes... rolls... crashes... breaks...

On the posters we saw there was going to be an automobile race after the fair on August 15. That would be sure to attract a lot of people, especially the English. My mother decided we'd stay on a while. We hadn't had much luck. The weather had been so bad in July that the ladies stayed home with their embroidery... That didn't help us to sell our bonnets and boleros, or even our needlework sets... If at least they had worked at it! But they never got through mending their drapes!... They yacked even worse at the seashore than in town... like all society women... always about maids and bowel movements...

They took it easy, they wallowed in idleness, they'd dawdle over our merchandise, pick things up a dozen times...

My father had lost hope. His letters were full of worry. We were done for in his opinion. We'd lost more than a thousand francs. My mother wrote him to dig into the inheritance. That was real heroism, all this could end very badly. I could already see myself getting blamed for the whole mess. He wrote back that he was coming. We waited for him in front of the church. He finally hove in sight with his bike all covered with mud.

I expected him to bawl the hell out of me, blame everything on me. I was all prepared for one of his headlong corridas... but not at all... Actually he seemed glad to be alive and glad to see us. He even congratulated me on my conduct and my red cheeks. I was really moved. He himself suggested a little walk in the port... He knew all about boats. He remembered his whole childhood... he was an expert on navigation. My mother went off with her bundles and we made for the docks. I remember a Russian three-master, all white. She had made for the harbor mouth on the afternoon tide.

For three days she'd been fighting the storm off Villers, rolling in the swell... her jibs were full of foam... She had an awful cargo of loose lumber, mountains of it, piled every which way on every deck. In the holds there was nothing but ice, enormous dazzling blocks, the top of a river. She'd brought it all the way from Archangel to sell in the cafés... She was listing badly and the crew weren't happy... My father and I and a lot of other people went over and followed her in from the harbor light to her berth. She was so drenched with spray that her mainyard was dragging in the water... I can still see the captain, an enormous roly-poly, shouting into his funnel, ten times louder than even Papa. His monkeys climbed up in the shrouds to roll up all the spars and canvas, all the gaffs and yards up to the big St. Andrew's cross at the masthead... During the night they'd expected her to be smashed against the rocks... The rescue squads had refused to put out, God had taken the day off... Six fishing smacks had been lost. Even the big buoy off the reef of Trotot had taken too much punishment and broken loose from its chain... That gives you an idea of the weather.

In front of the Saucy Trollop café they maneuvered her around the mooring buoy... The drift wasn't bad. But the hauling crew were so drunk they couldn't see straight... They hauled in the wrong direction... The bow smashed into the customs wharf... The "lady" on the prow, the beautiful sculptured figurehead, stove her tits in... It was a shambles... The sparks flew... The bowsprit went through the window... straight into the café... The jib scraped the bar.

Everybody was screaming and yelling... People came running. The curses volleyed and thundered... Finally, as gently as you please, the fine ship pulled alongside... Bristling with cables, she tied up at the dock... After a great deal of activity the last sail fell from the foremast... spread out on the deck like a seagull.

The stern hawser gives a last deep groan... The land embraces the ship. The cook comes out of his galley and empties out an enormous bowl for the squawking birds. The giants on board stand at the rail shaking their fists, the drunken longshoremen aren't in the mood to go up the gangplank. The companion ladders are dangling alongside.

The harbor master's clerk in a frock coat is the first to go aboard... The pulley swings a plank overhead... More insults fly... The rumpus goes on... the longshoremen swarm over the rigging... The hatch covers are taken off... Now we see the iceberg in sections... After the forest... Faster, coachman!... Here come the wagons... There's nothing more to see, the excitement is elsewhere.

We go back to the semaphore, they're expecting a collier. She comes in past Guignol Rock with her flag at half-mast.

The pilot in his boat dances and splashes from one wave to the next. He's fighting every inch of the way... he's thrown back... finally he grabs the ladder and climbs up the side. The old tub has been hammering into the storm all the way from Cardiff... She's rolling from rail to rail in a mountain of foam and spray... She's caught in the current, carried toward the breakwater... Finally the tide shifts a bit, sets her right, and drives her into the harbor mouth... Her whole hull is trembling as she pulls in, the waves are still chasing her. She grunts and rumbles and blows out steam. Her rigging screeches in the gale. Her smoke falls back on the crests of the waves, the ebb tide beats against the jetties.

Now you can make out the "helmets" in the Emblemeuse narrows... the little rocks come up at low tide...

Two cutters in trouble are trying to feel their way through... There's going to be a tragedy; we mustn't miss a mouthful... The fans collect at the end of the breakwater by the bell... They study the situation through binoculars... A man beside me lends me his... The squalls are getting so thick they gag you. You can't breathe... The wind blows up the water rougher than ever... it splashes in streams high up against the lighthouse... way up to the sky.

My father pulls his cap down... We wouldn't be going home before nightfall... Three dismasted fishing boats come in... You can hear the voices from the channel... They're calling each other... They get tangled up in each other's oars...

Mama was beginning to worry, she's waiting for us at the Little Mouse, the fishmongers' hangout... She hasn't sold much... But the two of us aren't interested in anything but ocean voyages.

Papa was a good swimmer, he was crazy about bathing. It didn't appeal to me. The beach at Dieppe is no good. But after all, this was vacation. And besides I was even filthier than in the Passage.

At the Tomtit we only had one little basin for the three of us. I got out of washing my feet. I was beginning to smell very bad, almost as bad as the sink.

Sea bathing takes a lot of courage. The crest of the wave seethes and foams, rises high in the air, roars, descends reinforced with thousands of pebbles. It catches me.

Chilled to the bone, bruised, the child totters and falls... A universe of pebbles beats my bones amid the flaking foam. First your head wobbles, sways, staggers, and pounds into the gravel... Every second is your last... My father in a striped bathing suit, between two roaring mountains, is shouting like mad. He bobs up in front of me... he belches, thrashes about, makes wisecracks. A roller knocks him over too, turns him upside down, there he is with his feet in the air... He's wriggling like a frog... He can't straighten himself out, he's done for... At this point a terrible volley of pebbles hits me in the chest... I'm riddled... drowned... It's awful... I'm crushed under the deluge... Then the wave carries me back and lays me down at my mother's feet... She tries to grab me, to rescue me... The undertow catches me, carries me out... She lets out a terrible scream... The whole beach comes running... But it!s no use... The bathers crowd around, all hysterical... The raging sea pounds me down to the bottom, then lifts me gasping to the surface... In a flashing moment I see that they're discussing my agony... There they are, every imaginable color: green... blue, parasols, lavender ones, lemon-yellow ones... I whirl about in pieces... And then I don't see a thing... A life preserver is strangling me... They haul me up on the rocks... like a whale... Brandy scorches my throat, they cover me all over with arnica... and those terrible rubdowns... I'm burning under the bandages... I'm strangled in three bathrobes...

All around me people are saying the sea is too rough for me! OK! That suits me fine. I hadn't expected as much... It was a sacrifice... on the altar of energetic cleanliness...

Already ten days had passed. Next week it would all be over. My father would have to go back to the office. It made us sick to think about it. There wasn't a single minute to waste.

We weren't selling much. All of a sudden business had got so slow that only a real moment of panic could have made us decide to go on that excursion... to take the boat to England, all three of us... It was the idea of going back so soon that sent us off our rockers, that drove us to extremes...

We started off at daybreak, hardly time for a cup of coffee... Grandma's nest egg... well... we'd already gone through half of it...

We went on board ahead of time... We had the cheapest seats, in the bow... they were fine... We had a wonderful view of the whole horizon... It was agreed that I'd be first to point out the foreign shores... The weather wasn't bad, but even so, as soon as we were a little way out and had lost sight of the lighthouses, it began to be kind of wet... The ship started to seesaw; this was real seafaring... My mother took refuge in the shelter where the life jackets were kept... She was the first to vomit across the deck and down into third class... For a moment she had the whole area to herself...

"Watch out for the child, Auguste," she had barely time to yelp... That was the surest way to infuriate him...

Some of the others began straining their guts over the side... In the rolling and pitching, people were throwing up any old place, without formality... There was only one toilet... in one corner of the deck... It was already occupied by four vomiters in a state of collapse, wedged in tight... The sea was getting steadily rougher... At every rising wave, oops... In the trough a dozen oopses, more copious, more compact... The gale blew my mother's veil away... it landed wringing wet on the mouth of a lady at the other end... who was retching desperately... All resistance had been abandoned. The horizon was littered with jam... salad... chicken... coffee... the whole slobgullion... it all came up...

My mother was down on her knees on the deck... she smiled with a sublime effort, she was drooling at the mouth...

"You see," she says to me in the middle of the terrible plummeting... "You see, Ferdinand, you still have some of that tuna fish on your stomach too..." We try again in unison. Bouah! and another bouah!... She was mistaken, it was the pancakes... With a little more effort I think I could bring up French fries... if I emptied all my guts out on deck... I try... I struggle... I push like mad... A fierce wave beats down on the rail, smacks against the deck, rises, gushes, rolls back, sweeps the steerage... The foam stirs up the garbage and spins it around between us... We swallow some of it... We spit it up again... At every plunge the soul flies away... at every rise you recapture it in a wave of mucus and stink... It comes dripping from your nose, all salty. This is too much!... One passenger begs for mercy... He cries out to high heaven that he's empty... He strains his guts... And a raspberry comes up after all!... He examines it, goggle-eyed with horror... Now he really has nothing left!... He wishes he could vomit out his two eyes... He tries, he tries hard... He braces himself against the mast... he's trying to drive them out of their sockets... Mama collapses against the rail... She vomits herself up again, all she's got... A carrot comes up... a piece of fat... and the whole tail of a mullet...

Up top by the captain, the first and second class passengers were leaning over the side to puke, and it came tumbling down on us... At every wave we caught a shower with whole meals in it... We were lashed with garbage, with meat fibers... The gale blows the stuff upward... it clings in the shrouds... Around us the sea is roaring... the foam of battle... Papa in a cap with a chin strap... supervises our misery... He's in the pink, lucky man, he's a born sailor... he gives us good advice, he wants us to lie even flatter... to crawl on the floor... A woman comes staggering... she wedges herself in beside Mama so as to throw up better... There's a sick mutt, too, so sick he shits on the ladies' skirts... He rolls over and shows us his belly... piercing screams are heard from the shithouse... Those four are still jammed in, they can't puke anymore, they can't pee, they can't shit... They're leaning over the toilet, pushing... They bellow, begging someone to shoot them... And the tub pitches still higher... steeper than ever... and plunges into the depths... into the dark green... And she rises again, the stinker, she picks you up again, you and the hole in your stomach...

A stocky little character, a wise guy, is helping his wife to throw up in a little bucket... he's trying to encourage her.

"Go on, Léonie... Don't hold back... I'm right here... I'm holding you." All of a sudden she turns her head back into the wind... The whole stew that's been gurgling in her mouth catches me full in the face... My teeth are full of it, beans, tomatoes... I'd thought I had nothing left to vomit... well, it looks like I have... I can taste it... it's coming up again... Hey, down there, get moving!... It's coming!... A whole carload is pushing against my tongue... I'll pay her back, I'll spill my guts in her mouth... I grope my way over to her... The two of us are crawling... We clutch each other... We embrace... we vomit on each other... My smart father and her husband try to separate us... They tug at us in opposite directions... They'll never understand...

Why bear grudges? It's nasty. Bouah!... That husband is a stupid brute!... Come on, sweetie, we'll vomit him up together!... I give his fair lady a complete hank of noodles... with tomato juice... a drink of cider three days old... She returns the compliment with Swiss cheese… I suck at the strings... My mother's snarled up in the ropes... she comes crawling after her vomit... The little dog is caught in her skirts. We're all tangled up with this brute's wife... They tug at me ferociously... He starts peppering my ass with his boot to get me away from her... He was a regular bruiser... My father tried to mollify him... he hadn't said two words when the other guy rams him in the breadbasket with his head and sends him sprawling against the winch… And that wasn't the end of it! The strong man jumps on him and starts hammering at his face... He bends down to finish him off... Papa was bleeding all over... The blood poured down into the vomit... He was slipping down the mast... In the end he collapsed... But the husband still wasn't satisfied... Taking advantage of a moment when the roll has sent me spinning he charges me... I skid... He flings me at the shithouse... like a battering ram... I smash into it… I bash the door in... I fall on the poor sagging bastards... I turn around... I'm wedged in the middle of them... They've all lost their pants... I pull the chain. We're half drowned in the flood. We're squashed into the bowl... But they never stop snoring... I don't even know if I'm dead or alive.

The siren woke everybody up. We climbed up and stuck our heads out the portholes. The jetties at the entrance to the harbor were like a lacework of wooden piles... We looked out on England as though disembarking in the other world...

Here too there were cliffs and then green... But much darker and rougher than on the other side... The sea was perfectly flat now... It was easy to vomit... but you didn't need to so much anymore.

Talk about shivering... it's a wonder our teeth didn't crack... My mother was weeping spasmodically from having vomited so much... I had bumps all over... A big silence fell in our ranks... everyone felt bashful, worried about going ashore. Corpses couldn't have been any more bashful.

The steamer tugged at the anchor, gave two, three jerks, and then we really stopped. We fished around for our tickets... Once we were through customs we tried to clean ourselves up. My mother had to wring her skirt, rivers of water ran out. My father"d taken such a beating a chunk of his moustache was missing. I pretended not to notice but he had some shiner. He dabbed at it with his hander-kerchief... Little by little we pulled ourselves together. The streets were still heaving pretty bad. We walked past the shops, little tiny ones the way they are over there, with striped shutters and little whitewashed stoops.

My mother did her best, she didn't want to hold us back, but she was limping way behind... We thought of going to a Hôtel, of taking a room right away so she could rest... just a little while... we'd never get to London, we were already too wet... We were sure to get sick if we tried to go any farther... And besides, our shoes wouldn't hold out. They were drinking up the mud, making a noise like a flock of sheep...

We identified a hôtel... The word was written on the front in gold letters... At the door we got scared and went past... The rain kept coming down harder and harder... We tried to figure out how much things would cost, the least little things... We were afraid of the currency... We went into a tearoom... they understood us all right... Once seated, we looked at our suitcase... It wasn't ours! In the confusion at the customs we'd taken the wrong one... We ran back p.d.q... ours was gone... we gave the one that didn't belong to us to the Stationmaster... So then we didn't have anything... We were really out of luck... Such things only happened to us... That was perfectly true in a way... My father didn't pass up the opportunity to point it out... We had no fresh clothes to put on... not even a shirt! Still, we had to see the sights... People began to notice us in the village, the three of us shivering in the rain. We definitely looked like gypsies. We thought we'd better take a road out of town... We took the first one we saw... after the last house...

"Brighton" said a signpost. Fourteen miles ahead... We were good walkers, that didn't scare us. But we couldn't keep together. My father was always way ahead... He wasn't very proud of us... Even there, soaked, muddy, half crippled, he kept as far away from us as possible... He couldn't stand us clinging to him... He kept his distance...

My mother was so fagged out she could hardly drag her leg. She was panting like an old hound.

The road wound along the cliffs. We pushed along in the downpour. Down below the ocean roared at the bottom of the chasm... full of clouds and landslides.

My father's yachting cap was oozing into his mouth. His dust coat clung so tight his ass looked like an onion.

Mama hobbles along... she abandons her hat, the one trimmed with swallows and little cherries. We gave it to a bush... The gulls running away from the storm are screeching all around us. They must have been surprised to see us in the clouds too... Under the gusts of rain we kept our foothold as best we could... On the side of the cliff, on hills like waves, another and still another... endless... The clouds had spirited my father away... He seemed to melt away in the downpour... Every time we saw him he was farther away, pressing on doggedly, always smaller, heading down the far slope.

"We'll just climb to the top of this one, Ferdinand... And then I've got to rest... Do you think he can see Brichetonne? Do you think it's still far?..." She was at the end of her rope. It was impossible to sit down. The embankments were pure mud... Her clothes had shrunk so that her arms stuck way out... Her shoes were swollen up like saddlebags... At that point my mother's leg buckled... It caved in under her weight... She toppled over into the ditch... her head was wedged in, stuck fast... She couldn't move... All she could do was make bubbles like a toad... The rain in England is like an ocean suspended in midair... little by little you drown... I shouted: "Papa!... help!..." at the top of my lungs... Mama had fallen head down. I pulled with all my might... it was like a tug-of-war. It was no good... But finally our explorer turns up after all. He's all dizzy with the clouds. We go at it together... we heave and we hoist. She moves. We extract her from the muck... She comes up smiling. My, was she happy to see her Auguste again! Was he all right? He hadn't had too bad a time? What had he seen from the end of the cliff? He didn't answer... He only said we'd better make it snappy... Get back to the port quick... Up and down, another hundred hills... breathless and panting. The storm had made such a mess of the road we couldn't recognize it on the way back... We caught a glimpse of lights... the port, the lighthouses... It was pitch dark... Crawling, staggering, we passed the same Hôtel... We hadn't spent a nickel... We hadn't met anybody... We hadn't a stitch of clothing to our name... we were all strips and tatters... We looked so worn out they were good to us on the boat... they let us move from third to second class... they told us to lie down... At the station in Dieppe we stretched out on the benches... We were going right back... In the train there was another big scene on account of Mama's constipation...

"You haven't gone in a week!... You'll never go again." "I'll go when we get home..."

The irregularity of her bowels was an obsession with him... it haunted him. Sea voyages are constipating. From then on he couldn't think of anything but her bowels. In the Passage we were finally able to dry ourselves. All three of us had colds. We got off easy. My father had a beautiful shiner. We said it was a horse, he just happened to be behind it when something exploded...

Madame Divonne was bubbling with curiosity, she wanted to hear all about it... every detail of our adventure... She'd been to England too, on her honeymoon. She was so eager to hear about it she stopped playing the piano... Right in the middle of the Moonlight Aria...

Monsieur Visios was also crazy about stories and discoveries... Édouard came by with Tom to hear the news... Mama and I had our little impressions too... But Papa wouldn't let us open our mouths... He hogged the floor... He had certainly seen some amazing, fantastic, stupendous, absolutely unexpected things... at the end of the road... way out beyond the cliffs... When he was in the clouds... between Brigetonne and the hurricane... Papa all alone, cut off from the world!... lost in the tempest... between heaven and earth...

Now it was over he stopped at nothing, he gave them all the wonders they could ask for... He shot off his mouth like a machine gun... Mama didn't contradict him... She was always happy to see him triumph... "Isn't that right, Clémence?" he'd ask her when his story was getting a bit too tall... She nodded, she backed up everything he said... Of course she knew he was overdoing it, but if it gave him pleasure...

"But what about London? You didn't get there?" asked Monsieur Lérosite, the optician from 37, who was completely senile and imported his lenses from over there...

"Oh, yes, but only the outskirts... We saw the best part!... The harbor!... When you come right down to it, that's the only thing that's really worth seeing! And the suburbs... We only had a few hours." Mama didn't bat an eyelash... Soon word got around that we'd been in a big shipwreck... that the women had been landed on the cliffs with a cable... He made it up as he went along... And the way we'd gone roaming around London with the other survivors... mostly foreigners... He stopped at nothing... He even imitated their accents.

There was a session every night after dinner... fantasies, new ones every time... Madame Méhon was beginning to boil and bubble again... in her den, she didn't come over... we were too mortally on the outs for that... She made her phonograph sing so as to interrupt my father... so as to make him stop... Mama closed the shop to give us a little peace and pulled the shutters all the way down... Then Madame Méhon came over and banged on the windows to needle Papa, to make him come out and start a riot... My mother wouldn't let him... The neighbors were all furious. They were all on our side... They were developing a taste for explorations... One night when we came home from our errands, we didn't hear Madame Méhon and her phonograph... Our usual visitors came in one by one... We settled ourselves in the back room... Papa started in on his story... it was something brand-new... Suddenly from the old battle-ax's place... boom!... a tremendous blast! And a whole string of firecrackers!... The flash is blinding. It explodes against the shop! The door crashes in! We see the old bag waving her arms... she's holding a torch and some rockets... She lights the fuses!... The rockets whistle and whirl! She'd dreamed up the whole act just to cramp my father's style! She flails around like a demon. She sets fire to her skirts. She's going up in flames. The people rush out. They smother her in curtains. They put out the blaze! But her shop's on fire, corsets and all. The firemen come running. We never saw the old witch again. They took her away to the bughouse in Charenton. She stayed there for good. Nobody wanted her back. They signed a petition from one end of the Passage to the other, saying she was insane and impossible.

Hard times were back again. No more talk of vacation or markets or England... The rains pounded down on our glass roof, the Passage was closed up tight with the sour smell of people and little stray dogs.

It was fall...

The thrashings were coming thick and fast again because I wanted to play instead of doing my homework. I didn't catch on very well in school. Once again my father made the discovery that I was really feeble-minded. The sea air had made me grow but had made me more listless than ever. I was always daydreaming. He flew into terrible tempers. He accused me of hopeless laziness. Mama was beginning to moan and groan again.

Her business was going from bad to worse. The styles never stopped changing. Batiste came in again. We dragged out our old bonnet tops. The ladies rolled them up like napkins and put them on their tits and in their hair. In the crisis Madame Héronde was always busy making things over. She invented boleros of Irish linen, made to last twenty years. Alas, it was only a passing fancy. After the Grand Prix we mounted them on wire, now they were lampshades . '. . Sometimes Madame Héronde was so worn-out she got her orders balled up, she gave us little embroidered bibs when we were expecting comforters... The scenes were something... The customer would split a gut and threaten to haul us into court. We were in despair, we paid for all the damage, which accounted for two months' worth of noodles... The day before my examination a volcano erupted in the shop, Madame Héronde had dyed a "négligé" cuckoo- yellow, when it was actually meant to be a bridal dress. People have been killed for less! A criminal blunder! The customer would skin us alive!... And it was all written plain as day in the order book!... Madame Héronde collapsed sobbing in my mother's arms. My father was upstairs bellowing.

"Ah, you'll always be the same! You'll always be soft. Haven't I warned you forty-six times? Didn't I tell you they'd ruin us... those seamstresses of yours... Ah! Suppose I made even half a mistake at La Coccinelle!... I can just imagine what they'd say in the front office!" The mere idea was so terrifying that he thought he was dead and buried... He blanched... We sat him down... The crisis passed... I went back to my arithmetic... He reviewed my lessons with me... And I couldn't think of anything to say, he got so balled up in his explanations that I couldn't see straight... I attacked the problem ass-backwards... I didn't know very much to begin with... I gave up... He started in on my failings... In his opinion I was incorrigible... For my money he was as nutty as a fruitcake... He started up again about my division... He tangled himself up to the square roots... He slapped my face... he pulled my ears... He accused me of grinning... of taking him for a fool...

My mother came in for a minute... That redoubled his fury... He bellowed that he wanted to die!

On the morning of my exam my mother closed the shop. She thought it would encourage me if she came along. The exam was held at the grade school next to Saint-Germain-l'Auxerrois, right in the entrance hall. On the way she tried to bolster up my self-confidence. It was a solemn occasion, she thought of Caroline. That made her whimper some more...

All the way around the Palais-Royal she made me recite my Fables and the list of departments... At eight o'clock sharp we were all outside the gate, waiting to have our names taken. The kids were all cleaned up and neatly dressed, but terribly nervous, the mothers too.

First there was dictation, then problems. It wasn't very hard, I remember, all you had to do was copy. This was a bunch that had flunked the previous fall. For almost all of us it was a matter of life and death... if you wanted to be taken on as an apprentice... When it came to the oral, I was lucky, I pulled a big fat little guy with warts all over his nose. He had a flowing bow tie, sort of like Uncle Arthur... he wasn't an artist, though... He'd been a pharmacist on the rue Gomboust. Some of the people there knew him. He asked me two questions about plants... I hadn't the faintest idea... He answered them himself. I was in a complete muddle... Then he asked me the distance between the sun and the moon and then between the earth and the other side... I was afraid to stick my neck out too far. He had to come to the rescue. When he asked me about the seasons, I knew a little more. I mumbled something kind of vague... He really wasn't hard to please... He finished all the answers for me.

Then he asked me what I was planning for the future if I got my diploma. "I'm going into business," I said without enthusiasm.

"It's a hard life, my boy," he said. "Couldn't you wait a while? Another year perhaps?"

I guess he didn't think I was very strong... Right away I thought I'd flunked... I thought of the return home, of the tempest I was going to unleash... I began to feel dizzy... I thought I was going to faint... I could feel the blows in advance... I clutched the desk... The old guy saw me turn pale...

"Come, come, boy," he said. "Don't worry. All that doesn't mean a thing. I'll pass you. You'll get your start in life. If you want it as badly as all that."

I went back and sat down on a bench, some distance away, by the wall... I was still mighty upset. I wondered if he hadn't been soft-soaping me, just to get rid of me. My mother was outside the church, on the little square. She was waiting for the results...

Everybody hadn't finished yet... there were still some kids waiting... I saw the others now... stammering their confessions across the table cover... the map of France, the continents... Since hearing those words about starting out in life, I looked at my little friends as if I'd never seen them... Their dread of failing made them strain against the desk, wriggling as if they were caught in a trap.

Was that what it meant to start out in life?... They were trying to stop being kids that very moment... struggling to arrange their faces, to look like men...

We all looked pretty much alike, all dressed the same way, in our school smocks. They were all like me, small shopkeepers' kids... or their parents did tailoring at home or sold stationery or something... They were all pretty puny... They opened their eyes big and round, they panted like puppies in their effort to answer the old guy...

Lined up along the wall, the parents watched the proceedings... The looks they shot at their offspring were fierce, electric, enough to cramp anybody's style.

The kids were wrong every time... They shrank up even smaller... The old man was untiring... he answered for everybody... The kids were all dunces... The mothers' faces were getting redder and redder... Thousands of thrashings threatened... There was a smell of impending massacre... Finally all the kids were through... It was all over, except for the list of successful candidates... And then miracle of miracles... everybody had passed! The government inspector made the announcement from the platform... He had a paunch with a chain on it, a great big watch charm that jiggled between sentences. He sort of bumbled and got all the names screwed up... It didn't matter...

He took advantage of the occasion to say a few words... they were really kind words... cordial and encouraging... He told us that if we conducted ourselves as valiantly in later life we had nothing to fear, we'd be rewarded.

I'd wet my pants and shat in them something awful too, I could hardly move. I wasn't the only one. None of the kids were able to walk right. But my mother caught a whiff while pressing me to her bosom... The stink was so terrible we had to make it fast. We couldn't stop to say good-bye to all my little friends... My studies were over... to get home even faster we took a cab...

We made a draft... The cab had funny windows that rattled all the way. She spoke of Caroline again. "How glad she'd have been to see you succeed! Ah! I only hope she has second sight!..."

My father was on the second floor with the lights out, waiting to hear the results. He was so excited he had taken in the sidewalk display and the lamps all by himself...

"Auguste! He passed!... Do you hear?... He passed... He came through with flying colors!"

He received me with open arms... He lit the lamp to get a good look at me. He gazed at me affectionately. I'd never seen him so moved... His whole moustache was trembling...

"That's splendid, my boy! You've given us a lot of trouble... But now I congratulate you... Now you'll be starting out in life... The future lies open before you... If only you take the right course... the straight and narrow!... Work hard!... Struggle..."

I begged his forgiveness for having always been bad. I hugged and kissed him with all my heart... Only I stank so bad he began to sniff...

"Ah! What's this?" He pushed me away. "Oh, the stinker... the little pig!... He's filled the whole place with shit! Ah, Clémence, Clémence! For God's sake take him upstairs before I lose my temper! He's revolting..." That was the end of his effusions.

They scrubbed me hard, they drenched me in cologne. The next day we went looking for a really respectable establishment where I could start my business career. A place where they wouldn't be too easy on me, where they wouldn't let me get away with anything.

If you really want to learn, you've got to be on the jump. That was Édouard's opinion. He had twenty years of experience. Everybody agreed with him.

In business it's absolutely essential to look your best. An employee who lets himself go is a disgrace to his firm... You're judged by your shoes... Never look down-at-the-heel!..."

The Prince Regent, near Les Halles, had been in business for a century... You couldn't hope for better. A lifelong reputation for ferocious pointed dress shoes... they were known as "duckbills." Your toenails are driven into your flesh, the man of fashion is a cripple! My mother bought me two pairs, guaranteed to last forever. Then we went across the street to the Deserving Classes clothing store... We took advantage of the sales, I needed a complete outfit.

She bought me three pairs of pants, of such good quality, so long-wearing, that we took them a little bigger, with a ten-year hem. I was still growing fast. The jacket was as somber as possible, besides I kept my arm band, my mourning for Grandma. I had to look thoroughly serious-minded. Collars are important too, you mustn't go wrong... a wide collar can atone for a multitude of sins when you're young and scrawny. The only flight of fancy permitted was a frivolous snap-on bow tie. Naturally there had to be a watch chain, but darkened too for mourning. I had the whole works. I looked respectable. I was all set. Papa wore a watch too, but his was gold, a precision instrument... He counted every passing second on it to the very end... The long hand fascinated him, the one that goes around fast. He'd sit there for hours looking at it...

My mother herself took me to introduce me to Monsieur Berlope, Ribbons and Trimmings, on the rue de la Michodière. just across the boulevard.

Being the soul of honesty, she had told him all about me in advance... That he'd have his hands full with me, that I'd be a hard row to hoe, that I was pretty lazy, disobedient by nature, and passably scatterbrained. That was her idea. I always did my best. In addition she warned them that I picked my nose incessantly, that it was a passion with me. She suggested that they try to shame me. She said they'd always been trying to better me, but it didn't help much... While listening to these details, Monsieur Berlope was slowly paring his nails... He looked thoughtful and grave. He was wearing a terrific vest sprinkled with golden bees... I remember his fan- shaped beard too, and his round embroidered skullcap that he didn't take off for us.

Finally he answered... He'd try to train me... He still hadn't looked at me... If I showed willingness, intelligence, and zeal... Well, he'd sec... After a few months behind the counter, maybe they'd send me out on the road... with a salesman... to carry the sample cases... I'd get to know the customers... But before taking any chances, he'd have to see what I was good for... If I had a business head!... If I was cut out for the job... if I had the competence... the loyalty…

After what my mother had said, all that seemed mighty doubtful…

While speaking, Monsieur Berlope ran a comb through his hair, spruced himself up, took a look at his profile, there were mirrors all over the place... He was doing us an honor in seeing us... Mama never tired of saying so… it was a big favor to be interviewed by the boss in person.

Berlope & Son didn't hire just anybody, not even on trial, not even without pay!

The next morning at seven o'clock sharp I was already on the rue Michodière, outside their iron shutter... I jumped to it... I helped the errand boy... I turned the crank for him... I wanted to show my zeal first thing...

Of course it wasn't Monsieur Berlope himself that broke me in, it was Monsieur Lavelongue... He was a real bastard, you could see that right away. He had his eye on you all day long, always trying to catch you off your guard... Wherever you went, he came pussyfooting along behind you... He slithered after you like a snake, from corridor to corridor... His arms dangling, ready to pounce, to crush you... on the lookout for a cigarette... for the least bit of a butt... for any poor tired bastard that sat down...

Before I'd finished taking my coat off, he gave me the lowdown. "I am your personnel director... What's your name?" "Ferdinand, sir."

"Well, you'd better get this straight... No monkey-shines around here... If you're not absolutely up to snuff in a month from now... I personally will fire you... Understand?... Have I made myself clear?"

Having made himself clear, he vanished like a ghost between the piles of boxes... He was always mumbling something or other... When you thought he was miles away, he was right on top of you... He was a hunchback. He'd hide behind the customers. The salesmen lived in terror of him from morning to night. He always had a smile on his face, but it was a special kind of a smile... Really poisonous...

Silk gets into a worse mess than any other kind of material. All the different widths and lengths, the samples and leftovers, get rumpled and twisted and scattered all over the place... By the end of the day it's a horrible sight... Enormous mounds, all tangled up like bushes.

From morning to night the store is full of dressmakers' errand girls, clucking and griping, never satisfied. They rummage, they complain, they splash around... the place is a nuthouse of silks and satins... wriggling and writhing with ribbons...

After seven o'clock we have to put it all away, what a mess!... There are too many of us... We suffocate in the stuff... An orgy of loose ends. Thousands and thousands of colors... moiré, satin, tulle... Where-ever those yak-yaks get a hand in, it's worse than a battlefield. There isn't a single box left. The numbers are all mixed up. We get the hell bawled out of us and then some... By every louse in the department! Fat salesmen with slicked-down hair or wigs à la Mayol.[103]

Cleaning up is the apprentices' job... Rolling up the spools, pinning up ends, turning the baby ribbon... the masses of felt... macramé, velvet... the riot of changeable silk... all the leftovers, the whole sickening avalanche of remnants... it's all for the apprentices. You've hardly got it straightened out when some more wreckers start in... making more havoc... ruining all your work...

They put on airs... they make idiotic remarks, they're so kittenish you want to puke... and always carrying their patterns around, looking for some other shade, the one we haven't got...

In addition to this I had my regular job that was pretty exhausting... running back and forth to the stockroom. About fifty times a day. It was on the eighth floor. I had to tote all the boxes. Whole carloads of tag ends, of mixed-up snippets or plain rubbish... All the returns were my job... The marquisettes, big pieces and little pieces, the styles of a whole season—I hauled them up seven flights. It was really a rough job. Enough to kill a mule. With all my hurry and effort my collar with the bow tie on it worked itself up around my ears. And yet it was double-starched.

Monsieur Lavelongue was very hard on me... and unfair. As soon as a customer came on the scene, he motioned me to beat it. I wasn't ever allowed to hang around. I wasn't fit to be seen... Naturally with all the layers of dust in the stockroom and the way I sweated, my face was one big smudge. But the moment I left he began to give me hell for disappearing. It was impossible to please him.

The other punks were in stitches at the way I was always running, the way I raced up the stairs. Lavelongue wouldn't let me rest a minute:

"A little sport is good for young people!..." That was his line. I'd hardly come down when they'd slip me another load!... "Get going, kid. You can't fool me."

Smocks were not worn in the garment district in those days, it wasn't considered proper.

With the kind of work I was doing my beautiful jacket was soon threadbare.

"You're going to wear out more than you make," my mother complained. That wasn't hard, because I wasn't paid at all. It's true that in some trades the apprentices had to pay to learn. In a way I was lucky... I was in no position to complain... I raced up to the stockroom with so much vigor that the other kids called me the Squirrel. Even so, Lavelongue always had it in for me. He couldn't forgive me for having been taken on by Monsieur Berlope. The mere sight of me gave him the gollywobbles. He couldn't stand my guts. He did everything he could to discourage me.

He even complained about my shoes, he said I made too much noise on the stairs. It's true I had a tendency to walk on my heels, my toes hurt something terrible, especially toward closing time they felt like hot coals.

---

[103] Wigs à la Mayol. Mayol was a popular cabaret singer (1872-1941), famous in part for the large tuft of hair over his forehead. This feature was imitated in the wigs bearing his name.

"Ferdinand!" he'd yell. "You're insufferable. You make more racket all by yourself than a whole bus line." That was an exaggeration.

My jacket was coming apart in several places. I was a bottomless pit for suits. They had to have another one made out of one of Uncle Édouard's old ones. My father was in a constant temper, he was having the worst kind of trouble at the office. While he was away on vacation, those bastards, the clerks, had taken advantage of his absence to slander him... Monsieur Lempreinte, his boss, believed every word they told him. His trouble was stomach cramps. When he was really in pain, he saw tigers on the ceiling... That didn't help.

I didn't know what to do to make a good impression at Berlope's. The harder I raced up the stairs, the more Lavelongue couldn't stand me. I really gave him a pain in the neck.

Along around five o'clock he went out for a cup of coffee, and I took the opportunity to take my shoes off for a minute up in the stockroom. I'd do it in the can too when nobody was there. So one day those cocksuckers go and tell the boss. Lavelongue did a hundred-yard dash, I was his obsession... He was there in two seconds flat.

"Will you come out of there, you little skunk? Is that what you call working?... Jerking yourself off in every corner you can find... Is that your way of learning the trade?... Flat on your ass with your dick in the air!... That's the younger generation for you!"

I found another place where I could give my dogs a little air. I'd hold them under the faucet. My shoes were always getting me in trouble... at home too... after making such a sacrifice, my mother would never have admitted that she had bought them too narrow. It was just my laziness again. My unwillingness. I was always in the wrong.

The stockroom where I took the boxes was little Andre's headquarters... His job was repairing the boxes and going over the numbers with a brush and blacking. He'd started in the year before. He lived miles away in the suburbs, he had a long way to travel... The hole he lived in was after Vanves, the neighborhood was called "the Coconut Palms."

He had to get up at five o'clock so as not to spend too much on streetcars. He brought a basket. His grub was in it. It was closed with a rod and padlock.

In the winter he didn't budge, he ate in the stockroom, but in summer he'd go out to the Palais-Royal and eat on a bench. He'd leave a couple of minutes ahead of time to be there at twelve sharp when the cannon went off. He liked that.

He never showed himself much, he always had a cold, he was always blowing his nose even in the middle of August.

His clothes were worse than mine, all patches. The other apprentices were always picking fights with him because he stuttered and didn't make sense... He preferred to stay upstairs, no one came up to bother him.

His aunt whopped the hell out of him too, especially when he peed in bed, terrible lickings, he described them in detail. Mine were nothing in comparison... He wanted me to go to the Palais-Royal with him, he wanted to show me the whores, he spoke to them, so he claimed. He had some sparrows too that would even fly down on his bread. But I couldn't go. I had to go straight home. My father had sworn he'd have me locked up in La Roquette if he caught me bumming around.

On the subject of women, my father was a holy terror... if he suspected me of wanting to see what it was like, he flew into a ferocious temper. It was enough that I jerked off. He brought it up every day on the slightest pretext. He was suspicious of little André... He had the instincts of the common people... He was a hoodlum's kid... With me it was entirely different, I had respectable parents and I shouldn't ever forget it, I was reminded every night when I got home from Berlope's, so tired I couldn't see straight. I'd get an old-time thrashing if I dared to talk back!... I'd better not keep bad company! I already had too many foul habits that I'd picked up God knows where... If I listened to little André, I'd be sure to end up a murderer. My father could swear to it. Actually he regarded my loathsome vices as a part of his misfortunes, of the terrible troubles that fate had heaped on him...

I did have terrible vices, it was undeniable, it was awful. That's the truth. He didn't know

how to go about saving me... And I didn't know how to go about making amends... Some children are simply untouchable.

Little André smelled bad, his smell was more acrid than mine, the smell of really poor people. He smelled up the whole stockroom. His aunt cropped his hair short with her own scissors, he looked like a lawn with a single tuft left in front.

With all the dust he breathed in, the snot in his nose turned to putty... it was stuck tight... His favorite pastime was prying out a chunk and quietly eating it. Since we blew our noses with our fingers in the middle of all the blacking and boogers and numbers, we ended up looking like niggers.

Little André handled about three hundred boxes a day... His eyes were always dilated from trying to see in that attic. He kept his pants on with strings and safety pins.

Now that I was doing the dumbwaiter work, he stopped coming in through the salesrooms. That was better for him, it spared him a lot of rough treatment. He came in through the court, slipped past the caretaker's lodge, and went up the outside stairs... If there were too many numbers, I'd stay late and help him. After hours I was able to take my shoes off.

When we wanted to shoot the shit, we had it pretty nice. On account of his nose we slipped into a little nook between two beams, sheltered from the drafts.

André was lucky with his feet, he had stopped growing. Two of his brothers were still living with another aunt in Les Lilas. His sisters were with his old man in Auber-villiers... His father read all the gas meters in the region... He hardly ever saw him, he didn't have time.

Sometimes we showed each other our pricks. Besides, I told him what was going on downstairs in the salesrooms, the guys who were going to be fired, because some were always getting the ax... That was how those punks spent their time... getting each other fired by spreading stories... vicious lies... We'd also talk about the different methods of getting a look at a customer's ass when she sat down for a minute.

Some of those errand girls were pretty wicked... Sometimes they'd put their feet up on a stool just to give you a view of their ass. Then they'd toddle away with a big grin... One of them showed me her garters as I was passing... And made sucking noises at me... I went upstairs to tell little André about it... We speculated... What would her crack be like? Was it very runny and what color? yellow? red? did it burn? And her legs... the top part? We made sounds too with our tongues and saliva, we imitated the kissing routine... Even so we knocked off twenty-five to thirty pieces an hour. Little André taught me the trick with the pin, which is the main thing to know when you're smoothing out the ends of the pieces... on the selvedge... the little rim of the satin. One on each side... that's where you stick them... You've got to be careful not to mess up the smooth side... You've got to wash your hands first. It's a real art.

At home they realized I wasn't going to last long at Berlope's, that I hadn't started out right... Lavelongue would run into Mama around the neighborhood when she was out shopping. He'd always make some nasty remark. "Ah, madame, that little boy of yours, he's not a bad sort, but what a scat-terbrain!... Ah, how right you were!... His head just isn't screwed on right!... I really don't know what we'll be able to do with him!... Everything he touches, he knocks it over!... Ah la la!..."

It was all a pack of lies... lousy injustice... I knew it perfectly well. I wasn't so innocent anymore! He told all those stinking lies so I'd go on working for nothing!... He took advantage of my parents... Let them go on feeding me!... He ran me down so he wouldn't have to pay me... There was nothing I could do about it... If I'd complained, they wouldn't have believed me... they'd only have yelled louder...

Even a poor little punk like André was making thirty-five francs a month. They couldn't exploit him any worse. My father tortured his imagination about my future... where could they send me? He was at his wits' end... I was no good for office work... Probably even worse than he was... I had no education at all... If I failed in business, it was the end... Right away he was at half-mast... He clamored for help... And yet I tried... I worked up enthusiasm... I got to work hours ahead of time... I was the last to leave... And even so they disapproved of me... I was always fouling things up... I was in a panic... Everything I did was wrong...

If you haven't been through that you'll never know what obsessive hatred really smells like... the hatred that goes through your guts, all the way to your heart...

Nowadays I'm always meeting characters who complain, who bristle with indignation... They're just poor bastards that aren't getting anywhere... jerks... dinner-table failures... that kind of rebellion is for weak sisters... they didn't pay for it, they got it for nothing... They're drips.

Where did they get it from?... no place... the *lycée* maybe... It's a lot of talk, hot air. Real hatred comes from deep down, from a defenseless childhood crushed with work. That's the hatred that kills you. There'll be more of it, so deep and thick there will always be some left, enough to go around... It will ooze out over the earth... and poison it, so nothing will grow but viciousness, among the dead, among men.

Every night when I came home, my mother asked me if I hadn't been given notice... She was always expecting the worst. At supper we talked about it some more. The subject was inexhaustible. Would I ever earn my living?...

With all that kind of talk I couldn't stand looking at the bread on the table. I was afraid to ask for any. I hurried through the meal. That drove my mother crazy, though she was a quick eater too. "Ferdinand! You're doing it again. You don't even see what you're eating. You gulp it all down without chewing. You bolt your food like a dog. And the way you look! You're transparent! You're green!... How do you expect to get any good out of your food! We do all we can for you! But you just waste your food."

Little André had a certain amount of peace in the stockroom. Lavelongue hardly ever went up. As long as he painted his numbers, nobody bothered him much.

André loved flowers, invalids often do. He brought them in from the country and stuck them in bottles... He decorated all the rafters with them... One morning he even brought in an enormous bunch of hawthorn... The others saw him coming in... They couldn't stand it... They talked about it so much in front of Lavelongue that he went up in person to have a look... He bawled hell out of André and threw the whole bundle out in the court...

Downstairs in the big showrooms they were all bastards, especially the shipping clerks; I've never known such stinkers, such a slimy lot of fishwives... They had nothing to think about but making packages.

One of these characters was Magadur, a big tall guy in the Paris shipping department... he was the worst bastard imaginable. He went to work on André and turned him against me... They often came in together from the Porte des Lilas... He told him all kinds of crap to poison him against me... It was easy, André was very impressionable. All alone in his corner, for hours on end in the stockroom, he was always mulling things over. All you had to do was hand him a line and get him worried... Once he was started, nothing could stop him... Any cock-and-bull story would do it... I come in and find him all in a dither.

"Is it true, Ferdinand?" he asks me. "Is it true? That you want to take my job?"

His attack took me by surprise... I was flabbergasted... I couldn't understand... He went on...

"Aw, go on! Save your breath. Everybody in the store knows all about it. I was the only one that didn't suspect... I'm a sap, that's all!"

He was always pretty pale, now he turned yellow; he he always looked horrible with his snot and the gaps in his teeth... when he got excited you couldn't stand to look at him... his face all covered with impetigo, the stubble on his head, the way he smelled... I couldn't bring myself to say anything... I was too much ashamed for him...

I'd a thousand times rather have been fired on the spot than have him suspect me of wanting to take his job... But then where would I go? That was a big decision to make... Much too big for me... All I could do was hang on, do my damnedest, try to clear myself... I tried to put him straight. But that bastard Magadur had really rubbed it in.

After that he didn't trust me at all. He never showed me his prick anymore. He was afraid I'd go and tell on him. He went to the crapper by himself to smoke in peace. He never even mentioned the Palais-Royal anymore...

Between two trips to the eighth floor, hauling all the bundles, I collapsed under the mansard roof. I took off my shoes and my coat and waited for it to pass...

André pretended not to see me, he had a copy of *Illustrated Adventure Stories*. He read it all by himself. He spread it out on the floor... If I spoke to him even at the top of my lungs, he pretended not to hear me. He brushed in his numbers. Everything I could say or do made him suspicious. In his opinion I was a traitor. If he were ever to lose his job, he had often told me, his aunt would give him such a licking he'd end up in the hospital... That was the story. I'd known it all along... But even so I couldn't stand having him take me for a rat.

"Say, André," I said to him at my wits' end. "You ought to know I don't want to get you fired..."

He still didn't answer, he went on mumbling over his pictures... He read to himself out loud... I took a look to see what it said... It was the story of King Krogold... I knew the story well... I'd always known it... since Grandma Caroline... She'd taught me to read with it... All he had was one old number...

"Say, André," I said. "I know the whole story by heart. I know how it goes on..." He still didn't answer. But I was getting somewhere... I'd caught his interest... He didn't have the next number...

"Here's how it goes," I said, grasping at the opportunity. "All the people of Christiania... the whole city... have taken refuge in the church... in the cathedral, under the vaulting, it's four times as big as Notre-Dame... They all go down on their knees... in there... Are you listening?

... They're afraid of King Krogold... They pray to heaven for forgiveness for having meddled in the war... for having protected Prince Gwendor... the traitor... They don't know where to go... There are a hundred thousand of them in the church... Nobody dares to leave... They're so scared they don't even know their prayers... They mumble a lot of gibberish... Old people, merchants, young people, mothers, priests, cowards, little children, beautiful dames, the archbishops, the constables, they're all shitting in their pants... They all lie flat in a heap... A terrible jumble... All grunting and moaning... The situation is so desperate they're even afraid to breathe... They entreat... they implore... that King Krogold won't burn the whole place... but only the suburbs a little... that he won't burn everything to punish them... they're attached to their market, the granaries, the weighing house, the presbytery, the courthouse, the cathedral... St. Christiania... the most magnificent in the whole world! Nobody knows where to put himself... they're so cowed... how to disappear...

"And then from down below, from beyond the walls, an enormous din is heard... It's King Krogold's advance guard... the clatter of heavy armor on the drawbridge... Ah, yes, they're coming all right! And the horsemen of his escort... King Krogold is at the gates... he rises up in his stirrups... The jangling of a thousand suits of armor is heard... The knights crossing the suburb of St. Stanislas... The enormous city seems deserted... There's nobody in the king's path... Here comes the train of servants... The gate isn't wide enough... The wagons will never get through... They rip down the high walls on both sides... Everything comes tumbling down... Wagons, legions, barbarians, rush through, catapults, elephants with upraised trunks pour in through the breach... In the city everything is silent, frozen... Belfries... convents... houses... market stalls... Nothing stirs...

"King Krogold has stopped on the first steps of the parvis... Around him his twenty-three mastiffs mount the steps, yelping and leaping... His pack is famous for their prowess in hunting the bear and the aurochs... they've torn whole forests to pieces... from the Elbe to the Carpathians... In spite of the tumult Krogold hears the sound of hymns... sung by that dense, hidden, harried crowd beneath the vaulting... their prayer... The vast doors swing on their hinges... And Krogold sees them all seething and writhing before him... In the depths of the shadow... Can the whole people be in hiding?... He fears treachery... He doesn't go in... The organs rumble... Their thunder pours out through the triple porch... Defiance!... This city is disloyal!... And always will be!... He orders the provost to clear the church at once... Three thousand henchmen storm in, bruising and battering... chopping and mauling... The crowd gives way, regroups around them... squashes against the doors... gathers in the aisles... The ruffians are sucked in... They charge and charge again... they aren't getting anywhere... Still in his saddle, the king waits... His charger, a huge, shaggy beast, paws the ground... The king is devouring a great big hunk of meat, a leg of mutton; he bites into it, he buries his fangs in it... He tears it to pieces, he's awful mad... What's this? No headway?... The king hoists himself up in his stirrups again... He's the biggest bruiser of them all... He whistles... He calls... He gathers his mastiffs around him... He brandishes his big hunk of meat over his crown... He chucks it way out... into the darkness... It falls in the middle of the church... in the middle of the cowering mass... The whole pack bounds forward, howling... they spring up everywhere... leaping at throats... tearing... crunching... The panic is terrible... The yapping grows louder... The whole terrified flood pours out the doors... pushing...

scrambling... a torrent, an avalanche... all the way to the drawbridges... They're dashed against the walls... Between the lances and the wagons... The king's path is open... The whole cathedral is his... He spurs his horse... He enters... He orders all to be silent... the dogs . . the people... the organ... the army... He rides another two lengths... He's passed the three porches... Slowly he unsheathes... his enormous sword... He makes a big sign of the cross with it... And then he hurls it away... far, far... It lands in the middle of the altar!... The war is over... His brother the bishop approaches... He falls on his knees... He sings his Credo..."

Say what you like, that makes an impression. Little André would really have liked me to go on... to throw in some more details... He liked nice stories... But he was afraid I'd begin to influence him... He fished around in his box... He jiggled his little pieces of zinc... his brushes... he didn't want me to cast a spell on him... he didn't want us to be friends like before...

The same afternoon I came back up again with another load... He still wouldn't speak to me... I was good and tired, I sat down... I really wanted him to talk to me. "Say, André," I said, "I know the next chapter too, when all the merchants go off to Palestine... With Thibaut on the crusade... And they leave the troubadour behind to guard the castle... and Wanda, the princess... You never heard about that? It's marvelous... especially Wanda's vengeance, the way she washes away her affront in blood... the way she humiliates her father..."

Little André pricked up his ears. He didn't want to interrupt me, but I heard faint sounds in the corridor... I didn't want to break the spell. Suddenly I saw Lavelongue's phizz in the little window... I jumped... He must have come up that very second to catch me... Of course somebody had tipped him off... I shot up... I put my shoes on... He just gives me a little sign...

"Splendid, Ferdinand. Splendid! We'll attend to this later. Stay right where you are, my boy!"

I didn't have to wait long. The next day I come home for lunch and my mother gives it to me...

"Ferdinand," she starts right in... already resigned, absolutely convinced... "Monsieur Lavelongue has just left... Yes, in person!... Do you know what he said?... He doesn't want you on the job anymore. Isn't that a fine how-do-you-do? He was dissatisfied before, but this was the last straw. He tells me you hide in the attic for hours on end!... Instead of getting ahead with your work!... And giving little André bad ideas... He caught you... Don't deny it... telling stories... disgusting stories... Don't try to tell me any different!... With a common child like that! A guttersnipe! Monsieur Lavelongue has known us for ten years, luckily, thank goodness! He knows we're not to blame. He knows how we work our fingers to the bone. Both of us, your father and I, to give you everything you need. He knows the kind of people we are... He respects us. He wants to treat us kindly. He's asked us to take you back. Out of consideration for us he won't dismiss you... He'll spare us the shame of it... Ah, when I tell your father... he's going to be sick!..."

Just then he comes home from the office. The moment he opened the door, she starts telling him the story... As he listened, he clutched the table... He couldn"t believe his ears... He looked me up and down and shrugged his shoulders... The two of them collapsed with dismay... A monster like me was past understanding... He didn't bellow... he didn't even hit me... He only wondered how he could bear it... He gave up. He rocked his chair... "Hm!... Hm!... Hm!" was all he said... back and forth... Then finally he spoke...

"So you're even more unnatural, more underhanded, more abject than I imagined, Ferdinand?"

Then he looked at my mother and called her to witness that there was nothing more they could do... that I was incorrigible...

I myself was crushed, I searched the depths of my soul, trying to figure out what enormous vices, what unprecedented depravities I could be guilty of... I couldn't get it straight... I couldn't make up my mind... I found a whole raft of them, but I wasn't sure of anything...

My father closed the session. He went up to his room, he wanted to be alone to think... I slept in a nightmare... The whole time I saw little André telling Monsieur Berlope awful things...

The following afternoon my mother and I went to get my reference... Monsieur Lavelongue gave it to us in person... Besides, he wanted to speak to me...

"Ferdinand," he said to me. "Out of consideration for your worthy parents I'm not going to dismiss you... They are taking you back... of their own free will! You see the difference? Believe me, I'm sorry to see you leaving us. But I've got to face the facts: your misconduct has undermined discipline in every department... And I'm responsible, you see... I have had to take measures, what's right is right!... But let this setback be a lesson to you. What little you've learned will surely be of use to you somewhere else! Experience is never wasted. You'll have other employers, maybe some will be even less indulgent... It was a lesson you needed... Well, Ferdinand, now you've had it... I only hope you benefit by it... At your age you can always make up for lost time..." He shook my hand with a good deal of conviction. My mother's emotion was indescribable... She dabbed at her eyes.

"Apologize, Ferdinand," she ordered me as we were getting up to go. "He's young, monsieur, he's young... Thank Monsieur Lavelongue for giving you an excellent reference after all you've done... You don't deserve it, you know!"

"Don't mention it, madame, it's nothing, nothing at all, I assure you. It's the least I could do. Ferdinand is not the first young man to start out on the wrong foot. Oh, no, far from it. Ten years from now he himself... I can assure you... will come to me and say: 'Monsieur Lavelongue, you did the right thing. You are a good man! Thanks to you, I found out what's what!'... But today he has it in for me... It's only natural." My mother protested. He tapped me on the shoulder. He showed us out.

The very next day they took on another apprentice for the stockroom... I heard about it... He didn't last three months... He flopped down on every landing... The work killed him.

But innocent or guilty, a lot of good it did me. I was getting to be a real headache for the whole family. Uncle Édouard began to look for another job for me, as a salesman, I'd have to start all over again. But it wasn't so easy for him this time... I'd have to try a different line...

I already had a past... It would be best not to mention it. And that's what we decided.

Once he'd recovered from the shock, my father started raving again... He drew up a complete inventory of all my faults, one by one... He searched for the vices hidden deep down in me like a scientist looking for mysterious phenomena... He let out diabolical screams... He was having his fits again... He was being persecuted by a whole carnival of demons... He really turned on the gas... He dragged everybody into it... Jews... schemers... social climbers... And most of all the Freemasons... I don't know what they had to do with it... He tracked his enemies to the ends of the earth... He got so lost in his apocalypse that in the end he forgot all about me...

He laced into Lempreinte, the monster with the stomach trouble... And Baron Méfaize, his managing director... Anybody and anything would do, as long as he could rave and splutter... He made a terrible hullabaloo, the neighbors were in stitches.

My mother dragged herself at his feet... He wouldn't stop bellowing... He remembered me and my future... He discovered the worst symptoms in me... The most abominable profligacy!

... Oh well, he washed his hands of me... Like Pontius Pilate... That's exactly what he said... His conscience was clear...

My mother looked at me... her "cross"... It was sad, but she resigned herself... She'd never abandon me... Obviously I was going to end on the gallows and she'd stick by me all the way...

We had only one thing in common in our family in the Passage, and that was our terror of going hungry. We all had plenty of that. It was with me from my first breath... They passed it right on to me... We were all obsessed with it... As far as we were concerned, the soul was fear. In every room the walls sweated fear of going without... It made us swallow the wrong way, it made us bolt our meals and run around town like mad... we zigzagged like fleas all over Paris, from the Place Maubert to the Étoile, for fear of being auctioned off, for fear of the rent, of the gas man, the tax collector... We were always in such a hurry I never had time to wipe myself properly.

Since my dismissal from Berlope's, I had in addition, all to myself, the fear of never getting anywhere in the world... I've known poor unemployed bastards, hundreds of them, here and all over the world, people who were only half a step from the poorhouse... They hadn't managed right.

To tell the truth, my main pleasure in life is being quicker than the boss when it comes to getting fired... I can see that kidney punch coming... I can smell it a mile off... I can tell when a job is folding... I've got some other little racket sprouting in my other pocket. Bosses are all stinkers, all they think about is giving you the gate... There's only one kind of real lowdown fear, the fear of being out on your ass, flat broke and no job... I've always had one on hand, some lousy meal ticket, it doesn't matter what kind... I nibble at it, kind of like vaccinating yourself... I don't give a shit what it is... I lug it through the streets, the mountains, and the muck... I've had such cockeyed ones they had neither shape, size, nor taste... It's all one to me... It's no skin off my ass. The sicker they make me, the less I worry...

I hate all jobs. Why should I make distinctions?... You won't catch me singing any hymns of praise... I'd shit on the whole lot of them if I could... That's what it is to work for hire...

Uncle Édouard was doing better and better in his hardware business. He mostly sold stuff for automobiles in the provinces, headlights and accessories. Unfortunately I was too young to go on the road with him. I'd have to wait a while... Besides, after what had happened I needed watching.

Uncle Édouard wasn't so pessimistic about me, he didn't think my case was so hopeless. If I was no good at a sedentary job, he said, maybe I'd make a first-class traveling salesman.

It seemed to be worth trying... Appearance was important, you had to have the right clothes ... To make me really acceptable they added a couple of years to my age, they got me an extra-stiff collar, I'd wrecked all the others. They got me spats too, nice and gray over my shoes, so my feet wouldn't look so enormous, so they wouldn't clutter up people's doormats. My father was skeptical, he had given up hope in my future. The neighbors put in their two cents' worth, they all gave advice... Not that they expected much of my career... Even the Passage caretaker was against me... When he went around lighting the lamps, he'd drop in at all the shops and bat the breeze. I'd turn out to be a screwball, that's what he told everybody, sort of like my father in his opinion, good for nothing except pestering people... Luckily there was Visios, the sailor, he had a soft spot for me, he realized I was doing my best and contradicted everybody. He said I wasn't a bad kid. There was a good deal of talk... but I was still high and dry... They still had to find me a job.

At that point they began to wonder what they should have me sell... My mother wanted me to be a jeweler. That was her fondest hope... It struck her as eminently respectable. A jeweler's staff had to be more than neat and spruce, they had to look really smart... And they handled treasures behind gleaming counters. But jewelers are tough when it comes to trusting anybody. They're always trembling for their jewels. They can't sleep, they're so scared of being burgled, strangled, and set on fire!... Christ!

One thing that was indispensable was scrupulous honesty! On that score we had nothing to fear. With parents like mine, so meticulous, so strict about honoring their business obligations, I had a terrific reference!... I could apply to any employer... the most obsessed... the most suspicious... With me he could rest easy. Never, as far back as anybody could remember, had there been a thief in our family, not a single one.

Once that was settled, we began to look around. Mama reconnoitered some, she went to see the people we knew... They didn't need anybody... In spite of my good intentions it was no cinch landing a job, even on trial.

They outfitted me again to make me more attractive. I was getting to be as costly as an invalid. I'd worn out my suit completely... I'd gone through my shoes... In addition to my matching spats they got me a new pair of shoes, Broomfields, the English brand, with enormous jutting soles... they looked like submarines. They got them twice too big, so they'd last a couple of years at least... They were awfully narrow, I thought I'd sprain my ankle, but I bore it with grim determination. I hobbled along on the Boulevards like a deep-sea diver.

Once I was patched up, my mother and I headed for the addresses we had. Uncle Édouard gave us the ones he got from his friends, we found the rest in the directory. Madame Divonne kept the shop every morning until noon while we went out job hunting. Believe me, we had no time for dawdling... We combed the whole Marais, door after door, and then the cross streets, rue Quin-campois, rue Galante, rue aux Ours, rue Vieille-du-Temple... We did the whole neighborhood, take my word for it, floor by floor...

My mother hobbled along behind... Tip-tap-plunk! Tip-tap-plunk!... She'd offer my services to every family, to little home artisans huddled behind their globes... She offered me ever so kindly... as an extra tool... a useful little drudge... not at all demanding... clever, eager, energetic... and best of all, a fast runner! All in all a good bargain... Well trained, obedient... At our timid ring on the bell, they'd open the door a crack... at first they were suspicious... Cigarette immobilized, expectant... they'd peer at me over their spectacles... They'd take a good look... Not very appetizing, they decided... In the face of their blousy wrinkled smocks, my mother would start her song and dance:

"You wouldn't be needing a young salesman, monsieur?... I'm his mother. I thought I'd better come along... all he asks is to give satisfaction... He's a very well-behaved young man... You can easily make inquiries about him... We've been in business for twelve years in the Passage des Bérésinas... The child has been raised in business... His father works for the Coccinelle Fire Insurance Company... You must have heard of it... We're not rich, either one of us, but we don't owe anybody a single penny... We honor our obligations... His father in the insurance company..."

We'd generally do twelve to fifteen of a morning, all kinds... Jewel setters, cutters, and polishers, chain makers, silversmiths, and even trades that have gone out of existence, like silver gilders and agate engravers.

They examine us some more... They put down their magnifying glasses to get a better look... to make sure we're not bandits... murderers... escaped convicts... Once reassured, they became friendly, even sympathetic... Except they don't need anybody... not for the moment. They couldn't afford any overhead... They made their own calls... The whole family was in the business, all together, in their tiny niches... The seven stories on the court were honeycombed with their burrows, their workshops were like little caves carved out of the walls of what had once been fashionable houses... They'd stopped trying to keep up appearances... They lived on top of each other, wife, kids, grandmother, all working together... At the most they'd take on an apprentice for the Christmas rush...

My mother ran out of arguments and suggested as a last inducement that they take me on without pay... that really made them jump. They'd clam up tight and slam the door in our faces. They were suspicious of anybody who'd work for nothing. It looked shady as hell. We'd have to start all over again. My mother concentrated on inspiring confidence, but it didn't seem to get us very far. She couldn't very well represent me as an apprentice in stone setting or machining fine metal... It was too late for that... I'd never be handy with my fingers... The most I could expect to be was a blabbermouth, an outside salesman, a common ordinary "young man"... My career had been bungled in every way...

When we got home, my father wanted to know what what was what... We were always empty-handed and it drove him nuts. All evening he'd thrash around in the most terrible nightmares... You could have furnished a dozen loonybins with the contents of his dome...

My mother's legs were all twisted from climbing stairs... She felt so funny she couldn't stop... She kept limping around the table making the most terrible faces... She had drawing pains in her legs... she was racked with cramps...

We'd race off bright and early to other addresses all the same... rue Réamur, rue Greneta... the Bastille, rue des Jeûneurs... and especially the Place des Vosges... after several months of begging and stair climbing, of puffing and pestering for nothing, my mother began to wonder whether people couldn't tell by the cut of my jib that I was nothing but an insubordinate little no- good... My father didn't doubt it for a moment... He'd known it for years... His certainty was reinforced every time we came home empty-handed... dazed, panting, dog-tired, wet from running, drenched inside and out with sweat and rain...

"It's harder to get that kid a job than to liquidate our whole stock... and I don't have to tell you, Clémence, that wouldn't be easy."

He hadn't been educated for nothing, he knew how to make comparisons, to draw inferences. My last suit was already sagging in all directions, with great big bags at the knees, stairs are death on clothes. Luckily I was able to borrow an old hat from my father. We wore the same size. It wasn't in very good shape, so I always held it in my hand. The part I wore out was the brim...

People were awfully polite in those days... .

It was high time Uncle Édouard found me a decent address. We were really out of luck. We didn't know what to do. And then one day the whole thing got straightened out... He came in at lunch time, beaming and burbling... He was absolutely positive. He'd gone to see this man, a master engraver. He was going to take me on. It was in the bag!

Gorloge was his name, he lived on the rue Elzévir, in an apartment on the sixth floor. He went in mostly for rings, brooches, embossed bracelets, and small repair jobs. He took anything that came his way. He struggled along from day to day. He didn't expect much. He tried to give satisfaction regardless.

Édouard infected us with his confidence. We couldn't wait to see him. We didn't even finish our cheese. In two seconds flat my mother and I were out in the street... A short bus ride, the Boulevards, the rue Elzévir... Five flights... They were still at table when we rang the bell.

They ate bread soup too, big bowls of it, and then noodles with cheese, and nuts for dessert. They'd been expecting us. My uncle had sung my praises. We had come at just the right moment

... They didn't gild the pill... They didn't try to hide anything... They were having a hell of a time with their engraved ornaments... They made no bones about it... for twelve years there hadn't been anything doing... They were still waiting for things to pick up... They were moving heaven and earth... but the resurrection didn't come... The customers had other things in mind. Ruin was staring them in the face.

Even so, Monsieur Gorloge was holding out, he was putting up a fight... He still had hope

... He dressed like Uncle Arthur... the happy artist, with a goatee, a flowing bow tie, long pointed shoes, and a baggy smock all covered with wine spots... He sat there at his ease. He was smoking, you couldn't even see him behind the eddies of smoke... He fanned it away with his hand.

Madame Gorloge sat across the table from him on a low stool. Her tits were squashed against the workbench, she was round all over, magnificent bulges... Her curves overflowed from her apron... she was cracking nuts with her fists... a staggering blow from way up, enough to split the table wide open. The whole workshop shook... She was quite a number... a former model... I found that out later... The type appealed to me.

As for wages, the subject didn't even come up. We didn't want to be indiscreet. That would come later... I didn't expect him to offer anything. But then he made up his mind after all, just as we were leaving. He said I could expect a regular wage... thirty-five francs a month... transportation included... And besides I had prospects... a sizable bonus if by my efforts I succeeded in reviving the engraver's craft. He thought me a little young, but that didn't matter because I had the sacred fire... because I'd grown up in the racket... because I'd been born in a shop!... It was a deal... all very heart-warming... one cheery remark after another...

We went home to the Passage full of enthusiasm... The rainbow at last. We finished our meal. We emptied the jam pots. Papa took three helpings of wine. He let a fine fart... like he'd almost stopped doing... We kissed Uncle Édouard... There was wind in our sails again after the awful famine.

The next day I went to the rue Elzévir bright and early to get my collection.

The way Monsieur Gorloge was lounging around when I came in, I thought he"d forgotten me... He was sitting at the wide-open window, looking at the rooftops. Between his knees he had a big bowl of coffee. He wasn't doing a damn thing, that was plain. The view amused him... the thousands of courtyards in the Petit Marais... He had a dazed dreamy look... That can be mighty fascinating, it can't be denied. The lovely lace-work of slate... the light playing over it… the intermingled colors... the way the gutters twist and twine. And the sparrows hopping about... And the wisps of smoke coiling over the deep chasms of shadow...

He motioned me to keep my trap shut and listen to things... to take in the scene... He didn"t like to be disturbed... He must have thought me rather uncouth. He gave me a sulky look.

All around the court, from top to bottom, at every window it was like a Punch and Judy show… heads popping out... bald ones, bushy ones, pale faces... squealing, griping, whistling... And then different noises... A watering can tips, falls, bounces down on the big cobblestones below... A pot of geraniums slips... and flops kerplunk on the concierge's lodge. It breaks into smithereens. The concierge comes bounding out of her grotto... flinging her cries out into space. Help!... Bloody murder!... The whole house is in an uproar... Every pest in the place rushes to the window... They spew fire... they spit at each other... They challenge each other across the void... They're all yelling at once... You can't make out who's in the right...

Monsieur Gorloge hangs out the window... He doesn't want to miss one crumb... He's crazy about these scenes... When things quiet down, he's heartbroken... He heaves a sigh... and then another... He goes back to his bread and butter... He pours himself another bowl... he offers me some coffee too...

"Ferdinand," he finally says, "I'd better tell you again that it's not going to be any sinecure selling my merchandise... I've had ten salesmen already... They were good boys, nothing wrong with them! And plenty of grit!... Actually you're the twelfth, because to tell you the truth, I've tried my hand at it too... Well, there you have it... Anyway, come back tomorrow. I'm not in form today... And... well no, hang around awhile... Monsieur Antoine will be coming in... Maybe I ought to introduce you... Oh well, you might as well be leaving at that... I'll tell him I've hired you... Won't he be surprised! He doesn't like salesmen! He's my first assistant... my foreman in fact... He's a tough customer... no doubt about that. You'll know that as soon as you lay eyes on him. But he's very helpful... yes, yes, I can't deny it... I want you to meet little Robert too, our apprentice... He's a good kid. You'll get along fine, I'm sure. He'll give you the collection... It's in the bottom of the closet... It's unique, see what I mean?... It's pretty heavy though... About thirty pounds... Nothing but models... Copper and lead... The earliest pieces date back to my father... He had some beautiful things! Unique! Unique! I remember seeing his Trocadéro!... All handcarved, mounted as a diadem. Can you imagine? It was worn twice... I still have the photograph. I'll show it to you one of these days..."

Gorloge was sick of explaining... He was disgusted again, fed up... He made a last effort ... He put his feet on the table... He let out a deep sigh... He was wearing embroidered slippers, I can still see them... with kittens running around on them...

"Well, Ferdinand, better go on home... Give your mother my best regards... On your way out would you tell the concierge to run over to the café at Number 26 and make a phone call for me... Tell her to call the Three Admirals Hotel and see if Antoine is sick... he's plumb crazy... to find out if anything has happened to him... He hasn't been in for two days now... She can yell up to me from the court... Tell her to look it up in the phone book... The Three Admirals... Tell her to send up some milk... The old lady isn't feeling very well... Tell her to send up the paper... any old paper... Well, maybe the *Sports News...*"

It wasn't next day, but the day after that I finally got to see the collection... Gorloge had understated... Thirty pounds!... It weighed at least twice that much... He had vaguely suggested certain "sales techniques"... but nothing very definite... He wasn't really sold on any of them... I could do exactly as I pleased... He relied on my initiative... I expected horrors but I've got to admit I had a sinking feeling when I saw that mess close up... It was unbelievable... Never had I seen such a lot of such disgusting monstrosities all at once... A challenge... A pocket inferno...

Everything we opened was horrible... nothing but gargoyles and bottle imps... made out of lead, turned and tortured, fussed and finicked... it turned your stomach... The whole Symbolist orgy... Chunks of nightmare... A putty "Samothrace"... more "Victories" in the shape of little clocks... Necklaces made out of Medusas, coils of snakes... More chimeras... Hundreds of allegorical rings, one crappier than the next... My work was cut out for me... All those things were supposed to be put on fingers, on belts, or stuck in ties. Or hung on somebody's ears... It was unbelievable!... Somebody was expected to buy them! Who? Great God, who? No form of dragon, demon, hobgoblin, or vampire was missing... A complete collection of nightmares... A whole world of sleepless nights... The manias of a whole insane asylum served up as trinkets... I was going from punk to horrible... Even in my grandmother's store on the rue Mont-orgueil the most moth-eaten white elephants were things of beauty by comparison...

I'd never be able to make a living with such garbage. I was beginning to see the point about the ten saps before me. They must have been floored... These nightmares weren't being sold anymore... Since the last of the Romantics people had tucked them away in terror... Maybe people were still passing them around in families... when somebody died... but taking plenty of precautions... It wouldn't be safe to show such loony stuff to people who hadn't been warned... They might feel offended. Even Gorloge was afraid to do it... in person, that is. He'd given up buffeting the tide of fashion... The heroism was for me!... I was the last salesman!... Nobody had stuck it out for more than three weeks...

He himself did nothing but prospect for small repair jobs... to keep the shop going until fashions should change... He had kept up a few connections in the trade... Friends from better days who wouldn't have wanted to let him starve. They sent jobs his way... settings and patchwork... disgusting toil... but he never touched a finger to it himself... He passed it all on to our Antoine. Gorloge was an engraver... He wasn't going to ruin his touch doing menial work… he wasn't going to lose his standing and reputation for a few sous. No, sir. On that score he was adamant.

At nine o'clock sharp I climbed the stairs on the rue Elzévir, I didn't wait for him to come down... I flung myself on Paris right away, armed with my zeal and my "few pounds" of samples... Seeing as I was the outside man, they gave me a good outing... I was used to it. From the Bastille to the Madeleine... Miles and miles... All the Boulevards... every single jewelry store, one by one... Not to mention the little side streets... There was no room in my heart for discouragement... To revive the customers' taste for engraved articles I'd have cut the moon into little pieces. I'd have eaten my dragons. Pretty soon I myself was executing all their grimaces as I walked... Frantically conscientious, I'd wait my turn on the salesmen's bench outside the buyers' room.

I ended up believing in the renaissance of the jewel engraver's art. I had the faith of a crusader. I didn't even see my competitors. They went into gales of laughter whenever they heard my name called. When it came my turn at the window, I'd put on my most winning smile, all sweetness and light. Quietly, from behind my back, I'd produce my little jewel case containing the least loathsome items... and put it on the counter... The beast didn't even bother to say anything... He just made a gesture meaning to clear out... that I was a dirty-minded brat...

I hurried on... farther and farther. A fanatic doesn't calculate. Dripping wet in my shell or consumed with thirst, according to the season, I tried the most insignificant little shops, the grimiest little watchmakers, cowering in their suburbs between lamp and globe...

From La Chapelle to Les Moulineaux, I did them all. I found a gleam of interest in a junk dealer in Pierrefitte and a ragpicker in Saint-Maur. I tried the shopkeepers who've been dozing all around the Palais-Royal ever since the days of Camille Desmoulins, under the Arcades Montpensier... the stalls in the Galeries des Pas-Perdus... shopkeepers who've lost all hope... grown stiff and sallow behind the counter... They don't want to live and they don't want to die. I galloped over to the Odéon... to the last of the Parnassian jewelers in the arcades around the theater. They weren't even starving anymore, they digested diist. They had their models too, all of lead, almost identical with mine, enough for a thousand coffins... and a whole raft of mythological necklaces... And mounds of amulets, a mass so dense that the counters were sinking into the ground... They were shoulder-deep in the rubbish... they were disappearing, turning into Egyptians... They didn't even answer when I spoke. Those guys really gave me a scare...

I went back to the suburbs... When I had ventured too far in my hunt for enthusiasm, when I was caught by nightfall and felt kind of lost, I'd hurry up and take a bus so as not to get home too late. My parents left me fifteen francs out of my monthly thirty-five... It melted away in fares. Without meaning to, by the sheer force of circumstances, I was getting pretty extravagant... Of course I should have walked... but then it goes out in shoe-leather.

Monsieur Gorloge even got around to the rue de la Paix looking for repair work. The ladies who ran the fashionable shops might have taken a shine to him, the only thing that prevented him from really making a hit was that he wasn't very clean. On account of his beard. It was always full of scabs... his "sycosis," as he called it...

I'd often catch sight of him in a doorway, scratching furiously. Then he'd walk away happy as a lark... He always had a few rings in his pocket to alter, to change the size. A brooch to weld... the one that never stays closed. A watch chain to shorten... some trinket or other... enough to keep his business running... He wasn't very demanding.

It was Antoine, his one assistant, who did all these little jobs. Gorloge never touched them. As I was going down the Boulevards, I'd run into him, I'd recognize him in the distance... He didn't walk like other people... He took an interest in the crowd... He looked in all directions... I could see his hat turning on its hinges. He also attracted attention by the polka dots on his vest... and his hearty manner... he made you think of a musketeer...

"Well, Ferdinand, how you doing? Still going strong? Still in there fighting? Everything all right? Everything OK?..."

"I'm fine, Monsieur Gorloge. Really fine."

I'd stand up straight to answer him despite the crushing weight of my saddlebags... My enthusiasm was undiminished. Except that what with making nothing, selling nothing, and hiking all day with that heavy collection, I was getting thinner and thinner... Except for my biceps of course. My feet were still growing. My soul was growing... and everything else... I was getting to be sublime...

When I got back from my selling tour, I'd run a few more errands for the shop. To some artisan's. To the wholesaler's for jewel cases. All that was in the same street.

Little Robert, the apprentice, was better off tinkering with little settings, filing openwork, or even sweeping out the joint. There was never much harmony in the Gorloge household. They yelled at each other at the top of their lungs, even louder than in our house. Especially between Antoine and the boss, there were terrible brawls. No more respect, especially on Saturday evening when they settled accounts. Antoine was never satisfied... Whether they figured by the piece, by the hour, by the week, regardless of the system, he always complained. And yet he was his own boss, there were no other helpers... "Your lousy joint... you can stick it up your ass! How many times do I have to tell you?..."

That was the tone they took with each other. You should have seen Gorloge's face... He scratched his beard... he was so upset he'd nibble at the scales.

Some days Antoine got so mad about money that he threatened to smash the glass globe on his head... Every time I expected him to leave... But not at all!... It was getting to be a regular habit, like with us at home...

But Madame Gorloge didn't get upset like Mama... The roaring and bellowing didn't interfere with her knitting. Whenever things began to look desperate, little Robert would crawl under the workbench... There he was safe... but he wouldn't miss a second of the corrida. He'd eat a slice of bread and butter...

When there wasn't a sou in the place to pay Antoine on Saturday, we'd always, at the last minute, find a few coins in the bottom of a drawer to round out the sum... There was always something... We even had our emergency fund in the big kitchen closet... our cargo of cameos... our stock of delirium... our mythological treasure... that was our last resort... It was no time for hesitation...

In the leanest weeks I'd unload them by weight, some place... any place... at the Village Suisse, across the street at the Temple... on the sidewalk at the Porte Kremlin... They'd always bring in five francs or so...

Never since engraving had gone out had a single gram of gold spent more than three days at Gorloge's. What repair work we picked up we'd deliver in hurry, the same week. Nobody was very trusting... Three or four times, on Saturdays, I took care of the deliveries, to the Place des Vosges, the rue Royale, as usual on the run. In those days nobody talked about hardship. It wasn't until much later that people began to realize how lousy rotten it was to be a worker. The suspicion was just dawning. About seven in the evening, in the middle of the summer, it wasn't cool on the Boulevard Poissonnière on my way back from my cross-country efforts. I remember that we'd stop at the fountain, under the trees by the Théâtre de l'Ambigu... and toss off two or three cups of water, we even had to wait in line... We'd sit down on the steps of the theater and rest a minute. There were stragglers from all over, still trying to get their breath... It was a perfect place for collectors of cigarette butts, sandwich men, pickpockets, bookmakers on the prowl, small-time pimps, and bums of every description, by the tens and dozens... You'd hear talk about hard times, about little bets you could make... horses that were sure to place... and news of the velodrome... We'd pass *La Patrie* from hand to hand for the races and the want ads...

The song hit at the time was "Matchiche"... Every-body'd whistle it while sauntering around the kiosk... waiting to take a leak... And then we'd cross the street and start off again... The dust was thickest on the rue du Temple, where the street was being ripped up... They were digging for the métro... Then came the square with the trees on it, a lot of alleys, the rue Greneta, the rue Beaubourg... The rue Elzévir is a long way... around seven in the evening. It's way at the other end of the district.

Little Robert the apprentice... his mother lived in Épernon, he sent her all his pay, twelve francs a week, plus his board... he slept under the workbench on a mattress that he rolled up himself in the morning. I watched my step with the kid. I was very careful, I didn't tell any stories, I'd decided to keep my nose clean...

Antoine, our skilled assistant, was awfully strict, he'd smack him for nothing at all. But he liked the job all the same, because after seven nobody bothered him. He could have fun on the stairs. The court was full of cats, he'd bring them scraps. On his way back upstairs he'd look through all the keyholes... That was his main amusement.

When we got to know each other better, he told me all about it. He showed me his system of looking into the can to see the women pissing, right on our landing, two holes in the door. He'd put little plugs in them when he was through. He'd seen them all, Madame Gorloge too, she was the biggest slob of the lot, he could tell by the way she picked up her skirts...

He was a peeping torn by instinct. It seemed she had thighs like monuments, enormous pillars, and so much hair on her pussy, the fur went up so high it covered her belly button... Robert had seen her right in the middle of her monthlies... It splattered up the whole shithouse... She had the most amazing ass... you can't imagine... He promised to show me. And something even worse, another hole he had bored... something really terrific... in the bedroom wall, right next to the bed. And there was still another way... If you climbed up on the stove... in the corner of the kitchen, you could look down through the transom... and see the whole bed.

Little Robert would get up at night just for that. Lots of times he'd watched the Gorloges fucking. The next day he told me all about it, except he could hardly stand up from jerking off so much...

Little Robert worked mostly with filigree... the rough polishing... He had a file no thicker than a hair that he stuck into the tiniest openings... He'd also put patina on the finished pieces... It was close work, those things were as fine as cobwebs... He'd squint at them until his eyes hurt... Then he'd stop and sprinkle the floor.

Antoine never let him get away with anything, he always had it in for him... He couldn't stand my guts either. We wanted to catch him laying Madame Gorloge. Apparently he did... Robert said so, but he wasn't really sure... Maybe it was a red herring. At the table during meals Antoine was insufferable, you had to watch your step. At the slightest word he'd fly off the handle and start packing up his tools. They'd promise him a raise... ten frances... maybe only five... "Go shit in your hat!" he'd say. Right to Gorloge's face. "You give me a good pain in the ass... How can you make promises when you haven't got a pair of shoes to your name!... Bullshit!"

"Don't get excited, Antoine! I assure you that things are going to pick up... One of these days... I'm positive... Soon... Sooner than you think..."

"Balls! They'll pick up when I'm an archbishop..."

That was the way they spoke to each other. The sky was the limit... The boss would stand for anything... he was so scared Antoine would pick up and leave. He didn't want to do anything by himself... he didn't want to ruin his hands. While waiting for the renaissance... his main pleasure in life was his cup of coffee and looking out the window smoking his pipe... The neighborhood panorama... He didn't like anybody to talk to him... You could do anything you pleased as long as you didn't bother him. He told us so perfectly frankly: "Just pretend I'm not here."

I still wasn't finding any takers, neither wholesale nor retail. I still had every one of my bats and chimeras on my hands... And yet I hadn't left a stone unturned... From the Madeleine to Belleville... I'd been everywhere, I'd tried everything... From the Bastille to Saint-Cloud there wasn't a single door that I didn't open sooner or later... Every junk dealer, every watchmaker from the rue de Rivoli to the cemetery of Bagneux... Every little Yid knew me... every punk... every goldsmith... All I got was the brush-off... They didn't want anything... This couldn't go on forever... Even bad luck gets tired...

Finally one day it happened. A miracle... on the corner of the rue Saint-Lazare... I'd been passing the place every day... And I'd never stopped... They sold Chinese bric-a-brac... Not a hundred yards from La Trinité. Funny I hadn't noticed before that they went in for grimaces too, and not little ones, great big ones! Whole windows full of them. And they weren't just kidding, they were real horrors. Pretty much like mine... Every bit as ugly... But they went in more for salamanders, flying dragons... Buddhas with enormous bellies... all gilded... furiously rolling their eyes... Smoke was coming up from behind the pedestal... like an opium dream... And rows of arquebuses and halberds all the way up the ceiling... with fringes and sparkling glass- beads. Real fun. Lots of snakes too, spitting fire... twined around columns... wriggling down toward the floor... And along the walls a hundred flaming parasols and next to the door a devil, life-size, surrounded by toads with wide-open eyes lit by thousands of lanterns...

Since they sold that kind of truck, the idea came to me —a real inspiration... that they might like my little things.

I screw up my courage. I push through the door… with my saddlebags... I unpack... of course I stammer a little at first... then finally the patter begins to flow.

The guy was a little character with slanting eyes and a voice like an old woman, as sly as they come... he was wearing a silk dress with a flower design, and clogs... in short he looked like a Chinese goblin except for his soft hat... At first he didn't say much... But I could see I was making an impression with my large selection of charms... my mandrakes... my knots of Medusas... my Samothrace brooches... For a Chink it was hot stuff!... You had to have come a long way to appreciate my collection...

Finally he thawed... In fact he was frankly excited... enthusiastic... exultant... He even stuttered with impatience... He came right out with it: "I believe, my dear little young man, that I shall be able to do something for you..." And he went on in his singsong...

He knew an art lover near the Luxembourg... A very respectable gentleman... A real scholar... who was crazy about high-class artistic ornaments... exactly my style... This guy was a Manchu, he was here on vacation... He filled me in... I mustn't talk too loud... He couldn't stand noise of any kind... He gave me his address... It wasn't a very good Hôtel, it was on the rue Soufflot... All the Chink on the rue Saint-Lazare wanted for himself was a little "present"... if I got the order... Only five percent... It wasn't too much... I signed his little paper... I didn't waste a second... I even jumped into the Odéon bus on the rue des Martyrs.

I tracked down my art lover. I show him my boxes, I introduce myself. I dig out my samples. He's even more slant-eyed than the other guy... He's wearing a long dress too. He's delighted with my stuff... He makes a whole speech... about his pleasure at discovering such beautiful things.

Then he shows me on the map where he came from... From the end of the world... even a little farther, way off in the left-hand margin... This was the mandarin on vacation... He wanted something beautiful to take home with him, except he wanted to have it engraved to order... He'd even selected his model, he just had to have it. He wanted me to make it up for him... A real order!... He explained where I could go to copy it... It was in the Galliera Museum, on the third floor, in the middle showcase... I couldn't go wrong, he made me a little sketch. He wrote the name in big letters: SA-KYAMUNI, it was called... the god of happiness... He wanted an exact copy of it for a tiepin, because back home, as he told me: "I dress in the European style. I'm the chief justice."

He'd got this idea. He was very trusting. He gave me two hundred francs just like that to buy the gold with... It was more convenient... that way we wouldn't lose any time…

I can swear I made a face like Buddha myself when I took those two bills... This weird way of doing things knocked me for a loop... I staggered on my way down the boulevard... I was so dizzy I almost got myself run over...

Finally I get to the rue Elzévir... I tell the whole story... What luck when we'd given up hoping!... Engraving was coming back... Gorloge had been right... We drank on it... Everybody hugged and kissed me... Everybody made up... We went out and changed the two hundred frances... There was only a hundred and fifty left...

Gorloge and I went to the museum to sketch the little Chink. He was mighty interesting in his little case, all alone, still as a mouse, on a little camp chair, laughing to himself, holding a shepherd's crook...

We took our time, we copied our sketch and reduced it one to a hundred... We made a little model... It all went off fine. Then Robert and I dashed over to the Comptoir Judéo-Suisse on the rue Francoeur for some eighteen-carat gold, a hundred francs' worth at one throw, and fifty francs' worth of solder... We put the little ingot away carefully, we double-locked the safe... That hadn't happened in four years... keeping metal overnight on the rue Elzévir... When the model was finished, we sent it to be cast... Three times they messed it up... they had to start all over again... Founders never know what they're doing... The time passed... We were getting annoyed... And then finally they caught on. All in all, it wasn't bad... The god was beginning to shape up... It only needed to be finished, polished, and engraved...

Then we had lousy luck... The cops come looking for Gorloge... The whole house is in an uproar... On account of his four weeks of military service... No further postponement was possible... He'd already had too many... He couldn't miss the big maneuvers... No two ways about it, he'd have to leave the "god of happiness" unfinished... It wasn't the kind of job you could do in a hurry... It needed fine finishing...

Since there was no way out, this is what Gorloge decided. Antoine would finish the job... he'd take his time... and I'd deliver it... There was only another hundred francs to collect... Gorloge would collect in person... he made that very clear... when he got back from his hitch... He was awfully suspicious.

If our Chinaman liked it, we'd make more, we'd make a whole pile of Sakya-Munis in solid gold! What could stop us? The future, as we saw it, was one glowing sunrise... Why wouldn't the renascence of engraved ornaments come to us from the Far East?... Why not? Our whole stairway... Stairway B... was buzzing with our story, all the little tinkers upstairs and downstairs were flabbergasted at our luck, they couldn't get over it! What a windfall! There were rumors that we were getting checks from Peking.

Gorloge hung around to the last minute. He was building up to a mess of trouble. He and Antoine took turns working on the little character. There were crazy details, things so small, so tiny you couldn't see them properly even with the magnifying glass. The little chair... the shepherd's crook... and especially his little puss... it was hard to catch that tiny little smile! They were still scraping away particles with a fine tool, as sharp as a fingernail... He was almost done... It was a perfect copy. But even so, maybe Antoine had better give it a little more thought... go back to it in four or five days... Then it would be really first-class...

Finally Gorloge made up his mind to get going, it was high time. The cops had been back again...

The next day when I got there, I saw him... He was dolled up like a soldier from top to toe... The enormous floating cape, with the two buttons so you could turn up the corners like a sack of French fries... the kepi with the green pompon and the bright-red pants that went with it... That's what he was wearing when he went downstairs... Little Robert carried his musette bag. It was packed mighty full... there were three camemberts, so much alive that everybody made remarks... And two quarts of white wine and some smaller bottles, an assortment of socks... and his woolen nightgown for sleeping in the open...

The neighbors all came trooping down in denims and slippers... They were all hawking like mad, spitting all over the doormats... They wished him luck. I took Gorloge to the station, I left him outside the Gare de l'Est, on the corner of the Boulevard Magenta. He was worried about having to leave right now, with this job on hand. He kept giving me instructions. It burned him up that he couldn't finish it himself... Finally he said good-bye... He told me to be good... He followed the sign... The whole place was full of soldiers... Some of the guys said we were blocking the traffic with our gabfest... I had to beat it...

When I got back to the rue Elzévir, I passed by the lodge. The concierge calls me:

"Hey," she says, "come in here a minute, Ferdinand. So he's gone? So he finally made up his mind! Well anyway, he won't be cold out there. They'll make it plenty hot for him. It's a good thing he took all those bottles. 'Cause they're going to make it mighty rough for him. Whew! The bastards! They'll make your cuckold sweat!"

She said all that to get me started, to make me talk. I didn't answer. I was fed up on gossip. That's God's truth. I was getting to be very cautious... I was right... But I wasn't cautious enough!... As I was soon to find out.

Once the boss was gone, little Robert couldn't contain himself. He was determined to see Antoine and the *patronne* fucking... He said it would happen, it was bound to... He was a natural-born peeping torn.

The first week we didn't see much... So's to keep the shop running it was me that went over to the rue de Provence and down the boulevard looking for repair work... I brought back what I found... It was barely enough... I didn't tote my collection around anymore. That would have made them throw me out.

Antoine went on fussing with the little priest, he was doing fine. He knew his business. About the second week the patronne suddenly began to change. She'd always been kind of standoffish... when Gorloge was there, she hardly ever spoke to me. All of a sudden she began to be friendly, ingratiating, intimate. At first I thought there was something phony about it. But I kept my suspicions to myself... I decided maybe it was because I was getting to be more useful... Because I was bringing in little jobs... Still, they weren't getting us any dough... not one of our bills had been paid...

Gorloge, who was always suspicious... had made it very clear that we weren't to collect a single bill! He'd do all that when he got back. He'd notified the customers.

One morning I came in early and found Madame Gorloge already up, roaming around the room... She pretended to be looking for something by the workbench... She was wearing a swishy dressing gown... For my money she was acting pretty weird... She comes close. She says to me:

"Ferdinand, on your way home from your errands this evening, be a good boy and bring me a little bunch of flowers. It'll cheer the place up..." She heaves a sigh. "Since my husband went away, I haven't had the heart to go out."

She waggled her ass around the room. She was putting on a seduction act. That was plain. The door to her bedroom was wide open. I could see her bed... I didn't bat an eyelash... I didn't make a move... Antoine and Robert came up from the café... I didn't breathe a word...

That evening I brought back three peonies. That was all I could afford. There wasn't any money left in the till. As far as I was concerned it was plenty. I knew I'd never be paid back.

And then Antoine gets polite too, almost palsy-walsy... when only a week before he'd done nothing but yell at us... He was perfectly charming... He didn't even want me to go out anymore, to go looking for work...

"Take it easy," he said. "Stick around the shop... Watch us work, you'll learn something... you'll make your rounds later..."

In spite of all our shilly-shallying the pin was finished... it came back from the polishers. It was my job to deliver it... Just then the *patronne* gets a letter from Gorloge... he said we shouldn't hurry... we should keep the pin a while... wait for him to get back. He'd take it to the Chinaman himself... Meanwhile if I felt like it, I could show it to some of our customers, the ones that would appreciate it...

Right away I began to feel worried. Everybody admired the little character, that's a fact... He looked real good on his little throne, Sakya-Muni in solid gold... eighteen carats after all... that meant something in those days. You couldn't have asked for anything finer... All our neighbors came around and complimented us... and some of them were connoisseurs... It was an honor to the house... Our customer could have no cause for complaint... Gorloge was going to be away for another ten days... That left me plenty of time to show it around the shops...

"Ferdinand," the *patronne* advised me, "why don't you leave it here at night, in your drawer? Nobody'll touch it, you know. You can pick it up again in the morning."

I preferred to keep it in my pocket and take it home with me. That struck me as much more conscientious... I even fastened it with safety pins, a great big diaper pin and two little ones, one on each side... Everybody laughed. "He won't lose it," they said.

The way our shop was situated, right under the tiles, it was awfully hot, even at the end of September the heat was so bad we were always drinking.

One afternoon Antoine went off his rocker from guzzling so much. He was singing so loud you could hear him all over the court as far as the concierge's lodge at the other end... He'd brought up some absinthe and a lot of little cakes. We all nibbled. Robert and I put all the little bottles out under the faucet on the landing to cool. We bought them on credit, whole baskets full... There was trouble though... The grocers got mean... It was crazy in a way... We'd all gone berserk, it was the hot weather and the freedom.

The *patronne* joined us. Antoine sat down right beside her. We laughed to see them necking. He went looking for her garters. He lifted her skirts up. She was giggling like a goat. She was irritating as hell, you wanted to sock her... He pulled out one of her tits. She just sat there beaming. He poured out the rest of the bottle. Robert and I finished it. We licked the glass. It was better than Ban-yuls... In the end everybody was crocked... the frenzy of the senses... Antoine hiked up her skirts completely... at one stroke... way over her head!... He got up too and just as she was, all bundled up in her skirts, he pushed her into the bedroom. She was still laughing... She had the giggles... They closed the door behind them... She went right on cackling...

The time had come for Robert and me to climb up on the kitchen stove and watch the show... It was a good place... ringside... You could see the whole bed... we couldn't miss a trick. Right away Antoine pushed the fat mama down on her knees... He was awfully brutal... She had her ass up in the air... He tickled and teased her... He couldn't find her dingbat... He tore her ruffles... he tore everything in sight... And then he attacked... He took out his cock... He began to charge her... And it was no make-believe... I hadn't expected he could be so wild... I couldn't get over it. He was grunting like a pig... She was making noises too... Louder and more piercing every time he charged. Robert had told me the truth about her ass... We could see it good now... All red... enormous, scarlet! Her fine lace panties were all in tatters... and sopping wet... Antoine was coming in like a battering ram... You could hear the smack... They wrestled like savages... The way he was going at her I was sure he'd kill her... His pants were dragging on the floor... His smock was still in his way, he ripped it off with one tug... It fell right next to us... He was naked now... Except he still had his slippers on, the boss's, the ones with the embroidered kittens... He was so excited he skidded on the carpet... He banged his head against the bar of the bed... he was madder than a hornet... he felt his head... he had bumps. He slipped out... He bounded back in a fury... "You stinking bitch!" he bellows at her. "You lousy whore!" He drives his knee into her ribs. She tries to get away, she begins to simper and moan...

"Antoine, oh, Antoine darling, I can't stand it... Stop, I implore you... Be careful... Don't make me a kid! I'm wringing wet."

That was for the birds, she was asking for more.

"Go on, you old cow, shut your trap. Open your basket."

He didn't listen to her. He put her back on again with three enormous clouts in the gizzard... Bam! they resounded... She gasped for breath, the stinker... She wheezed like a bellows... I wondered if he was going to kill her... finish her off on the spot!... He gave her another vicious clout... right while he was pumping... They were both roaring like wild animals... She was coming... Robert was green around the gills. We climbed down off our diving board... We went back to the workbench... We didn't say a word... We'd wanted a show... we'd had our money's worth... Except it was dangerous... The corrida was still going on. We went down to the court... to get the pail and brooms, supposedly to clean up... We went in to see the concierge, we thought that was a better place to be in case he strangled her...

There was no tragedy and no corpse... They came out beaming... we just had to get used to it...

The next few days we ordered provisions from all over, from three different grocers, on the rue des Écouffes and the rue Beaubourg, who didn't know us yet... We set up a whole food department and quite a cellar too, beer and sparkling Malvoisin, all on credit. We were going to the dogs...

I found excuses for not eating with my people at home. It was getting to be something on the rue Elzévir, we never stopped pouring it down. We didn't do a lick of work. In the afternoon, about four o'clock, Robert and I would wait for the corrida to start... We weren't scared anymore... It didn't excite us so much either.

Besides, Antoine was weakening, the fight had gone out of him, the least little effort was making him winded.

She began to resist... to fight him off. Then his fury came back... It was a regular circus... She was braying like a jackass... He kept skidding every time he tried... He couldn't get it in anymore... So he jumps out of bed and heads straight for the kitchen... Luckily, being as we were on top of the stove, he didn't see us, he was too hot and bothered... He went right by and began rummaging around the cupboard, just like that, mother-naked in his slippers... He was looking for the butter dish... his cock kept bumping into things:

"Ow ouch, oh oh ouch!" he kept yelping. We were in stitches... Christ, it was funny... we thought we'd explode... .

"The butter, damn it, the butter!..."

Finally he found his dish... He took a whole ladleful... He went back with a whole mess of it... He runs back to the bed quick... She was putting on airs again... wriggling and writhing... He buttered her treasure, the whole thing and all around it, slowly and very carefully, like a specialist... She was all shiny... He had no trouble... He took her by storm... It went in easy... The excitement was terrific... They let out piercing yells... They collapsed on their sides.

Then fiat on their backs... They went to sleep... It wasn't any fun anymore...

The first ones to make a stink were the grocers on the rue Berce... They refused to give us any more food on the cuff... They came around with their bills... We heard them coming up... We didn't answer...

They went back down to the concierge... They raised hell... Things were getting rough. So then Antoine and the *patronne* began going out all the time, they did their drinking on the outside, they ran up terrible bills in every joint in the neighborhood... I didn't breathe a word about all this at home... They'd have blamed it all on me... They'd have thought I was at the bottom of all the monkeyshines.

The main thing was the jewel case... That solid gold Sakya-Muni... I didn't let him run around, he didn't get out much. I kept him very carefully way down in the bottom of my pocket... and fastened with three diaper pins. I had stopped showing it to people, I didn't trust anybody anymore... I was waiting for the boss to come back.

In the shop Robert and I took it easy... Antoine hardly did a lick of work. After their parties he and the old bitch would come in and kid around with us. We turned the whole place into a shambles. Meanwhile in the afternoon they'd saw wood for hours... We were one happy family... as thick as thieves and twice as sticky.

But one night the ax fell. We hadn't bolted the door... It was dinner time... There was a lot of bustle on all the landings... So one of our enraged liquor suppliers, the meanest of the lot, comes dashing up the stairs, four at a time... We didn't hear him until it was much too late. He opens the door, he comes in... He finds the two of them in bed! Antoine and Her Fatness... He begins to yap like a dozen seals... His eyes were all bloodshot... He wanted to murder Antoine on the spot. He was brandishing his big hammer... I thought he was going to emboss him one...

It was true, we owed him plenty... for at least twenty-five bottles... white... rosé... cognac, and even vinegar... It degenerated into a pitched battle... It took eight of us to handle that gorilla... . We called in all our friends... Antoine was bleeding like a stuck pig... he had two enormous shiners... a blue one and a yellow one...

From downstairs in the court he went on threatening us. He was delirious. He called us every name in the book: "Crooks!... Scum!... Cocksuckers!..."

"You just wait, you lousy chiselers. You'll hear from me... Sooner than you think, you crumb-bums... You'll see when the police get here."

Things were getting sticky...

The next day, in the afternoon, I say to Robert: "Listen, kid. I got to go out. They came around again from Tracard's this morning asking for their brooch, it should have been delivered at least a week ago..." "OK," he says, "I got to go out too. I got a date with a guy on the corner outside the Matin."

The two of us race down the stairs... Neither Antoine nor the *patronne* had been home for lunch...

When we get to the third-floor landing, I hear her coming up... All out of breath, red in the face, incandescent... They must have been eating too much...

"Where are you going, Ferdinand?"

"Just a little errand... On the boulevard... to see a customer."

"Oh, don't go," she said. She seemed put out. "Come back upstairs a minute... I've got something to tell you."

OK. I go back upstairs with her. Robert runs off to his date.

The minute we get in she closes the door, she locks everything, she pushes both bolts... She steps in ahead of me, she goes into the bedroom... She motions me to come in too... I come closer... I wonder what's going to happen... She starts feeling me up... She blows up my nose... "Ah! Ah!" she goes. That excites her... I pet her a little too...

"Oh, what a little pig! I hear you look through keyholes... Is that right?... Oh!... tell me it isn't true..." With one hand she starts massaging me underneath...

"I'm going to tell your mama. Oh what a little pig! Oh, sweet little pig!..."

She begins to gnash her teeth... She begins to wriggle... She clutches me... She sticks in her tongue, à real lowdown kiss... I see stars... She makes me sit down beside her on the bed... She flops down backwards... Suddenly she hikes up her skirts...

"Touch me!" she says. "Touch me down there."

I put my hand on...

"Go ahead!" she insists... "Go ahead, angel dumpling... Go ahead... Call me Louison!

Your Louison! You slimy little pig! Call me... You will, won't you?..." "Yes, Louison," I say.

She sits up, she kisses me again. She takes everything off... blouse... corset... shift... I see her all naked . . her thingamajig so voluminous... spread out all over the place... It was too much... I was sick to my stomach... She grabs me by the ears... She pulls me down to mother nature... She bends me with all her might... My nose is in a hell of a state... It's dazzling and all runny... It's all over my neck... She makes me kiss it . . at first it tastes like fish, then like a dog's muzzle...

"Go on, little love. Go on, don't be bashful."

She manhandles me, she pesters the life out of me... I'm up to my ears in marmalade... I'm afraid to sniff too hard... I'm afraid of hurting her... She's shaking like an apple tree...

"Bite me, sweet little puppy... Bite into it! Go ahead," she encourages me. She's heaving like mad! She lets out little squeals... I plunge in deep... it smells like eggs and shit... My collar is strangling me... the celluloid... She pulls me out of the pit... I come up for air... My eyes are like covered with varnish, even my eyebrows are all sticky...

"Get undressed," she orders me. "Take all that stuff off. I want to see your cunning little body. Quick. Quick. You'll see, you little rascal. You a virgin? Tell me, angel. You'll see how I'm going to love you up... Oh, what a nasty little pig! I'll teach you to look through keyholes…"

She billowed and writhed while waiting for me... The whole bed was zigzagging... She was a regular vampire...

I didn't dare take off too much. Just the choker that was killing me... and my coat and vest... She hung them up beside the bed, on the back of the chair... I didn't want to take everything off... the way Antoine did... I knew my ass was shitty and my feet coal-black... I could smell myself... To keep her from insisting. I started up again as fast as I could... I played the ardent lover, I climbed, I squeezed, I grunted... I charged like Antoine, but much more gently... I felt my thingamajig sailing all around... I was lost in the foam... I didn't dare use my fingers, though that's what I should have done... I scrabbled around in her moustache... Finally it slipped right in... all by itself... She squashed me against her tits! She was having a hell of a good time... It was stifling... it was like a furnace... She wanted me to work harder... She didn't beg for pity like with that bastard... Oh, no, she wanted me to be more brutal...

"Deeper, angel. Deeper, don't be afraid. My, what a big fat one you've got... Ah... ah... you're ripping me apart, you big thug!... Oh, rip me... Are you coming?... Oh, say yes!... Oh, oh! You're killing me, you little bastard! My big little skunk! Isn't it good?" And bam, I plowed into her... I was done in. I lay down on the job... She blew in my face... I had a noseful... from her licking too... garlic... Roquefort... they'd been eating sausage...

"Swoon good, little pet! Oh, swoon... We'll die together!... Aren't you going to, little treasure!... You're killing me... There... Don't worry about me..." She swooned, she began to list... She turned over almost on top of me... I felt my chip coming...

Suddenly I say to myself: "Cheese it, kid." I was out cold, but just the same... One two three... I wrench myself loose... I pull it out... It gushes all over my belly... I try to squeeze… I get a handful...

"Oh, what a little beast!" she hollers. "Oh, what a slimy little toad!... Come quick and let me clean you up..." She goes for my pecker... She makes a meal of it... She likes the sauce... "Oh, what a delicious little dessert!" she squeals. She goes looking for it all over my legs... She pokes into the folds... She's really thorough... She's going to swoon again... She's down on her knees, clinging to my legs, she contracts, she relaxes... Fat ass and all, she's as nimble as a cat. She forces me down on her again... "I'll show you, you little louse," she says roguishly. She sticks two fingers into my opening. She forces me. What a scrimmage! The stinker, the way she's steamed up, she'll be at it all day!

"Oh," it suddenly occurs to her. "I've got to take a douche." With one jump she was out of the room. I hear her pissing in the kitchen... She's rummaging under the sink... "Wait for me, angel," she sings out... I've had enough. I jump into my suit... I grab the door, I push it open, I'm on the landing... I take the stairs four at a time... I take a good deep breath... I'm out in the street... It's time to think things over... I catch my breath... I walk slowly toward the boulevards.

When I got to the Ambigu, I finally sat down. I pick up a newspaper from the sidewalk. I'm just beginning to read... I don't know why... I feel my pocket... I did it without thinking... A sudden inspiration... I feel again... I can't find the bump... I feel the other... Same result. I haven't got it anymore... My jewel case is gone. I look for it harder and harder... I feel all my linings... My pants... inside... outside... nothing doing... I go to the can... I undress completely... I turn everything inside out... Nothing... I'm not blind... The blood boils in my veins... I sit down on the steps again... I'm cooked... and good!... I'm really screwed... I pull out my pockets again... And again... But I've given up hope... I remember perfectly... I'd pinned it all right...Way in the bottom of my inside pocket. I'd felt it before going out with Robert... The safety pins were gone... They hadn't come out all by themselves... All of a sudden I remembered the funny way she'd held me by the head the whole time... And on the other side of the chair... she'd been working with one hand... It all came to me in waves... Fright, terror welled up in me... straight up from my heart... It pounded worse than forty-nine truck horses... My whole head shook... That didn't do any good... I began to look again... The case couldn't have fallen... it couldn't have slipped out the way I'd pinned it... Impossible... Diaper pins don't open so easy... And there were three of them... They don't come open all by themselves! To make sure I wasn't dreaming I ran back toward the Place de la République... When I got to the rue Elzévir, there was nobody home... They'd all gone out... I waited on the stairs... until seven o'clock, to see if they'd come in... Nobody came...

I tried to put things together... words... snatches of talk... incidents. It all came to me little by little... Suppose Antoine had engineered it? And what about little Robert?... Maybe they were both in on it... in cahoots with the bitch... When I stood up, I couldn't feel my two legs... I went down the street like I was drunk... The people noticed me... I stayed a while in the little tunnel by the Porte Saint-Denis. I was afraid to come out... I saw the buses in the distance, swaying in the heat... I felt dizzy... I didn't get back to the Passage until late... I said I had a bellyache... That stopped them from asking questions... I had such cramps I didn't sleep all night... Next day I was out at the crack of dawn, I was in such a hurry to know...

When I got to the shop, I took a good look at all three of them... They didn't seem to be thinking anything... neither the bitch... nor Antoine... nor the kid... When I told them the pin had been lost, they gaped at me... they were flabbergasted...

"What's that, Ferdinand? You're sure? Have you taken a good look at home?... Turn your pockets inside out... We haven't found anything here... How about it, Robert?... You didn't see anything?" It was the kid who swept... "You'd better sweep again..."

The way they talked, they seemed so savage, so villainous that I began to bawl... I could see them in the mirror, making little signs to each other... Antoine avoided looking at me... He kept his back turned, he pretended to be cleaning his emery stone... She went on blowing hot air... trying to trip me up, to make me contradict myself.

"You don't remember at Tracard's... Didn't you say you were going there?... Maybe you left it there... Are you sure?..."

I was floundering in the soup... What a vicious rotten trick!... There wasn't a thing I could do... I was cooked... Nobody'd believe me if I told the truth... What was the use?

"The boss will be back the day after tomorrow... Try to find it before then... Robert will help you..." She was full of ideas. Any way you looked at it I was screwed... If I went into details, they'd call me an impostor, a horrible abject monster... trying to wriggle out by slandering the boss's wife, so good, so kind... Had I no shame?... What colossal gall!... what a preposterous calumny!... what monumental villainy!... I didn't even try to defend myself... I didn't even feel like it anymore... I couldn't eat... My head was all stuffed up... my mind, my mouth, my whole face...

My mother thought I was looking odd, she wondered what ailment I could be coming down with... My guts were all tied up with fear... I wanted to disappear... to get so thin there'd be nothing left...

My father made caustic remarks... "You wouldn't be in love by any chance? It wouldn't be spring fever?... You got pimples on your ass?..." He took me off to one side and asked me: "You wouldn't have a dose of clap?..." I didn't know which way to squirm.

Gorloge, who was late wherever he went, had come back by a route of his own, he had dawdled from one town to the next... He arrived on a Wednesday, we'd been expecting him since Saturday... The next morning when I went to work, he was in the kitchen, sharpening his files. I stood behind him for quite a while... in the hallway, I was afraid to move... I waited for him to speak to me. I had a shitless lump in my throat. I'd forgotten what I meant to say. He must have been told by then. I hold out my hand just the same. He kind of squints at me from the side... He doesn't even turn around... He goes back to his work. I wasn't even there anymore... So I run into the shop. I was so scared I left half my collection in the bottom of the closet so as to get out faster... Nobody called me back... They were all there in the room, concentrating on their thingamajigs... I left without a word... I didn't even know where I was going... Luckily I was used to that... I walked along in a dream... On the rue Reaumur I was in a terrible cold sweat... On the big terrace I went from one bench to another... In spite of everything I tried to go into a shop... But my hand trembled so on the door handle I never made it inside... I thought everybody was following me.

I spent hours like that... the whole morning. And the afternoon too, the whole time from one bench to another and so on, as far as the Square Louvois... always leaning against the house fronts... I couldn't walk anymore... I didn't want to go back to Gorloge's... Even my parents were better than that... It was just as awful... but at least it was nearer... Only a step from the Square Louvois... It's funny when you've got no place to breathe in but places that are all equally horrible...

I walked around the Bank of France once, twice, very slowly, with my disgusting junk... Then suddenly I pulled myself together and went back to the Passage... My father was on the doorstep... obviously waiting for me... The way he told me to go upstairs left no room for doubt... The storm was on... He began right away to stammer so bad and so loud that steam came out instead of words... I couldn't understand a thing... Except that he was blowing off rockets... His cap was buffeted by the storm... It flew in all directions... He rained blows on it... He jammed it down on his noodle... His face swelled up still worse... absolutely crimson... with livid furrows... He changed color. He went violet.

I was fascinated. Was he going to turn blue?... and then yellow? I was so drenched in his fury that I couldn't feel anything... He picked up some dohicky on the sideboard. He brandished it with a view to breakage... I thought he was going to tear the whole place to pieces... He bit his tongue so hard, so furiously, it swelled up like a stopper, a big lump of meat, wedged into his mouth and like to burst... But it didn't... He put down the hot plate... He gagged... He couldn't go on...

Suddenly he dashed out, he headed for the street, he ran through the Passage. I thought he was going to fly away, he was so blown up... so irresistible... so horrible...

My mother stayed with me... She trotted out the whole fool story, every detail of the disaster... And all her own little ideas... her timeworn certainties...

Monsieur Gorloge had been there, he had talked to them for two hours... He knew all about it... He'd told them everything... he had prophesied the whole Future. "That child will be your ruin... he's corrupt to the marrow... A wretch... I trusted him... He was beginning to get ahead..."

Those were his parting words... Mama had been scared he'd turn me in... that he'd have me arrested right away... She hadn't dared to answer... As far as she was concerned, there were no two ways about it... I'd been taken in... Why didn't I own up right away... at least that I'd lost it... instead of prevaricating... and turning my boss against me... That was the least revolting possibility... They'd pay him back little by little... and in any case my parents... That was already settled...

"Who set you such an example?" she asked me in tears. "What did you do with the pin?... Come, tell me, my boy. We won't eat you... I won't say a word to your father... I swear I won't!... There, you do trust me? We'll go see her together... If you gave it to a woman! Tell me right away, before he comes home! Maybe she'll give it back in exchange for a little money?

... Do you know her well?... Don't you think so?... That way it'll all come out all right in the end! We won't say a word to anybody!"

I waited for her to calm down some, then maybe I'd be able to explain... Just then my father comes in... He hadn't cooled off at all. He begins to pound the table and bang at the partitions as hard as he can... with both fists... all the time letting off jets of steam... When he stops for a second, it's only to kick at the furniture... His anger lifted him up, he was like a horse galloping through the air... bashing into the walls... The whole place was shaking... What an onslaught, the sideboard capsizes...

From blast to crash the scene went on all night... He'd bounce into the air in his fury and fall on all fours... He barked like a mastiff... Between fits and frenzies they bellowed the pros and cons... It was no time for me to try to say anything...

When she ran out of arguments, my mother came upstairs to see what she could do with me... I didn't answer... She wanted me to confess... She went down on her knees by my bed and cried as if I were already dead... She mumbled prayers... She went on imploring me... She wanted me to own up right away... to tell her if it was a woman!... We'd go and see her together...

"I tell you it was the boss's wife," I finally vomited up. I couldn't stand it anymore. Hell and damnation!

"Ah, be still, you little wretch... You don't realize how you're hurting us!"

It was no use insisting... How could you talk to such mugs!... They were stopped up worse than all the shithouses in all Asnières! That's my opinion.

It was a terrible blow all right. I stayed in my room a long time, five or six days without going out. They forced me to come down and eat... She called me a dozen times. In the end she came up and got me. I didn't want anything at all. Especially I didn't want to talk. My father talked to himself... He went off into monologues... Raging and fuming... he went on and on... about the forces of evil... his whole repertory... Destiny... The Jews... his rotten luck... The Exposition... Providence... The Freemasons...

As soon as he got home from his deliveries, he'd climb up to the attic... He'd started doing watercolors again, he really had to... We had pressing needs, Gorloge had to be paid back... But he couldn't concentrate... His mind wandered... The moment he picked up a brush he was so exasperated the stem would snap in his hands. He was so jumpy he'd smash his little India-ink pen to bits... and his paint pots too... the colors flowed all over... It was hopeless... The mere feeling that I was anywhere near him made him want to smash everything to pieces... And as soon as he was with my mother, he started up again... he redoubled his alarms and excursions.

"If you let him bum around the street all day on the pretext of learning the business, we haven't seen the end of our troubles. Believe you me. This is only the beginning. He won't content himself with being a thief. He'll be a murderer, see?... A murderer! I wouldn't give him six months before he murders some old woman for her money. He's on the downgrade all right. He isn't slipping. Take it from me. He's hurtling, he's galloping. Headlong. I can see it plain as day. Can't you? You don't believe me? You're blind! But not yours truly. Not on your life... not me..."

Here he took a deep breath. He was hypnotizing her...

"Will you finally listen to me?... You want me to tell you what's going to happen?... No?... You don't want to know..."

"No, Auguste, I implore you..."

"Ha! So you're afraid to listen?... So you know?"

He seized her by both wrists, he wouldn't let her get away... she had to listen to the bitter end.

"It's us, see? It's us he's going to rub out... one of these days... Yes, my dear, he'll settle our hash... That's the kind of gratitude you'll get from him... Don't say I didn't predict it... Don't say I didn't warn you... Christ almighty... My conscience is clear... Ah, godammit, godammit to hell! I've warned you in every key... I've shouted it from the rooftops! For years! Oh well! *Alea jacta!...*"

He got my mother so scared she began to foam at the mouth and bleat... and blow bubbles... she was out of her mind... He really knocked her for a loop...

"I don't mind being strangled... OK. But you can't pull the wool over my eyes, godammit ... Do what you like... You'll be responsible!"

In the face of these savage predictions, she didn't know what to say or do. Convulsed with grief, she kept chewing at her lips, she bled profusely. I was damned, there was no doubt about that. He started his Pontius Pilate act again, he splashed up the whole floor, I was dirt, and he washed his hands of me... the water flowed in jets... at high pressure... He said whole sentences in Latin. It came back to him at dramatic moments. Just like that, standing in the little kitchen, he'd hurl the anathema at me, he'd declaim in the ancient manner. He'd break off occasionally, pause to explain... because I had no education, no feeling for the "humanities"...

He knew everything. All I really knew was one thing, that I was untouchable, not fit to be handled with a ten-foot pole. I was despised on all sides, even by the Roman moralists, by Cicero, by the whole Empire, by all the Ancients... My papa knew all that... He didn't have a single doubt left... His certainty made him bellow like a polecat... My mother went right on bawling ... He played the scene so often it got to be a regular act... He'd pick up the laundry soap, the big heavy cake, and brandish it like mad... with wild, sweeping gestures... Now and then he'd put it down... perorating all the while... And pick it up again... And brandish it some more... The soap would slip out of his hand... and go bouncing under the piano... We'd all dive for it... We'd rummage around with the broom... we'd fish with the handle... Shit, piss, and corruption!... We'd bash our heads against the corners... There were wild collisions... We'd stick the broom handle in our eyes... It would end in a battle. They'd call each other every stinking name in the world. He'd make her hop around the table on one foot.

They'd forget me for a minute.

My mother was so terrified she lost all shame. She went all over the Passage retailing my villainies... she asked the other parents for advice... the ones that had trouble with their brats... that had got into messes on their jobs... How had they managed?...

"I'm perfectly willing to make more sacrifices," she added. "We'll see this thing through to the bitter end..."

All very eloquent, but it didn't get me out of the soup. I still had no work.

Even Uncle Édouard, so ingenious, with so many strings to his bow, was beginning to get upset. He found me a bit of a nuisance... He'd already pestered just about all his friends with my shenanigans, my hard luck... He was getting kind of sick of it... I stumbled over every obstacle... There was something wrong with me... I was beginning to get his goat.

The neighbors were mighty interested in my tragedy... Our customers too. As soon as they got to know me a little, my mother told them all about it... That didn't help matters... Even Monsieur Lempreinte at La Coccinelle finally got mixed up in it... It's true that my father didn't sleep anymore, that he was beginning to look like a corpse... He came to work so exhausted that he staggered in the hallways as he carried the mail from one floor to another... Besides, he'd lost his voice, he'd gone hoarse from bellowing his inanities...

"Your private life, my friend, doesn't concern me in the least. That's your business. But I expect you to do your work properly... Look at the face on you... You're falling apart... You've got to take care of yourself! What have you been doing on the outside? Aren't you getting enough rest?" That was the way he peppered him.

Then my father was scared and told him all about it... all his family troubles...

"Ah, my poor boy! Is that all? Lord, if only I had your stomach! Believe me, I wouldn't give a good godam... not much!... about all my neighbors and relations... about all my sons and cousins... my wife! my daughters! my eighteen fathers! If I was in your place, I'd piss on everybody. On the whole world. You hear what I say! You're soft, monsieur, that's all I can see."

That was how Lempreinte looked at things, on account of his ulcer, an inch away from the pylorus, eating into him, excruciating... The whole world for him was nothing but one mass of acid... The only thing left for him to do was to try to turn into bicarbonate... He worked at it all day... he took whole carloads of the stuff... He couldn't put out the fire. He had a poker at the bottom of his esophagus that was burning his guts... Soon there wouldn't be anything left but holes... The stars would shine through every time he belched... He and Papa were always offering to change places...

"I'd take your ulcer any day. Anything you please, if only you'll take my son off my hands! How about it?"

That was my father. He'd always put moral torment way above physical pain... It was more respectable... More essential. That's how it was with the Romans, and that's how he saw all the trials of existence... At peace with his conscience... Through thick and thin, come what may! Amid the worst calamities!... No compromise! No evasions! That was his law!... his *raison d'être!* My conscience is my own! My conscience! He shouted that in every key... when I stuck my fingers in my nose... if I upset the salt cellar. He opened the window on purpose to give the Passage a treat...

Seeing me down like that, my ears chewed off in every direction, Uncle Édouard finally took pity on me, he was a very good guy... I was up to my ears in shit... He got his connections moving again and found a way... A shrewd trick to get me out of there... the foreign-language routine...

Just like that he says I ought to know at least one... if I want a job in business... that it was being done nowadays... it was a necessity... The hardest part was getting my parents' consent … The suggestion floored them completely... Still, Édouard knew what he was talking about... We'd lost the habit in our shanty of hearing anything sensible... It came as a big surprise...

My uncle didn't believe in being strict all the time... He was for conciliation, he didn't believe in force... He didn't think it would get results... He told them so straight from the shoulder.

"If he does everything wrong, I don't think it's on purpose... His intentions aren't bad... I've been watching him for years... He's just dull-witted... He doesn't understand what people want of him... It must be adenoids... He ought to be out in the fresh air and stay quite a long time... Isn't that what your doctor told you?... If you ask me, I'd send him to England... We'd find a respectable boardingschool... not too expensive... or too far away... maybe we could make an arrangement for him to work for his board and lodging?... How does it strike you? When he comes back, he'll know the language... It'll be easy to find him a job... I could find him something in the retail trade... In a bookstore... Or in haberdashery... Some place where he isn't known. Gorloge would be forgotten... We'd never even mention it again..."

When my parents heard that, they were flummoxed. They pondered the pros and cons... It took them off their guard... There were so many dangers and what about the expense... There was nothing left of Caroline's legacy, only a few thousand francs... And that was Édouard's share... Right away he offered it. He put the money on the table... They'd give it back when they could... He wouldn't listen to any nonsense... He wouldn't even take an IOU. "Think it over," he said. "I'll be back tomorrow. By then I'll have some information..."

The excitement was at its peak!... My father wouldn't have anything to do with it... He was absolutely convinced that all that money would be thrown out the window, that it was sheer waste and madness to boot... That if I escaped from their vigilant supervision for so much as a week I'd turn into the worst of thugs... That was a certainty and you couldn't tell him any different... I'd murder somebody in England just as quickly as in Paris! No two ways about it. It was in the bag... All they had to do was turn me loose for a month... Were they asking for disaster?... Well, their prayers would be answered and then some. They'd be cooked... Up to their necks in debt! A son in the pen!... Extravagance all along the line!... And the consequences?... Unspeakable. Those people over there would never look sharp enough, they'd never be smart enough! The poor bastards! He'll put them through the mill. And what about the women? I'd rape every last one of them. It was plain as day: "Go on, tell me I don't know what I'm talking about!"

He had his penitentiary on the brain... No one could argue with him... To him that was the only remedy, the only palliative... the only way to hold me in check... Don't you learn anything from experience? Haven't we been through enough?... Berlope? Gor-loge? The clock? Hadn't I proved sufficiently that I was the scum of the earth? A disaster hanging over their heads!... I'd drag them all down with me in my ruin... He'd expected it from the start! Alea!... God's will be done! He gave us another load of Caesar... All by himself he defended Gaul!... He stopped up the kitchen door with his gestures and his ranting... He evoked the past and future, he shook the whole place...

He ran to the water faucet... He stuck his face in the jet and gulped... He was sopping wet and still yelling... He didn't dry himself, he ran around dripping in his hurry to acquaint us with the thousand pitfalls in wait for me... with every aspect of the situation... It was inconceivable! Frightful! Unheard-of. The unspeakable surprises that such an expedition would involve! It was diabolical foolishness, and that's that!

Two days later Uncle Édouard came back to the Passage with some first-class dope. He had located a school. What more could we want? From every point of view and in every way... just the thing for me, for my nature, my intractable disposition... On a hilltop. With plenty of fresh air, a garden, a river down below... Excellent food... Extremely moderate prices... No supplements, no surprises!... Last but not least, the strictest discipline... Supervision... It wasn't very far from the coast, in Rochester to be exact... Only an hour from Folkestone...

In spite of all these advantages, my father had his doubts... He'd see... He clung to his suspicions... He looked for niggers in the woodpile... He read the little ad a hundred times... He went right on insisting that we were headed for disaster... It was sure as shooting... First of all it was insane to contract any more debts... Even with Uncle Édouard... Even to pay back Gorloge would be a labor of Hercules... What with the rent! taxes! the seamstress!... They'd have to tighten their belts till they croaked! He had to pinch himself to believe they wanted to spend more money!... He was aghast to see Mama going out of her mind too... It was the height of damn foolishness... How's that? Wasn't she going to think it over a little more?... What's that you say? I'm making difficulties! Does that strike you as so unusual? My goodness! What am I expected to do? Say yes? Every single time? Just like that? To every crazy idea that comes into your head? Go on! I know what I'm doing. I'm responsible. Who's the father around here anyway? Édouard doesn't give a damn, that's a cinch. When the trouble breaks, he'll be miles away. He'll wash his hands of it. But I'll always be here. With a bandit on my neck. That's right. Yes, every bit of it. I exaggerate? Wah!... Go ahead, say it. Say I'm jealous. Go right ahead.

Damn it all. Go ahead and say it...

"Of course not, darling. Come, come..."

"Shut up, you simpleton, will you shut up? Let me finish and I'll prove it. I can't say anything around here anymore! Somebody else is always talking. What's that? That good-for- nothing! That little gangster! That pervert, who hasn't even felt the first glimmerings of remorse for his repulsive crime! For his infamous sneaky theft. There he is. Lounging around!... Defying us both! It's disgraceful, I tell you!... It's enough to make you dash your ass against the floor!

... It makes my hair stand on end!... Just because Édouard has deigned to open his mouth! That clown! That jumping jack! All you can think about is travel! Extravagance! Sure! Why not? New ways of spending our money! Pure tommyrot! Insanity! Madness... Has it ever entered your head, you poor addled thing, that we haven't even begun to pay his ransom!... You heard me... His ransom!... Why, it's unthinkable!... Abominable!... What are we coming to? I'm going out of my mind! Unspeakable! We're up to our necks in absurdity! I can't stand it! It's killing me!"

Uncle Édouard had taken a powder at the beginning of the session. He'd seen the storm coming... He'd left his prospectuses...

"I'll be back tomorrow afternoon... You'll have made up your minds by then..."

He was handling things as best he could, but there wasn't much he could do... My father was in full eruption. This plan for my departure upset his whole tragedy... He tried to save it by fussing over the conditions... He saw completely red... He paced the room like a wild animal... My mother hobbled along behind him... She went on about the advantages... the reasonable prices... the strict supervision... the splendid food... the fresh air... Lots of fresh air!

"You know Édouard is completely dependable... I know you don't think much of him... But you've got to admit he's no fool... He's not impulsive... He doesn't rush into things with his eyes closed... When he says something, that means it's so... You know that as well as I do... Admit it... Come along now, Auguste, my poor darling..." "I don't want to be beholden to anybody..."

"But he isn't just anybody!..."

"That's all the more reason. Jumping Jehoshaphat!" "We'll give him a note, as if he were a stranger!"

"You know what you can do with your notes, godammit to blinking hell!" "But he's never let us down... ."

"He gives me a swift pain in the balls... that damn brother of yours... do you hear me?... He gives me... I hope I've made myself clear... He's the biggest damn fool of the lot... And you two give me an even worse pain, do you hear me? The whole damn lot of you..."

He worked himself into such a lather that his whole head swelled up, he let off jets of steam, and in the end his words exploded like firecrackers. She latched onto him, she wouldn't give an inch. She was stubborn... She wrestled him into the corners... Her leg dragged so bad it got caught in all the chairs. She supported herself against the walls...

"Auguste! Oh, you're hurting me! You're so rough. Oh, my ankle! Now you've done it. I've twisted it!"

The screams went on for an hour...

He started up again. He kicked the chairs to pieces. He went raving mad. Even so, she pursued him wherever he went... even up the stairs... That drove him even wilder... Tip-tap- plunk, tip-tap-plunk, to hear her clumping on the stairs... He'd have gladly thrown her straight over the banister... Or crawled into a rathole... She'd make me little signs as she passed... meaning that he was beginning to weaken... He kept on losing his cap... He let her catch up with him... He couldn't keep up the pace... He fled as from a bad smell... "Leave me alone, leave me alone, please, Clémence... I beg you, leave me alone, godammit! You stinking bitch! Won't the two of you ever get sick of persecuting me! All you do is talk talk talk, I've got it up to here. Godammit to lousy stinking hell! Will you ever listen to me!"

My good mother didn't care what he said, she was worn to a frazzle, but wouldn't relax her grip. She grappled him by the neck, she kissed him on the moustache, she closed his eyes with kisses... She treated him to a convulsion. She spat supplications into his ears... In the end she had him gagging. His head was sopping wet with storms and caresses... He couldn't stand straight. He collapsed on the stairs. Then she began talking about his own health, his alarming condition... Everybody had been saying how pale he was... Then he was willing to listen... "You're going to make yourself really sick, my poor angel, working yourself up into such a state! If you come down, where will that get us? What will become of us?... I assure you it's better he should go away... His being here is making you sick... Édouard saw that... He told me so before he left..."

"What did Édouard tell you anyway?"

"Your husband won't last long. If he keeps on working himself up like that... He's wasting away... Everybody's noticed it in the Passage... Everybody's talking about it..."

"Were those his exact words?"

"Yes, angel. I assure you... He didn't want me to tell you... You see how tactful he is... You see, I assure you, you can't go on like this... You see? You agree, don't you?"

"To what?"

"To letting the child go... it'll give us a breathing spell... Just you and me together... Wouldn't you like that?"

"No, certainly not! Not so fast! God almighty! No! Not so fast!"

"Come along, Auguste. Just think. If you fret yourself to death, where will it get us?..." "Die? Me? Good Lord! Die! That's all I'm asking for. Die? Hurry hurry. Good grief! You think I give a damn! Why, it's all I want in the world... Ah! Christ! Christ!"

He disentangles himself, he shakes himself loose, he knocks my mother over. He begins to bellow again... He hadn't thought of that! Death!... Christ! His death!... He starts up again in a fine lather... He puts his whole soul into it! He jumps up... He runs for the sink... He wants a drink of water. Pum pum crash!... He skids... He somersaults... He sprawls on all fours : . . He plunges into the sideboard... he ricochets into the buffet... He hollers so the whole place echoes... He's bumped his nose... He tries to pick himself up... The whole shooting match comes down on us... All the china, the cutlery, the lamp... A waterfall, an avalanche... We're snowed under... We can't even see each other... My mother screams in the ruins... "Papa, papa, where are you? Papa, answer me!"... He was stretched out full length on his back... I see his shoes sticking out over the red varnished tiles in the kitchen...

"Papa, answer me. Answer me, darling..."

"Shit! Can't you leave me alone!... Godammit, am I asking you for anything?"

In the end he was worn down... He finally consented... My mother had her way... The fight had gone out of him... He said it was all one to him... He talked about suicide again... He went back to his office... He stopped thinking of anything but himself... He threw in the sponge ... He went out so as not to have to look at me. He left me alone with my mother... That was when she began to dish it out again... her grievances... her whole litany... All sorts of ideas cropped up in her head... and they had to come out, she wanted me to benefit by them, to get a whole bellyful before going away... Just because my father had given up didn't mean I should think I could do anything I pleased...

"Listen to me just a minute, Ferdinand! It's high time we had a little talk: I don't want to pester you, scold you, threaten you with one thing or another. That's not what a mother's for and it's not my way. But even so there are certain things a mother can't help noticing... I often seem to be daydreaming, but I see what's going on... I don't say much, but that doesn't keep me from thinking... It's a big risk we're taking... Of course it is. Just imagine! Sending you to England... Your father isn't crazy... He's a thoughtful man... Yes, he's nobody's fool... For poor folks like us it's sheer madness... sending you abroad... We're deep in debt... And the price of that pin to be paid back... And now two thousand francs to your uncle! Your father was talking about it only this morning, it's insane... And that's God's truth... I don't want to rub it in, but your father knows what's what... He's got eyes in his head! I'd like to know where we're going to find all that money! Two thousand francs!... Even if we move heaven and earth!... It doesn't grow on trees... Your father, you've only got to open yours eyes, is at the end of his tether... As for me, I'm all in, exhausted, I don't mention it to him, but I'm ready to collapse... You see my leg?... It's begun to swell up every night... Do you call this a life?... What have we done to deserve it? Are you listening, my boy? I'm not reproaching you... I just want you to realize... to look the situation in the face... to know what we've been through... Because you'll be away for several months now. You've made life very hard for us, Ferdinand. I've a right to tell you that, to let you know. I'm always inclined to be lenient with you... I'm your mother, after all... It's hard for me to judge you... But strangers, your employers... these people who've had you with them day after day... They haven't got the same weakness... Gorloge, for instance!... Only yesterday... I can still hear him... I told your father what he said... As he was leaving... he'd been here a whole hour... 'Madame,' he said, 'I see the kind of woman I'm talking to... Your boy... well, if you ask me, it's all perfectly simple... You're like so many mothers... You've spoiled him. He's rotten. That's all there is to it. You think you're being kind, you work yourselves to the bone! And you're ruining your children.' I'm telling you exactly what he said, word for word. With the best of intentions all you'll make of him is a lazy, pleasure-seeking egotist... I was flabbergasted, take it from me... I didn't say boo... I didn't bat an eyelash... As a mother, I wasn't going to tell him he was right!... But what do you suppose I was thinking?

... He was able to see clearly... With us it's not the same, especially with me... If you're not more affectionate, more reasonable, more hardworking, and especially more grateful... if you're not more considerate... if you don't try to help us more... in this hard life of ours... there's a reason, and I'm going to tell you what it is... I'm your mother, I understand because I'm a woman... It's because you're heartless... That's the whole trouble... I often wonder whom you can take after. I'm wondering right now where you get it from? Certainly not from your father or from me... Your father is all heart... his heart's too big, poor man... And me, I guess you saw the way I was with my mother... My heart's always been in the right place... We've been weak with you... We were too busy, we didn't want to face the facts... We thought things would straighten out all by themselves... And in the end you did a dishonest thing... How perfectly abominable!... We're all of us a little at fault... I've got to admit it... And this is what it's led to... 'He'll be your ruination!'... Ah, he made no bones about it. Lavelongue warned me long ago... He's not the only one who saw it, Ferdinand... Everybody who lives with you catches on after a while... Well, I won't rub it in... I don't want to paint you blacker than you are... Over there you'll be in entirely different surroundings... Try to forget your evil ways... to keep out of bad company... Don't go running around with little hoodlums... And most of all, don't imitate them... Think of us... Think of your parents... Try to mend your ways over there... Play in recreation time, but don"t play when you're supposed to be working... Try to learn the language quickly and then you'll come back... Improve your manners... Try to mold your character... Make an effort... The English always seem so correct... So clean! So nicely dressed! I don't know what to say, my boy, to make you behave a little better... It's the last try... Your father has explained it all to you... Life is a serious business at your age... You want to be a decent man... I can't tell you anymore..." That was God's truth, I'd heard just about all there was to hear... The whole business left me cold... All I wanted was to get out of there as quickly as possible and not to hear any more talk. The main thing isn't knowing whether you're right or wrong. That really doesn't matter... The main thing is to keep people from bothering you... The rest is eyewash...

When it came time to go, I felt bad after all, worse than I'd have expected. It's hard not to. As the three of us were standing on the platform in the Gare du Nord, we were a miserable sight... We hung on to each other's clothes, trying to keep together... As soon as we were in a crowd, we grew timid, furtive... Even my father, who hollered so loud in the Passage, was helpless outside... He shriveled up... It was only at home that he could wield thunder and lightning. Outside he blushed for fear of being noticed. He peered out of the corner of his eyes...

It took a lot of gumption to send me so far... all alone... just like that... All of a sudden we were scared... My mother, who was the most heroic, tried to find somebody who was going my way... Nobody had ever heard of Rochester... I went in to get a seat... They repeated all the necessary instructions... to be careful, very careful... not to get out before the train stopped... never to cross the tracks... To look in all directions... Not to play with the door handle... to watch out for drafts... not to get things in my eyes... To keep an eye on the baggage rack... because something can fall down and bash your brains in when the train jolts... I had a pack-jammed suitcase and in addition a blanket, sort of a carpet, an enormous oriental rug with colored checks, a green and blue "plaid""... We got it from Grandma Caroline. We'd never been able to sell it... I was taking it back to its home country. It would be fine for the climate, that's what we thought...

In the middle of all the racket I had to recite my lesson a last time, everything they'd been dinning into me for the last week... "Brush your teeth every morning... Wash your feet every Saturday... Ask to take sitz baths... You have a dozen pair of socks... Three nightgowns... Wipe yourself properly when you go to the toilet... Chew your food and eat slowly... You'll ruin your stomach... Take your worm syrup... Get rid of that habit of touching yourself..."

I was treated to many more precepts for my moral resurrection, my rehabilitation... They gave me everything before I left... I took it all away with me to England, good principles, excellent principles... and shame on account of my vicious instincts. I'd want for nothing. The price was all settled. Two months had been paid for in advance. I promised to be well behaved, obedient, courageous, attentive, sincere, grateful, scrupulous, never to lie, especially never to steal, not to stick my fingers up my nose, to come back completely changed, a model of good behavior, to put on weight, to know English, not to forget my French, to write every Sunday at the very least. I promised everything they asked... if only they'd let me leave right away... and cut the tragedy... We'd talked so much there was nothing left to say... It was time to get going... Nasty thoughts came to me, sinister feelings... There's something stupefying about all this loathsome confusion... the steam, the crowd, the whistles... In the distance I could see the rails disappearing into the tunnel. Soon I'd be disappearing too. I had some rotten presentiments, I wondered if the English weren't going to be meaner and crummier, a damn sight worse than the people around here...

I looked at my parents, they were trembling all over... They couldn't hold back the tears... I began to bawl too. I was terribly ashamed, I was breaking down like a girl, I didn't think much of myself. My mother clutched me in her arms... It was time to close the doors... They were shouting "All aboard!"... She hugged me so hard, with such a storm of emotion, that I reeled... On those occasions the tenderness that welled up from her misshapen carcass had the strength of a horse... The idea of parting drenched her in advance. A howling tornado turned her inside out, as if her soul were coming out her behind, her eyes, her belly, her bosom... it hit me in all directions, it lit up the whole station... She couldn't help it... it was something awful to look at.

"Calm yourself, Mama, please... The people are laughing at us..."

I begged her to control herself, I implored her amid the kisses, the blowing whistles, the racket... But it was too much for her... I extricated myself from her embrace, I jumped on the step, I didn't want her to start in again... I didn't dare to admit it, but in a way I was curious... I'd have liked to know how far she could go in her effusions... From what nauseating depths was she digging up all this slop?

With my father at least it was perfectly simple, he was nothing but a slobbering fool, there was nothing left in his dome but rubbish, pretense, and uproar... a clutter of idiocy... My mother was different... She kept her wits about her, her mind was still in one piece... Even in the lousiest situation... the slightest caress would send her into a tizzy... li..»; some broken machine, the piano of genuine unhappiness that had nothing left but a few sour notes... Even when I was up in the car, I was afraid she'd grab me again... I went in and out, pretending to be looking for something... I climbed up on the bench... I took down my blanket... I stepped on it... I was mighty glad when the train gave a jolt...

We pulled out in a roar of thunder... We had passed Asnières before I settled down like everybody else... I was still anxious...

When we got to Folkestone, they pointed out the head conductor, who was supposed to keep an eye on me and tell me when to get out. He was wearing a red shoulder strap with a little bag hanging in the middle of his back. I couldn't very well lose sight of him. In Chatham he motioned to me. I grabbed my suitcase. The train was two hours late, the people from my school, Meanwell College, had gone back home, they'd given me up. In a way that suited me. I was the only one getting out, the others were going on to London.

It was already dark, the place wasn't very well lighted. It was a raised station, propped up on piles... like stilts... It was elongated, a big wooden tangle in the mist, all covered with colored posters... When you walked on the platform, thousands of planks resounded...

I didn't want to be helped anymore, I was sick of it... I left by a side door and then a footbridge... Nobody asked me anything... I couldn't see my man anymore, a different one in a red and blue uniform who'd been pestering the life out of me. I looked around outside the station, the square was mighty dark. The town began right away. Little streets tumbling downhill, from one dim light to the next. The air was thick and sticky, swirling around the gas jets... The effect was spooky... From way down below came gusts of music... carried by the wind, I guess... Tunes... like a busted merry-go-round in the night...

It was a Saturday when I arrived, the streets were full of people, flocking past the shops. The streetcar, which looked like a fat giraffe, towered over the shanties, compressed the crowd, shook the windowpanes... The crowd moved in dense, brown waves, it smelled like muck and tobacco and anthracite, and also like toast and a little like sulphur for the eyes; it got thick and more enveloping, more suffocating the farther down I went, it closed in after the streetcar had passed, like fish after a dam...

In the eddies the people felt oilier, stickier than our people. My suitcase got tangled up in legs, I passed from one paunch to another. I took a gander at the food piled up in the shop windows. Little mountains of hams... Valleys of bologna... I was mighty hungry, but I was afraid to go in. I had a pound in one pocket and some change in the other.

After a lot of pushing and poking we ended up on the riverfront... The fog was pretty thick... You get used to stumbling... Mustn't fall in the river... The whole place was rigged up like a fair, with little booths and some regular stages... Thousands of lamps and what a mob!... Peddlers fished for suckers in the crowd... shouting themselves hoarse in their language... There were lots of stands all along the esplanade, to suit every taste... Fish and chips... mandolins, wrestlers, weight lifters, a sword swallower, a bicycle track, little birds... there was a terrific mob around the canary pecking the "future" in a box... There was something for everybody... nougat... whole barrels of currant jelly, dripping all over the place... A dense cloud comes down from the sky... it falls on the fair... for a moment it hides everything... blots out space... You can still hear all right, but you can't see a thing... neither the man nor his acetylene lamp... Ah, a gust of wind! There he is again... A real gentleman in a frock coat... He exhibits the moon for twopence... for three he gives you Saturn... it's written on his sign... There's the mist again, falling on the crowd, spreading out... Everything's muffled... The guy breaks off his spiel, folds up his telescope, curses, and clears out. The people are all laughing... You can't even move anymore... People lose each other, then they get together outside the stands where the light is really bright. Music drifts over from all directions... You think you're right in the middle of it... It's a kind of mirage... Like you were bathing in sound... That's a banjo... A nigger on a carpet right beside me, whimpering on the ground... he imitates a locomotive, he's going to run everybody over. We're all having a fine time, we can't see each other.

The fog lifts and blows away... I'm not in a hurry anymore... I can take my time about getting to Mean-well... This place on the riverfront suits me... the fair and the strangers in the haze... There's something very pleasant about a language you don't understand... It's like a fog swirling around in your thoughts... It's nice, it's like a dream, there's really nothing better... It's fine as long as the words stay in the dream... I sit down for a while quietly on my blanket, against a stone post, on the other side of the chains... I can lean back, I'm pretty comfortable... I watch the whole show passing... A whole string of sailors with lanterns on the end of long poles... They're funny guys... Confusion!

Fireworks!... They're all dead-drunk and happy... They push and shove and squeal like cats... They throw the whole crowd into a panic. They can't get ahead... Their snake dance gets tangled up in a lamp post... It winds and unwinds... One of them collapses in the gutter... They've knocked the nigger over... Shouts... challenges... insults... Suddenly they're roaring mad... They want to hang the nigger from the trolley pole... What a racket!... A mean fight starts up... The whole place is steaming and sizzling... The blows fall like drumbeats... terrible grunts and groans... Whistles blow... A troupe of extras come running... A screaming cloud... A whole squad of police, blue with pointed black helmets... They're in a terrible hurry... They pop out of the streets, out of the shadows, from all over... on the double... And the soldiers who've been strutting along the stands, dandling their riding whips, start running too... They plunge into the fray... Catcalls from the sarabande... They stagger and fall... Every color in the rainbow! A battle of samples... Jonquil... green... violet... A free-for-all... a scramble... The women escape into the corners with their acetylene lamps, the lights blend with the fog... all screaming something awful... terrified... skinned alive... Police reinforcements arrive... parrot color... Majestically they join in the dance... They're toppled over, their clothes are torn off. A battle in a bird-house... A welter of riding whips and plumes... A charabanc with four horses bounds out of an alley... It stops short in the middle of the riot... Some more bruisers pour out... They fling themselves on the mob like a ton of bricks... they're giants and they move fast... They nab the most truculent, the drunkest, the ones that are yelling loudest... They toss them into the van, completely upside down... The corpses pile up inside... The battle dies down... The ruckus is swallowed up in darkness... The wagon gallops away... And that's the end of the riot... The crowd flows back toward the bars, to the mahogany counters... to guzzle harder than ever... The roadway is clear... little carts go by... French fries... sausages... periwinkles... Glasses are clinked... Knives cutting into sausage... The swinging doors are in constant motion... right and left... A drunk stumbles and falls flat in the gutter... The procession circles around him... People dawdle past... A bevy of floozies... cackling and guffawing... sailors push them into the doorways... They talk... they belch... the bar absorbs them... The Scotsmen dash in...They'd like to fight some more, but they really can't...

I follow them in with my suitcase... Nobody asks me anything... They serve me first... A whole mugful of syrup, thick and black and frothy... it's bitter... it's beer! It tastes like stewed smoke... They give me back two coppers with the queen on them, the one that just died, with the face like a rear end... the fair Victoria... I can't finish their brew, it turns my stomach and I'm mighty ashamed. I go back to the procession. We pass the little carts again, with the lamps between the shafts... I hear a regular orchestra... I look around and locate it... It's right near the landing... It's coming out of a big tent, a blaring uproar... They're singing in chorus, completely out of tune... It's amazing the way they manage to torture their mouths, to dilate them, to blow them up like real trombones... And pull them in again... They're on their last legs... They're dying of convulsions... They're praying and singing hymns... There's this big tall battle-ax with only one eye, she's yodeling so hard it's like to pop out of her head... The way she's jigging and heaving, her bun starts sliding down over her nose, and her bonnet with the ribbons too... she thinks she's not making enough noise, she grabs her man's trombone and blows, she spits a whole lung into it... But it's a polka she's playing, a regular hornpipe... The gloom is over... The people begin to dance, they hug each other, they hop, they shake each other up... The guy in the uniform that's looking at her must be her brother, he looks just like her except for the beard, and besides he's got glasses and a nifty cap with an inscription. He seems to be sulking... He's got his nose in a book... All of a sudden he breaks into a fit too! He grabs the horn from his sister... He climbs up on the stool, spits a good oyster... and begins to jabber... The way he's waving his arms and beating his breast... working himself up into an ecstasy... I can sec it must be a sermon... His words come out sobbing... tortured... it's unbearable... The characters around them are laughing fit to kill... He defies them, challenges them, nothing can stop him... not even the whistles of the boats stemming the current... He goes right on thundering... Personally, he gives me a pain... He puts me to sleep... I sit down on my blanket... I cover myself, nobody can see me, I'm hidden by the sheds... The Salvation Army guy is still yelling, screeching his lungs out... He makes me tired... It's cold, but I wrap up good... I feel a little warmer... The mist is white, then blue. I'm right next to a sentry box... It's getting dark, little by little... I'm going to sleep... Over there, that's where the music is coming from... It's a merry-go-round... a barrel organ... From across the river... that's the wind... the lapping of the water...

A terrible groan from a boiler woke me with a start... A ship was coming up the river... fighting the current... The Salvation Army characters from before had cleared out... Niggers were jumping up and down on the stage... somersaulting in swallowtails... landing in the street... Their lavender coat-tails spun around behind them in the mud and the acetylene glare. "The Minstrels," it said on their big drum... They went on and on... a roll of the drum... a happy landing... a pirouette... A great big enormous siren rips through the echoes... The crowd stops in its tracks... They all move down to the edge to watch the ship landing... I wedge myself into the staircase right next to the waves...

A lot of brats in little boats were whirling around in the eddies looking for the hawser... The launch, the big fat one with the enormous copper boiler in the middle, was rolling like a top... She was bringing the papers. The East Indiaman was having a tough time with the current... She was still in midstream, in the middle of the blackness... She didn't want to come closer... with her green eye and her red one... Finally the wise guy came in after all, bashing against an enormous bundle of sticks that was hanging from the dock... It cracked like a pile of bones... She had her nose into the current, she roared in the rough water... She churned against the mooring buoy... a tethered monster... She let out one little howl... She was beaten... all alone in the glistening whirling water... We turned back to the merry-go-round, the one with the organs and the mountains... The party was still going on... I felt better after my nap... It was like magic... an entirely different world... fantastic... like a crazy picture... All of a sudden I felt they'd never catch me again... that I'd turned into a memory that no one would ever recognize... that I had nothing more to fear, that nobody'd ever find me again... I treated myself to a ride on the merry-go-round, I held out my change. I took three whole rides with three crazy floozies and some soldiers... They were cute, they had faces like dolls, eyes like blue candies... I was dizzy... I wanted to take another turn... I was afraid to show my dough... I went off a little way into the darkness... I tore open my lining, I wanted to take out my banknote, the whole pound. And then the smell of something frying steered me to a place right near the locks... It was fritters... I could smell them a mile away... on a cart with little wheels.

This kid that was messing with the batter... I can't say she was pretty... She had two teeth missing in front... She never stopped laughing... She had a fringed hat with a big pile of flowers on top... crushed under the weight... a regular hanging garden... and long muslin veils that hung down into her kettle... She took them out with a sweet smile... She seemed very young to be wearing such a thing even at that time of night... even under those cockeyed circumstances... that lid really sent me... I couldn't take my eyes off it. She was still smiling at me... The kid wasn't twenty, with pert little boobies and a wasp waist... and an ass the way I like them, taut, muscular, with a good split... I walked around her to get a good look. She was still absorbed in her grease... She wasn't proud or standoffish... I showed her my change... She served me enough fritters to stuff a whole family. All she took was one little coin... There was sympathy between us... She could see from my suitcase that I'd just got off the train... She tries to make me understand something... She tries to explain... She speaks very slowly... She pronounces each word separately... Well, then I begin to feel jumpy... I shrivel up... The poison runs through me... As soon as anybody starts talking to me I get mean... I didn't want any more gabfests... Save your breath! I've had enough!... I know what it leads to... you can't fool me... She gets politer, sweeter, more endearing than ever... Anyway that hole in her mouth when she smiles makes me sick... I make motions to show that I'm going for a walk over by the pubs... to have a little fun... I leave her my suitcase in exchange and my blanket... I put them down beside her camp chair... I make a sign for her to watch them... I go back to the crowd...

With nothing to weigh me down, I head for the shops... I stroll past the piles of grub... But I'm full up, I can't eat anymore... The clock strikes eleven... Drunks come out in waves and stream down the esplanade... this way and that way, crashing against the wall of the customs house... tumbling, roaring, spreading out, dispersing... The ones that are stewed but still swaggering step into the pub stiffly, rhythmically, buttoned crooked but buttoned, and head straight for the bar... There they stand speechless, transfixed, riveted by the mechanical din, the "valse d'amour." I've got piles of money left... I took two more helpings of beer soup, the kind that makes you piss...

I went out with a little thug and another burper with a little cat under his arm. He was miaowing between the two of us... I didn't get very far... I retreated into the next pub... I staggered through the swinging doors... I sat down on a bench... waiting for it to pass... with all the boozehounds... There was a crowd of dames in short jackets, in feathers and tarns and hard-brimmed straw hats... They were all talking like animals... barking and belching... They were dogs, tigers, wolves... crabs... I was beginning to itch...

Outside, through the window, fish were passing now... You could see them clear as anything... They were moving slowly... undulating past the glass... coming out into the light... They opened their mouths, little puffs of fog came out... There were mackerel and carp... They smelled like it too, they smelled of muck, honey, acrid smoke... everything... Another little slug of beer... and I'll never be able to get up again... That'll be fine... They drool, they chortle... all those bums... They're all fighting, they give each other clouts on the ass that would kill a mule... The stinkers!

But then the piano stops, the bartender in the apron throws us all out... I'm in the street again. I unbutton my collar... I feel lousy... I drag myself through the shadows... I can still see the two street lamps a little... not much... I see the water... I can see it lapping... Ah! I can even see the way down. I take the steps one by one... I lean on the rail, I'm very careful... I touch the drink... on my knees... I vomit on it... I make a violent effort... I feel better... An enormous burst comes down on me from above... a whole meal... I can see the guy leaning over... Seconds... A slimy mess... I try to stand up... Hell, I can't make it... I sit down again... I take the whole business... Oh well... it runs into my eyes... Another retch... Wah!... I see the water dancing... white... and black... It's really cold. I'm shivering, I tear my pants... I can't throw up anymore... I lie down again in a corner... The bowsprit of a sailboat passes over me... It just grazes my head... The guys are coming. A whole squadron of them... They're coming out of the fog. They're pulling at the oars... They pull up at the dock... The sails are furled at half-mast... I hear the mob coming, stamping along the dock, that's the fatigue squad...

I stay by the water's edge... I'm not quite so cold... My head's fuzzy... I'm all right here. Why not? I'm not bothering anybody... They're some kind of "tartans"... I know about boats... Still more of them coming... They crowd together... They settle in the waves... up to the rail... weighed down with food. Enough vegetables for an army... Red cabbage, onions, black radishes, mountains of turnips, whole cathedrals of them, heading into the stream, towed by a sailboat... They rise up out of the darkness... proud and graceful in the beam of the searchlights... The longshoremen have put the ladder in place... All at the same time they swallow their plugs. They hang their hats on their alpaca coats... They looked like a bunch of bookkeepers... They were even wearing cuffs... That's what longshoremen were like in those days... They toted baskets, enormous piles of them... balancing acts... the tops were lost in the darkness... They came back with tomatoes, they dug deep tunnels in the wall of cauliflowers... They vanished in the holds again... They came back out into the lamplight... with big loads of artichokes... the boat wasn't listing anymore, it was sinking under the weight of the gangplanks... Another batch of phony longshoremen tote some more of the cargo away...

That's funny, my teeth are chattering... I'm dying of the cold... literally. I'm not dizzy anymore... Suddenly I remember... Where did I leave my blanket? It all comes back to me... the kid with the fritters... I look from one stand to the next... Finally I find her. She was waiting for me. She'd put everything away, all the kettles, the big fork, folded up the whole shooting match... She was all ready to leave. She was glad to see me back... She'd sold her whole stock... She even showed me that all the dishes were empty... The French fries... the potato salad... All she had left was a piece of head cheese... She smeared it on bread with a knife, a good chunk, and we shared it... I was hungry again. She pulled up her veil to get a better look at me. She made scolding gestures, because I'd stayed away too long. She was jealous already!... She wouldn't let me help her pulling at the shafts... The shed where she kept her cart was in town... I carried the lantern... I hadn't seen all of her hat... There was more to see... streamers hanging down to her waist. A great big peacock feather was tied under her chin with a really magnificent scarf with a mauve and gold flower pattern.

In the shed we piled up the pots... We locked the door and went out bumming. She came closer to me... she wanted to talk to me seriously... But again I wouldn't give in... I played dumb. I showed her my address... "Meanwell College." I stopped under a lamp so she could read it... As it happened, she didn't know how to read... She went on gabbing the whole time... She kept repeating her name.

She tapped on her chest... Gwendoline! Gwendoline!... I heard her all right, I massaged her tits, but I didn't get the words... To hell with tenderness... sentiment! That stuff is like a family... At first you don't catch on, but it stinks, it's putrid, crawling... No Greasy Joan is going to drag any words out of me... Pleased to meet you, kid!... Go. shit in your hat!... Let her carry my bag... God bless your kind heart! Go right ahead! Anyway, she was stronger than me... She took advantage of the dark corners to smother me with caresses. She hugged me like a wrestler... There was no point in resisting... The streets were almost deserted… She wanted me to knead her... to press her... to squeeze her... She was hot stuff... demanding and curious... We hid behind the fog... I had to keep on kissing her, she wouldn't have given my stuff back... It was no use wriggling, I'd have looked like a dope... We were under a lamp... she had a crust on her... she took out my dick... it wasn't hard anymore... she hardens it up... I come... That really drives her crazy... She goes jumping around in the fog... She hikes up her skirt... she dances like a cannibal... I couldn't help laughing... It didn't seem like the right time of day... She wanted the whole works... Hell... She's running after me... She's getting mean... She catches me... She tries to eat me alive... with big sucking kisses... That kid liked foreigners...

The esplanade was empty, at the other end the jugglers were folding their tents... the little carts with candy and jam crossed the open space, jolting in the holes and ruts... They had trouble pushing... We came to a booth... the last woman in the place, a grandmother, was rolling up her hangings... She was dressed like a houri... She blew out her candles... She rolled up her oriental carpets... There were signs all around the entrance... showing the lines of the hand... She was yawning tremendously... enough to dislocate her jaw... Wah! Wah! she grunted out through the night. We came closer, me and my floozie. We interrupted her housecleaning. The two broads knew each other... They stop to chat... They must have been friends... They jabber a lot of stuff... They were both interested in me... The Fatima motions me to come up, to step into her shack. I couldn't refuse; the other one minded my things... The old bag takes my hand, she turns it over, she looks at my palms... Close up, under the lamp. She's going to tell my fortune... I catch on... They're curious about my future... Women always want to know everything... the minute you refuse to talk... I didn't give a damn, I was nice and comfortable on a pile of cushions... It was a damn sight warmer than outside... I just took it easy... They went on with their hocus-pocus... They were interested in my case... The Fatima was getting excited... she was cooking up my horoscope... My girl was frowning... My fate must have been sad... I let them work on my hands... It wasn't unpleasant. Anyway I had other things to worry out... I looked around me some... Their tent had stripes and stars on it, and on the ceiling embroidered moons and comets... It was too late to get up much interest... I couldn't understand a word of their gibberish... It was at least two o'clock... They kept at it, drawing things out... Now they were talking about the little furrow... They were conscientious souls... My hands were always dirty, that couldn't have helped much. And the nails... I could just as well have dropped off to sleep... Finally they were done... They didn't agree... My kid paid the old bag with her own money, two coins, I was looking... She had the cards laid out for her... And then we were through with the future... We went out under the curtains. The old bag climbed up on her counter and went back to her hangings.

From that moment on, my conquest, this Gwendoline, looked at me differently... I wasn't the same guy... I felt that she had presentiments... she thought me transfigured... She didn't pet me the same way anymore... My destiny must have been pretty sticky... I guess the cards showed the same as the furrows: pure grief...

I felt so sleepy I could have dropped on the spot, but it was too chilly. We had to keep tramping around on the dock... There really wasn't a soul, just a little dog that tagged around after us for a while. He trailed off toward the storehouses. We went into a shelter right by the water, we listened, we saw the tide lapping against the wall... chattering like tongues.... And then the sound of oars and the deep breathing of the guys...

My Greasy Joan dragged me away, I think she wanted me to go home with her... I wouldn't have minded sleeping on the sacks, there were big piles of them all the way up to the rafters... They cut the wind... She made motions to say she had a real room with a real bed... That didn't appeal to me... It meant intimacies... even then, in the depths of my weariness, she gave me the willies. I make a sign meaning no... I've got this address I want to get to... "Meanwell College"... if it comes to laying Gwendoline, I'd rather go back to school. Not that she was so ugly looking... she had charm in her way, even a kind of elegance... She had an ass on her and muscular thighs and cute little boobies... an ugly-looking puss, but it was dark... We could have done our business, we'd certainly have had a good time... But once we'd had our sleep out, then what?... Anyway I was too tired... And besides, it was impossible... It stirred up my gall... it cramped my cock to think of it... of all the treachery of things... as soon as you let anybody wrap you up... The whole stinking rotten business... And of my mother... Ah, the poor woman! And of Gorloge and Madame Méhon and the quotations! And the kitchen faucet! And Lavelongue! And little André! The whole lousy mess! Yes, damn it all, I had as much as I could take... a big stinking steaming load of shit up to here... See what I mean? Nothing doing!

I'd gladly have knocked hell out of this fritter baby, so innocent, so kind... an extra-special thrashing till she couldn't see straight... if I'd thought I was stronger... to teach her what was what... But she'd have knocked me for a loop, that was sure. She could take care of herself, she was built like a wrestler, she would have turned me like a pancake if I'd started getting real mean!... That's all I had on my mind in the little side streets while my cutie was unbuttoning me... She had the grip of a working girl, rough as a grater, and not at all bashful. Everybody was screwing me. O well...

Finally I got my address out. We'd have to find the place sooner or later. She couldn't read at all, so we went looking for a *policemanne...* Two or three times we went wrong. It was always some funny-looking fountain at a street crossing in the middle of the fog... We had a hell of a time finding one... We looked from dock to dock... We went stumbling over barrels and gangplanks... It was fun in spite of being so exhausted... She held me up and my suitcase too... She really had a good disposition. She was losing her bun... I even pulled her hair. That made her laugh too. The stray dog started following us again... Finally through the cracks in a shelter we saw real light... The watchman was slumped over, he jumped when he saw us. He had on at least three overcoats one on top of the other. He cleared his throat a long time... He came out in the fog, he shook himself like a duck... He was very obliging. He was able to read my address. He showed us... way up there, he pointed his finger, way at the end of the night... where Meanwell College was, on the hilltop after a string of lanterns that climbed up in a zigzag... He went back into his shack. He squeezed in through the door with all his layers.

Once we knew the way, we weren't in such a hurry... There was still a climb, a big long slope... Our adventure wasn't over... We climbed very slowly... She didn't want me to knock myself out... She was all kindness. She didn't dare to molest me anymore... She only kissed me a little when we stopped to rest. She made signs under the lamp that I was just her style... that she liked me fine... About halfway up the slope we sat down on a rock; from there you could see clouds of fog moving in the distance across the river... they came swooping down, blotting out the little boats on the smooth water... dousing their lights... then there was moonlight, and then clouds took over again... The kid made some more gestures... Wasn't I hungry? She offered to get me something to eat, her heart really seemed to be in the right place... Dazed as I was, I wondered if I'd have the strength to topple her off the edge with a good swift kick in the ass. Well, how about it?

Below us the cliff dropped sheer into the drink.

All of a sudden we hear voices, men, a whole gang, I recognize them with their lanterns, it was the "minstrels," phony niggers with blackened faces... They were coming up from the harbor too... pulling their cart in the fog. They're having a lot of trouble with it. It's heavy, all that setup of theirs, they'd taken it all apart... Their poles and instruments jiggle and clatter... They see us, they talk to Greasy Joan... They take time out, they settle down a while, they go into conference, they pile up all their coins on the end of the bench... trying to count them, but they can't make it... They're too tired... One at a time they go wash their faces in the waterfall nearby. They come back livid in the morning light... you'd think they were dead already... They raise their heads a moment, they sag, they sit down again in the gravel... They crack some more jokes with my cutie... Finally we all pick ourselves up, we leave together... We push the wheels of their contraption, we tug and pull to get them up the hill somehow. I still had quite a way to go. They didn't want to leave us... Meanwell College was over past the trees, then another turn, and then a slope and a garden...

By now things were blue. When we got to the gate, we were all pretty palsy-walsy. It was hard to find the right number. we scratched matches in two three different places... Finally we had it... The kid began to bawl. But we had to leave each other some time... I made gestures, signs... to tell her she shouldn't stay there, she should go on with the boys... I'd be seeing her again for sure... down below... in the port... one day... I made affectionate gestures... It was true, all in all I really wanted to. I gave her my blanket to make her believe me... I'd go and get it... She had trouble understanding... I didn't know what to do... She was kissing me like mad... Our pantomime sent the "minstrels" into stitches... They imitated our kisses...

In the narrow little street an icy wind was blowing... We were all so worn out... I could hardly stand up... But really our effusions were too funny... In the end we were all rocking with laughter... it was all so dumb... at that time of night... Finally she made up her mind... She didn't want to go on alone so she followed the minstrels... They all pushed off together behind the cart, the instruments, the bass drum... A nice litle stroll they were having... The kid waved some last good-byes from far off with her lantern... Finally they disappeared... in the trees, around the bend in the street.

Then I looked at the sign in front of me where I was supposed to go in... It was written plainly: "Meanwell College" and above that, in much redder letters: Director J. P. Merrywin. That was the place, I hadn't gone wrong. I lifted the little knocker: Tap! Tap! At first nothing happened... then I rang at the other door... still nobody answered... quite a while... Finally I heard somebody moving... I saw a light coming down the stairs... I could see through the curtains... It gave me a rotten feeling... For two cents I'd have cleared out... I'd have run after the kid... I'd have caught up with the other guys... I'd have never come back to the school... I was already turning on my heels... Bing, I bump right into this guy... a little man, all stooped over, in a dressing gown... He pulls himself up. He looks me over... He jabbers explanations... That must be the boss... He was all upset... He had side-whiskers... they were red... with a few white hairs. A little wig over his eyes. He repeated my name. He'd come out through the garden... taken me by surprise... That was a funny way to act... He must have been afraid of thieves... He sheltered his candle... He stood there in front of me, mumbling. It wasn't a very warm place for an interview. He couldn't find all the words he needed, the wind blew out his candle:

"Ferdinand... good... morning... I... am... glad... to see you... but... you are... very late... what happened?"

"I don't know," I said.

He didn't press the point... He went ahead. He took tiny little steps... Finally he opened the door... He jiggled with the lock. He was shaking so hard he couldn't get the key out... Once we were in the entrance he motioned me to wait... to sit on the chest... he was going to fix things upstairs. Right in the middle of the stairs he thought of something, he leaned down over the banister and pointed his finger at me:

"Tomorrow, Ferdinand! Tomorrow... I'll only talk English to you. Eh what?..." It made him laugh in advance...

"*Attendez-moi un moment!* Wait! Moment! There, you see! You're catching on, Ferdinand... Already..."

He was clowning...

It took him forever up there, poking around in drawers, closing doors, moving cupboards. I said to myself: "What does he think he's doing?... I'm going to sleep just like this..." I was still waiting.

At the end of the corridor I saw the gas jet flickering... it was turned low...

Little by little my eyes got used to the light and I saw the clock... a great big one... really magnificent... the dial was all copper and a tiny little frigate was dancing out the seconds... tic... toc... tic... toc... She went sailing right along... In the end I I was so tired it made me fuzzy...

The old codger was still fussing around... fighting with bric-a-brac... running the water... talking with a woman... Finally he came down... He had gone to a lot of trouble... Completely washed, shaved, dressed fit to kill... and some style!... like a lawyer... a flowing black cape... hanging from his shoulders... accordion pleats... and on the top of his dome a pretty little skull- cap with a big tassel... I figured it was for my benefit. He wants to impress me... He makes a little sign... I get up... I start moving... To tell the truth, I could hardly stand up... He cast about for some more phrases... something appropriate, about my trip... If I'd had trouble finding the place... I didn't answer... I followed him... First through the drawing room... around a piano... then through the laundry room... the washroom... the kitchen... Finally he opens another door... And what do I see?... A bed!... I didn't waste any time...

I didn't wait to be told... I jumped right on it... I spread myself flat... Right away the little crab gets all excited, he flies into a rage... He couldn't stand it. He hollers... he jumps up and down... he dances around the sack... He hadn't been expecting such a thing... He grabs me by the shoes... He tries to pull me off...

"*Chaussures! Chaussures!* Boots! Boots!" He was getting madder and madder. He was in a terrible state. My mud on his lovely bed.... on all those big flowers... That's what was upsetting him, sending him into an epileptic fit. "Go shit in your hat!" I was thinking. "'Go split a gut, you little asshole..." He was desperate... He ran up and down the hall... looking for reinforcements... If they'd touched a finger to me, I'd have gone wild... I'd have got right off that bed and given that little fart some thrashing... On the spot... I was exactly in the mood... I was all set... He was skinny and puny... He was getting on my nerves with his damn nonsense... I'd have turned him inside out like a glove... I was fed up... He went right on yapping, but I had no trouble falling asleep.

For fresh air and the view, you couldn't have asked for anything better than Meanwell College. The location was marvelous... From the garden and even from the windows of the study you could look out over the whole countryside. When the weather cleared, you could see for miles, the river, the three towns, the port, the docks huddled together by the shore... The railroad lines... the ships disappearing... and coming back into view a little way out... behind the hills past the meadows... toward the sea, past Chatham... The effect was magnificent... Only it was awfully cold at the time I got there, the place was so unprotected on top of the cliff it was impossible to keep warm. The wind hammered against the house... The squalls and storms came bounding over the hill... The wind roared through the rooms, the doors rattled day and night. We were living in the middle of a tornado. When the tempest began to roar, the kids yelled like deaf people, they couldn't hear each other... Nothing could stand up against that wind! It was bend or break. The trees were stooped over, they never straightened up, the lawns were in tatters, whole patches were ripped up. You can imagine...

In a rough, ravaged climate like that you get a ravenous appetite... It turns out husky kids, real bruisers. When there's enough to eat. But at Meanwell College the grub wasn't so hot. It was worse than middling. Their prospectus was a big lie. There were fourteen of us at table, including me. Plus the boss and his wife... In my opinion that was at least eight too many, considering what there was to eat... Six of us could have handled it... On days when the wind was blowing strong... the eats were very meager.

I was the biggest and the hungriest of the crew. I was growing like mad... it was almost time for me to stop. In a month I doubled in bulk. The violence of the elements created a revolution in my lungs and in my stature. The way I helped myself, the way I scraped all the platters without being asked, I got to be a regular pest at the table... The kids eyed my plate, they gave me dirty looks, I was the enemy... naturally... I didn't give a damn, I didn't say a word to anybody... I was still so hungry I'd even have eaten noodles if anybody'd asked me to... A school that gave you enough to eat would go bankrupt... They've got to watch their step... I made up for it on the porridge, there I was ruthless... I took advantage of my strength, and I was even worse with the marmalade... There was a little saucerful for four of us, I gobbled it up all by myself, straight out of the dish... I did away with it before anybody could see what was happening... The others could gripe all they pleased, I never answered... why should I have?... You could have all the tea you wanted, it warms you, it bloats you, it's perfumed water, not bad, but it makes you even hungrier. When the tempest went on for a long time, when the whole hilltop roared for days on end, I dug into the sugar bowl... with a tablespoon or even my bare hands. It was yellow and sticky, it gave me strength...

At meals Mr. Merrywin had the big platter right in front of him, he himself dished everything out... He tried to make me talk... No soap... Me, talk! The mere idea made me see red... I was a tough customer... Only his lovely wife had me kind of bewitched, she might have softened me... I sat next to her... She was really adorable. Absolutely. Her face, her smile, her arms, all her movements, everything. She was busy the whole time, trying to make little Jongkind eat, he was a freak, a retarded child. After every mouthful or pretty near she had to help him, clean him up and wipe away his slobber. It was rough work.

This idiot's parents were in India, they didn't even come to see him. A little screwball like that was a real nuisance, especially at mealtime, he'd swallow everything on the table, the spoons, the napkin rings, the pepper, the oil and vinegar bottles, even the knives... Swallowing things was his passion... He always had his mouth all dilated, distended, like a boa constrictor, he'd suck up all sorts of little objects, even off the floor, grunting and slobbering the whole time.

Mrs. Merrywin always stopped him, took the things away, always patient and gentle. Never a harsh word...

Aside from his swallowing act, the kid wasn't so bad. He was actually rather good-natured. He wasn't bad looking either, only his eyes were weird. He bumped into everything without his glasses, he was disgustingly near-sighted, he'd have collided with a mole, he needed thick lenses, like bottle stoppers. They made his eyes pop out, they were wider than the rest of his face. The least little thing frightened him, Mrs. Merrywin always comforted him with the same two words: *"No trouble, Jong-kind! No trouble..."*

He himself would repeat those words for days on end, for no rhyme or reason like a parrot.

After several months at Chatham that was all I remembered: *"No trouble, Jongkind."*

Two weeks, three weeks passed... They left me alone. They didn't try to force me... they'd have liked me to talk... for me to learn a little English. That was only natural. My father asked in his letters if I was making an effort... if I was applying myself to my studies... I didn't let them rope me in... Talk wasn't for me... I'd had enough... I only had to bring back my memories... the hullabaloo at home... my mother's blah-blah... all the applesauce people can serve you up in words... Hell no!... Not for me. I had my belly full... I'd had all the confessions, all the soft soap I could take... No, thank you... I had whole carloads... If I even thought of trying, the whole mess stuck in my throat.... They weren't going to catch me again. I'd had enough. I had a good excuse for keeping my mouth shut, a golden opportunity, and I was determined to take every advantage of it... to the bitter end... No appeals to sentiment, no fiddle-faddle... They made me want to throw up with all their talk... Maybe even worse than noodles... And believe me it gave me the creeps even to think of home...

Mr. and Mrs. Merrywin were at their wits' end, they wondered what made me so silent, so sullen and obstinate... It was mostly he that made overtures, the minute we sat down to table, on any subject he could think of... He really wanted me to learn... "Hello, Ferdinand!" he'd sing out... I wasn't greatly tempted... "Hello, hello," I'd answer, and that was all. It stopped right there. We began to eat. From behind his glasses he gave me a pained look. He had spells of melancholia, he must have said to himself: "That boy won't be with us long... He'll leave if he's unhappy." But he didn't dare to say any more... He'd blink his little cockhole eyes, his turned-up chin would twitch, and he'd raise his eyebrows, which shot off in different directions and weren't the same color either. He was the old-fashioned type, with side-whiskers and a little cosmetic moustache, very pointed at the ends... He looked rather jolly. He was always on the jump, playing games, and even racing around on a tricycle...

She, his wife, wasn't the same at all, she hadn't her equal for charm, I have to admit that she was a dream... she made a profound impression on me.

That refectory of theirs on the ground floor was a pretty miserable place. The walls were daubed a kind of snuff color all the way up to the ceiling. It looked out on a blind alley. The first time she came into the room with Jongkind... you can't imagine how beautiful she seemed to me... I had a feeling, something very unusual... I kept looking at her... I blinked both eyes... I felt dizzy... I buried my nose in my slobgullion... Nora was her name... Nora Merrywin...

At the beginning and end of the meals, we all went down on our knees while the old man said prayers... He commented at length on the Bible. The kids dug into their noses and wriggled in all directions...

Jongkind didn't want to wait, he wanted to eat the doorknob that was right in front of him, on a level with his mouth. The oldtimer really threw himself into his prayers, he liked to mumble... he'd bumble away for a good fifteen minutes, it rounded out the meal... In the end we'd get up, when he said *"ever and ever."*

Only the bottom half of the walls was painted brown, the rest was whitewashed. There were engravings of Bible stories... There was Job with his staff, all in rags, crossing a desert... Then there was Noah's Ark, crushed under the rain that was bouncing on the waves, on the foaming fury... Just like in Rochester... Our roof was the same way. I can bet the storms we had were much more violent... Even the double windows couldn't stand up to it... Later it was calm... Then everything was enchanted... an enormous realm of mist like another world... You couldn't see two steps away in the garden... There was nothing left but one big cloud, it crept softly into the rooms, it hid everything, it seeped in everywhere, into the classroom, in between the kids...

The sounds of the city, of the port, rose up like an echo... especially from the river below... It sounded like a tugboat coming straight into the garden... You could even hear it panting behind the house... It came back... And then it was gone again, down into the valley... All the railroad whistles coiled and twisted through the mists in the sky... It was a kingdom of phantoms... We even had to hurry back into the house... We would have fallen off the cliff...

While they were saying their prayers, I had dangerous sensations... As we knelt, I almost touched Nora. I breathed against her neck, into her hair. I had terrible temptations... It was a desperate moment, I had to hold myself back from doing something dumb... I wonder what she would have said if I had dared... I played with myself thinking of her, at night in the dormitory, very late, long after all the others, and in the morning I'd have a little more...

Her hands were marvels, tapering, pink and white, tender, the same gentleness as her face, just to look at them was like a glimpse of fairyland. What troubled me most, what moved me deep inside was the special charm she had, that lit iip on her face when she was speaking... her nose would tremble just a little, and her cheeks and the curve of her lips... I was really damned... It was sorcery... It intimidated me... I saw stars, I couldn't move... At the least smile, waves of magic ran through me... I was afraid to look at her. I stared at my plate the whole time. Her hair too, when she passed by the fireplace, was a pure play of light... Hell! She was turning into a fairy. That was plain. The part I mostly wanted to eat was the corner of her lip.

She was as kind to me as she was to the idiot, she translated every word for me, everything that went on at table, everything the little snotnoses said... She explained everything, first in French, she repeated everything very slowly... She took on work for two... Her old man went on twinkling behind his glasses... He didn't chirp very much anymore, he just acquiesced... "Yes, Ferdinand. Yes," he said approvingly... After that he entertained himself, he'd pick his teeth very slowly and then his ears, he'd play with his dental plate, unhook it, and pop it back into place. He'd wait till the kids were done, then he'd start up his prayers again.

Once we were back on our feet, Mrs. Merrywin, before we went back to school, made another stab at arousing my interest in things... "'The table, la table, now come along, Ferdinand...'" I resisted all her charms. I didn't answer one word. I let her go out ahead of me... Her buttocks fascinated me too. She had an admirable ass, not just a pretty face. Taut, compact, not too big, not too little, all in one piece under her skirt, a muscular banquet... A thing like that is divine, that's the way I feel about it... The witch, I'd have eaten every bit of her, gobbled her up, I swear... I kept my temptations to myself. I distrusted the other kids in the place like the plague. They were a bunch of little snotnoses, always looking for a fight, always shooting the shit, crazy and dumb as hell. I'd lost interest in that kind of foolishness... the way those kids made faces all the time, they made me sick... I was too old, I hadn't the patience. I couldn't stand school anymore... The stuff they do, the truck they recite... it's unbearable... when you think of what's waiting for you... the way you'll be treated as soon as you're out... If I'd felt like shooting my mouth off, I'd have mowed all those phony little bastards down with three words and a menacing gesture... Knocked them flat... Just to see them bouncing around the cricket field made my blood boil... At first they laid for me in corners, to break me in, as they put it... They'd decided they were going to make me talk, regardless... There were about a dozen of them... They swallowed their cigarettes... I pretended not to notice. I waited until I had them good and close. Then I went all out, I poked them smack in the eyes, I kicked them square in the shins, I sent them sprawling... It was a massacre, a pudding! They went over like tenpins... Days later they were still feeling their bones... After that they behaved better... They got to be soft- spoken, respectful... They came back for another sniff... I laid out two or three of them... After that they knew what was what.

I was really the strongest and maybe the meanest... French or English, kids are all the same kind of vermin... You've got to step on them quick... There's no point in using kid gloves, you've got to teach them right away or you never will. Give them a good shellacking. Otherwise you'll be the one to get stepped on... You'll be all washed up. Miss your chance and all you'll get is one good bellyache. If I'd started talking to them, naturally I'd have told them what *business* is really like... the realities of life... apprenticeship... I'd soon have wised those little phonies up... Those kids didn't know which way is up... They didn't know a damn thing... All they knew about was football... that isn't enough... and looking at their cocks...

There wasn't too much school, only in the morning.

Mr. Merrywin was in charge of the schoolwork, religion, and the different kinds of sports... he managed all by himself, there weren't any other teachers.

At the crack of dawn he came around himself in slippers and dressing gown to wake us up. He was already smoking his pipe, a little clay one. He waved his long cane over the bed, bringing it down once in a while, but never hard. *"Hello, boys, hello, boys!"* he'd cry with his little old woman's voice. We followed him to the washroom... There was a row of faucets, we used them as little as possible. It was too cold to soap yourself. And it never stopped raining. From December on we had a regular deluge. You couldn't see the least bit of the town anymore or the port or the river in the distance... Nothing but fog the whole time, a big mess of cotton... The rains made holes in it, you could see lights, then they disappeared... You could hear all the foghorns, the boats calling, from daybreak on there was always a noise... the grinding of winches, the little train along the waterfront... puffing and squealing...

When he came in, Merrywin turned up the gas jet so we could find our socks. After the washroom we ran, still sopping wet, down to the basement for our measly feed. A bit of prayer and then breakfast. That was the only place where they burned a little coal, the greasy, slippery kind that erupts like a volcano, that explodes and smells like asphalt. It's a pleasant smell, but then it gives off a whiff of sulphur that stings pretty bad.

On the table there were sausages on toast, but Lord were they small! They were mighty good, a delicacy, but there was never enough. I could have bolted the whole lot. Through the smoke, the flames threw reflections on the wall, on Job and the Ark... fantastic visions.

Not speaking the English language, I had plenty of time to look around... The old man chewed slowly. Mrs. Merrywin came in last. She had dressed Jongkind, she settled him in his chair, she moved the cutlery out of his reach, especially the knives, it was really a wonder he hadn't stuck his eye out yet... and greedy as he was... that he hadn't swallowed a coffeepot and bust... I looked furtively at Nora, Mrs. Merrywin, I listened to her like a song... Her voice was like the rest of her, enchanting gentleness... What interested me in her English was the music, the way it danced in and out of the firelight. I was living in a daze myself, a little like Jongkind. I was soft in the head, I was letting myself be bewitched. I had nothing to do. The stinker, she must have known. Women are scum. She was as lowdown as the rest of them. "What's the matter with you, Buster?" I said to myself. "You swallowed a kite? You sick? You off your rocker? Flying away? Watch yourself, kid. Pinch yourself. Pull yourself together. Before it's too late." So naturally I tightened up... I curled up like a hedgehog. The danger was past. I kept my trap shut.

I had to watch myself, my imagination was running away with me, it was a dreamy kind of place, with its opaque storms and its clouds all over. I had to hole up and keep patching my armor. One question kept coming back to me, how had she come to marry that little worm? That little rat with the cane! It seemed impossible. That goblin! That monster! With that mug! Even on a pipe bowl it would scare people out of their wits, it wouldn't sell for a dime! Oh well, it's her business.

She was always keeping after me. trying to make me converse: *"Good morning, Ferdinand! Hello! Good morning!"* I was all hot and bothered. Her expression was so adorable... Plenty of times I almost fell. But I'd pull myself together quick... I reminded myself of all the stuff I had on my mind... I saw Lavelongue's face, and Gorloge, all mixed up... I had plenty to choose from to make me puke... Madame Méhon... Sakya-Muni... I only had to sniff, my nose was always in the shit. I answered inside: "Go on talking, baby doll, go right ahead... you won't get a rise out of me... You can laugh your head off... smile like a dozen frogs... You won't catch me... I'm hardened, take it from me, I've had it up to here." I thought of my father... his scenes, the bilge he was always dishing out... all the shit that was waiting for me... the lousy jobs... the crummy customers, all the beans, the noodles, the deliveries... the bosses... all the thrashings I'd had... in the Passage... If I had any desire to kid around, that knocked it right out of me... I was convulsed with memories... I scraped my ass with them... I was so mad I tore off whole patches of skin... My bleeding ass! No, this skirt wasn't going to take me.

Maybe she was good, maybe she was marvelous! Let her be a thousand times more radiant and beautiful, you wouldn't catch me going soft on her... She wouldn't wring a single sigh out of me... She could cut her face in ribbons to please me, she could roll them around her neck, she could cut three fingers off her hand and stick them up my ass, she could buy herself a pure-gold pussy! I still wouldn't talk to her! Never!... I wouldn't even kiss her! All that was the bunk, more of the same. And that was that. I preferred to stare at her old man, to look him up and down... that kept me from having dumb ideas... I drew comparisons... He was part turnip... green diluted blood... part carrot too, on account of the squiggly hairs coming out of his ears and at the bottom of his cheeks... How had he ever got hold of this beauty?... It couldn't have been money... Then it must have been a mistake... Of course, you've got to remember, women are always in a hurry... They'll grow in anything... any old garbage will do... They're just like flowers... The more beautiful they are, the worse the manure stinks... The season is short. Bzing! And the way they lie all the time... I'd seen some horrible examples. They never stop. It's their perfume. That's the long and the short of it.

I should have talked to her? Beans! She'd have taken me for a ride. That was sure as shit... I'd have understood even less... Buttoning up built my character at least.

In school Mr. Merrywin tried to persuade me, he went to a lot of trouble, he put all the kids to work making me talk. He wrote whole sentences on the blackboard in capital letters... easy to decipher... and the translation underneath... The kids repeated them all together, in chorus... in cadence... over and over. I opened my mouth wide... I pretended something was coming... I was waiting for it to come out... Nothing came out... Not a syllable... I shut my mouth again… The try was over... They'd leave me alone for another twenty-four hours... *"Hello, Hello! Ferdinand!"* the old ape would sing out, crestfallen, at the end of his wits... When he did that, he really gave me a pain... I'd have made him swallow his big stick... I'd have put him on a spit… I'd have hung him up on the window by the ass... Ah! He caught on finally... He stopped pushing me... He suspected the kind of instincts I had. I frowned... I grunted when my name was called... I kept my overcoat on even in school, I slept in it...

I meant a lot to Merrywin, he didn't want to lose me, his school wasn't overcrowded, he didn't want me to go home before my six months were up. He was worried about my impulses. He kept on the defensive...

In the dormitory we kids were left to ourselves... once the prayers were over... We said them in our nightgowns, kneeling on the floor at the foot of the bed... Merrywin delivered a kind of sermon, we formed a circle around him... and then he went off to his room... We didn't see him anymore. After hurrying through our responses, we hit the sack quick, impatient to start playing with ourselves. It warms you up... Nora shut the idiot up in a special bed with a grating over it. He was always trying to get out... he walked in his sleep so bad that sometimes he upset the bed...

I'd made friends with a crazy little kid that jerked me off almost every night, he suggested a lot of other things, he had ideas, I had plenty of juice, more than the others... He was greedy, he made all the kids laugh with his clowning... He sucked two of the other kids... He pretended to be a dog... Woof! Woof! he'd bark... he'd crawl around like a puppy, he came when we whistled, he liked being ordered around... On the nights when the storm was really acting up, when the wind was howling in the alley under our windows, we made bets whether the wind would put out the lamp... the one that creaked so bad, that was hanging above the gate... I used to hold the bets, the ginger, the chocolate, the pictures, the cigarette butts... even a few lumps of sugar... and three matches. They trusted me... They put it all on my bed... The woof-woof dog often won... He had an instinct about stormy weather... On Christmas Eve there was such a cyclone that the lamp in the alley smashed to bits. I can still remember... Kid Woof-Woof and I ate up all the bets.

It was the style and tradition that in the afternoon everybody put on sport clothes, a green-and-yellow-striped uniform and a cap to match, all decorated with the college seals and blazons… I wasn't very eager to dress up like a jester and one of those outfits, I felt sure, must be mighty expensive... Especially the cleated shoes... I wasn't in the mood for toys... I didn't see any games in my future... It was just some more damn foolishness, made to order for little punks.

Right after lunch old man Merrywin himself took off his half-soutane, put on his Pied Piper coat and bzing!... out he went. All of a sudden he was full of beans, you wouldn't have known him... He'd go romping up and down the field like a pony... Under the squalls and showers he was especially happy... His little harlequin suit had a magical effect on him. He was comical, as jumpy as quicksilver.

Englishmen, you've got to admit, are a funny sight... A cross between a pastor and a little boy... Everything about them is ambiguous. Mostly they bugger each other... He was awfully keen on having them buy me a complete set of livery, so I could be rigged out like a champion from Meanwell College. So I wouldn't stick out like a sore thumb when we went for a walk, or on the football field... He even showed me a letter he'd written my father on the subject... Maybe there was something in it for him. Maybe he'd get a rake-off. There was something suspicious about the way he kept insisting... I didn't bat an eyelash when I saw the letter, but I had a little laugh to myself... "Go ahead and send it, you old fool, you don't know my parents. They don't give a good godam about sports." Obviously he had no idea... Obviously they'd tell him what for... They'd stick at the monkeysuit... any bets? There'd be hell to pay...

Well anyway, after lunch, rain or shine or earthquake, we all had to go out... Two by two we had to climb another hill behind ours, absolutely waterlogged, a chaos of bogs and torrents... I brought up the rear with Mrs. Merrywin and the idiot in between us... We brought his pail and shovel, so he could make mud pies, big mushy ones, that kept him quiet for a while... Umbrellas and raincoats were no use at all... nothing could resist the tornadoes... If it hadn't been for the slush that was thicker than lead, we'd have flown away with the birds...

I had the best position in the football game, I kept goal... that gave me a chance to meditate... I didn't like to be disturbed, I let almost everything through... When the whistle blew, the brats flung themselves into the battle, they plowed through the muck till their ankles cracked, they charged at the ball, full steam into the clay, they plastered themselves with it, their eyes were full of it, their whole heads were covered... When the game was over, our little angels were nothing but molded garbage, staggering hunks of clay... with big wads of pigeon shit sticking to them. The muddier they were, the shittier, the more hermetically sealed, the happier they felt... They were wild with joy under their crusts of ice, welded into their clay helmets.

Our only trouble was lack of competition... Rival teams were rare, especially nearby. Actually the only ones that played us regularly, every Thursday, were the kids from Pitwitt Academy, on the other side of the bridge at Stroud, a gang of miserable pimplefaces, foundlings, a charitable institution... They were mighty skinny, even lighter than our gang... Actually they didn't weigh anything. At the first violent charge downwind, they flew away just like the ball... The main thing was to hold them, to flatten then down... We used to beat them 12 to 4. Regularly. It was the custom... If there were any complaints, if we heard the slightest murmur, we didn't hesitate a second, we beat the shit out of them, we massacred them... That was the custom too. If they kicked so much as a single goal more than usual, our boys got really vicious... They said they'd been double-crossed... they began looking for the guilty parties... murder was in the air... When we got home in the evening, they went over the whole business again... after prayers, when the old man had closed the door... Hell broke loose for five minutes... Jongkind was to blame... The fool things he did, he was always responsible for the penalties we got... He got his punishment... It was epic... They lifted up the grating and spilled him out of his crib... First they spread him out on the floor like a crab, ten of them all together gave him a mean whipping with belts... even with the buckles... When he yelled too loud, they'd pin him under a mattress and everybody stamped on him... Then they went after his pecker... to teach him how to behave... till there wasn't any more... not a single drop.

Next day he couldn't stand up... Mrs. Merrywin was puzzled, she couldn't make the kid out... He didn't say *"No trouble"* anymore... He crumpled up at the table and in class... for three days he was a wreck... But he was incorrigible, you'd have had to tie him to make him keep still... You had to keep him away from the goal... The minute he saw the ball go in, he went off his rocker, he dashed in like a madman, jumped on the ball, wrenched it away from the goalkeeper... Before we could stop him, he'd run away with it... At times like that he was really out of his mind... He ran faster than anybody else... "Hurray, hurray, hurray!" he'd keep shouting all the way down the hill. It wasn't easy to catch him. He'd run all the way to town. Often we'd catch him in a shop... kicking the ball into shop windows, smashing signs... He was a demon athlete. He had funny ideas, you never knew what he was going to do next.

For three months I didn't say boo; I didn't say hip or hep or oof... I didn't say yes... I didn't say no... I didn't say anything at all... it took some heroism... I didn't speak to a living soul... That suited me fine...

In the dormitory everything went on as usual... the jerking and sucking... I wondered about Nora, but I didn't really know a thing...

Around January and February it was terribly cold and the fog was so thick we could hardly find our way home from the playing field... We groped our way...

The old man let me alone in school and on the hill, he'd stopped trying to argue with me. He caught on to my character... He thought I was thinking things over... that I'd come around after a while, if handled gently... That's not what interested me. What gave me the creeps was the thought of going back to the Passage. It gave me the shivers three months in advance. It drove me crazy just to think about it... Christ! Having to start talking again!...

On the physical side I had nothing to complain about, I was doing all right. I was feeling a good deal stronger... The rough climate, the glacial weather was just what I needed... It built me up more and more, if the eats had been better I'd have turned into a regular strong man... I'd have laid them all flat...

Another couple of weeks went by... That made four months of silence. Then all of a sudden Merrywin got kind of scared... One afternoon when we came in from sports, I saw him grabbing a sheet of paper. He begins to write my father, hysterically... a lot of bilge... It was a dumb thing to do...By return mail I got three big long letters that I can safely describe as vile... stupid, bristling with threats, bloodcurdling oaths, insults in Greek and Latin, warnings, prospective punishments, selected anathemas, infinite grief... My conduct was diabolical! Apocalyptic!... That got me down again... He writes me an ultimatum to plunge into the study of the English language, immediately, in the name of his terrible principles, of their extreme privations... of their twenty million sacrifices, of the horrible sufferings they had endured, all for my sake. Merrywin, the stupid bastard, stuttered and stammered... he was all upset, flummoxed at having brought on such a deluge... A lot of good it had done him! Now the dikes were broken... it was every man for himself... I can't begin to say how rotten sick it made me to see all my old man's damn foolishness right there on the table, spread out in black on white... It was even crummier in writing.

What an asshole he turned out to be... old Swallowtail Merrywin! Worse than all the brats lumped together... And ten times stupider and stubborner... I was sure he'd be my downfall with those glass eyes of his.

If he'd kept quiet and minded his business as agreed, I was good for another six months... Now that he'd put his foot in it, it was only a question of weeks... I locked myself up in my silence... I was very angry with him... If I picked up and left, he'd asked for it... It would be a disaster for the school. He'd brought it on himself. Meanwell College wasn't doing very well to begin with... Without me on the football team, they were all washed up, the team would never get through the season.

After Christmas vacation four kids left—that is, they didn't come back... The school would have one hell of a football team even if they let Jongkind play... It would be nonexistent... With only eight snotnoses left it was no use even lining up... They'd wipe the floor with us. Pitwitt would score whenever they felt like it... even if their kids had been lighter than feathers, even if they'd been twice as undernourished... Our boys would cut and run... They wouldn't wait for the massacre... Meanwell was washed up... No more football meant bankruptcy... The old man was scared shitless... He made a last despairing try... He questioned me in French... Did I have any complaints, was anything wrong?... Did the kids bully me?... I'd have liked to see them try! Did my feet get too wet?... Was there something special I'd like to eat? There was no sense in talking. I was ashamed to sulk and act like an ass in front of Nora... but self-respect wasn't the half of it... Once you've made up your mind, you got to go through with it... The more pupils they lost, the more indispensable I was getting... They were always making up to me... smiling... doing me favors... The kids knocked themselves out... Little Jack, the one that put on the puppy act at night, brought me candy... he even gave me some of his water-cress... the little tiny leaves... stiff as whiskers... that taste like mustard... and grow in special moldy boxes on the windowsill...

The old man had told them all to be nice... and try and keep me until Easter... for the sake of our sports, the honor of the school depended on it... If I left any sooner, the team would be shot... they wouldn't be able to play Pitwitt anymore...

To make things even nicer for me they let me off classes. In class I distracted everybody's attention... I was always banging my desk... or I'd go and look out the window... at the fog and the movement in the port... I had projects of my own, I did things with chestnuts and walnuts, I set up naval battles... I made big sailboats with matches... I prevented the others from learning anything...

The idiot behaved pretty well, except he kept sticking his penholder up his nose... Sometimes he put two or even four of them in one nostril... He pushed them way up and yelled... He drank the ink out of the inkwells... It was better he should take walks... The more he grew the harder it got to handle him... They took us out together... I missed the classroom a little... I didn't learn anything but I felt good, I didn't mind the sound of English... It's pleasant, elegant, supple... It's a kind of music, it comes from another planet... I had no talent for learning... It wasn't hard for me to resist... Papa always said I was stupid and opaque... There was nothing to be surprised about... My isolation suited me better and better... Obstinacy is my strong point... They had to give in, to stop bothering me... They flattered my instincts, my taste for bumming... They walked me all over the region, up hill and down village, with the idiot, his wheelbarrow, and all his toys...

As soon as school started, we lit out for the country, Jongkind, Mrs. Merrywin, and I... We often came back by way of Chatham, depending on the errands we had to do. We held the idiot by a rope fastened to his belt, so he wouldn't make off through the streets... He was always up to something... We'd mosey down to town, we'd saunter along the shop fronts, we'd have to watch out for the carriages, he was scared of horses, he'd practically jump under the wheels...

While doing the shopping, Mrs. Merrywin tried to teach me the signs on the shops... That way I'd learn without even trying, without the slightest effort... I let her talk... I just looked at her face, at the particular spot that fascinated me, her smile... that saucy little jigger... I'd have liked to kiss her right there... It was itching me something terrible... I went around behind her... I hypnotized myself on her waist, her movements, her undulations... On market day we took the big basket... it was like a cradle... Jongkind and I each held a handle. We brought back all the food for the whole week... Our shopping took all morning.

I saw Gwendoline, my Greasy Joan, in the distance. She was still cooking her fritters, she was wearing a different hat, it was even bigger, with more flowers... I refused to go in that direction... I'd never have extricated myself from all the explanations and gush. When we stayed home because Jongkind had a cold, Nora lay on the couch in the drawing room and began to read, there were books all over the place... Our blessed angel was a sensitive soul, poetic, imaginative... She didn't soil her hands, she never touched a finger to the food or the beds or the floors. There were two maids when I first came: Flossie and Gertrude. They seemed to be pretty hefty... How did they manage that? They must have kept all the grub for themselves, or maybe it was some disease... They were neither of them any spring chickens... You could hear them griping the whole time, they were always sniffing on the stairs. They'd shake their brooms at each other... But they didn't knock themselves out... It was filthy in the corners...

Flossie smoked on the sly, I caught her one day in the garden... No washing was done in the house, we took it all to town to a special laundry, at the end of the world, way past the barracks. On those days Jongkind and I didn't rest a minute, we went up and down the hill any number of times with enormous bundles... We'd have contests to see who could carry more and faster... That was a sport I understood... it reminded me of the days on the Boulevards... Our walks got to be wild adventures when the rain came down so heavy and wet... when the sky crashed against the roofs and burst into torrents and waterfalls. The three of us clung together to resist the tempest... The storm was so violent that Nora... her curves, her buttocks, her thighs... looked like solid water, everything was stuck together... We weren't making any headway... We couldn't take the stairs that went up our cliff... We had to go around by the park... to make a detour past the church. We stopped outside the chapel, under the portico... waiting for the storm to pass.

The rain drove the idiot crazy with excitement... He'd run out of his shelter... He tilted his head back and took the rain full in the face... With his mouth wide open... He gulped down the rivers, he was having a hell of a good time... He bobbed up and down, he flew into a frenzy... He danced a jig in the puddles, he jumped like a wood sprite... He wanted us to dance too... It was one of his fits... I was beginning to understand him, it was hard to calm him down... You had to pull his rope and hitch him to the foot of a bench.

I knew my parents. This business with the striped suit wasn't going to suit them one bit, I knew it all in advance... They answered after some delay, they still hadn't got over it, they yelled like stuck pigs, they thought I was trying to put one over on them, that the whole thing was a subterfuge to cover up my wild extravagance... They took advantage of the occasion to remark that if I wasted my time kicking a ball around, no wonder I wasn't learning two cents' worth of grammar... This was their final notice... my last chance... I needn't worry too much about the accent... any old accent would do... as long as I could make myself understood... I read the letter over again with Nora and her old man... it lay open on the table... There were some passages they didn't dig. The whole thing struck them as very strange and mysterious... I didn't do any explaining... I'd been there for four months, I wasn't going to let myself in for a lot of applesauce on account of a jacket... It upset them though. Even Nora seemed unhappy... that I didn't want to wear a sport uniform with the monkey jacket and the rainbow cap... Probably for roaming around town, it would be good publicity for Meanwell, especially me, because I was the biggest and gawkiest... the way I looked on the football field was a disgrace to the school... Finally they carried on so much that I softened a little... I accepted a compromise... Nora pieced together a rig out of two of her old man's castoffs... and I said I'd try it... Some combination... it made me look real cute... twice as grotesque... I had no shape or middle... But I didn't have to listen to their lamentations anymore... At the same time I inherited a cap, two tones, with a crest, a tiny little thing the size of half an orange... It looked weird on my enormous bean... But they thought all that stuff helped the prestige of their establishment... the honor of the school was saved... Now they made a point of taking me out... they didn't have to think of excuses anymore...

As long as we could roam around and no one tried to make me open my heart... it was OK with me... I couldn't hope for anything better... I'd even have worn a topper if they'd insisted… if it gave them pleasure... They wore them on Sunday when they went to sing hymns at their Protestant mass... That temple of theirs was like a drill ground: Stand up! Sit down!... Nobody asked me how I felt about it... they just took me along... they were afraid I'd be unhappy all alone in the house... In church, too... between the pews... we had to keep an eye on Jongkind, it was pretty rough. He kept fairly quiet between the two of us, Nora and me.

In church Nora seemed even more beautiful than outside, that's what I thought at least. With the sound of the organ and the half-tints of the windows, her profile was dazzling... I can still see her... It was years ago, but I can bring back her image whenever I please. At the shoulders her silk blouse forms lines, curves, miracles of flesh, agonizing visions, soft and sweet and crushing... Yes, I could have fainted away with delight while our kids were bawling the Psalms of Saul...

Sunday afternoon there'd be another hymn-singing session at home, I'd be kneeling beside her... The old geezer read something interminable, I had to hold my cock down with both hands, way at the bottom of my pockets. In the evening, after all the meditations, I was bursting with desire... The kid that came around to lap me up had his money's worth on Sunday night, he had his fill... But I wasn't satisfied, it was her I wanted, every last bit of her... Beauty comes back at you in the night... it attacks you, it carries you away... it's unbearable... I was soft in the head, from jerking off on visions... The less we had for meals, the more I masturbated... It was so cold in the house we put all our clothes back on as soon as the old geezer had cleared out...

The lamp under our window, the one we made bets about, creaked the whole time... To save a little warmth we went to bed two by two... We did each other up brown... I was ruthless, I couldn't stop, my imagination kept winding me up... I devoured Nora in all her beauty, every nook and cranny... I ripped up the bolster... I'd have ripped out her quiff if I'd really bit into her, her entrails, the juice of her marrow, I'd have drunk it all... I'd have sucked up every bit of her... left nothing... I'd have taken all her blood, every drop... Still it suited me better to ravage the bed, to chew up the sheets... than to let Nora or any other skirt take me for a ride. I'd caught on, believe me, I knew the score with women. Ass is a rat race, a suckers' caravan! An abyss, a bottomless pit, and that's that... My way was to strangle my dick... I was oozing like a snail... but I didn't let it come out... Not me... Cock that wets will suck eggs... To hell with all that stinking mush!... Yak! yak! I love you. I adore you! Sure, sure! Let her shit in your face! Why worry, it's a party. Bottoms up! It's so lovely! It's so innocent!... I'd wised up when I was a kid! Sentiment, hell! Balls!... Go jump in the lake... Go fly a kite!... I clutched my oil can. My fly was all twisted! Ding dong dell! You won't catch me dying like a sucker... with a poem on my lips! Ugh!

Aside from the business with the prayers, I had other tortures to put up with... The crafty demon of lechery walked every path, he was hiding behind every bush... I walked enormous distances with the idiot and my lovely and got to know every inch of the country around Rochester in every kind of weather...

We explored every valley, every path and bypath. I looked at the sky a good deal to distract my attention. It changed color with the tides... During calm spells pink clouds came up, on the land side and on the horizon... and then the fields turned blue...

The way the town was laid out, the roofs sloped down toward the river, it looked like an avalanche... an enormous herd of cattle, all black and pressed together in the mists that blew down from the open country... all steaming in the yellow and violet fog...

She was always making detours and arranging for long rests at propitious moments. It didn't get her anywhere, it didn't make me open my heart... Even when we spent hours coming home through little narrow streets... Even one evening when it was already dark on the bridge that goes to Stroud... We looked down at the river... A long time, the eddies swirling around the arches... we heard all the bells... from the villages... far far away in the distance... Then she took my hand and kissed it... just like that... I was all stirred up, I didn't react... I didn't move... No one could see us... I didn't say a word, I didn't bat an eyelash... She never suspected...

It wasn't easy to resist... The harder it was for me, the stronger I became... She wasn't going to soften me, the bloodsucker, even if she were a hundred times as pretty. Anyway, she was going to bed with that little ape! When you're young, it makes you puke to see the old fossils they shack up with... If I'd said anything, I'd have tried to find out why it was him... why him when he was so ugly? It was incongruous... Maybe I was slightly jealous. I guess I was. But it's true that he was horrible to look at and listen to... with his little short arms... flapping like stumps... all the time, for no reason... He waved them around so much he seemed to have ten of them... It made you scratch just to look at him... He was always snapping his fingers, clapping his hands, twirling his cane, crossing his arms... but just for a second... Bzing! He was off again... like a jumping jack... what a guy!... twitching and jerking... like a loony chicken...

She, on the contrary, emanated grace, every movement was lovely... She was a mirage of charm... When she left the room, you felt a void in your soul, your heart slipped down to the basement in sadness... She had every reason to be downcast, she might have shown signs of worry. During the first months I always saw her happy, patient, untiring with the snotnoses and the idiot... They weren't always a pleasure to handle... Her life was no joke... With her beauty, she should have been able to marry a bag of money... She must have been bewitched... or taken some kind of a vow. And he certainly wasn't rich. It stuck in my craw, in the end I couldn't think of anything else...

For Nora the idiot was an awful nuisance, she had every reason to be exhausted at the end of the afternoon... Just wiping his nose, taking him to pee, keeping him from getting run over, from swallowing everything in sight... it was really a rotten chore...

She was never in much of a hurry. As soon as the weather picked up a little, we stayed out even later, we dawdled around the village and by the riverbank... Jongkind didn't drool as much when we were out walking as at home, only he swiped things, matches for instance... The minute you left him alone for a second, he set fire to the curtains... Not to be bad... he'd come and tell us right away... He'd want us to see how pretty the little flames were...

The shopkeepers in town saw us passing so often they all got to know us... They were *"grocers"*... that's what they call them... something like *épiciers*... That's one word I actually learned... In their windows they piled up regular mountains of apples and beets, and whole valleys of spinach on their enormous counters... The stuff went all the way up to the ceiling... the hills ran from one shop to the next... cauliflower, margarine, artichokes... It made Jongkind happy to see those things. He'd jump up on a pumpkin, he'd bite into it like a horse...

328 | P a g e

The shopkeepers thought I was crazy too... They asked her how I was getting along... the minute I turned my back, they made motions to Nora... with their fingers, they'd tap their heads… *"Better? Better?"* they whispered. *"No, no!"* she answered sadly... I wasn't any *"better,"* dammit. I'd never be *"better"*... It gave me the creeps the way they carried on... So worried... so sympathetic...

When we went shopping, there was one little thing I'd always noticed... it puzzled me quite a lot... Those bottles of whiskey... In the course of a week we always brought back one and often two... And sometimes brandy too... And I never saw the stuff on the table... or in the parlor... or in the glasses... not a single drop... We always drank water, absolutely straight... So where did the booze go? Was there a tippler in the house? I had strong suspicions... I kept saying to myself... Somebody's lapping it up... There's one spoiled brat around here that doesn't feel the cold... The way he's pouring it down, he doesn't have to worry about rheumatism... that's a cinch.

The weather began to improve, the winter was over... It had passed in walks, games, cross-country races, storms, and masturbation...

To get a little more to eat, I did a little sleight-of-hand in the shops... They thought I was so simple they never suspected my tricks... I put on the innocent mischief act, I disappeared... I played peekaboo with Jongkind behind the posts and counters... I snitched a little sausage, an egg here and there, a few crackers, a banana or two... just a few odds and ends... Nobody ever bothered me...

In March we had another rainy spell, the sky was heavy, crushing, it gets on your nerves in the end after all those months... It weighs on everything, on the houses, the trees, it falls right down to the ground. You walk on it, you're sopping wet, you walk in the clouds, in mists that melt into slush, in the soup, on broken bottles... It's miserable!

The farthest we went on our walks was past Stroud, on paths, through woods and over hills, to an enormous estate where they raise pheasants. They weren't wild at all, they roamed around by the dozens. They pecked like chickens on a big lawn with some kind of monument in the middle, an enormous black block of coal, standing upright, tremendous, almost as big as a house. It dominated the landscape... We never went any farther... After that there wasn't any path...

One place I was sorry I couldn't go in the evening was the waterfront at the bottom of the town, especially on Saturday... Nora would have been delighted to please me by going there more often... But it was dangerous on account of Jongkind, he tripped over the ropes, half a dozen times he almost drowned himself... On the whole it was better for us to stick to the heights, and best of all, to the open country, where you see the dangers in the distance, big dogs, bicycles, and so on...

One afternoon, just by chance, as we were looking for something new, we climbed a different hill, the one that went up toward Bastion 15... on the other side of the cemetery... where Scotsmen, the 18th regiment, drilled every Thursday... we watched them drill, and they weren't fooling... They really gave themselves a workout, marching up and down behind their bagpipes and trumpets. They churned up the ground, they sank in deeper and deeper. They went right on parading, harder than ever... They were up to their shoulders...

Our walk wasn't over, we went on through the valley. Right in the middle of the fields we saw something being built... Lots of workmen... They were putting up a big house... We looked through the fence... there was an enormous sign... it was easy to decipher... They were building another school... A magnificent location between the fort and the villas... And a clearing for sports, at least four times as big as ours... The track had already been laid out and covered with cinders... the little flags were in place at all four corners... the goals were marked… Everything was just about ready... The builders didn't seem to be laying down on the job, they were almost finished... Three stories were done already... The place seemed to be swarming with workmen... The name was written in red letters: "The Hopeful Academy"—for boys of all ages. It was quite a shock.

Nora Merrywin was flabbergasted... She stood there gaping like a statue... Finally we left on the double. She was in a big hurry to report the news to the little stinker... I didn't give a damn about their business, but I realized that this was a real tragedy, a catastrophe... We didn't see either of them all day... It was I that fed Jongkind, at the table after the other kids...

Next day Nora was still white as a sheet, she was all upset. She, who was usually so charming, so playful, so mild-mannered, was making movements almost like him, snapping her fingers all the time. It looked like she hadn't slept, she couldn't sit still, she stood up, went upstairs, came down again to talk to him... And then she'd leave again...

The old geezer sat motionless, he'd even stopped blinking, he was in a daze. He stared into space. He didn't eat, he only drank his coffee... He kept pouring himself whole cups... Between gulps he'd smack his right palm with his left fist, with all his might... Smack! Smack! And that was all...

Two days later he went up with us as far as the Scotsmen... He wanted to see for himself... They were making great strides in fixing up the "Hopeful." They'd done the track over and mowed the cricket field... Besides, they had two tennis courts and even a miniature golf course... They were sure to open by Easter...

The overgrown kid went jumping up and down by the fence... He wanted to look over... He was a runt, he couldn't see much... He looked through the cracks... We found a ladder... He motioned us to keep on going, he'd catch up with us on our grounds... He did actually come back... He wasn't so frisky anymore. He sat down beside his wife, this thing had knocked him cold... He'd had an eyeful of the wonders of Hopeful College.

I could see what this competition meant. Our kids were taking it on the lam already... They thought Meanwell stank... And now?... What was to prevent them from leaving?... It was a hopeless catastrophe... I couldn't catch what the old folks were saying, but the tone was mighty gloomy... The three of us went back and looked at the scaffolding... They were building walls for kicking practice. The place was an orgy of luxury... While gazing at all the splendor, the old man stuck his fingers up his nose, three at a time in his confusion, trying to think... At the table he was in a trance. I guess he couldn't see much future ahead... He let the gravy get cold. He chewed so hard on his false teeth that they popped out... He put them on the table, right beside his plate... He didn't know what was going on... He kept mumbling snatches of prayers... and thoughts... Then he says Amen! Amen! Suddenly he gets up... He rushes to the door. He takes the stairs four at a time... The kids were in stitches... His teeth were still on the table. Nora didn't know which way to look... Jongkind came right over, he bent down, he was foaming at the mouth, he sucked up the false teeth... They'd never laughed so hard. We made him spit them out again.

Discipline was shot. The kids did what they felt like... The old man was afraid to say anything... Same with Nora, in the house or outside... To play all those strenuous games there were only ten of us left... to make up a team on Thursday we'd pick up brats on the road, anybody we ran into, little hoodlums we didn't even know... We had to hold out till Easter...

The days got a little longer... To keep my parents from getting impatient I wrote postcards, I made up fairy tales, I said I was beginning to talk... They all congratulated me... It was almost spring... Jongkind caught cold, he coughed for two weeks... We were afraid to take him so far after that. We spent whole afternoons outside the fortified castle, an old ruin full of echoes, caves, and dungeons... At the slightest shower we took refuge under the vaulting with the pigeons. That was their home, there were hundreds of them, very friendly and tame... they'd come and coo right in our hands, they're comical characters, they strut, they make eyes at you, they recognize you right away... What Jongkind liked best was the sheep... he played with them for all he was worth. He'd run after the young ones that stumble and topple over. He'd roll with them in the wet grass, he'd bleat when they bleated... He was in ecstasy... he turned into a regular animal... He went home wet to the skin... and coughed for another week...

There was lots of clear weather now... new breezes, sweet, enchanting smells. Daffodils and daisies quivered in every field... The sky went back where it belonged and kept its clouds to itself like everybody else. No more of that peasoup that never stops coming down, that pukes all over the country-side... Easter came in May, the kids were bursting with impatience... They were going home to see their parents... It would be time for me to leave too... My stay was coming to an end. I was quietly steeling myself... when we received a registered envelope, a letter from my uncle with money in it and a few words... He told me to stay on, to have patience for another three months... it would be much wiser... Uncle Édouard was a good guy! It was a marvelous surprise... He'd done it on his own hook... From sheer kindness of heart... He knew my father... He could imagine the tragedies that would break out if I came home like a dope, without any English to my name... It was sure to be pretty lousy...

All in all I was thoroughly recalcitrant, ungrateful, repulsive. I could have made a bit of an effort, it wouldn't have killed me... to give him pleasure... But just as I was about to give in, I felt the gall coming back in my throat... the whole rotten business rose up... the whole stinking mess... To hell with it... I'd be damned if I'd learn anything... I'd come home crummier than ever... I'd been buttoning up for months... Hah, that's the ticket, don't talk to anybody, not here and not over there... If you're little, you've got to be tough... Open your mouth, and they'll step on you. That's the stuff, if you ask me... You're not very big? So get hard. I could keep my trap shut for another few years! Absolutely! I only had to think of the Gorloges, of little André, of Berlope, and even old lady Divonne with her piano playing, her eighth notes, and her Moonlight... Balls! Time didn't do a bit of good... They came back at me sharper than ever, and even a damn sight sourer... Bah!... My head was still full of it—the thousands of beatings, the slaps, the swift kicks... Christ! And all their stinking rottenness, and my buddies and the fags and the floozies and all their lowdown tricks!... What was I supposed to do? Think about a lot of hooey? *"Ever and ever!"* like the little stinker?... Amen! Amen! Applesauce! I made faces. I imitated them all by myself. I made a face like Antoine when he was shitting in the can... I shat in his face... Language? Language? Speak? Speak? About what?...

I'd never seen Nora dressed in a light color, a tight-fitting blouse, pink satin... It brought her boobies right out... The movement of her hips was terrific too... The way they swayed, the mystery of the ass...

It was coming on to the end of April... She tried again to cheer me up, to win me over... One afternoon I see her coming out for our walk with a book... A great big one, some kind of Bible, to judge by the size and weight... We go to the usual place... we settle down... She opens the book on her knees... I can't help looking on... The effect on kid Jongkind was magical... He plunged his nose into it... he didn't budge... The colors fascinated him... This book was full of pictures, marvelous illustrations... I didn't need to know how to read it, I knew all about it... I could see the princes, the upraised lances, the knights... the purple, the greens, the scarlets, all the armor studded with rubies... The whole shooting match... It was a good job... Well done... I knew good work when I saw it, it was tops... She turned the pages slowly... She began telling the story. She wanted to read it to us word for word... Her fingers were terrific... like beams of light on every page that passed... I'd have liked to lick them... to suck them... I was under the spell... Just the same I didn't say boo... I looked at the book all by myself... I didn't ask a single question... I didn't repeat a word... what most amazed Jongkind was the beautiful gilt edges... they dazzled him, he went to pick daisies, he came back and strewed them all over us, he filled the margins with them... The two most marvelous pages were in the middle of the book... A whole battle spread all over . . an amazing turmoil... Dromedaries, elephants, Templars charging... A hecatomb of cavalry... All the barbarians routed!... It was really marvelous... I couldn't stop looking... I was almost going to talk... I was going to ask questions… . Bing!... I tighten up, I get sore... Rotten luck!... Another second!... But I didn't say boo... I clutched the grass... To hell with it, no more stories for me!... I was vaccinated... What about little André? Wasn't he the prize cocksucker?... Hadn't he screwed me good? Hadn't he?... Some skunk he turned out to be!... Didn't I remember plenty of legends? And my own damn foolishness? Am I right or am I wrong? Once you get into the habit, where does it get you?... So stop batting my brains out! Leave me alone!... Leave me to my bread and onions!... I'd rather be unhappy than listen to stories... OK, that does it. It's all settled... I even proved I was a man, I cleared out with Jongkind, I let her read her book by herself... completely flummoxed in the grass...

The idiot and I ran down to the river... We came up by way of the pigeons... When we got back, I looked at her face... She was on her way home with her pictures... She certainly thought I was pigheaded... She was certainly sad... She was in no hurry to get back... We started off very slowly... We stopped near the bridge... It had already struck six... She looked at the water… The Medway has a strong current... When the tides are high, it gets really wild... It comes down in big eddies. The bridge shakes in the whirlpools... The water is hoarse, it makes hollow sounds... it gasps in big yellow knots...

Nora leaned way over, then she quickly raised her head... She looked far away into the distance, at the day sinking behind the houses on the coast... It threw a light on her face... A sadness that made her features tremble... It grew stronger... she couldn't stand it, it made her all fragile... She had to close her eyes...

As soon as Hopeful Academy was finished, our kids began to leave. The ones that wanted to clear out didn't even wait until Easter... Six day-pupils left at the end of April, and four boarders, their old men came and got them... They didn't think Meanwell College was good enough anymore... They drew comparisons with that other dazzling place...

I've got to admit it, Hopeful Academy made quite a splash in the middle of its grounds... The building alone was worth the trip... All of red brick, it looked out over Rochester, you couldn't see anything else on the whole hillside... They'd put up an enormous flagpole on the lawn, they flew great big banners, every pavilion in the Maritime Register, and yards, shrouds, the whole works, for the kids that wanted to learn about rigging and seafaring and prepare for the naval academy.

That's how I lost little Jack, my little jerker-offer... He had to transship, his father wanted him to be a sailor... The Hopeful made a lot of fancy publicity about getting you ready for the navy...

We lost so many boarders that in the end there were only five of us at Meanwell, including Jongkind... The survivors weren't very happy, actually they were burned up... They must have been behindhand with their payments, they couldn't settle their bills, that's why they were stuck... The football team melted away in a week... The Pitwitt Pimplies, the charity palefaces, came around twice more, asking us to crush them. We tried to explain, to tell them it was all over... they didn't understand... They missed their "twelve to nothing." They couldn't understand... They had no rivals left... not a one... It depressed them something awful... They went home deep in gloom...

The Hopeful boys were too snooty, they wouldn't play them, they snubbed them like lepers... They said they were in a higher category... The Pitwitts were sunk... They had to match up with themselves...

At our table at Meanwell the tragedy was getting serious... bitter and grim... Nora Merrywin did wonders to keep the meals going. The maids left... First Gertrude, the older one, and then four days later, Flossie... A cleaning woman came... Nora hardly touched her food anymore... She left us all the marmalade, she didn't touch it, she didn't put any more sugar in her tea, she took her porridge without milk, that left more for the rest of us... But I was awfully ashamed just the same... When the pudding was passed on Sunday, there was such a rush we almost bent our spoons... We chipped all the platters... It was a wild scramble... Merry-win lost patience, he didn't say anything, but he wiggled all over, he fidgeted in his chair the whole time, he beat a tattoo on the table, he cut the prayers short so we'd get out quicker... Things were getting too ticklish in the dining room...

In class he did the same thing... He climbed up on his platform... He put on his pleated cape, his lawyer's robes... He sat behind his desk, all huddled up in his chair, staring at the class... He began to blink and wiggle all his fingers, waiting for the time to be up... He didn't talk to the pupils anymore... the kids could do as they pleased...

Merrywin was getting thin, he'd always had enormous protruding ears, now they looked like the wings of an airplane... The four kids that were left made enough rumpus for forty... and then they got sick of it and simply walked out... anywhere... to the garden... into the street... They left Merrywin all alone, they joined us on our walk. Later we'd meet him on the road... we'd pass him in the open country... we'd see him coming in the distance... he'd race toward us, perched on an enormous tricycle...

"Hello, Nora! Hello, boys!" he'd shout as he passed... He'd slow down a second... *"Hello, Peter!"* she answered ever so sweetly... They smiled at each other very politely... *"Good day, Mr. Merrywin,"* all the kids took up in chorus... He'd go racing on. We watched him as he left, pedaling away till he was out of sight. He was home before us...

The way things were going, I felt I'd be leaving very soon... I stopped writing again... I didn't know what to say, what to invent anymore... I'd thought up everything I could... I was fed up with all that bullshit... What was the use?... I preferred to enjoy the time that was left, not to be bothered with letters. But now that Jack was gone, it wasn't so much fun in the dormitory... the little stinker certainly knew how to suck...

I was jerking off for Nora too much, my cock was bone dry... in the silence I dreamed up some new ideas... much more ingenious, more amusing, more tempting... my fatigue was even making me affectionate... Before leaving Meanwell, I'd have liked to see the kid doing it with her old man... The idea got under my skin... suddenly I had a craving to see them together... it gave me a hard-on just to think of it. What would he do to her exactly?

I had experience at the racket... But it wasn't an easy trick to pull off...They had separate rooms... His was on the right side of the hall, right after the gas jet... That was handy enough... But to get a look in at Nora's room I'd have had to go out the other end of the dormitory and go up the stairs... it was after the washroom... It was difficult... complicated...

How did they fuck? Did they do it in his room? or hers? I made up my mind... This was something I had to see... I'd waited too long...

Now that there were only five boarders, it was much easier to move around... Besides, the old man had stopped coming in at night to say prayers... The kids went to sleep very quickly once they'd warmed themselves up good... I waited till they were sawing wood... once I heard their snores, I slipped into my pants, I pretended I was going to the can... and then I tiptoed...

When I got to the old man's door, I bent down. I looked through the keyhole... I was screwed... The key hadn't been taken out... I went on... like I had to take a leak... I come back quick... I lie down again... But that wasn't the end... It's now or never, I says to myself... There wasn't a sound in the whole place... I pretend I'm asleep... I lie there a couple of minutes, tingling but perfectly still... I wasn't nuts... I'd seen the light through the transom... Right over the door... It was the same layout as on the rue Elzévir... I says to myself: "If they catch you there, kid, you'll never hear the last of it." I took extreme precautions... I tote a chair into the hall... If they catch me, I figure I'll make out I've been walking in my sleep... I put my chair down right next to the door. I wait, I sit down a while... I flatten myself against the wall... I hear a kind of thud inside... Like two pieces of wood knocking together . , . Could that be coming from his bed?... I make sure the back of the chair is balanced all right... I climb up, an eighth of an inch at a time... I straighten up... even more slowly... I'm on a level with the pane... Ah! I've made it! Jeepers! I can see perfectly. I can see everything!... I see my man... He's all sprawled out in an armchair... But he's absolutely alone! No sign of the kid!... Ah! He's mother-naked... Say!... Stretched out by the fire, all glowing... He's positively scarlet! He's so hot that he's puffing... He's naked to the belly... He's kept on his drawers and cloak, the one with the pleats, his lawyer's robe... it's dragging on the floor behind him...

The fire's blazing hot... The whole room is crackling... The big dope is all lit up by the glow... He doesn't seem unhappy... he's kept his lid on, the little one with the tassel... Ah! The stinker, it tips, it topples... He catches it, he puts it back on... He's sadder than in the classroom

... He's playing all by himself... He's got a cup-and-ball... A big one! A colossus! He shakes it, he balances, he tries to catch the ball in the cup... He misses, he giggles... he doesn't get angry... His cap falls off again... his cloak too... He picks them up as best he can... He burps, he sighs... He puts his toy down for a minute... He pours himself a big glass of liquid... He sips it very slowly... So that's where the whiskey is!... He even has two bottles beside him on the floor... And two siphons... within easy reach... and a pot of marmalade... a whole pot!... He digs into it with a big spoon... he lifts it up... he gets it all over him... he's eating!... He goes back to his game... he empties another glass... The string gets caught, it winds up around the caster of the armchair... He tugs at it, gets all muddled... he grumbles... he lets out a big laugh... He can't find his hands... He's tied... It only makes him laugh, the damn fool... I've seen enough... I come down off my perch... I pick up my chair very quietly... I slip back down the hall... Nobody's stirred... I go back to bed...

We worried along until Easter vacation... We had to cut down something awful... on food... on candles... on heat... The last few weeks the kids, the ones that were left, didn't listen to anybody... They did what they pleased... The old man didn't even give classes anymore... He stayed in his room the whole time... or else he went out all alone on his tricycle... on long excursions...

The new maid came... She didn't even last a week... The kids were impossible, insufferable, they turned the whole kitchen upside down... A cleaning woman took the maid's place, but only in the morning. Nora helped her to do the rooms and the dishes too... She put on gloves for that... She protected her beautiful hair with an embroidered handkerchief, she made a kind of turban out of it...

In the afternoon I took the idiot for a walk, I did it all by myself. Nora couldn't come anymore, she had the cooking to do... She didn't tell us where to go... I was the boss... We took our time... We took all the same streets and sidewalks, and then down along the waterfront. I looked all over for the fritter kid, I'd have liked to run into her. She wasn't anywhere in town with her cart... Neither in the harbor nor in the market... nor around the new barracks... No sign of her...

We had some good times on our walks... Jongkind behaved pretty well... Except you had to be careful not to get him excited... When we passed soldiers, for instance, brass bands, loud music, you couldn't hold him... There were lots of them around Chatham... and sailors too... On their way home from drilling they played wild tunes, triumphant hornpipes... That sent Jongkind out of his mind... He ran right into the band like a dart... It knocked him for a loop... It had the same effect on him as football... He'd dive right into the boom-booms!

A regiment is a lively thing, the color, the rhythm... it stands out against the weather... The band was scarlet… They made a big splash against the sky and the dun-colored walls... The Scotsmen puff their cheeks out when they play; they're chesty and husky and strong when they play; winsome and stalwart, they play their bagpipes; their music has hair on its legs...

We followed them to their "barracks," their tents in the open fields... We discovered other parts of the country, past the soldiers... past Stroud and still further... on the other side of another river. We always came back by way of the school, the girls' school behind the station, we waited for them to come out... We didn't say anything, we just looked, we sopped up the vision… We came back down by way of the Arsenal, the special cinder field where the "pros" played, real tough guys, who practiced by the numbers, with narrow goals, for the Nelson Cup. They kicked so hard they split all their footballs...

We came home as late as possible... I waited until it was really dark, until I saw all the streets were lighted, then I took High Street, the one that ends by our steps... Often it was after eight o'clock... The old man was waiting for us in the hall, he was afraid to say anything, he was reading his paper...

As soon as we came in, we sat down to table... Nora waited on us... Merrywin didn't talk anymore... He didn't say anything to anybody... it was getting to be the easy life... As soon as Jongkind started his soup, he began to drool. We left him alone now. We didn't wipe him off until the meal was over.

None of the brats came back from Easter vacation. There was nobody left at Meanwell but Jongkind and me. The joint was a desert.

To save on housework they closed off a whole floor. The furniture had gone, they sold it piece by piece, first the chairs, then the tables, the two cupboards, and even the beds. There was nothing left but our two beds. They were really liquidating... There was more to eat though... Quantities of jam... all we wanted... we could take seconds on pudding... The food was plentiful, what a change... that was really something new... Nora did the heavy work, but she prettied up all the same. At the table she was perfectly charming, almost playful...

The old geezer didn't hang around long, he'd fill up in a hurry and start off again on his tricycle. Jongkind kept the conversation going, all by himself. *"No trouble!"* And he'd learned another word: *'No fear!"* He was proud of that, it made him jump with joy. He never stopped saying it. "Ferdinand! *No fear!"* he kept saying to me between mouthfuls.

Outside I didn't like to be noticed... I gave him a few kicks in the ass... He got the drift, he left me alone... As a reward I gave him pickles. I always took a supply with me, my pockets were full of them... They were his favorite delicacy, that way I made him behave... He'd let himself be torn limb from limb for pickles...

There wasn't much left in our living room... First the knickknacks went... then the upholstered pink couch, then the vases, then the curtains... For the last two weeks there was nothing left but the piano, the big black monumental Pleyel, all by itself in the middle of the room...

I wasn't very eager to get back, because we weren't very hungry anymore... We took precautions, we brought provisions along, we looted the kitchen before leaving. I wasn't in any hurry at all... Even when I was tired, I was happier roaming around...We took a rest whenever we felt like it... We'd treat ourselves to a last stop on the steps or on the rocks right beside our garden gate... The top of the big staircase that led up from the harbor was almost under our windows... Jongkind and I would sit there as late as possible, saying nothing...

From there you could see a lot of ships, coming in or passing each other in the harbor... It was like a magic game... all the reflections moving on the water... the portholes coming and going, glittering the whole time... The train burning, trembling, setting the little arches on fire as it passed... Nora always played the piano while she was waiting for us... She left the window ajar... You could hear her plainly from our hiding place... She even sang a little... in an undertone... She accompanied herself... Her singing wasn't loud at all... Actually it was no more than a murmur... a little ballad... I still remember the tune... I never knew the words... Her voice rose softly and floated down into the valley... It came back to us... The air over the river has a way of echoing and amplifying... Her voice was like a bird, beating its wings, the whole night was full of little echoes...

The people had all passed, the ones that were going home from work, the stairs were empty... *"No fear"* and I were all alone... We'd wait till she stopped, till she wasn't singing anymore, till she closed the piano... Then we went in.

The grand piano didn't last much longer. The movers came for it one Monday morning... They had to take it out piece by piece... Jongkind and I gave them a hand... First they put up a regular hoist over the window... They had trouble getting the piano through. All morning they were tinkering with ropes and pulleys in the living room... They lowered the big crate down to the veranda overlooking the garden... I can still see that big black cupboard rising into the air... over the view...

As soon as they started in, Nora went down to town, she stayed out the whole time... Maybe she had a call to make... She'd put on her best dress... She didn't get back until late... She was very pale...

The old geezer didn't come home until eight o'clock, just in time for dinner. He'd been doing that for several days. After dinner he went up to his room... He'd stopped shaving, he didn't even wash, he was filthy... He smelled very sour. He sat down beside me. He began to eat, but he didn't finish... He began to poke around in his pants, in the folds, in the cuffs... He pulled up his dressing gown... He looked all through his pockets... He was trembling all over... He belched a few times... He yawned... He grumbled... Finally he found his piece of paper. It was another letter, registered this time... This was at least the tenth we'd received from my father since Christmas... I never answered... Merrywin didn't either... What was there to say?... He opens it, he shows it to me... I read it just to be on the safe side... I wade through pages and pages... It was copious and thoroughly documented... I start all over again. It was a formal order to return home... It was nothing new for them to bawl me out... Far from it... But this time there was a ticket... an honest-to-God ticket home via Folkestone!

My father was beside himself. We knew his letters. The others had been almost the same, desperate, complaining, full of hooey and threats... After reading them, the old geezer piled them up in a special box... He filed them very carefully by date and subject... He took them all up to his room... He shook his head a little and blinked... There was no call for him to comment... He kept all the letters on file, that was enough... Sufficient unto the day is the evil thereof... and all the applesauce... Still, this was a new kind of ultimatum... This time there was a ticket... I had only to pack up and leave... Time to be going, son... Next week it would be... the month was almost up... My account was closed!

Nora didn't seem to know what was going on... She was completely absorbed... absent... The old geezer wanted her to know... He shouted loud enough to wake her up. She came up from her daydream... Jongkind began to bawl... Suddenly she jumped up and looked through the box, she wanted to read the letter again. She deciphered it out loud...

I have no further illusions about the future you hold in store for us—alas, we have had only too many occasions to experience all the ferocity, all the wickedness of your instincts, your terrifying selfishness... We all of us know your taste for idleness and dissipation, your well-nigh monstrous appetite for luxury and pleasure... We know what to expect... We realize that no amount of gentleness, no amount of affection will ever check or diminish your unbridled, implacable impulses... It seems to me that in that respect we have done our utmost, tried everything! And now we are at the end of our rope, there is nothing more we can do. We can spend no more of our slender resources trying to save you from your fate... We can only trust in God...

In this last letter I wished to warn you, as a father, as a friend, for the last time, before your homecoming, to put you on your guard before it is too late, against any useless bitterness, any surprise, and futile rebellion at the fact that in the future you must count on yourself alone, Ferdinand.

On yourself alone.' Count on us no longer, I implore you, for your daily keep, your subsistence. Your mother and I are at the end of our tether. There is nothing more we can do for you...

We are literally collapsing under the weight of our liabilities, both old and recent... On the brink of old age, our health, already undermined by continual anguish, back-breaking toil, reverses, perpetual worry, privations of all kinds, is failing, breaking... We are in extremis, my dear boy. Materially speaking, we have nothing left... Of the small sum we received from your grandmother, nothing remains... absolutely nothing... not a sou! On the contrary, we have gone into debt... under what circumstances, you are well aware... The two houses in Asnières are mortgaged to the hilt!... In her business, in the Passage, your mother is faced with new difficulties which I presume to be insurmountable... A change in the styles, an absolutely unforeseen caprice of fashion, has just annihilated our prospects of a relatively successful season... All our hopes have been shattered... For once in our lives we took a chance... At great expense, by scrimping on all our expenses and even on our food... we laid in a large stock of "Irish" boleros last winter. And then suddenly, without the slightest warning indication, our customers' taste took a radical swing, they began literally to shun this item in favor of other styles, other whims... It is beyond understanding! Destiny seems to have conspired against our frail bark... It seems likely that your mother will be unable to get rid of a single one of her boleros. Not at any price! She is now trying to convert them into lampshades for the new electrical appliances!... Futile efforts!... How long can this go on? Where are we headed? For my part, at La Coccinelle, I am subjected every day to the subtle, perfidious, treacherous attacks of a cabal of young clerks who have recently been taken on... Endowed with high university degrees (some of them have their Master's), taking advantage of their influence with the director, of their family ties and social connections, of their "modern" upbringing (a well-nigh total absence of scruples), these ambitious young men have a crushing advantage over mere rank-and- file employees like myself... No doubt they will succeed (and very quickly, it appears) not only in getting ahead of us, but in ousting us altogether from our modest positions... Without wishing to take too dark a view, it is only a question of months! On that score it is impossible to harbor any illusions.

For my part, I am trying to hold my own as long as possible... without losing all dignity and self-respect... I am doing my best to minimize the chances and risks of a scandal whose consequences I dread... all the consequences... I control myself... I restrain myself... I contain myself to avoid any possibility of a scene, a skirmish! Unfortunately, I am not always successful... In their misguided zeal these young opportunists provoke me deliberately... I have become the target, the butt of their malice... I feel pursued by their plots, their sarcasms, their incessant jibes... They amuse themselves at my expense... Why?... I am lost in conjectures... Is it the mere fact of my existence? As you can imagine, this persistent hostility, their very presence, is bitterly painful to me. Moreover, all things considered, I feel myself defeated in advance in this contest of smoothness, skulduggery, and malice!... What weapons have I to defend myself with? Without a fortune or family, with nothing more to my credit than a record of service honestly, scrupulously, rendered La Coccinelle over a period of two and twenty consecutive years, my blameless conscience, my perfect probity, my meticulous and unswerving sense of duty... What have I to expect? Obviously the worst... This ample inventory of sincere virtues will, I fear, be counted rather against me than to my credit on the day when my accounts are settled... Of that, my dear son, I have a clear presentiment!...

If my position proves untenable (as it is rapidly becoming), if I am discharged once and for all (any pretext will do, there is more and more talk of reorganizing the whole office)—what will become of us then? Your mother and I cannot think of this eventuality without a sense of the most terrible and justified anguish, without positive terror!

On an off chance, in a last impulse of self-defense, I have undertaken (a desperate measure) the task of learning to operate a typewriter, outside the office of course, taking advantage of the little time I can spare from deliveries and errands for the shop. We have rented the machine (an American make) for several months (one more expense). But here again I harbor no illusions... At my age, as you can well imagine, it is not easy to assimilate so novel a technique, new methods, new habits, new ways of thinking! Especially crushed as we are by continual misadventures... mercilessly tormented!... All this, my dear son, leads us to take the darkest view of our future. And beyond the slightest doubt or fear of exaggeration, we cannot afford the least mistake... not even the most trifling imprudence... if we, your mother and I, are not to end our existence in the most utter destitution!

We send you our love, my dear child. Once again your mother and I exhort you, adjure you, implore you, before your return from England (if not in our interest or for love of us, then at least in your own interest) to make a brave decision, to resolve above all to apply yourself body and soul to the success of your undertakings.

Your affectionate father,
Auguste.

P. S. Your mother asks me to inform you of the death of Madame Divonne last Monday at her haven in Kremlin-Bicêtre.

She had been confined to her bed for several weeks. She was suffering from emphysema and a heart ailment. She suffered little. The last few days she slumbered constantly... She was not aware of the approach of death. We had been to see her the day before, in the afternoon.

The next day, it must have been about noon, Jongkind and I were in the garden waiting for lunchtime... The weather was beautiful... Along comes a character on a bicycle... He stops, he rings at our gate... It was another telegram... I ran to take it, it was from my father... "Return immediately, mother worried. Auguste."

I run upstairs, I meet Nora on the landing, I pass her the wire, she reads it, she comes down, she dishes out our soup, we begin to eat... Bingo! She bursts into tears. She's bawling, she can't stop, she gets up, she leaves the room, she runs into the kitchen. I hear her sobbing in the hall... it threw me to see her acting like that. It wasn't her way... she never did that... Just the same, I didn't bat an eyelash... I stay where I am with the idiot, I finish feeding him... It was time for our walk... I wasn't in the mood... That incident had cramped my style.

And then I thought of the Passage. All of a sudden the idea began to haunt me... my arrival, all the neighbors... the search for some wonderful job... No more independence... no more silence... No more roaming around... My childhood would be starting in again, the whole stinking business, I'd have to start in again where I left off... I'd have to show enthusiasm! Oh, the lousy luck, the slimy horror of it all... The misery of working for people! The deserving young man!... Twelve dozen crappers! I couldn't stand thinking about it... The mere thought of my parents and my mouth was full of birdshit. My mother, her skinny stilt leg, my father with his bacchanalias, his hysterical damn foolishness...

Kid Jongkind was tugging at my sleeves. He didn't catch on. He still wanted us to go out. I looked at him: *"No trouble."* We'd be leaving each other soon... This little screwball that swallowed everything in sight... I guessed he'd miss me out of his world... I wondered how he actually saw me... As an ox? As a lobster?... He'd got really used to having me take him out, with his big round eyes, his perpetual cheerfulness... He was lucky in a way... He was pretty affectionate if you were careful not to get his goat... He didn't really like to see me thinking... I went over and looked out the window a second... Before I could turn around the little joker had jumped up on the table... He calms down, he pees! It splashes in the soup... He's done it before, I run over, I grab him, I make him come down... Just then the door opens... Merrywin comes in… He moves mechanically, his features are frozen... He walks like an automaton... First he goes around the table... twice, three times... He starts in again... He's wearing his fancy rig, the black lawyer's robes... but underneath he has on a whole sport outfit, golf pants, binoculars… a nifty nickel-plate flask, and a green smock belonging to his wife... He's still walking the same way, like a somnambulist... he goes down the steps in jerks and jolts... He roams around the garden a while... he even tries to open the gate... he hesitates, he comes back, he heads for the house... still completely in a dream... He passes in front of Jong-kind again... He salutes us majestically, with a sweeping gesture... His arm rises and falls... He bows a little each time... He's addressing a crowd far in the distance... He seems to be responding to a tremendous ovation... And then finally he goes back upstairs... very slowly... with perfect dignity... I can hear him closing the door...

These weird goings-on... this mechanical man... had frightened Jongkind... He couldn't keep still. He had to get out of there, he was in a panic. I clicked my tongue at him and shouted whoa!

whoa!... like you talk to a horse. Usually that quieted him... I finally had to give in... We went out across the fields...

Near the Scottish barracks, we ran into the Hopeful College kids who were out for a walk. They were on their way to the cricket field on the other side of the valley. They were carrying their bats and their wickets... we recognized all our old boys, they waved to us, all very friendly... Naturally they had filled out and grown... They were very gay... They seemed glad to see us... their new rig was orange and blue... their caravan looked mighty bright against the horizon.

We looked after them... We came home very early... Jongkind was still trembling.

We were at the top of Willow Walk, the path leading to the school, when we passed the truck, the big van with three horses... more movers...

They avoided the steep hill, they went all the way around by the garden, they took more things away. This time they really cleaned the place out... they took the scrapings... We looked inside, the flaps were rolled up... They had the two maids' beds, one of the kitchen cupboards, the little china closet, and the old geezer's tricycle... and a lot of other junk... They must have emptied the attic! The whole joint! There wouldn't be anything left!... They even took the bottles, you could hear them rolling around in the bottom of the crate... There wouldn't be much left the way they were going about it...

I began to be worried about my two or three scraps and my shoes. If they kept on looting this way, there was no limit, anything could happen... The inside of that van looked like a regular auction room. I took the stairs four at a time, I wanted to see the extent of the damage. And besides it was time to eat... The table was laid sumptuously... with the best silver... and the dishes with the flower patterns, and all the cut glass... It stood out beautifully in the naked room...

The meal consisted of potato salad, artichokes vinaigrette, cherries in brandy, a luscious cake, a whole ham... Real abundance, and in addition there were daffodils strewn over the tablecloth, in between the cups... It was really something. It was a real surprise.

I was amazed. Jongkind and I stood looking at the marvels... neither he nor she came down... We were both famished... First we take a little taste of everything... And then we make up our minds... we dive in, we gobble... we dig in with our fingers... nothing to it once you're started... It's delicious! Jong-kind was beside himself with pleasure, he was as happy as a king... We didn't leave much... Still nobody came down...

Once we were full, we went out into the garden... It was time for his business... I look around a little... Nothing but night, not a living soul... It was really weird... Upstairs I saw only a single light in the whole housefront, in the old geezer's room... He must have locked himself in again... I says to myself, I'm not going to waste any time, I'm sick of all this hanky- panky... As long as I've got my ticket, I'll pack up... Tomorrow morning I'll skedaddle by the first train at seven-thirty. Sure! Just like that! I won't wait for the end of the song. I never could stand good-byes.

Still, I'd have liked to lay my hands on a little dough, maybe a shilling or two for some ginger beer, it's good on a trip... First I put my idiot to bed, so he'll leave me alone... I jerk him off just a little, that usually kept him quiet... it sent him off to sleep... But that night he was frantic with all his fears of the day, he wouldn't close his eyes... I tried shouting whoa whoa!... He kept thrashing around, he jumped up and down in his cage, he growled like a wild animal. He may have been nuts, but he suspected something unusual was up... He suspected I was going to leave him in the middle of the night... He didn't like that. It scared him out of his wits to be left alone... Hell!

It's true the dormitory was a big place... For him that was an awful lot of space... There were only two of us left where there'd been twelve of us before, or even fourteen...

I collected my socks, hunted up my handkerchiefs, picked up my lousy underwear, it was all holes and tears... They'd have to outfit me again. There'd be another riot... A lovely prospect... my troubles weren't over... The future is no joke... The thought of the Passage, so close to me now, sent the grimy shivers through me...

I'd been gone for eight months... What would they be like now down there under the glass roof?... That wasn't hard to figure out... They'd be even dumber... worse pains than ever... The Rochester characters... well, probably I'd never be seeing them again! I took a last look at the view out the window, the big one that opens up and down like a guillotine... The weather was clear, marvelous... You could see all the paths on the hillside and the docks all lit up... the crisscrossing lights of the ships... all the colors moving in and out... like dots looking for each other at the end of the darkness... I'd seen lots of ships and passengers leaving... sailboats... steamboats... God knows where they were now... in Canada... and some in Australia... all sails unfurled... They were chasing whales... I'd never see all that... I'd be going to the Passage... to the rue Richelieu, the rue Méhul... I'd see my father cracking his collar... my mother picking up her leg... I was going looking for jobs... I'd have to talk, to explain why and how... I'd be cornered like a rat... They'd be waiting for me, lousy with questions... I'd have to take my medicine... It gave me the golly wobbles to think of it...

It was pitch-dark in the room, I'd blown out the candle... I stretched out on the bed all dressed, I relaxed... I decided to sleep as I was... I said to myself: "Don't peel, kid, that way you can beat it at the crack of dawn..." There was nothing more for me to do... all my junk was ready. I'd even taken some towels... Jong-kind finally falls asleep... I can hear him snoring... I won't say good-bye to anybody... Just beat it on the q.t.... . No effusions for me!... I'm beginning to doze... I play with myself just a little... I hear the door opening... My blood froze... I says to myself: "Watch out, kid. It's ten to one they're coming to say good-bye... You got your nerve with you, baby doll..."

I hear a light step, somebody slipping across the floor... It's her... breathing... I'm cooked... No time to run... she won't wait... She's down on me like a cyclone... she's on the bed in one jump... A fine kettle of fish!... I take the shock full in the ribs... She clutches me... I'm crushed, flattened under her caresses... I'm all ground up, there's nothing left of me... The whole weight of her has come down on my head... it's sticky... My face is wedged in, I'm suffocating... I protest... I implore... I'm afraid to yell too loud... The old geezer might hear!... I struggle... I try to wriggle out from under... I contract... I strain my muscles... I crawl under my own ruins... I'm caught again, flattened out, crushed again... An avalanche of tenderness... I collapse under her wild kisses, her licking, her tugging... My face is a mash... I can't find my openings to breathe by... "Ferdinand! Ferdinand!" she implores me... She sobs down my windpipe... She's out of her mind... I jam all the tongue I can produce down her throat to make her stop yelling like that... the old geezer in his room is bound to wake up... I'm terrified of cuckolds... some of them are ferocious...

I try to soothe her pain, to make her control herself... I caulk wherever I can... I knock myself out... I try my best... I try the subtlest tricks... But she's too much for me... She gives me some wicked holds... The whole bed is shaking... She flails around like crazy... I fight like a lion... My hands are all swollen from clutching her ass! I want to anchor her, to make her stop moving. There. That's it. She's stopped talking. Christ almighty! I plunge, I slip in like a breeze! I'm petrified with love... I'm one with her beauty... I'm in ecstasy... I wriggle... I bite right into her tit... She moans, she sighs... I suck her all over... On her face I go looking for the exact spot next to her nose... the one that tortures me, the magic of her smile... I'm going to bite her there too... especially... I stick one hand up her ass, I massage... I dig in... I wallow in light and flesh... I come like a horse... I'm full of sauce... She gives a wild leap... She breaks loose, she's gone, the bitch!... She jumps backward... Hell! She's on her feet... She's in the middle of the room... She's making a speech... I can see her in the white of the street lamp... in her nightgown... all pulled up... her hair flying loose... I'm lying there flummoxed with my cock in the air...

"Come on back," I say. I try to quiet her. All of a sudden she seems to be furious... She yells, she waves her arms... She moves back toward the door... The bitch, she hands me a line... *"Good-bye, Ferdinand!"* she yells, *"Good-bye! Live well, Ferdinand! Live well..."* What sense does that make?...

Another scene! Holy creepers! I jump off the bed!... I'll flatten her out! She'll be the last! Dammit to stinking hell! She doesn't wait, the slut! She's gone... I hear the downstairs door opening and slamming hard... I run to the window... I open it... I'm just in time to see her running out of the alley... under the street lamps... I see her movements, her nightgown fluttering in the wind... She dashes down the steps... She's crazy. Where the hell is she going?

It flashes through my mind that something terrible is going to happen... I says to myself: "This is it. You're in for it. This is going to be one sweet mess! And you're going to take the rap! That's sure as shit! Bloody murder! She's going to throw herself in the drink..." I knew it. She's off her rocker!... Dammit to hell... Could I catch her?... But it's none of my business... There's nothing I can do... The whole thing is beyond me... I listen... I look out through the hall door... to see if I can see her on the waterfront... She must be down by now... There she is again... still screaming... "Ferdinand! Ferdinand!" And then some more Ferdinands... her screams cut through the sky... That's her again, the bitch, yelling way from the bottom... She's got her nerve... Dammit to hell! I can hear her from the other end of the harbor... I'm scared... I stare... They'll say I knew something... They'll pinch me for sure... I'm in for it. It's the handcuffs for me... I'm in one hell of a dither... I go and shake the idiot in his crib... If I leave him alone for a minute and he gets panicky... he'll do some damn-fool thing... He'll set the place on fire... Christ! I wake him up... I pull him out of his cage... I drag him out in his kimono... I pull him helter-skelter down the stairs...

When we get out into the alley, I lean over the rocks, I try to look down as far as the bridge, under the lights... Where can she be? Ah, there she is, I see her... A spot... wavering through the shadows, a white spot, whirling... That's the kid all right, that's my loony! She flits from one lamp to the next... Like a butterfly, the stinker!... She's still yelling here and there, the wind brings back the echoes... And then for a second there's a terrible scream and then another, an awful scream that fills the whole valley... "Hurry up, boy," I tell the kid. "Our lady love has jumped in. We"ll never make it. We're in for a dip. You'll see, kid. You'll see."

I run like hell, I race down the steps, through space... Bing! Just like that. AU of a sudden... Right in the middle of the stairway... My blood froze... I'd had an idea. I stop. I'm trembling all over. That's enough! I'm not taking another step... It's for the birds! I pull myself together. I look back... I lean over the rail... I see... The place on the waterfront where the sound was coming from isn't very far... There's a big crowd now... People pouring in from all sides...

The esplanade is full of rescuers... There's more coming. They're talking it over... They're running around in all directions with poles, lifebelts, and canoes... All the whistles and sirens begin to blow at once... It's a hullabaloo, a riot... But they're working hard, they re knocking themselves out... They don't catch anything... The little white square in the waves... It's being carried out farther and farther...

I can still see her from where I am, clearly in the middle of the water... she passes out beyond the piers... I can even hear her choking... I can hear her gurgling... I can still hear the sirens... I hear her swallowing water... She's caught in the tide... She's caught in the eddies... The little white speck is passing the breakwater! O Christ! O holy shit! She's drunk up the ocean by now!... I got to get the brat home... I give him a poke in the ass... They mustn't catch us out... We've got to be out of here before they come back... That's for sure.

He's worn out from running... I push him... I throw him... He can't see a thing without his glasses... He can't even see the lamp posts. He starts bumping into everything... He whines like a dog... I grab him and pick him up, I carry him up the hill... I toss him into his bed... I run to the old man's door... I knock hard. No answer, not a word! Come on! I knock again, I pound!... Then I give a good push, I bash it in... He's there all right... Just the way I'd seen him... He's stretched out in front of his grate, all pink... He's stroking his belly, as peaceful as can be... He gives me a look as if I'd interrupted him... He blinks a little, his eyelids flutter... He don't know from nothing... "She's drowning! She's drowning!" I yell at him. I repeat it even louder... I shout my lungs out... I make motions... I imitate the glug-glug... I point down... into the valley... out the window! Down there! Down there! The Medway! *"River! River! Down there! Water!..."* He raises himself just a little... the effort makes him belch... He loses his balance, collapses on a stool... "Oh, nice Ferdinand," he says... "Nice Ferdinand!" He even holds out his hand... But his cup-and-ball gets all fouled up... It's stuck in the armchair... He tugs at it, he's exhausted, he has to stop... He upsets all the bottles... All the whiskey drips down... The marmalade, the jar tips over... Everything topples... like a waterfall... That hands him a laugh... he's convulsed... He tries to pick things up... the gravy... everything collapses … the plate too... he skids on the pieces... He slides under the bench... He doesn't move... He's wedged against the fireplace... He shows me how it's done... He ruminates... he grunts… He massages his belly with round strokes... He bunches up wads of fat and gives them a good going over... He kneads them slowly... He rubs and squeezes... he pushes them apart... he works into the furrows...

I've completely forgotten what I was going to say... What's the use?... I close the door, I go back to the dormitory... I says to myself: "You're going to clear out of here at the crack of dawn..." My bag is all ready... I lie down on the bed for a minute... but I get up a second later... I'm in a panic again... I don't know exactly why. I start thinking about the kid again... I look out the window... I listen... Not a sound... Nothing... There's not a soul on the waterfront... Had they all left so soon?

Then suddenly this thing begins to plague me, in spite of my terror, in spite of my tiredness... I couldn't resist... I wanted to go down and see if they'd pulled her out of the drink... I put on my coat and pants, my suit... The kid was sound asleep... I lock him up in the dormitory... I meant to come back right away... I make it quick... I'm down at the bottom of the stairs... I see a cop making his rounds... I see a sailor who calls out to me... That cools me off... I'm scared again... I stop still in my niche... Hell! It's too complicated for me. I'm not moving... I'm too exhausted anyway. I stay there quite a while... There's nobody around... Down below, that's the bridge she jumped from... I see the lights, red ones, a big long string of them, trembling in the reflections of the water... I say to myself. I'll be getting back now... It's not far... Maybe the cops are there by now... I begin wondering... imagining... I'm exhausted... I'm knocked out... I'm really not feeling very good... I'm all in... So help me, I can't move... I'll never make it back to Meanwell... I won't even try... I lean back... There's nothing I can do after all... This mess has nothing to do with me... not a thing... Just let me beat it out of here, all by myself... Slowly I head for the station... I wrap up tight in my overcoat... I don't want anybody to recognize me... I slide along the walls... I don't meet a soul... The waiting room is open... Good deal... I stretch out for a while on the bench... There's a stove right near... I'm doing fine... I'm in the dark... The first train for Folkestone is at five... I haven't got my stuff, not one damn thing... It was up there on the bed... To hell with it! I'll go home without it... I don't want to go back there... It can't be done... The one thing for me is to make myself scarce... I sit up so as to keep awake... I'm sure of making that five o'clock train... I'm sitting right under the bulletin board... I lie down right there... I stretch out. *"5 o'clock. Folkestone via Canterbury."*

Coming home that way without any of my stuff, I really expected to be welcomed with the broom handle. Not a bit of it... My folks seemed pleased, they were kind of glad to see me... They were just surprised that I hadn't brought back a single shirt, a single sock, but they didn't press the point... they didn't start up a scenario... They were too much absorbed by their own private worries...

In the eight months I'd been away they had changed a good deal... their whole appearance and bearing. I found them all shriveled up, with wizened faces and hesitant movements... My father's pants bagged at the knees, they fell down in big folds on all sides like an elephant. His face was livid, he'd lost all his hair on top, he disappeared under his sea captain's cap... His eyes were almost colorless now, they weren't even blue at all, but gray, all pale like the rest of his face... He was all wrinkles, they were a dark color, furrows running from the nose down to the mouth... He was falling apart... He didn't talk to me about anything much... He only asked me once or twice how come we'd stopped answering his letters to England... Were they dissatisfied with me at Meanwell College? Had I made progress?... Had I caught the accent?... Did I understand English when they talked fast?... I mumbled something vague... He didn't seem to expect any more...

He wasn't listening to me anyway... He was too panic-stricken to worry about things that were over and done with. He'd lost interest in arguing... Morose as his letters had been, they hadn't told me the whole story... Far from it... There was plenty more to come... Calamities— brand-new ones! So I heard it all, in every detail... They really had put themselves through the wringer to send me my keep for the first six months... It had been rough... The disaster with the boleros had sunk them completely... without exaggeration... My father's watch never left the pawnshop... Nor my mother's ring either... They'd taken out some mortgages in Asnières... on those beat-up houses...

Not having his watch drove father crazy... not having the time on him... that contributed to his collapse. He so punctual, so exact in everything he did, he was obliged to look at the clock in the Passage every minute... He'd go out on the doorstep... Every time Madame Ussel, the seamstress, would be waiting for him... Tic toc, tic toc... she'd say to get his goat... she'd stick out her tongue...

New difficulties cropped up... end to end like a string of sausages... They were too much for them... They huddled up in their misery, disintegrating, lacerating themselves with despair, shrinking so as to offer less surface... They tried to wriggle out from under their calamities... It didn't help! They got caught, they got the same going-over every time.

Madame Héronde, our seamstress, couldn't work anymore, she was in the hospital all the time... Madame Jasmin, who took her place, was completely unreliable... A spendthrift, always in debt! Her tastes ran to liquor. She lived in Clichy. My mother spent all her time on the bus, she went out there twice a day, morning and evening... She always found her in some bar... She was married to a colonel, she steeped herself in absinthe... The customers that gave us things to mend had to wait months for their doodads... They had terrible fits of rage and impatience... It was even worse than before... They were always in a fury about the delays and postponements... And when it came time to pay up, it was always the same song and dance, the same mists and monkeyshines... Whish!... Madame was gone... All of a sudden there was nothing but empty space... Or if they did cough up a little, they hollered and griped so much, they whittled down the tiny little bills, with such tirades... that in the end my mother didn't know what to say or do... She'd sweated blood, limping after that Jasmin woman and all the rest of them, just to be yelled at, treated like dirt... It wasn't worth it.

Anyway my mother was perfectly well aware, she had to admit it with tears in her eyes, that the taste for lovely things was dying out... you couldn't buck the stream... it was stupid to even try and fight, you were just wearing yourself out for nothing... Rich people had lost all their refinement... all their delicacy... their appreciation for fine work, for hand-made articles... all they had left was a depraved infatuation with machine-made junk, embroideries that unravel, that melt and peel when you wash them... Why insist on making beautiful things?... That's what the ladies wanted. Flashy stuff... gingerbread... horrors... rubbish from the bargain counter... Fine lace was a thing of the past... What was the use of fighting?... My mother had had to give in to the contagion... She'd filled the whole place with this cheap junk... real crap... in less than a month... That was a safe bet!... The window was full of it... To see every curtain rod and shelf in the place full of this trash, miles of it, didn't just make her unhappy, it gave her a real bellyache... But it was no use arguing... The Jews two steps away from us, on the corner of the rue des Jeûneurs, piled up enormous pieces of the same, the whole shop front was thrown open, and the counters were buried under the stuff like at the fair, by the bobbin, by the rod, by the pound!

It was a real comedown for anybody who had known the real stuff... my mother was overcome with shame at having to compete with such garbage... But she had no choice... She'd have preferred to abandon this line altogether and get along as best she could with other things, with her little pieces of furniture for instance, her marqueterie, her *poudreuses*, her kidney- shaped tables, her cabinets, or even the gewgaws people put in glass cases, the knickknacks, the little pieces of pottery, and even the Dutch globes that leave next to no profit and are so heavy to carry... But she wasn't strong enough... it was too hard with her bad leg... running all over Paris, she could never have carried a bigger load... It couldn't be done. But that's what you had to do if you wanted to find bargains. And hang around the auction rooms pointing like a hound dog for hours on end... And what about the store?... The two didn't go together... Our doctor, Dr. Capron from the Marché Saint-Honoré, had been to see us twice on account of her leg... He'd made himself very clear... He'd ordered her to take a complete rest... to stop running up and down stairs, loaded like three dozen mules... to give up the housework... even the cooking... He hadn't pulled any punches... He'd told her in so many words that if she kept overdoing it... he'd warned her... she'd get a real abscess inside the knee, he even showed her the place... From the continual strain the upper and lower part of her leg had gone stiff... they were riveted together... joint and all, they were frozen into a single bone. It looked like a stick with ridges running all along... They weren't muscles... When she moved her foot, they pulled on it like ropes... You could see them straining... It gave her excruciating pain... a terrible cramp. Especially in the evening when she was through, when she came home from running around... She showed me when we were alone... She put on hot compresses... She was careful not to let my father see her... She'd finally noticed what a temper it put him in to have her limping along behind him...

Since we were all alone again... and I was in the shop, waiting... she took advantage of the opportunity to repeat... very gently, very affectionately, but with absolute conviction, that it was really my fault if things were going so badly... on top of all their other troubles in the shop and the office... My conduct, all my misdeeds at Gorloge's and at Berlope's had hit them so hard they'd never get over it... They were still stunned... Of course they weren't angry with me... they didn't hold it against me... Let bygones be bygones... But at least I ought to realize what a state I'd put them in... My father was so shattered he couldn't control his nerves... He started up in the middle of the night... He woke up with nightmares... He'd pace back and forth for hours...

As for her, I had only to look at her leg... It was the worst of calamities... It was worse than a serious sickness, than typhoid or erysipelas... Again she repeated all her recommendations in the most affectionate tone... that I should try to be more reasonable with my new bosses... more settled in my ways, more courageous, persevering, grateful, scrupulous, obliging... to stop being scatterbrained, negligent, lazy... to try to have my heart in the right place... Yes, that's the main thing, the heart!... to remember always, and never forget, that they'd deprived themselves of everything, that they'd both of them worked their fingers to the bone for me ever since I was born... and now, only recently, sending me to England!... that if, by ill luck, I were to commit any more horrible crimes... well, it would be the end... my father wouldn't be able to take it... poor man, he'd be through. He'd come down with neurasthenia, he'd have to leave his office... For her part... if she had to go through any more agonies... over my conduct... it would affect her leg... there'd be one abscess after another and in the end they'd have to amputate... That's what Capron had said.

In Papa's case it was even more tragic on account of his temperament, his sensibility... He ought to take a rest, right away and for several months, what he needed was a long vacation in a quiet place, away from it all, in the country... That's what Capron had recommended... He'd examined his heart very carefully... it beat like a triphammer... Sometimes it even missed a beat... The two of them... Capron and Papa... were exactly the same age, forty-two years and six months... He'd even added that a man is even more delicate than a woman when the "menopause" sets in... that he should take a thousand precautions... His advice came at the wrong time... Right then my father was knocking himself out more than ever... You could hear him typing up on the fourth floor, the machine was an enormous contraption with a keyboard the size of a factory... When he'd been typing a long time, the clickety click of the keys buzzed in his ears a good part of the night... It kept him awake. He took mustard footbaths. That brought some of the blood down from his brain.

I began to realize that my mother would always regard me as an unfeeling child, a selfish monster, a little brute, capricious, scatterbrained... They had tried everything, done everything they could... it was really no use. There'd never be any help for my disastrous, innate, incorrigible propensities... She could only face the facts, my father had been perfectly right... During my absence their griping had got even worse, it had settled into a groove... They were so busy with their troubles they couldn't even bear the sound of my footsteps. My father made horrible faces every time I came upstairs.

The business with the lousy boleros had been the last straw... and the typewriter was driving him crazy, he'd never be able to work it... He spent hours making copies... He banged it like he was deaf... he ruined whole pages... Either he'd hit too hard or not hard enough... The little bell was ringing all the time... From my bed... I was right near him... I saw him struggling... missing the keys... getting tangled up in the connecting rods... He wasn't cut out for it... He'd get up all in a sweat... He'd reel off the most terrible blasphemies... At the office Monsieur Lernpreinte was still rubbing it in, persecuting him from morning to night. Obviously he was just looking for a pretext... "Those downstrokes... those curlicues... they take you all day. Ah, my poor friend! Take a look at your colleagues. They were done hours ago. You're a calligraphier, monsieur! You ought to set yourself up in business..." They really had it in for him... He began to look for another job... He saw he was on the skids... He went to see former associates... He knew an assistant cashier in a rival company... The Connivance Fire Insurance Company. They'd as good as promised him a tryout in January... But there he'd have to type... He went at it every night after his deliveries.

It was an antique contraption, absolutely unbreakable, specially made for rental, the bell rang at every comma. He'd hammer away frantically under the transom from suppertime to midnight.

My mother came up for a moment after she'd done the dishes, she propped up her leg on a chair and put on compresses... She couldn't chat, it bothered my father... We were dying of the heat... The beginning of summer was torrid that year.

It was a bad time to be looking for a job... Business was quiet just before the slack season. We put out a few feelers... We made inquiries here and there... with some agents we knew... They had no prospects to offer. There wouldn't be much doing until after summer vacation... not even in the foreign shops.

In a way it was lucky I had nothing to do, because I hadn't any clothes... they'd definitely have to outfit me before I could start making my rounds... But it wasn't going to be easy... The main trouble was lack of money... I'd simply have to wait till September for the shoes and the overcoat... I was mighty glad of the reprieve... It gave me time to breathe before trotting out my English... There'd be hell to pay when they began to catch on... Well, it wouldn't be right away... I had only one shirt to my name... I wore one of my father's... They decided they'd order a jacket and two pair of pants all at once... But not until next month... At the moment it couldn't be done... There was barely enough for grub and even that was touch and go... The rent came due on the eighth and they were behind with the gas... Not to mention taxes and Papa's typewriter... We were really in the soup... There were writs all over the place... all over the furniture, violet ones, red ones, and blue ones...

So I had a little respite. I couldn't go calling on prospective bosses in a threadbare suit, patched, frayed, with the sleeves only halfway down my arm... It was out of the question! Especially in novelties and haberdashery, where they all dress up like fashion plates.

My father was so preoccupied with his typing exercises and his dread of being fired from Coccinelle that even at supper he was deep in thought. He'd lost interest in me. He'd made up his mind about me once and for all... the idea was firmly anchored in his dome that I was villainy incarnate... a hopeless blockhead... and that was that... that I had no part in the worries, the anxieties of noble individuals... I wasn't the kind that would carry my suffering around with me in my flesh like a knife... And keep turning it as long as I lived... Far from it... And jerk the handle... And stick it in deeper! To heighten the pain... And bellow and broadcast every new step forward in my suffering! Of course not. And turn into a fakir in the Passage! Side by side with them! Sure, something miraculous, something people could worship! Something more and more perfect! That's it. A thousand times more anxious, more harassed, more miserable!... The saint engendered by hard work and family thrift... Sure, why not? More muddleheaded... Sure... A hundred times thriftier! Glory be! Something that had never been seen in the Passage or anywhere else... In the whole world... Christ! The child marvel... the marvel of all France... the wonder of wonders! But nothing like that could be expected of me... I had a depraved nature... It was inexplicable... There wasn't a speck or straw of honor in me... I was rotten through and through... repulsive, degenerate! I was unfeeling. I had no future... I was as dry as a salt herring... I was a hard-hearted debauchee... a dungheap... full of sullen rancor... I was life's disillusionment... I was grief itself. And I ate my lunch and supper there, not to mention my morning coffee... They did their Duty! I was their cross on earth!... I'd never have a conscience!... I was nothing but a bundle of debased instincts and a hollow that devoured my family's sorry pittance and all their sacrifices. In a way I was a vampire... It was no use thinking about it...

In the Passage des Bérésinas, in all the shopwindows, a lot of changes had taken place while I was gone... They were going in for the "modern style" with lilac and orange tints... Convolvulus and iris were all the rage... They climbed up the windows... done up into carved molding... Two perfume stores and a gramophone shop opened... There were still the same pictures outside our theater, the Plush Barn... the same posters in the stage entrance... They were still playing *Miss Helyett* and still with the same tenor—Pitaluga... He had a heavenly voice; every Sunday he bowled over his female admirers in the *Elevation* at Notre-Dame-des- Victoires... For twelve months every shop in the Passage was talking about the way this Pitaluga sang "Minuit Chrétien" at Saint-Eustache on Christmas... Every year he was more swooning, more wonderful, more supernatural...

There was talk of installing electricity in all the shops in the Passage. Then they'd get rid of the gas that started whistling at four o'clock in the afternoon from three hundred and twenty jets… it stank so bad in that confined space (added to the urine from the dogs, which were getting to be more and more plentiful) that along about seven o'clock some of the lady customers began to feel faint. There was even talk of tearing us down completely, of dismantling the whole gallery! Of removing our big glass roof and building a street eighty feet wide right where we were living… My oh my! But the rumors weren't very serious, actually it was poppycock, prison gossip. We were prisoners in a glass cage and prisoners we'd always be... Forever and regardless... No getting around it... The law of the jungle...

Once in a while the poor bastards got crazy ideas... fantastic fairy tales passed from mouth to mouth as they were standing outside their shops, especially in hot weather... Like bubbles oozing out of their brains... before the September storms. They'd dreamed up harebrained schemes, monumental rackets, all they could think of was big deals, wild swindles... Nightmares... they saw themselves expropriated, persecuted by the State! They worked themselves up, they went completely off their rockers, they were absolutely crackers, maddened with hokum. Ordinarily so pale, they went crimson...

Before going to bed, they'd pass around fantastic estimates, wild memoranda showing the staggering, but absolutely indispensable sums they'd demand if anybody mentioned moving. My oh my! By God, the authorities were in for a little trouble if they tried to turn them out... The Council of State didn't know what resistance meant! Don't you worry! And the chancellery and the whole damn government!... They'd shit in their pants. They'd see who they were talking to! Oh ho! And the Hall of Writs and Records... The whole rotten gang and then some! By my grandmother's crabs! The sparks would fly... It wasn't going to be any pushover, hell, no... Over their dead bodies... they'd lock themselves up in their rooms! In the end they'd have to disembowel the whole Bank of France to build them new shops... exactly the same! to the milligram! to two decimals! That's what we're asking, or the deal is off! We won't budge! Now you know the score! That's our last word!... Well, in a pinch they'd accept a settlement... A big one... They wouldn't say no... They might agree... But it's got to be on the level... An income for life! A nice juicy one, guaranteed to the hilt by the Bank of France, to be spent any way they pleased! They'd go fishing! For ninety years if they felt like it! And nightclubs day and night! And that wouldn't be the end of it! They'd have royalties and claims and country houses and other indemnities besides... astronomical... incalculable!

Well then? It was all a question of guts! The whole thing was perfectly simple, no use arguing... Stand up for your rights, don't weaken... That was their point of view... It was the heat, the terrible atmosphere, the electricity in the air... That way at least they weren't shouting at each other... They all got together on their "claims"... Everybody was in agreement... They were all hypnotized on the future... Everybody was hoping to be evicted.

All the neighbors in the Passage were flabbergasted at the dimensions I had assumed... I was getting to be a big bruiser. I'd almost doubled in bulk... That would cost even more when we went to the Deserving Classes for my outfit... I tried on my father's clothes They burst at the shoulders, I couldn't even get into his pants. I needed everything new. I'd just have to wait...

On her way home from her errands Madame Béruse, the glovemaker, dropped in just to see how [looked: "His mother can be proud of him," she finally concluded. "His stay abroad has done him good." She repeated that wherever she went. The others came in too to form an opinion of their own. The old caretaker of the Passage, Gaston the hunchback, who picked up all the gossip, found me changed, but in his opinion I was thinner. They couldn't really agree, everybody had his own idea. In addition, they wanted to know all about England. They asked me for details about how the Engleesh lived over there... I spent all my time in the shop, waiting for them to clothe me. Visios, the sailor, the one with the pipes, Charonne, the gilder, Madame Isard from the dry-cleaning shop, they all wanted to know what we ate at my school in Rochester. Especially about the vegetables. Was it really true they ate them raw, or hardly cooked? And the beer and the water? If I'd had whiskey? If the women had big teeth... kind of like horses? And what about their feet? A lot of applesauce. And their tits? Did they have any? All this with a lot of snide remarks and scandalized looks.

But what they really wanted was for me to say something in English. They were just dying to hear me, they didn't care if they understood or not... the effect was what they wanted... to hear me talk a little... My mother didn't make too much of a fuss, but all the same it would have made her mighty proud to have me display my talents... put all those busybodies in their place...

All I knew was: *"River... water... no trouble... no fear"* and maybe two or three more things... It really didn't amount to much. Anyway I didn't feel like it... I wasn't in the mood... It made my mother miserable to see I was just as stubborn as ever. I wasn't worthy of all their sacrifices. The neighbors were vexed too, they began to make long faces, they thought I was acting like a pigheaded mule... "He hasn't changed a bit," said Gaston, the hunchback. "He'll never change... he's still the same as when he used to piss on my gates... I could never make him stop."

He'd never been able to stomach me... "It's lucky his father isn't here," my mother consoled herself. "He'd feel so badly. He'd be beside himself, poor man... to see you so ungracious... so boorish... so antagonistic... so unfriendly... so horrid to everybody!... How do you expect to get ahead? Especially nowadays, the way things are in business... with all the competition? You think you're the only one that's looking for a job? Only yesterday he was saying: 'Good Lord, if only he lands on his feet! We're on the brink of disaster...'"

Just then Uncle Édouard turned up... he saved my life... He was in high good humor... He gave everybody in general a good hearty greeting... He'd just put on his beautiful checked suit for the first time, the new summer style, from England as a matter of fact, with a mauve derby, the latest thing, fastened to his buttonhole with a thin ribbon. He seized both my hands, he shook them heartily, a real knockdown, drag-out *"shake-hands."* He was wild about England... He'd always wanted to take a little trip over there... He kept putting it off because he wanted to learn the names for the things in his business first... pump, and so on. He was counting on me to teach him the language... My mother was still sniveling about my attitude, my repulsive, hostile ways... Far from siding with her he took my part right away... In two words he told all those insignificant cockroaches that they were dense, that they didn't know a thing about foreign influences... especially England... When you come from over there, it changes you completely! It makes you more laconic, more reserved, it gives you a certain aloofness, in a word, distinction.

And it's a good thing... Why, of course! In high-class business nowadays... especially when you're selling... the main thing is to hold your tongue... It's a sign of breeding... that's what counts in a salesman today... That's right... The old style is dead, through, washed up... your slobbering... obsequious... voluble salesman.... People are sick of them... That's all right for punks out in the sticks, for small-town jokers... In Paris you can't get away with it... If you try that stuff in the Sender quarter, they'll throw you out... It makes a crawling, servile impression... Got to keep up with the times... According to him I was dead right... That was the line he gave them...

His patter was a great comfort to my mother... it set her mind at rest... she heaved big sighs... she was really relieved... But the rest of them, the lousy stool pigeons, were still hostile... They had their ideas... and nobody could make them change their mind... They griped in accompaniment... I'd never get ahead with those kind of manners. It was out of the question.

Uncle Édouard did his best, he racked his brains and talked himself blue in the face... They stuck to their guns... They were stubborner than mules, they kept repeating that anywhere in the world... if you want to earn an honest living, you've got to be friendly and courteous... that's the first requirement.

Days and days passed and we hardly saw any more customers. It was midsummer and they'd all gone to the country. My mother finally decided that in spite of her bad leg and the doctor's orders, she'd go out to Chatou and try to sell a little something. I'd keep the shop while she was gone. We had no other alternative... we had to bring in some money. First to buy me a new suit and two pairs of shoes, and then to paint our whole shop front in attractive colors before the new season started.

Our windows looked heartbreaking beside the others... They were pearl-gray and greenish, while next door there was Vertune's dry-cleaning shop, all brand-new, a fancy yellow and sky- blue, and on the other side the Gomeuse stationery store, an immaculate white, decorated with scrolls and jiggers and a sweet little pattern of little birds on branches... All that meant a big outlay... And we'd have to do it.

She didn't say a word to my father, she just took the train with an enormous bundle weighing at least forty-five pounds.

Out in Chatou she got started right away... She scrounged a stand from behind the Town Hall and set herself up behind the station, a good location. She handed out all her cards to let people know about the shop. In the afternoon she began traipsing around again, loaded like a mule, all over town, looking for villas where some customers might be hiding... When she came home to the Passage in the evening, she was so done in she could hardly stand up, her leg was so tied up with cramps she could have screamed, her knee was swollen, and the worst of all was her dislocated ankle... She stretched out in my room while waiting for my father to come home... She put on soothing lotion... good cold compresses.

On her suburban tours she sold her stuff any old place dirt-cheap, so as to bring in a little cash... We needed it so bad... "So as not to haul it back home," she explained... Only two or three people came to the shop all the time she was gone... So it made more sense to close up completely... that way I could go with her to the suburbs and tote her biggest bundles. We didn't have Madame Divonne anymore to hold the shop down when we were absent. We hung out a sign saying: "Returning immediately." We took the door handle with us.

Uncle Édouard really loved his sister, no fooling, it got him down to see her so miserable, wasting away, getting more and more run-down from all her work and troubles... He was worried about her health and her morale... He thought of her all the time. The day after a trip to Chatou she couldn't stand up, her face was ravaged with the pain in her leg. She whined like a dog and lay all twisted on the linoleum... She'd flop on the floor as soon as my father went out. She said it was cooler than the bed. If he caught her like that when he came home from the office, wan and disheveled, massaging her leg in the dish-pan, her skirts hiked up to her chin, he beat it upstairs, he pretended he hadn't seen her, he raced past, he was gone in a flash. He'd plunge into his typewriting or his water-colors... We always sold a few, especially his "Sailboats," we had a whole collection of them, and the "Councils of Cardinals"... They had the liveliest colors... Really striking... Those things always look good in a room. And it was high time he got a wiggle on... It was coming on the end of the month... To make up for closing in the daytime during our wanderings through Chatou, we stayed open pretty late... People would go for a stroll after dinner... Especially if a storm came up... If a customer came in, my mother, quick as lightning, hid the basin and all her wads of cotton under the couch in the middle of the room... She'd pull herself up with a smile... She'd start her spiel... Around her neck, I remember well, she'd tie a big muslin cabbage-bow... They were all the rage at the time... It made her head look very big.

Uncle Édouard worked like a dog too, in his own way, but he had nothing to be sorry about, he got results... He was doing better and better in his line... bicycle accessories... That was getting to be a good business, very good in fact. Soon he was able to buy a share in a garage, on the edge of Levallois, with some reliable friends.

He was enterprising by nature and besides he was crazy about inventions... any kind of mechanical idea... Those things really sent him... Right away he'd invested the four thousand francs of his inheritance in a patent for a bicycle pump, the latest thing, it folded up so small you could keep it in your pocket... He always had two or three of them on him, ready to demonstrate. He'd blow them up people's noses . . He pretty near lost his four thousand francs. The sellers were crooks... He managed to wriggle out of it thanks to his quick wits and a telephone call... a conversation he'd overheard at the last minute... An amazing stroke of luck!... In another minute he'd have been cooked...

My mother admired my uncle. She wanted me to be like him... After all I needed a model... For want of my father, my uncle was somebody to look up to... She didn't say it straight out, but she dropped hints... In my father's opinion Édouard was a hell of an example, he was idiotic, absolutely unbearable, grasping, vulgar, always getting a kick out of something nonsensical... He got on my father's nerves... with his mechanical gadgets, his jalopies, his three-wheelers, his funny-looking pumps! Just hearing him talk irritated the hell out of him.

When my mother took it into her head to sing her brother's praises, to tell everybody about his plans, his success, his bright ideas, he'd always interrupt her... He wouldn't stand for it. Certainly not. He'd made up his mind once and for all... He put it all down to luck... "He's disgustingly lucky and that's all there is to it..." That was my father's verdict. He never went any further. He couldn't run him down anymore, we still owed him money and gratitude... But he had to hold himself in to keep from giving him a piece of his mind... Édouard must have known... It was perfectly obvious... He put up with my father's dislike, he didn't want to make trouble, he was always thinking of his sister.

He was very tactful, he just dropped in for a minute to see how we were getting along... wasn't Mama feeling a little better? He was alarmed about the way she looked and the monumental loads she peddled around... Afterwards her joints were so stiff she'd moan for days on end... It worried him more and more... She was getting worse... He finally decided to speak to my father... The three of them talked it over, and finally they agreed it was high time she took a rest... that this couldn't go on... But how could she rest? They hit on a plan... we'd take on a cleaning woman, maybe two three hours a day, even that would be a relief... She wouldn't have to climb stairs nearly so much... She wouldn't have to sweep under the furniture... she wouldn't need to go shopping... But how in our present circumstances could we spend all that money?... The whole thing was a pipe dream, sheer lunacy... It would be feasible only if I found work... Then, with my earnings, which would go into the till after all, maybe, once we'd paid the rent, we could think about a maid... That would make it easier for Mama... She wouldn't have to work so hard or run around so much... They'd thought this out all by themselves... They were delighted with their decision... They'd appeal to my better nature... they'd put me to the test. I wasn't going to be a perverse, self-centered screwball anymore... Now I too would have my role, my aim in life! To make things easier for my mama!... On the double, boy... Get in there and fight... find yourself a job! That's the ticket! As soon as they'd bought me my job-hunting suit... pronto, roll up your sleeves... do your stuff! No more mistakes! No more shilly-shallying! Down to business and no more questions! Show your mettle! Your perseverance! By God, I would! What a marvelous goal in life! It was already in the bag, I thought...

First I needed shoes. We went to the Prince Consort again... The Broomfields after all were a little too expensive... especially for two pairs with buttons... And yet, once you begin moving around, what you really need is three or four pairs.

For the suit and pants I had measurements taken at the Deserving Classes, near Les Halles, that was a gilt-edge firm, with a reputation going back a hundred years, especially for all sorts of cheviots and even for "dressy" goods, stuff that lasted practically forever... "Working-man's outfits" they called them... Only the price was steep. A terrible sacrifice!

It was still August, I was being outfitted for the winter... The warm weather doesn't last long... But at that particular moment the heat was stifling... Oh well, it wouldn't be long, I'd live through it... The cold, the bad weather, goes on and on... In the meantime, while I was looking around, suppose I suffocated to death... hell, I'd simply carry my coat over my arm. I'd put it on as I was ringing the bell... it was simple...

My mother hadn't said how much it would take out of our household funds to outfit me... from top to toe... Considering our resources, it was a staggering sum... We scraped the bottom of the drawers... She ran herself ragged, she racked her brains, she'd dash out to Le Vésinet and come back by the next train, hightail it to Neuilly, to Chatou on market days, hauling her whole stock, everything that wasn't too repulsive... that was more or less negotiable... She couldn't sell it... She couldn't make up the amount... It was a real headache... we were always twenty or twenty-five or thirty-five francs short... On top of the taxes that kept raining down on us and the seamstress's wages and the rent that was two months overdue... An avalanche, it was sickening... She didn't say a word to Papa... She kept looking for some new dodge... She took five of his best water-colors to the rue d'Aboukir, to old Madame Heurgon Gustave (a real filthy junk shop), for less than a quarter of the usual price. On consignment, so to speak... In short, she tried dozens of crummy expedients to scrape up the full amount... She wouldn't buy anything on credit... After desperate weeks and all sorts of plots and stratagems I was finally dressed, absolutely resplendent, good strong material, but very hot... When I saw myself dolled up brand- new, I lost some of my confidence! Hell! It made me feel funny. I still had the will, but nasty doubts began to crop up... Maybe I'd perspire too much in my winter suit? I was like a walking oven...

It was God's truth that I didn't feel the least bit pleased with myself anymore, or optimistic about the future... The immediate prospect of facing bosses... of reeling off my cock-and-bull stories, of shutting myself up in their rotten morgues, gave me a pain in the gizzard. Over in lousy England I'd got out of the habit of being shut in... I'd have to get used to it again. It was no joke... It knocked me for a loop just to look at a possible boss! It made me gag... Just figuring out how to get to places gave me the creeps... It was so hot the nameplates on the doors were melting... It was 102 in the shade.

Of course what my folks were saying was perfectly reasonable... that I was at the critical age, the turning point... this was the time to make a supreme effort... to force the gates of destiny... to start a career... it was now or never... All that was fine and dandy... But even if I took off my suit, my collar, my shoes, I couldn't stop sweating... The sweat ran down in streams... I took the itineraries I knew. I passed outside the Gorloge's place... It gave me the shivers to see their house and the big carriage door... Just thinking about that incident gave me a twinge in the asshole... Holy shit! Some sweet memory!

Faced with the enormity of my task... thinking it over, I lost heart, I just wanted to sit down... I hadn't much money to spend on bocks... even little glasses for ten centimes... I hung around in doorways... There was always plenty of shade and treacherous drafts... I sneezed something terrible... It got to be a habit while I was thinking... I kept thinking... I thought so much that in the end I almost agreed with my father... I realized... experience proved it... that I was worthless... I had disastrous impulses... I was completely thickheaded and lazy... I didn't deserve their great kindness... their terrible sacrifices... I felt absolutely unworthy, infectious, loathsome... I knew what I had to do and I struggled desperately, but I wasn't up to it... less than ever... I wasn't improving with age... And I was getting thirstier and thirstier... The heat in itself is a calamity... Looking for a job in August is the most thirsty-making thing in the world, on account of the stairs and the terror that parches your throat every time... while you're cooling your heels... I thought of my mother... of her leg and the cleaning woman we might be able to take on if I could get somebody to hire me... It didn't revive my enthusiasm... I lashed myself, I screwed up all my strength to rise to the ideal, I couldn't feel sublime anymore. Since Gorloge I had lost all my enthusiasm about work. It was pitiful! And in spite of all the sermons I'd had, I felt that I was more miserable than all the other bastards, more woebegone than the whole lot of them together... What disgusting egotism! All I cared about was my own troubles, and there they were, all of them horrible, they made me stink worse than a senile camembert... I was rotting in the heat, collapsing with sweat and shame, climbing stairs, oozing over the bells, I was falling apart, I'd lost all dignity, all character.

With nothing on my mind but a slight bellyache, I drifted through the old streets, rue du Paradis, rue d'Hautcville, rue des Jeûneurs, the Sentier quarter... in the end I took off not only my heavy jacket but also my extra-solid celluloid collar, it would have killed a dog, and besides it gave me pimples. I got dressed again on the landing. I looked up more addresses, I found them in the directory. At the post office I drew up lists. I hadn't any money left for a drink. My mother left her purse, the little silver one, knocking around on the furniture... I eyed it avidly... Such heat is demoralizing... Frankly, I came damn near swiping it... At a certain point... two steps from the fountain... I'd get mighty thirsty... I think my mother noticed, she gave me two francs more...

When I came back from my long wanderings, always futile and useless, up and down stairs and neighborhoods, I had to fix myself up before going back into the Passage, so I wouldn't look too miserable, too crestfallen at meals. That wouldn't have gone down at all. That was one thing my folks couldn't have taken, that they'd never been able to stomach, that they'd never understand, that I, their son, should be without hope and heroic fortitude... They wouldn't have stood for it... I had no right to my share of lamentations, certainly not... Tragedies and condolences were their private preserve... All that was for my parents... Children were thugs, hoodlums, ungrateful, thoughtless scum... The minute I dropped the slightest complaint, even the wee little beginning of a complaint, they both saw red... That was anathema! Sacrilege! Abomination!

"What's that, you little shitheel? What colossal nerve!" How, with youth on my side, could I put on such airs? What a beastly imposture! What diabolical impertinence! Ah! The effrontery of it! Heavens above! Didn't I have my best years ahead of me! All the treasures of existence! And I thought I was entitled to gripe... About my piddling little setbacks? Ah! Jumping Jehoshaphat! What monstrous insolence! What absolute degeneracy! What inconceivable rottenness! They'd have beaten me to a pulp to make me eat my blasphemies. Her bad leg, her abscesses, her horrible sufferings were forgotten... My mother leapt to her feet! "You little wretch! Right this minute! You heartless little reprobate! Take back those insults..."

I did as I was told. I couldn't exactly make out what the joys of youth were, but they seemed to know... They would have massacred me without hesitation if I hadn't recanted... If I expressed the slightest doubt or seemed to be running things down, they went right off the handle... They'd rather have seen me dead than hear me profane the gifts of heaven. My mother's eyes went white with fury when I let myself be carried away! She'd have bashed me in the nose with anything that was handy just to make me stop... My only right was to rejoice! to sing hymns of praise! I was born under a lucky star! Imagine a miserable worm like me having parents who dedicated themselves exclusively...

wasn't that enough?... to the worries, the troubles, the tragic fatalities of existence... I was just a brute and nothing else! Silence! An unconscionable family burden!... My business was to do as I was told... to fix everything up sweet and nice again! To make amends for my faults and nauseating propensities!... The misery was all for them! if there was any complaining to do, that was their department! They were the ones who understood life! They were the ones with sensitive souls! Who was it that suffered atrociously? Under the most excruciating circumstances? From outrageous fortune?... It was they. They alone, always and forever. They didn't want me meddling, even going through the motions of helping them... taking my small share... It was their absolute monopoly! That struck me as very unjust. We just couldn't see eye to eye.

They could talk and curse till they were blue in the face, I stuck to my convictions. I too felt myself to be a victim in every way. On the steps of the Ambigu, right near the Wallace fountain,[104] all these thoughts came back at me... It was all as plain as day!...

If I'd finished pounding the sidewalks, another day wasted, I frankly aired my dogs... I smoked skinny little butts... I'd question the boys a little, the bums that hung around there, they always had plenty of dope and phony tips... They were big talkers... They'd seen all the ads, they knew about all the odd jobs... One of them was a tattooer, he clipped dogs on the side... They knew all the crummy rackets... the food market, the slaughterhouse, the wine market... They were as grimy as a railroad station, down at heel, crawling with dirt, they passed their crabs back and forth... That didn't cramp their cock-and-bull stories... their bragging and bluffing... they'd split a gut telling about their connections... their triumphs, their fancy deals... One big delirious fantasy!... There was no limit to the dog they put on... and they were perfectly capable of pulling a knife... if anybody doubted they had a cousin in the Cabinet... or of chucking him in the Canal Saint-Martin... No claim was too wild... Even the cock-eyedest sandwichmen... had certain pet episodes in their lives that it wasn't healthy to laugh at... Fairy tales drive people to crime even worse than liquor... they were so moth-eaten they had no teeth left to chew with, they'd sold their glasses... That didn't prevent them from dishing out a line... You can't imagine such hokum... I could gradually see myself getting to be exactly like them...

It was about five in the afternoon when I suspended my efforts... called it a day... It was a good place to convalesce in, a regular resort... We'd give our feet a good rest... Ambigu Beach, catering to bums and down-and-outers. Some of them weren't so lazy, but they figured it was better to drink up their luck than drag around in the heat. Which is easy enough to understand... All along the theater front, under the chestnut trees, there was a fence... handy to hang your stuff on... we took it nice and easy... we exchanged mugs of beer... There was white sausage "à la mode" and garlic and red wine and Camembert... on the ramp and the stairs it was like an academy... All kinds... They hadn't changed much... since the days when I went out peddling for Gorloge... There were lots of little pimps, and dicks with plenty of time on their hands... stool pigeons of all ages... who made good money tipping off the cops... There'd always be a card game going on... And two or three bookies, trying to drum up trade... There were overage salesmen who'd turned in their sample cases... nobody was willing to hire them anymore... There were little fairies still too green for the Bois... One of them came around every day, his specialty was the urinals and especially the crusts of bread soaking in the drains... He told us his adventures... He knew an old Jew who was nuts about those babas... They'd go and eat the stuff together... One day they got caught... We didn't see him for a couple of months... He was changed beyond recognition when he got back... The cops had given him such a going-over he was fresh out of the hospital... That shellacking had turned him inside out... He'd moulted in the meanwhile... He had a big bass voice... He'd let his beard grow... He'd given up eating shit.

Another of the charms of the place was the procuress. She had a kid in long red stockings... she'd walk her up and down outside the Folies Dramatiques... They said she cost twenty francs... She'd have suited me fine... That was a fortune at the time... They didn't even look in our direction... we were too crummy... We whooped at them, but it didn't get us anywhere...

---

[104] Wallace fountain. After Sir Richard Wallace (1818-1890), an English philanthropist who in 1872 donated one hundred drinking fountains to the city of Paris.

We exchanged newspapers and the jokes we'd picked up on our rounds... The bad part of it was the crabs... Naturally I caught them too... Those cooties out in front of the Ambigu were a pestilence... The worst of all were the butt pickers that hung around the terraces of the cafés... A whole bunch of them would drop over to the Saint-Louis hospital for ointment... Then they'd go off together and rub it in...

I can still see my straw hat, the reinforced boater, I always had it in my hand, it must have weighed a good two pounds... It was supposed to last me two years, if possible three... I wore it till I was drafted, which was in 1912. I took my collar off one more time, it had left a terrible mark, completely scarlet... All men had that red furrow around their necks in those days, they kept it until their dying day. It was like a magic sign.

When we'd finished commenting on the ads, all those crazy come-ons, we'd start on the sports column, the try-outs at the Buffalo Stadium and the forthcoming six-day bicycle race, with Morin and pretty-boy Faber, who was the favorite... Those who preferred the horse races set up on the opposite corner... The little streetwalkers moseyed back and forth... They weren't interested in us, they went on walking... We weren't good for anything but talk, a bunch of no- soap artists...

The very first motor buses, the marvelous Madeleine-Bastille with the high top-deck, gave it the works at that point... set off all their explosives to make it up the hill... It was some show, an uproar! They dashed boiling water against the Porte Saint-Martin. The passengers on the balcony took part in the performance... They were nuts. They could have capsized the whole thing the way they all leaned over on the same side at once in their ecstatic excitement... They clutched the tassels, the bars and knobs that ran around the railing... They shouted and cheered... Horses were a thing of the past, it was plain as day... It was only on bad roads that they still had a chance... Uncle Édouard had always said so... well, in front of the Ambigu, between five and seven, I witnessed the coming of Progress... but I still didn't find a job... Every night I came home empty-handed... I couldn't seem to find the boss who'd give me a new start in life... They wouldn't take me as an apprentice, I was too old... And to be a- regular employee I was apparently much too young... I'd never get past the ungrateful age... And even if I talked English beautifully, it made no difference... They had no use for it... Foreign languages were only for the big shops... And there they didn't take beginners... I was out of luck all along the line... any way I went about it... it was always the same old shit...

Very gently, in small doses, I let my mother in on the ideas I'd been piling up... I told her my prospects didn't look too brilliant... She wasn't one to be discouraged... She'd begun to make other plans, this time for herself, something new, something more backbreaking than ever. She'd been thinking about it a long time and now she made up her mind... "You see, my boy, I won't tell your father, so keep this to yourself... The poor man, it would come as a terrible disappointment... He's suffering enough already to see me miserable... But between you and me, Ferdinand, I don't think our poor shop... sh-h... will ever pick up again... Hum, hum, I fear the worst. In our lace business... there's no denying it... the competition has become impossible to meet... Your father doesn't understand... He's not right in the thick of it, day in day out... luckily, thank God for that... What you need nowadays isn't a few hundred francs, but thousands and thousands, if you want to lay in a really up-to-date stock! Where can we find that kind of money? Who's going to give us credit, I ask you? It's only the big businesses that can afford it, the enormous stores... Our little shops are doomed... It's only a question of time... a few years... or months maybe... It's a desperate struggle for nothing... The big stores are crushing us... I've seen it coming for a long time... Even in Caroline's day things were getting harder and harder... it's nothing new... The slack season went on forever... longer each year... worse and worse... Well, my boy. one thing I've got is energy... you know that... We've got to get out of this mess!... Now here's what I'm going to try as soon as my leg is better... if I could even go out a little. I'm going to one of the big firms and ask for a card... I won't have any trouble... They've known me for years... They know I'm a go-getter... they know I've got plenty of gumption... They know your father and I are the soul of honesty... that they can trust us with anything... no matter what . . Yes, I don't mind saying it... Marescal!... Bataille!... Roubique!... they've known me for thirty years... as a saleswoman and shopkeeper... I won't have any trouble finding something... I don't need any other references... I don't like working for other people... But at present I have no choice... Your father won't suspect... not a thing... I'll tell him I'm going to see a customer... He won't be any the wiser...

I'll go out as usual and I'll always be back on time... Poor man, he'd hang his head for shame to think I was working for somebody else... He'd be humiliated... I want to spare him that... at all costs... He'd never get over it!... I wouldn't know how to buck him up... His wife working for strangers!... Good lord! Even with Caroline it was almost more than he could bear... Anyway, he won't know a thing!... I'll make my rounds regularly... One day one street, the next day another... It'll be a good deal simpler than this eternal balancing act... this acrobatics that's killing us... Always batting our brains out... figuring out how to stop up holes... It's infernal! It would be the end of us! We won't have nearly as much worry... Pay here! Pay there! Will we make it? How awful! It's torture... We won't make much, but it'll be regular... no more surprises, no more nightmares! That's what we've always needed... A steady income! It'll be a change from the last twenty years! What a rat race! Heavens above! Always running after five francs!... And the customers that never pay! You've hardly paid one bill when another one comes in... Oh yes, independence is all very fine! It was my dream, my mother's too! But I can't go on... We'll make ends meet, you'll see, if we all put our shoulders to the wheel... We'll have our cleaning woman! since that's what he wants... Besides, I need one. You couldn't call it a luxury."

That was just what my mother wanted... some horrible new thing to do... something inconceivably difficult... Nothing could be too hard, too grueling! If she'd had her own way she'd have done everybody's work. Run the shop... kept the whole family going all by herself... and the seamstress too.... She never tried to draw comparisons, to understand... As long as it was lousy work, as long as there was plenty of sweat and heartache, she was satisfied... That was her nature... Whether I ran myself ragged or not, it wouldn't make a particle of difference... With a maid I was positive she'd work fifty times harder... She was really attached to her horrible fate... It wasn't the same with me... I had a little worm in my conscience. But next to her I was a parasite... Maybe that came from my stay in Rochester, from doing nothing at the Merrywins... I'd got to be frankly lazy. Instead of chasing after work I'd just sit and think... When you come right down to it, my job hunting was pretty feeble... But when I saw a doorbell, I'd fold... I had no martyr's blood in my veins... Hell no! I didn't have the right attitude for a poor bastard... I kept putting things off till next day... I'd try a different neighborhood, not quite so hot, a little breezier... a little shadier... for my little bit of job hunting. I took a gander at the shops around the Tuileries... under those beautiful arcades... on the broad avenues... I thought I'd ask the jewelers if they could use a young man... I was baking in my jacket... They didn't need anybody... In the end I stayed in the Tuileries... I'd pass the time of day with the floozies that were wandering around... I spent hours in the greenery... not doing a damn thing, just like in England, except I'd have a cup of water now and then and work the waffle machines, the little dials on cylinders... There was also the fellow with the cocoanut drink and the mechanical band by the hobbyhorses...

That was all a long time ago... One evening I caught sight of my father... He was on the other side of the fence on his way to make his deliveries... To play it safe I stayed in the Carrousel... I hid between the statues... Once I went into the Louvre... It was free at the time… I didn't dig the pictures, but up on the fourth floor I discovered the Navy Museum. I couldn't drag myself away. I went regularly. I spent whole weeks there... I knew all the ship models by heart... I stood all alone by the showcases... I forgot all my troubles, all about jobs and bosses, the whole mess... There was nothing in my head but boats... Sailboats, even models of sailboats, send me frankly off my rocker... I'd have really liked to be a sailor... Papa too in his time... Our lives hadn't panned out right... I had a pretty fair idea of what was what...

When I came home at suppertime, he asked me what I'd been doing... why I was so late... Job hunting, I said... Mama had resigned herself. Papa grunted into his plate... He didn't press the subject.

They'd told my mother she could try her luck right away at the market in Le Pecq or even Saint-Germain, that now was just the time because of all the rich people... it was the new style … who were renting villas all over the hillside... They'd be sure to appreciate her lace for their bedroom curtains, their bedspreads, and those pretty little blinds... A golden opportunity...

She hightailed it out there quick. For a whole week she traipsed up and down all the roads with her whole caboodle... From Chatou station almost as far as Meulan... always on foot and limping... Luckily the weather was marvelous! Rain would have been a disaster. She was delighted, she'd sold a good part of her white elephants, fringed point-lace and heavy Spanish shawls that had been in drydock since the Empire. The people in the villas were developing a taste for our genuine curios. They were in a hurry to furnish their houses... They kind of lost their heads... The view of Paris from the hillside made them optimistic, enthusiastic... My mother pushed hard, she followed up on her luck. Except one fine morning her leg wouldn't move at all... That was the end of her foolishness, of her heroic treks... Even the other knee was on fire... It swelled up double...

Capron came running... All he could do was take note of her condition... He threw up his arms to high heaven... An abscess was forming, there was no room for doubt... The joint was affected, it was swollen... Her fighting spirit was no use at all... She couldn't move her rear end, she couldn't change sides or lift herself, not even an eighth of an inch... She let out piercing screams... She sighed the whole time, not so much from the pain, she was as tough as Caroline, but because her ailment had got her down.

It was a terrible defeat.

Naturally we had to take on a cleaning woman... Our habits changed... Everything was at loose ends... Mama lay on her bed, my father and I did most of the work before we left in the morning, the sweeping, the carpets, the sidewalk outside our door, the shop... All of a sudden my dawdling, my hesitation, my squirming were over... I had to get a wiggle on, to find some work in a hurry and p.d.q.

Hortense, the cleaning woman, came in for an hour in the afternoon and for two hours after supper. She worked all day in a grocery store on the rue Vivienne next to the post office. She was a reliable soul... She made a little extra working for us... She was down on her luck, she had to sweat double, her husband had lost all their money trying to set himself up as a plumber. Besides she had two kids and an aunt dependent on her... She couldn't ever sit down... My mother was riveted to her bed and had to listen to her whole story. One morning my father and I carried her down. We put her in a chair. We had to be very careful not to bump her on the stairs or drop her. We set her up in a corner of the shop, wedged in with cushions... so she could answer the customers... It was rough... And having to attend to her knee... and put on "vulnerary" compresses...

As for looks, Hortense, even though she worked like an ox, was pretty crunchy... She herself always said that she denied herself nothing, especially in the way of food, her trouble was sleep! She had no time to go to bed... It was eating that kept her going, especially café au lait... She'd take at least ten cups a day... In her grocery store she ate enough for an army. Hortense was a card, her stories even made my mother laugh on her bed of pain... It made my father mad to find me in the same room with her... He was afraid I'd lay her... It's true that I jerked off on account of her... who doesn't?... but it really didn't amount to much, nothing like England... I didn't put the same frenzy into it, the flavor was gone, we were really too miserable for me to do things right... Hell and damnation!... I wasn't in the mood anymore... It was awful to be on the rocks with the whole family... My head was pack-jammed full of worries… It was a worse headache finding me a job than before I went away... Seeing my mother's distress, I started out again... I went looking for more addresses... I did the Boulevards inside out, the Sen-tier quarter, the streets around the stock exchange... Around the end of August that's certainly the worst of neighborhoods... There's none stinkier, more stifling... I pounded the stairs again with my collar, my tie, my butterfly bow, my armored boater... I haven't forgotten a single nameplate… coming or going... Jimmy Blackwell and Careston, Exporters... Porogoff, Merchants... Tokima, Traders with Caracas and the Congo... Herito and Kugelprunn, commission merchants for India and the East Indies...

Once more I was knocked out, fed up, resolute. I ran my comb through my hair on my way into the building. I attacked the stairs. I rang at the first door and then at another... But all of a sudden everything went wrong when I had to answer questions... If they asked me for my references... or what kind of work I wanted to do... my actual aptitudes... my demands... That knocked the stuffings out of me... I stammered, I made bubbles... I panicked... I mumbled vague apologies and began to back out... The faces on those inquisitors scared me green... All of a sudden I had this queasy feeling... All the nerve trickled out of me. I was drained... I took my bellyache out of there... Even so, I started in again... I rang at the door across the way... It was always the same monsters... I'd do twenty like that before lunch... I even stopped going home to eat. I just had too much on my mind... My appetite was gone in advance... I was too fiendishly thirsty... For two cents I wouldn't have gone home at all. I knew by heart the scenes that were waiting for me. My mother and all her suffering. My father all tangled up in his typewriter, with his rages, his screwball ideas, his insane bellowing... A gloomy prospect... I knew the kind of compliments to expect... It caked my shit to think about it... I stayed out by the banks of the Seine, waiting for it to be two o'clock... I watched the dogs swimming... I didn't even have a system anymore... I just looked around at random... I searched the whole Left Bank... At the rue du Bac my Odyssey would start in again... rue Jacob, rue Tournon... I ran across businesses that were almost shut down... agencies for textile mills that had gone out of existence... in provinces that maybe France would recover some day... dealers in objects so dismal they left you speechless... Even so I put on the charm... I plugged for an interview at a shop that sold religious articles... I attempted the impossible... I put on a good show in a wholesale house for chasubles... It looked like they were going to hire me in a chandelier factory... I was out of my mind with joy... I was even beginning to like the stuff... And then everything collapsed! In the end the Saint-Sulpice quarter was a big disappointment to me... They were having their troubles too... Everybody turned me out...

From pounding all those pavements my tootsies were on fire... I took my shoes off wherever I could... I'd give them a quick dip in the toilet... I could slip out of my shoes in one second flat... That way I made the acquaintance of a waiter in a café whose dogs hurt him even worse than mine. He worked all day until past midnight on the enormous terrace of the German brasserie in the Cour de la Croix-Nivert... Sometimes his shoes hurt him so bad he stuck little pieces of ice inside... I tried it... It helps for a little while, but then it's even worse.

My mother stayed like that in the back of her shop with her leg stretched out for three weeks. There weren't many customers... That gave her one more reason to eat her heart out... She couldn't go out at all...

There were only the neighbors that came in now and then to bat the breeze and keep her company... They brought her all the gossip... They worked her up good... Especially in connection with me they dreamed up the stinkingest stuff... Those bastards couldn't stand to see me doing nothing. Why couldn't I find a job? they kept asking... It was inconceivable that I should be getting nowhere so fast after such efforts, such extraordinary sacrifices... It surpassed the understanding! It was a mystery! Seeing me on the rocks like that gave them a pain... Oh-ho, not on your tintype! They wouldn't be saps like my parents... They wouldn't make that mistake... They made that perfectly plain... You wouldn't catch them working their fingers to the bone... for kids that didn't give a shit... They wouldn't bleed themselves white for their brats... Hell, no! Where did it get you?... Especially teaching them languages! Christ almighty Jesus, some joke! It only turned them into tramps, that's all... it certainly didn't do any good... There's the living proof, one look at me was enough... A job? I'd never find one!... I didn't inspire confidence... I just didn't look right... They knew, they'd known me all my life... And that's a fact.

That song and dance crushed my mother completely, especially in the state she was in, with her painful abscess that was getting worse and worse... The whole side of her leg was swollen now... Usually she restrained herself a little from repeating all that rot... But with the excruciating pain she was in she couldn't control her reflexes... She repeated the whole business to my father, almost word for word... He hadn't had a tantrum in a long time... He jumped at the opportunity... He began to holler that I was skinning him alive and my mother too, that I was his shame and opprobrium, that everything was my fault! The worst disasters, past and future! That I was driving him to suicide... that I was an absolutely unprecedented type of murderer!... He didn't say why... He whistled, he blew out so much steam there was a cloud between us... He tore his hair... He dug his fingers into his scalp till he drew blood... He cracked his nails... He gesticulated so wildly that he banged into the furniture... He knocked the sideboard over... The shop was very small... There wasn't room enough for a lunatic... He bumped into the umbrella stand... He sent two vases crashing. My mother tried to pick them up and gave her leg a terrible twist... She let out a yell so piercing... so horrible... that the neighbors all came running.

She almost fainted... We gave her smelling salts... Little by little she came to... She began to breathe, she settled back on her chairs... "Ah!" she says. "It's burst." She meant her abscess... She was delighted, Visios came and squeezed the pus out. He was used to it. He'd done it often on shipboard.

I was very nicely dressed with my choker collar, my shoes polished fit to kill, but my mother, thinking it over in the room behind the shop, decided I still wasn't quite right... that I still didn't look serious enough in spite of my watch and my darkened chain... In spite of all their lectures there was still something of the hoodlum about me... The way I carried money, for instance, whole pockets full of change... That's what gave me my disreputable look... like a tough! A tout! Revolting!

She made up her mind on the spot... She sent Hortense to the Bazar Vivienne... for the ideal change purse... Good and solid, hand-stitched, with plenty of compartments, indestructible... In addition she made me a present of four fifty-centime pieces... But I wasn't to spend them… ever!... Those were my savings... to give me a taste for thrift! She put in my address too, in case of an accident in the street... It gave her pleasure. I raised no objection.

I quickly drank up the little nest egg in ten-centime bocks... The summer of 1910 was abominably hot... Luckily it was easy to wet your whistle around the Temple... It was cheap on the stands all along the street... whole sidewalks full of drinks... and the little bars in the street fairs...

I transferred my efforts to the jewel setters. That's a real trade after all and I knew something about it... I went back to the Marais... It was unbearable on the Boulevards... The people were packed like a parade in front of the Café du Nègre and the Porte Saint-Denis... Like being crowded into a furnace... With the loafers on the Square des Arts it was even worse... there was no use sitting down, the whole place was a dust bowl... just trying to breathe made you choke... All the peddlers from miles around collected there with their boxes and bundles... and the dumb kid that pushes their pushcarts... They all slumped down by the railing, waiting for it to be time to go up and face the boss... They were sad sacks... Business was so slow that summer they weren't selling anything at all... Even with ninety days' credit nobody wanted their stuff anywhere... They looked dazed... They were suffocating in the clouds of sand... They'd never get a single order before the fifteenth of October... That didn't encourage me very much… They could close their order books... Their misery paralyzed me...

I'd asked people right and left if they didn't know of a job, I'd pestered everybody, I'd looked at every name-plate in town, analyzed all the directories and telephone books. I went back to the rue Vieille-du-Temple... For at least a week I roamed along the Canal Saint-Martin, looking at the barges... the quiet movement of the locks... I went back to the rue Elzévir. I was so worried I woke up with a start in the middle of the night... I had an obsession that got stronger and stronger... It squeezed my head like a vise... I wanted to go back to Gorloge's... All of a sudden I felt a terrible pang of remorse, an irresistible sense of shame, a curse... I was getting ideas like a poor bastard, absolutely screwy... I wanted to go up to Gorloge's and frankly confess, accuse myself... in front of everybody... "It was I that stole..." I'd say... "It was I that took the beautiful pin! The pure-gold Sakya-Muni... It was I... Absolutely positively!" I worked myself up. Hell! Once I get it over with, I said to myself, my bad luck will leave me... I was under a spell... every fiber in my brain! The idea gave me such horrors I was always shivering... It got to be irresistible... Christ!... Well, in the end I actually went back to the house... in spite of the sizzling heat I had the cold shivers... I was in a panic! I catch sight of the concierge... She takes a good look at me, she recognizes me from far away... So I try to remember, to figure out why I'm guilty... I start for her den... First I'll tell her all about it!... Shit!... No, I can't do it... I've got the jitters... I about-face quick... I get out of there fast... I run down toward the Boulevards... what in hell's the matter with me?... I was acting like an ass! I was going nuts... all sorts of crazy crummy ideas... I stopped going home for lunch... I took bread and cheese with me... I was sleepy in the afternoon from sleeping so badly at night… Always being woken up by dreams... I had to keep walking the whole time or I'd fall asleep on a bench... I kept on batting my brains out... trying to figure out what I was guilty of. There must have been some reason... some damn good reason... I wasn't educated enough to puzzle it out... I covered so much ground I found another place to rest in the afternoon. At Notre-Dame- des-Victoires, by the little chapels on the left as you go in... you couldn't have found a cooler place... I felt cruelly persecuted by my stinking luck... You feel better in the dark... The flags are soothing on the feet... Nothing could be more refreshing... I'd stay there a long time... The candles are nice... like fragile bushes... the way they quiver in the deep velvet of the vaulting… They hypnotized me... Little by little they put me to sleep... I woke up to the sound of little bells. Naturally it never closes... It's the best place.

I kept finding excuses for coming home later and later... Once it was almost nine o'clock... I'd applied for a job way out in Antony... in a wallpaper factory. They were looking for salesmen in midtown... It was just the thing for my aptitudes... I went back two or three times... Their factory wasn't ready!... They hadn't finished building it... Anyway a lot of hooey!

I was scared shitless when I got back to the Passage. I'd spent all my carfare money on beer... So I walked more and more... It was a really unusual summer... It hadn't rained in two months!...

My father was twisting and turning like a tiger in front of his typewriter... In my bed right next door it was impossible to sleep, he cursed so much at the keyboard... At the beginning of September he developed a whole raft of boils, first on his arms, then on the back of his neck a really enormous one that turned into a carbuncle right away. In his case boils were really serious, they knocked him out completely... He went to the office anyway... But people looked at him in the street, all wound up in cotton. They turned around... He took quantities of brewer's yeast, but it didn't help...

My mother was terribly worried to see him all broken out like that... Her abscess was doing a little better, what with lying still and putting on compresses. It festered a good deal, but the swelling had gone down. It drained a little more... And then she got back on her feet, she wouldn't wait for the wound to heal, right away she got busy around the place, hobbling around the chairs and things... She tried to keep an eye on Hortense, she climbed the stairs, she wouldn't let us carry her anymore. She clutched the banister to climb the steps all by herself, she hoisted herself from one floor to the next while we were busy... She wanted to clean the house, to straighten out the shop, put the knickknacks where they belonged...

My father was so wrapped up in bandages he couldn't turn his head, he was suffocating in his boils, but that didn't prevent him from hearing my mother downstairs, bustling from room to room with her leg dragging behind her... That made him madder than anything else... He banged on his machine... He was in such a dither he scraped the skin off his fists. He yelled at her to watch what she was doing...

"Jumping Jesus, Clémence! You can hear me all right. Holy suffering catfish, will you lie down, godammit. You think we haven't trouble enough? Christ, what a stinking life!"

"Come, come, Auguste. Can't you leave me be... Let me attend to my business... Don't worry... I'm feeling fine."

She'd put on her angelic tone...

"It's easy to talk," he yelled. "It's easy to talk! Godammit to lousy stinking hell! Will you finally sit down?"

In the morning I notified my mother...

"Say, Mama, I won't be home for lunch today... I'm going out to Les Lilas again... see about that factory..."

"All right, Ferdinand," she says. "In that case, listen to me. I've been thinking... This evening I'd like Hortense to do the kitchen thoroughly... It's been in a disgusting state for the last two months at least, the pots, the sink, and all the brass... Since I've been sick, I haven't been able to attend to it... You can smell the grease all the way upstairs... If I send her shopping, she'll start dawdling again, she'll be out for hours, she's such a chatterbox... She hangs around the vegetable store... gabble gabble... You'll be near the Place de la République... so drop in at Carquois' and bring me seventy centimes' worth of their best ham for your father... the very best... you know the kind I mean?... absolutely fresh and not too fat... Take a good look at it before you buy it... There are some noodles left over for the two of us, we'll boil them up again... And at the same time you can bring me three portions of cream cheese and if you can remember a head of lettuce, not too wide open... That way I won't have to cook for dinner... You'll remember all that, won't you? We've got beer... Hortense will get some yeast... With your father and his boils I think salad is the best thing for the blood... Before you go, take a five- franc piece out of my purse on the mantelpiece in our room. Don't forget to count the change... And be sure to get back before dinner... Do you want me to write it all down? With this heat I'm afraid to give your father eggs... his digestion hasn't been right... or strawberries, for that matter... They give me a rash... so with his nerves... we'd better be careful..."

I'd had enough instructions, I was all set to go... I took the five francs... I left the Passage... I sat for a while in the Square Louvois, beside the fountain... thinking things over, on a bench... Lilas, my ass! But I had a little tip about a jobber, a fellow that made showease accessories at home, velvet pads, little wooden plaques. Somebody had told me about him... It was on the rue Greneta, at Number 8... just to have a clear conscience... It must have been about nine o'clock… It wasn't too hot yet... So I go there, very slowly... I come to the door... I climb up to the sixth floor... I ring, they open the door a crack... The job was taken... OK, no point arguing... That was a load off my chest... I went down maybe two flights... There on the fourth floor landing I sit down for a minute, I take off my collar... I do a little more thinking… After quite some thought it came to me that I still had another address, a dealer in de luxe leather goods way down at the end of the rue Meslay... There was no hurry about that either... I look around, I take in the setting. The place was really sumptuous... the floors were all worn down, it smelled terrible of mold and toilets... but what generous proportions, really magnifi-cent... must have belonged to some gravy riders in the seventeenth century... You could tell that by the decorations, the moldings, the wrought-iron railings, the marble and porphyry steps... Nothing phony about it... all handmade... I knew about style... Hell!... It was really magnificent… Not a single fixture was imitation!... It was like an enormous drawing room, where people would never stop again... They dashed straight through into the hovels, to their lousy jobs. I'd contemplated enough... I myself was a memory... a putrid smell...

There, right beside the water faucet I could see the whole landing, I was nice and comfortable... That's all I wanted... Even the panes of glass dated from the period... Little tiny ones, different-colored squares, violet, bottle-green, pink... So there I was, perfectly at peace, the people paid no attention to me... They were going to work... I pondered how I was going to spend the day... Hey! Suddenly I see an old friend coming up... a big six-footer with a goatee… holding on to the banister and panting... He was a salesman, not a bad guy... a real joker. I hadn't seen him since I was at Gorloge's... He sold watch chains and such... He recognized me on the landing... He shouts up to me... He tells me all about himself and asks me what I've been doing for the last year. I give him all the details... He didn't have time to listen, he was just leaving for his vacation... early in the afternoon... He was all pepped up with the prospect... So he leaves me pretty quick... He took the stairs four at a time... He ran in to see his boss and drop his sample case... He barely had time to dash to the Gare d'Orsay and take the train for Dordogne... He was going to be away for a week. He wished me plenty of luck... I told him to have a good time...

But that big palooka had got me down with his line about the country... Just like that, he'd punc-tured me completely. Hell, I wouldn't do a damn thing all day. That was a safe bet... I couldn't think of anything but skylarking, the open spaces, the country... Hell, he'd demoralized me... I was suddenly frantic to see greenery, trees, flowerbeds... I couldn't control myself... I was wild... Dammit to hell!... I says to myself: "I'll do my shopping for supper right away..." That was my idea... "Then I'll go out to the Buttes-Chaumont... First we'll get that out of the way! I won't go home until seven... I'll be free all afternoon!" Not bad!...

I run to the nearest place... Ramponneau's... I make it fast... on the corner of the rue Etienne-Marcel... a model delicatessen store... even better than Carquois'... Really luxurious for those days and clean... I buy the seventy centimes' worth of ham... The kind my father liked best, hardly a speck of fat... I bought the head of lettuce at Les Halles across the street... The cream cheese too... They even lend me a container.

So I start moseying down the Boulevard Sébastopol, then the rue de Rivoli... I've kind of lost track. It's so stifling you can hardly move... I drag myself through the arcades... along the shop fronts... "How about the Bois de Boulogne!" I says to myself... I kept on walking quite a while... But it was getting to be unbearable... unbearable... When I see the gates of the Tuileries, I turn off... across the street and into the gardens... There was a hell of a crowd already... It wasn't easy to find a place on the grass... Especially in the shade... It was full up…

I get pushed around some, I slide down an embankment near the big basin... It was nice and cool, really pleasant... But just then a red-faced mob appears on the scene, a compact mass, griping and greasy, pouring out of all fourteen adjoining quarters... Whole buildings disgorging their inhabitants on the spacious lawns, every last tenant and janitor, driven out by the heat, the bedbugs, the itch... They swept on in a sea of wisecracks, the gags burst like rockets... More hordes were on their way from the Invalides, you could hear their awful rumbling...

They tried to close the gates, to rescue the rhododendrons, the bed of daisies... The horde broke down the gates, bending the bars, tearing them up by the roots, they ruptured the whole wall... It was worse than a landslide, a cavalry charge over ruins... They howled bestially to make the storm burst at last over the Concorde... But not a drop of rain fell, so they rushed into the basins... rolling and wallowing, whole battalions of them, naked, in their underdrawers... They made it overflow, they drank up the last drop...

I was flat on my ass on the grassy bank, I really had nothing to complain about... I was safe... I had my provisions to the left of me, within easy reach... I could hear the stampeding herds trampling the flowerbeds... More were coming from all directions... The numberless legions of thirst... They were battling to lick the bottom of the pond... sucking mud, worms, slime... They'd plowed up the whole place, disemboweled the earth, dug deep crevices. There wasn't a single blade of grass left in the whole park... Only delirium, a chopped-up crater for three miles around, rumbling with disaster and drunks...

At the bottom of the crater, in the red-hot oven of hell, thousands of families were looking around for their pieces... Sides of meat, chunks of rump, kidneys gushing and spurting as far as the rue Royale and up into the clouds... The stink was merciless, tripe in urine, whiffs of corpse, decomposed liver patty... You got a mouthful with every breath... You couldn't get away from it... The terraces were inaccessible, blocked off by three impregnable bulwarks... Baby carriages piled as high as a six-story building...

But as the purple dusk fell, strains of song were wafted through the putrid breezes... Slumped on top of the martyrs, the monster with a hundred thousand cocks stirs up music in his guts... I had a couple of beers, swiped free of charge... and two more... and two more... which makes twelve... Why not?... I'd spent my five francs... I hadn't a red cent left... I snagged a quart of white wine... Nothing to it!... and a whole bottle of *mousseux*... Why wouldn't I do a little trading with that family on the bench?... Sure... I swap my cream cheese for a real live Camembert... Better watch out!... I change my sliced ham for a quart of red ink... There's no other word for it... Just then the mounted police attack... they're brutal... Some nerve!... The damn fools... They can't get anybody to move... In half a second they're toppled off their horses, disgraced... jerked off... beheaded... put to flight before you can count three!... They run for it, they scatter behind the statues!... The masses are in revolt!... A storm... that's what they're demanding... The crater rumbles, grumbles, thunders... Spewing empty bottles as far as the Étoile!

I break my salad in two, we eat it just like that, raw... I kid around with the young ladies... I sit there, drinking whatever I find on the corner of the bench. No more beer!... it doesn't quench your thirst... It actually heats up your mouth... Everything is scorching, the air, the girls' tits. You'd throw up if you moved, if you tried to get up... it's a fact, you can't move at all... My eyelids are drooping... my eyes are closing... Just then a sweet refrain passes through the air... "I know you're lovely..."

Bing! Rat-tat-tat! That's the street lamp, the big white globe breaking into smithereens. A vicious stone. A slingshot! They give a jump. They screech something awful. It's those toughs over there in the corner on the other side of the ditch, wise guys, bastards... They want it to be pitch-dark... The lousy little heels... I sprawl over on the guy next to me... He's a fat son of a bitch... He's snoring! It's terrible... Cut it out!... I'm comfortable, though!... His hullabaloo is putting me to sleep... A lullaby... I thought it was Camembert I had... It's cream cheese... I can see that... I've still got some in my breast pocket... I shouldn't have left any in the box... in the box... Here we are... here we stay... Seems like a breeze is coming up... The cream cheese is sleeping... It must be very late... Or even later... Like the cheese... Absolutely.

I was sleeping nicely. I wasn't bothering anybody... I'd slipped deep down into the ditch... I was wedged against the wall...

Then some fool comes stumbling around in the darkness... He bumps into my neighbor. He falls back on me, he knocks me over... He feels me up. I half open my eyes... I give a ferocious grunt... I look at the horizon... way in the distance... I see the dial... The one over the Gare d'Orsay, those great big clocks... It's one o'clock in the morning. Christ! Hell and damnation! Stinking mess! I start up. I disentangle myself... I've got two floozies crushing me, one on each side... I roll them over... All around me they're sawing wood and wheezing... Got to get up... Got to beat it home... I pick up my good jacket... But I can't find my collar... To hell with it. I was supposed to be home for dinner. Hell. My lousy luck. It was the heat too. Besides, I was in a daze, I wasn't all there. I was scared and I was drunk... I was still completely befuddled... Christ, was I drunk! Hell!

I remember the way all the same... I take the rue Saint-Honoré... then the rue Saint-Roch on the left... rue Gomboust... then straight ahead. I reach the Passage gate... It's not closed yet on account of the heat... All the neighbors are there... in their shirtsleeves with their collars open, outside their shops... taking the air... chewing the fat from chair to chair, astraddle, on their doorsteps... I'm still kind of tipsy... It's obvious that I can't walk straight... That throws them. I never got drunk... They'd never seen me that way... They're amazed... "Hey, Ferdinand!" they holler, "You land a job? The frogs having a party?... You run into a cloud? Been struck by a cyclone?..." A lot of hooey anyway... Visios was rolling up his awning, he called after me: "Say, Ferdinand. Your mother's been down here at least twenty times since seven o'clock, asking if we hadn't seen you. So help me. She's mad as a hornet... Where you been keeping yourself anyway?"

So I stagger over to the shop. It wasn't closed at all... Hortense was standing in the hall... She must have been waiting for me...

"Oh, if you could see your mother... the state she's in. Poor woman! It's dreadful. She's been out of her mind since six o'clock... They say there's been a riot in the Tuileries. She's sure you were in it... She went out this afternoon for the first time when she heard the rumors... She saw a runaway horse on the rue Vivienne... She came home more dead than alive. She was all in a tizzy. I've never seen her so upset!" Hortense herself was in a terrible state just telling me about it... Her face was all in a sweat and she was dabbing at it with her big filthy apron. It left her streaked with green and yellow and black... I took the stairs four at a time... I went to my room... My mother was there on the bed, prostrated, completely beside herself, her smock unbuttoned... her petticoats pulled up to her waist... She was still bathing her leg with Turkish towels. She rolled them up into big wads, the water dripped down on the floor... "Ah!" she starts up... "So there you are!" She'd thought they'd made hash of me...

"Your father's in a terrible rage. Oh, the poor man! He was just going to the police station. Where on earth have you been?"

Just then I hear my father coming out of the toilet. He comes slowly up the stairs, adjusting his suspenders... He straightens out the bandage on his boils... First he doesn't say a word... He pretends not to see me... He goes back to his typewriter... He types with one finger... He puffs like a porpoise, he sponges his forehead... It's stifling, that's a fact... absolutely suffocating... He stands up... He takes the towel from the nail... He splashes water all over his face... He's done in... He comes back... He gives me a cross-eyed look... He looks at my mother too, stretched out on the bed... "Good Lord, Clémence, cover yourself..." he bellows at her, furious on account of her leg... Here we go again... He motions at her. He thinks I'm looking at her bare legs... She doesn't see what he's excited about... She's innocent, she has no sense of shame... He raises his hands to high heaven... He's scandalized, outraged! She's naked up to her stomach... Finally she pulls her skirt down... She changes her position a little... She turns over on the mattress... I want to say something... something to put an end to the embarrassment... I'll say something about the heat... You can hear the cats screwing... way over there on the glass roof... chasing each other... jumping over chasms between tall chimneys…

A breath of air comes up... an honest-to-goodness breeze... Glory be! "It's cooling off," my mother says right away. "Well, it's none too soon... You know, Auguste, I can feel it in my leg that it's going to rain... I'm positive... It's always the same pain... A drawing pain in the ass... That's the sign all right, it never fails... Do you hear, Auguste, it's going to rain!..."

"Ah! Can't you shut up a minute! Let me work! Christ! Can't you stop gassing the whole time?"

"Why, Auguste, I haven't said a word. It's getting on to two o'clock. My goodness, child, and we aren't in bed yet."

"As if I didn't know it, Christ almighty asshole blazes. I know it's two o'clock. Is it my fault?... Pretty soon it'll be three. Hell fire! And four! And thirty-six! And twelve! Blast it to stinking hell! Why do I have to be badgered day and night? Is it right? Is it fair?" He gives his contraption a terrifying blow, enough to smash all the type, to flatten out the keyboard... He turns around. He's blue in the face... Now he turns on me... He gives it to me straight: "Wah!" he bellows. He roars at the top of his lungs: "You give me a pain in the ass, the whole lot of you. D'you hear me?... That's right. And you, you dirty little louse! You no-good bum! Where've you been again? Since eight o'clock this morning? Well? Are you going to answer me? Speak up, dammit..."

At first I didn't say a thing... All of a sudden I remember what I'd done with the stuff I'd bought. It was true, I hadn't brought home a thing! Jesus Christ! What a mess!

I'd forgotten all about the ham... I'd forgotten everything... Now I begin to catch the tune. Christ! "What about your mother's money?... And the food you were supposed to be bringing home?... Well? Ahh!" He was exultant. "You see, Clémence?... Your handiwork... Now do you see what you've done... with your idiotic leniency... your stupid blindness... You trust that little thug with money! Your unpardonable trustfulness! Your idiotic credulity!... You give him money... you hand him your purse! Why not give him everything? Give him the whole house. Why not?... Ah! Ah! I predicted it, didn't I!... He'll shit in your hand! Ah! Ah! He's drunk it all up! He's guzzled it all down!... He stinks of liquor. He's drunk! He's caught the syphilis! And the clap! He'll bring us the cholera! Then you'll be satisfied!... Ah! Well, you'll reap the fruits. You and nobody else, you hear me?... Whose fault is it if we've a stinker for a son? Yours! You can have him. All for yourself! Lousy, stinking, cock-sucking life!"

He winds himself up again... He surpasses himself. He goes all out... He rips his shirt open... He bares his chest...

"Thunderation asshole Jesus! Why, he's a scoundrel throngh and through! He'll stop at nothing!... It's high time you realized... you can't trust him with anything... not with a single centime! not with a sou!... You promised me a dozen times! twenty times! a hundred thousand times! But you had to start right in again! Ah! Ah! You're incorrigible!"

He bounces up from his stool... He comes clear across the room and shouts at me point- blank. He blows spit in my face, he puffs himself up like a balloon... two inches from my nose... Here comes his hurricane act!... I see his eyes right up against mine... Strangely revulsed...

Quivering in their sockets... It's a tempest between the two of us... He stammers so furiously that the spit flies thick and fast... he's drowning me! He clouds my vision, I'm dazed... He flails around so violently he tears the bandages off his neck. That only makes him thrash harder… He twists around and bellows at me... He grabs hold of me... I push him back and recoil... I've got my dander up too... I don't want the dirty bastard to touch me... That stops him for a second...

"What?" he goes. "What's this?... Ah, if I didn't control myself!..." "Go right ahead!" I say... I can feel the gall rising.

"Ah, you little skunk! You defy me? You little pimp! You swine! The insolence of it! The shame! Do you want to kill us? Is that it?... Why don't you say so right away?... You little coward! You bum!..." He fires all this in my face... And then some more incantations...

"Suffering asshole Christ almighty! My poor dear, what did we do to produce such vermin? As corrupt as three dozen jailbirds!... Profligate! Scoundrel! Idler! And then some! He's calamity personified! Good for nothing except to rob us and clean us out! A pestilence! Gouge us without mercy! That's all his gratitude!... for a whole life of sacrifice! Two lives of torment! We're nothing but a couple of old fools... We're the ones that get it in the neck! Every time!... Go on, say it again, say it, you poison toad! Come on, out with it. Admit you want to be the death of us... that you want us to die of grief... and misery! Let me hear you say it at least before you finish me off! Go on, you stinking scum!"

At this point my mother gets up and limps across the room, trying to come between us... "Auguste! Auguste! Listen to me, my goodness. Listen to me, I beg of you. Come, Auguste.

You're going to be laid up again. Think of me, Auguste. Think of all of us! You're going to make yourself sick. Ferdinand. Go away, child. Go outside! Don't stay here..."

I didn't budge. It was he who sat down again...

He mops himself off, he grunts... He strikes one or two keys... Then he starts to bellow again... He turns toward me, he points a finger at me... He takes a solemn tone...

"Ah yes. today I can admit it... How I regret it! I was weak. I'm to blame for not having disciplined you with a vengeance! Christ, yes! Disciplined you! Before it was too late! When you were twelve, do you hear, at the latest. That's when I should have collared you and locked you up good.

That's right. No later... locked you up in a reform school... That's the ticket! They'd have taught you a thing or two... And things wouldn't have come to such a pass... But now the die is cast... Our doom is sealed... Too late! Too late! Do you hear me, Clémence? Much too late! This blackguard is incorrigible! It's your mother that prevented me! And now you'll pay for it, my dear!"

He points at her as she limps around the room, sighing at every step. "It was your mother. Yes, your mother. If she'd listened to me, you'd never have sunk so low... Jumping Jesus, no! Ah, Christ almighty!..."

He pounds the keyboard again... wicked punches with both fists... He's going to demolish it for sure.

"Do you hear me, Clémence? Do you hear me? I've told you often enough!... Didn't I warn you? I knew how it was going to be!"

He's going to explode again... His rage is coming back... He puffs up all over... his head and his eyes are bulging... all you can see is the whites... She's stumbling in all directions, she can't stand up anymore. She climbs back on the bed. She collapses... She hikes her petticoats way up... She uncovers her thighs, the bottom of her belly... She writhes with pain... She gently massages herself... She's bent double...

"Jesus, cover up. Cover up, will you, it's disgusting!"

"Please, please, I beg you, Auguste. You're going to make us all sick..." She was at the end of her rope. She was besides herself...

"Sick? Sick?..." That shoots through him like a rocket. A magic word!... "Ho ho! Christ, that's the last straw!" He bursts out laughing... "That's a revelation!" He's off the handle again… "But it's him. Can't you see that, you poor innocent?... It's this little hoodlum... My Lord, can't you get it through your noodle... it's this infernal little villain that's making us all sick! This slimy viper! Hes after our hide. He's always been plotting against us! He wants us dead and buried! That's right! We're in his way! He doesn't even bother to hide it...'He wants the old folks to conk out... It's obvious. It's plain as day! And the sooner the better. His behavior is unbelievable. He's in a hurry! It's our wretched two cents he's after! Our miserable crust of bread he's got his eye on! You haven't noticed? That's it, all right. The little scum knows what he's doing! The scoundrel! The bloodsucker! He knows. He's got eyes in his head. He sees how we're wasting away! He's rotten through and through! Just take it from me! I know him if you don't! Even if he is my son!" He starts trembling again, his whole carcass is quaking, he's beside himself... He clenches his fists... His stool is creaking and dancing... He's winding up, he's going to lunge... He comes back blowing up my nose... more insults... more and more of them… I feel things coming up in me too... And the heat besides... I pass my two hands over my face... Suddenly everything looks cock-eyed... I can't see straight... Just one jump... I'm over him. I lift up the big heavy machine... I lift it way up. And wham!... I give it to him full in the face! He hasn't got time to parry... He goes over under the impact, the whole business topples... table, man, chair, the whole shebang in all directions... They fall on the floor and scatter... I'm caught up in the dance... I stumble, I fall... That does it, I've got to finish the stinking bastard! Bzing! He's down again... I'm going to smash his kisser!... So he can't talk anymore... I'm going to smash his whole face... I punch him on the ground... He bellows... He gurgles... That'll do. I dig into the fat on his neck... I'm on my knees on top of him... I'm tangled up in his bandages... both my hands are caught. I pull. I squeeze. He's still groaning... He's wriggling… I weigh down on him... He's disgusting... He squawks... I pound him... I massacre him... I'm squatting down... I dig into the meat... It's soft... He's drooling... I tug... I pull off a big chunk of moustache… He bites me, the stinker!... I gouge into the holes... I'm sticky all over… my hands skid... he heaves... he slips out of my grip. He grabs me around the neck. He squeezes my windpipe... I squeeze some more. I knock his head against the tiles... He goes limp... he's soft under my legs... He sucks my thumb... he stops sucking... Phooey! I raise my head for a minute... I see my mother's face on a level with mine... She's staring at me, her eyes twice their size... Her eyes are so big I start wondering where I am... I let go… Another head appears from the stairs... over the corner of the banister... That one's Hortense. Must be. It's her all right. She lets out a terrible scream: "Help! Help!"' She almost splits a gut... That does something to me. I let go my old man... One jump... and I'm on top of Hortense!... I'm going to strangle her! I want to see how she wriggles! She struggles... I daub her face... I close her mouth with the palms of my hands... The pus and blood from the boils squash on her face and drip down... She gurgles louder than Papa... I latch on to her... She struggles... She's hefty... I want to choke her too... It's amazing... It's a hidden world that spasms in your hands... It's life... Get a good feel of it... I knock her skull stubbornly against the banister... It thuds... There's blood in her hair... She yells! It's split. I dig a big finger into her eye... I haven't got the right hold... She breaks loose... She's up again... She gets away... She's a strong one... She clatters down the stairs... I can hear her yelling outside... raising hell... screaming at the top of her lungs... "Murder, murder!..."I hear echoes, voices. A crowd comes running... they gallop into the shop, they jostle at the bottom of the stairs... They push and shove on every landing... An invasion... I hear my name... Here they come... They go into a huddle on the third floor... I look out... Somebody's coming... It's Visios! He's the first one to pop out... He plunges in from the landing... There he is, firm, menacing, resolute... He points a revolver at me... straight at my chest... The other bastards come around behind me, encircle me, grunting, bawling the hell out of me... Hurling threats at me, insults... The old man is still out cold... still on the floor... with a little trickle of blood flowing from his head... I'm not angry anymore... I don't give a damn... Visios bends down, touches the bundle, Papa grunts and moans a little...

The bastards push me around, they're stronger... They're pretty brutal... They drag me down the stairs... they won't even listen to my mother... They push me into the room downstairs... I take the blows as they come... I've stopped resisting... I get some from everybody, especially in the balls... I can't fight back... The wickedest of the lot is Visios... I get a kick square in the stomach... I stagger... I don't double up... I stay put, glued to the wall... They leave, spitting in my face as they go... They lock me in.

I'm all alone... pretty soon I begin to tremble... My hands... my legs... my face... inside... all over... I have a lousy sick feeling, a panic in my kidneys... like everything was falling apart, coming off in shreds... like a hurricane was shaking me... My whole carcass is rattling, my teeth are chattering... I'm dead to the world... I've got a spasm in my asshole... I shit in my pants... My heart's pounding so hard I can't hear what's going on... I can't make out what they're doing... My knees are knocking together... I stretch out on the floor... I don't know what's what... I'm scared... I feel like yelling... I haven't knocked him off, have I? Shit! To hell with that... But my asshole is opening and closing... A spasm... it's awful.

I think of Papa again... The sweat's dripping off me and what's left is cold... I swallow it through my nose... I'm bleeding... The cocksucker scratched me... I wasn't very rough... I'd never have expected him to be so weak, so mushy... It's amazing... It was easy to squeeze... I remember how I was kneeling there with my fingers locked in front... the slobber... and the way he suckled my thumb... I can't stop shaking... I'm trembling all over... All you've got to do is squeeze!... My face is twitching all over... I groan! Now I can feel every one of those bastards' blows... I'm scared shitless... It's my asshole that hurts worst... It keeps on twisting and tightening... It aches like hell.

Shut up in that room, stretched out on the tiles, I kept on trembling a long while, banging against everything in sight... I bumped into the clothes cupboard... it sounded like castanets... I'd never have thought I could have such a tempest inside me... The jolting was unbelievable... I flapped around like a lobster... It came from way inside... "I've knocked him off!" I said to myself... I was more and more sure of it, and then for a moment I heard something like the sound of steps... people talking things over... And then they were pushing the bed upstairs...

"That's it! They're taking him away..." But a minute later I heard his voice... That was him all right!... He was only punch-drunk! "I must have bashed his head in," I began to think. "He'll conk out later. That'll be even worse..." He was still on my bed... I could hear the springs... Actually I didn't know a thing. And then my stomach heaved... I began to vomit... I even pushed to make it come up... That made me feel a lot better... I vomited up everything... The shivers started in again... They shook me so hard I didn't know who I was anymore... I was surprised at myself... I threw up the macaroni... I started in again... It did me a whole lot of good. Like I was getting rid of everything... I threw up everything I could all over the floor... I pushed and strained... I bent double to make myself puke still more and then came slime and then froth... It splattered, it spread under the door... I vomited up everything I'd eaten for at least a week and then diarrhea too... I wanted to call them to let me leave the room... I dragged myself to the pitcher that was standing by the fireplace... I shat into it... After that I couldn't keep my balance... My head was spinning... I collapsed again and let it all out on the floor... I shat some more... A flood of marmalade...

They must have heard me floundering around... They came and opened... They took one look at the room... They locked it up again... Maybe ten minutes later Uncle Édouard came in… He was all alone... I hadn't put my pants back on... I was covered with shit... He wasn't afraid of me... "Get dressed now," he says to me... "You go down first, I'm taking you away…" He had to hold me up. I was trembling so bad all over I couldn't button my pants... Finally I did what he said... I went down ahead of him... There was nobody on the stairs anymore or in the shop either. Everybody had cleared out... They must have gone home... They had plenty to talk about...

By the clock up there under the glass roof it was 4:15... It was dawning already...

At the end of the Passage we roused up the caretaker to open the gate. "So you're taking him away?" he asked my uncle...

"Yes, he'll sleep at my place."

"Well, I wish you luck. You'll need it, my dear monsieur. That's some number you've got on your hands..."

He double-locked the gate behind us. He went back to his shack. You could hear him grumbling in the distance: "Christ! That brat's got himself into a fine mess!"

My uncle and I went down the rue des Pyramides... We crossed the Tuileries... When we got to the Pont Royal I was still trembling... The wind from the river wasn't warm. As we were walking along, Uncle Édouard told me how they'd come for him... It seems to have been Hortense... He was sound asleep... His part of town wasn't exactly around the corner... It was beyond the Invalides, behind the École Militaire... on the rue de la Convention before you get to the rue de Vau-girard... I was afraid to ask for further details... We walked fast... I couldn't get warm... My teeth were still chattering...

"Your father's better," he said after a while… "But he'll surely be in bed for two or three days... He won't be going to the office. Dr. Capron came..." That's as much as he told me.

We took the rue du Bac and then turned right as far as the Champ de Mars... His place was at the end of the world... Finally we get there... There it is!... He shows me his home, a small house in the back of a garden... His pad was on the third floor... I didn't dare say anything about being tired... but I couldn't stand on my feet... I hung on to the banister. It was broad daylight by now... Upstairs a terrible wave of nausea came over me!... He took me to the shithouse himself... I threw up a long time... it kept coming… He takes a folding bed out of the closet... He takes a mattress off his bed... He sets me up in another room... He gives me a blanket too... I collapse... He undresses me... I spit up another flood of slime... Finally I fall asleep by fits and starts... A nightmare catches hold of me... I only slept off and on...

I never really found out how Uncle Édouard managed to make my father lay off... to make him leave me strictly alone... I think he must have given him to understand that his disciplinary routine, his idea of sending me to La Roquette, wasn't so very bright... That I wouldn't stay there forever... that maybe I'd escape right away... just to come and rub him out... and that this time I'd really finish the job... Anyway, he managed... He didn't confide in me... I didn't ask him to.

My uncle's place was nicely situated, it was cheerful, pleasant... It looked out over the gardens of the rue de Vaugirard and the rue Maublanc... There were rows of little copses and kitchen gardens in front and in back... The honeysuckle climbed all around the front windows... Everybody had his little plot between the houses, radishes, lettuces, even tomatoes... and grapevines! All that reminded me of my head of lettuce... It hadn't brought me much luck. I was terribly weak, like after an illness. But in a way I felt better. I didn't feel hunted at Uncle Édouard's place.

I began to breathe again...

The decoration in his room consisted of whole series of picture postcards, pinned up fanwise, in frescoes, in garlands... The "Kings of the Steering Wheel," the "Kings of the Handlebars," and the "Heroes of Aviation"... He bought them all, a few at a time... His ultimate plan was to have them form a tapestry that would cover the walls completely... It wouldn't be long now... Paulhan and his little fur cap... Rougier of the lopsided schnozzle... Petit-Breton with the legs of steel and the zebra-stripe jersey... Farman, the bearded... Santos-Dumont, the fearless fetus... Vicomte Lambert, the Eiffel

Tower specialist... Latham, the disillusioned... MacNamara, the "black panther"... Sam Langford, all thighs... And a hundred other celebrities... Boxing too of course...[105]

It wasn't a bad life... We managed pretty well... When my uncle came home from his business and all the chasing around connected with his pump, he talked to me about sporting events... He figured all the chances... He knew all the weaknesses, the idiosyncrasies, the tricks of the champions... We ate our meals on the oilcloth, we did the cooking together... We talked things over in every detail, the chances of all the favorites...

On Sunday we were full of beans... By ten o'clock in the morning we were in the big Gallery of Machines... it was a fantastic sight... We'd get there good and early... We'd take our places way up top, on the turn... We were never bored for a second... Uncle Édouard was always on the run, from one end of the week to the other... He never stopped going... His pump still wasn't exactly the way he wanted it... He was having a lot of trouble with patents... He didn't quite see what the difficulty was... It mostly had something to do with America... But whether he was in a good or a bad humor he never made speeches... He never moralized... That's what I liked best about him... Meanwhile he put me up. I lived in his second room. My fate was in suspense. My father never wanted to see me again... He was still gassing as usual... He'd have liked me to start my military service... But I wasn't old enough... I only heard about all this bit by bit... My uncle didn't like to talk about it... He preferred to talk about sports, his pump, boxing, gadgets... anything... Touchy subjects gave him a pain... me too...

Even so, he was a little more talkative on the subject of my mother... He brought me news... She couldn't move around at all anymore... I wasn't very eager to see her... What was the use?... She always said the same thing... Anyway, the time passed... A week, two weeks, three... This couldn't go on forever... I couldn't dig in here for good... My uncle was OK but that was just the trouble... And how was I going to live?... At his expense?... That was no good... I dropped a little suggestion... "We'll see about it later on." he said... there was no hurry... he was attending to it...

He taught me how to shave... He had a special contraption, tricky and modern... you could put it together in all directions and even backwards... Except it was so complicated it took an engineer to change the blade... This delicate little razor was another nest of patents, he explained to me, about twenty in all.

It was I who set the table and did the shopping... I kept on like that, waiting and doing nothing, for almost a month and a half... lounging around like a woman... That had never happened to me before... I did the dishes too. We didn't bother with too much cleaning... Then I went roaming around wherever I pleased... No kidding!... That was something... I had no fixed destination... I just wandered... Every day Uncle Édouard said the same thing before I went out: "Go take a walk. Go ahead, Ferdinand! Just follow your nose... Don't worry about a thing... Go wherever you like... If you've got some special place, that's the place to go. Sure. As far as the Luxembourg if you feel like it... Ah! If I only weren't so busy... I'd go and watch them playing tennis... I'm crazy about tennis... Get a little sunshine... You never look at anything, you're like your father..." He'd stop for a minute, he'd stand still, thinking. Finally he'd add: "And then you'll come home, but don't hurry... I'll be a little later than usual tonight..." And he'd give me a little extra dough, a franc and a half, two francs... "Take in a movie... if you're up on the Boulevards... You seem to like stories..."

Seeing him so generous... with me on his hands, I began to feel crummy... But I didn't dare to argue. I was afraid he'd take offense... After the latest ruckus I was always on the lookout for consequences... So I thought I'd wait a while for things to straighten themselves out... To spare expense I

---

[105] Paulhan. Early aviator. Already famous in 1910. Henri Rougier. Holder of the eleventh airplane pilot's license. Lucien Petit-Breton. Famous bicycle racer. Winner of the Tour de France in 1907 and 1908. Henri Farman (1874-1958) and his brother Maurice (1877- 1964). Aviators and airplane builders. Also engaged in tandem, motorcycle, and automobile racing, winning numerous prizes. Henri won the Grand Prix de l'Aviation. In 1908, first flight with passengers. Founded one of the earliest passenger lines in 1919. Maurice was French bicycle champion in 1895. Alberto Santos-Dumont (1873-1932). Brazilian aviator. Constructed several types of aircraft. In 1906 made the first world record in aviation, a flight of 220 meters, covered in 21 seconds. Vicomte Lambert. Aviator. Created an enormous sensation by flying over the Eiffel Tower in 1909. Hubert Latham (1883-1912). French aviator. Established altitude records. Made two unsuccessful attempts to fly across the English channel.

washed my own socks while he was out... The rooms in his place weren't strung in a row, but pretty far apart. The third, next to the stairs, was weird, it was like a small drawing room... But with hardly anything in it... a table in the middle, two chairs, and a single picture on the wall... an enormous reproduction of Millet's *Angelus*... I never saw such a wide picture... it took up the whole panel... "'Isn't it beautiful? What do you say, Ferdinand?" Uncle Édouard asked every time we passed in front of it on our way to the kitchen. Sometimes we stopped a moment to contemplate it in silence... We didn't talk in front of the Angelus... This wasn't any "Kings of the Handlebars"... It wasn't made to be gassed about!

I think my uncle had an idea it would do me a lot of good to look at a fine picture like that... that it was a kind of treatment for a rotten character like mine... that maybe it would soften me up... But he never made an issue of it... He understood these sensitive things perfectly... He didn't talk about them, that's all... Uncle Édouard wasn't only good at machinery... That would be the wrong idea... He was very sensitive, there's no denying it... Actually that was what made me feel so uncomfortable... It made me feel lousy to be sitting there like a sap, piling his groceries into my belly... I was a skunk and I had my nerve with me... Hell!... Enough was enough...

I asked him again... risked it... if there was any objection to my starting out again... having a look at the want ads... "You stay right here," he says to me. "Aren't you happy? Is anything eating you, kid? Go out for a walk. It'll be better for you. Don't worry about a thing... You'll only get mixed up with the same dopes... I'll find you a job... I'm working on it. Just leave me alone. Don't stick your nose in. You're still too jittery... You'll only bollix everything up... You're too nervous right now. Anyway I've arranged everything with your parents... Go roaming around some more... You won't always have the chance. Go out to Suresnes along the river. Or take the boat, come to think of it. Give yourself a change of air. There's nothing like those boats. Get off at Meudon if you feel like it. That'll clear your mind... I'll tell you in a few days... I'll have something very good for you... I can feel it... I'm sure of it... But we mustn't try to force things... And I hope you'll be a credit to me..." "Yes, Uncle."

You don't meet many men like Roger-Martin Courtial des Pereires... I was a good deal too young at the time, I've got to admit, to appreciate him properly. My uncle had the good fortune to meet him one day at the office of the *Genitron*, the favorite magazine (twenty-five pages) of the small artisan-inventors of the Paris district... in connection with his scheme for obtaining a patent, the best, the most airtight, for all kinds of bicycle pumps... folding, collapsible, flexible, or reversible.

Courtial des Pereires, let's get this straight right away, was absolutely different from the mob of petty inventors... He was miles above all the bungling subscribers to his magazine... that crawling mass of failures... Oh no! Roger-Martin Courtial wasn't in that class... He was a real master!... It wasn't just neighbors that came to consult him... but people from all over, from the departments of the Seine, the Seine-et-Oise, subscribers from the provinces, the colonies... even from foreign countries...

But the remarkable thing about it was that in private Courtial expressed nothing but contempt and ill-concealed disgust for all those small-fry, those weights around the neck of Science, those misled shopkeepers, those delirious tailors, those gadget peddlers... all those harebrained delivery boys, always being fired, hunted, cachectic, driving themselves nuts about perpetual motion or the squaring of the world... or the magnetic faucet... The whole miserable swarm of obsessed screwballs... of inventors of the moon!...

He had his bellyful of them right away, just from looking at them and especially when he had to listen to them... He had to put a good face on it in the interests of the paper... That was his routine, his bread and butter... But it was disgusting and embarrassing... It wouldn't have been so bad if he could have kept quiet... But he had to comfort them! flatter them! get rid of them gently... according to the case and the mania... and above all collect his fee... It was a race between all those maniacs, those dreary slobs, to see who could get away a little quicker... only five minutes more!... from his furnished room... his workshop, his bus or shed... just time to take a leak... and then dash to the Genhron... and collapse in front of des Pereires' desk, like a lot of escaped convicts... panting... haggard... tense with fright... to shake their dunce caps some more... to fire thousands of puzzlers at Courtial... about "solar mills," the junction of the "lesser radiations"... ways of moving the Cordilleras... of deflecting the course of comets... as long as they had a gasp of breath left in their dottering bagpipes... to the last twitch of their stinking carcasses... Courtial des Pereires, secretary, precursor, owner, founder of the *Genitron*, always had an answer to everything, he was never embarrassed or disconcerted, never maneuvered to gain time... His aplomb, his perfect competence, his irresistible optimism made him invulnerable to the worst assaults of the worst nitwits... Besides, he never put up with long conversations... Instantly he parried, he himself took over... Whatever was said, decided, settled... was settled once and for all... no use starting up again or he'd go purple with rage... He'd tug at his collar... He'd spray spit in all directions... Incidentally he had some teeth missing, three on one side... In every case his verdicts, the most tenuous, the most dubious, the most open to argument, became massive, galvanized, irrefutable, instantaneous truths... He had only to open his mouth... He triumphed instantly... There was no room for a comeback.

At the slightest sign of disagreement he gave free rein to his temper and the martyred consultant didn't have a chance... Instantly turned inside out, crushed, routed, massacred, volatilized forever... It was a regular fantasia, a trapeze act over a volcano... The poor insolent bastard saw stars... Courtial was so imperious when he got mad he would have made the most insatiable nut drop through the floor, he'd have made him crawl into a mousehole.

Courtial wasn't a big man, he was short and wiry, the small powerful type. He himself told you his age several times a day... He was past fifty... He kept in good shape thanks to physical culture, dumbbells, Indian clubs, horizontal bars, springboards... he did his exercises regularly, especially before lunch, in the back room of the newspaper office. He'd fixed up a regular gymnasium between two partitions. Naturally it was kind of cramped... But all the same he swung himself around on his apparatus... on the bars... with remarkable ease... That was the advantage of being little... he could pivot like a charm... Even so he collided now and then... good and hard... when he was swinging on the rings... He'd shake the walls of his cubbyhole like a bell clapper! Boom! Boom! You could hear him exercising. Never in the worst heat did I ever see him take off his pants or his frock coat or his collar... Only his cuffs and his ready- made tie.

Courtial des Pereires had a good reason to keep in perfect form. He had to watch out for his physique and keep limber... It was indispensable... In addition to being an inventor, an author, and a journalist, he often went up in a balloon... He gave exhibitions... Especially on Sundays and holidays... It usually went off all right, but occasionally there was trouble and plenty of excitement... And that wasn't all... He led a perilous life, full of unforeseen dangers and a hundred different kinds of surprises... That's how he'd always lived... It was his nature... He told me what he was aiming at...

"Muscles without mind, Ferdinand," he'd say, "aren't even horse meat. And intelligence without muscles is electricity without a battery! You don't know where to put it... It leaks out all over the place... It's a waste... It's a mess..." That was his opinion. He'd written several conclusive works on the subject: "The Human Battery and its Upkeep." He was gone on physical culture even before the word existed. He wanted a varied life... "I don't want to be a pen- pusher." That was the way he talked.

He was crazy about balloons, he'd been an aeronaut almost from birth, ever since his earliest youth... with Surcouf and Barbizet... highly instructive ascents... No records, no long-distance flights, no breathtaking performances. No, nothing showy, colossal, unusual... He had no use for the clowns of the atmosphere... Nothing but demonstration flights, educational ascents... Always scientific... That was his motto and he stuck to it. The balloon was good for his magazine, it rounded out his activities... Every time he went up it brought in subscribers. He had a uniform for climbing into the basket, he had an uncontested right to it, like a captain with three stripes, he was an "associated, registered, graduate" aeronaut. He couldn't even count his medals. They looked like a breastplate on his Sunday rig... He didn't give a damn about them, he wasn't a show-off, but it meant a lot to his audience, you had to keep up appearances.

To the last, Courtial des Pereires was a staunch defender of "lighter-than-air" craft. He was already thinking about helium. He was thirty-five years in advance of his times. And that's something. Between flights he kept the Enthusiast, his veteran, his big private balloon, in the cellar of the office, at 18 Galerie Montpensier. As a rule he only took it out on Friday before dinner to straighten out the rigging and fix up the cover with infinite care... the folds, the sleeve, the cords, filled the miniature gymnasium, the silk puffed up in the drafts.

Courtial des Pereires himself never stopped producing, imagining, conceiving, resolving, making claims... his genius tugged at his brains from morning to night... And even at night it didn't rest... He had to hold tight to resist the torrent of ideas... And be on his guard... It was incomparable torture... Instead of dozing off like other people, he was pursued by chimeras, new crazes, fresh hobbies... Bing! The whole idea of sleeping ran out on him, it was out of the question. He wouldn't have got any sleep at all if he hadn't rebelled against the torrent of inventions, against his own enthusiasm... This disciplining of his genius had cost him more trouble, more superhuman efforts, than all the rest of his work... He often told me so...

When he was overcome in spite of himself, when after no end of resistance he felt swamped by his own enthusiasm and began to see double... or triple... to hear queer voices... there was no other way of stopping the onslaughts, of falling back into his rhythm, of recovering his good humor, than a little trip in the clouds. He'd treat himself to an ascent. If he'd had more free time, he'd have gone up a lot more often, just about every day, but it wasn't compatible with the operation of his rag... He could only go up on Sunday... And even that wasn't so easy... The *Genitron* took up all his time, he had to be there... he couldn't fool around... Inventors are no joke... He always had to be on tap. He stuck to it bravely, nothing diminished his zeal or baffled his ingenuity... no problem, however stupendous, however colossal, however microscopic... He made faces but he put up with it... The "powdered cheese," the "synthetic azure," the "rocker valve," the "nitrogen lung," and the "collapsible steamship," the "compressed café au lait," or the "kilo-metric spring" that would take the place of fuel. No vital innovation in any of these far- flung fields was ever put into practice before Courtial had found occasion, not once but many times, to demonstrate its mechanisms, to stress its advantages, but also, without mercy, to point out its deplorable weaknesses and defects, its hazards and drawbacks.

All this of course brought him terrible jealousies, hatreds without quarter, long-lasting grudges... But he remained impervious to these trifling contingencies.

As long as he wrote for the paper, no technical revolution was recognized as worthwhile or even workable until he had said so and endorsed it in the columns of the *Genitron*. That gives you an idea of the authority he wielded. For every invention of any importance his verdict was decisive... The OK had to come from him. Take it or leave it. If Courtial wrote on his front page that an idea was no good... heavens above!... persnickety, cock-eyed, absolutely unsound, that was the end of it. The contraption was dead and buried... The project was sunk... But if his opinion was definitely favorable... the thing would be all the rage in no time... The subscribers came running...

In his office looking out over the gardens from under the arcades, Courtial des Pereires, thanks to his two hundred and twenty absolutely original handbooks, read all over the world, and thanks to *Genitron* magazine, exerted a peremptory and incomparable influence on the progress of the applied sciences. He directed, oriented, and multiplied the inventive effort of France, Europe, the universe, the whole vast ferment of the petty "certified" inventors...

Naturally all this took some doing, he had to attack people, defend himself, and watch out for underhanded tricks. He could make or break an inventor, you never could tell which, by word of mouth or a stroke of the pen, by a manifesto or a flea in somebody's ear. One day he'd almost started a riot with a series of talks on "the tellurian orientation and memory of swallows."... He was a wonder at writing digests, articles, lectures in prose, in verse, and sometimes, to attract attention, in puns... "Spare no effort to enlighten the family and educate the masses": that was the motto presiding over all his activities.

Genitron: Discussion, Invention, Aerostatics, that was the range of his interests, and actually those words were written all over the walls of his offices... on the title page and on the shop front... You couldn't go wrong... The most up-to-date muddled, complex controversies, the most daring, most subtly ingenious theories on physics, chemistry, electrothermics, or agricultural hygiene shriveled up like caterpillars at Courtial's command, and there wasn't another wiggle out of them... In two seconds flat he punctured them, knocked them cold... You could see their skeleton, their fabric... He had an X-ray mind... It took him only an hour's effort and furious concentration to knock the damnedest damnfoolish-ness, the most pretentious quadrature into shape for the *Genitron*, to make it accessible to the recalcitrant understanding of the most hopeless dolt, of the most boneheaded of his subscribers. It was magical work and he did it mar-velously, turning out definitive, incontrovertible explanations and digests of the most preposterous, hairsplitting, farfetched, and nebulous hypotheses... By sheer force of conviction he'd have made a flash of lightning pass through the eye of a needle and light up a cigarette lighter, he'd have put thunder into a tin whistle. That was his destiny, his training, his rhythm... to put the universe in a bottle, to cork it up, and then tell the masses all about it... Why! And how!... Later on when I was living with him, it was frightening to think of all the things I managed to learn in a twenty-four hour day... just by hints and snatches... For Courtial nothing was obscure, on one side there was matter, lazy and barbaric, and on the other the mind to understand between the lines... *Genitron: invention, discovery, inspiration, light...* That was the subtitle of the paper. At Courtial's we worked under the aegis of the great Flammarion,[106] his portrait with a dedication stood in the middle of the shopwindow, he was invoked like God almighty whenever the slightest argument came up, any pretext would do... He was the highest authority, providence, the shining light... we swore by him alone and maybe a little by Raspail. Courtial had devoted twelve manuals to summaries of astronomical discoveries and only four to the brilliant Raspail, to "nature healing."

One day Uncle Édouard got the brilliant idea of going up to the *Genitron* office to sound out the possibility of a little job for me. He had another reason, he wanted to consult him about his bicycle pump... He'd known des Pereires a long time, since the publication of his seventy- second handbook, the one that people still read more than any of the others, that was most widely distributed all over the world and had done the most for his reputation, his fame: *How to equip a bicycle in all latitudes and climates for the sum of seventeen francs ninety-five, including all accessories and nickel-plated parts.* At the time of which I am speaking this little manual published by the specialized firm of Berdouillon and Mallarmé, on the Quai des Augustins, was in its three-hundredth printing!... Today it is hard to conceive of the enthusiasm, the general craze that this piddling, insignificant work aroused when it came out... But around 1900 *How to Equip a Bicycle* by Courtial-Martin des Pereires was a kind of catechism for the neophtye cyclist, his bedside reading, his Bible... Still, Courtial never ceased to be shrewdly self-critical. A little thing like that didn't turn his head. Naturally his rising fame brought him bigger and bigger mountains of mail, more visitors, more tenacious pests, extra work, and more acrimonious controversies... Very little pleasure... People came to consult him from Greenwich and Valparaiso, from Colombo and Blankenberghe, on the various problems connected with the "oblique" or "flexible" saddle... how to avoid strain on the ball bearings... how to grease the axles... the best hydrous mixture for rust-proofing the handlebars... He was famous all right, but the fame he got out of bicycles stuck in his craw. In the last thirty years he had scattered his booklets like seeds throughout the world, he had written piles of handbooks that were really a good deal more worthwhile, digests and explanations of real value and stature... In the course of his career he had explained just about everything... the fanciest and most complex of theories, the wildest imaginings of physics and chemistry, the budding science of radio-polarity... sidereal photography... He'd written about them all, some more, some less. It gave him a profound feeling of disillusionment, real melancholy, a depressing kind of amazement to see himself honored, adulated, glorified for the stuff he had written about inner tubes and freewheeling... In the first place he personally detested bicycles... He'd never ridden one, he'd never learned how... And on the mechanical side he was even worse... He'd never have been able to take off a wheel, not to mention the chain... He couldn't do anything with his hands except on the horizontal bar and the trapeze... Actually he was the world's worst butterfingers, worse than twelve elephants... Just trying to drive a nail in he'd mash at least two of his fingers, he'd make hash of his thumb, it was a massacre the minute he touched a hammer. I won't even mention pliers, he'd have ripped out the wall, the ceiling, wrecked the whole room... There wouldn't have been anything left... He didn't have two cents' worth of patience, his thoughts moved too fast and too far, they were too intense, too deep... The resistance of matter gave him an epileptic fit... The result was wreckage... He could tackle a problem in theory... But when it came to practice, all he could do on his own was swing dumbbells in the back room... or on Sunday climb into the basket and shout "Let her go"... and roll up in a ball to land when he was through... Whenever he tried to do any tinkering with his own fingers, it ended in disaster. He couldn't even move anything without dropping it or upsetting it... or getting

---

[106] Camille Flammarion (1842-1925). Astronomer and author of popular works on astronomy.

it in his eye... You can't be an expert at everything... You've got to resign yourself... But among his vast panoply of achievements, there was one in particular that he took the greatest pride in... It was his soft spot... He'd tremble with emotion if you even mentioned it... If you came back to it regularly, you were his pal. As a digest, it won't be any exaggeration to call it an incomparable gem... a shattering triumph... *The Complete Works of Auguste Comte Reduced to the Dimensions of a Positivist Prayer in Twenty-two Acrostic Verses!*

For this unprecedented performance he had been hailed almost immediately all over America... Latin America, that is... as a great renovator. A few months later the Uruguayan Academy, assembled in plenary session, had elected him by acclamation *Bolversatore Savantissima* with the supplementary title of "life member"... The following month the city of Montevideo, not to be outdone, had proclaimed him *Citadinis Eternitatis Amicissimus.* With such a title and the triumph he'd been having, Courtial had hoped to achieve new glory, of a somewhat higher order... he'd thought he could really go to town... take over the leadership of a lofty philosophical movement... "The Friends of Pure Reason"... But not at all. Absolutely no soap. For the first time in his life he'd really put his foot in it... He'd loused himself up completely... The high fame of Auguste Comte was easily exported to the Antipodes, but couldn't make it back! It stuck to the River Plate, indelible, undetachable. It refused to come home again. It was "for the Americans," and there was nothing to be done about it, though for months and months he attempted the impossible... He tried everything he could think of, blackened whole columns of the *Genitron*, trying to give his "prayer" a winsome French flavor... he twisted it into a rebus, turned it inside out like a shirt, sprinkled it with flattery... he made it chauvinistic... Corneillian... violent, and in the end contemptible... It didn't do him a bit of good.

Even the bust of Auguste Comte, which had long occupied a place of honor... the customers were sick of seeing it there to the left of the great Flammarion, it had to be removed. It was bad for business. The subscribers complained. They didn't care for Auguste Comte. They liked Flammarion fine, Auguste Comte gave them the creeps. He loused up the shop window... That's the way it was. It couldn't be helped.

On certain evenings much later when Courtial was in the dumps, he said weird things... "Some day, Ferdinand, I'm going away... I'll go far away... you'll see... to the end of the world... All by myself... on my own... You'll see..."

And then he'd stay there in a dream... I didn't like to interrupt him. He'd have those spells from time to time... It made me very curious...

Before des Pereires took me on, my uncle had done everything in his power to find me a job, he'd moved heaven and earth, stopped at nothing, he'd exhausted just about all his leads... Wherever he went he spoke of me in glowing colors... he got no results... He was certainly glad to put me up in his apartment on the rue de la Convention, but after all he wasn't rich... This couldn't go on forever. It wasn't right for me to take advantage of him... Besides I was in the way... His pad wasn't exactly spacious... I pretended to be asleep when he brought a tomato home with him on tiptoes... but just my being there must have cramped his style.

For one thing he was extremely modest... You'd never have expected it, but about some things he was positively bashful... Even after he'd known Courtial for months, for instance, he wasn't really at his ease with him. He sincerely admired him and didn't dare to ask anything of him... He'd waited too long before telling him about me... though it was certainly on his mind... He felt responsible in a way... for my being left high and dry... without the slightest sign of a job...

One day he finally screwed up his courage... As they were batting the breeze, he slipped in his little question... Wouldn't he by some chance need a young secretary, just starting out in life, for his Bureau of Inventors or his aeronautics?... Uncle Édouard had no illusions about my aptitudes. He realized that I wasn't very hot at the usual kind of job... he had a pretty keen eye... that my type and temperament required something out of the way, some kind of fly-by-night racket, something on the screwy side... With Courtial's hare-brained schemes, his long-distance deals, I'd have a chance to make out... That was his idea.

Courtial dyed his hair jet-black and left his moustache and his goatee gray... His hair and his whiskers bristled like a cat, and his bushy rebellious eyebrows were even more ferocious, they were distinctly diabolical, especially the one on the left. He had small restless eyes, his pupils were always darting about deep in their caverns and then suddenly stopping dead when he had a bright idea. Then he'd laugh out loud, his whole belly would shake, he'd slap his thighs hard and then suddenly subside as though transfixed by thought, lost in admiration of his idea...

It was he, Courtial des Pereires, who had obtained the second driving license for racing cars issued in France. Over the desk we had his diploma in a gold frame and his photograph as a young man at the wheel of a monster, with the date and the rubber stamps. The end had been tragic... He often told me about it:

"I was lucky," he admitted. "Take it from me. We were coming into Bois-lc-Duc... the carburation was perfect... I didn't even want to slow down... I catch sight of the schoolteacher... she had climbed up on the embankment... She motioned to me... She'd read all my books... She waved her parasol... I didn't want to be rude... I threw on my brakes outside the school... In a minute I'm surrounded, feted... I take a drink... I wasn't supposed to stop again before Chartres... another ten miles... The last control station... I invite the young lady to come along... 'Climb in, mademoiselle,' I say... 'Climb in beside me. Come along.' She was cute. She hesitated, she shilly-shallied, she coquetted some... I pressed her... So she sits down beside me and off we go... All day long, at every control station, especially all through Brittany, there'd been cider and more cider... My machine was really humming, running fine... I didn't dare to make any more stops... But I needed to bad... Finally I had to give in... So I throw on the brakes... I stop the car, I stand up, I jump, I spot a bush... I leave the chick at the wheel. 'Wait for me,' I sing out, 'I'll be back in a second...' I'd hardly touched a finger to my fly when so help me I'm stunned! Lifted off my feet! Dashed through the air like a straw in a gale! Boom! Stupendous! A shattering explosion!... The trees, the bushes all around, ripped up! mowed down! blasted! The air's aflame! I land at the bottom of a crater, almost unconscious... I feel myself... I pull myself together... I crawl to the road... A total vacuum! The car?... Gone, my boy... A vacuum! No more car! Evaporated! Demolished! Literally! The wheels, the chassis... oak! pitch-pine! All ashes!... The whole frame... Oh well!... I drag myself around, I scramble from one heap of earth to the next... I dig... I rummage... A few fragments here and there... a few splinters... A little piece of fan, a belt buckle. One of the caps of the gas tank... A hairpin... That was all... A tooth that I've never been sure about... The official investigation proved nothing... explained nothing... What would you expect?... The causes of that terrible conflagration will remain forever a mystery... Almost two weeks later in a pond, six hundred yards from the spot, they found... after a good deal of dredging... one of the young lady's feet, half devoured by the rats.

"For my part, though I can't claim to be absolutely certain, I might in a pinch accept one of the numerous hypotheses advanced at the time to explain that fire, that incredible explosion... it's possible that imperceptibly, little by little, one of our 'long fuses' shook loose... When you come to think of it, it would suffice for one of those thin minium rods, shaken by thousands of bumps and jolts, to come into contact for only a second... for a tenth of a second... with the gasoline nipples... The whole shebang would explode instantly! Like melinite! Like a shell! Yes, my boy, the mechanism was mighty precarious in those days. I went back to the place a long time after the disaster... There was still a charred smell... At that critical stage in the development of the automobile, I might add, a number of these fantastic explosions were reported... almost as powerful! Everything pulverized! Horribly scattered in all directions! Propelled through the air for miles!... If pressed for a comparison, the only thing I can think of is certain sudden explosions of liquid air... And even there I have my reservations... Those things are commonplace! Perfectly easy to explain... from start to finish... beyond the shadow of a doubt. No mystery at all! Whereas my tragedy remains an almost complete mystery... We may as well admit it in all modesty. But what importance has that today? None whatever. Fuses haven't been used in ages. Such speculation only impedes progress... Other problems demand our attention... a thousand times more interesting! Ah, my boy, that was a long time ago... Nobody uses minium anymore... Nobody!"

Courtial hadn't, like myself, adopted the celluloid collar... He had his own method of making ordinary cloth collars wear-proof, dirt-proof, water-proof... It was a kind of varnish that you put on in two or three coats... It lasted at least six months... offering protection against the dirt in the air, fingermarks, and perspiration. It was a first-class product with a pure cellulose base. He'd been wearing the same collar for the last two years. Out of sheer coquetry he'd touch it up once a month... just a stroke of the brush. That gave it the patina, the tone, you could even say the orient, of old ivory... The same with his shirt front... But contrary to what it said in the prospectus, the fingers left distinct marks on the glazed collar... big spots one on top of the other... The result was a regular Bertillon[107] collection, the process wasn't quite perfected. He himself admitted it occasionally. Besides, he didn't have a name yet for this wonder product. He said he'd get around to it when the time was ripe.

When it came to height, Courtial wasn't too well fixed... He hadn't a quarter of an inch to spare... He wore very high heels... altogether, he was particular about his shoes... tan cloth uppers and little mother-of-pearl buttons... Only he was like me, his feet stank something awful... By Saturday afternoon the smell was rough... He'd wash on Sunday morning, he told me so. During the week he didn't have time. I knew all those things... I'd never seen his wife, he told me all about her. They lived in Montrctout... He wasn't the only one that had smelly feet... they were the curse of the period... When the inventors came around all in a sweat, usually from the other end of town, it was hard to listen till they were through, even with the door wide open on the big gardens of the Palais-Royal... The smells that came your way at times were inconceivable... They made me feel disgusted with my own dogs.

The disorder in the offices of the *Genitron* was something monstrous, in a class by itself... the place was a junk shop, absolute chaos... From the door of the shop to the ceiling of the second floor, every step of the stairs, every ledge, every piece of furniture, the chairs, the cupboards, were buried under papers, pamphlets, piles of returns, all topsy-turvy, a desperate hodgepodge, creviced and lacerated, the complete works of Courtial helter-skelter, in pyramids, a fallow field. In that loathsome muddle it was impossible to lay hands on the dictionary, the historical maps, the oleographed dissertations. You'd dig in at random, groping your way... sinking into garbage, a leaking bilge... a teetering cliff... Suddenly it would cave in... you were caught in a cataract... a landslide of blueprints and diagrams... ten tons of printed matter would fall on your face... That would start new avalanches, a frothing torrent of paper... a dust storm... a volcano of stinking filth... Every time we sold five francs' worth of merchandise the dikes threatened to burst...

But that didn't bother him... He didn't even sec anything wrong with it, he felt no desire to change things, to modify his methods... Not at all... He felt perfectly at home in the dizzy chaos... He never had to look very long for the book he was after... He'd reach in and there it was... He'd dive into any old pile... The tatters would go flying, he'd burrow vigorously into the heap and drill to the exact spot where the book was concealed... The miracle happened every time... He seldom went wrong... He had a feeling for disorder... He was sorry for anybody who didn't... Order is entirely in our ideas! In matter there's no trace of it!... When I ventured to remark that it was absolutely impossible for me to find my way in that chaos, that bedlam, he'd get mean... he'd blast me. He didn't even give me time to breathe... He'd attack instantly... "I'm not asking the impossible of you, Ferdinand. You've never had the instinct, the essential curiosity, the desire to learn... After all, you can't claim to be deprived of books around here... Did you ever wonder, my poor young friend, what the human brain looks like?... The mechanism that makes you think? Did you? No. Of course not. That doesn't interest you one bit... You'd rather look at girls. So of course you don't know. Because the first honest glance would convince you that disorder, yes, my boy, disorder, is the quintessence of your very life! of your whole physical and metaphysical being! Why, it's your very soul, Ferdinand! millions, trillions of intricate folds... plunging deep down into the gray matter, complex, subjacent, evasive... limitless! That's Harmony. Ferdinand. All nature! A flight into the imponderable! And nothing else! Put your wretched thoughts in order, Ferdinand! That's where to begin. Not with grotesque, material, negative, obscene substitutions, but with the essential, that's what I'm getting at. Are you going to assault the brain, correct it, scrape it, mutilate it, force it to comply with an assortment of stupid rules? carve it up geometrically? recompose it according to the rules of your excruciating idiocy?... Arrange it in slices? like an Epiphany cake?... With a prize in the middle. Tell me that. I'm asking you. Frankly? Would that be any good? Would it make sense? Heaven help us! There's no doubt about it, Ferdinand, your soul is overwhelmed by errors. It makes you, like so many others, a unanimous nonentity. Great

---

[107] Alphonse Bertillon (1853-1914). Devised the system of identifying criminals by anthropometric measurements and fingerprints.

instinctive disorder is the father of fertile thoughts! It's the beginning of everything... Once the propitious moment has passed, there's no hope... You. I'm afraid, will spend your whole life in the garbage pail of reason... So much the worse for you! You're a numbskull, Ferdinand, a nearsighted, blind, preposterous, deaf, one-armed dolt!... befouling my magnificent disorder with your vicious reflections... In Harmony, Ferdinand, resides the world's only joy! The only deliverance! The only truth!... Harmony! Find Harmony, that's the ticket!... This shop is in Har-mon-y... Do you hear me, Ferdinand? Like a brain, neither more nor less! Order! Pah! Order! Rid me of that word, that thing! Accustom yourself to Harmony and Harmony will reward you. You'll find everything you've been looking for so long on the highways of the world... And far more! Many other things, Ferdinand! A brain, Ferdinand, that's what the whole lot of you will find! Yes! The *Genitron* is a brain. Have I made myself clear? That's not what you're after? You and your kind? An inane ambush of pigeonholes! A barricade of brochures! A house of the dead! A Chartist necropolis! No, never! Here everything is in movement! Swarming with life! You're not satisfied? It stirs, it quivers! Just touch it! Put out your little finger. Everything comes to life. Everything trembles instantly. Asking only to surge up! to blossom! to shine! I don't live by destroying. I take life as it comes! Do you take me for a cannibal, Ferdinand? Never!... Bent on reducing it to my chickenshit concepts? Pah! Everything shakes? Everything topples? Splendid! I have no desire to count stars 1! 2! 3! 4! and 5! I'm not the kind that thinks he's entitled to do anything he pleases. The right to shrink! rectify! corrupt! prune! transplant!... No!... where would I get it?... From the Infinite?... From life itself? It's not natural, my boy! It's not natural! It's infamous meddling!... I prefer to keep on good terms with the Universe! I take it as I find it!... I'll never rectify it! No! The Universe is master of its own house! I understand it! It understands me! It gives me a hand when I ask it! When I'm through with it, I drop it! That's the long and the short of it... It's a cosmogonie question! I have no orders to give! You have no orders! He has no orders!... Bah! Bah! Bah!..."

He got sore as hell, like somebody who's definitely in the wrong...

Courtial's little handbooks were translated into a good many languages, they were sold even in Africa. One of his correspondents was a real nigger, the chief of a sultanate in Upper Ubanghi Shari-Chad. That boy was wild about elevators of every kind. They were his dream, his mania... We'd sent him all the literature... He'd never actually seen one. About 1893 Courtial had published a regular treatise, *On Vertical Traction* . He knew all the details, the many varieties, hydraulic, balistic, "'electro-recuperative"... It was an excellent work, absolutely irrefutable, but it constituted only a slight and modest fraction of his opus as a whole. His knowledge definitely embraced every possible field.

The official world disapproved of him, looked down its nose at him, but the crustiest pedant couldn't very well do without his handbooks. In a good many schools they were actually a part of the curriculum. You couldn't imagine anything handier, simpler, easier to assimilate, all pre- digested! You could remember it, you could forget it without the slightest effort. We reckoned by and large that in France alone, at least one family out of four owned a copy of his *Family Astronomy, Economy Without Usury, and How to Make Ions...* At least one in twelve had his *Color Poetry*, his *Roof Gardening*, his *Poultry Raising at Home.* So far I've been speaking only of his practical works... But he had to his credit a whole series of other volumes (in numerous fascicles) that were real classics. *Hindustani Revelation, The Story of Polar Voyages from Maupertuis to Charcot.* Ponderous tomes. Reading matter for several winters, pounds and pounds of stories...

Everybody had commented, examined, copied, paraphrased, ridiculed, and looted his famous *Be Your Own Doctor* , his *True Language of Herbs*, and his *Electricity Without a Bulb...* All of them brilliant, attractive, definitive popularizations of sciences which in their pure form are exceedingly difficult, complex, and hazardous and which without Courtial would have remained beyond the reach of the general public, in other words, highfalutin', hermetic, and, to sum up without undue flattery, as good as useless...

Little by little, what with living in the closest intimacy with Courtial, I really got to know his character... Way down deep it wasn't so hot. The fact is he was pretty mean, petty, envious, and sneaky... Still, to be fair, I've got to admit that the work he did was a nightmare, struggling desperately, year in year out, to hold his own against that gang of raving maniacs, the *Genitron*'s subscribers...

He spent ghastly, absolutely devastating hours... in a hotbed of asininity... And he had to bear up, to defend himself, to return blow for blow, to sweep away all resistance, to make a good impression on them, so they'd all go away happy and want to come back...

At first Courtial was reluctant to take me on. He didn't go for the idea... He thought me a little too tall, a little too broad-shouldered, a little too husky for his shop. Even without me, you couldn't move in all that mess... And yet I wasn't expensive. I was being offered without pay, just for board and lodging... My parents were perfectly satisfied. I didn't need money, they kept telling my uncle... I'd only put it to bad use... It was much more important that I shouldn't live with them anymore... That was the unanimous opinion of the whole family, of the neighbors too, and of all our acquaintances... that I be given something to do, no matter what! that I be kept busy at any price! no matter where, no matter how! As long as I wasn't left idle! and kept away!

From one day to the next, to judge by the way I had started out, I might set the Passage on fire! That was the general sentiment...

Of course there was always the army... My father asked nothing better... Only I still wasn't old enough... I lacked at least eighteen months... So Pereires and his valiant *Genitron* came in really handy, they were a gift from heaven...

But Courtial hesitated and shilly-shallied a good deal... He asked his wife what she thought about it. She raised no objection... Actually she didn't give a hoot in hell, she never came to the Galerie, she stayed out in Montretout in her cottage. Before he made up his mind, I'd been to see him at least ten times all by myself... He talked abundantly... always and incessantly... I was a very good listener... My father! England!... Everywhere I'd listened... By that time I was in the habit... It didn't bother me in the least. I didn't need to answer. That was how I won him over... By keeping my trap shut... Finally one evening he said:

"Well, my boy. I've kept you waiting quite a while, but now I've thought things over thoroughly. I'm going to keep you here with me. I think we'll get along... But you mustn't make any demands on me... Oh no! Not a sou! Not a centime! It can't be done. I should say not. Don't expect anything. Never expect anything. I'm already having a hell of a time making ends meet in these unpredictable times! covering the costs of the magazine, keeping the printer quiet! I'm harassed, crippled, exhausted! You understand? They dun me day and night. And surprises with the photographic plates... unforeseen expenses... It's out of the question. This isn't an industry... a business... some cushy monopoly... Far from it. It's a frail skiff sailing before the wind of the spirit... And what storms, my boy, what storms!... You want to join us? Good! I take you, I welcome you! Fine! Come aboard! But I'm telling you in advance! You won't find a single doubloon in the hold... Empty hands... little in your pocket... No bitterness... No rancor... You'll get lunch... You'll sleep on the mezzanine, I used to sleep there myself... in the Tunisian office... you'll make up the couch... It's perfectly comfortable... you'll be marvelously at peace... Lucky boy!... Wait and see, in the evening, how pleasant, how peaceful it is! After nine o'clock the Palais-Royal is all yours! You'll be happy, Ferdinand!... Just think of me, rain, thunder, or tempest, I still have to traipse out to Montretout! It's abject slavery. I'm expected! Ah, let me tell you, it's awful some days. When I see the locomotive, I'm so exasperated I could fling myself under the wheels! Ah! I restrain myself... for my wife's sake. And a little for my experiments. My radio-telluric garden! Well, all in all, I've no business complaining. She's been through a good deal. And she is charming. You'll see Madame des Pereires one of these days. She gets so much pleasure out of her garden... It's all hers... And she hasn't much in her life... That and her house... And myself too, a little. I'd forgotten myself. Ha! Ha! That's a good one. Well, we've joked enough. It's settled. Splendid! Shake on it! Then we understand each other? As man to man. Fine. In the daytime you'll run errands. You'll have plenty of them. But don't worry, Ferdinand, I mean to take you in hand too, to guide you, equip you, raise you to the heights of knowledge... No salary! Of course not! Not in cash, that is. But spiritual fare! Ah, Ferdinand, you don't realize what you stand to gain. No! no! no! You'll leave me some day, Ferdinand... inevitably..." Already there was sadness in his voice. "You'll leave me... You'll be rich! Yes, rich! I'm telling you!"

He had me flabbergasted, I stood there open-mouthed.

"You understand me, Ferdinand... Everything isn't in a pocketbook... No! There's nothing in a pocket-book! Nothing!"

I was of the same opinion...

"Well, as a starter, here's an idea. How about giving you a title? *A raison d'être!* It's indispensable in our line of business... an official label!... I'm going to put you on our stationery, on all our paper! 'Secretary in charge of Stock." What do you think of it? It sounds good to me... Is it all right with you? Not too pretentious? Not too vague?... OK?"

It was all right with me... Everything was all right with me... But there wasn't anything honorary about that title... the stock was real and it was hard work... He set me straight right away... My job was to do all the delivering with a pushcart... all the hauling to the printer's and back... In addition I was responsible for every tear in the big balloon... I had to keep tabs on all the hardware he left lying around, the barometers, the ropes, all the little gadgets... I had to mend the rips and the big bag... patch things up with cord and glue... and attend to all the knots in the cables and guy ropes... all the tackle that broke in midair... The *Enthusiast* was a venerable old balloon, even down there in the cellar sprinkled with moth flakes, it was eminently given to decay... thousands of grubs feasted in the folds... luckily the rubber repelled the rats... there were tiny little mice that nibbled at the silk. I'd locate the tears in the *Enthusiast,* the tiniest holes, and patch them like a pair of pants... with oversewing, hems, pleats, depending on the nature of the tear... It was in pretty bad shape all over, I mended for hours on end, after a while I got really absorbed...

At least in that cubbyhole of a gymnasium there was a little more elbowroom... And besides the customers in the shop weren't supposed to see me...

Some day, it was stipulated in our solemn agreement, I was to go up in the contraption, to an altitude of a thousand feet... Some Sunday... I'd be second in command... a different title... He told me that, I suppose, to make me mind my mending... The old buzzard was pretty sly under those shaggy eyebrows... He looked at me out of his mean little eyes... I was on to his game... As a soft-soap artist he had no equal... He was giving me a song and dance... But we ate pretty well in the back room... I wasn't too unhappy... Naturally he had to take me for a ride... or he wouldn't have been the boss.

At about four o'clock, when I was knee-deep in my sewing, he'd look in: "Ferdinand," he'd say, "I'm closing up... if anybody asks for me, tell them I stepped out five minutes ago. Anyway I'll make it fast. I won't be long."

Putting two and two together. I knew where he was going. He'd run down to the Insurrection, the little bar at the corner of the Passage Villedo and the rue Radziwill, for the racing results... That was the time they came out... He never told me anything definite... But I knew... When he had won, he came back whistling a Matchiche[108]... That wasn't very often... When he'd lost, he'd chew on his quid and spit in all directions... He'd check up in *Turf,* his dope sheet, that he always left lying around... He'd mark his ponies with blue pencil... This was the first vice I detected in him.

If he wasn't too eager to take me on. it was mostly on account of the horses... He was afraid I'd blab... go noising it around the neighborhood that he played in Vincennes... that the subscribers would get wind of it. He told me so later... He lost stupendously... he wasn't very lucky. Whether he tried a combination or bet with his eyes closed, he lost his money... Maisons, Saint-Cloud, or Chantilly, it was always the same story... A bottomless pit... All the subscription money went into the "classics"! And the dough he took in with the balloon was swallowed up in Auteuil... The Equine Race[109] was rolling in clover! Longchamp! La Porte! Arcueil-Cachan! Giddyap giddyup, and down the drain. I could see the cash drawer going down. There was no great mystery. Our petty cash was always running with the ponies... trotting! limping! to win! to place! to come in fourth!... simple or fancy, it made no difference... he'd never get back when he went to see about those proofs... We ate beans to try and mollify the printer... My veal stew had to last all week, and we ate on our knees with a napkin

---

[108] Matchiche. Popular dance of Spanish origin. Introduced to France from Brazil about 1904, it was all the rage for a few years.

[109] Equine Race. Society for the Improvement of the Equine Race *(Société pour l'amélioration de la race chevaline):* One of several organizations that supervise the French race tracks.

in the back of the shop... It didn't seem so very funny to me... When he'd lost heavily, he didn't explain, he never admitted it... But he'd get vindictive, touchy, aggressive with me... He'd abuse his power...

After a trial period of two months, he fully realized that I'd never be happy anywhere else... that the *Genitron* routine was right down my alley, that it suited me fine, that anywhere else or in any other racket I'd be impossible... That was my Destiny... When he chanced to win, he'd never put anything back in the till, he got stingier than ever, like he was trying to get even... He'd have curry-combed a penny... Always sly and deceitful, worse than a dozen false bosoms... He told me such whoppers they'd stick in my craw at night... They were so steep, so crummy, so indigestible, I'd mull them over... They woke me up with a start. Sometimes he really overdid it... he'd dream up any damn thing... so as not to pay me... But when he came home from the provinces, when he'd put on a good show with his balloon and made a sensation... when they'd bowled him over with compliments... and the *Enthusiast* hadn't split too many seams... there'd be an outburst of generosity... He'd spend like mad... He'd bring in piles of eats through the back door... whole baskets full... For a week we shoveled in so much we couldn't chew anymore... our suspenders were bursting... You had to make hay while the sun was shining, because soon there'd be famine... the ragouts would begin again... we'd stretch the stew with pickles... with sardines... with little onions... And around toward rent time there'd be strictly bread soup, with or without potatoes... He at least was lucky, he'd be getting another meal in the evening with his old lady. He wouldn't lose any weight... I wouldn't get beans.

From going hungry I began to wise up too... I operated with the subscriptions... The business didn't have any regular receipts... only expenses... He knocked himself out with his bookkeeping. He had to show his wife the books. Her supervision exasperated him... It put him into a vile temper... He'd sweat for hours... Nothing but loops and zeroes...

All the same there was one department where he never cheated me, never disappointed me, never once bluffed me or let me down. I'm referring to my scientific education... On that score he never weakened, never hesitated a second... He always came through... As long as I listened to him, he was always happy, delighted, overjoyed... He was always ready to give me an hour, two hours, and more, sometimes he'd spend whole days explaining something or other... Anything that can be understood, solved, communicated, in connection with the direction of the winds, the movements of the moon, the functioning of heating installations, the ripening of cucumbers, the reflections of the rainbow... Yes, teaching was really a consuming passion with him. He'd have liked to teach me everything in the world and from time to time play a mean trick on me! He couldn't help it... in either case! I used to think it all over in the back room, while mending his contraption... That was his nature... he was a man who had to work off his energy... He had to throw himself wholeheartedly in one direction or another, he never did things by halves. He wasn't boring! No, you could never accuse him of that. What I'd really have liked to do was to visit his home some day... He often spoke to me of his old lady, but he never let me see her. She never came to the office. She didn't care for the *Genitron*. She must have had her reasons.

When my mother was perfectly sure I was all set, that I wasn't going to pick up and leave, that I had a steady job with this des Pereires, she came over to the Palais-Royal in person, to bring me some underwear... It was really a pretext... she wanted to look around, to see what the place was like... She was as curious as a titmouse, she always wanted to see, to find out about everything... What was the *Genitron* like? And my lodgings? Was I getting enough to eat?

It wasn't very far from her shop to our place... No more than a fifteen minutes' walk...

Even so, she was groaning with fatigue when she got there... She was completely bushed... I saw her in the distance... from the end of the Galerie. I was talking with a subscriber. She was leaning on the shopwindows, resting without letting on, every fifty feet she'd stop... She looked awfully thin, and besides she'd gone sallow, her eyelids and cheeks had shriveled, she was all wrinkled around the eyes. She really looked sick... She gave me my socks, my underdrawers, and my big handkerchiefs, and then right away she started talking about Papa, though I hadn't asked... He'd feel the effects of my assault to his dying day, she sobbed. Twice already they'd brought him home from the office in a cab... He could hardly stand up... He had fainting spells all the time... He sent word that he gladly forgave me, but that he didn't want to see me again... not for a long time... not before my military service... until my looks and mentality had changed completely... when I got back from the army...

Courtial was just coming back from a stroll, probably to the Insurrection. Maybe he hadn't dropped as much as usual... in any case he was extremely polite all of a sudden, as charming and friendly as he could be... delighted to meet her... And about me? Reassuring. Right away he set out to charm my mother, he asked her upstairs for a chat... in his private office... on the "Tunisian" mezzanine... She had difficulty in following him... It was a horrible corkscrew staircase and to make matters worse it was littered with piles of garbage and papers that made you skid. He was mighty proud of his "Tunisian office." He wanted to show it to everybody. It was a devastating layout in the hyperpoky style, with "Alcazar" cabinets... You couldn't conceive of anything crummier... And then the Moorish coffeepot, the Moroccan ottomans, the fringed shaggy carpet that stored up a whole ton of dust all by itself... Nothing had ever been done about it... not even the slightest attempt at cleaning... Anyway the heaps of printed matter, the mountains, the cataracts of proof, of type, of newsprint lying around would have mocked any effort... Actually, there's no denying it, it would have been dangerous... To come around troubling the equilibrium would be taking a big risk... The only way was to leave it perfectly intact, to move things as little as possible... Better still, I soon found out, was to toss on new layers of litter as you went along. That gave the surface a certain freshness... a kind of gloss.

I heard them talking... Courtial told her frankly that he had discerned in me a real aptitude for the kind of journalism that was just what the *Genitron* needed... reporting... technical investigation... scientific research... objective criticism... that I was sure to get ahead... that she could go home with an easy mind and sleep soundly... that the future was already smiling on me... it would be all mine as soon as I'd acquired all the essential knowledge. It was a matter of simple routine and patience... He'd gradually teach me all I needed... But all that took time... Ah yes, he had no use for haste! Thoughtless precipitation!... No use trying to force matters... to go too fast... That would be idiotic waste! Anyway, according to his song and dance, I displayed a keen desire for education!... Moreover, I was learning to be clever with my hands. I did the little jobs that came my way to perfection... I was managing very nicely... I was getting to be as nimble as a monkey! Eager! Intelligent! Hardworking! Discreet! In short, a dream! He went on and on... It was the first time in her life that my poor mama had heard anybody speak of me in such glowing colors... She couldn't get over it... At the end of the interview, as she was leaving, he insisted on her taking a whole book of subscription blanks to distribute at random among her connections and acquaintances... She promised to do anything he pleased. She gaped at him in bewilderment... Courtial had no shirt on, only his varnished shirt front over his flannel vest, but the vest always went way up over his collar... he took an extra large size, it formed a kind of ruff, and of course it was completely filthy... In winter he wore two of them, one on top of the other... In the summer, even during hot spells, he wore his long frock coat, his lacquered collar down a little lower, no socks, and he brought out his boater. He took meticulous care of it… It was a unique item, a real masterpiece of the sombrero type, a gift from South America, a rare weave! Impossible to match... In short, it was priceless!... From the first of June to the fifteenth of September he kept it on his head. He hardly ever took it off... except for some extra- special reason... He was sure somebody'd steal it... That was his biggest worry on Sundays, before going up in his balloon... But there was no help for it, he had to exchange it for his cap, the tall one with the braid... That was part of his uniform... He entrusted his treasure to me... But the moment he'd touched the ground, the moment he'd rolled like a rabbit into the muck and come bouncing over the furrows, that was his first cry: "Hey, my panama! Ferdinand! My panama, dammit..."

My mother noticed the thickness of the flannel vest right off and the fine quality of the prize hat... He let her feel the weave, to give her an idea... For quite some time she was lost in admiration, exclaiming: "Oh! Ttt! Oh! Ttt!... Ah, monsieur, I can see that. It's the kind of straw they don't make anymore!" She was in ecstasy.

All this restored my mother's confidence... a good omen... She was particularly fond of flannel vests... they indicated solidity of character, she'd never gone wrong. After fond farewells, she gradually started on her way... For the first time in her life and mine I think she was a little less worried about my future and my fate.

It was perfectly true that I threw myself into my work. From morning to night I had no chance to loaf... In addition to my cargoes of printed matter, I had the *Enthusiast* in the cellar, the endless mending, and our pigeons that I had to look after two or three times a day... Those critters lived all week in the maid's room on the seventh floor, under the eaves... They cooed like, mad... They never felt gloomy. Their working day was Sunday, they'd be taken out in a basket for a ride in the balloon... At six or eight hundred feet Courtial would raise the lid... They'd be released... with messages... They'd all fly straight home... to the Palais-Royal!... The window'd be left open for them... They never dawdled on the way, they didn't care for the country, they didn't like to bum around... They flew back automatically... They loved their attic and their roo-coo-crooing. That's all they wanted. It never stopped... They were always home before us. I've never known pigeons less enthusiastic about traveling, so enamored of peace and quiet... And I left their windows wide open... It never occcurred to them to take a turn around the garden... to go calling on the sparrows... or the fat gray cooers gallivanting on the lawns... around the fountains... and once in a while on the statues... on Desmoulins[110]... or old Vick[111]... dropping their beauty marks... Not at all... they kept to themselves... they were perfectly happy in their attic, they left it only under duress, when they were tossed into their basket... They were pretty expensive though, on account of the grain... It takes quantities, pigeons eat a lot... They're pigs... you wouldn't expect them to eat so much... it's on account of their high body temperature, normally 107 and a few tenths... I swept up their droppings carefully... I made several little piles along the wall and I let them dry... That made up some for their food... It was excellent fertilizer... When I had a whole sack full, about twice a month, Courtial took it away, he used it in his garden... in Montretout on the hill... where he had his tony villa and his experimental garden... there's no better manure...

I got along fine with the pigeons, they reminded me a little of Jongkind... I taught them tricks... Naturally after they got to know me, they ate out of my hand... But I did a lot better than that, I got them to perch on a broomstick, all twelve of them at once... I even managed to carry them down to the shop... and back up again without their moving, without a single one of them deciding to fly away... They were really sedentary. When it came time to throw them in the basket and push off, they got terribly sad. They didn't coo at all. They hid their heads in their feathers. They hated it.

Two more months passed... Little by little Courtial gained confidence in me. He was convinced that we were made to get along... I had a lot of advantages, I wasn't very particular about food or pay or working hours... I never complained... As long as I was free in the evening, as long as nobody bothered me after seven o'clock, I felt I was well off...

From the moment he lit out for his train, I was the one and only boss of the shop and paper... I got rid of the inventors... I soft-soaped them... then I started out on a cruise, often heading for the shipping office on the rue Rambuteau, pulling the cart loaded with copies of the rag. At the beginning of the week I had to bring back proofs, the typos and plates and engravings. What with the pigeons, the *Enthusiast*, and a million other odds and ends, there was never a letup... He dropped everything and pushed off for the sticks... He had urgent work out there, so he said. Hm! Neo-agriculture... he said it with a straight face... but I was convinced it was hokum... Sometimes he forgot to come back, he'd stay out for two or three days... that didn't worry me... I'd take a little rest, I needed it... I'd feed the pigeons up in the attic, then I'd paste up a sign in the middle of the shopwindow: "Closed for the day"... I'd go take it easy on a bench, under the trees nearby... From there I watched the joint, the people coming and going... I saw them in the distance, always the same gang of dopes, the same lunatics, the same haggard faces, the old crowd of bellyachers, the disgruntled subscribers... They bunked into the sign, they massacred the door handle, they beat it... That was fine with me.

When his nibs came back from his spree, he had a screwy look... He eyed me curiously to see if I suspected anything...

"I was detained," he said. "The experiment wasn't quite perfected... I thought I'd never be through."

---

[110] Camille Desmoulins (1760-1794). Leader in the French Revolution, executed with Danton on April 5, 1794.
[111] Old Vick = Victor Hugo.

"That's too bad," I said. "I hope you made out all right in the end..."

Little by little he filled me in, he told me a little more each day, he gave me all the details about the beginnings of his racket... There were some pretty wild stories, gimmicks that could end you in the cemetery. How it had started, the ups and downs, the risky dodges, the shady little deals... He told me the whole story, which was pretty strange when you think of his rotten character, his innumerable suspicions, and all his calamities and hard luck... He wasn't the complaining kind... But the troubles and messes he'd been through were unbelievable... It was no rest cure monkeying around with inventors... Don't get the wrong slant... Oh no. Some of those boys were real savages, absolutely diabolical... they'd go off like dynamite if they felt they'd been taken... And naturally you can't hope to please everybody... the devil and his brother-in-law! That would be too sweet. I knew something about that myself... In that connection he gave me an example of malice that was really hair-raising... The lengths people will go to... In 1884 he'd got an order from Beaupoil and Brandon on the Quai des Ursulines, the publishers of *Epoch*, for a textbook intended for the second program of the Preliminary Schools… A concise work, of course, but carefully executed, elementary but compact. Specially condensed... *The Home Astronomer*, the little book was entitled, with the subtitle: *Gravitation, explained to the whole family*. So he goes to work... He dives right in... he might have contented himself with delivering a brief work on the specified date, a hurry-up job full of inept borrowings from foreign periodicals... slapdash, corrupt, garbled quotations, and in three shakes of a lamb's tail constructed a new cosmogony a thousand times lousier than all the other miniature handbooks, full of mistakes and absolutely senseless!... Utterly useless!... As everyone knew, that wasn't Courtial's way of doing things. He was conscientious. His chief concern when he sat down to a piece of work was to get tangible results... He wanted his reader to form his own ideas in person, by his own observations... about the most essential aspects of the work... the stars and gravitation... to discover the laws for himself... He wanted to force the always indolent reader to do real laboratory work and not just cajole him with flattering flimflam... He'd appended a little set of instructions: how to build a "family telescope"... A few squares of cardboard provided the darkroom... a few cheap mirrors... an ordinary lens... a few lengths of pliable wire... a cardboard packing tube... By strictly following the instructions you could do it for seventeen francs, seventy-two (reckoned to the centime)... for that price (in addition to the exciting and instructive work) you could obtain in your own home, not only a direct view of the principal constellations, but also photographs of most of the large stars of our zenith... "All sidereal observations made available to the family"... that was his formula... As soon as the booklet came out, more than twenty-five thousand readers started without a moment's delay to build the thing, the marvelous miniature photosidercal device…

I can still hear des Pereires telling me about all the trouble that ensued... The incomprehension of the competent authorities... their abject partiality... How painful, rotten, sickening it all was... All the libels he had received. Threats... Challenges... A thousand threatening letters... Summonses... How he'd been obliged to lock himself in, barricade himself in his apartment!... He'd been living on the rue Monge at the time... Then, more and more harassed, he'd fled to Montretout from the rage of all those insatiable, vicious peeping toms, disappointed by telescopy... The mess had gone on for six months... and it still wasn't over! Some of those angry stargazers, even pestier than the rest, would take advantage of their Sunday off... They'd come out to Montretout, they'd bring the whole family, to kick the boss in the ass… He hadn't been able to receive any visitors in almost a year... This "photosidereal" business was only a small example among many others of how the masses were capable of reacting the minute you tried to educate them, to uplift them, to wise them up...

"I can tell you, Ferdinand, that I've suffered for science... Worse than Flammarion, that's certain! worse than Raspail! worse even than Mongolfier![112] On a small scale, of course... I've done everything! And then some!" He used to repeat that often... I didn't answer... He gave me a sidelong look... suspicious... he wanted to see the impression he was making... Then he'd dive right into the chaos... looking for his file... He'd locate it by instinct under the enormous mound... He'd pat the dust off it... He'd change his mind... He'd cautiously open it up in front of me...

---

[112] Mongolfier. The Mongolfier brothers, paper manufacturers, pioneers in lighter-than-air aircraft.

"When I think it over, I'm sorry... Maybe I too have become a trifle bitter, carried away by memories... Perhaps I'm a little unjust... Good Lord. I've reason enough... I ask you! In the course of time I've forgotten... that was very wrong of me... not intentionally, to be sure! not intentionally!... the most touching, perhaps the most sincere, the most precious testimonials... Ah! They haven't all failed to appreciate me!... The whole human race isn't so absolutely depraved... No! A few noble souls here and there in the world... have been able to recognize my absolute good faith. Here! Here! And still another!" He pulled out letters and memoranda at random from his collection... "I'll read you one among many":

Dear Courtial, honored master and revered precursor: It is assuredly thanks to you, to your admirable and so scrupulous telescope (for the family) that yesterday at two o'clock on my own balcony I was able to view the whole moon, in its *complete* totality, with its mountains, its rivers, and even I believe, a forest... Perhaps even a lake! I hope to see Saturn too with my children in the course of the coming week, as it is indicated (in italics) on your "sidereal calendar" and also Bellegophorus a little later, in the last days of the autumn, as you yourself have written on page 242... Yours, dear, gracious, and benevolent master, yours in heart, body, and spirit, here below and in the stars.

One who has been transformed.

He kept all these admiring letters in his mauve and lavender portfolio. As for the others, unfavorable, menacing, draconic, vicious, he burned them on the spot. In this connection at least, he kept a certain amount of order... "The poison's going up in smoke." he told me every time he touched a match to one of those monstrosities... How much evil would be eliminated if everybody did the same. My idea is that he wrote the favorable ones himself... He showed them to visitors... He never actually admitted it to me... Now and then I smiled... There was a certain restraint in my approval... He half-suspected that I smelled a rat. Then he'd scowl at me… I'd go up to feed the pigeons or I'd go down to the *Enthusiast...*

By now I was laying his bets for him at the Insurrection on the corner of the Passage Radziwill. He preferred for me to do it on account of the customers, it could have been bad for business... On Cartouche and Lysistrata in the Vincennes gallops... and giddyup and away we go!

"You'll tell them it's your own sugar."... He owed all the bookies money. He had no desire at all to show his face... The character that took most of our bets between the saucers had a funny name, he was called Formerly... He had a way of stuttering, of garbling the names of the winners... He did it on purpose, I think, to give you a wrong steer... Afterwards he'd deny everything... He'd want to skip the number... I always made him write it down... we lost anyway.

I'd bring back the *Turf Echo* or *Racing Luck...* If he'd lost heavily, he had the crust to give me hell... He sent all the inventors away... He threw them all out with their models and diagrams... "Go wipe your ass, the whole lot of you. Those blueprints stink... You got a headache?... They smell of axle grease, margarine... You call that ideas? Innovations? Hell, I can piss better ideas than that... a whole potful!... three times a day... Aren't you ashamed of yourself? Don't you realize?... It's a disaster! You have the gall to bring that stuff here? To me? When I'm up to my neck in crap already... Get out of here! Christ! You lounge lizards! You loafers in body and soul!..."

The guy would leave all right, he'd run for the door, he'd fly with his roll of plans. Courtial was fed up with them. He wanted to think of something else... I was the scapegoat, he started in on me... any old baloney would do... "You, naturally, you suspect nothing! You have time to listen to everything! You've got nothing to do, is that it?... But I'm not exactly in that position… I can't look at things that way... I have preoccupations... metaphysical preoccupations!... Permanent! Ineluctable! That's right! They leave me no rest! Never! Even when I don't show it! When I'm talking to you about one thing and another, I'm haunted... harassed... tormented by riddles!... Well, there you have it! You didn't know! It comes as a surprise to you? You never suspected it?"

He stared at me again as if he hadn't ever really placed me... He straightened out his moustaches, he dusted off the dandruff... He went for a rag to pass over his shoes... All the while telling me what he thought of me...

"What can it matter to you? You just drift along. You don't give a good goddamn about the universal consequences that can flow from our most trifling acts, our most unforeseen thoughts… It's no skin off your ass... You're caulked... hermetically sealed... Nothing means anything to you... Am I right? Nothing. Eat! Drink! Sleep! Up there as cozy as you please... All warm and comfy on my couch... You've got everything you want... You wallow in well-being... the earth rolls on... How? Why? A staggering miracle... how it moves... the profound mystery of it... toward an infinite unforeseeable goal... in a sky all scintillating with comets... all unknown... from one rotation to the next... Each second is the culmination and also the prelude of an eternity of other miracles... of impenetrable wonders, thousands of them, Ferdinand! Millions! billions of trillions of years!... And you? What are you doing in the midst of this cosmologonic whirl? this vast sidereal wonder? Just tell me that! You eat! You fill your belly! You sleep! You don't give a damn... That's right! Salad! Swiss cheese! Sapience! Turnips! Everything! You wallow in your own muck! You loll around, befouled! Glutted! Satisfied! You don't ask for anything more! You pass through the stars... as if they were raindrops in May!... God, you amaze me, Ferdinand! Do you really think this can go on forever?..."

I didn't say a word... I had no set opinion about the stars or the moon, but I had one about him, the bastard. And the stinker knew it.

"Take a look some time in the little cabinet upstairs. Put them all together. I've received at least a hundred such letters. I wouldn't want them to be stolen... There's an idea, why don't you file them?... You like order so much... you'll get a kick out of it..." I saw through him... He was handing me a line... "You'll find the key on top of the gas meter... I'm going out for a while... you can close up..." He changed his mind. "No, you'd better stick around in case somebody comes in. Tell them I've gone away... far away! far far away! on an expedition... Tell them I've gone to Senegal! Pernambuco! Mexico!... any place you like... Christ, I've had enough for today!... It turns my stomach to see them coming in from the gardens... I'll puke if I see one more of them... Hell, I don't care... Tell them anything you please... Tell them I've gone to the moon... that it's no use waiting... And now open up the cellar... Hold the lid properly! Don't let it fall back on my head the way you did last time... I bet you did it on purpose..."

To those words I made no reply... He stepped into the hole. He went down two three rungs... He waited a moment. Then he said...

"You're not a bad kid, Ferdinand... your father's mistaken about you. You're not bad... You're unformed, that's it... pro-to-plas-mic! What month are you, Ferdinand? What month were you born in, I mean! February? September? March?"

"February, maître!"

"I'd have bet five francs on it. February! Saturn! What's going to become of you! Poor devil! Why, it's insane! Well, anyway, lower the trap. When I'm all the way down. All the way, see? Not before! And have me break both my legs. This ladder's a wreck! it sags in the middle!... I should have repaired it long ago... Let her go!..." He went on shouting from deep down in the cellar... "Whatever happens, don't let anybody in! No pests! No drunks! You hear me, I'm not here for anybody! I want privacy! Absolute privacy!... Maybe I'll be gone two hours... maybe two days... But I don't want to be disturbed. Don't worry about me. Maybe I'll never come up! If they ask you, you don't know a thing... I'm going into meditation... You understand?"

"Yes, maître!"

"Total, exhaustive meditation, Ferdinand! Exhaustive retirement!..." "Yes, maître..."

I let the thing slam full force in a volcano of dust. It thundered like a cannon... I pushed the newspapers over the trapdoor, it was completely camouflaged... you couldn't see the opening... I went up to feed the pigeons... I stayed quite a while... If he was still in his hole when I came back down, I began to wonder if anything was wrong... I waited a while longer... half an hour... three quarters of an hour... then I began to think the monkeyshines had been going on long enough... I lifted the trap a little and looked in... If I didn't see him, I made a racket... I banged the trapdoor... He had to answer... It brought him out of his nirvana... Nearly always he was sawing wood under the transom in the folds of the *Enthusiast*, in the rolling billows of silk... It took some doing to get him to move... Finally he'd surface... He'd reappear... rubbing his eyes... He'd brush off his frock coat... Back in the shop he'd be all befuddled...

"I'm dazzled, Ferdinand! How beautiful it is! Beautiful, like fairyland!"

He looked pasty, the talk had gone out of him, he had calmed down... He went "bdia, bdia, bdia" with his tongue... He went out... teetering from his nap... He walked slantwise like a crab... Port of call: the Pavillon de la Régence! The café that looked like a china birdcage, with pretty piers... in those days it was still in the middle of a moldering flowerbed... He slumped down the first place he found... at the table by the door... I had a good view of him from the shop... He started off with his usual absinthe... It was easy to see him... We still had our nifty telescope in the window... the one left from the big show... Maybe you couldn't see Saturn through it, but you could see des Pereires sugaring his pea soup[113]... Then he had an "anisette" and after that a vermouth... The colors were easy to make out... and just before taking off for his train a good stiff grog for the road.

After his terrible accident Courtial had taken a solemn vow that he'd never again, at any price, take the wheel in a race... That was all over... finished... He'd kept his promise... And even now, twenty years later, he had to be begged before he'd drive on some quiet excursion, or in an occasional harmless demonstration. He felt much safer out in the wind in his balloon...

His studies of mechanics were all contained in his books... Year in year out he published two treatises (with diagrams) on the development of motors and two handbooks with plates.

One of these little works had stirred up bitter controversies and even a certain amount of scandal. Actually it wasn't even his fault... It was all on account of some low-down sharpers who travestied his ideas in an idiotic money-making scheme... It wasn't at all in his style. Anyway here's the title:

An Automobile Made to Order for 322 Francs 25. Complete instructions for home manufacture. Four permanent seats, two folding seats, wicker body, 12 m.p.h., 7 speeds, 2 reverse gears. Done entirely with spare parts that could be picked up anywhere! assembled to the customer's taste... to suit his personality! according to the style and the season of the year! This little book was all the rage... from 1902 to 1905... It contained... which was a step forward... not only diagrams, but actual blue-prints on a scale of one to two hundred thousand. Photographs, cross-references, cross sections... all flawless and guaranteed.

His idea was to combat the rising peril of mass production... There wasn't a moment to be lost... Despite his resolute belief in progress, des Pereires had always detested standardization... From the very start he was bitterly opposed to it... He foresaw that the death of craftsmanship would inevitably shrink the human personality...

At the time of this battle for the "made to measure" automobile Courtial was practically famous in the world of innovators for his original and extremely daring studies on the "All-Purpose Cottage," the flexible, extensible dwelling, adaptable to families of every kind in all climates!... "Your own house," absolutely detachable, tippable (that is, transportable), shrinkable, instantly reducible by one or more rooms at will, to fit permanent or passing needs, children, guests, alterable at a moment's notice... to meet the requirements, the tastes of every individual... "An old house is a house that doesn"t move!... Buy young! Be flexible! Don't build. Assemble! To build is death! Only tombs can be built properly. Buy a living house! Live in a living house! The 'All-Purpose Cottage' keeps pace with life!..."

Such was the tone, the style of the manifesto written by Courtial himself just before the "Future of Architecture" exhibition held in June, '98, at the Gallery of Machines. Almost immediately his little book on home building created an enormous furore among men about to be pensioned, heads of families with insignificant incomes, homeless young couples, and colonial civil servants... He was bombarded with inquiries from all over France, from abroad, from the Dominions... His cottage, all set up with movable roof. 2,492 nails, 3 doors, 24 sections, 5 windows, 42 hinges, wood or muslin partitions according to the season, won a special prize, *"hors concours,"* unbeatable... It could be assembled in the desired dimensions with the help of two workmen, on any kind of ground, in seventeen minutes and four seconds!... The wear and tear was minimal... it would last forever!... "Only resistance is ruinous. A house in its entirety must have play, it has to adapt itself like a living organism! it has to give... it has to dodge the whirling winds! the gales and tempests, the paroxysms of nature! The moment you oppose... what utter folly!... the unleashed elements, disaster ensues!... Can a

---

[113] pea soup = absinthe

building... the most massive... the most galvanic... the most firmly cemented... be expected to defy the elements? Pure madness! One day or another, inevitably, it will be overturned, annihilated! If you wish to be convinced, you have only to pass through one of our beautiful, our fertile countrysides! Isn't our magnificent country interspersed from north to south with melancholy ruins? Once proud habitations! Haughty manors! Ornaments of our soil, what has become of you? Dust!"

"The 'All-Purpose Cottage,' on the other hand, is flexible, it adapts itself, it expands, it contracts according to necessity, according to the laws, the living forces of nature!"

"It bends enormously, but it never breaks..." The day his stand was inaugurated, after President Félix Faure had come through, after all the powwow and congratulations, the crowd broke through the barriers! the guards were swept away! The populace burst in so frantically between the walls of the cottage that the little marvel was instantly torn apart, washed away, swallowed up! The mob was so feverish, so avid, that it combusted all the materials... You couldn't say this one and only model was destroyed... it was sucked up, absorbed, digested on the spot... The evening the exhibition closed there wasn't a trace left of it, not a crumb, not a nail, not a shred of muslin... The amazing edifice had been absorbed like a pimple... As Courtial told me about all this fifteen years later, he was still in a daze...

"Of course I could have started in again... In that field, I can say without flattering myself, my ability was remarkable... When it came to drawing up a precise, a meticulous estimate for on-the-spot assembly, I had no rival... But other, more grandiose projects carried me away, kept me absorbed... I've never found the time to resume my calculations of the 'indices of resistance'

... And after all, in spite of the final disaster, I had proved what I set out to... By my boldness I had enabled certain schools, certain young enthusiasts, to step forward... to shout their opinions from the rooftops... to find their way... That and nothing else was my mission! I desired nothing more! My honor was intact! I asked for nothing, Ferdinand! Coveted nothing! Demanded nothing of the authorities! I went back to my studies... I didn't scheme or intrigue!... And now listen... Guess what I get... Practically one right after the other? The Nicham, and a week later the Academic Palms!... I was really offended! Whom did they take me for all of a sudden? Why not a tobacco counter? I wanted to send all that flimflam back to the minister! I told Flammarion about it: 'Don't do it,' he said, 'don't do anything of the kind. I've got them too!' Well, in that case I was in the clear. But even so they'd swindled me outrageously!... Oh, the skunks! My plans had been plagiarized, pirated, copied, do you hear, in a thousand revolting ways... and incompetently what's more... by so many swelled-headed, unprincipled, shameless official architects that I wrote to Flammarion... If they wanted to make amends, they owed me at least the Legion of Honor... if they'd wanted to butter me up with honors, I mean... He thought I was perfectly right, but he advised me to keep quiet and not make any more of a stink... it would even get him in trouble... to be patient... that the time wasn't quite ripe... that after all I was his disciple and I shouldn't forget it... Oh, I don't feel any bitterness, get me straight! Yes, those little things still make me feel sad... But nothing more! Absolutely not!... A melancholy lesson... That's all... I think of it now and then..."

I could tell when the architectural blues came over him... It usually happened in the country... and when he was getting ready to go up in his balloon... when he was climbing into the basket... His memories came back to him... Maybe he was a little scared and that was what made him talk... He looked at the country in the distance... Out there in the suburbs, especially at the housing lots, the shacks and shanties... He was overcome with emotion... it brought the tears to his eyes... Those shacks, all lopsided and cross-eyed, all cracked and rickety, rotting away in the muck, sinking into the slush, at the edge of the fields... beyond the highway... "You see all that," he'd say to me, "you see that stinking mess?" He'd make a sweeping gesture, embracing the horizon... The whole crawling swarm of shanties, the church and the chicken coops, the wash-house and the schools... The ramshackle tumbledown huts, gray, mauve, and mignonette... all the plaster thingamajigs...

"It's bad, eh? It's pretty crummy?... Well, it's a good deal my fault... I'm responsible!

You can put the blame on me... All that is mine, do you hear me?... Mine!..."

"Ah?" I said as though flabbergasted. I knew he was going into his routine... He threw his leg over the edge... He jumped into the wicker basket... If the wind wasn't too strong, he kept his panama on... he was much happier that way... but he tied it under his chin with a broad ribbon... I'd wear his cap... "Let her go!" She'd rise inch by inch, very slowly at first... and then a little faster... He'd have to get a move on to clear the roofs... He couldn't make up his mind to throw off ballast... But he had to rise somehow... We never inflated her completely... The stuff cost thirteen francs a bottle...

Some time after the adventure with the "Homemade Cottage" that the insane crowd had torn to pieces, Courtial des Pereires suddenly decided to change his whole tactics... "Capital first!" That's what he said... That was his new motto. "No more risks. Cold cash!..." He had mapped out a program based entirely on these principles... And fundamental reforms... all absolutely judicious and pertinent...

First of all he decided that come hell or high water the conditions of inventors had to be improved... He started from the premise that in this racket there'd never be any shortage of ideas... that they were actually too plentiful! But that capital, on the other hand, is disgustingly evasive! pusillanimous! retiring!... That all the misfortunes of the human race and his own in particular came from lack of funds... the distrustfulness of money... the hideous rarity of credit... But all that could be straightened out... All it would take to remedy this state of affairs was action... an ingenious idea... So one two three, right there on the Galerie Montpensier, behind the "Tunisian office," between the kitchen and the corridor, he founded an "Investors' Corner"... a very special little nook, furnished very simply: a table, a cupboard, a filing cabinet, two chairs, and to preside over deliberations, a fine bust of de Lesseps on the top shelf, between folders and more folders...

On the strength of the new statutes, any inventor willing to invest fifty-two francs (total payable in advance) could run an ad in our paper for three successive issues... saying anything he pleased about all his projects, even the wildest nonsense, the dizziest phantasmagorias, the most shameless impostures... Not bad! It filled up two full columns in the *Genitron* and we'd throw in a ten minutes' private consultation with Courtial, the director... And finally, to make the deal even more attractive, an oleo-graphed diploma, certifying him as a "member in good standing of the Eureka Research Center for the financing, study, equilibration, and immediate exploitation of discoveries conducive to the advancement of all the sciences and of industry..." It wasn't so easy to get them to cough up the fifty smackers... That was always slow going... Even giving them the song and dance... talking himself blue in the face... when it came to paying up, they nearly always balked... even the screwiest of them got to feeling worried... even in their delirium, they smelled a rat... they realized that this was dough they'd never be seeing again... "Registration fees" was the name we dreamed up for our gimmick...

The understanding was that from that moment on Courtial would take all the necessary steps, put out feelers, attend to all the calling and contacting, the interviews... the documentation... the meetings... the premonitory discussions, the arguments, in short everything that was needed to attract, propitiate, arouse, and reassure a consortium... All this, it went without saying, at the opportune moment... On that point we were adamant... Haste makes waste... easy does it... that was our way... Impatience can only mess everything up! Precipitation wrecks the best-laid plans! The most fruitful undertakings are those that ripen slowly!... We were radically opposed, implacably hostile, to all premature bungling... to all hysteria... "Your investor escapes on the wings of the swallow, he's a tortoise when it comes to forking up."

To interfere as little as possible with the negotiations, always so delicate, the inventor was advised to leave the field perfectly clear... to go straight home... to smoke his pipe and wait... and not worry about a thing. He'd be duly notified, summoned, acquainted with every detail as soon as things began to shape up... But it wasn't often that he'd stay home and mind his business... Hardly a week would pass before he came running... asking for news... bringing us new models... complementary projects... more blueprints... spare parts... we could yell ourselves blue in the face, he'd keep coming, he'd come more and more often... like shooting pains, worried, dispirited... As soon as he began to see the light, he'd start bellowing... kicking up a ruckus of varying proportions... And after that you'd never see him again. There were some... but not very many... who weren't so dumb, who threatened to raise hell, legal proceedings, to register a complaint with the police if we didn't return their dough... Courtial knew them all. He cleared out when he saw them coming. He recognized them a mile away... It's incredible what a piercing eye he had for spotting a rabid customer... They seldom caught him... He'd disappear into the back room and do a little turn with the dumbbells, but mostly he went down in the cellar... There it was even safer... He wasn't in... The old-timer who wanted his money back could split a gut, it didn't get him anywhere...

"Hold him, Ferdinand. Just hold him,'" the stinker would say. "Hold him while I think things over... I know that gasbag only too well! That drooling ape! Every time he comes here for an interview he stays two hours at least... He's made me lose the thread of my deductions a dozen times. It's shameful! It's scandalous! He's a plague! Kill him, I beseech you, Ferdinand! Don't let him contaminate the world anymore! Burn him!... Slaughter him! Scatter his ashes! I don't care what you do! But for God's sake, at any price, do you hear me, don't bring him to me. Tell him I'm in Singapore! in Colombo! in the Hesperides! Tell him I'm making elastic banks for the Isthmus of Suez and Panama. That's an idea!... Tell him anything! Anything will do, so long as I don't have to see him!... I beg you, Ferdinand, I beg you!"

So it was I that had to bear the brunt of the whole tempest sure as shit... I had my system, I admit... I was like the "Do-it-yourself Cottage," my approach was flexible... I put up no resistance... I bent in the direction of his fury... I went even further... I amazed the lunatic by the virulence of my hatred for the loathsome Pereires... I took him every time in nothing flat... with my hair-raising insults... In that province I was supreme... I flayed him! I stigmatized him!

I covered him with garbage, with pus! That abject villain! That mountain of shit! Twenty times worse! a hundred times! a thousand times worse than the customer had ever thought on his own!...

For his private delectation I turned Courtial... shouting at the top of my lungs... into a heap of soft, slimy, inconceivably sickening turds... How unbelievably loathsome he was!... He was in a class by himself! I went at it hammer and tongs!... I stamped on the trapdoor right over the cellar, in chorus with the nut... I outdid them all in violence... thanks to the intensity of my revolt! my sincerity! my destructive enthusiasm! my implacable tetanism!... my frenzy!... my anathematic writhing!... It was unbelievable what a paroxysm I could work myself up into in my total fury... I got all that from my dad... and the performances I'd been through... For temper tantrums I had no equal... The worst lunatics, the most delirious interpretive screwballs didn't stand a chance if I decided to take a fling, if I really wanted to bestir myself... Young as I was... they all left with their asses dragging... absolutely bewildered by the intensity of my hatred... my indomitable fury, the eternal thirst for vengeance that I harbored in my flanks... With tears in their eyes they entrusted me with the task of crushing that turd... that execrable Courtial... that sink of iniquity... of covering him with new and unpredictable kinds of excrement, slimier than the bottom of the shithouse!... a mass of unconscionable purulence!... of making a cake out of him, the most fetid that could ever be imagined... of cutting him up into balls... flattening him out into sheets, plastering the whole bottom of the crapper with him, all the way from the bowl to the sump... and wedging him in there once and for all... to be shat on for all eternity...

As soon as our friend was gone... as soon as he was far enough away... Courtial would come back to the trapdoor... He'd lift it up a little... He'd take a gander... Then he'd surface...

"Ferdinand! You've just saved my life... Ah, yes! My life! It's the truth. I heard it all. Ah! It's just as I feared! That ape would have torn me apart. Right then and there! Did you realize that?" Then he'd stop and think. He began to feel worried about what I'd been shouting... my little session with the visitor...

"But I do hope, Ferdinand, tell me now, that I haven't fallen as low as all that in your esteem? You'd tell me, wouldn't you? You wouldn't hide it from me, would you? I'll explain my position if you want me to. Go ahead... I do hope these little acts you put on have no effect on your feeling for me! That would be too dreadful. Your affection for me is unchanged? You can count on me to the hilt, you know that. I'm a man of my word. You do understand me? You're beginning to understand me, aren't you? Tell me you understand me."

'Yes, yes. Of course... I think... I think I'm beginning..."

"Then listen to me, my dear Ferdinand!... While that lunatic was raving, I was thinking .of thousands of things... while he was turning our stomachs... mouthing his delirium... I was saying to myself: My poor Courtial! All these scenes, this ranting, this infamous uproar is lacerating your existence abominably... without furthering your cause any! When I say cause, you understand, I don't mean money. I'm speaking of the great intangible treasure! Immaterial wealth! The great Decision! The eternal theme, the infinite acquisition! The idea that is worthy of our enthusiasm... You've got to understand me, Ferdinand... Quicker! Quicker! Time is passing! A minute! An hour! At my age, Ferdinand, that's eternity. You'll see... It's all one, Ferdinand, all one!" His eyes moistened... "Listen to me, Ferdinand. I hope you'll understand me fully one day... yes!... that you'll really appreciate me... When I'm not here to defend myself... Then it's you, Ferdinand, who will possess the truth!... You who will refute the calumnies... It's you, I'm counting on you, Ferdinand. I'm counting on you! If people come to you... from all four quarters of the world... and say : 'Courtial was nothing but a skunk, the crummiest bastard of them all! A swindler! There was never another like him...' What will you say, Ferdinand?... Just this... You hear me? 'Courtial made only one mistake. But that mistake was fundamental! He thought the world was waiting for the spirit... to help it change... The world has changed... That's a fact... But the spirit hasn't come to it!...' That's all you'll say... Absolutely... Not another word! You will add nothing!... The order of magnitudes, Ferdinand! The order of magnitudes! Maybe the infinitestimal can be inserted in the immense... But how are we to reduce the immense to the infinitesimal? Ah? Our misfortunes have no other source, Ferdinand! No other source! All our misfortunes!..."

When he'd had a big scare as he had that afternoon, he felt a touching solicitude for me. He didn't want to see me sulking...

"Go on out, Ferdinand!" he'd say... "Go take a walk... Go to the Louvre. It'll do you a world of good! Go up to the Boulevards! You like Max Linder. Our joint still stinks of that mammoth! Let's go, Ferdinand. Let's clear out. Shut up the shop. Hang out the sign. Join me at the Three Musketoons! It's on me. Take some money out of the drawer on the left... I won't leave with you... I'll sneak out through the hall... Take a look in at the Insurrection... You'll see Formerly... Ask him if there's anything new... You've placed a bet on Scheherazade, I hope? And did you put your winnings on Violoncelle? You're still betting for yourself, eh? You don't even know where I am... Understand?"

He began to dish out his Great Decision routine more and more often... He'd disappear into the cellar, supposedly to meditate, for hours on end... He'd take a big fat book with him and his big candle. He must have owed every bookie in the neighborhood money, and not just Kid Formerly at the Insurrection, but at the Musketoons, and even the Brasserie Vigogne on the rue des Blancs-Manteaux... That was a real dive... He gave orders that he wasn't to be disturbed... I wasn't always very happy about it... his shenanigans made it my business to deal with all our daily screwballs... our discontented subscribers... the harmless little characters with stupid questions... the thoroughbred maniacs... whole broadsides of them swept over me... I had them all on my neck... bellyachers of every description... the repulsive mob of deep thinkers... the fanatics of gadgetry... They kept pouring in . . coming and going... The bell was having fits... It rang the whole time... They were preventing me from repairing my *Enthusiast...* Courtial was cluttering up the cellar with his clowning... And that was my main job after all... I was responsible, I'd be to blame if he broke his neck... which was touch and go every time!... In other words, his act was for the birds... In the end I told him, on this count and several others, that this couldn't go on... that I was fed up... that I washed my hands of it... that we were heading for trouble... It was plain as day... But he hardly listened. It left him cold... He disappeared more and more. When he was in the cellar, he wouldn't let anybody disturb him... Even his candle bothered him... Sometimes he put it out so it wouldn't interfere with his meditations.

Finally I gave it to him straight... I was so griped that I couldn't control myself... I told him to try the sewer . . that was the ideal place to look for his Decision... That did it. He blasts me:

"Ferdinand," he shrieks. "What's that? Is that a way to talk to me? You, Ferdinand? To me? Stop right there. Merciful heavens, I beg you! Have pity! Call me whatever you please! Liar! Boa! Vampire! Skunk! if the words I utter are not the strict expression of the ineffable truth! You wanted to do away with your father, didn't you? So young! Heavens above! That's the truth! Is it a delusion? A phantasmagoria? No, it's the unbelievable, deplorable reality!... Whole centuries won't wipe out the shame of it! That's a fact! It's God's own truth! You don't deny it? I'm not making it up? Well then? And now what? Will you kindly tell me what you're after? To kill me in my turn? Why, it's obvious! It's plain as day! Biding your time!... Waiting for the propitious moment!... when I'm relaxed... unsuspecting... And do me in!... abolish me!... annihiliate me!... That's your program!... Where have I been keeping my wits? Ah, Ferdinand, heavens above! Your nature! your destiny! are darker than the darkest Erebus!... Oh, you're sinister, Ferdinand, though you don't look it! Your waters are troubled!

What monsters there are, Ferdinand, in the crannies of your soul! Slithering, evasive! I don't know them all!... They pass!... They sweep everything away!... Death! To me! To whom you owe a thousand times more than life! More than bread! More than air! than the sun itself! The power of Thought! Ah, reptile, is that what you're up to? Am I right? Relentless! Crawling! Mercurial! Chameleonlike! Unpredictable!... Violence... tenderness... passion... strength... I heard you the other day... You're capable of anything, Ferdinand! Everything! Only the outer coating is human! But I see the monster within! Do you know where you're headed? Was I warned? Yes, I had plenty of warning... guile!... affection!... and then suddenly, every syllable a revelation... homicidal frenzy! Yes, frenzy!... A cataract of base instincts! Ah yes, that's the sign, my friend. The mark of the criminal... The lightning that denounces the murderer, the congenital, innate pervert!... That's you, right here in front of me! So be it! You're not dealing with a coward, the weakling you may have been expecting to terrorize! You've got another think coming! I stand up to my destiny! I asked for it! I'll see it through to the bitter end! All right, kill me if you can!... Go ahead! I'm waiting! Undaunted! What are you afraid of?... I'm right here! I defy you, Ferdinand! You exasperate me! Do you hear? You're driving me out of my wits! I'm nobody's fool! I'm wide-awake! Are you afraid to look a Man in the whites of his eyes? I measured the risks the day I took you on! Let's call it my last act of daring! Go ahead! Strike! I defy my assassin! Hurry!..."

I let him drool... I looked away... at the trees... at the gardens in the distance... the lawns... the nursemaids... the sparrows hopping around the benches... the fountain bobbing in the breeze... That was better than answering... or even turning around to look at him... He'd hit the nail on the head without knowing it... for two cents I'd hit him over the head with the paperweight... the big greaser, Hippocrates... my hand was itching... it weighed at least six pounds... I had a rough time... I controlled myself... It was heroic of me... The bastard kept right on:

"The younger generation nowadays have murder in their bones! That kind of thing, take it from me, Ferdinand, will land you in La Santé! With a hood over your eyes! That's right, a hood! Merciful heavens! And I'll have been to blame!..."

I had a tongue in my head too... I felt the mustard rising... Enough was enough!... *"Maître,"* I said right then and there. "Go shit in your hat. And make it quick! Get away from me! I'm not going to kill you. I'm going to take your pants down. I'm going to tattoo your ass. Till it looks like thirty-six bunches of peonies... I'm going to bust open your asshole, stink and all! That's what's going to happen to you if I hear one more fucking word out. of you."

I was going to grab him for real... The stinker was quick, though... He beat it into the back room... He saw I meant business, that I'd put up with as much as I was going to... He stayed right there in his hole... fiddling with the parallel bars... He let me alone for a while... He'd gone far enough... A little later he came out... He passed through the shop... He took the corridor on the left... he went out... He didn't go up to his office... At last I could work without being bothered.

It was no rest cure to sew and darn and patch that rotten balloon cover, to fasten together the pieces that were coming apart... It was an awful chore... Especially because I used the carbide lamp so as to see what I was doing... which was pretty risky down there in the cellar... with all those adhesives... that are always lousy with benzine... It was trickling around all over the place... I could see myself a living torch!... The cover of the *Enthusiast* was a ticklish business, in a good many places it was a regular sieve... More rips! More tears! And worse every time he went up, every time he landed... from dragging through plowed fields!... from catching on the eaves... on whole rows of roofs, especially on days when the wind was from the north... She left big patches and little shreds in the forests, on the branches, between steeples... on the ramparts... She picked up tin chimneys! roofs! tiles by the ton! weather vanes on every trip! But the worst punishment, the most terrible rips were when she got impaled on a telegraph pole!... Half the time she'd split in two... To give the devil his due. you've got to admit that des Pereires took some pretty bad risks on his aerial tours. The ascent was wild enough... it was a wonder he made it with the thing only half-inflated... for reasons of economy... But what was really awful was bringing his moth-eaten contraption down... Luckily he had plenty of experience. He knew his business. All by himself, at the time when I met him, he had chalked up 1,422 balloon flights! Not counting captive balloons... That was an impressive total! He had all the medals, all the diplomas, all the licenses... He knew all the tricks, but what always dazzled me was his landings… It was marvelous the way he always landed on his feet. The second the end of the rope scraped over the ground, the second the thing slowed down... he rolled himself up in a ball at the bottom of the basket... when the wicker touched the muck... and the whole thing was about to bounce up again... he had a feeling for the exact moment... He shot up like a jack-in-the-box... he unwound like a spool... he fell like a regular jockey... in his tight-fitting frock coat... He seldom hurt himself... He didn't lose a button... He didn't waste a second... He ran straight ahead... He sped over the furrows... He didn't turn around... He chased after the *Enthusiast*, at the same time blowing the little bugle he had slung over his shoulder... He made his own music... what a guy! His cross-country race went on a long time, until the whole balloon settled... I can still see him sprinting... It was a beautiful sight, in his frock coat and panama... To tell the honest truth, my autoplastic sutures weren't so hot... but he wouldn't have done it himself... He hadn't the patience... he'd only have messed things up even worse... After all, that patching was an art! Despite my infinite stratagems and vast ingenuity, I often despaired of that beastly gasbag... She was thoroughly fed up... After being taken out for sixteen years regardless of conditions... in cloudbursts and tornadoes... she only held together by patches and weird darns... Every time we blew her up was a catastrophe... After she'd come down and dragged along the ground, it was worse... When a whole strip was missing, I'd borrow a piece of the *Archimedes*' old hide... She was all in pieces, a lot of rags, piled up every which way in the cellar... That was the balloon of his beginnings, a bright red captive, an enormous bag. She'd done the fairs for twenty years... I was mighty careful... infinitely meticulous... about pasting the whole thing together... I got some curious effects... When at the cry of "Let her go" the *Enthusiast* rose over the crowd, I could recognize my patches in the air... I could see them wobbling and shriveling... It didn't make me laugh.

But in addition there were the preparations, the preliminaries... The balloon racket was no rest cure... don't get that idea... You had to get ready, make arrangements, palaver for months in advance... We had to send out leaflets, photographs... saturate the whole of France with prospectuses!... get in touch with the local big shots... put up with the insults of the festival committees, all terrible tight-wads... So in addition to the inventors, we had these mountains of mail in connection with the *Enthusiast*.

Courtial had taught me to write letters in the official style. I didn't make out too badly... After a while I didn't make too many mistakes... We had special stationery for the balloon racket with a natty letterhead: "Paris Section of the Friends of the Dirigible Balloon."

At the end of winter we'd start selling the municipal authorities... The programs for the season were drawn up in the spring... In principle we expected to have all our Sundays booked up shortly before All Saints. We'd needle committee presidents over the phone. It was my job again, going to the post office. I'd go during rush hours... I tried to get away without paying. They'd catch me at the door...

We applied for every fair, convention, and carnival in all France... No town was too small. Anything was down our alley. But naturally if we had any choice, we tried not to go any farther than Seine-et-Oise... or Seine-et-Marne at the worst. It was shipping our equipment that ruined us, the sacks, the bottles of gas, the gear, all our crazy gadgets. For the game to be worth the candle, we had to be back at the Palais-Royal that same night. Otherwise it would run into money. Courtial cut his prices as low as possible... they were absolutely reasonable: two hundred and twenty francs... plus the cost of the gas, and pigeons released for two francs a piece... We made no mention of altitude... Our most famous rival, maybe the most immediate threat, was Captain Guy de Roziers, he asked a good deal more. He performed hazardous feats with his balloon, the *Intrepid*... He'd take his horse up with him and sit in the saddle in midair... at an altitude of 1,200 feet guaranteed!... His price was five hundred and twenty-five francs, return fare payable by the township. But the ones who beat us to the draw even more often than the equestrian were the Italian and his daughter, "Calagoni & Petita"... We ran into them wherever we went... They were immensely popular, especially in garrison towns! They were very expensive, they did all sorts of tricks up in the sky... Besides, they threw down bouquets, little parachutes, and cockades from a height of 1,800 feet! They asked eight hundred and thirty-five francs and a contract for two seasons... They really cornered the market...

Courtial didn't go for the showy stuff... that wasn't his style... No theatricals! Certainly not. His show was definitely scientific: an edifying demonstration. He explained everything in a neat little preparatory chat and wound up with pigeons, which he released ever so gracefully... He himself served notice in his brief introductory patter: "Ladies and gentlemen... if I'm still flying a balloon at my age, it's not out of vain bravado... you can take my word for that... out of any desire to impress the crowd... Take a look at my chest! You see before you all the best known, most highly prized, most envied medals for merit and courage! If I take to the air, ladies and gentlemen, it is for purposes of popular education... that is my life-long aim! Everything in my power to enlighten the masses! We are not appealing to any morbid passion, to sadistic instincts, to emotional perversity!... I appeal to your intelligence! Your intelligence alone!"

He said it again for my benefit, he wanted me to get it straight: "Ferdinand, never forget that we must preserve the character of our performances at any price... the mark of the *Genitron*... They must never degenerate into buffoonery! masquerades! aerial tomfoolery! empty-headed tricks! No, no, and again no! We must preserve the tone, the spirit of Physics! Of course we have to entertain... and never forget it! That's what we're paid for. It's only right and proper! But better still, if possible, we must fire the minds of these rustics with a desire for exact knowledge, for genuine enlightenment. Of course we have to go up. But we must also elevate those yokels you see standing around with their mouths open! Ah! it's not easy, Ferdinand..."

It's perfectly true that he would never have left the ground without first explaining all the details, the principles of aerostatics, in a cozy little talk. To command his audience, he balanced himself on the edge of the basket, resplendently decorated, in frock coat, panama, and cuffs, with one arm passed through the rigging... He explained the working of the valves, the guy rope, the barometers, the laws of weight and ballast. Then carried away by his subject, he embarked on other fields, expatiating, ad-libbing without order or plan, about meteorology, mirages, the winds, cyclones... He touched on the planets, the stars... Everything was grist for his mill: the zodiac, Gemini... Saturn... Jupiter... Arcturus and its contours... the moon... Bellegophorus and its relief... He pulled measurements out of his hat... About Mars he could talk at length... He knew it well... It was his favorite planet... He described all the canals, their shape and itinerary! their flora! as if he'd gone swimming in them! He was on the friendliest terms with the heavenly bodies. He was a big success.

While he was perched up there shooting the shit, spellbinding the masses, I took up a little collection... That was my little private racket. I took advantage of the circumstances, the excitement... I slipped into the crowd... I peddled the *Genitron* at two sous a dozen... returns... little autographed handbooks... commemorative medallions with a tiny balloon engraved on them... and for the ones I could spot that looked dirty-minded... whose hands went roaming in the crush... I had a little selection of funny, entertaining, spicy pictures, and transparents you could slide back and forth... It was a bad day when I didn't unload the lot... All in all, with a little luck, it brought in twenty-five smackers! That was good money in those days. When my stock was gone and I'd finished collecting, I'd give the master the high sign... He'd shut off steam... He'd turn off the blarney and climb down into his basket... He'd straighten his panama... batten down the hatches, unfurl the last sheet... and slowly push off. I only had to hold the last rope... It was I who sang out "Let her go"... He'd answer me with a blast from his bugle... With the guy rope dragging, the *Enthusiast* rose into the air... I never saw her go straight up... She was limp from the start. For a number of reasons we were very careful about blowing her up... As a result, she rose crooked... She careened over the roofs. With her colored patches she looked like a fat harlequin... She bobbed up and down in the air, waiting for a decent breeze... She could only puff out in a real wind... She was pathetic like an old petticoat on a clothesline... even the cowfloppiest yokels caught on... The whole crowd laughed to see her teetering over the roofs... I was a good deal less cheerful... I foresaw the horrible, decisive, disastrous rip! The final smashup... I made all kinds of motions to him... he should drop the sand right away... He was never in much of a hurry... He was afraid he'd go up too high... There wasn't much to fear . . '. Considering the state of the fabric, there wasn't a chance... My worry was that he'd flop in the middle of the village... that would have been the end... It was always a narrow squeak... or that he'd collide with the schoolhouse... or take the weathercock off the church... or get caught in the eaves... or settle on the Town Hall... or founder in the little clump of woods. He'd be doing all right if he got her up to 150 or 200 feet... I figured roughly... that was the maximum... Courtial's dream, in view of the state of his equipment, was never to go any higher than the second story... That was fairly safe... Higher was madness... In the first place we could never have pumped the bag full... With one or two bottles more it would have split for sure, from top to bottom... exploded like a bombshell from valve to valve... When he'd passed the last house, cleared the last fences, he'd throw out his sand... He'd make up his mind and unload the lot of it... When the ballast was all gone, he took a little hop... a leap of about thirty feet... Then it was time for the pigeons... He quickly opened their basket... They shot out like arrows... Then it was time for me to shake a leg... Believe me, I ran like hell... I had to stage a tragedy to get the yokels interested... to make them run after the balloon... and help us to fold up quick... the enormous ragbag... and tote the whole mess back to the station... to hoist her up on the derrick... We weren't through yet. We had to do something to prevent our audience from clearing out, the whole lot of them at once... Our best dodge was the disaster act... It worked every time... without it we were sunk... We'd have had to pay them to do any work... We'd have lost money... It was that simple...

I began to scream and yell! I lit out like a stuck pig! I ran lickety-split through the muck in the direction of the catastrophe... I heard his bugle... "Fire!... Fire!" I yelled. "Look! Look at the flame!... He's going to set the whole place on fire! She's over the trees!..." The mob got moving... They came on the gallop... They followed me... As soon as Courtial saw me with the peasantry at my heels, he opened all the valves... He disemboweled the whole contraption from top to bottom!... She collapsed in her rags... She lay down in the muck, crippled, exhausted, bushed... Courtial popped out of the basket... He landed on his feet... He blew another blast on the bugle to rally the pack... And he started another speech... The hicks were scared shitless, they expected the whole thing to burst into flame and set their haystacks on fire... They threw themselves on the bag to keep it from billowing... They folded her up... But she was a disgusting wreck... from catching on every branch in sight... She'd lost so much material there was nothing left but heartbreaking rags... She'd brought back whole bushes between the bag and the net... The rescuers were delighted, overjoyed, jumping up and down with excitement; they hoisted Courtial on their shoulders like a hero and carried him off in triumph... They took him to the taproom to celebrate... They drank plenty... All the work was left for me, the rottenest lousiest chore... Collecting all our junk out of the swamp before nightfall... from the fields and furrows... Recovering all our tackle, anchors, pulleys, and chains, all the wandering hardware... The mile and a half of guy rope... the log, the cleats, scattered far and wide in oats and pasture, the barometer, the aneroid pressure gauge... a little Morocco leather case... the nickel doodads that are so expensive.... A picnic, take it from me... Keeping those repulsive beggars happy with wisecracks and promises... And telling smutty jokes to make them handle those fifteen hundred pounds of exhausting junk all free gratis and for nothing! The gasbag that looked like a massacred shirt, the remains of the hideous catafalque! Getting them to toss the whole junk pile in the last freight car just as the train was pulling out! Hell! Believe me, it took some doing. When I finally squeezed through the corridors and found Courtial, the train was under way. I found my zebra in the third class. Calm as you make them, talking, showing off, handing his audience a brilliant lecture... The conclusions to be drawn from his adventure!... So attentive to the brunette on the opposite bench... considerate of youthful ears... watching his language... but the life of the party even so... drunk as a lord, throwing his chest and his medals around... And still drinking, the stinker! Jollity! High spirits! A slug of the red stuff all around! Hold out your glasses, everybody!... He was stuffing his face full of bread and butter... Why worry... He didn't ask about me... Take it from me, I was fed up... I put a crimp in his merriment.

"Ah, so it's you. Ferdinand? It's you?" "Yes, my dear Jules Verne!..."

"Sit down, boy. Tell me all about it... My secretary... My secretary." He introduced me.

"Well then, is everything all right in the freight car?... You've attended to everything?... You're satisfied?"

I made a very glum face, I wasn't the least bit satisfied... I didn't say a word... "Then it's not all right?... Is something wrong?..."

"It's the last time," I said. I didn't mince words. I was very dry and firm... "What's that? Why is it the last time? You're joking? What do you mean?..." "The thing can't be repaired anymore... And I'm not joking at all..."

A real silence fell... No more applause and sausage. You could hear the wheels... the creaking of the carriage... the glass of the lamp jiggling up top... He tried in the dim light to make out what I was thinking... if I wasn't kidding a little. But I didn't bat an eyelash... I kept my long face... I stuck to my guns...

"You really think so, Ferdinand? You're not exaggerating?" "If I say it, I mean it... I know what I'm talking about."

I'd got to be an expert on holes, I refused to be contradicted... He sat back gloomily in his corner... That was the end of our conference... We didn't say another word...

All the others, on their benches, wondered what was going on... Clankety-clank! Clankety-clank! from one jolt to the next. And the oil dripping from the top of the lamp... All the heads nodding... then drooping.

If there's one thing in the world that needs to be handled with care, it's perpetual motion... Don't touch it or you'll get your ringers burned...

Inventors in general can be classified according to their bugs... There are whole categories that are practically harmless... The ones who go in for mysterious radiations, "tellurism," for instance, or the "centripetals"... They're easy to handle, they'd eat breakfast out of your hand... The little household gadgeteers aren't very rough either... the cheese-graters... the Sino-Fin- nish kettles... the two-handled spoons... well, everything that's useful in the kitchen... Those boys like to eat... they know how to live... The ones who want to improve the subway?... Ah, there you'd better begin to watch your step. But the real screwballs, the wild men, the vitriol throwers, are mostly all of them in "Perpetual"... Those characters will go to any length to demonstrate the value of their discoveries... They'll turn your gizzard inside out if you express the slightest doubt... They're no good to fool with...

One of the boys I met at Courtial's, an attendant at the public baths, was a fanatic... He never talked about anything but his "pendulum," and then only in a whisper... with murder in his eyes... Another one who came to see us was a public prosecutor in the provinces... He came all the way from the southwest just to bring us his cylinder... an enormous ebonite tube with a centrifugal valve and an electric starter... It was easy to spot him in the street, even from far away, he always walked slantwise, like a crab, along the shop fronts... That was his way of neutralizing the influence of Mercury and the "ionic" radiations of the sun, that pass through the clouds... And he never took off the enormous muffler he wore around his shoulders, day and night, made of braided asbestos, lisle, and silk. That was his ray detector... When he walked into "interference"... right away he began to shiver... bubbles came out of his nose...

Courtial had known them for ages... he knew what to expect of them... He called a number of them by their first names. We were on pretty good terms with them... But one day he got the idea of organizing a contest for them... That was sheer lunacy... Right away I sounded the alarm... I let out a howl... Anything but that!... He wouldn't listen... He needed money bad, ready cash... It was perfectly true that we were having a hell of a time finishing out the month... that we owed at least six issues of the *Genitron* to Taponier, the printer... So we had plenty of extenuating circumstances... Besides, the balloon flights weren't paying off so well anymore... Airplanes were breaking our backs... By 1910 the yokels were all hopped up... they wanted to see flying machines... We were still writing letters like mad... incessantly... We de-defended every inch of ground... We pestered all the hicks... the archbishops... the prefects... the postmistresses... the druggists... and the horticulture societies... In the spring of 1909 alone we had more than ten thousand circulars printed... we fought to the last ditch... But I also have to admit that Courtial was playing the races again. He'd gone back to the Insurrection... He must have paid his debts to Formerly... Anyway, they were on speaking terms again... I'd seen them together... At one throw my boss had won six hundred francs at Enghien on Carrot... and then two hundred and fifty on Célimène at Chantilly... It had gone to his head... He began raising his bets...

The next morning he comes into the shop all steamed up... He starts in right off the bat... "Aha, Ferdinand! My luck's turned! This is it! I'm in luck... Do you hear me... After ten years... after losing almost uninterruptedly for ten long years... That's all over... My luck is running... And I'm holding on!... Take a look!..." He shows me the *Dingbat*, a new racing sheet... he had it all marked up in blue, red, green, and yellow. I said my piece right away...

"Watch out, Monsieur des Pereires! It's the twenty-fourth already... We've got fourteen francs in the till... Taponier has been very nice... very patient, I've got to admit, but even so, he says he won't print the rag anymore!... I might as well tell you right now! He's been biting my head off for the last three months every time I show my face on the rue Rambuteau... Don't count on me to go around there anymore! not even with the pushcart!"

"Don't bother me, Ferdinand. Don't bother me... You're driving me crazy. You depress me with your sordid gossip... I can feel it! I can feel it in my bones! Tomorrow we'll be out of the woods. This is no time to be quibbling. Go back and tell Taponier... Tell him from me... from me, do you understand! That bastard, when I think of it... He's grown fat at my expense... For twenty years I've been feeding him... he's piled up a fortune... several fortunes... on my paper. I've decided to do the stinker one last favor. Tell him! Tell him, do you hear me, to put his whole plant! his machines! his equipment! his apartment! his daughter's dowry! his new car! everything! his insurance policy! tell him not to forget anything! his son's bicycle! Everything! Remember! Everything! on Bragamance to win! To win, I say!... not to place! not to come in third! At Maisons, on Thursday!... That's it! That's the long and the short of it, son! I can see the finish! And 1,800 francs for five! Do you hear me, 1,887 to be exact... In your pocket... Remember that! With what's left of my winnings... that will be 53,498 francs for the two of us! Net!... Bragamance!... Maisons!... Bragamance!... Maisons!..."

He went on jabbering... He didn't hear my answers... He went out through the corridor... He was like a sleepwalker.

The next day I waited for him all afternoon... to show with the fifty-three grand... It was after five o'clock... Finally he turns up... I can see him across the garden... He doesn't look at anybody in the shop... He comes straight up to me... he grabs me by the shoulders... The hot air has all gone out of him... He's sobbing... "Ferdinand! Ferdinand! I'm a viper! A despicable scoundrel!... Talk of depravity!... I've lost everything, Ferdinand! Our month's earnings. Mine! Yours! My debts! Your debts! The gas bill! Everything! I still owe Formerly what I put on that horse!... I owe the binder eighteen hundred francs... I borrowed thirty francs more from the scrubwoman in the theater... I owe another hundred francs to the gatekeeper in Montretout!... I'll be running into him this evening!... You see the morass I'm stuck in... Ah, Ferdinand, you were right! I'm sinking into my own muck!..."

He disintegrated completely... He flayed himself... He added up the sum... He added it up again... How much did he actually owe?... It came to more each time... He unearthed so many debts I think he made some of them up... He went for a pencil... He was going to start in all over again. I stopped him. I was firm.

"See here, Monsieur Courtial," I said. "Calm down. You're making a spectacle of yourself.

Suppose some customers came in! What would they think? Better take a rest..."

"Oh, Ferdinand! How right you are! You're wiser than your master, Ferdinand! The stinking old fool! A wave of madness, Ferdinand! A wave of madness!..."

"It's unbelievable! Unbelievable!..." After a moment's prostration he opened the trapdoor… He vanished all alone... I knew his act!... It was always the same routine... When he'd made an ass of himself... first he'd lay on the applesauce, then came meditation... But what about eating, friend? I'd have to lay hands on some dough somehow!... Nobody gave me any credit... neither the butcher... nor the grocer... The bastard was counting on my having a little nest egg put by... He'd suspected that I'd take my little precautions... that I had some sense... I was the guy with foresight... I was the shrewd accountant... With the scrapings from the drawers I held out a whole month... No air bubbles with salt... And we didn't eat so badly... We had real meat!... plenty of French fries... and jam made out of pure sugar... That was my way of doing things.

He didn't want to put the bite on his wife... She didn't know a thing out there in Montretout.

Uncle Édouard came by one Saturday night... He'd been out of town, we hadn't seen him in a long time... He brought news from home, from my parents... Their luck was still running bad… In spite of all his efforts, my father hadn't been able to leave La Coccinelle... And that was his only hope... Even after he knew how to type, they hadn't wanted him at Connivance Fire Insurance... They thought he was too old for an underling's job... and that he seemed too bashful to deal with the public... So he'd had to give it up... and stick to the old grind... and butter up Lempreinte... It was a terrible blow... he wasn't sleeping at all anymore.

Baron Méfaize, the head of "Litigious Life," had got wind of my father's moves... he'd detested him from way back, he was always torturing him... He'd make him climb five flights of stairs on the other side of the yard to tell him what an ass he was... that he got all the addresses wrong... which was absolutely untrue...

While talking with me Uncle Édouard began wondering... he thought maybe it would give my folks pleasure to see me again for a minute... I could make up with my father... He'd had trouble enough, he'd suffered enough... It came from a good heart... But just thinking about it, the gall started coming up... I had vomit in my throat... I wasn't going to try again...

"OK, OK, I'm sorry for them and all that... But if I went back to the Passage, I can tell you right now, I wouldn't last ten minutes... I'd set the whole place on fire." There was no use trying…

"All right, all right," he said. "I can see how you feel."

He dropped the subject... He probably told them what I'd said... Anyway, his happy- homecoming gambit never came up again...

With Courtial, I've got to admit... I can't deny it... it was one holy mess from morning to night... a perpetual rat race... He played some rotten tricks on me... he was as sneaky as thirty- six bedbugs. It was only at night that I had any peace... Once he was gone I did what I felt like… I made my own plans... Until ten in the morning when he came back from Montre-tout I was the boss... And that's a good deal. Once I'd fed my pigeons, I was absolutely free... I always took a little rake-off on the sales of the *Genitron...* We had a racket with the returns... some of it was for yours truly... I put it aside... and I got something out of the balloon flights too... It was never more than twenty, twenty-five francs... but to me, for pocket money, it was a fortune!

The old crocodile would have been glad to know where I stashed my dough away... my cute little nest egg... He could look till doomsday... I was very careful... I'd learned a thing or two… My little treasure never left my pocket, actually it was a special pocket, carefully pinned, inside my shirt front... You couldn't say we trusted each other very much... I knew all his hiding places... he had three... One was under the floor... another behind the gas meter (a loose brick)... and a third right there in Hippocrates' head!... I dipped into them all... He never counted... In the end he began to have his suspicions... But he had no call to complain... He never gave me a penny in wages... And what's more, I fed him... Supposedly out of "general'" funds... The stuff wasn't too bad... and plenty of it... He realized that he couldn't say anything…

In the evening I didn't cook, I went all by myself to the Automatic on the corner of the rue de Rivoli... I took a bite standing up... I've always liked that best... it only took a minute... Then I went roaming around... I had my little circuit... rue Montmartre... the post office... rue Etienne-Marcel... I'd stop by the statue on the Place des Victoires and smoke a cigarette... It was a majestic square... I liked it fine... A quiet place to think things over... I've never been so happy as in those days on the *Genitron...* I made no plans for the future... But the present didn't seem too rotten... I'd be back by nine o'clock...

I still had plenty of work... There was always patching on the *Enthusiast...* bundles that were late in getting off... and letters for the provinces... So then about eleven o'clock I'd go out under the arcades again... That was the interesting time... Our neighborhood was full of whores… They did it for five francs... or even less... Every three or four columns there was one with one or two customers... They knew me well from seeing me all the time... Sometimes they were good company... I took them up in our office when there was a raid... They hid in between the files, eating up the dust... waiting for the cops to go away... We had some hot brawls in the investor's corner. I was entitled to all the ass I wanted... thanks to my eagle eye, because I watched all the approaches from my mezzanine... at the critical hour... When I saw the cops coming... they all piled in through the little side door... I was the gang's lookout... What people don't know won't hurt them... We expected the bulls a little before midnight... Sometimes I had ten or twelve of these tomatoes in the shambles on the second floor... We doused the candle... You couldn't make a sound... We heard their size tens passing on the flags and doubling back... The girls were scared stiff... They were like rats skulking in the corner... Later on we relaxed... The best part of it was the stories... They knew all about the Galerie... everything that went on... under the arches... in the attics... in the back rooms... I found out all about the business people in the neighborhood... all the ones who had themselves buggered… all the miscarriages... all the cuckolds... between eleven o'clock and midnight... I heard all about des Pereires, how the low-down swine would get flagellated at the Etruscan Urns at Number 216 in the alley across the way... near the exit of the Comédie Française... he liked a good shellacking… you could hear him bellowing behind the velvet curtains... and it cost him twenty-five francs a throw... cash on the line, naturally... and he seldom went a week without getting himself whipped three times in a row!

It made me good and sore too to hear such stories... I was beginning to see why we never had a penny in the till... what with the knout and the ponies, no wonder we couldn't make ends meet...

The one who told the best stories was Violette. She wasn't young anymore, she came from the North, she never wore a hat, she had a triple bun like a flight of stairs, and long "butterfly" pins. She was a redhead, she must have been forty... Always in a tight-fitting black skirt, a tiny pink apron, and high-laced white shoes with "spool" heels... She had a weakness for me... We all died laughing listening to her... she was a wonderful mimic. She had new ones every time... She wanted me to bugger her... She called me her "ferryboat" because of the way I bucked her… She was always talking about "her" Rouen... she'd been there for twelve years in the same house, hardly ever going out... When we went down in the cellar, I lit the candle for her... She sewed on my buttons... that was a job I hated... I tore off a good many... because of my struggles pushing that handcart around... I could sew anything at all... but not a button... never!... I couldn't stand them... She wanted to buy me socks... she wanted me to look nice... I hadn't worn any in a long time... Pereires didn't either, to tell the truth... When she left the Palais-Royal, she hiked up to La Villette... the whole way on foot... for the five-o'clock trade… She'd do pretty well up there too... She didn't want to be shut up in a house anymore... From time to time, though, she'd spend a month in the hospital... She'd send me a postcard... She'd hurry back. I knew her way of tapping on the windowpanes... We were good friends for almost two years... until we left the Galerie... Toward the end she was jealous, she had hot flashes... she was hard to get along with.

When vegetables were in season, we piled them in... I did them up in mixtures with chopped bacon... He brought in salads... beans by the basket... from Montretout. Bunches of carrots and turnips, and even peas...

Courtial went in for sauces. I'd learned all that from his cookbook... I could make any kind of stew, I knew all about browning and simmering... It's a very convenient method... You can dish it out all week. We had a powerful Sulfridor gas heater... slightly explosive... in the backroom-gymnasium... In the winter I made *pot-au-feu...* It was me that bought the meat, the margarine, and the cheese... We took turns bringing home the liquid refreshments...

Violette liked to take a snack around midnight... She liked cold veal on bread... But all that ran into money... On top of our wild expenses.

I argued against it... I predicted the most dire disaster... it was no use. We had to have a try at his perpetual-motion contest. It was a hurry-up scheme... We expected quick results. The situation was desperate!... The admission fee was twenty-five francs... The first prize was twelve thousand smackers, the winner to be selected by a "grand jury of the world's foremost authorities" and in addition there was a second, consolation prize... four thousand three hundred and fifty francs... We were no pikers!

We had customers right away... a flood... a tidal wave... an invasion!... Blueprints!... dissertations!... enormous monographs!... illustrated theses!... We ate better and better! But we weren't easy in our minds... Far from it! I was dead sure we'd be sorry... that we were in for every kind of headache and no kidding... that we'd pay through the nose for every cent we took in... for our beautiful dreams of two... three... maybe five thousand francs... that we were cooking up a mess of indignation that would come down on our noodles... and pretty damn quick.

Models of every description were entered in the contest... every taste, trend, craze was represented... There were pumps, dynamic flywheels, cosmo-terrestrial tubes, pendulums for dynamos... calorimetric clocks... sliding refrigerators, reflectors of Hertzian waves... You only had to reach into the pile, you were sure to get your money's worth... After two weeks the screwball contestants began to come around... in person... They wanted news... Ever since the contest started, they'd been on tenterhooks. They besieged the joint... They hammered on our door... Courtial appeared in the doorway... he made them a long speech... He put them off for a month... He told them one of our financiers had broken his arm while taking a walk on the Riviera... but he'd be better soon and would hurry back... he wanted to bring his mezuma in person... Everything was all right... just this little hitch... It wasn't a bad line... They left... but they were disgruntled... They moved away from the window... spitting their bile in all directions... some of them in solid lumps... something like tadpoles... Courtial had certainly stirred up a mean gang of maniacs... they were really dangerous... He himself began to have misgivings, but he wouldn't admit it... instead of admitting his mistake, he took it out on me...

After lunch, while waiting for me to worry the coffee through the strainer, he'd squeeze the end of his nose... he'd make little drops of grease ooze out. They came out like worms, then he'd squash them between his filthy, pointed nails... That was some schnozzola he had... a regular cauliflower... wrinkled... browned... and wormy... Besides, it was getting still bigger... I told him so.

We'd drink our mud and wait for the horde of lunatics to come back... those feverish Archimedeses... for them to begin cussing us out... lurching into the joint... On these occasions Courtial would light into me and try to humiliate me... That seemed to relieve him... He'd start in out of a clear sky... "One of these days, Ferdinand, I'll have to teach you something about certain major trajectories... certain essential ellipses... You don't know one thing about Gemini... or even the Big Dipper! Not a solitary thing!... I noticed it this morning when you were talking to that little louse... It was pitiful, shocking... Just imagine if some fine day one of our contributors, in the course of an interview, were to ask you a few questions about the Zodiac and its signs?... about Sagittarius... What would you have to say? Nothing, or just about. Nothing at all would be better... We'd be discredited, Ferdinand! And under the sign of Flammarion... That's right! It's too much! It's a howling mockery! Your ignorance! What's the sky to you? A hole, Ferdinand! One more hole! There you have it. That's what the sky is to Ferdinand!" He clutched his head in both hands... He'd swing it from left to right, he couldn't get over it... as if, sitting there with me, such a revelation, such an aberration, had suddenly become just too painful... as though he couldn't stand it another minute... He sighed so loud I could have knocked his block off.

"But let's get down to more pressing business," he'd snap out... "Hand me fifteen or twenty of those files. At random. Just reach in. I'm going over them right away... I'll annotate them tomorrow morning. We've got to get started, dammit. And don't let anybody disturb me, that's the main thing. Put a sign over the door: 'Preliminary meeting of the Prize Committee'... I'll be up on the second floor, do you hear me?... As for you, it's a nice day... go drop in on Taponard... Ask him how our supplement is coming along... First pass by the Insurrection. But don't go in. Don't let them see you. Just look into the back room and see if Formerly's there... If he's gone, go ask the waiter, but absolutely on your own hook... you understand... not a word about me... how much Siberia won last Sunday in the fourth of the Drags. Don't come back the front way. Slip around through the rue Dalayrac... And whatever you do don't let anybody disturb me... I'm not home to a million... I want to work in absolute silence and quiet..." He went up and settled down in his Tunisian office. He'd eaten too much and I knew damn well he was going to sleep... I still had addresses of small-town notables to make out... and letters to finish... I left the shop and sat down under the trees across the way... I hid behind the kiosk. The idea of going to the printer's didn't appeal to me... I knew in advance what he'd say... I had more urgent things to attend to. I had the two thousand labels and all the wrappers to stick for the next issue... if the printer released it... which we couldn't bank on... We'd taken in money in the last two weeks... the money orders for the contest... But we owed a lot more!... Three rent bills... gas bills for the last two months... and especially the shipping office...

As I was laying low out there, I saw the procession of contestants coming... They stormed the shop... They jumped up and down in front of the showease... They shook the door in their fury... I'd taken the handle with me... They'd have broken the whole place down... They exchanged information... and indignation... They hung around a long time... grumbling outside the door... Four, five hundred yards away, I could hear the hum... I gave no sign of life... I didn't show myself... They'd have all come galloping... They'd have drawn and quartered me... At seven o'clock new ones were still turning up... That punk up there in his sook must still have been sawing wood... Unless he'd shoved off... at the sound of the pack... through the handy little door on the street side...

Anyway, there was no hurry... I had time to think a while... It had been years since I left Berlope's... and little André... The little stinker must have grown... He must be working someplace else... for other bosses... Maybe he wasn't even in ribbons anymore... The two of us had come around here together quite a few times... right here by the fountain, on the bench on the left... waiting for the cannon to go off at noon... It was a long time since we'd been apprentices together... Hell! Doesn't a kid grow up fast! I looked around to see if little André might be somewhere around... One of the salesmen had told me he was working in the Sender quarter... as a junior clerk... Sometimes I thought I recognized him under the arcades... and then no, it wasn't him... Maybe he wasn't close-cropped anymore... his dome, I mean, like in those days... Maybe he'd lost his aunt... He was bound to be someplace, chasing after his pittance... and his fun... Maybe I'd never see him again... maybe he'd gone for good... swallowed up, body and soul, in the kind of stories you hear about... Ah, it's an awful thing... and being young doesn't help any... when you notice for the first time... the way you lose people as you go along... buddies you'll never see again... never again... when you notice that they've disappeared like dreams... that it's all over... finished... that you too will get lost someday... a long way off but inevitably... in the awful torrent of things and people... of the days and shapes... that pass... that never stop... All these assholes, these pests... all these bystanders and extras strolling under the arcades, with their pince-nez, their umbrellas, and their little mutts on the leash... you'll never see them again... Already they're passing... they're in a dream with the others... they're in cahoots... soon they'll be gone... It's really sad... it's rotten... all these harmless people parading along the shop fronts... A wild desire took hold of me... I was trembling with panic... I wanted to jump out on them... to plant myself in front of them... and make them stop where they were... Grab them by their coats... a dumb idea... and make them stop... and not move anymore... stay where they were, once and for all... and not see them going away anymore.

Maybe two three days later Courtial was called to the police station... A cop came to notify him... That happened fairly often... It was kind of a nuisance... But things always straightened out... I'd brush his clothes with great care for the occasion... He'd reverse his cuffs... Then he'd go off to clear himself... He'd be gone a long time... He always came back delighted... He had confounded them... He knew all the laws by heart... he had all the alibis up his sleeve, all the dodges of the chase... But this little joke wasn't so funny... It wasn't in the bag by a long shot... Those low perpetual-motion characters were pestering the *commissaires*... The one on the rue des Francs-Bourgeois was getting a dozen complaints a day... and the one on the rue de Choiseul had lost all patience... he was completely exasperated... he was threatening to raid us… He was new, they'd put him on in January... the old one, who'd been so obliging, had been transferred to Lyons... The new one was a bastard. He'd warned Courtial that if we started any more contest rackets, he'd issue a warrant that wouldn't be any joke at all... He wanted to make a name for himself with his vigilance and zeal... He came from some one-horse town at the end of the world... He was full of beans... Hell, he didn't have to pay our printer's bill, our rent, and the rest of it... All he wanted in life was to terrorize us... We didn't even have the phone anymore... They'd stopped it, I kept having to run over to the post office... It had been cut off for the last three months... Inventors with complaints had to come in person... We'd stopped reading our mail... There was too much... We'd been getting too nervous with these legal threats... When we opened a letter, we just took out the banknotes... We let the rest ride... It was each man for himself... It's easy to panic!...

Courtial could say what he pleased... The Choiseul *commissaire* had spoiled his appetite, this was a real ultimatum... He'd come back white as a sheet...

"Never, I tell you, never, Ferdinand! Never in all the thirty-five years I've been laboring in the sciences!... crucifying myself! yes, that's the word... to educate... to elevate the masses... never have I been treated like that scum treated me... It surpasses all indignation! That greenhorn!... That whippersnapper!... What does that crumb take me for?... A crooked cabdriver?... A ticket speculator? The blackguard! The insolence! He wants to raid us! Like a whorehouse! Raid, raid, that's all he can talk about! All right, let him come, the jackass! What will he find? Ah, it's easy to see that he's new. A greenhorn in the region! A provincial, I tell you! Must be a hayseed! Ambitious, that's what he is, the damn fool! Trying to show imagination! He can't control himself! Imagination! Ah, this will cost him more than it will me… That's right, dammit... The fellow on the rue d'Aboukir! He thought he'd come around! He had to have his raid! He came! He looked! They turned the whole place inside out! The rotten scum!... They wrecked the joint and then they left... *Veni, vidi, vici!* The stupid bastards!

That was two years ago. I remember all right. And what did that two-bit Vidocq[114] find... papers and plaster... My boy, they were covered with rubbish! The despicable bedbug! It was pitiful... They'd dug all over! They hadn't understood a word... The crawling cockroach!... Ah, the cocksuckers!... the poor bedraggled nitwits!... The legal donkeys... Shitass donkeys if you ask me..."

He pointed to the piles and piles of junk reaching up to the ceiling... the prodigious mounds

... regular ramparts, menacing promontories! Tottering!... He was probably right... that Choiseul *commissaire* was bound to be dismayed at the sight of those mountains... those suspended avalanches...

"A raid! A raid! Will you listen to them talk! Poor boy! Poor infant! Poor larva!..."

He put on a front, but just the same those threats got him down... He was plenty upset... He went back to see the young whippersnapper next day... To try to convince him that he'd got him wrong... From beginning to end! Completely!... That he'd been slandered... It was a matter of pride with him... That ape's tirade ate him up... He didn't even go near his dumbbells... It stuck in his craw... He sat there mumbling... He didn't talk to me about anything but that raid... For once he even neglected my scientific education... He wouldn't see anybody... he said it was no use. I hung up the little sign about the "Committee Meeting" and left it there.

It was about this time, when this talk about the place being searched came up, that he started in again about his future... About how overworked he was... that it was getting him down more and more...

"Ah, Ferdinand," he said while looking for files to take up to his little crow's nest... "You can see what I need... Another day lost! Sullied! spoiled! absolutely corrupted! annihilated by muddles!... by idiotic worries... If I only had a chance to meditate!... Really and truly... To get away from all this!... do you understand?... I'm tied hand and foot by the externals of life... corroded! scattered! dispersed!... My grandiose plans are clouded over, Ferdinand! I hesitate... That's right, clouded over! I hesitate... It's terrible! Don't you see? It's the worst of disasters... It's like going up in a balloon, Ferdinand... I rise... I'm crossing a little piece of infinity! I'm going to break through!... I pass through some more clouds... At last I'm going to see... Clouds again!... The lightning bewilders me!... More clouds! I'm frightened!... I don't see a thing!... No, Ferdinand!... I can't see one thing, I try my best... I'm distraught, Ferdinand... I'm distraught!" He poked around in his goatee... He straightened out his moustache... His hand was trembling... We'd stopped opening to anybody... even to the perpetual-motion maniacs... From banging on the door so much they'd given up hope... They .began to leave us alone... There wasn't any search... They didn't start any proceedings... But we'd had a good scare...

By now Courtial des Pereires was suspicious of everything... of his Tunisian office... of his own shadow! His private mezzanine was still too exposed, too easily accessible... They could creep up unexpectedly and jump him... He wasn't taking any more chances... At the mere sight of a customer, his face would turn to wax... he'd almost reel... This last Trafalgar had really affected him... He was much happier in his cellar... He spent more and more of his time down there... There he had a little peace... He could meditate at his ease... He holed up in the cellar for weeks on end... I kept the paper going... It was all routine... I took pages out of his handbooks... I cut them out carefully... I touched them up in spots... I fixed up the titles a little... With scissors, eraser, and paste I did all right. I left plenty of blank space for "letters from subscribers"... reproductions, I mean... I skipped the complaints... I stuck to the enthusiastic passages... I drew up a list of subscribers... I dressed it up good... Four loops after the zeros! . . I put in photographs. The one of Courtial in uniform, half-length with medals all over his chest... another of the great Flammarion, picking roses in his garden... That made an amusing contrast... If any inventors came around asking for information again and disturbing me at my work, I'd found a new stall...

"He's with the minister," I'd say before they could get a word in. "They sent for him last night... It must be for an expert opinion..." They didn't entirely believe it, but it gave them pause. Time enough for me to beat it to the gymnasium... "I'll go see if he's back."

---

[114] François-Eugène Vidocq (1775-1857). Adventurer, convict, spy, and detective, who became chief of the Paris Security Police. He inspired Balzac"s character Vautrin.

That was the last they saw of me.

Misfortunes never come singly... We had new headaches with the *Enthusiast...* she was getting so ripped and patched, so crippled, leaky and beat-up, she'd just lie down on her ropes.

The autumn came, it was getting windy. She staggered in the gale, the poor thing would crumple up right at the start instead of rising into the air... She ruined us in hydrogen and methane... But we kept on pumping and she'd take a little start after all... in two or three jumps she'd clear the first bushes well enough... if she snagged a fence, she'd plummet in the orchard... she'd start again with a jerk... she'd ricochet into the church... she'd carry away the weather vane... she'd head for the country... The squalls would bring her back... straight into the poplars... That was enough for des Pereires... He'd release the pigeons... He'd blow a big blast on his bugle... The whole gasbag was ripping... What little gas he had was evaporating... I had to pick him up in mortal peril all over Seine-et-Oise, in Champagne, and even in the Yonne department! He scraped all the beets in northeastern France with his ass. The lovely wicker basket had lost its shape... On the Orgemont plateau he spent two good hours completely submerged, stuck in the middle of the pond, a sea of liquid manure... frothing and bubbling, fantastic!... The farm boys laughed to split a gut... When we folded the *Enthusiast*, she stank so bad of hard and liquid substances, and Courtial too for that matter... he was completely caked, welded, upholstered with shit... that they wouldn't let us into the compartment... We had to travel in the freight car with the contraption, the rigging, and all the junk.

When we got back to the Palais-Royal, it wasn't over... Our lovely aerostat still stank so bad, even in the depths of the cellar, that all that summer we had to burn at least ten pots full of benzoin, sandalwood, and eucalyptus... and reams of Armenian paper... we'd have been evicted... Petitions were already circulating...

All that we could still manage... It was part of the risks and hazards of the trade... The worst thing, the death blow, was certainly the competition of the airplane... That's for sure... They took away all our customers... Even our most faithful committees... the ones that were almost sure to hire us... Péronne, Brives-la-Vilaine, for instance... Carentan-sur-Loing... Mézeaux... Reliable committees, absolutely devoted to Courtial... who'd known him for thirty- five years... Places where they'd always sworn by him... All those people suddenly found weird pretexts for putting us off till later... subterfuges!... cock-and-bull stories! Our business was melting away! Ruin was staring us in the face!... It was especially beginning in May and June- July, 1911, that things really went to pot... Candemare Julien, to mention only one, did us out of more than twenty customers with his *Dragonfly*.

And yet we'd made almost unbelievable reductions... We went further and further... We supplied our own hydrogen... the pump... the condensimeter... We went to Nuits-sur-Somme for a hundred and twenty-five francs! gas included! And we paid the shipping costs!... It was getting to be too much. The stinkingest holes... the most rancid county seats... all they cared about was cellules and biplanes... flying meets and Wilbur Wright...

Courtial knew it was a death struggle... He was determined to fight back... He attempted the impossible. Within two months he published twelve articles in his rag and four handbooks in quick succession, proving to the hilt that airplanes would never fly... that they were a perversion of progress!... an unnatural fad!... a technological monstrosity!... that all this would end in an atrocious shambles!... that he, Courtial des Pereires, with his thirty-two years of experience, washed his hands of the whole business! He ran his picture with the article... But his readers were way ahead of him... He was obsolete... submerged by the rising wave. The only answer he got to his diatribes, his virulent philippics, was insults, blistering broadsides, menacing threats... The inventor audience wasn't going along with des Pereires anymore... That's the plain truth... Still he persisted... he stuck to his guns... He even took the offensive... That was when he founded the "Feather-in-the-Wind Society"... at the most critical moment... "For the Defense of the Spherical, Much Lighter-than-Air Balloon." Exhibitions! Demonstrations! Lectures! Parties! Socials! Headquarters at the *Genitron* office. We never enrolled ten members. There was hunger in the air... I went back to my mending... I'd taken so much out of the Archimedes, our old captive, that there wasn't a decent piece left... All moldy rags... And the *Enthusiast* wasn't much better... There was nothing left but the ropes... You could see the warp all over... And I'm in a position to know...

Our last flight was one Sunday in Pontoise. We'd decided to risk it... They hadn't said yes and they hadn't said no... we'd drastically overhauled the old carcass, tucked in the frayed edges, turned her inside out... We'd reinforced her a little with patches of cellophane... rubber, fuse wire, and oakum! But in spite of all our efforts she was condemned, she had her last spasm in front of the Town Hall! We pumped a whole gasometer into her... but she was losing more than went in... It was a case of endosmosis, as Pereires immediately explained... And when we kept trying, the thing split... with a terrible farting noise... The foul smell spread... The people fled from the gas... It was a panic, a nightmare!... To make matters worse, the whole enormous cover flops down on the cops... it smothers them, they're stuck in the flounces... wriggling under the folds... They damn near suffocated... They were caught like rats... After struggling for three hours we got the youngest out... the rest had fainted... we weren't popular anymore... They cussed us out something terrible... The kids spat at us.

Even so, we folded up the wreck... we found some charitable souls... luckily the fairground wasn't far from the big lock... We hailed a barge... They let us come on board... They were going down to Paris... We threw all our crap down in the hold...

The trip was fine... It took about three days... One night we reached the Port à l'Anglais... That was the end of our balloon flights... We hadn't had a bad time on the barge... They were nice friendly people... Flemings from the North... we drank coffee the whole time, so much we couldn't sleep. They played the accordion fine... I can still see the laundry drying all along the deck... The liveliest colors... raspberry, saffron, green, and orange. You could take your pick... I taught their kids to make paper boats... They'd never seen them.

As soon as our old lady, Madame des Pereires, heard the fatal news, she descended on the office... she didn't let the grass grow under her feet... I'd never seen her in all the eleven months I'd been there... It took a real disaster to move her... She was happy in Montretout.

At first glance she looked so weird I thought she must be an "inventress"... that she'd come to talk about some contraption... She was in a terrible state... As she opened the door, she was so upset... that was plain... and in such a lather she could hardly get the words out. Her hat was all crooked, shimmying in all directions. She wore a thick veil... I couldn't see her face. What I remember mostly is her black velvet skirt with the big flares, the big embroidered pattern on her mauve, bolero-style waist sprinkled with beads of the same color... and a changeable-silk umbrella... The picture is still with me.

After a certain amount of palavering, I finally got her to sit down in the big visitor's armchair... I ask her to be patient... the master won't be long... But right away she sails into me...

"Ah! Why, you must be Ferdinand? Am I right? You are, aren't you? Then you know all about the tragedy?... Isn't it a disaster?... That zebra of mine!... He got what he was after!... He doesn't feel like working anymore, is that it?..." She kept her fists clenched on her hips. She sat there anchored in the chair. She started up again. She was brutal.

"So he wants to sit on his ass all day?... So he's sick of working?... He thinks there's no need of it? What does he expect us to live on? Our investments? Ah, the bum! the scoundrel! the stinker!... the slimy toad! Where's he keeping himself at this time of day?"

She looked in the back room...

"He's not there, madame! He's gone to see the minister..."

"Ha, the minister! What's that again? The minister!" That hands her a laugh. "Oh no, sonny, that won't go down with me. Not with me!... I know him better than you, the swine! Minister!

Oh no. A whorehouse, maybe! In the clink, you mean... in jail, yes. That I'm willing to believe. Anywhere! In Vincennes! In Saint-Cloud! Maybe... but that minister gambit? Oh no!"

She shakes her umbrella in my nose...

"You're an accomplice, Ferdinand! That's right, an accomplice! Do you hear? You'll end up in jail, the whole lot of you... That's where your schemes will land you... your slimy tricks... your dirty work... your rotten swindles!..."

She fell back in the chair, her elbows on her knees, she made no attempt to control herself... her ferocious harangues gave way to prostration... she mumbled and sobbed... She filled up her veil... She told me the whole story.

"Never mind, I know what's what... I never wanted to come... I knew how it would hurt me... I know he's incorrigible... I've been putting up with him for thirty years..."

Out there in Montretout she had peace and quiet... she could take care of herself. Her health was frail... She didn't like to go out, to leave her house... Long ago... Long ago... she'd knocked around a lot with des Pereires... in the early days of their marriage... Now she didn't care for change... She preferred to stay home... Especially on account of her shoulders and her back, they were so sensitive... If she was caught in the rain or took a chill, she'd suffer for months on end... excruciating rheumatism and everlasting bronchitis, a kind of catarrh... That's how it had been all last winter and the year before... On the business end, she told me, they hadn't finished paying for their house... Fourteen years of scrimping and saving... She spoke gently... She appealed to my reason...

"Dear little Ferdinand! Dear boy! Have pity on an old woman... Why, I could be your grandmother, and don't forget it. Please tell me... tell me, I beg of you... if the *Enthusiast* is really lost. With Courtial I never know, I can't trust him... I can't believe a thing he tells me... How could you expect me to?... He's such a liar!... He's gotten to be so lazy... But you, Ferdinand! You can see what a state I'm in!... You can understand how I feel!... You won't try to pull the wool over my eyes!... I'm an old woman... I've plenty of experience of life... I'm capable of understanding anything... I only want someone to explain I had to tell her again... I had to swear by my immortal soul that the *Enthusiast* was completely cracked up, rotten, finished... inside and out... That there wasn't one sound stitch in the whole cover... in the carcass or the basket... that nothing was left but stinking rubbish... loathsome junk... absolutely impossible to repair...

The more I talked, the more miserable it made her. But now she trusted me, she saw I wasn't lying... She started confiding in me some more... She told me all the details... about her life since the early days of her marriage... when she'd still been a certified first-class midwife... How she'd helped Courtial get ready for his balloon flights... how she'd given up her own career for him and his balloon... and never left him for a second... They'd spent their honeymoon in a balloon... from one fair to the next... In those days she'd gone up with her husband... They'd gone as far as Bergamo in Italy... even to Ferrara... to Trentino near Vesuvius... As she unloaded, I realized that that woman, in her heart and conviction, expected the *Enthusiast* to last forever!... And the fairs too! She expected them to go on and on!... She had a good reason, an absolutely imperative reason... Namely, the balance due on their dump! La Gavotte, at Montretout... They still owed six monthly payments plus arrears... Courtial had stopped bringing money home... They were actually two and a half months overdue and had been given notice five times... Just telling me about the disgrace of it tied her voice into knots... Which reminded me that our own rent on the shop was long overdue... And what about the gas?... And the telephone bill?... There wasn't a chance we'd ever pay it... Maybe the printer would deliver again, just this once... That son of a bitch Taponier knew what he was doing. He'd put a lien on the joint... He'd snap it up for a song... That was a sure thing... He was the crummiest of the lot... A fine pickle we were in!... I could feel a whole mountain of headaches... an avalanche of troubles coming down on me... The future and our lovely dreams were all screwed up... I couldn't kid myself... The old doll was moaning into her veil... She'd sighed so much that she thought she'd make herself a little more comfortable... She took off her hat... I could recognize her by the portrait and des Pereires' description of her... Even so I was taken aback... He'd told me about the moustache that she refused to have removed... And it wasn't any faint shadow... It had started growing after her operation... They'd taken everything out in one throw... both ovaries and the womb... At first they'd thought it was her appendix, but when they opened up the peritoneum, they'd found an enormous fibroma... She'd been operated on by Péan[115] himself...

Before being mutilated that way, Irène des Pereires had been a very pretty woman, attractive, affable, charming, and what have you... But since the operation and especially in the last four or five years, the male characteristics had got the upper hand... Regular moustaches had come out and even a sort of beard... They were bathed in tears, which flew copiously as she talked to me... Colored streams ran down from her makeup. She had powdered... plastered... and painted like mad! She'd

---

[115] Jules-Emile Péan (1830-1898). Eminent surgeon.

made odalisque's eyelashes, she'd given herself a complete overhauling before coming to town... She put her enormous lid back on. with its bed of hydrangeas... it started wobbling again in the storm... there was nothing to hold it... It slid back... She banged it straight... She put in long hatpins... and tied her veil again. For a minute I see her rummaging around in her petticoats... She takes out a big briar pipe... He'd told me about that too...

"Is it all right to smoke in here?" she asks.

"Yes, madame, of course. Only be careful about the ashes, because of the papers on the floor. They'd catch fire easily. Hee-hee!" A guy's got to laugh once in a while.

"You don't smoke, Ferdinand?"

"No. To tell you the truth, I'm afraid to try. I'm not careful enough. I wouldn't want to be a living torch. Hee-hee!"

She begins to puff... She spits on the floor... in all directions... She was a little calmer now... She puts her veil back on. She only lifted up one corner with her little finger. When she'd completely finished her pipe, she took out her tobacco pouch again... I thought she was going to fill another...

"Say, Ferdinand!" she fires at me... An idea had shot through her head, suddenly she jumps up... "You're sure he's not hiding upstairs?..."

I was afraid to be too definite... It was a ticklish situation... I wanted to avoid bloodshed...

"Ha!" She didn't wait. She gave a leap. "Ferdinand! You've been deceiving me! You're as big a liar as he is."

She wouldn't listen to any explanations... She brushes me aside... She dashes into the little winding staircase... She climbs up in a rage... He had no warning... She jumps him!... I listen... Right away hell breaks loose!... She gives him his money's worth... It starts out with a couple of clouts... then screams...

"Will you look at the sex fiend... the smut hound... the no-good!... That's how he spends his time... I suspected his filthy ways... It's good I came..." She must have caught him just as he was putting our postcards away in the album... the transparent ones that I sold on Sunday!... He often spent his time that way after lunch...

His troubles weren't over. She didn't listen to what he said. "Pornographer! False membrane! Anarchist! Dishrag! Cesspool!..." Those were some of the things she called him...

I went up, I risked a glance over the banister... When she couldn't think of anything more to say, she threw herself on him... He flopped on the couch... was she heavy and brutal!

"Down on your knees, you stinker! Ask your victim's forgiveness!" Finally he put up a bit of struggle... She lashed into his shirt front, but the material was so hard she cut her hands on it... She was bleeding... but she kept on squeezing...

"You don't like it, do you? You don't like it!" she shouted in the thick of the battle. "Ah! You like it, you infernal windbag... What do you say, you swill pail? Does it give you pleasure to see me angry?" She was square on top of him. She was bouncing up and down on his belly. "Wah! Wah! Wah!" he groaned. "You're suffocating me, you big bitch! You're killing me! You're strangling me!..." Then she let him go, she was bleeding too hard... She ran down the stairs... She went to the faucet... "Ferdinand! Ferdinand! Just imagine, it's been a whole week. All week I've been waiting for him! All week he hasn't been home once... He's eating my heart out! I'm wasting away!... He doesn't care!... He only sent me a postcard: 'Balloon ruined. No lives lost!' Not another word... I ask him what he means to do. Don't nag, he says... Total loss! Since then not a word. His lordship doesn't show up. Where is he? What's he doing? The Benoiton Loan Company is dunning me for the payments... Complete mystery! Ten times a day they ring the bell... The baker's at my heels... The gas has been shut off... Tomorrow they're going to cut off the water... His lordship is doing the town!... While I'm eating my heart out!... That rotten failure!... The pervert!... The criminal!... The infernal, diabolical beast!... The baboon!... Believe me, Ferdinand, I'd rather live with a real monkey... I'd understand him at least! He'd understand me! I'd know where I was at. But after almost thirty-five years with that lunatic I don't know what he's going to do from one minute to the next as soon as I have my back turned! Drunkard! Liar! Lecher! Thief! He's every one of them... You'll never know how I detest that swine!... Where is he? That's the question I ask myself fifty times a day... While I work my fingers to the bone all alone out there to keep him! to pay the bills!... saving candle ends...

his highness throws it to the winds... on every racetrack... and all those filthy whores! my money! the little I've been able to put aside!... by denying myself everything! Where does it go? Into the sink of degradation! Don't worry, I know! He can't hide it from me... Vincennes!... Pari-Mutuel!... Enghien!... rue Blondel... Boulevard Barbes, it's all one to him! He's not hard to please as long as it's depravity! Any stinkhole will do!... It's all grist for his mill. His highness wallows in vice! He throws money down the drain!... And meanwhile... I'm killing myself trying to save a sou... to save an hour on the cleaning woman's wages... I'm the one that does everything in spite of the condition you see me in!... I wear myself out! I scrub the floor! All of it, in spite of my hot flashes! even when my rheumatism comes on!... I can hardly stand up, that's the plain truth... I'm killing myself!... And that's not the end of it. When they attach the house!... Where are we going to sleep then? Can you tell me that? You beggar! You rotten nitwit! Gangster! Bandit!" She was shouting up at him. "Why, in a flophouse of course! Have you still got the addresses? You ought to remember, my fine-feathered friend!... That's where he went before we were married... And under the bridges, Ferdinand!... I should have left him there... That's right!... with his mange and his vermin... Why, he's poisoned my life... that's what he deserved... He'd have enjoyed himself!... I should have sent him to the venereal hospital! His highness likes to indulge his passions! He's a rake, Ferdinand! The worst kind of ruffian! Nothing holds him back! Neither dignity! Nor reason! Nor self-respect! Nor kindness!... Nothing!... That man has mocked me, made a fool of me, poisoned my whole existence!... Ah, what a daisy he turned out to be! Ho ho! You can say that again! I've been a hundred times too good... I've been a sap, Ferdinand! I could die laughing! It's a scream... And now he's fifty-five and then some... fifty-six, to be exact, next April... And what does the old clown do?... He ruins us!... He sends us to the poorhouse... absolutely... He's given up the fight... All he cares about is his vices... They've carried him away... He rolls in the gutter... And it's up to me to fish him out... to make ends meet, to wear myself to the bone!... His highness couldn't care less… he refuses to control himself... I've got to mend the pieces... I've got to pay his debts... How about it, you chimpanzee?... The balloon? He lets it go... He hasn't two cents' worth of guts... Do you want to know what he does at the Gare du Nord, instead of coming straight home?… Or maybe you've heard?... Where he wastes his vitality? In the toilet. Ferdinand! That's right! Everybody's seen him. They all recognized my hubby!... Seen him masturbating... They caught him in the waiting room and in the corridors... Exhibiting himself... his private parts... his nasty equipment... to all the little girls! That's right, to children! Yes, indeed, there've been complaints, I'm not making it up... Yes, you pervert!... They've had their eye on him for a long time... Right in the middle of the station, Ferdinand!... Swarming with people that know us... They come and tell me about it!... Who told me? You're not going to deny it, I hope... You're not going to tell me it was somebody else... The infernal gall of that man!... Why, it's the *commissaire* himself, my friend... he came to see me last night just for that... just to tell me about your slimy ways... He had a complete description of you and even your picture... You see they've got your number... Ah, and it's nothing new. He'd taken your papers! Well, am I telling the truth?... You knew all right... You scum, that's why you didn't come home!... You knew what to expect!... Anyway, he'd told you... Children is what he needs now... Babies! It's too awful... Gambling! Liquor! Lies!... Spendthrift! Crook! Women! Every known vice! Minors!… Sink of corruption!... Of course I knew all about it... I learned the hard way... I've been through hell... But now... little girls!... It's too much!..." She looked at him, she stared at him from the distance... He was still on the steps, on the winding staircase... He felt safer behind the bars... He didn't come any closer... He made me signs not to rile her up... to keep absolutely quiet... that it would pass... that I shouldn't say a word... And actually she did calm down slightly...

She sank back in the armchair... She fanned herself gently with a wide-open newspaper... She puffed... She blew her nose... Courtial and I managed to put in a few words... and then a little speech trying to explain the whys and wherefores of the catastrophe... We didn't say anything about the little girls... we stuck to the balloon... If nothing else, that varied the monotony... We went on about the cover... that it was really hopeless... He tried flattery...

"What you've got to realize, Ferdinand, is that my Irène is impressionable!... She's a model wife... the cream of the cream! I owe her everything, Ferdinand. Everything! No two ways about it! I can shout it from the rooftops!... Not for a minute would I think of denying her affection for me! The extent of her devotion! The immensity of her sacrifices! Certainly not!... But she's impetuous, quick-tempered... It's only the other side of her kind heart. Yes, impulsive... but not mean. Oh no! She's the soul of goodness... as soft as milk soup! Aren't you, Irène, my treasure?..." He came up to kiss her...

"Go away! Go away, you pig!"

He didn't take offense... He only wanted her to understand. But she persisted in her fury... He tried to tell her that we had attempted the impossible... put on ten thousand patches... mended... spliced the lining in every shape and color, that in spite of anything we could say or do, the *Enthusiast* was falling apart... that the moths had eaten the sleeves... the rats had gnawed the valves... that it simply wouldn't stick together... neither standing nor lying down! That it wouldn't even be any good as a strainer! a dishrag! a sponge! or an ass wiper!... that it was no good for anything... She still had her doubts... We went into every detail... we described every ailment... we did our damnedest, we swore, we perorated, we declaimed, we even exaggerated if that was possible... She shook her head... She didn't believe us... We showed her the letters we had, telling us off in black and white... they came from all over... Even without a fee, for what we could make by passing the hat... they turned us down... and not with kid gloves either... they couldn't even stand the sight of us anymore... The heavier-than-air craft were taking all the jobs... resorts... seaports... fairs... That was the honest truth!... Spherical balloons weren't wanted... not even at "pardons" in Brittany! A character in Finistère had given it to us straight when we kept on pestering him:

Monsieur, you and your contraption belong in a museum and we haven't got one at Kraloch-sur-Isle. I really wonder why they still let you out. The curator is neglecting his duties! Our young people here aren't interested in digging up dead bodies. They want to be amused. Try to get it through your head once and for all!... A word to the wise!...

Joël Balavais Local wag and Breton.

She rummaged through the files but she didn't get much out of it... She softened up though... She consented to go out with us... We took her into the gardens... We sat her down on a bench between us... She began to talk sensibly... But we couldn't shake her conviction that the *Enthusiast*, in spite of everything, could perfectly well be repaired... that we could still use her... for two or three fairs in the provinces... which would give us enough to placate the architect... they'd get another extension... the house would be saved... all we needed was courage and never say die... That was what she thought... She couldn't see it any other way... We packed her pipe for her... Courtial sat there chawing. That was mostly always his way of finishing his cigars...

The people, the passersby looked over at our group... they were kind of fascinated, especially by the old cutie... She seemed to listen to me even better than to her husband... I went on with my line... my tragic demonstration... I tried to give her an idea of the obstacles we had to contend with... how we were wearing ourselves out with hopeless, more and more futile efforts... She eyed me suspiciously... She thought I was trying to sell her a bill of goods... She started bawling again...

"You've no energy, I can see that, neither one of you. So it's up to me! I'll have to do it all by myself... I'll fly the balloon! You see if I don't get her up! If I don't get her up to four thousand feet!... if monkey shines at five thousand feet is what they like! Or six thousand! Anything they want! I'll do whatever they ask of me!"

"You're talking through your hat, my dear," Pereires stopped her... "You're talking pure blarney... With a bag like ours you won't get up thirty feet... That's in the first place... You'll fall into the watering trough... A lot of good that'll do us... And they wouldn't want you anyway... Even the captain with his *Friend of the Clouds* and his horse! The whole bag of tricks! And Rastoni and his daughter! His trapeze and his bouquets... They're not doing anything either... They're being turned down too... We're all in the same boat... It's not our fault. Irène... It's the times... the general crack-up... It's not just the *Enthusiast...*" He could talk himself blue in the face, he could swear by his grandmother's ghost... she wouldn't give in... She even started up again...

"It's you! You let them get you down! That airplane fad will be all over a year from now... You're just looking for excuses because the both of you are making in your pants... Why not face it? instead of telling me fairy tales... If you had any guts... why not admit it?... you'd be in there working instead of dishing out hooey... All this stuff you've been telling me is a lot of bunk! What about the house? Who's going to make our payments for us? We're three months behind already... Twice we've been given notice... You expect your filthy rag to do it? I'll bet you it's knee-deep in debt... And summonses up to there! You can't pull the wool over my eyes... You think I don't know these things? So you throw it all up, eh? You've made up your mind, haven't you? You shitface!... You've written it off! A whole house! Complete! Eighteen years' savings!... Purchased stone by stone... Centimeter by centimeter... You can say that again... and land that's going up every day... And you leave it all to the mortgage holders... You wash your hands of it... You don't care... That's where the crack-up is..." She tapped his head... "It's not the balloon, it's in there... I'm telling you... And now what... You want to end up under the bridges?... Go ahead! Who's keeping you? Filthy pervert! Swine! You're not even ashamed of yourself!... You'll go back with the other bums, you no-good tramp... That's where I found you... Yes, indeed!... I had a family, Ferdinand... He's wrecked my whole life! Ruined my career... He cut me off from my people... The vampire! The scum!... And my health... He's ravaged me... destroyed me completely! And now he wants me to die in dishonor... Ho ho! Men have it easy! It's incredible... Eighteen years' savings! eighteen years of continuous privation... of calamity... after all my sacrifices!..."

She was awfully violent. Listening to her curse that way, the starch went out of des Pereires... he wasn't cracking wise anymore... He began to cry... He burst into tears... He threw himself right into her arms... He implored her forgiveness... He knocked the pipe out of her mouth... They went into a feverish clinch... Right there in public... And they didn't break... But she went on yammering in his arms... The same words over and over...

"I'm going to mend it. Courtial! I'm going to mend it! Something tells me I'll be able to! I know she can hold up... I'm positive!... I'll bet on it... What about our *Archimedes?*... Didn't she hold her own for forty years?... Why, she'd still be in there fighting..."

"But she was only a captive... You see, sugarplum... it's not the same wear and tear..." "I'll go up myself... I'm telling you... I'll go up! If you two aren't in the mood..."

She was taking it hard... She kept looking for an out... Anything, so long as we didn't give up...

"All I want is to help you. You know that, Courtial, don't you?" "Of course I do, angel... That's not the question..."

"That's all I want... You know I'm not lazy... I'd even go back to midwifing if that would help... I'd start right in again if I could... I wouldn't wait... Even in Montretout... Good Lord, even in Colombes, as assistant to the one who took over my practice... I'd do anything at all... Just so they don't come and evict us... You see how I am... Actually I've been making inquiries all over... But I've lost my hand... And besides there's my face... It would hand them a laugh, I've got to admit... I've changed quite a lot... so they say... I'd have to fix myself up a little... Hell, I don't know... shave, I suppose... I refuse to pluck it out..." She lifted her veil. Frankly, she was quite a sight... in broad daylight... the caked powder... the rouge on her cheeks, her violet eyelids... those thick moustaches, and even a suggestion of side-whiskers... And eyebrows even bushier than Courtial's... Dense enough for an ogre, no kidding! With all that hair on her face, she'd scare her expectant mothers out of their wits... She'd need quite some fixing... she'd have to change her whole face... It gave you pause...

We stayed there a long while side by side in the gardens, telling each other stories, trying to comfort each other... The night fell very slowly... All of a sudden she began to cry again, so hard it was really the limit... A paroxysm of misery...

"Ferdinand," she implored me. "You won't leave us at least? Look at the condition we're in... I haven't known you long. But already I know that down deep you're a good boy, aren't you?... Besides, everything will come out all right... You can't tell me different... It's just a bad time we're going through... Don't worry, I've seen worse... This can't be the end... We'll just have to put our shoulders to the wheel... all three of us together... But first I've got to see what's what... I'll see what I can do by myself..."

She gets up... She goes back to the shop... She lights the two candles... We don't stop her... She opens the trapdoor... She starts down... She stays down there in the cellar by herself for quite a while... rummaging through the junk... unfolding the cover... tugging at the rubbish... seeing for herself how rotten it was... how absolutely decrepit and ragged... I was alone in the shop when she finally came up... She couldn't say a word... She was suffocating with real grief... She sat in the armchair like paralyzed, completely bushed... pooped... finished... Her lid flopping around on the floor... Seeing it with her own eyes had really stunned the old battle-ax... I thought she'd keep her trap shut now... that she had nothing more to say... But then she started up again... after maybe fifteen minutes... But this time it was lamentations... She spoke very softly... like in a dream...

"It's washed up, Ferdinand... I admit it... Yes... It's true... You were right... It's done for... It's awfully sweet of you, Ferdinand, not to leave us now... two old folks like us... You won't leave us, will you?... Anyway, not right away?... Eh, Ferdinand? Not right away... not for a few days at least... A few weeks... You'll stay on, won't you? What do you say, Ferdinand?"

"Yes, madame... Yes, of course!..."

Next morning when Courtial came in from Montretout around eleven o'clock, he was still pretty embarrassed.

"Well, Ferdinand? Anything new?"

"Oh no," I say. "Nothing unusual..." And I start questioning him in return. "Well? Is it all straightened out?"

"Straightened out? What?" He plays it stupid. "Ah, you're referring to yesterday?" And right away he starts handing me a line. "Listen to me, Ferdinand! I hope you don't take all that gossip for coin of the realm... No, you couldn't... She's my wife, yes, of course... I honor her above everything... there's never been a real quarrel between us... So much the better! But we might as well call a spade a spade... She has all the terrible drawbacks that go with so generous a nature... She's intransigent! Despotic! You see what I mean, Ferdinand?... Impetuous!... She's a volcano! She's dynamite!... Whenever anything goes wrong, she blows her top... Sometimes she frightens even me... There she goes... And she works herself up... she explodes... She splutters and stammers... She loses her head... And talks through her hat... It's not so bad when you're used to it... It doesn't throw you... I forget it as quickly as a shower at the races... But let me repeat, Ferdinand... in thirty-two years of marriage... emotional outbursts, yes. But never a real tempest... All couples have their quarrels... I'm even willing to admit that we're going through a nasty moment right now... Unquestionably... But it's not the first time... we've seen worse... It's not the end of the world... To say we're stone-broke on that account... destitute! evicted!... sold out! attached!... is pure imagination... I won't stand for it... The poor kitten! Naturally I'd be the last man in the world to hold it against her!... It can all be explained!... It's out there in the cottage that she cooks up these nightmares... alone all day... with nothing to do but think... it gets her down... in the end it carries her away... She works herself up!... She works herself up!... She loses track... She sees and hears things that never happened... Yes, since her operation she's been inclined to... imaginings... impulses... I'd go even further... Sometimes she's a little delirious... Ah yes, several times, I've been really taken aback.... Definite hallucinations... She's perfectly sincere... Like this thing about the complaint... My oh my! You understood, of course? You caught on right away?... Actually it was very funny... It was ludicrous... But she'd done it before... That's why it didn't get a rise out of me... I let her go on... I didn't seem surprised, did I? You noticed?... I acted as if she were perfectly normal... That's what you've got to do... Mustn't frighten her... That's it... Mustn't frighten her..."

"Yes, of course. I caught on right away..."

"Sure, that's what I thought... Ferdinand hasn't fallen for it... he's not that gullible... He must have realized... It's not that she drinks, poor thing! No, never!... She's the soul of temperance... Except for tobacco... In a way, she's more on the Puritan side... It's the operation that turned her inside out... Ah! She was a very different woman... If you'd only known her before!... in the old days..." He started looking under the piles of papers... "I wish I could find her picture when she was young... the enlargement from Turin... I ran across it only a few days ago... You wouldn't recognize her... It's been a revolution... In the old days, I assure you, before she was operated on... she was a marvel... her carriage! the roses in her cheeks!... Beauty personified!... And what charm, my boy!... And her voice!... A dramatic soprano!... All that was wiped out from one day to the next... with a scalpel... It's incredible... I can even tell you without vanity that she was unrecognizable! Sometimes it was almost embarrassing... especially while traveling... Especially in Spain and Italy... where they're such ladies' men... I remember it all clearly, I was rather touchy in those days... quick on the draw... I'd go off the handle for nothing at all... A hundred times I was on the verge of a duel..."

Memories were going through his mind... I respected his silence... and then he started off again...

"Well anyway, Ferdinand. We've got other worries... Let's get down to serious matters... Suppose you drop over to the printer's... And now listen and try to understand... In the villa... in the desk... I've found something that may help us out... If my wife comes back... if she asks… you haven't seen a thing!... you don't know a thing!... It's only a receipt for a charm and a bracelet... But they're solid gold... absolutely genuine... warranted eighteen carat... Here are the tickets from the Mont-de-Piété... We could give it a try... Go see Sorcelleux on the rue Grange-Batelière... Ask him what he'll give for them... Tell him it's for me... A favor... You know where it is... Fifth floor, staircase A... Get the concierge to show you the way... Ask him how much he'll give me for them... That would give us a little money ahead... If he says no, try Rotembourg... on the rue de la Huchette... Don't show him the ticket... Just ask him if he's interested... And I'll go around myself... He's the worst kind of crook!..."

For all his air of not caring one way or another, the *commissaire* on the rue des Bons-Enfants was a mean bastard. It was mostly his doing that they took action... And that the public prosecutor got mixed up in it... Not for very long, it's true... But long enough to give us a good pain in the ass... The office was full of cops... They went through the motions of searching the joint... What could they expect to find?... They were pretty sore when they left... They hadn't found anything to indict us on... There was no clear evidence of fraud... They tried to bluff us… But we had our alibis... We had no trouble clearing ourselves... Courtial trotted out some articles of the law that were entirely in our favor... After that they called him up to the Quai des Orfèvres almost every day. Just listening to his protestations... his cock-and-bull stories... the examining magistrate laughed for full five minutes. Right off the bat he said:

"Before presenting your defense, send back those money orders... Reimburse the contestants... It's a common confidence racket, out-and-out piracy."

Those words gave the old man a jolt... He defended himself tooth and nail, inch by inch, desperately...

"Reimburse what? Destiny is crushing me... I'm being driven to despair! Harried! Hounded! Ruined! Trampled! Persecuted in a thousand ways! And what does he want now? That's what I'd like to know? To gouge my last nickel out of me... To hell with them!... Imaginary offenses! They're out to get me! A hornets' nest! A sewer! I can't stand it!... The villainy of all those people! It would drive an angel to drink!... But I'm no angel! I defend myself, but how sickening it is!... I proclaim my innocence... I told him off all right, that jack- in-the-box! that beast! that scoundrel! that little shyster!... A whole life, monsieur, devoted to the service of Science, of truth... my intellect!... my courage!... one thousand two hundred and eighty-seven balloon flights... A whole life of peril... of relentless struggle... against the three elements... And my honeyed friends, where are they now? Ah! The ignorance! The prating!... Ah yes... for light... for the education of the masses!... And have it come to this!... Faugh!... to be hunted by a pack of hyenas... Constrained to cavil and quibble!... Flammarion will come and testify! He'll come! And then that no-good despicable snotnose stops me short... why, he was positively rude... 'Hold your tongue,' he says. 'Hold your tongue, des Pereires, I'm sick of listening to you... Let's get back to the subject. Your perpetual-motion contest... I've all the proofs right here... is nothing but a monstrous racket... If it were your first... but it's only the most flagrant... the most recent... the most barefaced of the lot!... An utter imposture!... A cynical shell game! You can't get around Article 222, Monsieur des Pereires!... Your rules don't make sense!... You'd do better to confess... Read your own prospectus over again... Look at your ads!... What phenomenal gall!... There's not a shred of honesty in the whole contest!... It's completely unjustifiable... Absolutely no way of checking up!... You just worm out of it!

… It's all eyewash! window dressing! You carefully frame the rules in such a way as to make the whole thing impossible!... A fine kettle of fish... It's an out-and-out swindle!... Pure fraud!... Theft in the most literal sense of the word... You're nothing but a leech, des Pereires, on the grand ideal of Science! You live by setting traps for enthusiasts... high-minded seekers after truth!... You're a despicable poacher on the preserves of Research... You're a jackal, des Pereires... a loathsome beast!... Your kind can only live in the deepest darkness... the most inextricable thickets! The least ray of light sends you scurrying! Light! That's just what I mean to throw on your low activities! Take care, you dangerous specimen... You putrid, slimy survivor of the fauna of the estragulums! Every day I send whole litters of crooks that are a lot more pardonable than you out to Rungis!...'

"But perpetual motion, I told that brute, is an ideal that runs through all human history... Michel-angelo! Aristotle! Leonardo da Vinci! Pico della Mirandola!...

"'So you're going to be the judge,' he fires back at me... 'You think you're eternal?... You'd have to be... you're aware of that... to judge that contest of yours fairly! Ha! I've caught you there! Am I right! Eternity?... You say you're eternal?... just like that! There you have it!

... It's as plain as day! When you started that contest, you had no intention of picking any winners!... Am I right? I've caught you red-handed, robbing those poor unfortunates? All right, just sign this, here at the bottom.' He held out his fountain pen! The bastard! The unmitigated gall! I hadn't said boo, and he hands me this paper!... I ask you!... I was thunderstruck... Naturally I turned him down flat... It was a trap!... A rotten low-down ambush, and I didn't mind telling him so... He couldn't get over it!... I walked out with my head high!

" 'See you tomorrow, des Pereires,' he said. 'It won't help you any to put it off.'

"'You think you're eternal?' No, really, I ask you, the crust of him! The unconscionable effron-tery!... Those savages think they're so clever just because brute force is on their side...

with their two cents' worth of whiskers and their big mouths. I've got to admit it, though, that was a pretty good crack... Absolutely novel and unprecedented!... Thundering asshole catacombs! A killer! But he'll need more than that to get me down! A little something more than asinine traps... believe you me!... His infernal insolence only strengthens my position! That's my impression! Come what may! Let them deprive me of food! drink! bed and board! Let them throw me in prison, torture me in every possible way! I snap my fingers at them! I have my conscience... and that's enough for me!... Never will I make a move without it! Or in opposition to it!... There you have it, Ferdinand! It's my lodestar!"

I knew the music... Papa had saturated me with it... You can't imagine how overworked con-science was in those days!... But it was no solution... The prosecutor was seriously thinking of locking him up... The crack about eternity was pretty clever though... It could be interpreted in different ways... They gave us a few adjournments... That gave us a chance to sell some crap... Old junk out of the cellar... Even wreckage from the balloon... The old bag came in from Montretout for that very purpose... She'd decided to take control, to run things her way, especially selling the doodads... eve-rything that was left of the balloon... We made one trip with the stuff on our backs and another with the pushcart... We unloaded most of it at the Temple... right in the middle of the floor... We had plenty of takers... People liked our little mechanical relics... And on Saturday we took whole job lots of books to the Flea Market... we sold it all wholesale, with little pieces of the *Enthusiast* thrown in... instru-ments... a barometer... and the ropes... In the end... after a good many trips... we got pretty near four hundred francs out of all that junk... It was pretty nice... It gave us a chance to soften up the printer some by giving him a decent slice on account... And they gave the Benoiton Loan Company enough for half an installment on the shack...

But after that there was nothing to justify the existence of our poor carrier pigeons... We hadn't been feeding them much in the last two months... Sometimes only every other day... and even so it ran into money... Grain is always expensive, even when you buy it wholesale... If we'd sold them, they'd have certainly come right back as I knew them... They'd never have got used to other masters... They were good little creatures, loyal and faithful... like members of the family... They'd wait for me up in the attic... As soon as they heard me move the ladder, they'd coo double! Courtial was talking about throwing them in the pot... But I wasn't willing to give them to just anybody... If they had to be bumped off, I preferred to do it myself... I tried to think of a way... Supposing like it was me, I said to myself... I wouldn't like it with a knife... no! I wouldn't want to be strangled... no!... I wouldn't want to be opened up... and have my insides taken out... and be cut in quarters!... I have to admit it made me kind of sad!... I knew them awfully well!... But you couldn't get around it... I had to do something... There hadn't been any grain in four days... So I went up one afternoon about four o'clock. They thought I was coming to feed them... They didn't suspect at all... They were gurgling like mad... "Come along, little glug-glugs," I say. "We're going to the fair. All aboard for the ride!..." They knew the routine... I open the pretty basket wide, the one we took them ballooning in... They all come running... I batten down the lid, I run a rope through the handles... I tie it in all directions... Finally it was ready... First I leave it in the hall. I pop downstairs a while... I don't say a thing to Courtial... I wait until he shoves off for his train... Violette taps on the windowpane... "Come back later, beautiful..." I say, "I've got to run an errand..." She hangs around... she mutters something...

"Ferdinand," she insists, "I got something to tell you..." "Scram!"

So I go upstairs for my animals... I bring them down. I balance the basket on my head... I go out by the rue Montpensier... I cross the Carrousel... When I get to the Quai Voltaire, I look for a good place... I don't see a soul... On the bank at the bottom of the stairs... I pick up a big cobblestone... I tie it on... I look around again... I pick it up in both hands and throw it in the drink... as far out as I can... It didn't make any noise... I did it automatic...

Next morning I gave it to Courtial straight... I didn't wait... I didn't beat about the bush... He had no comment to make... Angelface, who was in the shop too, didn't either... They could see by the way I looked that this was no time to fool with my ass.

If they'd left us alone, we'd probably have made out all right... We'd have saved our ante without any help from anybody... Our *Genitron* magazine, nobody could say any different, was getting along fine... It was read all over... Lots of people remember how interesting it was... Lively from cover to cover! From beginning to end! Always perfectly informed about everything connected with inventing and the interests of inventors.

On that end I'm not exaggerating... Nothing has ever taken its place... What knocked us for a loop was our joker with his racetrack fever... I knew he'd start playing again... even if he told me different. I saw the money orders coming in... fifteen francs for a new subscription... and whoopsy daisy!... if I wasn't careful to hide them p.d.q., they'd melt into thin air! In a flash! He was a regular prestidigitator!... No business can stand up under that kind of drainage... not even the Bank of Peru!... He must have been spending our dough someplace... He wasn't going to the Insurrection anymore... He must have got a new bookie... I'll find out who it is, I says to myself... That's when they started after us some more... More proceedings!... They call him back to the Préfecture... That little bastard on the rue des Bons-Enfants wouldn't let go his bone... He started up again... He had us in his clutches... He was out to get us... He found more victims... of that damn competition... he'd even gone poking around in the furnished rooms on the Avenue des Gobelins... He was stirring them up against us... getting them sore again. He persuaded them to put in new complaints... Our life wasn't worth living... It was time to shake the old gray matter and do something about it... We thought it over, and this is what we came up with: we'd have to divide and prosper... That was the only way... All those pests fell into two classes... On the one hand and mostly... the ones who were griping for the sake of form... the melancholies, the hard-luck boys... That was easy... we wouldn't refund those stinkers anything... On the other hand, the characters that were really in a temper and never came out of it... That's where the danger lay!... We'd have to get to those boys and smooth them down right away... talk things over with them... a little cash maybe... Naturally we weren't going to reimburse them completely... It was impossible... out of the question... But slip them a little present... say, five ten francs... That way they wouldn't be taking a total loss... They might be made to realize that this was an act of Fate... When it came to carrying out his lovely plan, Courtial went white as a sheet... The stuffing went out of him... Couldn't he do it himself?... Inconceivable!... How would it look for him to go ringing bells?... What about his authority? He'd lose face with the inventors... Better I should go spreading the good word... I had no standing, no dignity to lose... But what a smelly prospect! I could see that in advance! I'd have chickened out too, but then we were sunk... If we let things drift, the rag was through... That would be ruin, we'd be out in the street!... Things really had to be bad for me to take on such a rotten job...

In the end I took a good deep breath, I steeled myself. I rehearsed the stuff I had to say... a whole collection of bedtime stories... Why things had gone wrong... beginning with the preliminary tests... because of a grave disagreement among scientists on a highly controversial technical point... We'd try again next year... Well anyway, a ton of baloney... So there I go... into the fray!... Good luck, kid... First of all I was to give them back all their plans, their models, their blueprints, their cock-eyed knickknacks... along with our apologies...

I used the indirect approach... I began by asking them if they'd received my letter... announcing my visit... No?... That got a rise out of them... They thought they'd won the jackpot... If it was dinner time, they'd invite me to join them. If the whole family was there, my little mission got kind of delicate with all those people around... I needed plenty of tact... They'd had visions of gold... It was an ugly moment... After all, I had to disabuse them... That's what I'd come for... I tried to break it gently... They'd start gulping... they couldn't eat anymore... They'd stand up hypnotized, their eyes fixed in stupor... It was time for me to keep an eye on the cutlery... Stormy weather in the dishes!... I braced my back against the wall... I'd pick up the soup tureen for a sling... ready to block any aggressor!... I'd go on with my spiel. At the first halfway suspicious move, I'd let go! Right in the guy's face... But in most places my resolute attitude was protection enough... it made them think twice... It didn't end so badly... with gushing congratulations... and then, after a little wine, a chorus of sighs and belches... especially if I coughed up the ten francs!... But one time, in spite of my caution and long practice, I got a bad shellacking... It was on the rue de Charonne, I remember, Number 72 to be exact, the Hôtel is still there... This guy was a locksmith, he did his inventing in his room... believe me, I know... not on the third floor, on the fourth... If you ask me, this character's work was assembling kits of burglar's tools... Well, anyway, his invention for the perpetual- motion contest was a mill, something like a dynamo, with a "variable faradic" intake... The idea was to store up the energy of storms... After that it kept going from one equinox to the next...

So I go in, I see his porter, I give him the name: "It's on the fourth floor." I go up, I knock... I was worn-out... fed up... I spill the beans all at once! The guy doesn't even answer... I'd hardly looked at him... He was a heavyweight champ... I hadn't even finished talking... Not a word! Boom!... He charges me... He rams me!... I take it in the breadbasket... I stagger... I topple backward... a wild bull!... I fall... I cascade down all three flights... They pick me up on the sidewalk... I was all over bumps... a bloody mess... They took me home in a cab... Seeing as I'd passed out, the boys had gone through my pockets... I didn't even have my ten francs left...

After that little collision, I was even more careful... I didn't go into the rooms right away... I'd parley from outside the door... With complaints from the provinces we had a different method... We told them their dough had been sent by mail... that they'd be sure to get it soon... that the address had been wrong... the department... the first name... any old thing... the contest had brought such a rush of mail... In the end they got sick of corresponding in all directions... They were ruining themselves on postage...

With the wild ones, you know where you're at... it's a bullfight... The only problem is jumping the fence before they gore your insides out... But with the timid, the sensitive souls that lose their grip and want to commit suicide right away... you're in for trouble... The disappointment is too much for them... they can't bear it... They hang their heads in their soup and start mumbling... They don't understand... They break out in a sweat, their glasses fall off... Their faces go green, you can't stand to look at them... Those are the sad sacks... Some of them want to end it all... They sit down, they get up again... They mop themselves off... They can't believe their ears when you tell them their contraption didn't work right... You've got to say it over again slowly, you've got to slip them their plans... They abandon themselves to their misery... They don't want to live... they don't want to breathe anymore... They collapse...

From laying on words like poultices, I was getting pretty good at it. I knew the phrases that console... the *De Profundis* of hope... Sometimes after my visits we parted buddies... I gained their sympathy... Out by the Plaine Saint-Maur, I had a whole group... really enthusiastic about our studies... they appreciated what I'd done for them... From the Porte Villemomble to Vincennes I knew rafts of them... fine hands at drawing magical plans and not at all vindictive... And in the west suburbs too... In a corrugated-iron shack right after the Porte de Clignancourt... there are Portuguese living there now... I met two junk dealers who with hair, matches, a spiral spring, three violin strings, and a sleeve-joint had worked up a little compensatory system that really seemed to work... Hygrométrie power!... The whole thing fitted inside a thimble!... It was the only perpetual-motion device I ever saw that worked a little.

It's unusual for women to invent anything... But I met one... She was a bookkeeper for the railroad. In her leisure hours she decomposed water from the Seine with a diaper pin. She toted around a pile of equipment, a pneumatic pump, and a Ruhmkorff coil in a fish net. She had a flashlight too and a picrate battery... She recovered the essences right out of the water... and even the acids... She stationed herself for her experiments near the Pont-Marie, not far from the wash barge[116]... She was nuts about hydrolysis... Her build wasn't bad... Only she had a tic and she was cross-eyed... I came around one day, I said I was from the paper... First she thought like all the rest that she'd won the jackpot... She wouldn't let me go away... she went and got me some roses!... I talked myself blue in the face... she didn't understand... She wanted to take my picture... She had a camera that worked with infrared rays... She had to close the windows... I went back twice... She thought I was some good-looker... She wanted me to marry her right away. She kept on writing me... registered letters!... Mademoiselle Lambrisse her name was... Juliette.

I took a hundred francs off her once... and fifty another time... But that was very exceptional...

Jean Marin Courtial des Pereires wasn't so cocky anymore... In fact he was downright morose... He was scared of the oddballs and lunatics from the contest... He got anonymous letters that were no joke... The meanest and crankiest of the lot threatened to come back some time sure as shooting... and knock the shit out of him... flatten him out once and for all... so he'd never be able to swindle anybody again... Avengers!... So under his frock coat, over his flannel vest, he'd taken to wearing a coat-of-mail made out of tempered aluminum... one of the *Genitron's* patents that was still on our hands, "extra-light and bulletproof." But even that didn't reassure him completely... Any time he lamped a character that wasn't looking too well... that didn't seem to be entirely happy... coming in our direction with a scowl on his face, he ran straight down to the cellar... He didn't wait for the details...

"Open the trap, Ferdinand! Let me through quick. It's one of them! I can tell!... Tell him I'm gone... left the day before yesterday! that I'm never coming back!... to Canada! That I'm spending the whole summer there! Hunting weasels! sables! The great hawk! Tell him I never want to see him again! Not for all the gold in the Transvaal! Tell him to go away!... evaporate!... scatter!... Blow the bastard up!... Explode him!... Christ almighty Jesus!" Hermetically sealed in the cellar, he felt a little easier in his mind. It was empty now that we'd sold what was left of the balloon, all the gadgets... He could roam around from wall to wall as he pleased... He had plenty of room... He could do his gymnastics again... In addition he'd built himself a "blockhouse" in one corner... absolutely impregnable... where he couldn't be seen at all... in case of invasion... in among the crates and clothes racks... He'd stay there for hours on end... That way at least he didn't bother me... His disappearing act was all right with me... I had my hands full with the old cutie... she was spending all her time in the shop these days... She stuck like granulated glue... She was determined to run everything her way... the paper and the subscribers...

At two in the afternoon she'd breeze in from Montre-tout... She'd settle down in the shop in full battle dress, with her hydrangea hat, her veil, her parasol, and her pipe. You couldn't fool with her! She was all ready for the enemy... It gave them quite a shock when they came in and found her staring them in the face...

"Sit down," she'd say. "I am Madame des Pereires... I know the whole story... I wasn't born yesterday! Speak up! I'm listening! But be brief! I haven't a moment to lose! I'm expected at the dressmaker's..."

That was her routine... It threw them off almost every time... The brutal tone, the powerful voice... a little hoarse maybe, but cavernous and not easy to shout down... They'd stop and think a minute... standing there in front of the old bag... She'd lift her veil a little... They'd lamp the moustaches, the paint, the odalisque's eyes... And then she'd frown... "Is that all?" she'd say... And they'd pull out trembling... half the time backwards... As meek as Moses... "I'll call again, madame... I'll call again..."

So one afternoon she was giving her audience... She was finishing up her dish of compote on the corner of the table... it was about four o'clock... that was her afternoon snack... it was part of her diet... I remember the exact day, it was a Thursday... the fateful day when I had to go see the printer... It was very hot... The audience was drawing to a close... Madame had already bounced out a whole gang of jokers from the contest... the whole crowd of spluttering argumentative bellyachers... she'd punctured

---

[116] Wash barge. The *bateaux lavoirs* were floating laundries, formerly common in France.

them in record time... nothing to it!... when in comes a priest... That was nothing so unusual... We knew a few... Some of them were faithful subscribers... and delightful correspondents...

"Won't you sit down, Father..." Right away she puts on her company manners. He appropriates the big armchair... I look him over carefully... I'd never seen the guy... Definitely a neweomer... At first sight he seemed reasonable enough... or maybe even reserved would have been the right word... Perfectly calm and well behaved... He was toting an umbrella in spite of the weather, which was conspicuously sunny... He goes and leans it in a corner... He comes back, he gives a polite little cough... He was on the pudgy side... not the least bit emaciated... We were used to freaks... Nearly all our subscribers had tics, they made terrible faces... This one seemed mighty quiet... Then suddenly he opens his mouth... the words begin pouring out... and right away I could see the lay of the land... Some tripe! He'd come to talk about a contest... He read our *Genitron*, he'd been buying it at the stands... for years... "I travel a good deal! yes, a good deal!" He spoke in long bursts... You had to catch his words in full flight, the sentences came out in tangled bundles... full of knots, garlands, and throw-backs… and loose ends that went on forever... In the end, though, we made out that he didn't care for our perpetual-motion line... He didn't even want us to mention it! On no account! It would make him very angry! He had something very different in mind... It left him no peace... He wanted us to go in with him... Take it or leave it!... If you weren't with him you were against him!... He gave us fair warning! We should consider the consequences! Perpetual motion was out... An absurdity! A hoax!... Not for him!... His obsession was a horse of a different color... We finally found out... little by little... after thousands of circumlocutions... what was eating him… Submarine treasure!... A noble project!... The systematic salvage of all the ships that were ever wrecked... Of all the galleons and armadas lost beneath the waves since the beginning of time... of all the glitter... strewn and scattered over the bottom of the sea... Well, that was his craze in a nutshell... That's what he'd come to see us about... He urged us to get started... there wasn't a minute to lose... to organize a contest! a worldwide competition... for the best method... the most reliable, most efficient way of raising all those treasures... He offered us everything he had, his own little fortune, he was prepared to risk it all... He'd give us a thumping advance that would cover all our initial expenses... Naturally Madame and I were kind of leery... But he kept at it... This crazy sky pilot had his own idea, a diving bell that would go way down deep... say 6,000 feet... It would be able to crawl into the hollows... grab hold of objects... hook on to metal and disintegrate it... it would absorb safes by "special suction"... As far as he was concerned, the whole thing was perfectly simple... Our job would be to attract competitors through the paper... In that department we were supreme... unrivaled... He was trembling with impatience for us to get started... He didn't give us time to raise the slightest objection... or even the shadow of a doubt... Plunk! He lays a wad of bills right smack on the table... Six thousand francs!... He didn't even have time to look at them... I had them in my pocket!... Grandma Courtial let out a whistle... I decided to strike the iron... No shilly- shallying for me...

"Stay right where you are, Father... just a second... Half a second... while I go get the director... I won't be a minute..."

I run down to the cellar... I yell for the old man... I hear him snoring... I head straight for his hide-out... I shake him... He lets out a scream... He thinks they've come to arrest him... He was scared shitless... he was shaking in his boots...

"Come on," I say. "Get up. This is no time to swoon." In the trickle of light under the transom I show him the lettuce... Hell, this is no time to lose your voice!... In two words I fill him in... He takes another look at the wampum... He tolds it up to the light... He looks at the mint leaves one by one... He pulls himself together quick! He yawns and stretches, he sniffs at the bills... I clean him up! I pick the straw off him... He primps up his moustaches... He's ready. He emerges into the daylight... he makes a brilliant entrance... He had his outline all ready... absolutely eloquent and resounding!... On the subject of divers he had us dazzled in two seconds flat... He dished up the history of every system from Louis XIII to the present day! Dates and places, the first names of those precursors and martyrs... the bibliographic sources... the research that had been done at the School of Arts and Trades!... It was a dream... He had the sky pilot burping, jumping up and down with joy... His highest hopes were fulfilled... He was so delighted that just like that, in addition to his previous offer—we hadn't asked for anything— he guaranteed us two hundred thousand... cash on the line!... for the expenses connected with the contest!... He didn't want any skimping on the preliminary studies... the drawing up of estimates... No pettifoggery... No swindling... We agreed to everything... We wrote in our initials... we closed the deal... Now that we were all buddies, he pulled an enormous map of the ocean floor from under his soutane... So we could see right away where all the treasures were located... where all that staggering wealth had been swallowed up... twenty centuries ago or more...

We closed up the shop... We spread out the parchment between our two chairs and the table... That treasure map was a marvel... It really made you dizzy just to look at it... Especially when you consider when this cock-eyed Saviour turned up... the trouble we'd been having! And he wasn't kidding!... All that dough hidden in the drink was exactly marked on his map... It was a sure thing... And right near the coast... with the longitude written in... It was a cinch that if we found a bell that would go down to even 2,000 feet, we'd be rolling in clover... It was in the bag... We'd have all the treasures of the Armada right in our laps... We'd only have to bend down to pick them up... Literally! Only three nautical miles off Lisbon, in the mouth of the Tagus... there was an enormous cache!... That was an easy job... for beginners... If we put some gumption into it and perfected the technique a little, the thing would take on entirely different proportions... In three shakes of a lamb's tail we could expect to raise the treasure of "Saar Ozimput," swallowed up in the Persian Gulf two thousand years before Jesus Christ... Several rivers of unique gems! Necklaces! Emeralds of inconceivable splendor... worth a billion at the very least... The priest had marked the exact position of that shipwreck on his map... It had been established by hundreds of soundings made over the centuries... No mistake was possible!... Expenses aside, it was only a little question of oxy-hydrogen drills... They'd need perfecting... Well, yes, we might have a little trouble raising the treasures of the "Saar"... We thought about it all one day... And certain "imponderables" of Persian legislation had us stymied for a minute... But we had other jobs that were perfectly within our reach, accessible, pure velvet... in more clement seas, absolutely free of sharks! We had the divers to think of! Gracious! No tragedies, please!

The truth of the matter was that all the ocean bottoms in the world were full of inviolate coffers, of galleons stuffed with diamonds... Few were the straits, coves, bays, roadsteads, or river mouths that did not, on the map, harbor some colossal booty... only a few hundred feet down and perfectly easy to raise... All the treasures of Golconda... Galleys! Frigates! Caravels! Luggers! full to bursting with rubies and Koh-i-noors and "triple effigy" doubloons... The waters of Mexico in particular appeared to be positively indecent in this respect... The conquistadores seem to have literally filled them in and plugged them up with their ingots and precious stones... If you really put your mind to it and went down 3,000 feet, diamonds were a dime a dozen... Off the Azores, for instance, to mention only a single instance... the *Black Stranger*, a steamer from last century with a mixed cargo, a Transvaal courier, had more than a billion francs' worth of them on board... all by itself (according to the most conservative experts)... She was lying overhung on a rocky bottom at a depth of 4,472 feet... already split in two amidships... All you had to do was rummage through the hull!...

Our padre knew of plenty more, the choice was staggering... He knew all the salvageable wrecks... all of them perfectly simple to clean out... several hundreds actually... He'd riddled his chart with holes... those were the places to prospect in... It showed the most urgent salvage jobs... to the tenth of a millimeter... They were marked in black, green, or red, according to the size of the treasure... with little crosses...

It was only a question of technique, of ingenuity, of flair... It was up to us to demonstrate our talents... Odds bodkins, we didn't dawdle!... In a fever, before he had time to cool off, des Pereires seized his pen, a ream of paper, a ruler, an eraser, a blotter, and right there in front of us, accompanying himself in a loud voice, he wrote a regular proclamation... It was vibrant!... It was sincere!... And at the same time it was meticulous and honest!... That was the way he worked!... In less than five minutes, in a flurry of inspiration, he'd formulated the whole problem! It was a first-class job!... "Let's not put anything off until tomorrow!... This article has to appear at once... we'll make it a special number!" Those were his orders... The padre was delighted... jubilant... speechless...

I ran off to the rue Rambuteau... I took all the dough in my pocket... I left only fifty francs for the old cutie... Hell!... I'd had trouble enough!... If I'd left it in the till, I knew I'd never see it again... The old man looked pretty glum... He owed Formerly a pile... He'd already dreamed up a bet... He couldn't resist... It was better I should be the treasurer... Less risky... We'd spend very gradually...

and not one cent on the ponies, I'd see to that... I'd pay the bills... First Taponier, top priority, and the special number!... That printer was on his last legs... When he saw the cash, he could hardly believe his eyes... He took a good look at the bills though... he held them up to the light... Hard cash! He was absolutely groggy... He didn't know what to say... I paid him six hundred francs on our back debts and two hundred more for the special number and publicity for the contest... He moved fast all right... Two days later we received the papers... shipped, banded, pasted, stamped... the works!... I took them to the main post office in the pushcart with Courtial and Madame...

As the padre was leaving, we'd asked him to write out his address, his name, street, and so on... but he'd flatly refused... He wanted to be anonymous. That puzzled us... He was an oddball all right! But a lot less than a good many other people... He was a corpulent man, he looked very healthy, and he was neat and clean-shaven, about the same age as Courtial... but completely bald... In his spells of enthusiasm he stuttered like a machine gun... The way he writhed and wriggled, he almost fell off his chair!... He struck us as mighty optimistic... certainly eccentric... But one thing he'd proved was that he had plenty of dough... He was a real backer... The first we'd ever seen... Let him be a little weird...

On the way back from the main post office with the cart, we passed right in front of the police station on the rue des Bons-Enfants. "Stop a minute!" I say to the old man. "Dare me to go tell him?... I just want to let him know that everything's OK." I get this fool idea of pushing some weight around... of telling him we had plenty of cabbage... I run over, I open the door... The coppers recognize me:

"Hiya, Butch," says the one at the desk. "Watcha doing around here? Like to stay a while?" "Oh, no," I say. "No, sir... The clink's not for me. I was just passing by. I thought I'd drop in and show you a little currency..." And I take out my four bills... I wave them under his nose... "Take a look," I say... "And they're not stolen... I just wanted to tell you that it's for a new contest... The diving bell!"

"Dive, dive!" he says. "I'll dive you!... Are you trying to kid me, you little snot-nosed asshole?"

I ran out even faster than I came... I didn't want them to jug me... We had a good laugh in the street... We galloped a ways with the cart... We made it fast as far as the rue du Beaujolais...

Naturally that kind of a competition, to recover sunken treasure, was going to draw a crowd... Our share as the organizers was fixed at sixteen percent of everything that was brought up... That wasn't unreasonable! Even so, on the Armada alone, reckoning it close without forcing the figures, that made about three million for us... Not bad!...

I've got to admit that the old cutie didn't think it was all in the bag... She smelled a slight rat... She still had her suspicions... Even so, she didn't dare to say anything... After all it was a miracle... She wasn't swept off her feet... She just kept her eye on the cash...

Courtial threw himself into the thing body and soul... head over heels... He could already see those sparklers piled up on the beach, emeralds by the fistful... mountains of gold dust... ingots... The whole treasure of the Incas, pumped from the galleys... "We are the looters of the deep," he'd roar through the house... He skipped and gamboled over the piles of paper... And then suddenly he'd stop, he'd tap his head. "Wait a minute, my sugar bun! We haven't divided it up yet..." He'd lay out four columns in red ink... He was very strict about sharing the spoils... Fiercely meticulous... he foresaw the worst kind of trouble. This was no laughing matter... He took every possible precaution. He drew up an agreement!

"Never mind, angel pudding, you don't know them... You don't know what they're capable of... I deal with them every day, I know what we're up against... I've seen backers... and inventors too, I know what I'm talking about... I've been handling them for forty years... And now I'm caught between two fires... Ah! Exactly!... I don't want to be crushed!... fleeced!... drawn and quartered! just when things start popping... at that very moment! Oh no, hell no, not on your tintype... Hell's bells!... The pen in one hand, Ferdinand. Quick! And in the other the scales! And across my knees a carbine! That's it. There's Courtial for you! To the life! Justice! Respect! Presence! I've seen my brilliant inventors... as sure as I'm here talking to you... create marvels... absolutely stupefying wonders... throughout my long career! And nearly always... take it from me... for beans! For cheese! For glory! For less than nothing!... Genius is left to rot! That's the exact truth! It doesn't sell! It goes begging! It's *gratis pro Deo*. Cheaper than matches... But suppose you try to be nice, with your heart on your sleeve! You want to do something for them, an unprecedented kindness! Sure! You believe in this bozo's song and dance! You want to encourage the scientist... dress the martyr's wounds... you come around in all innocence, bringing a small sardine... The martyr jumps sky-high! It's an affront... Everything's changed... revolutionized... Everything collapses! A flash of lightning and hell opens... Your genius turns jackal! Vampire! Leech! The hounds are unleashed... carnage!... an atrocious massacre! To get the money out of you they disembowel you on the spot!... crucify you! vaporize you! No quarter given! The soul is forgotten! Nothing counts but gold! Gold! So be careful! Take it easy, take it easy, pal! You want to search the depths? Why, for a hundred francs divided up wrong, I know those zebras, they'd blow up the terrestrial globe! That's right... so help me... I'm not exaggerating! I'm in a good position to know... To our documents! To our documents, Ferdinand! Keep your powder dry! Letter-perfect documents! notarized! initialed! deposited before noon with Maître Van Crock on the rue des Blancs-Manteaux... An excellent notary! in triplicate... Our share first! And stipulated in capitals! Airtight! Oleographic! No dubious arguments! No underhanded finagling! No, never! Oh providential padre, you'll soon have plenty to dive with! Ah, the poor innocent! He hasn't the faintest idea! Diving bells!... Why, before the month is out, they'll be bringing in three or four a day! What am I saying? A dozen. And meeting our specifications!... Two thousand feet?... Four thousand?... Six thousand?... I'm not the least bit worried. Oh no, I won't breathe a word... No snap judgments… I've got to be impartial... I don't want to seem prejudiced... I'll wait for the day of the trials… Very well!... But unless my memory deceives me, I've already written some very well-documented articles on that very question... Let's see... Maybe I'll remember the exact dates… It was before we were married... Around '84 or '86... Just before the Amsterdam Congress… the Submersible Exhibition... Maybe I can lay hands on them... They must be around somewhere... I explained it all... It was in the Supplement... Say, it all comes back to me!... It was in *The World Upside Down...* I can see that bell plain as day... Reinforced of course... with triple bolts... and double-guaranteed walls and a ferromagnetic top... So far it's perfectly simple... Cushions threaded to the thousandth of a centimeter around the ballast... That's it! Irido-bronze rivets... absolutely impervious to the action of the sea water... Not a single acid spot after years in the water!... Tempered in chlorido-sodium! À galvanoplastie overstress on a cen-trifugal pin!... A simple matter of computation... The factors involved are child's play... Radio-diffus-ible lighting with a Valladon projector!... My word, all it takes is a little spunk and initiative... No need to bat your brains out... A big circular prehensible grab will do the trick... That may be a little more ticklish... I'd attach it to the outer face... How about 23-25?... That's an excellent caliber... Retrobascule valves for still greater security... The drop chain is simple… A Rotterdam-Durtex with one-inch links... And if they want something even stronger... to be absolutely on the safe side... the guaranteed maximum... they can take special cable plaited from copper and rope, a 28-34 while they're about it! See what I mean?... Rastrata is tops... I haven't any shares in the firm... Reinforced pneumatic hood... the Lestragone patent... And about portholes?... Ah!" He was assailed by doubt. "If I were in their shoes, I'd steer clear of that packing they turn out in the arsenals... that Tromblon-Parmesan stuff... It hasn't worked too well on submarines. It's a Hop!... They haven't told the whole story... At the ministry of course they defend it tooth and nail... but I'll stick to my guns... I foresaw it!... At medium pressures it does all right... Up to twenty kilos to the square centimeter, all right... But starting with twenty tenths'?... It's tissue paper, my boy... The fish pass right through it... That's my opinion and you won't make me change it... Anyway, they'll think of that... I've no right to influ-ence them... I won't even mention my article... Certainly not!... Hell! I will too... Sure I'll quote it... *in toto...* After all it's my duty... Don't you agree, Irène darling? And you, Ferdinand? Don't you think I ought to speak out? After all it's a critical moment... It's now or never... I'm in this thing... I'm in charge... I've got to tell them what I think, don't I? Today, and not in ten years... My opinions are worth something, aren't they? But enough phrasemongering!... It's all very well to give advice, to play the sage, the academician, the know-it-all... But it's not enough... Not by a long shot!... I've always done my share!... Here!… There! Everywhere! Irène can bear me out... I've never sidestepped a danger!... Never... By what right?... Why, I'll go down in their contraption myself... Maybe not the first try, but certainly the second!... Nobody can stop me!... It's my duty!... my right! Obviously! I'd even say it was indispensable... My eye, my authority, will be their only real security! Make no mis-take!"

"Oh no!" the old lady screeches as if somebody'd taken a bite out of her ass. "Nothing doing! I'd sooner cut the rope! As I live and breathe! This is the payoff! Never, you hear me! I'll never let you go down! Haven't you made an ass of yourself long enough! Go down in that contraption! You're not a fish, are you?... Let the lunatics dive! It's their business, not yours!... Certainly not!"

"Lunatics! Lunatics! You haven't a grain of sense! Where's your logic?... Didn't you pester the life out of me to make me go up in the air? Yes or no? Weren't you all for the balloon? You were nuts about it, out of your mind! 'The *Enthusiast!* The *Enthusiast!*' You couldn't think of anything else! And I'm not a bird!..."

"Bird, bird! Now you're insulting me! You're picking a fight!... All right! I see what you're up to, you dog!... I know, you want to clear out!... You want to go gallivanting around again!"

"Where? On the bottom of the sea?" "Bottom of the sea, my foot!..."

"Oh, leave me alone! Leave me alone, Irène! How do you expect me to think? You're always balling everything up!... with your idiotic outbursts... your insane frenzies!... Let me think in peace and quiet!... The circumstances, it seems to me, are solemn enough... Ferdinand! You hold down the shop... And whatever you do, don't say another word to me!"

He was giving orders again... He was recovering his tone, his color... and his crust for that matter... He started whistling his charmer's tune, the "Sole Mio" of happier days...

"Yes, I'd better go out! Take a breath of air... You've still got a hundred francs, haven't you, kid?... I'll go pay the telephone bill... That'll give me a chance to stretch my legs... It's high time they turned it on again... Wouldn't you say so? We need it..."

He hung around the doorstep... He was undecided... He looked out toward the arcades... He started off to the left... that probably meant the Insurrection. If he'd gone right, it would have been the Urns and his cat-o'-nine-tails... As soon as things begin to look up a little, all people can think of is piggishness...

The sale of that number was a real orgy, there's no getting around it... They came in a steady stream... They took the joint by storm... Even after nine at night subscribers came around asking for their supplement... All day long it was a riot... The shop shook under the weight of the mobs... The doorstep was all worn down from their trampling... Des Pereires harangued them... He'd stand on the counter, handing out papers by the armful... I was running around the whole time … pestering the printer... chasing back and forth... with the hod... The cart was too slow on the Faubourg Montmartre... I'd bring them back in batches as they came off the press...

The old cutie made up the wrappers for shipment to the provinces... That was important too... The diving-bell contest was being talked about far and wide... It was getting to be an event... Naturally Uncle Édouard heard about it... He dropped over to the Galerie... He came in through the side door... He was mighty glad our rag was picking up... He'd been worried... He expected me to be out on my ass again... looking for another job... And just then our popularity skyrocketed... We really had the wind in our sails... It was terrific...

The hope for treasure is real magic. There's nothing like it... At night after my errands, when I came back from the Automatic, I'd have more bundles to tie up... until eleven o'clock... Violette gave it to me straight:

"You're working too hard! You're a sap! You think they appreciate it?... If you knock yourself out, who's going to take care of you? Not your boss, I bet! Buy me a *menthe*, kid!... I'll sing you The Girl from Mostaganem'... It'll drive you crazy, you'll see..." For that little number she'd hike up her skirt front and back... She didn't wear any panties, so it was a real belly dance... She'd do it right out in the open... in the middle of the Galerie... The other floozies would come running... usually with three or four customers each... Bums, jerkoffs, bankrupt peepers... "Do your stuff, Suzy! Don't piss crooked!" She sure threw her twot around... You could see it bobbing up and down... The crowd clapped and cheered, that Tunisian dance of hers was some excitement... It always drew a crowd. When it was over, I'd buy her her *menthe*... We'd all end up at the Insurrection...

Violette's stand was over by the scales, behind the thickest column, in the Galerie d'Orléans … It didn't take her two minutes to do a job... If she hooked a real sucker, she'd take him up to the Pelican only a few steps away... across from the Louvre... The room cost two francs... She liked her pernod straight... We'd get her to sing her song:

The enchanted Orient came And sat in my caravansar-ee...
His ass was bare and from his belly A great big eye looked out at me.

That didn't do my work for me... Sometimes she'd hang around chewing the fat for hours... When I wanted to get rid of her, there was only one way.

"Let's go in," I'd say. "Come on, kid. You can help me tie up some bundles."

"Let me suck just one more... Wait for me, little chickadee!... I got to finish my night's-work..."

I could never count on her... Right away she'd look for the back door... She'd chicken out... Except for sewing on buttons, which was her weakness, I never got any real work out of her... She faded the minute I brought it up... It was surefire.

Hardly a week later the plans and solutions began to pour in at a terrific rate... about a hundred a day. Our rules had specified *ad libitum...* They hadn't let hard reality faze them!... They'd given their fancy free rein... All in all, at first glance, their expositions and plans were as dopey as they come... Our geniuses had really knocked themselves out!...

On the balistic side their ideas were wild... but some of the detail was good... We'd get something out of it... Generally speaking, when they used small sheets of paper, the size of the writing paper they give you in cafés, it was almost always to advertise some colossal device, a bell bigger than the Opéra... and when the plans were enormous, sprawled over eighteen octavo pages, you could bet they were selling some little sounding device about five inches long.

In that hobby parade there was everything you could ask for... every imaginable system, invention, and subterfuge for treasure hunting... Some of the caissons suggested were shaped like an elephant... Others were more like a hippopotamus... The majority, as we might have expected, looked like fishes... Some had a human aspect... regular people with faces... One, the inventor told us, was actually his landlady, a very faithful likeness, with eyes that would shine when they got down below two thousand feet... revolving in concentric circles... to attract all the fauna of the deep seas...

In every mail a fresh load of brilliant solutions turned up... they were somersaulting all over his desk... All we had to do now was wait for our sky pilot. He'd promised to be back the last Thurday of the month... It was all arranged and settled... We were right there at our posts... He was supposed to bring us ten thousand francs... an advance on our share... That would give us a chance to pay our most urgent debts in the neighborhood, to get the telephone turned on, and to run some beautiful pictures in an "extra-special number" devoted entirely to the diving bell... Already the big dailies were talking about us in connection with salvaging submarines, not just recovering the fabulous treasures of the deep... It was the year after the *Farfadet* disaster... The excitement hadn't died down... We had a sure chance of winning the gratitude of the nation...

But all those prospects didn't turn the old cutie's head... In fact she was looking pretty glum. She wanted to see that priest again before taking another step... Sometimes she'd ask me a dozen times an hour if I didn't see him coming... at the far end of the Galerie... And what about the boss? Where could he be keeping himself again? Painting the town?... Wasn't he down in the cellar?... No?... He'd been out since morning... All sorts of people were asking for him... It was getting worrisome... "Wait a minute," I tell the old lady. "I'll look in at the Insurrection..." I'd hardly stepped out when I see his nibs taking it easy, strolling through the gardens... making eyes at the nursemaids... without a care in the world... He's whistling, the stinker! He's got his arms full of bottles... I hightail it over to him...

"Well, well, Ferdinand! You look mighty anxious... Is the house on fire?... Is something wrong?... Has he turned up?"

"No," I say, "he's not there..."

"He won't be long," he says calmly... "Anyway, here's some Banyuls... and a bottle of Amer Picon... some anisette... and cookies... How do I know what the priest likes?... What do priests drink anyway?... Everything, I hope..." He wanted to celebrate the success of our venture. "I sincerely believe, Ferdinand, that we've hit the royal road... Ah yes! Things are shaping up... I was looking at the plans this morning... my oh my, what a shipment again! A torrent of ideas, my boy... Once the avalanche has subsided... I'm going to do some big-time sorting... On one side everything that looks promising... and on the other, the stuff we'd better forget... He wouldn't be able to do that... I expect him to give me carte blanche. No hit-or-miss methods!... It takes knowledge! We'll talk it over this afternoon... And that's not all, you know... There's the question of surety... I can't go into this thing with my eyes closed... Oh no! That would be too easy! Not at my age! Certainly not!... First of all a bank account... That's the main thing! And two hundred thousand on the line! And joint signatures... him and me! I send for the builders... we place the order... Then we can talk... We'll know where we're at... After all we're not babes in the woods!" Still, a shadow of doubt grazed his mind... "You think he'll be pleased with all this?"

"Ah," I say, "I'm positive." I hadn't the slightest doubt.

And so, chatting away, we get back to the office... We wait another little while... Still no priest in sight. It was getting kind of sticky... Madame des Pereires was all wrought up, she was trying to make a little order... so the place wouldn't look too much like a barn... It was a terrible shambles even in normal times, and now with this rush there wasn't an inch of space anywhere!... An enormous dungheap! A sow wouldn't find her kittens... Garbage in full eruption... absolutely sickening... from floor to roof... torn papers, disemboweled books, putrid manuals, manuscripts, memoranda, all reduced to streamers... clouds of flying confetti... The bindings all ripped, thrown in all directions... Those hoodlums had even made off with our beautiful statues... They'd decapitated Flammarion! They'd stuck blotting paper on Hippocrates, lovely violet moustaches... After an inconceivable lot of trouble we managed to extricate three chairs, the table, and the big armchair from the mess. We threw out the customers... We cleared a space to receive the holy man in.

On the stroke of half past five, only half an hour late... there he comes... I spy him coming down the Galerie d'Orléans... He was carrying a black briefcase, stuffed to the gills... He comes in... We greet him. He puts his load down on the table... Everything's OK. He mops his brow... he must have been walking fast... He catches his breath... The conversation starts up... Courtial takes over... The old lady goes up to the Alcazar... she comes back with a few folders, the most remarkable... quite a neat little assortment... She puts them down beside his briefcase... He seems satisfied... He leafs vaguely through them... picks out one or two at random... He doesn't seem terribly interested... We wait... we're afraid to stir a muscle... for him to say something... We breathe with care... He rummages through a few more pages... Then he screws up his whole face... A nervous tic!... And then another! A hideous grimace! Lord, it's an attack! A regular convulsion comes over him... He takes the whole load of papers and throws them into the showcase... Then he clutches his head... He rubs it with both hands... He kneads it, he mangles it... He pinches himself, he massages his chin... and his fat cheeks, his nose too, and his ears... A satanic convulsion!... He gouges his eyes, he scrapes his scalp... And then all of a sudden he leans over... He bends down and there he is on the floor... Plunging his head into the papers... He sniffs at the piles... He grunts, he puffs and blows... He picks up a whole armful and... whoops!... he tosses them up in the air... He flings them at the ceiling... It all comes raining down... papers, folders, plans, pamphlets... They're all over... We can't see each other... Once... twice... and then he does it again! All the time howling with joy... jubilant... He squirms... he digs in again... The people collect outside the door... He turns his briefcase upside down... He takes out more newspapers, a lot of clippings, whole armfuls... He scatters them too... In among them, I see them all right... there's a lot of bank notes... I see them in with the papers... I see them flying away... I dive to pick them up... I know how it's done... Just then two plug-uglies come charging up... They bang into the door with their shoulders... They push the crowd aside. They barge in... They jump the padre... They collar him from behind, they rough him up, they knock him over, they pin him to the floor... Ah, the poor bastard's suffocating... He crawls under the table, groaning... "Police," they inform us... They pull him out by the dogs... They sit on the poor guy...

"Have you known him long?" they ask us... They're inspectors... The meanest of the two pulls out his card... We tell them quick that we've got nothing to do with it... Absolutely nothing! The sky pilot is still wriggling... still struggling... He manages to get up on his knees... He starts sniveling... "Forgive me! Forgive me!" he begs us... "It was for my poor! My blind!... My poor little deaf-mutes..." All he wants in life is to go on collecting funds...

"Shut up! Who's asking you!... The dirty bastard's nuts!... When are you going to stop horsing around?" The one who had shown us his card gives the sky pilot such a clout that he goes "quack" and folds up... He wasn't talking anymore... They put the handcuffs on him right away… They wait a minute... They catch their breath... They kick him to make him get up. It's not over yet. Courtial still has to sign a statement and then some other paper on both sides. One of the bulls, the one that's not so mean as the other one, tells us a little about this screwball... He really was a priest... he was even an honorary canon!... Monsieur le Chanoine Fleury!... That's what he called himself... This wasn't his first fling or his first run-in with the law... He'd already taken every member of his family for thousands and thousands of francs... His cousins... his aunts... the Little Sisters of Saint-Vincent-de-Paul... He'd touched everybody... the churchwardens of the diocese... the beadle... and even the chair attendant... He owed her at least two thousand francs!... All for screwy schemes without any rhyme or reason... Lately he'd been burglarizing the sacraments chest... They'd caught him at it twice... with his hand in the chest... They'd found the whole of Joan-of-Arc's-Pence in his room, broken open with a chisel… He had treasure on the brain... They'd noticed it too late... Now they were going to lock him up... His bishop in Libourne had insisted on having him interned...

There was a crowd under our arcades... They were having a hell of a good time, enjoying the show... There were plenty of comments... A lot of thinking was going on... They saw the lettuce scattered around the place... But I'd seen it too... I'd had presence of mind... I'd already saved four or five bills and a fifty-franc piece... They did a lot of exclaiming...Those lugs outside the window had been watching me... The bulls pushed our priest into the gymnasium... He was still resisting... They had to go around in back to load him into a cab... He held on with all his might... He just didn't want to go...

"My poor! My poor poor!..." he kept yelling. Finally after a lot of trouble the cab came... They hauled him in... They had to tie him down, to rope him to the seat... Even so, he didn't keep still... He threw us kisses... It was shameful the way they tortured him... The cab couldn't get going, the people were standing in front of the horse... They wanted to look inside… They wanted to have the canon brought out... Finally with the help of some more cops they managed to get the carriage clear... So then the whole crowd of pests stream back in front of the shop... They couldn't make head nor tail of it! They kept cursing at us...

All those insults got the old cutie's dander up... She wasn't going to stand for it another minute... She didn't think twice... She leapt to the door... She opens it, she goes out, she stands there facing them...

"Well?" she says. "What's the matter with you?... You lousy suckers! You creeps! You're a lot of crummy snotnoses! Go chase yourselves! Louts! Hoodlums! What have you got to complain about?... Was that crook a friend of yours?" She had guts all right... But it didn't work... They cussed her even worse... They bellowed harder than ever. They spat all over our window. They threw gravel... It looked like a massacre coming on... We had to beat it out of there quick... by the back way...

After that Trafalgar we didn't know what to do... How were we going to quiet those lunatics now? This deep-sea diving-bell contest was getting as wild as our perpetual-motion runaround... The place was humming all day long... Often they'd wake me up in the middle of the night with their screeching... A procession of screwballs with their eyes popping out half a mile, ripping their shirts off outside the door, swollen, bloated with certainties, with implacable solutions... It wasn't a pleasant sight... More and more of them kept coming...They were blocking the traffic… A sarabande of lunatics!...

There was such a seething mass of them in the shop... tangled up in the chairs, clinging to the junk piles, submerged in the papers... that you couldn't get in when you needed something… All they wanted was to hang around and argue a little more, to bowl us over with some new and conclusive detail...

If at least we'd owed them something... if they'd all coughed up an advance, a rake-off, or a registration fee, we could have understood maybe what they had to be unhappy about, why they were peevish and disgruntled... But that wasn't the case... For once in our lives we didn't owe them a nickel! That was the payoff! Couldn't they give us credit?... Couldn't they see we weren't out for lucre?... that all we cared about was honor and fair play!... that we were quits… But nothing of the kind!... It was exactly the opposite! They were rioting for the hell of it... just to get us down... They were a thousand times angrier... a thousand times crummier, gripier, than on previous occasions when we'd bled them white... They were regular demons... Every single one yelled like at the Stock Exchange in honor of his gadget... And all of them together… The racket was something awful!...

None of them could wait... Every damn one wanted us to get his screwball invention under construction this minute... this second!... Hurry, hurry... get it working!... Christ, were they impatient to dive to the bottom of the ocean... Each for his own private treasure… They all wanted to be first! They said it was in the rules. They brandished our prospectus... We shouted back that we were sick of their stinking shenanigans and listening to their racket... we told them it was all a lot of hooey... Courtial climbed up on the winding staircase to tell them the whole truth... He shouted at the top of his lungs... The occasion was so solemn he'd put his topper on… He made a clean breast of it, I was there... He was perfect, a show like that could only happen once... He told them straight from the shoulder that we'd lost our backer... that the whole contest was dead and buried... No more millions than butter on his ass!... He explained that the bulls had locked him up... this fellow we were expecting to... this priest... that he'd never get out, they'd put him into a straightjacket, that the whole business was gone overboard!... "Overboard, overboard!" At these words they stamped with enthusiasm... They took up the chorus: "Overboard! Courtial! Lower the bell!..." They kept coming back. There were more of them every time, bringing new projects... They laughed in your face if you tried to reason with them... It didn't take... Their minds were made up... They all knew that you've got to suffer if you've got the faith! The faith that moves mountains, that upsets the seas... Theirs was sensational! When it came to faith, they were in a class by themselves! Besides they were convinced we wanted to keep all the mezuma for ourselves instead of sharing it with them... So they camped outside the door... They watched the exits... They settled down along the fence... They lay down, they made themselves at home... They weren't in any hurry... They had their conviction... it was solid rock!... No use trying to shake it... They would have massacred us on the spot at the slightest sign of contradiction... They were getting more and more ferocious... The slyest and sneakiest of the lot came around in back... They slipped in through the gymnasium... They'd motion us to join them... Whispering with us in the corner, they'd suggest terms, an increase in our cut... forty percent instead of ten for us on the first spoils raised... if we'd take care of them right away, ahead of the rest... They thought we were mighty greedy... They tried to bribe us... They held out prospects of golden grease...

Courtial refused to look at their stuff, he wouldn't say a word or even listen to them... He didn't even feel like going out anymore... He was afraid they'd spot him... The best place as usual was the cellar.

"You'd better take the air" was his advice to me. "They'll rub you out! Go sit under the trees… on the other side of the fountain . , . They better not see us together... Let them wear themselves down ... Let them holler till they're blue in the face... It's just a momentary riot... It'll die down in a week or ten days..."

He was way off. It went on much longer...

Luckily we'd saved a little nest egg... what I'd swiped off the canon... almost about two thousand francs... Our idea was that once the storm had subsided we'd take a powder one night with our dough... We'd take our stuff and give ourselves a change of air... move to a different neighborhood... Around here it was getting too hot... We'd start another Genitron along entirely new lines... with different inventors... We wouldn't even mention the diving bell... It seemed perfectly feasible... why not?... The hard part was putting up with their guff for two three weeks.

Meanwhile I had a rough time convincing the old cutie that she'd better stay home in her cottage in Montretout... and wait for the storm to blow over... She wouldn't listen, she didn't see the danger... I knew our customers... She riled them up with her manner, her pipe, her veil… I heard them passing mean remarks... Besides, she stood up to them... You couldn't tell what would happen... They were perfectly capable of skinning her alive... Inventors get terrible waves of fury, they see red... They disembowel everything in their path! She wouldn't have chickened out, that was sure... She'd have fought like a lioness, but why ask for trouble?... We had nothing to gain... That wouldn't save their cottage... In the end, after a lot of gulping and heartrending sighs, she saw it my way...

She hadn't come that day... Courtial was sawing wood in the cellar... We'd had lunch together at Raoul's Escargot on the corner of the Faubourg Poissonnière... not bad, I've got to admit... He'd done all right for himself... I didn't hang around the shop... I came right out and settled down as usual at a healthy distance on a bench across the way, behind the rotunda... From there I could watch the approaches... I could even step in if the situation got really rough... But it was a quiet day... Nothing special... Just the usual ferment... groups talking things over, chewing the fat... that's how it had been since the beginning of last week... Really nothing out of the way... No call to be scared... no fireworks... They were only simmering... Along about four o'clock a kind of calm settled... They sat down in a straggle... Their talk was no louder than a murmur... They must have been all in... They were strung out in a line along the shop fronts... You could smell how tired they were... They'd have to give up pretty soon... I was beginning to think of the prospects... we'd have to move and dream up another racket... find a fresh batch of suckers... start up a new line of business... We had our little nest egg. But how long could it last? Hell! Two thousand francs melt away easy... if we wanted to start the paper up again and make the payments on their cottage... Actually it wouldn't be possible to do both at once... Anyway, I was off in my daydreams... really absorbed... when far in the distance... in the Impasse du Beaujolais... I see a big lug all by himself making a terrible uproar... waving his arms in all directions... He comes charging up right in front of our joint... He grabs the handle… He shakes the door like an apple tree... He yells for des Pereires... Say, that boy is stark raving mad, he's off his rocker... He raises hell a while... Nobody answers... He takes a brush and daubs the whole shop front with green paint... Smut, I guess... He shoves off, still raving... Oh well, that didn't amount to much... I'd feared a lot worse...

Another hour or two go by... The sun was beginning to go down... The clock strikes six... That was the nastiest time, the time I dreaded most... the stinking hour, made to order for riots and disturbances... especially with our customers... the crummy time of day when all the shops disgorge their little maniacs, their extra-clever employees... That's when the lunatics are on the loose... the spawn of the offices and factories... They come out in droves, bareheaded... they run after the bus... the artisans stung by the radiations of Progress. They take advantage of the last few minutes of daylight... They leap, they bound... They're the sober kind, water drinkers… They run like zebras... This was the battle hour!... I could feel them coming... it gave me a bellyache... This was the time they regularly landed on us... we were their aperitif...

I pondered a little while longer... I began to think about our dinner too... I'd go and wake Courtial up... he'd asked me for fifty francs. But suddenly I give a start... A terrible noise is coming at me! Through the Galerie d'Orléans... swelling, coming nearer... It was more than a hum... It was a rumble! A storm!... Thunder under the glass roof!... I jump up... I run over to the rue Gomboust, where the worst of the ruckus seemed to be coming from... I bump into a horde of haggard maniacs, roaring frothing brutes... There must be at least two thousand of them bellowing in the chasm... And more keep gushing out of the adjoining streets... They're compressed, squeezed against a big heavy cart... looks like a gun carriage... Just as I get there, they're busy demolishing the double garden-fence... They uproot it at one blow... That flat cart made a terrible battering ram... They smash both arcades... Blocks of stone are falling like marbles... crashing, collapsing, bursting into smithereens right and left... It was terrifying . . They come down like thunder, harnessed to their infernal machine... The earth was trembling half a mile away... They're bouncing in the gutters... They're all delirious... bobbing and jumping around their catafalque, carried on by the fury of the charge!... I couldn't believe my eyes!... They're berserk!... There's at least a hundred and fifty of them pulling at the shafts... galloping under the arches with that enormous load behind them!

More lunatics roaring, tangling, tearing each other apart, trying to get a better hold on the shaft... the keel... the axles... I come closer... Christ! It's our inventors!... I see pretty near all of them!... I recognize them one by one… There's De la Greuze, the café waiter... he's still got his slippers on... And Carvalet the tailor... He's having trouble running... He's losing his pants... There's Bidigle and Juchère, the two who do their inventing together... who spend their nights at Les Halles... carrying baskets... I see Bizonde! I see Gratien, the one with the invisible bottle! There's Cavendou... There's Lanémone with his two pairs of glasses... the one who invented the mercury heating system... I see the whole gang of punks... all yelling blue murder! Christ, are they mad!... I climb up on the fence! Above the tumult... I get a good look at the character in the driver's seat, the big guy with the curly hair that's egging them on, the ringleader… I see the monumental contraption! It's a cast-iron shell... a fantastic mess! It's Verdunat's diving bell! Armored to the hilt!... That's it all right, I've seen the model a hundred times... his famous project... I'd know it in the dark! With the luminous portholes and the diverging searchlight beams... Hell's bells!... There's Verdunat himself, half-naked... Riding his monster... He's climbed up on top of it! He's shouting!... mustering his lousy troops... haranguing them!... getting ready for a new charge!...

I have to admit that he'd warned us. He'd told us categorically that he was going to have it built at his own expense, in spite of our opinions... He was going to put all his savings into it... We refused to take him seriously... He wouldn't have been the first to hand us a line... The Verdunats were dry cleaners in Montrouge, from father to son... He's brought the whole family along... There they are, the whole lot of them, dancing around the bell... holding each other's hands... doing a square dance... mama, grandpa, and the small-fry... They've brought us their invention... He'd promised... and we wouldn't believe him... They'd hauled the monster all the way from Montrouge! The whole screwy tribe! The unholy alliance!... I patch up all my courage... I foresee the worst... They recognize me... They howl at me... The fury is general... They have it in for my guts... They all spit up at me... They vomit at me!...

"I beg your pardon!" I say. "Please listen to me just a minute." Silence. "You don't seem to understand."

"Come on down, you little stinker... so we can knock the shit out of you once and for all... Cock-sucker! Chameleon! Baboon! Where's the old wise-guy? We just want to twist his guts a little..."

That was the way they listened... There wasn't any point in my going on... Luckily I was able to give them the slip... I hid behind the kiosk. I shouted "help" with all my might... But it was too late... Nobody could hear me in the gardens with all the thunder and lightning... Outside our door the carnage was at its height... It was like I'd stirred them up with my words, made them madder than ever... This was the climax...They undo the harness... They come out from the shaft... They aim the infernal machine straight across the sidewalk... with the tip against our shop front... The clamor redoubles... The lunatics from all the Galeries and environs rally around the bell... The whole mob brace themselves... "One... two... And yoop! Heave-ho!" The crowd heaves... With one swing they drive the whole catapult through the window... Everything flies into smithereens... The woodwork gives way, cracks, scatters... The whole place is wrecked!... An avalanche of glass!... The monster drives in, forces its way, vacillates, crashes! A torrent of plaster! The whole *Genitron* caves in!... Our winding staircase, the investors' corner, the Tunisian mezzanine... There's barely time to see it all collapsing in a cataract of papers, followed by an explosion of dust... Then an enormous cloud flies up, the gardens, all four Galeries are filled with whiteness... The hordes are choking, enveloped in plaster... They spit, they cough, they gag! That doesn't prevent them from propelling their monster... The ironwork... the mirrors... the ceilings join the cascade! The bell staggers! The floor gives way, cracks, gapes open... The horrible machine teeters, dances at the edge of the precipice... tips... falls to the bottom... Christ! It's the end of the world! Thunder all the way up to the sky! Suddenly a blast of awful piercing screams stops the mob in their tracks!... The gardens are veiled in dense dust... Finally the police turn up... they grope their way to the scene... They draw a cordon around the wreckage... More bulls come running... They charge... The rioters break up... scatter... Over by the restaurant they start galloping again... They're all shivering with the excitement...

The cops clear the onlookers away from the disaster site... I knew all the rioters... I could turn in the whole lot of them... It would be a cinch... I know who is the meanest of the whole gang... the rottenest, the most violent... the biggest stinker of them all... I know some who'd be in for ten years! That's right! But I don't go for vengeance much! It would only make things a little lousier than they are... that's all... Better attend to urgent business... I run into the crowd, I pass from group to group... I make myself known to the cops... "Have you seen the boss? Courtial des Pereires?" I ask in all directions.

Nobody's seen him. I'd left him at noon... Suddenly I catch sight of the *commissaire*... the one from the rue des Bons-Enfants... The exact same little punk that had been running us ragged... I go up to him... I tell him the boss has disappeared... He listens... He's skeptical... "You think so?" he says... He doesn't believe me. "I'm positive!" So he climbs down one side of the crevice with me... We both of us search... I yell... I call... "Courtial! Courtial!... Get up!" The cops yell too... Once, twice... ten times... I go around the edge of every hole... I lean down over the abyss... "If you ask me," the jerk says, "he's at the whorehouse." They were going to give up... when suddenly I hear a voice!

"Ferdinand! Ferdinand! You got a ladder?"

It's him! It's him all right! He surfaces from a deep pile of rubble... He fights his way out... His face is full of flour... We throw him a strong rope... He catches hold... we hoist! We pull him out of the crater!... Unharmed, he assures us... He was only taken by surprise, wedged, squeezed, absolutely blocked between the bell and the wall... But we can't find his lid. That vexes him at first... He blusters... His frock coat has suffered... He doesn't press the point... He refuses any kind of first aid... He refuses to go to the pharmacy... Then he gets snotty with the cops... "I shall bring action, gentlemen," he says just like that... Then without waiting for an answer, he climbs over the rail and the beams and the wreckage... We're outside. "Make way!

... Make way!..." He pushes through the crowd. His frock coat has lost its tails... He's completely defrocked... He's all powdery, he looks like a Pierrot. The stuffing drops out as he runs... he only runs harder... He drags me toward the exit on the Louvre side... He clutches my sleeve. He's trembling something awful... He's not the old high and mighty...

"Come on, come on, Ferdinand! Make it snappy! Take a look behind us. Nobody's followed us?... You're sure? Keep on moving, boy!... We'll never come back here... Not to this joint... It's an infamous trap! You can take my word for it! It's an obvious conspiracy... I'll write a letter to the landlord."

Now that our office was all smashed up, I had no place to sleep... So we decided I'd move out to Montretout... We looked in at the Insurrection... He couldn't take the train with his coat in rags... The owner was kind enough to lend him an old coat... We had a little chat with two screwballs... Courtial's pants were full of holes... They had to be mended... Everybody'd seen the riot, heard the screams and all the commotion... they were all excited... Even Formerly joined in... He wanted to do something for us, to take up a collection... I told him we didn't need it... It would have given me a pain to accept... I said we had some money left! He'd made a pretty pile out of my old man... He could afford to be generous... So he paid for the drinks, another round, and then still another.

It was getting kind of hot... It was the end of June... With all that awful dust and talking so much our throats were mighty parched... we must have drunk at least ten twelve bottles... We were zigzagging as we left... It was very late... We were still pretty excited... We just barely caught the last train out of the Gare du Nord.

In Montretout luckily the sky was full of stars... and even a little moonlight. We could almost see the way... Even so, to keep from going wrong on the pathways of Montretout, especially up on the hill, you had to be mighty careful... At that time street lamps or road signs were unheard-of... It was only by dead reckoning, by instinct, by the feel of it that you could steer your way in among the shacks... It was mighty dangerous... There were always nearly four or five murders every year as a result of tragic blunders... People that got lost... or wise guys... that picked the wrong house... that went up to the gate and rang the bell when they shouldn't have... The poor stupid bastards would get themselves riddled with bullets... from service revolvers, from Lebel carbines... and in two seconds flat the neighborhood dogs would finish them off... It was a ruthless collection of the most ferocious carnivorous mongrels... horribly aggressive, trained specially for the purpose... They'd bound to the kill... There wouldn't be anything left of the poor devil... I'd better explain, though, that this was just when the Bonnot gang[117] were doing their stuff, they'd been terrorizing the whole northwestern suburbs for the last six months, and they were still at large...

Everybody was in a panic, suspicious as hell... Once the door was shut, those people didn't know father or mother... It was no time to be getting lost...

Your worried cottager, your rich miser would spend the night peering out through the blinds, sleeping with one eye, clutching his gun!

---

[117] Bonnot gang *(Bande à Bonnot)*. A group of anarchists led by Joseph Bonnot (1876-1912). Specialized in bank robberies for the benefit of the cause. Bonnot and three others were killed at the time of their arrest in 1912.

At the first sign, the crafty burglar, the shifty tramp could consider himself strung up, rubbed out, extinguished... They'd have needed a miracle (o get their balls out of there... Those people were vigilant all right, and the darkness was murder...

Under the station shelter Courtial didn't feel easy in his mind... He was thinking about the hike ahead of us... the assorted ambushes... He stopped to think a minute... Then "Let's go!

..." After the first few steps on the road he began to whistle good and loud... kind of like yodeling... That was his rallying tune... It was supposed to identify us in the danger spots... We plunged into the night... The road got very soft, full of holes and mush... We could vaguely make out shapes in the darkness... the outlines of shacks... At every fence the dogs barked and bayed and howled at us... We walked as fast as possible, but then it began to rain... A sea of molasses! The road climbed in zigzags.

"We're heading for the top of Montretout," he informed me. "The summit... Wait till you see the view."

Their house, La Gavotte was the highest point in the region. He'd often told me, it looked out over the whole countryside... He could see the whole of Paris from his bedroom... He began to be out of breath... Still, the mud wasn't thick... Supposing it was winter! Then a little farther, after the bend, I made out signals, a lamp moving... up and down... "That's my wife," he cries out... She's talking to me in code: S... T... I... N... One down! Two up." Anyway, we knew we were on the right road... We were still climbing though... We went faster and faster... Pooped and panting, we come up to the house... Our old battle-ax with her lantern comes running down from her platform... she jumps on the boss... She was good and mad... she wouldn't let me get a word in... She'd been making signals after every train since eight o'clock and then some... She was really in a dither... And besides, what was I doing there... I wasn't expected... What was the big idea?... She kept firing questions at us... all of a sudden she noticed that he'd changed his rig... We were too dog-tired to break it to her gently... Balls!... We go in... We sit down in the first room...We give it to her straight... Naturally, when he was so late she'd been expecting some kind of trouble... But now this total disaster, we couldn't have told her anything worse... bang, right square in the puss... It knocked her cold... her whole face began to tremble, even her moustache... She couldn't get out a sound... Finally the tears unwound her...

"So it's all over, Courtial?... Tell me, is it all over?" She collapsed onto her chair... I thought she was going to conk out... The two of us were standing there... we got ready to lay her out on the floor... I got up to open the window... But she comes to... She's frantic... She jumps up from her chair, quivering all over... She pulls herself together... She hadn't been out for long... She's up again... She wobbles a bit on her pins... She steadies herself... She gives a hefty clout on the table... on the oilcloth...

"Christ almighty! It's too much," she yells all of a sudden.

"Too much! Too much! You said it!..." He's off the handle too. He stands right up to her... He's not going to take it lying down... He clucks like a rooster.

"Ah, it's too much! Too much, you say? Well, my dear, I regret nothing! No, absolutely! Nothing, nothing!"

"Ah, you miserable stinker! You regret nothing?... You're perfectly happy, aren't you? And what about the house?... Have you thought about the payments? They'll be coming back on Saturday, my friend... Saturday, not a day more... Have you got those twelve hundred francs? Have you got them on you?... We promised... They're expecting them... They're coming at twelve!... Have you got them on you?... Not at one o'clock, at twelve!"

"Balls and counterballs! To hell with your cottage... You know what you can do with it... The events have set me free... Do you understand that, you blockhead?... No bitterness or rancor! No debts or protests!... To hell with it all! Do you hear? I shit on the whole business; I..."

"Shit! Shit! Debts! Debts! All I want to know is whether you've got the money on you, you big jerk... Ferdinand, he's got six hundred smackers in all, I know that... Have you got the money, Ferdinand?... You haven't lost it? It's twelve hundred francs they're coming for, not six... Can't you get it through your head?"

"Bah! Foo! Never a step backward!... Gangrene!... You want to defend gangrene?... It's got to be amputated!... Don't you know that, you big hunk of baloney! It's got to be amputated high up! Say, have you been drinking up all the white wine? I can smell it from here. High up! Garlic! What do you want to save? Say, your breath stinks! The rotten stump? The maggots? The flies? The bubo? No putrid flesh for me! I won't make another move! Not one, you hear me?... Never, you fishwife, as long as I live... Defeat! Recantation! Guile! Oh no! My toe! Do you expect me to jerk off my executioners?... Me? Never!... Do you hear me, Ferdinand?... Profit from what you see! Observe! Try to recognize grandeur when you see it, Ferdinand! You won't see much of it in this world!"

"My goodness, it's you that's been drinking... Why, you've both been drinking... They come here drunk, the rotters!... And then they have the gall to cuss me out!"

"Grandeur, detachment, you simpleton! I'm going away! Did you know that?... You know nothing!... Far away! Even farther! I'm telling you! I despise their provocations, even the foulest... the most sickening! What unspeakable vileness germinates in those unclean goatskins?... those mangy curs?... What is the measure of my essence? Nobility, you old bag... Do you hear? You who stink of garliacic acid! Do you get me, you shallot? Nobility! Are you listening? Shit on your Gavotte and double shit! Nobility! Light! Ineffable wisdom!... Ah! O delirious bandits! Demons of pillage!... O Marignan! O debacle, poor little Ferdinand! I can't believe my eyes! nor my own voice! I'm magical! I'm carried away! O turn of events!... Only yesterday at my zenith! Overloaded with favors! Adulated! Plagiarized! Pursued! Feted like a god! What am I saying? Consulted from all over the world! You've seen it, you've read about it! And today? Crash bang! Nothing! The bolt has struck... Nothing... Anatom... The atom, it is I!... But the atom, Ferdinand, is everything... Exile, Ferdinand!... Exile?" His voice was drowned in sadness... "Yes! That's it! I am finding myself! Destiny is opening its gates! Exile? So be it! You and I... I've been praying for it too long! And now it's come! The blow has fallen, transcendent... Hosannah... irrevocable!... Villainy has thrown off her mask... At last... She owed me that... All these years she's been tracking me, undermining me, exhausting me!... But now, compensation!... She shows herself! I uncover her! And I ravish her... to the full! Ah yes! She is forced to my will, seething! On the public square!... What a vision, Ferdinand!... What a spectacle!... O Irène, all my desires are fulfilled!... Frothing, bleeding, howling! Do you hear me?... This very afternoon we saw her attacking our proud journal! Assaulting the human spirit! Ferdinand here is my witness! Wounded, bruised, mutilated!... And yet I collect myself, I pull myself together, I wrench myself away from the nightmare! Oh, what a foul battle! But the bladder has burst! The gall has gushed in all directions!... hit me square in the eyes! But my spirit is intact. Oh, the pure, the proud reward! Oh! And above all, no compromise! Get that through your heads, the whole lot of you! You expect me to cajole my executioners? Give me cold steel instead! Or fire!... Anything, but not that! Bah!... The gods are conspiring! So be it!... They honor me with the bitterest of gifts! Hatred, the hatred of vultures!... Exile?... Will I refuse it? I? You don't know me... They're putting me to the test! Let them!..." That handed him a laugh. "They choose to put me to the test?... I'm flattered... I could roar with pride!... Too cruel?... Hum, hum! we'll see! It's an affair between gods and men!... You want to know how I'll manage, Ferdinand?... Don't worry, friend! Don't worry... You won't be bored! See here, Ferdinand, you who like to roam around, you know the Panthéon?... Tell me, poor muddlehead, haven't you ever noticed anything? You've never seen the Thinker? He's there on his pedestal... He's there... And what's he doing? Eh, Ferdinand? He's thinking, my boy. That's right. Nothing else. He's thinking. Well, Ferdinand! He's alone!... There you have it! I'm alone too!... He's naked! I'm naked too... What can you do for me, you poor little creatures?..." He was feeling sorry for us, the old cutie and me... "Nothing! You in a pinch!... poor child, benighted by your endocrine glands, tormented by growing pains, in short invertebrate! Poor gastropod, destroyed by the slightest dream... As for my old goblin here, what useful or useless thing could she give me? A touching echo of years long dead... Trials! Forgotten hardships! Worm-eaten winters! Carrion!..."

"What's that you called me?... Say it again... Say it again quick so I can hear you." She hadn't liked those last words. "Are you trying to make a fool of me? Just tell me that, you flyspeck!"

She didn't care for allusive language... She threatened him with a vase, she demanded further details...

"Don't listen to him, Ferdinand! Don't listen to him!... He's just telling more lies! Nothing else comes out of his mouth... What have you been doing in the kitchen? Tell me this minute!... What's become of my marsh-mallow root?... You don't know?... He's stolen that too!... And on my washstand... The bicarbonate? You don't know that either?... You took an enema with it!

... Don't try to deny it! And my Vais water? Where did you put it?... He respects nothing! I'd bought it specially to take on Sunday..."

"Leave me alone, can't you? Let me think. You molest me, you harass me, you exasperate me!... How obtuse you are, my good darling, my sweet little cherub!..."

At that she tears her hat off, sniffs up her snot, and toys with the back of the big heavy chair...

"Answer me," she menaces, "what have you done with my marshmallow root?"

He has no answer... she begins to lift the chair... she's clutching the two struts... He sees her... He lunges over to the sewing table... picks it up under the drawer... They're both nicely armed... This is going to be quite an argument... I take refuge in the chimney corner... He parleys...

"My sweet angel, please! My sugarplum, I beg you! Listen to me! Just a word before you get excited... Listen to me!... Don't break anything... I sold it! God! I've sold it all!"

"Sold? Sold? What have you sold?"

"Everything! Yes, everything! Only this morning! I've been standing on my head trying to tell you! To the Lémenthal Bank... to Monsieur Rambon! You know him... The lawyer. There was nothing else to do! It's all over! Liquidated! Washed up! Down the drain! Do you understand? Do you understand me now, you stupid old goose! That takes the wind out of your sails, eh? It calms you down, doesn't it? Tomorrow, see! They're coming tomorrow morning!..."

"Tomorrow? Tomorrow? Tomorrow morning?..." she echoed. She was still in a dream. "Yes, tomorrow. It's all settled. All you have to do is sign the papers."

"Oh, the blackguard! The monster! He's tearing out my entrails! I'd never have thought it possible... Oh, what a numbskull I've been..."

She drops the chair, she slumps down on it... she lets her arms dangle, she's out for the count... She sniffles and that's all... She really wasn't the stronger party, he'd got what he wanted... She looks across the table at him... that beastly lout over there in the distance... the way you'd look at a slimy octopus, a hideous monster in an aquarium... an incredible nightmare from another world... She couldn't believe her eyes... There really wasn't a thing she could do. It was no use trying... She gave up, she was completely beaten... She gave in to her grief... She sobbed so violently, she beat her head so hard against the sideboard that the dishes came tumbling out on the floor... A little thing like that couldn't faze him... He pressed his advantage… He consolidated his position...

"Well now, Ferdinand? What do you say? Do you see? Do you realize... Now perhaps you're beginning to understand what passionate intrepidity is... You see what I mean? Ah, my decision wasn't made yesterday... it matured slowly, by God, and wisely... Examples? Epigones? We have plenty to offer you, madame. How many? Rafts of them. Illustrious examples! Take Marcus Aurelius! That's right! What did that old bugger do? In very similar situations! Harassed! Maligned! Traduced! On the brink of succumbing under the welter of abject plots... of murderous perfidies... What did he do in such a case?... He withdrew, Ferdinand!... He abandoned the steps of the Forum to the jackals! Yes! In solitude! In exile! That's where he sought his balm! That's where he found new courage!... That's right!... He took counsel of himself! And no one else!... He didn't ask the mad dogs for their opinion!... No! Faugh! Ah, despicable recantation!... And what about Vergniaud?[118] The pure, ineffable Vergniaud! At the hour of carnage, when the vultures gathered over the charnel house? When the sickening smell rose up? What did he do, that man who was purest of the pure?... the very heart of wisdom... in those ravaged minutes where every lie means life?... Did he take back his words? Recant? Eat dirt?... No, he mounted his calvary alone... Alone, he rose above the crowd... He withdrew... Alone, he ushered in the great silence! He was silent! There you have it, Ferdinand... I too will be silent, dammit all!..."

Des Pereires wasn't a very big man. He pulled himself up to his full height to harangue me better... But he was wedged in between the stove and the big sideboard... He didn't have much room... He looks over at the two of us... He keeps on looking... An idea was budding in his brain...

---

[118] Pierre-Victurnien Vergniaud (1753-1793). Girondist deputy who voted for the death of Louis XVI. Arrested with other leaders of the Gironde party, he was executed in 1793. The basis of Courtial's reflections is obscure.

"Wouldn't you like to... go out?" he says... "to take a little stroll?... I want to be alone... Just for a minute... There's something I've got to do... Please! I beg of you! Just for a second!"

That was a mighty odd proposition, especially at that time of night! Standing there in the door-way, all shriveled in her shawl, the old girl looked pretty mean.

"So now you're throwing us out?... Say, you're completely nuts."

"Give me at least ten minutes. I don't ask more. It's indispensable! Imperative! Urgent! It's just a little favor I'm asking of you... Leave me in peace for a second! All alone for just a second... You won't? It won't be any trouble... Take a turn around the garden... It's much nicer outside than in... Go on, go on! I'll call you. Can't you understand?"

He kept at it. He didn't have any big cellar like at the *Genitron* for his meditations... He only had three little rooms to pace around in... They were so stubborn, so obstinate, so contradictious I could see they were going to tear each other's hair out if I didn't take the old girl away... She was the worse hothead of the two... So I take her out in the hall...

"We'll come back in five minutes," I tell her... "Leave it to me... Let him stew in his juice... He's a pain in the neck... Anyway, I want to talk to you..."

She insisted on taking her lantern... It wasn't a very good time for a stroll... It was pretty chilly out... She was tearing mad, take it from me... She was really broken up... She kept wailing the whole time.

"Imagine his doing this to me! The swine! The pervert! The scoundrel! To me, Ferdinand! To me!..."

Gesticulating, she skirted the fence... She stumbled a little with her lantern... She kept mumbling insults... We came to some garden frames... There she stopped... Still wailing and sniffling, she wanted to show me... she lifted the big pulleys... She wanted me to take a good look at the shoots and the little blades that were coming up... and the fine soil...

"I planted it all myself, Ferdinand... All by myself... He didn't do it, oh no! rest assured..." I had to look again... The little turnips... and the little slugs... and the saucer for the pumpkin... She lifted all the lids... all the frames... There was enough chicory for an army... We went around every bed... Then she was exhausted... She told me, as we went along, about all the trouble she had in times of drought... It was she who pumped the water, she who carried the pitchers... from over there... from the faucet at the end of the walk... Her misery took her words away... She sat down, she stood up... I had to go look at the big rain barrel and see for myself that it wasn't big enough...

"Oh yes," she jumps up again. "You haven't seen his system... It's mighty cute... His precious invention... You really haven't heard about it?... Well, believe me it's a nightmare... He outdid him-self! Of course I was against it... what would you expect?... My oh my! I gave him a good piece of my mind! I raised hell! But it was hopeless! Absolutely hopeless. He's as stubborn as thirty-six mules! He slugged me! Well, I didn't exactly pet him either, believe you me! And what for? So he could destroy the whole good side of the fence... And eighteen rows of carrots! Yes, eighteen!... And twenty-four artichokes!... For what purpose? To build a shed!... You should see the state it's in... A sow wouldn't find her eggs... A garbage can, I tell you... a cesspool! That's what he did to my garden..."

We started off in that direction, she guided me with her light...

It actually was a little shanty... dug into the ground, almost entirely buried... only the roof stuck out... Inside I looked under the tarps... nothing but rubbish... a lot of broken-down instruments... all in a complete mess... and a big dynamo, completely clogged and rusted... a gas tank bottomside up... a bent flywheel... and a one-cylinder motor... That was Courtial's invention... I knew a little something about it... The "Wave Generator"!... It was supposed to make plants grow... It was one of his ideas... There'd been a whole special number of the *Genitron* devoted to "The Future of Agriculture Thanks to Radiotel-lurism"... He'd written three manuals and a whole string of articles (with eighty dia-grams)... explaining its use... In addition he'd given two lectures in Le Perreux and one in Juvisy to convince small farmers... It hadn't gone over... And yet, according to des Perei-res, with the help of a "Polarimeter" it was child's play to radiate the roots of this or that vegetable or plant with those clusters of telluric rays which are otherwise ridiculously scattered, dispersed, and lost to the world!... "I bring you," he said to them, "my subracinal spray, infinitely more useful than any water! An electric shower! Providential for beans!" According to him nothing was easier, with a small amount of equipment, than to make a salsify swell up to the size of a large turnip... The whole gamut of fructi-fying infra-terrestrial magnetism was made fully available!... Vegetables grown to meet the needs of every individual! In season! Out of season!... It was really quite an idea!

Unfortunately, harassed as he was by so many daily cares, by all the snags and setbacks con-nected with the operation of the *Genitron*, he had been unable to perfect the system... Especially the condensers... They didn't synchronize properly... They needed watching... He couldn't run them more than two or three hours on Sunday... That didn't provide enough waves... On weekdays he had other fish to fry... He was busy with the rag and his various contests... Madame des Pereires had no faith whatever in this telluric jazz... "I told him a million times... I was wasting my breath... 'That thing of yours will never work! It's impossible! You'll only make one more mess... You're going to cave the house in with your trenches... That's all the vegetables we'll ever have... Electric currents... if that's what you want... don't stay in the ground... they fly through the air, you dope... Everybody knows that. What about storms? Or just take a look at the roads... Why do they spend all that money on telephone lines? And what about lightning rods? The government isn't nuts, I hope... They wouldn't go to all that expense if they could help it!...' I'd have said any old thing to keep him from digging up my garden! 'You're talking through your hat!' He always insults me when he knows I'm right... He won't give in! He'd rather bust! Oh, I know my little man! Pretentious! Proud! Hell, a peacock is nothing!... Having to listen to that tommyrot day in day out!... For twenty-eight years I've been putting up with him... and this is what I get... this is my reward... You'll never know how bad I feel... But it's no use... He's selling us out!... Absolutely! That man would sell his shirt! He'd sell yours, Ferdinand! He'd sell anything!... When he gets the bug and feels he needs a change, he's not a man anymore, he's a rattle! It's the fairs that ruined him! The older he grows the screwier he gets... He's completely cracked... I can see it, I'm nobody's fool! He's diabolical, Ferdinand!... It's not just a disease with him, it's a disaster... But I can't go along with him anymore... Nothing doing... I gave him a piece of my mind when he told me about his system... 'Courtial,' I said, 'you're always monkeying with things that are none of your business... What do you know about agriculture? No more than you do about elevators and piano factories!...' But he always thinks he knows it all... That's his special vice... Knowing it all! Poking his nose into every crack! He's the original busybody! He's too big for his shoes, that's what's wrong with him! One day he comes home and it's chemistry... The next day it's sewing machines... The day after it's beets... Always something new... Naturally he doesn't get any-where... The thing for him is balloons. I've thought so all along. I've always told him so... 'Courtial, your balloon, Courtial, your balloon! That's the one thing you know how to do! With anything else you'll come to grief. It's stupid to keep trying! Your business is ballooning! It's our only hope. If you keep on with these brainstorms of yours, you'll come to grief. We'll end up in the poorhouse, making paper flowers.' I've told him a thousand times, I've repeated it over and over again. But it's go chase yourself, you old battle-ax! The balloon? He gets so stupid when those pig-headed spells come on he won't even let me mention it! I know what I'm talking about. I've got to bear the brunt. His highness is a 'writer,' I don't understand such things. He's a 'scientist,' an 'apostle'! Hell, I can tell you what he is! He's a loafer... a crook!... A buffoon!... He's a crumb... a four-flusher... Yes, à bum, that's what he is! He's unscrupulous! He wants to dive, does he? Well, he's heading straight for the bottom... a flophouse crawling with lice, that's what he deserves! And that's what he'll get! What a jerk he turned out to be!... He's coming apart at the seams! He doesn't know where the next nickel is coming from... He thinks I don't know... He can gas all day, he won't fool me. I know the score!... But he won't get away with it... no, sir... He'd better not kid himself! He'd better watch his step! I won't stand for it!..."

She came back to her obsession... She talked about the *Enthusiast* some more... about the early days of her married life, expeditions with the balloon... Even then it wasn't easy to pump her up full... They never had enough gas... The bag was fragile and not very airtight... But they'd been young and those were the good old days... On Sundays she'd gone up with des Pereires... During the week she'd worked as a midwife . , She'd applied cups, wet ones and dry ones... little nursing jobs... She'd known Pinard well, who'd delivered the Czarina... It got her all excited to talk about him... an obste-trician of worldwide fame... I was beginning to feel chilly in among the vegetables... The sky and the country all around were turning bluish... I was shivering and stamping my feet... We came back up the little path for the hundredth time... We went down again... She talked some more about mortgages... Their house was made of millstone grit... It must have been worth quite a lot... Did I think he'd really sold out?... I had no way of knowing... He was sly and secretive... I didn't even know this Monsieur Rambon!... I'd never seen him... And the Lémenthal Bank... I'd never heard of it... Actually I didn't know anything...

Looking into the distance, I could begin to make out the shapes of the other shacks... And past the big empty lots there were tall chimneys... the factory in Arcueil... that smelled so strong of cinnamon over the vineyards and the pond... By now I could see the villas all around... All sizes... Little by little the colors came out... a regular battle... all ugly as hell, fighting in the fields... All kinds... rocky, flattened, arrogant, bandy-legged... pale, half-finished ones, skinny, emaciated... staggering... reeling on their frames... A massacre in yellow, brick-red, and semi-piss color... Not a one that can stand up right... A collection of toys plunked down in the shit!

In the lot next door there was a regular little monument, a miniature fretwork church something like Notre-Dame, a cabinet-maker's fancy... He kept rabbits in it...

The old bag went on talking, drooling, explaining... In the end she ran down... she lost the thread of her thoughts... she'd had enough... We'd been out there in the gale for two full hours...

"That'll do! Who does he take us for?... I'm sick and tired of his nonsense... Hell, why shouldn't he come out too?... I'm going to give that brute a piece of my mind... Come, Ferdinand... This way, by the kitchen door... He's going too far... What if I come down with pleurisy?..." She hightails it up to the terrace... Just as she opens the door, des Pereires appears... He pops out of the darkness, he was coming to get us... Some cock-eyed rig he had on... He was all wrapped up in the big tablecloth... He'd made a hole for his head and pinned it up with safety pins and a rope around the waist... He comes down the five steps, he grabs me by the arm... He looks completely absorbed... really deep in something... He drags me out to the end of the garden, over by the last frame... He bends down, he pulls up a radish, he shows it to me, he puts it under my nose...

"You see?" he says... "Take a good look!... You see?... You see how big it is?... And this leek? You see it? And how about this fellow?..."

It's some funny-looking vegetable I don't recognize... "Do you see it?"

"Yes," I say, "of course."

"Then come over here! Quick, quick!" He drags me to the other end of the garden... He bends over... He gets down on his knees, he crawls, he puts his whole arm through the fence... He puffs and blows... He pokes around in the neighbor's garden... He pulls up another radish... He brings it back... He presents it to me... He wants me to compare... He's triumphant... The other guy's radish is really very little... infinitesimal... almost nonexistent... And pale! He thrusts both of them under my nose, his and the stunted one...

"Compare, Ferdinand, compare. I'm not trying to influence you. Decide for yourself... I don't know what Madame des Pereires may have been telling you... but just take a look... Scrutinize them... Feel their weight!... Don't let anything cloud your judgment... The big one is mine! Thanks to tellurism! Look at it. His, without tellurism, infinitesimal! Compare! That's all! I add nothing! Why confuse you?... What interests me is conclusions! Conclusions!... What can be done... what must be done... *with* tellurism... And mark my words, in this field, so inhospitable in its texture, all I have to work with is a mere telluric auxiliary!... Auxiliary, I repeat!... Not the big 'Tornado' model... Of course, I must add, there are certain all-important requirements... The roots have to be bearing roots! Ah yes, bearing roots! And the soil has to be 'ferro-calcic'... if possible with a certain magnesium content... Otherwise you won't get anywhere... So now judge for yourself... You understand? No?... You don't understand?... You're like her... You understand nothing!... Yes, yes, exactly! You're blind, both of you! But what about that big radish? You see it, don't you? Right there in the palm of your hand? And the little one? You see it too, don't you? Stunted! Dwarfed! This miserable puny radish!... A radish is a perfectly simple matter, isn't it? No, it's not simple? Ah, you disarm me!... And a giant radish, Ferdinand? Imagine an enormous radish!... Say as big as your head!... Suppose I take this ludicrous little radish and blow it up to enormous size with telluric blasts... Well? Like a balloon! Ah? And suppose I make a hundred thousand of them... a hundred thousand radishes! More and more voluminous!... And each year as many as I please... Five hundred thousand... enormous radishes!... As big as pears!... As big as pumpkins!... Radishes such as nobody has ever seen!... Why, it's automatic... I eliminate the small radish... I wipe small radishes off the face of the earth!... I corner the market, I erect a monopoly! All your measly undersized vegetables are finished! Unthinkable! Through! All these baubles! These small-fry! No more tiny bunches! No more piddling shipments! If they keep, it's only by miracle... It's wasteful, my friend... anachronistic... shameful!... Enormous radishes, that's what I want to see! And here's our slogan: The future belongs to the radish... my radish... And what's going to stand in my way?... My market? The whole world!... Is my radish nutritious? Tremendously!... Radish flour is fifty percent richer than the other kind... 'Radicious bread' for the army!... Far superior to all the wheat of Australia!... The analyses bear me out!... Well, what do you think of it?... Is it beginning to dawn on you? You're not interested! Neither is she... But I am... If I devote myself to the radish... I'm only taking the radish as an example, I might have chosen the turnip... But let's take the radish! The shock value will be greater. So there you are! I'm going into it! To the hilt!... to the hilt, do you hear... You catch my meaning?"

He's still clutching me, he drags me off toward the view, on the south side... From there, it's perfectly true, you could see the whole of Paris... The city was like an enormous animal, sprawled across the horizon... It's black, it's gray... it changes... it smokes... it makes a sad sound, a soft rumbling... it's like a shell... notches, holes, spines catching at the sky... Des Pereires doesn't give a hoot, he's still talking... He harangues the scenery... He hoists himself up on the rail... He deepens his voice... It carries far away... It rolls over quarries and landslides...

"Look, Ferdinand, look!..." I open my eyes as wide as they'll go... I make a last effort... I'm really awfully tired... I wish he wouldn't start in again...

"Farther, Ferdinand! Farther... Do you see the city now? At the end! Do you see Paris? The capital?..."

"Yes... yes... yes!... that's it all right..." "They eat, don't they?"

"Yes, Monsieur Courtial!" "Every day, don't they?" "Yes, yes... yes!"

"Good! Then listen to me!"

Silence... He stirs up the air magnificently... He spreads his wings... He opens his cape a little... His gestures are really something... Is he going to fling challenges again?... He smiles in anticipation... He's sardonic... He dispels a vision... a phantom... he brushes it aside... He taps his dome... Yes, indeed... Good Lord, he'd been mistaken! He'd been deceiving himself all along! Ah! A big mistake! He questions me... He calls me to witness:

"So then they eat, Ferdinand?... they eat... yes indeed, they eat... And I, poor fool! Where have I been?... Oh futile courage! But I've been punished! Cut to the quick!... I bleed! And it serves me right! Forget? Not I! Oh ho! I'm going to take them as they are!... and where they are! In their bellies! Customers by and for the belly... I will address their bellies, Ferdinand!..."

He addresses the city too... all of it, rumbling over yonder in the mist...

"Whistle, you bitch! Mutter and roar! Grunt!... I hear you!... Gluttons!... Bottomless pits... All that's going to change, Ferdinand!... Gluttons, I tell you!..."

He calms down. Confidence returns... He smiles at me... He smiles to himself...

"Ah, that's a thing of the past! I'll lay to that! You can trust me! You will be my witness! You can tell the old lady! Ah, the poor darling! Our troubles are over now! I've seen the light! It's all settled. The spirit is victimized!... They scoff at the spirit! They persecute me! They spit at me! In the heart of Paris! Good! Very well! So be it! They can all go shit in their hats!... They can rot with leprosy! They can stew in a million kettles full of snot and cockroaches... I'll stir them myself! Let them pickle! Let them whirl in gangrene! It's too good for the stinkers! If they ask for me, I won't be there!... I'm through with the spirit! That's dead and buried!... The bowels are the thing, Ferdinand!... The gastric ferments!... Faugh!... I'm going to wallow in their bowel movements... Phoo!... It's going to be an orgy! You challenge me? Here I stand! I Courtial! Winner of the Popincourt Prize! The Nicham and all the rest!... one thousand seven hundred and twenty-two balloon flights!... What do I fire my garden with? With radishes! That's right! I'll show you! You too will see me! O zenith! O my Irène! O my jealous fury!... We haven't a moment to lose!..." He pondered a while.

"In this alluvial gravel?... This sandy soil? Never! Here? Bah! I've proved my point! Small-scale farming! I've had enough of it!... No time to waste on that!" He started chortling again at the mere thought!... It was just too funny!

"My oh my! Take it away..." He swept the poor cottage off the map.

"To the country! That's the ticket! The country, that's for me! Open spaces? Forests?... Present!... Cattle? Udders? Hay? Poultry? If you will!... But above all, radishes!... Take my word for it! And we'll have all the waves!... Every last one, do you hear?... Real waves! You'll see, Ferdinand... You'll see it all... The whole works! Orgies of waves!..."

The old girl was out on her feet. She had braced herself against the fence... She'd dozed off... I shook her so's she'd come in too...

"I'll make you a cup of coffee... I think there's some left..." That's what she said... but there was no use looking... he'd drunk it all up, the stinker!... and eaten all the leftovers... There was nothing left in the cupboard... Not even a crumb of bread! Almost a whole Camembert... While the rest of us were starving... He'd even finished off the beans in the pot... Balls! That really pissed me off...

We yelled at him to come in... "I've got to send a wire," he answered from the distance... "I've got to send a wire..." He was out on the road already... He wasn't crazy.

We slept all day... We were supposed to leave the day after... It was perfectly true that he'd sold the shack! With a part of the furniture thrown in!... The contractor who'd bought it had even coughed up a small advance to make us clear out quicker... he was scared shitless we'd wreck the joint before leaving...

That same day while we were eating lunch, he started pacing up and down in front of our gate. We wouldn't let him in... We'd kicked him out several times... He should let us finish, dammit! That bastard couldn't keep still! He was a horrible sight... He was so frantic he'd rumpled up his hat and was eating the brim... tearing out pieces... He started roaming around again, clutching his hands behind his back... Humped over and scowling. He came and went like an animal in a cage... when he had the whole road to himself! And every five minutes he'd yell in at us: "Don't go smashing up my crapper! I've seen the bowl! It was in good condition! Watch out for my sink! A new one costs two hundred francs!..."

Suddenly he couldn't stand it anymore... He came into the garden... He took three steps up the path... We all went charging down... We put him out again... He had no right! Courtial was outraged at his unspeakable impudence...

"You will take possession at six this evening and not a minute sooner... At nightfall, my dear sir, at nightfall!... That was clearly specified in our deal..." It was enough to make you lose control...

The guy went back to his rounds... He got to grumbling more and more... It was so bad we had to close the window so we could discuss our own affairs in private... How were we going to get out of there? What would be the best place to go... better than someplace else?... How much money had we? Between us, Courtial's and mine?...

Des Pereires' agricultural plans, his radio-terrestrial contraption were bound to cost us a pretty penny... He swore it wouldn't be expensive... Anyway, it was a venture... We had to take his word for it... He'd already picked a place for his experiment... On the fringe of the Seine-et-Oise department... not too far from Beauvais... A splendid bargain. Still according to him... a farm they'd let us have for a song... Anyway, he'd just about settled with the agency... The rotter was wrapping us up! He'd conned us into this thing... He'd wired... He showed us an ad out of some paper, *The Echo of the Soil*. He got a kick out of watching our faces as we listened to him... The old cutie and I weren't looking very good... "Lot for several tenants, southern exposure. Market gardening preferred but not required... Buildings in perfect repair, etc... "

"Chin up! Chin up, dammit! What did you expect me to find? A chalet in the Bois de Boulogne?... In Bagatelle?... You should have told me... Why, this was a stroke of luck... On the Property for Sale page..." He was delighted at the prospect... He knew how to read between the lines... It was now or never...

In the course of our lunch the buyer of our cottage got noisier than ever, he clutched the gate... We really felt sorry for him with his eyes popping out of his head... slithering down over his cheeks. He'd hollered so much he couldn't close his mouth... He was coming all over bubbles... He'd never hold out till six o'clock... His greed was something awful... "Have pity! Have pity!" he begged...

Courtial had to hurry through his cheese and run over to the telegraph office to confirm his "option." We let our buyer in. The poor bastard was so grateful he licked the terrace steps...

Madame des Pereires and I began to pack up... to collect all the clothes, the pots and pans, the mattresses... all the stuff that hadn't been sold... everything we were taking away with us on our venture... In addition, under cover of darkness, I was to do a little reconnoitering around the Arcades Montpensier... to see if maybe there wasn't something I could salvage... to try and rescue our brand-new mimeograph machine... our pride and joy... and really indispensable... And the little Mirmidor oil stove... and maybe three or four gross of old pamphlets... Especially the cosmogonies on alfa paper that Courtial set so much store by... Maybe those brutes hadn't had the time or chance to destroy everything... to wreck the whole place... Maybe a little something was left under the rubble... And the miniature altimeter... a gift from South America... Courtial would feel very badly if that couldn't be saved... Anyway, I'd give it a try… It was all right with me... The part I didn't like was that she wanted to come along... she didn't quite trust me. She wanted to see for herself... In case there was something to be saved, she thought I'd better not be alone... "I'll go too, Ferdinand! I'll go with you!" She hadn't seen the disaster with her own eyes... She still had some hope... Maybe she thought we were pulling a fast one...

Courtial came back from the post office. Me and Madame des Pereires went to the bedroom to empty the last cupboards... Now it was his turn to argue with that drip... who kept protesting that we were breaking the contract... We almost had to fight to recover our clothes and a few extra towels... Taking possession had made him bumptious. We threw him out again to teach him good manners. Then the lug begins shaking the bars so hard that the whole gate fell down... He got wedged under it... He was caught like a rat... I'd never seen a man in such awful convulsions! He was some buyer!... He was so fouled up he didn't even notice when the old lady and I shoved off... We took a local...

It was very late when we got to Paris... We made it fast... We didn't see a soul in the arcades of the Palais... The neighboring shops were all closed up tight... Ours was nothing but a hole... an enormous yawning chasm... a pit with big wobbly beams across it... Finally the old lady got it through her head that this was a real disaster... that nothing was left of the *Genitron*… that we hadn't been kidding... All a rotten stinking mess... We bent down over the hole and took a good look at the wreckage... We even managed to recognize some big chunks of our Alcazar... the investors' corner... under the huge avalanche of cardboard and garbage... That terrible bell was there to! The catapult! It had sunk in sideways... between the scaffolding and the cellar... Actually it plugged up the whole crevasse... When old lady Courtial saw that, she still wanted to go down under and take a look... She was sure we'd find something worth saving… I warned her of the danger... one touch could bring down the whole mountain, she'd be squashed flat... She insisted... She did a balancing act on a loose joist... I held her by the hand from up top... Watching her swaying over the void, my cock went limp... She'd hiked up her skirts and tied them around her waist. She saw a crack between the wall and the bell... She slipped in all by herself... She disappeared in the darkness... I heard her rummaging around at the bottom of the abyss... Then I sang out... I was too scared... My voice echoed like in a cave… She didn't answer... Half an hour later she appeared in the opening... She called me to come and help her... Luckily I managed to grab her by the handles of her smock... I hoisted with all my might... She came up. She was tangled up in a pile of truck... all one enormous bundle... I hoisted the whole thing up on the edge... It was very hard going... There was plenty of resistance... I saw she was pulling one more thing behind her... A big chunk of balloon, a whole slice of the *Archimedes*... a big wide flap... the red strip I'd taken patches out of... I knew that rag well... I'd hidden it myself between the gas meter and the transom... She had a wonderful memory... She was as happy as a lark...

"It'll come in handy, you know," she said briskly. "It's real rubber, no cheap imitation... you can't imagine how strong it is..."

"Sure," I said, "of course..." I knew all right. I'd taken enough hunks out of it to patch up the other one with... In any case it was heavy and bulky... Even folded as small as it would go, it was quite a package... as tall and almost as heavy as a man... She refused to abandon it... We had to take it with us...

"Well anyway, we'd better hurry," I say... She was mighty strong, she hoisted it up on her back and carried it... I took her as far as the rue Radziwill in a big hurry... When we got there, I said:

"You go ahead, madame, but don't hurry anymore. Take your time... Stop on every corner.

Watch out for the traffic. You've got plenty of time. I'll join you on the rue Lafayette. I've got to look in at the Insurrection... It's just as well they don't see you... I left a key with the waiter... the key to the attic... I'd like to take another look up there..."

This was only a pretext for going back awhile... I wanted to look around under the arcades... I thought maybe I'd run across Violette... Lately she'd been hanging out mostly over by the Galerie Coloniale... past the scales... She sights me from a distance... "Yoo hoo," she goes and comes running over... She'd seen me with the old lady... She'd been afraid to show herself... So then we had a good chance to talk and she told me all the dirt... everything that had been going on since we left... since the disaster... What a mess!... Trouble trouble the whole time... The cops had been asking thousands of questions... even of the whores... the screwiest stuff about our habits... Did we sell junk?... Did we get ourselves buggered?... Were we taking bets?... Did we sell dirty pictures? Did foreigners come around? Did we have any revolvers? Were we seeing anarchists?... The girls were scared pink... They were afraid to hang around near our wreckage... They were doing the other Galeries now... They were scared of having their cards taken away... That's what it meant to them... Everybody was complaining... All the shopkeepers in the neighborhood were sore too... They really had it in for us... you can't imagine... they were in a boiling lather... A petition had been sent to the prefect of the Seine department... to have the Palais-Royal cleaned up... They were sick of living in a hotbed of debauchery... Their business was ruined already... They didn't want to be corrupted by extra- bad eggs like us... Violette liked me fine, she'd have liked me to stay on... But she was convinced that if we came back in the neighborhood there'd be an awful stink and we'd be snagged in two seconds flat... that was definite and no use arguing... The only thing we could do was clear out, make ourselves scarce... Why ask for trouble?... That's what I thought too... We just had to blow... But what about me, what was I going to do? What kind of work? She was kind of worried about that... I couldn't tell her much... I didn't know myself... Except it would be in the country, that was sure... when she heard that, she said right away that she'd manage to come and see me... especially if she got sick again... It happened now and then... Then she always had to go away for at least two three weeks, not just on account of her sickness, but for her lungs too... She'd been spitting blood... In the country she stopped spitting... It was perfect... She gained a couple of pounds a day... So that's how we left it... that's what we agreed between us... But I was to write her first in care of General Delivery... Circumstances prevented me... We had so much trouble... I didn't keep my word... I always kept putting off my letter until the following week... I didn't go back to the Palais until years later... That was during the war... I didn't find her with the other girls... I asked them all... Even her name, Violette, didn't register... Nobody remembered... They were all new...

So that night I left her on the run... I had to make it fast, that's a sure thing... I wanted to drop by the Passage Bérésinas to tell my folks I was leaving town with des Pereires... so they wouldn't start acting up and put the bulls on my trail...

When I got there, my mother was still in the shop straightening out her junk, she'd come home from peddling her selection around Les Ternes... My father came downstairs... He'd heard us talking... I hadn't seen him in two years... Gaslight always makes people look green, but his pallor was something awful... On account of the surprise maybe, he began to stammer so bad he had to stop talking... He couldn't say a single word more... He couldn't understand either... what I was trying like mad to explain. That I was going away to the country... He wasn't against it... Not in the least!... They didn't care what happened... As long as I didn't go broke on their hands... As long as I made some kind of a living, here or somewhere else, it didn't matter how! It was all one to them, in the île de France or the Congo... It was no skin off their ass...

My father looked lost in his old clothes... Especially his pants had nothing to hold on by... He'd got so thin, his head was so shrunk his big cap floated around on his bean... it slid down over his eyes... He looked at me from underneath... He couldn't catch the meaning of what I was saying... I kept repeating that I thought there was a future for me in farming... "Ah! Ah!" he said... He wasn't even surprised...

"Say, Clémence... I had a bad headache this afternoon... That's a funny thing... It wasn't hot, was it?"

That still had him puzzled... He thought of nothing but his ailments... He couldn't take any interest in whether I stayed or went, or where to... He had trouble enough... especially since his bad setback at Connivance Fire Insurance... He couldn't stop mulling it over... He was still going through hell at Coccinelle... they were always stepping on his feet... it was as bad as ever... He was so miserable that some weeks he didn't shave at all... He was too shaken... He refused to change his shirt...

They hadn't eaten yet when I got there... She told me about the hard times, the trouble they were having in the store... She set the table... She limped kind of differently, maybe a little less... Even so she had a good deal of pain but mostly in the left leg now... She kept sniffling and making sounds with her mouth... the minute she sat down to ease her pain. He'd just come back from his errands, from making a few deliveries... He was very weak... He was sweating more and more... He sat down with us... He didn't talk, he didn't burp; all he did was eat very slowly... There were leeks... From time to time, by fits and starts, he'd come to life a little... Actually it happened only twice while I was there... He'd start muttering hoarse, low curses into his plate... "Christ almighty! Shit, piss, and corruption!..." He'd grumble some more... He'd get up... He left the table, he went off teetering... as far as the little partition that separated us from the kitchen... It was as thin as an onion peel... He'd haul off and hit it two three times... That was the best he could do... He'd retreat backward... He'd flop on his stool, looking down at the tiles... way down below... his arms dangling... My mother gently put his cap straight... She motioned me to look away... She was used to it now. Actually it couldn't have bothered him anymore... He didn't really catch on... He was too wrapped up in his troubles at the office... There was no room in his dome for anything else... For the last two months he hadn't been sleeping more than an hour a night... His head was all tied up with worry like a bundle... he wasn't interested in anything else... He didn't even care what went on in their business... He didn't want to hear about it... That suited my mother fine... I really didn't know what to do... I felt like a sore finger, I was afraid to move! Even so I tried to tell them a little about myself... my little adventures... Not the whole truth... just a few things to entertain them, a little innocent horseplay to break the embarrassment... Christ, what a face they made... just because I was joking... The effect was exactly the opposite... Hell, that griped me... I was beginning to get sore too... I had my troubles too, dammit all! I was in a jam too, just as bad as they were... I hadn't come to beg... either for dough or for food... I wasn't asking them for anything... Only I didn't want to join in their lousy bellyaching . . I didn't feel like crying into the soup or grazing on their troubles... I hadn't come to be comforted... Or to complain either... I'd simply come to say good-bye... Shit and period!... They might have been pleased...

One time just as a joke I said: "I'll send you some morning-glory seeds from the country... They'll grow fine up in the attic... they'll climb over the glass roof..."

I was saying anything that came into my head...

"Ah, it's easy to see that you're not the one that toils and struggles around here... that you don't have to work your fingers to the bone trying to meet our obligations. Ah, it's a fine thing to be care-free..."

Balls! Ah the hardship and misery, all the sickening trials were for them. Mine didn't exist by comparison. If I got into a jam it was all my fault... according to them, the stinkers... oh, the shame of it! They had their nerve with them! Balls and counterballs! Whereas they were innocent victims! Martyrs forever... There was no comparison... It was all very well to be young, but I'd better watch my step... or I'd go wrong for good... My business was to listen... and to profit by their example!... Forever and ever! Hell's bells and never a moment's doubt!... Just watching me there at table in front of my beans (there was Swiss cheese afterwards) the whole past came back to Mama... She had a hard time holding back the tears, her voice cracked... and anyway she preferred not to say anything... That was a real sacrifice... I'd have gladly asked forgiveness for all my faults, my capricious behavior, my unspeakable debauchery, my disastrous crimes!... if that could have cheered her up... if that was the only thing that made her start moaning again... if that was all that was breaking her heart... I'd have begged her forgiveness and shoved off right away... I'd have ended up by admitting that I was incredibly lucky, that I was too spoiled for words, that I spent my time having fun... Sure! I'd have said anything at all to get it over with... I was looking toward the door... But she motioned me to stay... He went up to his room... He wasn't feeling at all well... He clutched the banister... It took him at least five minutes to climb the three flights... And then, once we were alone, her miseries started up worse than ever... She gave me all the details... What she was doing now to make ends meet... Her new racket... She went out every morning for a lace house... in three months she'd made almost two hundred francs in commissions... In the afternoon she doctored herself, she stayed in the store with her leg on a chair... She wouldn't see Capron anymore... He went on telling her to keep still... Why, she had to keep moving... It was all she had to live for... She preferred to treat herself by the Raspail method... She'd bought his book... She knew all the herb teas... all the mixtures and infusions... And she had oil of mignonette to massage her leg with at night... She got boils even so, but the pain was bearable and the swelling wasn't too bad. They burst almost immediately. They didn't keep her from walking, that was the main thing... She showed me her leg... The flesh was all creased, as if it had been wound around a stick, from the knee down... and yellow... with big scabs and places that were running... "It's nothing once they begin to drain... It's a relief, it feels better... but before that it's terrible, while they're still all purple... while they're closed... Luckily I have my poultice... without it I don't know what I'd do... You can't imagine what a help it is... Without it I'd be an invalid..." And then she told me some more about Auguste... how he was making a wreck of himself... he'd lost control of his nerves... and his terrors at night... The worst was his fear of being fired... it woke him up in a panic... He'd jump out of bed... "Help! Help!" he'd scream... the last time so loud that all the people in the Passage had started up... For a moment they'd thought it was a fight... that I'd come back to strangle him... They'd all come running!... When Papa had his fits, he didn't know what was going on... They'd had a time getting him back into bed... They'd had to put cold towels on his head for several hours... Ever since he began having those fits... they were getting more and more exhausting... life had been a torment!... He never came out of his nightmare... He didn't know what he was saying... He didn't recognize people anymore... He couldn't tell the neighbors apart... He was terribly afraid of cars... Often in the morning when he hadn't slept at night, she'd take him to the door of the insurance company... at 34 rue de Trévise... But her troubles weren't over... She'd have to go in and ask the concierge if there was anything new... if he hadn't heard anything... about my father... if he hadn't been dismissed... He couldn't distinguish between real and imaginary anymore... If not for her it was perfectly certain... he'd never have gone back... But then he'd have gone crazy... loony with despair... beyond the shadow of a doubt... It took a terrible balancing act to keep him from going under completely... And she did all the acrobatics... screwing his knob back on again... She couldn't let the grass grow under her feet... And what with the meals in addition... they didn't cook themselves... And then she had to go running to the other end of Paris... with her lace... finding customers, hurry-hurry... With all that she still managed to open our store... for a few hours in the afternoon... She didn't mind if things were slow in the shop, as long as it didn't go under completely... And at night the whole thing to start over again... So his fears wouldn't get any worse, so his terror wouldn't increase... she put a little lamp on a table in the middle of the room, turned down low. And besides, so's he could go to sleep a little faster, she plugged his ears with little wads of cotton dipped in vaseline... He started up at the slightest sound... if anybody walked through the Passage... And it started in again early in the morning with the milkman... It echoed terribly on account of the glass roof... But with the wads of cotton it was a little better... He said so himself...

Naturally, it's not hard to see, my mother was more awfully worn-out than ever from having to keep holding my father up all the time day and night... She was always at her post... bolstering his morale... warding off his obsessions... Well, actually she didn't feel too sorry for herself... If I hadn't been cussed... if I'd shown some sign of repentance... of acknowledging all my vices... my stinking ingratitude... it would have been balm for her... That was plain... She'd have been comforted... She'd have said to herself: "Ah, my boy, you've still a chance or two left... All hope isn't lost... His heart isn't all stone! He's not so debased, so absolutely incurable... Maybe he'll snap out of it..." It would have been a light in her distress... a delicious consolation... But I wasn't in the mood... Even if I'd done my damnedest, I'd never have gotten it out... I couldn't have made it... Of course I felt sorry... Of course I saw how unhappy she was! That was God's truth. If I felt bad, it wasn't to go blabbing it out! And especially not to her... And besides... after all... when I was a kid in their house and didn't know from nothing... who always got it in the neck?... It wasn't just her... It was me too... Me the whole time... I got the lickings... Childhood! Shit!... Yes, sure, she was always devoted, she sacrificed herself... OK, OK... it made me sick to be thinking of all that so hard... But hell! It was her fault too...

I never thought about it all by myself... That was the worst part of it, worse than all the rest of the crummy business... It was no use my trying to say something... She turned on me with a look of distress, as though I'd beaten her... It was best I clear out... We'd start fighting again... But I let her pour her heart out... I didn't open my mouth... Sure, help yourself... it's free of charge... She took a good slice... She gave me plenty of advice... All those excellent precepts, I heard them again... Everything that was indispensable to uplift my morality... To make me stop giving in to my low instincts... to make me learn from good examples and imitate them... She saw I was holding myself in, that I didn't want to answer... So she changed her tune... She was afraid of making me mad, she tried cajolery... She went to the sideboard and brought out a bottle of syrup... It was for me, to take to the country... as long as I was going... And then a bottle of tonic to build me up... She couldn't help harping on my terrible habit of eating too fast... I'd ruin my stomach... And finally she asked me if I didn't need money... for the trip or something else... "No, no," I said... "We've got all we need..." I even showed her the capital... I had it all in hundred-franc bills... See?... In conclusion I promised to write, to let them know... how our farming panned out... She didn't understand about such things... That was an unknown world... She put her trust in my boss... I was right next to the stairs, I got up, I tied up my bundle...

"Maybe after all it's better not to wake your father up now... What do you think?... Maybe he's asleep... Don't you think so? You saw how the slightest excitement upsets him... I'm afraid it'll throw him off again to see you leave... Doesn't it seem wiser... Suppose he had another attack like three weeks ago... I'd never get him to sleep again... I'd do anything to prevent that from happening..."I was of the same opinion... It struck me as perfectly reasonable… to clear out quietly... while the wind was right... We whispered good-bye... She gave me a little advice about my underwear... I didn't listen to the end... I slipped into the Passage and then galloped out to the street.

I hightailed it... I was late, very late in fact!... It was exactly midnight by the gilded dial of the Crédit Lyonnais... Courtial and his old cutie had been waiting for me for two solid hours outside the church of Saint-Vincent-de-Paul... with their pushcart... I climbed the whole length of the rue d'Hauteville in high... I could see them in the distance under a gas lamp... It was an honest-to-God moving... He'd brought the whole works. He'd really sweated for once in his life… He must have cleaned out the homestead regardless and notwithstanding... He'd had to murder the old punk (not for real!)... The cart was so loaded full of junk it was sagging... The dynamo and the motor were under the mattresses and the clothes... The double curtains, the whole kitchen... He'd saved as much as possible... You had to hand it to him... He was wearing a new frock coat I'd never seen... I wondered where he'd found it... It was pearl-gray… I remarked on it... it was from his younger days... He'd pinned up the tails. The old lady wasn't wearing her hydrangea-and-cherry hat... It was perched on top of the cart... for safekeeping... Instead she'd put on a real pretty Andalusian shawl, all embroidered in bright colors... It looked good under the street lamp... She told me it was really the best thing for long trips... it protected the hair.

Well, there we were finally... After some discussion about an obsolete timetable we started off very slowly... Frankly, I was happy!... The rue Lafayette is steep... especially between the church and the corner drugstore... We couldn't lay down on the job... Des Pereires had harnessed himself to the cart... The old bag and I pushed from behind... And "Come on, kid!" and "I know you got it in you!..." And "keep her rolling..." And "Never say die!" The only trouble was that we'd lost too much time... We missed our train... It was my fault... We could forget about the twelve-forty... now it was the two-twelve... the first of the day... So now we were ahead of time, pretty near fifty minutes... We had plenty of time to take our dolly apart... it was the folding reversible type... and load all our stuff... again!... into the freight car at the tail of the train. After that we still had time enough to blow ourselves to some mud, two cups with milk, a *mazagran*, and a "breakfast coffee," all in a row! At the spiffy Terminus... We were nuts about coffee all three of us... really gone... And I had the treasury.

We got out in Persant-la-Rivière... It was a sweet little village between two hills and some woods... A chateau with turrets provided the finishing touch... The dam below the houses made a majestic roar... All in all, it was very pretty... We could have picked worse, even for a vacation... I said as much to the old battle-ax… But she was out of sorts... We had a hell of a time with our stuff, getting our motor out of the freight car... We had to ask for help...

The Stationmaster looked our paraphernalia over... He thought we were itinerants... come for the fair... to put on movie shows... He judged by our rig... For the fair we'd have to come back another time... It was over two weeks ago... Des Pereires didn't like leaving him with the wrong idea... He put the little jerk straight right away... told him all about our projects... He wanted to speak to the notary! Immediately!... This was no laughing matter, it was an agricultural revolution... A crowd of yokels started poking into our stuff... They clustered around the tarp... They made a lot of remarks about our apparatus. On the road the three of us by ourselves couldn't make it... The cart was too damn heavy... We'd noticed that on the rue Lafayette... And our agricultural hole was too far away... We needed a horse at least... Right away those hicks put up a remarkable show of inertia... Finally we were able to start out...

Once settled on the seat, our cutie lit up a good pipe... Our hangers-on laid bets that she was a man dressed like a woman...

To reach our property at Blême-le-Petit it was still seven miles... with plenty of hills...

They warned us at Persant... Des Pereires had already collected piles of dope, going around from one group to another... It hadn't taken him long to sign all the papers... he'd hurried the notary

… Now he was prospecting the green hills from the top of the cart... We'd given one of the peasants a lift... With the map spread out on his knees, Courtial never stopped talking once the whole time... He commented on every rise, every roll in the ground... He searched for every last brook... in the distance with his hand over his eyes... He didn't always find them... He gave us a regular lecture that went on at least two solid hours, bumpity-bump, on the potentialities, the lag in development, the agricultural splendors and weaknesses of a region whose "metallo-geodisic infrastructure" didn't entirely suit him... Oh no!... He told us right off and several times over... He'd have to make his analyses before throwing himself into this thing… It was a beautiful day.

At Blême-le-Petit things weren't exactly the way the notary had said. It took us two whole days to find out...

The farm was plenty run-down... That much had been stated in the papers... The old man who'd had it last had died only two months before and nobody in the whole family had wanted to take over... It seemed that nobody wanted the land, or the shanty, or even the village... We looked over some of the other shacks a little farther on... We knocked at all the doors... We went into the barns... There was no sign of life... Finally near the watering trough, in some kind of a shed, we found two old customers so old they couldn't leave the place... They were almost blind... and completely deaf... They kept pissing on each other... That seemed to be their only amusement... We tried to talk to them... They couldn't think of anything to say... They made signs that we should go away and leave them alone... They'd lost the habit of anybody coming to see them... We frightened them.

It didn't look very promising to me... That deserted village... All those half-open doors... Those two old folks who didn't like us... And the owls all over the place...

Des Pereires, on the contrary, thought it was perfectly splendid... He felt invigorated by the country air... First thing he wanted to dress the part... He'd lost his panama, so he had to borrow a hat from our old sweetie... An enormous soft-straw number with a chin strap... He kept on his frock coat, the beautiful gray one... plus a soft shirt and a pair of wooden shoes (that he never really got used to)... When he took a long walk through the fields, he always came home barefoot... and so's to look really like a tiller of the soil, he never forgot his spade... He carried it jauntily over his right shoulder... Spade at the ready, we went out every afternoon to inspect the fallow fields, looking for a suitable place to plant radishes.

Madame des Pereires kept busy on her own hook... She did the errands and kept house... and most of all she went to the market in Persant twice a week... She did the cooking... She repaired things and made the place halfway livable... Cooking in the hearth was an awful business, we wouldn't have eaten if not for her... just to make an omelet you had to light the fire so many times... the logs, the embers... you lost your appetite...

The two of us, Pereires and me, didn't get up very early, I've got to admit... Even that made her gripe... She always wanted us to be getting a move on... to be doing something really useful… But once we'd gone out, we didn't feel like coming back... Then she got mad again, poor old thing, wondering what we were doing so long outside... Des Pereires enjoyed our big excursions… Every day he discovered new aspects of the countryside... and in the afternoon again, thanks to his map, he could be as instructive as hell... Now and then, at the edge of the woods... or on some slope... we'd make ourselves comfortable... as soon as a little heat came on... We always had a few bottles of beer... Pereires was free to meditate... I didn't bother him much...

He talked to himself... with his spade in the ground, dug in right beside us... The time passed pleasantly... It was a real change... the peace... the quiet of the woods... But the dough was going out fast... She was getting worried... She went over the accounts every night...

In the matter of dress I wasn't long in adapting myself... Little by little the soil gets you... You forget about the nonessentials... In the end I worked out a rugged little outfit consisting of bicycle pants and a spring overcoat with the tails cut to half length that I tucked into my baggy pants... kind of warm but comfortable... I could be recognized a mile away... The whole thing decorated with lengths of string... with ingenious props. The old cutie came around to our way of thinking, she wore pants too like a man... She didn't have a skirt to her name anyway. She thought it was handier... She went to market that way too. The school kids waited for her on the way into town. They hooted at her, they bombarded her with cowflop and broken bottles and big stones... It ended in a fight... She didn't take it lying down... The cops stepped in... They asked for her papers... She was very high and mighty: "I'm an honest woman, messieurs... You can follow me home!..." They weren't in the mood.

It was a beautiful summer... You really couldn't imagine it would ever end... The heat makes for idleness... Des Pereires and I, after his pousse-café, we'd head for the fields... and all afternoon we'd wander aimlessly over hill and furrow. If we ran into a yokel, we'd give him a polite "good-day"... Our life was mighty pleasant... It reminded us of the happy days with the balloon... But we had to be careful not to talk about our stratospheric setbacks in front of Madame des Pereires... or about the *Enthusiast* or the *Archimedes!*... Or she'd burst into tears... She couldn't contain her grief... She treated us like dirt... We mostly talked about one thing and another... We couldn't stir up the past... And we had to watch our step with the future... We could only mention it with kid gloves... The future was ticklish too... Ours was vague... it didn't stand out very clearly... Courtial was still hesitating... He preferred to wait a little longer, he didn't want to dive in until he felt perfectly sure... Between meditations, in the course of our afternoon wanderings, he'd prospect around with his spade... He'd bend down to examine, weigh, scrutinize the fresh earth he'd stirred up... He'd crush it into a powder... He'd filter it between his fingers as if looking for gold... Finally he'd clap his hands and blow on them hard... It would all fly away... He'd frown... "Tt, tt... This soil isn't so hot, Ferdinand. It's not rich. Hm! hm! I'm mighty scared about radishes . '. . Hm! Maybe artichokes... And even then I wouldn't be too sure... My oh my! There's an awful lot of magnesium in it..." We'd start off again, undecided.

At table his wife asked us for the hundredth time if we'd picked our vegetable... if we'd finally made up our minds... if maybe it wasn't high time... She suggested beans... she didn't put it very tactfully, I've got to admit... Hearing a thing like that made Courtial jump sky-high...

"Beans?... Beans?... Here?... In these rifts?... Did you hear that, Ferdinand?... Beans? In a soil without manganese! Why not peas?... Or eggplant while you're at it... Oh, this is too much!" He was scandalized... "Vermicelli! That's the thing!... Or truffles!... Say, what about truffles?"

He'd thump around the house for hours grumbling like a bear... The indignation aroused by an unwarranted suggestion was good for a long session... On that score he was uncompromising... Free deliberation! Scientific selection!... She'd go off to bed all alone in her windowless cubbyhole, a kind of alcove she'd fixed up for herself, far from the murderous drafts, between the threshing machine and the kneading trough... You could hear her sobbing through the partition... He was pretty rough on her.

You couldn't say she was ever short on courage or perseverance... or self-abnegation... Not once... She did wonders reclaiming that old shack... She never stopped fixing... Nothing worked... neither the pump nor the mill that was supposed to run the water... The hearth crumbled into the soup... She had to putty all the chinks in the walls, plug up all the holes... all the cracks in the fireplace... patch up the shutters, put on new tiles... She climbed up on the eaves... But at the first storm a lot of rain came into the rooms irregardless... through the holes in the roof... We put glasses underneath... one for each stream... All those repairs and alterations were a rough job, no petty tinkering... She changed the enormous hinges on the big barn door... Carpentry... locksmithing... nothing fazed her...

She got to be real good at it... a regular mechanic... And in addition of course all the housekeeping and cooking were her department... She said so herself, no line of work bothered her except the laundry... There got to be less and less of that... Our wardrobe was rock bottom... Hardly any shirts... and no shoes at all...

Plugging the chinks in those thick walls she kind of fouled up... her plaster wasn't right... Des Pereires was critical, he thought we should do it over... but we had other worries... Anyway we certainly had her to thank if that mangy den finally began to look like something more or less. It was a ruin even so... Whatever you did to patch it up, it kept falling apart...

Our old lady was heroic all right, but that operation with her ovaries kept bothering her more and more... Maybe the overwork... She sweated like a waterfall... her moustache dripped... she was all flushed and congested... By the end of the day she was so het up, exasperated from waiting... that at the least misplaced word... bam!... the storm broke... She'd blow her top... She'd be waiting there all tensed up... She'd explode over nothing... The tirades were endless...

What we mostly had to avoid was the slightest allusion to the good old days in Montretout... She had that on her esophagus... It gnawed at her like a tumor... If a single word escaped us on the subject, she called us every name in the calendar, she said it was a plot... she called us bloodsuckers, homos, vampires... We had to put her to bed by force...

Des Pereires' problem was still making up his mind about his precious vegetable... We had to think of something else... We were beginning to have our doubts about radishes... What vegetable would we try?... Which would be right for radiotellurism?... And grow to ten times its normal bulk?... And where to plant?... That was no small question... It would require minute investigation... We'd already spaded up samples of every field for ten miles around... We weren't going into this thing with our eyes closed... We were thinking it over, that's all...

One day in the course of our explorations we came across a really sweet little village in the opposite direction from Persant, on the way south... Saligons-en-Mesloir... It was pretty far on foot... at least two good hours from Blême-le-Petit... That was one hideout where our old lady wouldn't ever think of tracking us down... The soil around Mesloir, Courtial discovered right away, was much richer than ours in "radio-metallic" content and consequently, he figured, infinitely more fertile... it would yield quicker results... We came back to study it almost every afternoon... The remarkable thing about that soil was its "cadmio-potassic" and its special calcium... You could tell by the feel and even more by the smell... Its composition seems to have been simply amazing... des Pereires sniffed it out right away... Thinking it over, he even began to wonder if it mightn't be too rich in telluric catalyst... if we mightn't get concentrations so powerful as to make our vegetables burst... to make their pulp explode... That was the danger, the one questionable point... He had a hunch... In that case we'd have to give up the idea of growing small early vegetables in this ground that was really too rich... choose something coarse, something vulgar and resistant... Pumpkins for instance... But who'd buy them?... A single pumpkin for a whole city?... A monumental pumpkin?... The market wouldn't absorb them all... It was time we put our heads together! New problems to face! It's always like that with action.

In this burg of Saligons they served mostly cider in the cafés... and it didn't taste like piss, which, you've got to admit, is very unusual way out in the sticks... It went to your head kind of, especially the sparkling kind... We got to drinking quite a lot of it on our prospecting tours... That was in the Big Ball, the only tavern in the place... We got to going there more and more, it was conveniently located right near the cattle market... We learned about local customs from listening to the hicks...

Des Pereires made a beeline for the *Paris-Sport...* He'd been deprived of it for a long time... He talked to everybody... In exchange for advice about farming... little lessons about livestock... he was able to give them dope, some really ingenious pointers about placing bets in Vincennes... even from miles away... He made some fine connections... This was a hangout for cattlemen... I let him talk... The maid suited me fine... Her ass was so muscular it was almost square. Her tits too, you can't imagine how hard they were... The more you shook them, the harder they got... They were solid rock... Nobody'd ever licked her crack... I showed her the whole business... all I knew... It was magnetic... She wanted to throw up her job, at the bar and come back to the farm with us... That wouldn't have gone down with old lady des Pereires... especially as she was beginning to smell something fishy... It seemed to her that we were spending a lot of time around this Mesloir... It didn't look kosher... She asked us some tough questions... We were stumped... She set less and less store by our prospecting for vegetables... She was getting persnickety... The summer was getting ahead fast... it would be harvest time pretty soon... Hell!

At the Big Ball a sudden change came over the peasants, they got mighty weird... Between drinks they read the *Paris Racing News*... Des Pereires was kept busy... He sent their little bets, never more than five francs each, to his old pal in an envelope... Fifty francs was the limit... he wouldn't take more... Tuesday, Friday, Saturday... always through Formerly at the Insurrection... We kept twenty-five centimes a bet... that was our little rake-off. I taught the maid, the ironclad Agathe, how to keep from having babies... I showed her that it's even more terrific from behind... After that she was really crazy about me... She wanted to do everything for me... I passed her on some to Courtial to show him how well I'd trained her... She was willing... She'd have gone into a house if I'd only said the word... It couldn't have been my clothes that sent her, we'd have scared sparrows away... Nor my dough... We never gave her a cent... It was the prestige of Paris... That's the long and the short of it.

But when we got back at night, the hullabaloo was worse and worse... Irène was no joke... We got in later and later... We were in for some wild tantrums... horrible sessions... She tore out her hair to the blood... by the handful, by the bucket... because he couldn't make up his mind about the "right" vegetable... and his maximum soil... The old girl had started working in the fields all by herself... She spaded up the ground pretty good... She still couldn't make a furrow quite straight... but for application she was tops... She'd get there... She was mighty good at clearing brush... If she wanted to build up her muscles, there was plenty of room... just about anywhere... In Blême-le-Petit there was nothing to stand in your way... the whole region was fallow... to the right, to the north, south or left... There were no neighbors on the west either... The whole place was a desert... parched... perfectly arid...

"You're wearing yourself out, angel pie," Courtial would sing out in the middle of the night when we'd find her on the job, still spading up the ground... "You're wearing yourself out... It's no use... This soil is hopeless! I keep trying to tell you... Even the peasants have gradually given up... My feeling is that they'll shift to cattle... But even there... I don't know... Cattle on these plains... With the marly subsoil... the calcico-potassic seams... I can't see them getting anywhere... It's a perilous undertaking... beset with enormous hazards... abominable difficulties... I can see it all... Irrigate such gook?... My oh my..."

"What about you, you big lug... who's going to irrigate you? Will you tell me that? Go on... I'm listening..." He refused to say another word... He dashed into the house... I still had work to do. Every night when we got in I had to classify the day's samples... on separate boards... strewn around the kitchen in little bags... They dried all over the place... samples of the whole country for fifteen miles around... There'd be plenty to choose from when the time came... but our richest selection was certainly from Saligons.

Little by little we'd gotten popular at the Big Ball... Our friendly drunks had developed a keen taste for the races... We even had to preach moderation... They didn't care how they risked their dough... They'd put fifteen francs on a single pony... Those kind of bets we turned down flat... We didn't want to get any more people too down on us... We played it safe and cautious... Agathe, the maid, was having a fine time... She was really enjoying herself... turning into a whore right there on the premises... What bothered us more was our battle-ax's spells... Her fits and ultimatums were more than we could take... She was getting on our nerves... On one little point, though, des Pereires had changed his tactics... He stopped ragging her when he found her toiling... He encouraged her to dig... he egged her on... And actually, patch by patch, week by week, she spaded up enormous areas... Sure she was a holy terror... but if ever she stopped working, it was a damn sight worse... She was fed up with our shilly-shallying, she did the deciding: potatoes... We couldn't stop her... In the long run, she decided, that was the ideal vegetable... She got to work right away. She didn't ask for our opinion... Once her tubers were planted, huge fields of them, she went telling everybody in Persant... on her way in, on the way back... that we were experimenting with "giant potatoes," obtained with electrical waves... The news traveled like gunpowder...

At the Big Ball in the afternoon they bombarded us with questions... up to that point they'd liked us fine, we'd minded our own business at the other end of the county... the local hicks had welcomed us and treated us all right... they'd even expected us every afternoon... And now they began to give us the cold stare... This farming of ours looked fishy to them... They were jealous right away... "'Spuds" they started calling us.

We couldn't goof off anymore. The old cutie had gradually turned into a real terror... Now that she'd spaded up several acres of land all by herself, she was really leading us a life... We were afraid to say a word to her... She threatened to follow us if we went out bumming, if we didn't get to work within twenty-four hours... Our vacation was over... We had to get started, to haul the motor and the dynamo out from under the tarp... We cleaned the rust off the big flywheel... We started her up a little... We drew up a nifty-looking "table of resistances"... We let it go at that... Anyway we saw we wouldn't have wire enough... We needed a hell of a lot of it, spools and spools to zigzag back and forth between the rows of potatoes all over the plantation... Fifteen hundred feet wouldn't be enough... We needed miles... Otherwise it would never work... Without wire no radiotellurism... no intensive cultivation! no cathode rays... Wire was absolutely indispensable... Actually it wasn't so bad... At first we thought that lousy wire would be the perfect excuse, the airtight alibi, that the price of the stuff would scare our old lady out of this vital purchase... that she'd stop to think and leave us alone a while... But nothing doing, on the contrary... If anything it made her madder... She threatened that if we farted around anymore... if we kept letting things ride, she'd go to Saligons on her own and set up as a midwife... no later than next week... love had flown out the window! She was bluffing... But even with the best of intentions, we hadn't enough money left for such expensive purchases... Great God, they'd ruin us... And who'd give us credit?... It was no use trying...

On the other hand, we couldn't very well let the old girl in on our exact situation... Especially we couldn't tell her we'd just blown our last little reserves, what was left from the sky pilot, playing the races by mail... Well, anyway we'd lost it... It was certainly a terrible blow... the end of our scheme... an intolerable cataclysm... We were really in a jam... Now that she was sold on potatoes, she was getting absolutely fanatical and intolerant... It was getting to be exactly the same as the balloon... or her cottage in Montretout... She couldn't be budged... Once she threw herself into something, she latched onto it like a rivet, you had to tear the whole house down... It was very painful...

"That's what you said, isn't it?... You're not going to deny it?... I heard you, didn't I?... You told me ten times... a hundred times... that you were going to run your lousy electrical contraption? I wasn't seeing things, was I?... That's what we all came here for, isn't it?... I'm not making it up?... That's why we sold the house for a song... And threw up your paper... That's why you dragged us all here like it or not by force into this swamp... this pigsty... this muck! Am I right?"

"Yes, my love."

"Good!... Well, I want to see it, understand? I want to see it... I want to see every bit of it... I've sacrificed everything! My whole life!... My health... My future!... Everything!... I haven't anything left!... I want to see them grow!... Understand?... Grow!"

She planted herself there defiantly, she handed it to him full in the face... Her hard labor had given her biceps that were no joke... they looked like hams... She chewed tobacco in the fields... She only smoked her pipe in the evening and when she went to market... Eusèbe, the postman, who hadn't delivered in our neck of the woods for years, had to start in again... He came around two or three times a day... The news had spread around the country like wildfire that certain agriculturists were doing wonders, performing real miracles raising potatoes with magnetic waves...

Our old crowd of inventors had picked up our track... They all seemed mighty happy to hear that the three of us were safe and sound... They besieged us with new projects... They bore us no grudge at all... The postman was good and sick of it... Three times a week he had to tote whole sacks of manuscripts... His pouch was so heavy his frame had caved in... He'd been using a double chain... his bike had folded up... He'd put in to the department for a new one... From the very start des Pereires had taken to meditating again... He really took advantage of his solitude and leisure... He finally felt equal to the hazards of fate... all of them... He was deep in his meditations! Absolutely determined! The great Decision!... He'd face up to his Destiny... Not overconfident... not overcautious... just forewarned!...

"Ferdinand! See here and take note!... Events are shaping up pretty much as I predicted... But they've got a little ahead of themselves... The rhythm has been a little hasty... which wasn't what I wanted... Nevertheless, you'll see... Observe... Don't lose a scrap! Not one luminous atom!... Behold, my child, how Courtial is going to crush, to tame, to chain, to subjugate rebellious Fortune!... Behold with wonderment! Open your ears! Try to be fearless, ready at a moment's notice! The second I catch her, I'll pass her on to you! And go to it! Clutch her! Strangle her! It will be your turn! Kiss her! Mangle the bitch! My strictly private needs are those of an ascetic! I shall soon be replete! Stuffed! Submerged in abundance! Yours to bleed her. Drain her to the gills!... You're at an age for follies! Take advantage! Overdo it! Gods above! Shine! Do what you please with her! For me there'll always be too much and to spare... Embrace me... Lord, how lucky we are!"

It wasn't easy to do any embracing on account of my overcoat that was solidly moored with strings inside my pants... It curtailed my movements but kept me good and warm... It was necessary... The winter was on us... In spite of the fireplace and the caulking the main building was lousy with drafts... it kept in all the winds and very little heat... It was a strainer for the cold... It was really a very old house.

This inspiration that des Pereires had after all his meditations at the Big Ball and in the woods was really terrific... His ideas were even bolder and more farsighted than usual... He fathomed the needs of the world...

"The individual is washed up!... You won't get anything out of individuals... It's to the family, Ferdinand, that we'll have to turn! Once and for all, to the family! Everything for and by the family!"

His grand appeal was addressed to the "Anguished Fathers of France." To those whose sovereign preoccupation was the future of their dear little ones... To those who were slowly being crucified by daily life in corrupt, putrid, unhealthy cities!... To those who were ready to attempt the impossible to save their poor little cherubs from the atrocious fate of slavery in a shop... from bookkeeper's tuberculosis... To the mothers who dreamed of a wholesome spacious existence for their little darlings, absolutely in the open air... far from the city's putrefaction... of a future fully secured by the fruits of wholesome labor... in the country... of great sunlit joys, peaceful and complete!... Des Pereires solemnly guaranteed all that and a good deal more... He and his wife would take complete care of those lucky little tikes, their primary education, their secondary "rationalistic" education too... and finally of their higher learning, "positivistic, zootechnie, and horticultural..."

In two shakes of a lamb's tail our "radio-telluric" farm was transformed, with the help of our subscribers, into the "Renovated Familistery for the Creation of a New Race"... That's what we called our farm in our prospectus... In a few days our appeals (all sent out by Taponier) had covered several Paris neighborhoods... the most populous, the most congested... and for the hell of it a few of the slum districts out by Achères, where it stinks... We had only one worry... that the invasion would start too soon! We dreaded overenthusiasm like the plague... We knew all about it!

With our radiotellurism plentiful fare would be no problem... All in all, there was only one thing to worry about... The market would be glutted with our "undige-nous" potatoes... We'd think about that in due time... We'd raise pigs... millions of them... We'd have plenty of poultry too... The pioneers would eat chicken... Courtial was all in favor of a mixed diet... Meat is good for growth... Obviously we'd have no trouble clothing our little charges in the linen we raised on our farm... woven in choral cadence on long winter evenings... Sounds pretty good... All very promising! A beehive of agricultural industry! But under the aegis of Intelligence! not of mere instinct! Ah yes! That distinction meant a good deal to Courtial! He wanted his hive to be rhythmical!... flowing!... intuitive! That was how he summed up the situation. Playing all the while, learning on every hand, building their lungs, the children of the "New Race" would at the same time joyfully provide a spontaneous labor force... quickly trained and stable, absolutely free of charge... Without constraint they would harness their youthful vigor to the needs of "neo-pluri-radiant" agriculture... This great reform was rooted in the depths, in the very sap of the countryside! It would flourish in the heart of nature! We'd all bask in its perfume! Courtial sniffed in advance... We were especially counting on our charges, on their zeal and enthusiasm, to pull out weeds! to uproot them! to clear more ground!... A perfect pastime for kids... The worst torture for adults... Relieved of the petty tasks of common farming by this industrious afflux, des Pereires would be free to devote himself entirely to the delicate regulation, the endless adjustments of his "polarizer complex"... He'd rule the waves... He wouldn't do anything else... He'd flood our subsoil, he'd overwhelm it with telluric torrents!...

Our pamphlet looked good... We had ten thousand of them sent to various neighborhoods... It must have responded to a good many secret desires, unspoken longings... Anyway, we almost immediately received a deluge of answers... with truculent comments... almost all of them extremely flattering... What seems to have struck most of our subscribers in particular was the extreme modesty of our terms... It's true that we'd cut our prices to rock bottom... We could hardly have done better... To carry a pupil from early childhood (minimum age, seven) to the draft board, to provide him with board and lodging for thirteen consecutive years, to develop his character, his lungs, his mind, and his arms, to inculcate the love of nature, to teach him a magnificent trade, and last but not least to give him, when he left the phalanstery, the magnificent and valid diploma of a "Radio-geometric Engineer," all we asked of the parents, everything included, was the lump, global, and definitive sum of four hundred francs... This sum, these immediate receipts were to enable us to buy our wire and set up our circuits... our underground currents. We weren't expecting the impossible... Four carloads of potatoes a month would do for a starter.

The moment an undertaking begins to shape up, it becomes *ipso facto* the butt of a thousand hostile, treacherous, subtle, and untiring intrigues... Nobody can say different... A tragic fatality penetrates its very fibers... slowly lacerates its warp, so profoundly that, when you come right down to it, the shrewdest captains, the snootiest conquerors can only hope to escape disaster, to keep from cracking up, by some cock-eyed miracle... Such is the nature and the burden, the true upshot of the most admirable ventures... It's in the cards... Human genius is out of luck... The Panama disaster... it's the same old lesson... ought to bring the most outrageous blowhards to their senses... make them do some tall thinking about the perfidy of fate... the murky harbingers of Hard Luck! Foo! The slings and arrows!... Destiny eats prayers like a toad eats flies... It jumps on them! crushes them! mangles them! swallows them! It feasts on them and shoots them out in tiny little turds, ex-votive spitballs for the bride to be.

Making due allowances, we in Blême-le-Petit got it liberally in the neck from the very beginning of our operation... First the notary in Persant... He descended on us pretty near every afternoon... in the most menacing terms... to make us pay his balance... He'd read a sensational story in the paper about our magnificent experiments... He thought we had secret funds... He thought we were loaded... He demanded immediate payment for his beat-up farm and his swampy acreage... And our creditors from the Palais-Royal were all bursting with impatience... Taponier too... He'd been so nice at first, now he was getting to be the crummiest of the lot... He read the papers too... The jerk thought we were getting subsidized... drawing gravy from the Ministry of Education...

In addition to quantities of manuscripts relating to the "research" that would surely be required, we were riddled with court orders... of all kinds... we were practically attached before we'd even seen the color of our first potato! The constabulary jumped on the pretext for a little jaunt out our way, to get an eyeful of our astonishing mugs, to give us the once-over... Our clever prospectus in behalf of the "Race" had kind of upset the legal authorities... The Inspector of Schools, another envious character, naturally, had expressed certain doubts about our right to open an educational institution... Doubting was his business... In the end they were only average mean. They merely took the opportunity, which was to be expected, to give us a not unfriendly warning that all things considered we'd better content ourselves with something of the nursery, summer camp... or sanatorium type... that if we carried the educational aspect too far we'd inevitably fall foul of the authorities... the whole lot of them...

A delicate dilemma if ever there was one!... To perish or to teach?... We thought it over... We hadn't really made up our minds... when a bunch of snoopy parents came hiking out one Sunday afternoon around four o'clock to see for themselves... They carefully examined the farm, all the outbuildings, the general look of the place... We never saw them again...

Nuts! We were beginning to lose hope... So many adverse winds... Such rotten incomprehension!... Such deep-seated malevolence!... It was really too much... And then one fine day, the sky finally cleared... Almost all at once we received eighteen enthusiastic registrations!... Ah, these were really conscientious parents, who frankly cursed the city and its pestilential air! They frankly agreed with us... They subscribed immediately to our "New Race" reform... They sent us their kids with an advance on the fee, to be incorporated immediately in the agricultural phalanx... A hundred francs here, two hundred there... the rest to follow... All we got was advances, never the full sum... They promised to send the rest later on... Plenty of goodwill in any case... their enthusiasm was genuine... but kind of obscure... Economy, foresight... and a big helping of suspicion...

Anyway the kids came... fifteen in all... nine boys and six girls... Three didn't show up. It seemed best to pay a little attention to the judge's advice... a word to the wise... We'd play it cagey for a starter... A little caution wouldn't hurt us... Later on, when the experiment had proved a success, things would take care of themselves... They'd come begging... We'd unfurl our banner: "The New Race, Flower of the Furrows."

With the dough that first batch of kids brought us, we couldn't buy much... not even all the beds we needed! not even mattresses!... We all slept in straw... in perfect equality!... The girls on one side, the boys on the other... After all we couldn't send them back to their parents... that chickenfeed didn't last a week... It was already speculated in all directions... It was gone in no time... The notary alone claimed three-quarters of it... The rest went for wire... Maybe about five spools... but the large size... mounted on a trestle, ready to unroll.

Right at the beginning our old cutie, foreseeing trouble, had planted some kind of super- potato that grew even in the wintertime... There's no hardier spud in existence... If the worst came to the worst and Courtial's waves didn't yield all we expected... we'd still have a crop... He couldn't very well prevent them from growing... that would be mighty weird, in fact unheard-of. We all got down to work... We strung wire wherever he told us... With a little extra encouragement, to be on the safe side, we'd have wound three or four copper garlands around the roots of every plant... It was a memorable job!... Especially the way we were situated on the hillside... full in the north wind... Even in the most biting gale our kids were happy. All they cared about was being out-of-doors the whole time... never a minute in the house. Most all of them came from the suburbs... They weren't obedient. Especially a skinny little character, Dudule, who wanted to feel up all the girls... We had to sleep him between us... They began to cough... Luckily our old honeybun knew a little something about medicine, she covered them with poultices from head to toe... They didn't even mind having their skin ripped off... as long as they weren't shut in... They wanted to be outside come hell and high water... We ate out of the big kettle... enormous quantities of soup...

After three weeks of toil the immense potato field was one network of wire, strung just below the surface with a thousand joints in dotted lines... It was real needle-prick work... Turn her on!... Des Pereires had only to shoot the juice through the fibers... He started his contraption... Right away he gave those spuds a series of terrible shocks... of powerful, intensely telluric discharges... with a few little bursts of "alternating" in between... He even got up in the middle of the night to give them a little extra, to stimulate them more completely, to stir them up to the maximum. It worried the old sugarbun to have him going out in the cold like that... She woke with a start... She yelled at him to put something on.

We'd been worrying along for about a month when all of a sudden our Courtial began casting about for excuses... That was a very bad sign...

"I'd have preferred," he said "to try leeks..." He kept saying that more and more often in front of the old lady... He wanted to see her reaction... "What would you say to radishes?..." His wife gave him a cross-eyed look, she pushed up her dip in front... she didn't care for his insinuations... Hell, he'd made his bed, he shouldn't try to wriggle out of it...

Our pioneers were thriving, they made the most of their freedom... We didn't hem them in, they did what they pleased... they even attended to their own discipline... Terrible thrashings they gave each other... The littlest was the worst, the same old Dudule, he was seven and a half... The oldest of the flock was practically a young lady: Mésange Rimbot, the blonde with the green eyes, she had a nice billowy ass and her tits stuck out sharp... Madame des Pereires wasn't exactly a simple soul, she didn't trust our little wench around the corner, especially when she had her period... She'd fixed her up a special bunk in a corner of the barn, so she could sleep all by herself when she fell off the roof... That didn't keep her from monkeying around with the brats... nature, nature. That ornery postman caught her one night behind the chapel at the end of the village, doing it with Tatave, Jules, and Julien... All four of them were together...

This Eusèbe, the postman, had it in for us on account of the distances we made him travel... The department hadn't given him his bike... It would take two years... He wasn't entitled to it... He couldn't stand our guts... He wanted us to supply him with shoes, we didn't have any for ourselves... Naturally, moseying along on foot, he saw everything that went on. The day he caught the kids having fun, he doubled back extra, just to tell us what he thought of us... after he'd seen it all... as if it was our fault. Peeping toms are always like that... first they get a good eyeful... they don't miss an atom... And then when the party's over, they're all indignation... We told him off... We had more serious things to worry about.

In our beat-up hamlet there hadn't been any traffic for going on twenty years... Once this potato jazz got around, it was an invasion... a parade of sightseers from morning to night. The whole department was full of false rumors... The people from Persant and Saligons took the front row, they wanted all kinds of specimens and explanations. You couldn't put them off... They wanted to know if it was dangerous... if our system mightn't blow up and "start the earth vibrating"... As the expériment went ahead, as time passed, des Pereires was getting more and more cautious... He dropped "ifs" and "maybes" that sounded really ominous... lots of them... more and more... It was worrisome... He'd hardly ever said "if" and "maybe" at the Palais- Royal... About a week later he had to stop the dynamo and the motor... It was getting a little risky, he told us at that point, to pour on more waves and current... we'd better stop a while... we could start up again later... after a breathing spell. Waves of the telluric variety were perfectly capable of engendering certain individual disorders... you never could tell... absolutely unforeseeable repercussions detrimental to the physiology... Personally des Pereires was feeling the effects of saturation... He was having dizzy spells...

Hearing these remarks, the farmers and sightseers began to get suspicious. They shoved off, plenty worried. New complaints came in... The cops dropped in again... but there wasn't much they could say about our phalanstery... The kids had nothing wrong with them... none of them had taken sick... We'd only lost our seven rabbits... A rough case of epizootic! Maybe it was the climate... or the food... Finally the cops went away... Not long after that our cunning little pioneers got fed up on our Spartan fare... They griped something awful... They were insubordinate... They had to build up their strength, didn't they?... They'd have eaten the whole county... They found a way... It was their idea... One day they came home with three bunches of carrots... and the next day a crate of turnips. A ton of beans! All for the soup. The chow was looking up... Then came a dozen eggs and three pounds of butter and some bacon... It's perfectly true, we were out of all those things... This looting wasn't for the hell for it, it wasn't from wickedness... Madame des Pereires couldn't hardly go out anymore since we'd started our intensive farming, she was busy all the time with the "circuits," patching them up so the juice would go through... She only got to Persant once a week. At table nobody batted an eyelash... We dove right in... It was a case of "compelling circumstances"... The next day they brought home an old hen... all plucked... It turned into soup fast... As banquets go, we could have used a little wine... We didn't exactly suggest it... nevertheless and regardless we had wine on the table the following days... several different vintages... Where the kids found all that we didn't ask... We let well enough alone... A wood fire is mighty pretty but not very convenient. It's a nuisance to keep up, it burns too fast, you've got to keep stirring it up... They found some briquettes... They hauled them through the fields in a wheelbarrow... We had a beautiful fire... But it was getting risky... We counted on our potatoes to straighten everything out... our honor and all that... To dodge the worst reprisals...

We went out to look at the spuds, we watched them like gems, we dug one up every hour... to see what was going on... We started the wave machine up again... It was purring almost day and night... It used up a lot of gas, we didn't see much results... The spuds the kids brought home, their hot vegetables, were always a good deal better looking...

Des Pereires had noticed that. He was more puzzled than ever... In his opinion our wire wasn't right... The conductivity wasn't as good as we'd originally thought... or needed... That was perfectly possible.

We went back to the Big Ball... Only once, just to look in... We'd better hadn't... Some reception we got! Agathe, the maid, wasn't there anymore, she'd gone off with the town drummer, a married man with children... They'd shacked up for the sheer ass of it... Moral turpitude, they put the blame on me... Everybody was down on me in the village and environs... when the whole lot of them had screwed her!... So help me! They said I'd debauched her. They wouldn't have anything to do with either of us... They refused to gamble with us... They wouldn't listen to our Chantilly "starters"... They were laying their bets with the barber across from the post office... He'd taken over our whole system, envelopes, stamps, and all...

Those people at the Big Ball knew plenty more about our smelly ways... They knew, in particular, that we were living off the land... All those chickens that had disappeared for fifteen miles around... Same with the butter and carrots... We were the gypsies... They didn't say it in so many words, because they were hypocrites... But they made some mighty pointed remarks about buckshots in the ass that certain people had coming to them... about a bunch of no-goods that would certainly end up in the pen, amen and so be it!... Well anyway, disagreeable remarks... We left without saying good-bye... It was a good two-hour hike back to Blême... Time enough to meditate on our cool welcome...

Things weren't doing so hot... Our affairs weren't cooking with gas... Des Pereires knew it... I thought he was going to talk about it... but he talked about entirely different things on the road... About the stars again and the heavenly bodies... about their distances and satellites... about the magical dances they spin while we're mostly asleep... About constellations so dense you'd take them for clouds of stars.

We'd been walking quite a while... he was getting winded... He always got too excited when he got talking about the sky and the cosmogonie trajectories... It went to his head... We had to slow down... We climbed up on a bank... He was panting... We sat down.

"You see, Ferdinand, I can't manage it anymore... I can't do two things at once... when I used to be always doing three or four... Ah, it's no joke, Ferdinand... it's no joke... I don't mean life, Ferdinand, it's Time I mean... Life is ourselves, it's nothing... Time is everything... Look at the little stars of Orion... You see Sirius? right next to the Snake?... They pass... they pass... They're heading over yonder to join the great galaxies of Antiope..." He was done in... his arms fell back on his knees... "You see, Ferdinand, on a night like this I could have located Betelgeuse again... a night for vision, a really crystalline night... Maybe with the telescope we still could... It's the telescope I'm not likely to find so soon... Ah, Christ, what a stinking muddle when I think of it... Can you imagine, Ferdinand! Can you imagine! Say, you really went for it, didn't you?"

It made him laugh to think of it... I didn't answer... I didn't feel like gilding his pill anymore... When he got his optimism back, he always did something idiotic... He went on talking about one thing and another...

"Ferdinand, you see, my boy... I wish I were some place else... some place completely different... Somewhere... I don't know..." He made some more gestures, he described parabolas... He moved his hands through the milky ways... high, high up in the atmosphere... He discovered another twinkler... a little thing to explain... He wanted to talk some more... but he couldn't... His words scraped too hard... His chest was bothering him... "The fall gives me asthma," he said... So then he was quiet... He dozed off for a while... huddled up in the grass... I woke him on account of the cold... maybe half an hour later... we started off again very slowly.

Nobody has ever seen kids thrive like ours... growing so fast, getting so strong and muscular... since we'd been eating with no holds barred... We had enormous stews, we really put it away... and all the brats were on wine... They wouldn't take any reprimands or advice... They said we shouldn't worry about them, they were doing all right...

Our headache was Mésange... supposing one of the little thugs knocked her up... Sometimes she'd get a dreamy look that boded no good... Madame des Pereires had it on her mind... She marked crosses on the calendar to show when she was due.

All day long our pioneers sniped and snaffled around in the barns and farmyards... They got up again at night when they felt like it... It depended on the moon... They told us a certain amount... Our agricultural labors were mostly in the morning... When it came to bringing home the bacon, our little angels had gotten remarkably enterprising and ingenious... They were everywhere at once, in everybody's fields... But nobody ever saw them... They played Indians for real... They were crafty... After six months of scouting and fancy trailing in every kind of terrain, they'd learned to get their bearings by dead reckoning, they could do it in their sleep... they knew the most labyrinthine pathways, the most secret hideouts... the position of every clod of earth... better than the native hares... They'd catch them by surprise... That'll give you an idea.

Without them, I don't mind telling you, we'd have starved... We were stone-broke... they stoked us to the gills, it gave them a kick to see us get fat. All they ever heard from us was compliments...

Our old cutie was champing at the bit... She'd have liked to say something... It was too late... The food problem comes first... With the kids gone we'd have croaked... The country is merciless... We never issued a word of command... The initiative was all theirs... Raymond's father, a lampman on the railroad in the Levallois sector, was the only one who came to see us the first winter... It was easier for him because he had a railroad pass... He hardly knew his Raymond... he'd got so big and strong... the kid had always been frail, now he was a champ... We didn't tell him the whole story... Raymond was a wonder, for swiping eggs he was in a class by himself... He'd snitch them out from under the hen... without making her squawk... the velvet touch... The father was the honest kind, he wanted to settle his debt... Now that his kid was so husky, so perfectly built, he talked of taking him back to Levallois. He thought he looked well enough... We wouldn't hear of it... We put up stiff resistance... We made him a present of his dough, he still owed us three hundred smackers... on the sole condition that he'd leave the kid with us until he'd learned all there was to know about agriculture... That kid was worth his weight in gold... We sure didn't want to lose him... And he was glad to stay with us... He wasn't looking for a change... So our life was getting organized... We were detested for fifteen miles around, they hated us tooth and nail, but tucked away all by ourselves in Bléme-le-Petit it was hard for them to catch us red-handed...

The old cutie got fatter than anybody else on the fruits of the kids' larceny. So she couldn't say a thing... Her field didn't feed her! or her hat! or her pants! She heaved some comical sighs after sipping her brandy... She couldn't get over it the way little by little she'd got used to this unspeakable piracy... She'd taken to drink... maybe from repressed sorrow... A nip... another… and pretty soon she couldn't do without her pousse-café... "Let fate take its course," she sighed... "seeing as you're no good for anything." She was talking to Courtial.

We stored our victuals in our attic, in our basement, and in a corner of the barn... The kids had contests to see who could bring back the most in a day... We could have held out six months… gone through several honest-to-God sieges... We were fixed... Groceries, beer, margarine! Absolutely everything!... But we were eighteen at table, sixteen of whom were growing! A crowd like that can put it away, especially when "stationed" in the country...

Two of our pioneer girls, aged eleven and twelve, had brought home pretty near fourteen cans of gasoline for the boss's motor. He was beaming. The next day was his birthday, the other kids came back from Condoir-Ville, five miles away, with a big basket of babas, éclairs, and wafers... all kinds of cream buns and an assortment of aperitifs! In addition, to make it even funnier, they brought us stamped receipts... That was really sharp... They'd paid cash for the whole business... our clever little angels! They were swiping money now in the open fields... where it doesn't lie around. It was kind of miraculous! This time again we didn't say boo. We'd lost our authority. But those little tricks leave traces... Two days later the cops came around asking for big Gustave and little Leone... They hauled them off to Beau-vais... We couldn't protest... They'd got themselves pinched picking up a billfold... It was a common ordinary trap… on a windowsill... An ambush if ever there was one... A report had been made on the spot... There'd been four witnesses... The thing couldn't be denied... and it couldn't be fixed... The best was to make a show of surprise, amazement... horror! We made a show.

They arrested our Lucien, the curlyhead, four days later... on pure hearsay... Something about a chicken coop... the farmer had turned him in... The following week they came for Glass-eye Philippe... But there were no proofs against him, they had to return him to us... Even so it was a hecatomb... It was getting pretty plain that those hicks, always so slow to make up their minds, had finally sworn to wreck our whole business... They hated our guts!... Actually they were threatening to burn the whole house down with us in it... Eusèbe had tipped us off... To be roasted like rats, wouldn't that be nice?... They wanted to stop our racket...

The old cutie was the first to feel the fury of the insurgent populace... They'd run her out of the market in Persant... She'd tried to do a little business, to pass off a whole basket of lovely "secondhand" eggs... It didn't wash... They'd recognized where they came from... They got mean, they were delirious with hate and rage... She beat it out of there fast! In another minute they'd have beaten the shit out of her... She was in a terrible state when she got home... Right away she cooked herself up a big coffeepot full of her mixture, a concoction of verbena and mint plus pretty near a third of banyuls... She was developing a taste for strong stuff... especially distilled wines... sometimes she even drank liniment... That set her up quickly... It was a mixture recommended by a number of midwives at the time... they said it was the best thing for night nurses...

We were all gathered around her, talking about this assault, examining the consequences... The bottles were out on the table... In comes the sergeant... Right away he starts cussing us out... He tells us not to move.

"We'll come and get you at the end of next week. This circus has been going on long enough... We're fed up and then some. You've been given plenty of warning... Saturday we're taking you up to the county seat... we've got a clear case against the whole lot of you... If I catch a single one of your little gallows birds on the loose... If they set foot outside this village... they'll be picked up immediately! Immediately! Understand? Have I made myself clear?"

It seems the public prosecutor had enough evidence against us to put us in the pen for twenty years... Courtial, Madame, and myself... There were plenty of charges: Kidnapping... moral turpitude... obscene practices... illegal gambling... fraudulent tax returns... vice... burglary... abuse of confidence... nocturnal marauding... concealment of minors... Anyway a whole waterfall, a complete assortment... That sergeant was giving us a pain in the neck... Only Madame des Pereires, though shaken at first... what would you expect?... perked up pretty soon... She didn't bat an eyelash... She bounced up like one man... She stood right up to him... She leapt to her feet with an impetus so violent, so bristling with indignation, so fired with rage, that the sergeant wavered under the charge... He couldn't believe his ears... He blinked... She had him hypnotized, there's no other word for it. She answered in terms that nobody could have refuted. That dumb farmer couldn't have imagined... She came back at him, she accused him of personally fomenting the whole yokels' rebellion... the whole abominable *jacquerie*. He was the guilty party. Flummoxed! lashed! flayed, he was trembling in his boots... Contemptuous and sardonic, she called him a "poor bastard"... He was on the defensive... He hadn't one word to say for himself... She put her hat on... High above him she swayed from side to side, glaring like a cobra... She forced him backward... she threw him out. He skedaddled like a canary. He climbed on to his bicycle and rode away, zigzagging all over the road... He reeled through the night with his little red lamp... We watched him disappearing... He couldn't keep straight.

One of our campfire girls, Camille, for all she was a smart little number, got nabbed three days later in the garden of the presbytery in Landrezon, a stinkhole on the other side of the forest. She was just slipping out of the kitchen with a parmesan cheese, a couple of crawfish, and some sloe gin... two bottles... She'd taken everything she could lay hands on... Plus the altar cruets... That was the most serious, they were solid silver... She'd been caught in the act... They'd all chased her... They'd cornered her on the bridge... Poor little kitten, she'd never be back. They'd locked her up in Versailles!... That snake-in-the-grass postman hurried over with the news... He'd gone out of his way... Our situation was getting cock-eyed... a mean balancing act... You didn't need to be very smart to realize at that point that all the kids in our phalanstery were sunk... one by one they'd be caught foraging... even if they were ten times as careful... even if they went out only at night...

We tightened our belts, we were more and more cautious... We didn't have much margarine or oil or sardines... we were nuts about sardines... It was the shortage of tuna fish and sardines that really got us down... We couldn't make any more French fries... We holed up behind the blinds... We watched the approaches... We were afraid some hayseed would try to pick us off in the dusk... They came around now and then... They passed outside our windows on bikes with their guns... We had a blunderbuss too, an old double-barreled shotgun... and a police pistol... The former tenant had left them... They were still hanging in the kitchen, on a nail over the fireplace.

One night when there was nothing to do and we couldn't even go out, des Pereires took down the old blunderbuss... He started cleaning it... running a rag dipped in kerosene through the two barrels with a string... working the trigger... I could feel the state of siege coming.

We had only seven left... four boys, three girls... We wrote their parents, asking if they wouldn't like to take them back... our agricultural experiment had been disappointing in certain respects...

unforeseen circumstances obliged us to dismiss some of our pupils... temporarily... Those crummy parents didn't even answer... Absolutely no conscience... Only too glad to leave their headaches to us... So then we asked the kids if they wouldn't like us to deposit them in some charitable institution... at the county seat maybe... Hearing those few words, they came back at us so aggressive, so absolutely furious, for a minute I expected a massacre... They wanted no part of it... We threw in the sponge right away... We'd given those brats too much freedom and initiative... it was too late to get them back in line... Hell!... They didn't mind running around in rags and eating once in a blue moon... but they wouldn't stand for interference… they got nasty mean... They didn't even try to understand... They didn't give a shit about the circumstances... We tried to explain that life is like that... that we all have our obligations... that law and order screw you in the long run... that if you go snaffling right and left you always get caught sooner or later... that one fine day you come to a very bad end... They told us to jerk off with our rotten bullshit... For their money, we were pisspots... miserable drips... They wouldn't do anything we said... they wouldn't listen... Some New Race they turned out to be. Dudule, the youngest of the gang, went out looking for eggs... Raymond was afraid, he was getting too big... Little Dudule was our "Raft of the Medusa"... We hoped, we prayed... all the time he was out... that he'd come home safe, sound, and bringing something... He brought back a pigeon, we ate it practically raw with carrots... He knew the country better than any hunting dog... You couldn't see him six feet away... He'd lie in wait for hours to nab his bird... Without cord, ball, or string! With two little fingers... Crick! Crick!... He showed me how he did it... It was subtle, it was neat... "Betcha a dime I catch her... and you won't hear nothing!…" It was true. You didn't hear a thing.

Two of our windows were smashed the same week... Yokels passing lickety-split on their bikes... They stoned us more and more... They'd hide, they'd come back again... Christ, were they mean!... And we were on our good behavior... We didn't fight back... And we should have... they gave us plenty of provocation... A good volley of buckshot in the ass... Our pioneers were keeping out of sight... They only went out before dawn, maybe an hour or two in the gloaming... in the first streaks of daylight, so's to have some idea what they were doing... The farmers had stationed mutts in every yard in the county... wild, vicious, ferocious monsters!…

In addition we were sadly lacking in shoes for those awful hikes over rocky paths... It was torture... With all their practice the kids often cut themselves... At daybreak in the rain, especially now it was coming on November, their rags looked like comical patches of bandages… They were coughing more and more... Sure, they were tough little bandits... but they weren't immune to bronchitis... They sank in up to their ass in the deep furrows... When the dry cold set in, they were through... They couldn't make it without shoes... Their feet would have fallen off... In the winter our plateau came in for plenty of gales... it was swept by the north wind... We warmed up all right at night, but it was stifling in the room, the smoke came back at us from the fireplace... We had nothing but damp wood, there hadn't been any coal for weeks... We couldn't stand it... we put the whole business out... We were afraid it would start up again... we threw water on the coals... There was nothing for the kids to do but go to bed...

Pretty often around midnight Courtial would get up... He couldn't sleep... He'd take his muffled lamp and head for the barn, he'd fiddle around with his contraption... he'd start it up for a few minutes... His wife would jump up in her straw and go out too, to see for herself... I could hear them cussing each other at the far end of the yard...

She'd come running back... She woke me up... She wanted to show me the spuds... They weren't pretty... Those spuds growing in the waves... They were pimply, repulsive... Hell! She called me to witness... They weren't getting very fat... that was plain as day... I didn't dare to say so, to agree with her too much... but I couldn't disagree either... They were gnawed, shriveled, loathsome, and putrid... and in addition they were full of maggots... Courtial's potatoes... We couldn't even eat them ourselves... not even in our own soup... And we weren't hard to please... Madame des Pereires was dead sure the experiment had been a failure...

"And that, Ferdinand, is what he thinks he's going to send to market! What do you think, eh?… Who's he expect to sell them to?... It's too much. It's a disaster!... What I'd like to know is… where's the sap that's going to buy such garbage?... Just tell me where that nitwit is keeping himself so I can send him a basket of flowers... My oh my, there's a man I want to see... That dodo of mine is nuts... Say, come to think of it, who does he take me for?"

It's true they were disgusting... Yet those spuds were meticulously cared for... choice seeds... coddled day and night... They were completely moldy... crawling with vermin, with grubs and centipedes... and the smell was really nasty, infinitely sickening in spite of the bitter cold... That wasn't normal either... an unusual phenomenon... It was the smell that stymied me... A stinking potato is something very rarely seen... This was a very strange variety of hard luck...

"Sh-sh," I went... "You'll wake up the kids..."

She went back to the experimental field... She took her lantern and her spade... The temperature was around fifteen... She picked out the wormiest, she dug them up one by one... as many as she could, until dawn...

It was really impossible to keep that invasion of vermin a secret very long... The whole field was alive, even on the surface... The rot was spreading... we weeded, uprooted, hoed more and more, it didn't do a bit of good... In the end the news got around... The hicks came snooping... They dug up our potatoes to see for themselves... They sent samples of our produce to the prefect... with a police report on our strange goings-on... They even sent whole basketfuls, completely chock-full of grubs, to Paris, to the Museum Director... It was getting to be big news... Horrible rumors started up... we were the criminal originators of a brand-new agricultural pestilence... an unprecedented garden blight!...

By the effect of intensive waves, of malignant "inductions," by the diabolical instrumentality of a thousand wire networks, we had corrupted the earth... stirred up the jinni of the grubs... in the innocent bosom of nature... There, in Blême-le-Petit, we had given birth to a special race of absolutely vicious, unbelievably corrosive maggots, which attacked every kind of seed, every conceivable plant and root... trees! harvests! the peasants' houses! the very structure of the land! even dairy products! sparing absolutely nothing... Corrupting, sucking, dissolving... encrusting the plowshares!... absorbing, digesting stone, flint as well as beans! demolishing everything in their path! on the surface, under the ground! Corpses and potatoes alike! Everything without exception! And thriving, mind you, in midwinter... Drawing strength from the bitter cold... propagating in swarms, in vast myriads!... more and more insatiable... crossing mountains! plains! valleys... with the speed of electricity!... thanks to the waves generated by our machines!... Soon the whole district around Blême would be one enormous field of rot... a noisome bog!... an immense sewer of maggots!... a seism of swarming grubs!... Then it would be the turn of Persant!... and then of Saligons!... Such was the outlook... It was still too soon to predict how and when it would all end!... whether it would ever be possible to circumscribe the disaster!... Only the analyses would show... It might perfectly well spread to all the roots in France... consume the whole countryside... until our national soil in its entirety was nothing but stones... Our maggots might well make the whole of Europe unfit for cultivation... one big desert of rot!... Well, if that happened, believe you me, they'd talk about the Great Plague of Blême-le-Petit down through the ages... the way we nowadays talk about the ones in the Bible..."

It wasn't funny anymore... Courtial said so to the postman when he came... It was perfectly natural that this bikeless Eusèbe should spew a little poison... "It's damn-well fucking possible," was his answer. He added nothing. Anyway that stinker was getting more and more stinking. We didn't have a drop of anything left... we had nothing to offer him... He was really pissed off... Ten miles without a drink!... He was probably putting the evil eye on us... He came out from Persant three times a day! Just for our mail!... People were writing us from all over, it wasn't our fault...

Our mail had multiplied by ten... People who wanted to know all about it... who wanted to come out for an interview... And rafts of anonymous characters who told us off good for the price of a stamp... Cartloads of insults...

"OK, OK, the spirit's fermenting... Look at all those lovely letters! A hundred thousand times more verminous than all the soil in the planet... And God knows it's crawling... It's lousy with them. You want to know what putrefaction is? You want me to tell you? It's all the shit we have to put up with..."

We thought maybe if we cooked them over a very slow fire... putting cheese on them... frying them in fat... if we cajoled them... in some clever way, we'd gradually be able to make them edible after all... We tried all the stratagems of cookery... Absolutely nothing worked... The whole mess turned to jelly at the bottom of the pot... At the end of an hour... maybe an hour and a half... all we had was one enormous grub cake... And still that terrifying smell... Courtial spent a long time sniffing at the result of our cooking...

"It's ferrous hydrate of alumina! Make a note of that name, Ferdinand. Remember it well... You see that meconium-like substance?... Our land is saturated with it... literally!... I don't even need an analysis... Precipitated by sulphides... That's our main trouble... undeniably... Look at that yellowing crust... I'd always suspected as much!... Those potatoes... that's an idea!... they'd make a splendid fertilizer... Especially with the potash in them... You see the potash? That's our salvation! Potash! Potash! It's remarkably adhesive... They're all supercharged with it... See how they glisten... you observe the scales? That coating on every radicle?... All those infinitesimal crystals?... shimmering green? and violet?... Do you see them clearly?... Those, Ferdinand, my dear boy, are the transfers... Yes!... The transfers of hydrolysis!... Yes, yes indeed... neither more nor less... conveyed by our currents... Yes, my boy!... Absolutely!... The telluric signature!... That's it all right... Take a good look now... Open your eyes to the maximum! No clearer demonstration is possible! No need of further proof! What proof? There it is... the best! Exactly as I foresaw!... This is a current that nothing can stop, disseminate, or refract! But it shows... I've got to admit that... a slight excess of alumina... And there's another little drawback... but it's temporary... very temporary!... The question of temperature! The optimum for alumina is 12.05 degrees centigrade... Aha! Remember that, O-five... For our purposes! You follow me?"

Another two weeks passed... We rationed our bit of fat so strictly that we only made soup once a day... There was no question of going out... It rained enormously... The country was having a rough time too... flattened out by winter... The trees had the shivers… like ghosts rowing in the wind... As soon as we'd emptied our plates, we went back to our straw ticks to keep warm... We lay sprawled for whole days... all bunched up together... without opening our mouths... without saying a word... Even a wood fire doesn't help when you're that cold... We had terrible coughing spells... And we were getting thin... our legs were like matchsticks... and so weak we couldn't move... or chew... or anything... Starvation is no joke... The postman stopped coming... He must have had orders... We wouldn't have been so depressed if we'd had some butter... or even a little margarine... It's indispensable in the winter... About then Courtial began to have terrible nausea... when the cold got so intense and we were eating less and less... He had some kind of enteritis, really very bad... He had awful bellyaches... He writhed in the straw... It wasn't from food... He talked it over with the old girl and they took up the question of enemas... Should he take one?... or mightn't it be better if he didn't?... "But you haven't got anything in your bowels," she said... "How can you have rumblings? Colic doesn't start up all by itself."

"I tell you I can feel it going through! Jesus! It was twisting my bowels all night... It's a dry colic... It ties my guts up in knots... Oh! Oh!..."

"It's the cold, you poor dope!" "It's not the cold..."

"Then it's hunger..."

"No, I'm not hungry... I feel like throwing up..." "Oh, you don't know what you want..."

He didn't answer... He burrowed into his straw... He didn't want to be talked to...

In the agricultural line there was really nothing more he could do... There was no more gas in the shed, not even a single can to start the thing up with...

Two more days passed... in waiting and prostration... Our old ladylove, huddled in a corner, muffled in curtains, couldn't stand it anymore, her teeth were chattering fit to crack... She climbed up to the loft and got some more sacks... She cut herself out a kind of smock like the kids wore and a good stiff kilt. She put them on over her pants and padded herself out with cotton waste... It made her look like a Zulu... She thought it was funny-looking herself... The cold makes you laugh something awful... She was still cold, so she started cavorting around... clattering her wooden shoes, hey nonny nonny, around the big heavy table. The kids split a gut watching her... They joined her in a kind of snake dance... They ran after her... They hung on her shirttails... She sang a little song:

See the miller's daughter Dancing with the boys—

The poor thing's lost her garter, Her garter, her garter...

These kittenish spells didn't come over Ma Courtial very often... It took a special occasion... She had nothing left to chew... Courtial had taken all the tobacco... She started griping a little about her pipe... The kids tore her apart at the seams... They pushed her down in the straw...

"Godammit to blazes!" she hollered at them: "Shove off, the whole lot of you! You swivel- eyed, mangy snot-noses! Leeches... floozies!..." That made them laugh still harder...

"Courtial, listen..." He wouldn't listen... He burrowed his head in his hole... He sighed... He groaned... it was his belly and the roughhouse... The kids jumped on him, the four boys and the three girls... He still wouldn't answer.

A little later we began wondering what had become of Dudule... He'd been out a good two hours... supposedly relieving himself... We were all good and worried... It was nightfall by the time he got back... He was loaded to the gunwales... He'd covered seven miles... to Persant station and back in high... He'd raised a real windfall on the freight platform... What a deal... A shipment of groceries... He'd brought us butter, a huge chunk... two complete strings of sausages... three baskets of eggs... bologna, jam, and *foie gras...* He'd even taken their wheelbarrow... He'd snaffled the whole business outside the baggage room while the men were over in the switch house trying to get warm... It hadn't taken Dudule two minutes to walk off with his whole cargo... The only thing missing was bread... but that didn't keep us from throwing a banquet... a real spread!... We built our fire way up high... We threw on pretty near a whole tree...

When he heard what was going on, des Pereires woke up completely... He got up to eat... He started guzzling so fast it took his breath away. He was holding his belly in both hands... "Oh my oh my oh my!" he sighed from time to time... The old cutie didn't need to be asked twice either... In a few minutes she was so stuffed she had to lie down... She rolled over on the ground... from her belly to her back... very slowly... "Oh, gracious goodness, goodness gracious, Courtial! It won't go down! Mm, was I hungry!..." The kids kept going off to vomit in the corners... Then they came back and funneled in some more... Dudule's dog was so bloated up he was howling blue murder... "Ah! my children!" des Pereires kept saying, "Ah, the dear little angels! Ah, my dear darlings! Oh my oh my! It was high time! Ah, there's nothing like it..." He was in seventh heaven... "Ah, it was high time! Oh my oh my!... There's nothing like it!..." That was all he could say. He couldn't get over the miracle...

It must have been about five o'clock... there was no sign of daylight... when I heard Courtial stirring in the hay... He was getting up... I figured the time by the fireplace... the fire was almost out... I says to myself: "There he goes, he's hungry... He can't take the cold... He's going to make himself some coffee... We'll all have some... *Bueno!...*" He actually did make for the kitchen... That was perfectly natural... I hear him fiddling with the coffeepots... I felt like joining him and tossing down a cup... But between my nest and the door the kids were all sleeping... bunched up together, with their heads every which way... I was afraid of stepping on them... So I stayed in my hole... After all I wasn't too cold... I was sheltered by the wall... I was catching less breeze than the old-timer. I was only frozen stiff. I waited for him to come back with the coffeepot, I'd stop him on the way... But he was taking his time... He was padding around in the distance... For a long time I heard him clattering pots and pans... And then I heard him opening the door onto the road... The thought passed through my mind: "He's gone out to take a leak..." I didn't get it... I kept waiting for him to come back... I was worried for a second... I almost got up... And then I fell back asleep... I was in a torpor...

And then I had a nightmare... Deep in the bottom of my sleep I was fighting with the old bag... She was having things her own way... I broke loose... She grabbed me again... What a battle!... What a ruckus!... I couldn't disentangle myself... The noise was awful... She had me in a drowning-man's grip... She was cracking my head with her questions... I tried to shake her off, to cover up with straw... but the bitch was holding me, she latched onto my head... And she yelled! And she bellowed!... She twisted my ears in her fists... She wouldn't let go... Where was her Courtial? she yelled in all fifteen keys... She'd just come back from the kitchen... she'd wanted some coffee... There wasn't a drop left... So she'd started raising hell... Everything was empty... He'd swilled it all up, the swine!... every last cup, the three coffeepots, all by himself... before going out... Hadn't he said anything to me? She kept at me...

"No, no! Not a word!"

"Which way did he go?" Had I seen him in the yard?

"No! No!" I hadn't seen a thing... Mésange jumped up with a bang and started blubbering

... She'd had a crazy dream... She'd seen the boss, Courtial, riding on an elephant... This was no time to fall for such hooey... We tried to remember what he'd said that evening... He'd eaten enough for a regiment... we remembered that... Maybe he'd been sick... maybe he'd passed out... It was mighty cold out there... We started listing the possibilities... A stroke?... We didn't waste any time, we went looking for him with the kids... We searched all through the straw... every corner of the house... the outbuildings, the two barns... and the experiment shed... He wasn't anywhere... We went out across the fields... the immediate vicinity... and then a little farther... Some went up toward the hillside, searching every gully and clump of trees... The rest combed the plateau like they were picking berries... We sent out Dudule's dog... No hair or hide of Courtial... We reassembled... We searched the little woods, bush by bush... He often went roaming around through there... Just then one of the kids noticed something written on the big panel of the front door... "Good luck! Good luck!"... in chalk... in big capital letters... That was his handwriting all right...

At first the old lady couldn't make head or tail of it... She kept mumbling: "Good luck! Good luck!" She couldn't stop...

"What does it mean?... Why, good Lord! Why, he's blown!" Suddenly it hit her between the eyes. "Say, who does he take me for!... Heavens above!... Good luck!... What's that again? Good luck? He wishes me... good luck?... He says that to me?... Say... that's stinking! Oh!"

She was outraged... absolutely furious...

"Why, it's monstrous!... His highness blows... He steps out... He takes a little trip... His highness trots off to town for a binge! The skunk! The scoundrel! The no-good!... Good luck and that's that!... And I'm supposed to shut up and like it!... So the eight ball's all for me, is that it?... So I'm knee-deep in shit?... Well, climb on out, you old bag!... Just shake your ass! And good luck! And I'm expected to take it lying down!... What do you say, Ferdinand? What do you think?... Of all the rotten stinking gall!..."

The kids were doubled up listening to her raving... I didn't want to stir up the explosion... I let her cool off some... But I says to myself inside... "The poor bastard was sick of us... He was fed up on farming too... He's cleared out fast and far... We won't be seeing him again so soon..." That was my hunch... I remembered some of the things he said... They pinched me hard... Sure he talked a lot of hooey... But maybe all the same he'd finally gone through with his Great Decision... the skunk... leaving us to sink... up to our necks in shit... That was his way... He was plenty underhanded, vindictive, deceitful... worse than thirty-six bears... It was no surprise to me... I'd always known it... "The details are unimportant... They clutter up our lives... Decision is what counts... The Great Decision, Ferdinand! The Great Decision! You hear me?..."I heard him... It was all a lot of gas... But suppose he'd really cleared out once and for all!... Wouldn't that be stinking! Wouldn't that below-down!... How were the rest of us going to get out of this mess?... The old lady was dead-right... What could we do with this telluric junk?... Not a thing!... If they all came around accusing us of stinking up the whole earth... what would we have to say for ourselves?... We'd be out on our ass!... He with his glib tongue... maybe he could bamboozle the cannibals... maybe he could spellbind them... But us?... We didn't have a chance.

We were knocked for a loop... We tried to figure it out... Gradually the old lady calmed down... The kids searched the joint again... They went up in the loft... They turned over all the hay... Will he come back? Won't he come back? That was the chorus.

In Blême he didn't have his cellar to hide in like at the Palais-Royal... Maybe he hadn't gone far... Maybe it was just some fool idea... A little spell of lunacy... Where would we and the kids go if he didn't come back at all?... What with thinking it over, the old girl began to feel more optimistic... She told herself that it couldn't be... he had some heart after all... it was just some idiotic trick... he'd be back soon... We began to take hope... for no good reason... except there was nothing else to do...

The morning was getting along, it must have been about eleven... The lousy postman shows... I saw him first... I was looking out the window kind of... He comes up... He doesn't come in... He just stands outside the door... He motions me to come out... he's got something to tell me... I should hurry... I beat it out... He's waiting under the arch, he whispers to me, he's all excited...

"Quick, quick... Go see your old man... He's down there on the road, after you cross the Druve... on the way up to Saligons... You know the little wooden footbridge?... That's where he is, he's killed himself... The farmers at Les Plaquets heard him... Jeanne Arton and the kid... It was just after six o'clock... With his gun... the big one... They said to tell you... So you can take him away if you want to... I haven't seen a thing, understand?... They haven't either... They heard the shot, that's all... Say, here are two letters... They're both for him..." He didn't even say good-bye... He beat it along the wall... He hadn't taken his bicycle, he cut across the fields... I saw him coming out of the woods by the road up top, the one that goes to Brion.

I whispered the whole story in her ear... so the kids wouldn't hear... She made one bound to the door... She ran out full tilt... She raced over the gravel... I didn't even have time to finish... I had to quiet the kids down... They suspected a disaster...

"Don't get excited... Don't show your mugs outside... I'm going to catch the old bag... You keep on looking for Courtial... I'll bet he's still here... hidden someplace... He hasn't gone up in smoke... Turn over all the straw... bale by bale... He's sleeping underneath... We're going to see the cops in Mesloirs... they've sent for us... That's what the postman came about... We won't be long... Don't shit in your pants!... Stay right here and keep quiet... We'll be back by two... Don't let them hear you from outside... Don't go out... Search the loft... Take a look in the stable... We didn't look in the bins..."

The kids were scared stiff of the cops... That way I knew they wouldn't trail me... They smelled a herring all right... but where?... they had no idea...

"Keep the doors closed whatever you do," I told them. I tried to locate the old lady out of the window... She was miles away... I shook a leg... I had a hell of a time catching her... She was cutting across field and forest in high... Well anyway, I followed her... Hell, it took' all I had just to keep her in sight... All the same I put my thoughts together... I'm running blue blazes... And in the fever of the chase a rotten suspicion comes up in me... "Hell," I says to myself, "what a business!... You're a sucker again, kid... it's a frame-up... a swindle... that stuff about the footbridge!... Nuts!... It's a big hoax... a stinking lie... a sinister trap, that's all!" I strongly suspected it... A crummy trick of the postman's!... It was just like him, the stinker... And all those cannibals!... I wouldn't put it past them. That's what I was thinking in the middle of running... And where was our old man at that exact moment?... while we were breaking our necks running after his corpse?... Where could he be? Maybe he was only at the Big Ball... playing cards and sopping up anisette... We were the suckers again... I wouldn't put it past him... It didn't take a suspicious nature to know him for a mean sly bastard!... We were the fall guys... That was a cinch...

After a long level stretch through soft fields, there was a steep climb up the hillside... Up top you discovered the whole countryside so to speak... The old lady and I were puffing like oxen... We sat down for a second on the bank to see better... The poor old thing's eyesight wasn't very good... But mine was really piercing... You couldn't hide a thing from me ten miles away as the crow flies... From up top there... all the way down the slope... the Druve flowing at the bottom.... the little bridge and then the bend of the road... That was the place, I could see it plain as day... right in the middle of the road, kind of a big bundle... I was dead sure... Maybe two miles away it stood out against the gravel... And right that minute, the second I saw it, I knew who it was... By the frock coat... the gray one... and the rusty yellow pants... We beat it lickety-split... We ran down the hill... "Keep on going!" I said... "Go straight ahead... I'm going to turn off... I'll take the path..." It was a big shortcut... I was there in no time... Right on the spot... Two steps away... He was all shrunk... all shriveled up in his pants... It was him all right... But the head was a mess... He'd blown it all to hell... He'd hardly any skull left... Point-blank... He was still holding his gun... He was hugging it in his arms... The double barrel went in through his mouth and passed straight through his head... It was like hash on a skewer... shreds, chunks, and sauce... Big blood clots, patches of hair... He had no eyes at all... They'd blown out... His nose was wrong-side out... nothing but a hole in his face... all sticky around the edges... and plugged up in the middle with a lump of coagulated blood... a big mash... and trickles oozing all across the road... It was flowing mostly from the chin, which was like a sponge... Even in the ditch there was blood... puddles in the ice... The old lady took a good look... She just stood there... She didn't say boo... So then I decided to do something... "We'll move him up on the bank," I said... The two of us went down on our knees... First we tug at the bundle... We try to dislodge it... We tug a little harder... I pull on the head... It wouldn't come loose... We weren't getting anywhere... It was stuck too solid... Especially the ears were welded fast... The whole thing made a solid block with the ice and gravel... We could have unfastened the trunk and the legs by pulling hard enough... But not the head... the hash... It was one solid brick with the stones on the road... It couldn't be done... The body bent crooked like a Z... the head impaled on the gun barrel... First you'd have to straighten him and get the gun out... His back was all bent, his ass was wedged between his heels... He'd spasmed as he fell... I looked around... I see a farm down below... Maybe that was the one the postman had mentioned... Les Plaquets... I says to myself: "That's it... that's the place all right..."

"Hey, you stay right here," I tell the old witch. "I'm going to get help... I'll be back in a minute... They'll give us a hand... Don't move... That must be Jeanne's farm... They're the ones that heard it."

So I come up to the house... First I knock on the door, then on the shutters... Nobody seems to notice... I try again... I double back to the stables... I go right into the yard... I knock... I knock some more... I yell... Still no sign of life... But I could feel there was somebody around... The chimney was smoking... I shake the door with all my might... I tap, I clatter on the windowpanes... I'll tear the shutters down if they don't come... And then a face peeps out after all... It's the Arton kid... by a first marriage... He's not taking any chances... He just barely shows himself... I tell him what I want... Could they give me a hand carrying him?... Just those few words send her sky-high... She won't allow it... she comes to life... She wouldn't even think of touching it... She won't even let her lousy brat answer me... She won't even let him go out... He's going to stay right there with his mother... If I can't get him off the road, why don't I call the police?... "That's what they're there for..." The Artons aren't going to get mixed up in this... not for anything in the world... They haven't seen a thing... or heard anything... They don't even know what I'm talking about...

Old lady des Pereires up there on the embankment watched me parleying... She let out terrible screams... She was making a disgusting stink... That was the way she was... After the first shock you couldn't hold her... I pointed her out to the two savages... the poor woman in despair...

"Do you hear that? I suppose you can't hear her?... Her terrible grief!... We can't leave her husband out there in the muck, can we?... What are you afraid of? Good God, it's not a dog... he hasn't got rabies... It's not a calf... he hasn't got hoof-and-mouth disease... He's killed himself and that's that... He was perfectly healthy... He hasn't got the glanders... The least we can do is shelter him in the barn for a while... till they can come and take him away... Before the traffic starts up... They'll run him over..." Those shitheels were adamant... The more I tried, the more pigheaded they got... "No, no!" they yelled. Certainly not, they wouldn't take him in... not on their property... never, never!... they wouldn't even open the door for me... they told me to beat it... They were burning me up... So I says to this rotten bitch:

"All right, all right! That'll do, madame. I see. You won't help. That's your last word? You're sure? All right, It's your ass... In that case I'm going to stay right here... That's right... I'll stay a week! I'll stay a month! I'll stay as long as I have to! I'll yell until they come!... I'll yell so everybody can hear me, I'll tell them it was you... that you engineered the whole thing!..." That got them... Christ, were they scared! They were shitless!... And I went right on... I wasn't going to stop... Those scums made me so mad I'd have thrown an epileptic fit to show them... They didn't know how to make me shut up... The old lady up on the bank was shouting louder and louder... She told me to hurry... "Ferdinand, hey, Ferdinand... Bring hot water... Bring a sack... a cloth!..." The only thing those two bastards were willing to do... in the end after my song and dance and to make me let go their blind... was lend me their wheelbarrow on condition that I'd positively bring it back that same day... rinsed, cleaned... and scrubbed with Javel water... They said it over and over... They repeated it twenty times... So I toted the thing up the hill... I had to come back down to ask for a trowel... to pry the ear loose... to break up the lumps... Little by little we made it... But then the blood began to gush again, it flowed profusely... His flannel vest was one big jelly, a pudding inside his frock coat... the gray was all red... But the worst was getting the gun out... The barrel stuck so hard to the enormous plug of meat and brains... it was so completely wedged into the mouth and skull... that it took the two of us... She held the head on one end and I pulled at the butt on the other... When the brain let loose', it gushed out even harder... it dripped down sideways... steaming, it was still hot... a stream of blood spurted from the neck... He'd impaled himself completely... He'd fallen on his knees... He'd collapsed like that... with the barrel deep in his mouth... He'd stove his whole head in...

Once we got him loose, we turned him over on his back... belly and face up... but he folded again... He was still like a Z... Luckily we managed to squeeze him in between the sides of the wheelbarrow... We still had trouble though with the neck, the stump of the head... It kept dangling against the wheel... The old girl took off her petticoat and her heavy kilt... to bundle up his head in... so it wouldn't drip so hard... But the minute we started moving again, with the bumps and jolts, it started gushing thicker than ever... They could have followed our tracks... It was slow going... we took little short steps. I stopped every two minutes... Those four miles took us at least three hours... I saw the gendarmes way in the distance... or rather their horses… right outside the farm... They were waiting for us... There were four of them plus the sergeant... And besides there was one in civilian clothes, a big guy I didn't know... I'd never seen him before... We were crawling... I wasn't in any hurry at all... But we finally got there… They'd seen us coming... all the way down from the ridge... They must have spotted us even before we went into the woods...

"OK! Leave the wheelbarrow in the doorway, you little stinker! This way, both of you... The inspector'll be here in a little while... Put the handcuffs on him... and her too..." They shut us up in the barn. One of the cops guarded the door.

We waited several hours in the hay... I could hear the mob collecting in front of the farm. The village was crowding up... They were pouring in from all directions... Some of the hicks must have been right there under the arch... I could hear them talking... The inspector hadn't come yet... The sergeant came and went, getting madder and madder... He was making a show of activity while waiting for the orders... He was dishing out orders to his men...

"Push back the crowd. And bring me the prisoners..." He'd already questioned all the kids… He had us brought in to him and then he sent us back to the barn... After a while he hauled us out for good... The bastard browbeat us... He was eager-beavering... He threw his weight around, trying to terrorize us... probably so's to make us talk... so we'd confess right away... He had another think coming... He said we had no right to tote the body around... That was a felony in itself... We shouldn't have touched it... It was doing fine on the road... that now he wouldn't be able to make his report... What do you think of that?... and that twenty-five years in the pen would teach us a thing or two! Hell! that boy didn't like us... Anyway, the worst kind of bullshit... a lot of stupid cocksucking bellowing...

The old lady wasn't acting up much since we'd come back... She just sat there crying, huddled against the door. Once in a while she let out a hiccup, followed by the same two three laments...

"I'd never have expected it, Ferdinand... Oh, it's too much... Too much misery, Ferdinand... I haven't the strength... No!... I can't go on... I can't believe it... I can't believe it's true, Ferdinand... What do you think?... Is it really true? Do you think it's true?... Oh no, it can't be…" She was really stunned... She was out for the count... she was goofy cross-eyed... But when that cop started in again, calling us criminals in his stupid hayseed accent... that stirred her up... Worn-out as she was, she bridled at the affront... Christ!... She bounded like a tiger... She was in form again.

"What's that? What's that?" she flung at him... "I don't quite follow you... What's that you say?..." She shoved her face into his... "What's that you're telling me?... That I did him in?... Why, you've been drinking, my good man!... You've got your nerve with you!... Or are you crazy, the whole lot of you?... What's that? You're accusing me?... Of killing that scoundrel? That gallows bird?... I'll remember that one... Oh, it's rich... I'll have to write it down... That stinker who's been my misfortune... and nothing else but... He's the murderer... He's been murdering me for years... Vampire? He's the vampire!... And not just once! not ten times! not a hundred times! but a thousand times! Two thousand!... Why, he was murdering me every single day before you were even born... I ran myself ragged for that man!... tore my guts out!... I went hungry for weeks on end so they wouldn't take him away to Rungis... All my life, you hear? Tortured... abused... that's right... crushed! Yes, all my life for that skunk!... I did everything in my power to save him... Everybody knows that... Why don't you keep your questions for them, for the people who know... who know us... who saw what I did?... Go to the Palais-Royal... Go to Montretout... They know me... They know all I did... all I went through... Ferdinand can tell you... He's young, but he understands... I performed miracles, monsieur, to keep him from falling back into the gutter... miracles... and dishonor... That was his nature... He wallowed lower than a pig if you turned your back for half a minute... He fell into every cesspool... He couldn't help it... That's right... I'm not afraid to say it... He was a dungheap... I've nothing to hide... Anyway, everybody knows it... He had no shame, heavens above... Every evil instinct... every last one... the vilest... things you gendarmes are too young to understand... You're even too young to hear about them!"

She looked the cops up and down... Her hair was loose, it fell down over her eyes in scraggly gray wisps... She was sweating hard... She reeled a little, she sat down.

"You fellows think it's decent the way he ended up?... Is that all you've got to say?... Treat me like a whore?... That's my reward!... If you knew about the debts!... Ah?... That's news to you?... He didn't give a good god damn... Bills, bills, bills... You go pay them, you old crab!... And always new ones pouring in... Break your back, that's what you're good for... Double-talk! Cock-and-bull stories! Sleighrides! Hokum! Liquor!... That's how he lived! That's all he knew! Swindling and low living! He hadn't an ounce of feeling!..." She was convulsed with misery, bellowing between spasms...

"It was me! me that saved his house to the bitter end! If I hadn't fought for it, it would have been sold centuries ago... He couldn't control himself... The dirty bastard took advantage of my being so sick just then that I didn't know what was going on... He unloaded... he drank it all up… he sold us out bag and baggage! Ask if it's not true... if I'm a liar... He never spared me anything! Never! He couldn't... It was second nature with him... He had to torture me... All for his whores! For his vices! His horses! His races! His damn foolishness! His drinking, and I don't know what else... Generous?... He gave to strangers... It was all the same to him, as long as it went out fast... It slipped through his fingers... I could be on my deathbed, he didn't care… That's what he always wanted... Thirty years it went on... Thirty years I put up with it... Thirty years isn't five minutes... So now I get accused!... After all the vilest affronts... after all I've suffered... Oh no, it's too much!..." The enormity of the thing sent her into hysterics again. "What's that? What's that? It can't be! So now he disfigures himself... He shoves off... He makes hash of himself, and I'm the guilty party? My oh my, that takes the cake!... It's enough to make your hair stand on end! What a filthy business! To the very end that stinking rotten clown has poisoned my existence... you can say that again!... But I'm not going to take it lying down!... I'm still here!... It's up to you!... Hold the fort, you old mule! There won't be anything left! Not a crumb! Nothing but debts! Nothing but debts! He doesn't give a damn... as long as he can spend... He took everything I had... Ferdinand knows all about it... He saw how the land lay... He saw how I toiled and struggled and racked my brains to the very last minute... so as not to leave Montretout... so as not to come to this stinking hole... and bury myself with his potatoes... All in vain!... He was dead set on disaster... Ferdinand knows that too!... I've wasted my life... I've lost everything for that jack-in-the-box... that unbelievable scoundrel! My position, my career! my profession, my friends!... Everything! my parents!... Nobody wanted to see us anymore... except a bunch of cut-throats! A gang of crazy hoodlums... escaped from the bughouse... I ruined my health... First my operation... And I've aged twenty years in the last six months... Before that I never had anything wrong with me... I didn't know what a cold was... I could digest anything... I had a stomach like an ostrich... But what with one disaster after another... That's all he ever brought home... And there was never an end to it... We'd hardly finished one... Whoops!... He'd dream up another... loonier than the last... It undermined my resistance... That's not hard to understand... I was operated, it was bound to happen... They warned me at Péan's: 'Don't keep on with that kind of life, Madame des Pereires… it'll turn out very badly... Take it easy! Take care of yourself!... Avoid worry!...' Ah, go shit in your hat! It got worse from year to year! Never a moment's peace... Nothing but lawsuits, summonses... Green papers... yellow papers... Creditors at every door!... Persecuted!... That's the life I've had... Persecuted day and night! Exactly! Hunted like a criminal! For his sake... always for him!... Who could bear up under that?... I haven't had a good night's sleep in twenty years... if you want to know... That's the honest truth... Everything's been taken away from me... My sleep, my appetite, my savings... I've got such flashes I can't stand up... I can't take a bus anymore... I'm sick to my stomach right away... Any time I try to hurry, even on foot, I see stars... And now they tell me I'm the murderer... That's the prize package!... My advice to you is to think it over before you say such things..."

She led them out under the arch, the four cops and the sergeant... She went up to the body... she lifted the pants leg...

"You see those socks?... Take a good look... Well, he's got the only pair... There's not another in the house... The rest of us haven't got any... Never did... Neither Ferdinand nor the kids..." She hiked up her own pants to show the cops..."I'm barefoot myself... Go on, see for yourself... We always went without just for him... for him and nobody else... He took everything... We gave him everything we had . . He had everything... Always did!... Two houses... a magazine... at the Palais-Royal!... motors... thousands of gadgets and infernal majugguses... God knows how much they cost... the skin off your ass... The whole works... just to satisfy his whims... I can't even begin to tell you... I never crossed him... Don't worry, that's not why he bumped himself off... He was spoiled!... He was rotten!... That's right... rotten!... You want electrical jiggers?... All right, son, here you are... You think we should go to the country?... OK, we'll go... You want some more potatoes?... Sure, go right ahead... It never stopped... Never a moment's doubt... it was cut-and-dried... His highness couldn't wait... Wouldn't you want the moon by any chance?... Splendid, my love, you'll have it... Always more fancy ideas... new crazes!... You couldn't be more indulgent with a six-month-old baby... He had everything he wanted... before he could even open his mouth! Ah, that was my weakness... Well, I've got my punishment... Ah, if I'd only known... if I'd known what you people were going to say... Believe me, I'd never have brought him back... I don't know how the kid felt about it... But as far as I'm concerned, take it from me, I'd have sooner chucked him in the ditch! Then you wouldn't come around maligning me... That's where he ought to be... The rotten filthy scum! That's all he deserves! I don't give a shit about going to prison... It's all one to me... I won't be worse off than anywhere else... But Christ almighty Jesus, no! Hell, no! I'm not such a sucker..."

"That'll do! Come over here... You can tell all that to the judge! First answer my questions... We've heard enough talk... You say you don't know the gun he killed himself with?... But you brought it back... And the kid? Had he seen it?... He'd rammed it into his head, eh? That's how you found it, isn't it? The two of you pulled it out, eh?... How did it happen according to you?"

"Why, I never said that, I never said I didn't know the gun... It was up there over the fireplace... We'd all seen it the whole time... Ask the kids..."

"Pipe down! I've had enough of your idiotic remarks... Let's get down to brass tacks... name and destination... First the victim... Date, place of birth... What was his name anyway?... Courtial? Courtial what? And where was he born?... Reputation? Occupation?"

"His name wasn't Courtial at all," she answered point-blank... "It wasn't even des Pereires... or Jean... or Marin... He made that name up... It was like everything else... One more invention!... A lie... what a liar he was! Always! Everywhere! Still!... His name was Léon... Léon Charles Punais!... That's his honest-to-God name... It's not quite the same, is it?... Like me, my name is Honorine Beauregard, not Irène!... That was just another name he dug up for me... He had to change everything... I can prove it... I've got the proof all right!... I'm not trying to pull the wool over your eyes. I never go anywhere without it... I've got my family booklet... I'll go get it... He was born in Ville-d'Avray in 1852... September 24th... That was his birthday... I'll go over and get it for you... It's in my reticule... Come with me, Ferdinand..."

The sergeant was writing it out... "Escort the prisoners!" he ordered the two bulls... We passed in front of the wheelbarrow... We came back again. "Can we take it in now?" one of the cops asked... he shouted from under the arch.

"Take what in?"

"The body, sergeant... There's people all around it."

He had to think it over...

"OK, bring it in... Put it in the kitchen..." So then they took him out of the wheelbarrow... They lifted him very gingerly... They carried him in... They laid him down on the tiles... But he was still all crooked... He wouldn't unbend... The old lady went down on her knees to look at him up close... She was sobbing hard... Her tears flowed in rivers... she caught hold of me with her handcuffs... She was overcome with grief... You'd honestly have thought she'd just noticed there was nothing left of him but hash

"Oh! Oh! Look, Ferdinand..." She forgot the family booklet... she forgot about getting it… she just slumped there...

"Oh God, he hasn't any head!... He hasn't any head, Ferdinand! My darling! My darling! Your head!... It's gone..." She implored, she dragged herself at the gendarmes' feet... She crawled between their boots... she rolled on the floor...

"A placenta!... It's a placenta!... I know... His head!... His poor head!... It's a placenta!... Have you seen it, Ferdinand?... Do you see?... Look!... Oh! Oh! Oh!" she screamed like her throat had been cut...

"Oh! All my life!... Oh!... All my life!... Oh! Oh!..." More and more piercingly.

"I didn't do it, messieurs... It's not me, how could it be?... I swear it!... I swear it!... I gave him my whole life!... To bring him a little happiness!... to make him comfortable... He needed me... day and night... believe me... I'm not lying... Tell them, Ferdinand... Tell them if it isn't true... All my sacrifices!... He hasn't any head!... Oh, why are you all against me?... There's nothing left for him!... Good luck!... Good luck!... he says... the poor darling... good luck!... Oh God! You saw it? . . It was written... It was him, wasn't it?... It's written in his writing! It wasn't me! Good luck! That's him! All by himself! You can tell his handwriting! Oh! it wasn't me!... It's obvious!... Isn't it obvious?"

She'd thrown herself full length on the ground... Her whole body hit the packed earth... She pressed close to Courtial... She was shivering...

"Courtial, I implore you... Courtial, speak to me... Tell me, my angel... Why did you do it?... Why did you do such an awful thing?... Eh? Tell me, my dumpling, my treasure!..." She turned toward the cops...

"It's him! It's him! It's a placenta!..." She threw another fit... She started eating her hair… she was bellowing so loud we couldn't hear each other in the room... The snoopers at the window climbed up on each other's backs... She bit right into her handcuffs. She flailed around on the floor, possessed. The gendarmes picked her up by main force, they carried her into the barn... She yelled like a stuck pig... She clutched the door... She fell... she charged back against it... "I want to see him... I want to see him!" she screamed... "'Let me see him!... They want to take him away!... Murderers!... Help, help! My angel! My angel!... Not you, Ferdinand! Not you!... You're not my angel!... I want to see him!... Have pity!... I want to see him!..." This went on for an hour. They had to go back and take off the handcuffs... Then she calmed down a little... They didn't take mine off... though I promised to behave.

In the afternoon another cop came out on a bicycle... He'd been sent specially from Persant… He told the sergeant again that we mustn't touch anything... that the prosecutor was coming… and not the inspector... Those were the orders from above... He also told us to get the kids' stuff ready, they'd all be leaving next day, first thing in the morning... They were expected in Versailles at a juvenile welfare home, the S.P.C.C… . Those were the orders... By ten a.m. there wasn't to be one kid left on the premises... Two special people were coming from Beauvais to get them... to take them to the station...

We passed the orders on to the brats who were out in the yard... after all, we had to let them know that the jig was up... dead and buried... They didn't exactly get it... They tried to figure out what was going on, where they were being taken... They wondered if the whole thing wasn't a gag... I tried to explain that our show was over... the record was busted... they didn't get it… I told them the judge had sent orders to close up shop... and send the "New Race" home... that they were closing down our "wave" farm too... they were good and sick of it... that they were a lot of savages... perfectly ruthless... that it was finished... that they were looking for their parents... and this time they'd find them...

It was all Greek to them... They weren't used to being treated like kids anymore... They were too emancipated... They'd forgotten about obedience and those kind of things... It wasn't much trouble collecting their duds... Actually they had nothing but their bones and their pants… They had a few "bent" shoes that were never the right size. Half the time they only wore one... Mostly they went barefoot... All the same they managed to collect a whole pile of junk... thousands of nails, hooks, bird traps, slings, ends of string, nooses... shears, spiral springs, whole sets of graters, razor blades fastened to long sticks... two complete jimmies... Only Dudule had nothing... He worked with his fingers... The kids thought they were being taken someplace where their equipment would come in handy... They didn't realize... though I'd told them a dozen times... They didn't take the whole thing very seriously... though they'd seen the old man with his face blown off... They could hear the old lady wailing behind the door... But that didn't frighten them...

"If you ask me," said Dudule, "I betcha we'll be back on Thursday!"

"You don't know them, kid," I said... "And for Christ's sake don't pull any rough stuff... They'll lock you up for life... They got terrible sweatboxes... Watch your step, behave . . ; Keep your traps shut, the whole lot of you..." Even Mésange thought she was smart: "Aw go on, Ferdinand! That's a lot of hooey! They're sending us away so we won't see the funeral... It's the bunk... We'll be back on Sunday... when it's all over..." I'd have asked nothing better... They packed all their little odds and ends... There was an argument about dividing up... They all wanted the rubber bands... the big thick ones... They could peg a sparrow every time... They took lots of wire... pretty near two rolls... It was plenty heavy... But hell, there was still a whole trunkful in the shed...

The two lady social workers turned up earlier than we expected... Kind of like nuns... No coifs, but high-necked gray dresses, both exactly the same, and fingerless gloves... and funny voices, too soft and very insistent... It wasn't dark yet...

"So here we are, my dear children..." said the skinnier of the two. "We'll have to hurry a little... I hope you'll all be very well behaved... We'll have a lovely trip together..." They lined them up two by two... But Dudule was all by himself in front... It was certainly the first time they'd ever been put in order... They asked them all their names...

"And now we mustn't talk any more... We're all good little children... And what's your name, my dear?"

"Mésange Sweetiepie..." It was perfectly true that the others called her that. They were still nine in all... five boys, four girls. Dudule left us his mutt... They didn't want him in Versailles... All of a sudden they all broke ranks... They'd forgotten the old lady... She was still in her barn... They ran over and kissed her good-bye... Naturally they cried some... It wasn't a very cheerful leave-taking... considering the circumstances... Mésange cried the most...

"Good-bye, Ferdinand... Good-bye... See you soon," they shouted back from the other end of the yard... The ladies rounded them up again...

"My goodness, children, goodness me... Come along, little girls..." Their last cries came to me from way down the road... "So long, pal... so long..."

Balls! Balls! I knew the score... Getting older is a crummy trick... Kids are like years, you never see them again. We locked up Dudule's dog with the old bag. The two of them cried together. He yammered the hardest. That day, honestly, take it from me, was one of the rotten-est in my whole life. Balls!

Once the kids were gone, the sergeant settled down in the kitchen with his men. They saw I was perfectly quiet, they took off my handcuffs... The body was next door... There wasn't anything to do, because we had to wait for the prosecutor, who was coming next day... There'd be a "preliminary investigation," they said. The bulls talked it over... Anyway, they'd stopped bawling us out... And besides they were hungry... They looked through the cupboards... for food... They felt like gargling too... But there wasn't a drop of wine... We lit the fire... It was raining into the fireplace... It was bitter cold again. February is the littlest month but the meanest too... The first part of the winter hadn't been so bad... but now it was getting even... The bulls were talking it all over... they were peasants deep down... They clumped all over in their boots... I looked at their mugs up close... They were smoking their pipes... they were sitting around our table... There was plenty of time to look them over... They had a thick layer of blubber from their eyes down. Their cheeks were completely armored... and they had rolls of fat all around their necks up to their ears... They were all beef and pretty thick in the middle, especially one that was twice the size of the others... They wouldn't be easy to fill... Their two- pronged hats were piled up in a pyramid in the middle of the table... Their boots were the real seven-league kind... steamboats... When all five of them stood up and dragged their sabers around, you can't imagine the clatter... But they were getting thirstier and thirstier... They went and got some cider from the old folks at the end of the village... Later, maybe about eight o'clock, another bull showed up... he'd come from their barracks... He'd brought some wine and a bite to eat... five mess cans... We still had some coffee. I said we could make them some if they'd let us grind it. They were willing. The old lady came out of her barn. They opened up for her. Her fit of rage had passed... It was mighty hard on those giants having no more than that to eat... a little mess can apiece... and one bread ration for all five... The old girl, I knew, still had some bacon tucked away... And some lentils in a special hiding place of her own, and some turnips, and maybe half a pound of margarine...

"I could make you some soup," she said... "now the kids are gone... Maybe I can feed the lot of you..." They were delighted... They slapped their thighs... But she started sniveling again... We had a big kettle... it held at least fifteen mess cans... Some more wine arrived... all the way from Persant... The sergeant's wife sent a kid out with it with a letter and a newspaper... We sat down with them... Naturally we took our share... We hadn't had a bite to eat in twenty-four hours... The gendarmes asked for seconds... We emptied the whole kettle... First they only talked among themselves... Gradually they livened up... They shoveled it in... They unbuttoned without ceremony... One of the five... not the sergeant, one that was all bald... seemed more curious than the rest... He asked the old lady what line of business the deceased had been in before taking up farming... He was interested... She tried to answer, but she didn't do very well... She gagged on every word... She broke into sobs... She blew her nose in her plate... She sneezed into the pepper... In the end they were all laughing... Besides, the soup took the skin off your tongue... she'd had a heavy hand with the seasoning... Whew! Hoo! Oof!... The room was hot too... The fire was drawing fine... When the wind was right, it was enough to burn the house down... but when it changed, it blew back into the room... You suffocated in the smoke... It's always like that in the country...

At the end of the bench the sergeant couldn't take the heat anymore... He peeled off his tunic... The others followed suit... The big shots from the courthouse couldn't get there until morning... so there was nothing to worry about... They all wondered why the inspector had backed down... That question really got them excited... And especially why the prosecutor was coming in person!... And why in such a hurry?... There must have been some tangle between the prosecutor's office and the police... That was the conclusion they came to... If they were locking horns, we were sure to get it in the neck... that's what I was thinking. The sergeant, little by little, started eating again... All by himself he wolfed down pretty near a whole Camembert... enormous slabs of bread... washed down with the red stuff... A mouthful... a drink... A mouthful... another drink... I watched him... he winked at me... He was kind of sozzled... He got real friendly... He asked the old bag, not at all brutally, without the least malice, what her Courtial had done before they came to Blême... She heard him all wrong... she was all befuddled from crying. "Rheumatism" was her answer... she was way off... She started bugling again... Her tears got the best of her... She begged him, implored him, to let her stay in the kitchen... next door... just a little while... to sit with the body... until midnight for instance... We were all out of oil and kerosene... there was nothing but candles, but plenty of those... The kids swiped them all over the place, every time they went out... whenever they dropped into a farm. They'd brought back every known caliber... there were plenty to choose from... The old lady wanted to light two... The sergeant was sick of her yapping...

"Go on, go on... But come back quick... right away... And don't set the place on fire... And don't touch the old man, eh?... or I'll lock you up in the barn again... For good!"

She went out... A minute later when she didn't come back, one of the gendarmes got up to go see... "What in hell's she doing?..." they wondered... I went with him... She was down on her knees, bent over the body...

"Can't I cover him?..." "Nothing doing!" the bull said. "It's not that he scares me... But you're going to have to wrap him up... They can't take him away like this... I won't move him, I promise you... I don't need to touch him... I'd only like to put a cloth around him... That's all... A cloth under him and over his head..."

I wondered what she was meaning to use... Sheets?... We hadn't any... We'd never had any in Blême... We had blankets, but they were rags... completely rotted away... We hadn't been using them in a long time... we slept in our clothes... They were all falling apart... The gendarme wanted no part of it... He told her to ask the sergeant for permission herself... But the sergeant was asleep... He'd collapsed on the table... We could see him through the door... The other yokels were playing cards...

"Wait, I'll go," he said finally... "Don't touch him before I get back..." But she couldn't wait...

"Ferdinand, you go. Hurry up, son. Go look in my tick... you know... in the slit where I put the straw in... Stick your arm in at the foot end and rummage around... you'll find the big piece

... you know... out of the *Archimedes*... the red one... bright red... It's big enough... It'll be big enough... It'll go all around him... Go get it quick... I'll be right here... Hurry up, quick!" It was perfectly true... I found it right away... It stank of rubber... It was the piece she'd saved from under the ruins the night of the disaster... She unfolded it in front of me... she spread it out on the ground... It was still good canvas... only the color had changed... It wasn't scarlet anymore... it had turned all brown. She wouldn't let me help her to roll Courtial up in it... She did it all by herself... She was careful not to move him... She slipped the cloth all flat under the corpse... very gently I've got to admit... She had all the yardage she needed to wrap him up completely... And the hash where the head was, was all closed in too... The sergeant watched us... The other one had woken him up... So then he yelled through the door... "Say, you hiding him again?... Are you off your rocker?"

"Oh, don't scold me, sir... don't scold me, I beg of you... I've done my best..." She turned toward him on her knees. "I haven't done any harm! Come and see! I haven't done any harm! Come and see for yourself! He's still there... Believe me... believe me... I beg of you, Mr. Engineer..." she started calling him that all of a sudden, Mr. Engineer... She was screaming again...

"He went up, Mr. Engineer... You people didn't see him... Naturally you don't believe me... But Ferdinand saw him... Didn't you, Ferdinand?... How beautifully he went up!... You remember, son?... Tell him... They don't believe me... Mercy! Sweet Jesus! I'm going to say a prayer! Ferdinand! Mr. Engineer! Holy Mary! Mary! Lamb of heaven! Pray for us! Ferdinand! I conjure you! Tell the gentlemen! will you?... Come and pray! Come quick! Come here! It's the truth, isn't it?... In the name of the Father! the Son! and the Holy Ghost!... You know that one, don't you, Ferdinand?... You know your prayers?..."

She was horrified... Her eyes gaped white... "You don't know it?... Sure you know it... Forgive us our trespasses... Come along! Together! There! As I'll forgive you... Come! As I forgive you!... Say it after me, dammit... you little punk!..."

At this she gives me a big clout... The cops next door were in stitches.

"Oh, so you do know it... after all... He went up, Mr. Engineer, he went up... it was marvelous... He went up to six thousand feet... I went up with him wherever he went... Yes... I went up... You can trust me... It's the honest truth... I swear... I swear it..." She tried crossing herself... She couldn't make it... she got tangled up in her rags...

"In the hydrogen! In the hydrogen, dear sirs... You can ask anybody... I'm not lying..."

She prostrated herself beside the body, she threw herself square on top of it... She pleaded... "My poor darling!... My poor love!... They won't believe you anymore. Oh!... It's too awful... They won't believe you... I don't know how to tell them... I don't know what to do... I don't know how he went up... I don't know how far... I'm a hateful woman... It's all my fault!... It's my fault, Mr. Engineer... Oh yes, yes!... I did it all!... I did nothing but harm! He went up two hundred times... a hundred times!... I can't remember, my love!... Two hundred!... Six!... Six hundred times... I don't know... I don't know anything anymore... It's terrible... Mr. Engineer!... Three hundred!... More!... Much more!... I don't know!..." She threw her arms around him in the balloon cover... she clutched him convulsively... "Courtial! Courtial! I've forgotten everything!..." She clutched her throat... She started in on her head again, tearing out her hair by handfuls, rolling on the ground... She ransacked her memory...

"Three thousand!... Ten thousand!... Jesus!... Ferdinand! Can't you say anything?... It's too much!... Holy fucking God!..." She lost herself in figures again...

"Lieutenants!... Ferdinand!... Lieutenants!" That's what she was calling them now... "In heaven's name! Ah! I've got it!..." She raised herself on her elbows... "Two hundred and twenty-two times!... Yes, that's it... Two hundred and twenty-two..." She fell back again. "Nuts! I've forgotten everything!... My life! My life!..." The bulls had to pick her up... They took her back to the barn... They closed the door on her. All alone like that, she gradually resigned herself... she even fell asleep... Later on I went in to see her with the gendarmes. She started talking to us perfectly reasonably. She wasn't off her nut at all anymore.

We waited all morning... The old lady was still in the straw... She was sound asleep... Around noon they arrived from the prosecutor's office... The examining magistrate, a little fat guy all bundled up in his fur coat, lisped in the steaming air, he had coughing spells... He got out of his carriage with another character, a redhead. This one had a cap all pulled down over his eyes. He was the medical examiner. The gendarmes recognized him right away.

It was really bitter cold... They were chilled to the bone... They'd come from Persant station...

"Bring them here!" he ordered the gendarmes the minute he set foot on the ground... "Bring them to me in the big room!... Both of them! The woman and the little shitass! We'll take a look at the body later!... Nobody's moved it?... Wherc'd you put it?... And bring me the exhibits!... What was there?... A gun?... And the witnesses!... Were there any witnesses?..."

A few minutes later two more carriages drove up... One was full of cops, plainclothesmen... and the other, a big covered van, was pack-jammed with reporters... Right away they took millions of snapshots... every aspect of the farm... the interior... the surroundings... Those newspapermen were pests, a damn sight worse than the hicks... And so active... They absolutely insisted... they went into hysterics... on taking a flashlight picture of my mug... and then the old lady from every angle... She had no way of hiding... She was forced to stay right between the two bulls... But we couldn't move much, the crowd was too thick... the prosecutor was madder than a hornet! He was being stepped on... He ordered the cops to clear the room... They didn't waste any time... They sent the mob flying... The premises were cleared right away... the whole yard too...

The character with the lisp was shivering in his furs. He was in a hurry to get it all over with, that was plain... He was sore at the cops... His clerk was looking for a pen, he'd broken his own... The Lisp wasn't comfortable on the bench... The room was too big and damp, the fire was out... He beat his hands together... He took his gloves off to blow on them. He sucked his fingers... His nose was all amethyst... He put his gloves back on... He wriggled his ass... He stamped his feet... He couldn't get warm... The papers were all in front of him... He blew on them, they flew away... The clerk went chasing after them... They didn't write anything at all... He wanted to see the gun. He said to the newspapermen: "Take my picture with this weapon while you're at it..." He said to the sergeant: "Tell me the whole story!" So then the big cocksucker didn't talk big like with us... In fact he stammered... Actually he didn't know much... I saw that right away... He went out with the magistrate... They paced up and down the whole length of the yard... When they were through gassing, they came back inside... The Lisp sat down... Then it was my turn to talk... I told them the whole story right away... all I knew, that is... He didn't listen much: "What's your name?..." I told him "Ferdinand, born in Courbevoie." "Your age?..." I told him. "And what do your parents do?" I told him that too... "Good," he said... "Stay right where you are... And you?..." It was the old lady's turn...

"Tell me your story and make it fast..." He'd stood up... He couldn't sit still... He piddled up and down... He couldn't feel his dogs... Stamping didn't help... An earth floor is cold as hell... especially ours, it was so damp...

"Oh, Doctor! My feet!... Don't they ever make a fire around here?..." We were all out of wood... The gendarmes had burned every last stick... He cut the old lady short...

"Hell! I thee you don't know very much... Never mind! Never mind! We'll thee about all that later... Beauvais will be thoon enough... OK, OK leth get out of here!... Doctor, you've had a good look at the body?... What thay?... Well, what do you think?... What thay?" The two of them left the room to take another look... In the kitchen next door they talked it over... They were maybe ten minutes... They came back...

"Well, then," said the Lisp... "You, the wife... Madame Courtial... No... Des Pereires... No?... Nuts!... You're free for the present. But you'll have to come to Beauvais... My clerk will let you know... I'll send for the body tomorrow..." Turning toward the reporters: "You can call it suicide until further notice. After the autopsy we'll see... Maybe you'll be perfectly free... Anyway, we'll see... You, Bozo!" That was me... "You can go... You can leave... Go straight home... to your parents... Give the clerk your address... I'll send for you if I need you... OK, let's go! Sergeant, you will leave one of your men here... Only one... until the ambulance gets here... Let's go... Make it quick, clerk... Let's get going... Finished, the fourth estate? All reporters will please leave... Nobody can stay but the family and the officer... OK men, that'll do it for the night... You won't allow anybody to enter...

to touch anything... to leave... Have I made myself clear?... You've all got it?... Good... Let's get going!...

Quick... Step on it! All aboard, Doctor..."

He was still stamping his feet... He was bouncing up and down in front of his carriage... He couldn't stand it a minute longer... He was frozen stiff in spite of his overcoat and the sheepskin that went all the way up to his eyebrows... to his derby... As he set foot on the step:

"Driver! Driver! Listen here! You'll make it fast, won't you? And stop at Cerdance, at the little bar on the left... after the grade crossing... you know the place I mean?... Oh, Doctor, I've never had such shivers in all my life... I'm going to be laid up for a month... again, like all last winter... My! What wouldn't I give for a grog!... Christ, they've murdered me in this dump... Did you ever see such an icebox?... It's the limit... It's better outside... It's unbelievable... Ah! Never fear, the stiff will keep!..."

As they were starting, he stuck his head out again from under the big top... He took in the whole farm... The gendarmes at attention... "Whip 'em up, driver!" They drove off in a hurricane, heading for Persant... The bulls, the clerk, the plainclothesmen didn't let the grass grow... They beat it too about five minutes later... The reporters came back... They took some more pictures... They'd been around, they knew the score... They were nobody's fools... They knew all the dodges...

"Hell," they told me, "don't worry... Anybody can see you had nothing to do with it... It's all a lot of red tape... dumb routine... window dressing... Don't mind them... They won't hold you half a minute... they've got to go through the motions... that's all." The old girl was glum all the same...

"We know those characters... It's not the first time we've seen this guy on the job... If he had any real suspicions, he'd have hung around longer... Besides, he'd have arrested you sure as shit... Oh, no, he wouldn't have hesitated. We know him. One shred of presumption and hoop-la, he throws you in the clink! That's for sure!... Doubt is that boy's middle name . . He's got his feet on the ground... He's a shrewd article... You can't mess with him!"

"Then, my dear sirs, you're quite sure he won't come back?... that it wasn't just the cold drove him away?"

"The cold doesn't scare him!... You've got nothing to worry about... Hell, no, it's all a lot of moonshine... hocus-pocus... Baloney... If I were you, I'd relax... He came out here for beans, that's all... So what? So he's sore!" They were all of the same opinion...

They got back in their carriage... They were talking about women already... They had to push off slowly... The axles were creaking hard... There were too many of them, all in a pile... Two of the reporters had made the trip all the way from Paris just on our account... They were sorry they'd come... The old lady pestered them so bad with questions, in the end they started bellowing in chorus:

There ain't no crime... bingo bing! There ain't no crime... bingo bing.

Thumping their heels like to crack the floor... Actually they were having a fine time. They sang dirty songs... As they drove off, they were singing the one about the bishop who went up in a balloon:

High in the sky as he sailed around,
The skin of his balls dragged on the ground...

The gendarme who'd stayed there on guard found another shanty in the village, completely empty, near the watering trough, where he could put his horse inside. He liked that better... Our stable was a wreck... all the rain came in... and the drafts whistled like an organ... His plug wasn't happy in there... She staggered... her legs were folding with the cold... So he moved her... And then he came back... maybe an hour before suppertime... He had something to tell us...

"See here, you two jokers, can you keep your shirt on awhile? I've got to go to Tousne..." That was a village pretty far away on the other side of Berlot Forest... "I've got to get some oats... There's none left in my saddlebags... My sister-in-law's over there, she's got the tobacco store... Maybe I'll stay for supper... I'll be back a little later... But no later than ten... So don't get smart, you two... I haven't a grain of oats... While I'm at it, I'll take the nag... She's lost a shoe... I'll stop in at the blacksmith's... Then I can ride back... that'll be quicker... You understand?... You won't let anybody in?..." We understood perfectly... He was bored out there with us... He thought he'd take a little time off... We wished him a fair wind... He passed in front of the farm, leading his plug by the bridle... I saw him disappearing in the distance... It was getting dark...

The old lady and I lay low... We waited for it to be really dark to go out for wood... Then I made it quick... I pulled three slats at once off the fence... I broke them up into kindling... but naturally they smoked... they were too damp... I went back in with the old lady... I was glad we had a chance to get warm... We needed it... But we had to keep our eyes closed... it stung too bad... She had calmed down after her session... But she was still kind of worried...

"Do you think it's true?..." she asked me. "You think the cops won't bother us anymore? You don't think they've got some trick up their sleeves?... You heard the way they suspected me?... all of them!... The very first thing... you saw them... Weren't they disgusting?... Oh my oh my!"

"Who? The cops?" "That's right, the cops."

"Oh, the sergeant's nothing but a big yokel!... The way he lost his tongue, bzing, in front of the persecutors!... in two seconds flat... He dropped out... He didn't know what had hit him... He hadn't a word to say for himself... The sap, what'd you expect him to talk about?... he hadn't seen a thing... The reporters said the same thing... you heard them... They'd have noticed... they know the ropes... They'd certainly have warned us... They don't like that guy with the lisp... All they had was presumptions... hot air... They wouldn't have farted out of here so fast if they'd thought they had anything on us... Hell no... Those bulls would still be here, it's perfectly obvious... and then some!... You heard him, the Lisp himself, on his way out... what he said to the others: 'It's suicide.' That's all. Don't go looking for complications... The doctor said so too... I heard him telling the little guy: 'It was fired upward, my friend, upward...' That was clear enough... he wasn't spoofing... That's all there is to it... No use looking for trouble... We got plenty..."

"Yes, I guess you're right," she very softly. But she wasn't convinced... She wasn't very confident...

"How are they going to bury him?... First they do the autopsy, don't they? And then what? And what for anyway?... Do you know?... Are they still looking for something?..." "I couldn't tell you..."

"While they're about it, I wish they could take him back to Montretout... But it's too far now... if they take him to Beauvais... Is that where the funeral will be?... I'd have liked to have services... I'll ask them... Do you think they'll be willing?..." That was something else I didn't know...

"I wonder what a little service would cost in Beauvais... only in a chapel... the cheapest class for instance... It can't cost more than anywhere else... He wasn't religious, you know, but even so... They've tortured him enough. A little respect wouldn't hurt... What are they going to do to him now?... Can't they see well enough as it is?... He hasn't anything in his body, the poor man... It's all in his head, isn't it?... Anybody can see that... Oh, it's so awful!..." She started wailing again.

"Ah, Ferdinand, my little friend... When I think that they could think such a thing... Oh well, while they were at it, they couldn't use kid gloves, could they?... Oh, it's all the same to me... now... But what about you?... Do you think it's finished?... With you it's not the same... You've got to make your way... you've got your whole life ahead of you... It's not the same... You had nothing to do with all this... Goodness, no... They ought to leave you alone... Are you coming to Beauvais with me?..."

"I'd go... if I could... But I can't. There's nothing for me to do in Beauvais... Remember what the Lisp said... 'You'll go back to your parents.' He said it twice..."

"Well, in that case no monkey business... Go, my boy, go. What'll you do when you get there?... Look around for something?..."

"Naturally..."

"I'll have to look too... that is... if they let me go... Ah, Ferdinand... while it's on my mind..." She had an inspiration... "Come over here... I want to show you something..." She takes me to the kitchen... She climbs up on the stepladder... the little one... she disappears up the chimney to the waist, she pokes around in one of the niches... She dislodges the big brick... A lot of soot comes down... She shakes another stone, it moves, it jiggles... she takes it out... From the hole she takes some bills... and even some change... I hadn't known about that hiding place... And Courtial hadn't either, that was a safe bet... There were a hundred and fifty smackers and a few five-franc pieces... Right away she gives me a fifty-franc bill... She kept the rest...

"I'll take the hundred francs and the change... All right?... That'll cover my trip at least... and maybe my expenses at the church... if I'm there five, six days... It can't take any longer than that, can it?... that'll be plenty, don't you think?... But what about you? You've still got your addresses?... Do you remember all your bosses?..."

"I'll go see the printer right away," I said. "I'd rather start in that direction..."

She rummaged in the hole some more, she took out another twenty-franc piece, she gave it to me... Then she talked some more about Courtial... but she wasn't so excited anymore...

"Ah, my little Ferdinand, you know... The more I think of it... the more it comes back to me... how fond he was of you... He didn't show it, that's a fact... You know that too... It wasn't his way... his nature... he wasn't demonstrative... he wasn't a flatterer... You know that... But he was always thinking of you... In the worst situations he often told me so... Only a week ago... 'You know, Irène, Ferdinand is somebody I've got faith in... He'll never do us dirt... He's young... He's scatterbrained... But there's a kid that's as good as his word... He'll keep a promise... And that, Irène, that's rare...' I can still hear him saying that... Ah, he appreciated you all right... He was sincerer than a friend... Take it from me . . , And the poor man, believe me, he had plenty to be distrustful about... He'd seen a thing or two... and how he'd been deceived... In thousands of ways, one more disgraceful than the last... He could have been embittered... Never did he say an unfavorable word about you... Never the least unpleasantness... Nothing but compliments... He'd have liked to spoil you... But as he said one time when we were having a little chat... 'Wait just a little while... Patience... I'll make that kid's fortune yet...' Ah, how well he understood you... You can't imagine how fond he was of you..."

"Me too, madame, me too..."

"I know, Ferdinand, I know... But with you it's not the same... Youre still a kid luckily... Nothing is so sad at your age... Now you'll be starting out in life... You're only beginning... You can't understand..."

"He loved you too." I said... "He often told me... how terribly fond he was of you... that he couldn't do without you... without you he didn't exist... 'Take my wife,' he'd say..." I laid it on pretty thick... I was trying to console her... I did my best... So then she gushes like a fountain...

"Don't cry, madame! Don't cry... This is no time... You've got to harden yourself... You're not through yet... You'll have to talk... when you get to Beauvais... maybe you'll have to defend yourself! It gets on their nerves when you cry... You've noticed... I'll have to look out for myself too. You said so yourself..."

"Yes, you're right, Ferdinand... Boo hoo! You're right... I'm stupid... I'm nothing but an old crazy-woman..." She tried to control herself... she wiped her eyes...

"But he was really fond of you... Ah, believe me, Ferdinand... I'm not saying it to flatter you... You knew that, didn't you?... He knew what a good heart you had deep down... even if he was hard sometimes... even if he was a little hard on us..."

"Oh yes! I knew, madame..."

"And now that he's killed himself... It's so awful! Can you imagine?... I can't believe it... It's incredible..." She couldn't tear herself away from the terrible thought...

"Ferdinand," she started up again... "Ferdinand, listen..." She tried to find the exact right words... they wouldn't come... "Ah, yes... He trusted you, Ferdinand... and I trust you... And you know... he didn't believe in anybody anymore..."

Our wood wasn't burning at all... It smoked up the whole room _... It popped, it flew up in the air... it was going out... I tell the old lady... "I'm going to get some more that'll burn." I start for the barn... maybe I'd find a dry faggot... I could rip out a piece of the wall... the inside wall... I start across the yard... I turn to one side to pass around the well, I look across the plain... I see something moving... looked like a man!... "It can't be the gendarme," I says to myself... "He wouldn't be back so soon... It's some tramp... Some guy prowling around... Well," I say, "if he's looking for trouble... Hey," I shouted, "hey there... What are you looking for around here?" He doesn't answer... He disappears... So right there I turned back, I didn't even go so far as the barn... I had a feeling something fishy was going on. "Hell and damnation!" I says to myself. "Beat it, kid..." Quick I tear off a hunk of fence... "That'll do," I says to myself... I run over... I go in... I ask the old bag:

"You haven't seen anybody?" "No," she says... "No."

At that very moment, in the windowpane, not two yards away... I see a face staring at me... a great big face... I see the hat too... through the glass... and the lips moving... But I can't hear the words... I move up with the candle, I throw the window wide open... That was brave of me!... I recognize him right away... Christ, if it isn't our canon... Fleury!... It's him all right

... the nut! Him and nobody else... Shit!... How'd he get here? Where on earth did he come from? He starts spluttering... He sprays me with spit... He gesticulates like mad... He seems beside himself with joy to have found us... his friends!... his brothers!... He steps through the little window... There he is inside... He's jubilant... He prances... He wiggle-waggles all around the table... The old lady didn't remember his phizz, or his name, or the circumstances... A little lapse of memory...

"It's Fleury... Look, it's Fleury!... The one with the diving bell? Don't you remember? Take a good look..."

"Ah, my goodness, it's true!... Why, yes, yes, it's him... Oh, Father!... oh, forgive me... Ah! So you've heard? Ah, why of course it's you... Oh, I'm going out of my mind! Ah, I didn't recognize you... You haven't heard the awful thing?"

It took more than that to stop him... He kept on prancing... hopping... skipping... He didn't pay attention... He did a big leap and then some little jumps... he jerked backward... He jumped up on the table... He wiggled around some more... He jumped down, bam!... His cassock was all caked and armored with muck and cowflop... up to the armpits... up to the ears... Sure, it was him I'd seen out in the field just now... We'd both scared each other... My, was he harnessed!... Some load he had on his back... A whole soldier's outfit... two musette bags! two canteens! three mess kits! and on top a hunting horn... an enormous magnificent thing, slung over his shoulder... The whole business clanked every time he moved... and he never stopped moving... What bothered him most was his hat... it slid down over his eyes... a big straw affair like a fisherman... And the guy had decorated himself too... admirably... his whole soutane was full of orders and medals... and several Legions of Honor... They were all caked with muck, and a big heavy crucifix, an ivory Jesus, dangling on a long chain... He was so wet, this fine canon of ours, he dripped all over the room... He was a walking watering can... His soutane was ripped from top to bottom in back... You could still see the briars...

The old lady tried to make him stop moving... She wanted to convince him... She just had to!... I motioned her not to work him up... maybe he'd leave of his own accord... no use getting him excited... But she didn't want to understand... She was glad to see him again. She crowded him into corners... which made him growl like a wild animal... He backed plunk against the wall with his head down, ready to charge... He didn't listen to her... He pressed his fingers to his mouth... "Sh-sh" he went... He darted looks in all directions, and they weren't very friendly... This bozo was on the lam...

"Didn't you know, Monsieur le Chanoine?... I see you don't know... Oh, if you could only have seen... Oh, if you knew what's happened!..."

"Hush, hush!... Monsieur des Pereires!" Now he was asking for him... "Where is he? Where's Monsieur des Pereires?..." He grabbed her by the shoulders, he snorted into her face... A tic convulsed his whole mouth... It stayed twisted... Then in little spasms he relaxed...

"I haven't got him, Father... Oh no... I haven't got him!... You really don't know?... The poor man's not here... He's gone, poor soul... Come, come... Didn't they tell you?..."

"Hurry!... Hurry!" He shook her violently.

"But gracious, he's dead... He's passed away... Haven't I told you?..." She'd met up with somebody that was even more pigheaded than she was...

"I want to see him... I've got to see him..." He had this obsession and he wouldn't let go

... "It's urgent!... Sh-sh... Sh! Hurry, hurry..." He tiptoed around the table... He looked on top and underneath, he looked up the chimney... He opened both cupboards... He tore out the keys

... He battered the wood box... he broke off the hinges... He was frantic... He couldn't stand being crossed... His tic made his whole lip curl...

"Father!... Father!... Don't do that!..." She kept trying to convince him...

"Ferdinand! I implore you! Tell Father Fleury... Isn't he dead, boy?... Tell him!..." She latched on to his musette bag...

"Go look on the door, it's written there... Tell him if it's not true, Ferdinand... 'Good luck'..." She grabbed him by the hunting horn... He dragged the whole place after him... The old bag, the table, the chairs, the dishes...

"Enough! Enough of your insolence!... You're insolent whelps, the whole lot of you!... I want the director!... *Genitron* Courtial!... Can't you hear me?... Him and nobody else!... Heavens! He's expecting me!... He wants to see me immediately!... We have an appointment!... an appointment!..." He threw her off in his rage... She went careening into the wall... "Enough! Enough! I want to talk to him!... You can't stop me... Who's going to stop me?..." He hiked up his soutane... He rummaged through his pockets... He took out little scraps of paper... crumbs, newspaper clippings... He stayed like that on his knees in feverish confusion for a long time... He spluttered, he counted the papers one by one... he smoothed them out... he flattened them... He rolled some of them into little spitballs...

"Hush! Hush!" he started in again. He didn't want us to move. "There it is... It's authentic! What? Haven't you any eyes in your head?... It's a genuine Pharaoh manuscript!... This here!..." He hands me a pinch of it...

"There you are, my boy..." He pressed a spitball... two spitballs... into the hollow of my hand... "The director! The director!..."

Hell, there he goes again... his fury was mounting... He reared up... he jumped back on the table... he shouted for Courtial at the top of his lungs... He put the hunting horn to his lips... He blew one big blast and several raucous farts... and then a few squeaks and short hiccups...

"He's coming... He hears me..." Ten times, twenty times in succession... He grabs me by the coat, he slobbers in my face, he blows in my eyes... Christ, does he stink!... In gusts he tells me how he'd got there... He'd got off at Vry-Controvert, the whistle-stop on the narrow-gauge line, twelve miles from Blême... "They" were after him... He pesters the life out of me, trying to prove it...

"Hush, hush," he says again... "The Powers!... Yes indeed!" He goes back to the window... He looks out to see if they're coming... He hides behind the shutter, growling... He bounces out again... He scans the approaches... He pisses in the fireplace... He doesn't button his pants... He comes back to the blind... He must have seen the Powers... He mulls... He grunts like a wild boar...

"Grrr! Grrr!" he goes... "Never!... Grrr! Grrr!... Never!..." He turns on me... He shakes his fists in my face... He's certainly changed since the Palais-Royal!... How ferocious he's gotten to be!... They must have given him scorpions to eat... in the nuthouse... Hell! He's wild!... He's been drinking vitriol!... He never stops!... He lunges in all directions... He bangs into the walls... He threatens... he challenges... The old lady and I have given up trying to say anything... We're licked... That loony padre is beginning to give me a pain... I wouldn't mind laying him out with a clout from behind... I catch sight of a nifty pole beside the window... We use it as a poker... with a big long tip and a nice cast-iron handle... That would settle his hash... We'd have another crime on our hands... I motion the old lady to get out of the way... just for a second... to stand against the wall... Shit!... If only he'd shut up... so I wouldn't have to lay hands on him... Christ, what a rotten cocksucker!... What an ugly stupid bastard! Why can't the stinker pipe down?... Why can't the screwball leave us alone?... He won't believe us... He thinks we're hiding him... Hell, this is infernal... I tell the old lady:

"It can't be helped... This has gone too far! I'm fed up... I'm going to show him..." "Don't, Ferdinand!... Don't do it... I beg you..."

"Oh yes, I will... Maybe that'll straighten him out... Maybe he'll understand... The damn fool has this bee in his bonnet... He's screwy... he's bats... Then we'll throw him out..." He was still thrashing around, knocking into everything... He lifted up the whole table... and take it from me, that table was a monument... That Hottentot was strong!...

"The director! The director!" he started bellowing again... "I've given all I had..." He went down on his knees again, he kissed his crucifix... He crossed himself a thousand times... He stayed there in an ecstasy... his arms stretched out on both sides... He made a crucifix of himself... And then up like a spring... And off again on tiptoes... his eyes fixed on the ceiling... He started up again with the applesauce...

She tugged at me, she didn't want me to show him the stiff in the kitchen... She made motions... "No, no!" This malarky had been going on long enough... I had it up to here...

"Come this way..." I grabbed him by the hunting horn... and bam... I dragged him to the kitchen... Ah, the stinker... he won't believe us... Well, he's going to get an eyeful... All nuts are the same... They thrive on opposition... "Let's go! Come on, you lug!" I give him a kick in the ass... That makes him bounce... It's his turn to say uncle... I can get mean too... He gripes... he grumbles... I push him down the hallway...

"Upsy-daisy!... Take the candle, madame, take two... Let him have a good look... an eyeful... We don't want him coming back for seconds..." When we get to the kitchen, I go down on my knees... and a little lower... I show him the body in the balloon cover right under his nose... It's right there in front of him... I put the other candle down beside it...

"There you are... can you see all right?... What do you say now, you dumb cluck?... You going to stop wasting our time?... Is it him all right?... You recognize him?... You don't?..." He comes close... he sniffs... he's suspicious... He blows all up and down the legs... He lowers his head... He says a prayer... He goes on and on... Then he turns around... He looks at me some more... He starts praying again...

"Well? Did you get a good look?... D'you finally catch on. you jerk?... You going to behave?... You going to beat it like a good boy?... You going to shove off and take your train?..." But he kept right on grunting and sniffing at the corpse... So I grab him by the arm... I try to take him away... I try to make him get up... He goes into one of his tantrums... He gives me a terrible poke with his elbow... right square in the knee... Ah, the bum! Say, that hurts... I see stars... For two cents I'd have brained him then and there... the crazy bastard... I'd have wiped him out... The old lady kept at it though... She appealed to his kind heart... to his good intentions... She tried to smooth him down...

"You see, Father, you can see he's dead... You're making all of us miserable... That's all you're doing... He's gone, poor man... The gendarme forbade us... He told us not to let anybody in... We promised him! You're going to get us in trouble... both of us, Ferdinand and me... What good will that do?... You wouldn't want that, would you?..."

At this point I says to myself: "Balls! If he won't believe us, I'll show him the head... If he thinks we're hiding him... And then I'll throw him out quick..." So I lift up a corner of the cover... I bring the candle still closer... I show him the whole mulligatawny... "Take a good look!..." so he can really see what's what... He kneels down for a close-up... I try again:

"OK, you old souse? You coming?..." I tug at him... He doesn't want to move... He's adamant... He doesn't want to leave... He sniffs full in the meat... "Hm! Hm!" He starts howling! He works himself up... He throws another fit... His whole body is shaking... I try to cover the head up again... "That'll do!..." But he pulls at the canvas... He's in a frenzy... stark raving mad!... He won't let me cover him... He sticks his fingers into the wound... He plunges both hands into the meat... he digs into all the holes... He tears away the soft edges... He pokes around... He gets stuck... His wrist is caught in the bones... Crack!... He tugs... He struggles like in a trap... Some kind of pouch bursts... The juice pours out... it gushes all over the place... all full of brains and blood... splashing... He manages to get his hand out... I get the sauce full in the face... I can't see a thing... I flail around... The candle's out... He's still yelling... I've got to stop him!.... I can't see him... I lose my head... I lunge at him... by dead reckoning... I hit him square... The stinker goes over... he crashes against the wall... smash! boom!... I've got my momentum... I'm coming after him... but I straighten out... I brake, I get away from him... I'm very careful... Hell!... I don't want him conking out on account of me... I wipe my eyes... I keep my presence of mind... I try to get him up... I don't want him lying on the floor... I give him a good kick in the ribs... He lifts up a little... That's better!... I give him a good smack in the puss... That gets him all the way up... the old lady empties a whole basin of water... it was plenty cold... over his dome... He starts sighing and whimpering again... Isn't that lovely!... But then he folds up all in a piece... The rotten stinker!... Bam!... He collapses... He quivers like a rabbit... then he stops moving completely... The louse!... He can't take it... I give a look out the door... Then the two of us tote him out to the side of the road... We didn't want to have him around and get blamed for him too... Hell no!... Have the cop find him in the house... out like a light... completely at our mercy!... Wouldn't that be sweet!... We'd be cooked to a crisp!... They mustn't even know we've had him in the house... What people don't know won't hurt 'em... We're no suckers... OK... out with him... hurrah for the fresh air... unconscious or not!... He started grunting a little after all... He sniffed around in the muck... The rain was coming down in buckets... We ran back in... We bolted the door... The wind was coming in blasts... I says to the old lady:

"We're not going to move... even if he calls... We don't hear a thing... When the cop comes back, we play it dumb... We haven't seen a damn thing... If he bumps into him, that's his business..." OK. She caught on... So that was that...

Maybe an hour goes by... Maybe a little more... I fix up the kitchen... The old lady keeps a watch at the window...

"Don't look over here, madame!... Don't turn around... Don't worry about the housecleaning... Watch what's going on outside..." I stretch out the corpse... I tidy up the straw... Rivers of blood were coming through the canvas... I get a little more hay... I scatter it around... I mop up the puddles as best I can... I put some fresh straw under the head... a good thickness like a pillow... But the hardest part was the splashes... There were spots all the way up to the ceiling... And whole blood clots sticking to the wall... It really looked lousy... I tried to rinse it all off... I ran the sponge over it again... But the marks got worse each time... Hell, I couldn't stay there all night... I take the candles... I leave the room... We wait next door, the old lady and me... Boy, the jitters I had!... It was terrible... They kept coming back at me... Suppose this cop should notice?... Suppose he got wind of that brawl!... What a mess!... How were we going to wriggle out of that one?... Especially if he found the sky pilot out cold on the road... New evidence!... Hell!... The lousy cop didn't come and he didn't come... He must have screwed his sister-in-law for dessert... Some nerve!... We lay down on the ground... We'd thrown down some hay too... I didn't talk... I was thinking... The night would never be over... I could never have fallen asleep in the state I was in... I don't think I'd ever been so scared... Suddenly I hear a fanfare... Christ almighty Jesus!... There we go!... It's the hunting horn!... And it came from the plain... from nearby! I says to myself: "It's him!... Oh, the louse!" I recognized every squeak. He starts up again, an encore!... Oh. the stinker!... Oh, the rotten skunk!... He drowned out the wind... he drowned out the roar of the gale with his raucous trumpet... Christ! Enough was enough! He blew with all his heart and soul!... Some porpoise he turned out to be!... Imagine a priest being such a whack!... Christ, what a racket! Oh, that bum! That dirty dog! That pain in the ass!... I made up my mind... But then hell's bells, no! Better he should be gargling, horrible as it was... It showed he'd recovered... He seemed to be happy... It proved he hadn't conked out... Lord, what a monster! "Bellow away, queen of the cows!" And there he goes again with his damn trombone! His wind was doing fine... Not a thing wrong with him!... Tally-ho! Tally-ho! Oh, my bleeding ass! Ta-ta-ta, he's sure giving us our money's worth!... It was better than kicking off though... Hell, you got to admit that! But those belches, that brass bellyache was horrible all the same... The master of the hunt was making some pest of himself out there with his sewer pipe... He never stopped... He'd subside for half a second and right away he'd start up again... Louder and louder... Oh, you couldn't go wrong... It was our screwball all right... His concert went on until half past six at least... The day was breaking when somebody tapped on the window... It was our cop!... He'd just got back... in the nick of time... He'd slept in Blême, supposedly... in with his horse, so he said... He couldn't get him shod in Tousnes... it had been too late... he hadn't found the blacksmith's place...

"Say, who was playing the horn around here all night?..." he asked us right away... "You didn't hear anything?..."

"No!" we said. "The horn?... Oh no... Certainly not, we didn't hear a thing." "That's funny... The old folks told me..."

He went and opened the window... The priest was right out in front... He jumped in like a goat... He'd been waiting for the chance... He flopped down on his knees in the middle of the room... He started in "Our Father which art in heaven... Thy Kingdom come!..." He said it again... He kept repeating it like a phonograph... He hammered his ribs with both fists... He was trembling all over... He bounced around on his shins... He took a lot of punishment... He didn't stop for a second... He grimaced with pain... he was playing the martyr... "Thy Kingdom come!..." he shouted at the top of his lungs... "Thy Kingdom come!..."

"Say, what is this?... Say. what is this?" The gendarme hadn't ever seen such a number, he was flummoxed... "Ah, it's a party!..." He didn't know what to think... It threw him for several loops... The old lady was busy in the kitchen, she was heating up coffee for us... It didn't seem like the right time... Our supplicant St. Anthony broke off his prayers when he saw the mud coming in... He made a dive for a cup... He tried to drink out of all the bowls... He was very active! He sucked the spout of the coffeepot... He burned his mouth... He puffed like a locomotive... The cop was in stitches... "My goodness, the man must be crazy... Why, he's not normal!... that's a sure thing... Not that I give a damn... It's no skin off my ass... Nuts aren't in my line of duty... They're no business of mine... That's for the Public Welfare department… But I don't think he's a priest... He don't look it... Wherc'd he come from?... Escaped from the nuthouse?... Or maybe he's been to a ball?... Isn't he drunk?... Maybe it's a disguise... Anyway, it's not my line... But supposing he's a deserter!... That would be my line... I'd have to look into it... But hell, he's overage... Say, Pop, how old are you?... You won't tell me?..."

The shady character didn't say a word... He was draining the bottoms of the cups...

"Say, isn't he clever? He can even drink with his nose! Hey, Pop... Say, ain't that horn pretty?... Say, that's a handsome instrument... Say, I wonder where he came from..."

Later that morning a whole army of sightseers descended on our village... I wondered where they could all have come from... In that deserted region it was really a mystery... From Persant? There'd never been so many people there... or in Mesloirs either... So they came from much farther... from other counties... other districts... The crowd was so dense they overflowed onto our garden... They were packed so tight the road wouldn't hold them all... They stamped through the fields, both embankments caved in under the weight of the populace... They wanted to see everything at once... they wanted to know everything and knock everything over... The rain was splashing down... That didn't bother them in the least... They hung around, all plastered with cowflop... In the end they invaded our yard... They gave off a raucous rumble…

In the front row, right against our windows, there was a whole slew of grandmothers... What a sight! They fastened on to the shutters, there were maybe at least fifty of them... They croaked louder than anybody else... They fought among themselves with umbrellas...

At last the promised ambulance turned up... It was the very first time they'd risked it out of town... The driver tipped us off... The big hospital in Beauvais had just acquired it... Some breakdowns he'd had... Three punctures in a row... two leaks in the gas line... Now he'd have to hurry to be back before nightfall... We slipped out the stretcher, each of us took a shaft... There wasn't a second to be lost... The driver had another worry too... that his motor would stall... He couldn't stop... not for a minute!... not for a second!... He had to keep it running even when the car was standing still... But that was dangerous too on account of the little flames that shot out when it backfired... We went in for Courtial... The mob rushed the doorways... They pushed so hard... they blocked the arch and the little hallway so thoroughly that even clouting them, even charging them with the cop, it was like going through a rolling mill... We came back quick with the stretcher, we slipped the shafts into the grooves made specially for the purpose... it went all the way back... it fitted perfectly... We drew the big curtains... black oilcloth... That was that... The peasants stopped talking... They took off their caps... The women... young ones, old ones... crossed themselves like mad... standing ankle-deep in the mud... The rain came down in buckets... They mumbled all their prayers... Lord, was it raining!... The ambulance driver climbed up on his seat... He retarded the spark... Pip! Pop! Tap! Pip! Pop! Tap! Pip! Pip! Terrible hiccups... The engine was wet... It snorted from every cylinder... Finally it makes up its mind... It gives a jerk... another... He throws in the clutch… It moves a little way... When Canon Fleury sees the shebang leaving, he lights out... He does a hundred-yard dash... He bounds into the air... He jumps on the mudguard... We had to run after him and pull him off by main force! He fought like a lion... We locked him up in the barn. So far so good... But once the motor had stalled, it didn't want to start again... We all had to push it up the hill... to give it momentum... Then the new ambulance clanks down the slope, coughing and jerking and spluttering… almost two miles... Some sport!... We went back to the farm... We sat down in the kitchen... We waited a while for the people to get bored and clear out... There was nothing more to see, that was a cinch... but they didn't budge... The ones without umbrellas settled down in the yard... in the middle shed... they'd brought their lunch. We closed our shutters.

We looked through our stuff, the little we had left, to see if there was anything wearable we could take with us... frankly there wasn't much... The old lady found a shawl... Naturally she still had her pants on, she always dressed like the rest of us. She hadn't a skirt to her name... As for food, there was still a bit of rind in the pickling jar... enough to make a meal for the mutt... We were taking him with us to the station... We fed him. Luckily I found a little corduroy jacket in the back of the closet... a gamekeeper's rig with horn buttons... The kids had swiped it... They hadn't told anybody...

Plus my overcoat it would help to keep me warm... I still had my bicycling pants... The underwear department was nonexistent... not even a shirt!... When it came to shoes... mine were still holding out, I'd split them open some because they were too narrow... and patched them up with sandals underneath... that made them flexible but cold... The old lady had slippers stuffed into rubbers... she'd have trouble lasting out the trip... They kept all the water in... She bundled them up in old newspapers and string... to make them like real boots, so her feet wouldn't rattle around inside... Persant was pretty far... And Beauvais was still farther... There was no hope of getting a ride... We ran a little more coffee through the grounds... Then we got together with the cop... He was going to escort us... He was holding his plug by the bridle that still hadn't been shod... The priest wanted to come too... I'd rather have ditched him... locked him in behind us... But he made a terrible racket the minute he thought he was alone... So that was no solution... Suppose we left him locked up in the house... and he wrecked the joint... Suppose that screwball escaped and climbed up on the roof... And suppose he fell off and broke two or three limbs... Well, who'd be on the spot?... Who'd they accuse?... Us again naturally... Who'd get thrown in the clink?... We would, beyond any shadow of a doubt... So I went and opened the door for him... He threw himself into my arms... He loved me madly... But we couldn't find the mutt... We wasted at least an hour looking for him... in the shed, in the barn... That fleabite wasn't anywhere... Finally he showed... We were ready to go...

All those hayseeds waiting outside didn't say a thing when we left... They didn't say boo... Not a word... We passed right under their noses... The ditches were full of them... Hicks and more hicks... So we shot off down the road... Shot isn't exactly the word... we walked pretty gingerly... Only the lunatic ran... He gamboled about, this way and that way... The padre was curious about our itinerary... "Will we see Charlemagne?" he asked us in a loud voice... He didn't understand a word of our answers, but he didn't want to leave us... Shaking him was hopeless... Hiking set him up... He put his hunting horn to his lips... he blew a little tally-ho... And just as we were getting into town, he raced back and joined the main body... He ran like a zebra... We came to the first houses... on the way into Persant... with the music going strong... The gendarme turned off to the left... that was the end of his assignment... We could shift for ourselves... He wasn't keen on our company... he wasn't going out way... We headed for the station... Right away we asked about the trains... The old lady's train for Beauvais was leaving in ten minutes... an hour before the one to Paris... She'd have to cross over to the other platform... It was time to say good-bye... We didn't say anything much... We didn't make any promises... We kissed each other...

"My goodness, Ferdinand, you're prickly..." She meant my beard. That was a joke!... She was being brave... That was pretty good in such a rotten situation... She didn't know where she was going... Neither did I for that matter... We'd been sharing the bad luck for a long time now... This time it had really laid us out... That was pretty well to be expected... There wasn't much more to say...

In the station the padre was kind of scared right away... He shriveled up in a corner... Only he kept his eyes fastened on me... He just stared at me on the platform... The people around us wondered what on earth we were up to... Especially him and his horn... the old bag in her pants... me and my coat done up with strings... They were afraid to come too close... Then the dame at the tobacco counter looked out and recognized us... "It's the nuts from Blême," she sang out... They kind of panicked... The Beauvais train pulled in... luckily... It made for a diversion... The old honeybun hightailed it... she climbed in on the wrong side... She stood in the doorway with Dudule's little mutt... She waved me good-bye... I waved back... As the train was pulling out, the distress came over her... something awful... She made terrible faces in the window... She went rrrah! rrrah! like her throat was being cut... like some kind of animal...

"Ferdinand! Ferdinand!" she hollered across the tracks... over all the racket... The train beat it into the tunnel... We never saw each other again... the old lady and I... I found out much later that she'd died in Salonika, they told me in the Val-de-Grâce military hospital in 1916. She'd gone out there as a nurse on a troop transport. She died of some kind of epidemic, I think it was exanthematic typhus. So the two of us, the canon and I, were on the other platform, the Paris- bound side. He still had no idea what we were there for... But at least he'd stopped playing his horn... He was only scared I'd leave him in the lurch... As soon as the train pulled in, he jumped in too, right behind me... He stuck to me all the way to Paris... I lost him for a second on the way out of the station... The bastard caught me right away... I lost him again on the rue Lafayette... right across from the drugstore... I took advantage of the crush... I jumped into a trolley in between all the traffic... I got out again a little later... on the Boulevard Magenta... I wanted to be alone for a while... to think and figure out what I was going to do...

My rig was mighty weird... hardly presentable in a city... The people stared at me curiously... the shops and offices were just closing... It must have been a little after seven... I was quite a sensation with my abbreviated raglan... I hid in a doorway... The hardest to take was my overcoat... all bloused out in my pants... it gave me an amazing shape!... And I couldn't change there... Besides, I didn't have a hat either... I had Dudule's little one, a patent- leather Jean-Bart hat.[119] I'd worn it out there... Here it wouldn't do... I chucked it behind the door... There were still too many people for me to venture out on the sidewalk in my fancy dress… I thought I'd wait for the crowd to thin out... I watched the street go by... What struck me first was the new-type buses without an upper story, and the new motor taxies... There were more of them than hansom cabs... They made a terrible ruckus... I wasn't used to heavy traffic anymore... It made my head spin... I was kind of sick to my stomach too. I bought a croissant and a bar of chocolate... It was time to eat... I put them in my pocket... The air always seems muggy when you get back from the country... It's the wind you miss... And then I began to wonder if I'd go home to the Passage... And would I go directly?... Supposing the bulls came looking for me?... Maybe the Lisp would send them...

Farther up the Boulevard Magenta I ran into the rue Lafayette... If I took it, it wouldn't be very complicated... rue Richelieu, the Stock Exchange... I only had to follow the lights... Oh, I knew the way all right... But if I turned right, I'd end up at the Châtelet, the bird vendors... the Quai aux Fleurs, the Odéon... That would take me toward my uncle's... Finding a bed someplace wasn't the worst part... I could make up my mind at the last moment... But what about landing a job?... That would be rough... How was I going to get a new outfit?... I could hear the music already... And whom would I go to see?... I came out of my hiding place... But instead of taking the Boulevard, I turned into a little side street... I stop outside a shopwindow… I'm looking at a hard-boiled egg... it's all red... I says to myself: "I'll buy it..." I count my money in the light... I still had more than thirty-five francs and I'd paid for my railroad ticket and the padre's too... I peel the egg on the counter, I bite into it... I spit it out... I couldn't swallow anything... Hell, it wouldn't go down... Christ, I says to myself, I'm sick... I was seasick... I go out in the street... Everything was swaying... the sidewalk... the gas lamps... the shops... And I must have been teetering myself... A cop's heading my way... I speed up some... I cross the street... I hide in another doorway... I didn't feel like moving anymore... I sit down on the door-mat... I'm feeling a little better... I says to myself: "What's the matter, kid?... You can't be as lazy as all that?... Haven't you got the strength to move?..." And still sick to my stomach... The street put me in a panic... seeing it up ahead of me... on the sides... on the right and left... All those housefronts, so closed, so black. Nuts! so uninviting... it was even worse than Blême... not even a turnip to nibble on... I had the heebiejeebies all over... especially in my stomach... and my head. I wanted to vomit... Damn! I couldn't move at all! I was stuck to the house-front... With my back to the wall like that... no kidding... I had a good chance to remember... how the poor old lady had knocked herself out keeping us all body and soul together... You can hardly imagine... Hell, now I was all alone... Honorine was gone... Balls!... She was a good old battle-ax... she had guts... she'd really struggled for us... We were all fucked now... I was sure I'd never see her again... Positive... It hit me all of a sudden… it made me feel awful... I was sick to my stomach again... I found another doormat... I threw up in the gutter... The passersby were noticing... I had to beat it... Anyway I had to move on...

---

[119] Jean-Bart hat. A hat with a wide turned-up brim, formerly worn by children. In his best-known portraits Jean Bart (1651-1702), the famous privateer, is not wearing anything of the kind. "Hefty" *(Gros-Frère)*, slang for cuirassier.

I stopped again at the end of the rue Saint-Denis... I couldn't go any further, I found a niche where I couldn't be seen at all... I felt better once I was sitting down... it was walking that turned my stomach... When I began to feel dizzy, I looked up in the air... It relieved my nausea to look up... The sky was very clear... I think I've never seen it so plainly... I was astonished that evening to see it so cloudless... I recognized all the stars... Well, pretty near all of them... I knew all the names... The old clown had pestered me enough with his trajectory orbits... Funny how I'd remembered them... I hadn't made much of an effort, I've got to admit. Caniope and Andromeda... they were right there on the rue Saint-Denis... right over the roof across the street... A little further right the Waggoner, that kind of blinks in the direction of Libra... I knew them all right... It's a little harder to get Ophiuchus straight... You could easily mistake it for Mercury except for the asteroid... That's a neat trick... But you pretty near always get the Cradle and Berenice mixed up... Pelleas is a hard one to pick out... That night you couldn't miss it... That was Pelleas to a T... north of Bacchus... a nearsighted ape could have found it... Even the "great nebula of Orion" was clear as day... between the Triangle and Ariadne... You couldn't go wrong... A unique, exceptional opportunity... in Blême we'd only seen Orion once all year... And we'd looked for it every night... Kid Spyglass would have been mighty glad of the chance to observe it so distinctly... he was always going on about it... He'd published a guide about the "Asteroidal References"... there was even a whole chapter about the nebula of Antiope... It was really a surprise to be seeing it in Paris... where the sky is famous for being so smutty and opaque... I could hear Courtial raving about it... I could hear him gassing away beside me on a bench...

"You see, my boy, the one that trembles?... that's not even a planet... it's a fake... It's not even a point of reference, not even an asteroid... It's nothing but a vagabond... see what I mean?... So watch your step... A vagabond... Wait another two million years, maybe then it will give off a profuse light... Maybe then you'll be able to get a picture... Right now it's a phony and you'll ruin your whole plate... That's all the good it'll do you... And those vaporids are deceptive, my boy... It's not even a periodic comet... Don't let them fool you, Antonio... The stars are a lot of floozies... Look before you leap!... They're no little white elves... Watch your dynameter... A quarter of a second's exposure!... A quarter tenth and your film is shot! Oh, they're fierce... they're incorrigible... Watch your step, Lolita... They don't give plates away at the Flea Market... Not by a long shot, my dear bishop..." I could hear all the old blarney... "Once you've looked at a thing, you ought to remember it forever... Don't force your intelligence... it's reason that gums everything up... Give your instinct a chance... Once it gets a good look, the game is won... It'll never deceive you..." My reason had taken a powder... all I had left was blotting paper in my legs... I kept on walking though... And then I found another bench... I crumpled against the back... It wasn't exactly warm anymore... it seemed to me that the old boy was there on the other end, turning his back to me. I was seeing things... I shot the shit in his place... his exact own words... I wanted to hear him talk... to remember everything he'd said... He was in front of me on the pavement... "Ferdinand! Ferdinand! Ingenuity is man!... Don't waste yourself on low thoughts..." He told me all his fairy tales, and I remembered them all together... I was talking out loud... The people stopped to listen... They must have thought I was drunk... So then I shut my trap... But it stirred me up just the same... my dome was all full of it... Those memories really had a hold on me... I couldn't believe the old clothespin was dead... And yet I could see him with his head all marmalade... the meat still twitching... and messing all over the road... Hell! And the farm at the bottom of the hill!... and that Arton bitch and her kid!... and the trowel!... and the wheelbarrow!... and me and the old lady wheeling him down the road... Ah, the bastard! He wouldn't let go! He went bouncing through my memory... I thought of all those things... the Insurrection bar... Formerly... the *commissaire* on the rue des Bon-Enfants... his cock-eyed rays... And all those putrid potatoes... Ah, it was stinking when you think of it... the way that bastard lied to us... And now he was starting in again... He was right there in front of me... next to the bench... His meat smell was there... My nose was full of it... That's the presence of death for you... when you do their talking for them... All of a sudden I stood up... I couldn't stand it... I was going to let out one terrible yell... and get myself pinched good and proper... I lifted up my eyes... so as not to see the housefronts... They made me too sad... I saw his face too much on the walls... behind all the windowpanes... in the darkness... Up there Orion-tes had disappeared... I'd lost my landmark in the clouds... But I managed to find Andromeda... I kept looking... I looked for Caniope... the one that blinks at the Dipper... Naturally I got dizzy... I started walking again anyway...

I went down the Grands Boulevards... I came back to the Porte Saint-Martin... I was dead on my feet... I was zigzagging... I knew it myself... I was scared pink of the cops... They thought I was tight too... In front of the clock at the Nègre I went "pst, pst" to a cab... He took me in...

"To Uncle Édouard's," I said. "Uncle Édouard? Where's that?"

"Rue de la Convention... 14..." I was bound to get picked up if I kept wandering around like that... feeling so rotten dizzy... It was getting awfully risky... If the cops had questioned me... I was all mixed up in the first place... I'd never know what to say... The ride in the cab did me good... It really picked me up a little... Uncle Édouard was home... He didn't seem very surprised... He was glad to see me... I sit down at his table... I take off my coat... I only had the little corduroy jacket under it...

"That's some rig!" he remarked... He asked me if I'd had dinner. "No, I'm not hungry," I said. "So you've lost your appetite?"

He went right on talking... He told me all about himself... He had his troubles... He'd just come back from Belgium, he'd been in a terrible mess... He'd finally unloaded his little "extra- collapsible" pump on a manufacturing combine... the terms weren't so hot... He was damn sick of lawsuits and claims... in connection with the "multiple" and "reversible" patents... He was fed up... He didn't go for lawyers and headaches... With this little spot of cash he was going to buy some simple straight-forward business... something in the mechanical line... a going concern... repairing small cars... sec-ond-hand jalopies... That's always a profitable deal... In addition he'd take back his customers' lamps and horns... that was down his alley... He'd modernize them... There's always a demand for little nickel and copper accessories... All you've got to do is keep up with the styles... You fix them up... and then you find a customer good for a three hundred percent profit... that's business for you! He wasn't worrying... He knew all the tricks... If he hadn't quite made up his mind, it was on account of the premises... He still wanted to think it over... The lease wasn't very clear... They were asking plenty for the goodwill... He smelled a slight rat... They weren't giving the equipment away either... He was letting the negotiations drag out... He'd learned his lesson... He'd almost bought into some kind of company that was building a regular factory for body accessories... not a hundred yards from the Porte de Vanves... Nothing had come of it... They'd been screwing him in the contract... At the last moment he'd got cold feet... He hadn't trusted his partners... And he hadn't been wrong... He always stopped to think... It was too good to be honest... Pretty near forty-seven percent... Hell, they had to be ban-dits... He didn't regret it much... He'd have been taken sure as shit with those kind of gangsters... So anyway he spilled his story... he told me everything that had happened in his business from the time we'd gone to Blême to the present moment... Then it was my turn... I started off very slowly... He listened all the way...

"My Lord! Well, kid... say, that's rough..." He was flabbergasted... "Say, that's unbelievable... Say, it's no wonder you're skinny as a rail... Say, you've been through the mill... Hell... That'll teach you... You see, kid... that's how it is in the country... If you come from Paris, you'd better stay there... I've often been offered little agencies, garages and stuff in the sticks... It sounds good... Selling bicy-cles, tires, and so on... Your own master... free as the air... that's the old oil... They never took me in... Never, believe you me... All those country rackets, you got to know what you're doing... You've got to be born to their sticky ways... You go out there to the woods... as innocent as the day you were born... Imagine!... You're raring to go... They take you the minute you get off the train... You're a sitting duck and no two ways about it... Everybody fleeces you... They have the time of their lives... You're sunk... Profits?... Don't make me laugh!... Not a sou... They screw you all along the line... How are you going to stop them?... You're lost before you start... You've got to learn their ways with your mother's milk... Then you're all right... Otherwise you're a sucker from the word go... How can you expect to succeed?... You don't learn those things overnight... Artichokes aren't invented... You haven't a chance in ten thousand... And hell, the way you went about it!... With centrifugal farming... That's a hot one... You were looking for trouble... Naturally you got screwed... What would you ex-pect?... But say, kid, are you skinny! It's incredible... Do you like tapioca soup?..." He rummaged around the kitchen... It must have been at least nine o'clock... "You've got to build yourself up... Here you're going to eat, I can promise you that... You're going to put it away... No two ways about it..."

He took another look at me... the cut of my jacket made him smile a little... and my combination pants... with the string seat...

"You can't run around in rags... I'll go get you a pair of pants... Wait a second... I'll find something..." He went to the next room and brought me a whole suit, out of his closet with the sliding door... in perfect condition... and a bearskin coat... big and shaggy... "You can wear these for the time being..." He also gave me a cap with flaps and a suit of flannel underwear... I was all set up...

"So you're not hungry?... Not at all?" I couldn't have eaten a thing... I felt sick... There was something mean going on inside me... My bowels were aJJ gurgling... No kidding, I was in bad shape...

"What's the matter, kid?..." I was beginning to worry him. "Nothing... nothing at all..." I was trying to keep hold of myself. "Have you caught cold?... Say, you must have the grippe..."

"Oh no... I don't think so," I said. "But if you feel like it, Uncle, when you're through eating... maybe we could take a little walk..."

"You think that would make you feel better?" "Oh yes, Uncle... Yes, I think so..."

"Do you feel sick to your stomach?" "Yes, just a little, Uncle."

"Say, that's a good idea... Let's go right away... I'll eat later... I'm a little like your mother, you know... subito, presto, don't put things off!" He didn't finish his supper... We strolled, very slowly, to the café on the corner... He sat us down on the terrace and ordered mint tea for me... He talked about one thing and another... I asked him for news... Had he seen my parents?...

"As I was leaving for Belgium... that was two months ago yesterday... I dropped in at the Passage... I haven't seen them since... They were really racking their brains over your letters... They studied them word for word... They couldn't figure out what had become of you... Your mother wanted to go see right away... I dissuaded her... I told her I had news... I said you were getting along fine... but you didn't have a minute to spare on account of the sowing... Anyway a lot of blarney... She postponed her trip... Your father was still sick... He was absent from the office several days in succession this winter... They were both afraid that this time would be it... that Lempreinte and the other guy wouldn't wait... that they'd fire him... But in the end they took him back... But they docked him in full for the time of his absence!... Imagine!... For illness!... A company with a capital of a hundred million... with real estate all over the place! Isn't it disgraceful?...

Isn't it disgusting?... Well, that's the whole trouble... The bigger they are, the more they want... They're insatiable... They've never got enough... All that dough only makes them crummier... Companies are horrible... I see it in my own little business... They're bloodsuckers the whole lot of them... they're wild beasts, vampires... It's hard to imagine... but it's true... That's how people get rich... it's the only way!"

"Yes, Uncle..."

"Anybody that gets sick on the job can go to hell!" "Yes, Uncle..."

"It's the final shindig,[120] son, those are the things you've got to find out... and the sooner the better... Watch out for millionaires... And say, I forgot to tell you... There's something new... about their ailments... Your father refuses to see a doctor anymore... Not even Capron, who wasn't bad... and really not dishonest... He didn't force his calls on you... Your mother too... she won't have him... She just doctors herself... And I assure you she limps... I don't know how she manages... Plasters and poultices the whole time... with mustard, without mustard... hot, cold, hot, cold!... And she never stops working... And she runs herself ragged... She's got to go looking for customers... She's found some new ones for the new Embroidery House... Bulgarian lace they sell... Good God!... Your father of course doesn't know anything about it... Her territory is the whole Right Bank... That's a lot of mileage... If you could see her face when she comes home from those treks... Ah, you wouldn't believe it!... I'd have taken her for a corpse... She really frightened me the other day... I saw her in the street... She was coming home with her boxes... At least forty pounds, I'll bet... Forty pounds, do you hear?... Holding it all up... That crap is heavy... She didn't even see me... Exhaustion will be the death of

---

[120] The final shindig = "The final conquest" in l'Internationale, the Socialist—later Communist— hymn.

her... You won't last long either if you're not more careful... Take it from me... In the first place you eat too fast... Yourparents were always telling you that... They were right for once..."

All that was perfectly possible... But it didn't matter... anyway not very much... I didn't want to contradict him... I didn't want to start an argument... What troubled me while he was talking... was that I wasn't even listening very well... That was on account of my bellyache... My guts were all twisted... He went on talking...

"What are you going to do now?... Have you got something in mind?... After you've put a little flesh on your bones?..." He was kind of worried about my future too...

"What I'm saying, son, isn't to hurry you... Not at all... Take your time before you start applying... Get your bearings... Don't go for any old thing... You'll only be making trouble for yourself... Naturally you've got to go looking, but easy does it... Watch your step... A job is like food... It's got to be the right kind... Think it over... use your judgment... Ask me... Feel around... Look in all directions... And don't make up your mind until you're sure... Then you'll tell me... There's no fire... Not yet... Don't take any damn thing... just to please me... No little two-week jobs... Nothing doing!... You're not a kid anymore... No more screwball schemes... You'll get hurt in the end... You'll get a bad reputation."

We started back toward his place... We walked around the Luxembourg[121]... He talked some more about jobs... It was on his mind, kind of, trying to figure how I was going to make out... Maybe in the bottom of his kind heart he was wondering if I'd ever get over my disastrous instincts... my jailbird tendencies... I let him bubble a while... I didn't know what to say... I didn't answer right away... I was really too tired and I had a rotten ache in the temples... I was only listening with half an ear... When we got to the Boulevard Raspail, I couldn't even walk straight... I was looping all over the sidewalk... He noticed... We stopped again... I was thinking of something entirely different... I was resting... Uncle Édouard was driving me crazy with his prospects... I looked up in the sky again... "Say, Uncle Édouard, do you know the Veils of Venus... and the Hive of Shooting Stars?..." They were just coming out of the clouds... all that Stardust... "And Amarine... and Proliscrpe?" I'd spotted them one right after the other, the white one and the pink one... "'Wouldn't you like me to show you?" Uncle Édouard had known his constellations in the old days... At one time he'd even known the whole Great Boreal Zenith... from the Triangle to Sagittarius, almost by heart... He'd known his whole Flammarion... and his Pereires too naturally... But he'd forgotten it all... He didn't remember a single one... He couldn't even find Libra!

"Ah, my poor boy, I've lost my eyesight... I'll take your word for it... You look at them for me... I can't even read my paper anymore... I'm getting so nearsighted these days I wouldn't know a star if it was two feet away... I wouldn't see the sky if I was right in the middle of it... I'd mistake the sun for the moon . He was kidding.

"Oh, that doesn't matter," he went on... "But you're mighty smart, it seems to me... You're sharp as a razor... Say, you're really getting ahead... That's something... You didn't eat much out there... but you sucked up knowledge... You're as brainy as they come... You really crammed that big noodle of yours, didn't you, kid?... Say, you're full of science, no fooling..." I handed him a laugh... We talked some more about Courtial... He wanted to hear about the end... He asked me a few questions... Christ! I couldn't stand hearing him talk about it... It threw me into a tizzy... I panicked almost like the day before... I couldn't stop bawling... Hell!... That looked lousy... It shook my bones... And I was pretty tough... It must have been the terrible tiredness...

"Come, what's the matter, my poor old-timer?... You're all broken up... Come now, don't take it so hard... All that stuff about a job was just to be saying something... I wasn't serious... why should you be?... You wouldn't let that kind of flumdiddle throw you... You know me well enough... Don't you trust your uncle?... I wasn't saying that to get rid of you... Come along, you big sap, don't you understand!... Stop that blubbering and make it quick... You look like a little girl... OK, kid, you going to stop?... A man doesn't cry... You can stay as long as you please... There, that's better... First you're

---

[121] The Luxembourg. Quite a stroll. The reader is advised to locate the Luxembourg Gardens and the rue de la Convention on a map of Paris.

going to get your strength back... I want to see you stuffed... puffed... bloated... Nobody'd take you like this, I hope you realize... You wouldn't get anywhere... They're not looking for featherweights... They want big bruisers... You'll give it to them in the kisser... Boom!... And down they go! Right, left... Bam!... Waiter! Yes sir? Bring us an order of biceps..."He comforted me as best he could, but I couldn't stop the flow. I was gushing like a fountain.

"I want to go away, Uncle... I want to go away... far away..."

"What do you mean go away?... Where?... China?... What do you mean far?..."

"I don't know, Uncle... I don't know..." It was pouring out worse and worse... I stood up... I was suffocating... But when I was up, I started reeling... He had to prop me up... When we got back to his place, he really didn't know what to do or say...

"Well, kid... my oh my!... Let's forget about all that... Let's suppose I haven't said a word... It's not your fault, poor kid... Come now! You had nothing to do with it... You know what Courtial was like... An extraordinary man... A magnificent scientist!... I wouldn't deny that for a minute... I was always the first to say so... And I think he had a good heart... But he was an adventurer... Extremely bright, that's a fact... Extremely capable and what have you... He suffered a thousand injustices... Good, I'll subscribe to that too... But that wasn't the first time he went walking on precipices... Ah, he was a glutton for risks... He was always on the brink of catastrophe... People who play the races in the first place... it's because they like to get it in the neck... They can't change... And you can't stop them... They can't help heading for disaster!... Well, there you have it: they like to take chances... All the same I feel very bad about it... Believe me, it touches me a good deal... I admired him... I even felt sincere friendship... He was a unique mind... Ah, I know all that... he was a man of worth... I seem to be dumb, but I understand... Only it's no reason because he's dead that you should forget about everything else and waste away... Christ almighty! It won't do!... Do you think you can make your living in the state you're in?... You don't ruin your health at your age because you've run into some trouble... You're not going to brood over it the rest of your life... It's not your last calamity... you'll see plenty more... Leave the wailing to the dames, it don't stop their bladders... They get a kick out of it... But you're a man and you're an up-and-comer... Aren't you an up-and-comer, sonny boy?... You wouldn't want to drown in your waterworks?... Ha-ha!... Suppose it fell in your soup... Say, wouldn't that be a scream?..." He gave me a couple of gentle pokes... He tried to make me laugh...

"Say, will you look at that weeping willow!... That's how he comes back from the country... frazzled... washed-out... kerflooey... Come along, puppy boy... brace up... I won't say another word about your going away... You'll stay with me... You won't take a job anywhere... It's settled... It's a deal... There, do you feel better now?... Say, why not?... I'll take you on in my garage... Maybe it's not the best thing in the world to be apprenticed to your uncle... But hell, what can we do?... Health comes first... Who cares what people think?... The rest will take care of itself... Health, that's the ticket... I'll train you, OK, little pal?... First I want you to put on some weight... Oh, I know, it kills you to go looking for jobs... I could see that when you were back home... It doesn't come easy to you, you haven't the temperament... If that's what gives you the willies, nobody's going to force you... You'll stay with me the whole time... You won't ring any more doorbells... You wouldn't be a good salesman... Hell no!... What more can I say?... You don't like applying for jobs?... Fine!... That's what gets you down?... OK."

"No, Uncle, it's not exactly that... I want to go away..."

"Go away! Go away! Where to?... That's eating you, isn't it, little chickadee?... I don't get it!... You want to go back to the sticks?... You want to grow carrots?"

"Oh no, Uncle, not that... I'd like to enlist."

"Where'd you get that idea all of a sudden?... Say, that's a corker!... Enlist?... Where?... Why?... There's plenty of time for that, son... You'll go with your age group... What's the hurry?... The military vocation, is that it?... Say, that's a good one!" He scrutinized me... He found me very odd... He examined me carefully...

"That's just a bug, bunny boy... Like wanting to take a leak... You get over it the same way... You want to turn out like Courtial?... You want to be a flibbertigibbet?... What about your parents?... Have you thought of that?... The squawk they'll let out... My oh my, some serenade that will be!... I'll never hear the last of it... They'll say it's all my fault... Take it easy... they'll say I put funny ideas in your head... that you're as screwy as your boss..."

He wasn't one bit happy about it... I wanted to confess everything... right then and there... anything at all... it didn't matter what...

"But Uncle, I don't know how to do anything... I'm no good... I'm not sensible..."

"Who says you're no good, you big dope... I know you in and out... You're perfectly sensible..."

I couldn't stop bawling... "No, Uncle, I'm a fraud..."

"Not at all... not at all, angel child... You're a little sap, that's all... I tell you you're OK... You haven't a deceitful hair on your head... You're just an all-around sucker... The old scoundrel took you in... can't you see that, little bunny? That's what you can't stomach?... He put one over on you..."

"No! No!..." I was frantic... I didn't want to hear any explanations. I begged him to listen to me... "I only made everybody unhappy!" I told him over and over again... Oof! And then I was sick to my stomach... And then I talked some more... I'd always made everybody unhappy... That was my awful certainty.

"You've really thought it over?..."

"Yes, Uncle... Yes, honest... I've thought it over... I want to go away... Tomorrow... please... tomorrow..."

"Come, come! The house isn't on fire... I won't have it... Rest up awhile... You can't go away just like that... on the spur of the moment... You won't be signing up for one day... it's for three years, friend... A thousand and eighty-five days... not to mention the time you have to make up."

"Yes, Uncle..."

"Come, you're not a bad boy... Nobody's trying to get rid of you... Nobody's accusing you of anything... You're not so badly off here, are you?... I've never mistreated you, have I?"

"No, it's me, Uncle... I'm bad... I'm no good... You don't realize, Uncle... you just don't realize..."

"Here we go again! Why, you're nuts working yourself up like that, you poor little devil!... You're going to make yourself really sick..."

"I can't stand it, Uncle... I can't stand it... I'm old enough, Uncle... I've got to go away ... I'll go tomorrow... All right?"

"Not tomorrow, pal! Not tomorrow! Right away! Sure... right away!..." He was getting excited... "Christ, how stubborn can you be!... You're going to wait two weeks... Or a month for that matter... Two weeks to please me... We'll see... anyway they wouldn't take you the way you are now... I can guarantee that in advance... You'd scare the medics... First you've got to build yourself up... that's the main thing... They'd throw you out like a leper... What's the matter with you?... You think they enlist skeletons?... You'll have to put on a few pounds... At least twenty, see... I know what I'm saying... Twenty for a starter... Or else... vamoose... You want to go to war?... Say, you'd blow away!... Who's sent me this soldier who's as skinny as a rail?... Come on, we'll see about it later... Come along, little matchstick, button up those moans... Well, anyway... they won't be bored... they'll have a good laugh at the recruiting station when you come in all skin and bones... And on guard duty!... They'll split a gut... Hi, Private Crybaby!... Wouldn't you rather be in the Engineers?... What branch are you going to enlist in anyway?... You don't know yet?... Well, you'd better make up your mind..."

It was all the same to me. "I don't know, Uncle..."

"You don't know?... You never know anything.

"I like you fine, Uncle... But I can't stay... I just can't... You're mighty good to me... I don't deserve it, Uncle... I don't deserve it..."

"Why don't you deserve it?... Speak up, you little dope?"

"I don't know, Uncle... I make you unhappy too... I want to go away... I want to enlist tomorrow..."

"Oh, all right, then it's settled... Shake on it... I agree... OK... But that still doesn't tell us what regiment you've picked... All I can say is you'd better hurry..." He was making fun of me...

"You wouldn't want to join the footsloggers?... You don't favor the Queen of Battles?... No?... Well, I can understand that... you'd rather not carry anything... those sixty-five pounds... That doesn't appeal to you, does it, daisy boy?... You'd rather be carried... Take cover, dammit... You're not in the mood?... Under that manure pile over there on the left... And the parades!... Hup hoop hip hore!... And don't you care for our lovely maneuvers?... How about it, my bullyboy?... Take advantage of the terrain!... You ought to be good at that... You've seen plenty of terrain... you know what it's like... The leeks... and all the muck around them... How about it?... But you preferred the stars... Ah, so you're changing your mind?... It didn't take you very long... Maybe you'd like to be an astronomer?... Good!... You'll join the First Telescopes... Moon Regiment... No?... You don't go for anything I offer... Say, you're hard to please... I can see you'd rather be in Infantry after all... Are you a good hiker?... Boy, will you have blisters!... "Them boots are heavy in my pack. Them boots..." Or would you rather have boils on your ass?... OK, make it the cavalry... Extended order, that's the stuff... Or how about the mountain boys![122]...

There's a drop to drink up yonder, There's a drop to drink...

He made a bugle with his mouth: "Ta ra ta ta ta! Ta ta ta..."

"Oh, don't do that, Uncle... Don't!" It reminded me of that character.

"How sensitive you are, you poor lummox... What would you do in one of those nasty battles?... Wait... You haven't really thought it over... Stay where you are... You can spare another five minutes... Stay with me a little while longer... Maybe two three weeks... until you begin to see what's what... Say, why not a month?"

"No, Uncle... I'd rather go right away..."

"Good Lord, you're just like your mother... Once you get a bee in your bonnet... Hell, I'm just about out of ideas... How about the Cuirassiers?... A big fatso like you wouldn't look bad on a horse... They won't even be able to see you under your breastplate... You'll be the regimental ghost... Say, a lance couldn't even hit you... Good deal!... Say, that's a marvelous idea!... But even so you'd have to put on weight... there's not even enough of you for a ghost... You poor lug, you're at least twenty pounds short... And I'm not exaggerating... it's still the same twenty pounds... You think that's a better idea?..."

"Yes, Uncle."

"I can see you charging..." I didn't see a damn thing... "Yes, Uncle... Yes, I'll wait..."

"The Hefties! Ferdinand the Hefty!... The nursemaid's dream! The footslogger's friend!

The terror of the artillery! That'll give us a little bit of everything in the family...

"I can't see you in the navy... You're seasick already... See what I mean?... And your

father who was in for five years!... What's he going to say?... He was on the heavy guns... We'll have a sampling of everything in the family... The whole army... The Fourteenth of July at home, eh?... Taratata! Ta ta ta!..."

Still trying to cheer me up, he took his kepi, it was on the mantelpiece, on the right next to the mirror... I can still see his pompon, a little yellow chick... He slapped it on sideways...

"There you are, Ferdinand! The whole army!..." That was a happy ending.

"Nuts!" he reflected. "All that's the bunk... You're not through changing your mind... You haven't got your marching orders yet, son... you haven't even got a serial number... You've got plenty of time ahead of you, soldier boy..." He heaved a sigh. "It's never too late to make an ass of yourself... Right now you're upset... That's understandable... You've been crying like a waterfall... You must be pretty thirsty... You want some brandy... I've got some first-class calvados... I'll give you some sugar with it... It doesn't appeal to you?... How about some plain red wine?... I could warm it up for you... Or some camomile?... Or a spot of anisette?... I guess you'd rather hit the sack... I see how it is... A little shut-eye for a starter... That's not a bad idea... I guess I'm the one that's been talking rot... What you need is ten good hours of sleep... All right, my dear nephew, get a wiggle on... We've chewed the fat long enough... Let's get out the baby's bed... Poor kid... He's had a rough time... The country doesn't agree with you... I could have told you that, son... You just stay with me from now on..."

---

[122] "Mountain boys." The French word *"mataf"* is argot for "sailor." But the following song belongs to the mountain troops. Possibly "mataf" was a misunderstanding for Bat d'Af, Bataillon d'Afrique. Or possibly, as Celine's then-secretary suggests, he chose it for the sound.

"I'd like to, Uncle... I'd really like to... But honest, I can't... Later some time... Later... is that all right?... I wouldn't do anything decent right now... I couldn't... You'll let me go, won't you, Uncle?... You'll ask Papa, won't you?... I'm sure he won't mind..."

"No! Nothing doing!" I was making him sore... "My Lord, are you stubborn!... You're as obstinate as Clémence... My goodness, it runs in the family... You're wearing yourself out for the hell of it... The army isn't what you think, son... It's even rougher than a job... You don't realize... Especially at your age... The others are twenty-one, that's an advantage in itself... You're not strong enough... You'll be all worn-out..."

"I know, Uncle, but it's best I should try..."

"Say, you're plumb crazy... Come along now... We're going to bed... You're talking a lot of hot air now, we'll think about it some more tomorrow... In my opinion you're all in... This idea of yours is like a fever... you're raving, and I've had enough of it... Say, they've really cut you down with their pruning hooks... It was high time you came home... Those farmers have really fixed you... It's the payoff!... And now you're off your rocker... Well, my boy, I'm going to patch you up... And you're going to put it away, I'm warning you right now... Every day starches, buttter, and meat... and the best quality... no measly chops... And chocolate every morning... And cod-liver oil by the glassful... Don't worry, I know how it's done... No more empty plates and wind dumplings... That's right, puppy child... No more starvation... And now upsy-daisy, to bed with you... That's all a lot of rot... You're just upset... That's my private opinion... You're all inside-out... At your age it doesn't take long to get over that... You just have to stop thinking about it... Think of something else... And eat enough for four... for thirty-six… In a week you'll be hunky-dory... Guaranteed by the Bank of France and the Higgledy-Piggledy pharmacy!"

We took the bed out of the closet... The folding contraption that squeaked all over... It had shrunk something awful... When I tried to stretch out, I got tangled up in the bars... I preferred the mattress on the floor... He gave me another off his own bed... I was still shaking like a leaf… He gave me more blankets... My teeth were still chattering... He covered me all up, he buried me under a pile of overcoats... I had all his bearskins on top of me... There was a whole selection in the closet... I kept on shivering all the same... I looked at the walls of the room... They'd got smaller too... It was the middle room, the one with the *Angelus* in it...

"I can't put on anymore... What do you think, you old crocodile?... you wouldn't want me to smother you... Imagine!... suppose I couldn't find you again... Wouldn't that be a fine kettle of fish!... My oh my!... Some soldier boy you'd be!... Squashed under a pile of blankets… I can hear the hue and cry!... Wouldn't I be sitting pretty!... Think what they'd say in the Passage!... My goodness!... The dear child!... The little treasure!... And me trying to explain… Squashed in his own juice, the little devil! Squish! Absolutely! My oh my!... What a mess!… Stop it, emperor, I've had enough..."I spasmed, trying to laugh with him... He went to his room... He called out from far away...

"Listen, I'm leaving my door open... If you need anything, don't be afraid to sing out... It's no disgrace to be sick... I'll come right away... If you get the runs, do you know where the can is?... The little hallway on the left... Don't take the stairs by mistake... The lamp is on the table... You needn't blow it out... And in case you need to throw up... wouldn't you like a chamberpot?..."

"Oh, no, Uncle... I'll go out there..."

"Good. But if you get up, put on an overcoat... Just reach into the pile, it doesn't matter which... You'd catch your death out in the hall... There's no shortage of coats..."

"No, Uncle."

OTHER TITLES

Classipublica presents:

THE TWO
MASTERPIECES

Animal Farm

Nineteen Eighty-Four

Classipublica

www.omniapublica.com

CPSIA information can be obtained
at www.ICGtesting.com
Printed in the USA
LVHW021937010520
654881LV00006B/260